SLUGGY FR[...]
MEGATOME V[...]
LITTLE EVILS

BY PETE ABRAMS
HATHERLEIGH PRESS * NEW YORK

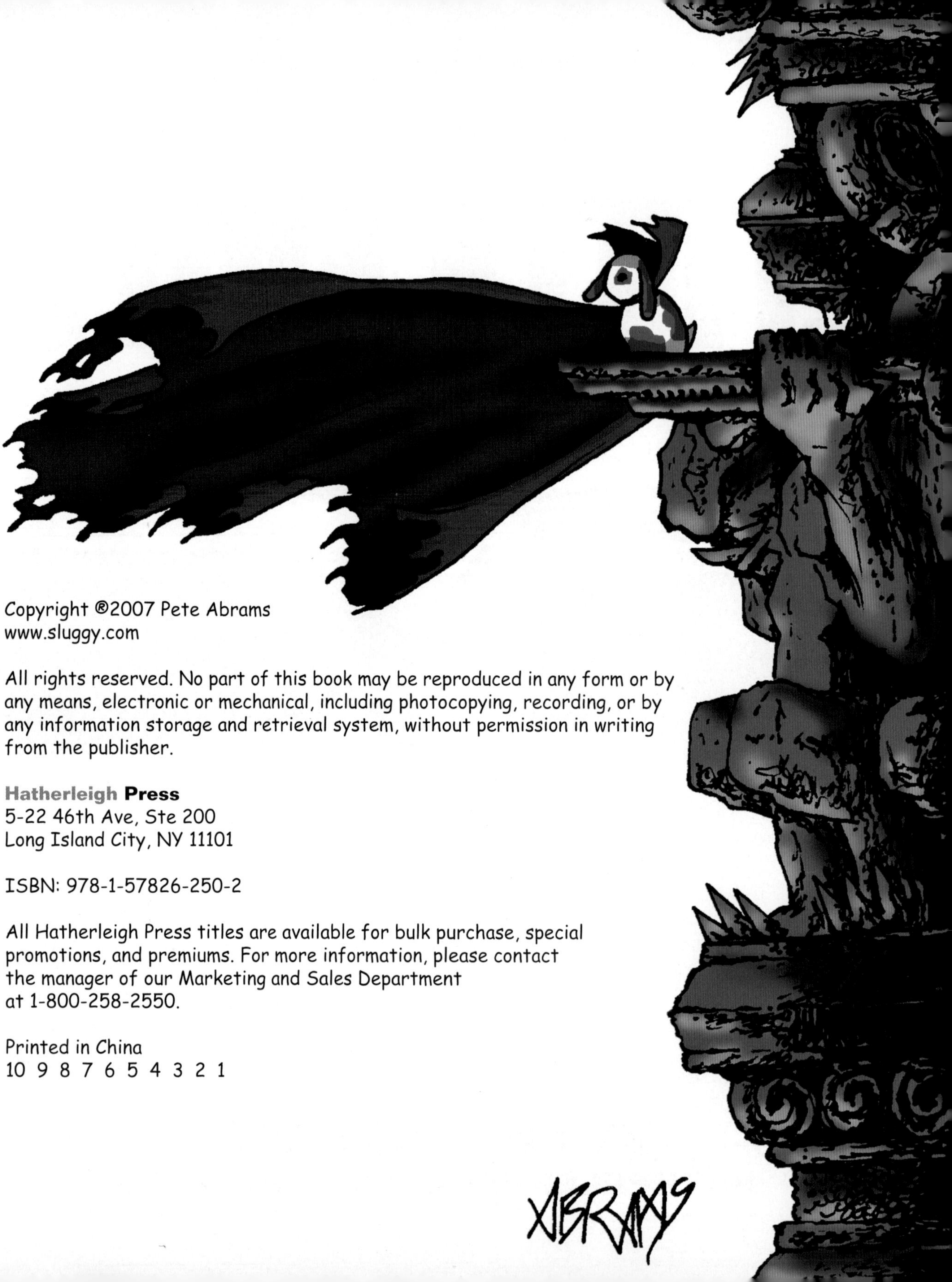
ABRAMS

Hatherleigh Press
5-22 46th Ave, Ste 200
Long Island City, NY 11101

ISBN: 978-1-57826-250-2

All Hatherleigh Press titles are available for bulk purchase, special promotions, and premiums. For more information, please contact the manager of our Marketing and Sales Department at 1-800-258-2550.

Printed in China
10 9 8 7 6 5 4 3 2 1

Table of Contents

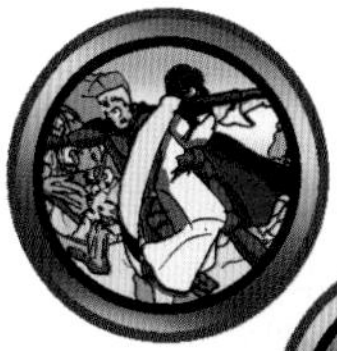
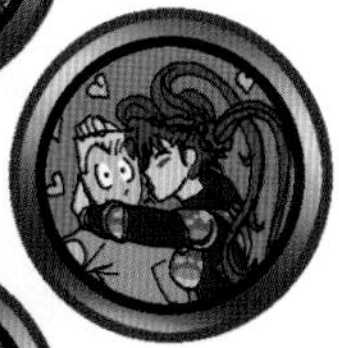
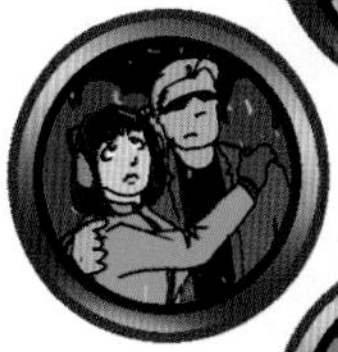
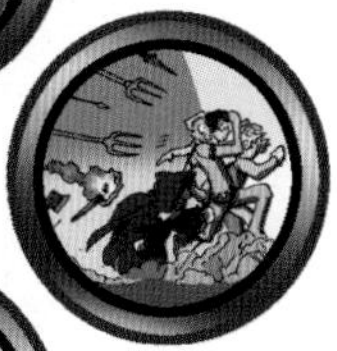
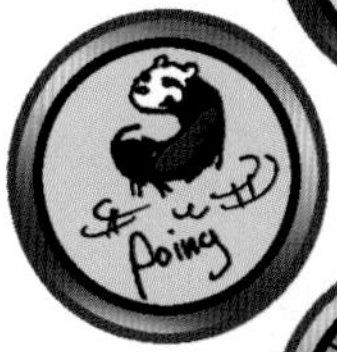
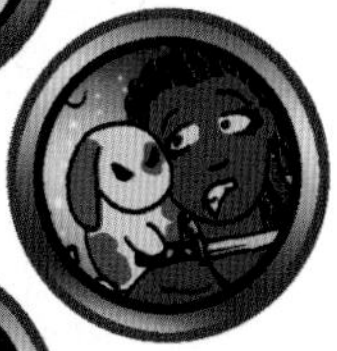
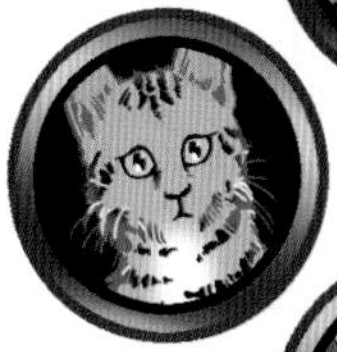
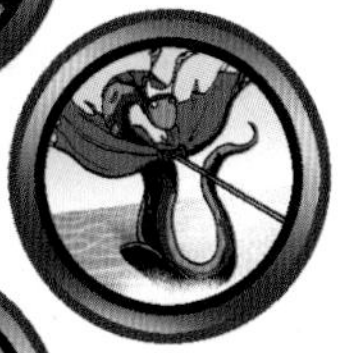
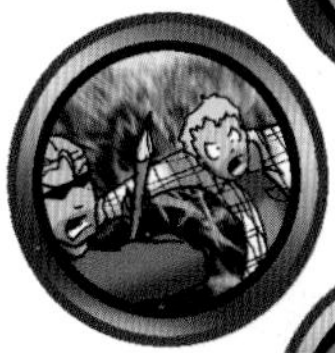
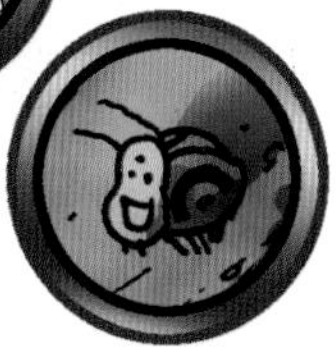

Dedication

Sluggy Freelance Book 4 is dedicated to:
Leah.

Sluggy Freelance Book 5 is dedicated to:
Tom and Kim. Thanks for dealing with all that evil!

Sluggy Freelance Book 6 is dedicated to:
my in-laws, Jules and Sandy. Thanks for the daughter!

Introduction

Welcome, dear readers, to the second book installment of the wildly popular webcomic Sluggy Freelance. Inside these pages, you will be introduced to a world that is like and yet unlike our own, if our world contained talking animals, puns galore, aliens, vampires, alternate dimensions, spoofs on popular movies, television shows, and real life events—and a mad scientist who just won't stop inventing. Are you ready?

Little Evils has been a long time coming. Each strip enclosed here was originally released, one each day, on the website www.sluggy.com. Now, for the first time, you are able to hold in your hands almost two years of Sluggy and devour it in one sitting. Instead of being tied to a computer screen and waiting those agonizing months and years as Sluggites in the past have, you can simply turn the page.

If you are new to Sluggy, now is the perfect time to join in. The stories in *Little Evils* are considered some of the most memorable of all of Sluggy's history. Their adventures are just beginning and you can climb on for the ride. New characters will be introduced in these pages, and you'll be there right at the start.

THE INTERNET. MORE THAN JUST FUN AND GAMES, IT HAS BECOME THE GLOBAL SOURCE OF PRACTICAL USES!
GACK!
FOR EXAMPLE, LETS SEE HOW RIFF MAKES USE OF THE INTERNET!
I'M TRYING TO SUMMON THE DEVIL ON-LINE.
PROVES MY POINT. IN THE NEW MILLENNIUM YOU'LL BE ABLE TO SELL YOUR SOUL IN A NANOSECOND!
Um...BUT WOULDN'T IT BE EASIER TO JUST E-MAIL HIM?
YES! SPAM SATAN!
ABRAMS

The first Sluggy Freelance comic. August 25th, 1997.

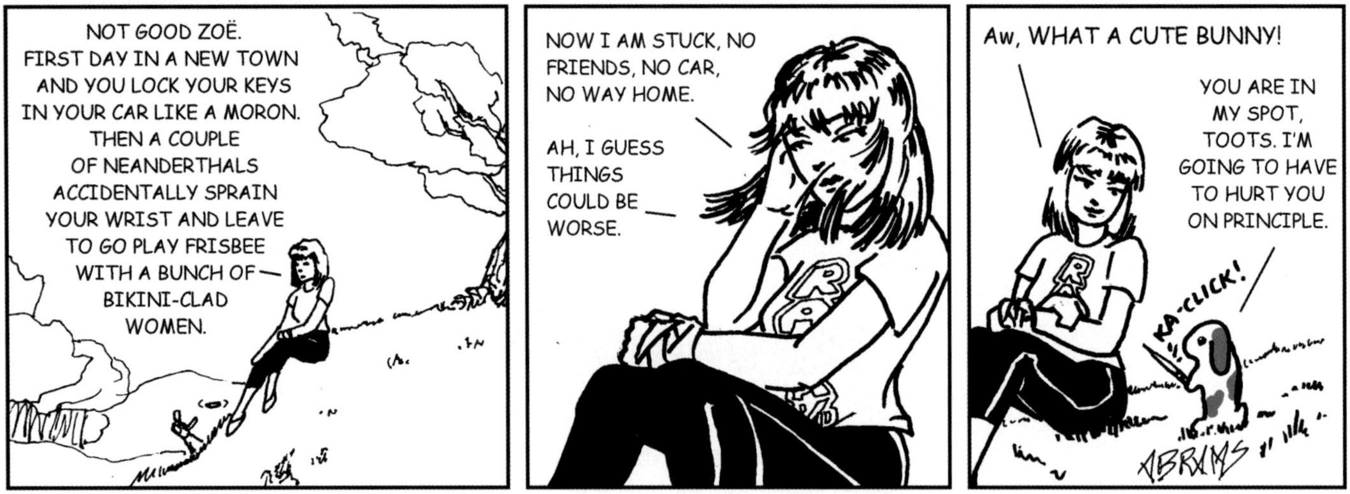
NOT GOOD ZOË.
FIRST DAY IN A NEW TOWN AND YOU LOCK YOUR KEYS IN YOUR CAR LIKE A MORON. THEN A COUPLE OF NEANDERTHALS ACCIDENTALLY SPRAIN YOUR WRIST AND LEAVE TO GO PLAY FRISBEE WITH A BUNCH OF BIKINI-CLAD WOMEN.
NOW I AM STUCK, NO FRIENDS, NO CAR, NO WAY HOME.
AH, I GUESS THINGS COULD BE WORSE.
Aw, WHAT A CUTE BUNNY!
YOU ARE IN MY SPOT, TOOTS. I'M GOING TO HAVE TO HURT YOU ON PRINCIPLE.
KA-CLICK!
ABRAMS
The third appearance of Zoë. September 26th, 1997.

If you're already familiar with Sluggy, what you hold in your hands is a compilation of the early years, as well as some new and never-before-released strips you've never had a chance to see anywhere else. Here's your chance to read it all in one go, without the 24-hour wait for the next strip. You'll also find new material: bonus chapters throughout.

No matter how familiar you are with the Sluggy universe, there's one guarantee we can make—you will laugh. So sit back, curl up with *Little Evils*, and discover what a fun ride Sluggy can be!

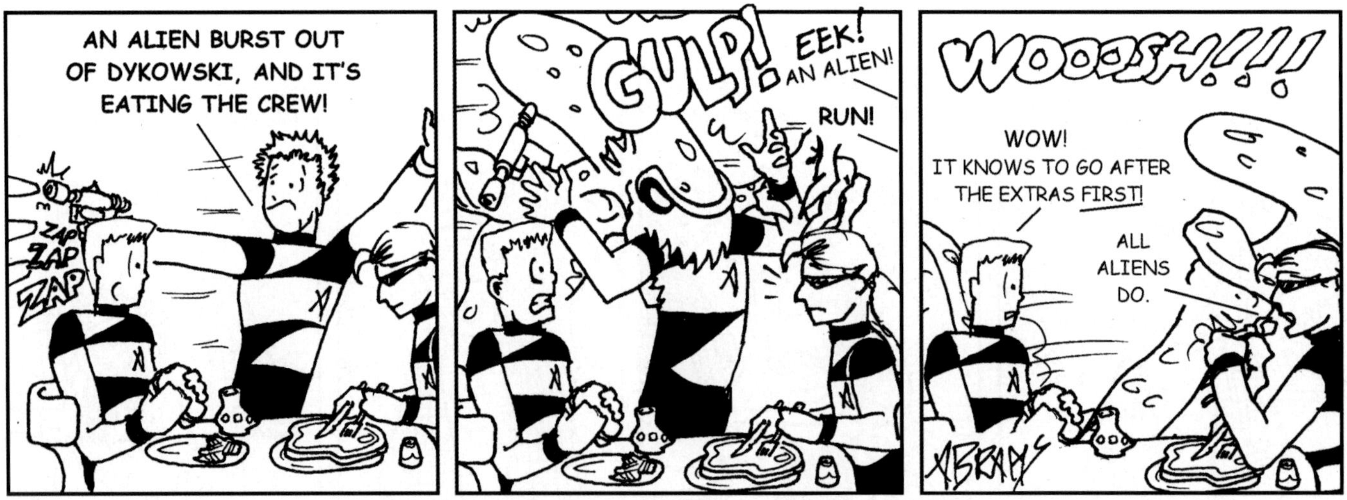
AN ALIEN BURST OUT OF DYKOWSKI, AND IT'S EATING THE CREW!
ZAP
ZAP
ZAP
GULP!
EEK! AN ALIEN!
RUN!
WOOOSH!!!!
WOW! IT KNOWS TO GO AFTER THE EXTRAS FIRST!
ALL ALIENS DO.
ABRAMS
The first appearance of Aylee, October 14th, 1997.

All about Sluggy Freelance

Sluggy Freelance celebrated its tenth year of daily comics on August 25th, 2007. It's been a long journey, and the strip's popularity has increased dramatically since its initial release, now garnering over 100,000 daily readers.

The strip began initially as a series of short adventures taken by the three main protagonists (Torg, Riff and Zoë), but gradually became more plot-oriented as the storylines became longer and more serious. The characters constantly find themselves in strange and usually dangerous circumstances and surroundings, and the cast has been expanded to include their pets (Kiki and Bun-Bun) as well as their acquaintances and enemies (Gwynn, Sam, Oasis, Santa Claus, the entire Dimension of Pain).

While it's always ideal to starting at the beginning of the adventures, Sluggy Freelance is set up so a new reader would be able to enjoy a storyline without knowing the entire picture.

There have been several series of Sluggy Freelance books released. The first nine books were self-published over the past ten years as small volumes that contained black and white art and limited page counts. The Mega-tomes are compilations of three of those original publications. The first self-published Megatome, *Born of Nifty*, contains Books 1 through 3. *Little Evils* contains Books 4 through 6.

Born of Nifty is a finalist for the prestigious Lulu Blooker Award.

All about the Author

Pete Abrams is the writer and illustrator of the comic strip Sluggy Freelance, now in its tenth year. Educated and trained at the Joe Kubert School of Cartoon and Graphic Art, established in 1976, he began Sluggy Freelance as a creative outlet. It eventually became so successful that it is now his full-time job. He is reputed to be the first person to make a living at drawing web-comics. He has attended conventions across the United States, including Dragon*Con and San Diego Comic-Con. He resides in northern New Jersey.

SLUGGY FREELANCE BOOK 4
GAME CALLED ON ACCOUNT OF NAKED CHICK
by Pete Abrams

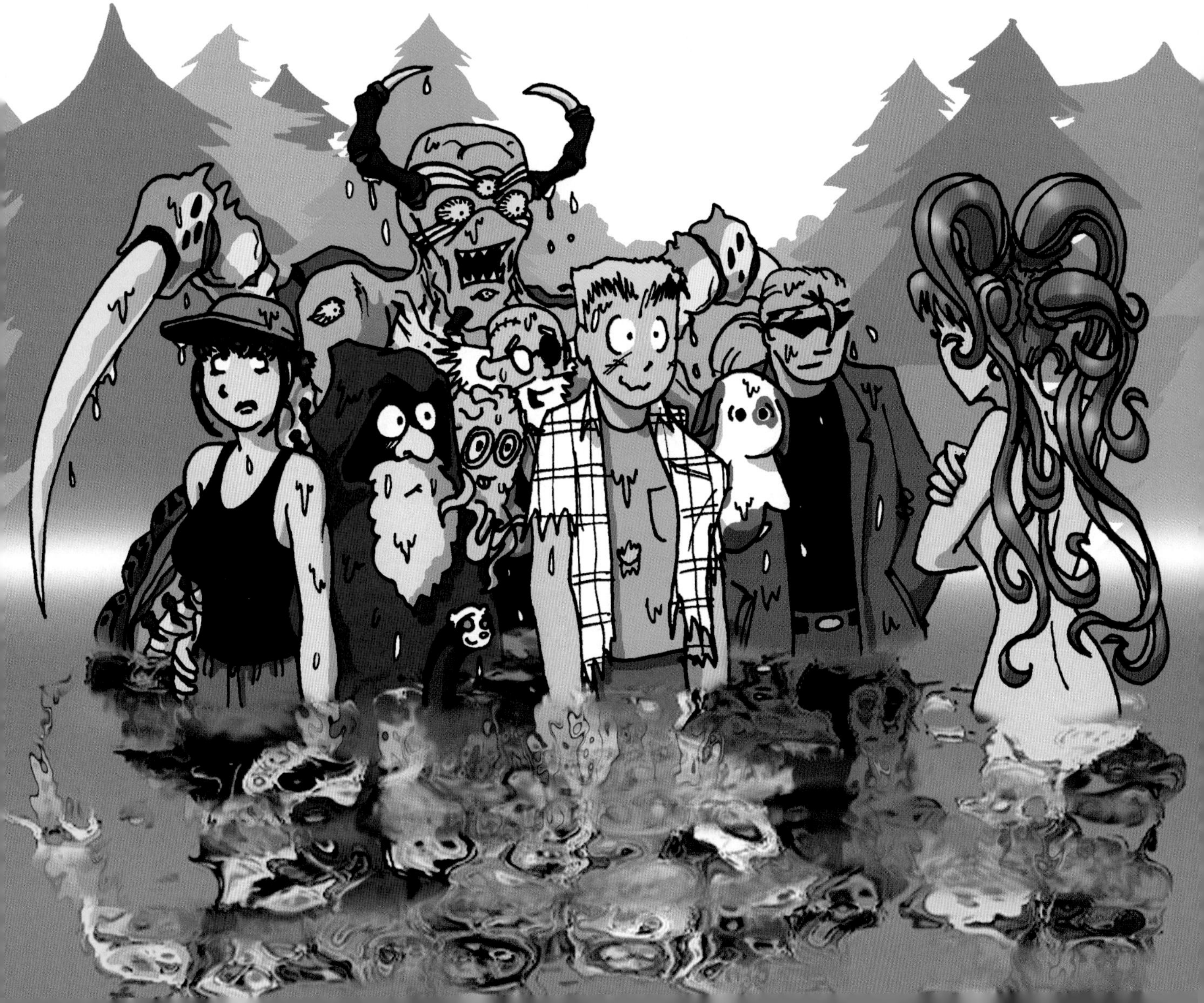

PREVIOUSLY ON SLUGGY FREELANCE

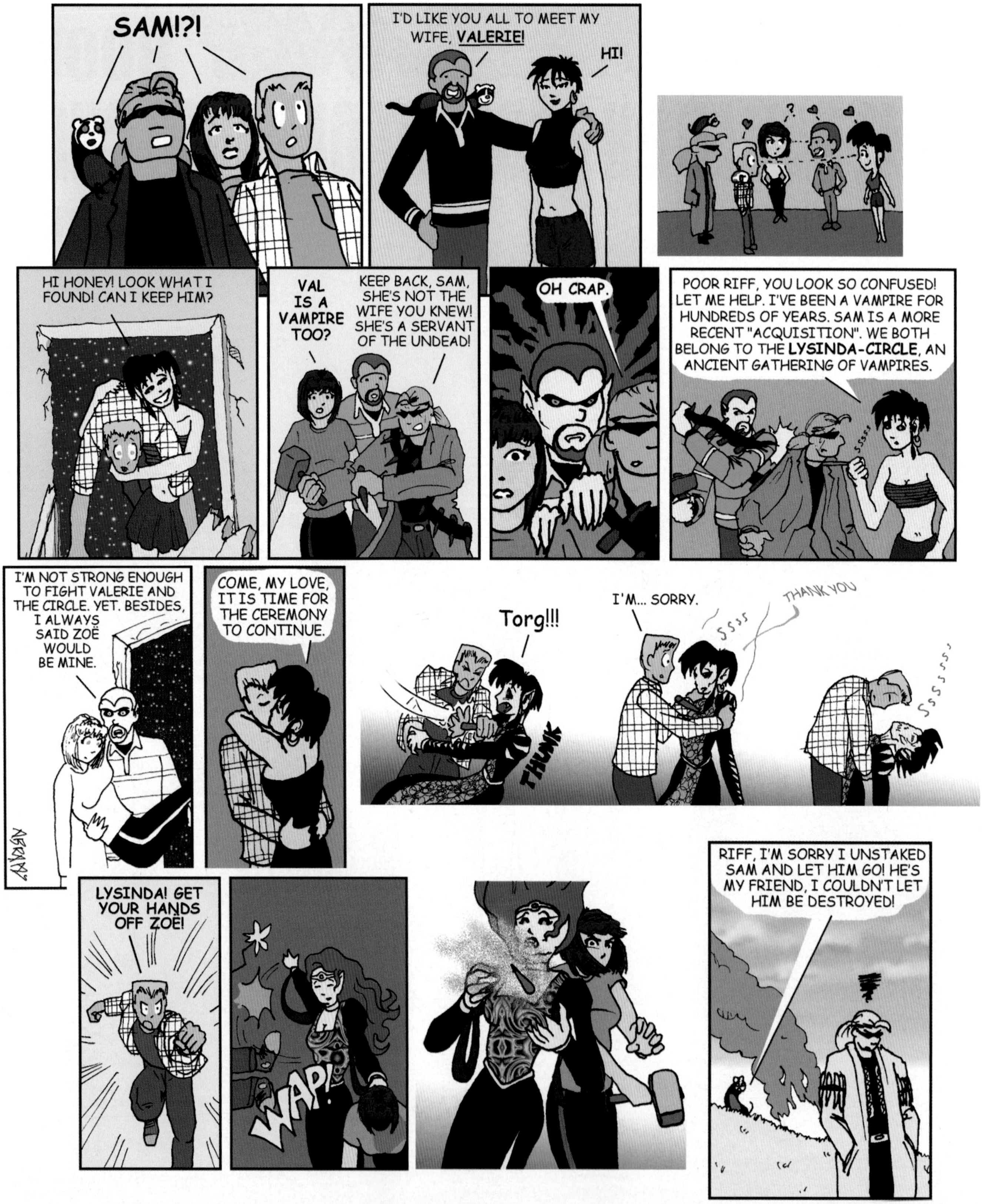

SAM!?!
I'D LIKE YOU ALL TO MEET MY WIFE, VALERIE!
HI!
HI HONEY! LOOK WHAT I FOUND! CAN I KEEP HIM?
VAL IS A VAMPIRE TOO?
KEEP BACK, SAM, SHE'S NOT THE WIFE YOU KNEW! SHE'S A SERVANT OF THE UNDEAD!
OH CRAP.
POOR RIFF, YOU LOOK SO CONFUSED! LET ME HELP. I'VE BEEN A VAMPIRE FOR HUNDREDS OF YEARS. SAM IS A MORE RECENT "ACQUISITION". WE BOTH BELONG TO THE LYSINDA-CIRCLE, AN ANCIENT GATHERING OF VAMPIRES.
I'M NOT STRONG ENOUGH TO FIGHT VALERIE AND THE CIRCLE. YET. BESIDES, I ALWAYS SAID ZOË WOULD BE MINE.
COME, MY LOVE, IT IS TIME FOR THE CEREMONY TO CONTINUE.
Torg!!!
THUNK
I'M... SORRY.
THANK YOU
LYSINDA! GET YOUR HANDS OFF ZOË!
WAP!
RIFF, I'M SORRY I UNSTAKED SAM AND LET HIM GO! HE'S MY FRIEND, I COULDN'T LET HIM BE DESTROYED!

PREVIOUSLY ON SLUGGY FREELANCE

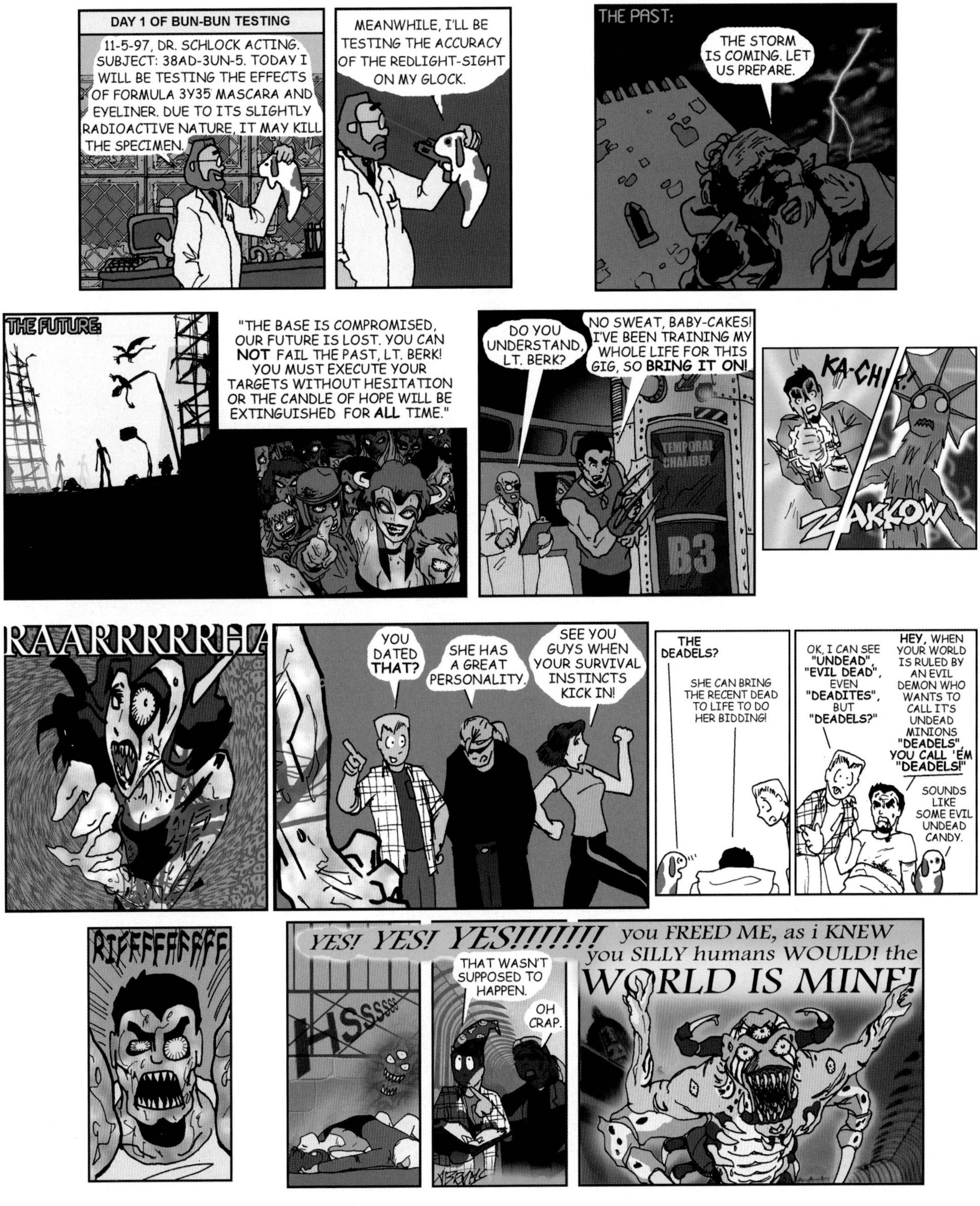

DAY 1 OF BUN-BUN TESTING
11-5-97, DR. SCHLOCK ACTING. SUBJECT: 38AD-3UN-5. TODAY I WILL BE TESTING THE EFFECTS OF FORMULA 3Y35 MASCARA AND EYELINER. DUE TO ITS SLIGHTLY RADIOACTIVE NATURE, IT MAY KILL THE SPECIMEN.
MEANWHILE, I'LL BE TESTING THE ACCURACY OF THE REDLIGHT-SIGHT ON MY GLOCK.
THE PAST:
THE STORM IS COMING. LET US PREPARE.
THE FUTURE:
"THE BASE IS COMPROMISED, OUR FUTURE IS LOST. YOU CAN NOT FAIL THE PAST, LT. BERK! YOU MUST EXECUTE YOUR TARGETS WITHOUT HESITATION OR THE CANDLE OF HOPE WILL BE EXTINGUISHED FOR ALL TIME."
DO YOU UNDERSTAND, LT. BERK?
NO SWEAT, BABY-CAKES! I'VE BEEN TRAINING MY WHOLE LIFE FOR THIS GIG, SO BRING IT ON!
TEMPORAL CHAMBER
B3
KA-CHIK!
ZAKKOW
RAARRRRRRHA
YOU DATED THAT?
SHE HAS A GREAT PERSONALITY.
SEE YOU GUYS WHEN YOUR SURVIVAL INSTINCTS KICK IN!
THE DEADELS?
SHE CAN BRING THE RECENT DEAD TO LIFE TO DO HER BIDDING!
OK, I CAN SEE "UNDEAD", "EVIL DEAD", EVEN "DEADITES", BUT "DEADELS?"
HEY, WHEN YOUR WORLD IS RULED BY AN EVIL DEMON WHO WANTS TO CALL IT'S UNDEAD MINIONS "DEADELS", YOU CALL 'EM "DEADELS!"
SOUNDS LIKE SOME EVIL UNDEAD CANDY.
RIFFFFFFFFF
YES! YES! YES!!!!!!!! you FREED ME, as i KNEW you SILLY humans WOULD! the WORLD IS MINE!
HSSSSSSS
THAT WASN'T SUPPOSED TO HAPPEN.
OH CRAP.

PREVIOUSLY ON SLUGGY FREELANCE

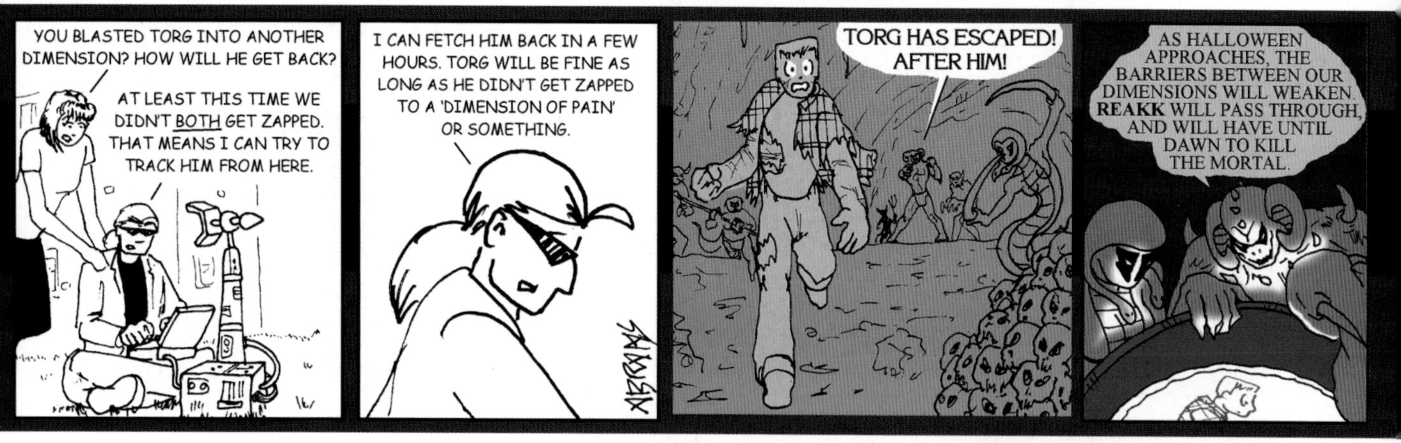

YOU BLASTED TORG INTO ANOTHER DIMENSION? HOW WILL HE GET BACK?
AT LEAST THIS TIME WE DIDN'T BOTH GET ZAPPED. THAT MEANS I CAN TRY TO TRACK HIM FROM HERE.
I CAN FETCH HIM BACK IN A FEW HOURS. TORG WILL BE FINE AS LONG AS HE DIDN'T GET ZAPPED TO A 'DIMENSION OF PAIN' OR SOMETHING.
TORG HAS ESCAPED! AFTER HIM!
AS HALLOWEEN APPROACHES, THE BARRIERS BETWEEN OUR DIMENSIONS WILL WEAKEN. REAKK WILL PASS THROUGH, AND WILL HAVE UNTIL DAWN TO KILL THE MORTAL.

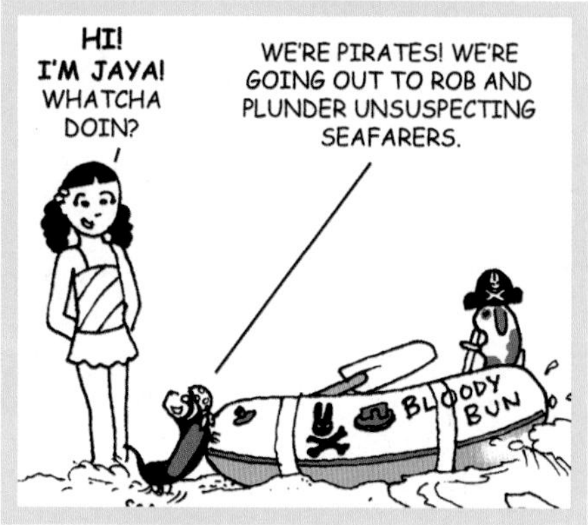

HI! I'M JAYA! WHATCHA DOIN?
WE'RE PIRATES! WE'RE GOING OUT TO ROB AND PLUNDER UNSUSPECTING SEAFARERS.
BLOODY BUN

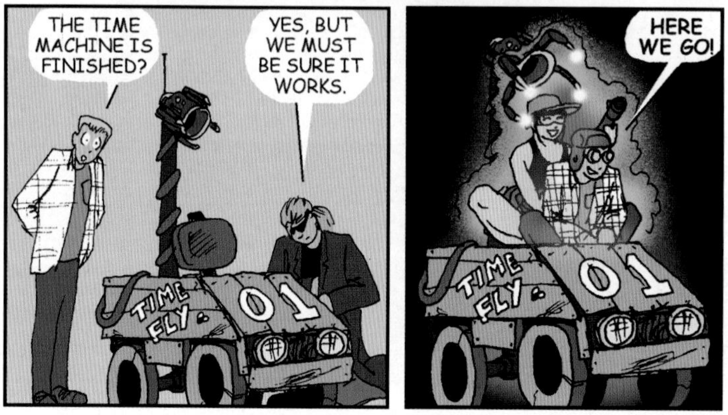

THE TIME MACHINE IS FINISHED?
YES, BUT WE MUST BE SURE IT WORKS.
TIME FLY 01
HERE WE GO!
TIME FLY 01

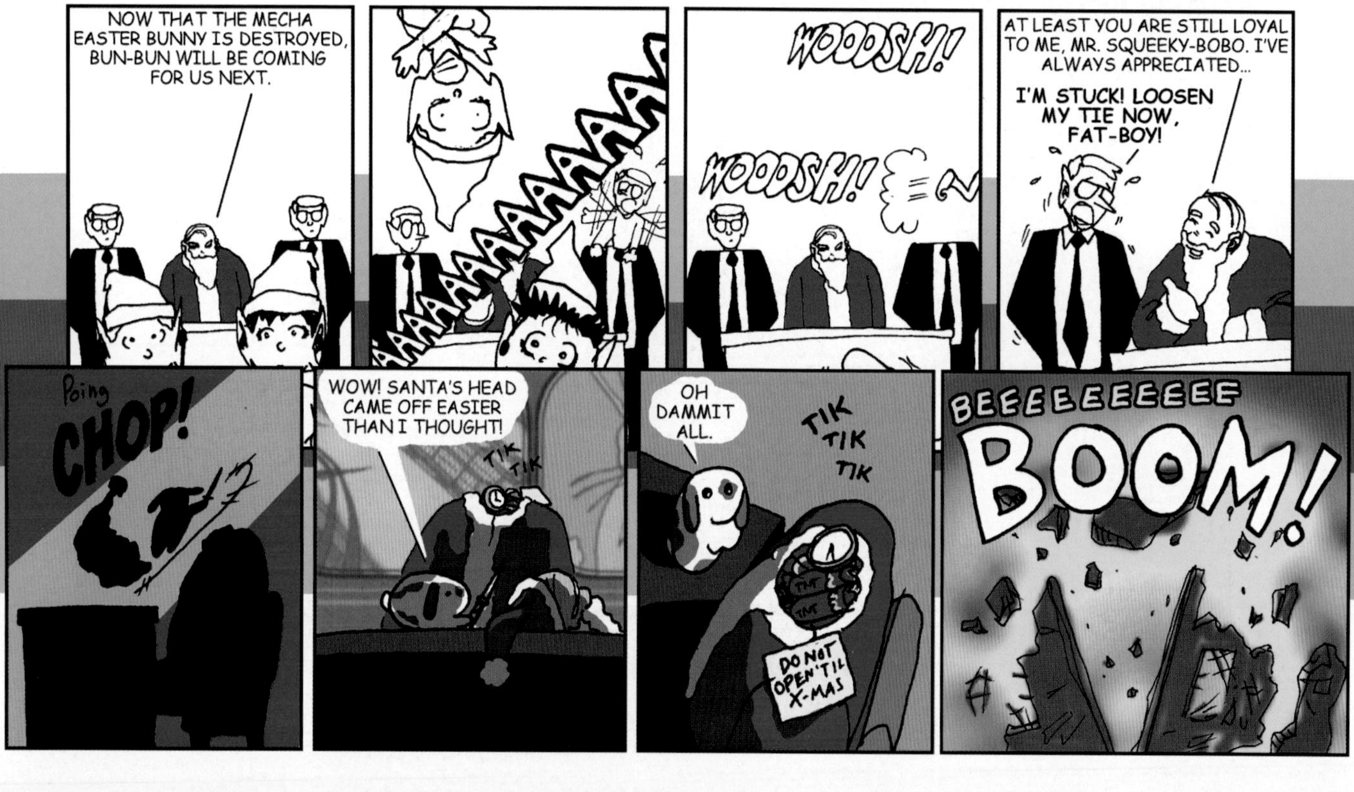

NOW THAT THE MECHA EASTER BUNNY IS DESTROYED, BUN-BUN WILL BE COMING FOR US NEXT.
WOOOSH!
WOOOSH!
AT LEAST YOU ARE STILL LOYAL TO ME, MR. SQUEEKY-BOBO. I'VE ALWAYS APPRECIATED...
I'M STUCK! LOOSEN MY TIE NOW, FAT-BOY!
Poing
CHOP!
WOW! SANTA'S HEAD CAME OFF EASIER THAN I THOUGHT!
TIK TIK
OH DAMMIT ALL.
TIK TIK TIK
DO NOT OPEN 'TIL X-MAS
BEEEEEEEEEEE
BOOM!

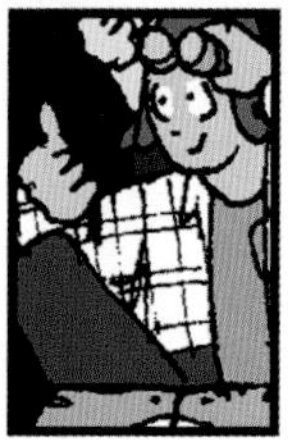

NAME: TORG
DESC.: FREELANCE WEB DESIGNER.

SITUATION: TEST DROVE RIFF'S TIME MACHINE TO THE **YEAR 2000.** THE TIME MACHINE WAS NOT **"Y2K COMPATIBLE".**
CURRENT CONDITION:
TRAPPED IN THE PAST.
SCREWED!

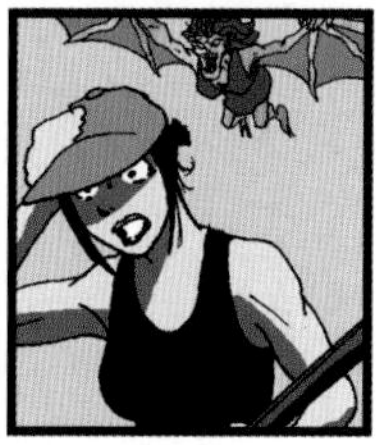

NAME: ZOË
DESC.: COED, COMMUNICATIONS MAJOR.

SITUATION: TEST DROVE RIFF'S TIME MACHINE TO THE **YEAR 2000.** THE TIME MACHINE WAS NOT **"Y2K COMPATIBLE".**
CURRENT CONDITION:
TRAPPED IN THE PAST.
SCREWED!

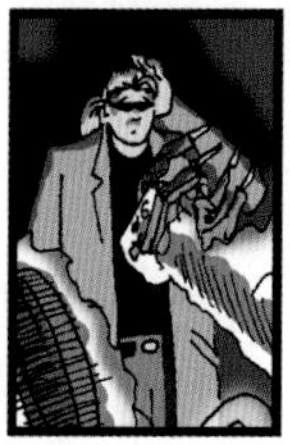

NAME: RIFF
DESC.: FREELANCE BUM, INVENTOR.

SITUATION: ACCIDENTALLY TRAPPED HIS FRIENDS SOMEWHERE IN TIME, NO IDEA HOW TO BRING THEM BACK.
CURRENT CONDITION:
ALL BUMMED OUT.

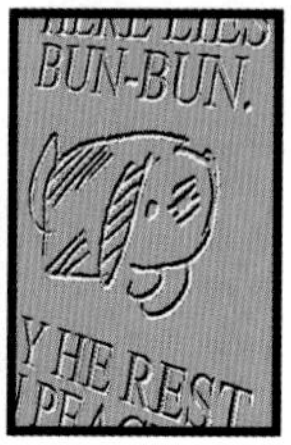
BUN-BUN.

NAME: BUN-BUN
DESC.: OFFICIAL CUTE TALKING ANIMAL.

SITUATION: BLOWN UP WHILE TRYING TO KILL SANTA CLAUS.
CURRENT CONDITION:
UNKNOWN, PRESUMED DEAD.

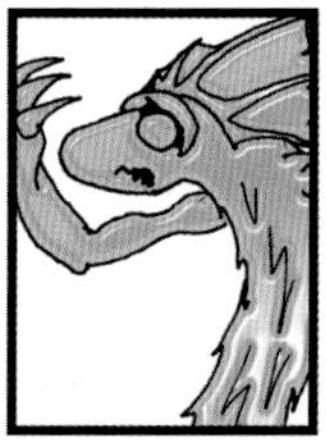

NAME: AYLEE
DESC.: ALIEN FROM ANOTHER DIMENSION/ SECRETARY

SITUATION: FROZEN IN TIME AND SOLD AS A STATUE.
CURRENT CONDITION:
UNKNOWN.

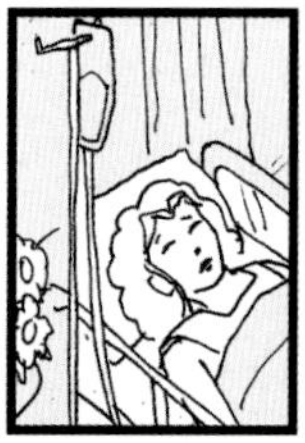

NAME: GWYNN
DESC.: FRIEND OF ZOË, PREVIOUS RELATIONSHIP WITH RIFF.

SITUATION: POSSESSED BY THE DEMON K'Z'K. HER SOUL WAS TAKEN WHEN THE DEMON WAS EXORCISED AND SENT TO THE PAST.
CURRENT CONDITION:
SOULLESS VEGETABLE.
COMATOSE.

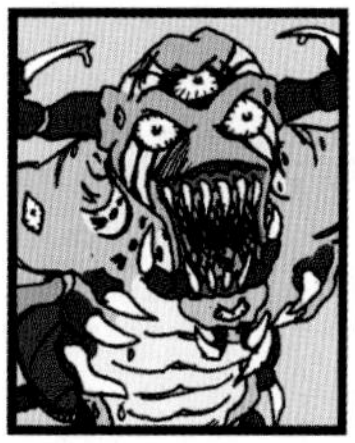

NAME: K'Z'K
(KIZKE)
DESC.: DEMON. "THE SOUL COLLECTOR".

SITUATION: UNLEASHED ON THE EARTH BUT BLASTED INTO THE PAST BY TORG AND RIFF. WOULD HAVE CONQUERED THE FUTURE, MAY STILL CONQUER THE PAST.
CURRENT CONDITION:
F R E E .

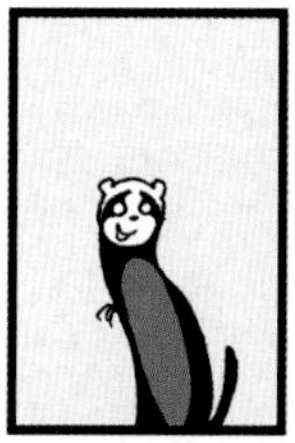

NAME: KIKI
DESC.: RIFF'S PET FERRET. EASILY DISTRAC... OOOOH! WHAT'S THAT?

SITUATION: CURRENTLY POINGING AROUND RIFF'S LAB AND...***OOOOH! WHAT'S THIS?***
CURRENT CONDITION:
OOOOOH!

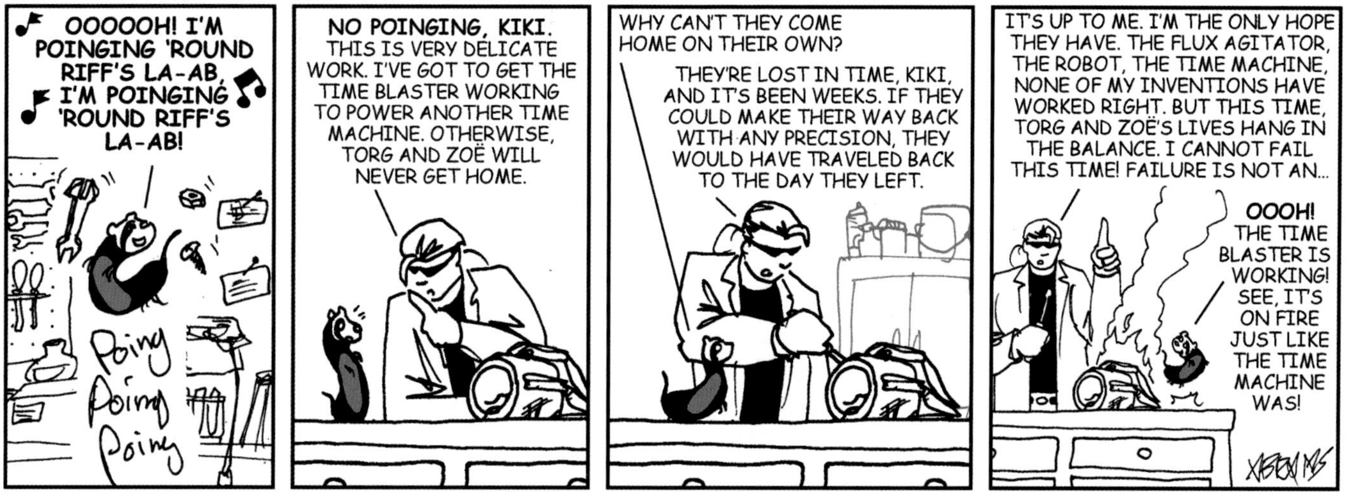
OOOOOH! I'M POINGING 'ROUND RIFF'S LA-AB, I'M POINGING 'ROUND RIFF'S LA-AB!
Poing Poing Poing
NO POINGING, KIKI. THIS IS VERY DELICATE WORK. I'VE GOT TO GET THE TIME BLASTER WORKING TO POWER ANOTHER TIME MACHINE. OTHERWISE, TORG AND ZOË WILL NEVER GET HOME.
WHY CAN'T THEY COME HOME ON THEIR OWN?
THEY'RE LOST IN TIME, KIKI, AND IT'S BEEN WEEKS. IF THEY COULD MAKE THEIR WAY BACK WITH ANY PRECISION, THEY WOULD HAVE TRAVELED BACK TO THE DAY THEY LEFT.
IT'S UP TO ME. I'M THE ONLY HOPE THEY HAVE. THE FLUX AGITATOR, THE ROBOT, THE TIME MACHINE, NONE OF MY INVENTIONS HAVE WORKED RIGHT. BUT THIS TIME, TORG AND ZOË'S LIVES HANG IN THE BALANCE. I CANNOT FAIL THIS TIME! FAILURE IS NOT AN...
OOOH! THE TIME BLASTER IS WORKING! SEE, IT'S ON FIRE JUST LIKE THE TIME MACHINE WAS!

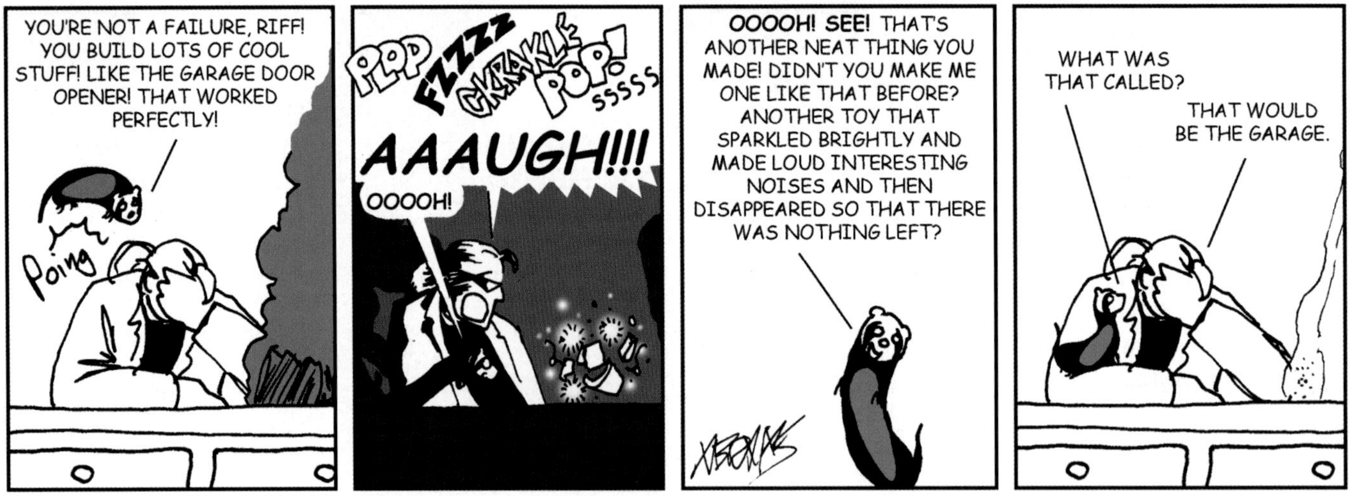
YOU'RE NOT A FAILURE, RIFF! YOU BUILD LOTS OF COOL STUFF! LIKE THE GARAGE DOOR OPENER! THAT WORKED PERFECTLY!
Poing
POP
FZZZZ
CKRAKLE POP!
SSSSS
AAAUGH!!!
OOOOH!
OOOOH! SEE! THAT'S ANOTHER NEAT THING YOU MADE! DIDN'T YOU MAKE ME ONE LIKE THAT BEFORE? ANOTHER TOY THAT SPARKLED BRIGHTLY AND MADE LOUD INTERESTING NOISES AND THEN DISAPPEARED SO THAT THERE WAS NOTHING LEFT?
WHAT WAS THAT CALLED?
THAT WOULD BE THE GARAGE.

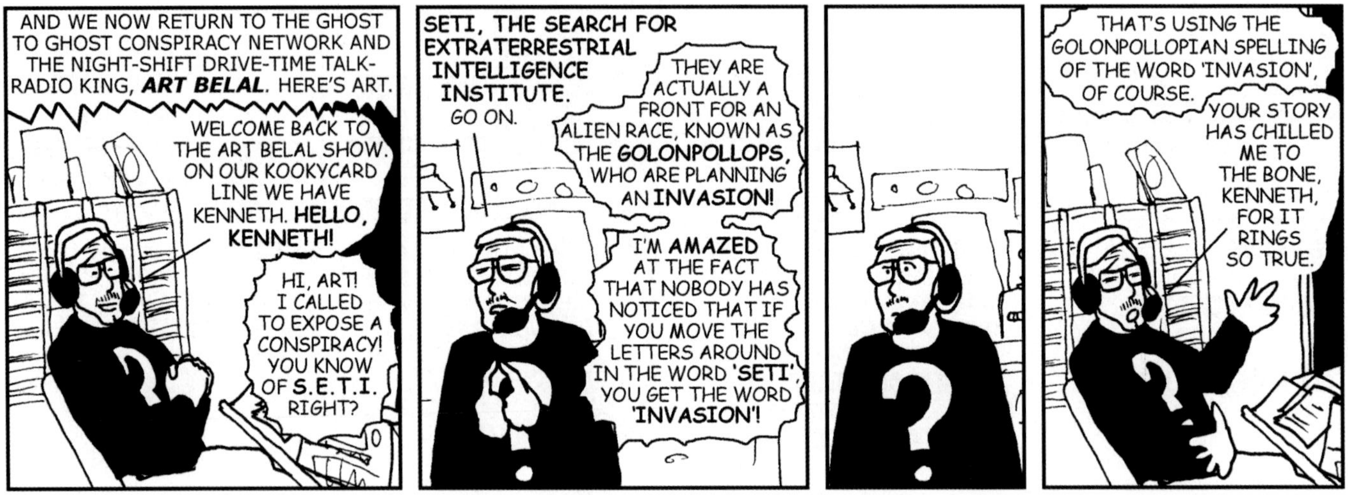
AND WE NOW RETURN TO THE GHOST TO GHOST CONSPIRACY NETWORK AND THE NIGHT-SHIFT DRIVE-TIME TALK-RADIO KING, ART BELAL. HERE'S ART.
WELCOME BACK TO THE ART BELAL SHOW. ON OUR KOOKYCARD LINE WE HAVE KENNETH. HELLO, KENNETH!
HI, ART! I CALLED TO EXPOSE A CONSPIRACY! YOU KNOW OF S.E.T.I. RIGHT?
SETI, THE SEARCH FOR EXTRATERRESTRIAL INTELLIGENCE INSTITUTE.
GO ON.
THEY ARE ACTUALLY A FRONT FOR AN ALIEN RACE, KNOWN AS THE GOLONPOLLOPS, WHO ARE PLANNING AN INVASION!
I'M AMAZED AT THE FACT THAT NOBODY HAS NOTICED THAT IF YOU MOVE THE LETTERS AROUND IN THE WORD 'SETI', YOU GET THE WORD 'INVASION'!
THAT'S USING THE GOLONPOLLOPIAN SPELLING OF THE WORD 'INVASION', OF COURSE.
YOUR STORY HAS CHILLED ME TO THE BONE, KENNETH, FOR IT RINGS SO TRUE.

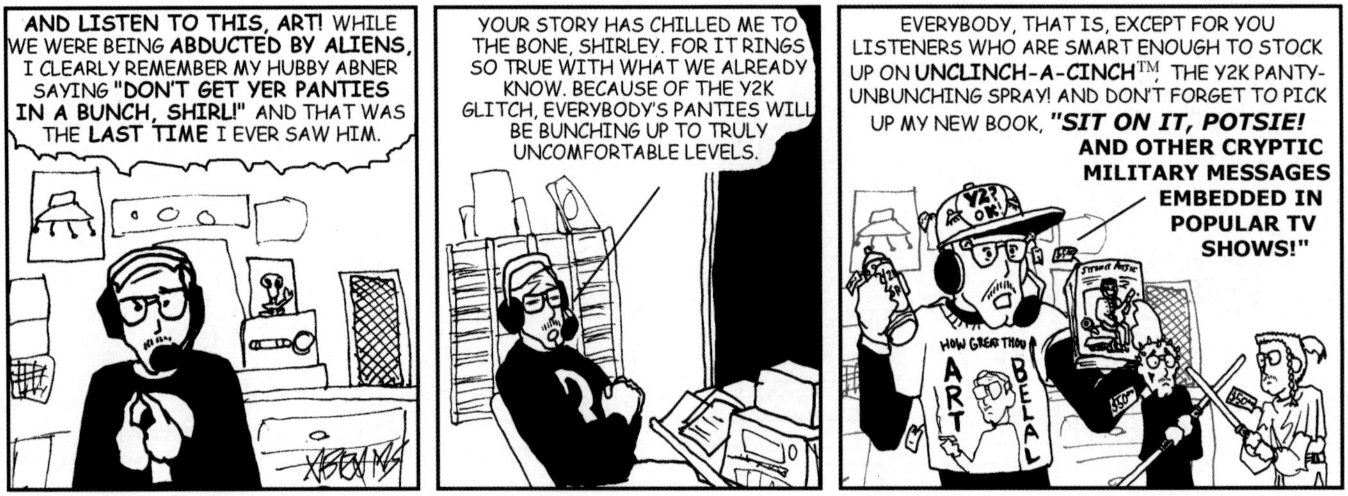
AND LISTEN TO THIS, ART! WHILE WE WERE BEING ABDUCTED BY ALIENS, I CLEARLY REMEMBER MY HUBBY ABNER SAYING "DON'T GET YER PANTIES IN A BUNCH, SHIRL!" AND THAT WAS THE LAST TIME I EVER SAW HIM.
YOUR STORY HAS CHILLED ME TO THE BONE, SHIRLEY. FOR IT RINGS SO TRUE WITH WHAT WE ALREADY KNOW. BECAUSE OF THE Y2K GLITCH, EVERYBODY'S PANTIES WILL BE BUNCHING UP TO TRULY UNCOMFORTABLE LEVELS.
EVERYBODY, THAT IS, EXCEPT FOR YOU LISTENERS WHO ARE SMART ENOUGH TO STOCK UP ON UNCLINCH-A-CINCH™, THE Y2K PANTY-UNBUNCHING SPRAY! AND DON'T FORGET TO PICK UP MY NEW BOOK, "SIT ON IT, POTSIE! AND OTHER CRYPTIC MILITARY MESSAGES EMBEDDED IN POPULAR TV SHOWS!"
Y2? OK!
HOW GREAT THOU ART BELAL

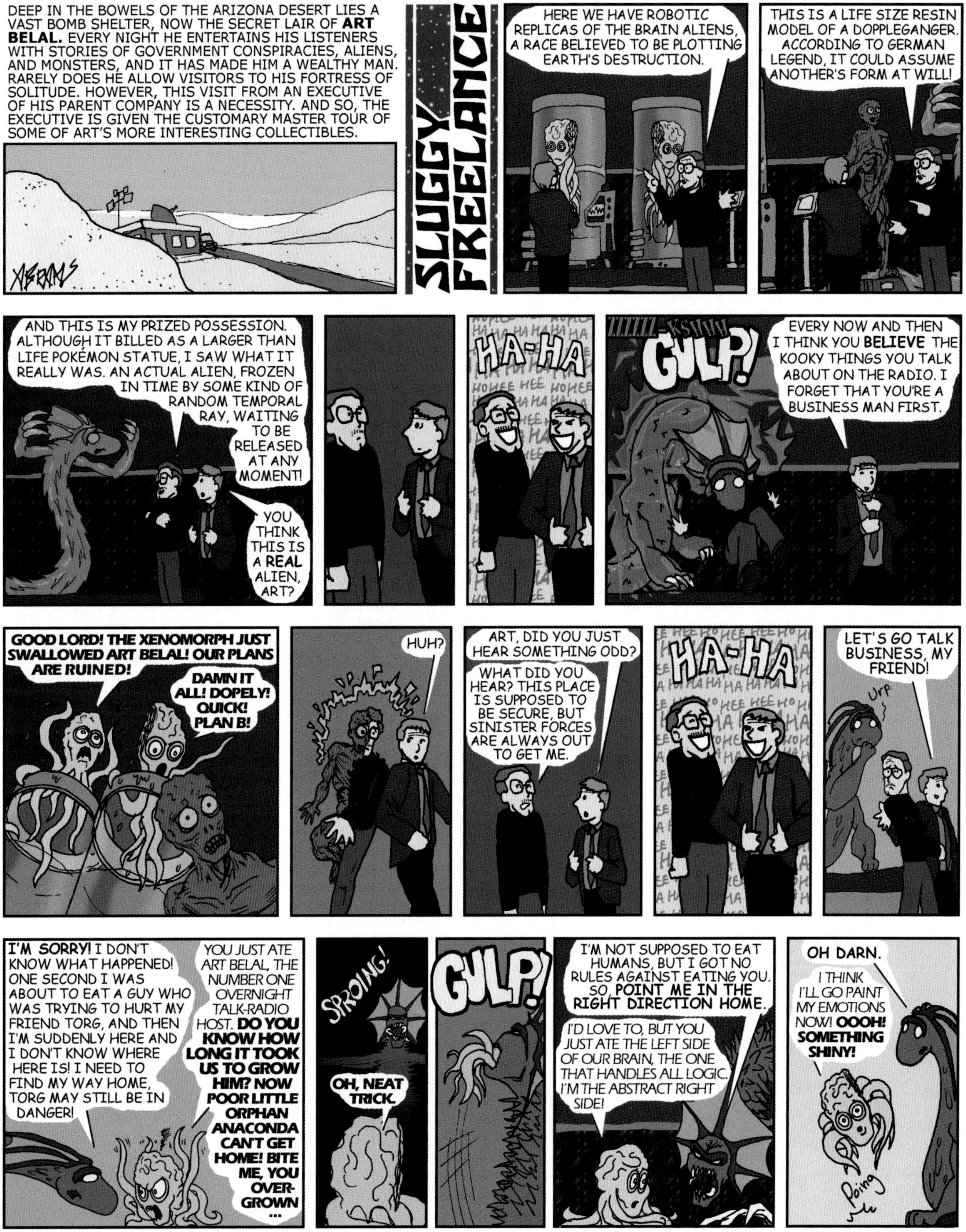
DEEP IN THE BOWELS OF THE ARIZONA DESERT LIES A VAST BOMB SHELTER, NOW THE SECRET LAIR OF **ART BELAL.** EVERY NIGHT HE ENTERTAINS HIS LISTENERS WITH STORIES OF GOVERNMENT CONSPIRACIES, ALIENS, AND MONSTERS, AND IT HAS MADE HIM A WEALTHY MAN. RARELY DOES HE ALLOW VISITORS TO HIS FORTRESS OF SOLITUDE. HOWEVER, THIS VISIT FROM AN EXECUTIVE OF HIS PARENT COMPANY IS A NECESSITY. AND SO, THE EXECUTIVE IS GIVEN THE CUSTOMARY MASTER TOUR OF SOME OF ART'S MORE INTERESTING COLLECTIBLES.
SLUGGY FREELANCE
HERE WE HAVE ROBOTIC REPLICAS OF THE BRAIN ALIENS, A RACE BELIEVED TO BE PLOTTING EARTH'S DESTRUCTION.
THIS IS A LIFE SIZE RESIN MODEL OF A DOPPLEGANGER. ACCORDING TO GERMAN LEGEND, IT COULD ASSUME ANOTHER'S FORM AT WILL!
AND THIS IS MY PRIZED POSSESSION. ALTHOUGH IT BILLED AS A LARGER THAN LIFE POKÉMON STATUE, I SAW WHAT IT REALLY WAS. AN ACTUAL ALIEN, FROZEN IN TIME BY SOME KIND OF RANDOM TEMPORAL RAY, WAITING TO BE RELEASED AT ANY MOMENT!
YOU THINK THIS IS A **REAL** ALIEN, ART?
HA-HA
GULP!
EVERY NOW AND THEN I THINK YOU **BELIEVE** THE KOOKY THINGS YOU TALK ABOUT ON THE RADIO. I FORGET THAT YOU'RE A BUSINESS MAN FIRST.
GOOD LORD! THE XENOMORPH JUST SWALLOWED ART BELAL! OUR PLANS ARE RUINED!
DAMN IT ALL! DOPELY! QUICK! PLAN B!
HUH?
ART, DID YOU JUST HEAR SOMETHING ODD?
WHAT DID YOU HEAR? THIS PLACE IS SUPPOSED TO BE SECURE, BUT SINISTER FORCES ARE ALWAYS OUT TO GET ME.
HA-HA
Urp.
LET'S GO TALK BUSINESS, MY FRIEND!
I'M SORRY! I DON'T KNOW WHAT HAPPENED! ONE SECOND I WAS ABOUT TO EAT A GUY WHO WAS TRYING TO HURT MY FRIEND TORG, AND THEN I'M SUDDENLY HERE AND I DON'T KNOW WHERE HERE IS! I NEED TO FIND MY WAY HOME, TORG MAY STILL BE IN DANGER!
YOU JUST ATE ART BELAL, THE NUMBER ONE OVERNIGHT TALK-RADIO HOST. **DO YOU KNOW HOW LONG IT TOOK US TO GROW HIM? NOW POOR LITTLE ORPHAN ANACONDA CAN'T GET HOME! BITE ME, YOU OVER-GROWN ...**
SPROING!
OH, NEAT TRICK.
GULP!
I'M NOT SUPPOSED TO EAT HUMANS, BUT I GOT NO RULES AGAINST EATING YOU. SO, **POINT ME IN THE RIGHT DIRECTION HOME.**
I'D LOVE TO, BUT YOU JUST ATE THE LEFT SIDE OF OUR BRAIN, THE ONE THAT HANDLES ALL LOGIC. I'M THE ABSTRACT RIGHT SIDE!
OH DARN.
I THINK I'LL GO PAINT MY EMOTIONS NOW! **OOOH! SOMETHING SHINY!**
Poing

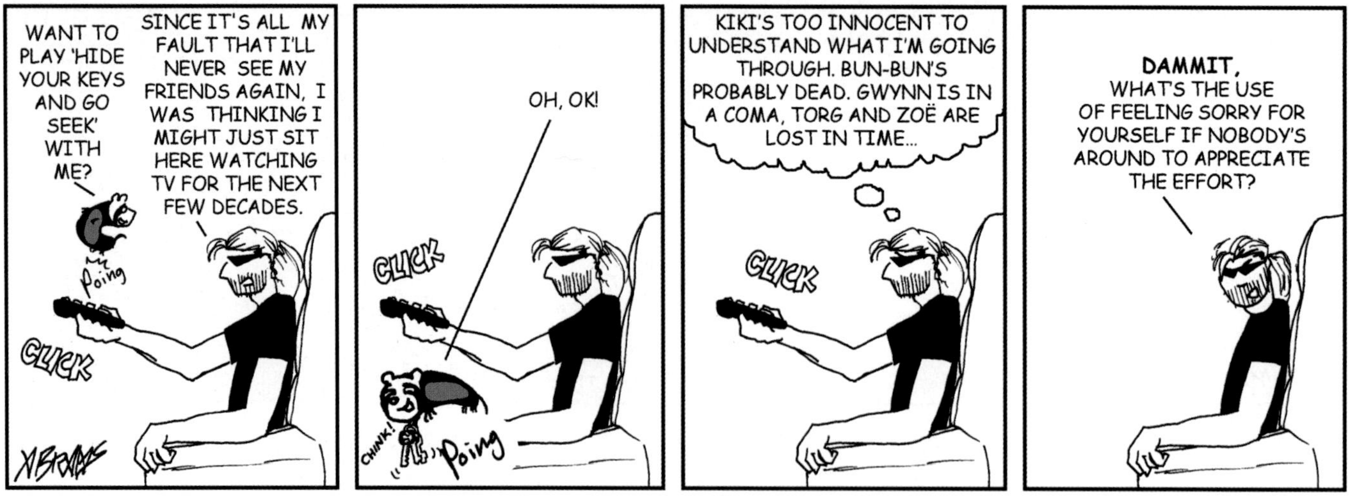
WANT TO PLAY 'HIDE YOUR KEYS AND GO SEEK' WITH ME?
SINCE IT'S ALL MY FAULT THAT I'LL NEVER SEE MY FRIENDS AGAIN, I WAS THINKING I MIGHT JUST SIT HERE WATCHING TV FOR THE NEXT FEW DECADES.
Poing
CLICK
CLICK
OH, OK!
CHINK!
Poing
KIKI'S TOO INNOCENT TO UNDERSTAND WHAT I'M GOING THROUGH. BUN-BUN'S PROBABLY DEAD. GWYNN IS IN A COMA, TORG AND ZOË ARE LOST IN TIME...
CLICK
DAMMIT, WHAT'S THE USE OF FEELING SORRY FOR YOURSELF IF NOBODY'S AROUND TO APPRECIATE THE EFFORT?

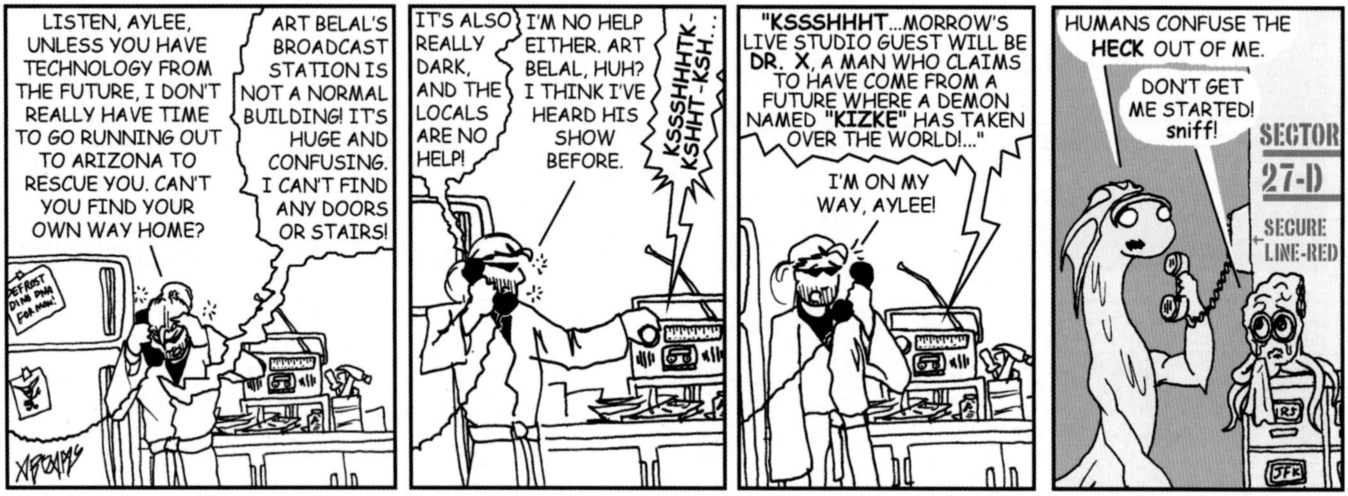
LISTEN, AYLEE, UNLESS YOU HAVE TECHNOLOGY FROM THE FUTURE, I DON'T REALLY HAVE TIME TO GO RUNNING OUT TO ARIZONA TO RESCUE YOU. CAN'T YOU FIND YOUR OWN WAY HOME?
ART BELAL'S BROADCAST STATION IS NOT A NORMAL BUILDING! IT'S HUGE AND CONFUSING. I CAN'T FIND ANY DOORS OR STAIRS!
DEFROST DINO DNA FOR MOM!
IT'S ALSO REALLY DARK, AND THE LOCALS ARE NO HELP!
I'M NO HELP EITHER. ART BELAL, HUH? I THINK I'VE HEARD HIS SHOW BEFORE.
KSSSHHHTK-KSHHT-KSH...
"KSSSHHHT...MORROW'S LIVE STUDIO GUEST WILL BE DR. X, A MAN WHO CLAIMS TO HAVE COME FROM A FUTURE WHERE A DEMON NAMED "KIZKE" HAS TAKEN OVER THE WORLD!..."
I'M ON MY WAY, AYLEE!
HUMANS CONFUSE THE HECK OUT OF ME.
DON'T GET ME STARTED! sniff!
SECTOR 27-D
SECURE LINE-RED
JFK

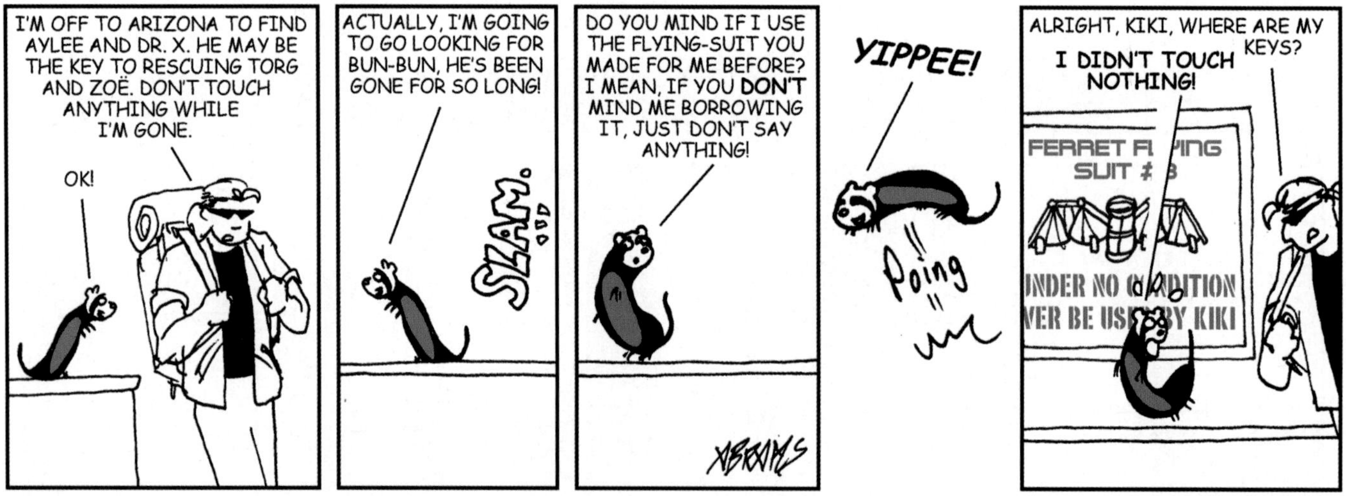
I'M OFF TO ARIZONA TO FIND AYLEE AND DR. X. HE MAY BE THE KEY TO RESCUING TORG AND ZOË. DON'T TOUCH ANYTHING WHILE I'M GONE.
OK!
ACTUALLY, I'M GOING TO GO LOOKING FOR BUN-BUN, HE'S BEEN GONE FOR SO LONG!
SLAM
DO YOU MIND IF I USE THE FLYING-SUIT YOU MADE FOR ME BEFORE? I MEAN, IF YOU DON'T MIND ME BORROWING IT, JUST DON'T SAY ANYTHING!
YIPPEE!
Poing
ALRIGHT, KIKI, WHERE ARE MY KEYS?
I DIDN'T TOUCH NOTHING!

WHILE RIFF HEADS OFF TO ARIZONA TO SAVE AYLEE, KIKI TAKES FLIGHT TO FIND BUN-BUN, WITH BUT ONE THOUGHT ON HER MIND: **"WEEEE! LOOP-DE-LOOP!** UM, I MEAN, ...**OOOOH!** THAT'S A PRETTY BIRD! DARN, I HAVE TO PEE! **SORRY, MA'AM!** UM...I HOPE BUN-BUN IS OK!"

MEANWHILE, IN THE DIMENSION OF PAIN...

LORD HORRIBUS, I BRING GREAT NEWS! WE HAVE A SOUL OF ONE RECENTLY SLAIN IN AN EXPLOSION, A SOUL FROM THE LAND OF TORG!

A TRANSDIMENSIONAL SOUL? HOW RARE!

HE SEEMED MYSTERIOUSLY DRAWN TO US! AND WHAT IS MORE IMPORTANT, HE HAS KNOWLEDGE OF TORG, THE ONE WHO ESCAPED US!

VERY WELL, BRING THE HUMAN TO ME.

BUT HE IS NOT A HUMAN, MY LORD!

DO YOU THINK HE CAN BE OF HELP TO US?

MOST DEFINITELY. I SHALL FETCH HIM AT ONCE!

LORD HORRIBUS! I PRESENT TO YOU THE ONE WHO HAS COME TO US, AND IS WILLING TO HELP US RECLAIM TORG IN EXCHANGE FOR REVENGE OF HIS MURDER. I PRESENT TO YOU...

SANTA'S ELF, MR. SQUEEKY-BOBO.

YOU KNOW OF TORG, LITTLE ELF?

I KNOW HIS PET RABBIT, BUN-BUN! SEE, BUN-BUN AND MY DEAR BOSS SANTA CLAUS WERE HAVING A LITTLE WAR. SANTA BLEW UP BUN-BUN, BUT DIDN'T SEEM TO MIND THE FACT THAT **I WAS STILL IN THE WAREHOUSE!** I'LL HELP YOU FIND TORG IF YOU HELP ME SEEK REVENGE ON SANTA!

I'D GIVE **ANYTHING** TO SEE THAT LARD ASS IN PAIN-PAIN-PAIN-PAIN-**PAIN!**

PATIENCE, ELF! IT MIGHT BE SOME TIME BEFORE OUR ATTACK. AND DO YOU NOT WANT REVENGE AGAINST THIS "BUN-BUN" AS WELL?

"BUN-BUN SURVIVED THE EXPLOSION? THAT'S IMPOSSIBLE! NOTHING COULD HAVE SURVIVED!"

MOM, CAN I PLAY WITH MR. FUZBUTT YET?

THE VET SAYS HE STILL NEEDS REST, MOLLY!

MOM, CAN I NOT PLAY WITH **MR. FUZBUTT** 'CAUSE HE HURT HIS HEAD?

HEAD TRAUMA, MOLLY. THE VET THOUGHT HE MIGHT HAVE SOME... PROBLEMS, BUT EVERYTHING'S OK, HE'S ACTING JUST LIKE A NORMAL BUNNY. HE'S BEEN THROUGH A LOT.

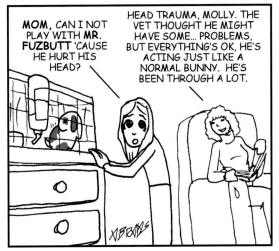

REMEMBER WHEN YOU FIRST FOUND HIM, MOLLY? ALL BROKEN AND BURNED, NO FUR AND ON THE VERGE OF DYING?

THANKS TO YOUR LOVE AND COMPASSION, MOLLY, MR. FUZBUTT WILL BE A HEALTHY HAPPY BUNNY!

HE'S BORING. CAN WE TRADE HIM IN FOR A FERRET?

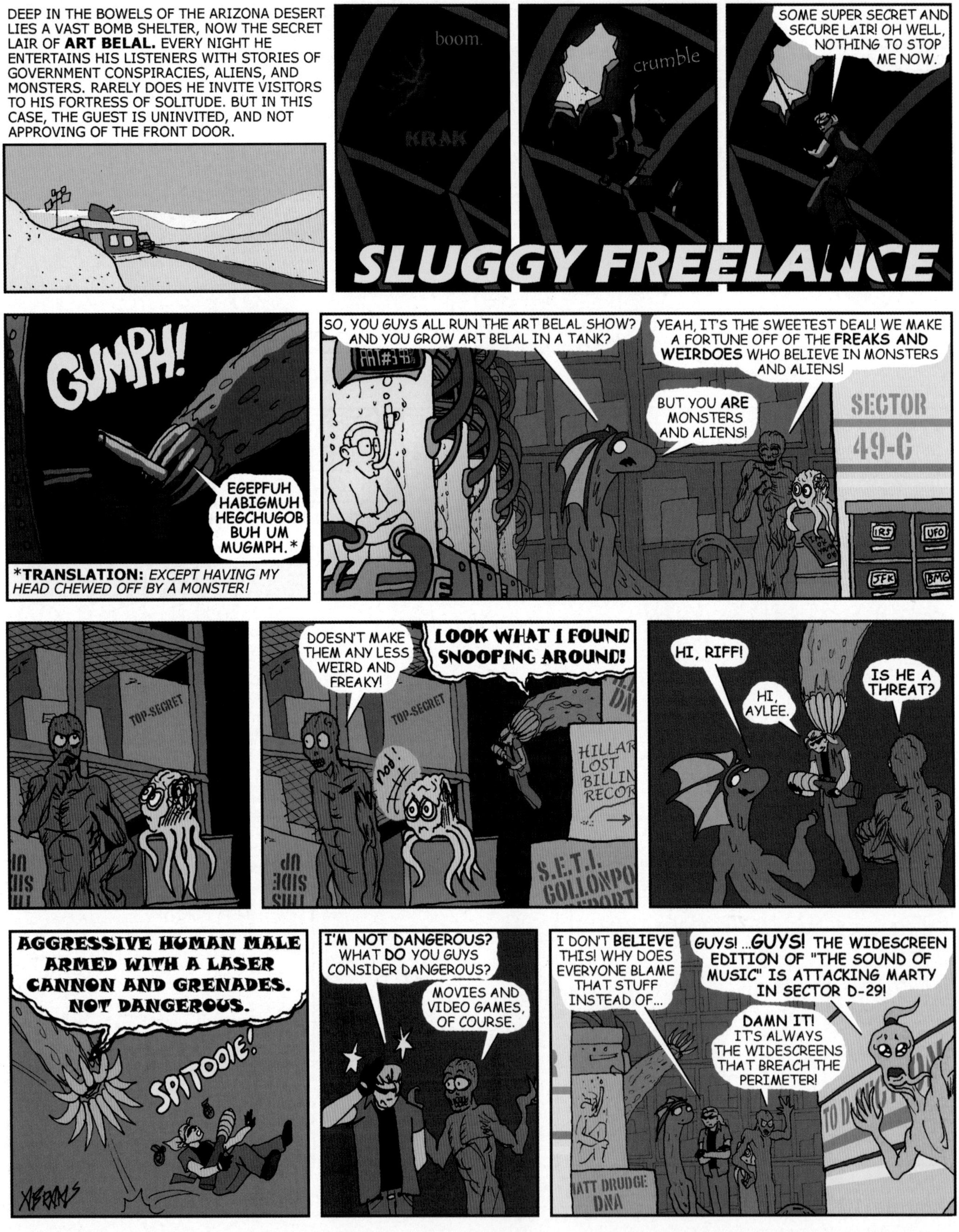
DEEP IN THE BOWELS OF THE ARIZONA DESERT LIES A VAST BOMB SHELTER, NOW THE SECRET LAIR OF ART BELAL. EVERY NIGHT HE ENTERTAINS HIS LISTENERS WITH STORIES OF GOVERNMENT CONSPIRACIES, ALIENS, AND MONSTERS. RARELY DOES HE INVITE VISITORS TO HIS FORTRESS OF SOLITUDE. BUT IN THIS CASE, THE GUEST IS UNINVITED, AND NOT APPROVING OF THE FRONT DOOR.
boom.
KRAK
crumble
SOME SUPER SECRET AND SECURE LAIR! OH WELL, NOTHING TO STOP ME NOW.
SLUGGY FREELANCE
GUMPH!
EGEPFUH HABIGMUH HEGCHUGOB BUH UM MUGMPH.*
*TRANSLATION: EXCEPT HAVING MY HEAD CHEWED OFF BY A MONSTER!
SO, YOU GUYS ALL RUN THE ART BELAL SHOW? AND YOU GROW ART BELAL IN A TANK?
YEAH, IT'S THE SWEETEST DEAL! WE MAKE A FORTUNE OFF OF THE FREAKS AND WEIRDOES WHO BELIEVE IN MONSTERS AND ALIENS!
BUT YOU ARE MONSTERS AND ALIENS!
SECTOR
49-C
IRS
UFO
JFK
BMG
TOP-SECRET
DOESN'T MAKE THEM ANY LESS WEIRD AND FREAKY!
LOOK WHAT I FOUND SNOOPING AROUND!
nod!
HI, RIFF!
HI, AYLEE.
IS HE A THREAT?
AGGRESSIVE HUMAN MALE ARMED WITH A LASER CANNON AND GRENADES. NOT DANGEROUS.
SPITOOIE!
I'M NOT DANGEROUS? WHAT DO YOU GUYS CONSIDER DANGEROUS?
MOVIES AND VIDEO GAMES, OF COURSE.
I DON'T BELIEVE THIS! WHY DOES EVERYONE BLAME THAT STUFF INSTEAD OF...
GUYS! ...GUYS! THE WIDESCREEN EDITION OF "THE SOUND OF MUSIC" IS ATTACKING MARTY IN SECTOR D-29!
DAMN IT! IT'S ALWAYS THE WIDESCREENS THAT BREACH THE PERIMETER!
DNA

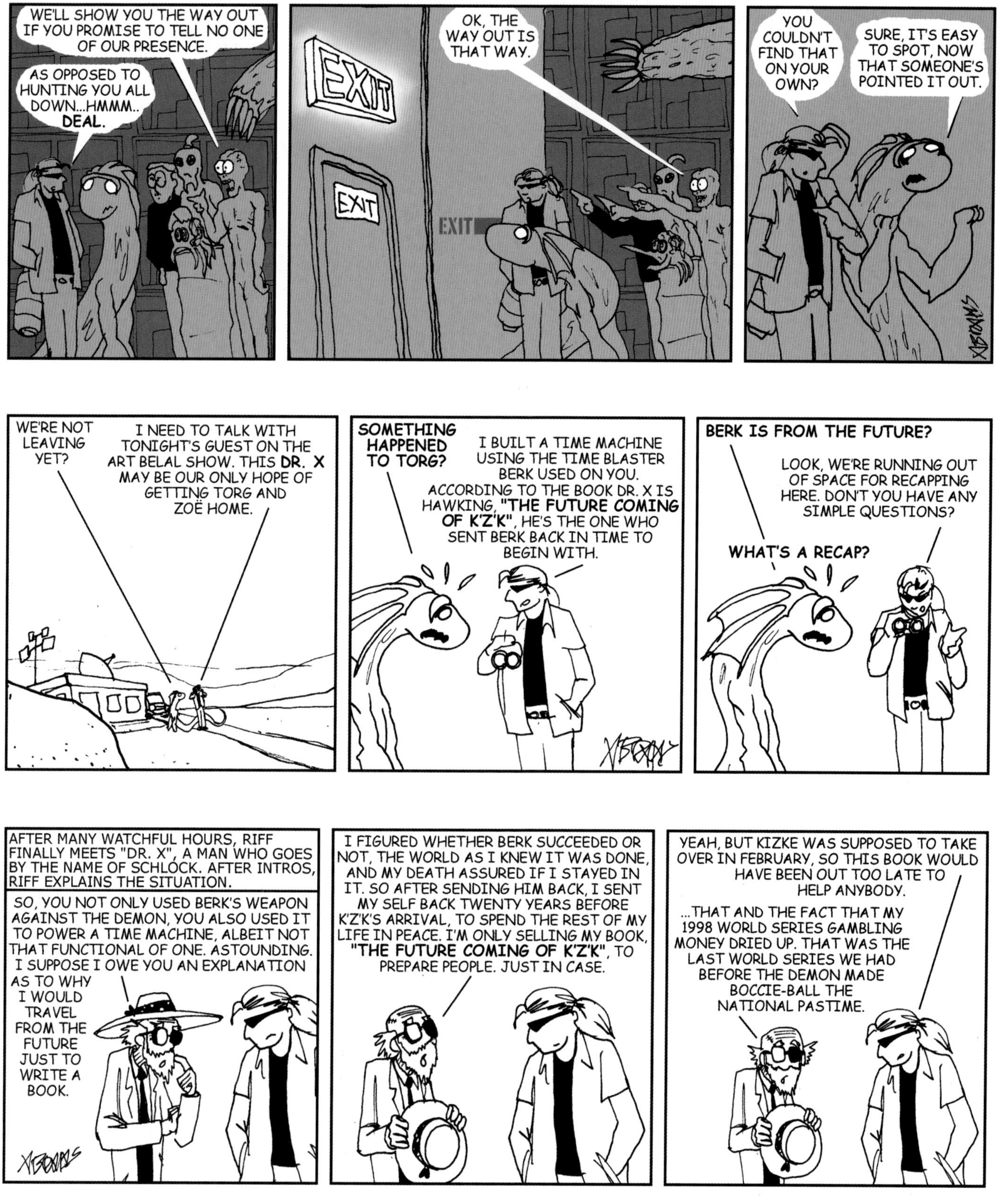
WE'LL SHOW YOU THE WAY OUT IF YOU PROMISE TO TELL NO ONE OF OUR PRESENCE.
AS OPPOSED TO HUNTING YOU ALL DOWN...HMMM.. DEAL.
EXIT
EXIT
EXIT
OK, THE WAY OUT IS THAT WAY.
YOU COULDN'T FIND THAT ON YOUR OWN?
SURE, IT'S EASY TO SPOT, NOW THAT SOMEONE'S POINTED IT OUT.
WE'RE NOT LEAVING YET?
I NEED TO TALK WITH TONIGHT'S GUEST ON THE ART BELAL SHOW. THIS DR. X MAY BE OUR ONLY HOPE OF GETTING TORG AND ZOË HOME.
SOMETHING HAPPENED TO TORG?
I BUILT A TIME MACHINE USING THE TIME BLASTER BERK USED ON YOU. ACCORDING TO THE BOOK DR. X IS HAWKING, "THE FUTURE COMING OF K'Z'K", HE'S THE ONE WHO SENT BERK BACK IN TIME TO BEGIN WITH.
BERK IS FROM THE FUTURE?
LOOK, WE'RE RUNNING OUT OF SPACE FOR RECAPPING HERE. DON'T YOU HAVE ANY SIMPLE QUESTIONS?
WHAT'S A RECAP?
AFTER MANY WATCHFUL HOURS, RIFF FINALLY MEETS "DR. X", A MAN WHO GOES BY THE NAME OF SCHLOCK. AFTER INTROS, RIFF EXPLAINS THE SITUATION.
SO, YOU NOT ONLY USED BERK'S WEAPON AGAINST THE DEMON, YOU ALSO USED IT TO POWER A TIME MACHINE, ALBEIT NOT THAT FUNCTIONAL OF ONE. ASTOUNDING. I SUPPOSE I OWE YOU AN EXPLANATION AS TO WHY I WOULD TRAVEL FROM THE FUTURE JUST TO WRITE A BOOK.
I FIGURED WHETHER BERK SUCCEEDED OR NOT, THE WORLD AS I KNEW IT WAS DONE, AND MY DEATH ASSURED IF I STAYED IN IT. SO AFTER SENDING HIM BACK, I SENT MY SELF BACK TWENTY YEARS BEFORE K'Z'K'S ARRIVAL, TO SPEND THE REST OF MY LIFE IN PEACE. I'M ONLY SELLING MY BOOK, "THE FUTURE COMING OF K'Z'K", TO PREPARE PEOPLE. JUST IN CASE.
YEAH, BUT KIZKE WAS SUPPOSED TO TAKE OVER IN FEBRUARY, SO THIS BOOK WOULD HAVE BEEN OUT TOO LATE TO HELP ANYBODY.
...THAT AND THE FACT THAT MY 1998 WORLD SERIES GAMBLING MONEY DRIED UP. THAT WAS THE LAST WORLD SERIES WE HAD BEFORE THE DEMON MADE BOCCIE-BALL THE NATIONAL PASTIME.

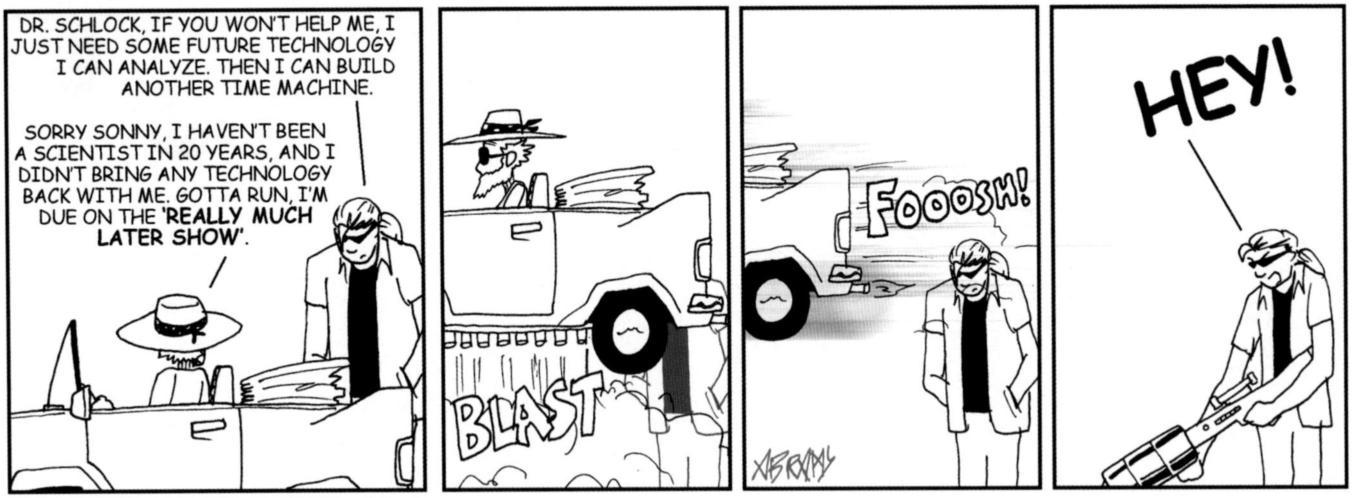

DR. SCHLOCK, IF YOU WON'T HELP ME, I JUST NEED SOME FUTURE TECHNOLOGY I CAN ANALYZE. THEN I CAN BUILD ANOTHER TIME MACHINE.
SORRY SONNY, I HAVEN'T BEEN A SCIENTIST IN 20 YEARS, AND I DIDN'T BRING ANY TECHNOLOGY BACK WITH ME. GOTTA RUN, I'M DUE ON THE **'REALLY MUCH LATER SHOW'**.
BLAST
FOOOSH!
HEY!

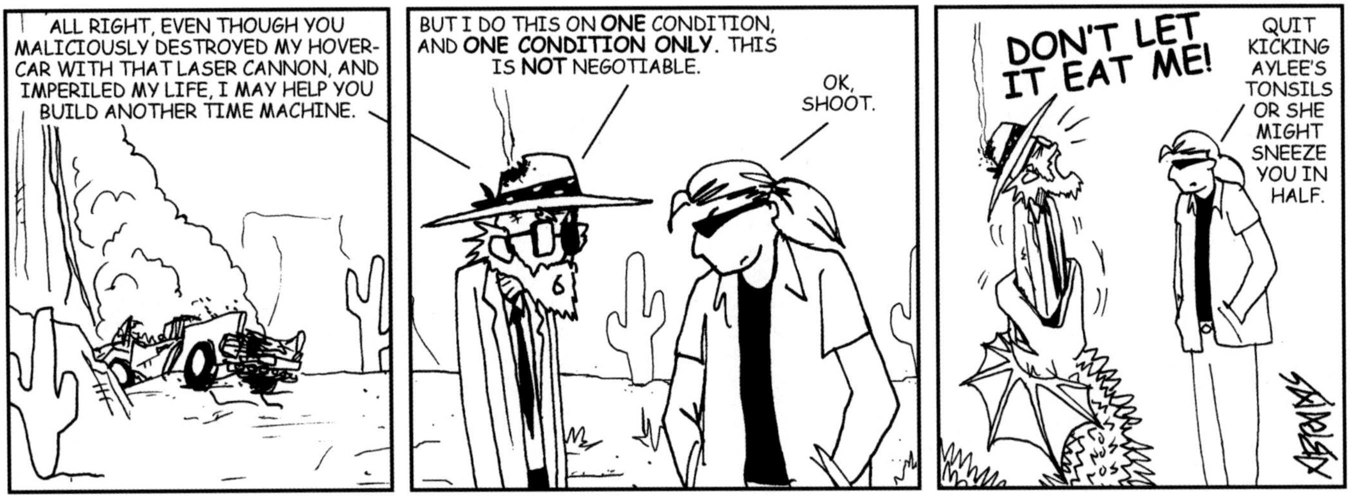

ALL RIGHT, EVEN THOUGH YOU MALICIOUSLY DESTROYED MY HOVER-CAR WITH THAT LASER CANNON, AND IMPERILED MY LIFE, I MAY HELP YOU BUILD ANOTHER TIME MACHINE.
BUT I DO THIS ON **ONE** CONDITION, AND **ONE CONDITION ONLY**. THIS IS **NOT** NEGOTIABLE.
OK, SHOOT.
DON'T LET IT EAT ME!
QUIT KICKING AYLEE'S TONSILS OR SHE MIGHT SNEEZE YOU IN HALF.

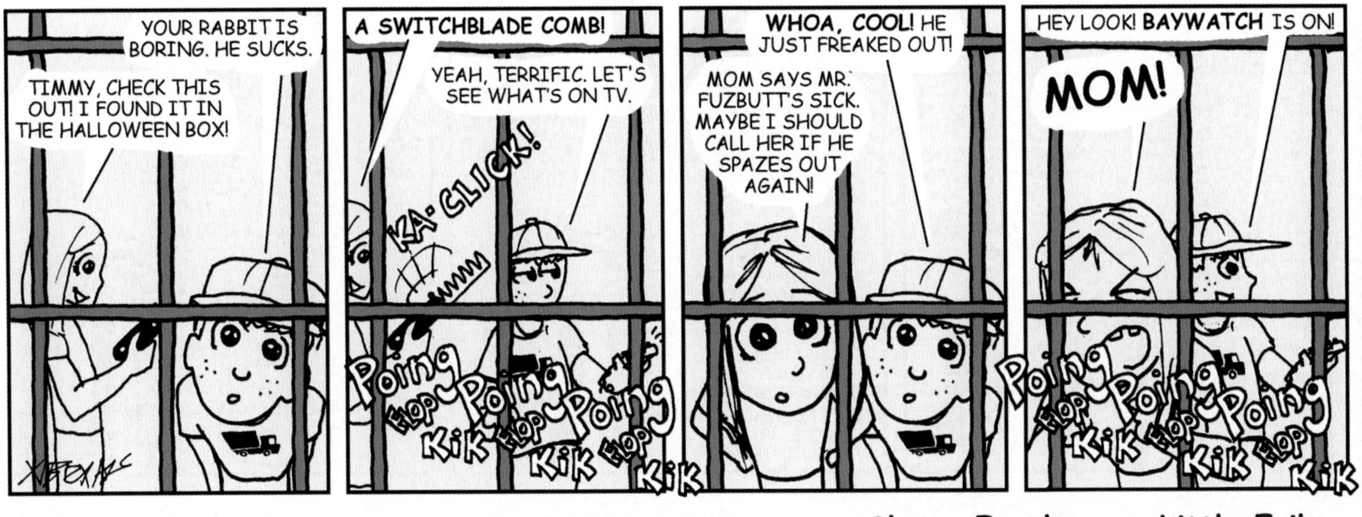

YOUR RABBIT IS BORING. HE SUCKS.
TIMMY, CHECK THIS OUT! I FOUND IT IN THE HALLOWEEN BOX!
A SWITCHBLADE COMB!
YEAH, TERRIFIC. LET'S SEE WHAT'S ON TV.
KA-CLICK!
Poing Flop Poing Flop Poing Kik Kik Flop Kik
WHOA, COOL! HE JUST FREAKED OUT!
MOM SAYS MR. FUZBUTT'S SICK. MAYBE I SHOULD CALL HER IF HE SPAZES OUT AGAIN!
HEY LOOK! **BAYWATCH** IS ON!
MOM!
Poing Flop Poing Flop Poing Kik Kik Flop Kik

SLUGGY FREELANCE

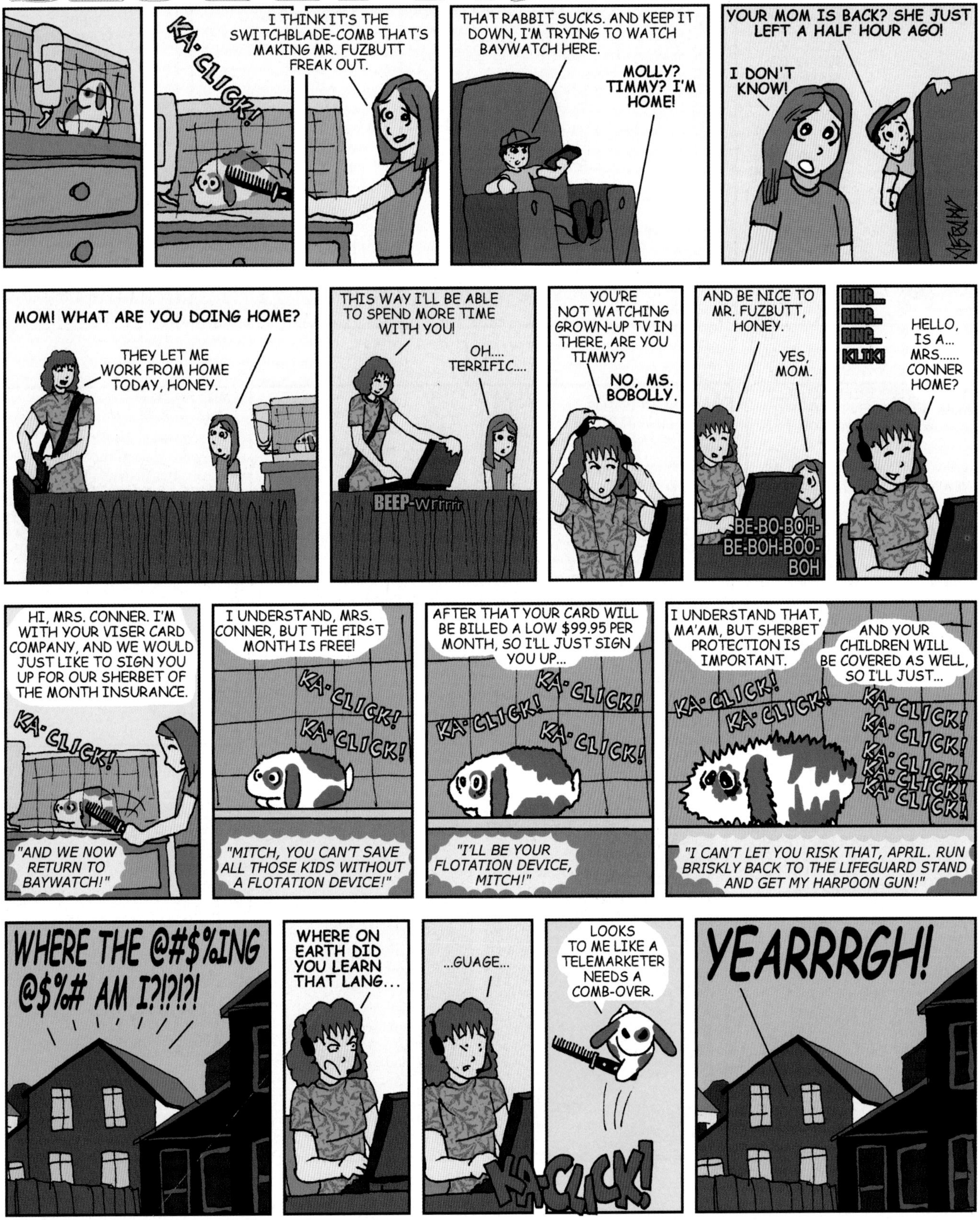
KA-CLICK!
I THINK IT'S THE SWITCHBLADE-COMB THAT'S MAKING MR. FUZBUTT FREAK OUT.
THAT RABBIT SUCKS. AND KEEP IT DOWN, I'M TRYING TO WATCH BAYWATCH HERE.
MOLLY? TIMMY? I'M HOME!
YOUR MOM IS BACK? SHE JUST LEFT A HALF HOUR AGO!
I DON'T KNOW!
MOM! WHAT ARE YOU DOING HOME?
THEY LET ME WORK FROM HOME TODAY, HONEY.
THIS WAY I'LL BE ABLE TO SPEND MORE TIME WITH YOU!
OH.... TERRIFIC....
BEEP-Wrrrrr
YOU'RE NOT WATCHING GROWN-UP TV IN THERE, ARE YOU TIMMY?
NO, MS. BOBOLLY.
AND BE NICE TO MR. FUZBUTT, HONEY.
YES, MOM.
BE-BO-BOH-BE-BOH-BOO-BOH
RING... RING... RING... KLIK!
HELLO, IS A... MRS...... CONNER HOME?
HI, MRS. CONNER. I'M WITH YOUR VISER CARD COMPANY, AND WE WOULD JUST LIKE TO SIGN YOU UP FOR OUR SHERBET OF THE MONTH INSURANCE.
KA-CLICK!
"AND WE NOW RETURN TO BAYWATCH!"
I UNDERSTAND, MRS. CONNER, BUT THE FIRST MONTH IS FREE!
KA-CLICK! KA-CLICK!
"MITCH, YOU CAN'T SAVE ALL THOSE KIDS WITHOUT A FLOTATION DEVICE!"
AFTER THAT YOUR CARD WILL BE BILLED A LOW $99.95 PER MONTH, SO I'LL JUST SIGN YOU UP...
KA-CLICK! KA-CLICK! KA-CLICK!
"I'LL BE YOUR FLOTATION DEVICE, MITCH!"
I UNDERSTAND THAT, MA'AM, BUT SHERBET PROTECTION IS IMPORTANT.
AND YOUR CHILDREN WILL BE COVERED AS WELL, SO I'LL JUST...
KA-CLICK! KA-CLICK! KA-CLICK! KA-CLICK! KA-CLICK! KA-CLICK! KA-CLICK!
"I CAN'T LET YOU RISK THAT, APRIL. RUN BRISKLY BACK TO THE LIFEGUARD STAND AND GET MY HARPOON GUN!"
WHERE THE @#$%ING @$%# AM I?!?!?!
WHERE ON EARTH DID YOU LEARN THAT LANG...
...GUAGE...
LOOKS TO ME LIKE A TELEMARKETER NEEDS A COMB-OVER.
KA-CLICK!
YEARRRGH!

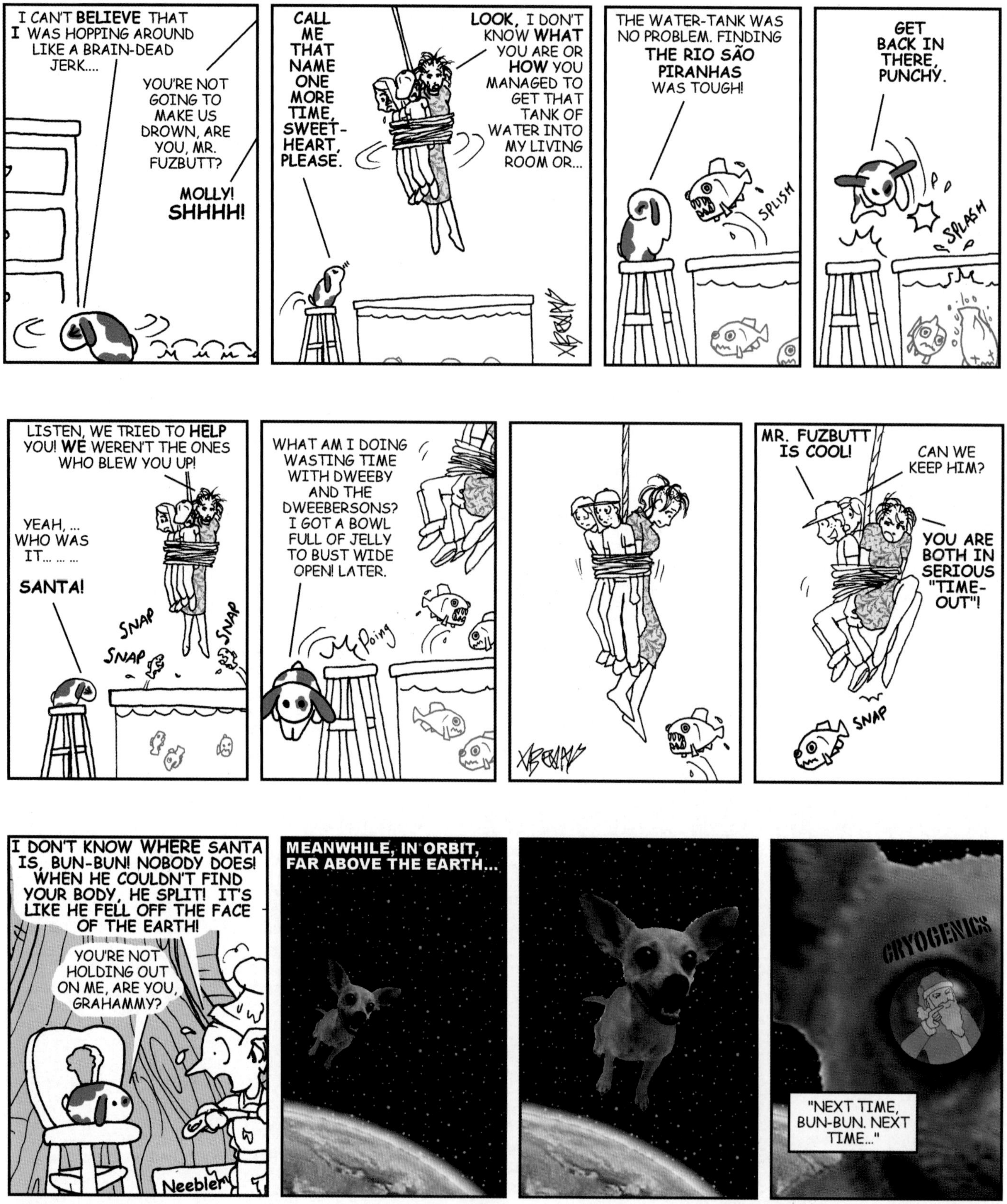
I CAN'T **BELIEVE** THAT **I** WAS HOPPING AROUND LIKE A BRAIN-DEAD JERK....
YOU'RE NOT GOING TO MAKE US DROWN, ARE YOU, MR. FUZBUTT?
MOLLY! SHHHH!
CALL ME THAT NAME ONE MORE TIME, SWEET-HEART, PLEASE.
LOOK, I DON'T KNOW WHAT YOU ARE OR HOW YOU MANAGED TO GET THAT TANK OF WATER INTO MY LIVING ROOM OR...
THE WATER-TANK WAS NO PROBLEM. FINDING THE RIO SÃO PIRANHAS WAS TOUGH!
SPLISH
GET BACK IN THERE, PUNCHY.
SPLASH
LISTEN, WE TRIED TO HELP YOU! WE WEREN'T THE ONES WHO BLEW YOU UP!
YEAH, ... WHO WAS IT... ... ...
SANTA!
SNAP
SNAP
SNAP
WHAT AM I DOING WASTING TIME WITH DWEEBY AND THE DWEEBERSONS? I GOT A BOWL FULL OF JELLY TO BUST WIDE OPEN! LATER.
Poing
MR. FUZBUTT IS COOL!
CAN WE KEEP HIM?
YOU ARE BOTH IN SERIOUS "TIME-OUT"!
SNAP
I DON'T KNOW WHERE SANTA IS, BUN-BUN! NOBODY DOES! WHEN HE COULDN'T FIND YOUR BODY, HE SPLIT! IT'S LIKE HE FELL OFF THE FACE OF THE EARTH!
YOU'RE NOT HOLDING OUT ON ME, ARE YOU, GRAHAMMY?
Neebler
MEANWHILE, IN ORBIT, FAR ABOVE THE EARTH...
CRYOGENICS
"NEXT TIME, BUN-BUN. NEXT TIME..."

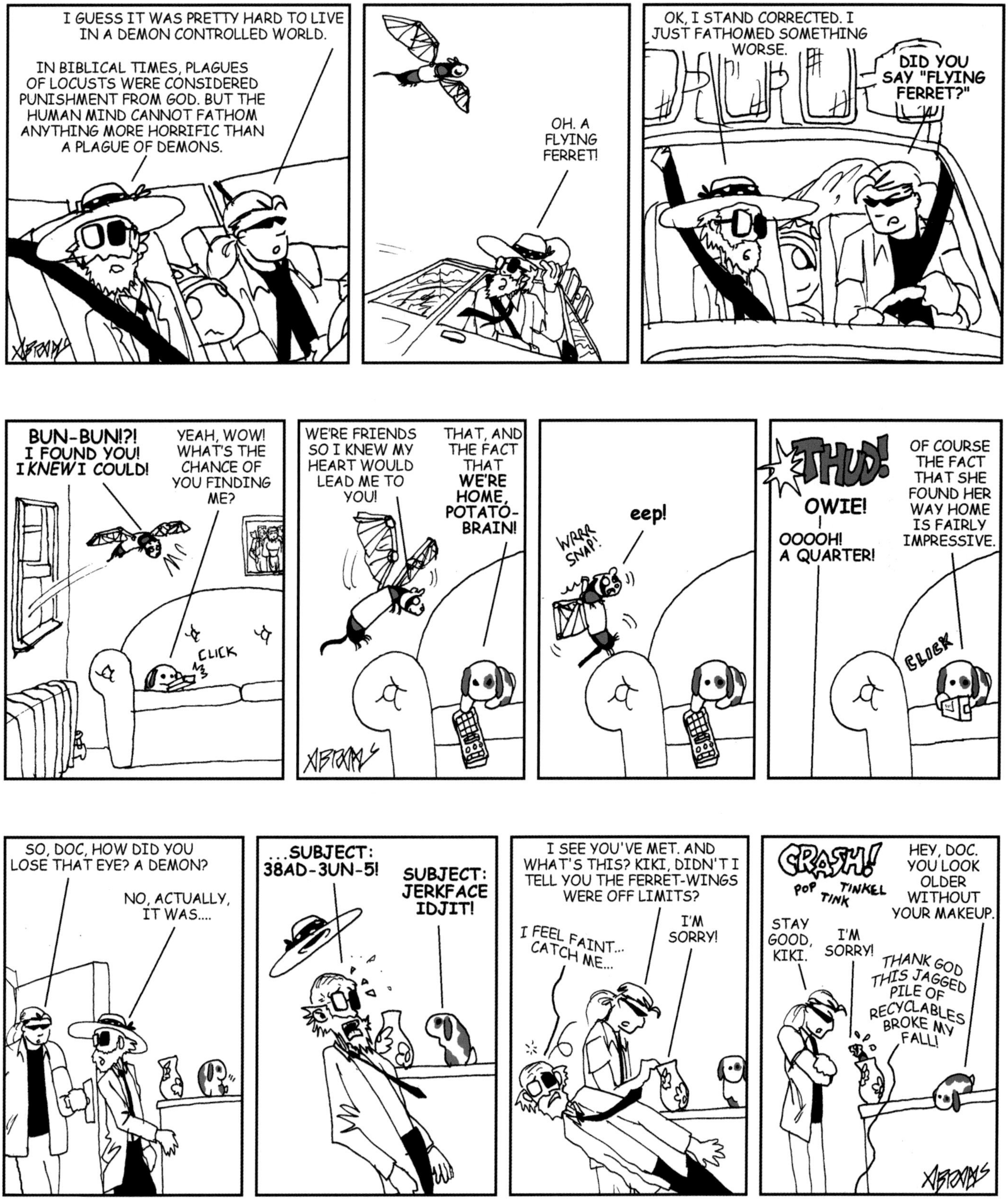
I GUESS IT WAS PRETTY HARD TO LIVE IN A DEMON CONTROLLED WORLD.
IN BIBLICAL TIMES, PLAGUES OF LOCUSTS WERE CONSIDERED PUNISHMENT FROM GOD. BUT THE HUMAN MIND CANNOT FATHOM ANYTHING MORE HORRIFIC THAN A PLAGUE OF DEMONS.
OH. A FLYING FERRET!
OK, I STAND CORRECTED. I JUST FATHOMED SOMETHING WORSE.
DID YOU SAY "FLYING FERRET?"
BUN-BUN!?! I FOUND YOU! I KNEW I COULD!
YEAH, WOW! WHAT'S THE CHANCE OF YOU FINDING ME?
CLICK
WE'RE FRIENDS SO I KNEW MY HEART WOULD LEAD ME TO YOU!
THAT, AND THE FACT THAT WE'RE HOME, POTATO-BRAIN!
WRRR SNAP!
eep!
THUD!
OWIE!
OOOOH! A QUARTER!
OF COURSE THE FACT THAT SHE FOUND HER WAY HOME IS FAIRLY IMPRESSIVE.
CLICK
SO, DOC, HOW DID YOU LOSE THAT EYE? A DEMON?
NO, ACTUALLY, IT WAS....
...SUBJECT: 38AD-3UN-5!
SUBJECT: JERKFACE IDJIT!
I SEE YOU'VE MET. AND WHAT'S THIS? KIKI, DIDN'T I TELL YOU THE FERRET-WINGS WERE OFF LIMITS?
I FEEL FAINT... CATCH ME...
I'M SORRY!
CRASH!
POP TINK TINKEL
HEY, DOC. YOU LOOK OLDER WITHOUT YOUR MAKEUP.
STAY GOOD, KIKI.
I'M SORRY!
THANK GOD THIS JAGGED PILE OF RECYCLABLES BROKE MY FALL!

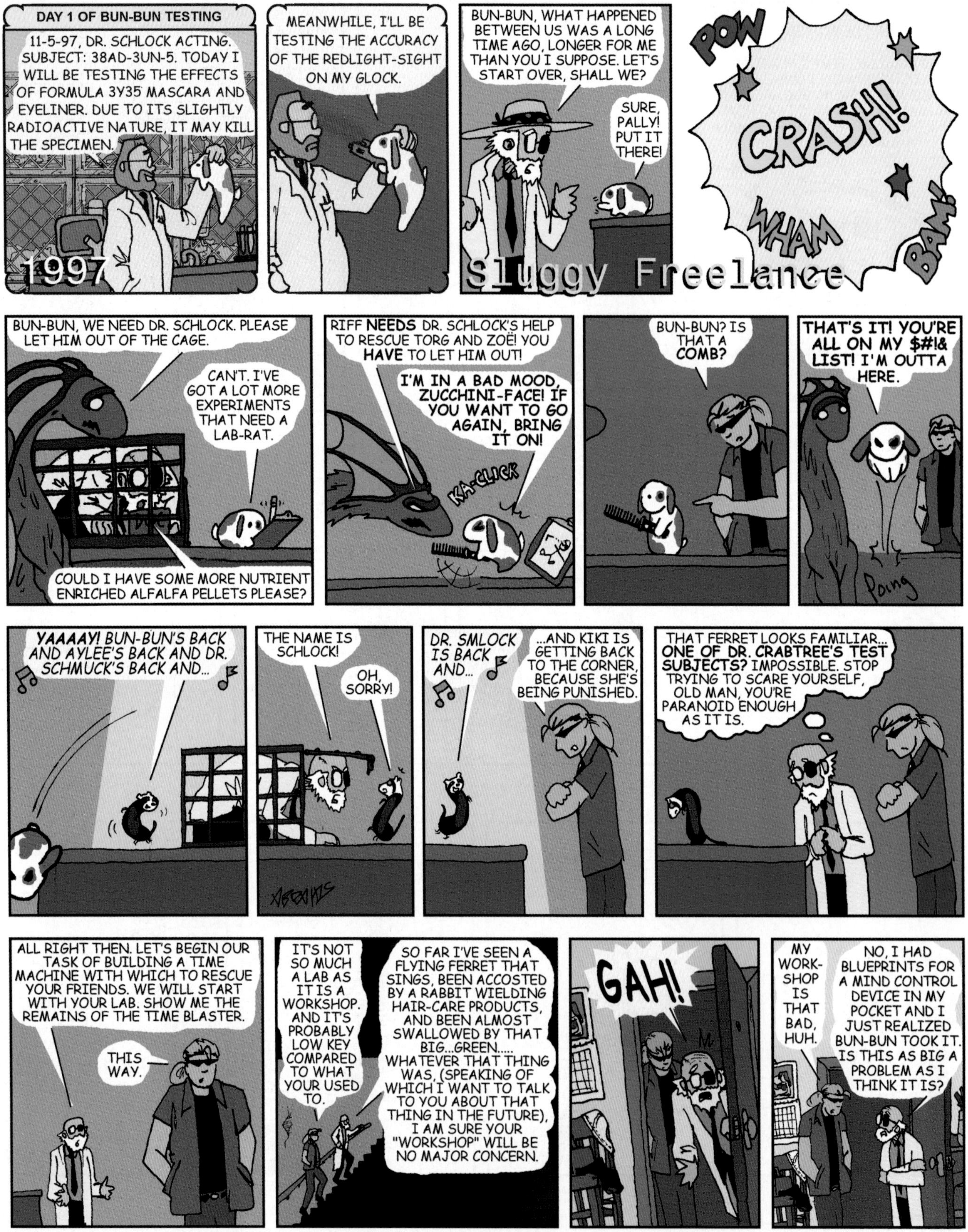

DAY 1 OF BUN-BUN TESTING
11-5-97, DR. SCHLOCK ACTING. SUBJECT: 38AD-3UN-5. TODAY I WILL BE TESTING THE EFFECTS OF FORMULA 3Y35 MASCARA AND EYELINER. DUE TO ITS SLIGHTLY RADIOACTIVE NATURE, IT MAY KILL THE SPECIMEN.
1997
MEANWHILE, I'LL BE TESTING THE ACCURACY OF THE REDLIGHT-SIGHT ON MY GLOCK.
BUN-BUN, WHAT HAPPENED BETWEEN US WAS A LONG TIME AGO, LONGER FOR ME THAN YOU I SUPPOSE. LET'S START OVER, SHALL WE?
SURE, PALLY! PUT IT THERE!
Sluggy Freelance
POW
CRASH!
WHAM
BAM!
BUN-BUN, WE NEED DR. SCHLOCK. PLEASE LET HIM OUT OF THE CAGE.
CAN'T. I'VE GOT A LOT MORE EXPERIMENTS THAT NEED A LAB-RAT.
COULD I HAVE SOME MORE NUTRIENT ENRICHED ALFALFA PELLETS PLEASE?
RIFF NEEDS DR. SCHLOCK'S HELP TO RESCUE TORG AND ZOË! YOU HAVE TO LET HIM OUT!
I'M IN A BAD MOOD, ZUCCHINI-FACE! IF YOU WANT TO GO AGAIN, BRING IT ON!
KA-CLICK
BUN-BUN? IS THAT A COMB?
THAT'S IT! YOU'RE ALL ON MY $#!& LIST! I'M OUTTA HERE.
Poing
YAAAAY! BUN-BUN'S BACK AND AYLEE'S BACK AND DR. SCHMUCK'S BACK AND...
THE NAME IS SCHLOCK!
OH, SORRY!
DR. SMLOCK IS BACK AND...
...AND KIKI IS GETTING BACK TO THE CORNER, BECAUSE SHE'S BEING PUNISHED.
THAT FERRET LOOKS FAMILIAR... ONE OF DR. CRABTREE'S TEST SUBJECTS? IMPOSSIBLE. STOP TRYING TO SCARE YOURSELF, OLD MAN, YOU'RE PARANOID ENOUGH AS IT IS.
ALL RIGHT THEN. LET'S BEGIN OUR TASK OF BUILDING A TIME MACHINE WITH WHICH TO RESCUE YOUR FRIENDS. WE WILL START WITH YOUR LAB. SHOW ME THE REMAINS OF THE TIME BLASTER.
THIS WAY.
IT'S NOT SO MUCH A LAB AS IT IS A WORKSHOP. AND IT'S PROBABLY LOW KEY COMPARED TO WHAT YOUR USED TO.
SO FAR I'VE SEEN A FLYING FERRET THAT SINGS, BEEN ACCOSTED BY A RABBIT WIELDING HAIR-CARE PRODUCTS, AND BEEN ALMOST SWALLOWED BY THAT BIG...GREEN..... WHATEVER THAT THING WAS, (SPEAKING OF WHICH I WANT TO TALK TO YOU ABOUT THAT THING IN THE FUTURE), I AM SURE YOUR "WORKSHOP" WILL BE NO MAJOR CONCERN.
GAH!
MY WORK-SHOP IS THAT BAD, HUH.
NO, I HAD BLUEPRINTS FOR A MIND CONTROL DEVICE IN MY POCKET AND I JUST REALIZED BUN-BUN TOOK IT. IS THIS AS BIG A PROBLEM AS I THINK IT IS?

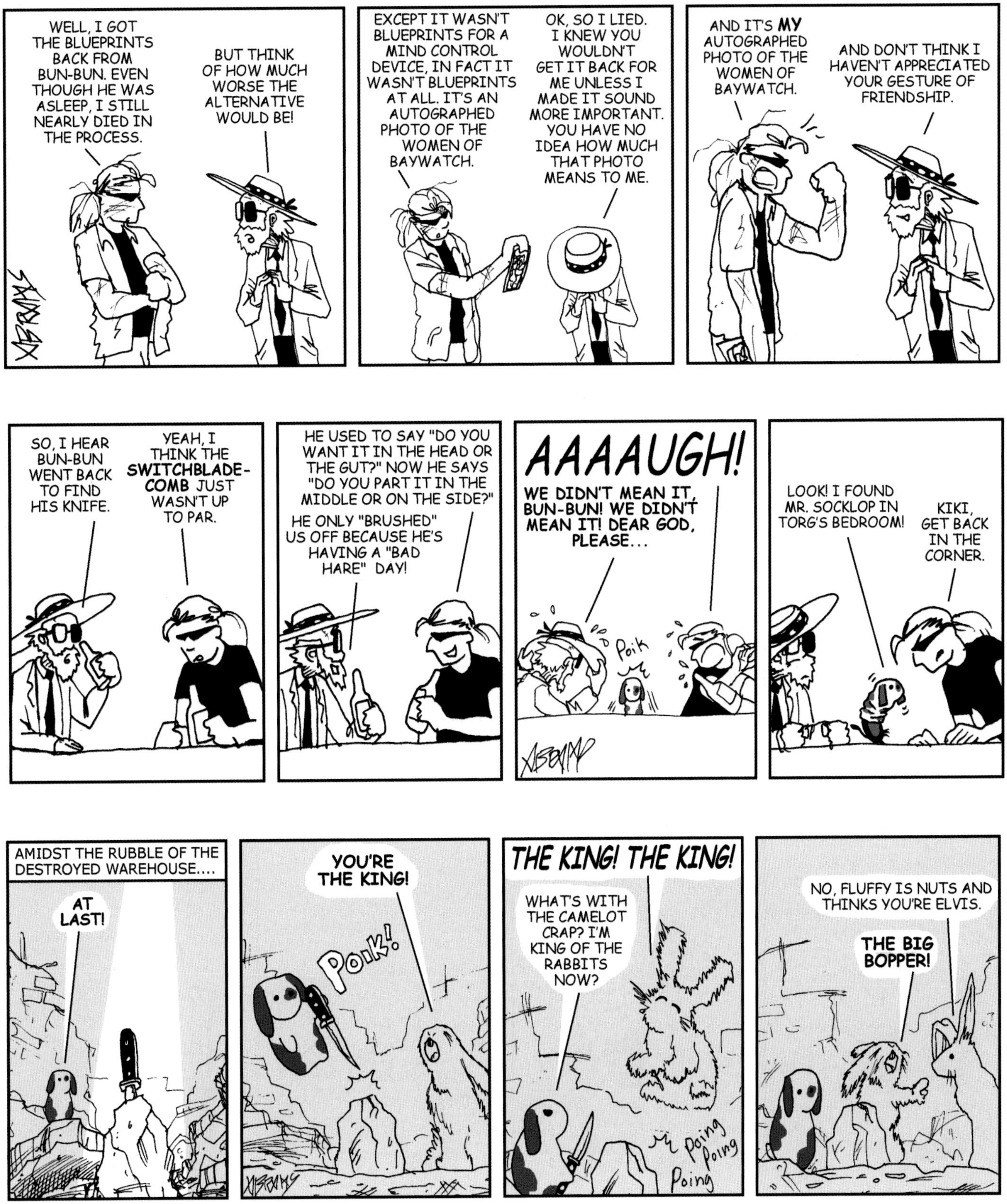
WELL, I GOT THE BLUEPRINTS BACK FROM BUN-BUN. EVEN THOUGH HE WAS ASLEEP, I STILL NEARLY DIED IN THE PROCESS.
BUT THINK OF HOW MUCH WORSE THE ALTERNATIVE WOULD BE!
EXCEPT IT WASN'T BLUEPRINTS FOR A MIND CONTROL DEVICE, IN FACT IT WASN'T BLUEPRINTS AT ALL. IT'S AN AUTOGRAPHED PHOTO OF THE WOMEN OF BAYWATCH.
OK, SO I LIED. I KNEW YOU WOULDN'T GET IT BACK FOR ME UNLESS I MADE IT SOUND MORE IMPORTANT. YOU HAVE NO IDEA HOW MUCH THAT PHOTO MEANS TO ME.
AND IT'S **MY** AUTOGRAPHED PHOTO OF THE WOMEN OF BAYWATCH.
AND DON'T THINK I HAVEN'T APPRECIATED YOUR GESTURE OF FRIENDSHIP.
SO, I HEAR BUN-BUN WENT BACK TO FIND HIS KNIFE.
YEAH, I THINK THE **SWITCHBLADE-COMB** JUST WASN'T UP TO PAR.
HE USED TO SAY "DO YOU WANT IT IN THE HEAD OR THE GUT?" NOW HE SAYS "DO YOU PART IT IN THE MIDDLE OR ON THE SIDE?"
HE ONLY "BRUSHED" US OFF BECAUSE HE'S HAVING A "BAD HARE" DAY!
AAAAUGH!
WE DIDN'T MEAN IT, BUN-BUN! WE DIDN'T MEAN IT! DEAR GOD, PLEASE...
Poik
LOOK! I FOUND MR. SOCKLOP IN TORG'S BEDROOM!
KIKI, GET BACK IN THE CORNER.
AMIDST THE RUBBLE OF THE DESTROYED WAREHOUSE....
AT LAST!
YOU'RE THE KING!
POIK!
THE KING! THE KING!
WHAT'S WITH THE CAMELOT CRAP? I'M KING OF THE RABBITS NOW?
Poing Poing Poing
NO, FLUFFY IS NUTS AND THINKS YOU'RE ELVIS.
THE BIG BOPPER!

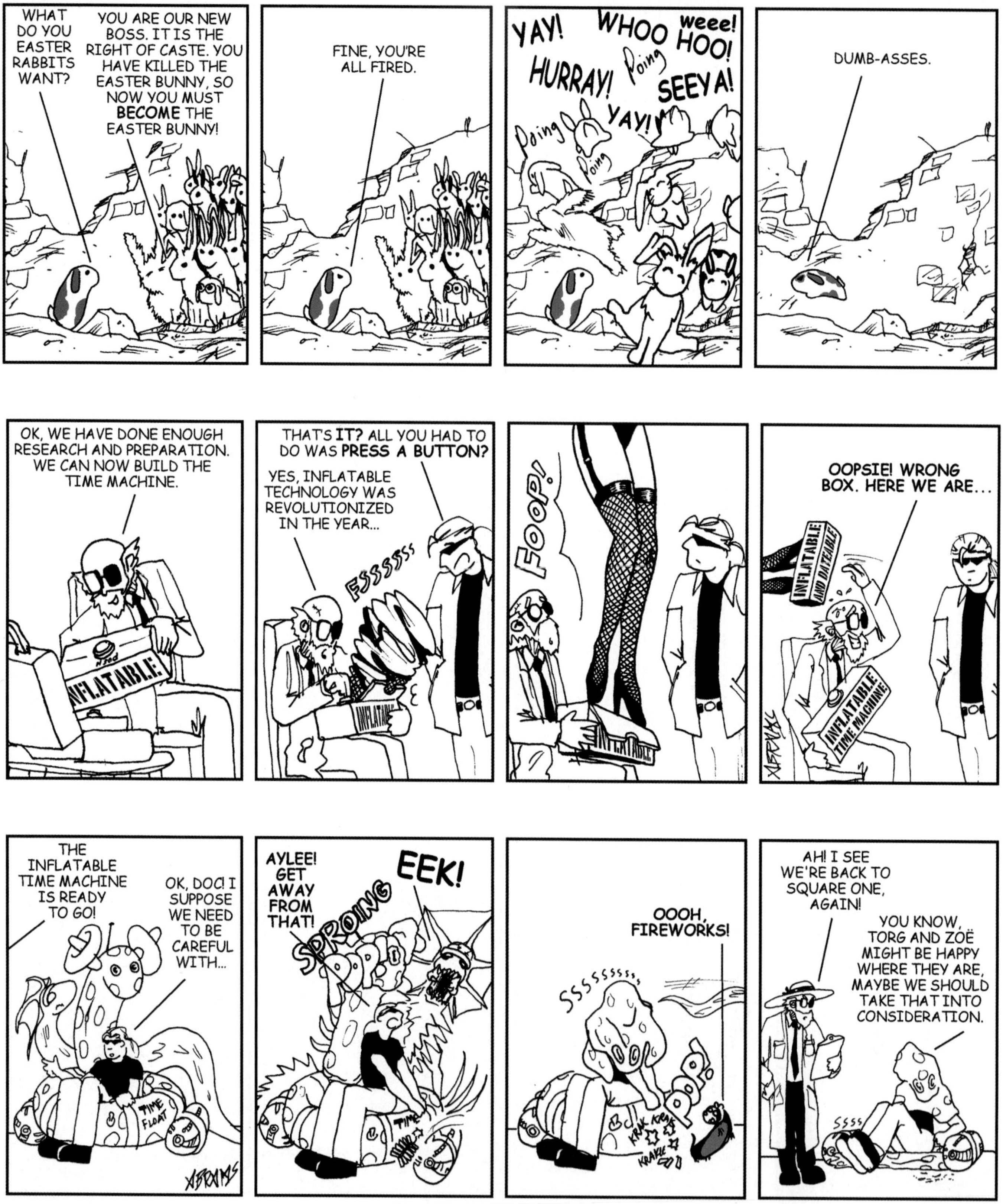
WHAT DO YOU EASTER RABBITS WANT?
YOU ARE OUR NEW BOSS. IT IS THE RIGHT OF CASTE. YOU HAVE KILLED THE EASTER BUNNY, SO NOW YOU MUST BECOME THE EASTER BUNNY!
FINE, YOU'RE ALL FIRED.
YAY!
WHOO HOO!
weee!
HURRAY!
Poing
SEEYA!
Poing
YAY!
Poing
DUMB-ASSES.
OK, WE HAVE DONE ENOUGH RESEARCH AND PREPARATION. WE CAN NOW BUILD THE TIME MACHINE.
INFLATABLE
THAT'S IT? ALL YOU HAD TO DO WAS PRESS A BUTTON?
YES, INFLATABLE TECHNOLOGY WAS REVOLUTIONIZED IN THE YEAR...
FSSSSSS
INFLATABLE
FOOP!
INFLATABLE
OOPSIE! WRONG BOX. HERE WE ARE...
INFLATABLE AND DATEABLE
INFLATABLE TIME MACHINE
THE INFLATABLE TIME MACHINE IS READY TO GO!
OK, DOC! I SUPPOSE WE NEED TO BE CAREFUL WITH...
TIME FLOAT
AYLEE! GET AWAY FROM THAT!
EEK!
SPROING
POP!
OOOH, FIREWORKS!
SSSSSSSS
POP!
KRAK KRAK
KRAKLE
AH! I SEE WE'RE BACK TO SQUARE ONE, AGAIN!
YOU KNOW, TORG AND ZOË MIGHT BE HAPPY WHERE THEY ARE, MAYBE WE SHOULD TAKE THAT INTO CONSIDERATION.
SSSS

The
Storm
Breaker
Saga

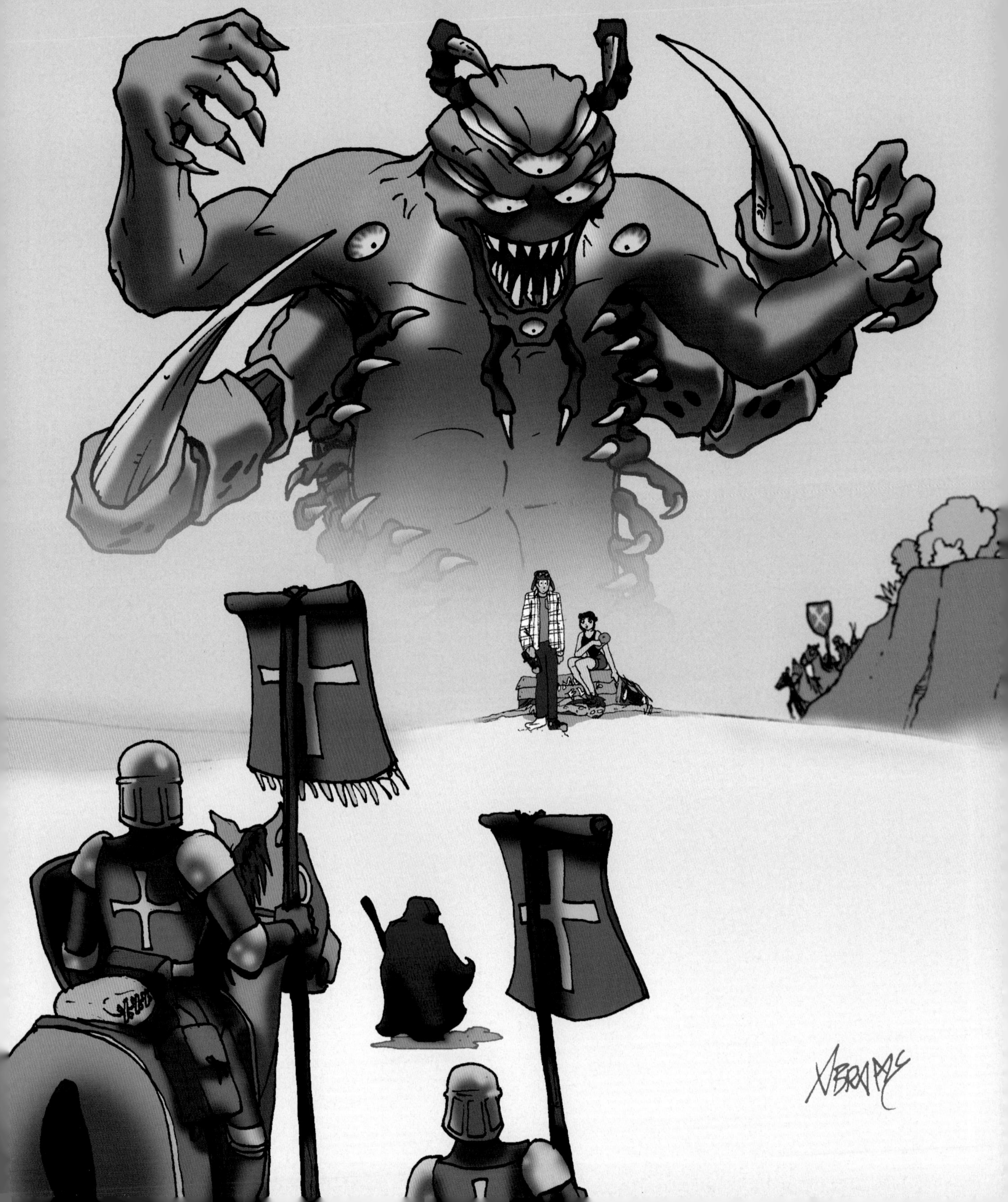

"MY NAME IS TORG. AND I'M A PRISONER."
"A DEMON NAMED KIZKE TOOK MY FRIEND GWYNN, AND THEN TOOK MY HAND."
"SO I TRADED UP FOR A CHAINSAW."
BZZZZZ
"I MANAGED TO BLAST KIZKE INTO THE PAST USING THE BOOK OF E-VILLE...."
"....BUT IT TOOK ME WITH IT."
TORG VS. THE ARMY OF K'Z'K
THAT'S NOT HOW IT HAPPENED!
WHO'S TELLING THIS STORY?
SHE'S RIGHT. YOU DON'T HAVE A CHAINSAW FOR A HAND.
YOU DON'T EVEN KNOW WHAT A CHAINSAW IS, BUDDY!
UNLESS THE WORD "CHAIN -SAW" MEANS "HANDS LIKE A LADY"
HEY!
TORG, QUIT THE HOLLYWOOD EMBELLISHING AND TELL IT STRAIGHT.
"WHATEVER. WE ARE FROM THE FUTURE. WE HAD THIS TIME MACHINE, AND IT MALFUNCTIONED AND SENT US HERE INSTEAD OF THE YEAR 2000."
OH, THIS VERSION IS BELIEVABLE.
OK, HOW ABOUT: "WE'RE FROM A FAR AWAY LAND SENT HERE BY LEPRECHAUNS."
WHAT EVER.
"THERE WERE MEN ON HORSES WAITING FOR US, LIKE WE WERE EXPECTED."
"OUT OF NOWHERE, MASKED RIDERS SCOOPED US UP AND RODE OFF WITH US."
KILL THE MERCIANS!
BE CAREFUL, KING SIGHARD! YOU MIGHT HIT THE "STORM BREAKER"!
OSRIC, YOU FORGET YOUR PLACE. DID YOUR PROPHECY INCLUDE HER BEFRIENDING MY MORTAL ENEMY? CONSORTING WITH THE WARLORD OF MERCIA?
FIRE!
TORG!
ZOË!
HE'S TRYING TO LEAP FROM THE HORSE! HAS HE GONE DAFT?
CAREFUL HOW YOU REFER TO OUR RULER. WE MUST BRING HIM HOME!
THEY HAVE ELUDED US, MY KING.
AT LEAST I HAVE THIS ONE TO VENT MY ANGER UPON!
SHE IS THE STORM BREAKER! AS FORETOLD SHE WILL DO BATTLE WITH THE DEMON KIZKE, WHO PLAGUES OUR LAND!
THIS BEGGAR WOMAN WILL DO BATTLE WITH THE EXECUTIONER'S AXE!
SLUGGY FREELANCE PRESENTS
The Storm Breaker Saga
I
THE WARLORD

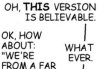

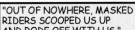

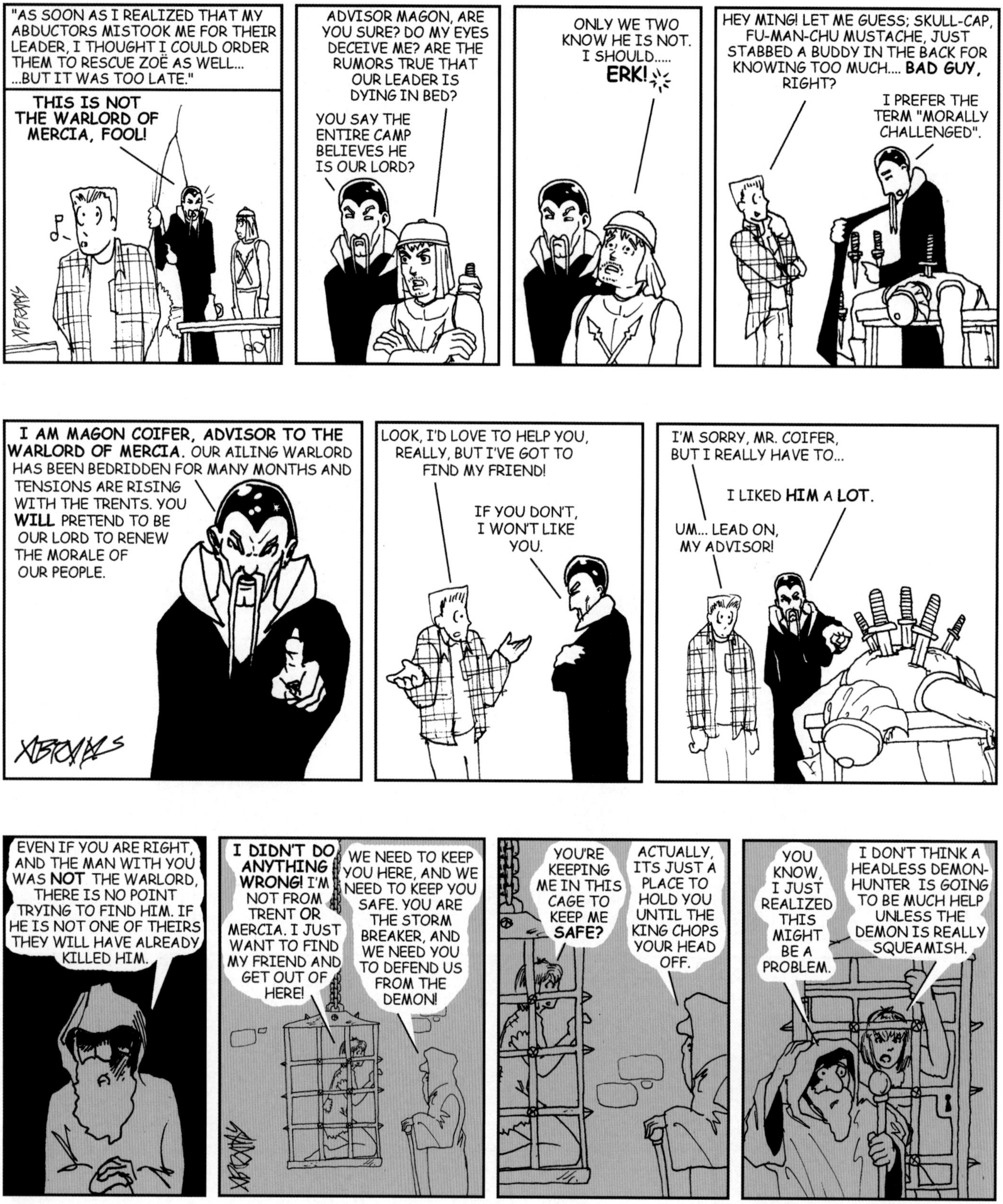
"AS SOON AS I REALIZED THAT MY ABDUCTORS MISTOOK ME FOR THEIR LEADER, I THOUGHT I COULD ORDER THEM TO RESCUE ZOË AS WELL... ...BUT IT WAS TOO LATE."
THIS IS NOT THE WARLORD OF MERCIA, FOOL!
ADVISOR MAGON, ARE YOU SURE? DO MY EYES DECEIVE ME? ARE THE RUMORS TRUE THAT OUR LEADER IS DYING IN BED?
YOU SAY THE ENTIRE CAMP BELIEVES HE IS OUR LORD?
ONLY WE TWO KNOW HE IS NOT. I SHOULD.....
ERK!
HEY MING! LET ME GUESS; SKULL-CAP, FU-MAN-CHU MUSTACHE, JUST STABBED A BUDDY IN THE BACK FOR KNOWING TOO MUCH.... BAD GUY, RIGHT?
I PREFER THE TERM "MORALLY CHALLENGED".
I AM MAGON COIFER, ADVISOR TO THE WARLORD OF MERCIA. OUR AILING WARLORD HAS BEEN BEDRIDDEN FOR MANY MONTHS AND TENSIONS ARE RISING WITH THE TRENTS. YOU WILL PRETEND TO BE OUR LORD TO RENEW THE MORALE OF OUR PEOPLE.
LOOK, I'D LOVE TO HELP YOU, REALLY, BUT I'VE GOT TO FIND MY FRIEND!
IF YOU DON'T, I WON'T LIKE YOU.
I'M SORRY, MR. COIFER, BUT I REALLY HAVE TO...
I LIKED HIM A LOT.
UM... LEAD ON, MY ADVISOR!
EVEN IF YOU ARE RIGHT, AND THE MAN WITH YOU WAS NOT THE WARLORD, THERE IS NO POINT TRYING TO FIND HIM. IF HE IS NOT ONE OF THEIRS THEY WILL HAVE ALREADY KILLED HIM.
I DIDN'T DO ANYTHING WRONG! I'M NOT FROM TRENT OR MERCIA. I JUST WANT TO FIND MY FRIEND AND GET OUT OF HERE!
WE NEED TO KEEP YOU HERE, AND WE NEED TO KEEP YOU SAFE. YOU ARE THE STORM BREAKER, AND WE NEED YOU TO DEFEND US FROM THE DEMON!
YOU'RE KEEPING ME IN THIS CAGE TO KEEP ME SAFE?
ACTUALLY, ITS JUST A PLACE TO HOLD YOU UNTIL THE KING CHOPS YOUR HEAD OFF.
YOU KNOW, I JUST REALIZED THIS MIGHT BE A PROBLEM.
I DON'T THINK A HEADLESS DEMON-HUNTER IS GOING TO BE MUCH HELP UNLESS THE DEMON IS REALLY SQUEAMISH.

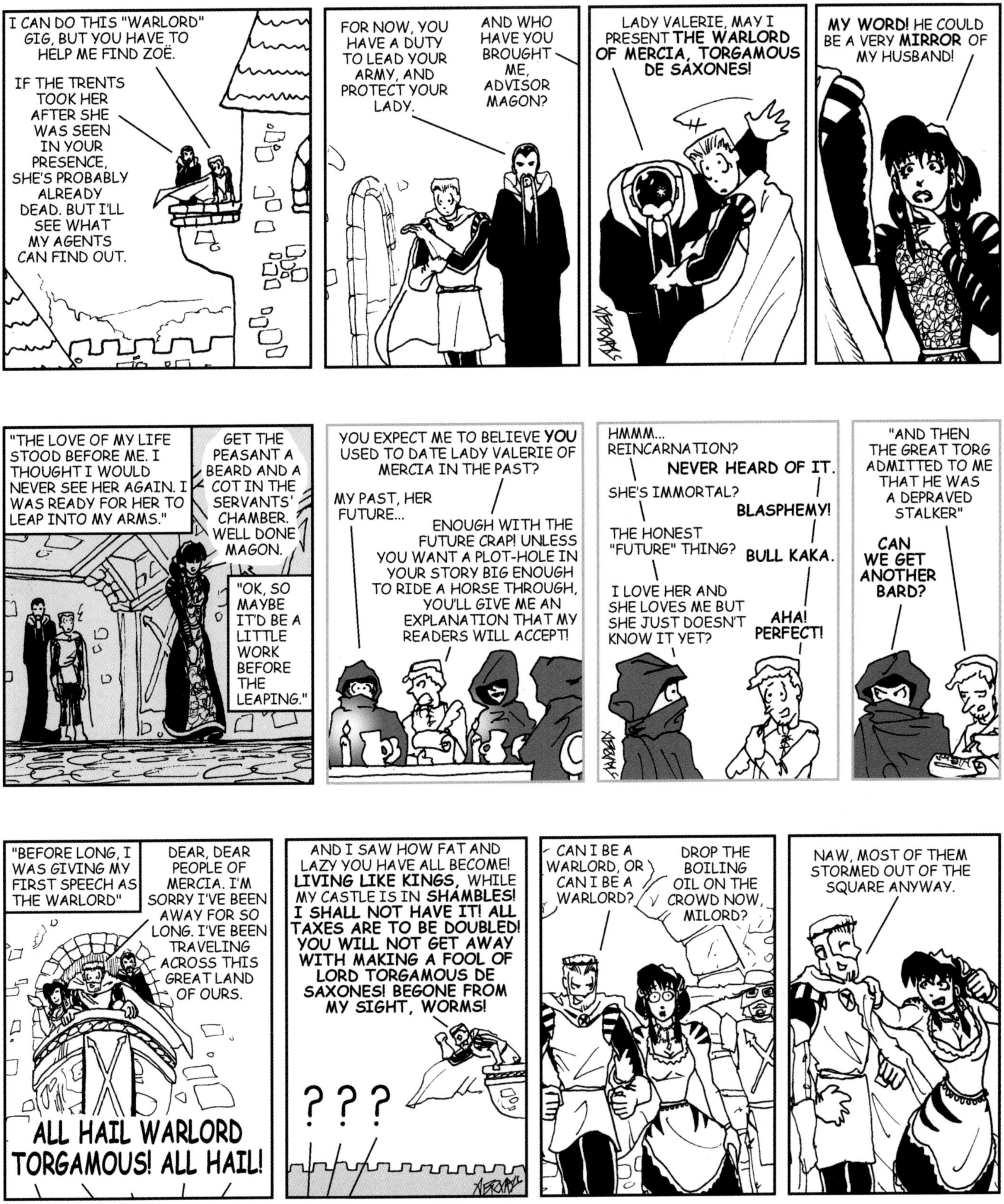
I CAN DO THIS "WARLORD" GIG, BUT YOU HAVE TO HELP ME FIND ZOË.
IF THE TRENTS TOOK HER AFTER SHE WAS SEEN IN YOUR PRESENCE, SHE'S PROBABLY ALREADY DEAD. BUT I'LL SEE WHAT MY AGENTS CAN FIND OUT.
FOR NOW, YOU HAVE A DUTY TO LEAD YOUR ARMY, AND PROTECT YOUR LADY.
AND WHO HAVE YOU BROUGHT ME, ADVISOR MAGON?
LADY VALERIE, MAY I PRESENT THE WARLORD OF MERCIA, TORGAMOUS DE SAXONES!
MY WORD! HE COULD BE A VERY MIRROR OF MY HUSBAND!
"THE LOVE OF MY LIFE STOOD BEFORE ME. I THOUGHT I WOULD NEVER SEE HER AGAIN. I WAS READY FOR HER TO LEAP INTO MY ARMS."
GET THE PEASANT A BEARD AND A COT IN THE SERVANTS' CHAMBER. WELL DONE MAGON.
"OK, SO MAYBE IT'D BE A LITTLE WORK BEFORE THE LEAPING."
YOU EXPECT ME TO BELIEVE YOU USED TO DATE LADY VALERIE OF MERCIA IN THE PAST?
MY PAST, HER FUTURE...
ENOUGH WITH THE FUTURE CRAP! UNLESS YOU WANT A PLOT-HOLE IN YOUR STORY BIG ENOUGH TO RIDE A HORSE THROUGH, YOU'LL GIVE ME AN EXPLANATION THAT MY READERS WILL ACCEPT!
HMMM... REINCARNATION?
NEVER HEARD OF IT.
SHE'S IMMORTAL?
BLASPHEMY!
THE HONEST "FUTURE" THING?
BULL KAKA.
I LOVE HER AND SHE LOVES ME BUT SHE JUST DOESN'T KNOW IT YET?
AHA! PERFECT!
"AND THEN THE GREAT TORG ADMITTED TO ME THAT HE WAS A DEPRAVED STALKER"
CAN WE GET ANOTHER BARD?
"BEFORE LONG, I WAS GIVING MY FIRST SPEECH AS THE WARLORD"
DEAR, DEAR PEOPLE OF MERCIA. I'M SORRY I'VE BEEN AWAY FOR SO LONG. I'VE BEEN TRAVELING ACROSS THIS GREAT LAND OF OURS.
ALL HAIL WARLORD TORGAMOUS! ALL HAIL!
AND I SAW HOW FAT AND LAZY YOU HAVE ALL BECOME! LIVING LIKE KINGS, WHILE MY CASTLE IS IN SHAMBLES! I SHALL NOT HAVE IT! ALL TAXES ARE TO BE DOUBLED! YOU WILL NOT GET AWAY WITH MAKING A FOOL OF LORD TORGAMOUS DE SAXONES! BEGONE FROM MY SIGHT, WORMS!
? ? ?
CAN I BE A WARLORD, OR CAN I BE A WARLORD?
DROP THE BOILING OIL ON THE CROWD NOW, MILORD?
NAW, MOST OF THEM STORMED OUT OF THE SQUARE ANYWAY.

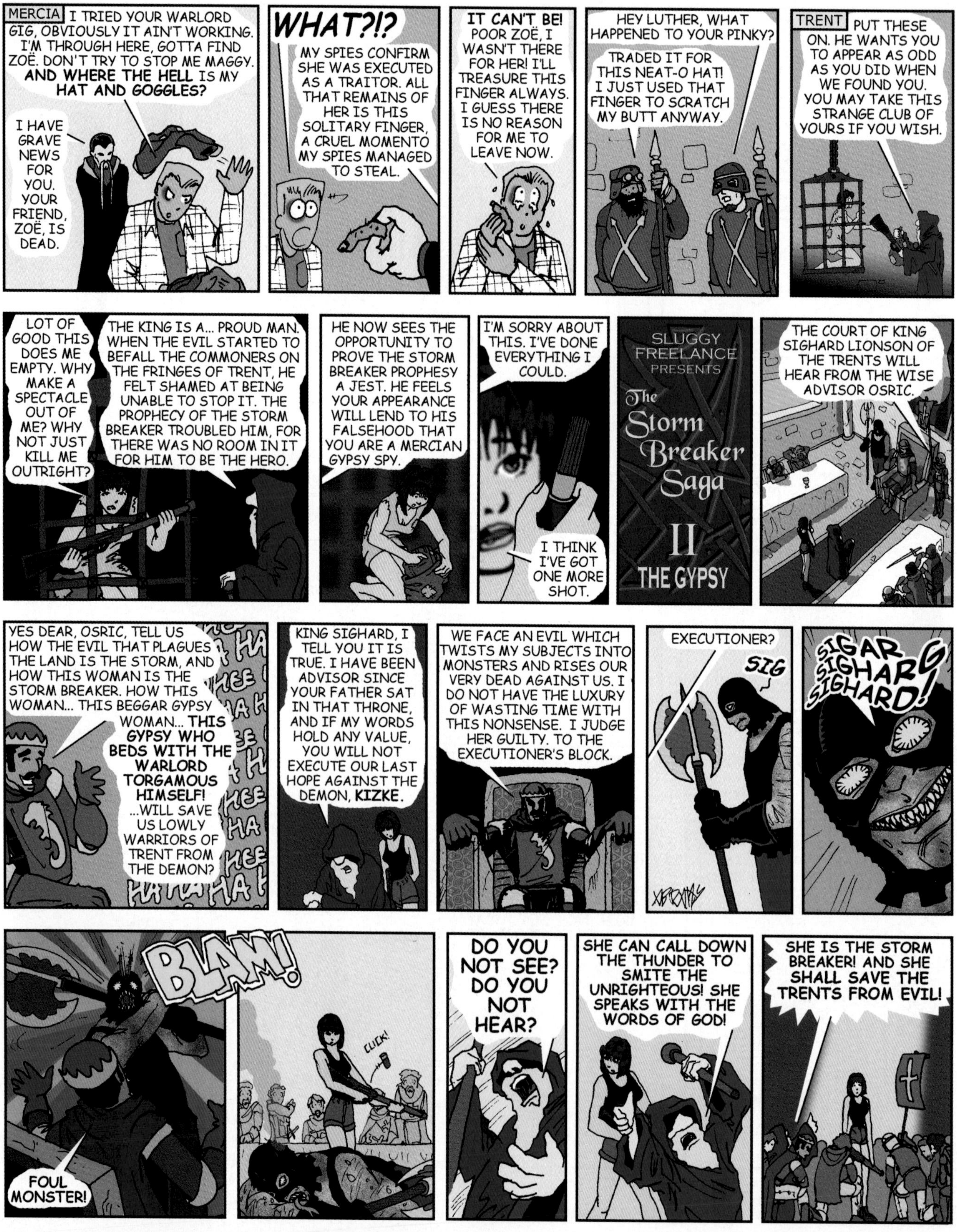

MERCIA
I TRIED YOUR WARLORD GIG, OBVIOUSLY IT AIN'T WORKING. I'M THROUGH HERE, GOTTA FIND ZOË. DON'T TRY TO STOP ME MAGGY. AND WHERE THE HELL IS MY HAT AND GOGGLES?
I HAVE GRAVE NEWS FOR YOU. YOUR FRIEND, ZOË, IS DEAD.
WHAT?!?
MY SPIES CONFIRM SHE WAS EXECUTED AS A TRAITOR. ALL THAT REMAINS OF HER IS THIS SOLITARY FINGER, A CRUEL MOMENTO MY SPIES MANAGED TO STEAL.
IT CAN'T BE! POOR ZOË, I WASN'T THERE FOR HER! I'LL TREASURE THIS FINGER ALWAYS. I GUESS THERE IS NO REASON FOR ME TO LEAVE NOW.
HEY LUTHER, WHAT HAPPENED TO YOUR PINKY?
TRADED IT FOR THIS NEAT-O HAT! I JUST USED THAT FINGER TO SCRATCH MY BUTT ANYWAY.
TRENT
PUT THESE ON. HE WANTS YOU TO APPEAR AS ODD AS YOU DID WHEN WE FOUND YOU. YOU MAY TAKE THIS STRANGE CLUB OF YOURS IF YOU WISH.
LOT OF GOOD THIS DOES ME EMPTY. WHY MAKE A SPECTACLE OUT OF ME? WHY NOT JUST KILL ME OUTRIGHT?
THE KING IS A... PROUD MAN. WHEN THE EVIL STARTED TO BEFALL THE COMMONERS ON THE FRINGES OF TRENT, HE FELT SHAMED AT BEING UNABLE TO STOP IT. THE PROPHECY OF THE STORM BREAKER TROUBLED HIM, FOR THERE WAS NO ROOM IN IT FOR HIM TO BE THE HERO.
HE NOW SEES THE OPPORTUNITY TO PROVE THE STORM BREAKER PROPHESY A JEST. HE FEELS YOUR APPEARANCE WILL LEND TO HIS FALSEHOOD THAT YOU ARE A MERCIAN GYPSY SPY.
I'M SORRY ABOUT THIS. I'VE DONE EVERYTHING I COULD.
I THINK I'VE GOT ONE MORE SHOT.
SLUGGY FREELANCE PRESENTS
The Storm Breaker Saga
II
THE GYPSY
THE COURT OF KING SIGHARD LIONSON OF THE TRENTS WILL HEAR FROM THE WISE ADVISOR OSRIC.
YES DEAR, OSRIC, TELL US HOW THE EVIL THAT PLAGUES THE LAND IS THE STORM, AND HOW THIS WOMAN IS THE STORM BREAKER. HOW THIS WOMAN... THIS BEGGAR GYPSY WOMAN... THIS GYPSY WHO BEDS WITH THE WARLORD TORGAMOUS HIMSELF! ...WILL SAVE US LOWLY WARRIORS OF TRENT FROM THE DEMON?
HA HA HEE HA HA HEE HA HEE HA HA HA
KING SIGHARD, I TELL YOU IT IS TRUE. I HAVE BEEN ADVISOR SINCE YOUR FATHER SAT IN THAT THRONE, AND IF MY WORDS HOLD ANY VALUE, YOU WILL NOT EXECUTE OUR LAST HOPE AGAINST THE DEMON, KIZKE.
WE FACE AN EVIL WHICH TWISTS MY SUBJECTS INTO MONSTERS AND RISES OUR VERY DEAD AGAINST US. I DO NOT HAVE THE LUXURY OF WASTING TIME WITH THIS NONSENSE. I JUDGE HER GUILTY. TO THE EXECUTIONER'S BLOCK.
EXECUTIONER?
SIG
SIGAR SIGHARG SIGHARD!
BLAM!
FOUL MONSTER!
CLICK!
DO YOU NOT SEE? DO YOU NOT HEAR?
SHE CAN CALL DOWN THE THUNDER TO SMITE THE UNRIGHTEOUS! SHE SPEAKS WITH THE WORDS OF GOD!
SHE IS THE STORM BREAKER! AND SHE SHALL SAVE THE TRENTS FROM EVIL!

MAGON, YOU **TRAITOROUS MAGGOT!** YOU'VE BEEN INSTRUCTING THAT **PEASANT** TO GRIND OUR PEOPLE INTO THE DIRT!

HE HAS TO BE FIRM IF THE PEOPLE ARE TO BELIEVE HE ACTUALLY IS LORD TORGAMOUS.

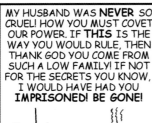

MY HUSBAND WAS **NEVER** SO CRUEL! HOW YOU MUST COVET OUR POWER. IF **THIS** IS THE WAY YOU WOULD RULE, THEN THANK GOD YOU COME FROM SUCH A LOW FAMILY! IF NOT FOR THE SECRETS YOU KNOW, I WOULD HAVE HAD YOU **IMPRISONED!** BE GONE!

CRASH!

HEY MAGGY! LOOKS LIKE VAL IS SMASHING VASES AGAIN.

SHE WAS JUST EXPRESSING HAPPINESS OVER YOUR NEW ORDER FOR THE APPROPRIATION OF FARMLANDS FOR THE NEW CASTLE.

OH! I GUESS SHE MUST HAVE **REALLY** LIKED MY IDEA ABOUT BANNING PUBLIC GATHERINGS!

I'M SO PROUD!

LOOK, MAGGY, I'M TRYING MY BEST TO BE A GOOD WARLORD, BUT I JUST DON'T LIKE HAVING TO BE MEAN ALL THE TIME!

BUT YOU HAVE DONE EXCELLENTLY! YOUR ONLY FLAW IS THAT YOU LACK THE POISE OF A TRUE WARLORD. WE SHALL PRACTICE. UP AHEAD IS THE GYPSY SEER WHOM LADY VALERIE CONFIDES IN. LET US PRACTICE YOUR FORMAL GREETING.

LORD TORGAMOUS, MAY I PRESENT TO YOU THE GYPSY SEER LYSINDA.

MY LORD.

"IT WAS **LYSINDA,** VAMPIRE QUEEN, PRETENDING TO BE A SIMPLE GYPSY FORTUNE TELLER. I REALIZED TWO THINGS; THAT WE WERE ALL IN GREAT DANGER, AND THAT I HAD A CHANCE, A **REAL** CHANCE, TO CHANGE THE FUTURE. TO SAVE VALERIE. AS SHE LOOKED AT ME, I COULD FEEL HER STUDYING ME. I WONDERED IF SHE KNEW I RECOGNIZED HER FOR WHAT SHE WAS."

THIS IS **NOT** POISE!

MAGON COIFER, WHY DO YOU WATCH LADY VALERIE FROM THE SHADOWS?

I HAVE NO TIME FOR YOU, GYPSY WENCH.

THE LADY BELIEVES YOU ARE TELLING THE FALSE LORD TO DO THE THINGS YOU WISH, ALLOWING YOU TO RULE IN PROXY.

SHE TELLS YOU SUCH THINGS?

I BELIEVE DIFFERENTLY. YOU ARE ORDERING THE FALSE LORD TO BE UNJUSTLY CRUEL, SO THE REBELLION YOU ARE FUNDING, WITH THE INCREASED TAXATION, WILL GATHER THE SUPPORT OF THE PEOPLE AND PLACE YOU ON THE THRONE OF MERCIA.

IT WOULD MEAN VALERIE WOULD LOSE HER EMPIRE, AND I HAVE PLANS FOR HER. THIS MIGHT RUIN THOSE PLANS.

AND WE CAN'T HAVE THAT.

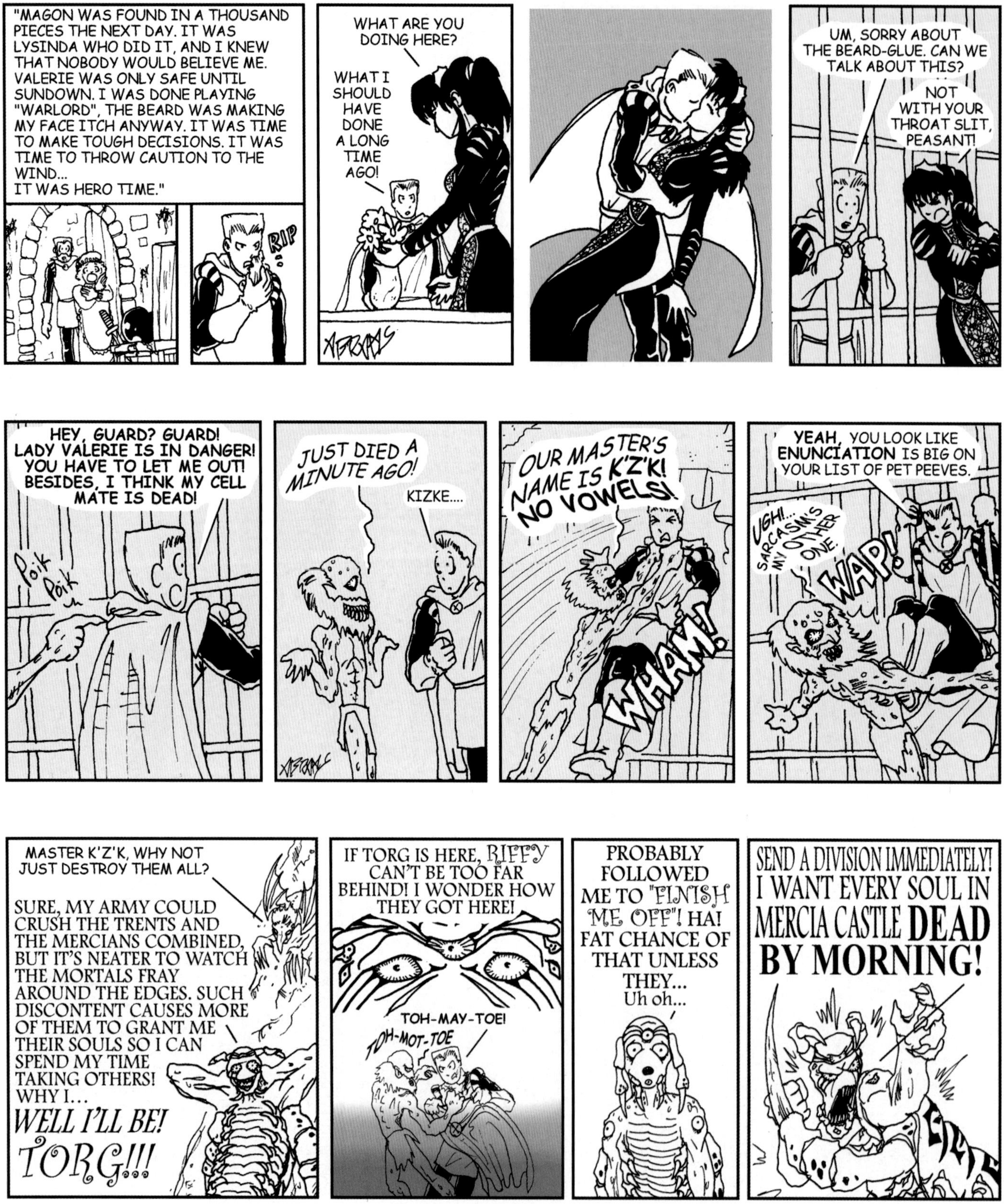
"MAGON WAS FOUND IN A THOUSAND PIECES THE NEXT DAY. IT WAS LYSINDA WHO DID IT, AND I KNEW THAT NOBODY WOULD BELIEVE ME. VALERIE WAS ONLY SAFE UNTIL SUNDOWN. I WAS DONE PLAYING "WARLORD", THE BEARD WAS MAKING MY FACE ITCH ANYWAY. IT WAS TIME TO MAKE TOUGH DECISIONS. IT WAS TIME TO THROW CAUTION TO THE WIND...
IT WAS HERO TIME."
RIP
WHAT ARE YOU DOING HERE?
WHAT I SHOULD HAVE DONE A LONG TIME AGO!
UM, SORRY ABOUT THE BEARD-GLUE. CAN WE TALK ABOUT THIS?
NOT WITH YOUR THROAT SLIT, PEASANT!
HEY, GUARD? GUARD! LADY VALERIE IS IN DANGER! YOU HAVE TO LET ME OUT! BESIDES, I THINK MY CELL MATE IS DEAD!
Poik Poik
JUST DIED A MINUTE AGO!
KIZKE....
OUR MASTER'S NAME IS K'Z'K! NO VOWELS!
WHAM!
YEAH, YOU LOOK LIKE ENUNCIATION IS BIG ON YOUR LIST OF PET PEEVES.
UGH!... SARCASM'S MY OTHER ONE.
WAP!
MASTER K'Z'K, WHY NOT JUST DESTROY THEM ALL?
SURE, MY ARMY COULD CRUSH THE TRENTS AND THE MERCIANS COMBINED, BUT IT'S NEATER TO WATCH THE MORTALS FRAY AROUND THE EDGES. SUCH DISCONTENT CAUSES MORE OF THEM TO GRANT ME THEIR SOULS SO I CAN SPEND MY TIME TAKING OTHERS! WHY I...
WELL I'LL BE! TORG!!!
IF TORG IS HERE, RIFFY CAN'T BE TOO FAR BEHIND! I WONDER HOW THEY GOT HERE!
TOH-MAY-TOE!
TOH-MOT-TOE
PROBABLY FOLLOWED ME TO "FINISH ME OFF"! HA! FAT CHANCE OF THAT UNLESS THEY...
Uh oh...
SEND A DIVISION IMMEDIATELY! I WANT EVERY SOUL IN MERCIA CASTLE DEAD BY MORNING!

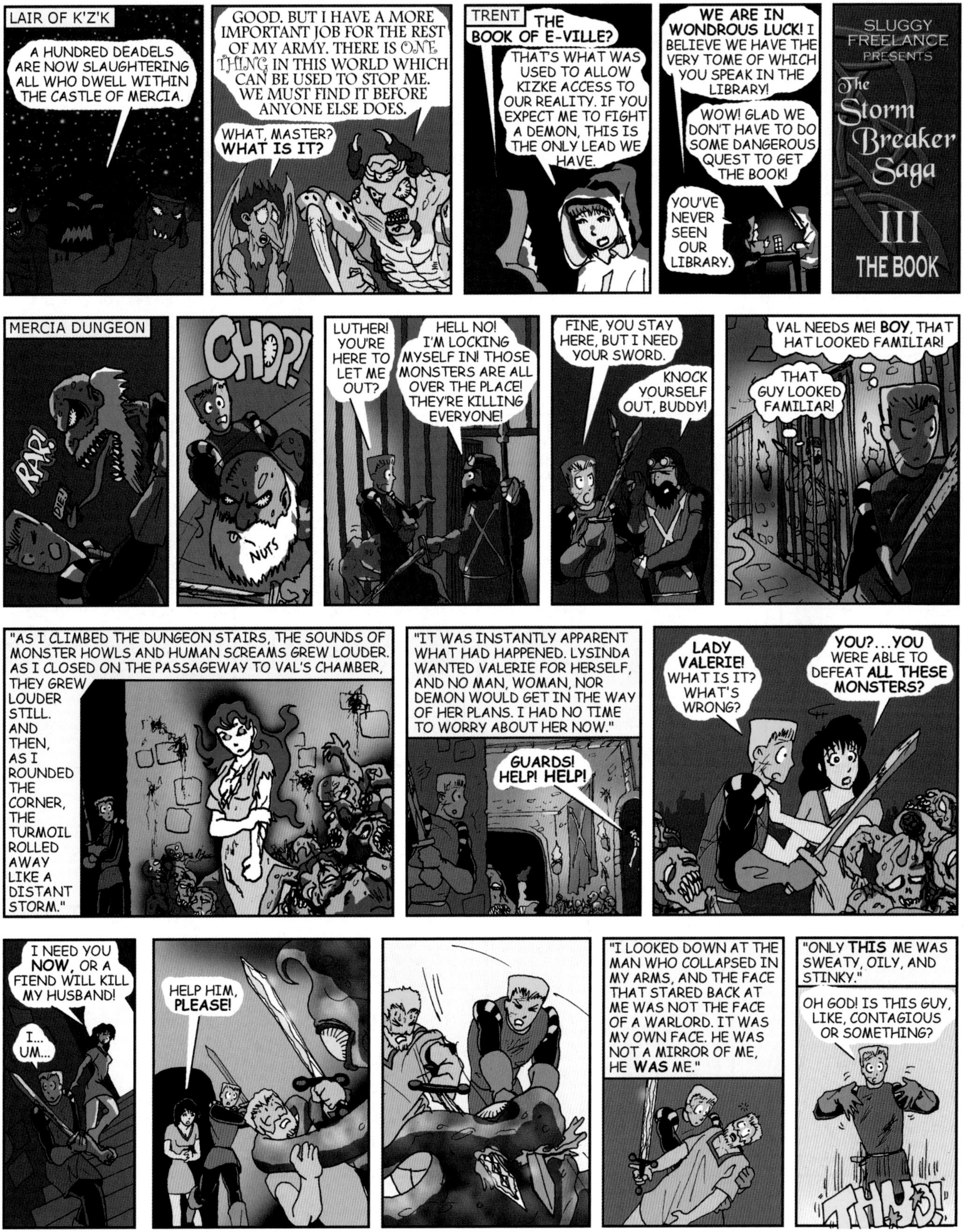

LAIR OF K'Z'K
A HUNDRED DEADELS ARE NOW SLAUGHTERING ALL WHO DWELL WITHIN THE CASTLE OF MERCIA.
GOOD. BUT I HAVE A MORE IMPORTANT JOB FOR THE REST OF MY ARMY. THERE IS ONE THING IN THIS WORLD WHICH CAN BE USED TO STOP ME. WE MUST FIND IT BEFORE ANYONE ELSE DOES.
WHAT, MASTER? WHAT IS IT?
TRENT
THE BOOK OF E-VILLE?
THAT'S WHAT WAS USED TO ALLOW KIZKE ACCESS TO OUR REALITY. IF YOU EXPECT ME TO FIGHT A DEMON, THIS IS THE ONLY LEAD WE HAVE.
WE ARE IN WONDROUS LUCK! I BELIEVE WE HAVE THE VERY TOME OF WHICH YOU SPEAK IN THE LIBRARY!
WOW! GLAD WE DON'T HAVE TO DO SOME DANGEROUS QUEST TO GET THE BOOK!
YOU'VE NEVER SEEN OUR LIBRARY.
SLUGGY FREELANCE PRESENTS
The Storm Breaker Saga
III
THE BOOK
MERCIA DUNGEON
RAR!
DIE!
CHOP!
NUTS
LUTHER! YOU'RE HERE TO LET ME OUT?
HELL NO! I'M LOCKING MYSELF IN! THOSE MONSTERS ARE ALL OVER THE PLACE! THEY'RE KILLING EVERYONE!
FINE, YOU STAY HERE, BUT I NEED YOUR SWORD.
KNOCK YOURSELF OUT, BUDDY!
VAL NEEDS ME! BOY, THAT HAT LOOKED FAMILIAR!
THAT GUY LOOKED FAMILIAR!
"AS I CLIMBED THE DUNGEON STAIRS, THE SOUNDS OF MONSTER HOWLS AND HUMAN SCREAMS GREW LOUDER. AS I CLOSED ON THE PASSAGEWAY TO VAL'S CHAMBER, THEY GREW LOUDER STILL. AND THEN, AS I ROUNDED THE CORNER, THE TURMOIL ROLLED AWAY LIKE A DISTANT STORM."
"IT WAS INSTANTLY APPARENT WHAT HAD HAPPENED. LYSINDA WANTED VALERIE FOR HERSELF, AND NO MAN, WOMAN, NOR DEMON WOULD GET IN THE WAY OF HER PLANS. I HAD NO TIME TO WORRY ABOUT HER NOW."
GUARDS! HELP! HELP!
LADY VALERIE! WHAT IS IT? WHAT'S WRONG?
YOU?...YOU WERE ABLE TO DEFEAT ALL THESE MONSTERS?
I NEED YOU NOW, OR A FIEND WILL KILL MY HUSBAND!
I... UM...
HELP HIM, PLEASE!
"I LOOKED DOWN AT THE MAN WHO COLLAPSED IN MY ARMS, AND THE FACE THAT STARED BACK AT ME WAS NOT THE FACE OF A WARLORD. IT WAS MY OWN FACE. HE WAS NOT A MIRROR OF ME, HE WAS ME."
"ONLY THIS ME WAS SWEATY, OILY, AND STINKY."
OH GOD! IS THIS GUY, LIKE, CONTAGIOUS OR SOMETHING?
THUD!

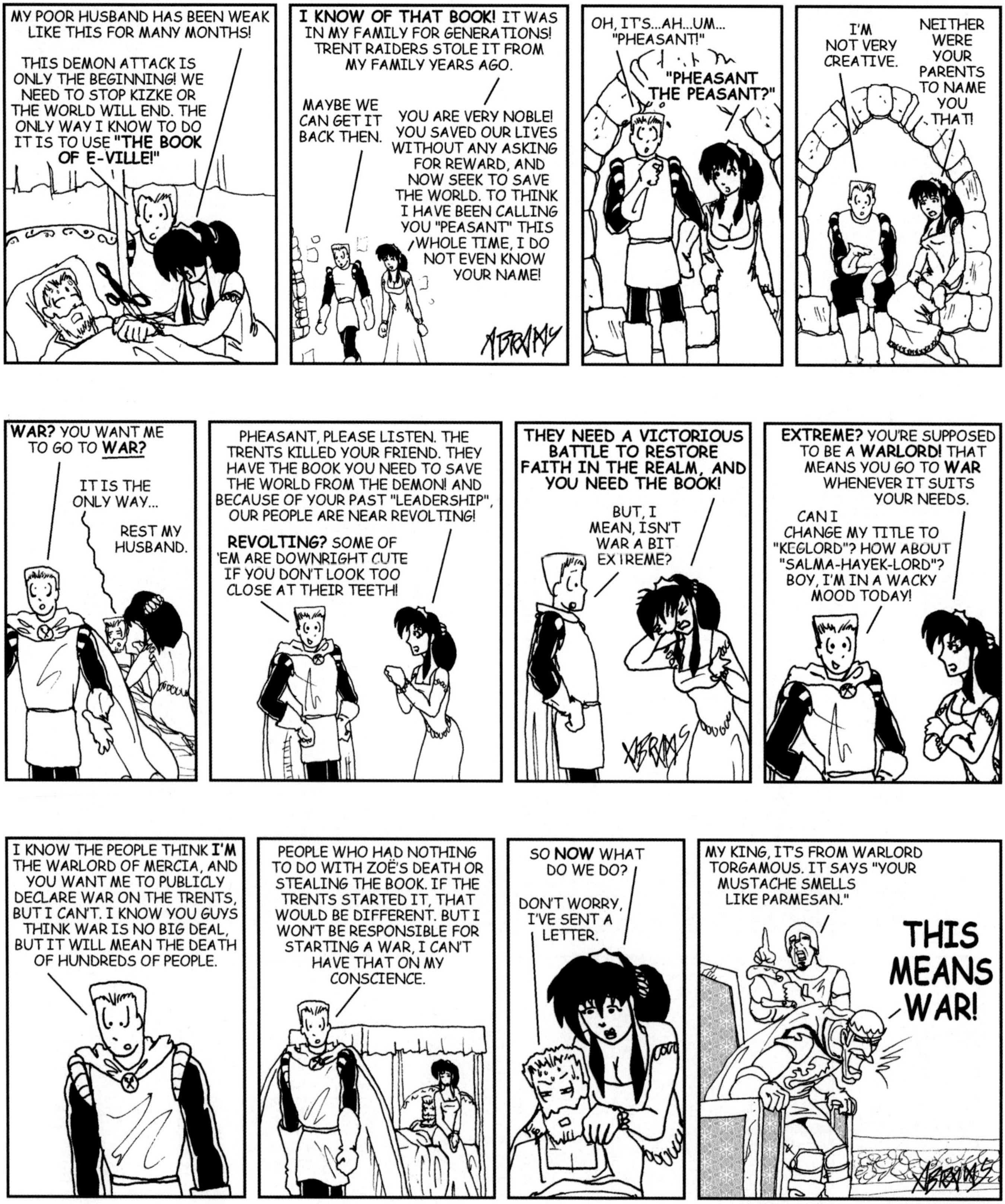

MY POOR HUSBAND HAS BEEN WEAK LIKE THIS FOR MANY MONTHS!
THIS DEMON ATTACK IS ONLY THE BEGINNING! WE NEED TO STOP KIZKE OR THE WORLD WILL END. THE ONLY WAY I KNOW TO DO IT IS TO USE "THE BOOK OF E-VILLE!"
I KNOW OF THAT BOOK! IT WAS IN MY FAMILY FOR GENERATIONS! TRENT RAIDERS STOLE IT FROM MY FAMILY YEARS AGO.
MAYBE WE CAN GET IT BACK THEN.
YOU ARE VERY NOBLE! YOU SAVED OUR LIVES WITHOUT ANY ASKING FOR REWARD, AND NOW SEEK TO SAVE THE WORLD. TO THINK I HAVE BEEN CALLING YOU "PEASANT" THIS WHOLE TIME, I DO NOT EVEN KNOW YOUR NAME!
ABRAMS
OH, IT'S...AH...UM... "PHEASANT!"
"PHEASANT THE PEASANT?"
I'M NOT VERY CREATIVE.
NEITHER WERE YOUR PARENTS TO NAME YOU THAT!
WAR? YOU WANT ME TO GO TO WAR?
IT IS THE ONLY WAY...
REST MY HUSBAND.
PHEASANT, PLEASE LISTEN. THE TRENTS KILLED YOUR FRIEND. THEY HAVE THE BOOK YOU NEED TO SAVE THE WORLD FROM THE DEMON! AND BECAUSE OF YOUR PAST "LEADERSHIP", OUR PEOPLE ARE NEAR REVOLTING!
REVOLTING? SOME OF 'EM ARE DOWNRIGHT CUTE IF YOU DON'T LOOK TOO CLOSE AT THEIR TEETH!
THEY NEED A VICTORIOUS BATTLE TO RESTORE FAITH IN THE REALM, AND YOU NEED THE BOOK!
BUT, I MEAN, ISN'T WAR A BIT EXTREME?
ABRAMS
EXTREME? YOU'RE SUPPOSED TO BE A WARLORD! THAT MEANS YOU GO TO WAR WHENEVER IT SUITS YOUR NEEDS.
CAN I CHANGE MY TITLE TO "KEGLORD"? HOW ABOUT "SALMA-HAYEK-LORD"? BOY, I'M IN A WACKY MOOD TODAY!
I KNOW THE PEOPLE THINK I'M THE WARLORD OF MERCIA, AND YOU WANT ME TO PUBLICLY DECLARE WAR ON THE TRENTS, BUT I CAN'T. I KNOW YOU GUYS THINK WAR IS NO BIG DEAL, BUT IT WILL MEAN THE DEATH OF HUNDREDS OF PEOPLE.
PEOPLE WHO HAD NOTHING TO DO WITH ZOË'S DEATH OR STEALING THE BOOK. IF THE TRENTS STARTED IT, THAT WOULD BE DIFFERENT. BUT I WON'T BE RESPONSIBLE FOR STARTING A WAR, I CAN'T HAVE THAT ON MY CONSCIENCE.
SO NOW WHAT DO WE DO?
DON'T WORRY, I'VE SENT A LETTER.
MY KING, IT'S FROM WARLORD TORGAMOUS. IT SAYS "YOUR MUSTACHE SMELLS LIKE PARMESAN."
THIS MEANS WAR!
ABRAMS

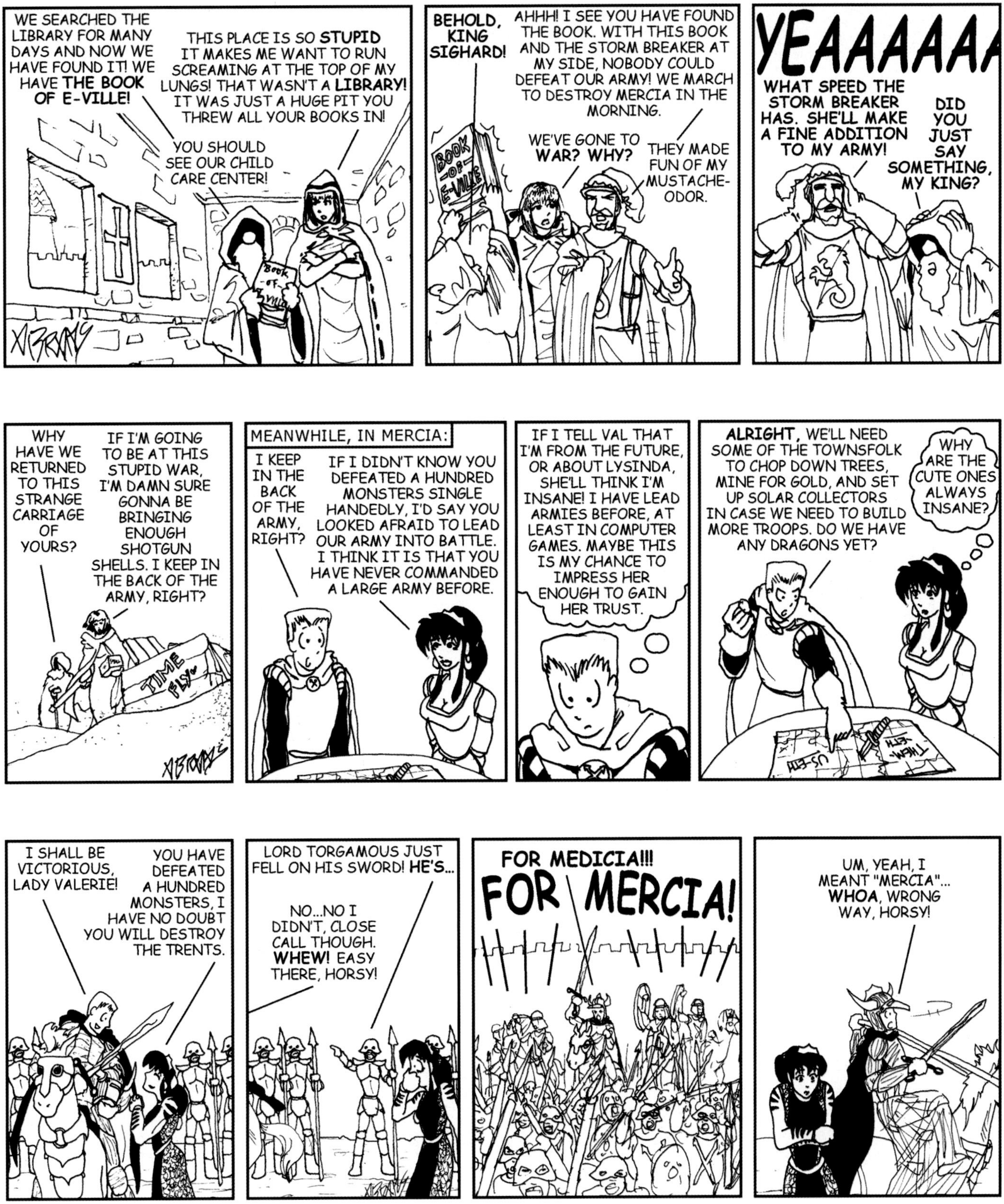
WE SEARCHED THE LIBRARY FOR MANY DAYS AND NOW WE HAVE FOUND IT! WE HAVE THE BOOK OF E-VILLE!
THIS PLACE IS SO STUPID IT MAKES ME WANT TO RUN SCREAMING AT THE TOP OF MY LUNGS! THAT WASN'T A LIBRARY! IT WAS JUST A HUGE PIT YOU THREW ALL YOUR BOOKS IN!
YOU SHOULD SEE OUR CHILD CARE CENTER!
BEHOLD, KING SIGHARD!
AHHH! I SEE YOU HAVE FOUND THE BOOK. WITH THIS BOOK AND THE STORM BREAKER AT MY SIDE, NOBODY COULD DEFEAT OUR ARMY! WE MARCH TO DESTROY MERCIA IN THE MORNING.
WE'VE GONE TO WAR? WHY?
THEY MADE FUN OF MY MUSTACHE-ODOR.
BOOK OF E-VILLE
YEAAAAAA
WHAT SPEED THE STORM BREAKER HAS. SHE'LL MAKE A FINE ADDITION TO MY ARMY!
DID YOU JUST SAY SOMETHING, MY KING?
WHY HAVE WE RETURNED TO THIS STRANGE CARRIAGE OF YOURS?
IF I'M GOING TO BE AT THIS STUPID WAR, I'M DAMN SURE GONNA BE BRINGING ENOUGH SHOTGUN SHELLS. I KEEP IN THE BACK OF THE ARMY, RIGHT?
TIME FLY
MEANWHILE, IN MERCIA:
I KEEP IN THE BACK OF THE ARMY, RIGHT?
IF I DIDN'T KNOW YOU DEFEATED A HUNDRED MONSTERS SINGLE HANDEDLY, I'D SAY YOU LOOKED AFRAID TO LEAD OUR ARMY INTO BATTLE. I THINK IT IS THAT YOU HAVE NEVER COMMANDED A LARGE ARMY BEFORE.
IF I TELL VAL THAT I'M FROM THE FUTURE, OR ABOUT LYSINDA, SHE'LL THINK I'M INSANE! I HAVE LEAD ARMIES BEFORE, AT LEAST IN COMPUTER GAMES. MAYBE THIS IS MY CHANCE TO IMPRESS HER ENOUGH TO GAIN HER TRUST.
ALRIGHT, WE'LL NEED SOME OF THE TOWNSFOLK TO CHOP DOWN TREES, MINE FOR GOLD, AND SET UP SOLAR COLLECTORS IN CASE WE NEED TO BUILD MORE TROOPS. DO WE HAVE ANY DRAGONS YET?
WHY ARE THE CUTE ONES ALWAYS INSANE?
I SHALL BE VICTORIOUS, LADY VALERIE!
YOU HAVE DEFEATED A HUNDRED MONSTERS, I HAVE NO DOUBT YOU WILL DESTROY THE TRENTS.
LORD TORGAMOUS JUST FELL ON HIS SWORD! HE'S...
NO...NO I DIDN'T, CLOSE CALL THOUGH. WHEW! EASY THERE, HORSY!
FOR MEDICIA!!!
FOR MERCIA!
UM, YEAH, I MEANT "MERCIA"... WHOA, WRONG WAY, HORSY!

SLUGGY FREELANCE PRESENTS
The Storm Breaker Saga
IV
THE WAR
LET THE BLOOD OF THE MERCIANS RUN LIKE RAIN!
GET BENT, TRENTS! KICK ASS!
...ZOË?
TORG?
ZOË!

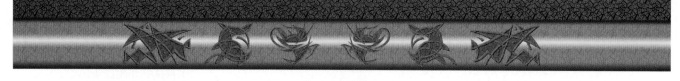

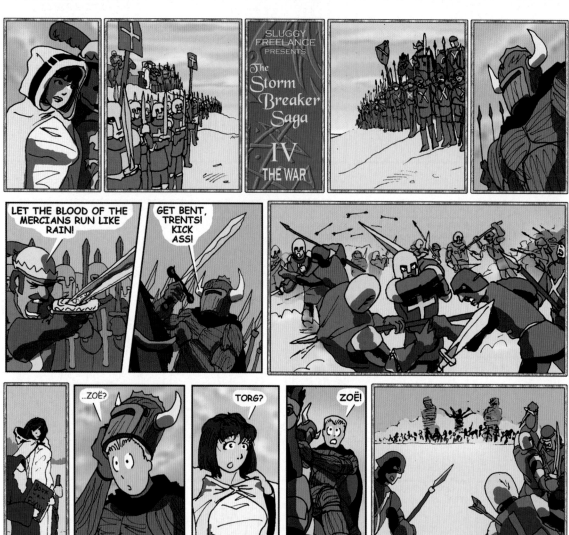

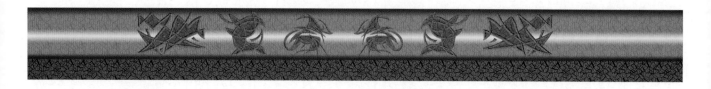

HOWDY-HO NEIGHBORS!
COULD WE BORROW THE BOOK OF E-VILLE, AND ALL OF YOUR SOULS?
DON'T GET UP, WE'LL HELP OURSELVES!

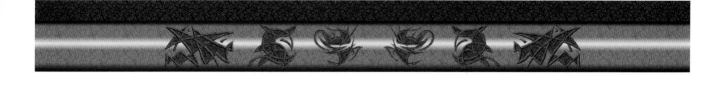

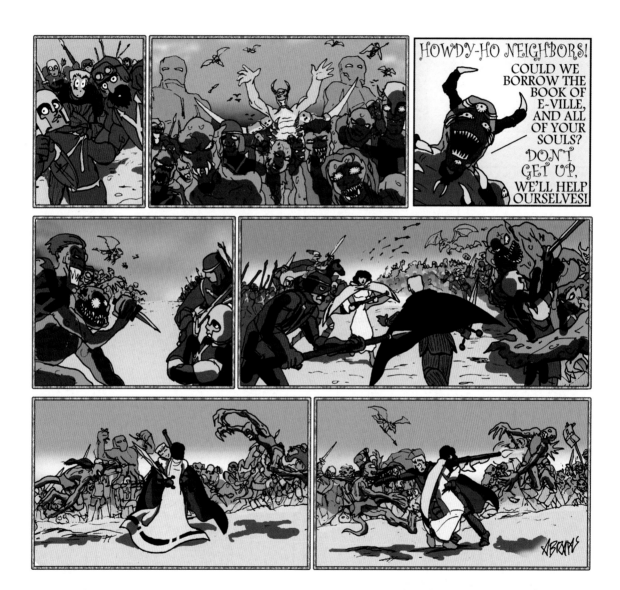

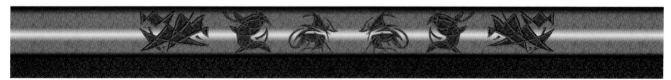

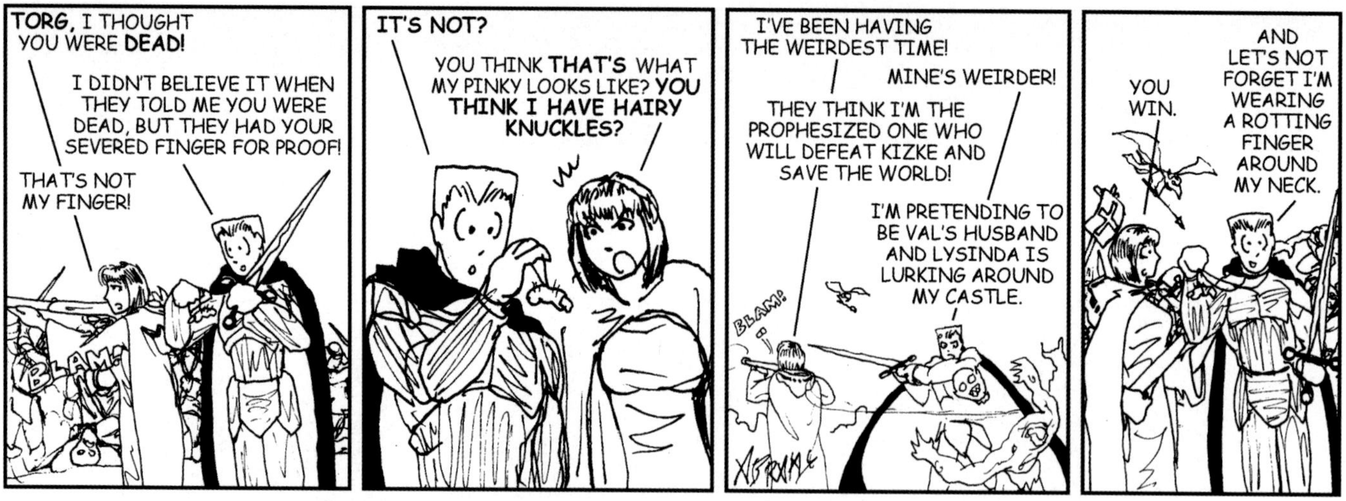
TORG, I THOUGHT YOU WERE DEAD!
I DIDN'T BELIEVE IT WHEN THEY TOLD ME YOU WERE DEAD, BUT THEY HAD YOUR SEVERED FINGER FOR PROOF!
THAT'S NOT MY FINGER!
BLAM!
IT'S NOT?
YOU THINK THAT'S WHAT MY PINKY LOOKS LIKE? YOU THINK I HAVE HAIRY KNUCKLES?
I'VE BEEN HAVING THE WEIRDEST TIME!
MINE'S WEIRDER!
THEY THINK I'M THE PROPHESIZED ONE WHO WILL DEFEAT KIZKE AND SAVE THE WORLD!
I'M PRETENDING TO BE VAL'S HUSBAND AND LYSINDA IS LURKING AROUND MY CASTLE.
BLAM!
YOU WIN.
AND LET'S NOT FORGET I'M WEARING A ROTTING FINGER AROUND MY NECK.

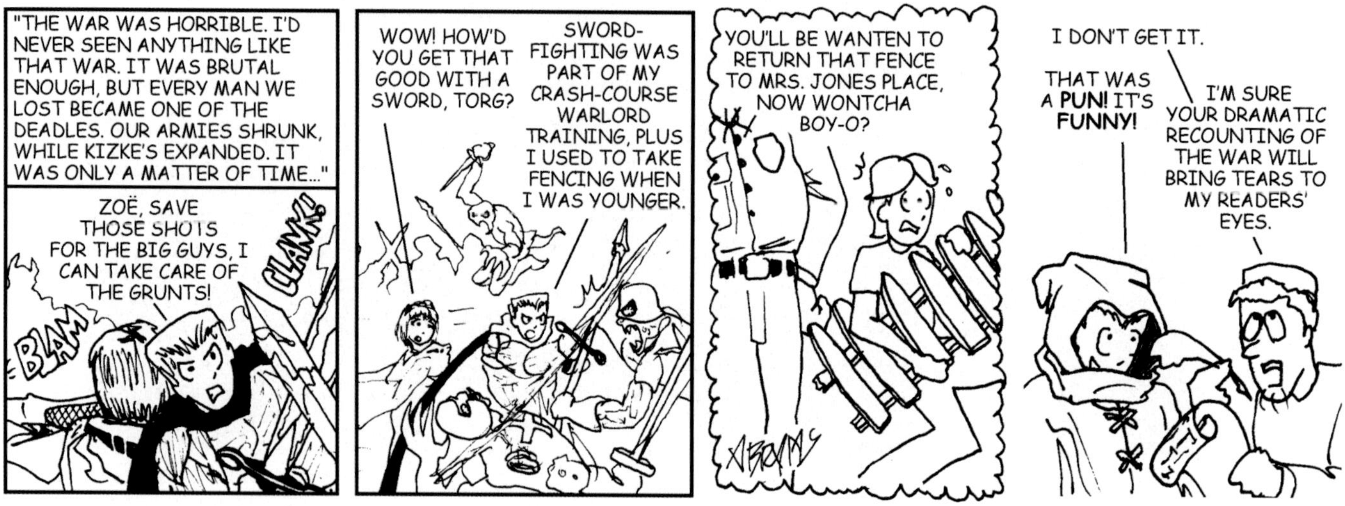
"THE WAR WAS HORRIBLE. I'D NEVER SEEN ANYTHING LIKE THAT WAR. IT WAS BRUTAL ENOUGH, BUT EVERY MAN WE LOST BECAME ONE OF THE DEADLES. OUR ARMIES SHRUNK, WHILE KIZKE'S EXPANDED. IT WAS ONLY A MATTER OF TIME..."
ZOË, SAVE THOSE SHOTS FOR THE BIG GUYS, I CAN TAKE CARE OF THE GRUNTS!
CLANK!
BLAM!
WOW! HOW'D YOU GET THAT GOOD WITH A SWORD, TORG?
SWORD-FIGHTING WAS PART OF MY CRASH-COURSE WARLORD TRAINING, PLUS I USED TO TAKE FENCING WHEN I WAS YOUNGER.
YOU'LL BE WANTEN TO RETURN THAT FENCE TO MRS. JONES PLACE, NOW WONTCHA BOY-O?
I DON'T GET IT.
THAT WAS A PUN! IT'S FUNNY!
I'M SURE YOUR DRAMATIC RECOUNTING OF THE WAR WILL BRING TEARS TO MY READERS' EYES.

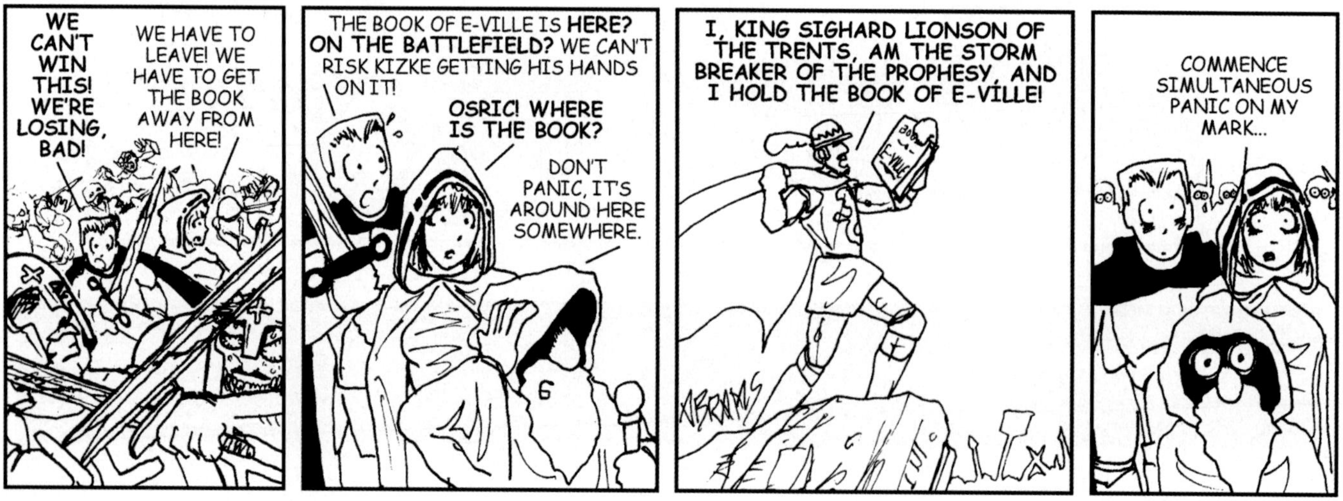
WE CAN'T WIN THIS! WE'RE LOSING, BAD!
WE HAVE TO LEAVE! WE HAVE TO GET THE BOOK AWAY FROM HERE!
THE BOOK OF E-VILLE IS HERE? ON THE BATTLEFIELD? WE CAN'T RISK KIZKE GETTING HIS HANDS ON IT!
OSRIC! WHERE IS THE BOOK?
DON'T PANIC, IT'S AROUND HERE SOMEWHERE.
I, KING SIGHARD LIONSON OF THE TRENTS, AM THE STORM BREAKER OF THE PROPHESY, AND I HOLD THE BOOK OF E-VILLE!
E-VILLE
COMMENCE SIMULTANEOUS PANIC ON MY MARK...

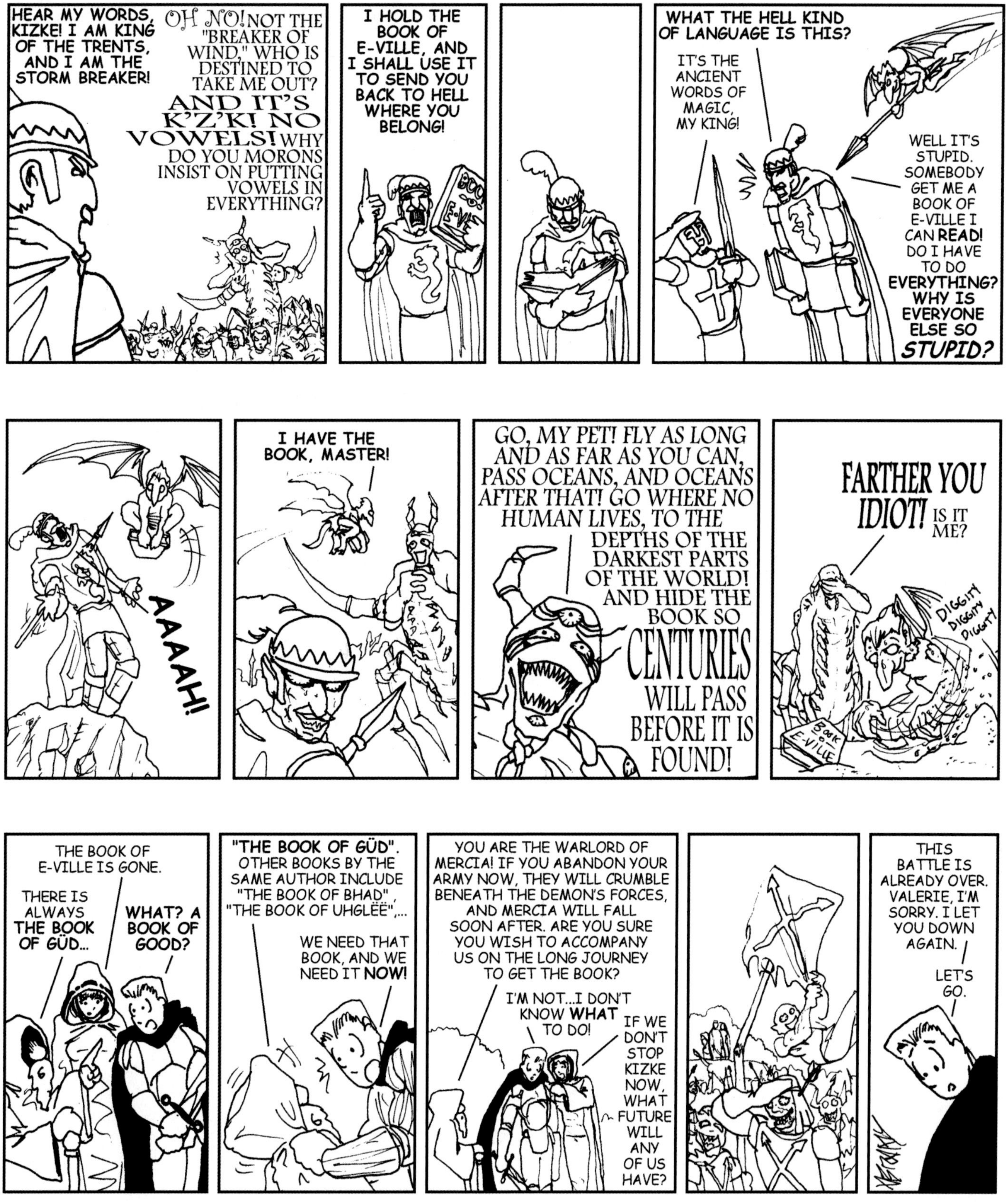
HEAR MY WORDS, KIZKE! I AM KING OF THE TRENTS, AND I AM THE STORM BREAKER!
OH NO! NOT THE "BREAKER OF WIND," WHO IS DESTINED TO TAKE ME OUT? AND IT'S K'Z'K! NO VOWELS! WHY DO YOU MORONS INSIST ON PUTTING VOWELS IN EVERYTHING?
I HOLD THE BOOK OF E-VILLE, AND I SHALL USE IT TO SEND YOU BACK TO HELL WHERE YOU BELONG!
WHAT THE HELL KIND OF LANGUAGE IS THIS?
IT'S THE ANCIENT WORDS OF MAGIC, MY KING!
WELL IT'S STUPID. SOMEBODY GET ME A BOOK OF E-VILLE I CAN READ! DO I HAVE TO DO EVERYTHING? WHY IS EVERYONE ELSE SO STUPID?
AAAAH!!
I HAVE THE BOOK, MASTER!
GO, MY PET! FLY AS LONG AND AS FAR AS YOU CAN, PASS OCEANS, AND OCEANS AFTER THAT! GO WHERE NO HUMAN LIVES, TO THE DEPTHS OF THE DARKEST PARTS OF THE WORLD! AND HIDE THE BOOK SO CENTURIES WILL PASS BEFORE IT IS FOUND!
FARTHER YOU IDIOT! IS IT ME?
DIGGITY DIGGITY DIGGITY
BOOK E-VILLE
THE BOOK OF E-VILLE IS GONE.
THERE IS ALWAYS THE BOOK OF GÜD...
WHAT? A BOOK OF GOOD?
"THE BOOK OF GÜD". OTHER BOOKS BY THE SAME AUTHOR INCLUDE "THE BOOK OF BHAD", "THE BOOK OF UHGLËE",...
WE NEED THAT BOOK, AND WE NEED IT NOW!
YOU ARE THE WARLORD OF MERCIA! IF YOU ABANDON YOUR ARMY NOW, THEY WILL CRUMBLE BENEATH THE DEMON'S FORCES, AND MERCIA WILL FALL SOON AFTER. ARE YOU SURE YOU WISH TO ACCOMPANY US ON THE LONG JOURNEY TO GET THE BOOK?
I'M NOT...I DON'T KNOW WHAT TO DO!
IF WE DON'T STOP KIZKE NOW, WHAT FUTURE WILL ANY OF US HAVE?
THIS BATTLE IS ALREADY OVER. VALERIE, I'M SORRY. I LET YOU DOWN AGAIN.
LET'S GO.

SLUGGY FREELANCE PRESENTS

The Storm Breaker Saga

V

THE QUEST

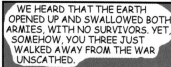

WE HEARD THAT THE EARTH OPENED UP AND SWALLOWED BOTH ARMIES, WITH NO SURVIVORS. YET, SOMEHOW, YOU THREE JUST WALKED AWAY FROM THE WAR UNSCATHED.

THERE WERE A FEW OTHER SURVIVORS, WE DO NOT LIE.

ONCE K'Z'K HAD THE BOOK OF E-VILLE, HE DIDN'T CARE ABOUT THE WAR ANYMORE, SO WE DID JUST WALK OFF THE BATTLEFIELD.

SO, WHY STOP ON YOUR NOBLE QUEST TO SHARE YOUR TALE WITH A LOWLY BARD IN AN UNNAMED TAVERN?

OSRIC SAYS THAT YOU'LL GIVE US INFORMATION IN EXCHANGE FOR OUR STORIES.

WHAT KIND OF INFORMATION?

WE ARE SEEKING THE BOOK OF GÜD. ACCORDING TO OUR RESEARCH, IT IS THE ANTITHESIS TO THE BOOK OF E-VILLE, AND CAN BE USED TO DESTROY THE DEMON WHO PLAGUES OUR LAND.

AND FOR THAT, YOU NEED TO FIND THE HERMIT-WARRIOR OF ASCETIA. HE IS THE ONLY ONE WHO KNOWS THE WAY TO THE CAVE OF YFFI, IN WHICH LIES THE BOOK OF GÜD.

THAT IS OUR QUEST, YES.

AND YOU THINK I KNOW HOW TO FIND HIM.

THAT IS WHAT WE HAVE HEARD.

THIS STORY IS NOT WORTH MAKING A SONG OUT OF FOR ANY BARD, LET ALONE ONE OF MY CALIBER!

THAT'S IT! THIS BARD IS USELESS! LET'S GO.

MY GOD! YOU'D LOOK JUST LIKE THE WARLORD OF MERCIA IF YOU HAD A BEARD!

YEAH, THAT WAS SORT OF A BIG PART OF THE STORY. WEREN'T YOU PAYING ATTENTION?

CRASH!

HOWDY-DO! I'M SIGHARD, KING OF TRENT, AND I'M HERE TO BREAK A STORM-BREAKER! HEY! THERE'S ONE!

RUN!

EEK!

THE KING OF THE TRENTS, A PUPPET OF THE DEMON? ALL YOU HAVE TOLD ME IS TRUE? EVERYTHING?

OF COURSE IT'S TRUE! IF YOU DIDN'T BELIEVE IT, WHY DID YOU WRITE IT ALL DOWN?

I DIDN'T! SEE, I'VE JUST BEEN TRYING TO LAYOUT SOME LANDSCAPING. A KOI POND WOULD JUST MAKE THE YARD PERFECT.

IT'LL BE A PAIN TO MAINTAIN. WHY NOT BUILD AN ARBOR THERE? GET SOME SHADE ON THOSE HOT SUMMER DAYS.

GUYS!

THUNK

STAY!

DON'T BE SNIPPY MISSY!

WATCH YOUR WORDS! KIZKE CAN HEAR AND SEE THROUGH HIS MONSTERS.

BUT...BUT THAT IS THE KING OF THE TRENTS!

NOT ANY MORE.

BARD, CAN YOU HELP US FIND THE MAN WE SEEK?

ARE YOU IN OR OUT?

I'M IN, I CAN HELP.

BLAM

AND COULD YOU ALL START THIS STORY OVER FROM THE BEGINNING?

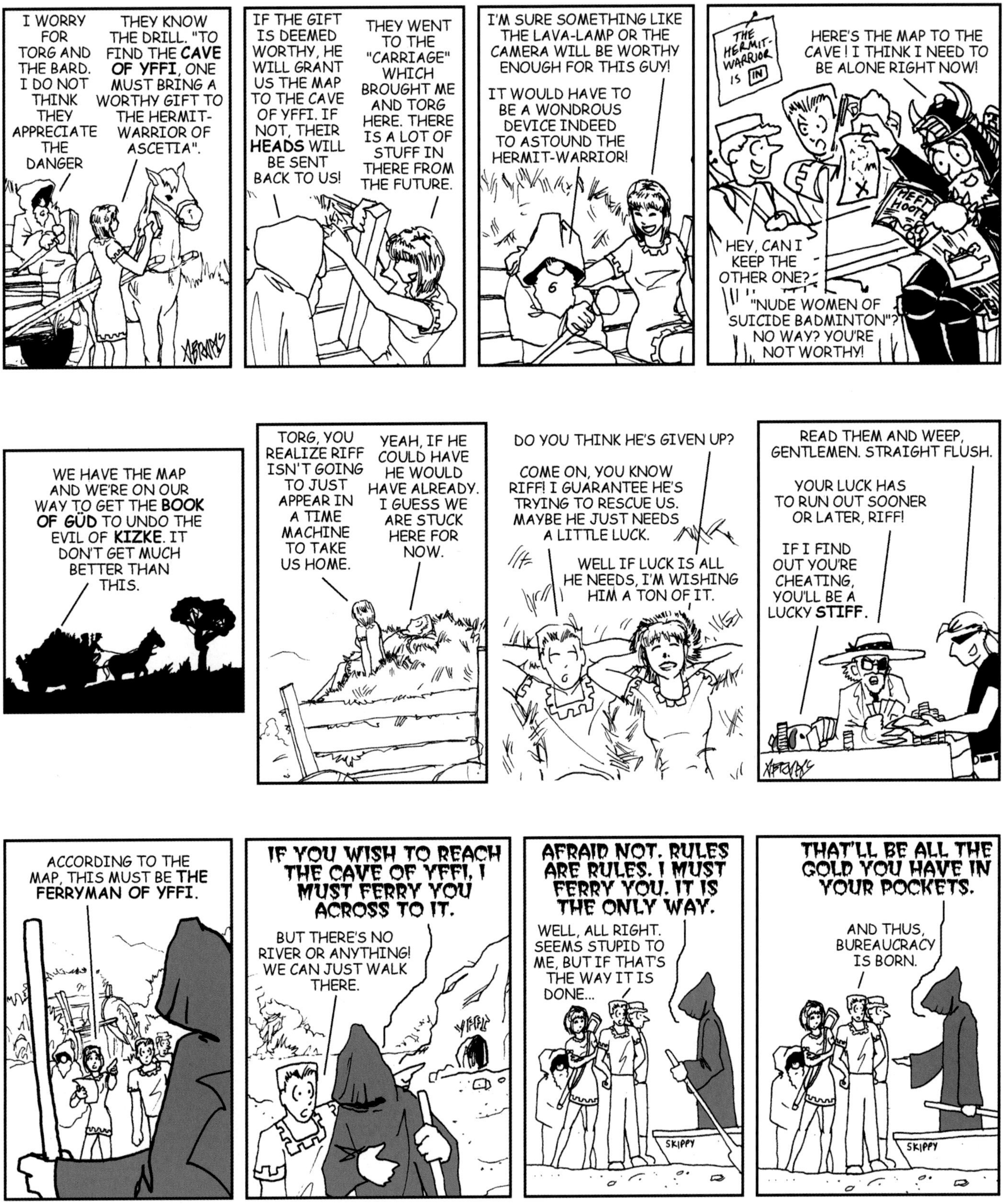
I WORRY FOR TORG AND THE BARD. I DO NOT THINK THEY APPRECIATE THE DANGER
THEY KNOW THE DRILL. "TO FIND THE **CAVE OF YFFI**, ONE MUST BRING A WORTHY GIFT TO THE HERMIT-WARRIOR OF ASCETIA".
IF THE GIFT IS DEEMED WORTHY, HE WILL GRANT US THE MAP TO THE CAVE OF YFFI. IF NOT, THEIR **HEADS** WILL BE SENT BACK TO US!
THEY WENT TO THE "CARRIAGE" WHICH BROUGHT ME AND TORG HERE. THERE IS A LOT OF STUFF IN THERE FROM THE FUTURE.
I'M SURE SOMETHING LIKE THE LAVA-LAMP OR THE CAMERA WILL BE WORTHY ENOUGH FOR THIS GUY!
IT WOULD HAVE TO BE A WONDROUS DEVICE INDEED TO ASTOUND THE HERMIT-WARRIOR!
THE HERMIT-WARRIOR IS IN
HERE'S THE MAP TO THE CAVE! I THINK I NEED TO BE ALONE RIGHT NOW!
HEY, CAN I KEEP THE OTHER ONE?
"NUDE WOMEN OF SUICIDE BADMINTON"? NO WAY? YOU'RE NOT WORTHY!
WE HAVE THE MAP AND WE'RE ON OUR WAY TO GET THE **BOOK OF GÜD** TO UNDO THE EVIL OF **KIZKE**. IT DON'T GET MUCH BETTER THAN THIS.
TORG, YOU REALIZE RIFF ISN'T GOING TO JUST APPEAR IN A TIME MACHINE TO TAKE US HOME.
YEAH, IF HE COULD HAVE HE WOULD HAVE ALREADY. I GUESS WE ARE STUCK HERE FOR NOW.
DO YOU THINK HE'S GIVEN UP?
COME ON, YOU KNOW RIFF! I GUARANTEE HE'S TRYING TO RESCUE US. MAYBE HE JUST NEEDS A LITTLE LUCK.
WELL IF LUCK IS ALL HE NEEDS, I'M WISHING HIM A TON OF IT.
READ THEM AND WEEP, GENTLEMEN. STRAIGHT FLUSH.
YOUR LUCK HAS TO RUN OUT SOONER OR LATER, RIFF!
IF I FIND OUT YOU'RE CHEATING, YOU'LL BE A LUCKY **STIFF**.
ACCORDING TO THE MAP, THIS MUST BE **THE FERRYMAN OF YFFI**.
IF YOU WISH TO REACH THE CAVE OF YFFI, I MUST FERRY YOU ACROSS TO IT.
BUT THERE'S NO RIVER OR ANYTHING! WE CAN JUST WALK THERE.
YFFI
AFRAID NOT. RULES ARE RULES. I MUST FERRY YOU. IT IS THE ONLY WAY.
WELL, ALL RIGHT. SEEMS STUPID TO ME, BUT IF THAT'S THE WAY IT IS DONE...
SKIPPY
THAT'LL BE ALL THE GOLD YOU HAVE IN YOUR POCKETS.
AND THUS, BUREAUCRACY IS BORN.
SKIPPY

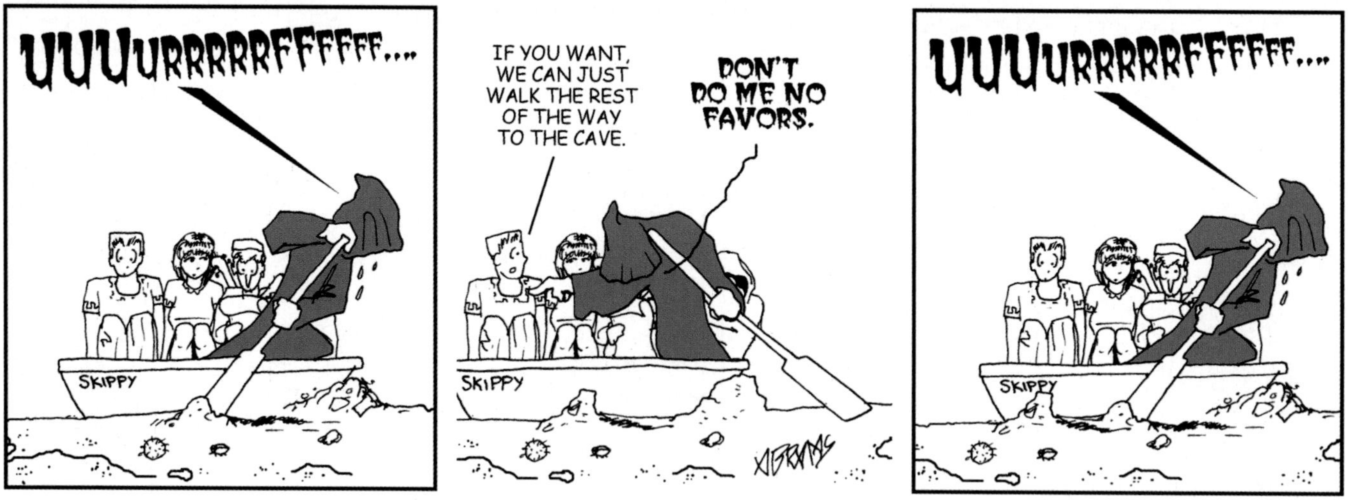
UUUURRRRRFFFFFF....
IF YOU WANT, WE CAN JUST WALK THE REST OF THE WAY TO THE CAVE.
DON'T DO ME NO FAVORS.
SKIPPY
UUUURRRRRFFFFFF....

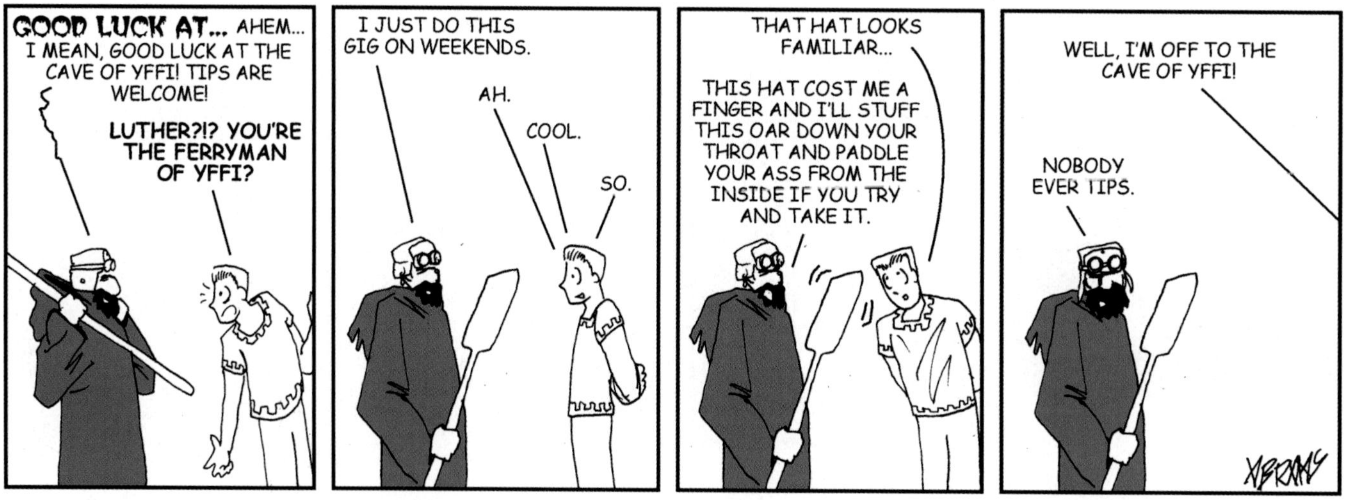
GOOD LUCK AT... AHEM... I MEAN, GOOD LUCK AT THE CAVE OF YFFI! TIPS ARE WELCOME!
LUTHER?!? YOU'RE THE FERRYMAN OF YFFI?
I JUST DO THIS GIG ON WEEKENDS.
AH.
COOL.
SO.
THAT HAT LOOKS FAMILIAR...
THIS HAT COST ME A FINGER AND I'LL STUFF THIS OAR DOWN YOUR THROAT AND PADDLE YOUR ASS FROM THE INSIDE IF YOU TRY AND TAKE IT.
WELL, I'M OFF TO THE CAVE OF YFFI!
NOBODY EVER TIPS.

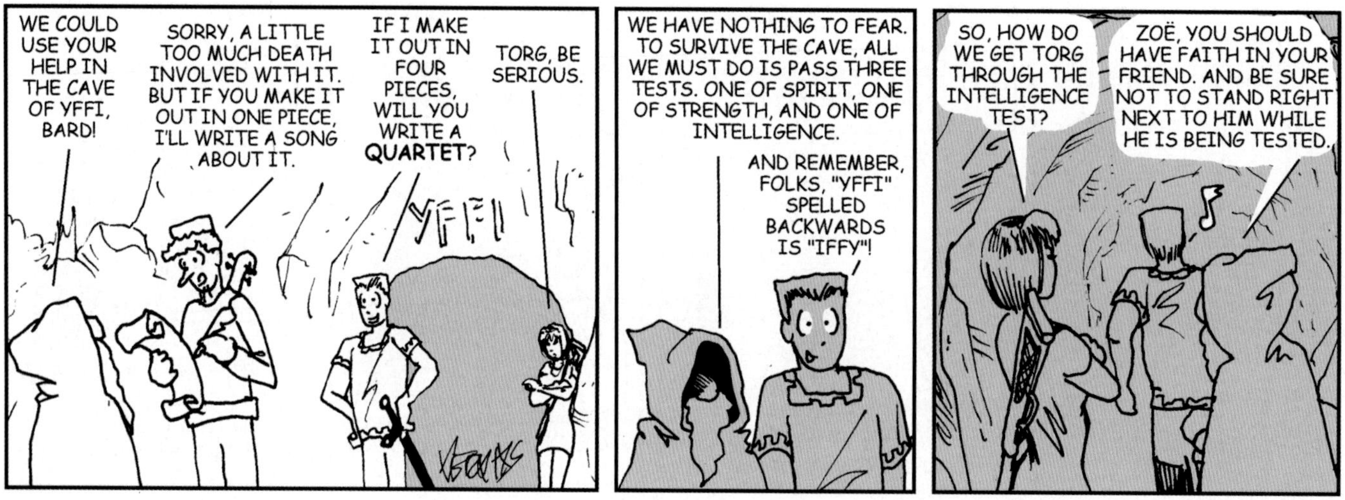
WE COULD USE YOUR HELP IN THE CAVE OF YFFI, BARD!
SORRY, A LITTLE TOO MUCH DEATH INVOLVED WITH IT. BUT IF YOU MAKE IT OUT IN ONE PIECE, I'LL WRITE A SONG ABOUT IT.
IF I MAKE IT OUT IN FOUR PIECES, WILL YOU WRITE A QUARTET?
TORG, BE SERIOUS.
YFFI
WE HAVE NOTHING TO FEAR. TO SURVIVE THE CAVE, ALL WE MUST DO IS PASS THREE TESTS. ONE OF SPIRIT, ONE OF STRENGTH, AND ONE OF INTELLIGENCE.
AND REMEMBER, FOLKS, "YFFI" SPELLED BACKWARDS IS "IFFY"!
SO, HOW DO WE GET TORG THROUGH THE INTELLIGENCE TEST?
ZOË, YOU SHOULD HAVE FAITH IN YOUR FRIEND. AND BE SURE NOT TO STAND RIGHT NEXT TO HIM WHILE HE IS BEING TESTED.

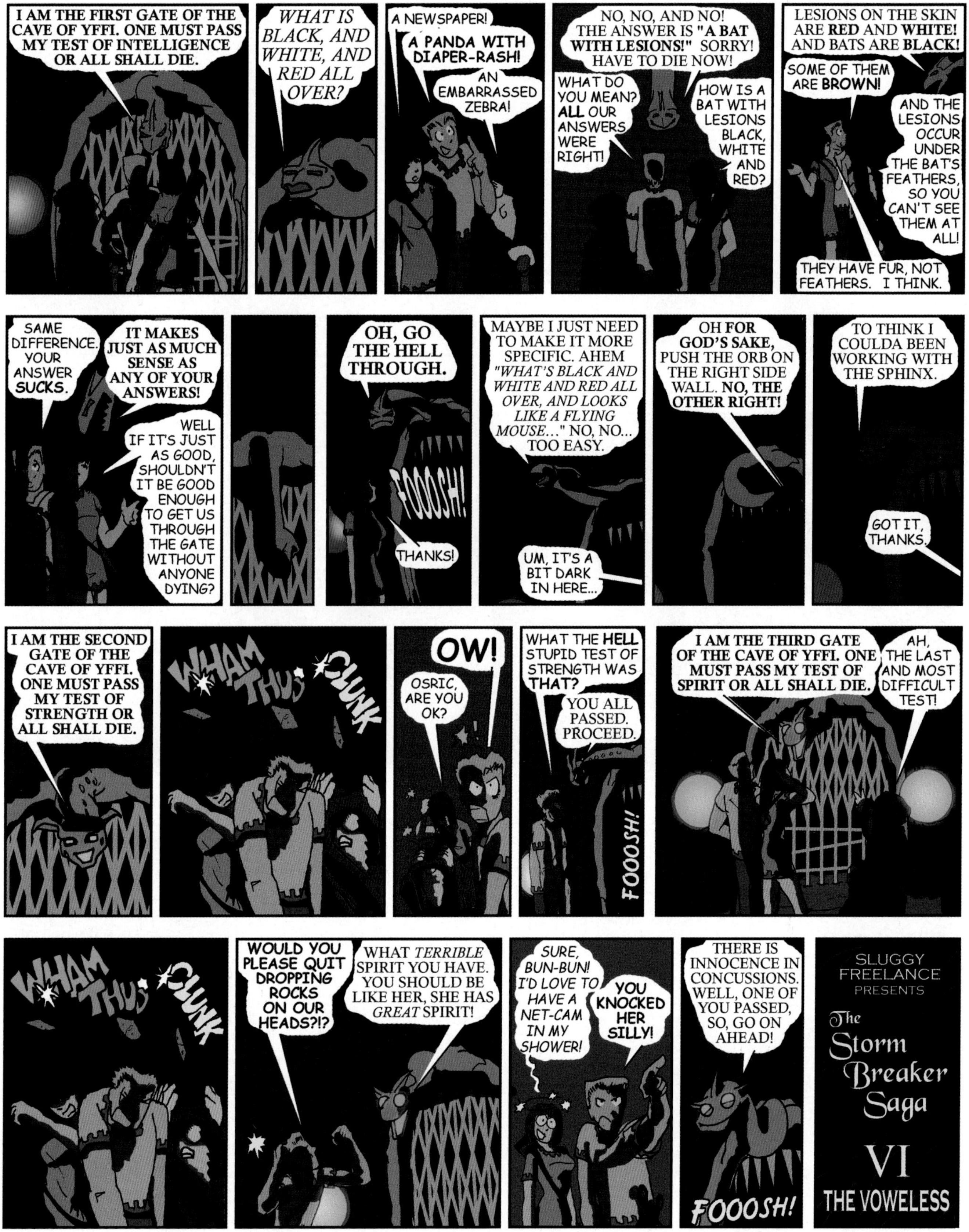
I AM THE FIRST GATE OF THE CAVE OF YFFI. ONE MUST PASS MY TEST OF INTELLIGENCE OR ALL SHALL DIE.
WHAT IS BLACK, AND WHITE, AND RED ALL OVER?
A NEWSPAPER!
A PANDA WITH DIAPER-RASH!
AN EMBARRASSED ZEBRA!
NO, NO, AND NO! THE ANSWER IS "A BAT WITH LESIONS!" SORRY! HAVE TO DIE NOW!
WHAT DO YOU MEAN? ALL OUR ANSWERS WERE RIGHT!
HOW IS A BAT WITH LESIONS BLACK, WHITE AND RED?
LESIONS ON THE SKIN ARE RED AND WHITE! AND BATS ARE BLACK!
SOME OF THEM ARE BROWN!
AND THE LESIONS OCCUR UNDER THE BAT'S FEATHERS, SO YOU CAN'T SEE THEM AT ALL!
THEY HAVE FUR, NOT FEATHERS. I THINK.
SAME DIFFERENCE. YOUR ANSWER SUCKS.
IT MAKES JUST AS MUCH SENSE AS ANY OF YOUR ANSWERS!
WELL IF IT'S JUST AS GOOD, SHOULDN'T IT BE GOOD ENOUGH TO GET US THROUGH THE GATE WITHOUT ANYONE DYING?
OH, GO THE HELL THROUGH.
FOOOSH!
THANKS!
MAYBE I JUST NEED TO MAKE IT MORE SPECIFIC. AHEM "WHAT'S BLACK AND WHITE AND RED ALL OVER, AND LOOKS LIKE A FLYING MOUSE..." NO, NO... TOO EASY.
UM, IT'S A BIT DARK IN HERE...
OH FOR GOD'S SAKE, PUSH THE ORB ON THE RIGHT SIDE WALL. NO, THE OTHER RIGHT!
TO THINK I COULDA BEEN WORKING WITH THE SPHINX.
GOT IT, THANKS.
I AM THE SECOND GATE OF THE CAVE OF YFFI. ONE MUST PASS MY TEST OF STRENGTH OR ALL SHALL DIE.
WHAM THUS CLUNK
OW!
OSRIC, ARE YOU OK?
WHAT THE HELL STUPID TEST OF STRENGTH WAS THAT?
YOU ALL PASSED. PROCEED.
FOOOSH!
I AM THE THIRD GATE OF THE CAVE OF YFFI. ONE MUST PASS MY TEST OF SPIRIT OR ALL SHALL DIE.
AH, THE LAST AND MOST DIFFICULT TEST!
WHAM THUS CLUNK
WOULD YOU PLEASE QUIT DROPPING ROCKS ON OUR HEADS?!?
WHAT TERRIBLE SPIRIT YOU HAVE. YOU SHOULD BE LIKE HER, SHE HAS GREAT SPIRIT!
SURE, BUN-BUN! I'D LOVE TO HAVE A NET-CAM IN MY SHOWER!
YOU KNOCKED HER SILLY!
THERE IS INNOCENCE IN CONCUSSIONS. WELL, ONE OF YOU PASSED, SO, GO ON AHEAD!
FOOOSH!
SLUGGY FREELANCE PRESENTS
The Storm Breaker Saga
VI
THE VOWELESS

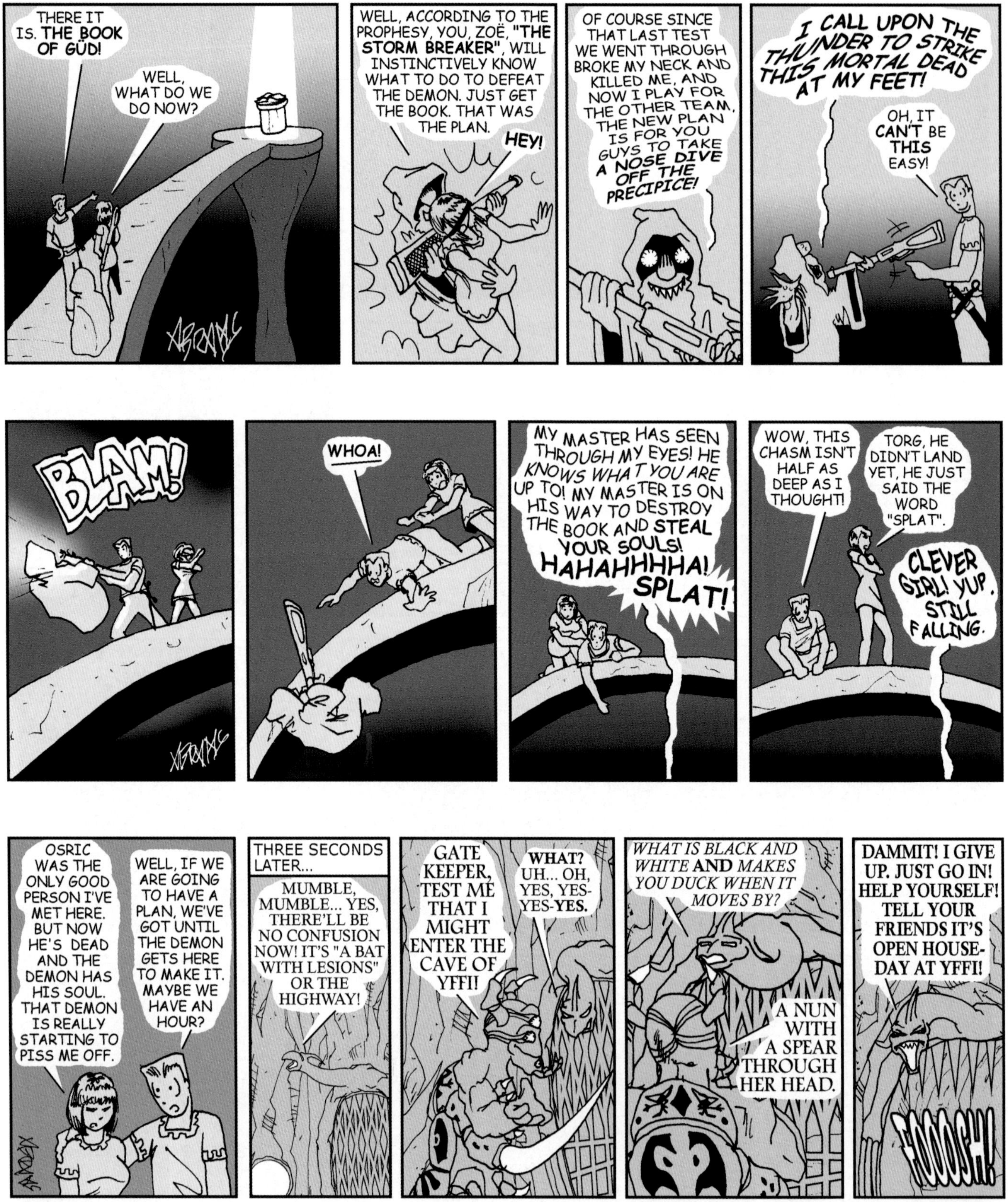
THERE IT IS. THE BOOK OF GÜD!
WELL, WHAT DO WE DO NOW?
WELL, ACCORDING TO THE PROPHESY, YOU, ZOË, "THE STORM BREAKER", WILL INSTINCTIVELY KNOW WHAT TO DO TO DEFEAT THE DEMON. JUST GET THE BOOK. THAT WAS THE PLAN.
HEY!
OF COURSE SINCE THAT LAST TEST WE WENT THROUGH BROKE MY NECK AND KILLED ME, AND NOW I PLAY FOR THE OTHER TEAM, THE NEW PLAN IS FOR YOU GUYS TO TAKE A NOSE DIVE OFF THE PRECIPICE!
I CALL UPON THE THUNDER TO STRIKE THIS MORTAL DEAD AT MY FEET!
OH, IT CAN'T BE THIS EASY!
BLAM!
WHOA!
MY MASTER HAS SEEN THROUGH MY EYES! HE KNOWS WHAT YOU ARE UP TO! MY MASTER IS ON HIS WAY TO DESTROY THE BOOK AND STEAL YOUR SOULS! HAHAHHHHA!
SPLAT!
WOW, THIS CHASM ISN'T HALF AS DEEP AS I THOUGHT!
TORG, HE DIDN'T LAND YET, HE JUST SAID THE WORD "SPLAT".
CLEVER GIRL! YUP. STILL FALLING.
OSRIC WAS THE ONLY GOOD PERSON I'VE MET HERE. BUT NOW HE'S DEAD AND THE DEMON HAS HIS SOUL. THAT DEMON IS REALLY STARTING TO PISS ME OFF.
WELL, IF WE ARE GOING TO HAVE A PLAN, WE'VE GOT UNTIL THE DEMON GETS HERE TO MAKE IT. MAYBE WE HAVE AN HOUR?
THREE SECONDS LATER...
MUMBLE, MUMBLE... YES, THERE'LL BE NO CONFUSION NOW! IT'S "A BAT WITH LESIONS" OR THE HIGHWAY!
GATE KEEPER, TEST ME THAT I MIGHT ENTER THE CAVE OF YFFI!
WHAT? UH... OH, YES, YES-YES-YES.
WHAT IS BLACK AND WHITE AND MAKES YOU DUCK WHEN IT MOVES BY?
A NUN WITH A SPEAR THROUGH HER HEAD.
DAMMIT! I GIVE UP. JUST GO IN! HELP YOURSELF! TELL YOUR FRIENDS IT'S OPEN HOUSE-DAY AT YFFI!
FOOOSH!

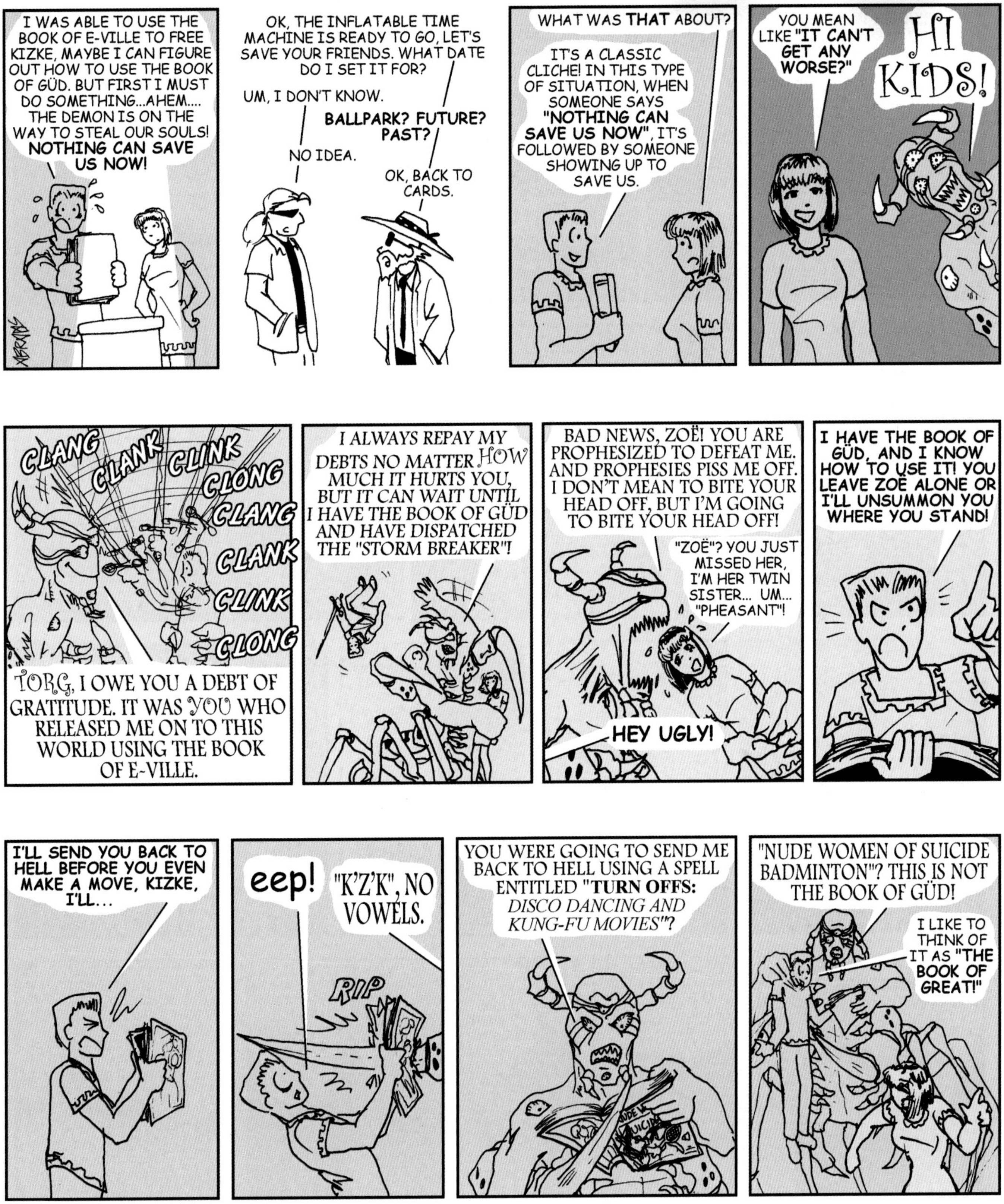
I WAS ABLE TO USE THE BOOK OF E-VILLE TO FREE KIZKE, MAYBE I CAN FIGURE OUT HOW TO USE THE BOOK OF GÜD. BUT FIRST I MUST DO SOMETHING...AHEM.... THE DEMON IS ON THE WAY TO STEAL OUR SOULS! NOTHING CAN SAVE US NOW!
OK, THE INFLATABLE TIME MACHINE IS READY TO GO, LET'S SAVE YOUR FRIENDS. WHAT DATE DO I SET IT FOR?
UM, I DON'T KNOW.
BALLPARK? FUTURE? PAST?
NO IDEA.
OK, BACK TO CARDS.
WHAT WAS THAT ABOUT?
IT'S A CLASSIC CLICHE! IN THIS TYPE OF SITUATION, WHEN SOMEONE SAYS "NOTHING CAN SAVE US NOW", IT'S FOLLOWED BY SOMEONE SHOWING UP TO SAVE US.
YOU MEAN LIKE "IT CAN'T GET ANY WORSE?"
HI KIDS!
CLANG CLANK CLINK CLONG CLANG CLANK CLINK CLONG
TORG, I OWE YOU A DEBT OF GRATITUDE. IT WAS YOU WHO RELEASED ME ON TO THIS WORLD USING THE BOOK OF E-VILLE.
I ALWAYS REPAY MY DEBTS NO MATTER HOW MUCH IT HURTS YOU, BUT IT CAN WAIT UNTIL I HAVE THE BOOK OF GÜD AND HAVE DISPATCHED THE "STORM BREAKER"!
BAD NEWS, ZOË! YOU ARE PROPHESIZED TO DEFEAT ME. AND PROPHESIES PISS ME OFF. I DON'T MEAN TO BITE YOUR HEAD OFF, BUT I'M GOING TO BITE YOUR HEAD OFF!
"ZOË"? YOU JUST MISSED HER, I'M HER TWIN SISTER... UM... "PHEASANT"!
HEY UGLY!
I HAVE THE BOOK OF GÜD, AND I KNOW HOW TO USE IT! YOU LEAVE ZOË ALONE OR I'LL UNSUMMON YOU WHERE YOU STAND!
I'LL SEND YOU BACK TO HELL BEFORE YOU EVEN MAKE A MOVE, KIZKE, I'LL...
eep!
"K'Z'K", NO VOWELS.
RIP
YOU WERE GOING TO SEND ME BACK TO HELL USING A SPELL ENTITLED "TURN OFFS: DISCO DANCING AND KUNG-FU MOVIES"?
"NUDE WOMEN OF SUICIDE BADMINTON"? THIS IS NOT THE BOOK OF GÜD!
I LIKE TO THINK OF IT AS "THE BOOK OF GREAT!"

"NUDE WOMEN OF SUICIDE BADMINTON"! NICE BOOK, BUT IT IS THE BOOK OF GÜD THAT I TRULY WANT. WAS THIS A DECOY? DID YOU TRY TO DECOY ME?
bobble bobble bobble
THAT'S RIGHT, CAPTAIN CONSONANT! MY JOB WAS TO DISTRACT YOU LONG ENOUGH FOR ZOË TO USE THE BOOK.
NUDE WOMEN OF SUICIDE BADMINTON
GET HIM, ZOË!
I...
...I...
...I CAN'T READ IT!
SLUGGY FREELANCE PRESENTS
The Storm Breaker Saga
VII
LAST CALL
AH-HAHAHAHAHAHA
SWIPE
OF COURSE YOU CAN'T, THIS BOOK WAS NOT MEANT FOR BUGS LIKE YOU! NOW I WILL SEND THIS BOOK WHERE I SENT THE OTHER AND... and... ....
my eyes!
I COULDN'T READ IT BECAUSE THERE ARE NO WORDS. ONLY PICTURES.
oh! ooh! oooooh, you little mother...
SQUISH!
PICTURES? PICTURES DID THAT?
IT'S MORE THAN JUST PICTURES, THEY'RE LIKE MAGIC PICTURES! THEY STIR SOMETHING DEEP INSIDE!
LIKE THE PICTURES IN "THE NUDE WOMEN OF SUICIDE BADMINTON"?
THEY CAUSE PEACE AND SERENITY THAT THE FOOLISH CANNOT SEE, AND THAT EVIL CANNOT STAND UP TO.
PRETTY!
SO, THAT IS IT?
WE SHOULD LEAVE THE BOOK HERE AND GO.
WHAT WAS THE WHOLE DEAL WITH YOU BEING THE "STORM BREAKER?" IT NEVER EVEN RAINED!
SYMBOLISM. KIZKE WAS THE STORM THAT WOULD HAVE SWEPT THE WORLD, AND I STOPPED HIM.
IF I WAS A PROPHET I WOULDN'T WASTE TIME WITH VAGUE SYMBOLISM! I'D HAVE PROPHESIED YOU THE "BUG SQUISHER!" THEN YOU WOULD OF KNOWN TO WEAR BIG BOOTS! THAT WAY YOU WOULDN'T HAVE DEMON-GUTS BETWEEN YOUR TOES RIGHT NOW!
AND THUS, THE SERENITY RUNS AWAY FROM ME FASTER THAN A BLIND DATE.

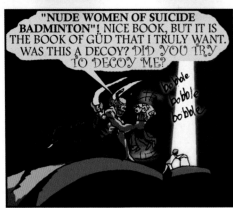

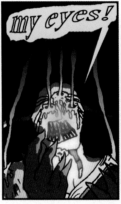

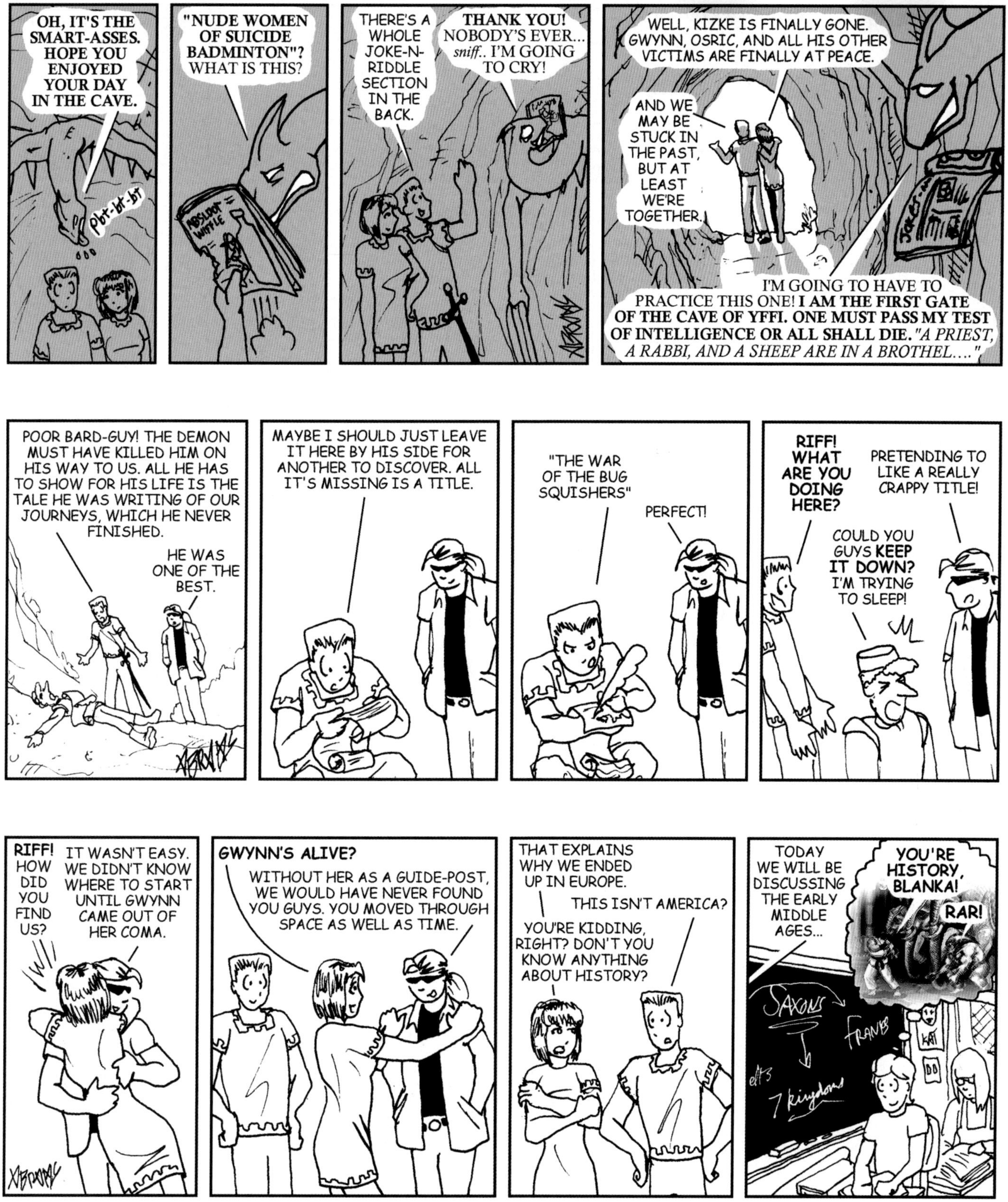
OH, IT'S THE SMART-ASSES. HOPE YOU ENJOYED YOUR DAY IN THE CAVE.
plbt-bt-bt
"NUDE WOMEN OF SUICIDE BADMINTON"? WHAT IS THIS?
THERE'S A WHOLE JOKE-N-RIDDLE SECTION IN THE BACK.
THANK YOU! NOBODY'S EVER... *sniff*.. I'M GOING TO CRY!
WELL, KIZKE IS FINALLY GONE. GWYNN, OSRIC, AND ALL HIS OTHER VICTIMS ARE FINALLY AT PEACE.
AND WE MAY BE STUCK IN THE PAST, BUT AT LEAST WE'RE TOGETHER.
I'M GOING TO HAVE TO PRACTICE THIS ONE! **I AM THE FIRST GATE OF THE CAVE OF YFFI. ONE MUST PASS MY TEST OF INTELLIGENCE OR ALL SHALL DIE.** *"A PRIEST, A RABBI, AND A SHEEP ARE IN A BROTHEL...."*
POOR BARD-GUY! THE DEMON MUST HAVE KILLED HIM ON HIS WAY TO US. ALL HE HAS TO SHOW FOR HIS LIFE IS THE TALE HE WAS WRITING OF OUR JOURNEYS, WHICH HE NEVER FINISHED.
HE WAS ONE OF THE BEST.
MAYBE I SHOULD JUST LEAVE IT HERE BY HIS SIDE FOR ANOTHER TO DISCOVER. ALL IT'S MISSING IS A TITLE.
"THE WAR OF THE BUG SQUISHERS"
PERFECT!
RIFF! WHAT ARE YOU DOING HERE?
PRETENDING TO LIKE A REALLY CRAPPY TITLE!
COULD YOU GUYS **KEEP IT DOWN?** I'M TRYING TO SLEEP!
RIFF! HOW DID YOU FIND US?
IT WASN'T EASY. WE DIDN'T KNOW WHERE TO START UNTIL GWYNN CAME OUT OF HER COMA.
GWYNN'S ALIVE?
WITHOUT HER AS A GUIDE-POST, WE WOULD HAVE NEVER FOUND YOU GUYS. YOU MOVED THROUGH SPACE AS WELL AS TIME.
THAT EXPLAINS WHY WE ENDED UP IN EUROPE.
THIS ISN'T AMERICA?
YOU'RE KIDDING, RIGHT? DON'T YOU KNOW ANYTHING ABOUT HISTORY?
TODAY WE WILL BE DISCUSSING THE EARLY MIDDLE AGES...
YOU'RE HISTORY, BLANKA!
RAR!
SAXONS
FRANKS
7 kingdoms

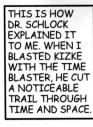

THIS IS HOW DR. SCHLOCK EXPLAINED IT TO ME. WHEN I BLASTED KIZKE WITH THE TIME BLASTER, HE CUT A NOTICEABLE TRAIL THROUGH TIME AND SPACE.

MR. TIME LINE

WHEN GWYNN'S SOUL WAS FREED, IT RUSHED TO MEET HER WAITING BODY.

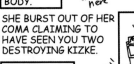

SHE BURST OUT OF HER COMA CLAIMING TO HAVE SEEN YOU TWO DESTROYING KIZKE.

WHEN MY TIME MACHINE MALFUNCTIONED, YOU WENT SPINNING OFF INTO THE CONTINUUM AND RODE KIZKE'S TRAIL LIKE A BOBSLED.

AND IT WASN'T LONG BEFORE DR. SCHLOCK COULD SEND ME TO FOLLOW HER TRAIL BACK TO YOU.

NOW I GET IT!

HEY, WHO DREW ALL OVER MY SCROLL?

MUST HAVE BEEN THAT DARN DEMON.

sniff! DEMONS CAN BE SO CRUEL!

YOU GUYS GO BACK TO OUR TIME. I'M STAYING.

WHAT?!?

NOW THAT WE'VE "SAVED THE FUTURE", THERE'S STILL A CHANCE I CAN SAVE VAL FROM LYSINDA. I HAVE TO TAKE THAT CHANCE. TELL EVERYONE I'M GOING TO MISS THEM. EVEN BUN-BUN.

VAL AND LYSINDA ARE HERE? NOW?

LONG STORY. TORG, PLEASE COME BACK HOME WITH US! WE HAVE OUR LIVES THERE! I HAVE FINALS, YOU HAVE YOUR BUSINESS TO TAKE CARE OF...

UM... WE'RE RETURNING TO MID-AUGUST, YOU MISSED YOUR FINALS.

AAAAAAAH! DO MY PARENTS KNOW? LEAVE ME HERE!

TORG, THIS IS AN INFLATABLE TIME MACHINE! IT'S VERY UNSTABLE! ANY SHARP THING COULD POP IT, STRANDING US HERE! AN ACORN! A ROCK, ANYTHING!

PLEASE LEAVE! IF PEOPLE FROM MY TIME WERE TO ACTUALLY MEET YOU, IT WOULD RUIN THE HEROIC QUALITY OF MY EPIC!

PLEASE TORG, LET'S GO HOME NOW!

COME ON, BUDDY!

LET'S GO!

PLEASE!

COME ON, TORG!

COME ON!

CHICKEN?

ALL RIGHT, BUT I DON'T THINK I LIKE THIS.

I'D LIKE TO UPDATE MY LIST OF SHARP THINGS TO INCLUDE SWORDS!

ZAP-POW!

Sluggy Freelance: Little Evils

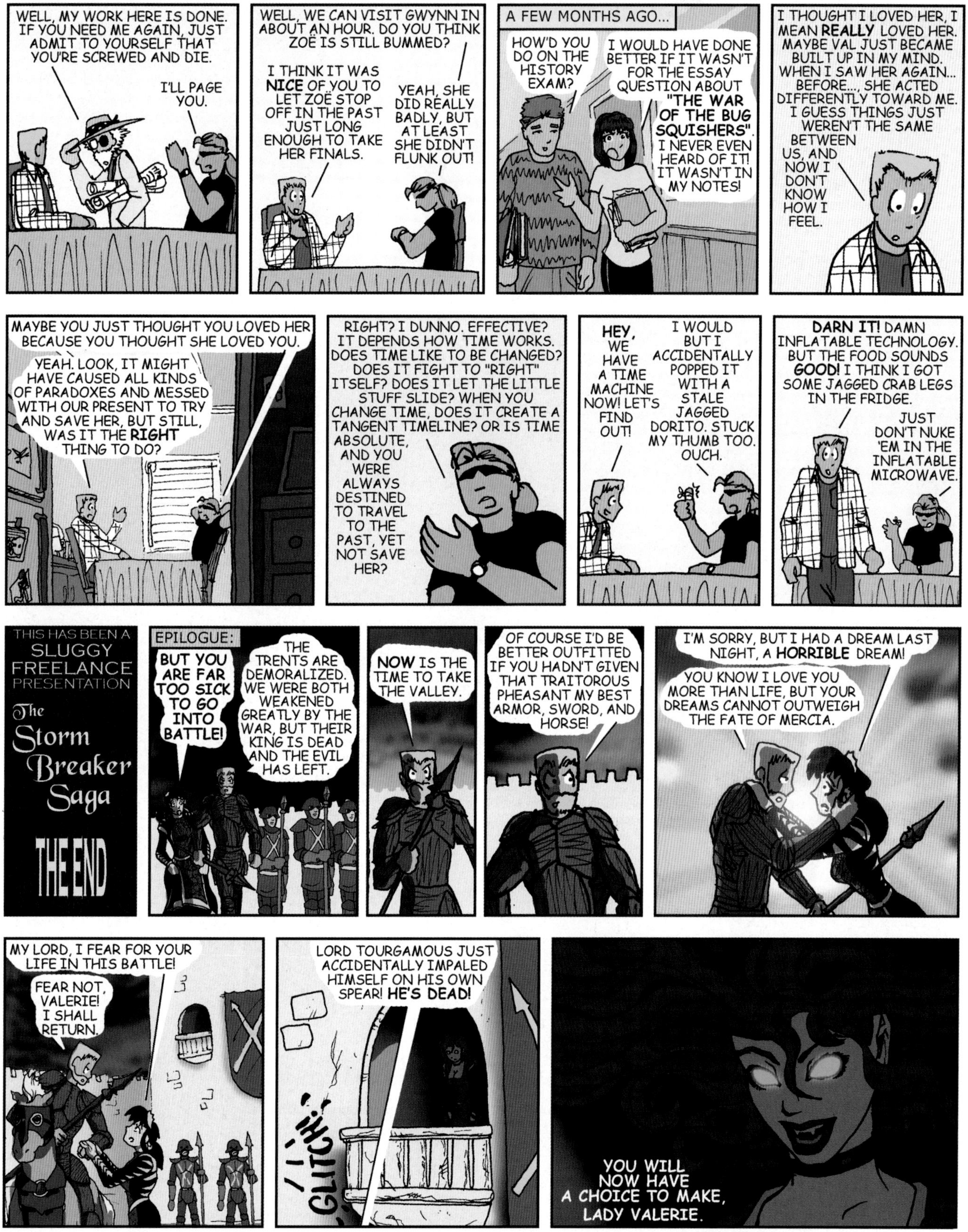

WELL, MY WORK HERE IS DONE. IF YOU NEED ME AGAIN, JUST ADMIT TO YOURSELF THAT YOU'RE SCREWED AND DIE.
I'LL PAGE YOU.
WELL, WE CAN VISIT GWYNN IN ABOUT AN HOUR. DO YOU THINK ZOË IS STILL BUMMED?
I THINK IT WAS NICE OF YOU TO LET ZOË STOP OFF IN THE PAST JUST LONG ENOUGH TO TAKE HER FINALS.
YEAH, SHE DID REALLY BADLY, BUT AT LEAST SHE DIDN'T FLUNK OUT!
A FEW MONTHS AGO...
HOW'D YOU DO ON THE HISTORY EXAM?
I WOULD HAVE DONE BETTER IF IT WASN'T FOR THE ESSAY QUESTION ABOUT "THE WAR OF THE BUG SQUISHERS". I NEVER EVEN HEARD OF IT! IT WASN'T IN MY NOTES!
I THOUGHT I LOVED HER, I MEAN REALLY LOVED HER. MAYBE VAL JUST BECAME BUILT UP IN MY MIND. WHEN I SAW HER AGAIN... BEFORE..., SHE ACTED DIFFERENTLY TOWARD ME. I GUESS THINGS JUST WEREN'T THE SAME BETWEEN US, AND NOW I DON'T KNOW HOW I FEEL.
MAYBE YOU JUST THOUGHT YOU LOVED HER BECAUSE YOU THOUGHT SHE LOVED YOU.
YEAH. LOOK, IT MIGHT HAVE CAUSED ALL KINDS OF PARADOXES AND MESSED WITH OUR PRESENT TO TRY AND SAVE HER, BUT STILL, WAS IT THE RIGHT THING TO DO?
RIGHT? I DUNNO. EFFECTIVE? IT DEPENDS HOW TIME WORKS. DOES TIME LIKE TO BE CHANGED? DOES IT FIGHT TO "RIGHT" ITSELF? DOES IT LET THE LITTLE STUFF SLIDE? WHEN YOU CHANGE TIME, DOES IT CREATE A TANGENT TIMELINE? OR IS TIME ABSOLUTE, AND YOU WERE ALWAYS DESTINED TO TRAVEL TO THE PAST, YET NOT SAVE HER?
HEY, WE HAVE A TIME MACHINE NOW! LET'S FIND OUT!
I WOULD BUT I ACCIDENTALLY POPPED IT WITH A STALE JAGGED DORITO. STUCK MY THUMB TOO. OUCH.
DARN IT! DAMN INFLATABLE TECHNOLOGY. BUT THE FOOD SOUNDS GOOD! I THINK I GOT SOME JAGGED CRAB LEGS IN THE FRIDGE.
JUST DON'T NUKE 'EM IN THE INFLATABLE MICROWAVE.
THIS HAS BEEN A SLUGGY FREELANCE PRESENTATION
The Storm Breaker Saga
THE END
EPILOGUE:
BUT YOU ARE FAR TOO SICK TO GO INTO BATTLE!
THE TRENTS ARE DEMORALIZED. WE WERE BOTH WEAKENED GREATLY BY THE WAR, BUT THEIR KING IS DEAD AND THE EVIL HAS LEFT.
NOW IS THE TIME TO TAKE THE VALLEY.
OF COURSE I'D BE BETTER OUTFITTED IF YOU HADN'T GIVEN THAT TRAITOROUS PHEASANT MY BEST ARMOR, SWORD, AND HORSE!
I'M SORRY, BUT I HAD A DREAM LAST NIGHT, A HORRIBLE DREAM!
YOU KNOW I LOVE YOU MORE THAN LIFE, BUT YOUR DREAMS CANNOT OUTWEIGH THE FATE OF MERCIA.
MY LORD, I FEAR FOR YOUR LIFE IN THIS BATTLE!
FEAR NOT, VALERIE! I SHALL RETURN.
LORD TOURGAMOUS JUST ACCIDENTALLY IMPALED HIMSELF ON HIS OWN SPEAR! HE'S DEAD!
GLITCH!
YOU WILL NOW HAVE A CHOICE TO MAKE, LADY VALERIE.

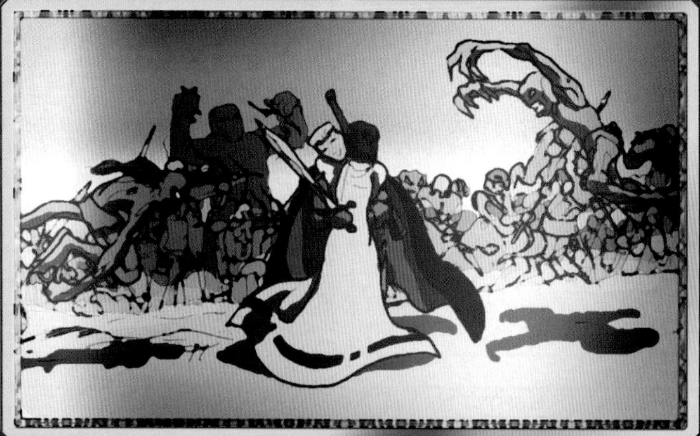

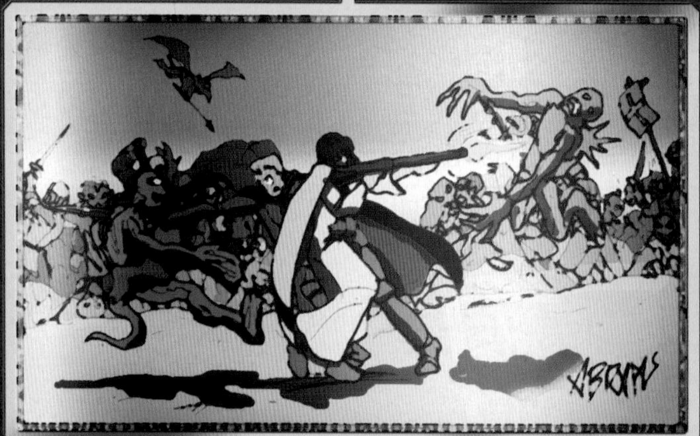

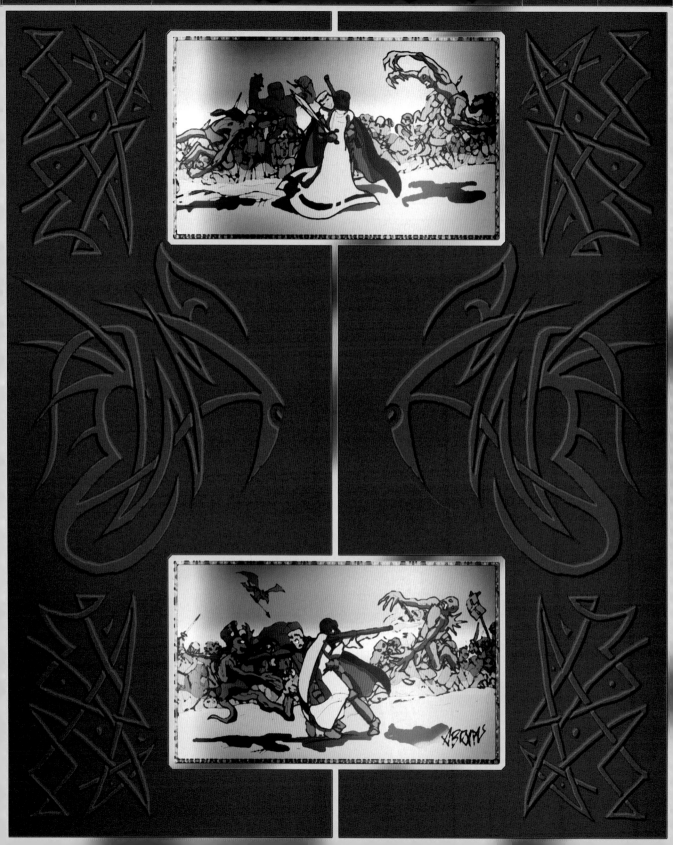

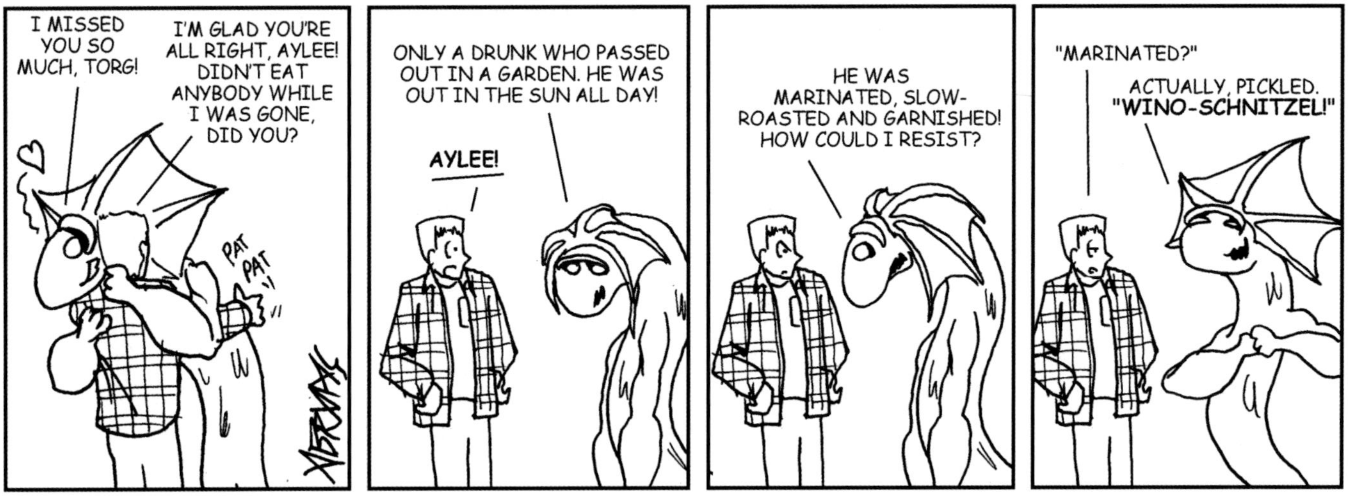
I MISSED YOU SO MUCH, TORG!
I'M GLAD YOU'RE ALL RIGHT, AYLEE! DIDN'T EAT ANYBODY WHILE I WAS GONE, DID YOU?
PAT PAT
AYLEE!
ONLY A DRUNK WHO PASSED OUT IN A GARDEN. HE WAS OUT IN THE SUN ALL DAY!
HE WAS MARINATED, SLOW-ROASTED AND GARNISHED! HOW COULD I RESIST?
"MARINATED?"
ACTUALLY, PICKLED. "WINO-SCHNITZEL!"

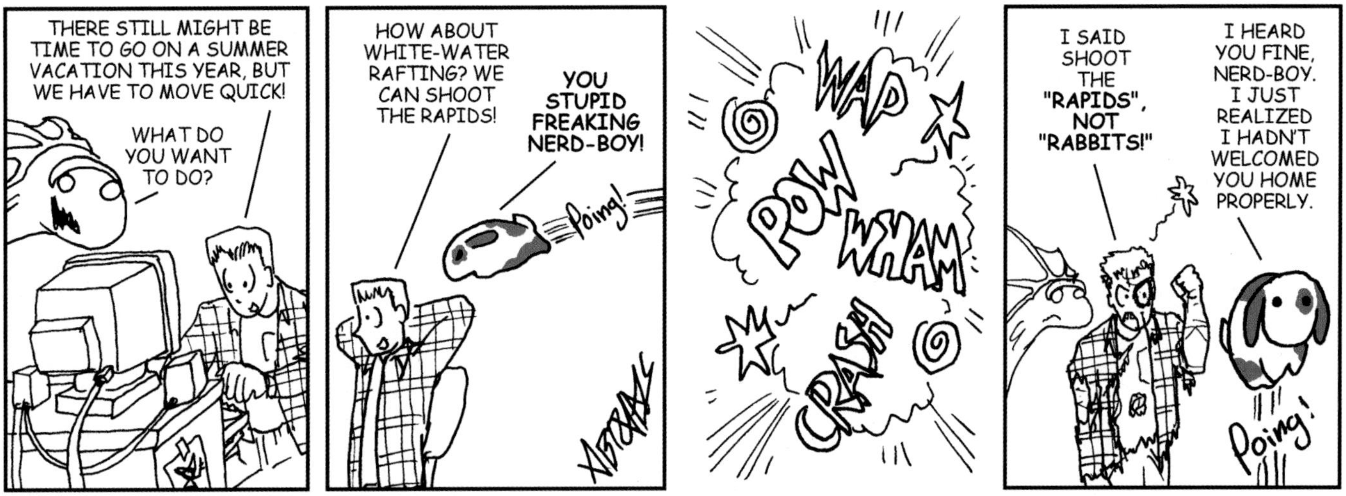
THERE STILL MIGHT BE TIME TO GO ON A SUMMER VACATION THIS YEAR, BUT WE HAVE TO MOVE QUICK!
WHAT DO YOU WANT TO DO?
HOW ABOUT WHITE-WATER RAFTING? WE CAN SHOOT THE RAPIDS!
YOU STUPID FREAKING NERD-BOY!
Poing!
WAP
POW
WHAM
CRASH
I SAID SHOOT THE "RAPIDS", NOT "RABBITS!"
I HEARD YOU FINE, NERD-BOY. I JUST REALIZED I HADN'T WELCOMED YOU HOME PROPERLY.
Poing!

OFFICIAL SLUGGY FREELANCE SECOND ANNIVERSARY COMIC

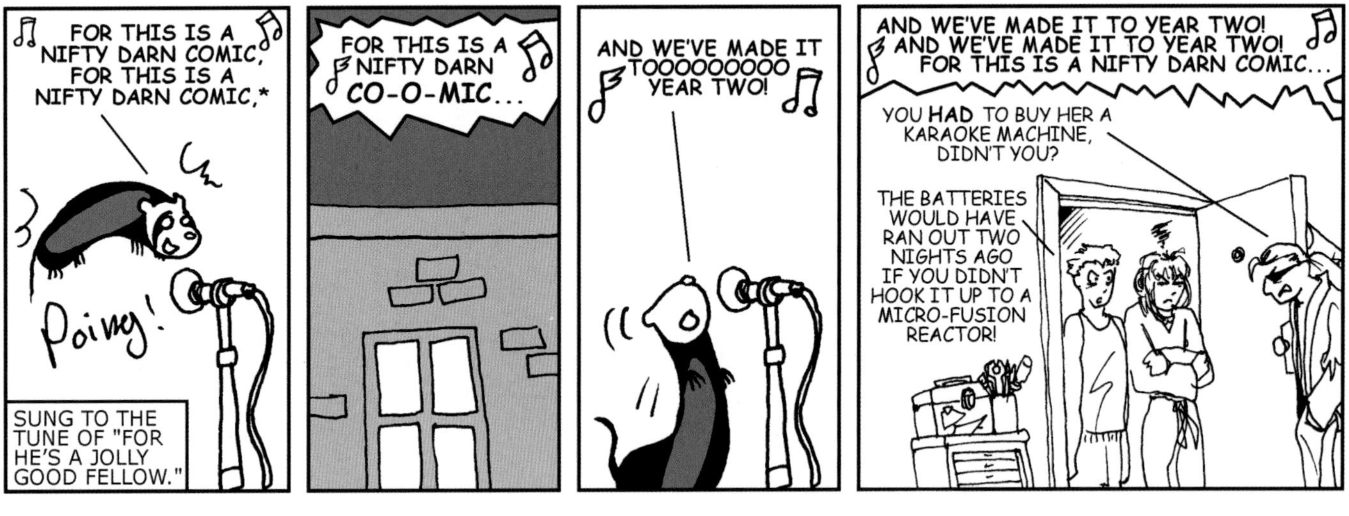
FOR THIS IS A NIFTY DARN COMIC, FOR THIS IS A NIFTY DARN COMIC,*
Poing!
SUNG TO THE TUNE OF "FOR HE'S A JOLLY GOOD FELLOW."
FOR THIS IS A NIFTY DARN CO-O-MIC...
AND WE'VE MADE IT TOOOOOOOOOO YEAR TWO!
AND WE'VE MADE IT TO YEAR TWO! AND WE'VE MADE IT TO YEAR TWO! FOR THIS IS A NIFTY DARN COMIC...
YOU HAD TO BUY HER A KARAOKE MACHINE, DIDN'T YOU?
THE BATTERIES WOULD HAVE RAN OUT TWO NIGHTS AGO IF YOU DIDN'T HOOK IT UP TO A MICRO-FUSION REACTOR!

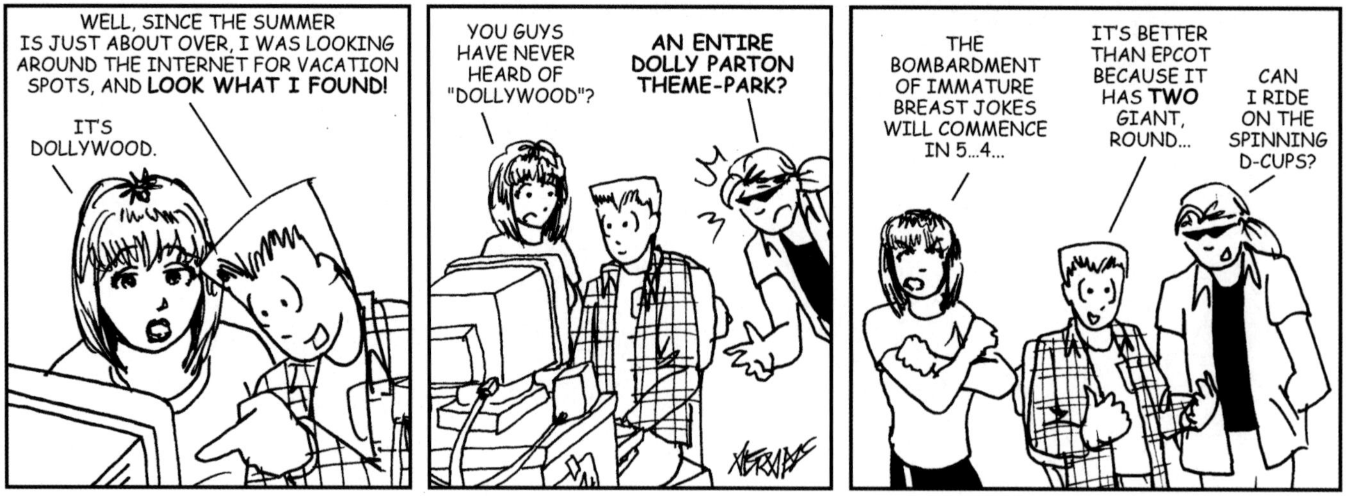
WELL, SINCE THE SUMMER IS JUST ABOUT OVER, I WAS LOOKING AROUND THE INTERNET FOR VACATION SPOTS, AND **LOOK WHAT I FOUND!**
IT'S DOLLYWOOD.
YOU GUYS HAVE NEVER HEARD OF "DOLLYWOOD"?
AN ENTIRE DOLLY PARTON THEME-PARK?
THE BOMBARDMENT OF IMMATURE BREAST JOKES WILL COMMENCE IN 5...4...
IT'S BETTER THAN EPCOT BECAUSE IT HAS **TWO** GIANT, ROUND...
CAN I RIDE ON THE SPINNING D-CUPS?

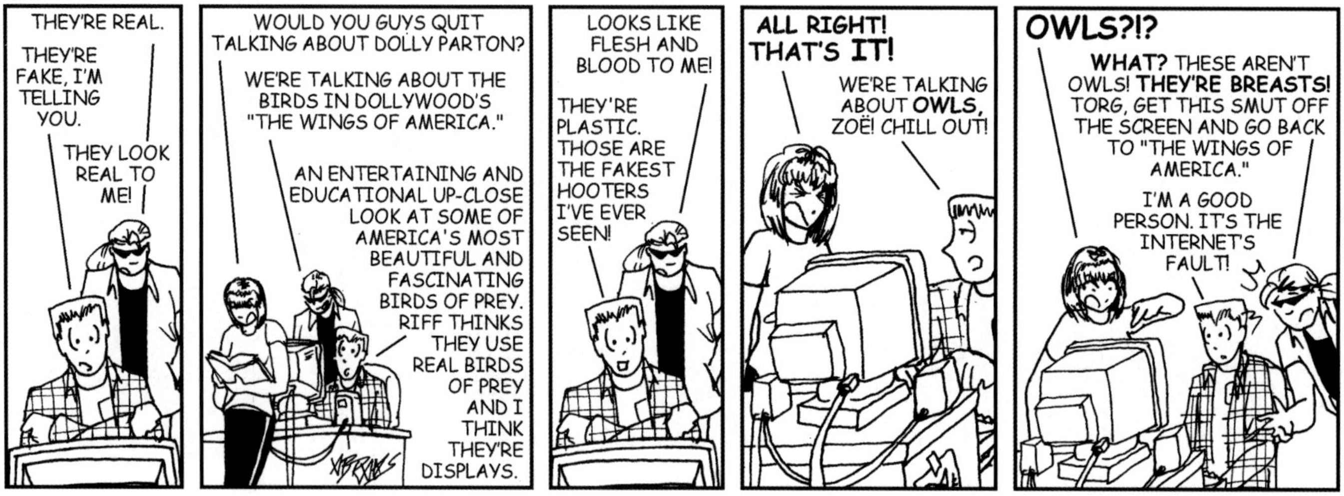
THEY'RE REAL.
THEY'RE FAKE, I'M TELLING YOU.
THEY LOOK REAL TO ME!
WOULD YOU GUYS QUIT TALKING ABOUT DOLLY PARTON?
WE'RE TALKING ABOUT THE BIRDS IN DOLLYWOOD'S "THE WINGS OF AMERICA."
AN ENTERTAINING AND EDUCATIONAL UP-CLOSE LOOK AT SOME OF AMERICA'S MOST BEAUTIFUL AND FASCINATING BIRDS OF PREY. RIFF THINKS THEY USE REAL BIRDS OF PREY AND I THINK THEY'RE DISPLAYS.
LOOKS LIKE FLESH AND BLOOD TO ME!
THEY'RE PLASTIC. THOSE ARE THE FAKEST HOOTERS I'VE EVER SEEN!
ALL RIGHT! THAT'S IT!
WE'RE TALKING ABOUT **OWLS,** ZOË! CHILL OUT!
OWLS?!?
WHAT? THESE AREN'T OWLS! **THEY'RE BREASTS!** TORG, GET THIS SMUT OFF THE SCREEN AND GO BACK TO "THE WINGS OF AMERICA."
I'M A GOOD PERSON. IT'S THE INTERNET'S FAULT!

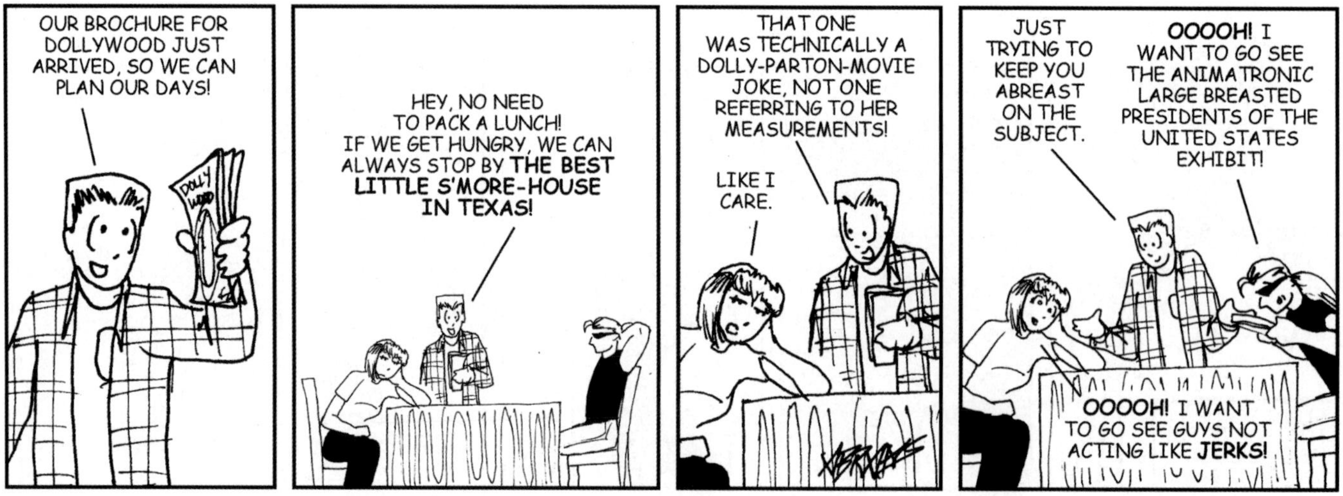
OUR BROCHURE FOR DOLLYWOOD JUST ARRIVED, SO WE CAN PLAN OUR DAYS!
DOLLY WOOD
HEY, NO NEED TO PACK A LUNCH! IF WE GET HUNGRY, WE CAN ALWAYS STOP BY **THE BEST LITTLE S'MORE-HOUSE IN TEXAS!**
THAT ONE WAS TECHNICALLY A DOLLY-PARTON-MOVIE JOKE, NOT ONE REFERRING TO HER MEASUREMENTS!
LIKE I CARE.
JUST TRYING TO KEEP YOU ABREAST ON THE SUBJECT.
OOOOH! I WANT TO GO SEE THE ANIMATRONIC LARGE BREASTED PRESIDENTS OF THE UNITED STATES EXHIBIT!
OOOOH! I WANT TO GO SEE GUYS NOT ACTING LIKE **JERKS!**

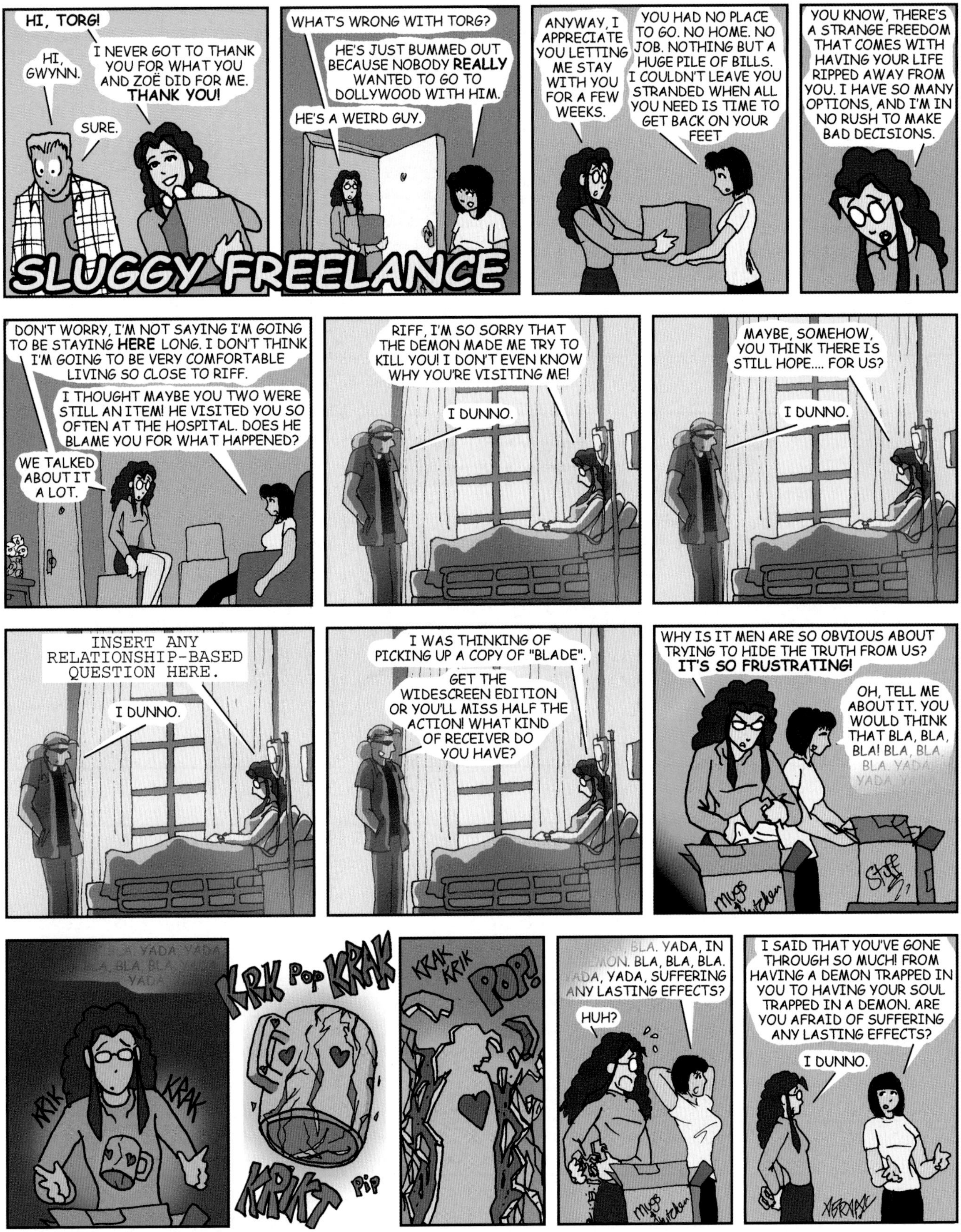
HI, TORG!
HI, GWYNN.
I NEVER GOT TO THANK YOU FOR WHAT YOU AND ZOË DID FOR ME. THANK YOU!
SURE.
SLUGGY FREELANCE
WHAT'S WRONG WITH TORG?
HE'S JUST BUMMED OUT BECAUSE NOBODY REALLY WANTED TO GO TO DOLLYWOOD WITH HIM.
HE'S A WEIRD GUY.
ANYWAY, I APPRECIATE YOU LETTING ME STAY WITH YOU FOR A FEW WEEKS.
YOU HAD NO PLACE TO GO. NO HOME. NO JOB. NOTHING BUT A HUGE PILE OF BILLS. I COULDN'T LEAVE YOU STRANDED WHEN ALL YOU NEED IS TIME TO GET BACK ON YOUR FEET
YOU KNOW, THERE'S A STRANGE FREEDOM THAT COMES WITH HAVING YOUR LIFE RIPPED AWAY FROM YOU. I HAVE SO MANY OPTIONS, AND I'M IN NO RUSH TO MAKE BAD DECISIONS.
DON'T WORRY, I'M NOT SAYING I'M GOING TO BE STAYING HERE LONG. I DON'T THINK I'M GOING TO BE VERY COMFORTABLE LIVING SO CLOSE TO RIFF.
I THOUGHT MAYBE YOU TWO WERE STILL AN ITEM! HE VISITED YOU SO OFTEN AT THE HOSPITAL. DOES HE BLAME YOU FOR WHAT HAPPENED?
WE TALKED ABOUT IT A LOT.
RIFF, I'M SO SORRY THAT THE DEMON MADE ME TRY TO KILL YOU! I DON'T EVEN KNOW WHY YOU'RE VISITING ME!
I DUNNO.
MAYBE, SOMEHOW, YOU THINK THERE IS STILL HOPE.... FOR US?
I DUNNO.
INSERT ANY RELATIONSHIP-BASED QUESTION HERE.
I DUNNO.
I WAS THINKING OF PICKING UP A COPY OF "BLADE".
GET THE WIDESCREEN EDITION OR YOU'LL MISS HALF THE ACTION! WHAT KIND OF RECEIVER DO YOU HAVE?
WHY IS IT MEN ARE SO OBVIOUS ABOUT TRYING TO HIDE THE TRUTH FROM US? IT'S SO FRUSTRATING!
OH, TELL ME ABOUT IT. YOU WOULD THINK THAT BLA, BLA, BLA! BLA, BLA, BLA. YADA, YADA, Y...
Mugs Kitchen
Stuff
...LA. YADA, YADA ...LA, BLA, BLA. YADA YADA
KRIK
KRAK
KRK Pop KRAK
KRIKT Pip
KRAK KRIK POP!
...BLA. YADA, IN ...MON. BLA, BLA, BLA. ...ADA, YADA, SUFFERING ANY LASTING EFFECTS?
HUH?
I SAID THAT YOU'VE GONE THROUGH SO MUCH! FROM HAVING A DEMON TRAPPED IN YOU TO HAVING YOUR SOUL TRAPPED IN A DEMON. ARE YOU AFRAID OF SUFFERING ANY LASTING EFFECTS?
I DUNNO.

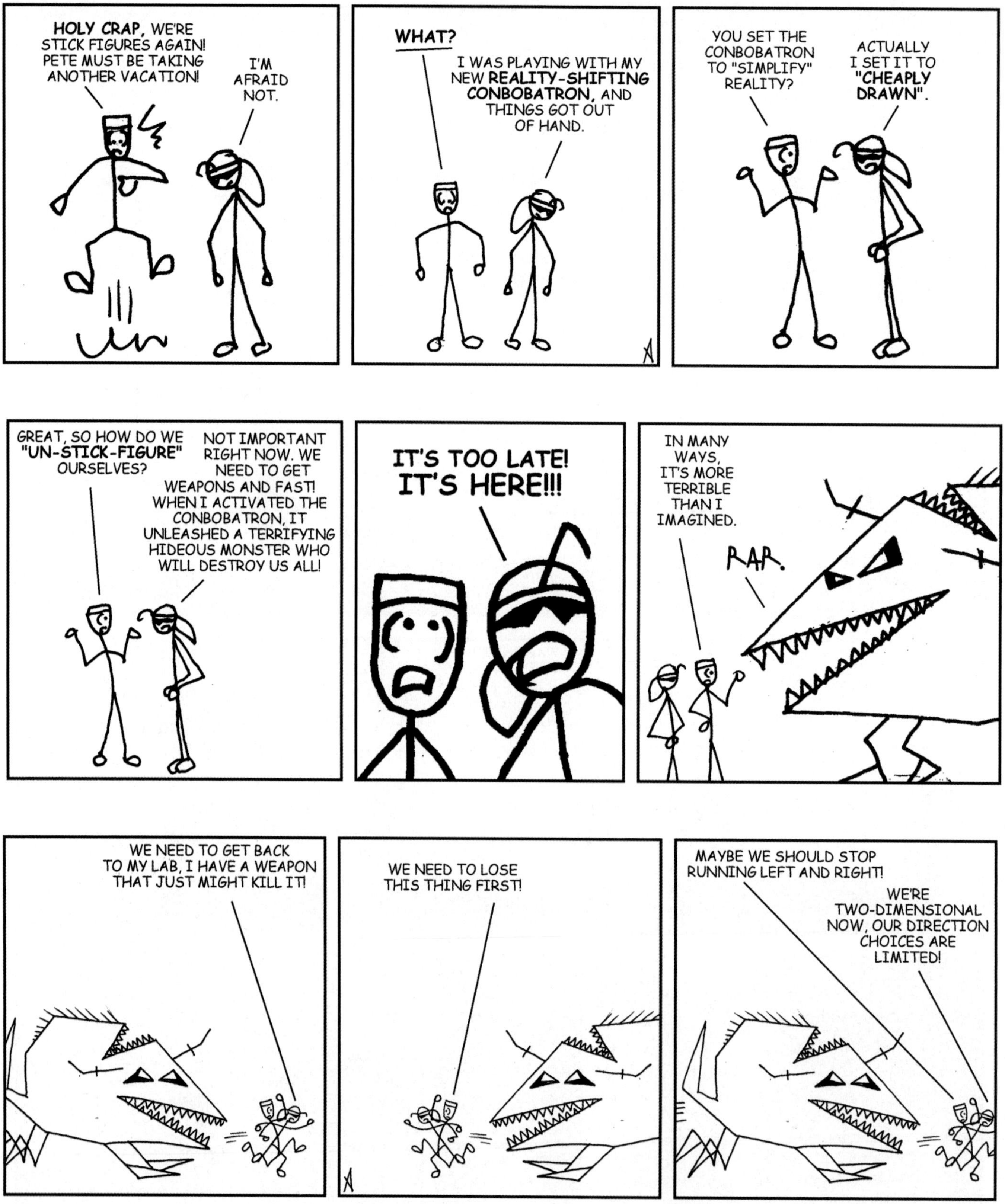
HOLY CRAP, WE'RE STICK FIGURES AGAIN! PETE MUST BE TAKING ANOTHER VACATION!
I'M AFRAID NOT.
WHAT?
I WAS PLAYING WITH MY NEW REALITY-SHIFTING CONBOBATRON, AND THINGS GOT OUT OF HAND.
YOU SET THE CONBOBATRON TO "SIMPLIFY" REALITY?
ACTUALLY I SET IT TO "CHEAPLY DRAWN".
GREAT, SO HOW DO WE "UN-STICK-FIGURE" OURSELVES?
NOT IMPORTANT RIGHT NOW. WE NEED TO GET WEAPONS AND FAST! WHEN I ACTIVATED THE CONBOBATRON, IT UNLEASHED A TERRIFYING HIDEOUS MONSTER WHO WILL DESTROY US ALL!
IT'S TOO LATE! IT'S HERE!!!
IN MANY WAYS, IT'S MORE TERRIBLE THAN I IMAGINED.
RAR.
WE NEED TO GET BACK TO MY LAB, I HAVE A WEAPON THAT JUST MIGHT KILL IT!
WE NEED TO LOSE THIS THING FIRST!
MAYBE WE SHOULD STOP RUNNING LEFT AND RIGHT!
WE'RE TWO-DIMENSIONAL NOW, OUR DIRECTION CHOICES ARE LIMITED!

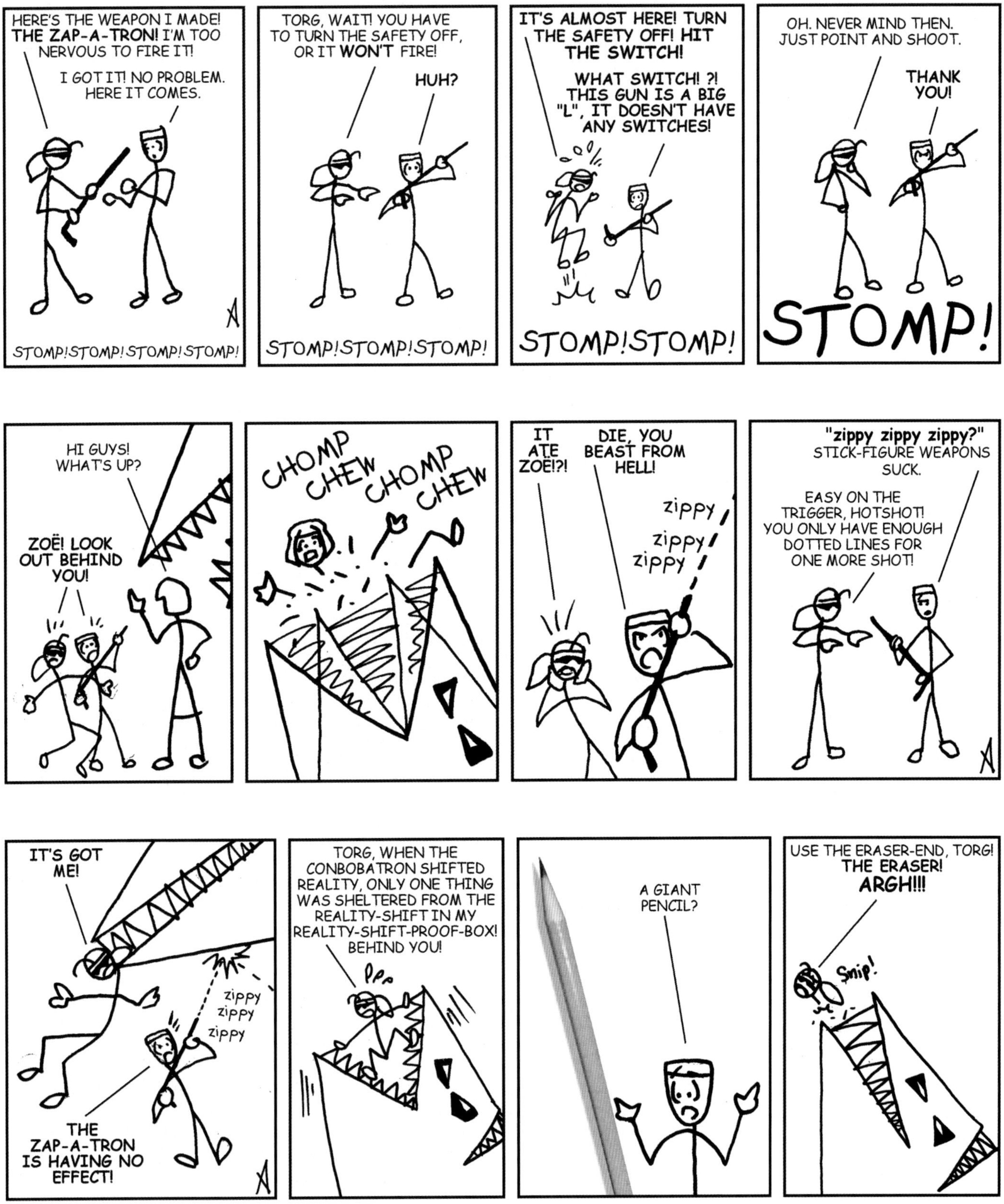
HERE'S THE WEAPON I MADE! THE ZAP-A-TRON! I'M TOO NERVOUS TO FIRE IT!
I GOT IT! NO PROBLEM. HERE IT COMES.
STOMP!STOMP!STOMP!STOMP!
TORG, WAIT! YOU HAVE TO TURN THE SAFETY OFF, OR IT WON'T FIRE!
HUH?
STOMP!STOMP!STOMP!
IT'S ALMOST HERE! TURN THE SAFETY OFF! HIT THE SWITCH!
WHAT SWITCH! ?! THIS GUN IS A BIG "L", IT DOESN'T HAVE ANY SWITCHES!
STOMP!STOMP!
OH. NEVER MIND THEN. JUST POINT AND SHOOT.
THANK YOU!
STOMP!
HI GUYS! WHAT'S UP?
ZOË! LOOK OUT BEHIND YOU!
CHOMP CHEW CHOMP CHEW
IT ATE ZOË!?!
DIE, YOU BEAST FROM HELL!
zippy zippy zippy
"zippy zippy zippy?" STICK-FIGURE WEAPONS SUCK.
EASY ON THE TRIGGER, HOTSHOT! YOU ONLY HAVE ENOUGH DOTTED LINES FOR ONE MORE SHOT!
IT'S GOT ME!
zippy zippy zippy
THE ZAP-A-TRON IS HAVING NO EFFECT!
TORG, WHEN THE CONBOBATRON SHIFTED REALITY, ONLY ONE THING WAS SHELTERED FROM THE REALITY-SHIFT IN MY REALITY-SHIFT-PROOF-BOX! BEHIND YOU!
A GIANT PENCIL?
USE THE ERASER-END, TORG! THE ERASER! ARGH!!!
Snip!

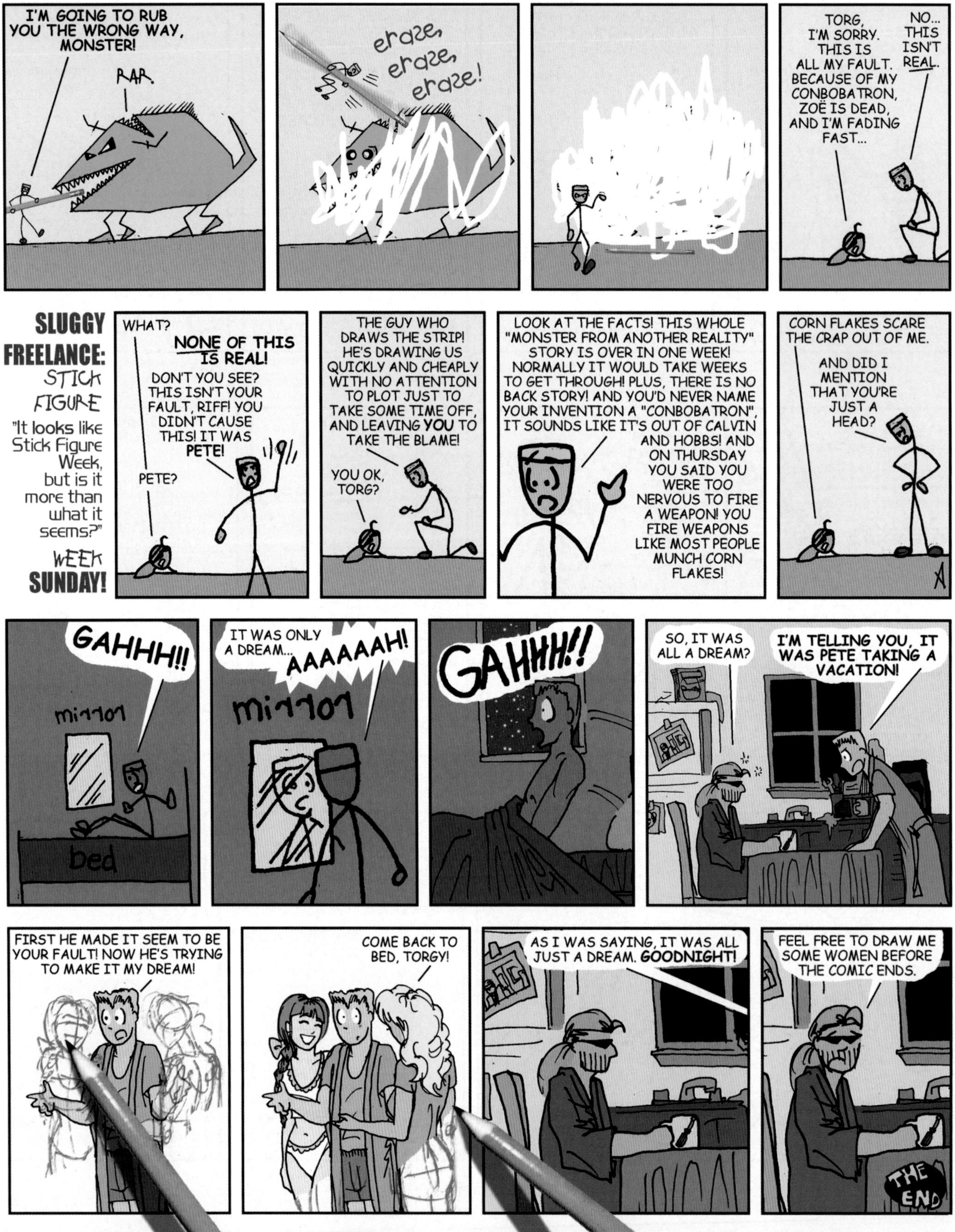
I'M GOING TO RUB YOU THE WRONG WAY, MONSTER!
RAR.
erase, erase, erase!
TORG, I'M SORRY. THIS IS ALL MY FAULT. BECAUSE OF MY CONBOBATRON, ZOË IS DEAD, AND I'M FADING FAST...
NO... THIS ISN'T REAL.
SLUGGY FREELANCE: STICK FIGURE
"It looks like Stick Figure Week, but is it more than what it seems?"
WEEK SUNDAY!
WHAT?
NONE OF THIS IS REAL!
DON'T YOU SEE? THIS ISN'T YOUR FAULT, RIFF! YOU DIDN'T CAUSE THIS! IT WAS PETE!
PETE?
THE GUY WHO DRAWS THE STRIP! HE'S DRAWING US QUICKLY AND CHEAPLY WITH NO ATTENTION TO PLOT JUST TO TAKE SOME TIME OFF, AND LEAVING YOU TO TAKE THE BLAME!
YOU OK, TORG?
LOOK AT THE FACTS! THIS WHOLE "MONSTER FROM ANOTHER REALITY" STORY IS OVER IN ONE WEEK! NORMALLY IT WOULD TAKE WEEKS TO GET THROUGH! PLUS, THERE IS NO BACK STORY! AND YOU'D NEVER NAME YOUR INVENTION A "CONBOBATRON", IT SOUNDS LIKE IT'S OUT OF CALVIN AND HOBBS! AND ON THURSDAY YOU SAID YOU WERE TOO NERVOUS TO FIRE A WEAPON! YOU FIRE WEAPONS LIKE MOST PEOPLE MUNCH CORN FLAKES!
CORN FLAKES SCARE THE CRAP OUT OF ME.
AND DID I MENTION THAT YOU'RE JUST A HEAD?
GAHHH!!
mirror
bed
IT WAS ONLY A DREAM...
AAAAAAH!
mirror
GAHHH!!
SO, IT WAS ALL A DREAM?
I'M TELLING YOU, IT WAS PETE TAKING A VACATION!
FIRST HE MADE IT SEEM TO BE YOUR FAULT! NOW HE'S TRYING TO MAKE IT MY DREAM!
COME BACK TO BED, TORGY!
AS I WAS SAYING, IT WAS ALL JUST A DREAM. GOODNIGHT!
FEEL FREE TO DRAW ME SOME WOMEN BEFORE THE COMIC ENDS.
THE END

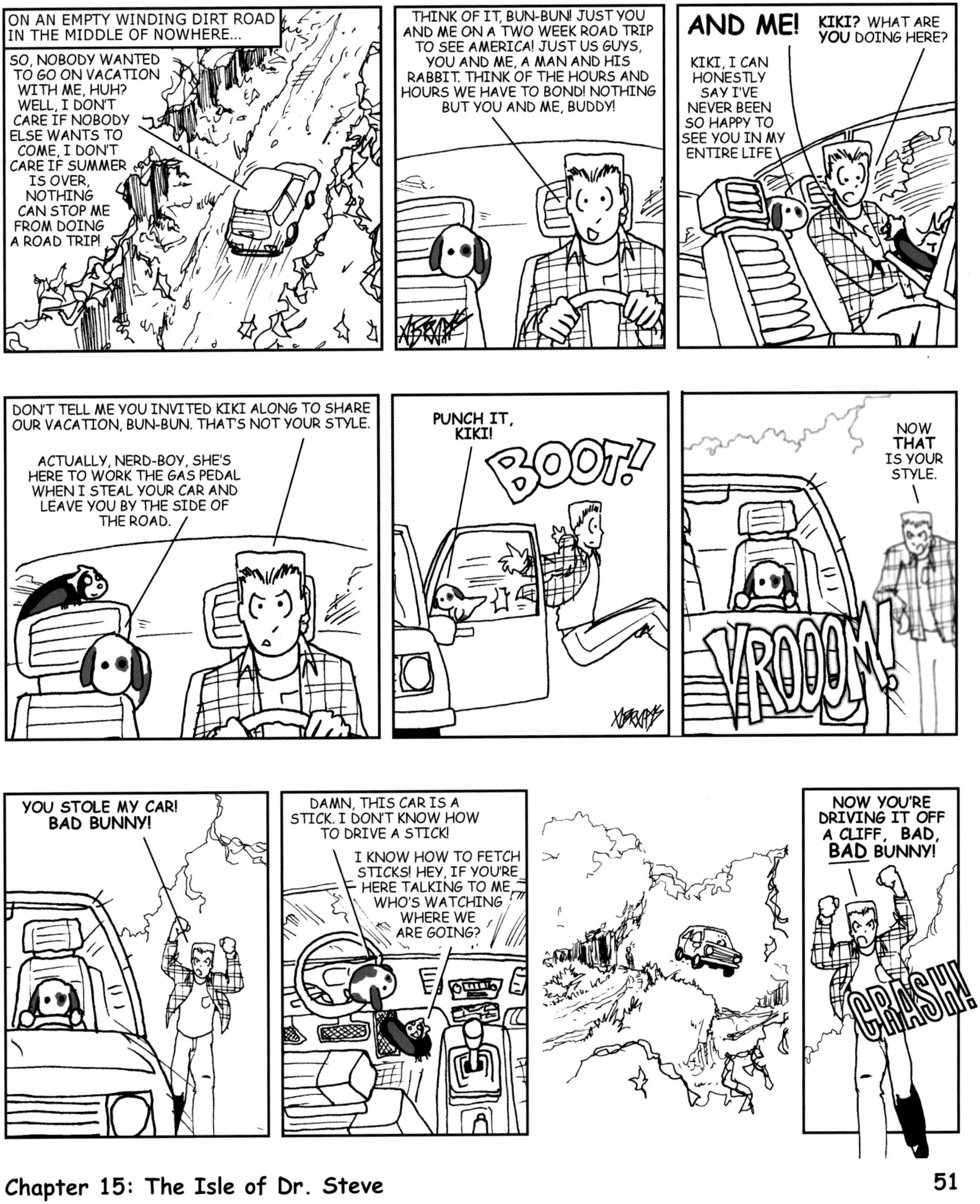
ON AN EMPTY WINDING DIRT ROAD IN THE MIDDLE OF NOWHERE...
SO, NOBODY WANTED TO GO ON VACATION WITH ME, HUH? WELL, I DON'T CARE IF NOBODY ELSE WANTS TO COME, I DON'T CARE IF SUMMER IS OVER, NOTHING CAN STOP ME FROM DOING A ROAD TRIP!
THINK OF IT, BUN-BUN! JUST YOU AND ME ON A TWO WEEK ROAD TRIP TO SEE AMERICA! JUST US GUYS, YOU AND ME, A MAN AND HIS RABBIT. THINK OF THE HOURS AND HOURS WE HAVE TO BOND! NOTHING BUT YOU AND ME, BUDDY!
AND ME!
KIKI? WHAT ARE YOU DOING HERE?
KIKI, I CAN HONESTLY SAY I'VE NEVER BEEN SO HAPPY TO SEE YOU IN MY ENTIRE LIFE
DON'T TELL ME YOU INVITED KIKI ALONG TO SHARE OUR VACATION, BUN-BUN. THAT'S NOT YOUR STYLE.
ACTUALLY, NERD-BOY, SHE'S HERE TO WORK THE GAS PEDAL WHEN I STEAL YOUR CAR AND LEAVE YOU BY THE SIDE OF THE ROAD.
PUNCH IT, KIKI!
BOOT!
NOW THAT IS YOUR STYLE.
VROOOM!
YOU STOLE MY CAR! BAD BUNNY!
DAMN, THIS CAR IS A STICK. I DON'T KNOW HOW TO DRIVE A STICK!
I KNOW HOW TO FETCH STICKS! HEY, IF YOU'RE HERE TALKING TO ME, WHO'S WATCHING WHERE WE ARE GOING?
NOW YOU'RE DRIVING IT OFF A CLIFF, BAD, BAD BUNNY!
CRASH!

WOW, THAT WAS NEAT! CAN WE DO THAT AGAIN?
I GUESS YOU BEING RUBBER-LIKE HELPED YOU BOUNCE AROUND UNHURT.
YOU THINK MY BODY IS LIKE RUBBER?
I MEANT YOUR HEAD! AND WHY THE HELL DIDN'T THE AIRBAG GO OFF?
WAP
Poing!
FWUMP!
THUD!
OOOH! SNUGGLY!
HEY GUYS! WOW, GOOD THING FOR YOU I HAD AIRBAGS! INSTALLED
NO WHEELS, NO FOOD, NO CELL PHONE, THIS SUCKS.
COME ON, GUYS, LET'S GO.
WHY DON'T WE WAIT BY THE ROAD?
WE HAVEN'T SEEN A CAR ON IT IN HOURS. BESIDES, HIGHWAY ISN'T FAR IF WE CUT THROUGH THE WOODS IN A STRAIGHT LINE.
IT SHOULD ONLY TAKE US A COUPLE OF HOURS. BUT JUST IN CASE WE HAVE TO CAMP OUT FOR THE NIGHT, I HAVE A LOT OF CAMPING GEAR. AND HEY, I DID WANT A VACATION! MAYBE THIS IS AS GOOD A PLACE AS ANY!
[INSERT OMINOUS THUNDER HERE.]
AND LOOK! I CAN TAPE THE WHOLE TRIP ON YOUR VIDEO CAMERA! I'LL DO AN OBITUARY ON US!
IT'S CALLED A DOCUMENTARY, RUBBER-HEAD, NOT AN OBITUARY.
I SENSE SOME MORE OMINOUS THUNDER COMING.
[INSERT INAUSPICIOUS THUNDER HERE.]
HOW WILL WE GET WATER WHEN WE'RE THIRSTY? AND I'M THIRSTY!
AHEM... NO NEED TO FEAR LACK OF WATER WHEN IN THE WOODS! ALL YOU NEED TO DO IS LOCATE A STREAM OR RIVER OR CREEK OF SOME KIND.
HERE WE SEE A BABBLING BROOK, ALLOWING US TO FILL OUR CANTEENS AND SCOOP UP THIS FRESH, CRYSTAL CLEAR WATER...
HEY, THIS WATER IS WARM!
BUN-BUN?!?
DOWNSTREAM!
WHAT?

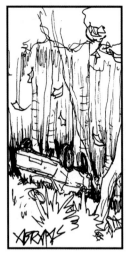

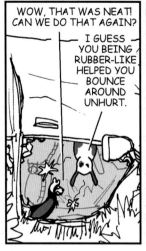

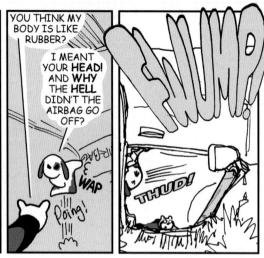

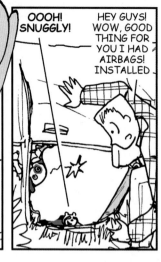

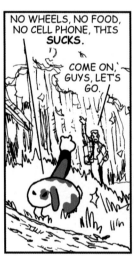

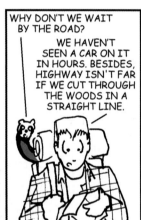

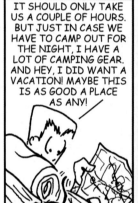

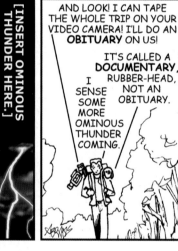

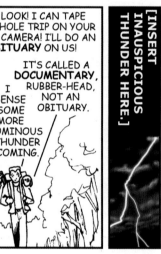

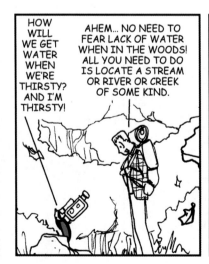

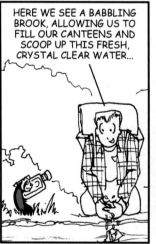

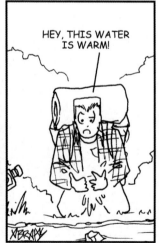

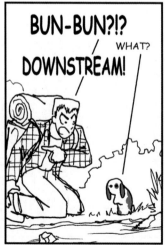

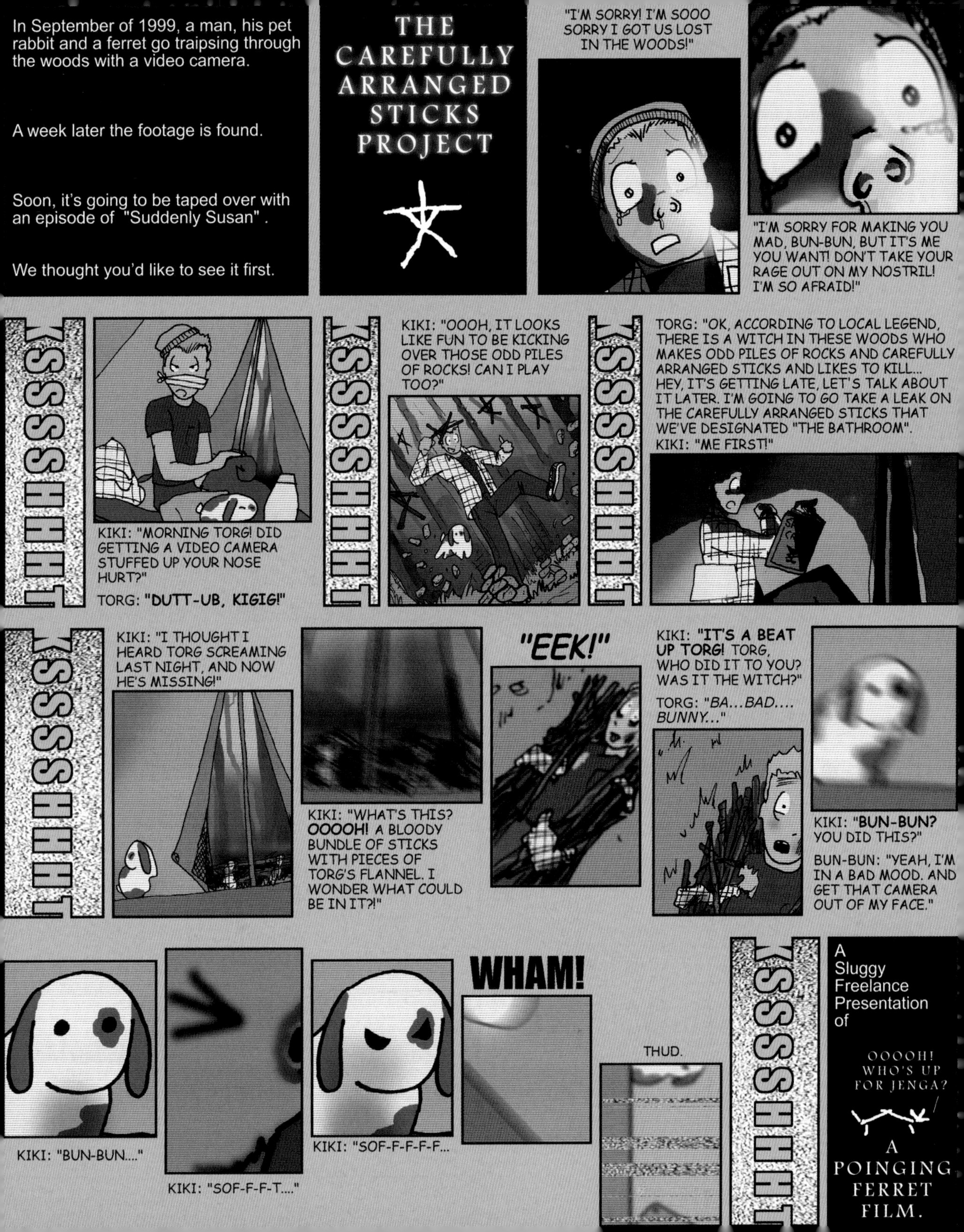
In September of 1999, a man, his pet rabbit and a ferret go traipsing through the woods with a video camera.
A week later the footage is found.
Soon, it's going to be taped over with an episode of "Suddenly Susan".
We thought you'd like to see it first.
THE CAREFULLY ARRANGED STICKS PROJECT
"I'M SORRY! I'M SOOO SORRY I GOT US LOST IN THE WOODS!"
"I'M SORRY FOR MAKING YOU MAD, BUN-BUN, BUT IT'S ME YOU WANT! DON'T TAKE YOUR RAGE OUT ON MY NOSTRIL! I'M SO AFRAID!"
KSSSSHHHT!
KIKI: "MORNING TORG! DID GETTING A VIDEO CAMERA STUFFED UP YOUR NOSE HURT?"
TORG: "DUTT-UB, KIGIG!"
KSSSSHHHT!
KIKI: "OOOH, IT LOOKS LIKE FUN TO BE KICKING OVER THOSE ODD PILES OF ROCKS! CAN I PLAY TOO?"
KSSSSHHHT!
TORG: "OK, ACCORDING TO LOCAL LEGEND, THERE IS A WITCH IN THESE WOODS WHO MAKES ODD PILES OF ROCKS AND CAREFULLY ARRANGED STICKS AND LIKES TO KILL... HEY, IT'S GETTING LATE, LET'S TALK ABOUT IT LATER. I'M GOING TO GO TAKE A LEAK ON THE CAREFULLY ARRANGED STICKS THAT WE'VE DESIGNATED "THE BATHROOM".
KIKI: "ME FIRST!"
KSSSSHHHT!
KIKI: "I THOUGHT I HEARD TORG SCREAMING LAST NIGHT, AND NOW HE'S MISSING!"
KIKI: "WHAT'S THIS? OOOOH! A BLOODY BUNDLE OF STICKS WITH PIECES OF TORG'S FLANNEL. I WONDER WHAT COULD BE IN IT?!"
"EEK!"
KIKI: "IT'S A BEAT UP TORG! TORG, WHO DID IT TO YOU? WAS IT THE WITCH?"
TORG: "BA...BAD.... BUNNY..."
KIKI: "BUN-BUN? YOU DID THIS?"
BUN-BUN: "YEAH, I'M IN A BAD MOOD. AND GET THAT CAMERA OUT OF MY FACE."
KIKI: "BUN-BUN...."
KIKI: "SOF-F-F-T...."
KIKI: "SOF-F-F-F-F...
WHAM!
THUD.
KSSSSHHHT!
A Sluggy Freelance Presentation of
OOOOH! WHO'S UP FOR JENGA?
A POINGING FERRET FILM.

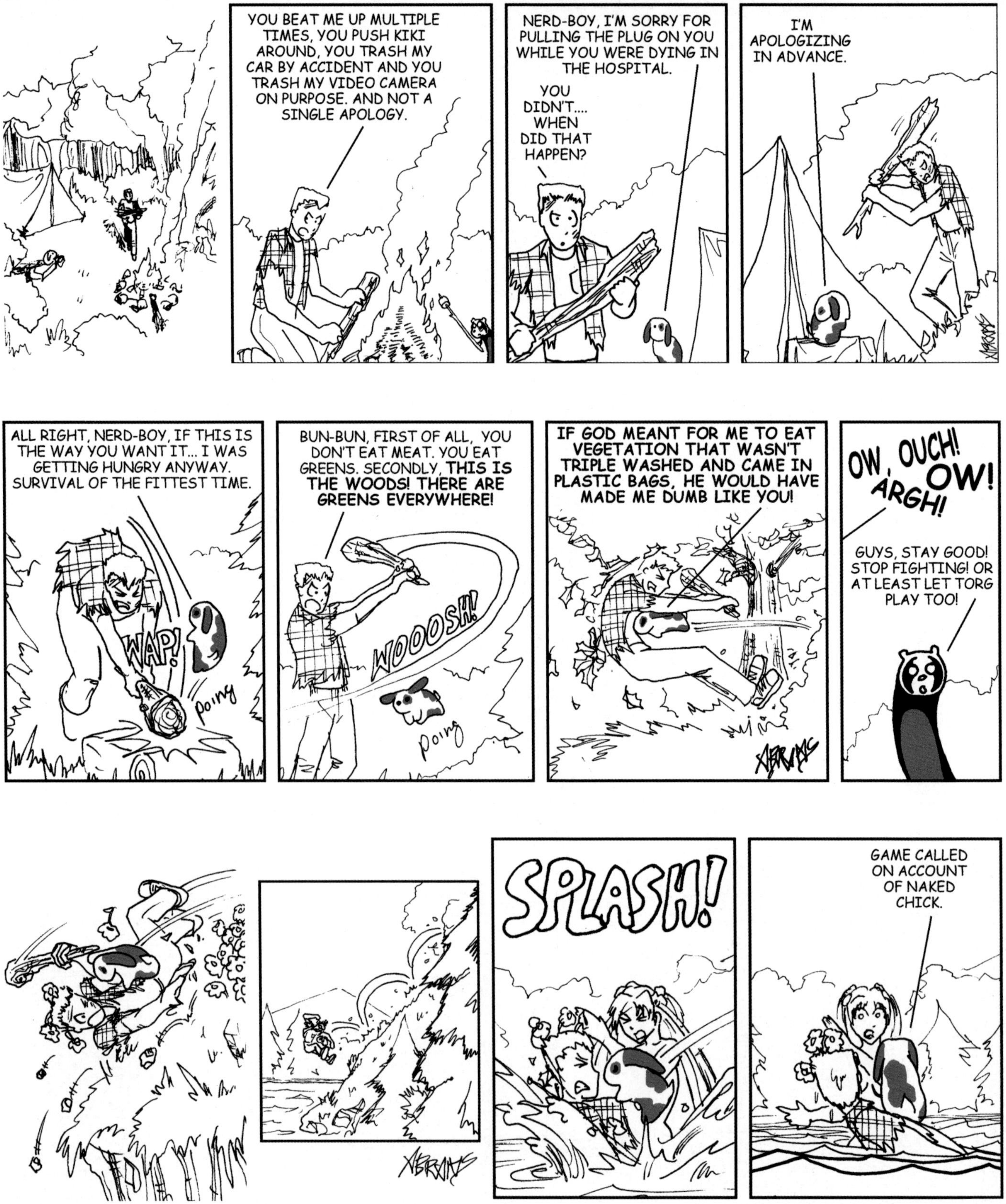
YOU BEAT ME UP MULTIPLE TIMES, YOU PUSH KIKI AROUND, YOU TRASH MY CAR BY ACCIDENT AND YOU TRASH MY VIDEO CAMERA ON PURPOSE. AND NOT A SINGLE APOLOGY.
NERD-BOY, I'M SORRY FOR PULLING THE PLUG ON YOU WHILE YOU WERE DYING IN THE HOSPITAL.
YOU DIDN'T.... WHEN DID THAT HAPPEN?
I'M APOLOGIZING IN ADVANCE.
ALL RIGHT, NERD-BOY, IF THIS IS THE WAY YOU WANT IT... I WAS GETTING HUNGRY ANYWAY. SURVIVAL OF THE FITTEST TIME.
WAP!
poing
BUN-BUN, FIRST OF ALL, YOU DON'T EAT MEAT. YOU EAT GREENS. SECONDLY, THIS IS THE WOODS! THERE ARE GREENS EVERYWHERE!
WOOOSH!
poing
IF GOD MEANT FOR ME TO EAT VEGETATION THAT WASN'T TRIPLE WASHED AND CAME IN PLASTIC BAGS, HE WOULD HAVE MADE ME DUMB LIKE YOU!
OW, OUCH! OW! ARGH!
GUYS, STAY GOOD! STOP FIGHTING! OR AT LEAST LET TORG PLAY TOO!
SPLASH!
GAME CALLED ON ACCOUNT OF NAKED CHICK.

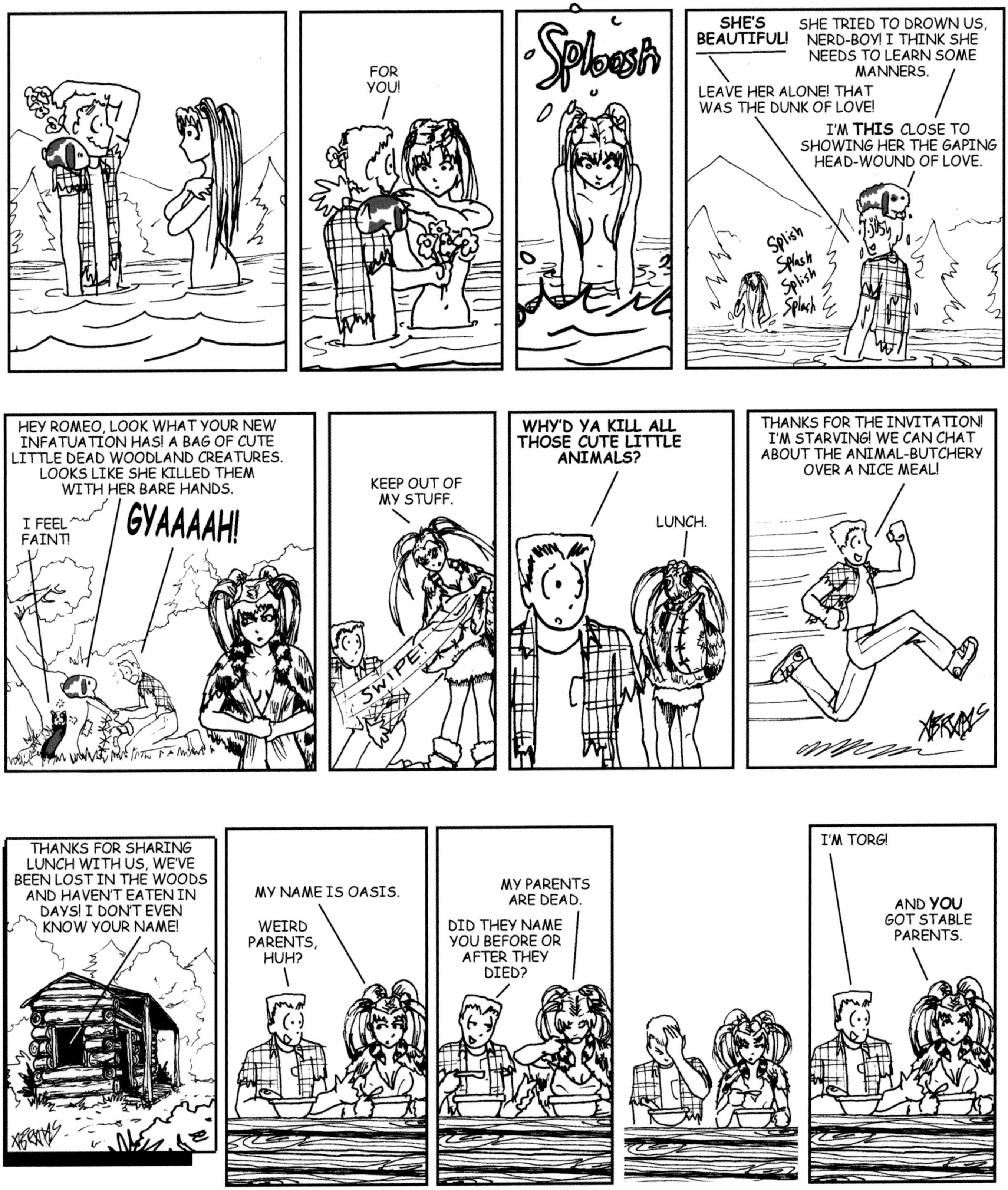
FOR YOU!
Sploosh
SHE'S BEAUTIFUL!
SHE TRIED TO DROWN US, NERD-BOY! I THINK SHE NEEDS TO LEARN SOME MANNERS.
LEAVE HER ALONE! THAT WAS THE DUNK OF LOVE!
I'M THIS CLOSE TO SHOWING HER THE GAPING HEAD-WOUND OF LOVE.
Splish Splash Splish Splash
HEY ROMEO, LOOK WHAT YOUR NEW INFATUATION HAS! A BAG OF CUTE LITTLE DEAD WOODLAND CREATURES. LOOKS LIKE SHE KILLED THEM WITH HER BARE HANDS.
I FEEL FAINT!
GYAAAAH!
KEEP OUT OF MY STUFF.
SWIPE!
WHY'D YA KILL ALL THOSE CUTE LITTLE ANIMALS?
LUNCH.
THANKS FOR THE INVITATION! I'M STARVING! WE CAN CHAT ABOUT THE ANIMAL-BUTCHERY OVER A NICE MEAL!
THANKS FOR SHARING LUNCH WITH US, WE'VE BEEN LOST IN THE WOODS AND HAVEN'T EATEN IN DAYS! I DON'T EVEN KNOW YOUR NAME!
MY NAME IS OASIS.
WEIRD PARENTS, HUH?
MY PARENTS ARE DEAD.
DID THEY NAME YOU BEFORE OR AFTER THEY DIED?
I'M TORG!
AND YOU GOT STABLE PARENTS.

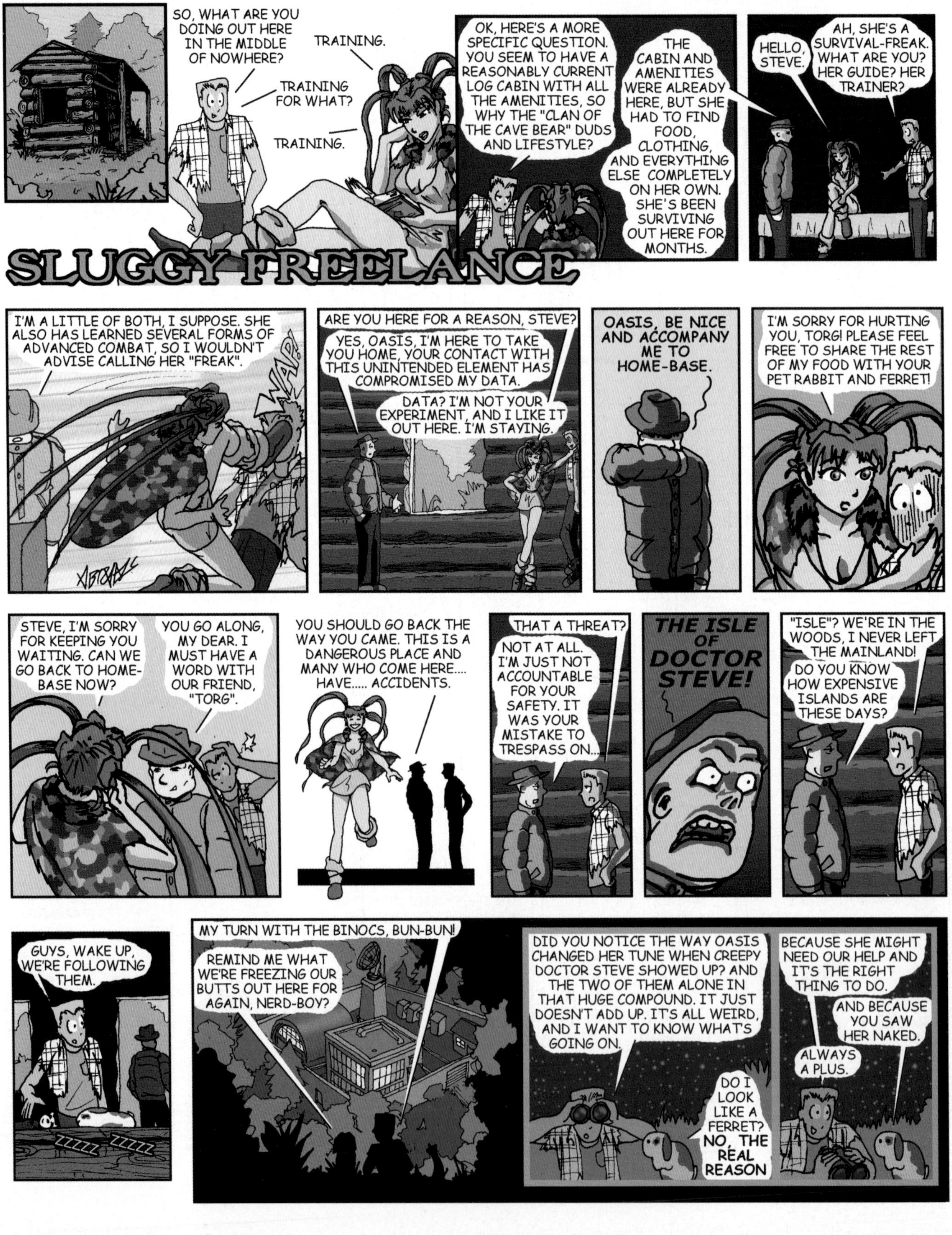
SO, WHAT ARE YOU DOING OUT HERE IN THE MIDDLE OF NOWHERE?
TRAINING.
TRAINING FOR WHAT?
TRAINING.
OK, HERE'S A MORE SPECIFIC QUESTION. YOU SEEM TO HAVE A REASONABLY CURRENT LOG CABIN WITH ALL THE AMENITIES, SO WHY THE "CLAN OF THE CAVE BEAR" DUDS AND LIFESTYLE?
THE CABIN AND AMENITIES WERE ALREADY HERE, BUT SHE HAD TO FIND FOOD, CLOTHING, AND EVERYTHING ELSE COMPLETELY ON HER OWN. SHE'S BEEN SURVIVING OUT HERE FOR MONTHS.
HELLO, STEVE.
AH, SHE'S A SURVIVAL-FREAK. WHAT ARE YOU? HER GUIDE? HER TRAINER?
SLUGGY FREELANCE
I'M A LITTLE OF BOTH, I SUPPOSE. SHE ALSO HAS LEARNED SEVERAL FORMS OF ADVANCED COMBAT, SO I WOULDN'T ADVISE CALLING HER "FREAK".
WAP!
ARE YOU HERE FOR A REASON, STEVE?
YES, OASIS, I'M HERE TO TAKE YOU HOME, YOUR CONTACT WITH THIS UNINTENDED ELEMENT HAS COMPROMISED MY DATA.
DATA? I'M NOT YOUR EXPERIMENT, AND I LIKE IT OUT HERE. I'M STAYING.
OASIS, BE NICE AND ACCOMPANY ME TO HOME-BASE.
I'M SORRY FOR HURTING YOU, TORG! PLEASE FEEL FREE TO SHARE THE REST OF MY FOOD WITH YOUR PET RABBIT AND FERRET!
STEVE, I'M SORRY FOR KEEPING YOU WAITING. CAN WE GO BACK TO HOME-BASE NOW?
YOU GO ALONG, MY DEAR. I MUST HAVE A WORD WITH OUR FRIEND, "TORG".
YOU SHOULD GO BACK THE WAY YOU CAME. THIS IS A DANGEROUS PLACE AND MANY WHO COME HERE.... HAVE..... ACCIDENTS.
THAT A THREAT?
NOT AT ALL. I'M JUST NOT ACCOUNTABLE FOR YOUR SAFETY. IT WAS YOUR MISTAKE TO TRESPASS ON...
THE ISLE OF DOCTOR STEVE!
"ISLE"? WE'RE IN THE WOODS, I NEVER LEFT THE MAINLAND!
DO YOU KNOW HOW EXPENSIVE ISLANDS ARE THESE DAYS?
GUYS, WAKE UP, WE'RE FOLLOWING THEM.
ZZZZZ
ZZZZZ
MY TURN WITH THE BINOCS, BUN-BUN!
REMIND ME WHAT WE'RE FREEZING OUR BUTTS OUT HERE FOR AGAIN, NERD-BOY?
DID YOU NOTICE THE WAY OASIS CHANGED HER TUNE WHEN CREEPY DOCTOR STEVE SHOWED UP? AND THE TWO OF THEM ALONE IN THAT HUGE COMPOUND. IT JUST DOESN'T ADD UP. IT'S ALL WEIRD, AND I WANT TO KNOW WHAT'S GOING ON.
DO I LOOK LIKE A FERRET?
NO, THE REAL REASON
BECAUSE SHE MIGHT NEED OUR HELP AND IT'S THE RIGHT THING TO DO.
AND BECAUSE YOU SAW HER NAKED.
ALWAYS A PLUS.

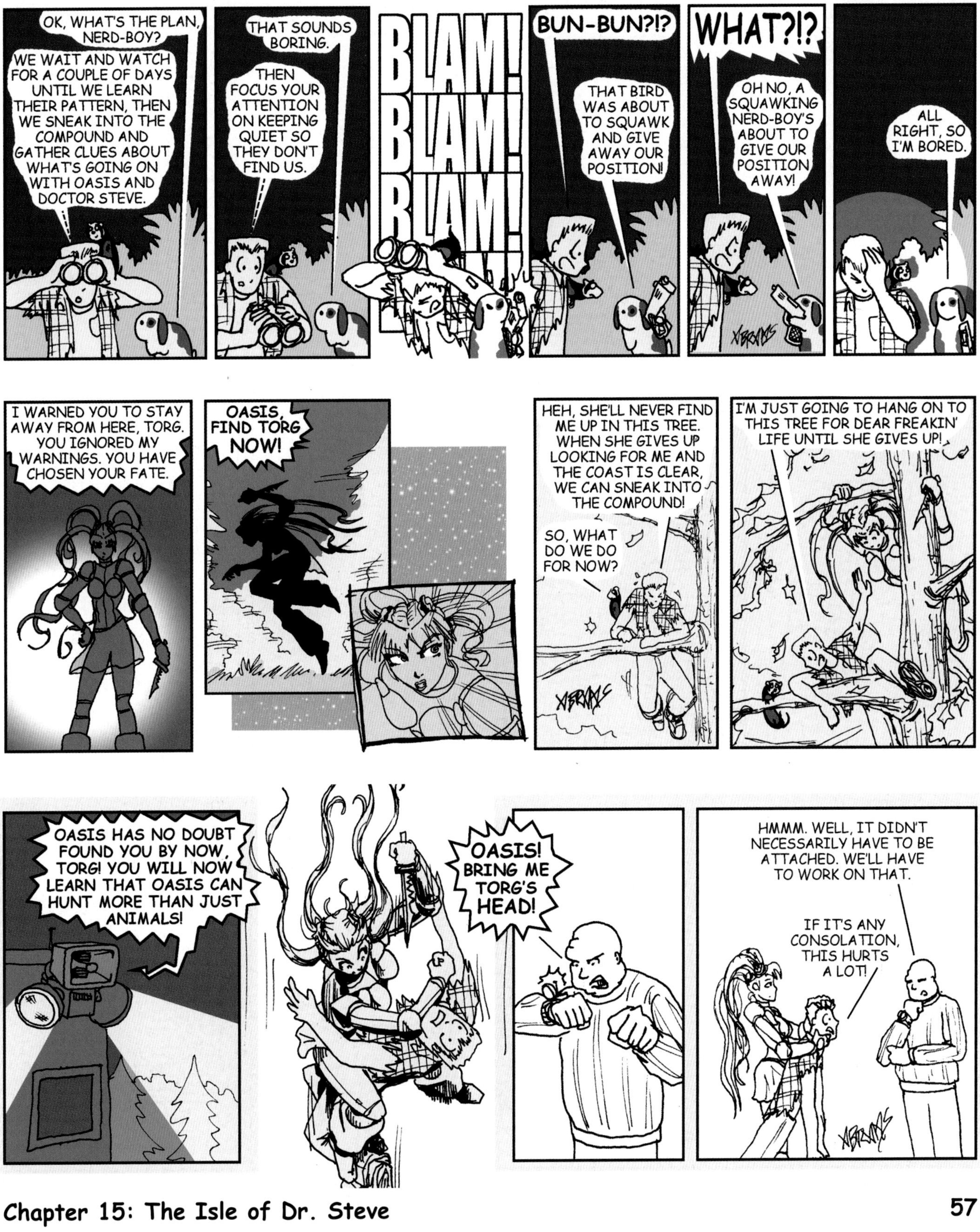
OK, WHAT'S THE PLAN, NERD-BOY?
WE WAIT AND WATCH FOR A COUPLE OF DAYS UNTIL WE LEARN THEIR PATTERN, THEN WE SNEAK INTO THE COMPOUND AND GATHER CLUES ABOUT WHAT'S GOING ON WITH OASIS AND DOCTOR STEVE.
THAT SOUNDS BORING.
THEN FOCUS YOUR ATTENTION ON KEEPING QUIET SO THEY DON'T FIND US.
BLAM! BLAM! BLAM!
BUN-BUN?!?
THAT BIRD WAS ABOUT TO SQUAWK AND GIVE AWAY OUR POSITION!
WHAT?!?
OH NO, A SQUAWKING NERD-BOY'S ABOUT TO GIVE OUR POSITION AWAY!
ALL RIGHT, SO I'M BORED.
I WARNED YOU TO STAY AWAY FROM HERE, TORG. YOU IGNORED MY WARNINGS. YOU HAVE CHOSEN YOUR FATE.
OASIS, FIND TORG NOW!
HEH, SHE'LL NEVER FIND ME UP IN THIS TREE. WHEN SHE GIVES UP LOOKING FOR ME AND THE COAST IS CLEAR, WE CAN SNEAK INTO THE COMPOUND!
SO, WHAT DO WE DO FOR NOW?
I'M JUST GOING TO HANG ON TO THIS TREE FOR DEAR FREAKIN' LIFE UNTIL SHE GIVES UP!
OASIS HAS NO DOUBT FOUND YOU BY NOW, TORG! YOU WILL NOW LEARN THAT OASIS CAN HUNT MORE THAN JUST ANIMALS!
OASIS! BRING ME TORG'S HEAD!
HMMM. WELL, IT DIDN'T NECESSARILY HAVE TO BE ATTACHED. WE'LL HAVE TO WORK ON THAT.
IF IT'S ANY CONSOLATION, THIS HURTS A LOT!

OASIS, THROW TORG IN A CELL UNTIL I FIGURE OUT HOW TO KILL HIM!
CRASH!!
KA-SMASH!
TINKLE
tinkle
TINKLE
tinkle
A BIT TOO LITERAL, AND SEVERAL FEET SHORT. NICE DISTANCE THOUGH. DIDN'T THINK YOU'D MAKE THE RACK OF DISHWARE.
OASIS, PLACE TORG GINGERLY IN A CELL AND BRING HIM SOME BAND-AIDS.
medic!
I'VE DECIDED TO JUST SHOOT YOU AND GET THIS OVER WITH.
BUT WAIT, DON'T YOU WANT TO REVEAL YOUR MASTER PLAN TO ME ?
NO.
IF YOU WERE A **REAL** VILLAIN, YOU'D TELL ME YOUR MASTER PLAN BEFORE KILLING ME.
HMMMM...
AFTER YOU TELL ME YOUR MASTER PLAN, YOU CAN STRAP ME TO A TABLE AND CUT ME IN HALF WITH A LASER!
HOW ABOUT I TIE YOU TO A CHAIR AND BLIND YOU WITH A PEN-LIGHT?
DEAL!
LET'S DO IT!
DR. STEVE, YOUR MASTER PLAN IS TO DATE **DAPHNE ZUNIGA?**
WELL, ONCE I RULE THE WORLD, SHE'LL HAVE TO SAY YES!
BUT WHAT DOES RULING THE WORLD HAVE TO DO WITH OASIS?
NOTHING, BUT YOU ASKED ME WHAT MY **MASTER** PLAN IS. GOTTA START SMALL. IN ANY CASE, YOU KNOW TOO MUCH. GOODBYE, TORG.
CLICK
thud.
ISN'T THIS TRAP DOOR SUPPOSED TO BE DEEPER?
LIKE I GOT NOTHING BETTER TO DO THAN TO DIG PITS. OASIS, PLEASE ESCORT "MR. PICKY" TO HIS CELL.

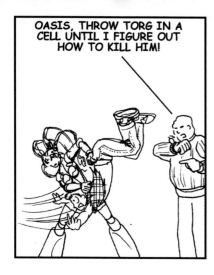

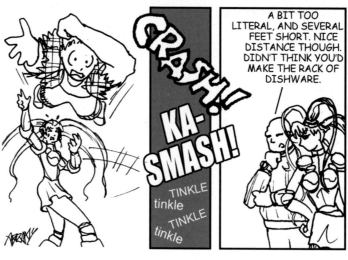

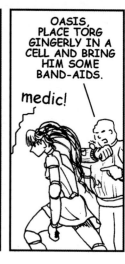

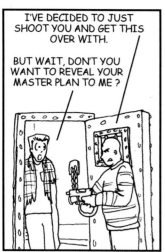

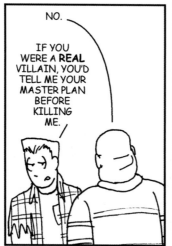

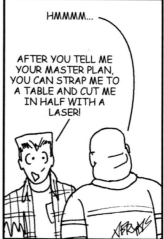

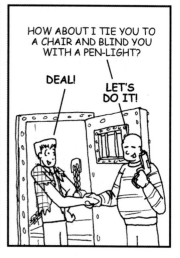

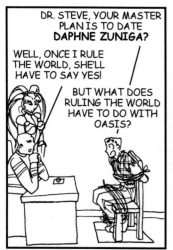

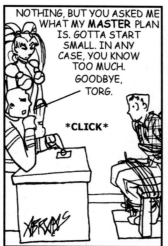

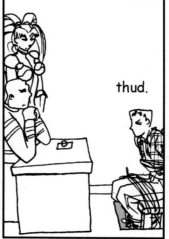

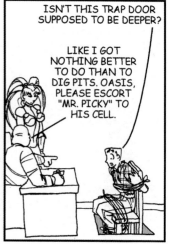

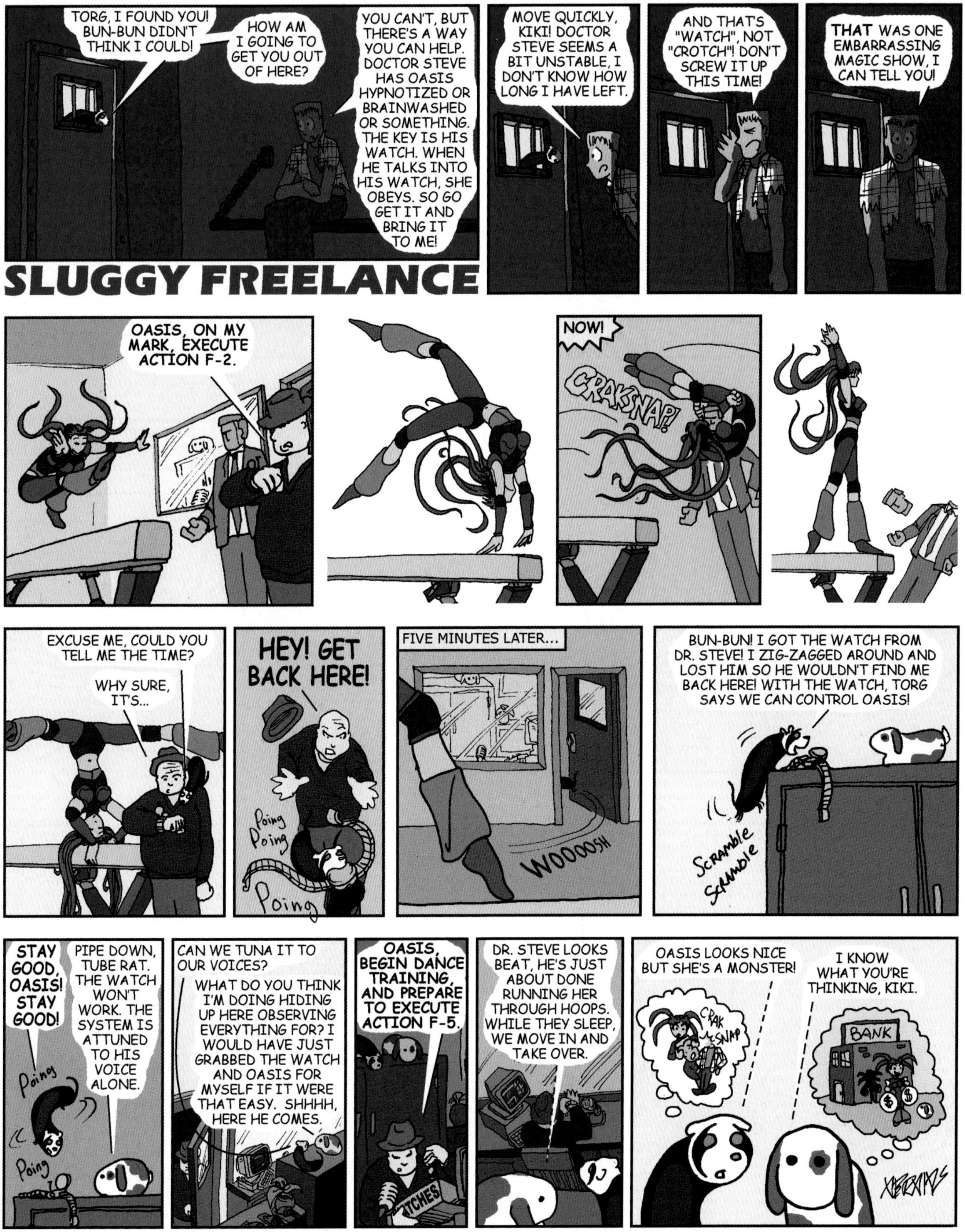

TORG, I FOUND YOU! BUN-BUN DIDN'T THINK I COULD!
HOW AM I GOING TO GET YOU OUT OF HERE?
YOU CAN'T, BUT THERE'S A WAY YOU CAN HELP. DOCTOR STEVE HAS OASIS HYPNOTIZED OR BRAINWASHED OR SOMETHING. THE KEY IS HIS WATCH. WHEN HE TALKS INTO HIS WATCH, SHE OBEYS. SO GO GET IT AND BRING IT TO ME!
SLUGGY FREELANCE
MOVE QUICKLY, KIKI! DOCTOR STEVE SEEMS A BIT UNSTABLE, I DON'T KNOW HOW LONG I HAVE LEFT.
AND THAT'S "WATCH", NOT "CROTCH"! DON'T SCREW IT UP THIS TIME!
THAT WAS ONE EMBARRASSING MAGIC SHOW, I CAN TELL YOU!
OASIS, ON MY MARK, EXECUTE ACTION F-2.
NOW!
CRAKSNAP!
EXCUSE ME, COULD YOU TELL ME THE TIME?
WHY SURE, IT'S...
HEY! GET BACK HERE!
Poing Poing
Poing
FIVE MINUTES LATER...
WOOOOSH
BUN-BUN! I GOT THE WATCH FROM DR. STEVE! I ZIG-ZAGGED AROUND AND LOST HIM SO HE WOULDN'T FIND ME BACK HERE! WITH THE WATCH, TORG SAYS WE CAN CONTROL OASIS!
Scramble Scramble
STAY GOOD, OASIS! STAY GOOD!
PIPE DOWN, TUBE RAT. THE WATCH WON'T WORK. THE SYSTEM IS ATTUNED TO HIS VOICE ALONE.
Poing
Poing
CAN WE TUNA IT TO OUR VOICES?
WHAT DO YOU THINK I'M DOING HIDING UP HERE OBSERVING EVERYTHING FOR? I WOULD HAVE JUST GRABBED THE WATCH AND OASIS FOR MYSELF IF IT WERE THAT EASY. SHHHH, HERE HE COMES.
OASIS, BEGIN DANCE TRAINING, AND PREPARE TO EXECUTE ACTION F-5.
DR. STEVE LOOKS BEAT, HE'S JUST ABOUT DONE RUNNING HER THROUGH HOOPS. WHILE THEY SLEEP, WE MOVE IN AND TAKE OVER.
OASIS LOOKS NICE BUT SHE'S A MONSTER!
CRAK SNAP
I KNOW WHAT YOU'RE THINKING, KIKI.
BANK

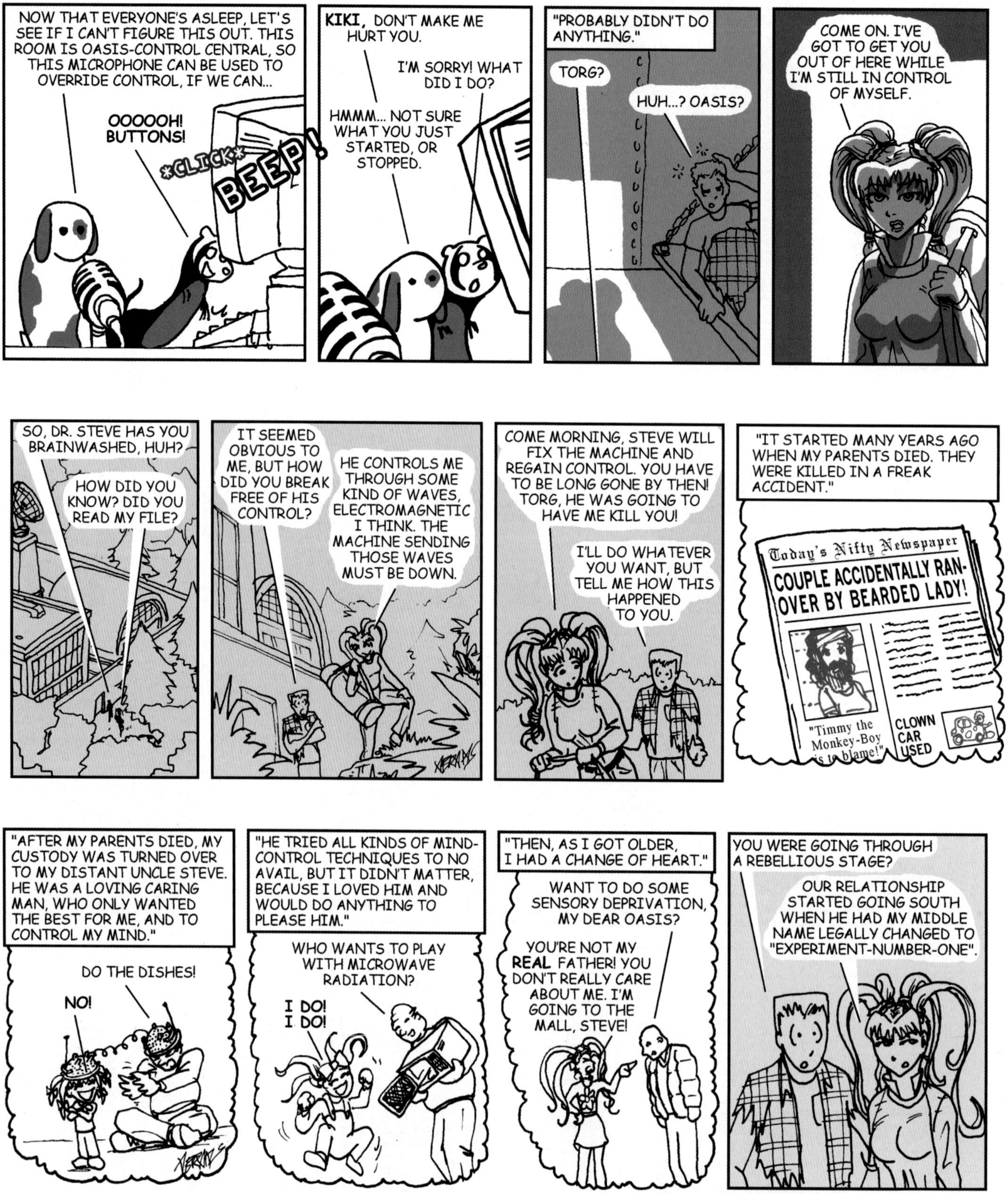
NOW THAT EVERYONE'S ASLEEP, LET'S SEE IF I CAN'T FIGURE THIS OUT. THIS ROOM IS OASIS-CONTROL CENTRAL, SO THIS MICROPHONE CAN BE USED TO OVERRIDE CONTROL, IF WE CAN...
OOOOOH! BUTTONS!
CLICK
BEEP!
KIKI, DON'T MAKE ME HURT YOU.
I'M SORRY! WHAT DID I DO?
HMMM... NOT SURE WHAT YOU JUST STARTED, OR STOPPED.
"PROBABLY DIDN'T DO ANYTHING."
TORG?
HUH...? OASIS?
COME ON. I'VE GOT TO GET YOU OUT OF HERE WHILE I'M STILL IN CONTROL OF MYSELF.
SO, DR. STEVE HAS YOU BRAINWASHED, HUH?
HOW DID YOU KNOW? DID YOU READ MY FILE?
IT SEEMED OBVIOUS TO ME, BUT HOW DID YOU BREAK FREE OF HIS CONTROL?
HE CONTROLS ME THROUGH SOME KIND OF WAVES, ELECTROMAGNETIC I THINK. THE MACHINE SENDING THOSE WAVES MUST BE DOWN.
COME MORNING, STEVE WILL FIX THE MACHINE AND REGAIN CONTROL. YOU HAVE TO BE LONG GONE BY THEN! TORG, HE WAS GOING TO HAVE ME KILL YOU!
I'LL DO WHATEVER YOU WANT, BUT TELL ME HOW THIS HAPPENED TO YOU.
"IT STARTED MANY YEARS AGO WHEN MY PARENTS DIED. THEY WERE KILLED IN A FREAK ACCIDENT."
Today's Nifty Newspaper
COUPLE ACCIDENTALLY RAN-OVER BY BEARDED LADY!
"Timmy the Monkey-Boy is to blame!"
CLOWN CAR USED
"AFTER MY PARENTS DIED, MY CUSTODY WAS TURNED OVER TO MY DISTANT UNCLE STEVE. HE WAS A LOVING CARING MAN, WHO ONLY WANTED THE BEST FOR ME, AND TO CONTROL MY MIND."
DO THE DISHES!
NO!
"HE TRIED ALL KINDS OF MIND-CONTROL TECHNIQUES TO NO AVAIL, BUT IT DIDN'T MATTER, BECAUSE I LOVED HIM AND WOULD DO ANYTHING TO PLEASE HIM."
WHO WANTS TO PLAY WITH MICROWAVE RADIATION?
I DO! I DO!
"THEN, AS I GOT OLDER, I HAD A CHANGE OF HEART."
WANT TO DO SOME SENSORY DEPRIVATION, MY DEAR OASIS?
YOU'RE NOT MY REAL FATHER! YOU DON'T REALLY CARE ABOUT ME. I'M GOING TO THE MALL, STEVE!
YOU WERE GOING THROUGH A REBELLIOUS STAGE?
OUR RELATIONSHIP STARTED GOING SOUTH WHEN HE HAD MY MIDDLE NAME LEGALLY CHANGED TO "EXPERIMENT-NUMBER-ONE".

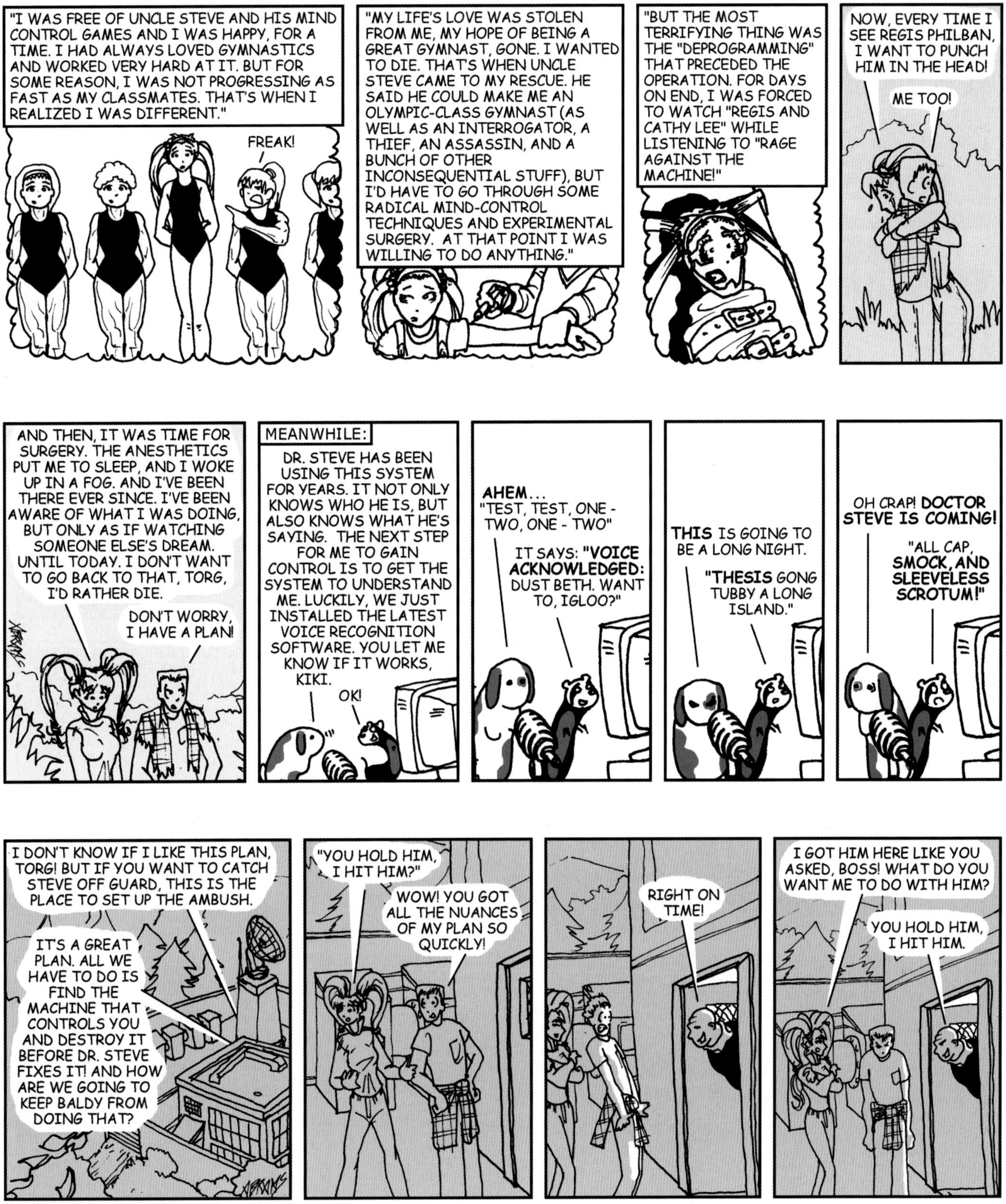
"I WAS FREE OF UNCLE STEVE AND HIS MIND CONTROL GAMES AND I WAS HAPPY, FOR A TIME. I HAD ALWAYS LOVED GYMNASTICS AND WORKED VERY HARD AT IT. BUT FOR SOME REASON, I WAS NOT PROGRESSING AS FAST AS MY CLASSMATES. THAT'S WHEN I REALIZED I WAS DIFFERENT."
FREAK!
"MY LIFE'S LOVE WAS STOLEN FROM ME, MY HOPE OF BEING A GREAT GYMNAST, GONE. I WANTED TO DIE. THAT'S WHEN UNCLE STEVE CAME TO MY RESCUE. HE SAID HE COULD MAKE ME AN OLYMPIC-CLASS GYMNAST (AS WELL AS AN INTERROGATOR, A THIEF, AN ASSASSIN, AND A BUNCH OF OTHER INCONSEQUENTIAL STUFF), BUT I'D HAVE TO GO THROUGH SOME RADICAL MIND-CONTROL TECHNIQUES AND EXPERIMENTAL SURGERY. AT THAT POINT I WAS WILLING TO DO ANYTHING."
"BUT THE MOST TERRIFYING THING WAS THE "DEPROGRAMMING" THAT PRECEDED THE OPERATION. FOR DAYS ON END, I WAS FORCED TO WATCH "REGIS AND CATHY LEE" WHILE LISTENING TO "RAGE AGAINST THE MACHINE!"
NOW, EVERY TIME I SEE REGIS PHILBAN, I WANT TO PUNCH HIM IN THE HEAD!
ME TOO!
AND THEN, IT WAS TIME FOR SURGERY. THE ANESTHETICS PUT ME TO SLEEP, AND I WOKE UP IN A FOG. AND I'VE BEEN THERE EVER SINCE. I'VE BEEN AWARE OF WHAT I WAS DOING, BUT ONLY AS IF WATCHING SOMEONE ELSE'S DREAM. UNTIL TODAY. I DON'T WANT TO GO BACK TO THAT, TORG, I'D RATHER DIE.
DON'T WORRY, I HAVE A PLAN!
MEANWHILE:
DR. STEVE HAS BEEN USING THIS SYSTEM FOR YEARS. IT NOT ONLY KNOWS WHO HE IS, BUT ALSO KNOWS WHAT HE'S SAYING. THE NEXT STEP FOR ME TO GAIN CONTROL IS TO GET THE SYSTEM TO UNDERSTAND ME. LUCKILY, WE JUST INSTALLED THE LATEST VOICE RECOGNITION SOFTWARE. YOU LET ME KNOW IF IT WORKS, KIKI.
OK!
AHEM... "TEST, TEST, ONE - TWO, ONE - TWO"
IT SAYS: **"VOICE ACKNOWLEDGED:** DUST BETH. WANT TO, IGLOO?"
THIS IS GOING TO BE A LONG NIGHT.
"THESIS GONG TUBBY A LONG ISLAND."
OH CRAP! **DOCTOR STEVE IS COMING!**
"ALL CAP, **SMOCK, AND SLEEVELESS SCROTUM!"**
I DON'T KNOW IF I LIKE THIS PLAN, TORG! BUT IF YOU WANT TO CATCH STEVE OFF GUARD, THIS IS THE PLACE TO SET UP THE AMBUSH.
IT'S A GREAT PLAN. ALL WE HAVE TO DO IS FIND THE MACHINE THAT CONTROLS YOU AND DESTROY IT BEFORE DR. STEVE FIXES IT! AND HOW ARE WE GOING TO KEEP BALDY FROM DOING THAT?
"YOU HOLD HIM, I HIT HIM?"
WOW! YOU GOT ALL THE NUANCES OF MY PLAN SO QUICKLY!
RIGHT ON TIME!
I GOT HIM HERE LIKE YOU ASKED, BOSS! WHAT DO YOU WANT ME TO DO WITH HIM?
YOU HOLD HIM, I HIT HIM.

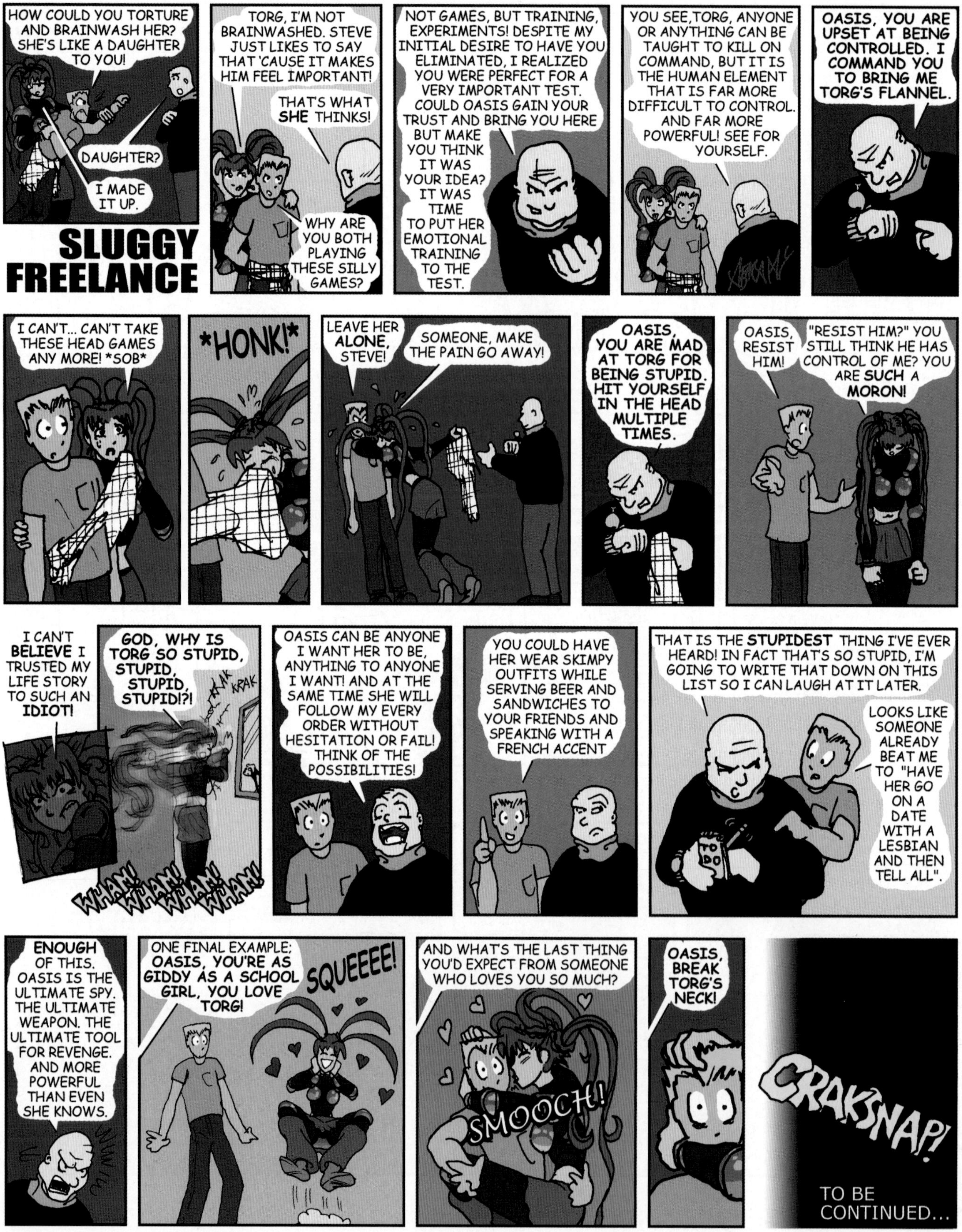
HOW COULD YOU TORTURE AND BRAINWASH HER? SHE'S LIKE A DAUGHTER TO YOU!
DAUGHTER?
I MADE IT UP.
SLUGGY FREELANCE
TORG, I'M NOT BRAINWASHED. STEVE JUST LIKES TO SAY THAT 'CAUSE IT MAKES HIM FEEL IMPORTANT!
THAT'S WHAT SHE THINKS!
WHY ARE YOU BOTH PLAYING THESE SILLY GAMES?
NOT GAMES, BUT TRAINING, EXPERIMENTS! DESPITE MY INITIAL DESIRE TO HAVE YOU ELIMINATED, I REALIZED YOU WERE PERFECT FOR A VERY IMPORTANT TEST. COULD OASIS GAIN YOUR TRUST AND BRING YOU HERE BUT MAKE YOU THINK IT WAS YOUR IDEA? IT WAS TIME TO PUT HER EMOTIONAL TRAINING TO THE TEST.
YOU SEE, TORG, ANYONE OR ANYTHING CAN BE TAUGHT TO KILL ON COMMAND, BUT IT IS THE HUMAN ELEMENT THAT IS FAR MORE DIFFICULT TO CONTROL. AND FAR MORE POWERFUL! SEE FOR YOURSELF.
OASIS, YOU ARE UPSET AT BEING CONTROLLED. I COMMAND YOU TO BRING ME TORG'S FLANNEL.
I CAN'T... CAN'T TAKE THESE HEAD GAMES ANY MORE! *SOB*
HONK!
LEAVE HER ALONE, STEVE!
SOMEONE, MAKE THE PAIN GO AWAY!
OASIS, YOU ARE MAD AT TORG FOR BEING STUPID. HIT YOURSELF IN THE HEAD MULTIPLE TIMES.
OASIS, RESIST HIM!
"RESIST HIM?" YOU STILL THINK HE HAS CONTROL OF ME? YOU ARE SUCH A MORON!
I CAN'T BELIEVE I TRUSTED MY LIFE STORY TO SUCH AN IDIOT!
GOD, WHY IS TORG SO STUPID, STUPID, STUPID, STUPID!?!
KRAK
WHAM! WHAM! WHAM! WHAM!
OASIS CAN BE ANYONE I WANT HER TO BE, ANYTHING TO ANYONE I WANT! AND AT THE SAME TIME SHE WILL FOLLOW MY EVERY ORDER WITHOUT HESITATION OR FAIL! THINK OF THE POSSIBILITIES!
YOU COULD HAVE HER WEAR SKIMPY OUTFITS WHILE SERVING BEER AND SANDWICHES TO YOUR FRIENDS AND SPEAKING WITH A FRENCH ACCENT
THAT IS THE STUPIDEST THING I'VE EVER HEARD! IN FACT THAT'S SO STUPID, I'M GOING TO WRITE THAT DOWN ON THIS LIST SO I CAN LAUGH AT IT LATER.
TO DO
LOOKS LIKE SOMEONE ALREADY BEAT ME TO "HAVE HER GO ON A DATE WITH A LESBIAN AND THEN TELL ALL".
ENOUGH OF THIS. OASIS IS THE ULTIMATE SPY. THE ULTIMATE WEAPON. THE ULTIMATE TOOL FOR REVENGE. AND MORE POWERFUL THAN EVEN SHE KNOWS.
ONE FINAL EXAMPLE; OASIS, YOU'RE AS GIDDY AS A SCHOOL GIRL, YOU LOVE TORG!
SQUEEEE!
AND WHAT'S THE LAST THING YOU'D EXPECT FROM SOMEONE WHO LOVES YOU SO MUCH?
SMOOCH!
OASIS, BREAK TORG'S NECK!
CRAKSNAP!
TO BE CONTINUED...

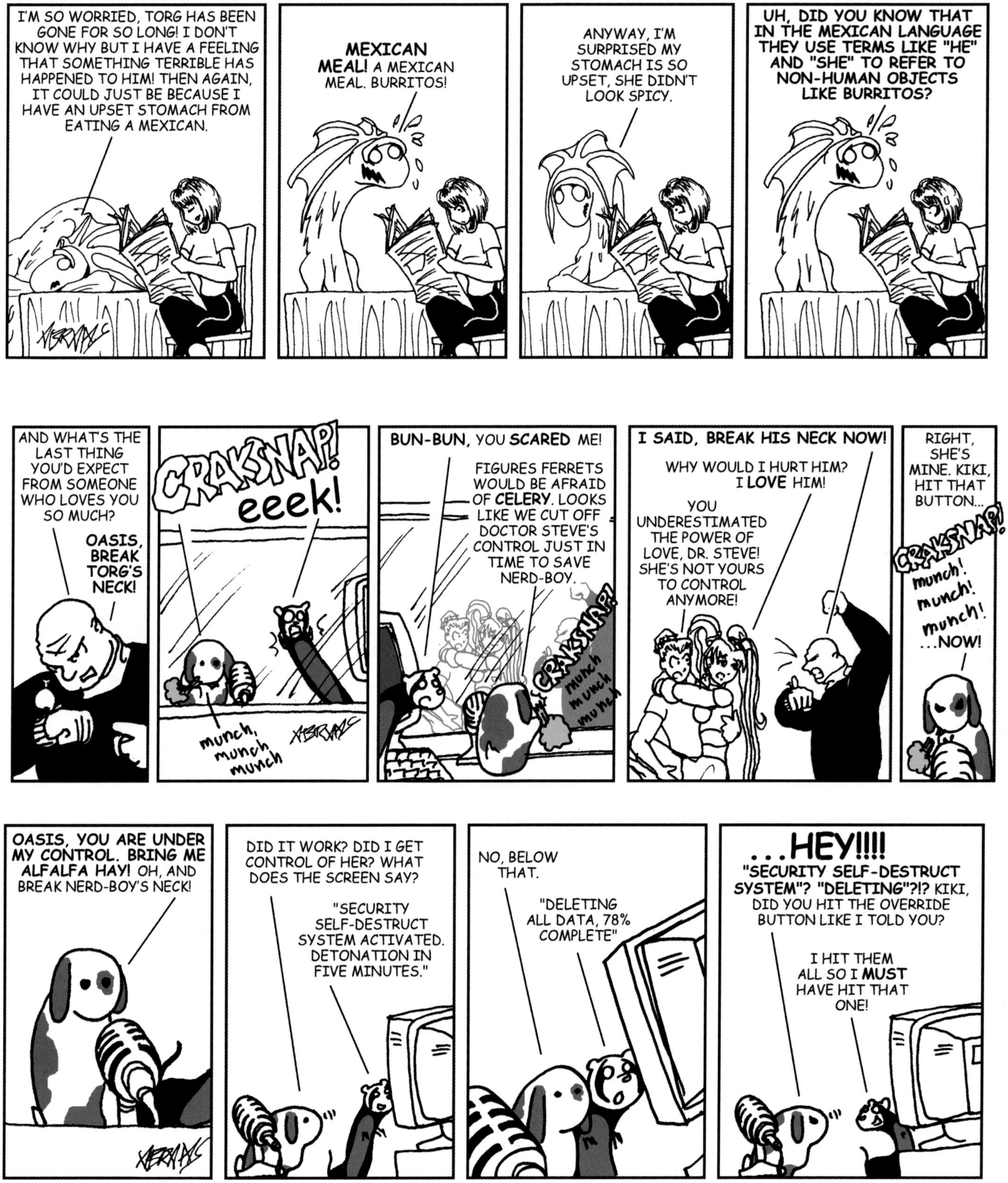
I'M SO WORRIED, TORG HAS BEEN GONE FOR SO LONG! I DON'T KNOW WHY BUT I HAVE A FEELING THAT SOMETHING TERRIBLE HAS HAPPENED TO HIM! THEN AGAIN, IT COULD JUST BE BECAUSE I HAVE AN UPSET STOMACH FROM EATING A MEXICAN.
MEXICAN MEAL! A MEXICAN MEAL. BURRITOS!
ANYWAY, I'M SURPRISED MY STOMACH IS SO UPSET, SHE DIDN'T LOOK SPICY.
UH, DID YOU KNOW THAT IN THE MEXICAN LANGUAGE THEY USE TERMS LIKE "HE" AND "SHE" TO REFER TO NON-HUMAN OBJECTS LIKE BURRITOS?
AND WHAT'S THE LAST THING YOU'D EXPECT FROM SOMEONE WHO LOVES YOU SO MUCH?
OASIS, BREAK TORG'S NECK!
CRAKSNAP!
eeek!
munch, munch munch
BUN-BUN, YOU SCARED ME!
FIGURES FERRETS WOULD BE AFRAID OF CELERY. LOOKS LIKE WE CUT OFF DOCTOR STEVE'S CONTROL JUST IN TIME TO SAVE NERD-BOY.
CRAKSNAP!
munch munch munch
I SAID, BREAK HIS NECK NOW!
WHY WOULD I HURT HIM? I LOVE HIM!
YOU UNDERESTIMATED THE POWER OF LOVE, DR. STEVE! SHE'S NOT YOURS TO CONTROL ANYMORE!
RIGHT, SHE'S MINE. KIKI, HIT THAT BUTTON...
CRAKSNAP!
munch! munch! munch!
...NOW!
OASIS, YOU ARE UNDER MY CONTROL. BRING ME ALFALFA HAY! OH, AND BREAK NERD-BOY'S NECK!
DID IT WORK? DID I GET CONTROL OF HER? WHAT DOES THE SCREEN SAY?
"SECURITY SELF-DESTRUCT SYSTEM ACTIVATED. DETONATION IN FIVE MINUTES."
NO, BELOW THAT.
"DELETING ALL DATA, 78% COMPLETE"
...HEY!!!!
"SECURITY SELF-DESTRUCT SYSTEM"? "DELETING"?!? KIKI, DID YOU HIT THE OVERRIDE BUTTON LIKE I TOLD YOU?
I HIT THEM ALL SO I MUST HAVE HIT THAT ONE!

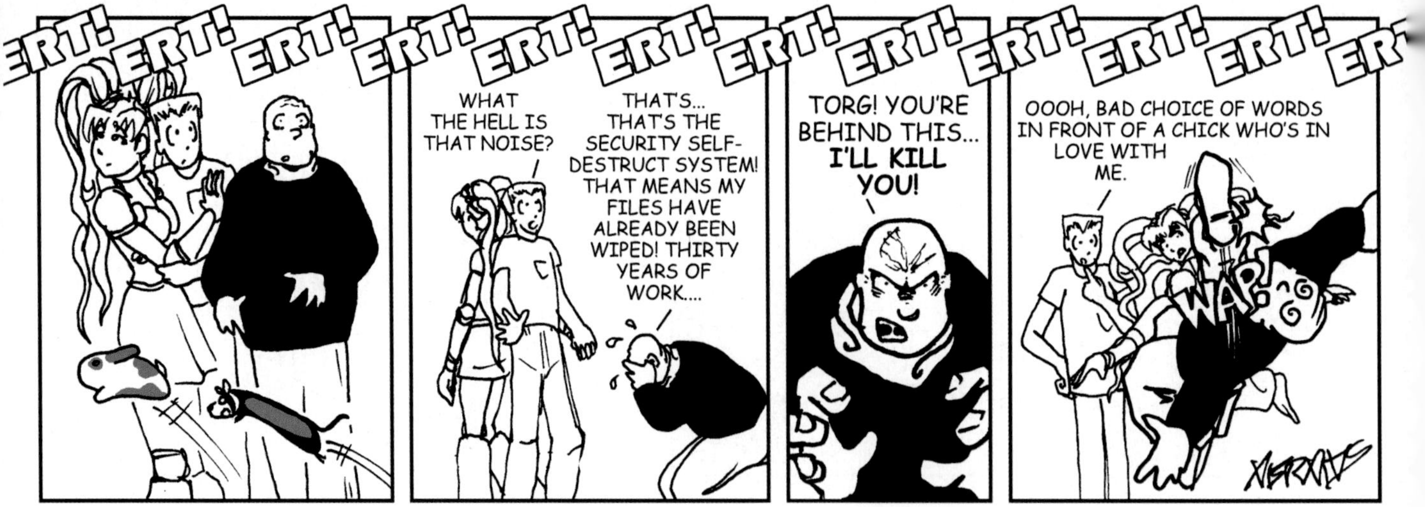
ERT! ERT! ERT! ERT! ERT! ERT! ERT! ERT! ERT! ERT! ERT!
WHAT THE HELL IS THAT NOISE?
THAT'S... THAT'S THE SECURITY SELF-DESTRUCT SYSTEM! THAT MEANS MY FILES HAVE ALREADY BEEN WIPED! THIRTY YEARS OF WORK....
TORG! YOU'RE BEHIND THIS... I'LL KILL YOU!
OOOH, BAD CHOICE OF WORDS IN FRONT OF A CHICK WHO'S IN LOVE WITH ME.
WAP!

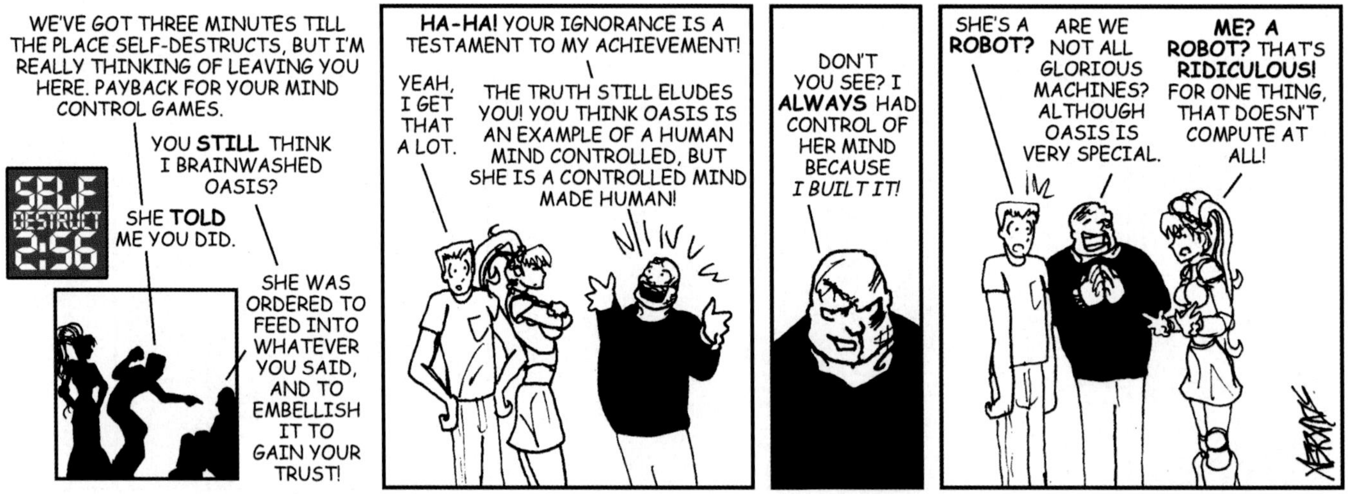
WE'VE GOT THREE MINUTES TILL THE PLACE SELF-DESTRUCTS, BUT I'M REALLY THINKING OF LEAVING YOU HERE. PAYBACK FOR YOUR MIND CONTROL GAMES.
YOU STILL THINK I BRAINWASHED OASIS?
SELF DESTRUCT 2:56
SHE TOLD ME YOU DID.
SHE WAS ORDERED TO FEED INTO WHATEVER YOU SAID, AND TO EMBELLISH IT TO GAIN YOUR TRUST!
HA-HA! YOUR IGNORANCE IS A TESTAMENT TO MY ACHIEVEMENT!
YEAH, I GET THAT A LOT.
THE TRUTH STILL ELUDES YOU! YOU THINK OASIS IS AN EXAMPLE OF A HUMAN MIND CONTROLLED, BUT SHE IS A CONTROLLED MIND MADE HUMAN!
DON'T YOU SEE? I ALWAYS HAD CONTROL OF HER MIND BECAUSE I BUILT IT!
SHE'S A ROBOT?
ARE WE NOT ALL GLORIOUS MACHINES? ALTHOUGH OASIS IS VERY SPECIAL.
ME? A ROBOT? THAT'S RIDICULOUS! FOR ONE THING, THAT DOESN'T COMPUTE AT ALL!

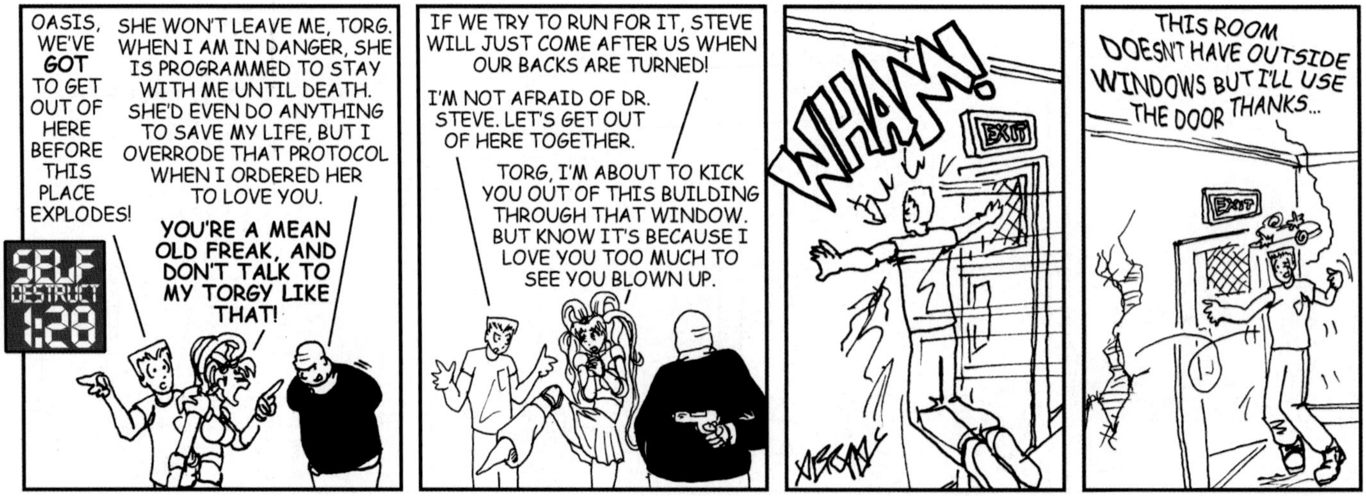
OASIS, WE'VE GOT TO GET OUT OF HERE BEFORE THIS PLACE EXPLODES!
SHE WON'T LEAVE ME, TORG. WHEN I AM IN DANGER, SHE IS PROGRAMMED TO STAY WITH ME UNTIL DEATH. SHE'D EVEN DO ANYTHING TO SAVE MY LIFE, BUT I OVERRODE THAT PROTOCOL WHEN I ORDERED HER TO LOVE YOU.
YOU'RE A MEAN OLD FREAK, AND DON'T TALK TO MY TORGY LIKE THAT!
SELF DESTRUCT 1:28
IF WE TRY TO RUN FOR IT, STEVE WILL JUST COME AFTER US WHEN OUR BACKS ARE TURNED!
I'M NOT AFRAID OF DR. STEVE. LET'S GET OUT OF HERE TOGETHER.
TORG, I'M ABOUT TO KICK YOU OUT OF THIS BUILDING THROUGH THAT WINDOW. BUT KNOW IT'S BECAUSE I LOVE YOU TOO MUCH TO SEE YOU BLOWN UP.
WHAM!
EXIT
THIS ROOM DOESN'T HAVE OUTSIDE WINDOWS BUT I'LL USE THE DOOR THANKS...
EXIT

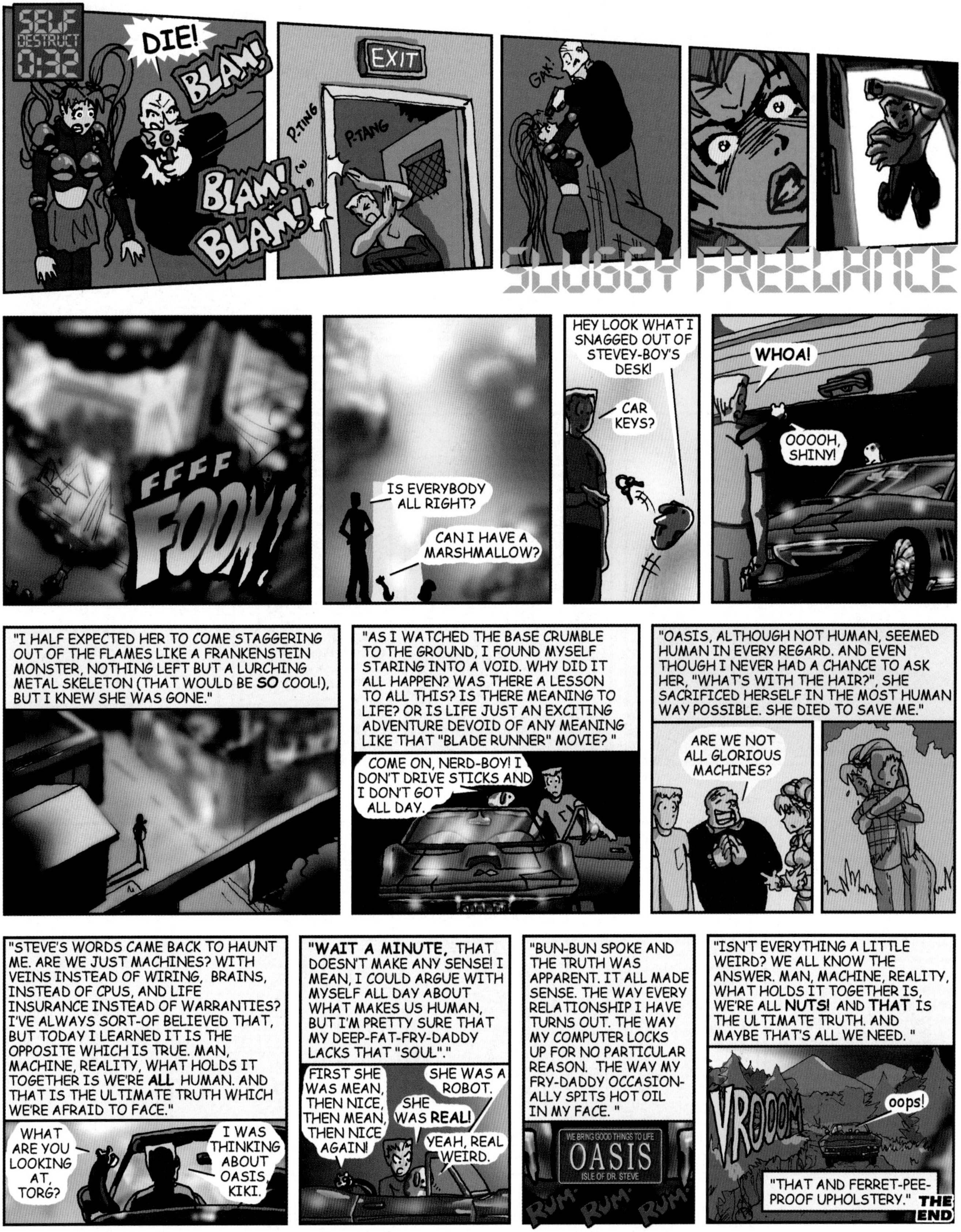
SELF DESTRUCT 0:32
DIE!
BLAM!
BLAM!
BLAM!
EXIT
P-TING
P-TANG
GAK!
SLUGGY FREELANCE
FFFF FOOM!
IS EVERYBODY ALL RIGHT?
CAN I HAVE A MARSHMALLOW?
HEY LOOK WHAT I SNAGGED OUT OF STEVEY-BOY'S DESK!
CAR KEYS?
WHOA!
OOOOH, SHINY!
"I HALF EXPECTED HER TO COME STAGGERING OUT OF THE FLAMES LIKE A FRANKENSTEIN MONSTER, NOTHING LEFT BUT A LURCHING METAL SKELETON (THAT WOULD BE SO COOL!), BUT I KNEW SHE WAS GONE."
"AS I WATCHED THE BASE CRUMBLE TO THE GROUND, I FOUND MYSELF STARING INTO A VOID. WHY DID IT ALL HAPPEN? WAS THERE A LESSON TO ALL THIS? IS THERE MEANING TO LIFE? OR IS LIFE JUST AN EXCITING ADVENTURE DEVOID OF ANY MEANING LIKE THAT "BLADE RUNNER" MOVIE? "
COME ON, NERD-BOY! I DON'T DRIVE STICKS AND I DON'T GOT ALL DAY.
"OASIS, ALTHOUGH NOT HUMAN, SEEMED HUMAN IN EVERY REGARD. AND EVEN THOUGH I NEVER HAD A CHANCE TO ASK HER, "WHAT'S WITH THE HAIR?", SHE SACRIFICED HERSELF IN THE MOST HUMAN WAY POSSIBLE. SHE DIED TO SAVE ME."
ARE WE NOT ALL GLORIOUS MACHINES?
"STEVE'S WORDS CAME BACK TO HAUNT ME. ARE WE JUST MACHINES? WITH VEINS INSTEAD OF WIRING, BRAINS, INSTEAD OF CPUS, AND LIFE INSURANCE INSTEAD OF WARRANTIES? I'VE ALWAYS SORT-OF BELIEVED THAT, BUT TODAY I LEARNED IT IS THE OPPOSITE WHICH IS TRUE. MAN, MACHINE, REALITY, WHAT HOLDS IT TOGETHER IS WE'RE ALL HUMAN. AND THAT IS THE ULTIMATE TRUTH WHICH WE'RE AFRAID TO FACE."
WHAT ARE YOU LOOKING AT, TORG?
I WAS THINKING ABOUT OASIS, KIKI.
"WAIT A MINUTE, THAT DOESN'T MAKE ANY SENSE! I MEAN, I COULD ARGUE WITH MYSELF ALL DAY ABOUT WHAT MAKES US HUMAN, BUT I'M PRETTY SURE THAT MY DEEP-FAT-FRY-DADDY LACKS THAT "SOUL"."
FIRST SHE WAS MEAN, THEN NICE, THEN MEAN, THEN NICE AGAIN!
SHE WAS A ROBOT.
SHE WAS REAL!
YEAH, REAL WEIRD.
"BUN-BUN SPOKE AND THE TRUTH WAS APPARENT. IT ALL MADE SENSE. THE WAY EVERY RELATIONSHIP I HAVE TURNS OUT. THE WAY MY COMPUTER LOCKS UP FOR NO PARTICULAR REASON. THE WAY MY FRY-DADDY OCCASION-ALLY SPITS HOT OIL IN MY FACE. "
WE BRING GOOD THINGS TO LIFE
OASIS
ISLE OF DR STEVE
RUM RUM RUM
"ISN'T EVERYTHING A LITTLE WEIRD? WE ALL KNOW THE ANSWER. MAN, MACHINE, REALITY, WHAT HOLDS IT TOGETHER IS, WE'RE ALL NUTS! AND THAT IS THE ULTIMATE TRUTH. AND MAYBE THAT'S ALL WE NEED. "
VROOOM
oops!
"THAT AND FERRET-PEE-PROOF UPHOLSTERY."
THE END

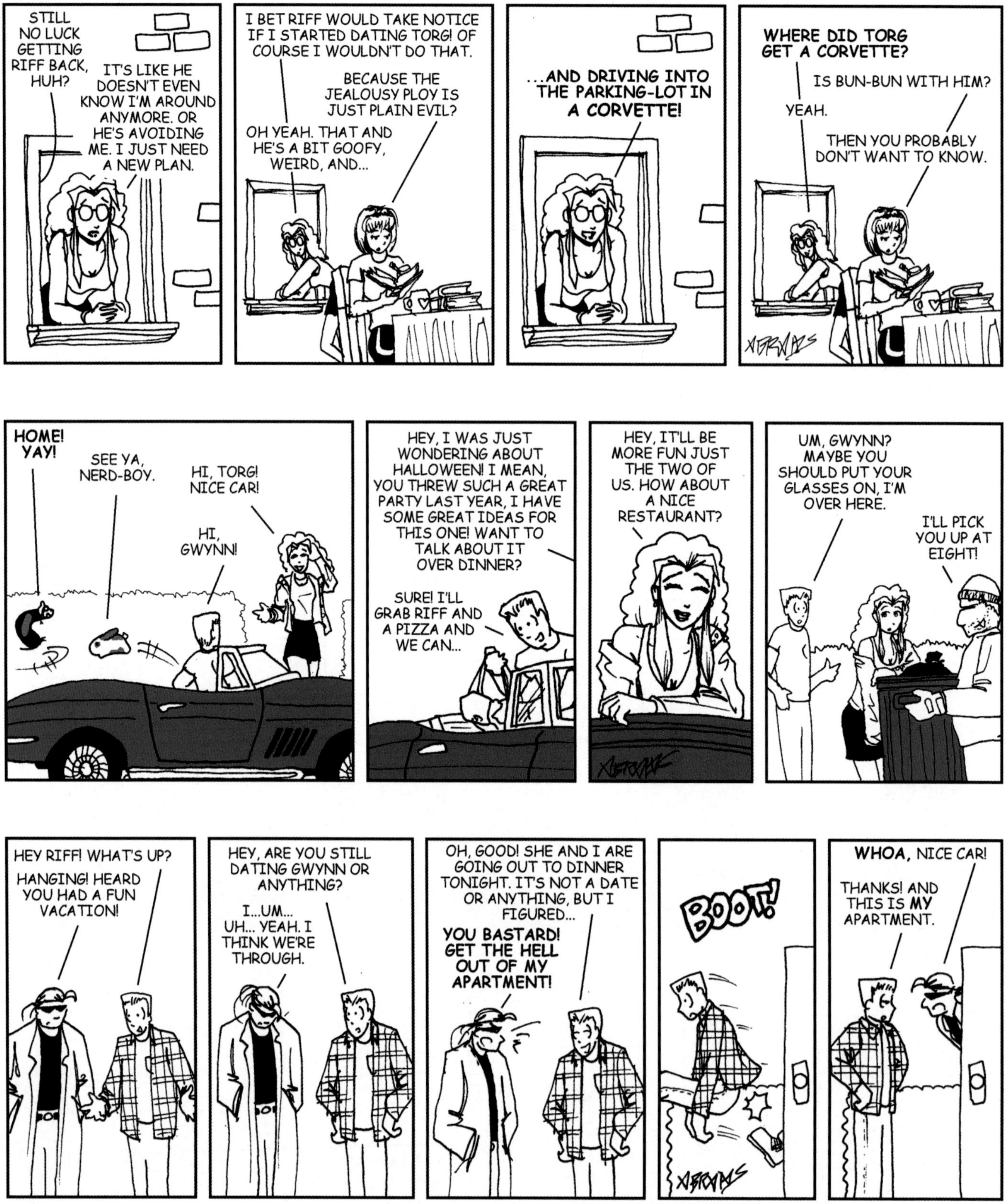
STILL NO LUCK GETTING RIFF BACK, HUH?
IT'S LIKE HE DOESN'T EVEN KNOW I'M AROUND ANYMORE. OR HE'S AVOIDING ME. I JUST NEED A NEW PLAN.
I BET RIFF WOULD TAKE NOTICE IF I STARTED DATING TORG! OF COURSE I WOULDN'T DO THAT.
BECAUSE THE JEALOUSY PLOY IS JUST PLAIN EVIL?
OH YEAH. THAT AND HE'S A BIT GOOFY, WEIRD, AND...
...AND DRIVING INTO THE PARKING-LOT IN A CORVETTE!
WHERE DID TORG GET A CORVETTE?
IS BUN-BUN WITH HIM?
YEAH.
THEN YOU PROBABLY DON'T WANT TO KNOW.
HOME! YAY!
SEE YA, NERD-BOY.
HI, TORG! NICE CAR!
HI, GWYNN!
HEY, I WAS JUST WONDERING ABOUT HALLOWEEN! I MEAN, YOU THREW SUCH A GREAT PARTY LAST YEAR, I HAVE SOME GREAT IDEAS FOR THIS ONE! WANT TO TALK ABOUT IT OVER DINNER?
SURE! I'LL GRAB RIFF AND A PIZZA AND WE CAN...
HEY, IT'LL BE MORE FUN JUST THE TWO OF US. HOW ABOUT A NICE RESTAURANT?
UM, GWYNN? MAYBE YOU SHOULD PUT YOUR GLASSES ON, I'M OVER HERE.
I'LL PICK YOU UP AT EIGHT!
HEY RIFF! WHAT'S UP?
HANGING! HEARD YOU HAD A FUN VACATION!
HEY, ARE YOU STILL DATING GWYNN OR ANYTHING?
I...UM... UH... YEAH. I THINK WE'RE THROUGH.
OH, GOOD! SHE AND I ARE GOING OUT TO DINNER TONIGHT. IT'S NOT A DATE OR ANYTHING, BUT I FIGURED...
YOU BASTARD! GET THE HELL OUT OF MY APARTMENT!
BOOT!
WHOA, NICE CAR!
THANKS! AND THIS IS MY APARTMENT.

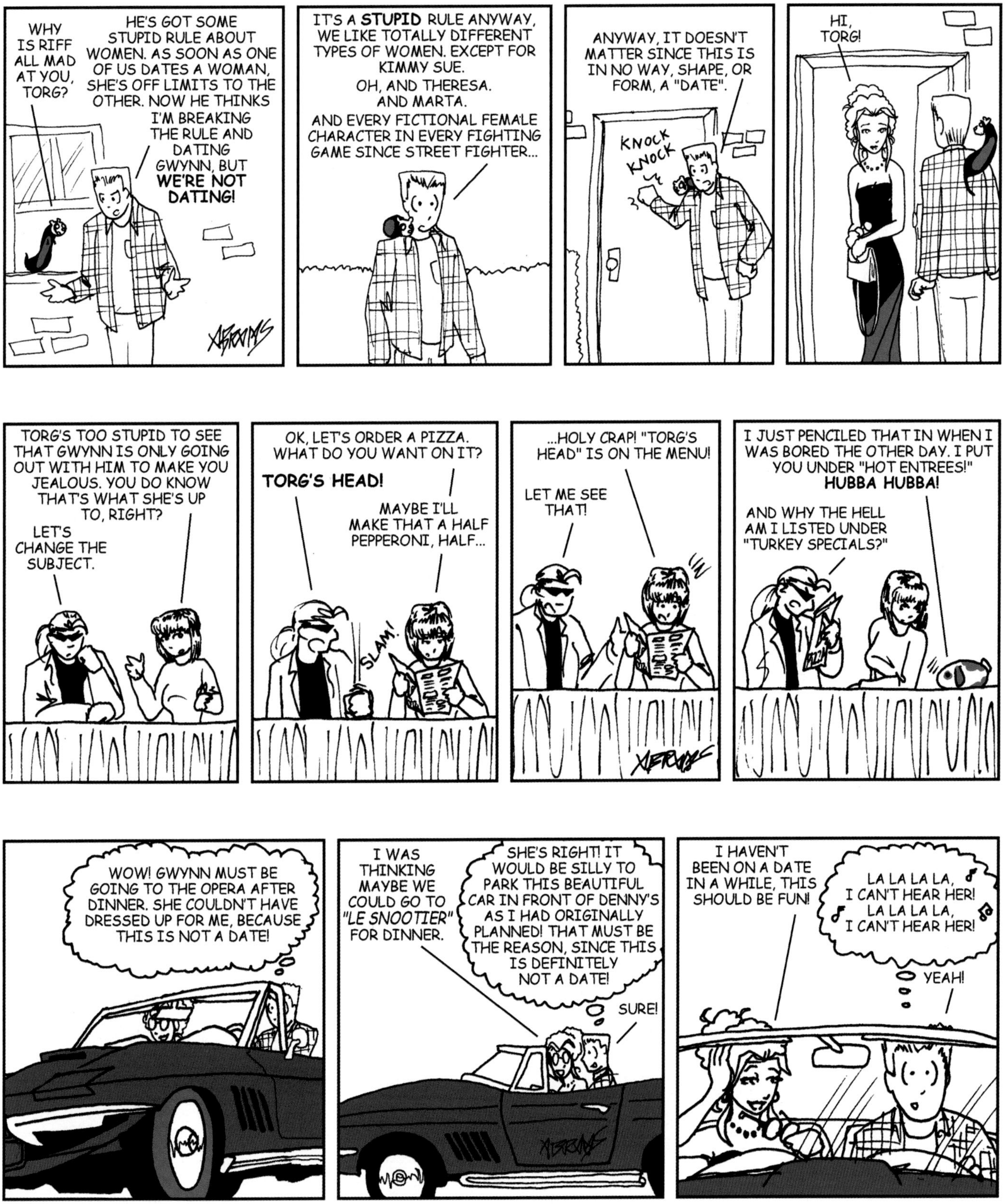
WHY IS RIFF ALL MAD AT YOU, TORG?
HE'S GOT SOME STUPID RULE ABOUT WOMEN. AS SOON AS ONE OF US DATES A WOMAN, SHE'S OFF LIMITS TO THE OTHER. NOW HE THINKS
I'M BREAKING THE RULE AND DATING GWYNN, BUT **WE'RE NOT DATING!**
IT'S A **STUPID** RULE ANYWAY, WE LIKE TOTALLY DIFFERENT TYPES OF WOMEN. EXCEPT FOR KIMMY SUE.
OH, AND THERESA.
AND MARTA.
AND EVERY FICTIONAL FEMALE CHARACTER IN EVERY FIGHTING GAME SINCE STREET FIGHTER...
ANYWAY, IT DOESN'T MATTER SINCE THIS IS IN NO WAY, SHAPE, OR FORM, A "DATE".
KNOCK KNOCK
HI, TORG!
TORG'S TOO STUPID TO SEE THAT GWYNN IS ONLY GOING OUT WITH HIM TO MAKE YOU JEALOUS. YOU DO KNOW THAT'S WHAT SHE'S UP TO, RIGHT?
LET'S CHANGE THE SUBJECT.
OK, LET'S ORDER A PIZZA. WHAT DO YOU WANT ON IT?
TORG'S HEAD!
MAYBE I'LL MAKE THAT A HALF PEPPERONI, HALF...
SLAM!
...HOLY CRAP! "TORG'S HEAD" IS ON THE MENU!
LET ME SEE THAT!
I JUST PENCILED THAT IN WHEN I WAS BORED THE OTHER DAY. I PUT YOU UNDER "HOT ENTREES!" **HUBBA HUBBA!**
AND WHY THE HELL AM I LISTED UNDER "TURKEY SPECIALS?"
WOW! GWYNN MUST BE GOING TO THE OPERA AFTER DINNER. SHE COULDN'T HAVE DRESSED UP FOR ME, BECAUSE THIS IS NOT A DATE!
I WAS THINKING MAYBE WE COULD GO TO *"LE SNOOTIER"* FOR DINNER.
SHE'S RIGHT! IT WOULD BE SILLY TO PARK THIS BEAUTIFUL CAR IN FRONT OF DENNY'S AS I HAD ORIGINALLY PLANNED! THAT MUST BE THE REASON, SINCE THIS IS DEFINITELY NOT A DATE!
SURE!
I HAVEN'T BEEN ON A DATE IN A WHILE, THIS SHOULD BE FUN!
LA LA LA LA, I CAN'T HEAR HER! LA LA LA LA, I CAN'T HEAR HER!
YEAH!

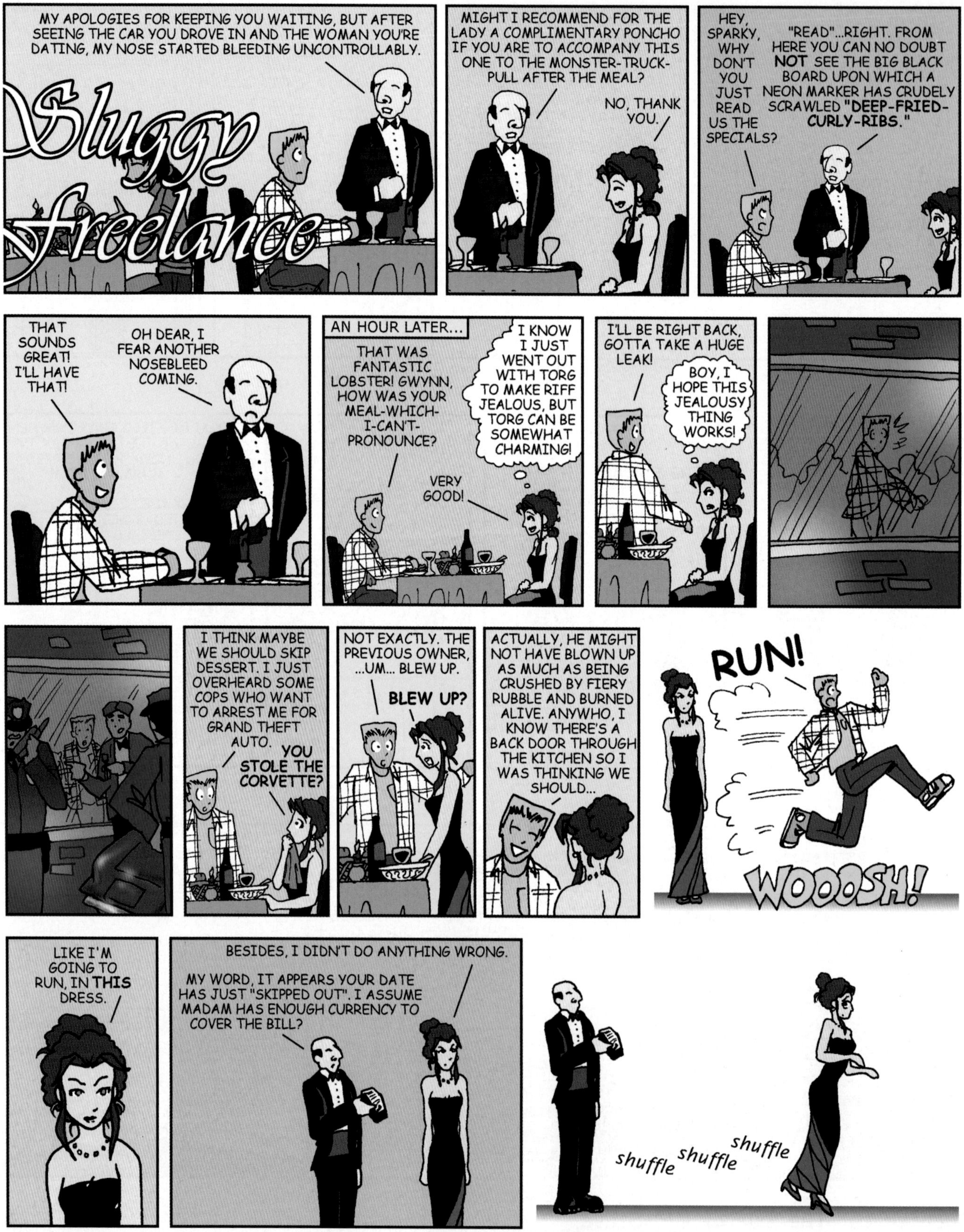

Sluggy Freelance
MY APOLOGIES FOR KEEPING YOU WAITING, BUT AFTER SEEING THE CAR YOU DROVE IN AND THE WOMAN YOU'RE DATING, MY NOSE STARTED BLEEDING UNCONTROLLABLY.
MIGHT I RECOMMEND FOR THE LADY A COMPLIMENTARY PONCHO IF YOU ARE TO ACCOMPANY THIS ONE TO THE MONSTER-TRUCK-PULL AFTER THE MEAL?
NO, THANK YOU.
HEY, SPARKY, WHY DON'T YOU JUST READ US THE SPECIALS?
"READ"...RIGHT. FROM HERE YOU CAN NO DOUBT **NOT** SEE THE BIG BLACK BOARD UPON WHICH A NEON MARKER HAS CRUDELY SCRAWLED **"DEEP-FRIED-CURLY-RIBS."**
THAT SOUNDS GREAT! I'LL HAVE THAT!
OH DEAR, I FEAR ANOTHER NOSEBLEED COMING.
AN HOUR LATER...
THAT WAS FANTASTIC LOBSTER! GWYNN, HOW WAS YOUR MEAL-WHICH-I-CAN'T-PRONOUNCE?
I KNOW I JUST WENT OUT WITH TORG TO MAKE RIFF JEALOUS, BUT TORG CAN BE SOMEWHAT CHARMING!
VERY GOOD!
I'LL BE RIGHT BACK, GOTTA TAKE A HUGE LEAK!
BOY, I HOPE THIS JEALOUSY THING WORKS!
I THINK MAYBE WE SHOULD SKIP DESSERT. I JUST OVERHEARD SOME COPS WHO WANT TO ARREST ME FOR GRAND THEFT AUTO.
YOU STOLE THE CORVETTE?
NOT EXACTLY. THE PREVIOUS OWNER, ...UM... BLEW UP.
BLEW UP?
ACTUALLY, HE MIGHT NOT HAVE BLOWN UP AS MUCH AS BEING CRUSHED BY FIERY RUBBLE AND BURNED ALIVE. ANYWHO, I KNOW THERE'S A BACK DOOR THROUGH THE KITCHEN SO I WAS THINKING WE SHOULD...
RUN!
WOOOSH!
LIKE I'M GOING TO RUN, IN **THIS** DRESS.
BESIDES, I DIDN'T DO ANYTHING WRONG.
MY WORD, IT APPEARS YOUR DATE HAS JUST "SKIPPED OUT". I ASSUME MADAM HAS ENOUGH CURRENCY TO COVER THE BILL?
shuffle shuffle shuffle

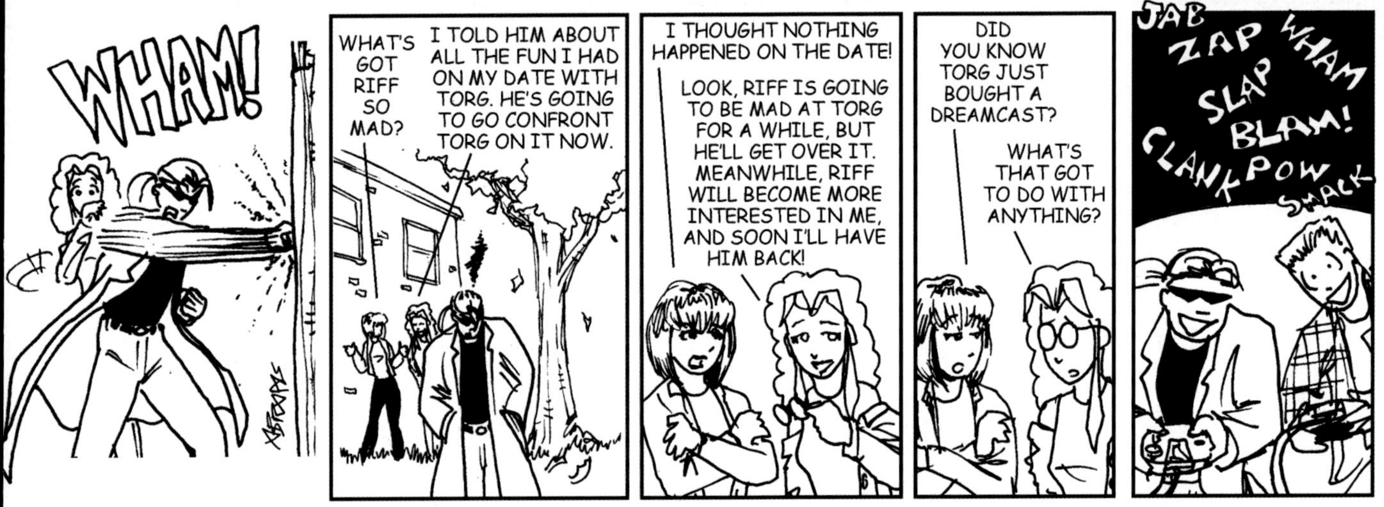
WHAM!
WHAT'S GOT RIFF SO MAD?
I TOLD HIM ABOUT ALL THE FUN I HAD ON MY DATE WITH TORG. HE'S GOING TO GO CONFRONT TORG ON IT NOW.
I THOUGHT NOTHING HAPPENED ON THE DATE!
LOOK, RIFF IS GOING TO BE MAD AT TORG FOR A WHILE, BUT HE'LL GET OVER IT. MEANWHILE, RIFF WILL BECOME MORE INTERESTED IN ME, AND SOON I'LL HAVE HIM BACK!
DID YOU KNOW TORG JUST BOUGHT A DREAMCAST?
WHAT'S THAT GOT TO DO WITH ANYTHING?
JAB ZAP WHAM SLAP BLAM! CLANK POW SMACK

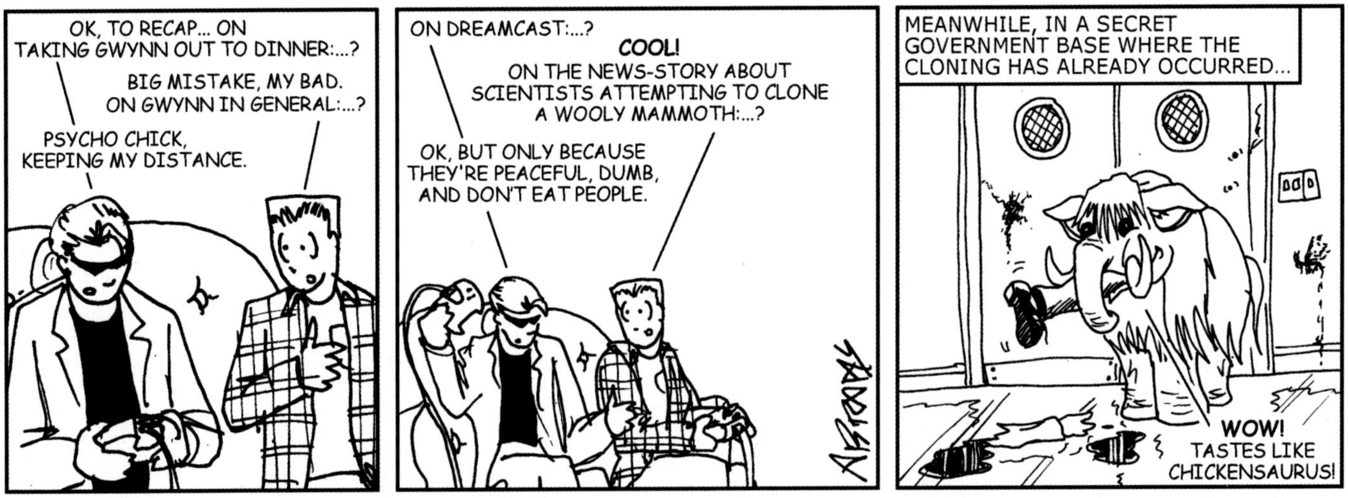
OK, TO RECAP... ON TAKING GWYNN OUT TO DINNER:...?
BIG MISTAKE, MY BAD. ON GWYNN IN GENERAL:...?
PSYCHO CHICK, KEEPING MY DISTANCE.
ON DREAMCAST:...?
COOL! ON THE NEWS-STORY ABOUT SCIENTISTS ATTEMPTING TO CLONE A WOOLY MAMMOTH:...?
OK, BUT ONLY BECAUSE THEY'RE PEACEFUL, DUMB, AND DON'T EAT PEOPLE.
MEANWHILE, IN A SECRET GOVERNMENT BASE WHERE THE CLONING HAS ALREADY OCCURRED...
WOW! TASTES LIKE CHICKENSAURUS!

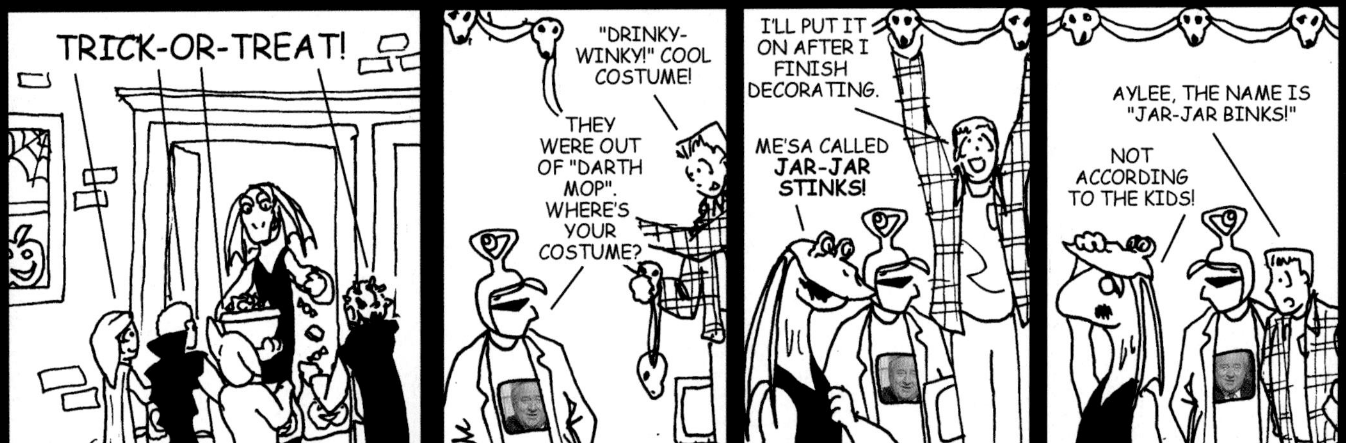
TRICK-OR-TREAT!
"DRINKY-WINKY!" COOL COSTUME!
THEY WERE OUT OF "DARTH MOP". WHERE'S YOUR COSTUME?
I'LL PUT IT ON AFTER I FINISH DECORATING.
ME'SA CALLED JAR-JAR STINKS!
AYLEE, THE NAME IS "JAR-JAR BINKS!"
NOT ACCORDING TO THE KIDS!

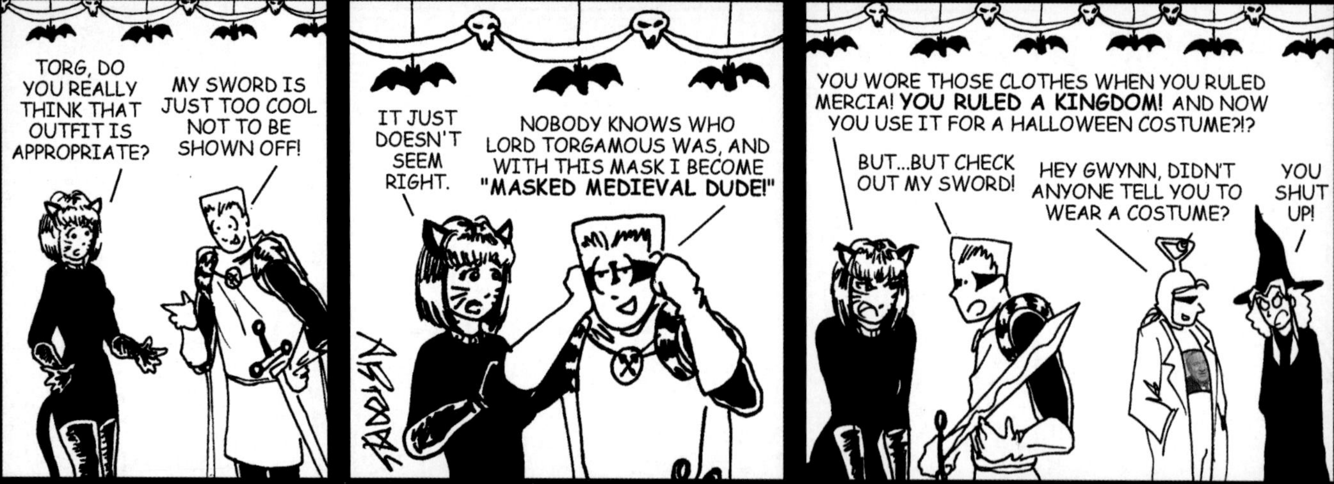
TORG, DO YOU REALLY THINK THAT OUTFIT IS APPROPRIATE?
MY SWORD IS JUST TOO COOL NOT TO BE SHOWN OFF!
IT JUST DOESN'T SEEM RIGHT.
NOBODY KNOWS WHO LORD TORGAMOUS WAS, AND WITH THIS MASK I BECOME "MASKED MEDIEVAL DUDE!"
YOU WORE THOSE CLOTHES WHEN YOU RULED MERCIA! YOU RULED A KINGDOM! AND NOW YOU USE IT FOR A HALLOWEEN COSTUME?!?
BUT...BUT CHECK OUT MY SWORD!
HEY GWYNN, DIDN'T ANYONE TELL YOU TO WEAR A COSTUME?
YOU SHUT UP!

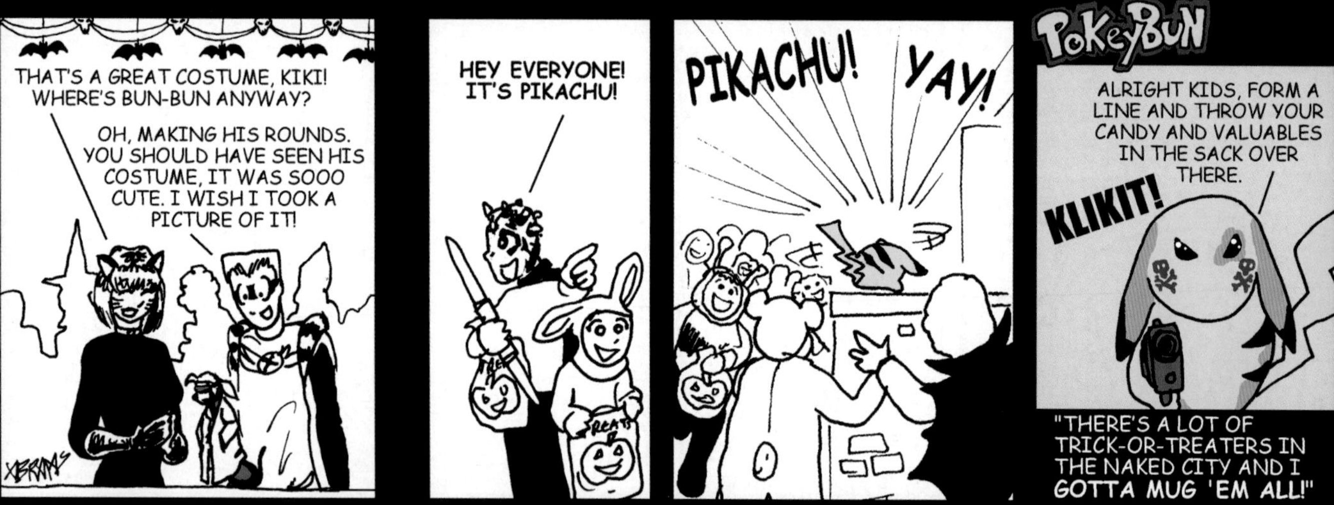
THAT'S A GREAT COSTUME, KIKI! WHERE'S BUN-BUN ANYWAY?
OH, MAKING HIS ROUNDS. YOU SHOULD HAVE SEEN HIS COSTUME, IT WAS SOOO CUTE. I WISH I TOOK A PICTURE OF IT!
HEY EVERYONE! IT'S PIKACHU!
PIKACHU!
YAY!
POKEYBUN
ALRIGHT KIDS, FORM A LINE AND THROW YOUR CANDY AND VALUABLES IN THE SACK OVER THERE.
KLIKIT!
"THERE'S A LOT OF TRICK-OR-TREATERS IN THE NAKED CITY AND I GOTTA MUG 'EM ALL!"

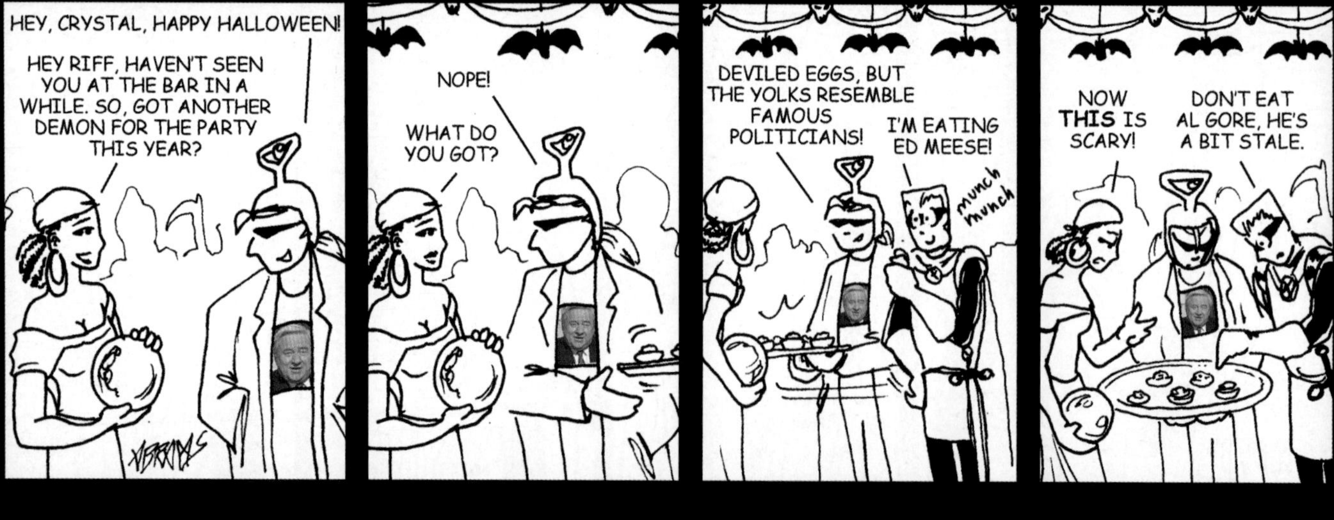
HEY, CRYSTAL, HAPPY HALLOWEEN!
HEY RIFF, HAVEN'T SEEN YOU AT THE BAR IN A WHILE. SO, GOT ANOTHER DEMON FOR THE PARTY THIS YEAR?
NOPE!
WHAT DO YOU GOT?
DEVILED EGGS, BUT THE YOLKS RESEMBLE FAMOUS POLITICIANS!
I'M EATING ED MEESE!
munch munch
NOW THIS IS SCARY!
DON'T EAT AL GORE, HE'S A BIT STALE.

HI DEX!

HI ZOË! THANKS FOR INVITING ME! CHECK OUT MY COSTUME!

I'M AUSTIN POWERS BABY! OH, BEHAVE, BABY! AREN'T YOU A NAUGHTY KITTY!

OH BABY! YEAH! YEAH!

THIS COULD BE A LONG NIGHT.

Sluggy Freelance

AND MEET MY SHAGADELIC GIRLFRIEND, ANGELA, DRESSED AS FELICITY SHAGWELL!

HI!

THIS **WILL** BE A LONG NIGHT.

HEY, THIS PARTY IS SLOWING DOWN. WE NEED TO DO SOMETHING.

HOW ABOUT GHOST STORIES?

I KNOW THIS GREAT ONE ABOUT THIS GUY WHO HAD A DEVILED EGG SHAPED LIKE JANET RENO FOR A **HAND**! AND HE ONLY SPOKE IN **IAMBIC PENTAMETER**!

HOW ABOUT A SEANCE?

YEAH, CRYS! YOU'RE ALL DRESSED FOR IT!

I WOULDN'T MESS WITH SEANCES. THERE ARE THINGS OUT THERE... LET'S JUST SAY IT'S BETTER IF THEY DON'T FIND YOU.

WHAT ARE WE TALKING ABOUT HERE, GWYNN?

POSSESSION. TERROR. DEATH. ETERNAL TORMENT.

"MY NAME IS GWYNN. A LONG TIME AGO I WAS TAKEN AND POSSESSED BY A DEMON. IT CAUSED ME TO LOSE MY LOVE, MY JOB, MY LIFE."

I DON'T KNOW HOW TO DO A REAL SEANCE ANYWAY.

THEN LET'S DO A FAKE ONE LIKE IN THE MOVIES.

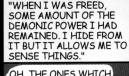

"WHEN I WAS FREED, SOME AMOUNT OF THE DEMONIC POWER I HAD REMAINED. I HIDE FROM IT BUT IT ALLOWS ME TO SENSE THINGS."

OH, THE ONES WHICH **ALWAYS** CAUSE POSSESSION, TERROR, AND DEATH?

YEAH BUT THE TORMENT ONLY LASTS ABOUT AN HOUR AND A HALF.

"FOR SOME REASON, TONIGHT I CAN ALMOST HEAR THE FOOTSTEPS, AND IT SCARES ME."

OH, SPIRITS, HEAR US! BLA, BLA, BLA.

"I TRIED TO WARN THEM, NOT TO DO ANYTHING TO ATTRACT ATTENTION, BUT I HEAR IT WALKING THIS WAY."

GIVE US A SIGN, YADA, YADA, YADA.

"IT'S RUNNING THIS WAY!"

"I HAD NEVER MET HER, BUT I KNEW HER FROM THE STORIES RIFF AND ZOË TOLD ME."

"AND FROM THE WAY SHE LOOKED AT THE CROWD AND SAW ONLY TORG WITH EMPTY EYES."

"THE ONE WHO LOVED TORG MOST, AND WHO DIED BY HIS HAND."

"VAL."

Die for me, love.

DIE YOU DEAD UNDEAD GHOST-BEAST!

ZAP ZAP ZAP

RIFF, YOU CAN'T KILL A GHOST WITH LASERS!

I RECALIBRATED THE LASER TO EFFECT GAMMA-GOZER-WAVES MAKING ECTOPLASM VULNERABLE.

ZAPPO!

AND WHEN, EXACTLY, DID YOU DO THAT?

WELL, I WOULD HAVE IF I KNEW SHE WAS COMING.

ZAP ZAP ZAP

GUYS! RIFF! WE'RE ON THE OTHER SIDE OF THE GHOST! QUIT SHOOTING!

UM,... HI, VAL!

I am cast into hell.

WHOA! SORRY TO HEAR IT!

I have led a good life yet am cast into hell. For crimes not in life but in death. Unfair.

YUP! WELL! UM.... SO! WHAT BRINGS YOU HERE?

Only your love can save me. And until you do...

None shall leave here!

SLAM!

SLAM!

Slam!

SLAM!

Slam!

SLAM!

ALL THE DOORS HAVE CLOSED AND LOCKED!

INCLUDING THE BATHROOM!

DAMN! NOW I HAVE TO GO, AND THE CONTINUOUS DRIPPING CAUSED BY THE WALLS BLEEDING AIN'T HELPING ANY!

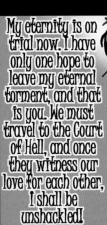

My eternity is on trial now. I have only one hope to leave my eternal torment, and that is you. We must travel to the Court of Hell, and once they witness our love for each other, I shall be unshackled!

OK. HOW DO WE GET TO THE "COURT OF HELL?"

I can bring your soul there, but first you must perform a ceremony to remove your soul from your body.

TIME OUT! I SORT OF LIKE MY SOUL WHERE IT IS. COULD I JUST INITIAL A STATEMENT OR SOMETHING?

YOU CAN'T DO THIS ONE THING FOR ME WHEN I DIED FOR YOU?

YOU DIDN'T DIE FOR ME! I KILLED YOU!

And I betcha feel guilty about it, dontcha?

YEAH, ALL RIGHT, I'LL DO IT.

The first step of the ceremony is to whack yourself in the face a few times with this axe...

TIME OUT AGAIN!

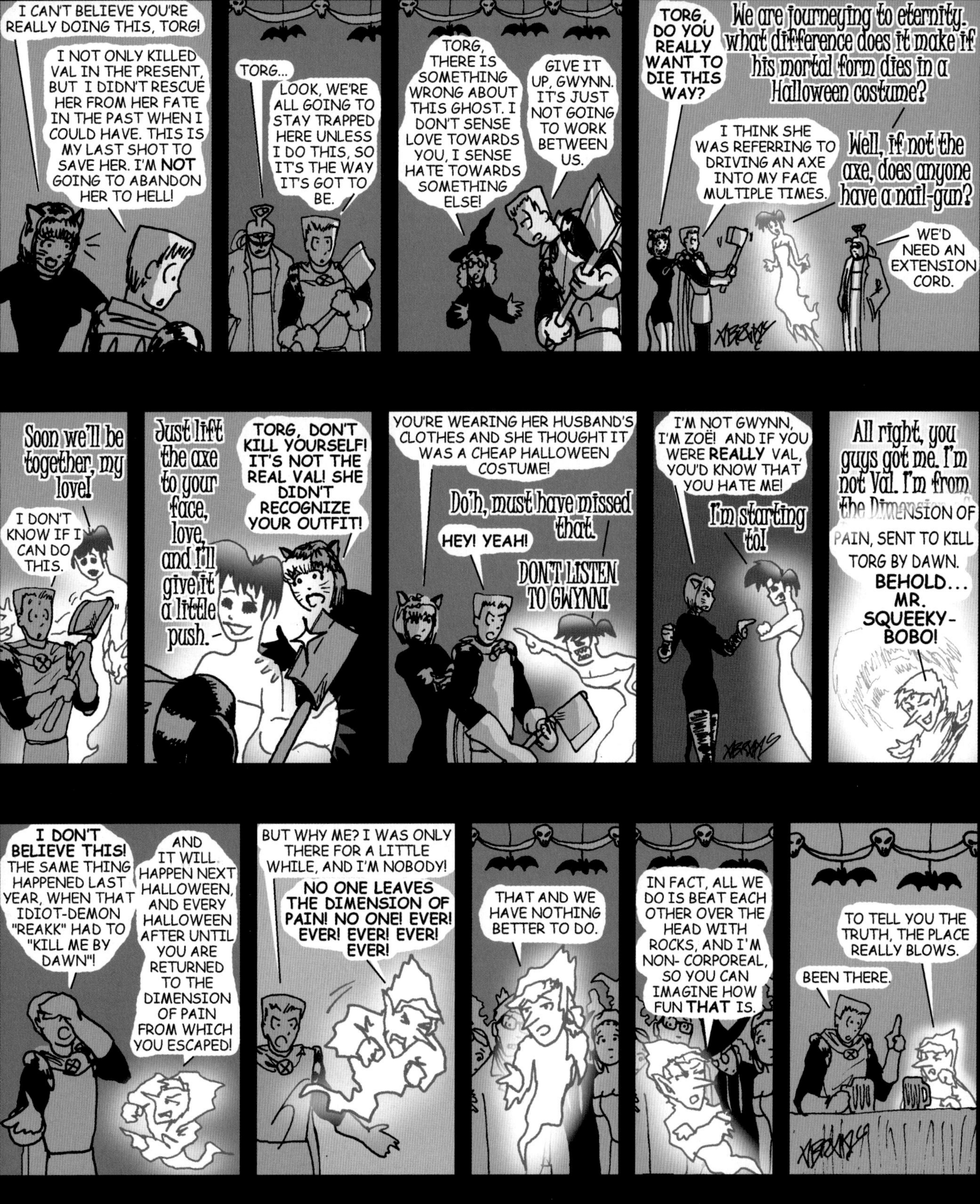
I CAN'T BELIEVE YOU'RE REALLY DOING THIS, TORG!
I NOT ONLY KILLED VAL IN THE PRESENT, BUT I DIDN'T RESCUE HER FROM HER FATE IN THE PAST WHEN I COULD HAVE. THIS IS MY LAST SHOT TO SAVE HER. I'M NOT GOING TO ABANDON HER TO HELL!
TORG...
LOOK, WE'RE ALL GOING TO STAY TRAPPED HERE UNLESS I DO THIS, SO IT'S THE WAY IT'S GOT TO BE.
TORG, THERE IS SOMETHING WRONG ABOUT THIS GHOST. I DON'T SENSE LOVE TOWARDS YOU, I SENSE HATE TOWARDS SOMETHING ELSE!
GIVE IT UP, GWYNN. IT'S JUST NOT GOING TO WORK BETWEEN US.
TORG, DO YOU REALLY WANT TO DIE THIS WAY?
We are journeying to eternity. what difference does it make if his mortal form dies in a Halloween costume?
I THINK SHE WAS REFERRING TO DRIVING AN AXE INTO MY FACE MULTIPLE TIMES.
Well, if not the axe, does anyone have a nail-gun?
WE'D NEED AN EXTENSION CORD.
Soon we'll be together, my love!
I DON'T KNOW IF I CAN DO THIS.
Just lift the axe to your face, love, and I'll give it a little push.
TORG, DON'T KILL YOURSELF! IT'S NOT THE REAL VAL! SHE DIDN'T RECOGNIZE YOUR OUTFIT!
YOU'RE WEARING HER HUSBAND'S CLOTHES AND SHE THOUGHT IT WAS A CHEAP HALLOWEEN COSTUME!
Do'h, must have missed that.
HEY! YEAH!
DON'T LISTEN TO GWYNN!
I'M NOT GWYNN, I'M ZOË! AND IF YOU WERE REALLY VAL, YOU'D KNOW THAT YOU HATE ME!
I'm starting to!
All right, you guys got me. I'm not Val. I'm from the DIMENSION OF PAIN, SENT TO KILL TORG BY DAWN.
BEHOLD... MR. SQUEEKY-BOBO!
I DON'T BELIEVE THIS! THE SAME THING HAPPENED LAST YEAR, WHEN THAT IDIOT-DEMON "REAKK" HAD TO "KILL ME BY DAWN"!
AND IT WILL HAPPEN NEXT HALLOWEEN, AND EVERY HALLOWEEN AFTER UNTIL YOU ARE RETURNED TO THE DIMENSION OF PAIN FROM WHICH YOU ESCAPED!
BUT WHY ME? I WAS ONLY THERE FOR A LITTLE WHILE, AND I'M NOBODY!
NO ONE LEAVES THE DIMENSION OF PAIN! NO ONE! EVER! EVER! EVER! EVER! EVER!
THAT AND WE HAVE NOTHING BETTER TO DO.
IN FACT, ALL WE DO IS BEAT EACH OTHER OVER THE HEAD WITH ROCKS, AND I'M NON- CORPOREAL, SO YOU CAN IMAGINE HOW FUN THAT IS.
TO TELL YOU THE TRUTH, THE PLACE REALLY BLOWS.
BEEN THERE.

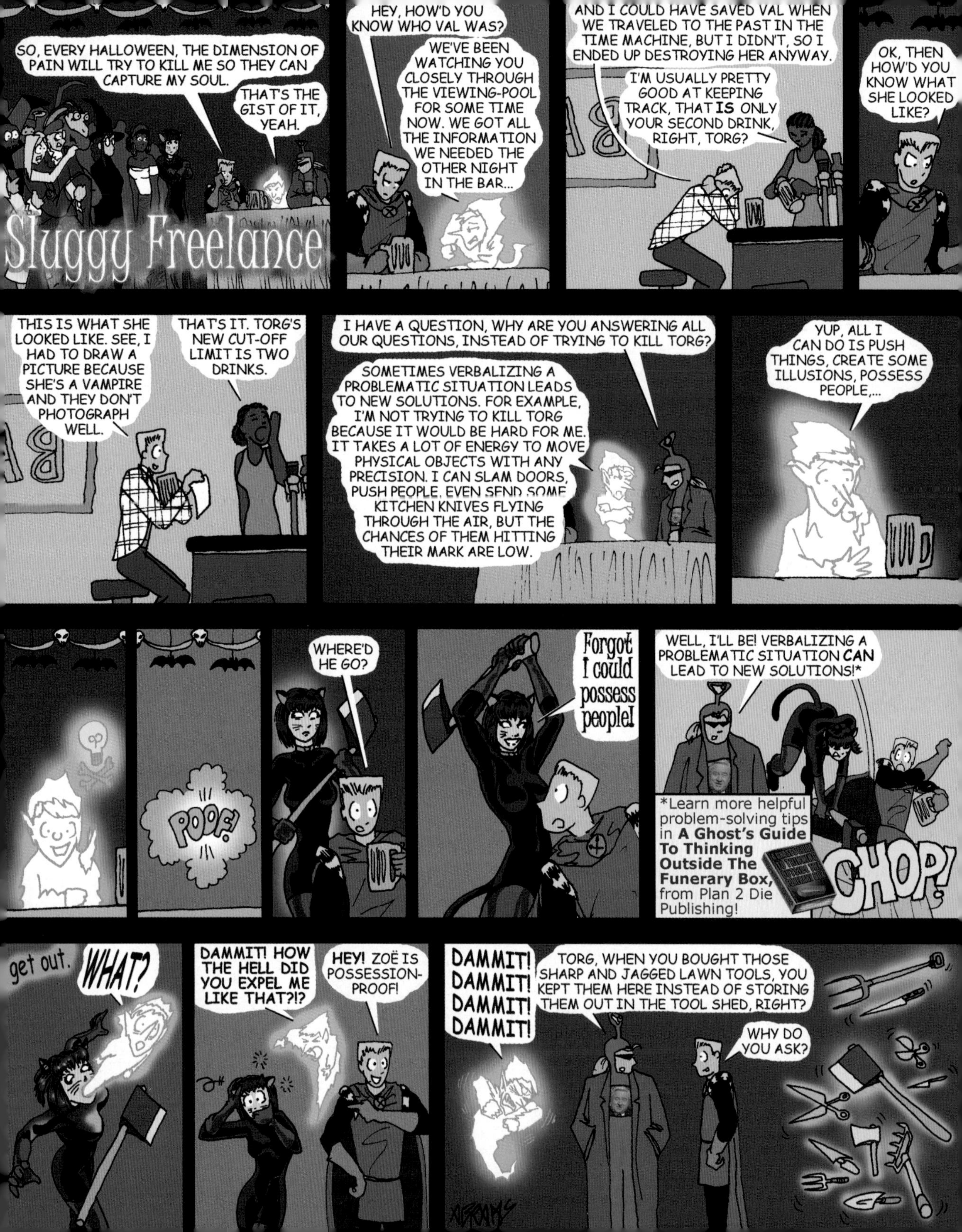
Sluggy Freelance
SO, EVERY HALLOWEEN, THE DIMENSION OF PAIN WILL TRY TO KILL ME SO THEY CAN CAPTURE MY SOUL.
THAT'S THE GIST OF IT, YEAH.
HEY, HOW'D YOU KNOW WHO VAL WAS?
WE'VE BEEN WATCHING YOU CLOSELY THROUGH THE VIEWING-POOL FOR SOME TIME NOW. WE GOT ALL THE INFORMATION WE NEEDED THE OTHER NIGHT IN THE BAR...
AND I COULD HAVE SAVED VAL WHEN WE TRAVELED TO THE PAST IN THE TIME MACHINE, BUT I DIDN'T, SO I ENDED UP DESTROYING HER ANYWAY.
I'M USUALLY PRETTY GOOD AT KEEPING TRACK, THAT **IS** ONLY YOUR SECOND DRINK, RIGHT, TORG?
OK, THEN HOW'D YOU KNOW WHAT SHE LOOKED LIKE?
THIS IS WHAT SHE LOOKED LIKE. SEE, I HAD TO DRAW A PICTURE BECAUSE SHE'S A VAMPIRE AND THEY DON'T PHOTOGRAPH WELL.
THAT'S IT. TORG'S NEW CUT-OFF LIMIT IS TWO DRINKS.
I HAVE A QUESTION, WHY ARE YOU ANSWERING ALL OUR QUESTIONS, INSTEAD OF TRYING TO KILL TORG?
SOMETIMES VERBALIZING A PROBLEMATIC SITUATION LEADS TO NEW SOLUTIONS. FOR EXAMPLE, I'M NOT TRYING TO KILL TORG BECAUSE IT WOULD BE HARD FOR ME. IT TAKES A LOT OF ENERGY TO MOVE PHYSICAL OBJECTS WITH ANY PRECISION. I CAN SLAM DOORS, PUSH PEOPLE, EVEN SEND SOME KITCHEN KNIVES FLYING THROUGH THE AIR, BUT THE CHANCES OF THEM HITTING THEIR MARK ARE LOW.
YUP, ALL I CAN DO IS PUSH THINGS, CREATE SOME ILLUSIONS, POSSESS PEOPLE,...
POOF!
WHERE'D HE GO?
Forgot I could possess people!
WELL, I'LL BE! VERBALIZING A PROBLEMATIC SITUATION **CAN** LEAD TO NEW SOLUTIONS!*
*Learn more helpful problem-solving tips in **A Ghost's Guide To Thinking Outside The Funerary Box,** from Plan 2 Die Publishing!
CHOP!
get out.
WHAT?
DAMMIT! HOW THE HELL DID YOU EXPEL ME LIKE THAT?!?
HEY! ZOË IS POSSESSION-PROOF!
DAMMIT! DAMMIT! DAMMIT! DAMMIT!
TORG, WHEN YOU BOUGHT THOSE SHARP AND JAGGED LAWN TOOLS, YOU KEPT THEM HERE INSTEAD OF STORING THEM OUT IN THE TOOL SHED, RIGHT?
WHY DO YOU ASK?

DAMMIT! DAMMIT! DAMMIT! DAMMIT! DIE, TORG!

THOCK! THOCK! Thock Thock! THOCK! Thock! THOCK! Thock

WOW, YOU **ARE** A CRAPPY SHOT.

THIS JOB PISSES ME OFF.

Poing

KIKI, WHAT'S WITH THE MOB RUNNING FROM THE APARTMENT? WHAT DID I MISS?

UGH. I'M NOT KIKI. I'M RIFF. UGH.

DON'T MAKE ME HURT YOU, TUBE-RAT!

WELL THIS GHOST SHOWE UP TO KILL TORG, AND IT WAS VAL BUT THEN IT WAS A DWARF NAMED SQUEEKER RRIES WHO SLAMMED DOO D MADE A MESS AND SCAR ! EVERYBODY WAS LOCKED ND WE ALL HAD TO USE TH THROOM BUT I KNEW WHE HE SECRET BATHROOM WA EHIND THE COUCH! THEN TH DWARF GHOST TRIED TO OSSESS ZOË AN HI ULDN'T HE GOT A SHOOK AND C N ALL TH S RO TR AN T HU T TO S TH VE ERRIES S AD A CRYED AND SAID BAD WOR

KIKI? BE RIFF.

I DUNNO. UGH.

ALL RIGHT, WHAT DID I MISS?

BUN-BUN!

Poing

YES, IT IS I, BACK FROM THE DEAD TO AVENGE MY DEATH! DAWN APPROACHES, SO I MUST RETURN TO THE DIMENSION OF PAIN, BUT REST ASSURED, AS SOON AS I GIVE THEM TORG, THEY WILL GIVE ME **YOU**!

YOU ARE ON MY LIST, BUN-BUN, ENJOY WHAT YOU CAN OF LIFE.

DO I KNOW YOU?

YOU KNOW MR. SQUEEKY-BOBO!

ONE OF GRAHAMMY'S FRIENDS? YOU'RE A NEEBLER ELF, RIGHT!

WHO THE %$#@ IS "GRAHAMMY?" I'M MR. SQUEEKY-BOBO, MOTHER %$#@ER! I'M SANTA'S...

POOF!

DAMN UNDEAD NEEBLER ELVES.

I THOUGHT HE WAS A HAUNTED LAWN-GNOME.

Chapter 15: The Isle of Dr. Steve

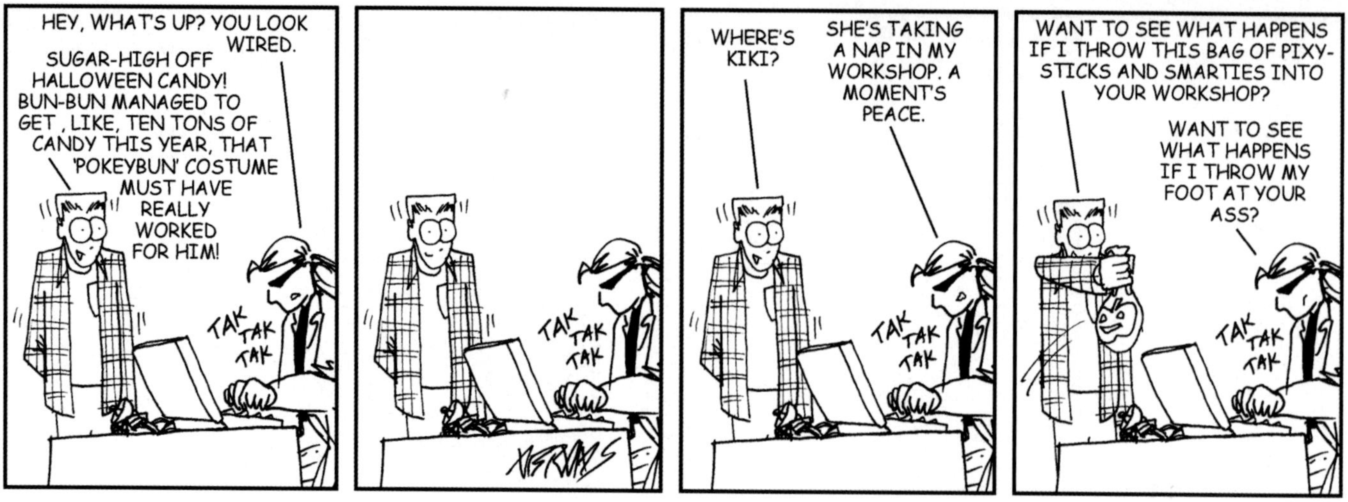
HEY, WHAT'S UP? YOU LOOK WIRED.
SUGAR-HIGH OFF HALLOWEEN CANDY! BUN-BUN MANAGED TO GET , LIKE, TEN TONS OF CANDY THIS YEAR, THAT 'POKEYBUN' COSTUME MUST HAVE REALLY WORKED FOR HIM!
TAK TAK TAK
TAK TAK TAK
WHERE'S KIKI?
SHE'S TAKING A NAP IN MY WORKSHOP. A MOMENT'S PEACE.
TAK TAK TAK
WANT TO SEE WHAT HAPPENS IF I THROW THIS BAG OF PIXY-STICKS AND SMARTIES INTO YOUR WORKSHOP?
WANT TO SEE WHAT HAPPENS IF I THROW MY FOOT AT YOUR ASS?
TAK TAK TAK

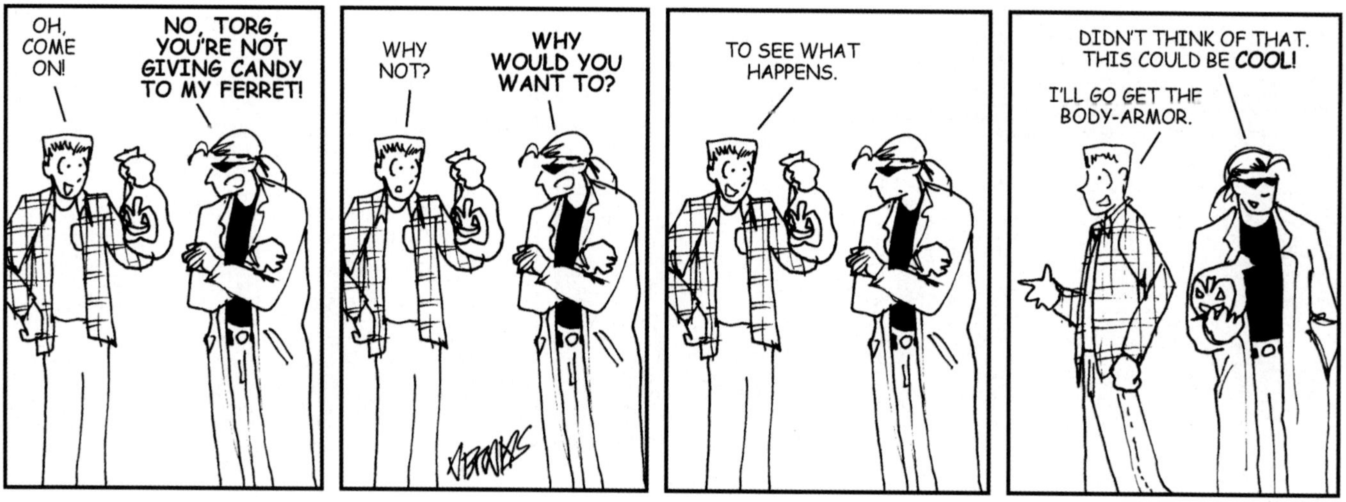
OH, COME ON!
NO, TORG, YOU'RE NOT GIVING CANDY TO MY FERRET!
WHY NOT?
WHY WOULD YOU WANT TO?
TO SEE WHAT HAPPENS.
DIDN'T THINK OF THAT. THIS COULD BE COOL!
I'LL GO GET THE BODY-ARMOR.

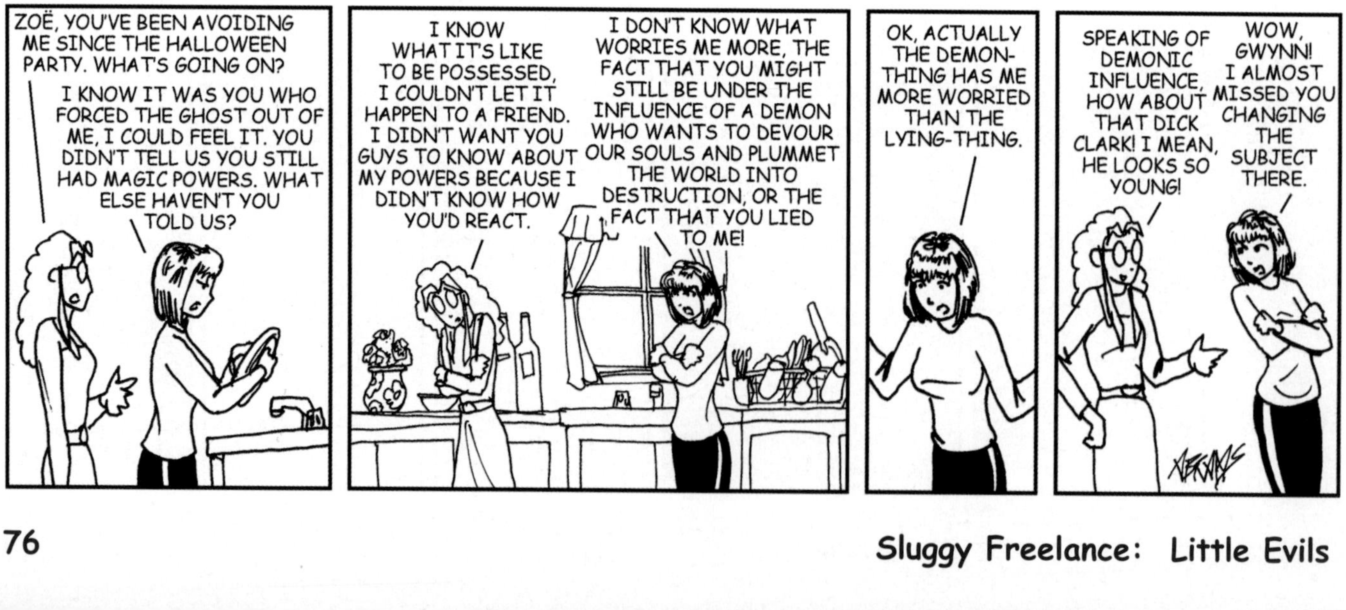
ZOË, YOU'VE BEEN AVOIDING ME SINCE THE HALLOWEEN PARTY. WHAT'S GOING ON?
I KNOW IT WAS YOU WHO FORCED THE GHOST OUT OF ME, I COULD FEEL IT. YOU DIDN'T TELL US YOU STILL HAD MAGIC POWERS. WHAT ELSE HAVEN'T YOU TOLD US?
I KNOW WHAT IT'S LIKE TO BE POSSESSED, I COULDN'T LET IT HAPPEN TO A FRIEND. I DIDN'T WANT YOU GUYS TO KNOW ABOUT MY POWERS BECAUSE I DIDN'T KNOW HOW YOU'D REACT.
I DON'T KNOW WHAT WORRIES ME MORE, THE FACT THAT YOU MIGHT STILL BE UNDER THE INFLUENCE OF A DEMON WHO WANTS TO DEVOUR OUR SOULS AND PLUMMET THE WORLD INTO DESTRUCTION, OR THE FACT THAT YOU LIED TO ME!
OK, ACTUALLY THE DEMON-THING HAS ME MORE WORRIED THAN THE LYING-THING.
SPEAKING OF DEMONIC INFLUENCE, HOW ABOUT THAT DICK CLARK! I MEAN, HE LOOKS SO YOUNG!
WOW, GWYNN! I ALMOST MISSED YOU CHANGING THE SUBJECT THERE.

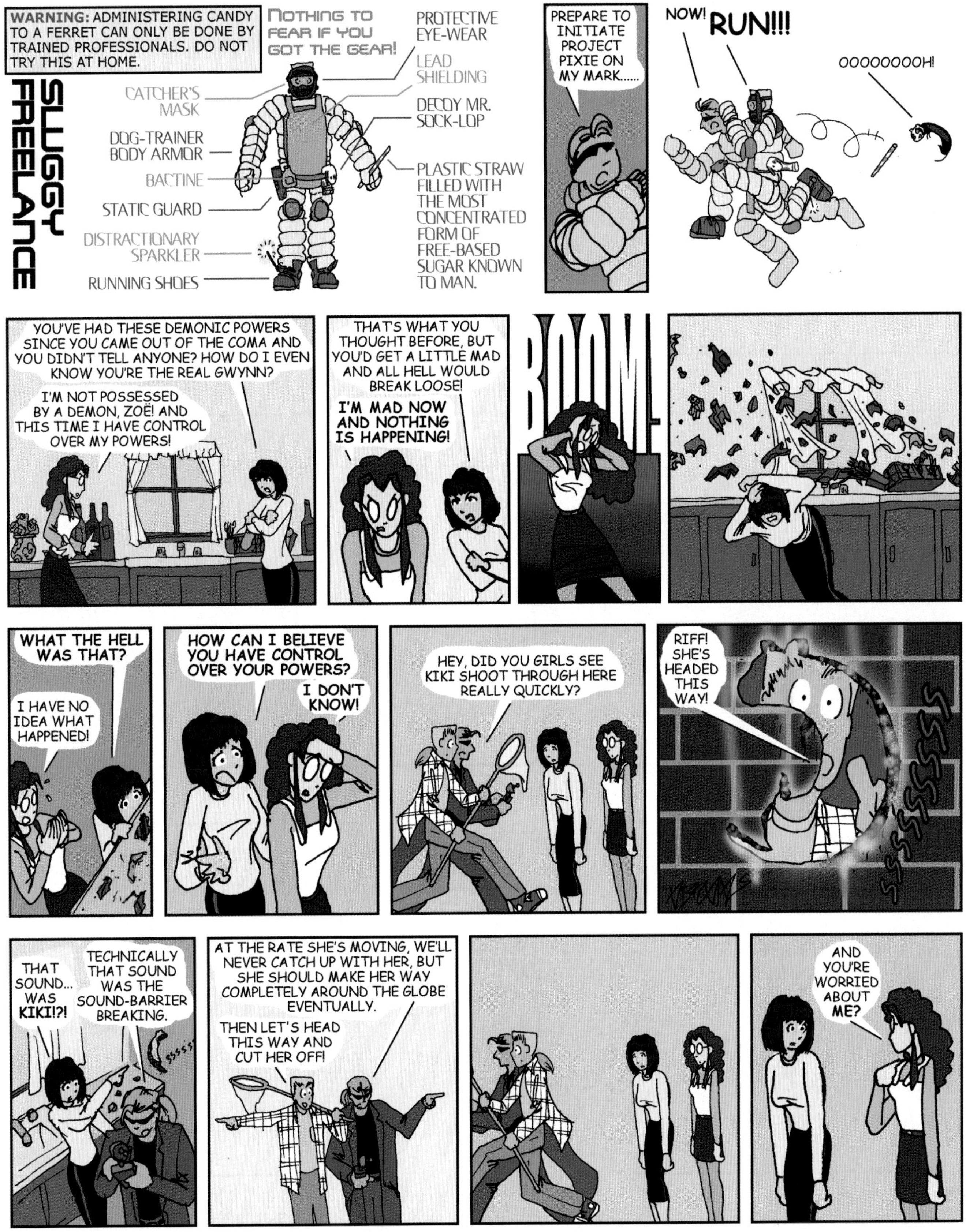
WARNING: ADMINISTERING CANDY TO A FERRET CAN ONLY BE DONE BY TRAINED PROFESSIONALS. DO NOT TRY THIS AT HOME.
SLUGGY FREELANCE
NOTHING TO FEAR IF YOU GOT THE GEAR!
PROTECTIVE EYE-WEAR
LEAD SHIELDING
CATCHER'S MASK
DECOY MR. SOCK-LOP
DOG-TRAINER BODY ARMOR
BACTINE
PLASTIC STRAW FILLED WITH THE MOST CONCENTRATED FORM OF FREE-BASED SUGAR KNOWN TO MAN.
STATIC GUARD
DISTRACTIONARY SPARKLER
RUNNING SHOES
PREPARE TO INITIATE PROJECT PIXIE ON MY MARK......
NOW!
RUN!!!
OOOOOOOOH!
YOU'VE HAD THESE DEMONIC POWERS SINCE YOU CAME OUT OF THE COMA AND YOU DIDN'T TELL ANYONE? HOW DO I EVEN KNOW YOU'RE THE REAL GWYNN?
I'M NOT POSSESSED BY A DEMON, ZOË! AND THIS TIME I HAVE CONTROL OVER MY POWERS!
THAT'S WHAT YOU THOUGHT BEFORE, BUT YOU'D GET A LITTLE MAD AND ALL HELL WOULD BREAK LOOSE!
I'M MAD NOW AND NOTHING IS HAPPENING!
BOOM!
WHAT THE HELL WAS THAT?
I HAVE NO IDEA WHAT HAPPENED!
HOW CAN I BELIEVE YOU HAVE CONTROL OVER YOUR POWERS?
I DON'T KNOW!
HEY, DID YOU GIRLS SEE KIKI SHOOT THROUGH HERE REALLY QUICKLY?
RIFF! SHE'S HEADED THIS WAY!
THAT SOUND... WAS KIKI!?!
TECHNICALLY THAT SOUND WAS THE SOUND-BARRIER BREAKING.
AT THE RATE SHE'S MOVING, WE'LL NEVER CATCH UP WITH HER, BUT SHE SHOULD MAKE HER WAY COMPLETELY AROUND THE GLOBE EVENTUALLY.
THEN LET'S HEAD THIS WAY AND CUT HER OFF!
AND YOU'RE WORRIED ABOUT ME?

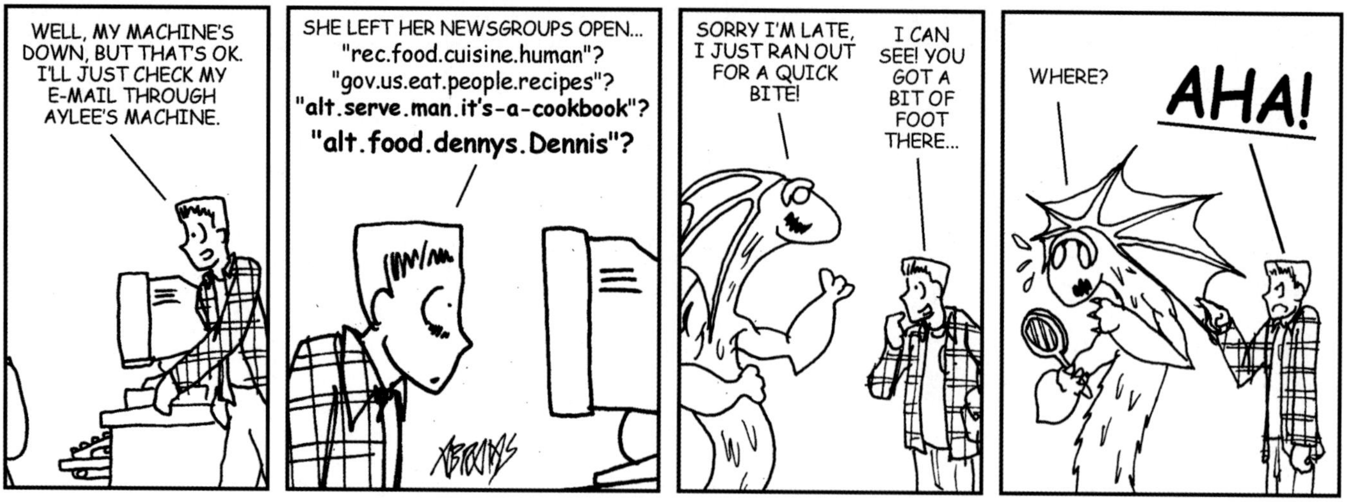
WELL, MY MACHINE'S DOWN, BUT THAT'S OK. I'LL JUST CHECK MY E-MAIL THROUGH AYLEE'S MACHINE.
SHE LEFT HER NEWSGROUPS OPEN... "rec.food.cuisine.human"? "gov.us.eat.people.recipes"? "alt.serve.man.it's-a-cookbook"? "alt.food.dennys.Dennis"?
SORRY I'M LATE, I JUST RAN OUT FOR A QUICK BITE!
I CAN SEE! YOU GOT A BIT OF FOOT THERE...
WHERE?
AHA!

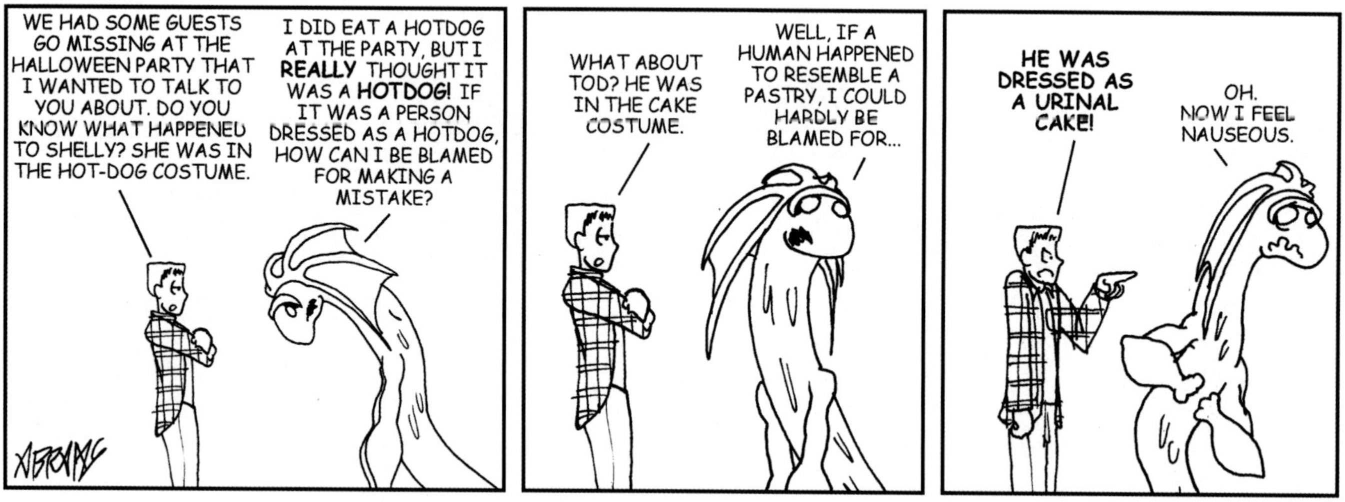
WE HAD SOME GUESTS GO MISSING AT THE HALLOWEEN PARTY THAT I WANTED TO TALK TO YOU ABOUT. DO YOU KNOW WHAT HAPPENED TO SHELLY? SHE WAS IN THE HOT-DOG COSTUME.
I DID EAT A HOTDOG AT THE PARTY, BUT I REALLY THOUGHT IT WAS A HOTDOG! IF IT WAS A PERSON DRESSED AS A HOTDOG, HOW CAN I BE BLAMED FOR MAKING A MISTAKE?
WHAT ABOUT TOD? HE WAS IN THE CAKE COSTUME.
WELL, IF A HUMAN HAPPENED TO RESEMBLE A PASTRY, I COULD HARDLY BE BLAMED FOR...
HE WAS DRESSED AS A URINAL CAKE!
OH. NOW I FEEL NAUSEOUS.

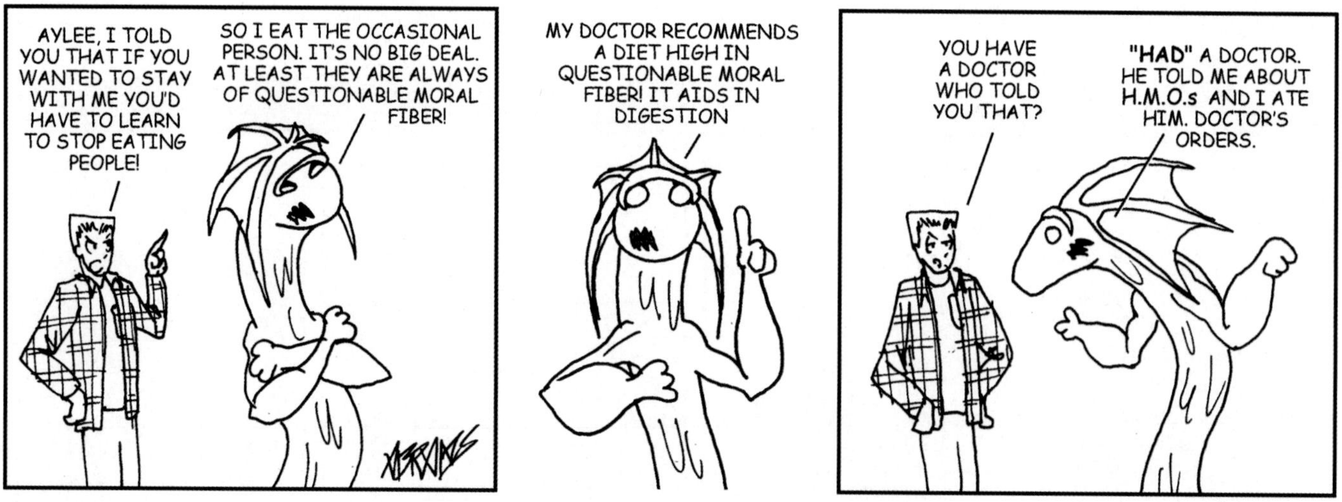
AYLEE, I TOLD YOU THAT IF YOU WANTED TO STAY WITH ME YOU'D HAVE TO LEARN TO STOP EATING PEOPLE!
SO I EAT THE OCCASIONAL PERSON. IT'S NO BIG DEAL. AT LEAST THEY ARE ALWAYS OF QUESTIONABLE MORAL FIBER!
MY DOCTOR RECOMMENDS A DIET HIGH IN QUESTIONABLE MORAL FIBER! IT AIDS IN DIGESTION
YOU HAVE A DOCTOR WHO TOLD YOU THAT?
"HAD" A DOCTOR. HE TOLD ME ABOUT H.M.O.s AND I ATE HIM. DOCTOR'S ORDERS.

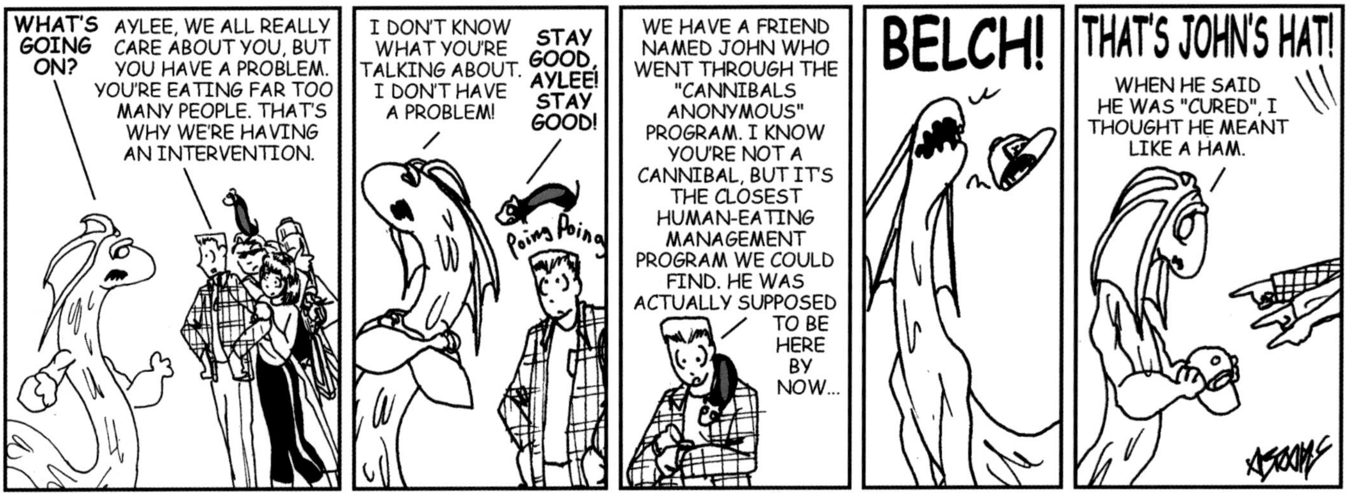
WHAT'S GOING ON?
AYLEE, WE ALL REALLY CARE ABOUT YOU, BUT YOU HAVE A PROBLEM. YOU'RE EATING FAR TOO MANY PEOPLE. THAT'S WHY WE'RE HAVING AN INTERVENTION.
I DON'T KNOW WHAT YOU'RE TALKING ABOUT. I DON'T HAVE A PROBLEM!
STAY GOOD, AYLEE! STAY GOOD!
Poing Poing
WE HAVE A FRIEND NAMED JOHN WHO WENT THROUGH THE "CANNIBALS ANONYMOUS" PROGRAM. I KNOW YOU'RE NOT A CANNIBAL, BUT IT'S THE CLOSEST HUMAN-EATING MANAGEMENT PROGRAM WE COULD FIND. HE WAS ACTUALLY SUPPOSED TO BE HERE BY NOW...
BELCH!
THAT'S JOHN'S HAT!
WHEN HE SAID HE WAS "CURED", I THOUGHT HE MEANT LIKE A HAM.

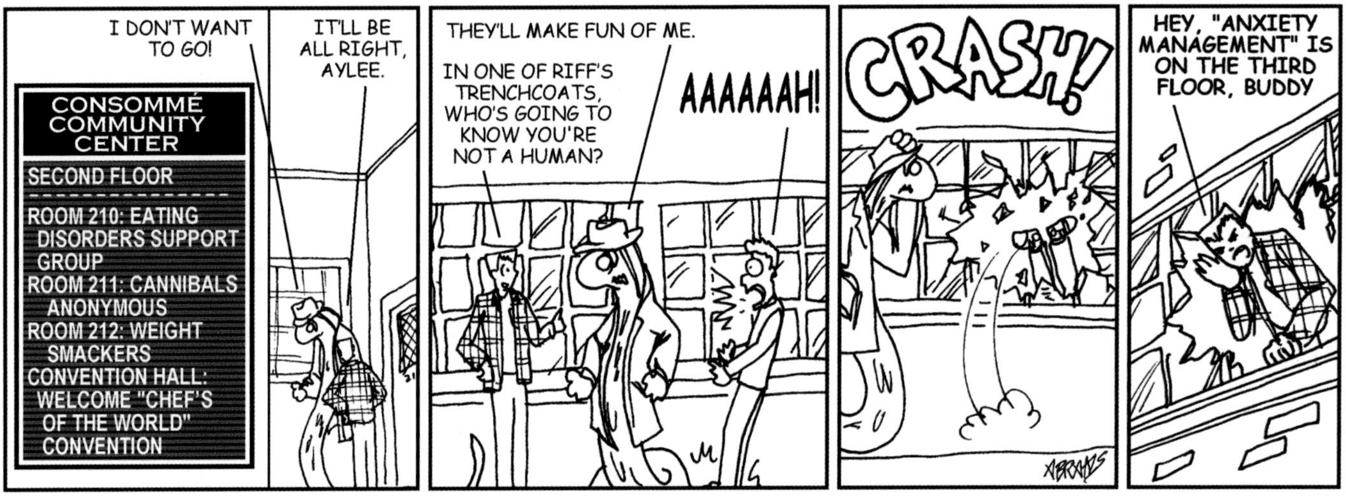
I DON'T WANT TO GO!
CONSOMMÉ COMMUNITY CENTER
SECOND FLOOR
ROOM 210: EATING DISORDERS SUPPORT GROUP
ROOM 211: CANNIBALS ANONYMOUS
ROOM 212: WEIGHT SMACKERS
CONVENTION HALL: WELCOME "CHEF'S OF THE WORLD" CONVENTION
IT'LL BE ALL RIGHT, AYLEE.
THEY'LL MAKE FUN OF ME.
IN ONE OF RIFF'S TRENCHCOATS, WHO'S GOING TO KNOW YOU'RE NOT A HUMAN?
AAAAAAH!
CRASH!
HEY, "ANXIETY MANAGEMENT" IS ON THE THIRD FLOOR, BUDDY

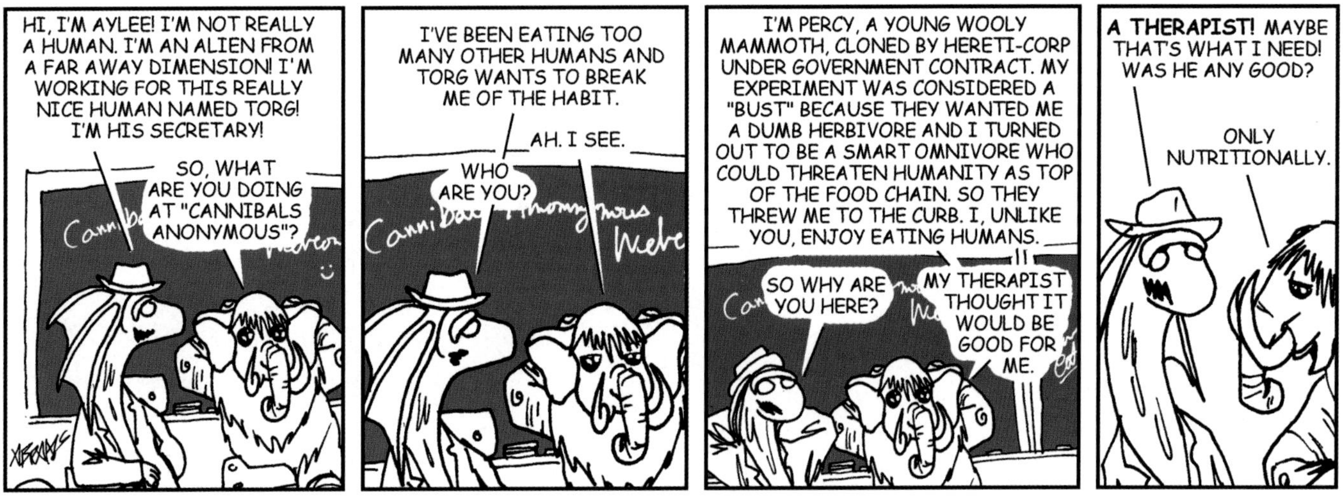
HI, I'M AYLEE! I'M NOT REALLY A HUMAN. I'M AN ALIEN FROM A FAR AWAY DIMENSION! I'M WORKING FOR THIS REALLY NICE HUMAN NAMED TORG! I'M HIS SECRETARY!
SO, WHAT ARE YOU DOING AT "CANNIBALS ANONYMOUS"?
I'VE BEEN EATING TOO MANY OTHER HUMANS AND TORG WANTS TO BREAK ME OF THE HABIT.
WHO ARE YOU?
AH. I SEE.
I'M PERCY, A YOUNG WOOLY MAMMOTH, CLONED BY HERETI-CORP UNDER GOVERNMENT CONTRACT. MY EXPERIMENT WAS CONSIDERED A "BUST" BECAUSE THEY WANTED ME A DUMB HERBIVORE AND I TURNED OUT TO BE A SMART OMNIVORE WHO COULD THREATEN HUMANITY AS TOP OF THE FOOD CHAIN. SO THEY THREW ME TO THE CURB. I, UNLIKE YOU, ENJOY EATING HUMANS.
SO WHY ARE YOU HERE?
MY THERAPIST THOUGHT IT WOULD BE GOOD FOR ME.
A THERAPIST! MAYBE THAT'S WHAT I NEED! WAS HE ANY GOOD?
ONLY NUTRITIONALLY.

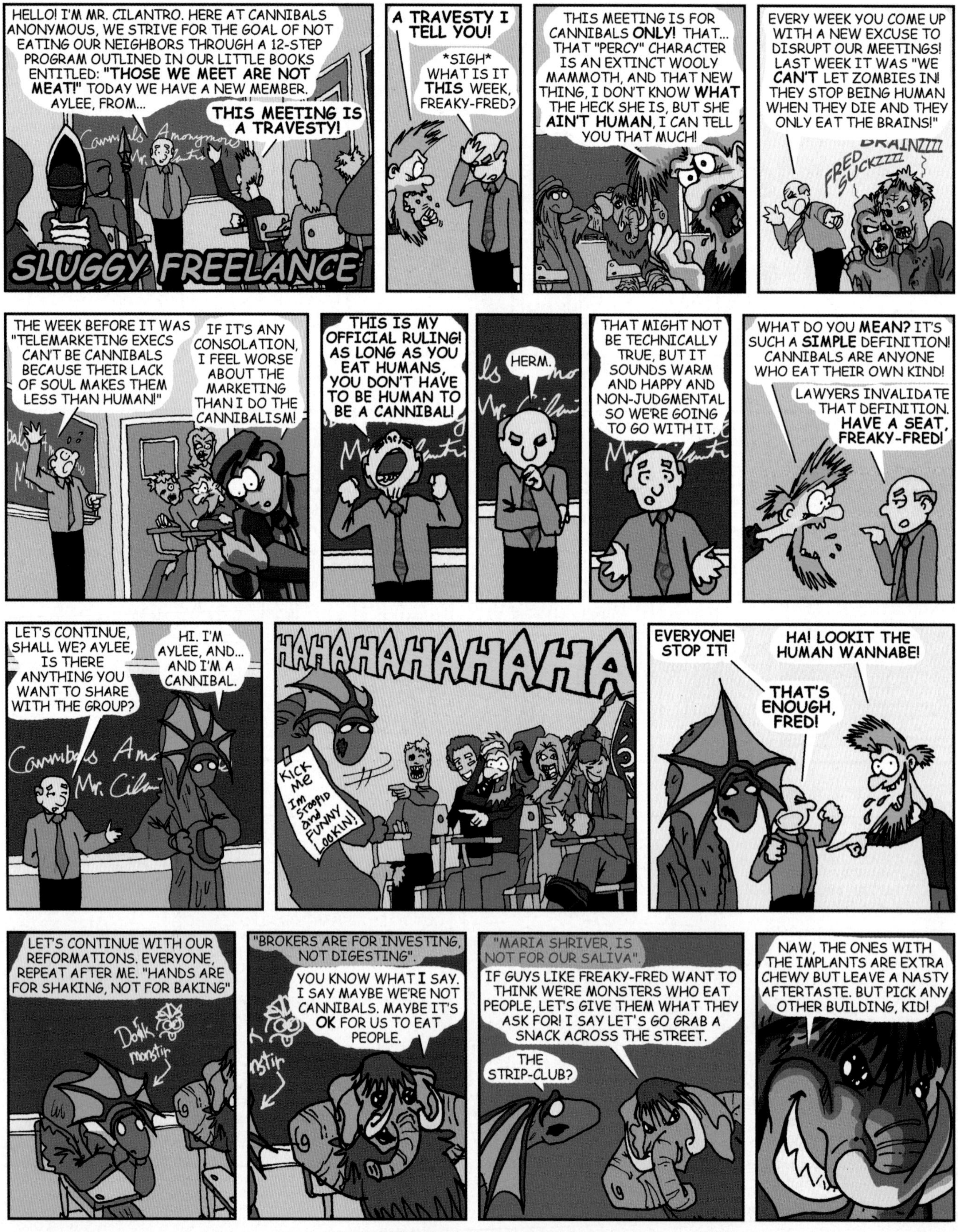
HELLO! I'M MR. CILANTRO. HERE AT CANNIBALS ANONYMOUS, WE STRIVE FOR THE GOAL OF NOT EATING OUR NEIGHBORS THROUGH A 12-STEP PROGRAM OUTLINED IN OUR LITTLE BOOKS ENTITLED: "THOSE WE MEET ARE NOT MEAT!" TODAY WE HAVE A NEW MEMBER. AYLEE, FROM...
THIS MEETING IS A TRAVESTY!
SLUGGY FREELANCE
A TRAVESTY I TELL YOU!
SIGH WHAT IS IT THIS WEEK, FREAKY-FRED?
THIS MEETING IS FOR CANNIBALS ONLY! THAT... THAT "PERCY" CHARACTER IS AN EXTINCT WOOLY MAMMOTH, AND THAT NEW THING, I DON'T KNOW WHAT THE HECK SHE IS, BUT SHE AIN'T HUMAN, I CAN TELL YOU THAT MUCH!
EVERY WEEK YOU COME UP WITH A NEW EXCUSE TO DISRUPT OUR MEETINGS! LAST WEEK IT WAS "WE CAN'T LET ZOMBIES IN! THEY STOP BEING HUMAN WHEN THEY DIE AND THEY ONLY EAT THE BRAINS!"
BRAINZZZZ
FRED SUCKZZZZ
THE WEEK BEFORE IT WAS "TELEMARKETING EXECS CAN'T BE CANNIBALS BECAUSE THEIR LACK OF SOUL MAKES THEM LESS THAN HUMAN!"
IF IT'S ANY CONSOLATION, I FEEL WORSE ABOUT THE MARKETING THAN I DO THE CANNIBALISM!
THIS IS MY OFFICIAL RULING! AS LONG AS YOU EAT HUMANS, YOU DON'T HAVE TO BE HUMAN TO BE A CANNIBAL!
HERM.
THAT MIGHT NOT BE TECHNICALLY TRUE, BUT IT SOUNDS WARM AND HAPPY AND NON-JUDGMENTAL SO WE'RE GOING TO GO WITH IT.
WHAT DO YOU MEAN? IT'S SUCH A SIMPLE DEFINITION! CANNIBALS ARE ANYONE WHO EAT THEIR OWN KIND!
LAWYERS INVALIDATE THAT DEFINITION. HAVE A SEAT, FREAKY-FRED!
LET'S CONTINUE, SHALL WE? AYLEE, IS THERE ANYTHING YOU WANT TO SHARE WITH THE GROUP?
HI. I'M AYLEE, AND... AND I'M A CANNIBAL.
HAHAHAHAHAHAHAHA
KICK ME
IM STOOPID AND FUNNY LOOKIN!
EVERYONE! STOP IT!
HA! LOOKIT THE HUMAN WANNABE!
THAT'S ENOUGH, FRED!
LET'S CONTINUE WITH OUR REFORMATIONS. EVERYONE, REPEAT AFTER ME. "HANDS ARE FOR SHAKING, NOT FOR BAKING"
Dork monstir
"BROKERS ARE FOR INVESTING, NOT DIGESTING".
YOU KNOW WHAT I SAY. I SAY MAYBE WE'RE NOT CANNIBALS. MAYBE IT'S OK FOR US TO EAT PEOPLE.
"MARIA SHRIVER, IS NOT FOR OUR SALIVA".
IF GUYS LIKE FREAKY-FRED WANT TO THINK WE'RE MONSTERS WHO EAT PEOPLE, LET'S GIVE THEM WHAT THEY ASK FOR! I SAY LET'S GO GRAB A SNACK ACROSS THE STREET.
THE STRIP-CLUB?
NAW, THE ONES WITH THE IMPLANTS ARE EXTRA CHEWY BUT LEAVE A NASTY AFTERTASTE. BUT PICK ANY OTHER BUILDING, KID!

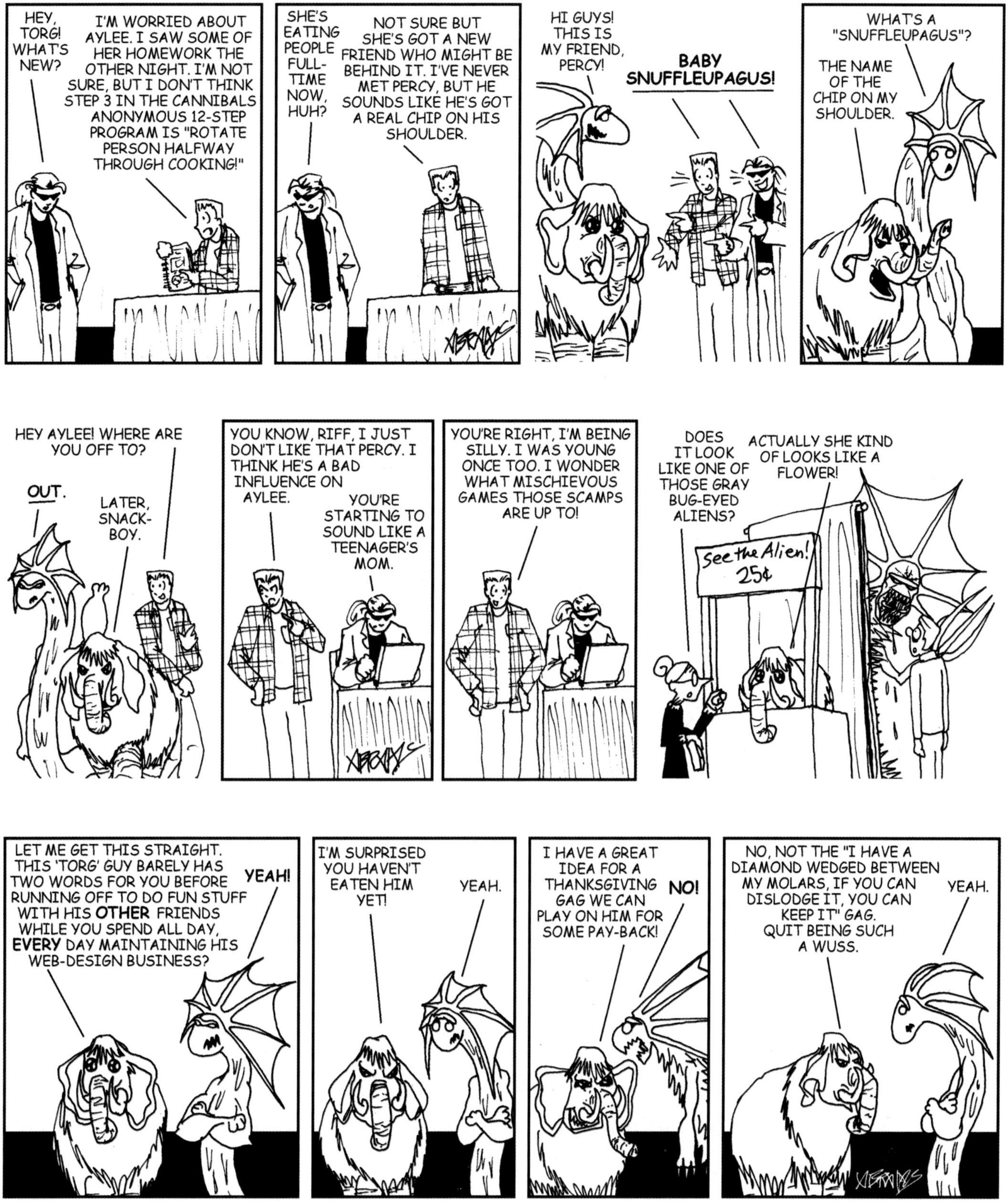
HEY, TORG! WHAT'S NEW?
I'M WORRIED ABOUT AYLEE. I SAW SOME OF HER HOMEWORK THE OTHER NIGHT. I'M NOT SURE, BUT I DON'T THINK STEP 3 IN THE CANNIBALS ANONYMOUS 12-STEP PROGRAM IS "ROTATE PERSON HALFWAY THROUGH COOKING!"
SHE'S EATING PEOPLE FULL-TIME NOW, HUH?
NOT SURE BUT SHE'S GOT A NEW FRIEND WHO MIGHT BE BEHIND IT. I'VE NEVER MET PERCY, BUT HE SOUNDS LIKE HE'S GOT A REAL CHIP ON HIS SHOULDER.
HI GUYS! THIS IS MY FRIEND, PERCY!
BABY SNUFFLEUPAGUS!
WHAT'S A "SNUFFLEUPAGUS"?
THE NAME OF THE CHIP ON MY SHOULDER.
HEY AYLEE! WHERE ARE YOU OFF TO?
OUT.
LATER, SNACK-BOY.
YOU KNOW, RIFF, I JUST DON'T LIKE THAT PERCY. I THINK HE'S A BAD INFLUENCE ON AYLEE.
YOU'RE STARTING TO SOUND LIKE A TEENAGER'S MOM.
YOU'RE RIGHT, I'M BEING SILLY. I WAS YOUNG ONCE TOO. I WONDER WHAT MISCHIEVOUS GAMES THOSE SCAMPS ARE UP TO!
See the Alien! 25¢
DOES IT LOOK LIKE ONE OF THOSE GRAY BUG-EYED ALIENS?
ACTUALLY SHE KIND OF LOOKS LIKE A FLOWER!
LET ME GET THIS STRAIGHT. THIS 'TORG' GUY BARELY HAS TWO WORDS FOR YOU BEFORE RUNNING OFF TO DO FUN STUFF WITH HIS OTHER FRIENDS WHILE YOU SPEND ALL DAY, EVERY DAY MAINTAINING HIS WEB-DESIGN BUSINESS?
YEAH!
I'M SURPRISED YOU HAVEN'T EATEN HIM YET!
YEAH.
I HAVE A GREAT IDEA FOR A THANKSGIVING GAG WE CAN PLAY ON HIM FOR SOME PAY-BACK!
NO!
NO, NOT THE "I HAVE A DIAMOND WEDGED BETWEEN MY MOLARS, IF YOU CAN DISLODGE IT, YOU CAN KEEP IT" GAG. QUIT BEING SUCH A WUSS.
YEAH.

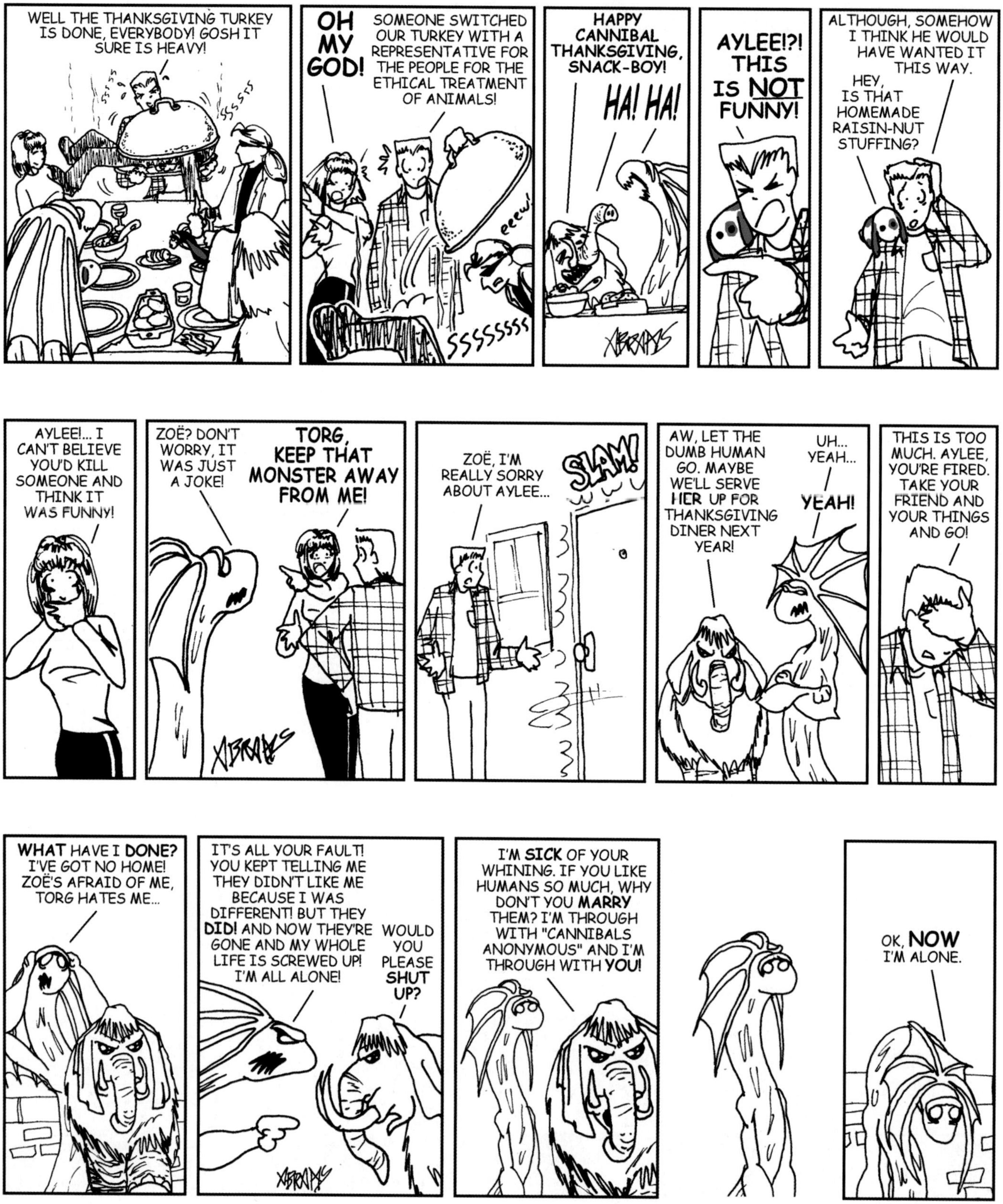
WELL THE THANKSGIVING TURKEY IS DONE, EVERYBODY! GOSH IT SURE IS HEAVY!
OH MY GOD!
SOMEONE SWITCHED OUR TURKEY WITH A REPRESENTATIVE FOR THE PEOPLE FOR THE ETHICAL TREATMENT OF ANIMALS!
eeew!
SSSSSSSS
HAPPY CANNIBAL THANKSGIVING, SNACK-BOY!
HA! HA!
AYLEE!?! THIS IS NOT FUNNY!
ALTHOUGH, SOMEHOW I THINK HE WOULD HAVE WANTED IT THIS WAY.
HEY, IS THAT HOMEMADE RAISIN-NUT STUFFING?
AYLEE!... I CAN'T BELIEVE YOU'D KILL SOMEONE AND THINK IT WAS FUNNY!
ZOË? DON'T WORRY, IT WAS JUST A JOKE!
TORG, KEEP THAT MONSTER AWAY FROM ME!
ZOË, I'M REALLY SORRY ABOUT AYLEE...
SLAM!
AW, LET THE DUMB HUMAN GO. MAYBE WE'LL SERVE HER UP FOR THANKSGIVING DINER NEXT YEAR!
UH... YEAH...
YEAH!
THIS IS TOO MUCH. AYLEE, YOU'RE FIRED. TAKE YOUR FRIEND AND YOUR THINGS AND GO!
WHAT HAVE I DONE? I'VE GOT NO HOME! ZOË'S AFRAID OF ME, TORG HATES ME...
IT'S ALL YOUR FAULT! YOU KEPT TELLING ME THEY DIDN'T LIKE ME BECAUSE I WAS DIFFERENT! BUT THEY DID! AND NOW THEY'RE GONE AND MY WHOLE LIFE IS SCREWED UP! I'M ALL ALONE!
WOULD YOU PLEASE SHUT UP?
I'M SICK OF YOUR WHINING. IF YOU LIKE HUMANS SO MUCH, WHY DON'T YOU MARRY THEM? I'M THROUGH WITH "CANNIBALS ANONYMOUS" AND I'M THROUGH WITH YOU!
OK, NOW I'M ALONE.

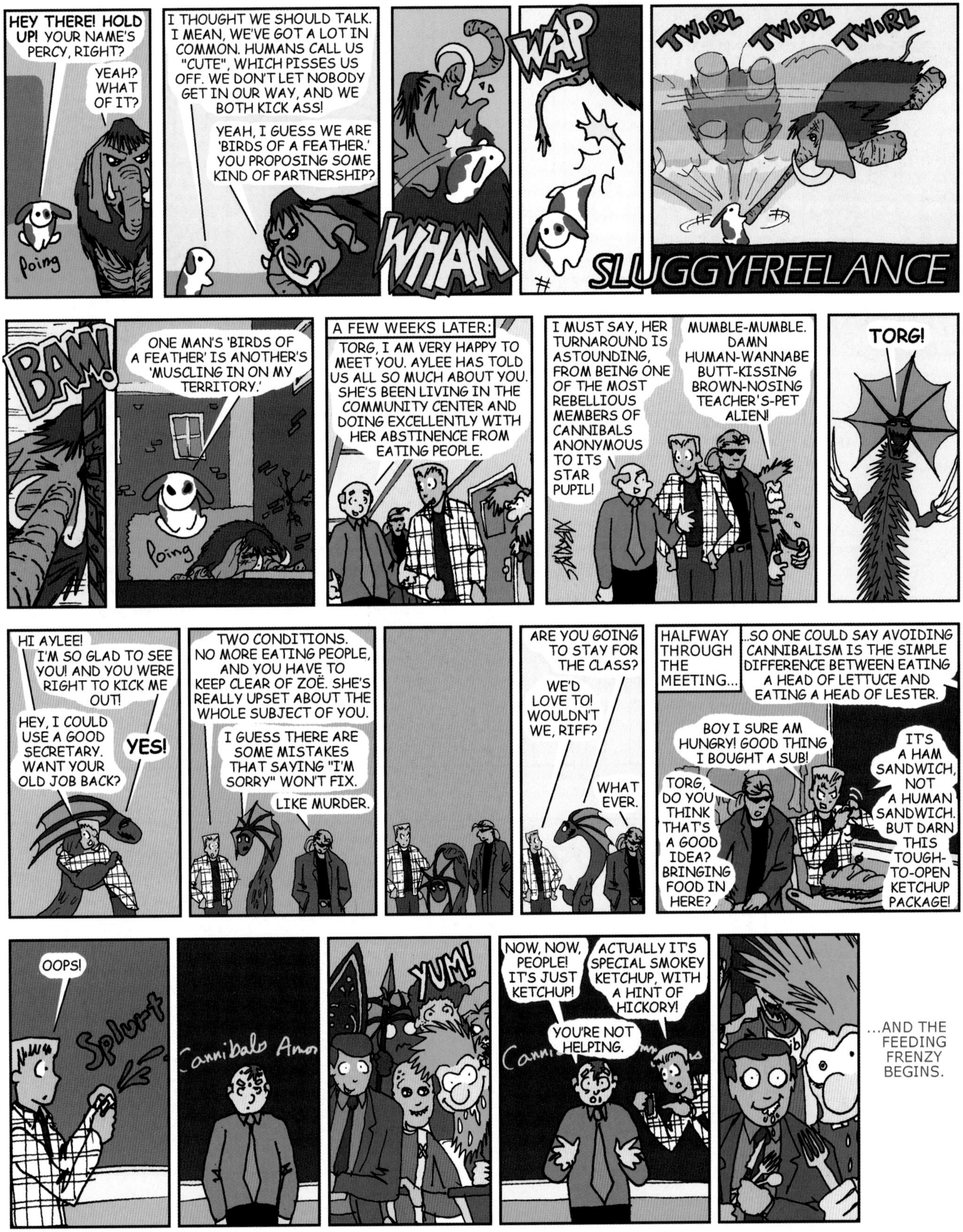
HEY THERE! HOLD UP! YOUR NAME'S PERCY, RIGHT?
YEAH? WHAT OF IT?
POING
I THOUGHT WE SHOULD TALK. I MEAN, WE'VE GOT A LOT IN COMMON. HUMANS CALL US "CUTE", WHICH PISSES US OFF. WE DON'T LET NOBODY GET IN OUR WAY, AND WE BOTH KICK ASS!
YEAH, I GUESS WE ARE 'BIRDS OF A FEATHER.' YOU PROPOSING SOME KIND OF PARTNERSHIP?
WHAM
WAP
TWIRL TWIRL TWIRL
SLUGGYFREELANCE
BAM!
ONE MAN'S 'BIRDS OF A FEATHER' IS ANOTHER'S 'MUSCLING IN ON MY TERRITORY.'
POING
A FEW WEEKS LATER:
TORG, I AM VERY HAPPY TO MEET YOU. AYLEE HAS TOLD US ALL SO MUCH ABOUT YOU. SHE'S BEEN LIVING IN THE COMMUNITY CENTER AND DOING EXCELLENTLY WITH HER ABSTINENCE FROM EATING PEOPLE.
I MUST SAY, HER TURNAROUND IS ASTOUNDING, FROM BEING ONE OF THE MOST REBELLIOUS MEMBERS OF CANNIBALS ANONYMOUS TO ITS STAR PUPIL!
MUMBLE-MUMBLE. DAMN HUMAN-WANNABE BUTT-KISSING BROWN-NOSING TEACHER'S-PET ALIEN!
TORG!
HI AYLEE!
I'M SO GLAD TO SEE YOU! AND YOU WERE RIGHT TO KICK ME OUT!
HEY, I COULD USE A GOOD SECRETARY. WANT YOUR OLD JOB BACK?
YES!
TWO CONDITIONS. NO MORE EATING PEOPLE, AND YOU HAVE TO KEEP CLEAR OF ZOË. SHE'S REALLY UPSET ABOUT THE WHOLE SUBJECT OF YOU.
I GUESS THERE ARE SOME MISTAKES THAT SAYING "I'M SORRY" WON'T FIX.
LIKE MURDER.
ARE YOU GOING TO STAY FOR THE CLASS?
WE'D LOVE TO! WOULDN'T WE, RIFF?
WHAT EVER.
HALFWAY THROUGH THE MEETING...
...SO ONE COULD SAY AVOIDING CANNIBALISM IS THE SIMPLE DIFFERENCE BETWEEN EATING A HEAD OF LETTUCE AND EATING A HEAD OF LESTER.
BOY I SURE AM HUNGRY! GOOD THING I BOUGHT A SUB!
TORG, DO YOU THINK THAT'S A GOOD IDEA? BRINGING FOOD IN HERE?
IT'S A HAM SANDWICH, NOT A HUMAN SANDWICH. BUT DARN THIS TOUGH-TO-OPEN KETCHUP PACKAGE!
OOPS!
SPLURT
CANNIBALS ANON
YUM!
NOW, NOW, PEOPLE! IT'S JUST KETCHUP!
ACTUALLY IT'S SPECIAL SMOKEY KETCHUP, WITH A HINT OF HICKORY!
YOU'RE NOT HELPING.
...AND THE FEEDING FRENZY BEGINS.

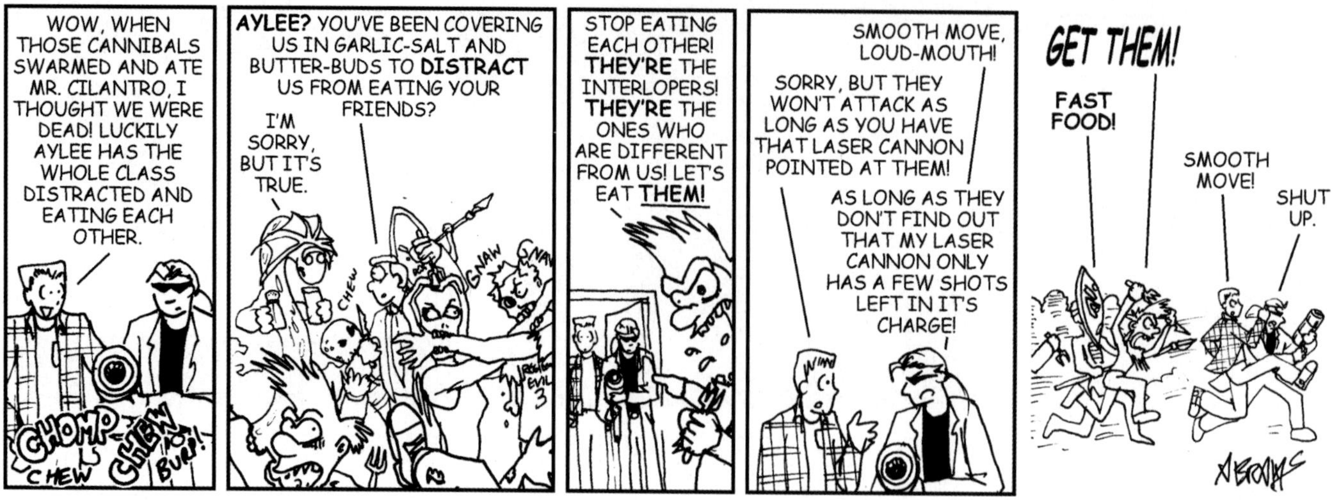
WOW, WHEN THOSE CANNIBALS SWARMED AND ATE MR. CILANTRO, I THOUGHT WE WERE DEAD! LUCKILY AYLEE HAS THE WHOLE CLASS DISTRACTED AND EATING EACH OTHER.
CHOMP CHEW CHEW BURP!
AYLEE? YOU'VE BEEN COVERING US IN GARLIC-SALT AND BUTTER-BUDS TO DISTRACT US FROM EATING YOUR FRIENDS?
I'M SORRY, BUT IT'S TRUE.
CHEW
GNAW GNAW
STOP EATING EACH OTHER! THEY'RE THE INTERLOPERS! THEY'RE THE ONES WHO ARE DIFFERENT FROM US! LET'S EAT THEM!
SMOOTH MOVE, LOUD-MOUTH!
SORRY, BUT THEY WON'T ATTACK AS LONG AS YOU HAVE THAT LASER CANNON POINTED AT THEM!
AS LONG AS THEY DON'T FIND OUT THAT MY LASER CANNON ONLY HAS A FEW SHOTS LEFT IN IT'S CHARGE!
GET THEM!
FAST FOOD!
SMOOTH MOVE!
SHUT UP.

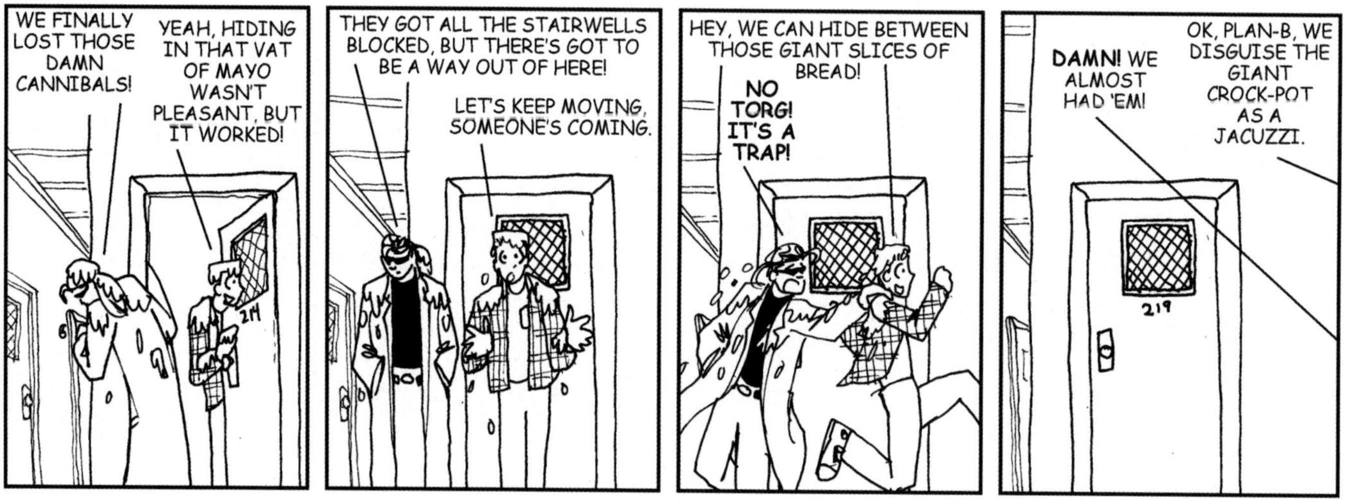
WE FINALLY LOST THOSE DAMN CANNIBALS!
YEAH, HIDING IN THAT VAT OF MAYO WASN'T PLEASANT, BUT IT WORKED!
214
THEY GOT ALL THE STAIRWELLS BLOCKED, BUT THERE'S GOT TO BE A WAY OUT OF HERE!
LET'S KEEP MOVING, SOMEONE'S COMING.
HEY, WE CAN HIDE BETWEEN THOSE GIANT SLICES OF BREAD!
NO TORG! IT'S A TRAP!
DAMN! WE ALMOST HAD 'EM!
OK, PLAN-B, WE DISGUISE THE GIANT CROCK-POT AS A JACUZZI.
219

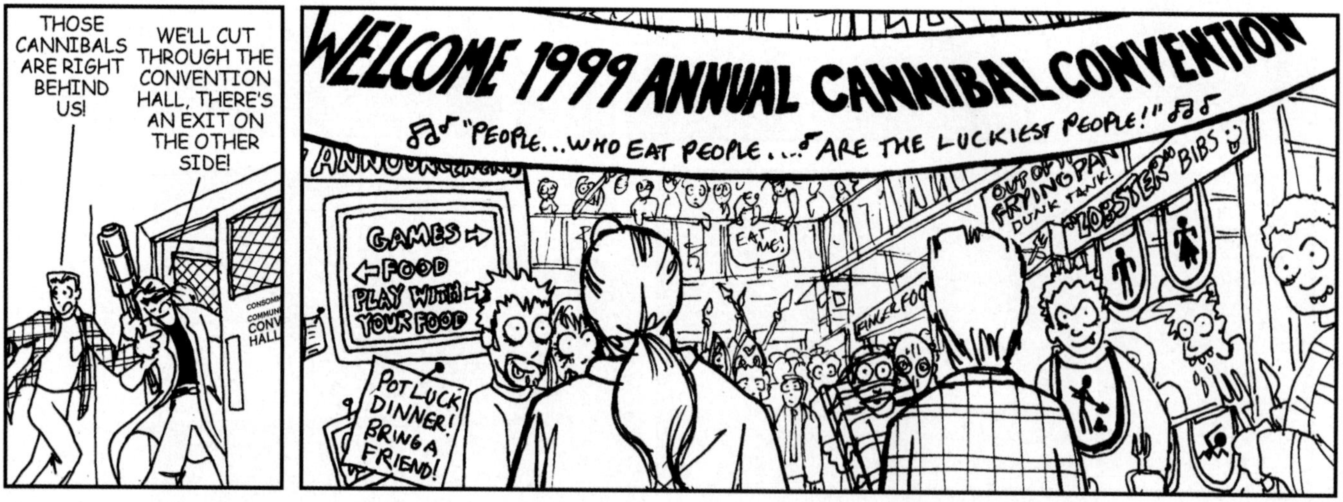
THOSE CANNIBALS ARE RIGHT BEHIND US!
WE'LL CUT THROUGH THE CONVENTION HALL, THERE'S AN EXIT ON THE OTHER SIDE!
CONV HALL
WELCOME 1999 ANNUAL CANNIBAL CONVENTION
"PEOPLE... WHO EAT PEOPLE... ARE THE LUCKIEST PEOPLE!"
GAMES →
← FOOD
PLAY WITH YOUR FOOD →
EAT ME!
OUT OF THE FRYING PAN DUNK TANK!
LOBSTER BIBS
POT LUCK DINNER! BRING A FRIEND!

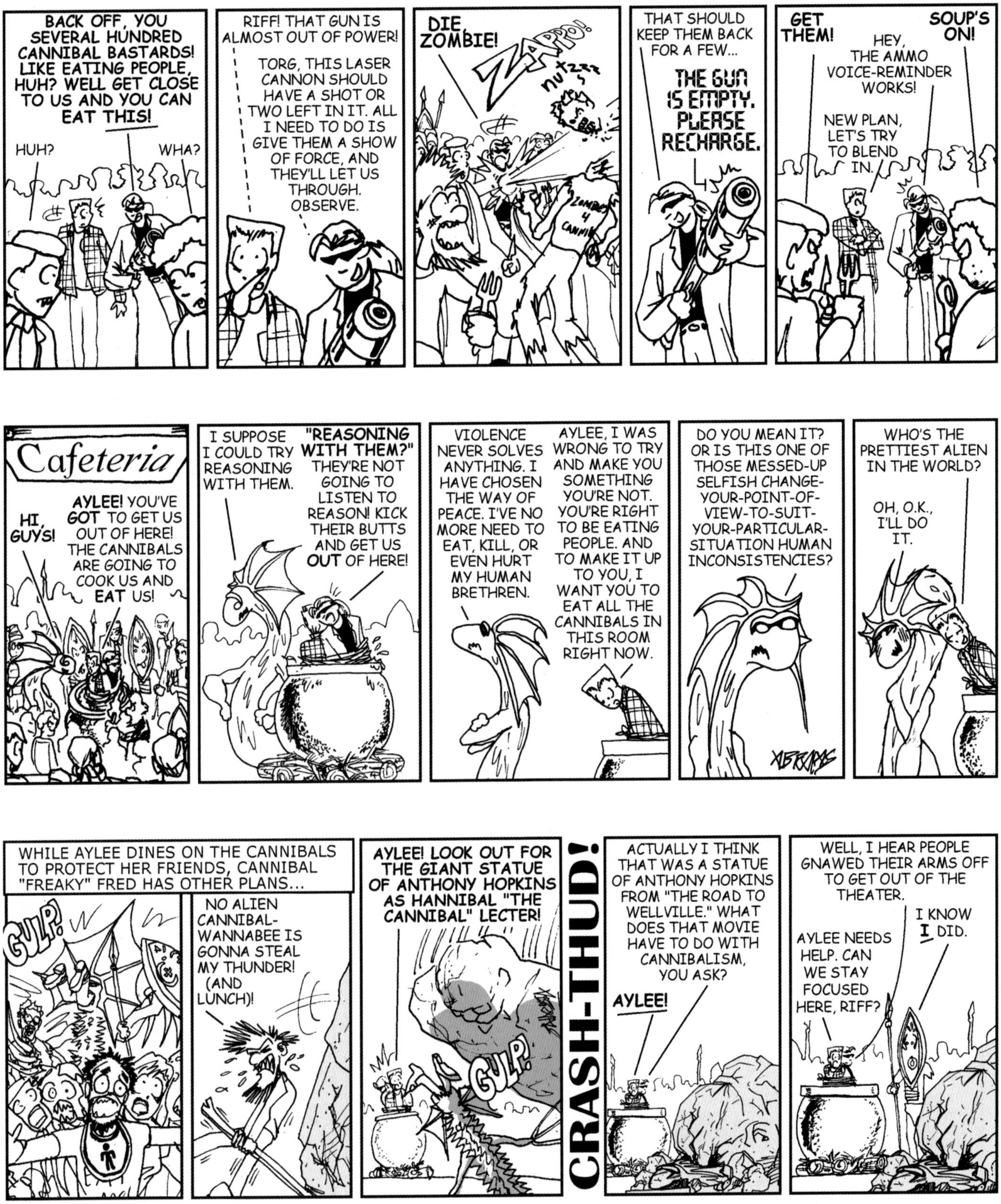
BACK OFF, YOU SEVERAL HUNDRED CANNIBAL BASTARDS! LIKE EATING PEOPLE, HUH? WELL GET CLOSE TO US AND YOU CAN EAT THIS!
HUH?
WHA?
RIFF! THAT GUN IS ALMOST OUT OF POWER!
TORG, THIS LASER CANNON SHOULD HAVE A SHOT OR TWO LEFT IN IT. ALL I NEED TO DO IS GIVE THEM A SHOW OF FORCE, AND THEY'LL LET US THROUGH. OBSERVE.
DIE, ZOMBIE!
ZAPPO!
THAT SHOULD KEEP THEM BACK FOR A FEW...
THE GUN IS EMPTY. PLEASE RECHARGE.
GET THEM!
SOUP'S ON!
HEY, THE AMMO VOICE-REMINDER WORKS!
NEW PLAN, LET'S TRY TO BLEND IN.
Cafeteria
HI, GUYS!
AYLEE! YOU'VE GOT TO GET US OUT OF HERE! THE CANNIBALS ARE GOING TO COOK US AND EAT US!
I SUPPOSE I COULD TRY REASONING WITH THEM.
"REASONING WITH THEM?" THEY'RE NOT GOING TO LISTEN TO REASON! KICK THEIR BUTTS AND GET US OUT OF HERE!
VIOLENCE NEVER SOLVES ANYTHING. I HAVE CHOSEN THE WAY OF PEACE. I'VE NO MORE NEED TO EAT, KILL, OR EVEN HURT MY HUMAN BRETHREN.
AYLEE, I WAS WRONG TO TRY AND MAKE YOU SOMETHING YOU'RE NOT. YOU'RE RIGHT TO BE EATING PEOPLE. AND TO MAKE IT UP TO YOU, I WANT YOU TO EAT ALL THE CANNIBALS IN THIS ROOM RIGHT NOW.
DO YOU MEAN IT? OR IS THIS ONE OF THOSE MESSED-UP SELFISH CHANGE-YOUR-POINT-OF-VIEW-TO-SUIT-YOUR-PARTICULAR-SITUATION HUMAN INCONSISTENCIES?
WHO'S THE PRETTIEST ALIEN IN THE WORLD?
OH, O.K., I'LL DO IT.
WHILE AYLEE DINES ON THE CANNIBALS TO PROTECT HER FRIENDS, CANNIBAL "FREAKY" FRED HAS OTHER PLANS...
GULP!
NO ALIEN CANNIBAL-WANNABEE IS GONNA STEAL MY THUNDER! (AND LUNCH)!
AYLEE! LOOK OUT FOR THE GIANT STATUE OF ANTHONY HOPKINS AS HANNIBAL "THE CANNIBAL" LECTER!
GULP!
CRASH-THUD!
ACTUALLY I THINK THAT WAS A STATUE OF ANTHONY HOPKINS FROM "THE ROAD TO WELLVILLE." WHAT DOES THAT MOVIE HAVE TO DO WITH CANNIBALISM, YOU ASK?
AYLEE!
WELL, I HEAR PEOPLE GNAWED THEIR ARMS OFF TO GET OUT OF THE THEATER.
AYLEE NEEDS HELP. CAN WE STAY FOCUSED HERE, RIFF?
I KNOW I DID.

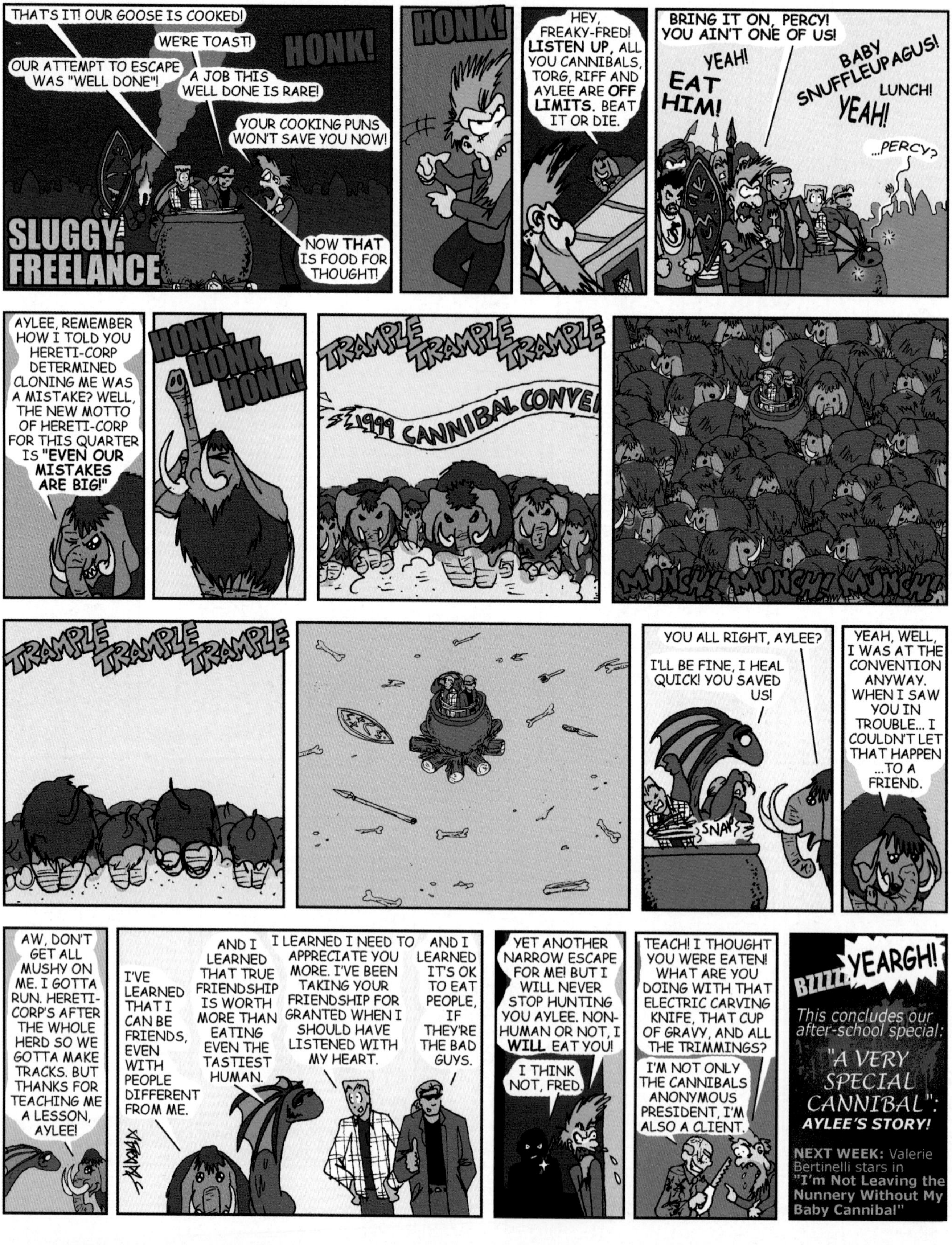
THAT'S IT! OUR GOOSE IS COOKED!
WE'RE TOAST!
OUR ATTEMPT TO ESCAPE WAS "WELL DONE"!
A JOB THIS WELL DONE IS RARE!
HONK!
YOUR COOKING PUNS WON'T SAVE YOU NOW!
SLUGGY, FREELANCE
NOW **THAT** IS FOOD FOR THOUGHT!
HONK!
HEY, FREAKY-FRED! **LISTEN UP,** ALL YOU CANNIBALS, TORG, RIFF AND AYLEE ARE **OFF LIMITS.** BEAT IT OR DIE.
BRING IT ON, PERCY! YOU AIN'T ONE OF US!
YEAH!
EAT HIM!
BABY SNUFFLEUPAGUS!
LUNCH!
YEAH!
...PERCY?
AYLEE, REMEMBER HOW I TOLD YOU HERETI-CORP DETERMINED CLONING ME WAS A MISTAKE? WELL, THE NEW MOTTO OF HERETI-CORP FOR THIS QUARTER IS **"EVEN OUR MISTAKES ARE BIG!"**
HONK, HONK, HONK!
TRAMPLE TRAMPLE TRAMPLE
1999 CANNIBAL CONVE
MUNCH! MUNCH! MUNCH!
TRAMPLE TRAMPLE TRAMPLE
YOU ALL RIGHT, AYLEE?
I'LL BE FINE, I HEAL QUICK! YOU SAVED US!
SNAP
YEAH, WELL, I WAS AT THE CONVENTION ANYWAY. WHEN I SAW YOU IN TROUBLE... I COULDN'T LET THAT HAPPEN ...TO A FRIEND.
AW, DON'T GET ALL MUSHY ON ME. I GOTTA RUN. HERETI-CORP'S AFTER THE WHOLE HERD SO WE GOTTA MAKE TRACKS. BUT THANKS FOR TEACHING ME A LESSON, AYLEE!
I'VE LEARNED THAT I CAN BE FRIENDS, EVEN WITH PEOPLE DIFFERENT FROM ME.
AND I LEARNED THAT TRUE FRIENDSHIP IS WORTH MORE THAN EATING EVEN THE TASTIEST HUMAN.
I LEARNED I NEED TO APPRECIATE YOU MORE. I'VE BEEN TAKING YOUR FRIENDSHIP FOR GRANTED WHEN I SHOULD HAVE LISTENED WITH MY HEART.
AND I LEARNED IT'S OK TO EAT PEOPLE, IF THEY'RE THE BAD GUYS.
YET ANOTHER NARROW ESCAPE FOR ME! BUT I WILL NEVER STOP HUNTING YOU AYLEE. NON-HUMAN OR NOT, I **WILL** EAT YOU!
I THINK NOT, FRED.
TEACH! I THOUGHT YOU WERE EATEN! WHAT ARE YOU DOING WITH THAT ELECTRIC CARVING KNIFE, THAT CUP OF GRAVY, AND ALL THE TRIMMINGS?
I'M NOT ONLY THE CANNIBALS ANONYMOUS PRESIDENT, I'M ALSO A CLIENT.
BZZZZ
YEARGH!
This concludes our after-school special:
"A VERY SPECIAL CANNIBAL": AYLEE'S STORY!
NEXT WEEK: Valerie Bertinelli stars in **"I'm Not Leaving the Nunnery Without My Baby Cannibal"**

Hi gang! This week I thought I'd answer some recent e-mail I've gotten involving plots and whatnot. Why do it in this forum instead of just replying to the e-mailer, you ask? Well, e-mail the question to me, and you may see the answer here! (OK, so it's all a plot to make my life easy this week. So sue me!)

-The Management

"WHAT HAPPENED WHEN KIKI WAS ON THAT SUGAR BUZZ? YOU NEVER FOLLOWED IT UP!"
-SUSIE, AUSTIN TX

Well Suzie, she ran really, really fast for a while and was hyper for a while and then slowed down.

Then she took a nap.

Poing
Poing
Poing
Poing

-YAWN
zzz

AND NOW YOU KNOW!

"DID KIKI HAVE ANY INTERESTING EXPERIENCES WHILE CIRCLING THE GLOBE ON HER SUGAR BUZZ?"
-JOHN, SPRINGFIELD, ID

Well, Jack, she did hear a really good knock-knock joke.

RIFF, I KNOW THIS REALLY FUNNY KNOCK-KNOCK JOKE! SAY "KNOCK-KNOCK!"

KNOCK-KNOCK.

OOOOH! I'LL GET THE DOOR!

And we'll never know what it was.

AND NOW YOU KNOW!

"WHAT'S ZOË BEEN UP TO ALL THIS TIME? HAVEN'T SEEN/HEARD FROM HER IN A LONG TIME, IT SEEMS..."
-NANCY RENNETT

Zoë is not having a good time.

She is angry and afraid of Aylee and her habit of eating people.

She is angry and afraid of her own roommate, Gwynn, unsure of if she is controlling her demonic powers, or under their control.

She is angry and has a crush on her college classmate Dex, who "doesn't know she's alive".

And she is overall sad. Her grades are down and she's almost out of money.

But she's looking forward to her Holiday Break and at least this week she's dressed as Oasis!

I'M NOT COMING OUT DRESSED LIKE THIS!

Now I'm overall sad.

AND NOW YOU KNOW!

Chapter 15: The Isle of Dr. Steve

"WHAT ABOUT GWYNN'S MAGIC POWERS? YOU KIND OF FORGOT ABOUT GWYNN'S MAGIC POWERS DURING THE WHOLE CANNIBALISM THING... ARE GWYNN'S MAGIC POWERS STILL GOING TO BE AN ISSUE?"
-REV. VICTOR W.
PROUD INVENTOR OF THE WHEEL.

Gwynn has become a classic Shakespearean tragic hero, walking a line between embracing her power, hiding from it, and getting Laser Eye Surgery.

GOOD
BAD
KRIIK
GLASSES-FREE

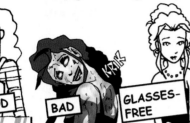

Before you try to guess which path she will take, remember the problems laser eye surgery caused Hamlet. I can say no more, for I have already said too much.

ZAP ZAP ZAP ZAP

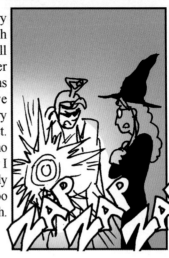

Alright, I'll say this much, dating Riff appears to have turned her off to the laser eye surgery for now.

AND NOW YOU KNOW!

"WHEN ARE YOU BRINGING OASIS BACK? **PLEASE PLEASE *PLEASE* BRING OASIS BACK! PRETTY PLEASE?"**
- MATT ELLIOT (ME.)

Herm.....

HEY GUYS! LOOK WHO'S BACK!
SSSSSSSSS

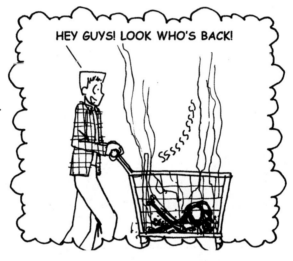

No comment.

WHATEVER HAPPENED TO SAM AFTER THE 'VAMPIRE BAKER' STRIP?
-PETE (NO RELATION)

"AS I PROWL THE CITY, I PROWL NOT FOR THE INNOCENT, AS MY VAMPIRIC URGES LEAD ME, BUT I PROWL ON THOSE WHO PROWL FOR THE INNOCENT. THOSE WHO CROSS MY PATH ARE..."
HEY BABES! WANT TO COME PARTY WITH SAM?
BITE ME, CREEP!
TOUCH ME AND YOU'RE DEAD!
"THE CURSE UPON MY VAMPIRE SOUL MEANS I MUST GO ON ALONE. LOOK OUT, PROWLERS, SAM THE VAMPIRE'S A PROWLER'S PROWLER. FOR I AM A VAMPIRE WHO..."
WHOA! I JUST THOUGHT OF THE COOLEST COMEBACKS TO THOSE LINES! I GOTTA GO FIND THOSE CHICKS AGAIN!

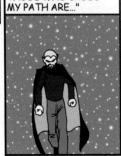

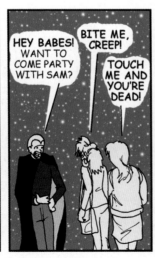

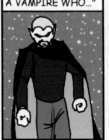

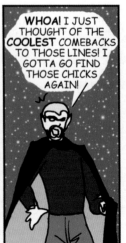

Well Pete, I actually have no idea what happened to Sam. But wherever he is, whatever he's doing, you know he's kickin' it "Sam-Style".

AND NOW YOU KNOW!

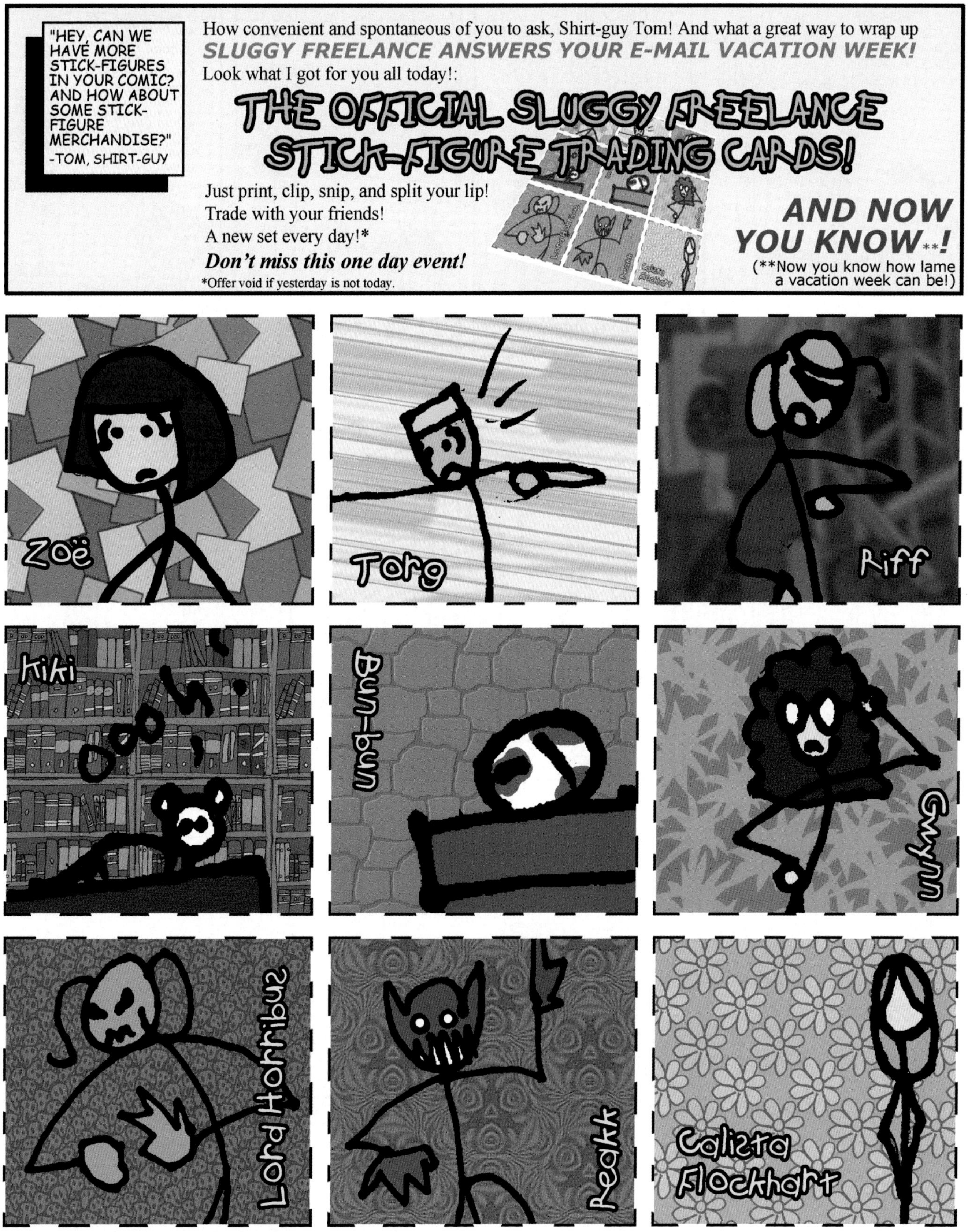

"HEY, CAN WE HAVE MORE STICK-FIGURES IN YOUR COMIC? AND HOW ABOUT SOME STICK-FIGURE MERCHANDISE?" -TOM, SHIRT-GUY
How convenient and spontaneous of you to ask, Shirt-guy Tom! And what a great way to wrap up
SLUGGY FREELANCE ANSWERS YOUR E-MAIL VACATION WEEK!
Look what I got for you all today!:
THE OFFICIAL SLUGGY FREELANCE STICK-FIGURE TRADING CARDS!
Just print, clip, snip, and split your lip!
Trade with your friends!
A new set every day!*
Don't miss this one day event!
*Offer void if yesterday is not today.
AND NOW YOU KNOW**!
(**Now you know how lame a vacation week can be!)
Zoë
Torg
Riff
Kiki
Bun-bun
Gwynn
Lord Horribus
Reakk
Calista Flockhart

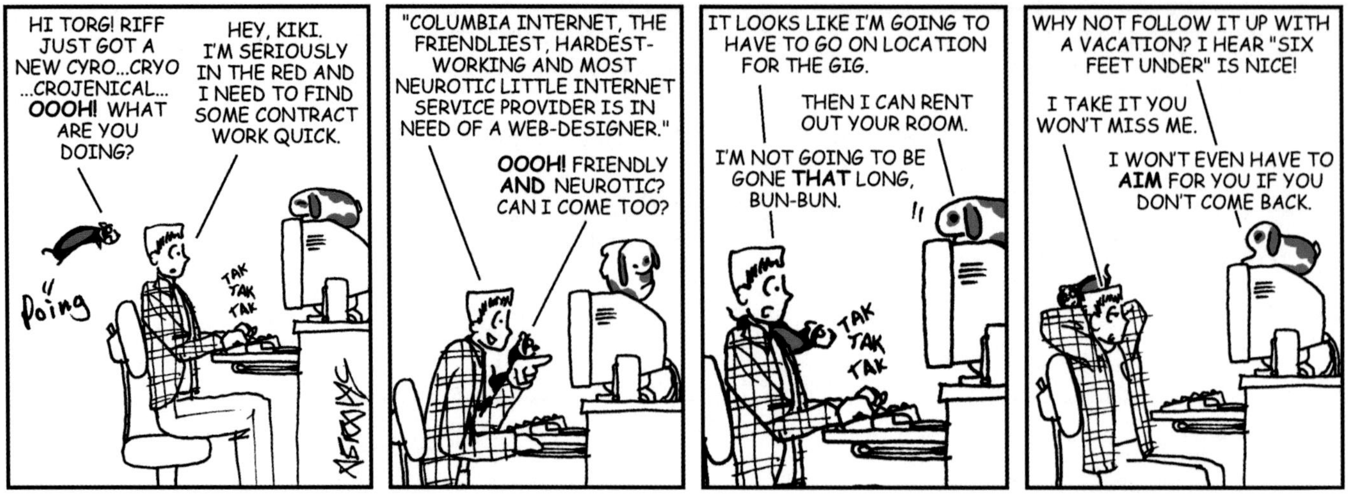
HI TORG! RIFF JUST GOT A NEW CYRO...CRYO ...CROJENICAL... OOOH! WHAT ARE YOU DOING?
HEY, KIKI. I'M SERIOUSLY IN THE RED AND I NEED TO FIND SOME CONTRACT WORK QUICK.
Poing
TAK TAK TAK
"COLUMBIA INTERNET, THE FRIENDLIEST, HARDEST-WORKING AND MOST NEUROTIC LITTLE INTERNET SERVICE PROVIDER IS IN NEED OF A WEB-DESIGNER."
OOOH! FRIENDLY AND NEUROTIC? CAN I COME TOO?
IT LOOKS LIKE I'M GOING TO HAVE TO GO ON LOCATION FOR THE GIG.
THEN I CAN RENT OUT YOUR ROOM.
I'M NOT GOING TO BE GONE THAT LONG, BUN-BUN.
TAK TAK TAK
WHY NOT FOLLOW IT UP WITH A VACATION? I HEAR "SIX FEET UNDER" IS NICE!
I TAKE IT YOU WON'T MISS ME.
I WON'T EVEN HAVE TO AIM FOR YOU IF YOU DON'T COME BACK.

A.J. (c) J.D. "Illiad" Frazer of UserFriendly.Org

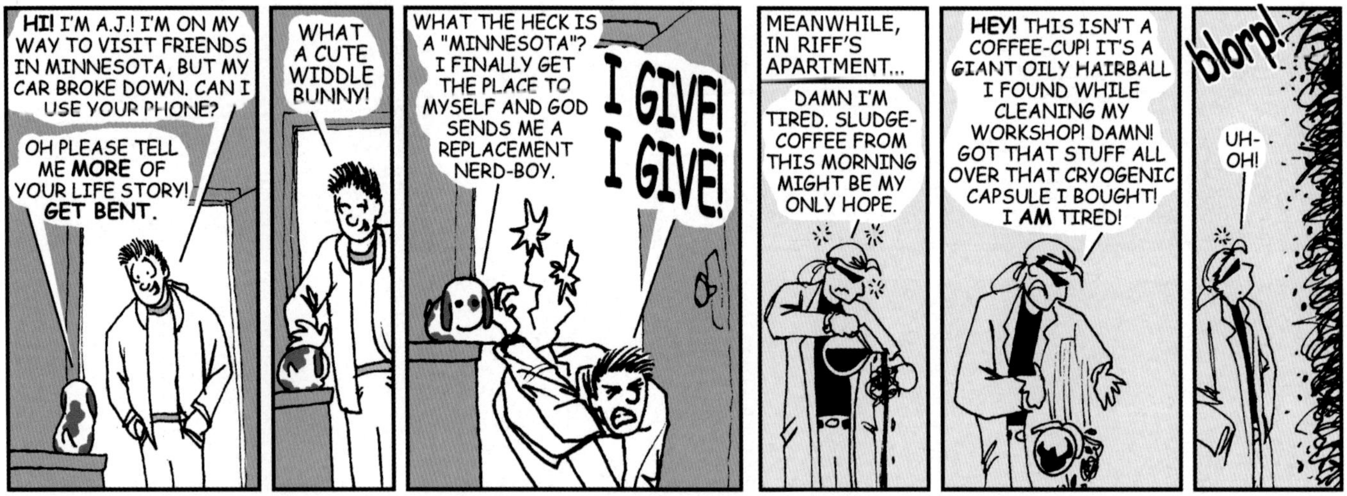
HI! I'M A.J.! I'M ON MY WAY TO VISIT FRIENDS IN MINNESOTA, BUT MY CAR BROKE DOWN. CAN I USE YOUR PHONE?
OH PLEASE TELL ME MORE OF YOUR LIFE STORY! GET BENT.
WHAT A CUTE WIDDLE BUNNY!
WHAT THE HECK IS A "MINNESOTA"? I FINALLY GET THE PLACE TO MYSELF AND GOD SENDS ME A REPLACEMENT NERD-BOY.
I GIVE! I GIVE!
MEANWHILE, IN RIFF'S APARTMENT...
DAMN I'M TIRED. SLUDGE-COFFEE FROM THIS MORNING MIGHT BE MY ONLY HOPE.
HEY! THIS ISN'T A COFFEE-CUP! IT'S A GIANT OILY HAIRBALL I FOUND WHILE CLEANING MY WORKSHOP! DAMN! GOT THAT STUFF ALL OVER THAT CRYOGENIC CAPSULE I BOUGHT! I AM TIRED!
blorp!
UH-OH!

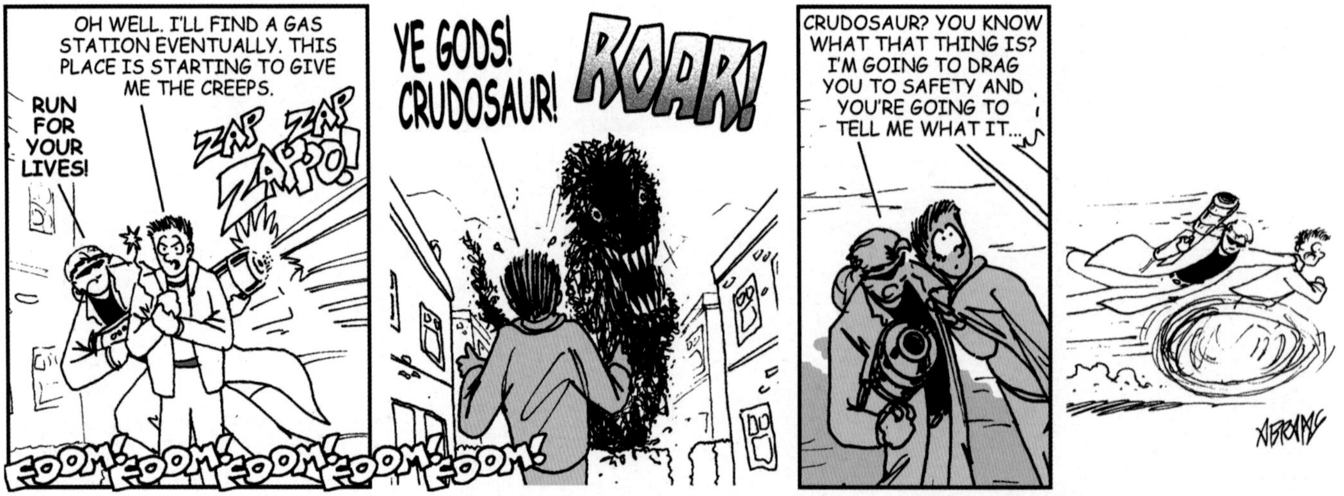
OH WELL. I'LL FIND A GAS STATION EVENTUALLY. THIS PLACE IS STARTING TO GIVE ME THE CREEPS.
RUN FOR YOUR LIVES!
ZAP ZAP ZAPPO!
FOOM! FOOM! FOOM! FOOM! FOOM!
YE GODS! CRUDOSAUR!
ROAR!
CRUDOSAUR? YOU KNOW WHAT THAT THING IS? I'M GOING TO DRAG YOU TO SAFETY AND YOU'RE GOING TO TELL ME WHAT IT...

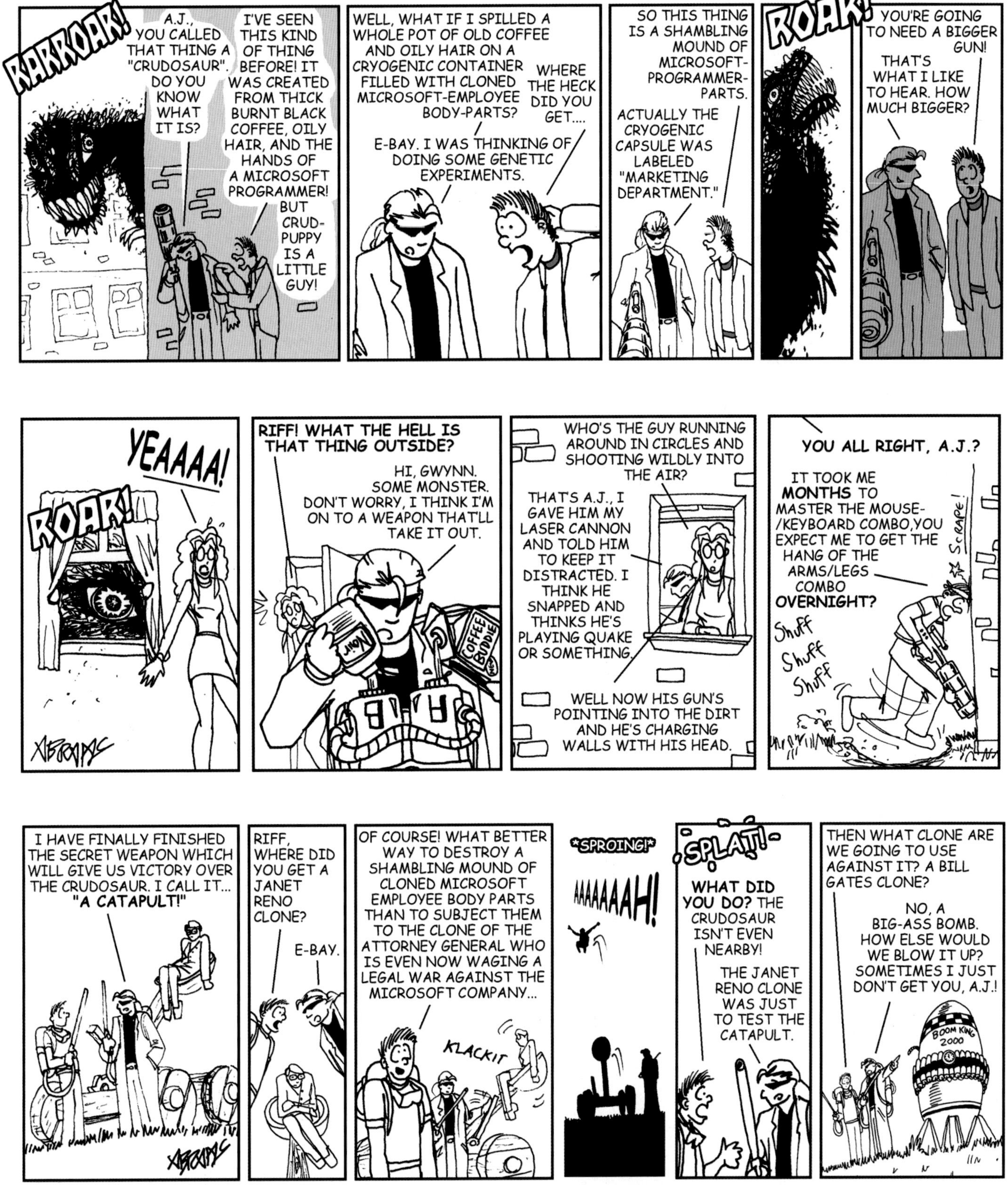
KARROAR!
A.J., YOU CALLED THAT THING A "CRUDOSAUR". DO YOU KNOW WHAT IT IS?
I'VE SEEN THIS KIND OF THING BEFORE! IT WAS CREATED FROM THICK BURNT BLACK COFFEE, OILY HAIR, AND THE HANDS OF A MICROSOFT PROGRAMMER!
BUT CRUD-PUPPY IS A LITTLE GUY!
WELL, WHAT IF I SPILLED A WHOLE POT OF OLD COFFEE AND OILY HAIR ON A CRYOGENIC CONTAINER FILLED WITH CLONED MICROSOFT-EMPLOYEE BODY-PARTS?
WHERE THE HECK DID YOU GET....
E-BAY. I WAS THINKING OF DOING SOME GENETIC EXPERIMENTS.
SO THIS THING IS A SHAMBLING MOUND OF MICROSOFT-PROGRAMMER-PARTS.
ACTUALLY THE CRYOGENIC CAPSULE WAS LABELED "MARKETING DEPARTMENT."
ROAR!
YOU'RE GOING TO NEED A BIGGER GUN!
THAT'S WHAT I LIKE TO HEAR. HOW MUCH BIGGER?
YEAAAA!
ROAR!
RIFF! WHAT THE HELL IS THAT THING OUTSIDE?
HI, GWYNN. SOME MONSTER. DON'T WORRY, I THINK I'M ON TO A WEAPON THAT'LL TAKE IT OUT.
COFFEE BUDDIE
WHO'S THE GUY RUNNING AROUND IN CIRCLES AND SHOOTING WILDLY INTO THE AIR?
THAT'S A.J., I GAVE HIM MY LASER CANNON AND TOLD HIM TO KEEP IT DISTRACTED. I THINK HE SNAPPED AND THINKS HE'S PLAYING QUAKE OR SOMETHING.
WELL NOW HIS GUN'S POINTING INTO THE DIRT AND HE'S CHARGING WALLS WITH HIS HEAD.
YOU ALL RIGHT, A.J.?
IT TOOK ME MONTHS TO MASTER THE MOUSE-/KEYBOARD COMBO,YOU EXPECT ME TO GET THE HANG OF THE ARMS/LEGS COMBO OVERNIGHT?
SCRAPE!
Shuff Shuff Shuff
I HAVE FINALLY FINISHED THE SECRET WEAPON WHICH WILL GIVE US VICTORY OVER THE CRUDOSAUR. I CALL IT... "A CATAPULT!"
RIFF, WHERE DID YOU GET A JANET RENO CLONE?
E-BAY.
OF COURSE! WHAT BETTER WAY TO DESTROY A SHAMBLING MOUND OF CLONED MICROSOFT EMPLOYEE BODY PARTS THAN TO SUBJECT THEM TO THE CLONE OF THE ATTORNEY GENERAL WHO IS EVEN NOW WAGING A LEGAL WAR AGAINST THE MICROSOFT COMPANY...
KLACKIT
SPROING!
AAAAAAAH!
SPLAT!
WHAT DID YOU DO? THE CRUDOSAUR ISN'T EVEN NEARBY!
THE JANET RENO CLONE WAS JUST TO TEST THE CATAPULT.
THEN WHAT CLONE ARE WE GOING TO USE AGAINST IT? A BILL GATES CLONE?
NO, A BIG-ASS BOMB. HOW ELSE WOULD WE BLOW IT UP? SOMETIMES I JUST DON'T GET YOU, A.J.!
BOOM KING 2000

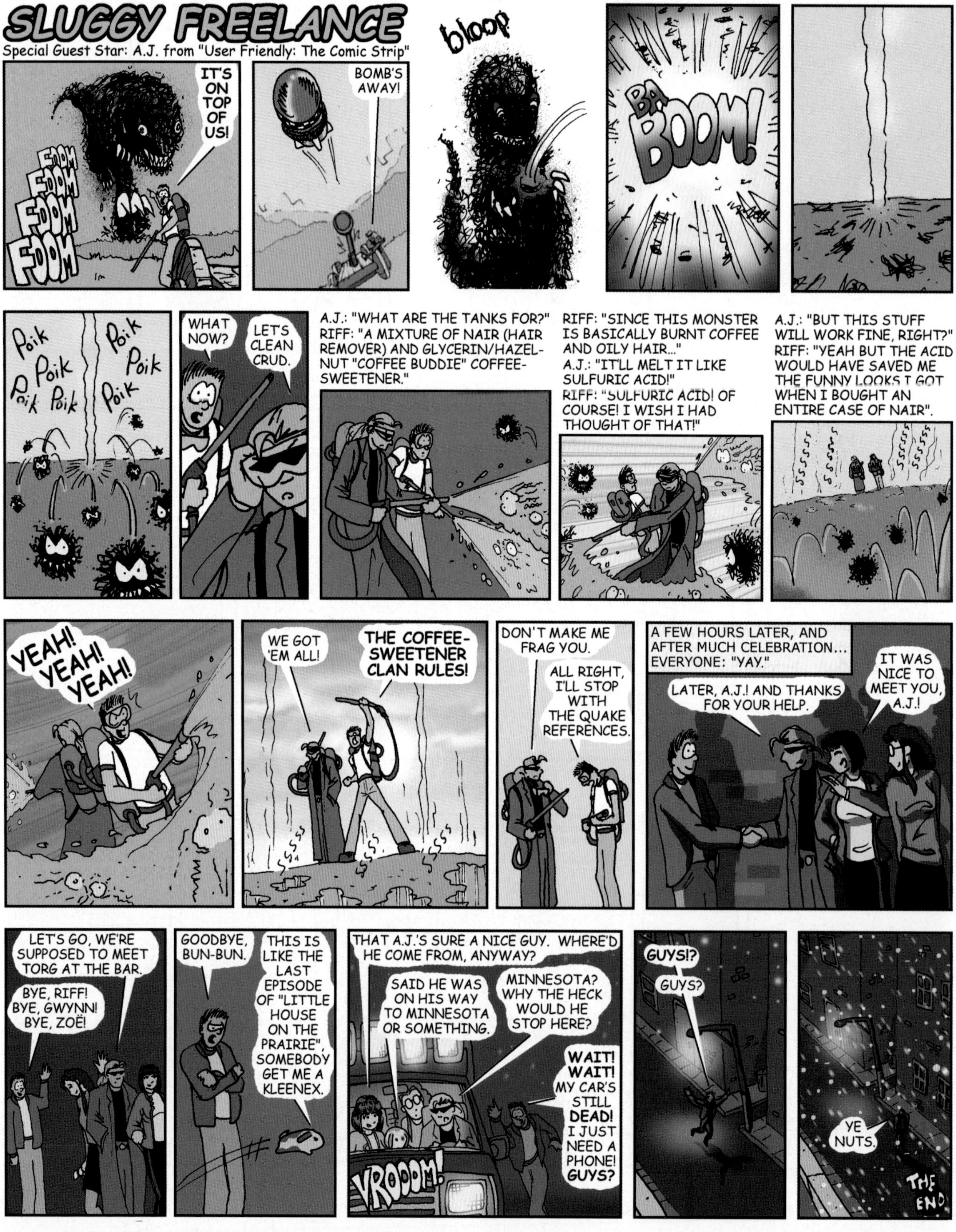
SLUGGY FREELANCE
Special Guest Star: A.J. from "User Friendly: The Comic Strip"
FOOM FOOM FOOM FOOM
IT'S ON TOP OF US!
BOMB'S AWAY!
bloop
BA BOOM!
Poik Poik Poik Poik Poik Poik Poik
WHAT NOW?
LET'S CLEAN CRUD.
A.J.: "WHAT ARE THE TANKS FOR?" RIFF: "A MIXTURE OF NAIR (HAIR REMOVER) AND GLYCERIN/HAZEL-NUT "COFFEE BUDDIE" COFFEE-SWEETENER."
RIFF: "SINCE THIS MONSTER IS BASICALLY BURNT COFFEE AND OILY HAIR..." A.J.: "IT'LL MELT IT LIKE SULFURIC ACID!" RIFF: "SULFURIC ACID! OF COURSE! I WISH I HAD THOUGHT OF THAT!"
A.J.: "BUT THIS STUFF WILL WORK FINE, RIGHT?" RIFF: "YEAH BUT THE ACID WOULD HAVE SAVED ME THE FUNNY LOOKS I GOT WHEN I BOUGHT AN ENTIRE CASE OF NAIR".
YEAH! YEAH! YEAH!
WE GOT 'EM ALL!
THE COFFEE-SWEETENER CLAN RULES!
DON'T MAKE ME FRAG YOU.
ALL RIGHT, I'LL STOP WITH THE QUAKE REFERENCES.
A FEW HOURS LATER, AND AFTER MUCH CELEBRATION... EVERYONE: "YAY."
LATER, A.J.! AND THANKS FOR YOUR HELP.
IT WAS NICE TO MEET YOU, A.J.!
LET'S GO, WE'RE SUPPOSED TO MEET TORG AT THE BAR.
BYE, RIFF! BYE, GWYNN! BYE, ZOË!
GOODBYE, BUN-BUN.
THIS IS LIKE THE LAST EPISODE OF "LITTLE HOUSE ON THE PRAIRIE", SOMEBODY GET ME A KLEENEX.
THAT A.J.'S SURE A NICE GUY. WHERE'D HE COME FROM, ANYWAY?
SAID HE WAS ON HIS WAY TO MINNESOTA OR SOMETHING.
MINNESOTA? WHY THE HECK WOULD HE STOP HERE?
WAIT! WAIT! MY CAR'S STILL DEAD! I JUST NEED A PHONE! GUYS?
VROOOM!
GUYS!?
GUYS?
YE NUTS.
THE END

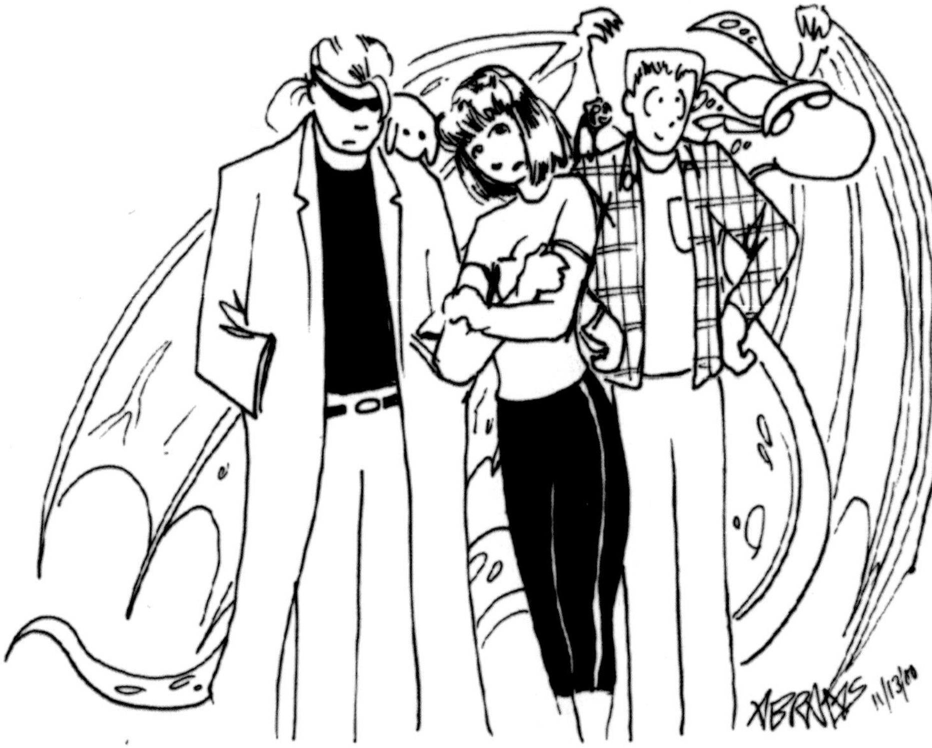

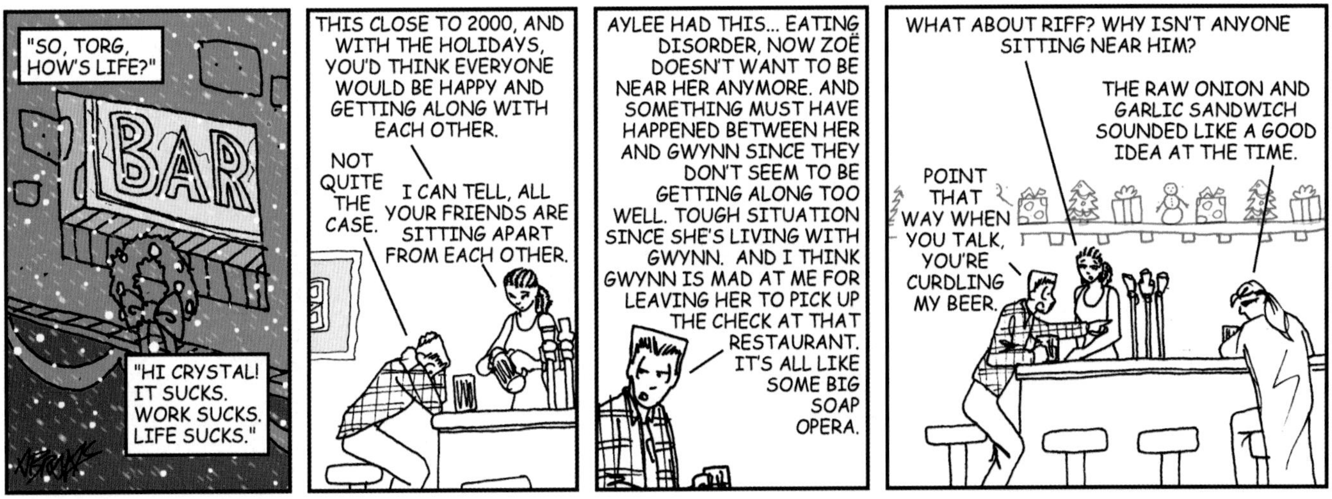
"SO, TORG, HOW'S LIFE?"
BAR
"HI CRYSTAL! IT SUCKS. WORK SUCKS. LIFE SUCKS."
THIS CLOSE TO 2000, AND WITH THE HOLIDAYS, YOU'D THINK EVERYONE WOULD BE HAPPY AND GETTING ALONG WITH EACH OTHER.
I CAN TELL, ALL YOUR FRIENDS ARE SITTING APART FROM EACH OTHER.
NOT QUITE THE CASE.
AYLEE HAD THIS... EATING DISORDER, NOW ZOË DOESN'T WANT TO BE NEAR HER ANYMORE. AND SOMETHING MUST HAVE HAPPENED BETWEEN HER AND GWYNN SINCE THEY DON'T SEEM TO BE GETTING ALONG TOO WELL. TOUGH SITUATION SINCE SHE'S LIVING WITH GWYNN. AND I THINK GWYNN IS MAD AT ME FOR LEAVING HER TO PICK UP THE CHECK AT THAT RESTAURANT. IT'S ALL LIKE SOME BIG SOAP OPERA.
WHAT ABOUT RIFF? WHY ISN'T ANYONE SITTING NEAR HIM?
THE RAW ONION AND GARLIC SANDWICH SOUNDED LIKE A GOOD IDEA AT THE TIME.
POINT THAT WAY WHEN YOU TALK, YOU'RE CURDLING MY BEER.

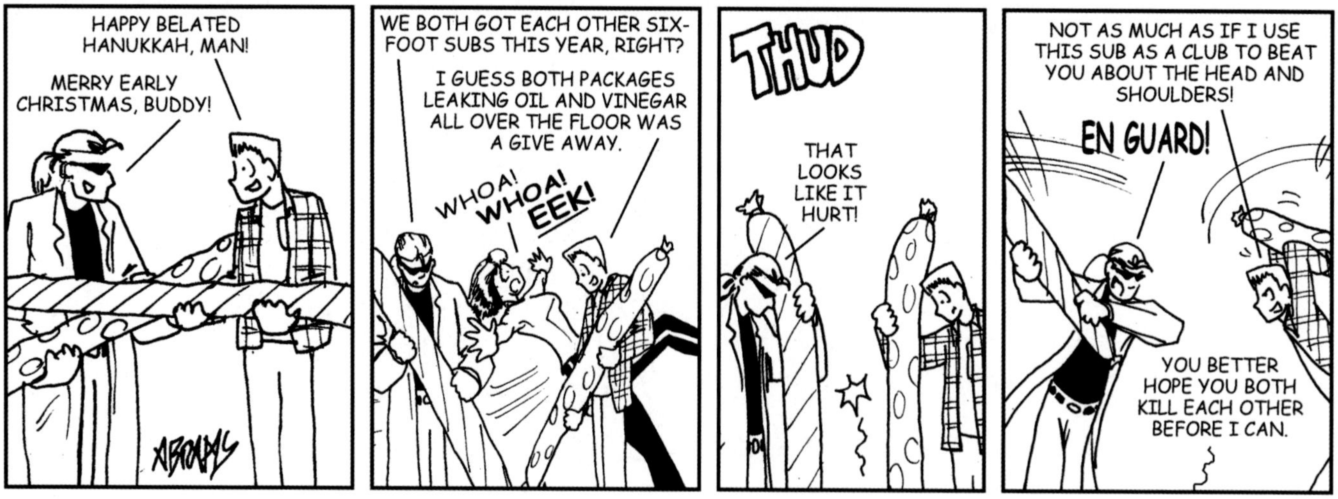
HAPPY BELATED HANUKKAH, MAN!
MERRY EARLY CHRISTMAS, BUDDY!
WE BOTH GOT EACH OTHER SIX-FOOT SUBS THIS YEAR, RIGHT?
I GUESS BOTH PACKAGES LEAKING OIL AND VINEGAR ALL OVER THE FLOOR WAS A GIVE AWAY.
WHOA! WHOA! EEK!
THUD
THAT LOOKS LIKE IT HURT!
NOT AS MUCH AS IF I USE THIS SUB AS A CLUB TO BEAT YOU ABOUT THE HEAD AND SHOULDERS!
EN GUARD!
YOU BETTER HOPE YOU BOTH KILL EACH OTHER BEFORE I CAN.

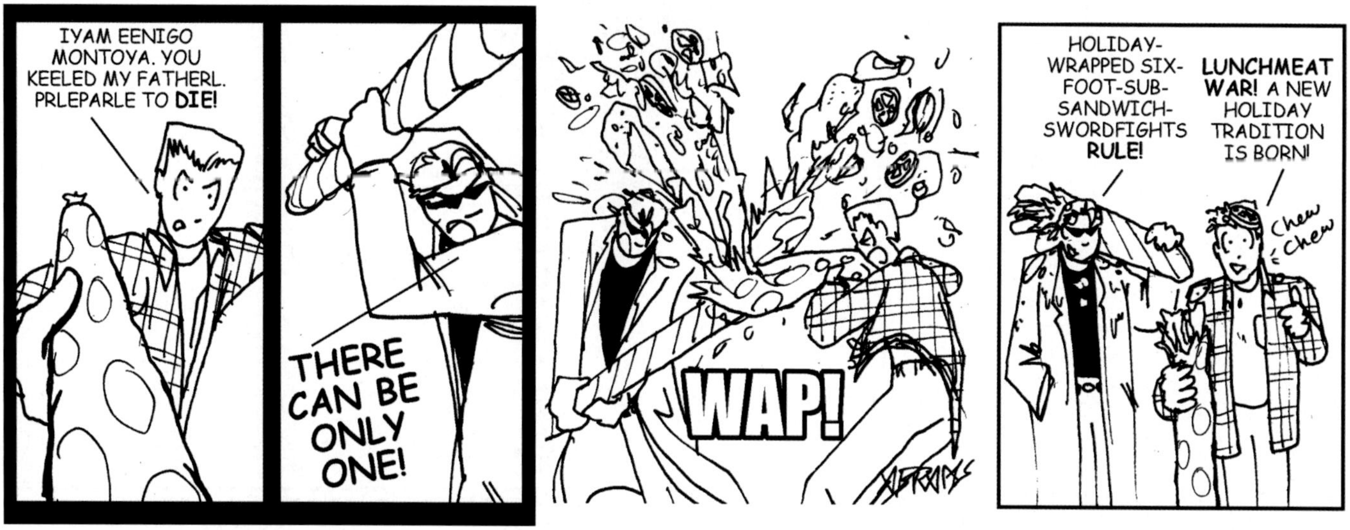
IYAM EENIGO MONTOYA. YOU KEELED MY FATHERL. PRLEPARLE TO DIE!
THERE CAN BE ONLY ONE!
WAP!
HOLIDAY-WRAPPED SIX-FOOT-SUB-SANDWICH-SWORDFIGHTS RULE!
LUNCHMEAT WAR! A NEW HOLIDAY TRADITION IS BORN!
Chew Chew

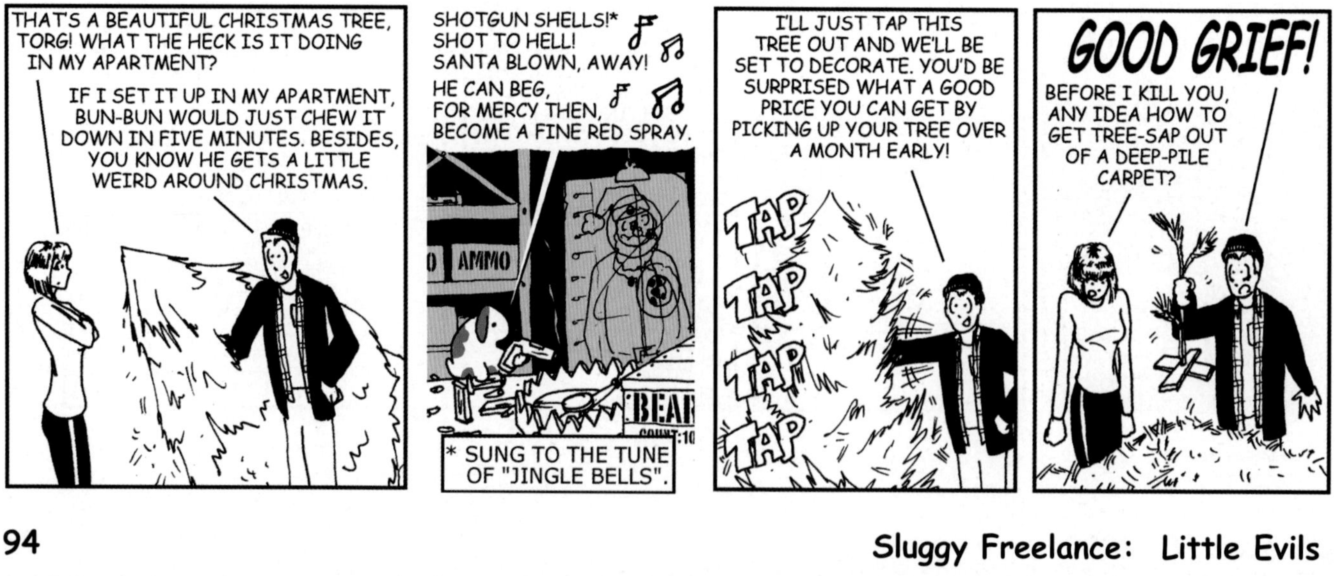
THAT'S A BEAUTIFUL CHRISTMAS TREE, TORG! WHAT THE HECK IS IT DOING IN MY APARTMENT?
IF I SET IT UP IN MY APARTMENT, BUN-BUN WOULD JUST CHEW IT DOWN IN FIVE MINUTES. BESIDES, YOU KNOW HE GETS A LITTLE WEIRD AROUND CHRISTMAS.
SHOTGUN SHELLS!* SHOT TO HELL! SANTA BLOWN, AWAY!
HE CAN BEG, FOR MERCY THEN, BECOME A FINE RED SPRAY.
AMMO
* SUNG TO THE TUNE OF "JINGLE BELLS".
I'LL JUST TAP THIS TREE OUT AND WE'LL BE SET TO DECORATE. YOU'D BE SURPRISED WHAT A GOOD PRICE YOU CAN GET BY PICKING UP YOUR TREE OVER A MONTH EARLY!
TAP TAP TAP TAP
GOOD GRIEF!
BEFORE I KILL YOU, ANY IDEA HOW TO GET TREE-SAP OUT OF A DEEP-PILE CARPET?

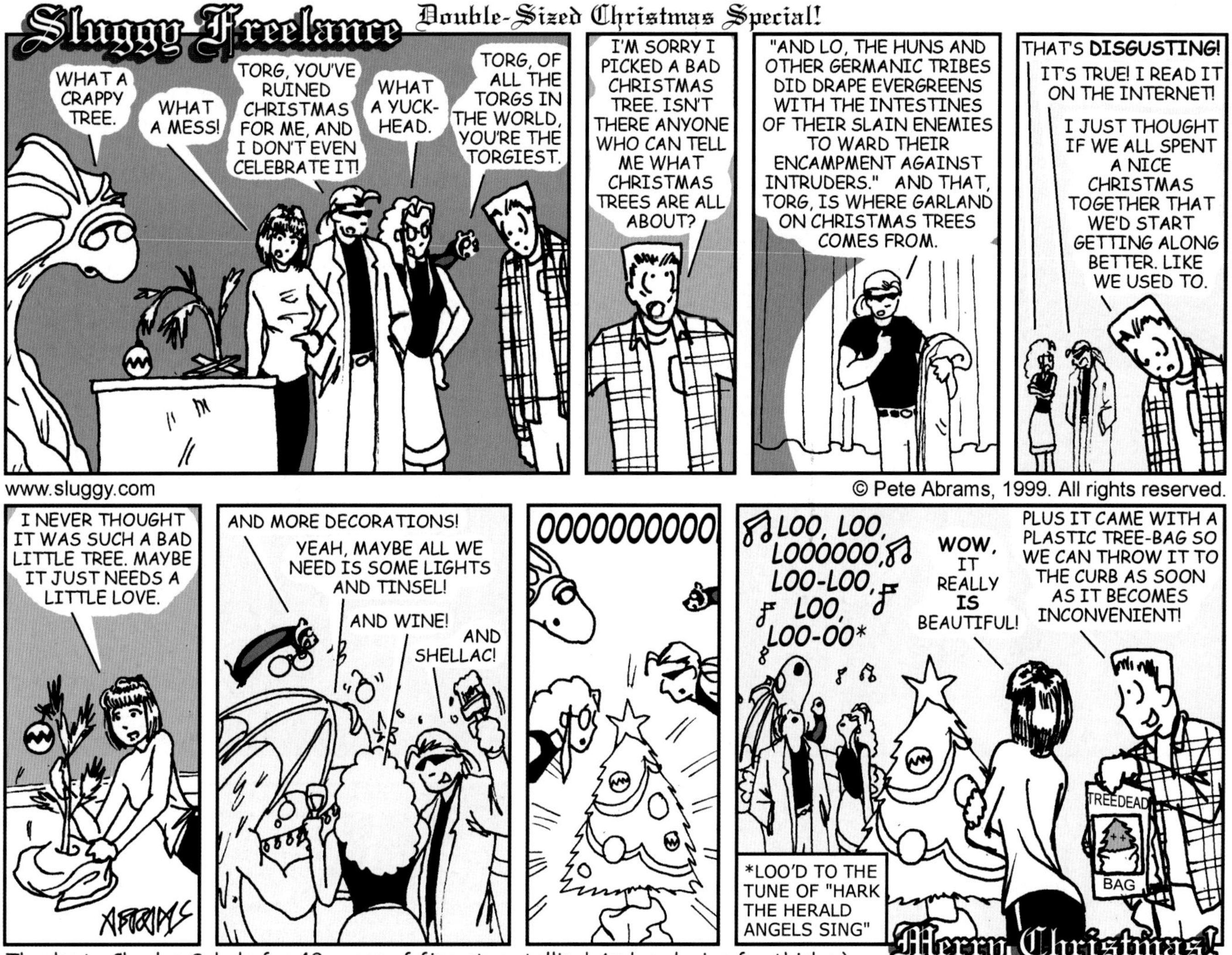
Sluggy Freelance
Double-Sized Christmas Special!
WHAT A CRAPPY TREE.
WHAT A MESS!
TORG, YOU'VE RUINED CHRISTMAS FOR ME, AND I DON'T EVEN CELEBRATE IT!
WHAT A YUCK-HEAD.
TORG, OF ALL THE TORGS IN THE WORLD, YOU'RE THE TORGIEST.
I'M SORRY I PICKED A BAD CHRISTMAS TREE. ISN'T THERE ANYONE WHO CAN TELL ME WHAT CHRISTMAS TREES ARE ALL ABOUT?
"AND LO, THE HUNS AND OTHER GERMANIC TRIBES DID DRAPE EVERGREENS WITH THE INTESTINES OF THEIR SLAIN ENEMIES TO WARD THEIR ENCAMPMENT AGAINST INTRUDERS." AND THAT, TORG, IS WHERE GARLAND ON CHRISTMAS TREES COMES FROM.
THAT'S DISGUSTING!
IT'S TRUE! I READ IT ON THE INTERNET!
I JUST THOUGHT IF WE ALL SPENT A NICE CHRISTMAS TOGETHER THAT WE'D START GETTING ALONG BETTER. LIKE WE USED TO.
www.sluggy.com
© Pete Abrams, 1999. All rights reserved.
I NEVER THOUGHT IT WAS SUCH A BAD LITTLE TREE. MAYBE IT JUST NEEDS A LITTLE LOVE.
AND MORE DECORATIONS!
YEAH, MAYBE ALL WE NEED IS SOME LIGHTS AND TINSEL!
AND WINE!
AND SHELLAC!
OOOOOOOOOO
LOO, LOO, LOOOOOO, LOO-LOO, LOO, LOO-OO*
WOW, IT REALLY IS BEAUTIFUL!
PLUS IT CAME WITH A PLASTIC TREE-BAG SO WE CAN THROW IT TO THE CURB AS SOON AS IT BECOMES INCONVENIENT!
TREEDEAD BAG
*LOO'D TO THE TUNE OF "HARK THE HERALD ANGELS SING"
Merry Christmas!

Thanks to Charles Schulz for 49 years of fine story telling! And apologies for this! :)

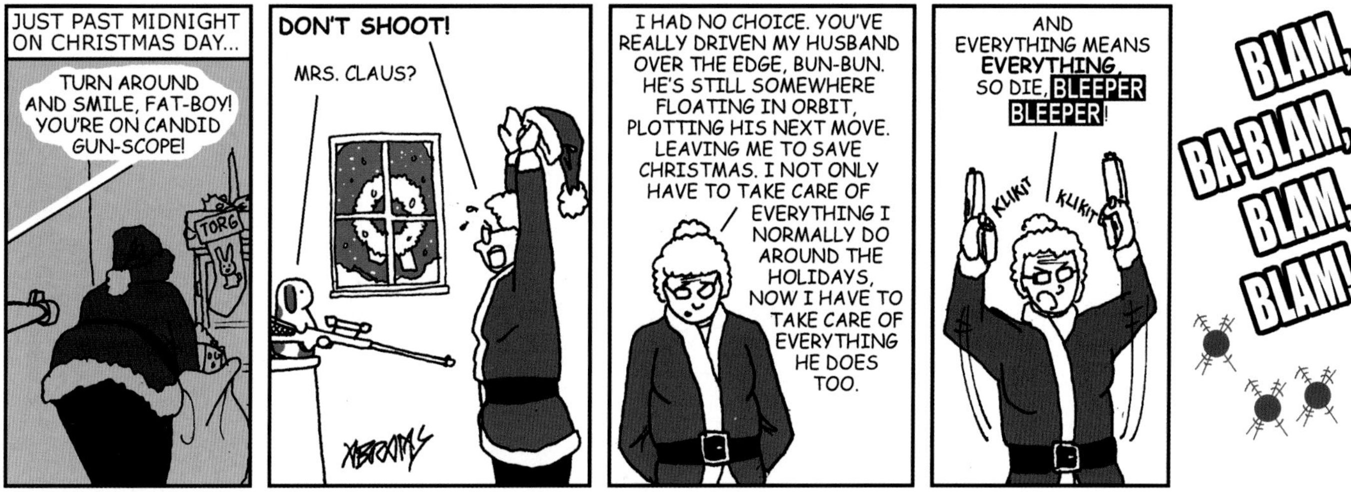
JUST PAST MIDNIGHT ON CHRISTMAS DAY...
TURN AROUND AND SMILE, FAT-BOY! YOU'RE ON CANDID GUN-SCOPE!
TORG
DON'T SHOOT!
MRS. CLAUS?
I HAD NO CHOICE. YOU'VE REALLY DRIVEN MY HUSBAND OVER THE EDGE, BUN-BUN. HE'S STILL SOMEWHERE FLOATING IN ORBIT, PLOTTING HIS NEXT MOVE. LEAVING ME TO SAVE CHRISTMAS. I NOT ONLY HAVE TO TAKE CARE OF EVERYTHING I NORMALLY DO AROUND THE HOLIDAYS, NOW I HAVE TO TAKE CARE OF EVERYTHING HE DOES TOO.
AND EVERYTHING MEANS EVERYTHING, SO DIE, BLEEPER BLEEPER!
KLIKIT
KLIKIT
BLAM, BA-BLAM, BLAM, BLAM!

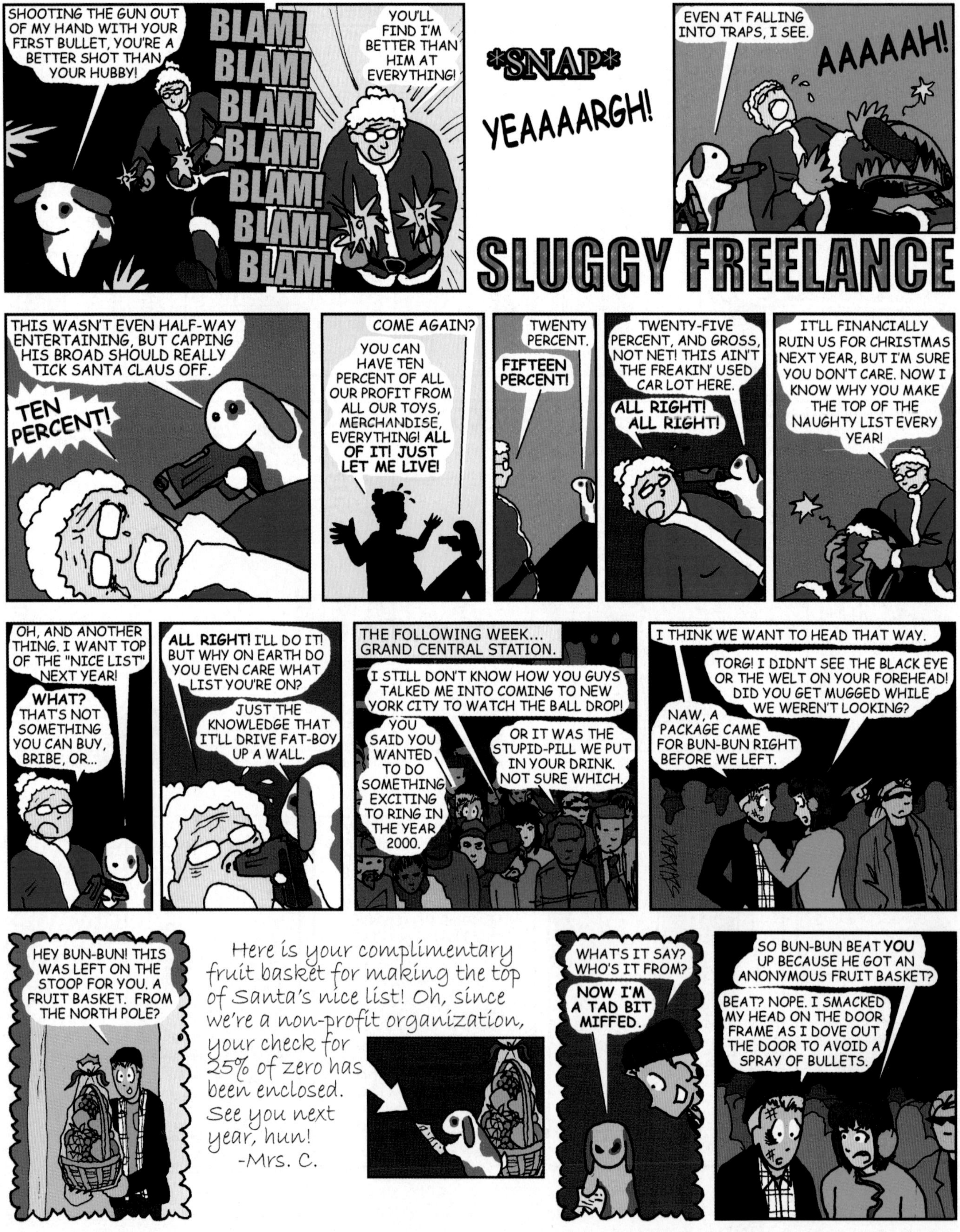
SHOOTING THE GUN OUT OF MY HAND WITH YOUR FIRST BULLET, YOU'RE A BETTER SHOT THAN YOUR HUBBY!
BLAM! BLAM! BLAM! BLAM! BLAM! BLAM! BLAM!
YOU'LL FIND I'M BETTER THAN HIM AT EVERYTHING!
SNAP
YEAAAARGH!
EVEN AT FALLING INTO TRAPS, I SEE.
AAAAAH!
SLUGGY FREELANCE
THIS WASN'T EVEN HALF-WAY ENTERTAINING, BUT CAPPING HIS BROAD SHOULD REALLY TICK SANTA CLAUS OFF.
TEN PERCENT!
COME AGAIN?
YOU CAN HAVE TEN PERCENT OF ALL OUR PROFIT FROM ALL OUR TOYS, MERCHANDISE, EVERYTHING! ALL OF IT! JUST LET ME LIVE!
TWENTY PERCENT.
FIFTEEN PERCENT!
TWENTY-FIVE PERCENT, AND GROSS, NOT NET! THIS AIN'T THE FREAKIN' USED CAR LOT HERE.
ALL RIGHT! ALL RIGHT!
IT'LL FINANCIALLY RUIN US FOR CHRISTMAS NEXT YEAR, BUT I'M SURE YOU DON'T CARE. NOW I KNOW WHY YOU MAKE THE TOP OF THE NAUGHTY LIST EVERY YEAR!
OH, AND ANOTHER THING. I WANT TOP OF THE "NICE LIST" NEXT YEAR!
WHAT? THAT'S NOT SOMETHING YOU CAN BUY, BRIBE, OR...
ALL RIGHT! I'LL DO IT! BUT WHY ON EARTH DO YOU EVEN CARE WHAT LIST YOU'RE ON?
JUST THE KNOWLEDGE THAT IT'LL DRIVE FAT-BOY UP A WALL.
THE FOLLOWING WEEK... GRAND CENTRAL STATION.
I STILL DON'T KNOW HOW YOU GUYS TALKED ME INTO COMING TO NEW YORK CITY TO WATCH THE BALL DROP!
YOU SAID YOU WANTED TO DO SOMETHING EXCITING TO RING IN THE YEAR 2000.
OR IT WAS THE STUPID-PILL WE PUT IN YOUR DRINK. NOT SURE WHICH.
I THINK WE WANT TO HEAD THAT WAY.
TORG! I DIDN'T SEE THE BLACK EYE OR THE WELT ON YOUR FOREHEAD! DID YOU GET MUGGED WHILE WE WEREN'T LOOKING?
NAW, A PACKAGE CAME FOR BUN-BUN RIGHT BEFORE WE LEFT.
HEY BUN-BUN! THIS WAS LEFT ON THE STOOP FOR YOU. A FRUIT BASKET. FROM THE NORTH POLE?
Here is your complimentary fruit basket for making the top of Santa's nice list! Oh, since we're a non-profit organization, your check for 25% of zero has been enclosed. See you next year, hun! -Mrs. C.
WHAT'S IT SAY? WHO'S IT FROM?
NOW I'M A TAD BIT MIFFED.
SO BUN-BUN BEAT YOU UP BECAUSE HE GOT AN ANONYMOUS FRUIT BASKET?
BEAT? NOPE. I SMACKED MY HEAD ON THE DOOR FRAME AS I DOVE OUT THE DOOR TO AVOID A SPRAY OF BULLETS.

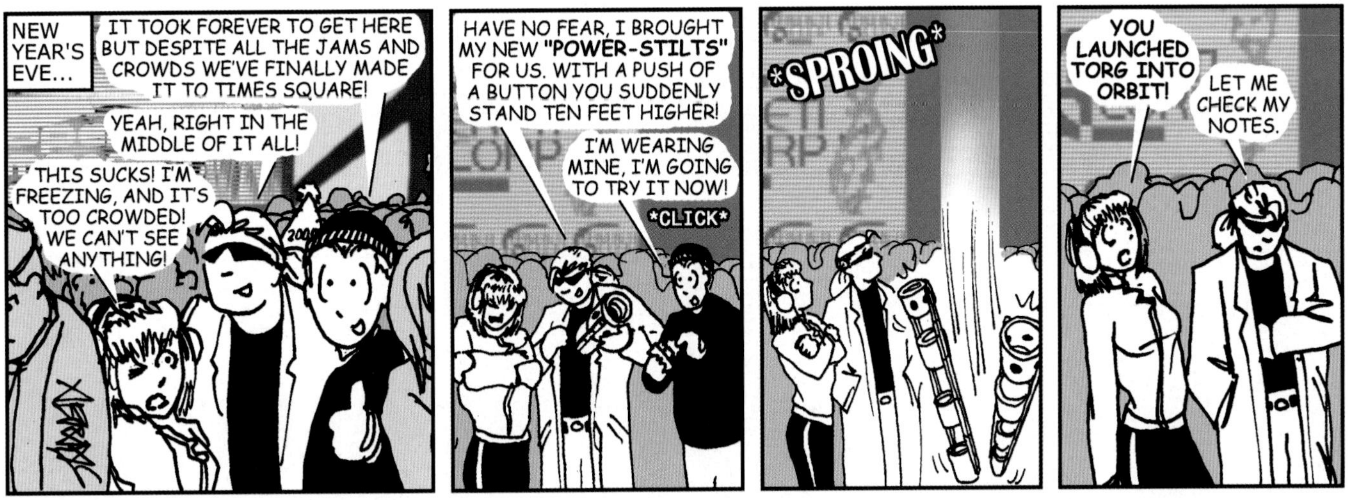
NEW YEAR'S EVE...
IT TOOK FOREVER TO GET HERE BUT DESPITE ALL THE JAMS AND CROWDS WE'VE FINALLY MADE IT TO TIMES SQUARE!
YEAH, RIGHT IN THE MIDDLE OF IT ALL!
THIS SUCKS! I'M FREEZING, AND IT'S TOO CROWDED! WE CAN'T SEE ANYTHING!
HAVE NO FEAR, I BROUGHT MY NEW "POWER-STILTS" FOR US. WITH A PUSH OF A BUTTON YOU SUDDENLY STAND TEN FEET HIGHER!
I'M WEARING MINE, I'M GOING TO TRY IT NOW!
CLICK
SPROING
YOU LAUNCHED TORG INTO ORBIT!
LET ME CHECK MY NOTES.

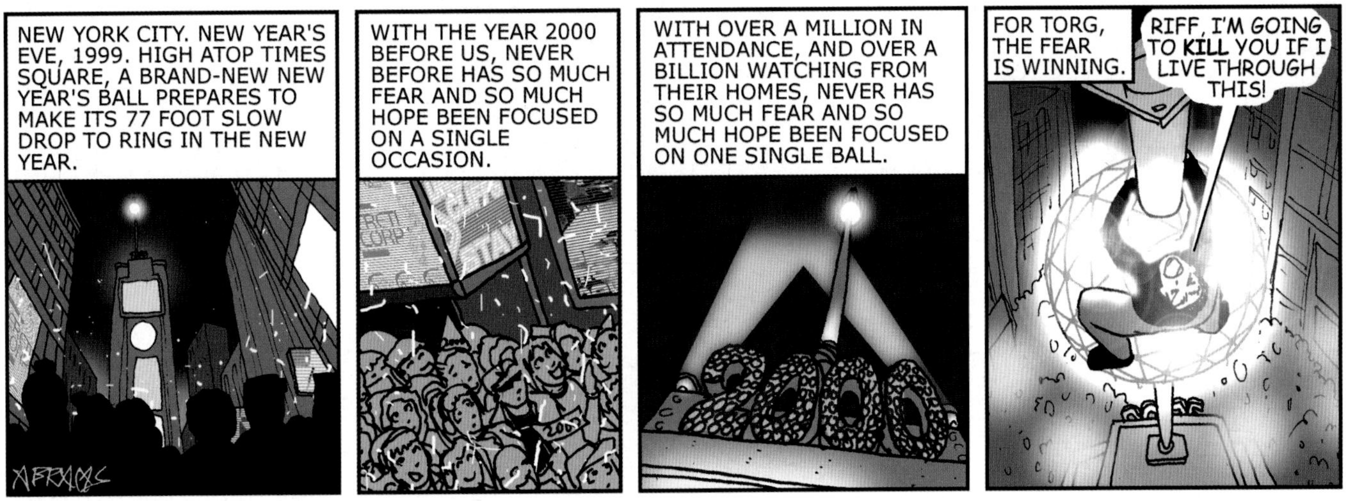
NEW YORK CITY. NEW YEAR'S EVE, 1999. HIGH ATOP TIMES SQUARE, A BRAND-NEW NEW YEAR'S BALL PREPARES TO MAKE ITS 77 FOOT SLOW DROP TO RING IN THE NEW YEAR.
WITH THE YEAR 2000 BEFORE US, NEVER BEFORE HAS SO MUCH FEAR AND SO MUCH HOPE BEEN FOCUSED ON A SINGLE OCCASION.
WITH OVER A MILLION IN ATTENDANCE, AND OVER A BILLION WATCHING FROM THEIR HOMES, NEVER HAS SO MUCH FEAR AND SO MUCH HOPE BEEN FOCUSED ON ONE SINGLE BALL.
FOR TORG, THE FEAR IS WINNING.
RIFF, I'M GOING TO KILL YOU IF I LIVE THROUGH THIS!

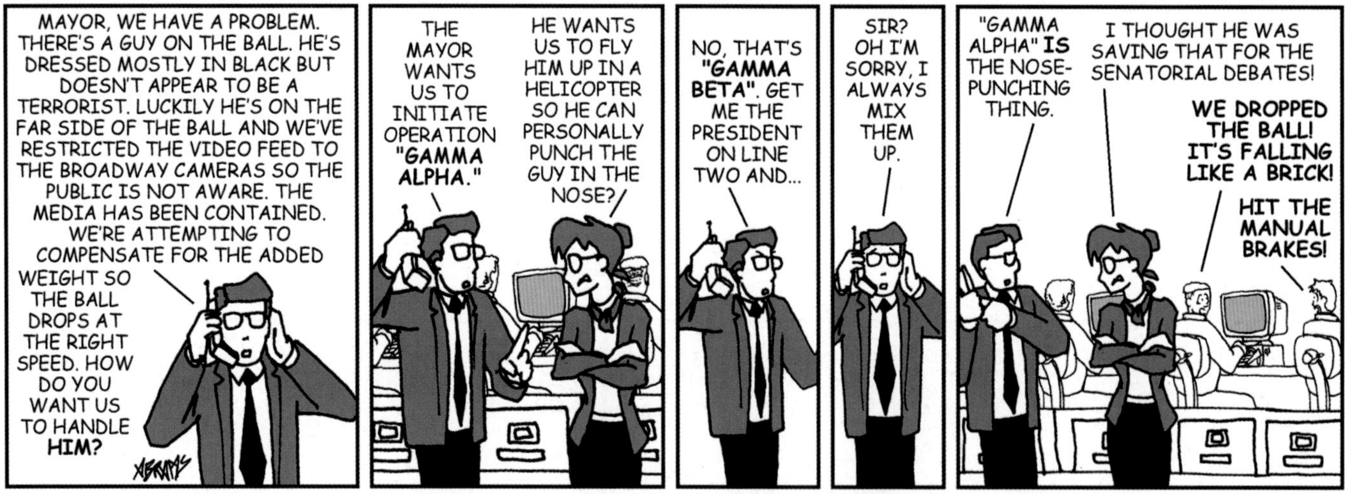
MAYOR, WE HAVE A PROBLEM. THERE'S A GUY ON THE BALL. HE'S DRESSED MOSTLY IN BLACK BUT DOESN'T APPEAR TO BE A TERRORIST. LUCKILY HE'S ON THE FAR SIDE OF THE BALL AND WE'VE RESTRICTED THE VIDEO FEED TO THE BROADWAY CAMERAS SO THE PUBLIC IS NOT AWARE. THE MEDIA HAS BEEN CONTAINED. WE'RE ATTEMPTING TO COMPENSATE FOR THE ADDED WEIGHT SO THE BALL DROPS AT THE RIGHT SPEED. HOW DO YOU WANT US TO HANDLE **HIM?**
THE MAYOR WANTS US TO INITIATE OPERATION **"GAMMA ALPHA."**
HE WANTS US TO FLY HIM UP IN A HELICOPTER SO HE CAN PERSONALLY PUNCH THE GUY IN THE NOSE?
NO, THAT'S **"GAMMA BETA"**. GET ME THE PRESIDENT ON LINE TWO AND...
SIR? OH I'M SORRY, I ALWAYS MIX THEM UP.
"GAMMA ALPHA" **IS** THE NOSE-PUNCHING THING.
I THOUGHT HE WAS SAVING THAT FOR THE SENATORIAL DEBATES!
WE DROPPED THE BALL! IT'S FALLING LIKE A BRICK!
HIT THE MANUAL BRAKES!

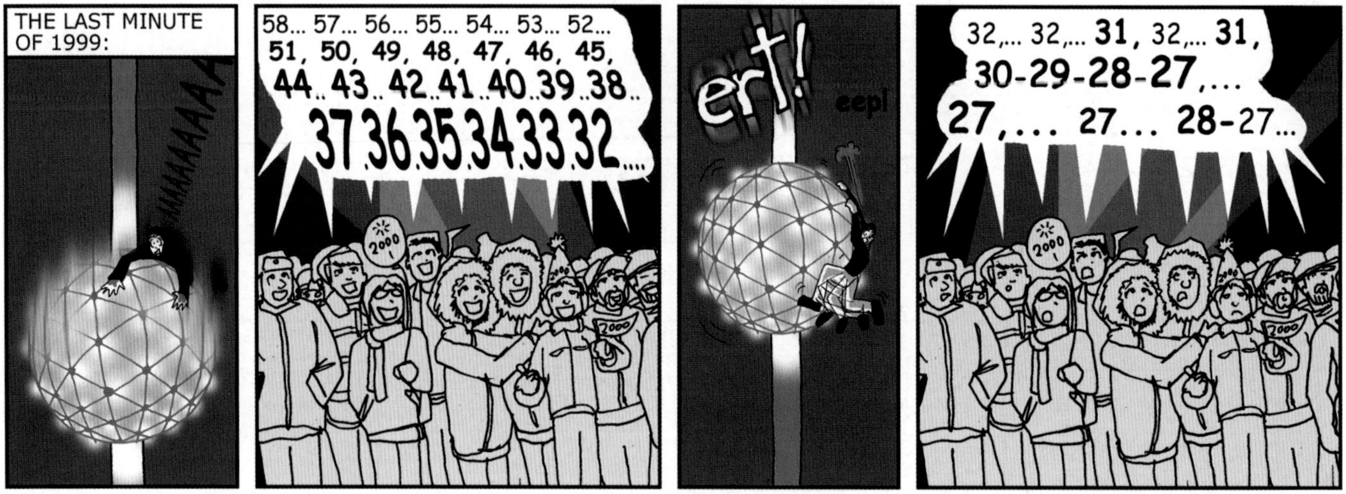
THE LAST MINUTE OF 1999:
58... 57... 56... 55... 54... 53... 52...
51, 50, 49, 48, 47, 46, 45,
44.. 43.. 42..41..40..39..38..
37 36 35 34 33 32....
ert!
eep!
32,... 32,... **31**, 32,... **31**,
30-29-28-27,...
27,... 27... 28-27...

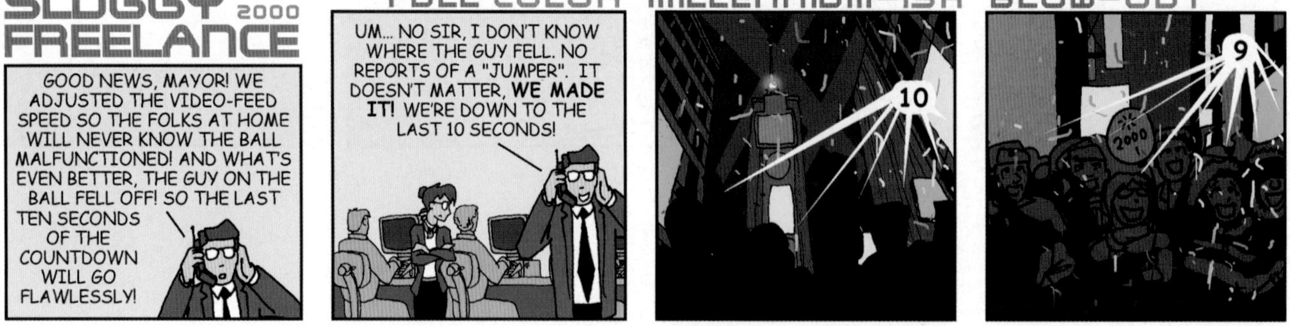
SLUGGY FREELANCE 2000
FULL COLOR MILLENNIUM-ISH BLOW-OUT
GOOD NEWS, MAYOR! WE ADJUSTED THE VIDEO-FEED SPEED SO THE FOLKS AT HOME WILL NEVER KNOW THE BALL MALFUNCTIONED! AND WHAT'S EVEN BETTER, THE GUY ON THE BALL FELL OFF! SO THE LAST TEN SECONDS OF THE COUNTDOWN WILL GO FLAWLESSLY!
UM... NO SIR, I DON'T KNOW WHERE THE GUY FELL. NO REPORTS OF A "JUMPER". IT DOESN'T MATTER, **WE MADE IT!** WE'RE DOWN TO THE LAST 10 SECONDS!
10
9

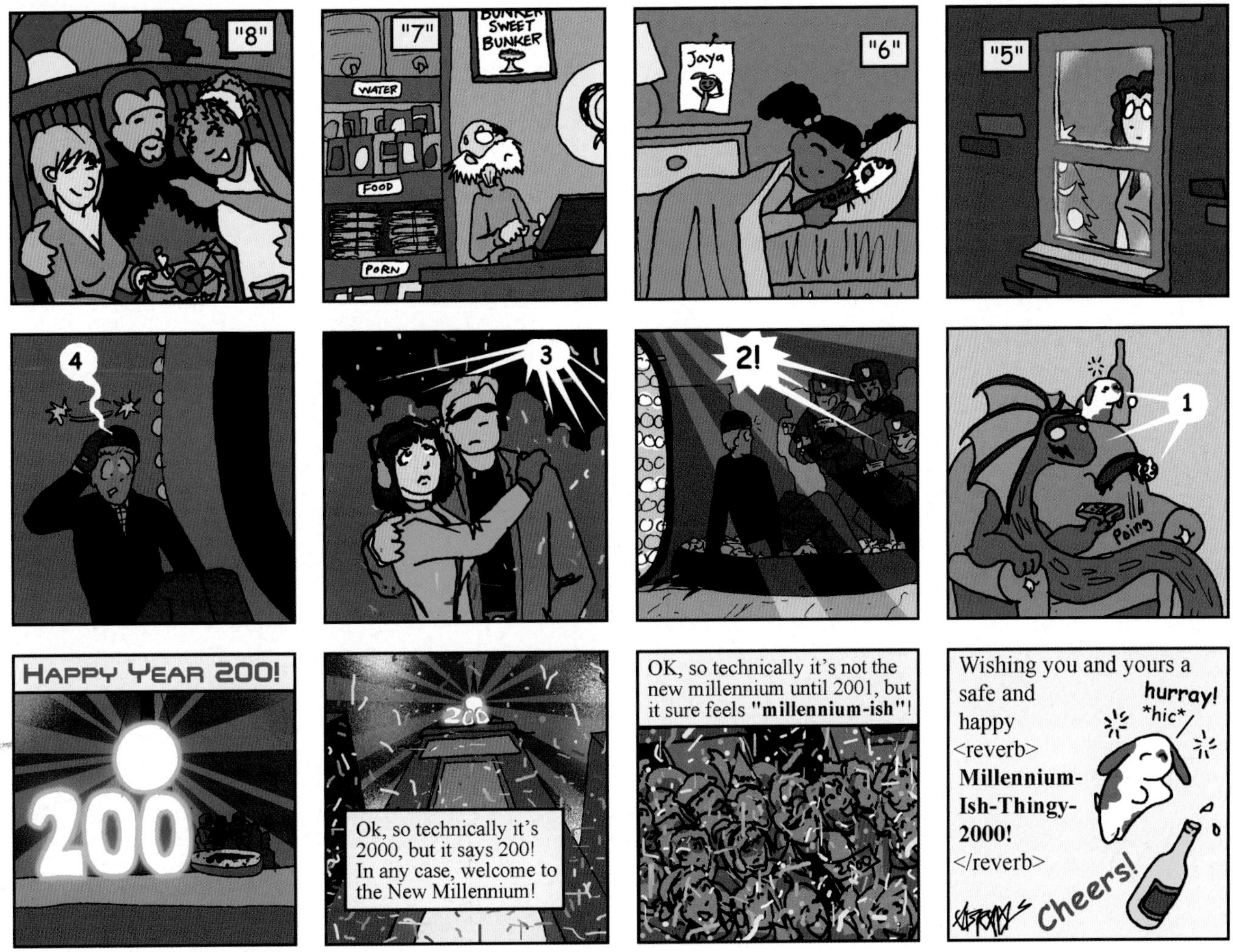
"8"
"7"
BUNKER SWEET BUNKER
WATER
FOOD
PORN
"6"
Jaya
"5"
4
3
2!
1
Poing
HAPPY YEAR 200!
200
Ok, so technically it's 2000, but it says 200! In any case, welcome to the New Millennium!
OK, so technically it's not the new millennium until 2001, but it sure feels **"millennium-ish"**!
Wishing you and yours a safe and happy <reverb> **Millennium-Ish-Thingy-2000!** </reverb>
hurray!
hic
Cheers!

SLUGGY FREELANCE

SORRY, THERE IS NO COMIC FOR TODAY DUE TO THE FACT THAT THE Y2K BUG HAS CAUSED THE PENCIL I USE TO LOCK-UP WHEN I TRY TO DRAW WITH IT. I AM WORKING VERY HARD TO GET THE PENCIL TO PAPER DESPITE THE BUG, BUT IT IS A LONG HUGE UPHILL BATTLE. THIS IS NOT... I REPEAT.. IS **NOT** A CHEAP TRICK TO GET OUT OF DOING THE COMIC FOR TODAY SO I MIGHT SPEND NEW YEAR'S EVE AND DAY WITH FRIENDS AND FAMILY. HOW MEAN OF YOU TO THINK OF SUCH A THING!

GOOD GOLLY, I JUST REALIZED I HAVEN'T CHECKED TO MAKE SURE MY PINK PEARL ERASER IS Y2K COMPATIBLE!

www.sluggy.com

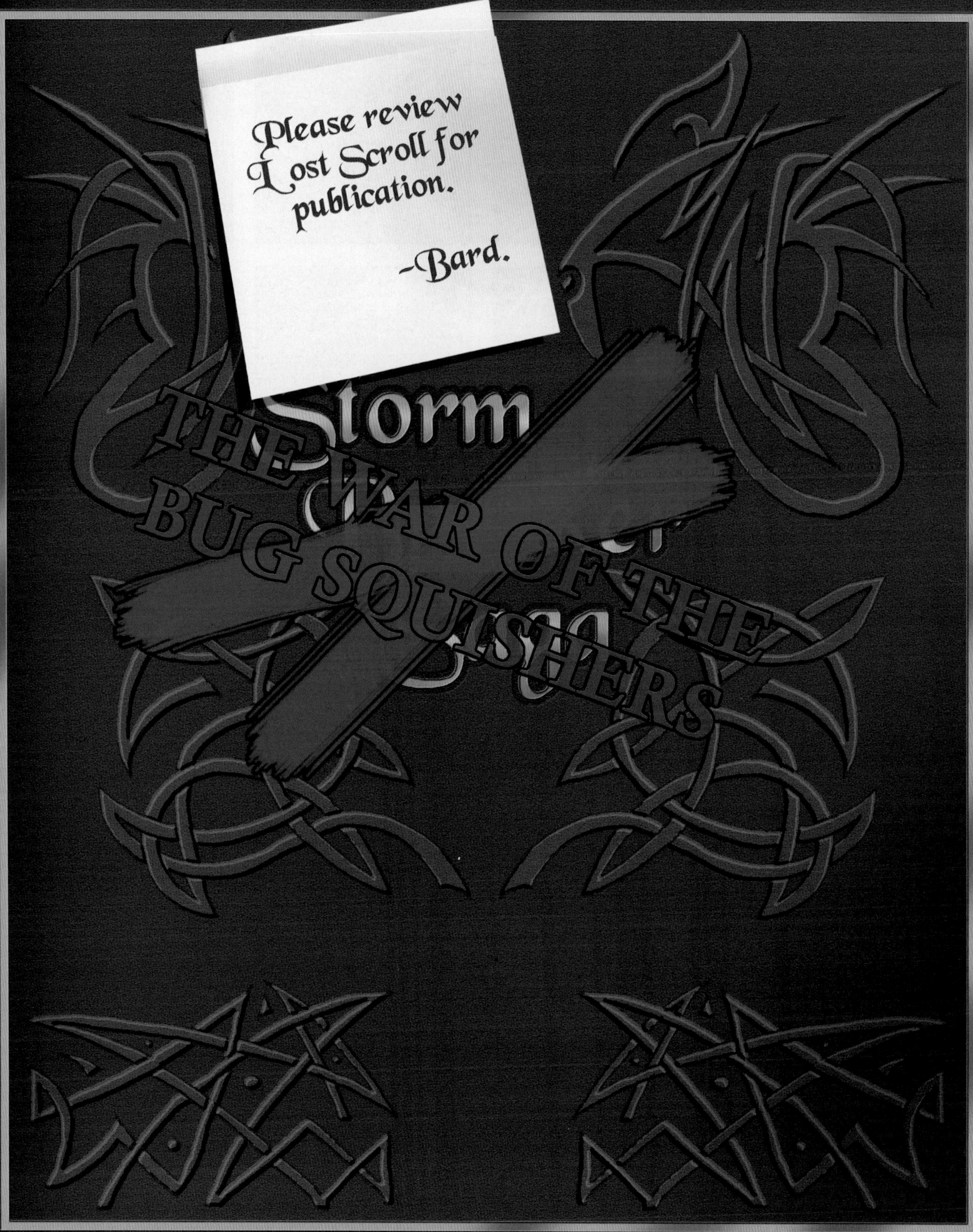
Please review
Lost Scroll for
publication.
-Bard.
Storm
THE WAR OF THE
BUG SQUISHERS

ALTHOUGH EVERYONE KNOWS THE HISTORICAL EPIC "THE WAR OF THE BUG SQUISHERS", MOST HAVE NOT HEARD OF THE LEGEND OF THE "LOST SCROLL". EACH SCROLL OF THE EPIC WAS CLEARLY ANNOTATED AND NUMBERED, AND MOST SCHOLARS AGREE THAT THERE WAS A MISSING SCROLL, CHRONOLOGICALLY PLACED BETWEEN THE BARD'S JOINING THE QUEST, AND THE HERMIT WARRIOR OF ASCETIA. WAS THIS MISSING SCROLL A SIMPLE CLERICAL ERROR BY THE BARD? WAS IT STOLEN TO HIDE SOME SECRETS IT CONTAINED? NOW THE TRUTH CAN BE TOLD AS THE LOST SCROLL HAS BEEN FOUND, REVEALING THE LOST CHAPTER OF THE EPIC, NOW AND FOREVER KNOWN AS...

THE FLIGHT FROM OHMELET

"THE ONE KNOWN AS "TORG", LADY ZOË, COURT ADVISOR OSRIC, AND MYSELF WERE TRYING TO REACH THE HERMIT-WARRIOR OF ASCETIA, IN ORDER TO GET THE MAP TO THE CAVE OF YFFI, AND END OUR QUEST. BUT ASCETIA WAS FAR TO THE EAST. A BIT **TOO** FAR."

WELCOME TO THE HAMLET OF OHMELET. NO ONE HERE SHOULD KNOW WHAT LORD TORGAMOUS LOOKS LIKE, SO YOUR IDENTITY SHOULD BE SAFE, M'LORD.

WE'LL NEVER REACH ASCETIA ON FOOT.

AND WE'RE OUT OF FOOD!

WELL, WE'RE GOING TO NEED A HORSE AND CART, BUT WE'RE DOWN TO OUR LAST TWO COINS.

I'LL PICK UP SOME SUPPLIES, YOU GUYS SEE WHAT SOURCES OF INCOME YOU CAN FIND AROUND HERE.

YE OLDE STUFFED MICRO-DRAGONS

THIS BOX!

EXCUSE ME?

I'VE HELD THIS BOX FOR FORTY YEARS, AND I WAS INSTRUCTED TO GIVE IT TO SOMEONE SPECIAL. AND THAT SOMEONE IS **YOU**! I KNOW, FOR I CAN SEE THE FUTURE!

YOU CAN TELL I'M FROM THE FUTURE?!?

NO, I SEE A FUTURE TIME IN WHICH THE WORD "SPECIAL" REFERS TO SOMEONE WITH SOME TYPE OF HANDICAP, MENTAL DEFICIENCY IN YOUR CASE. HOWEVER, NOW THAT I THINK ABOUT IT, BEING STUPID IS NOT A HANDICAP, AT LEAST NOT IN THE SENSE THAT IT ALLOWS YOU TO GET BETTER "PARKING". IN THE FUTURE, "PARKING" HAS NOTHING TO DO WITH "PARKS", BUT WITH...

ALL RIGHT! ALL RIGHT! GIVE ME THE DAMN BOX!

THAT'LL BE A COIN!

I THOUGHT YOU WERE GIVING ME THE BOX.

THAT'S ONLY 'CAUSE I THOUGHT YOU WERE GIVING ME A COIN!

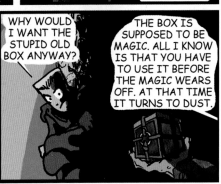

WHY WOULD I WANT THE STUPID OLD BOX ANYWAY?

THE BOX IS SUPPOSED TO BE MAGIC. ALL I KNOW IS THAT YOU HAVE TO USE IT BEFORE THE MAGIC WEARS OFF. AT THAT TIME IT TURNS TO DUST.

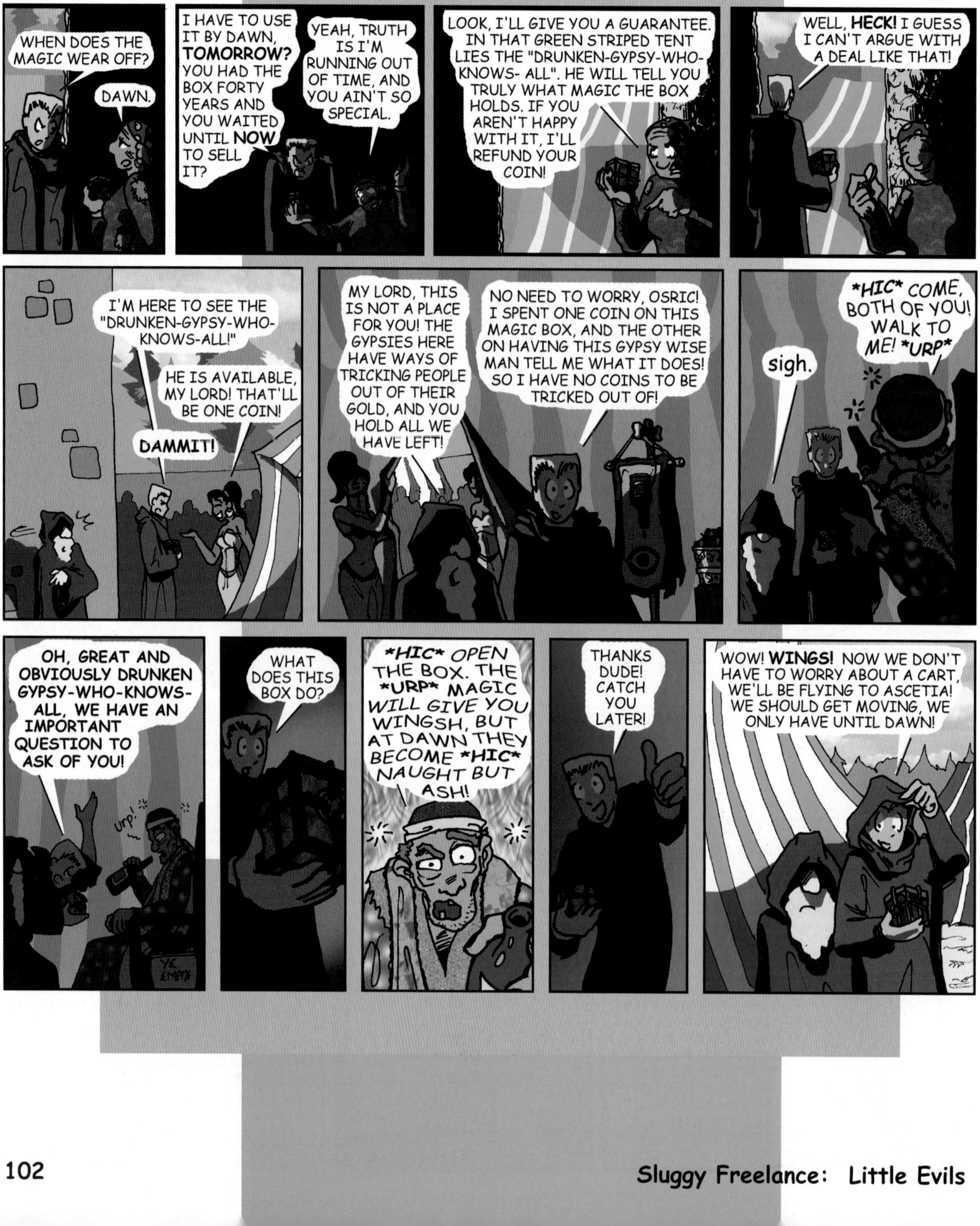
WHEN DOES THE MAGIC WEAR OFF?
DAWN.
I HAVE TO USE IT BY DAWN, TOMORROW? YOU HAD THE BOX FORTY YEARS AND YOU WAITED UNTIL NOW TO SELL IT?
YEAH, TRUTH IS I'M RUNNING OUT OF TIME, AND YOU AIN'T SO SPECIAL.
LOOK, I'LL GIVE YOU A GUARANTEE. IN THAT GREEN STRIPED TENT LIES THE "DRUNKEN-GYPSY-WHO-KNOWS- ALL". HE WILL TELL YOU TRULY WHAT MAGIC THE BOX HOLDS. IF YOU AREN'T HAPPY WITH IT, I'LL REFUND YOUR COIN!
WELL, HECK! I GUESS I CAN'T ARGUE WITH A DEAL LIKE THAT!
I'M HERE TO SEE THE "DRUNKEN-GYPSY-WHO-KNOWS-ALL!"
HE IS AVAILABLE, MY LORD! THAT'LL BE ONE COIN!
DAMMIT!
MY LORD, THIS IS NOT A PLACE FOR YOU! THE GYPSIES HERE HAVE WAYS OF TRICKING PEOPLE OUT OF THEIR GOLD, AND YOU HOLD ALL WE HAVE LEFT!
NO NEED TO WORRY, OSRIC! I SPENT ONE COIN ON THIS MAGIC BOX, AND THE OTHER ON HAVING THIS GYPSY WISE MAN TELL ME WHAT IT DOES! SO I HAVE NO COINS TO BE TRICKED OUT OF!
sigh.
HIC COME, BOTH OF YOU! WALK TO ME! *URP*
OH, GREAT AND OBVIOUSLY DRUNKEN GYPSY-WHO-KNOWS-ALL, WE HAVE AN IMPORTANT QUESTION TO ASK OF YOU!
urp!
WHAT DOES THIS BOX DO?
HIC OPEN THE BOX. THE *URP* MAGIC WILL GIVE YOU WINGSH, BUT AT DAWN THEY BECOME *HIC* NAUGHT BUT ASH!
THANKS DUDE! CATCH YOU LATER!
WOW! WINGS! NOW WE DON'T HAVE TO WORRY ABOUT A CART, WE'LL BE FLYING TO ASCETIA! WE SHOULD GET MOVING, WE ONLY HAVE UNTIL DAWN!

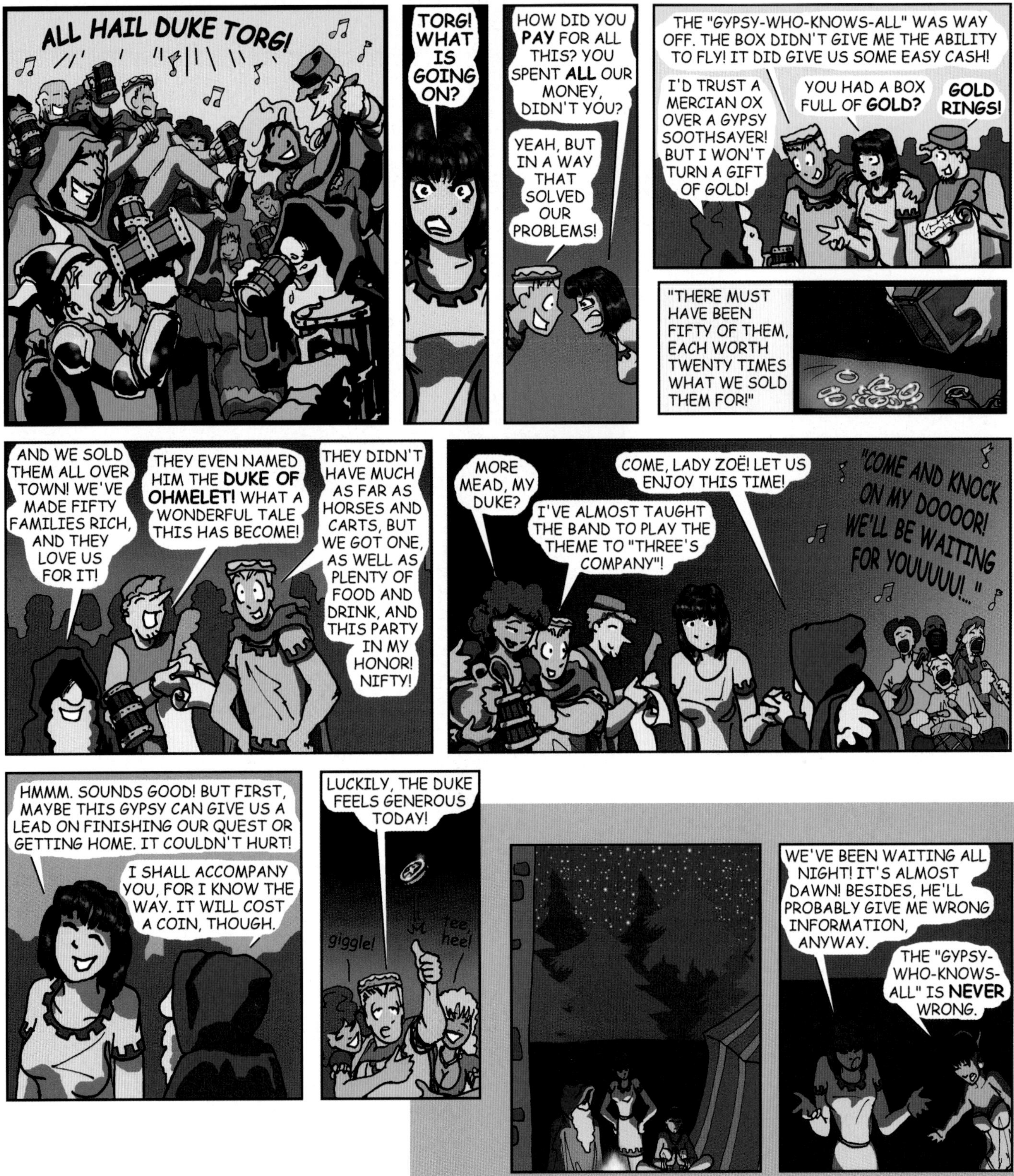
ALL HAIL DUKE TORG!
TORG! WHAT IS GOING ON?
HOW DID YOU PAY FOR ALL THIS? YOU SPENT ALL OUR MONEY, DIDN'T YOU?
YEAH, BUT IN A WAY THAT SOLVED OUR PROBLEMS!
THE "GYPSY-WHO-KNOWS-ALL" WAS WAY OFF. THE BOX DIDN'T GIVE ME THE ABILITY TO FLY! IT DID GIVE US SOME EASY CASH!
I'D TRUST A MERCIAN OX OVER A GYPSY SOOTHSAYER! BUT I WON'T TURN A GIFT OF GOLD!
YOU HAD A BOX FULL OF GOLD?
GOLD RINGS!
"THERE MUST HAVE BEEN FIFTY OF THEM, EACH WORTH TWENTY TIMES WHAT WE SOLD THEM FOR!"
AND WE SOLD THEM ALL OVER TOWN! WE'VE MADE FIFTY FAMILIES RICH, AND THEY LOVE US FOR IT!
THEY EVEN NAMED HIM THE DUKE OF OHMELET! WHAT A WONDERFUL TALE THIS HAS BECOME!
THEY DIDN'T HAVE MUCH AS FAR AS HORSES AND CARTS, BUT WE GOT ONE, AS WELL AS PLENTY OF FOOD AND DRINK, AND THIS PARTY IN MY HONOR! NIFTY!
MORE MEAD, MY DUKE?
I'VE ALMOST TAUGHT THE BAND TO PLAY THE THEME TO "THREE'S COMPANY"!
COME, LADY ZOË! LET US ENJOY THIS TIME!
"COME AND KNOCK ON MY DOOOOR! WE'LL BE WAITING FOR YOUUUUU!..."
HMMM. SOUNDS GOOD! BUT FIRST, MAYBE THIS GYPSY CAN GIVE US A LEAD ON FINISHING OUR QUEST OR GETTING HOME. IT COULDN'T HURT!
I SHALL ACCOMPANY YOU, FOR I KNOW THE WAY. IT WILL COST A COIN, THOUGH.
LUCKILY, THE DUKE FEELS GENEROUS TODAY!
giggle!
Tee, hee!
WE'VE BEEN WAITING ALL NIGHT! IT'S ALMOST DAWN! BESIDES, HE'LL PROBABLY GIVE ME WRONG INFORMATION, ANYWAY.
THE "GYPSY-WHO-KNOWS-ALL" IS NEVER WRONG.

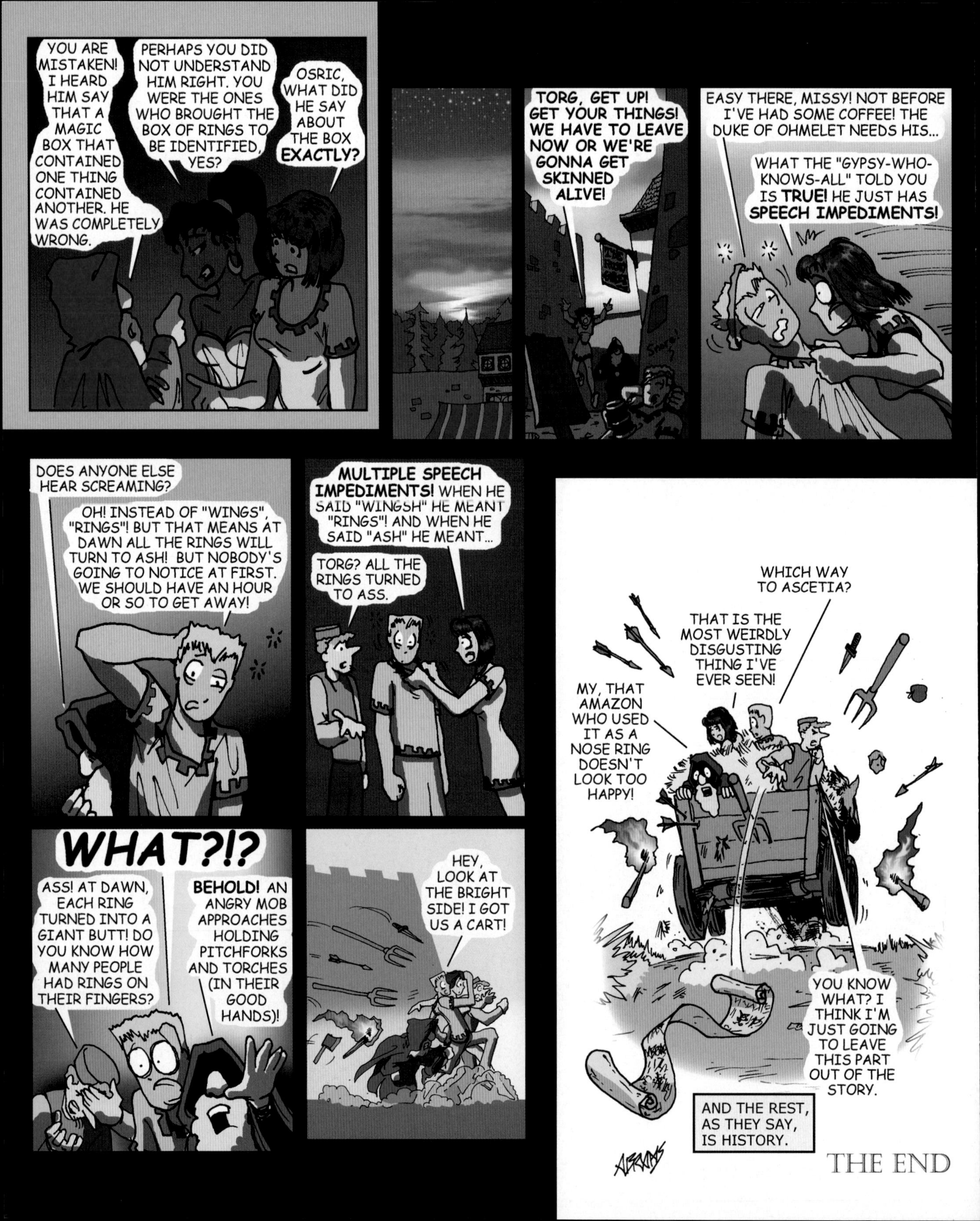

YOU ARE MISTAKEN! I HEARD HIM SAY THAT A MAGIC BOX THAT CONTAINED ONE THING CONTAINED ANOTHER. HE WAS COMPLETELY WRONG.
PERHAPS YOU DID NOT UNDERSTAND HIM RIGHT. YOU WERE THE ONES WHO BROUGHT THE BOX OF RINGS TO BE IDENTIFIED, YES?
OSRIC, WHAT DID HE SAY ABOUT THE BOX EXACTLY?
TORG, GET UP! GET YOUR THINGS! WE HAVE TO LEAVE NOW OR WE'RE GONNA GET SKINNED ALIVE!
EASY THERE, MISSY! NOT BEFORE I'VE HAD SOME COFFEE! THE DUKE OF OHMELET NEEDS HIS...
WHAT THE "GYPSY-WHO-KNOWS-ALL" TOLD YOU IS TRUE! HE JUST HAS SPEECH IMPEDIMENTS!
DOES ANYONE ELSE HEAR SCREAMING?
OH! INSTEAD OF "WINGS", "RINGS"! BUT THAT MEANS AT DAWN ALL THE RINGS WILL TURN TO ASH! BUT NOBODY'S GOING TO NOTICE AT FIRST. WE SHOULD HAVE AN HOUR OR SO TO GET AWAY!
MULTIPLE SPEECH IMPEDIMENTS! WHEN HE SAID "WINGSH" HE MEANT "RINGS"! AND WHEN HE SAID "ASH" HE MEANT...
TORG? ALL THE RINGS TURNED TO ASS.
WHAT?!?
ASS! AT DAWN, EACH RING TURNED INTO A GIANT BUTT! DO YOU KNOW HOW MANY PEOPLE HAD RINGS ON THEIR FINGERS?
BEHOLD! AN ANGRY MOB APPROACHES HOLDING PITCHFORKS AND TORCHES (IN THEIR GOOD HANDS)!
HEY, LOOK AT THE BRIGHT SIDE! I GOT US A CART!
WHICH WAY TO ASCETIA?
THAT IS THE MOST WEIRDLY DISGUSTING THING I'VE EVER SEEN!
MY, THAT AMAZON WHO USED IT AS A NOSE RING DOESN'T LOOK TOO HAPPY!
YOU KNOW WHAT? I THINK I'M JUST GOING TO LEAVE THIS PART OUT OF THE STORY.
AND THE REST, AS THEY SAY, IS HISTORY.
THE END

SLUGGY FREELANCE BOOK 5
YIPPY SKIPPY, THE EVIL!
by Pete Abrams

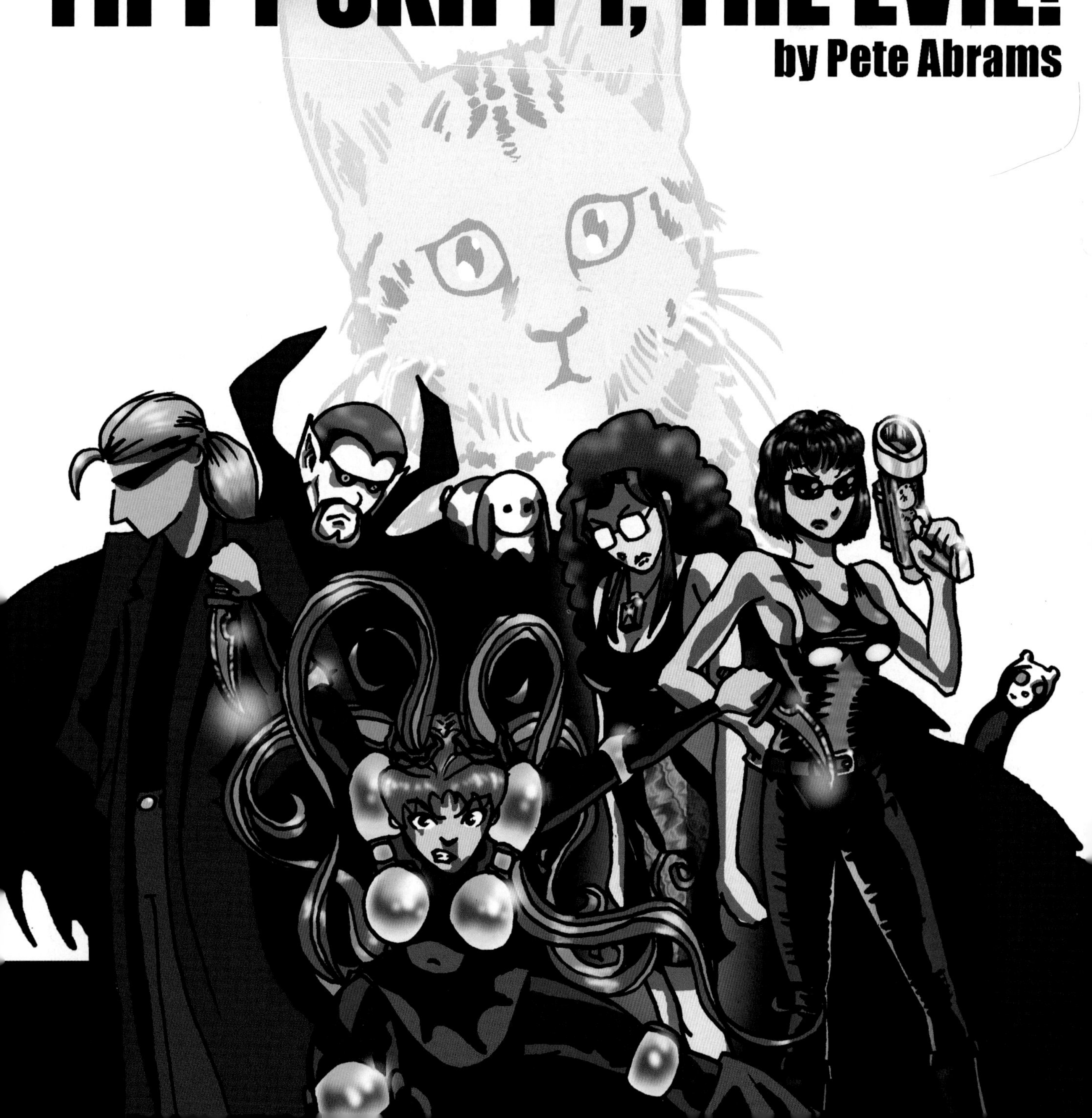

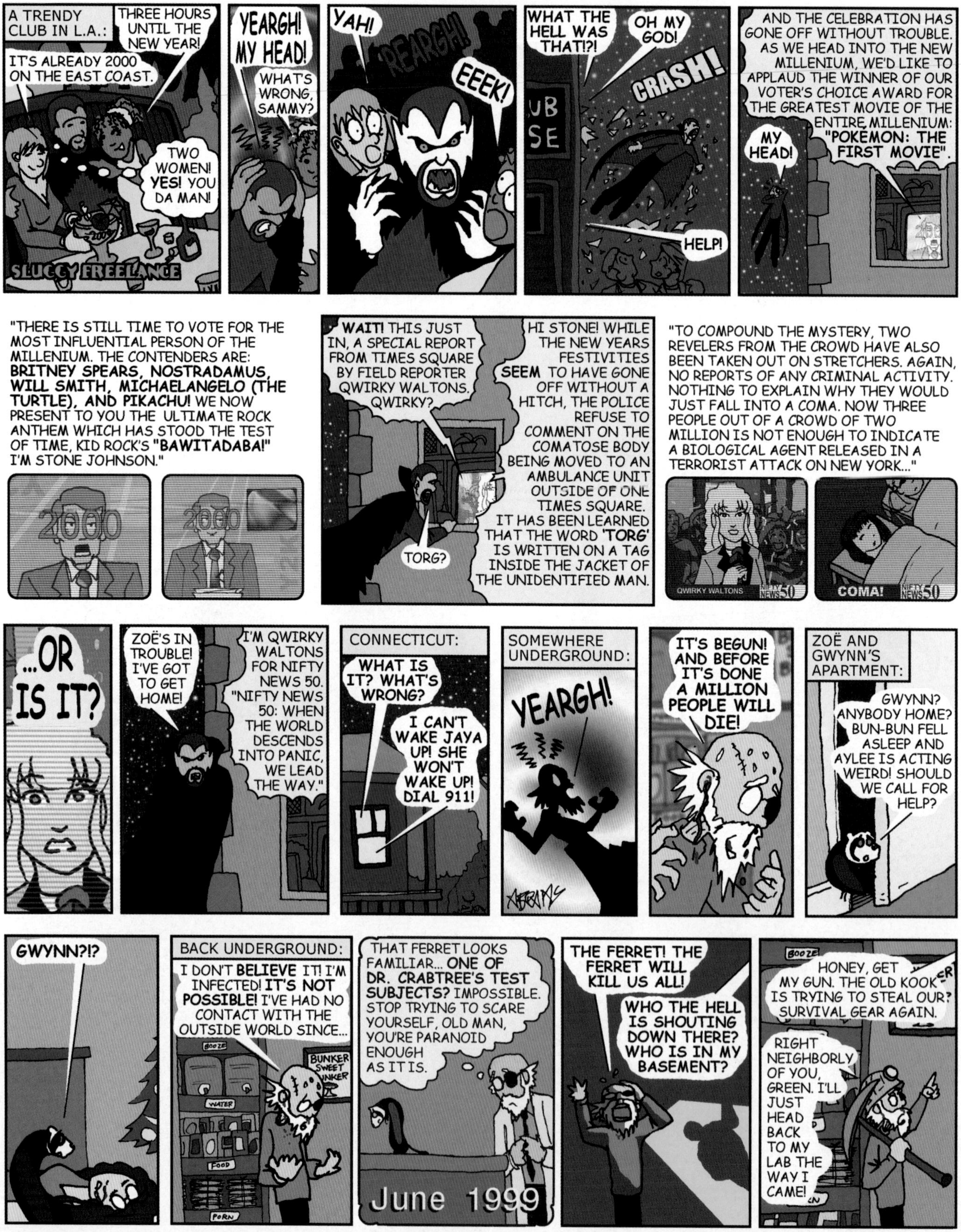

A TRENDY CLUB IN L.A.:
THREE HOURS UNTIL THE NEW YEAR!
IT'S ALREADY 2000 ON THE EAST COAST.
TWO WOMEN! YES! YOU DA MAN!
SLUGGY FREELANCE
YEARGH! MY HEAD!
WHAT'S WRONG, SAMMY?
YAH!
REARGH!
EEEK!
WHAT THE HELL WAS THAT!?!
OH MY GOD!
CRASH!
HELP!
AND THE CELEBRATION HAS GONE OFF WITHOUT TROUBLE. AS WE HEAD INTO THE NEW MILLENIUM, WE'D LIKE TO APPLAUD THE WINNER OF OUR VOTER'S CHOICE AWARD FOR THE GREATEST MOVIE OF THE ENTIRE MILLENIUM: "POKEMON: THE FIRST MOVIE".
MY HEAD!
"THERE IS STILL TIME TO VOTE FOR THE MOST INFLUENTIAL PERSON OF THE MILLENIUM. THE CONTENDERS ARE: BRITNEY SPEARS, NOSTRADAMUS, WILL SMITH, MICHAELANGELO (THE TURTLE), AND PIKACHU! WE NOW PRESENT TO YOU THE ULTIMATE ROCK ANTHEM WHICH HAS STOOD THE TEST OF TIME, KID ROCK'S "BAWITADABA!" I'M STONE JOHNSON."
2000
WAIT! THIS JUST IN, A SPECIAL REPORT FROM TIMES SQUARE BY FIELD REPORTER QWIRKY WALTONS. QWIRKY?
HI STONE! WHILE THE NEW YEARS FESTIVITIES SEEM TO HAVE GONE OFF WITHOUT A HITCH, THE POLICE REFUSE TO COMMENT ON THE COMATOSE BODY BEING MOVED TO AN AMBULANCE UNIT OUTSIDE OF ONE TIMES SQUARE. IT HAS BEEN LEARNED THAT THE WORD 'TORG' IS WRITTEN ON A TAG INSIDE THE JACKET OF THE UNIDENTIFIED MAN.
TORG?
"TO COMPOUND THE MYSTERY, TWO REVELERS FROM THE CROWD HAVE ALSO BEEN TAKEN OUT ON STRETCHERS. AGAIN, NO REPORTS OF ANY CRIMINAL ACTIVITY. NOTHING TO EXPLAIN WHY THEY WOULD JUST FALL INTO A COMA. NOW THREE PEOPLE OUT OF A CROWD OF TWO MILLION IS NOT ENOUGH TO INDICATE A BIOLOGICAL AGENT RELEASED IN A TERRORIST ATTACK ON NEW YORK..."
QWIRKY WALTONS
NIFTY NEWS 50
COMA!
NIFTY NEWS 50
...OR IS IT?
ZOË'S IN TROUBLE! I'VE GOT TO GET HOME!
I'M QWIRKY WALTONS FOR NIFTY NEWS 50. "NIFTY NEWS 50: WHEN THE WORLD DESCENDS INTO PANIC, WE LEAD THE WAY."
CONNECTICUT:
WHAT IS IT? WHAT'S WRONG?
I CAN'T WAKE JAYA UP! SHE WON'T WAKE UP! DIAL 911!
SOMEWHERE UNDERGROUND:
YEARGH!
IT'S BEGUN! AND BEFORE IT'S DONE A MILLION PEOPLE WILL DIE!
ZOË AND GWYNN'S APARTMENT:
GWYNN? ANYBODY HOME? BUN-BUN FELL ASLEEP AND AYLEE IS ACTING WEIRD! SHOULD WE CALL FOR HELP?
GWYNN?!?
BACK UNDERGROUND:
I DON'T BELIEVE IT! I'M INFECTED! IT'S NOT POSSIBLE! I'VE HAD NO CONTACT WITH THE OUTSIDE WORLD SINCE...
BOOZE
WATER
FOOD
PORN
BUNKER SWEET
THAT FERRET LOOKS FAMILIAR... ONE OF DR. CRABTREE'S TEST SUBJECTS? IMPOSSIBLE. STOP TRYING TO SCARE YOURSELF, OLD MAN, YOU'RE PARANOID ENOUGH AS IT IS.
June 1999
THE FERRET! THE FERRET WILL KILL US ALL!
WHO THE HELL IS SHOUTING DOWN THERE? WHO IS IN MY BASEMENT?
BOOZE
HONEY, GET MY GUN. THE OLD KOOK IS TRYING TO STEAL OUR SURVIVAL GEAR AGAIN.
RIGHT NEIGHBORLY OF YOU, GREEN. I'LL JUST HEAD BACK TO MY LAB THE WAY I CAME!

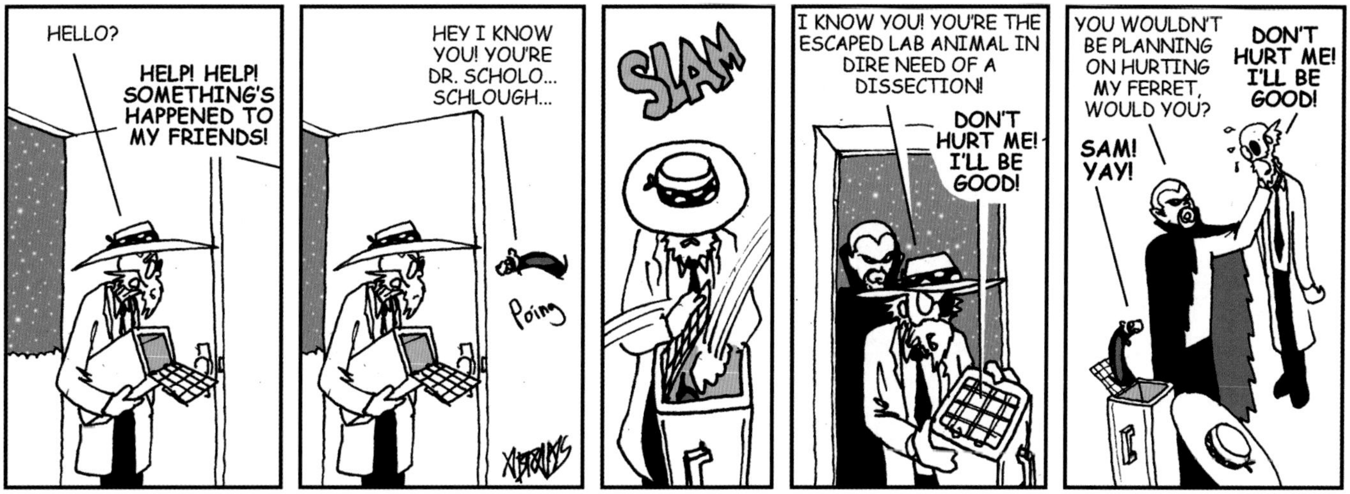
HELLO?
HELP! HELP! SOMETHING'S HAPPENED TO MY FRIENDS!
HEY I KNOW YOU! YOU'RE DR. SCHOLO... SCHLOUGH...
Poing
SLAM
I KNOW YOU! YOU'RE THE ESCAPED LAB ANIMAL IN DIRE NEED OF A DISSECTION!
DON'T HURT ME! I'LL BE GOOD!
YOU WOULDN'T BE PLANNING ON HURTING MY FERRET, WOULD YOU?
DON'T HURT ME! I'LL BE GOOD!
SAM! YAY!

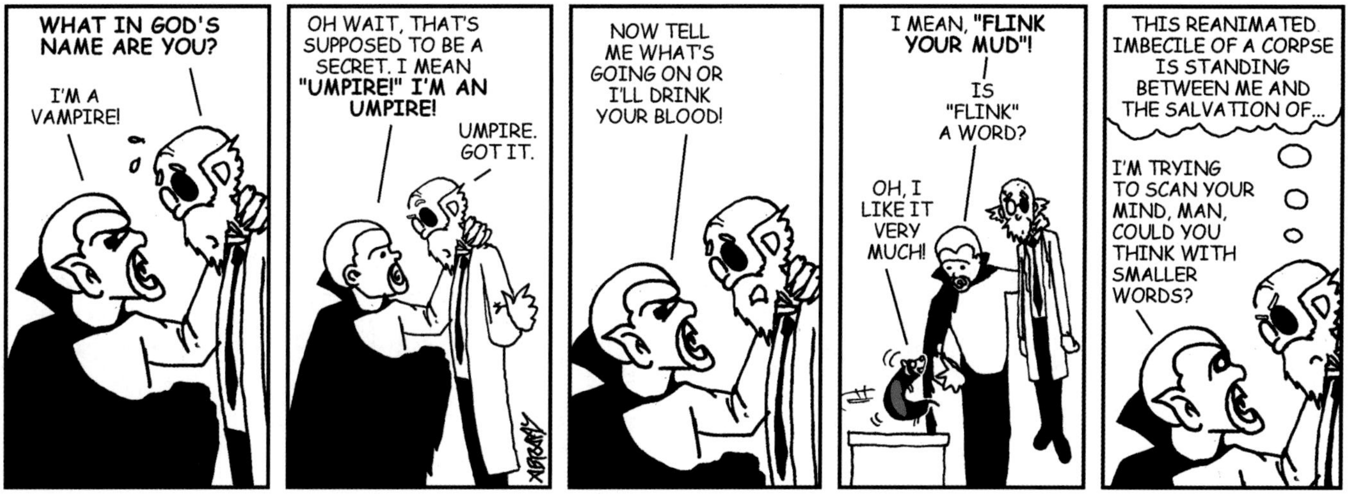
WHAT IN GOD'S NAME ARE YOU?
I'M A VAMPIRE!
OH WAIT, THAT'S SUPPOSED TO BE A SECRET. I MEAN "UMPIRE!" I'M AN UMPIRE!
UMPIRE. GOT IT.
NOW TELL ME WHAT'S GOING ON OR I'LL DRINK YOUR BLOOD!
I MEAN, "FLINK YOUR MUD"!
IS "FLINK" A WORD?
OH, I LIKE IT VERY MUCH!
THIS REANIMATED IMBECILE OF A CORPSE IS STANDING BETWEEN ME AND THE SALVATION OF...
I'M TRYING TO SCAN YOUR MIND, MAN, COULD YOU THINK WITH SMALLER WORDS?

I'M FROM THE FUTURE, AN ALTERNATE TIMELINE NOW, AND I'VE SEEN THIS DISEASE FIRST HAND. THE DISEASE HIT DURING THE HEIGHT OF OUR WAR WITH THE DEMON, JUST AFTER THE START OF THE YEAR 2000, WHICH IS WHERE IT GOT THE NICKNAME **"THE Y2K BUG"**. AN INANE YET PROFOUND NICKNAME AS IT TURNS OUT. OVER A MILLION PEOPLE DIED. WE THOUGHT THE DISEASE WAS PART THE DEMON'S PLAN OF WORLD DOMINANCE, BUT AFTER SOME RESEARCH, WE FOUND THE DISEASE HAD NOTHING TO DO WITH THE DEMON AT ALL.

WE CREATED A VACCINE OF SORTS, BUT IT WAS TOO LATE TO HELP ANYONE. THE DISEASE HAD RUN ITS COURSE. WE KNEW WHAT IT WAS, BUT WE NEVER NEW WHY IT WAS. WE NEVER KNEW THE REASON FOR IT. AND WE NEVER KNEW THE SOURCE.

THIS IS WHAT WE **DID** KNOW. SOMETHING INFECTED A COUPLE DOZEN PEOPLE WITH A DISEASE THAT CAUSED THEM TO FALL INTO A COMA THAT LASTED A WEEK OR SO. THOSE INFECTED AWOKE AS CARRIERS THEMSELVES, BUT THE DISEASE HAD CHANGED ITS MODUS OPERANDI ENTIRELY. INSTEAD OF INDUCING COMAS, IT SIMPLY SPREAD, AND SPREAD, AND SPREAD. WITHIN 48 HOURS, A MILLION PEOPLE WERE INFECTED, AND 48 HOURS AFTER THAT, THEY WERE ALL DEAD.

I'M INFECTED NOW, AND WOULD BE IN A COMA IF NOT FOR THE VACCINE WE CREATED IN THE FUTURE, BUT I HAVE NO IDEA HOW SAFE I'LL BE WHEN THE DISEASE HITS PHASE 2 IN A WEEK. BUT NOW... NOW THAT I KNOW THE CAUSE, I MAY BE ABLE TO STOP A GRIM HISTORY FROM TAKING PLACE.

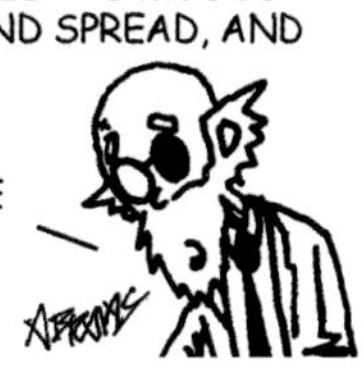

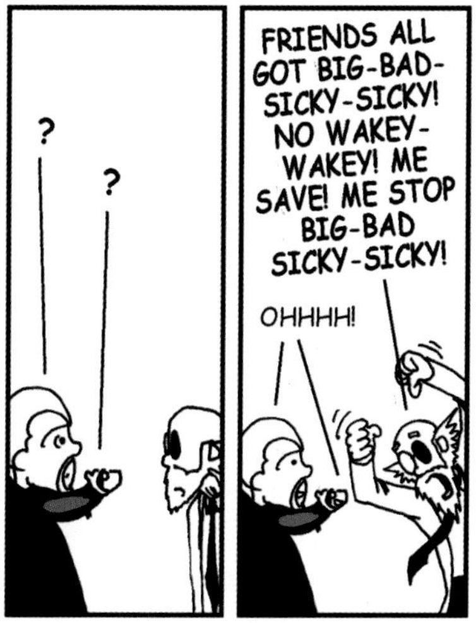
?
?
FRIENDS ALL GOT BIG-BAD-SICKY-SICKY! NO WAKEY-WAKEY! ME SAVE! ME STOP BIG-BAD SICKY-SICKY!
OHHHH!

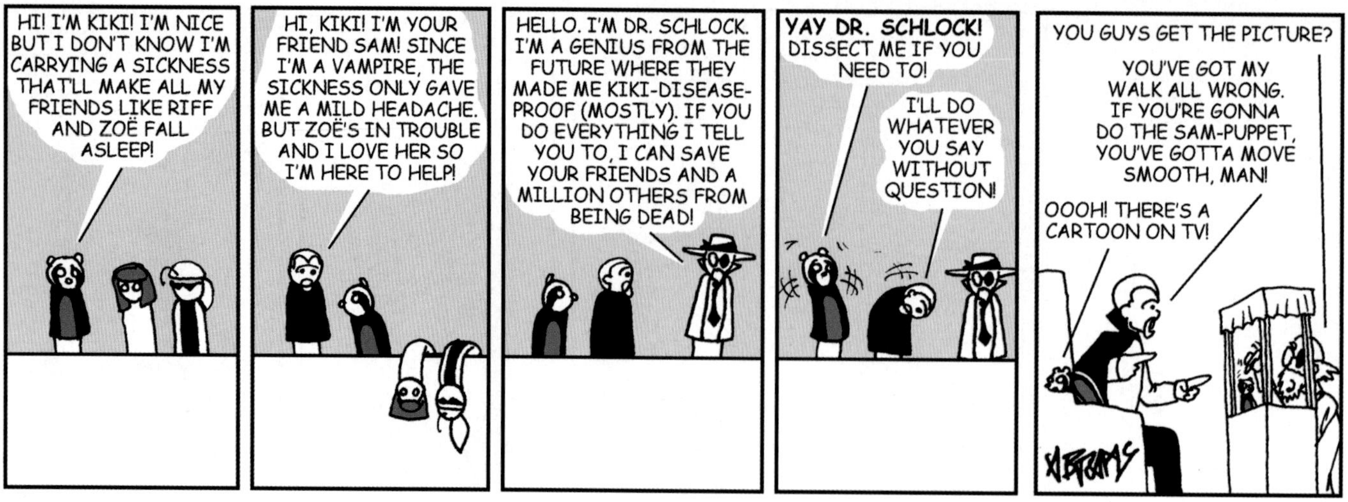
HI! I'M KIKI! I'M NICE BUT I DON'T KNOW I'M CARRYING A SICKNESS THAT'LL MAKE ALL MY FRIENDS LIKE RIFF AND ZOË FALL ASLEEP!
HI, KIKI! I'M YOUR FRIEND SAM! SINCE I'M A VAMPIRE, THE SICKNESS ONLY GAVE ME A MILD HEADACHE. BUT ZOË'S IN TROUBLE AND I LOVE HER SO I'M HERE TO HELP!
HELLO. I'M DR. SCHLOCK. I'M A GENIUS FROM THE FUTURE WHERE THEY MADE ME KIKI-DISEASE-PROOF (MOSTLY). IF YOU DO EVERYTHING I TELL YOU TO, I CAN SAVE YOUR FRIENDS AND A MILLION OTHERS FROM BEING DEAD!
YAY DR. SCHLOCK! DISSECT ME IF YOU NEED TO!
I'LL DO WHATEVER YOU SAY WITHOUT QUESTION!
YOU GUYS GET THE PICTURE?
YOU'VE GOT MY WALK ALL WRONG. IF YOU'RE GONNA DO THE SAM-PUPPET, YOU'VE GOTTA MOVE SMOOTH, MAN!
OOOH! THERE'S A CARTOON ON TV!

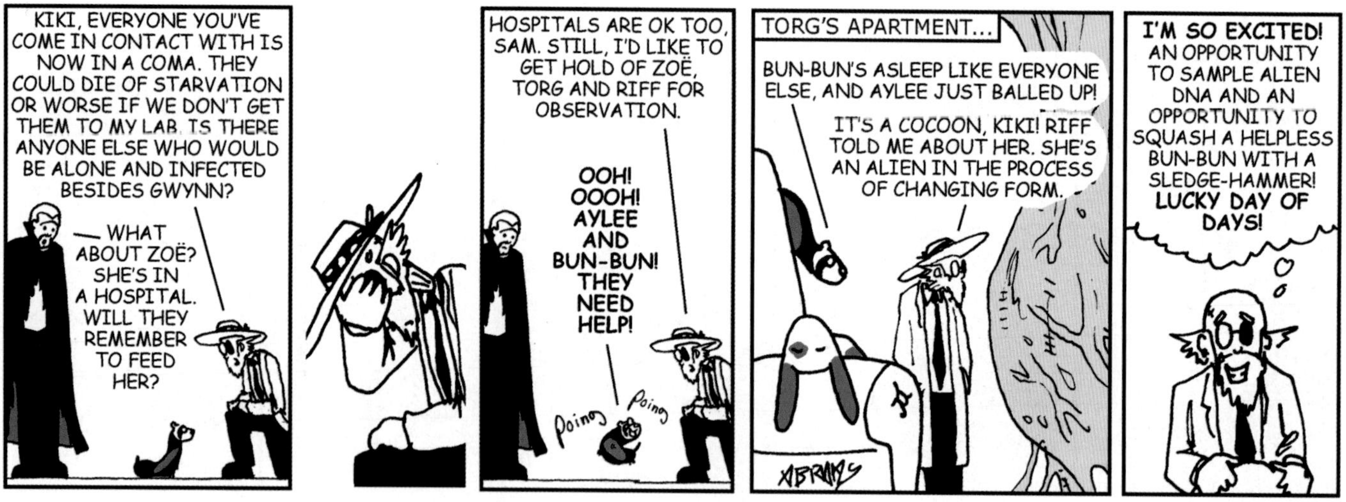
KIKI, EVERYONE YOU'VE COME IN CONTACT WITH IS NOW IN A COMA. THEY COULD DIE OF STARVATION OR WORSE IF WE DON'T GET THEM TO MY LAB. IS THERE ANYONE ELSE WHO WOULD BE ALONE AND INFECTED BESIDES GWYNN?
— WHAT ABOUT ZOË? SHE'S IN A HOSPITAL. WILL THEY REMEMBER TO FEED HER?
HOSPITALS ARE OK TOO, SAM. STILL, I'D LIKE TO GET HOLD OF ZOË, TORG AND RIFF FOR OBSERVATION.
OOH! OOOH! AYLEE AND BUN-BUN! THEY NEED HELP!
Poing Poing
TORG'S APARTMENT...
BUN-BUN'S ASLEEP LIKE EVERYONE ELSE, AND AYLEE JUST BALLED UP!
IT'S A COCOON, KIKI! RIFF TOLD ME ABOUT HER. SHE'S AN ALIEN IN THE PROCESS OF CHANGING FORM.
I'M SO EXCITED! AN OPPORTUNITY TO SAMPLE ALIEN DNA AND AN OPPORTUNITY TO SQUASH A HELPLESS BUN-BUN WITH A SLEDGE-HAMMER! LUCKY DAY OF DAYS!

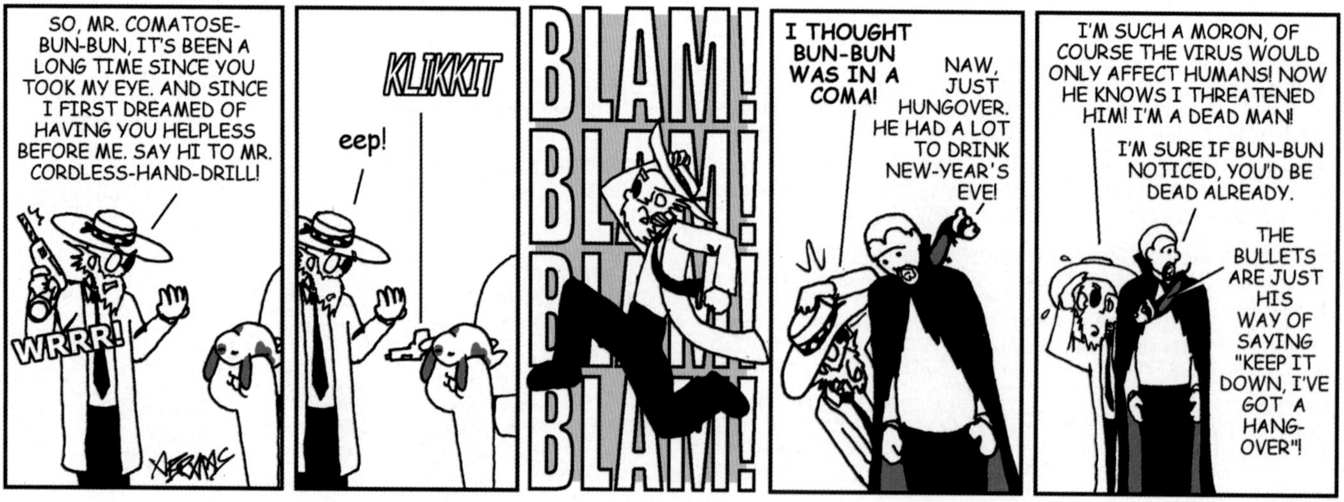
SO, MR. COMATOSE-BUN-BUN, IT'S BEEN A LONG TIME SINCE YOU TOOK MY EYE. AND SINCE I FIRST DREAMED OF HAVING YOU HELPLESS BEFORE ME. SAY HI TO MR. CORDLESS-HAND-DRILL!
WRRR!
KLIKKIT
eep!
BLAM! BLAM! BLAM! BLAM!
I THOUGHT BUN-BUN WAS IN A COMA!
NAW, JUST HUNGOVER. HE HAD A LOT TO DRINK NEW-YEAR'S EVE!
I'M SUCH A MORON, OF COURSE THE VIRUS WOULD ONLY AFFECT HUMANS! NOW HE KNOWS I THREATENED HIM! I'M A DEAD MAN!
I'M SURE IF BUN-BUN NOTICED, YOU'D BE DEAD ALREADY.
THE BULLETS ARE JUST HIS WAY OF SAYING "KEEP IT DOWN, I'VE GOT A HANG-OVER"!

DR. SCHLOCK'S LAB, JANUARY 3RD, 2000:

KIKI! FOR THE HUNDREDTH TIME, YOU **HAVE** TO TRY TO REMEMBER WHAT HAPPENED TO YOU WITH DR. CRABTREE.

DR. CRAB-TREE!?!?

SLUGGY FREELANCE

NOooooooooo

WOOOOSH!

LEAVE HER ALONE.

SAM, I NEED YOU TO DO SOMETHING FOR ME. ZOË, TORG, AND RIFF ARE ALL BEING KEPT IN A HIGHLY SECURE HOSPITAL UNDER VERY HEAVY GUARD. IT'S VERY IMPORTANT THAT WE GET THEM HERE BEFORE THEY HIT **PHASE 2** OR THEY'LL **DIE!** IT'S VERY DANGEROUS AND WILL TAKE CAREFUL AND THOUGHTFUL PLANNING...

SAY NO MORE! SAM'S ON THE BALL AND THE KING OF 'EM ALL!

NEAT TRICK, DOC. YOU MENTION ZOË-IN-TROUBLE TO SAM AND YOU GET HIM OUT OF YOUR HAIR FOR A WHILE. HE MIGHT ACTUALLY RESCUE THEM. VAMPIRES ARE UNSTOPPABLE IF YOU'RE NOT PREPARED.

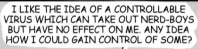

I LIKE THE IDEA OF A CONTROLLABLE VIRUS WHICH CAN TAKE OUT NERD-BOYS BUT HAVE NO EFFECT ON ME. ANY IDEA HOW I COULD GAIN CONTROL OF SOME?

I'M NOT SURE I'D TELL YOU IF I KNEW.

HOW ABOUT YOU START BY TELLING ME THE TRUTH ABOUT THE VIRUS?

I **DID** TELL YOU THE TRUTH.

REPEAT THE PART ABOUT DR. CRABTREE AGAIN.

Poing

WE'VE BEEN OVER THIS! DR. JOSEPH CRABTREE WAS AN ASSOCIATE OF MINE WHO WAS TRYING TO CREATE A CONTROLLABLE STRAIN OF THE **TYPE PT109 FLU** VIRUS. HE WAS DRIVEN LIKE NO-ONE I'VE EVER SEEN. A YEAR BEFORE MY FIRST ENCOUNTER WITH YOU, HE LEFT THE COMPANY TO JOIN THE MILITARY, THE BIO-WEAPONS DEPARTMENT, I BELIEVE.

AND YOU HAVE ABSOLUTELY NO IDEA HOW TO FIND HIM.

I'M FROM THE FUTURE, BUN-BUN. I HAVEN'T SEEN JOSEPH IN OVER FORTY YEARS. FEEL FREE TO TRY AND FIND HIM IF YOU THINK YOU CAN.

THAT'S RIGHT. YOU'RE FROM THE FUTURE, MEANING THE YOUNGER YOU IS STILL AROUND. MAYBE HIS MEMORY WOULD BE A LITTLE MORE FRESH. DO YOU KNOW HIS PHONE NUMBER?

IN MY VERSION OF JANUARY 3RD, 2000, THE DEMON IS ALREADY CAUSING GREAT TURMOIL. I'M RUNNING FOR MY **LIFE** THERE! IN THIS VERSION OF THE PRESENT, I HAVE NO IDEA HOW TO CONTACT YOUNG ME.

THEN WHAT'S WITH THIS MESSAGE ON HIS ANSWERING MACHINE?

DR. IRVING SCHLOCK, I KNOW YOU KNOW THIS VOICE. I CAN'T TALK LONG, THIS CALL MIGHT BE TRACED. DO NOT TALK TO ANYONE ABOUT YOUR WORK IN 1997, AND ESPECIALLY ABOUT DR. CRABTREE. WAIT BY THE PAYPHONE ON THE CORNER OF...

BLA, BLA BLA. GEE, THAT SURE SOUNDED LIKE YOU, IRVING!

WHERE DID YOU GET THAT MACHINE?!?

FUNNY THING IS, EVEN BEFORE YOUR CALL, YOUR YOUNGER SELF STILL DIDN'T RECOGNIZE THE NAME **JOSEPH** CRABTREE. HE **DID** KNOW A DR. **"CATHERINE"** CRABTREE THOUGH! HE WORKED IN THE LAB NEXT TO HERS IN 1997. ONE OF HER TEST SUBJECTS WAS A FERRET NAMED KIKI, AND SHE WAS **VERY** CONCERNED WHEN SHE FOUND OUT KIKI WAS LOOSE. AND HER WORK HAD NOTHING TO DO WITH THE FLU. OR VIRUSES. NOT AT ALL.

I... I MADE JOSEPH UP, I ADMIT IT! BUT WHAT HAVE YOU **DONE** WITH **HIM**... ME? I MUST SPEAK WITH HIM!

SURE THING DOC, HE'S RIGHT HERE! HEY KIKI! LOOK! ITS A YOUNG DR. SCHLOCK!

mphfmfmphf!

HI! I'M KIKI! YOU LOOK FAMILIAR!

NO!

Poing

KIKI! GET AWAY FROM HIM! EVERYONE YOU COME INTO CONTACT WITH FALLS INTO A COMA!

I'M SORRY!

YOU DID THAT ON PURPOSE! NOW PHASE 2 WILL KILL ME!

I ALREADY KNOW WHERE DR. CATHERINE CRABTREE IS. AND YOU KNOW WHAT HER LITTLE BACKFIRED EXPERIMENT WILL DO, AND HOW TO EXPLOIT IT. I'M THE ONLY KEY TO THE PAST, YOU'RE THE ONLY KEY TO THE FUTURE. I THINK AN INFORMATION EXCHANGE IS IN ORDER.

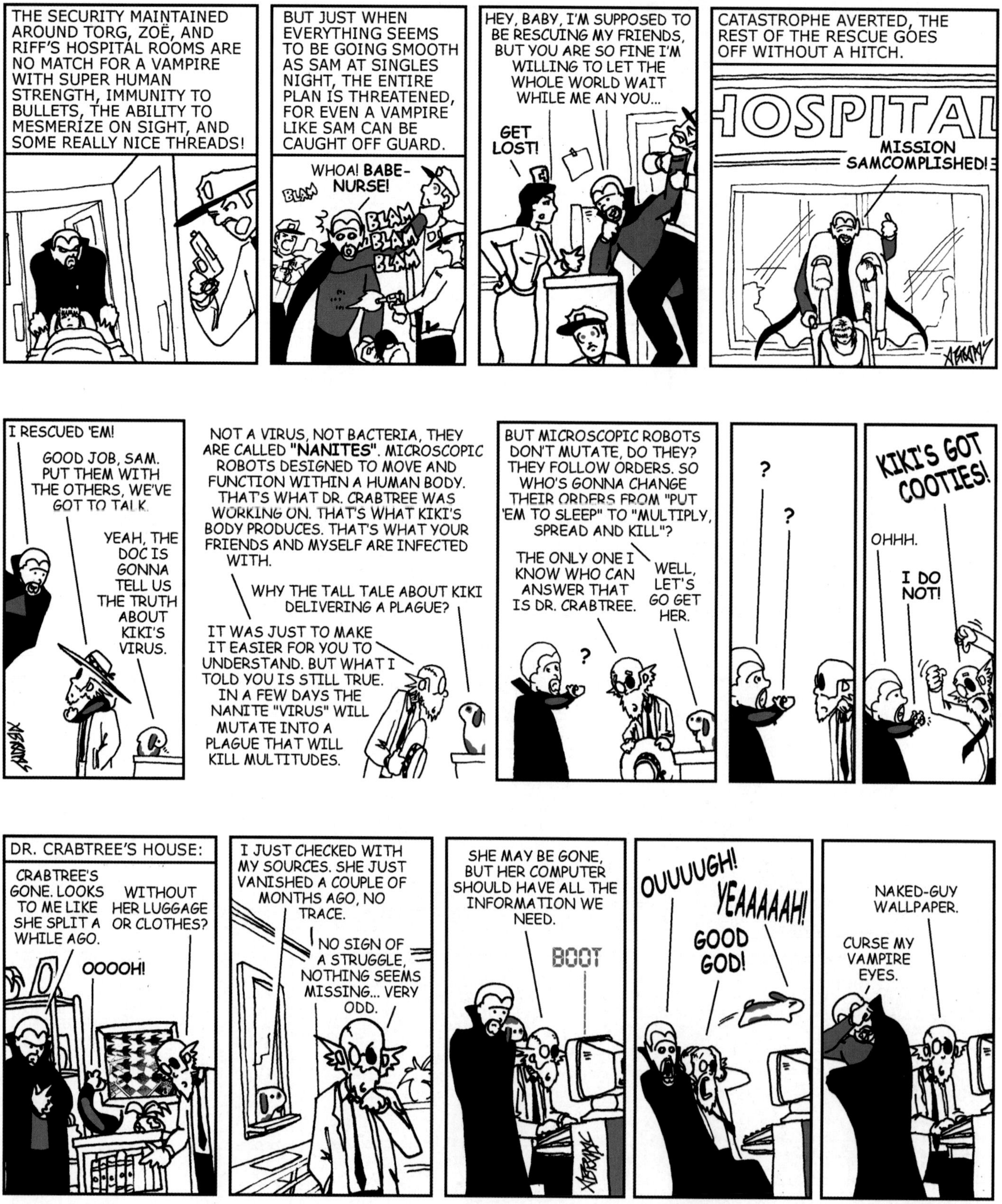

THE SECURITY MAINTAINED AROUND TORG, ZOË, AND RIFF'S HOSPITAL ROOMS ARE NO MATCH FOR A VAMPIRE WITH SUPER HUMAN STRENGTH, IMMUNITY TO BULLETS, THE ABILITY TO MESMERIZE ON SIGHT, AND SOME REALLY NICE THREADS!
BUT JUST WHEN EVERYTHING SEEMS TO BE GOING SMOOTH AS SAM AT SINGLES NIGHT, THE ENTIRE PLAN IS THREATENED, FOR EVEN A VAMPIRE LIKE SAM CAN BE CAUGHT OFF GUARD.
BLAM
WHOA! BABE-NURSE!
BLAM BLAM BLAM
HEY, BABY, I'M SUPPOSED TO BE RESCUING MY FRIENDS, BUT YOU ARE SO FINE I'M WILLING TO LET THE WHOLE WORLD WAIT WHILE ME AN YOU...
GET LOST!
CATASTROPHE AVERTED, THE REST OF THE RESCUE GOES OFF WITHOUT A HITCH.
HOSPITAL
MISSION SAMCOMPLISHED!
I RESCUED 'EM!
GOOD JOB, SAM. PUT THEM WITH THE OTHERS, WE'VE GOT TO TALK.
YEAH, THE DOC IS GONNA TELL US THE TRUTH ABOUT KIKI'S VIRUS.
NOT A VIRUS, NOT BACTERIA, THEY ARE CALLED "NANITES". MICROSCOPIC ROBOTS DESIGNED TO MOVE AND FUNCTION WITHIN A HUMAN BODY. THAT'S WHAT DR. CRABTREE WAS WORKING ON. THAT'S WHAT KIKI'S BODY PRODUCES. THAT'S WHAT YOUR FRIENDS AND MYSELF ARE INFECTED WITH.
WHY THE TALL TALE ABOUT KIKI DELIVERING A PLAGUE?
IT WAS JUST TO MAKE IT EASIER FOR YOU TO UNDERSTAND. BUT WHAT I TOLD YOU IS STILL TRUE. IN A FEW DAYS THE NANITE "VIRUS" WILL MUTATE INTO A PLAGUE THAT WILL KILL MULTITUDES.
BUT MICROSCOPIC ROBOTS DON'T MUTATE, DO THEY? THEY FOLLOW ORDERS. SO WHO'S GONNA CHANGE THEIR ORDERS FROM "PUT 'EM TO SLEEP" TO "MULTIPLY, SPREAD AND KILL"?
THE ONLY ONE I KNOW WHO CAN ANSWER THAT IS DR. CRABTREE.
WELL, LET'S GO GET HER.
?
?
?
KIKI'S GOT COOTIES!
OHHH.
I DO NOT!
DR. CRABTREE'S HOUSE:
CRABTREE'S GONE. LOOKS TO ME LIKE SHE SPLIT A WHILE AGO.
WITHOUT HER LUGGAGE OR CLOTHES?
OOOOH!
I JUST CHECKED WITH MY SOURCES. SHE JUST VANISHED A COUPLE OF MONTHS AGO, NO TRACE.
NO SIGN OF A STRUGGLE, NOTHING SEEMS MISSING... VERY ODD.
SHE MAY BE GONE, BUT HER COMPUTER SHOULD HAVE ALL THE INFORMATION WE NEED.
BOOT
OUUUUGH!
YEAAAAAH!
GOOD GOD!
NAKED-GUY WALLPAPER.
CURSE MY VAMPIRE EYES.

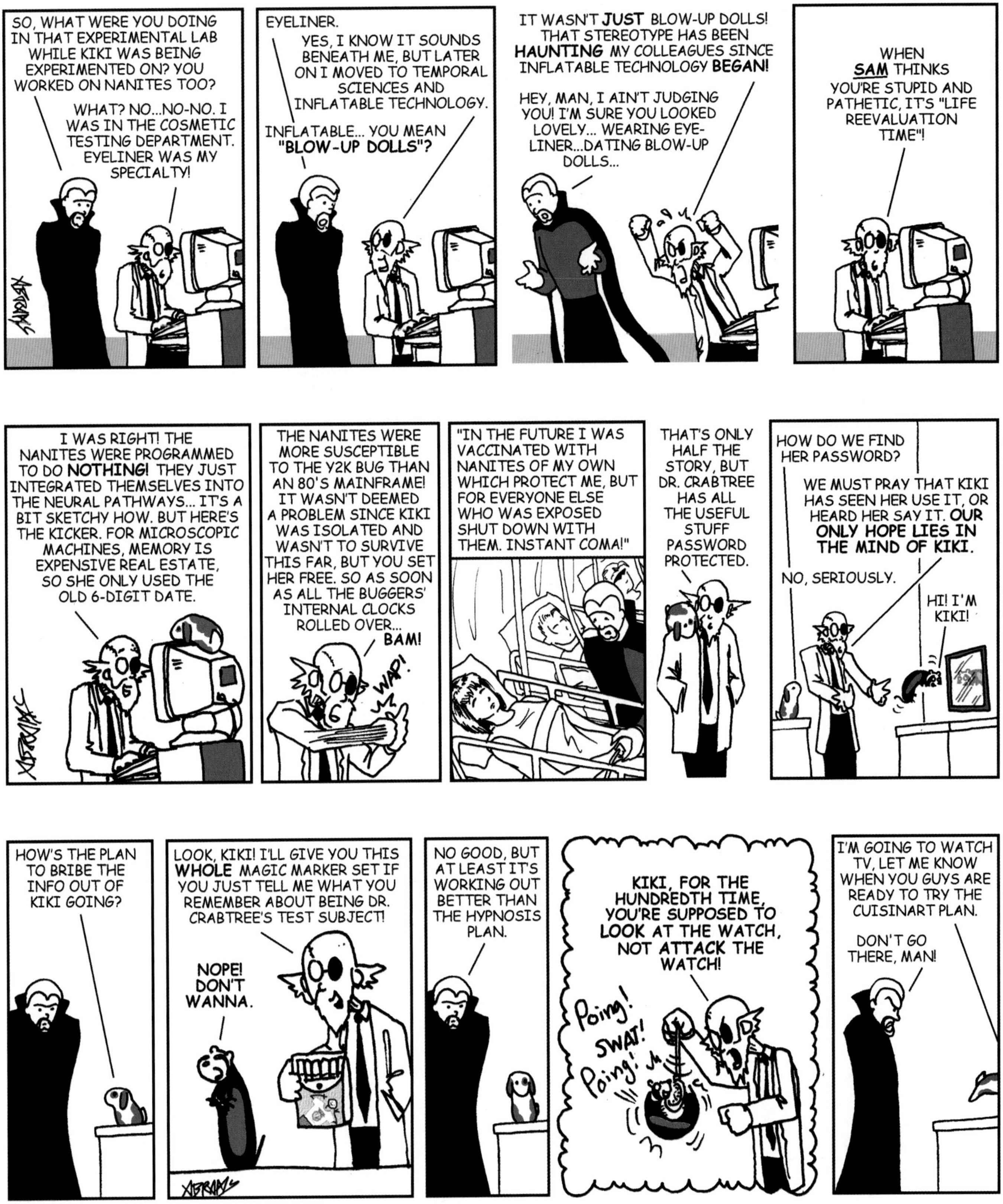

SO, WHAT WERE YOU DOING IN THAT EXPERIMENTAL LAB WHILE KIKI WAS BEING EXPERIMENTED ON? YOU WORKED ON NANITES TOO?
WHAT? NO...NO-NO. I WAS IN THE COSMETIC TESTING DEPARTMENT. EYELINER WAS MY SPECIALTY!
EYELINER.
YES, I KNOW IT SOUNDS BENEATH ME, BUT LATER ON I MOVED TO TEMPORAL SCIENCES AND INFLATABLE TECHNOLOGY.
INFLATABLE... YOU MEAN "BLOW-UP DOLLS"?
IT WASN'T JUST BLOW-UP DOLLS! THAT STEREOTYPE HAS BEEN HAUNTING MY COLLEAGUES SINCE INFLATABLE TECHNOLOGY BEGAN!
HEY, MAN, I AIN'T JUDGING YOU! I'M SURE YOU LOOKED LOVELY... WEARING EYE-LINER...DATING BLOW-UP DOLLS...
WHEN SAM THINKS YOU'RE STUPID AND PATHETIC, IT'S "LIFE REEVALUATION TIME"!
I WAS RIGHT! THE NANITES WERE PROGRAMMED TO DO NOTHING! THEY JUST INTEGRATED THEMSELVES INTO THE NEURAL PATHWAYS... IT'S A BIT SKETCHY HOW. BUT HERE'S THE KICKER. FOR MICROSCOPIC MACHINES, MEMORY IS EXPENSIVE REAL ESTATE, SO SHE ONLY USED THE OLD 6-DIGIT DATE.
THE NANITES WERE MORE SUSCEPTIBLE TO THE Y2K BUG THAN AN 80'S MAINFRAME! IT WASN'T DEEMED A PROBLEM SINCE KIKI WAS ISOLATED AND WASN'T TO SURVIVE THIS FAR, BUT YOU SET HER FREE. SO AS SOON AS ALL THE BUGGERS' INTERNAL CLOCKS ROLLED OVER...
BAM!
WAP!
"IN THE FUTURE I WAS VACCINATED WITH NANITES OF MY OWN WHICH PROTECT ME, BUT FOR EVERYONE ELSE WHO WAS EXPOSED SHUT DOWN WITH THEM. INSTANT COMA!"
THAT'S ONLY HALF THE STORY, BUT DR. CRABTREE HAS ALL THE USEFUL STUFF PASSWORD PROTECTED.
HOW DO WE FIND HER PASSWORD?
WE MUST PRAY THAT KIKI HAS SEEN HER USE IT, OR HEARD HER SAY IT. OUR ONLY HOPE LIES IN THE MIND OF KIKI.
NO, SERIOUSLY.
HI! I'M KIKI!
HOW'S THE PLAN TO BRIBE THE INFO OUT OF KIKI GOING?
LOOK, KIKI! I'LL GIVE YOU THIS WHOLE MAGIC MARKER SET IF YOU JUST TELL ME WHAT YOU REMEMBER ABOUT BEING DR. CRABTREE'S TEST SUBJECT!
NOPE! DON'T WANNA.
NO GOOD, BUT AT LEAST IT'S WORKING OUT BETTER THAN THE HYPNOSIS PLAN.
KIKI, FOR THE HUNDREDTH TIME, YOU'RE SUPPOSED TO LOOK AT THE WATCH, NOT ATTACK THE WATCH!
Poing!
SWAT!
Poing!
I'M GOING TO WATCH TV, LET ME KNOW WHEN YOU GUYS ARE READY TO TRY THE CUISINART PLAN.
DON'T GO THERE, MAN!

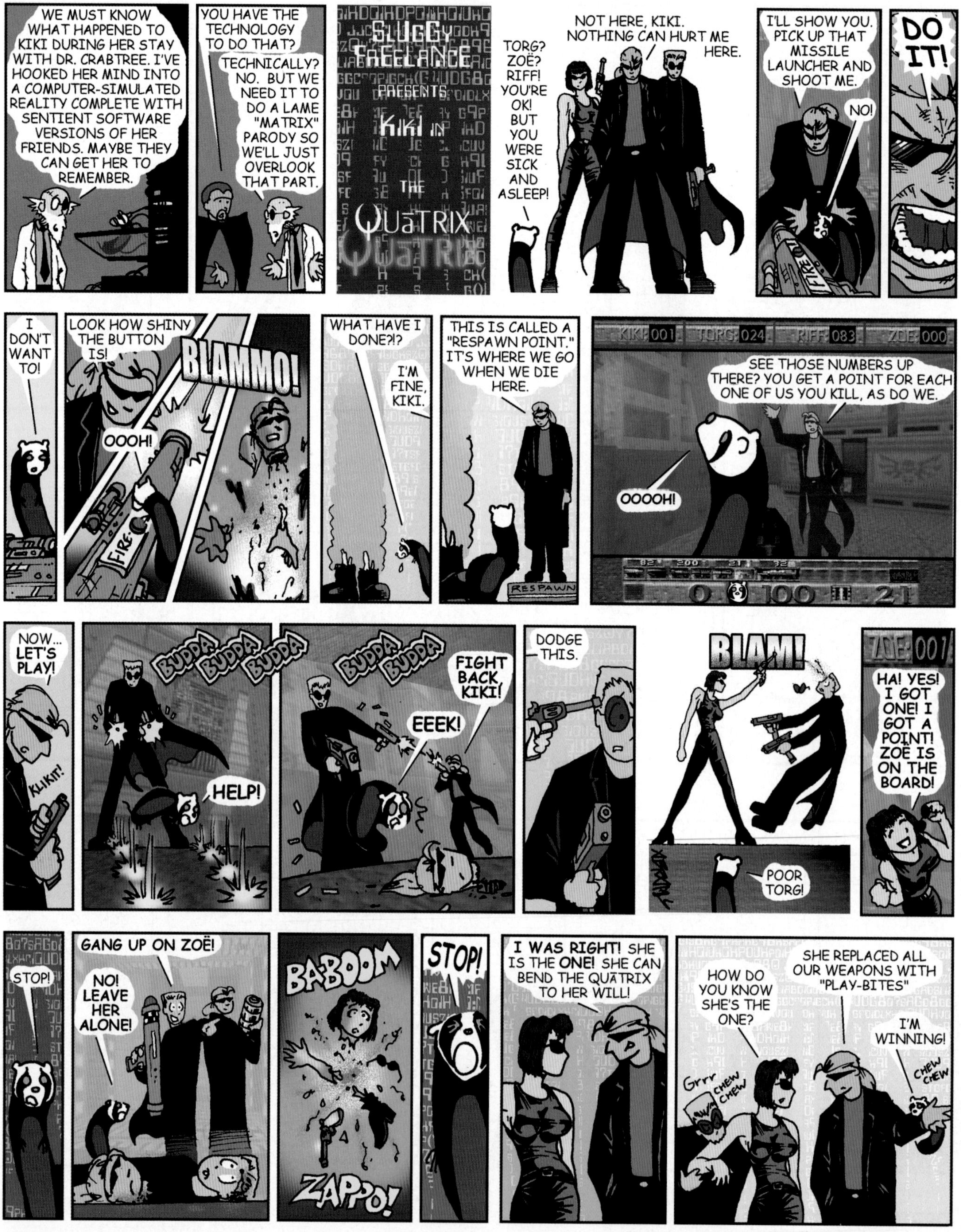
WE MUST KNOW WHAT HAPPENED TO KIKI DURING HER STAY WITH DR. CRABTREE. I'VE HOOKED HER MIND INTO A COMPUTER-SIMULATED REALITY COMPLETE WITH SENTIENT SOFTWARE VERSIONS OF HER FRIENDS. MAYBE THEY CAN GET HER TO REMEMBER.
YOU HAVE THE TECHNOLOGY TO DO THAT?
TECHNICALLY? NO. BUT WE NEED IT TO DO A LAME "MATRIX" PARODY SO WE'LL JUST OVERLOOK THAT PART.
SLUGGY FREELANCE
PRESENTS
KIKI IN
THE
QUaTRIX
TORG? ZOË? RIFF! YOU'RE OK! BUT YOU WERE SICK AND ASLEEP!
NOT HERE, KIKI. NOTHING CAN HURT ME HERE.
I'LL SHOW YOU. PICK UP THAT MISSILE LAUNCHER AND SHOOT ME.
NO!
FIRE
DO IT!
I DON'T WANT TO!
LOOK HOW SHINY THE BUTTON IS!
BLAMMO!
OOOH!
FIRE
WHAT HAVE I DONE?!?
I'M FINE, KIKI.
THIS IS CALLED A "RESPAWN POINT." IT'S WHERE WE GO WHEN WE DIE HERE.
RESPAWN
KIKI 001 TORG 024 RIFF 083 ZOE 000
SEE THOSE NUMBERS UP THERE? YOU GET A POINT FOR EACH ONE OF US YOU KILL, AS DO WE.
OOOOH!
0 100 21
NOW... LET'S PLAY!
KLIKIT!
BUDDA BUDDA BUDDA
HELP!
BUDDA BUDDA
FIGHT BACK, KIKI!
EEEK!
DODGE THIS.
BLAM!
POOR TORG!
ZOE 001
HA! YES! I GOT ONE! I GOT A POINT! ZOË IS ON THE BOARD!
STOP!
GANG UP ON ZOË!
NO! LEAVE HER ALONE!
BABOOM
ZAPPO!
STOP!
I WAS RIGHT! SHE IS THE ONE! SHE CAN BEND THE QUaTRIX TO HER WILL!
HOW DO YOU KNOW SHE'S THE ONE?
SHE REPLACED ALL OUR WEAPONS WITH "PLAY-BITES"
I'M WINNING!
Grrr
CHEW CHEW
CHEW CHEW

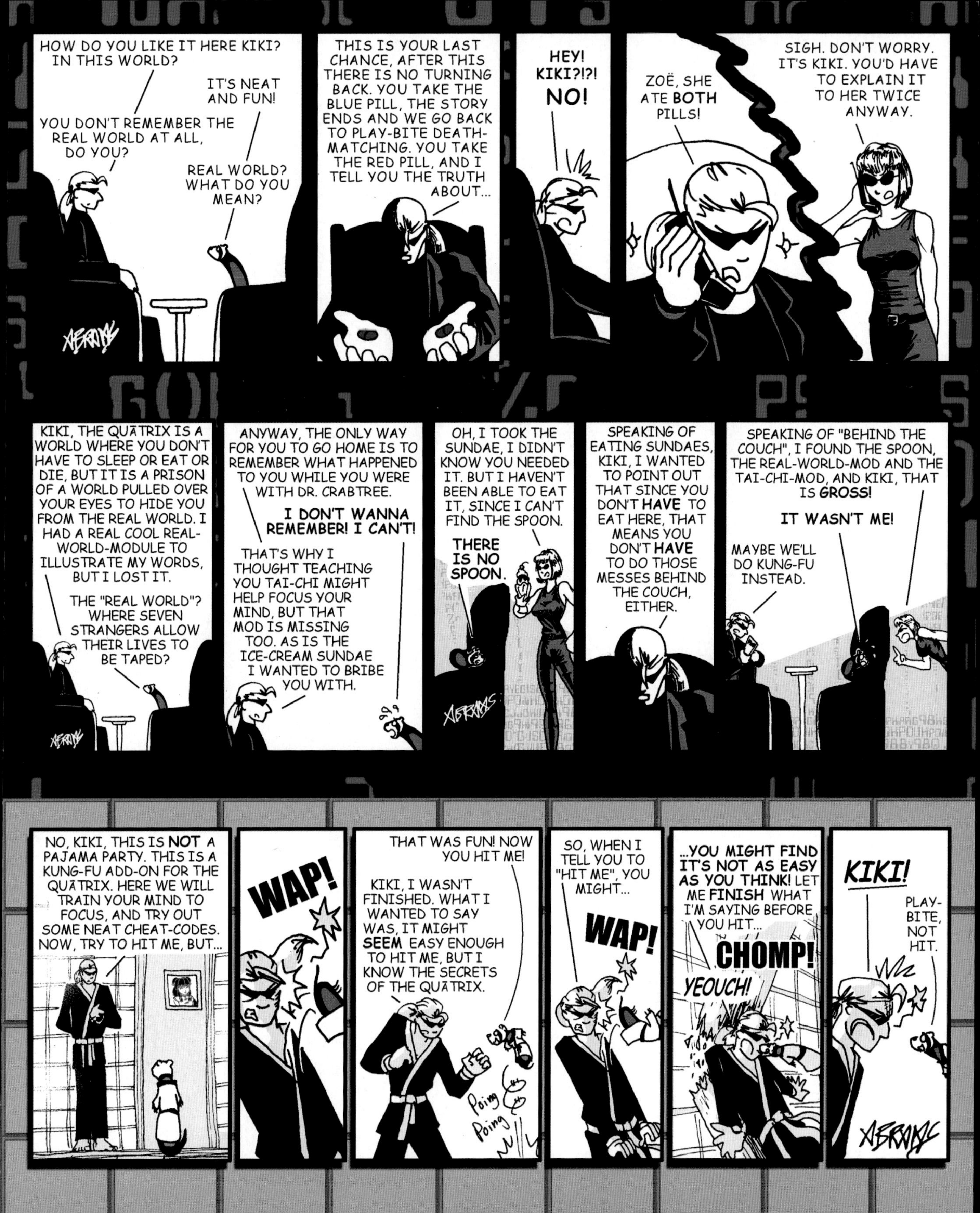

HOW DO YOU LIKE IT HERE KIKI? IN THIS WORLD?
IT'S NEAT AND FUN!
YOU DON'T REMEMBER THE REAL WORLD AT ALL, DO YOU?
REAL WORLD? WHAT DO YOU MEAN?
THIS IS YOUR LAST CHANCE, AFTER THIS THERE IS NO TURNING BACK. YOU TAKE THE BLUE PILL, THE STORY ENDS AND WE GO BACK TO PLAY-BITE DEATH-MATCHING. YOU TAKE THE RED PILL, AND I TELL YOU THE TRUTH ABOUT...
HEY! KIKI?!?! NO!
ZOË, SHE ATE BOTH PILLS!
SIGH. DON'T WORRY. IT'S KIKI. YOU'D HAVE TO EXPLAIN IT TO HER TWICE ANYWAY.
KIKI, THE QUĀTRIX IS A WORLD WHERE YOU DON'T HAVE TO SLEEP OR EAT OR DIE, BUT IT IS A PRISON OF A WORLD PULLED OVER YOUR EYES TO HIDE YOU FROM THE REAL WORLD. I HAD A REAL COOL REAL-WORLD-MODULE TO ILLUSTRATE MY WORDS, BUT I LOST IT.
THE "REAL WORLD"? WHERE SEVEN STRANGERS ALLOW THEIR LIVES TO BE TAPED?
ANYWAY, THE ONLY WAY FOR YOU TO GO HOME IS TO REMEMBER WHAT HAPPENED TO YOU WHILE YOU WERE WITH DR. CRABTREE.
I DON'T WANNA REMEMBER! I CAN'T!
THAT'S WHY I THOUGHT TEACHING YOU TAI-CHI MIGHT HELP FOCUS YOUR MIND, BUT THAT MOD IS MISSING TOO. AS IS THE ICE-CREAM SUNDAE I WANTED TO BRIBE YOU WITH.
OH, I TOOK THE SUNDAE, I DIDN'T KNOW YOU NEEDED IT. BUT I HAVEN'T BEEN ABLE TO EAT IT, SINCE I CAN'T FIND THE SPOON.
THERE IS NO SPOON.
SPEAKING OF EATING SUNDAES, KIKI, I WANTED TO POINT OUT THAT SINCE YOU DON'T HAVE TO EAT HERE, THAT MEANS YOU DON'T HAVE TO DO THOSE MESSES BEHIND THE COUCH, EITHER.
SPEAKING OF "BEHIND THE COUCH", I FOUND THE SPOON, THE REAL-WORLD-MOD AND THE TAI-CHI-MOD, AND KIKI, THAT IS GROSS!
IT WASN'T ME!
MAYBE WE'LL DO KUNG-FU INSTEAD.
NO, KIKI, THIS IS NOT A PAJAMA PARTY. THIS IS A KUNG-FU ADD-ON FOR THE QUĀTRIX. HERE WE WILL TRAIN YOUR MIND TO FOCUS, AND TRY OUT SOME NEAT CHEAT-CODES. NOW, TRY TO HIT ME, BUT...
WAP!
THAT WAS FUN! NOW YOU HIT ME!
KIKI, I WASN'T FINISHED. WHAT I WANTED TO SAY WAS, IT MIGHT SEEM EASY ENOUGH TO HIT ME, BUT I KNOW THE SECRETS OF THE QUĀTRIX.
Poing Poing
SO, WHEN I TELL YOU TO "HIT ME", YOU MIGHT...
WAP!
...YOU MIGHT FIND IT'S NOT AS EASY AS YOU THINK! LET ME FINISH WHAT I'M SAYING BEFORE YOU HIT...
CHOMP!
YEOUCH!
KIKI!
PLAY-BITE, NOT HIT.

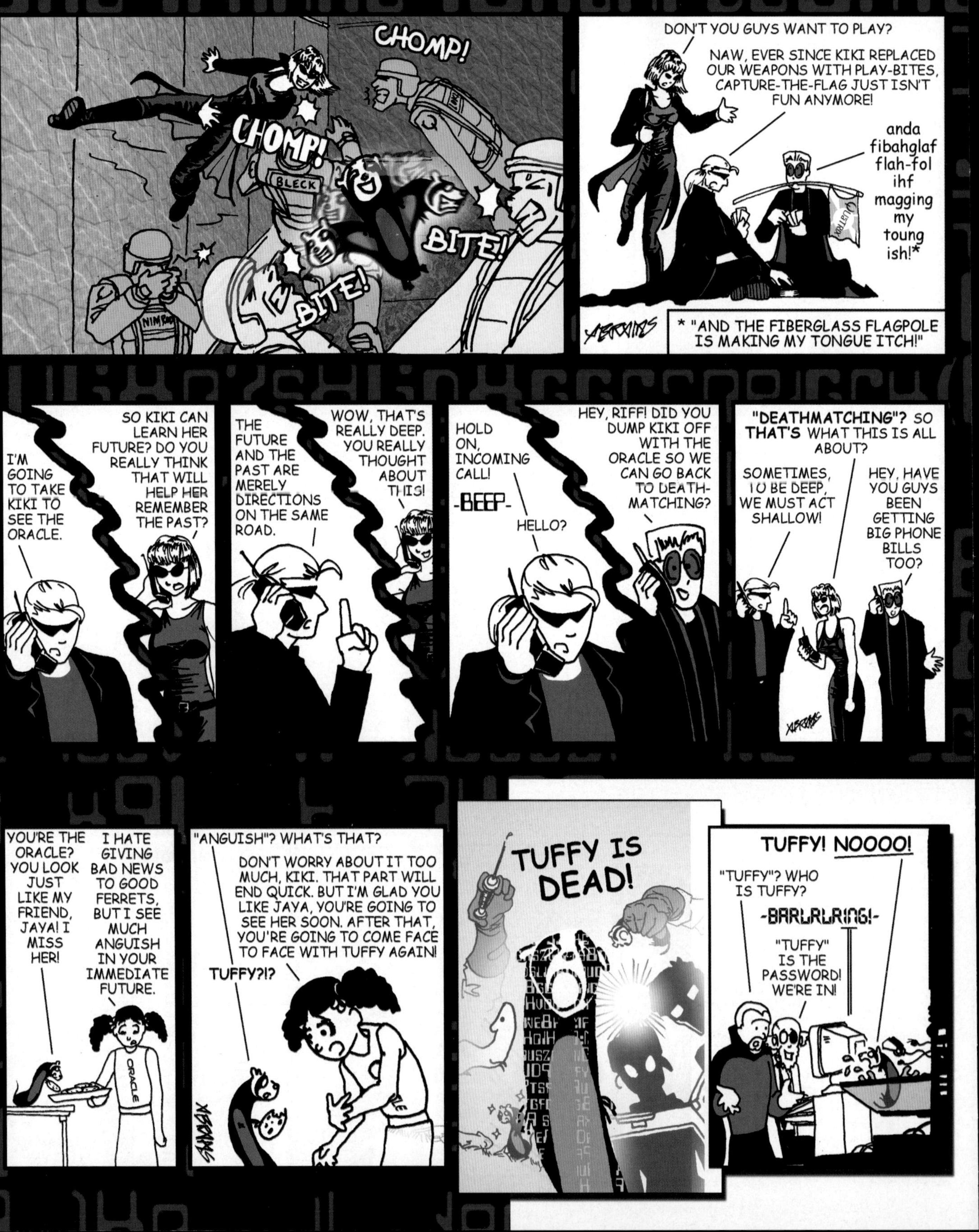
CHOMP!
CHOMP!
BLECK
BITE!
BITE!
NIMROD
DON'T YOU GUYS WANT TO PLAY?
NAW, EVER SINCE KIKI REPLACED OUR WEAPONS WITH PLAY-BITES, CAPTURE-THE-FLAG JUST ISN'T FUN ANYMORE!
anda fibahglaf flah-fol ihf magging my toung ish!*
* "AND THE FIBERGLASS FLAGPOLE IS MAKING MY TONGUE ITCH!"
I'M GOING TO TAKE KIKI TO SEE THE ORACLE.
SO KIKI CAN LEARN HER FUTURE? DO YOU REALLY THINK THAT WILL HELP HER REMEMBER THE PAST?
THE FUTURE AND THE PAST ARE MERELY DIRECTIONS ON THE SAME ROAD.
WOW, THAT'S REALLY DEEP. YOU REALLY THOUGHT ABOUT THIS!
HOLD ON, INCOMING CALL!
-BEEP-
HELLO?
HEY, RIFF! DID YOU DUMP KIKI OFF WITH THE ORACLE SO WE CAN GO BACK TO DEATH-MATCHING?
"DEATHMATCHING"? SO THAT'S WHAT THIS IS ALL ABOUT?
SOMETIMES, TO BE DEEP, WE MUST ACT SHALLOW!
HEY, HAVE YOU GUYS BEEN GETTING BIG PHONE BILLS TOO?
YOU'RE THE ORACLE? YOU LOOK JUST LIKE MY FRIEND, JAYA! I MISS HER!
I HATE GIVING BAD NEWS TO GOOD FERRETS, BUT I SEE MUCH ANGUISH IN YOUR IMMEDIATE FUTURE.
ORACLE
"ANGUISH"? WHAT'S THAT?
DON'T WORRY ABOUT IT TOO MUCH, KIKI. THAT PART WILL END QUICK. BUT I'M GLAD YOU LIKE JAYA, YOU'RE GOING TO SEE HER SOON. AFTER THAT, YOU'RE GOING TO COME FACE TO FACE WITH TUFFY AGAIN!
TUFFY?!?
TUFFY IS DEAD!
TUFFY! NOOOO!
"TUFFY"? WHO IS TUFFY?
-BARLRLRING!-
"TUFFY" IS THE PASSWORD! WE'RE IN!

BLAST! THAT PSYCHO CRABTREE HID ALL THE REAL IMPORTANT STUFF BEHIND ANOTHER PASSWORD! KIKI, YOU HAVE TO TELL US EVERYTHING YOU CAN REMEMBER, IT'S OUR ONLY HOPE!
I'LL... I'LL TRY!
SLUGGY FREELANCE
A LONG TIME AGO I MET TUFFY.
HI! I'M KIKI!
HI! I'M TUFFY!
Poing Poing
OOOH! SOMEONE'S COMING TO FEED US! I WANT TO SAY HI!
SHHH! DON'T TALK TO DR. CRABTREE! SHE HATES IT. IT CONFUSES HER.
WE CAN TALK MORE LATER!
TUFFY AND I WERE ALWAYS TOGETHER, AND ONE DAY WE MOVED!
TUFFY? WHY DID THEY MOVE US TO THIS NEW CAGE? IT'S SCARY!
LAST TIME I WAS HERE, I HAD A FRIEND NAMED BURRO, BEFORE YOU CAME. THE DOCTOR CAME FOR HIM, AND HE NEVER CAME BACK! I COULDN'T FIND HIM!
SOLATION CAGE 3
IF THE DOCTOR COMES FOR ME, WILL YOU FIND ME, KIKI?
SURE I WILL! YOU'RE MY BEST FRIEND
THEN, THAT NIGHT, BAD THINGS HAPPENED.
ZZZ
NO!
KIKI?
LEAVE ME ALONE!
THEN... THEN...
KIKI! YOU'VE COME BACK!
HI TUFFY! I DON'T FEEL GOOD.
TUFFY? WHAT'S WRONG?
Whump!
SOMEBODY HELP TUFFY!
DAMN IT ALL! ANOTHER DEAD FERRET. THE NANITES ARE SUPPOSED TO FEED ANALYTICAL DATA TO THE MACHINE, NOT KILL THE SUBJECT!
CRABTREE
WE NEED TO SEE PROGRESS, DR. CRABTREE. AND ON HUMAN SUBJECTS.
I THINK I CAN GET YOU HUMAN INTEGRATION BY DEADLINE. HUMAN ANALYSIS IS THE PUZZLE.
AREN'T YOU GOING TO HELP TUFFY?
THEN, AFTER MORE TESTS, I MET A NEW FRIEND!
BLAM! BLAM! BLAM!
ATTENTION ALL YOU TUBE RATS, TOILET DRINKERS, RABBITS, CATS AND DUNG FLINGERS! THE EXIT IS THAT WAY, LET'S CLEAR THE CAGES IN AN ORDERLY FASHION 'CAUSE I FASHION TO STUFF THEM WITH ORDERLIES!
KLIK KLIK KLIK
Poing Poing Poing
HEY, LOOKS LIKE THEY PUT YOU IN THE SPECIAL CAGE! KEEP YOUR HEAD DOWN.
BLAM! BLAM! BLAM!
OH THANK YOU SO...
HEY! THANK YOU! YOU'RE NICE!
HEY KIKI, LET'S GET OUT OF HERE!
Poing
AND I NEVER WENT BACK. POOR TUFFY!
IF I EVER FIND THAT DR. CRABTREE, I'M GOING TO RIP HER IN TWO!
UNLESS SHE'S A BABE OR SOMETHING. THEN I'D BE REALLY STERN WITH HER. YOU KNOW. AFTERWARDS.

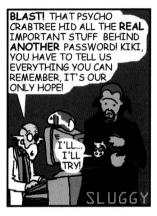

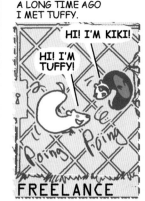

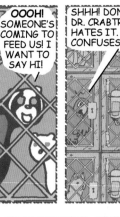

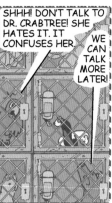

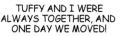

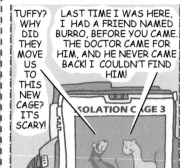

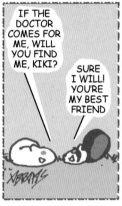

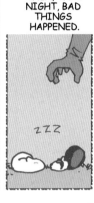

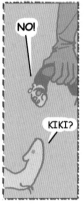

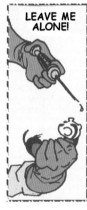

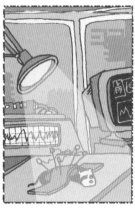

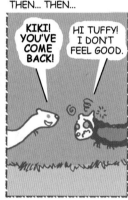

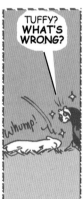

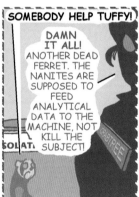

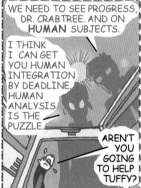

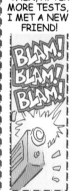

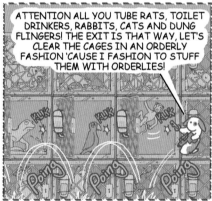

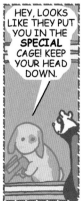

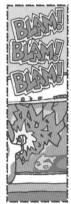

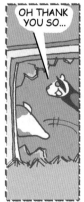

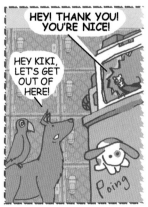

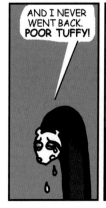

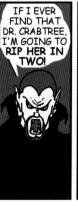

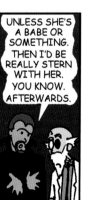

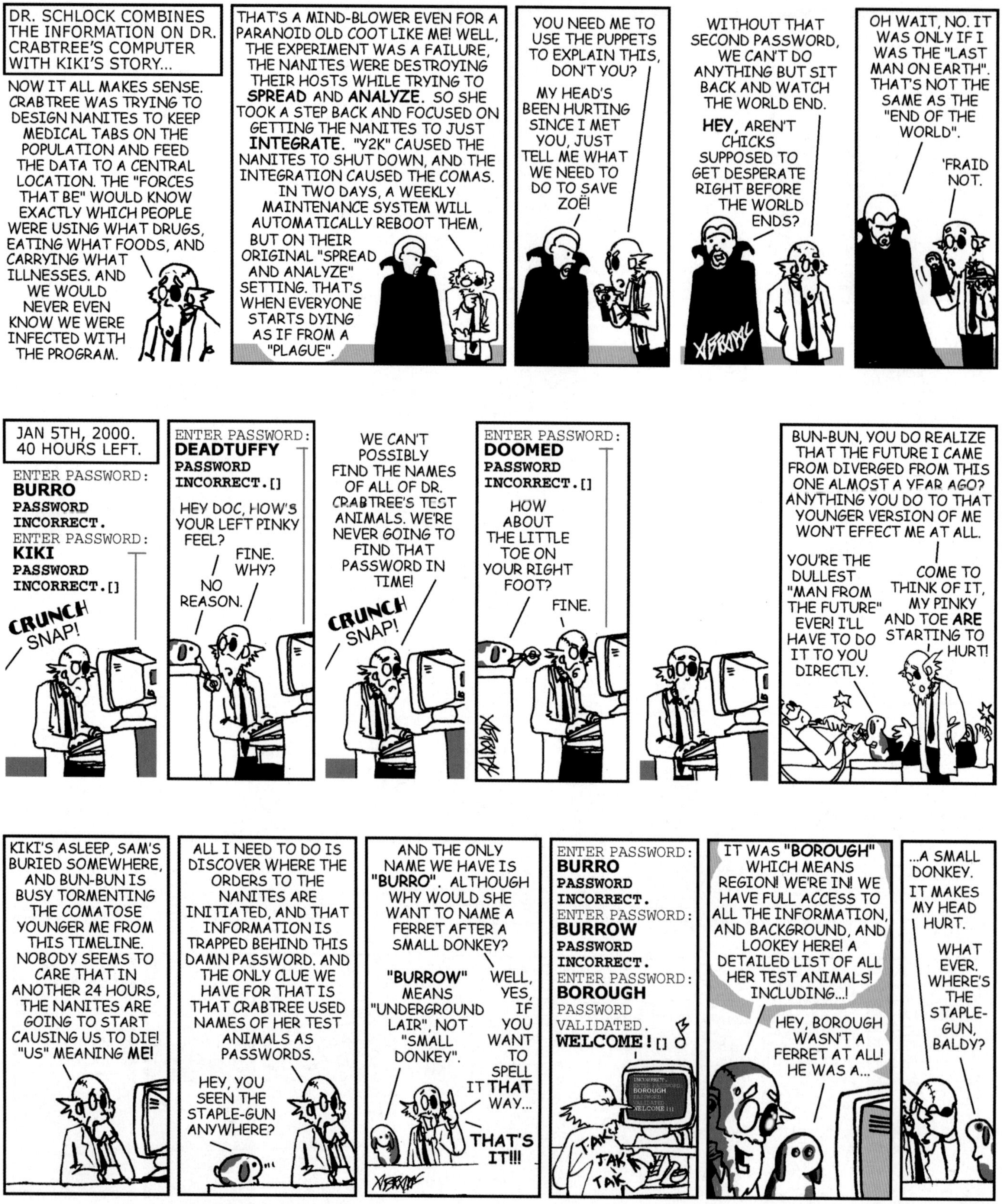
DR. SCHLOCK COMBINES THE INFORMATION ON DR. CRABTREE'S COMPUTER WITH KIKI'S STORY...
NOW IT ALL MAKES SENSE. CRABTREE WAS TRYING TO DESIGN NANITES TO KEEP MEDICAL TABS ON THE POPULATION AND FEED THE DATA TO A CENTRAL LOCATION. THE "FORCES THAT BE" WOULD KNOW EXACTLY WHICH PEOPLE WERE USING WHAT DRUGS, EATING WHAT FOODS, AND CARRYING WHAT ILLNESSES. AND WE WOULD NEVER EVEN KNOW WE WERE INFECTED WITH THE PROGRAM.
THAT'S A MIND-BLOWER EVEN FOR A PARANOID OLD COOT LIKE ME! WELL, THE EXPERIMENT WAS A FAILURE, THE NANITES WERE DESTROYING THEIR HOSTS WHILE TRYING TO **SPREAD** AND **ANALYZE.** SO SHE TOOK A STEP BACK AND FOCUSED ON GETTING THE NANITES TO JUST **INTEGRATE.** "Y2K" CAUSED THE NANITES TO SHUT DOWN, AND THE INTEGRATION CAUSED THE COMAS. IN TWO DAYS, A WEEKLY MAINTENANCE SYSTEM WILL AUTOMATICALLY REBOOT THEM,
BUT ON THEIR ORIGINAL "SPREAD AND ANALYZE" SETTING. THAT'S WHEN EVERYONE STARTS DYING AS IF FROM A "PLAGUE".
YOU NEED ME TO USE THE PUPPETS TO EXPLAIN THIS, DON'T YOU?
MY HEAD'S BEEN HURTING SINCE I MET YOU, JUST TELL ME WHAT WE NEED TO DO TO SAVE ZOË!
WITHOUT THAT SECOND PASSWORD, WE CAN'T DO ANYTHING BUT SIT BACK AND WATCH THE WORLD END.
HEY, AREN'T CHICKS SUPPOSED TO GET DESPERATE RIGHT BEFORE THE WORLD ENDS?
OH WAIT, NO. IT WAS ONLY IF I WAS THE "LAST MAN ON EARTH". THAT'S NOT THE SAME AS THE "END OF THE WORLD".
'FRAID NOT.
JAN 5TH, 2000. 40 HOURS LEFT.
ENTER PASSWORD: **BURRO** **PASSWORD INCORRECT.**
ENTER PASSWORD: **KIKI** **PASSWORD INCORRECT.[]**
CRUNCH SNAP!
ENTER PASSWORD: **DEADTUFFY** **PASSWORD INCORRECT.[]**
HEY DOC, HOW'S YOUR LEFT PINKY FEEL?
FINE. WHY?
NO REASON.
WE CAN'T POSSIBLY FIND THE NAMES OF ALL OF DR. CRABTREE'S TEST ANIMALS. WE'RE NEVER GOING TO FIND THAT PASSWORD IN TIME!
CRUNCH SNAP!
ENTER PASSWORD: **DOOMED** **PASSWORD INCORRECT.[]**
HOW ABOUT THE LITTLE TOE ON YOUR RIGHT FOOT?
FINE.
BUN-BUN, YOU DO REALIZE THAT THE FUTURE I CAME FROM DIVERGED FROM THIS ONE ALMOST A YEAR AGO? ANYTHING YOU DO TO THAT YOUNGER VERSION OF ME WON'T EFFECT ME AT ALL.
YOU'RE THE DULLEST "MAN FROM THE FUTURE" EVER! I'LL HAVE TO DO IT TO YOU DIRECTLY.
COME TO THINK OF IT, MY PINKY AND TOE **ARE** STARTING TO HURT!
KIKI'S ASLEEP, SAM'S BURIED SOMEWHERE, AND BUN-BUN IS BUSY TORMENTING THE COMATOSE YOUNGER ME FROM THIS TIMELINE. NOBODY SEEMS TO CARE THAT IN ANOTHER 24 HOURS, THE NANITES ARE GOING TO START CAUSING US TO DIE! "US" MEANING **ME!**
ALL I NEED TO DO IS DISCOVER WHERE THE ORDERS TO THE NANITES ARE INITIATED, AND THAT INFORMATION IS TRAPPED BEHIND THIS DAMN PASSWORD. AND THE ONLY CLUE WE HAVE FOR THAT IS THAT CRABTREE USED NAMES OF HER TEST ANIMALS AS PASSWORDS.
HEY, YOU SEEN THE STAPLE-GUN ANYWHERE?
AND THE ONLY NAME WE HAVE IS **"BURRO".** ALTHOUGH WHY WOULD SHE WANT TO NAME A FERRET AFTER A SMALL DONKEY?
"BURROW" MEANS "UNDERGROUND LAIR", NOT "SMALL DONKEY".
WELL, YES, IF YOU WANT TO SPELL IT **THAT** WAY...
THAT'S IT!!!
ENTER PASSWORD: **BURRO** **PASSWORD INCORRECT.**
ENTER PASSWORD: **BURROW** **PASSWORD INCORRECT.**
ENTER PASSWORD: **BOROUGH**
PASSWORD VALIDATED. **WELCOME! []**
TAK TAK TAK
IT WAS **"BOROUGH"** WHICH MEANS REGION! WE'RE IN! WE HAVE FULL ACCESS TO ALL THE INFORMATION, AND BACKGROUND, AND LOOKEY HERE! A DETAILED LIST OF ALL HER TEST ANIMALS! INCLUDING...!
HEY, BOROUGH WASN'T A FERRET AT ALL! HE WAS A...
...A SMALL DONKEY.
IT MAKES MY HEAD HURT.
WHAT EVER. WHERE'S THE STAPLE-GUN, BALDY?

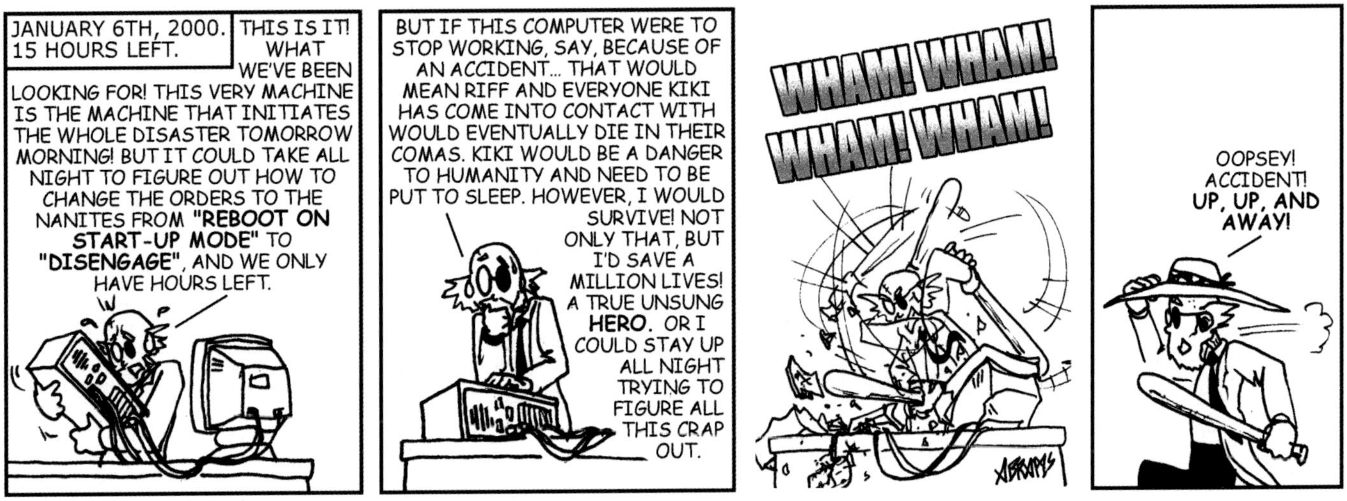
JANUARY 6TH, 2000. 15 HOURS LEFT.
THIS IS IT! WHAT WE'VE BEEN LOOKING FOR! THIS VERY MACHINE IS THE MACHINE THAT INITIATES THE WHOLE DISASTER TOMORROW MORNING! BUT IT COULD TAKE ALL NIGHT TO FIGURE OUT HOW TO CHANGE THE ORDERS TO THE NANITES FROM "REBOOT ON START-UP MODE" TO "DISENGAGE", AND WE ONLY HAVE HOURS LEFT.
BUT IF THIS COMPUTER WERE TO STOP WORKING, SAY, BECAUSE OF AN ACCIDENT... THAT WOULD MEAN RIFF AND EVERYONE KIKI HAS COME INTO CONTACT WITH WOULD EVENTUALLY DIE IN THEIR COMAS. KIKI WOULD BE A DANGER TO HUMANITY AND NEED TO BE PUT TO SLEEP. HOWEVER, I WOULD SURVIVE! NOT ONLY THAT, BUT I'D SAVE A MILLION LIVES! A TRUE UNSUNG HERO. OR I COULD STAY UP ALL NIGHT TRYING TO FIGURE ALL THIS CRAP OUT.
WHAM! WHAM! WHAM! WHAM!
OOPSEY! ACCIDENT! UP, UP, AND AWAY!

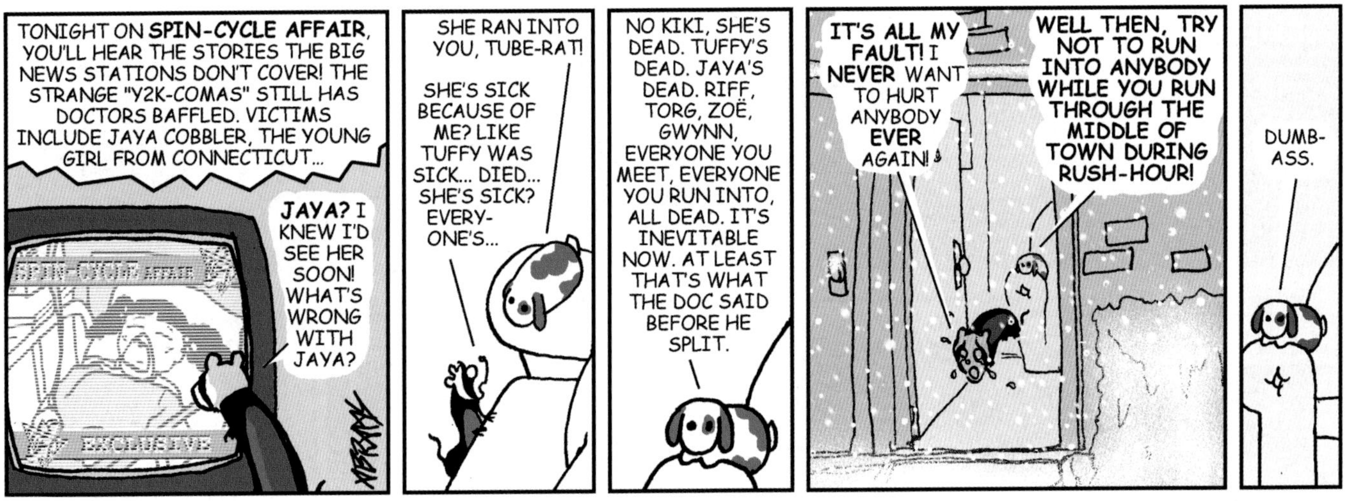
TONIGHT ON SPIN-CYCLE AFFAIR, YOU'LL HEAR THE STORIES THE BIG NEWS STATIONS DON'T COVER! THE STRANGE "Y2K-COMAS" STILL HAS DOCTORS BAFFLED. VICTIMS INCLUDE JAYA COBBLER, THE YOUNG GIRL FROM CONNECTICUT...
JAYA? I KNEW I'D SEE HER SOON! WHAT'S WRONG WITH JAYA?
SHE RAN INTO YOU, TUBE-RAT!
SHE'S SICK BECAUSE OF ME? LIKE TUFFY WAS SICK... DIED... SHE'S SICK? EVERY-ONE'S...
NO KIKI, SHE'S DEAD. TUFFY'S DEAD. JAYA'S DEAD. RIFF, TORG, ZOË, GWYNN, EVERYONE YOU MEET, EVERYONE YOU RUN INTO, ALL DEAD. IT'S INEVITABLE NOW. AT LEAST THAT'S WHAT THE DOC SAID BEFORE HE SPLIT.
IT'S ALL MY FAULT! I NEVER WANT TO HURT ANYBODY EVER AGAIN!
WELL THEN, TRY NOT TO RUN INTO ANYBODY WHILE YOU RUN THROUGH THE MIDDLE OF TOWN DURING RUSH-HOUR!
DUMB-ASS.

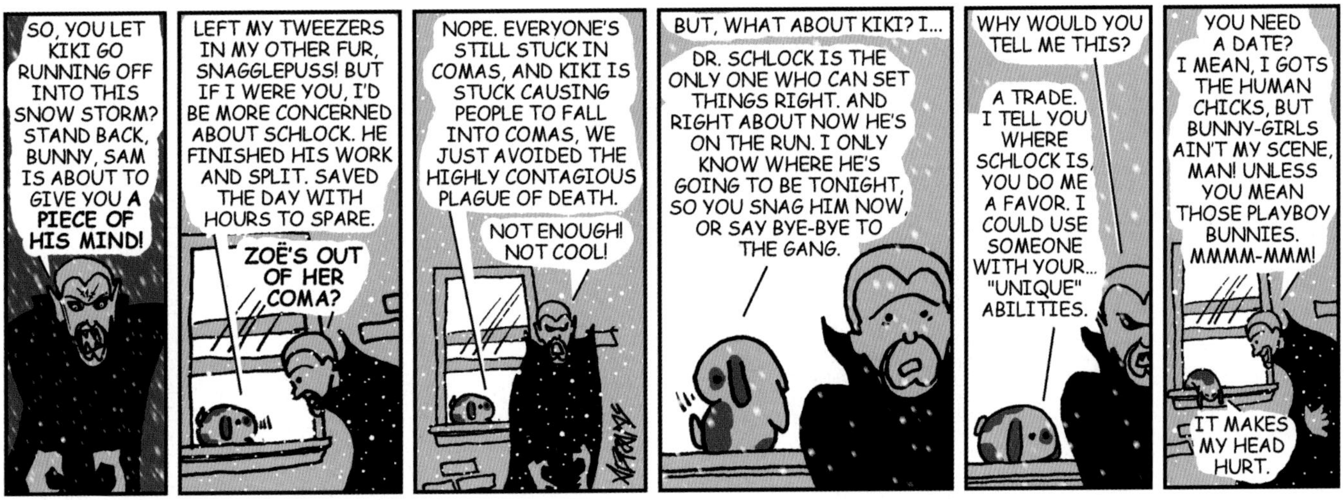
SO, YOU LET KIKI GO RUNNING OFF INTO THIS SNOW STORM? STAND BACK, BUNNY, SAM IS ABOUT TO GIVE YOU A PIECE OF HIS MIND!
ZOË'S OUT OF HER COMA?
LEFT MY TWEEZERS IN MY OTHER FUR, SNAGGLEPUSS! BUT IF I WERE YOU, I'D BE MORE CONCERNED ABOUT SCHLOCK. HE FINISHED HIS WORK AND SPLIT. SAVED THE DAY WITH HOURS TO SPARE.
NOT ENOUGH! NOT COOL!
NOPE. EVERYONE'S STILL STUCK IN COMAS, AND KIKI IS STUCK CAUSING PEOPLE TO FALL INTO COMAS, WE JUST AVOIDED THE HIGHLY CONTAGIOUS PLAGUE OF DEATH.
BUT, WHAT ABOUT KIKI? I...
DR. SCHLOCK IS THE ONLY ONE WHO CAN SET THINGS RIGHT. AND RIGHT ABOUT NOW HE'S ON THE RUN. I ONLY KNOW WHERE HE'S GOING TO BE TONIGHT, SO YOU SNAG HIM NOW, OR SAY BYE-BYE TO THE GANG.
WHY WOULD YOU TELL ME THIS?
A TRADE. I TELL YOU WHERE SCHLOCK IS, YOU DO ME A FAVOR. I COULD USE SOMEONE WITH YOUR... "UNIQUE" ABILITIES.
YOU NEED A DATE? I MEAN, I GOTS THE HUMAN CHICKS, BUT BUNNY-GIRLS AIN'T MY SCENE, MAN! UNLESS YOU MEAN THOSE PLAYBOY BUNNIES. MMMM-MMM!
IT MAKES MY HEAD HURT.

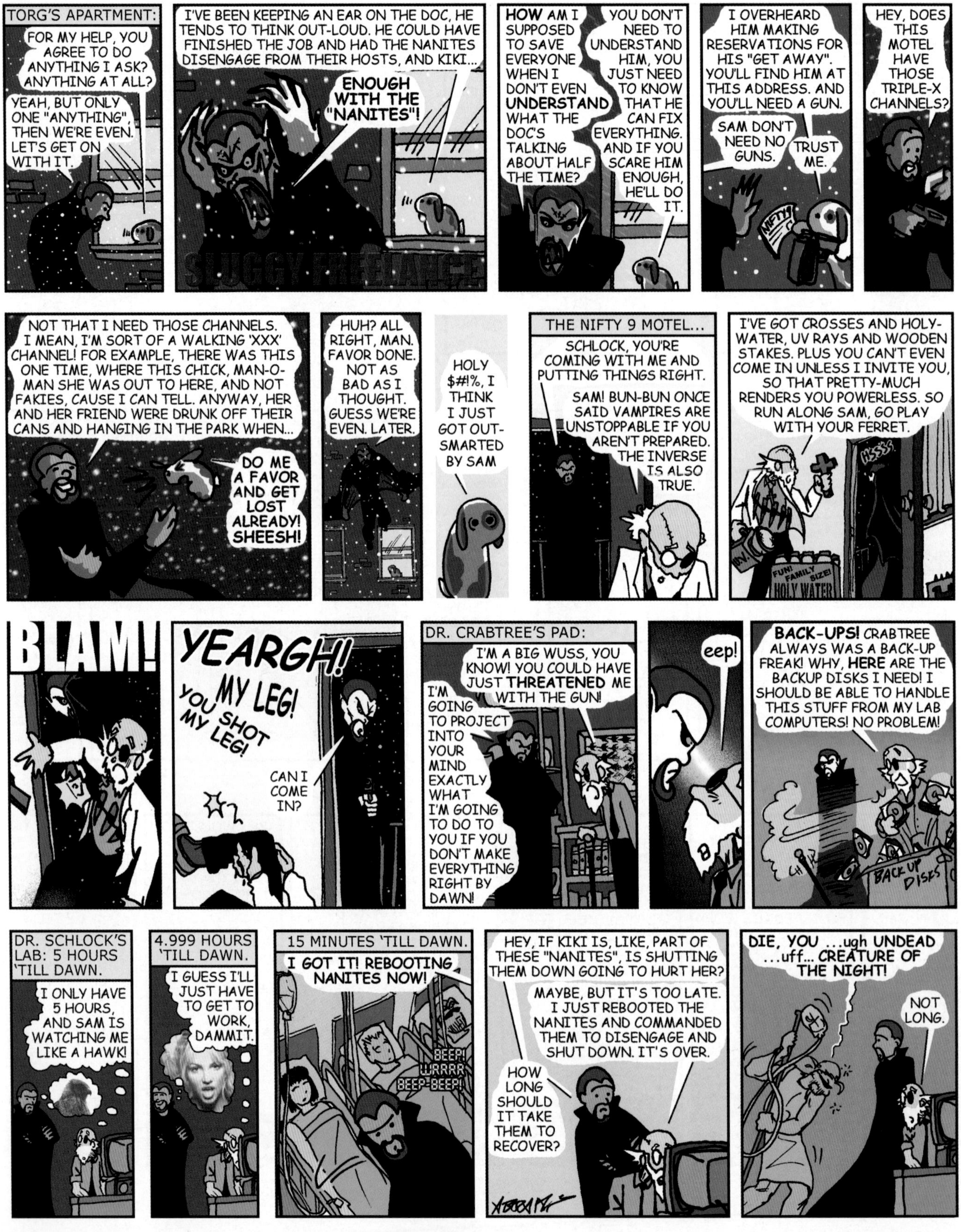
TORG'S APARTMENT:
FOR MY HELP, YOU AGREE TO DO ANYTHING I ASK? ANYTHING AT ALL?
YEAH, BUT ONLY ONE "ANYTHING", THEN WE'RE EVEN. LET'S GET ON WITH IT.
I'VE BEEN KEEPING AN EAR ON THE DOC, HE TENDS TO THINK OUT-LOUD. HE COULD HAVE FINISHED THE JOB AND HAD THE NANITES DISENGAGE FROM THEIR HOSTS, AND KIKI...
ENOUGH WITH THE "NANITES"!
SLUGGY FREELANCE
HOW AM I SUPPOSED TO SAVE EVERYONE WHEN I DON'T EVEN UNDERSTAND WHAT THE DOC'S TALKING ABOUT HALF THE TIME?
YOU DON'T NEED TO UNDERSTAND HIM, YOU JUST NEED TO KNOW THAT HE CAN FIX EVERYTHING. AND IF YOU SCARE HIM ENOUGH, HE'LL DO IT.
I OVERHEARD HIM MAKING RESERVATIONS FOR HIS "GET AWAY". YOU'LL FIND HIM AT THIS ADDRESS. AND YOU'LL NEED A GUN.
SAM DON'T NEED NO GUNS.
TRUST ME.
NIFTY 9
HEY, DOES THIS MOTEL HAVE THOSE TRIPLE-X CHANNELS?
NOT THAT I NEED THOSE CHANNELS. I MEAN, I'M SORT OF A WALKING 'XXX' CHANNEL! FOR EXAMPLE, THERE WAS THIS ONE TIME, WHERE THIS CHICK, MAN-O-MAN SHE WAS OUT TO HERE, AND NOT FAKIES, CAUSE I CAN TELL. ANYWAY, HER AND HER FRIEND WERE DRUNK OFF THEIR CANS AND HANGING IN THE PARK WHEN...
DO ME A FAVOR AND GET LOST ALREADY! SHEESH!
HUH? ALL RIGHT, MAN. FAVOR DONE. NOT AS BAD AS I THOUGHT. GUESS WE'RE EVEN. LATER.
HOLY $#!%, I THINK I JUST GOT OUT-SMARTED BY SAM
THE NIFTY 9 MOTEL...
SCHLOCK, YOU'RE COMING WITH ME AND PUTTING THINGS RIGHT.
SAM! BUN-BUN ONCE SAID VAMPIRES ARE UNSTOPPABLE IF YOU AREN'T PREPARED. THE INVERSE IS ALSO TRUE.
I'VE GOT CROSSES AND HOLY-WATER, UV RAYS AND WOODEN STAKES. PLUS YOU CAN'T EVEN COME IN UNLESS I INVITE YOU, SO THAT PRETTY-MUCH RENDERS YOU POWERLESS. SO RUN ALONG SAM, GO PLAY WITH YOUR FERRET.
HSSS
FUN! FAMILY SIZE! HOLY WATER
BLAM!
YEARGH!
MY LEG!
YOU SHOT MY LEG!
CAN I COME IN?
DR. CRABTREE'S PAD:
I'M A BIG WUSS, YOU KNOW! YOU COULD HAVE JUST THREATENED ME WITH THE GUN!
I'M GOING TO PROJECT INTO YOUR MIND EXACTLY WHAT I'M GOING TO DO TO YOU IF YOU DON'T MAKE EVERYTHING RIGHT BY DAWN!
eep!
BACK-UPS! CRABTREE ALWAYS WAS A BACK-UP FREAK! WHY, HERE ARE THE BACKUP DISKS I NEED! I SHOULD BE ABLE TO HANDLE THIS STUFF FROM MY LAB COMPUTERS! NO PROBLEM!
BACK UP DISKS
DR. SCHLOCK'S LAB: 5 HOURS 'TILL DAWN.
I ONLY HAVE 5 HOURS, AND SAM IS WATCHING ME LIKE A HAWK!
4.999 HOURS 'TILL DAWN.
I GUESS I'LL JUST HAVE TO GET TO WORK, DAMMIT.
15 MINUTES 'TILL DAWN.
I GOT IT! REBOOTING NANITES NOW!
BEEP! WRRRR BEEP-BEEP!
HEY, IF KIKI IS, LIKE, PART OF THESE "NANITES", IS SHUTTING THEM DOWN GOING TO HURT HER?
MAYBE, BUT IT'S TOO LATE. I JUST REBOOTED THE NANITES AND COMMANDED THEM TO DISENGAGE AND SHUT DOWN. IT'S OVER.
HOW LONG SHOULD IT TAKE THEM TO RECOVER?
DIE, YOU ...ugh UNDEAD ...uff... CREATURE OF THE NIGHT!
NOT LONG.

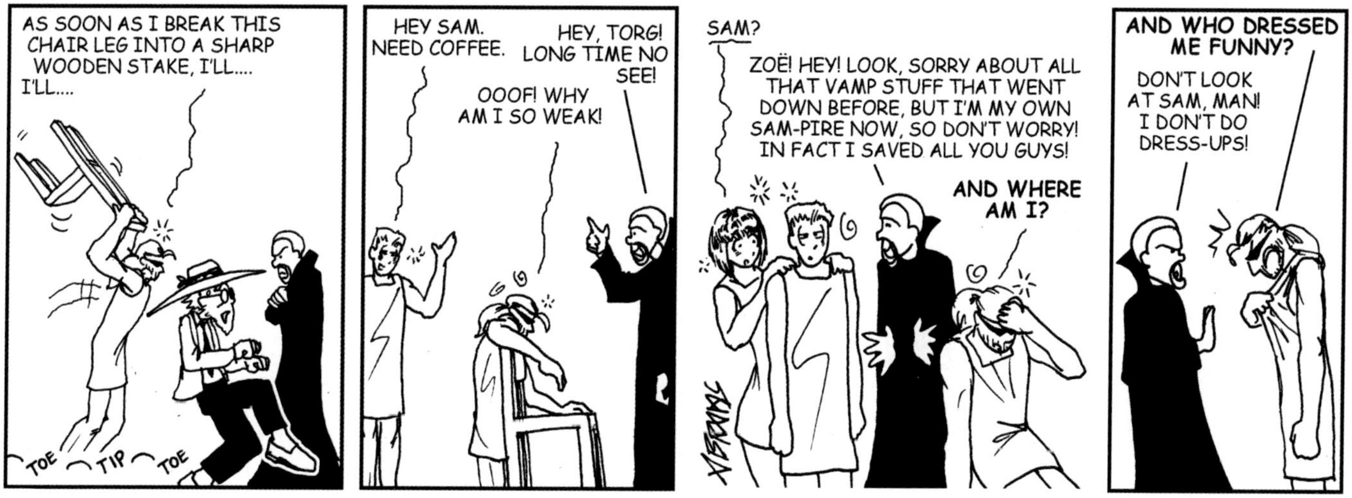
AS SOON AS I BREAK THIS CHAIR LEG INTO A SHARP WOODEN STAKE, I'LL.... I'LL....
TOE TIP TOE
HEY SAM. NEED COFFEE.
HEY, TORG! LONG TIME NO SEE!
OOOF! WHY AM I SO WEAK!
SAM?
ZOË! HEY! LOOK, SORRY ABOUT ALL THAT VAMP STUFF THAT WENT DOWN BEFORE, BUT I'M MY OWN SAM-PIRE NOW, SO DON'T WORRY! IN FACT I SAVED ALL YOU GUYS!
AND WHERE AM I?
AND WHO DRESSED ME FUNNY?
DON'T LOOK AT SAM, MAN! I DON'T DO DRESS-UPS!

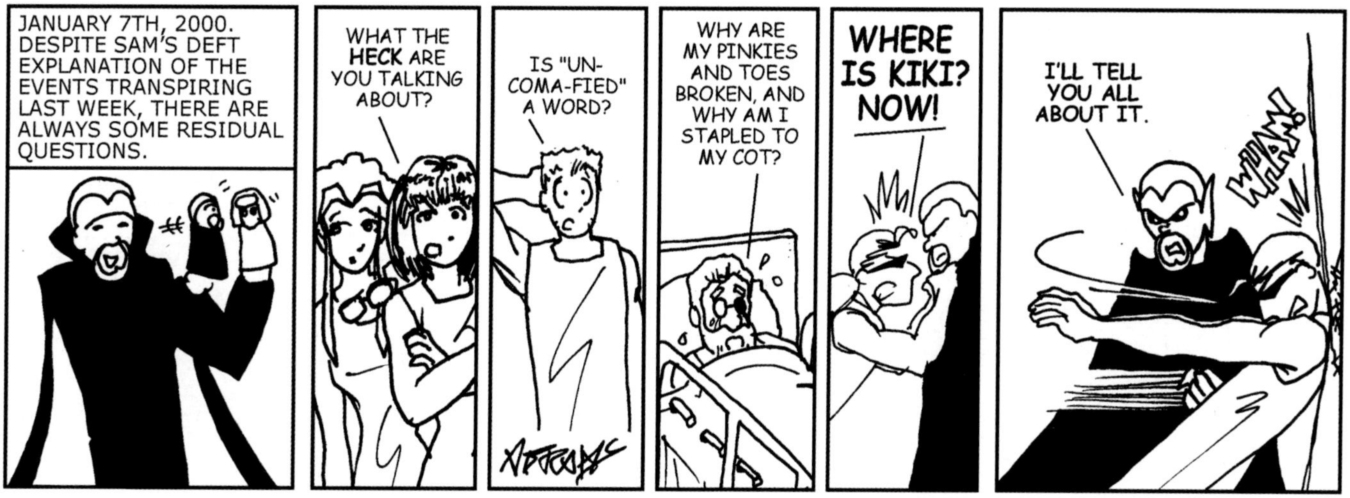
JANUARY 7TH, 2000. DESPITE SAM'S DEFT EXPLANATION OF THE EVENTS TRANSPIRING LAST WEEK, THERE ARE ALWAYS SOME RESIDUAL QUESTIONS.
WHAT THE HECK ARE YOU TALKING ABOUT?
IS "UN-COMA-FIED" A WORD?
WHY ARE MY PINKIES AND TOES BROKEN, AND WHY AM I STAPLED TO MY COT?
WHERE IS KIKI? NOW!
I'LL TELL YOU ALL ABOUT IT.
WHAM!

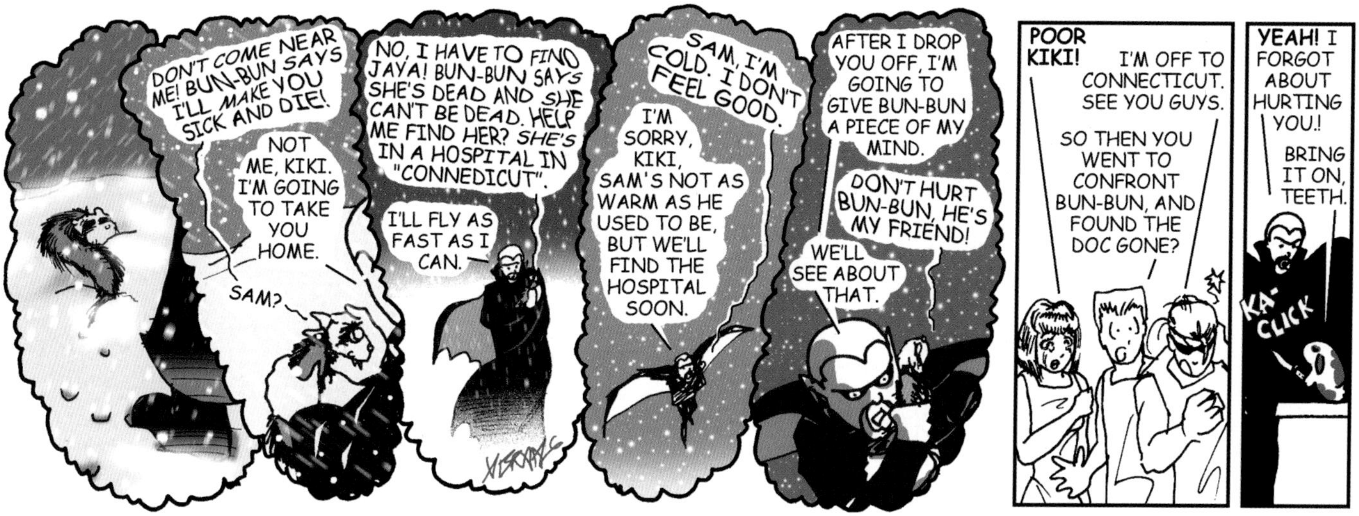
DON'T COME NEAR ME! BUN-BUN SAYS I'LL MAKE YOU SICK AND DIE!
NOT ME, KIKI. I'M GOING TO TAKE YOU HOME.
SAM?
NO, I HAVE TO FIND JAYA! BUN-BUN SAYS SHE'S DEAD AND SHE CAN'T BE DEAD. HELP ME FIND HER? SHE'S IN A HOSPITAL IN "CONNEDICUT".
I'LL FLY AS FAST AS I CAN.
SAM, I'M COLD. I DON'T FEEL GOOD.
I'M SORRY, KIKI, SAM'S NOT AS WARM AS HE USED TO BE, BUT WE'LL FIND THE HOSPITAL SOON.
AFTER I DROP YOU OFF, I'M GOING TO GIVE BUN-BUN A PIECE OF MY MIND.
DON'T HURT BUN-BUN, HE'S MY FRIEND!
WE'LL SEE ABOUT THAT.
POOR KIKI!
I'M OFF TO CONNECTICUT. SEE YOU GUYS.
SO THEN YOU WENT TO CONFRONT BUN-BUN, AND FOUND THE DOC GONE?
YEAH! I FORGOT ABOUT HURTING YOU.!
BRING IT ON, TEETH.
KA-CLICK

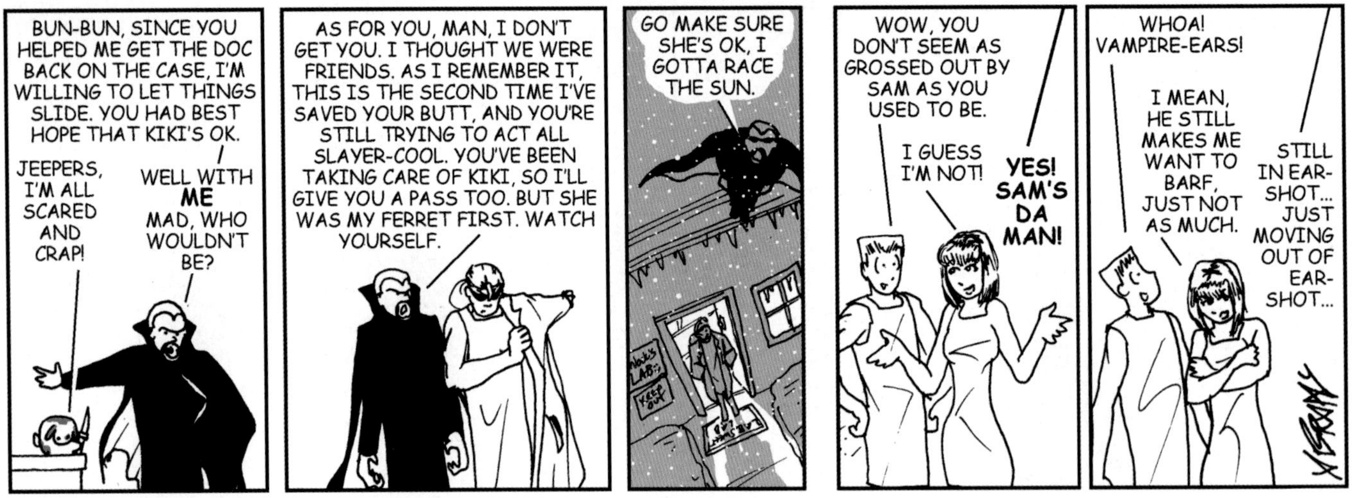
BUN-BUN, SINCE YOU HELPED ME GET THE DOC BACK ON THE CASE, I'M WILLING TO LET THINGS SLIDE. YOU HAD BEST HOPE THAT KIKI'S OK.
JEEPERS, I'M ALL SCARED AND CRAP!
WELL WITH ME MAD, WHO WOULDN'T BE?
AS FOR YOU, MAN, I DON'T GET YOU. I THOUGHT WE WERE FRIENDS. AS I REMEMBER IT, THIS IS THE SECOND TIME I'VE SAVED YOUR BUTT, AND YOU'RE STILL TRYING TO ACT ALL SLAYER-COOL. YOU'VE BEEN TAKING CARE OF KIKI, SO I'LL GIVE YOU A PASS TOO. BUT SHE WAS MY FERRET FIRST. WATCH YOURSELF.
GO MAKE SURE SHE'S OK, I GOTTA RACE THE SUN.
WOW, YOU DON'T SEEM AS GROSSED OUT BY SAM AS YOU USED TO BE.
I GUESS I'M NOT!
YES! SAM'S DA MAN!
WHOA! VAMPIRE-EARS!
I MEAN, HE STILL MAKES ME WANT TO BARF, JUST NOT AS MUCH.
STILL IN EAR-SHOT... JUST MOVING OUT OF EAR-SHOT...

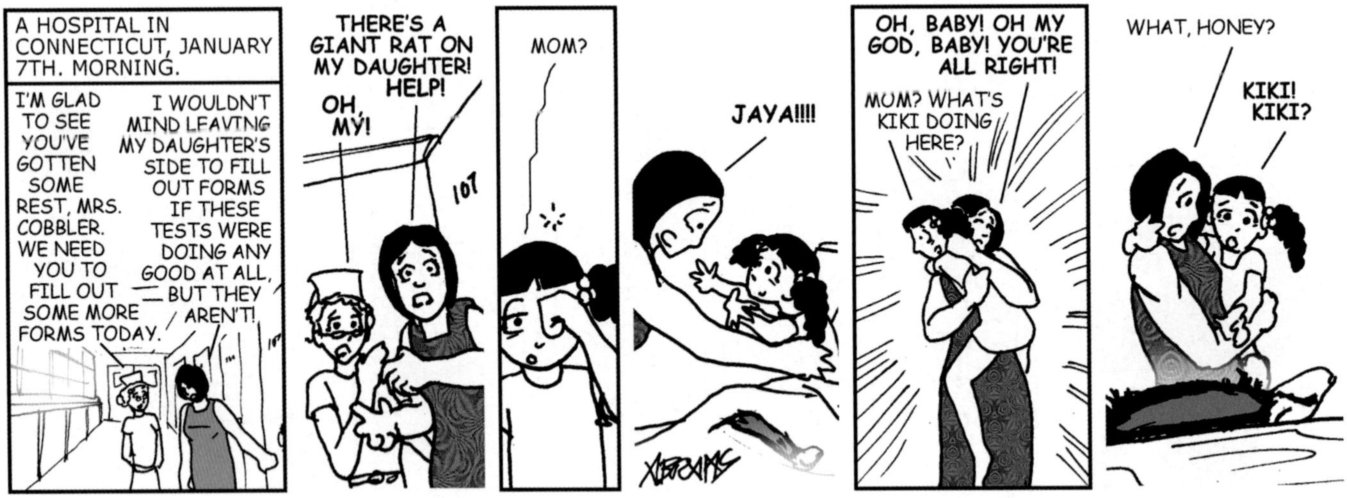
A HOSPITAL IN CONNECTICUT, JANUARY 7TH. MORNING.
I'M GLAD TO SEE YOU'VE GOTTEN SOME REST, MRS. COBBLER. WE NEED YOU TO FILL OUT SOME MORE FORMS TODAY.
I WOULDN'T MIND LEAVING MY DAUGHTER'S SIDE TO FILL OUT FORMS IF THESE TESTS WERE DOING ANY GOOD AT ALL, BUT THEY AREN'T!
THERE'S A GIANT RAT ON MY DAUGHTER! HELP!
OH, MY!
107
MOM?
JAYA!!!!
OH, BABY! OH MY GOD, BABY! YOU'RE ALL RIGHT!
MOM? WHAT'S KIKI DOING HERE?
WHAT, HONEY?
KIKI! KIKI?

"Make them bring Kiki back! Make them bring Kiki back!"

"Honey, the orderlies had to take it, it was dead. The poor thing."

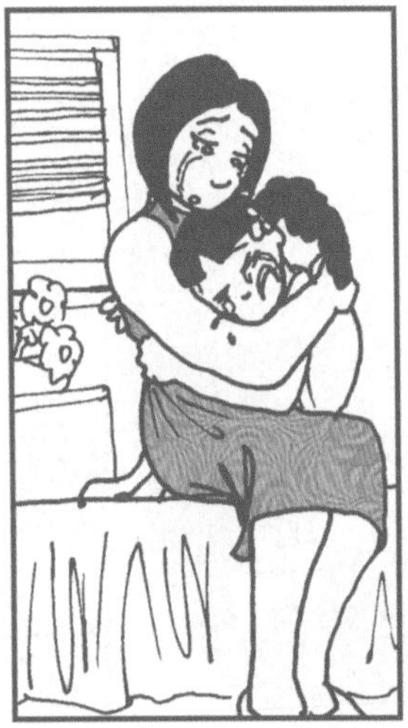

"No! Not Kiki!"

"Honey, I know it's hard, but please listen. That poor ferret couldn't have been the ferret you played with two summers ago."

"It was! It was Kiki!"

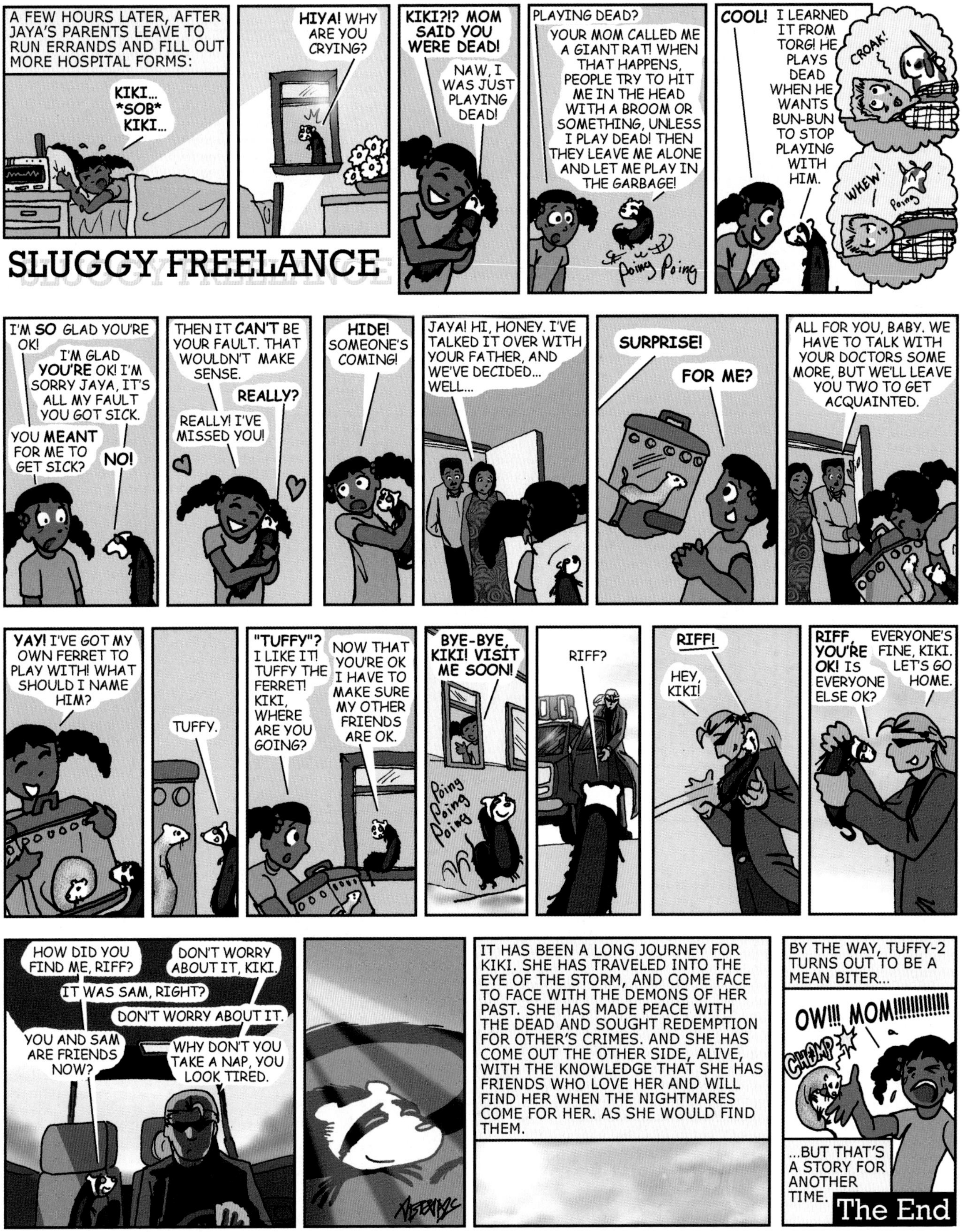
A FEW HOURS LATER, AFTER JAYA'S PARENTS LEAVE TO RUN ERRANDS AND FILL OUT MORE HOSPITAL FORMS:
KIKI... *SOB* KIKI...
HIYA! WHY ARE YOU CRYING?
KIKI?!? MOM SAID YOU WERE DEAD!
NAW, I WAS JUST PLAYING DEAD!
PLAYING DEAD?
YOUR MOM CALLED ME A GIANT RAT! WHEN THAT HAPPENS, PEOPLE TRY TO HIT ME IN THE HEAD WITH A BROOM OR SOMETHING, UNLESS I PLAY DEAD! THEN THEY LEAVE ME ALONE AND LET ME PLAY IN THE GARBAGE!
Poing Poing
COOL!
I LEARNED IT FROM TORG! HE PLAYS DEAD WHEN HE WANTS BUN-BUN TO STOP PLAYING WITH HIM.
CROAK!
WHEW!
Poing
SLUGGY FREELANCE
I'M SO GLAD YOU'RE OK!
I'M GLAD YOU'RE OK! I'M SORRY JAYA, IT'S ALL MY FAULT YOU GOT SICK.
YOU MEANT FOR ME TO GET SICK?
NO!
THEN IT CAN'T BE YOUR FAULT. THAT WOULDN'T MAKE SENSE.
REALLY?
REALLY! I'VE MISSED YOU!
HIDE! SOMEONE'S COMING!
JAYA! HI, HONEY. I'VE TALKED IT OVER WITH YOUR FATHER, AND WE'VE DECIDED... WELL...
SURPRISE!
FOR ME?
ALL FOR YOU, BABY. WE HAVE TO TALK WITH YOUR DOCTORS SOME MORE, BUT WE'LL LEAVE YOU TWO TO GET ACQUAINTED.
YAY! I'VE GOT MY OWN FERRET TO PLAY WITH! WHAT SHOULD I NAME HIM?
TUFFY.
"TUFFY"? I LIKE IT! TUFFY THE FERRET! KIKI, WHERE ARE YOU GOING?
NOW THAT YOU'RE OK I HAVE TO MAKE SURE MY OTHER FRIENDS ARE OK.
BYE-BYE, KIKI! VISIT ME SOON!
Poing Poing Poing
RIFF?
RIFF!
HEY, KIKI!
RIFF, YOU'RE OK! IS EVERYONE ELSE OK?
EVERYONE'S FINE, KIKI. LET'S GO HOME.
HOW DID YOU FIND ME, RIFF?
DON'T WORRY ABOUT IT, KIKI.
IT WAS SAM, RIGHT?
DON'T WORRY ABOUT IT.
YOU AND SAM ARE FRIENDS NOW?
WHY DON'T YOU TAKE A NAP, YOU LOOK TIRED.
IT HAS BEEN A LONG JOURNEY FOR KIKI. SHE HAS TRAVELED INTO THE EYE OF THE STORM, AND COME FACE TO FACE WITH THE DEMONS OF HER PAST. SHE HAS MADE PEACE WITH THE DEAD AND SOUGHT REDEMPTION FOR OTHER'S CRIMES. AND SHE HAS COME OUT THE OTHER SIDE, ALIVE, WITH THE KNOWLEDGE THAT SHE HAS FRIENDS WHO LOVE HER AND WILL FIND HER WHEN THE NIGHTMARES COME FOR HER. AS SHE WOULD FIND THEM.
BY THE WAY, TUFFY-2 TURNS OUT TO BE A MEAN BITER...
OW!!! MOM!!!!!!!!!!!
CHOMP
...BUT THAT'S A STORY FOR ANOTHER TIME.
The End

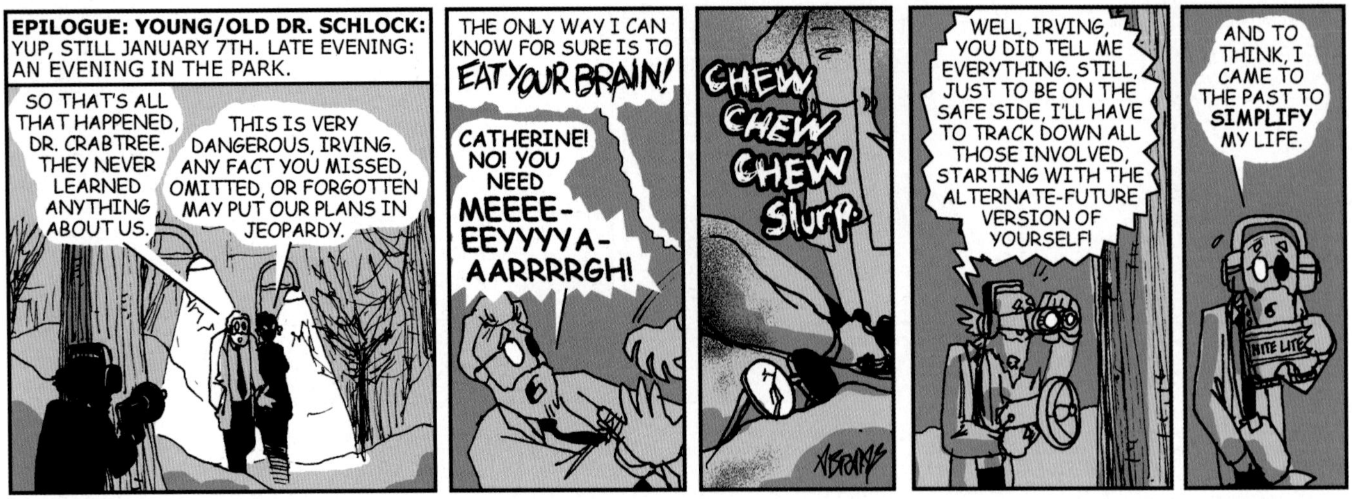
EPILOGUE: YOUNG/OLD DR. SCHLOCK:
YUP, STILL JANUARY 7TH. LATE EVENING: AN EVENING IN THE PARK.
SO THAT'S ALL THAT HAPPENED, DR. CRABTREE. THEY NEVER LEARNED ANYTHING ABOUT US.
THIS IS VERY DANGEROUS, IRVING. ANY FACT YOU MISSED, OMITTED, OR FORGOTTEN MAY PUT OUR PLANS IN JEOPARDY.
THE ONLY WAY I CAN KNOW FOR SURE IS TO EAT YOUR BRAIN!
CATHERINE! NO! YOU NEED MEEEE-EEYYYYA-AARRRRGH!
CHEW CHEW CHEW Slurp
WELL, IRVING, YOU DID TELL ME EVERYTHING. STILL, JUST TO BE ON THE SAFE SIDE, I'LL HAVE TO TRACK DOWN ALL THOSE INVOLVED, STARTING WITH THE ALTERNATE-FUTURE VERSION OF YOURSELF!
AND TO THINK, I CAME TO THE PAST TO SIMPLIFY MY LIFE.
NITE LITE

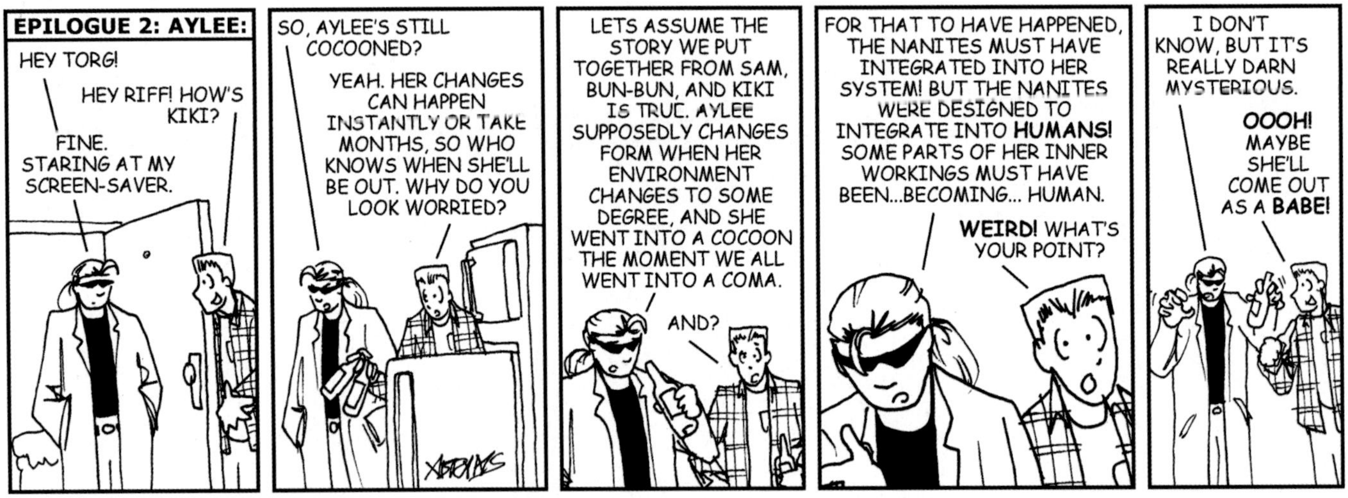
EPILOGUE 2: AYLEE:
HEY TORG!
HEY RIFF! HOW'S KIKI?
FINE. STARING AT MY SCREEN-SAVER.
SO, AYLEE'S STILL COCOONED?
YEAH. HER CHANGES CAN HAPPEN INSTANTLY OR TAKE MONTHS, SO WHO KNOWS WHEN SHE'LL BE OUT. WHY DO YOU LOOK WORRIED?
LETS ASSUME THE STORY WE PUT TOGETHER FROM SAM, BUN-BUN, AND KIKI IS TRUE. AYLEE SUPPOSEDLY CHANGES FORM WHEN HER ENVIRONMENT CHANGES TO SOME DEGREE, AND SHE WENT INTO A COCOON THE MOMENT WE ALL WENT INTO A COMA.
AND?
FOR THAT TO HAVE HAPPENED, THE NANITES MUST HAVE INTEGRATED INTO HER SYSTEM! BUT THE NANITES WERE DESIGNED TO INTEGRATE INTO HUMANS! SOME PARTS OF HER INNER WORKINGS MUST HAVE BEEN...BECOMING... HUMAN.
WEIRD! WHAT'S YOUR POINT?
I DON'T KNOW, BUT IT'S REALLY DARN MYSTERIOUS.
OOOH! MAYBE SHE'LL COME OUT AS A BABE!

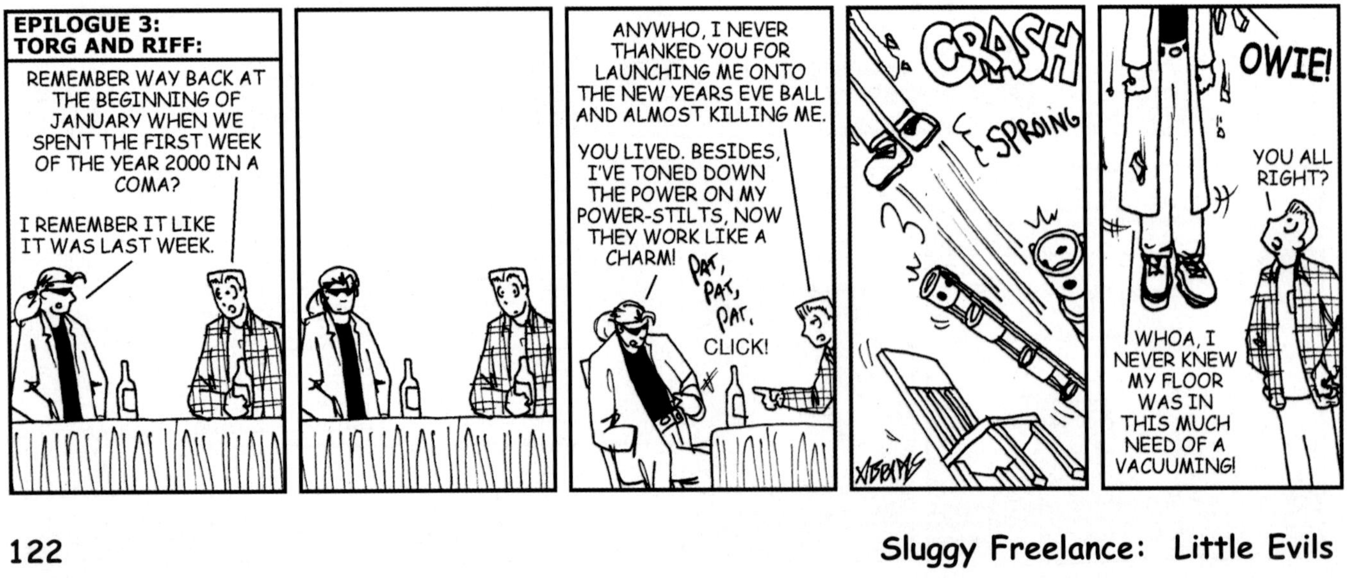
EPILOGUE 3: TORG AND RIFF:
REMEMBER WAY BACK AT THE BEGINNING OF JANUARY WHEN WE SPENT THE FIRST WEEK OF THE YEAR 2000 IN A COMA?
I REMEMBER IT LIKE IT WAS LAST WEEK.
ANYWHO, I NEVER THANKED YOU FOR LAUNCHING ME ONTO THE NEW YEARS EVE BALL AND ALMOST KILLING ME.
YOU LIVED. BESIDES, I'VE TONED DOWN THE POWER ON MY POWER-STILTS, NOW THEY WORK LIKE A CHARM!
PAT, PAT, PAT, CLICK!
CRASH
SPROING
OWIE!
YOU ALL RIGHT?
WHOA, I NEVER KNEW MY FLOOR WAS IN THIS MUCH NEED OF A VACUUMING!

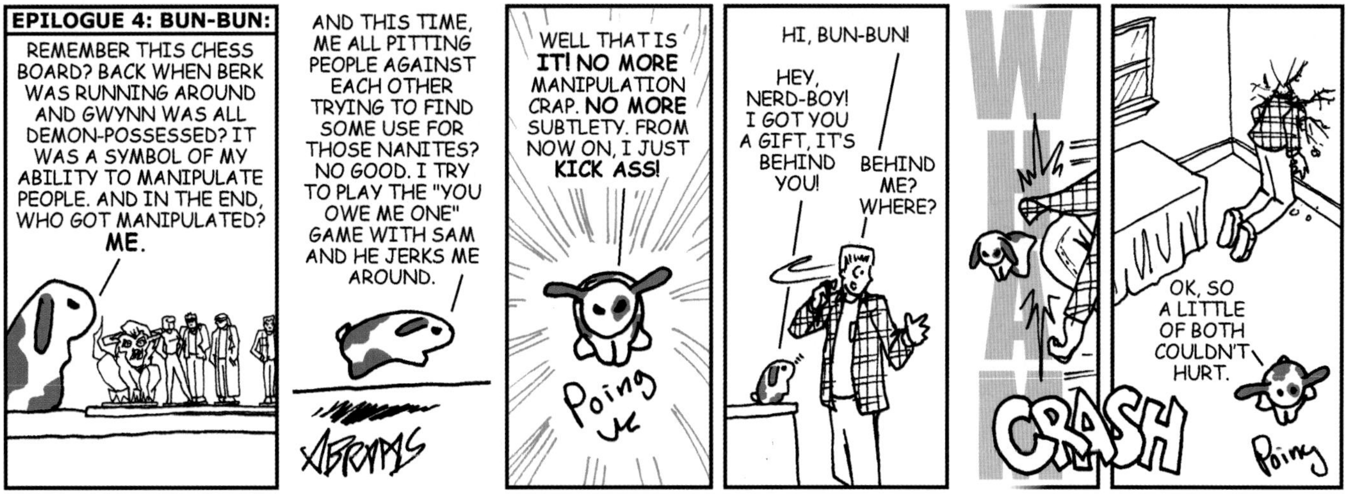
EPILOGUE 4: BUN-BUN:
REMEMBER THIS CHESS BOARD? BACK WHEN BERK WAS RUNNING AROUND AND GWYNN WAS ALL DEMON-POSSESSED? IT WAS A SYMBOL OF MY ABILITY TO MANIPULATE PEOPLE. AND IN THE END, WHO GOT MANIPULATED? **ME**.
AND THIS TIME, ME ALL PITTING PEOPLE AGAINST EACH OTHER TRYING TO FIND SOME USE FOR THOSE NANITES? NO GOOD. I TRY TO PLAY THE "YOU OWE ME ONE" GAME WITH SAM AND HE JERKS ME AROUND.
WELL THAT IS **IT! NO MORE** MANIPULATION CRAP. **NO MORE** SUBTLETY. FROM NOW ON, I JUST **KICK ASS!**
Poing
HI, BUN-BUN!
HEY, NERD-BOY! I GOT YOU A GIFT, IT'S BEHIND YOU!
BEHIND ME? WHERE?
WHAM
CRASH
OK, SO A LITTLE OF BOTH COULDN'T HURT.
Poing

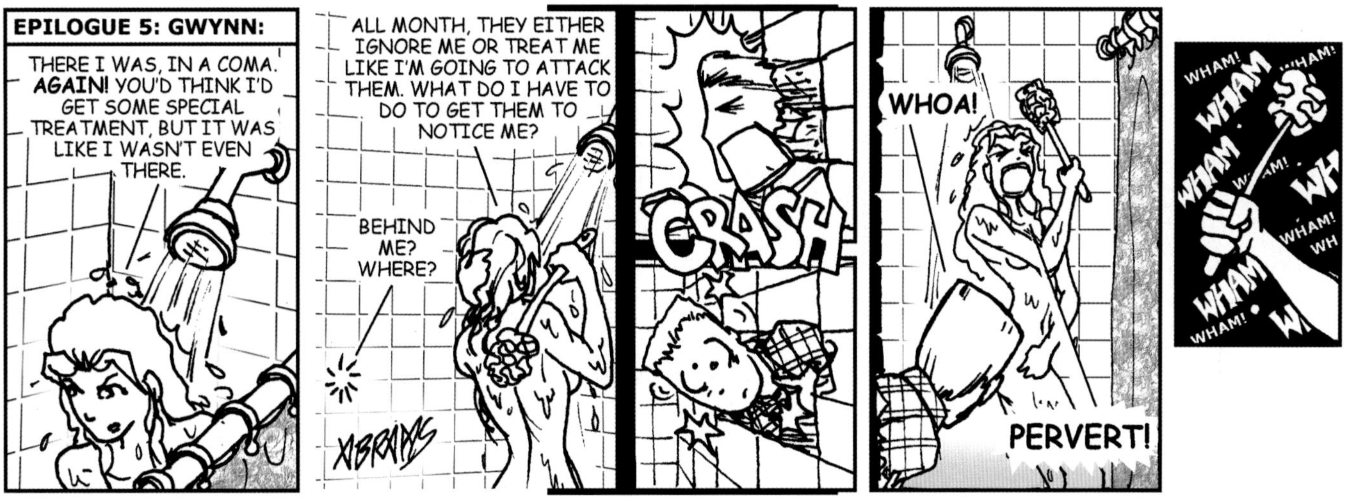
EPILOGUE 5: GWYNN:
THERE I WAS, IN A COMA. **AGAIN!** YOU'D THINK I'D GET SOME SPECIAL TREATMENT, BUT IT WAS LIKE I WASN'T EVEN THERE.
ALL MONTH, THEY EITHER IGNORE ME OR TREAT ME LIKE I'M GOING TO ATTACK THEM. WHAT DO I HAVE TO DO TO GET THEM TO NOTICE ME?
BEHIND ME? WHERE?
CRASH
WHOA!
PERVERT!
WHAM!
WHAM!
WHAM
WHAM
WHAM!
WHAM!
WHAM!

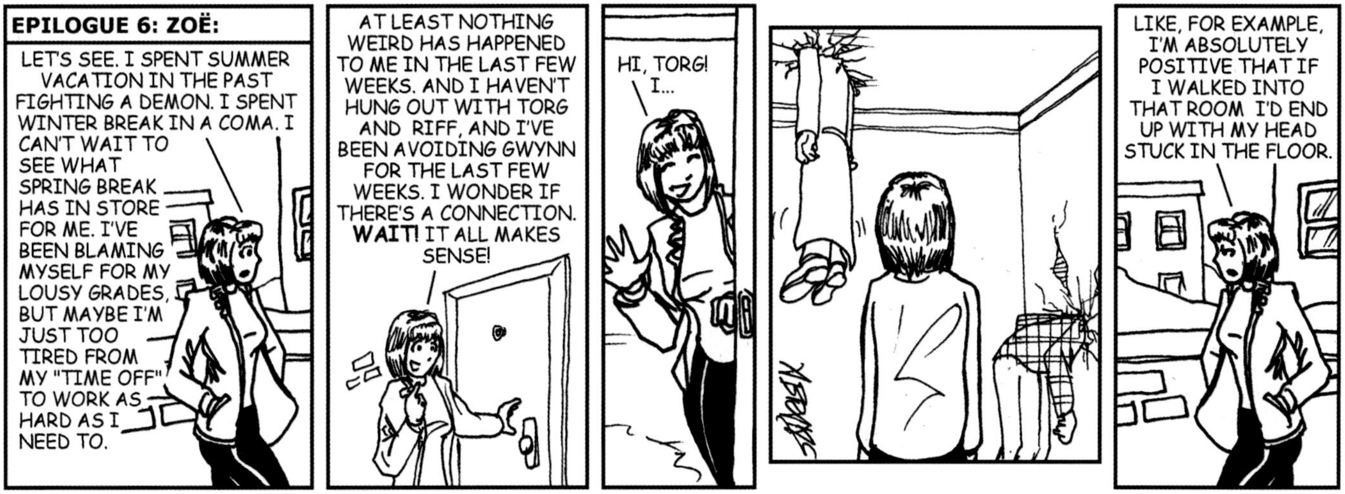
EPILOGUE 6: ZOË:
LET'S SEE. I SPENT SUMMER VACATION IN THE PAST FIGHTING A DEMON. I SPENT WINTER BREAK IN A COMA. I CAN'T WAIT TO SEE WHAT SPRING BREAK HAS IN STORE FOR ME. I'VE BEEN BLAMING MYSELF FOR MY LOUSY GRADES, BUT MAYBE I'M JUST TOO TIRED FROM MY "TIME OFF" TO WORK AS HARD AS I NEED TO.
AT LEAST NOTHING WEIRD HAS HAPPENED TO ME IN THE LAST FEW WEEKS. AND I HAVEN'T HUNG OUT WITH TORG AND RIFF, AND I'VE BEEN AVOIDING GWYNN FOR THE LAST FEW WEEKS. I WONDER IF THERE'S A CONNECTION. **WAIT!** IT ALL MAKES SENSE!
HI, TORG! I...
LIKE, FOR EXAMPLE, I'M ABSOLUTELY POSITIVE THAT IF I WALKED INTO THAT ROOM I'D END UP WITH MY HEAD STUCK IN THE FLOOR.

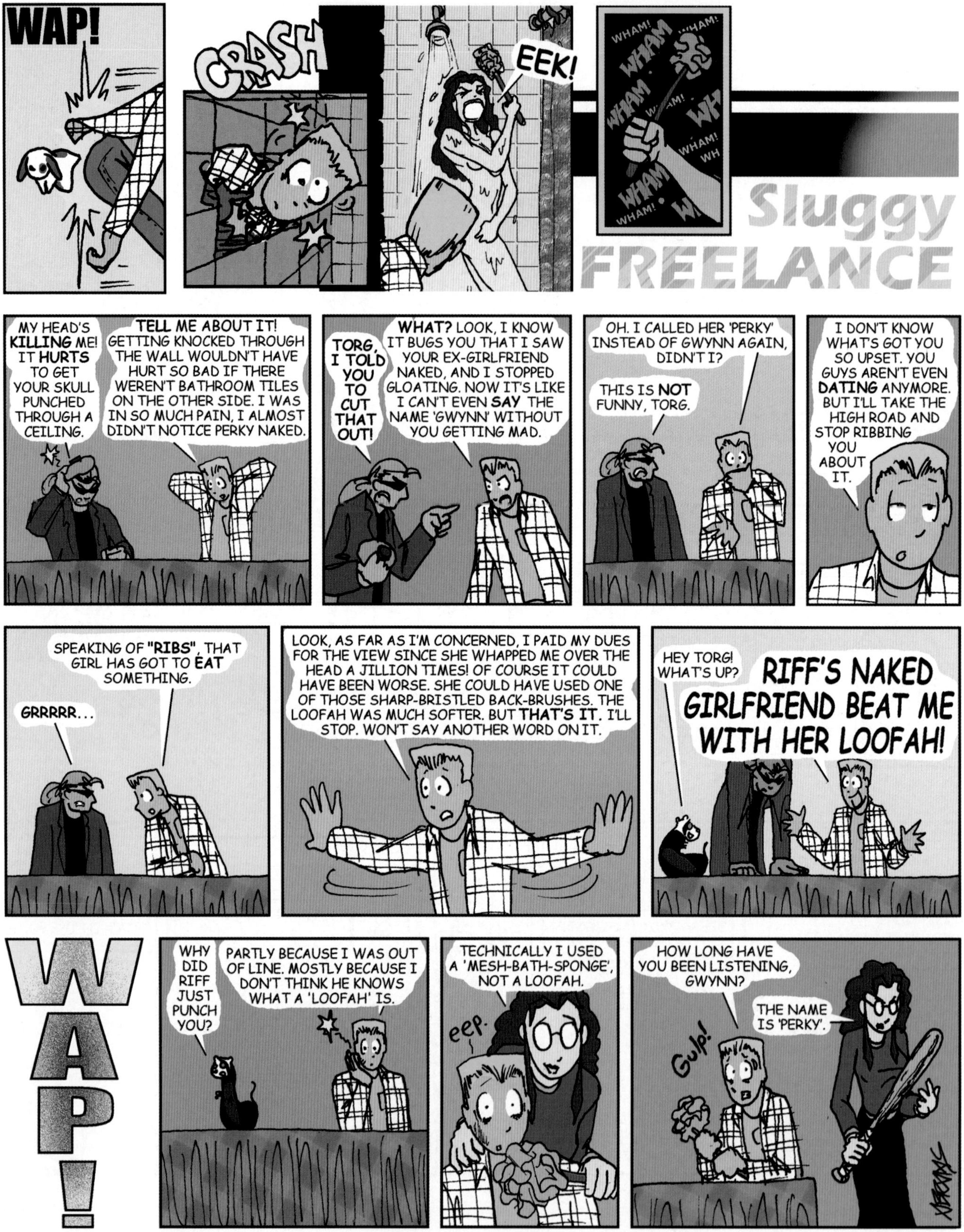
WAP!
CRASH
EEK!
WHAM! WHAM! WHAM! WHAM! WHAM! WHAM! WHAM! WHAM! WHAM!
Sluggy FREELANCE
MY HEAD'S KILLING ME! IT HURTS TO GET YOUR SKULL PUNCHED THROUGH A CEILING.
TELL ME ABOUT IT! GETTING KNOCKED THROUGH THE WALL WOULDN'T HAVE HURT SO BAD IF THERE WEREN'T BATHROOM TILES ON THE OTHER SIDE. I WAS IN SO MUCH PAIN, I ALMOST DIDN'T NOTICE PERKY NAKED.
TORG, I TOLD YOU TO CUT THAT OUT!
WHAT? LOOK, I KNOW IT BUGS YOU THAT I SAW YOUR EX-GIRLFRIEND NAKED, AND I STOPPED GLOATING. NOW IT'S LIKE I CAN'T EVEN SAY THE NAME 'GWYNN' WITHOUT YOU GETTING MAD.
OH. I CALLED HER 'PERKY' INSTEAD OF GWYNN AGAIN, DIDN'T I?
THIS IS NOT FUNNY, TORG.
I DON'T KNOW WHAT'S GOT YOU SO UPSET. YOU GUYS AREN'T EVEN DATING ANYMORE. BUT I'LL TAKE THE HIGH ROAD AND STOP RIBBING YOU ABOUT IT.
SPEAKING OF "RIBS", THAT GIRL HAS GOT TO EAT SOMETHING.
GRRRRR...
LOOK, AS FAR AS I'M CONCERNED, I PAID MY DUES FOR THE VIEW SINCE SHE WHAPPED ME OVER THE HEAD A JILLION TIMES! OF COURSE IT COULD HAVE BEEN WORSE. SHE COULD HAVE USED ONE OF THOSE SHARP-BRISTLED BACK-BRUSHES. THE LOOFAH WAS MUCH SOFTER. BUT THAT'S IT. I'LL STOP. WON'T SAY ANOTHER WORD ON IT.
HEY TORG! WHAT'S UP?
RIFF'S NAKED GIRLFRIEND BEAT ME WITH HER LOOFAH!
WAP!
WHY DID RIFF JUST PUNCH YOU?
PARTLY BECAUSE I WAS OUT OF LINE. MOSTLY BECAUSE I DON'T THINK HE KNOWS WHAT A 'LOOFAH' IS.
TECHNICALLY I USED A 'MESH-BATH-SPONGE', NOT A LOOFAH.
eep.
HOW LONG HAVE YOU BEEN LISTENING, GWYNN?
Gulp!
THE NAME IS 'PERKY'.

In the middle of producing the Kiki virus storyline I ironically became quite sick! Luckily my friends Tom Ricket (aka Shirt-Guy Tom) and Mike Scandizzo came in with a glorious rescue-week of content. I've shifted it to the end so as not to interrupt the story.

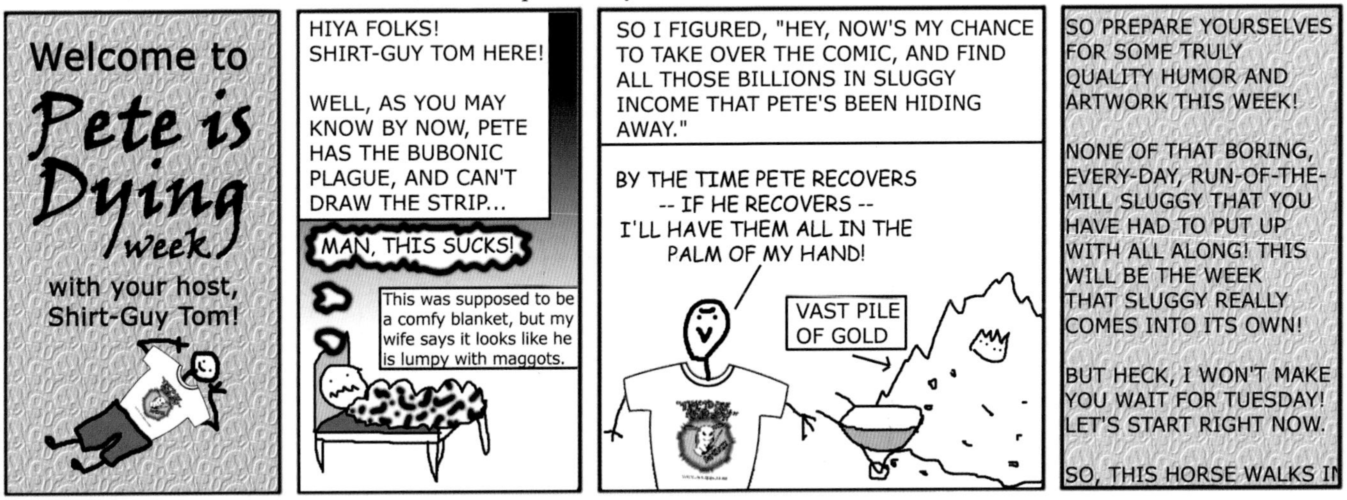

Welcome to Pete is Dying week with your host, Shirt-Guy Tom!
HIYA FOLKS! SHIRT-GUY TOM HERE!
WELL, AS YOU MAY KNOW BY NOW, PETE HAS THE BUBONIC PLAGUE, AND CAN'T DRAW THE STRIP...
MAN, THIS SUCKS!
This was supposed to be a comfy blanket, but my wife says it looks like he is lumpy with maggots.
SO I FIGURED, "HEY, NOW'S MY CHANCE TO TAKE OVER THE COMIC, AND FIND ALL THOSE BILLIONS IN SLUGGY INCOME THAT PETE'S BEEN HIDING AWAY."
BY THE TIME PETE RECOVERS -- IF HE RECOVERS -- I'LL HAVE THEM ALL IN THE PALM OF MY HAND!
VAST PILE OF GOLD
SO PREPARE YOURSELVES FOR SOME TRULY QUALITY HUMOR AND ARTWORK THIS WEEK!
NONE OF THAT BORING, EVERY-DAY, RUN-OF-THE-MILL SLUGGY THAT YOU HAVE HAD TO PUT UP WITH ALL ALONG! THIS WILL BE THE WEEK THAT SLUGGY REALLY COMES INTO ITS OWN!
BUT HECK, I WON'T MAKE YOU WAIT FOR TUESDAY! LET'S START RIGHT NOW.
SO, THIS HORSE WALKS IN

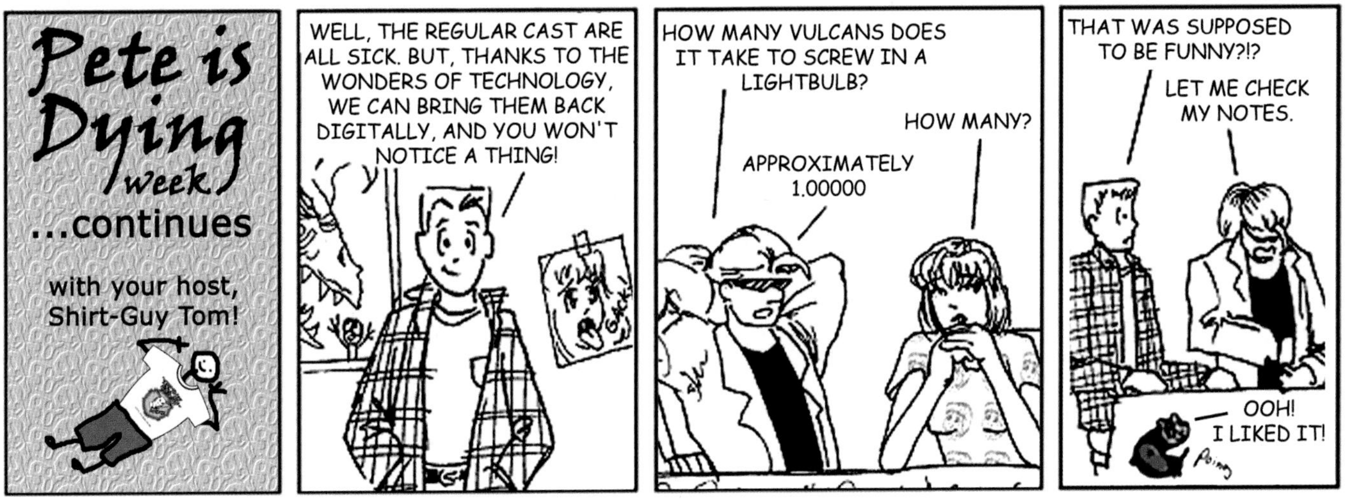

Pete is Dying week ...continues with your host, Shirt-Guy Tom!
WELL, THE REGULAR CAST ARE ALL SICK. BUT, THANKS TO THE WONDERS OF TECHNOLOGY, WE CAN BRING THEM BACK DIGITALLY, AND YOU WON'T NOTICE A THING!
GACK!
HOW MANY VULCANS DOES IT TAKE TO SCREW IN A LIGHTBULB?
HOW MANY?
APPROXIMATELY 1.00000
THAT WAS SUPPOSED TO BE FUNNY?!?
LET ME CHECK MY NOTES.
OOH! I LIKED IT!
Poing

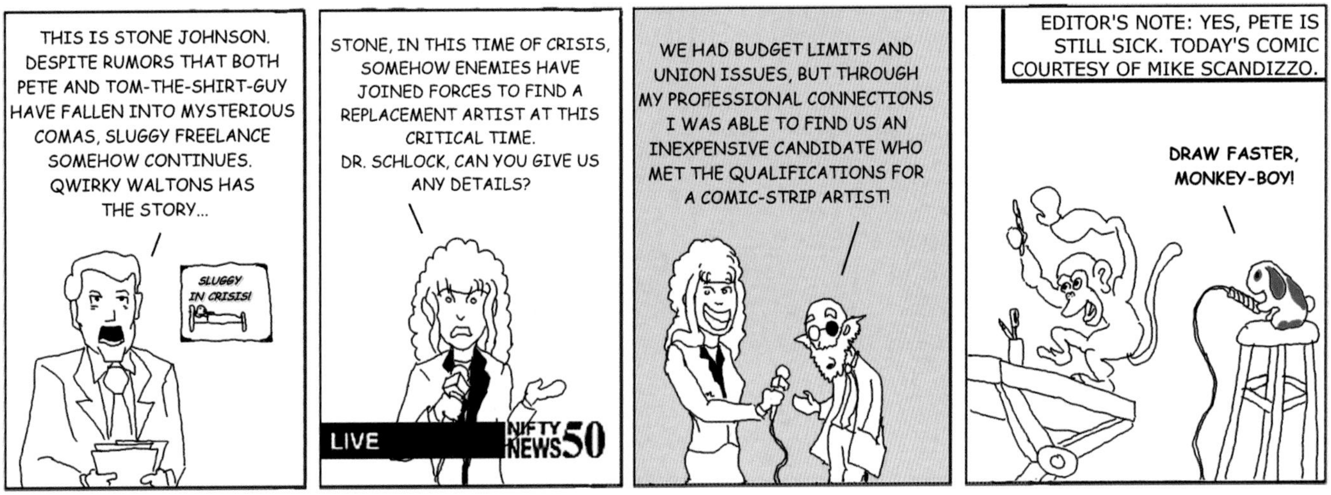

THIS IS STONE JOHNSON. DESPITE RUMORS THAT BOTH PETE AND TOM-THE-SHIRT-GUY HAVE FALLEN INTO MYSTERIOUS COMAS, SLUGGY FREELANCE SOMEHOW CONTINUES. QWIRKY WALTONS HAS THE STORY...
SLUGGY IN CRISIS!
STONE, IN THIS TIME OF CRISIS, SOMEHOW ENEMIES HAVE JOINED FORCES TO FIND A REPLACEMENT ARTIST AT THIS CRITICAL TIME. DR. SCHLOCK, CAN YOU GIVE US ANY DETAILS?
LIVE
NIFTY NEWS 50
WE HAD BUDGET LIMITS AND UNION ISSUES, BUT THROUGH MY PROFESSIONAL CONNECTIONS I WAS ABLE TO FIND US AN INEXPENSIVE CANDIDATE WHO MET THE QUALIFICATIONS FOR A COMIC-STRIP ARTIST!
EDITOR'S NOTE: YES, PETE IS STILL SICK. TODAY'S COMIC COURTESY OF MIKE SCANDIZZO.
DRAW FASTER, MONKEY-BOY!

MONKEY FREELANCE OO OO AH AH!

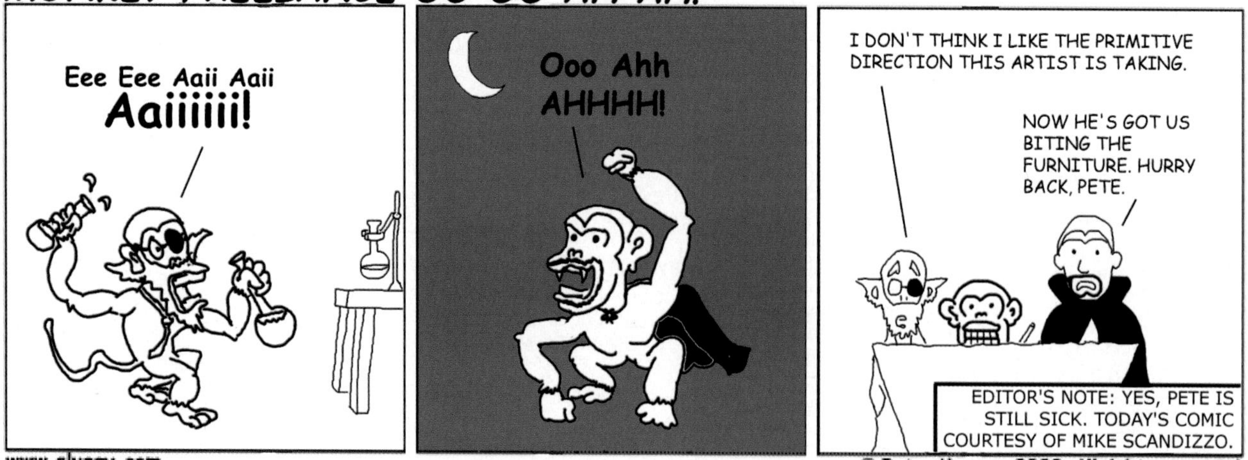
Eee Eee Aaii Aaii
Aaiiiiii!
Ooo Ahh
AHHHH!
I DON'T THINK I LIKE THE PRIMITIVE DIRECTION THIS ARTIST IS TAKING.
NOW HE'S GOT US BITING THE FURNITURE. HURRY BACK, PETE.
EDITOR'S NOTE: YES, PETE IS STILL SICK. TODAY'S COMIC COURTESY OF MIKE SCANDIZZO.

COMATOSE FREELANCE

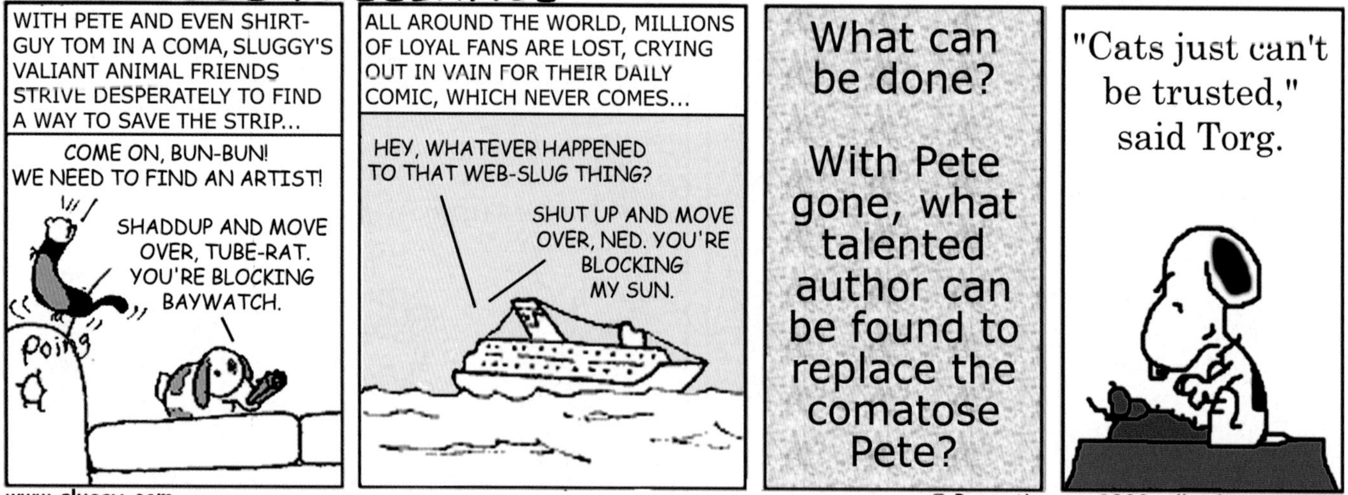
WITH PETE AND EVEN SHIRT-GUY TOM IN A COMA, SLUGGY'S VALIANT ANIMAL FRIENDS STRIVE DESPERATELY TO FIND A WAY TO SAVE THE STRIP...
COME ON, BUN-BUN! WE NEED TO FIND AN ARTIST!
SHADDUP AND MOVE OVER, TUBE-RAT. YOU'RE BLOCKING BAYWATCH.
Poing
ALL AROUND THE WORLD, MILLIONS OF LOYAL FANS ARE LOST, CRYING OUT IN VAIN FOR THEIR DAILY COMIC, WHICH NEVER COMES...
HEY, WHATEVER HAPPENED TO THAT WEB-SLUG THING?
SHUT UP AND MOVE OVER, NED. YOU'RE BLOCKING MY SUN.
What can be done?
With Pete gone, what talented author can be found to replace the comatose Pete?
"Cats just can't be trusted," said Torg.

SHIRT-GUY FREELANCE

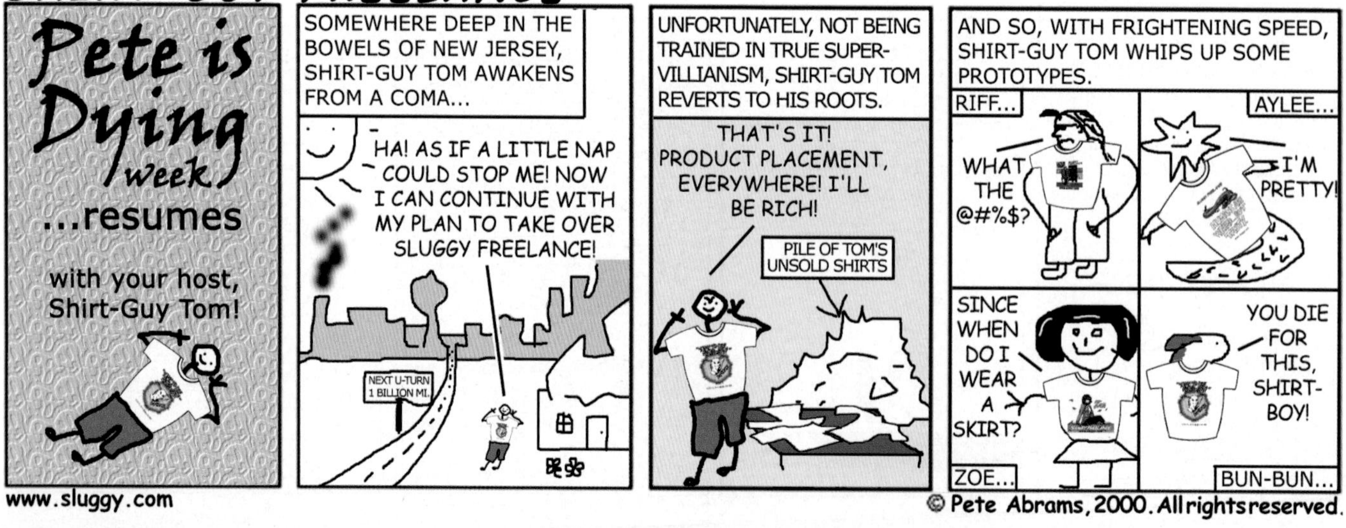
Pete is Dying week ...resumes
with your host, Shirt-Guy Tom!
SOMEWHERE DEEP IN THE BOWELS OF NEW JERSEY, SHIRT-GUY TOM AWAKENS FROM A COMA...
HA! AS IF A LITTLE NAP COULD STOP ME! NOW I CAN CONTINUE WITH MY PLAN TO TAKE OVER SLUGGY FREELANCE!
NEXT U-TURN 1 BILLION MI.
UNFORTUNATELY, NOT BEING TRAINED IN TRUE SUPER-VILLIANISM, SHIRT-GUY TOM REVERTS TO HIS ROOTS.
THAT'S IT! PRODUCT PLACEMENT, EVERYWHERE! I'LL BE RICH!
PILE OF TOM'S UNSOLD SHIRTS
AND SO, WITH FRIGHTENING SPEED, SHIRT-GUY TOM WHIPS UP SOME PROTOTYPES.
RIFF...
WHAT THE @#%$?
AYLEE...
I'M PRETTY!
SINCE WHEN DO I WEAR A SKIRT?
ZOE...
YOU DIE FOR THIS, SHIRT-BOY!
BUN-BUN...

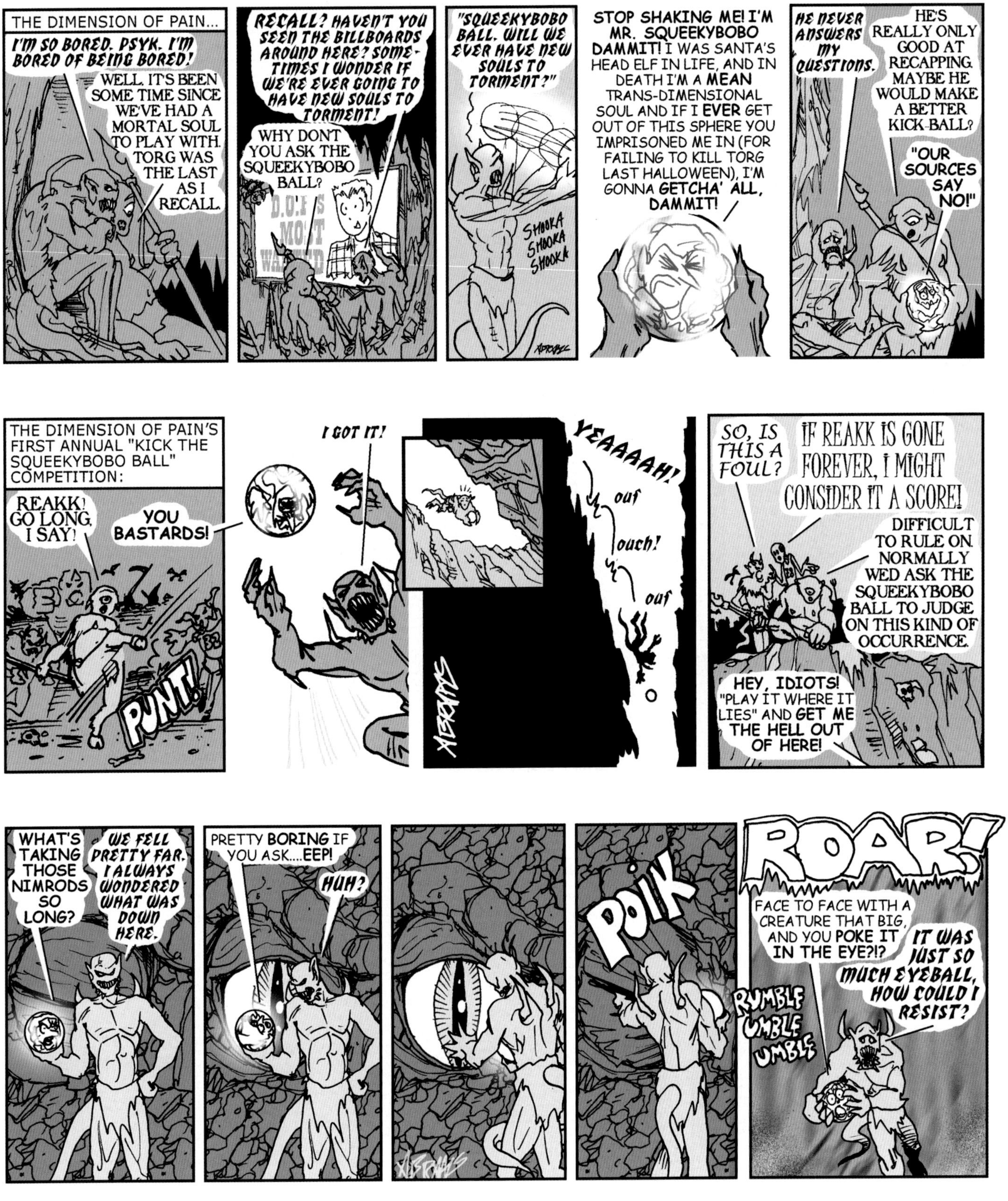

THE DIMENSION OF PAIN...
I'M SO BORED. PSYK. I'M BORED OF BEING BORED!
WELL, IT'S BEEN SOME TIME SINCE WE'VE HAD A MORTAL SOUL TO PLAY WITH. TORG WAS THE LAST AS I RECALL.
RECALL? HAVEN'T YOU SEEN THE BILLBOARDS AROUND HERE? SOMETIMES I WONDER IF WE'RE EVER GOING TO HAVE NEW SOULS TO TORMENT!
WHY DONT YOU ASK THE SQUEEKYBOBO BALL?
D.O.P.'S MOST WANTED
"SQUEEKYBOBO BALL. WILL WE EVER HAVE NEW SOULS TO TORMENT?"
SHOOKA SHOOKA SHOOKA
STOP SHAKING ME! I'M MR. SQUEEKYBOBO DAMMIT! I WAS SANTA'S HEAD ELF IN LIFE, AND IN DEATH I'M A MEAN TRANS-DIMENSIONAL SOUL AND IF I EVER GET OUT OF THIS SPHERE YOU IMPRISONED ME IN (FOR FAILING TO KILL TORG LAST HALLOWEEN), I'M GONNA GETCHA' ALL, DAMMIT!
HE NEVER ANSWERS MY QUESTIONS.
HE'S REALLY ONLY GOOD AT RECAPPING. MAYBE HE WOULD MAKE A BETTER KICK-BALL?
"OUR SOURCES SAY NO!"
THE DIMENSION OF PAIN'S FIRST ANNUAL "KICK THE SQUEEKYBOBO BALL" COMPETITION:
REAKK! GO LONG, I SAY!
YOU BASTARDS!
PUNT!
I GOT IT!
YEAAAAAH!
ouf
ouch!
ouf
SO, IS THIS A FOUL?
IF REAKK IS GONE FOREVER, I MIGHT CONSIDER IT A SCORE!
DIFFICULT TO RULE ON. NORMALLY WED ASK THE SQUEEKYBOBO BALL TO JUDGE ON THIS KIND OF OCCURRENCE.
HEY, IDIOTS! "PLAY IT WHERE IT LIES" AND GET ME THE HELL OUT OF HERE!
WHAT'S TAKING THOSE NIMRODS SO LONG?
WE FELL PRETTY FAR. I ALWAYS WONDERED WHAT WAS DOWN HERE.
PRETTY BORING IF YOU ASK....EEP!
HUH?
POIK
ROAR!
RUMBLE UMBLE UMBLE
FACE TO FACE WITH A CREATURE THAT BIG, AND YOU POKE IT IN THE EYE?!?
IT WAS JUST SO MUCH EYEBALL, HOW COULD I RESIST?

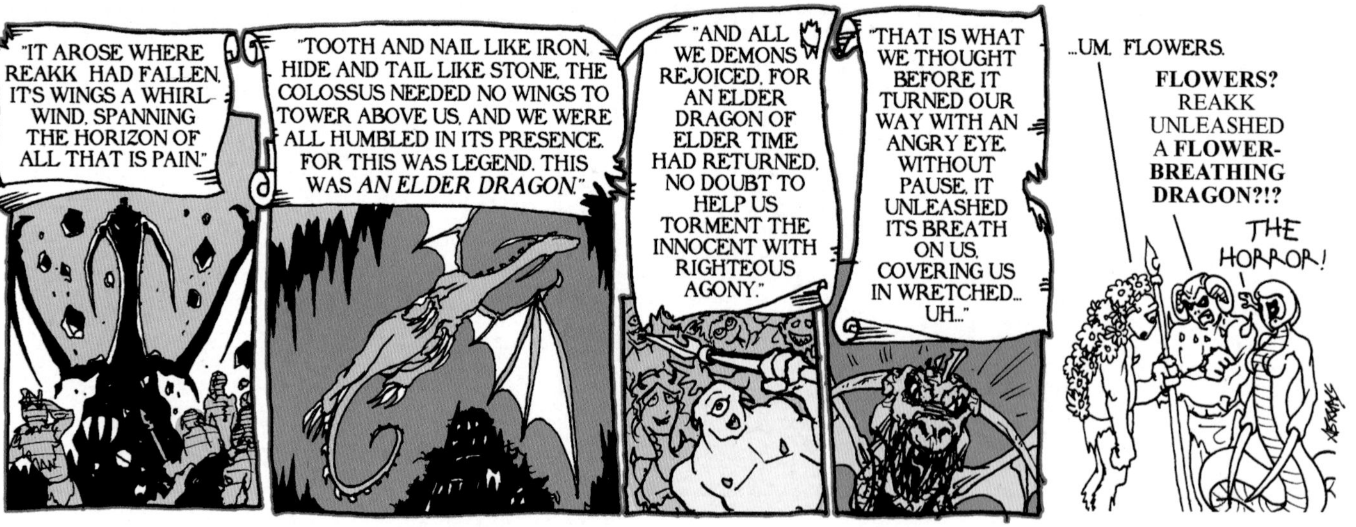
"IT AROSE WHERE REAKK HAD FALLEN. IT'S WINGS A WHIRLWIND, SPANNING THE HORIZON OF ALL THAT IS PAIN."
"TOOTH AND NAIL LIKE IRON, HIDE AND TAIL LIKE STONE, THE COLOSSUS NEEDED NO WINGS TO TOWER ABOVE US, AND WE WERE ALL HUMBLED IN ITS PRESENCE. FOR THIS WAS LEGEND. THIS WAS *AN ELDER DRAGON.*"
"AND ALL WE DEMONS REJOICED, FOR AN ELDER DRAGON OF ELDER TIME HAD RETURNED, NO DOUBT TO HELP US TORMENT THE INNOCENT WITH RIGHTEOUS AGONY."
"THAT IS WHAT WE THOUGHT BEFORE IT TURNED OUR WAY WITH AN ANGRY EYE. WITHOUT PAUSE, IT UNLEASHED ITS BREATH ON US, COVERING US IN WRETCHED... UH..."
...UM. FLOWERS.
FLOWERS? REAKK UNLEASHED A **FLOWER-BREATHING DRAGON?!?**
THE HORROR!

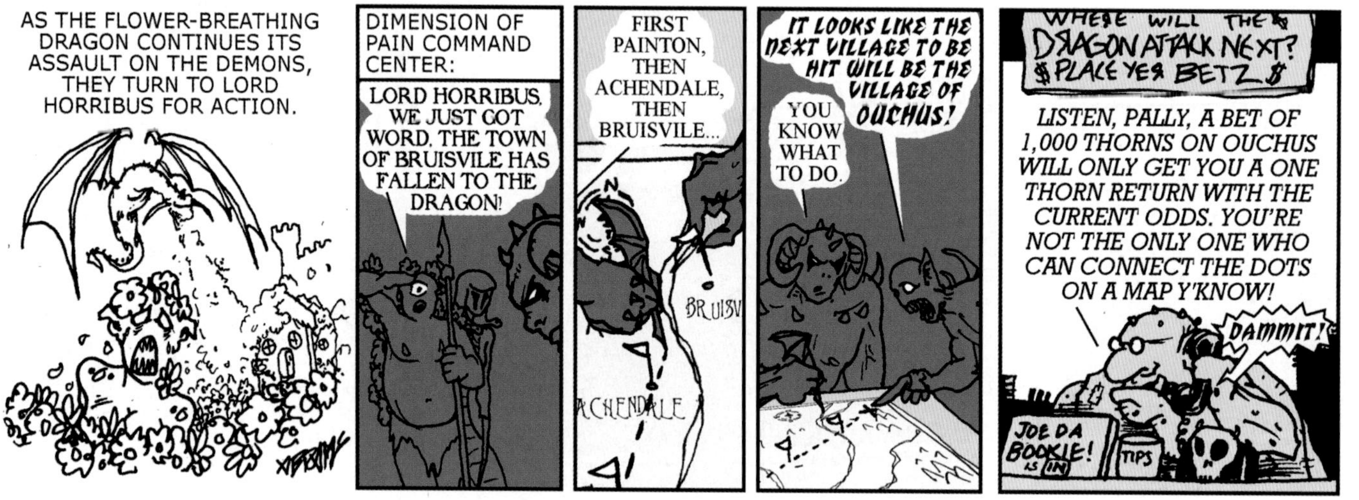
AS THE FLOWER-BREATHING DRAGON CONTINUES ITS ASSAULT ON THE DEMONS, THEY TURN TO LORD HORRIBUS FOR ACTION.
DIMENSION OF PAIN COMMAND CENTER:
LORD HORRIBUS, WE JUST GOT WORD, THE TOWN OF BRUISVILE HAS FALLEN TO THE DRAGON!
FIRST PAINTON, THEN ACHENDALE, THEN BRUISVILE...
ACHENDALE
IT LOOKS LIKE THE NEXT VILLAGE TO BE HIT WILL BE THE VILLAGE OF OUCHUS!
YOU KNOW WHAT TO DO.
WHERE WILL THE DRAGON ATTACK NEXT? $ PLACE YER BETZ $
LISTEN, PALLY, A BET OF 1,000 THORNS ON OUCHUS WILL ONLY GET YOU A ONE THORN RETURN WITH THE CURRENT ODDS. YOU'RE NOT THE ONLY ONE WHO CAN CONNECT THE DOTS ON A MAP Y'KNOW!
DAMMIT!
JOE DA BOOKIE! IS IN
TIPS

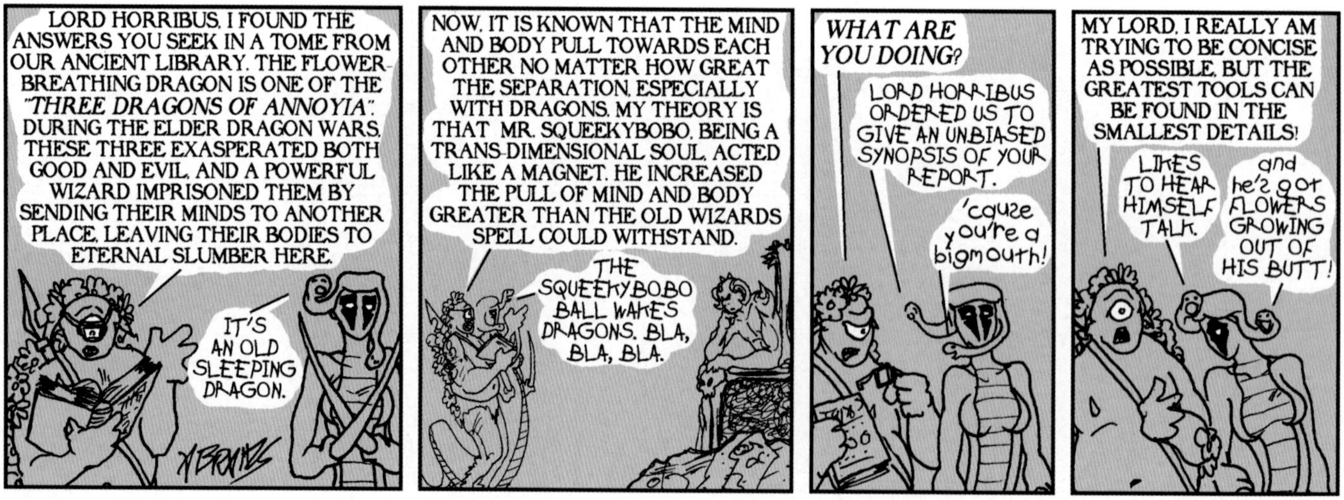
LORD HORRIBUS, I FOUND THE ANSWERS YOU SEEK IN A TOME FROM OUR ANCIENT LIBRARY. THE FLOWER-BREATHING DRAGON IS ONE OF THE *"THREE DRAGONS OF ANNOYIA"*. DURING THE ELDER DRAGON WARS, THESE THREE EXASPERATED BOTH GOOD AND EVIL, AND A POWERFUL WIZARD IMPRISONED THEM BY SENDING THEIR MINDS TO ANOTHER PLACE, LEAVING THEIR BODIES TO ETERNAL SLUMBER HERE.
IT'S AN OLD SLEEPING DRAGON.
NOW, IT IS KNOWN THAT THE MIND AND BODY PULL TOWARDS EACH OTHER NO MATTER HOW GREAT THE SEPARATION, ESPECIALLY WITH DRAGONS. MY THEORY IS THAT MR. SQUEEKYBOBO, BEING A TRANS-DIMENSIONAL SOUL, ACTED LIKE A MAGNET. HE INCREASED THE PULL OF MIND AND BODY GREATER THAN THE OLD WIZARDS SPELL COULD WITHSTAND.
THE SQUEEKYBOBO BALL WAKES DRAGONS. BLA, BLA, BLA.
WHAT ARE YOU DOING?
LORD HORRIBUS ORDERED US TO GIVE AN UNBIASED SYNOPSIS OF YOUR REPORT.
'cause you're a bigmouth!
MY LORD, I REALLY AM TRYING TO BE CONCISE AS POSSIBLE, BUT THE GREATEST TOOLS CAN BE FOUND IN THE SMALLEST DETAILS!
LIKES TO HEAR HIMSELF TALK.
and he's got FLOWERS GROWING OUT OF HIS BUTT!

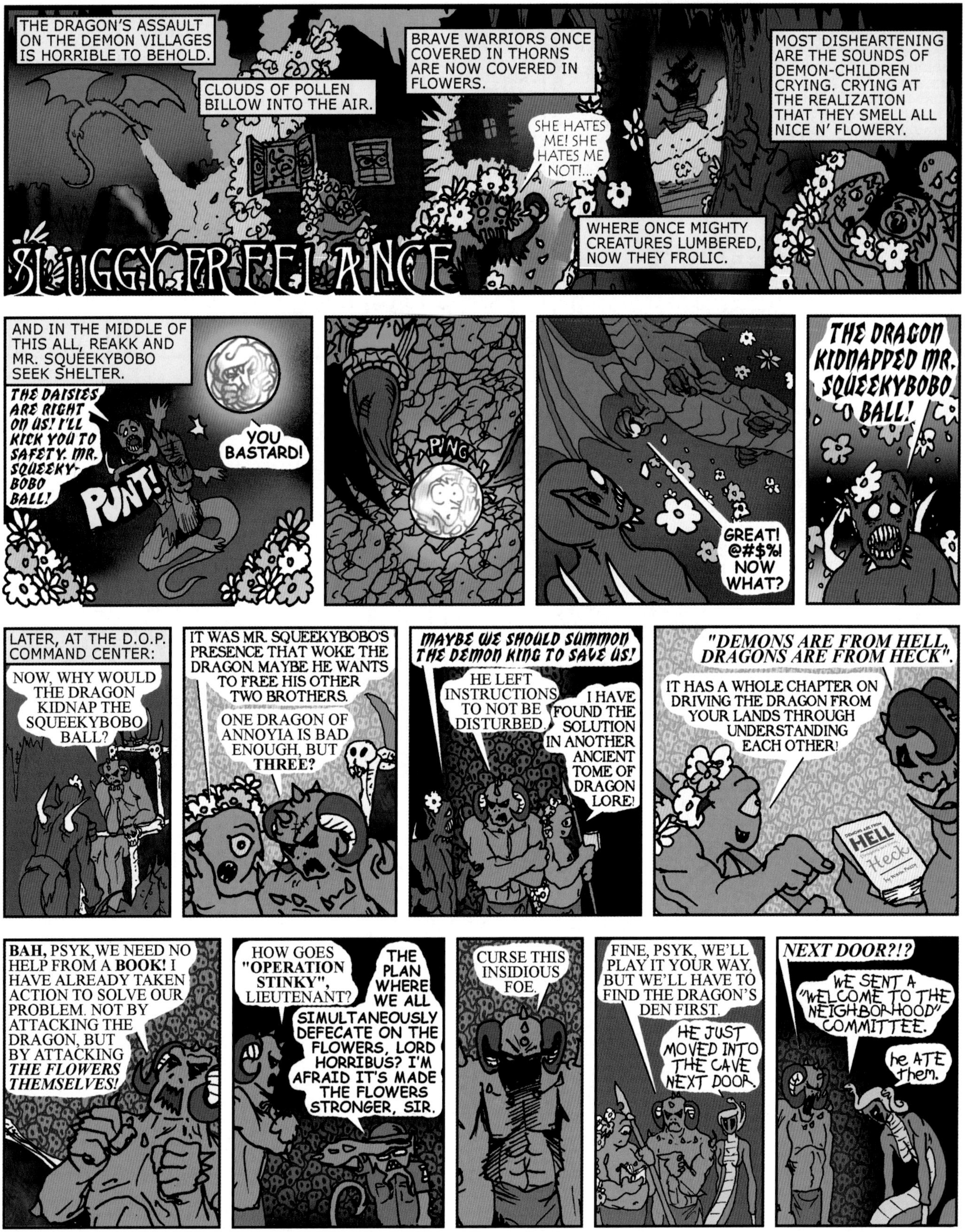

THE DRAGON'S ASSAULT ON THE DEMON VILLAGES IS HORRIBLE TO BEHOLD.
CLOUDS OF POLLEN BILLOW INTO THE AIR.
BRAVE WARRIORS ONCE COVERED IN THORNS ARE NOW COVERED IN FLOWERS.
SHE HATES ME! SHE HATES ME NOT!...
WHERE ONCE MIGHTY CREATURES LUMBERED, NOW THEY FROLIC.
MOST DISHEARTENING ARE THE SOUNDS OF DEMON-CHILDREN CRYING. CRYING AT THE REALIZATION THAT THEY SMELL ALL NICE N' FLOWERY.
SLUGGY FREELANCE
AND IN THE MIDDLE OF THIS ALL, REAKK AND MR. SQUEEKYBOBO SEEK SHELTER.
THE DAISIES ARE RIGHT ON US! I'LL KICK YOU TO SAFETY. MR. SQUEEKY-BOBO BALL!
YOU BASTARD!
PUNT!
PING
GREAT! @#$%! NOW WHAT?
THE DRAGON KIDNAPPED MR. SQUEEKYBOBO BALL!
LATER, AT THE D.O.P. COMMAND CENTER:
NOW, WHY WOULD THE DRAGON KIDNAP THE SQUEEKYBOBO BALL?
IT WAS MR. SQUEEKYBOBO'S PRESENCE THAT WOKE THE DRAGON. MAYBE HE WANTS TO FREE HIS OTHER TWO BROTHERS.
ONE DRAGON OF ANNOYIA IS BAD ENOUGH, BUT THREE?
MAYBE WE SHOULD SUMMON THE DEMON KING TO SAVE US!
HE LEFT INSTRUCTIONS TO NOT BE DISTURBED.
I HAVE FOUND THE SOLUTION IN ANOTHER ANCIENT TOME OF DRAGON LORE!
"DEMONS ARE FROM HELL, DRAGONS ARE FROM HECK".
IT HAS A WHOLE CHAPTER ON DRIVING THE DRAGON FROM YOUR LANDS THROUGH UNDERSTANDING EACH OTHER!
HELL
Heck
BAH, PSYK, WE NEED NO HELP FROM A BOOK! I HAVE ALREADY TAKEN ACTION TO SOLVE OUR PROBLEM. NOT BY ATTACKING THE DRAGON, BUT BY ATTACKING THE FLOWERS THEMSELVES!
HOW GOES "OPERATION STINKY", LIEUTENANT?
THE PLAN WHERE WE ALL SIMULTANEOUSLY DEFECATE ON THE FLOWERS, LORD HORRIBUS? I'M AFRAID IT'S MADE THE FLOWERS STRONGER, SIR.
CURSE THIS INSIDIOUS FOE.
FINE, PSYK, WE'LL PLAY IT YOUR WAY, BUT WE'LL HAVE TO FIND THE DRAGON'S DEN FIRST.
HE JUST MOVED INTO THE CAVE NEXT DOOR.
NEXT DOOR?!?
WE SENT A "WELCOME TO THE NEIGHBORHOOD" COMMITTEE.
he ATE them.

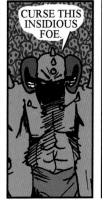

Method 1: Self Actualization

Freeing your kingdom from a dragon is a simple matter of talking, and more importantly, listening. Sounds easy, right? It is! The Dragons of today are not evil, merely repressed. On the inside they are frightened children, just looking for support. Be that supportive victimized townsfolk, not the codependent victimized townsfolk who only contribute to the problem. Just follow the outline weve provided.

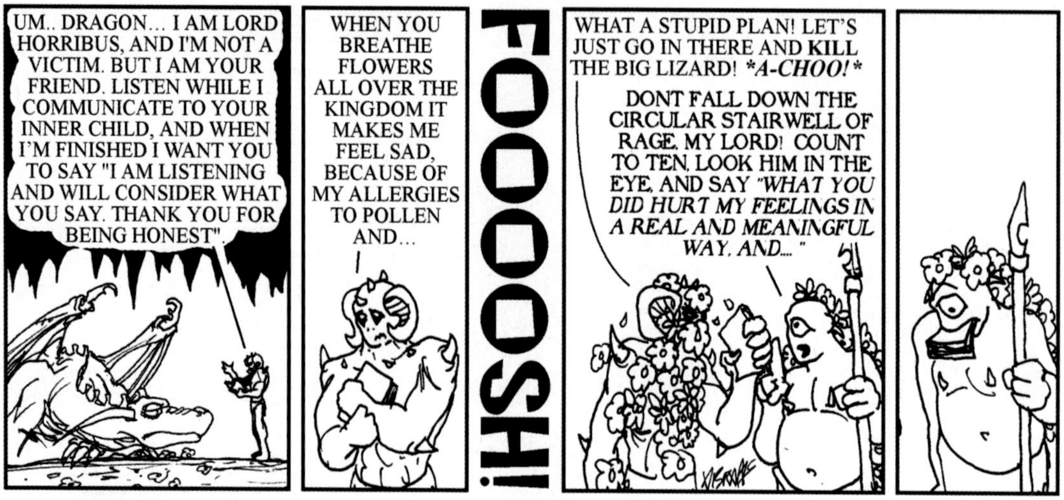

UM.. DRAGON... I AM LORD HORRIBUS, AND I'M NOT A VICTIM. BUT I AM YOUR FRIEND. LISTEN WHILE I COMMUNICATE TO YOUR INNER CHILD, AND WHEN I'M FINISHED I WANT YOU TO SAY "I AM LISTENING AND WILL CONSIDER WHAT YOU SAY. THANK YOU FOR BEING HONEST".
WHEN YOU BREATHE FLOWERS ALL OVER THE KINGDOM IT MAKES ME FEEL SAD, BECAUSE OF MY ALLERGIES TO POLLEN AND...
FOOOOSH!
WHAT A STUPID PLAN! LET'S JUST GO IN THERE AND **KILL** THE BIG LIZARD! **A-CHOO!**
DONT FALL DOWN THE CIRCULAR STAIRWELL OF RAGE, MY LORD! COUNT TO TEN, LOOK HIM IN THE EYE, AND SAY *"WHAT YOU DID HURT MY FEELINGS IN A REAL AND MEANINGFUL WAY. AND...."*

Method 2: Respect

Some dragons are too out of touch for self actualization. However, many dragon attacks may be caused by a simple misunderstanding. Try being humble and tactful before the dragon. Remember, even though you are equal partners in the universe, respectful praise may open the heavy doors of communication.

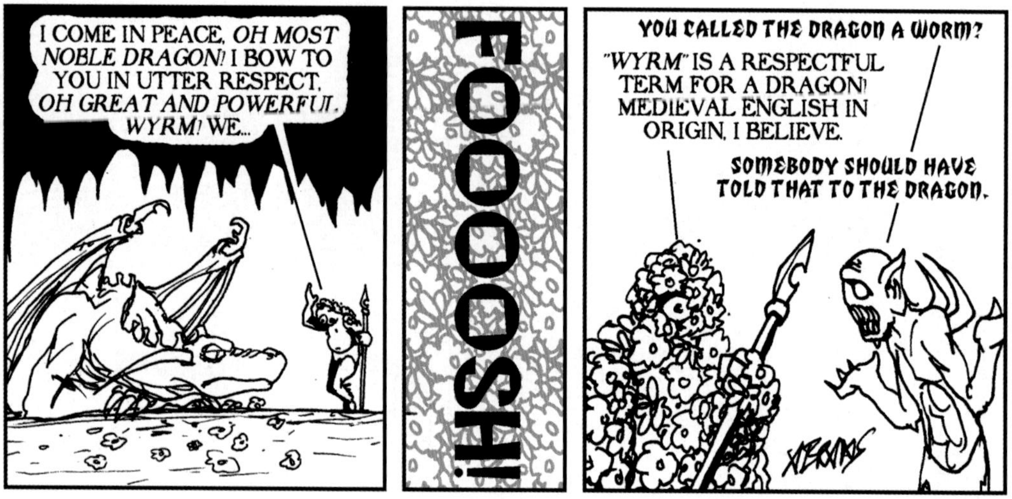

I COME IN PEACE, *OH MOST NOBLE DRAGON!* I BOW TO YOU IN UTTER RESPECT, *OH GREAT AND POWERFUL WYRM!* WE...
FOOOOSH!
YOU CALLED THE DRAGON A WORM?
"WYRM" IS A RESPECTFUL TERM FOR A DRAGON! MEDIEVAL ENGLISH IN ORIGIN, I BELIEVE.
SOMEBODY SHOULD HAVE TOLD THAT TO THE DRAGON.

Method 3: The Virgin

If the dragon won't listen to reason, try a tribute! A virgin maiden usually does the trick!

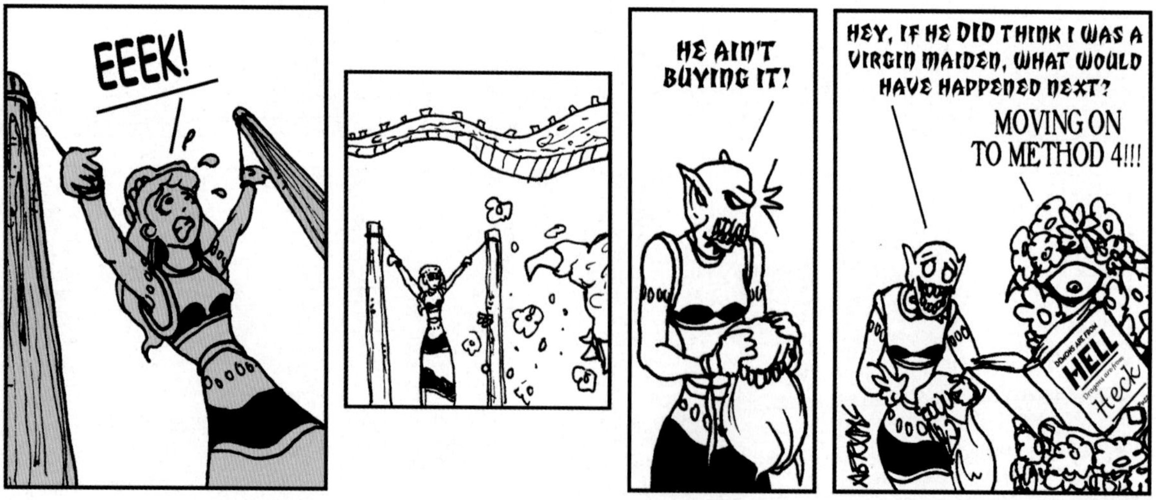

EEEK!
HE AIN'T BUYING IT!
HEY, IF HE **DID** THINK I WAS A VIRGIN MAIDEN, WHAT WOULD HAVE HAPPENED NEXT?
MOVING ON TO METHOD 4!!!
DEMONS ARE FROM HELL
Heck

Method 4: Riddles

All dragons respect the game of riddles. Present the dragon with a challenging riddle. If he cannot guess the answer, you may win the right to ask him to leave your kingdom. If he answers correctly, you will be given a riddle. If you do not answer, you...well... get eaten, but if you get it right, you are free to ask another riddle. And the contest continues until one answers wrongly. **What fun!**

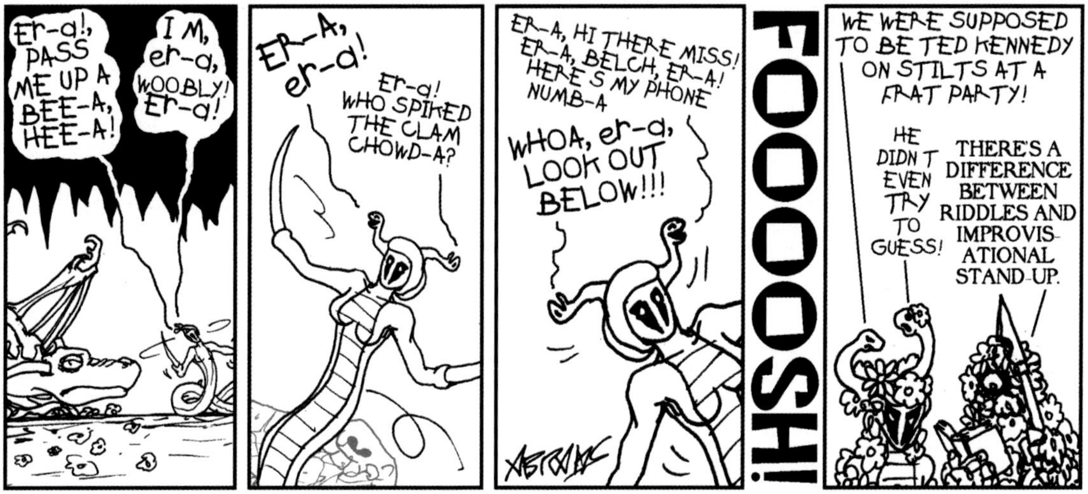

Er-a! PASS ME UP A BEE-A, HEE-A!
I M, er-a, WOOBLY! Er-a!
ER-A, er-a!
Er-a! WHO SPIKED THE CLAM CHOWD-A?
ER-A, HI THERE MISS! ER-A, BELCH, ER-A! HERE'S MY PHONE NUMB-A
WHOA, er-a, LOOK OUT BELOW!!!
FOOOOSH!
WE WERE SUPPOSED TO BE TED KENNEDY ON STILTS AT A FRAT PARTY!
HE DIDN'T EVEN TRY TO GUESS!
THERE'S A DIFFERENCE BETWEEN RIDDLES AND IMPROVIS-ATIONAL STAND-UP.

Method 5: Just Kill the Stupid Thing!

If all the other methods fail, the dragon must be a fluke! This book is so good that normal dragons would have caved by method 2, so just **kill the damn dirty fluke-dragon!** The dragon has a flaw in its defenses where the head meets the neck at the base of the skull. Just hop on the back of the dragon and attack with a demon-spear. *Easy!*

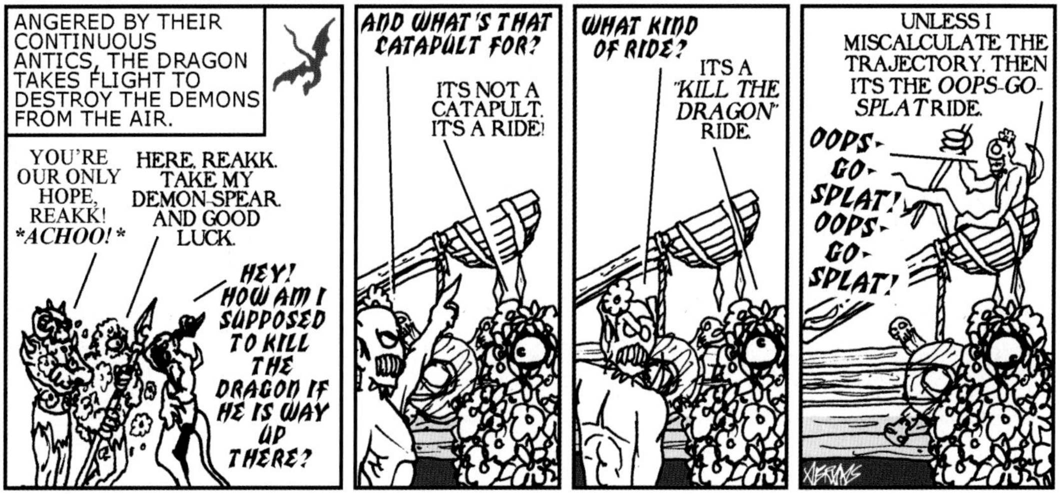

ANGERED BY THEIR CONTINUOUS ANTICS, THE DRAGON TAKES FLIGHT TO DESTROY THE DEMONS FROM THE AIR.
YOU'RE OUR ONLY HOPE, REAKK! *ACHOO!*
HERE, REAKK. TAKE MY DEMON-SPEAR. AND GOOD LUCK.
HEY! HOW AM I SUPPOSED TO KILL THE DRAGON IF HE IS WAY UP THERE?
AND WHAT'S THAT CATAPULT FOR?
IT'S NOT A CATAPULT. IT'S A RIDE!
WHAT KIND OF RIDE?
IT'S A "KILL THE DRAGON" RIDE.
UNLESS I MISCALCULATE THE TRAJECTORY. THEN IT'S THE OOPS-GO-SPLAT RIDE.
OOPS-GO-SPLAT! OOPS-GO-SPLAT!

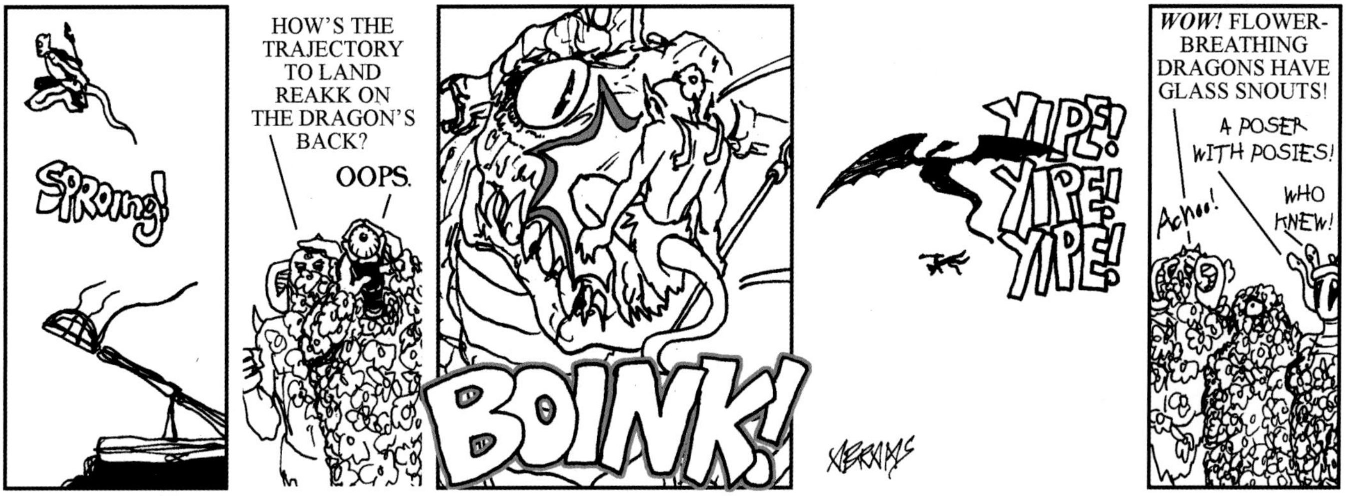

SPROING!
HOW'S THE TRAJECTORY TO LAND REAKK ON THE DRAGON'S BACK?
OOPS.
BOINK!
YIPE! YIPE! YIPE!
WOW! FLOWER-BREATHING DRAGONS HAVE GLASS SNOUTS!
A POSER WITH POSIES!
Achoo!
WHO KNEW!

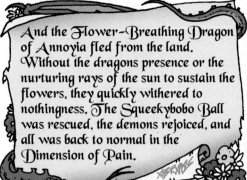

And the Flower-Breathing Dragon of Annoyia fled from the land. Without the dragons presence or the nurturing rays of the sun to sustain the flowers, they quickly withered to nothingness. The Squeekybobo Ball was rescued, the demons rejoiced, and all was back to normal in the Dimension of Pain.

SLUGGY FREELANCE

HEY PSYK! WHAT ARE YOU DOING?

I'M RECORDING OUR ENCOUNTER WITH THE DRAGON, NOTING THINGS LIKE THE IRONY OF YOUR FALL FROM THE HEAVENS BEING CUSHIONED BY THE FLOWERS WE WERE FIGHTING AGAINST.

WHERE IT SAYS THAT MY BODY "SMASHED" AGAINST THE DRAGON'S NOSE, YOU SHOULD REPLACE "SMASHED" WITH "BOINKED".

"BOINKED"?

YEAH, EVERYBODY HEARD THE BIG AUDIBLE "BOINK" WHEN I NAILED IT!

WE FEEL THAT WE CAN USE THE WORD "BOINK" TO HELP IDENTIFY REAKK, HELP HIM STAND APART FROM THE OTHER DRAGON SLAYERS.

WHO IS HE?

HE'S MY BARD! I'VE BECOME QUITE TALKED ABOUT SINCE DEFEATING THE DRAGON AND FIGURED I NEEDED A BARD TO CHRONICLE MY ADVENTURE.

OOOOOO

"TH' FLOWER-BREATHING DRAGON CAME AND PLUNGED US INTO DAISIES, EVEN OLD LORD HORIBBUS'S ALLERGIES LEFT HIM HAZY, THE DEMONS CRIED "WHO'D SAVE US", AS IF ANYBODY COULD, BUT REAKK, HE BOINKED THAT DRAGON, AND BOY, HE BOINKED HIM GOOD."

"REAKK THE DRAGON BOINKER, HE BOINKS THEM ALL THE TIME! REAKK THE DRAGON BOINKER, HE'S GOT BOINKING ON HIS MIND! YA WANT'YER SHEEP AND CHICKENS BOINKED? MOST ANY MAN WILL DO, BUT REAKK THE DRAGON BOINKER, HE'S A BOINKER THROUGH AND THROUGH!"

THE SECOND STANZA IS MOST OF THE WAY DONE, I JUST NEED TO FIND A WORD THAT RHYMES WITH "BASS-BOINKER."

OH SQUEEKYBOBO BALL, WILL THE SONG "REAKK THE DRAGON BOINKER" BE A BIG HIT?

SHOOKA SHOOKA SHOOKA

^%$#@! STOP THE $%#ING SHAKING ALL THE TIME ALREADY! @#$%! RESCUED FROM ONE BIG IDIOT JUST TO BE IMPRISONED BY A BUNCH OF LITTLE ONES! @#$%!

WANTED

WELL, I'M BORED AGAIN.

YES, THAT DRAGON ALMOST DESTROYED US, BUT FOR THE FIRST TIME IN YEARS I WASN'T BORED!

HEY, WASN'T THERE SUPPOSED TO BE TWO MORE DRAGONS OF ANNOYIA?

AND THE SQUEEKYBOBO BALL IS THE KEY!!!

THE DIMENSION OF PAIN'S FIRST ANNUAL KICK-THE-SQUEEKYBOBO-BALL-DRAGON-QUEST:

THERE'S A RANDOM CRACK IN THE EARTH! LET'S KICK HIM DOWN THERE!

"REAKK LIKES TO KICK HIS BALLS, HE KICKS THEM REAL HIGH. THE ONLY THING HE LIKES BETTER IS TO GRAB THEM FROM THE SKY..."

did he just sing the words "THIS GUY"?

PUNT!

I'M GONNA KILL YOU! @#$%! I'M GONNA KILL YOU ALL!

And that is the way it ends... for now.

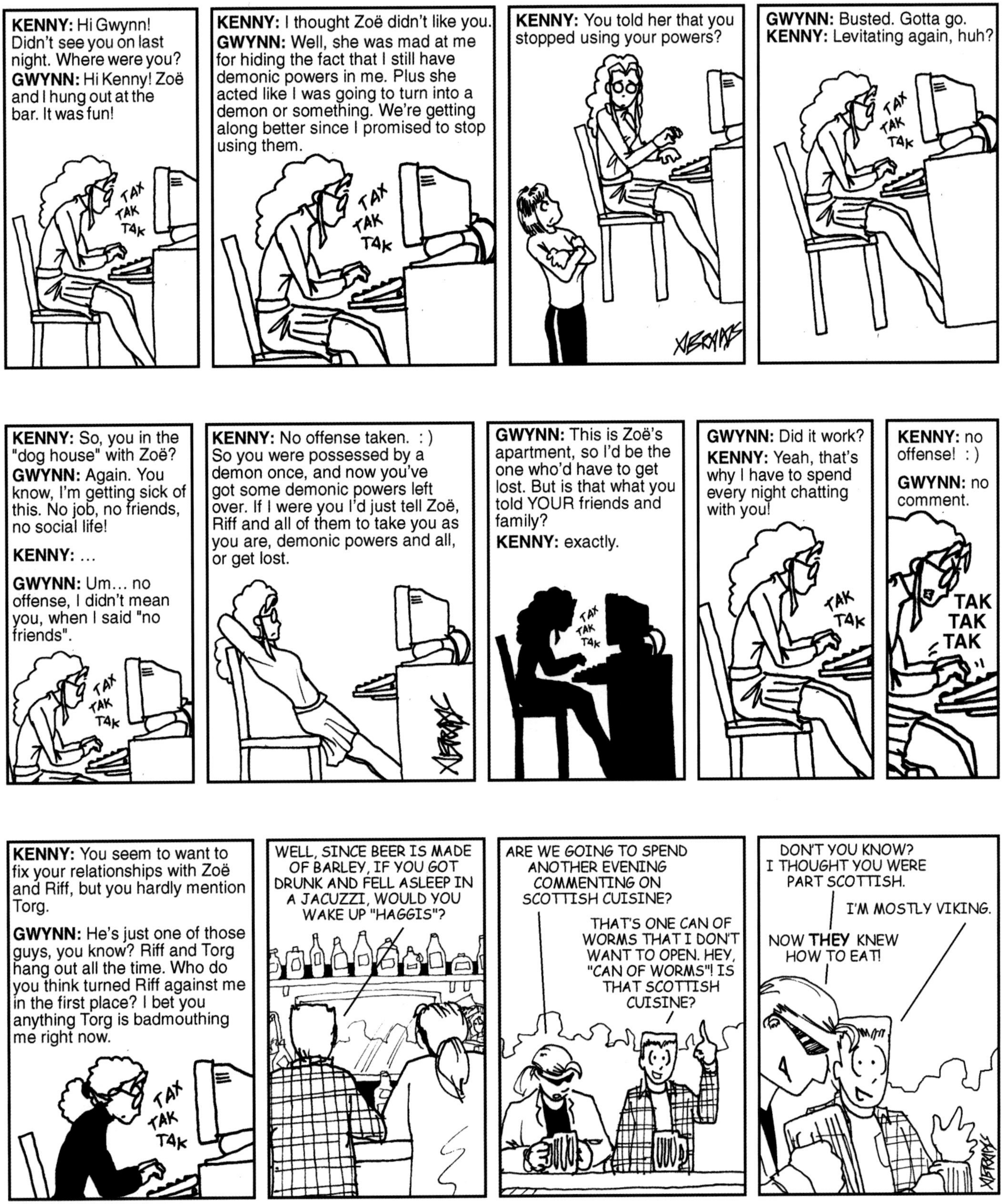
KENNY: Hi Gwynn! Didn't see you on last night. Where were you?
GWYNN: Hi Kenny! Zoë and I hung out at the bar. It was fun!
TAX TAK T4K
KENNY: I thought Zoë didn't like you.
GWYNN: Well, she was mad at me for hiding the fact that I still have demonic powers in me. Plus she acted like I was going to turn into a demon or something. We're getting along better since I promised to stop using them.
TAX TAK T4K
KENNY: You told her that you stopped using your powers?
GWYNN: Busted. Gotta go.
KENNY: Levitating again, huh?
TAX TAK T4K
KENNY: So, you in the "dog house" with Zoë?
GWYNN: Again. You know, I'm getting sick of this. No job, no friends, no social life!
KENNY: …
GWYNN: Um… no offense, I didn't mean you, when I said "no friends".
TAX TAK T4K
KENNY: No offense taken. :) So you were possessed by a demon once, and now you've got some demonic powers left over. If I were you I'd just tell Zoë, Riff and all of them to take you as you are, demonic powers and all, or get lost.
GWYNN: This is Zoë's apartment, so I'd be the one who'd have to get lost. But is that what you told YOUR friends and family?
KENNY: exactly.
TAX TAK T4K
GWYNN: Did it work?
KENNY: Yeah, that's why I have to spend every night chatting with you!
TAK T4K
KENNY: no offense! :)
GWYNN: no comment.
TAK TAK TAK
KENNY: You seem to want to fix your relationships with Zoë and Riff, but you hardly mention Torg.
GWYNN: He's just one of those guys, you know? Riff and Torg hang out all the time. Who do you think turned Riff against me in the first place? I bet you anything Torg is badmouthing me right now.
TAX TAK T4K
WELL, SINCE BEER IS MADE OF BARLEY, IF YOU GOT DRUNK AND FELL ASLEEP IN A JACUZZI, WOULD YOU WAKE UP "HAGGIS"?
ARE WE GOING TO SPEND ANOTHER EVENING COMMENTING ON SCOTTISH CUISINE?
THAT'S ONE CAN OF WORMS THAT I DON'T WANT TO OPEN. HEY, "CAN OF WORMS"! IS THAT SCOTTISH CUISINE?
DON'T YOU KNOW? I THOUGHT YOU WERE PART SCOTTISH.
I'M MOSTLY VIKING.
NOW **THEY** KNEW HOW TO EAT!

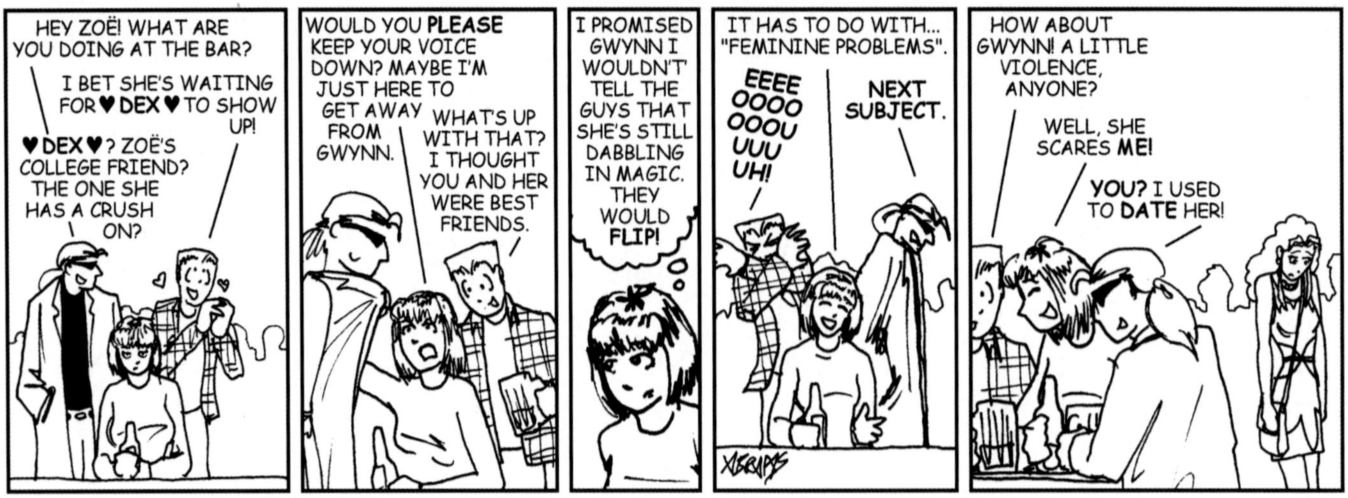
HEY ZOË! WHAT ARE YOU DOING AT THE BAR?
I BET SHE'S WAITING FOR ♥DEX♥ TO SHOW UP!
♥DEX♥? ZOË'S COLLEGE FRIEND? THE ONE SHE HAS A CRUSH ON?
WOULD YOU PLEASE KEEP YOUR VOICE DOWN? MAYBE I'M JUST HERE TO GET AWAY FROM GWYNN.
WHAT'S UP WITH THAT? I THOUGHT YOU AND HER WERE BEST FRIENDS.
I PROMISED GWYNN I WOULDN'T TELL THE GUYS THAT SHE'S STILL DABBLING IN MAGIC. THEY WOULD FLIP!
IT HAS TO DO WITH... "FEMININE PROBLEMS".
EEEE OOOO OOOU UUU UH!
NEXT SUBJECT.
HOW ABOUT GWYNN! A LITTLE VIOLENCE, ANYONE?
WELL, SHE SCARES ME!
YOU? I USED TO DATE HER!

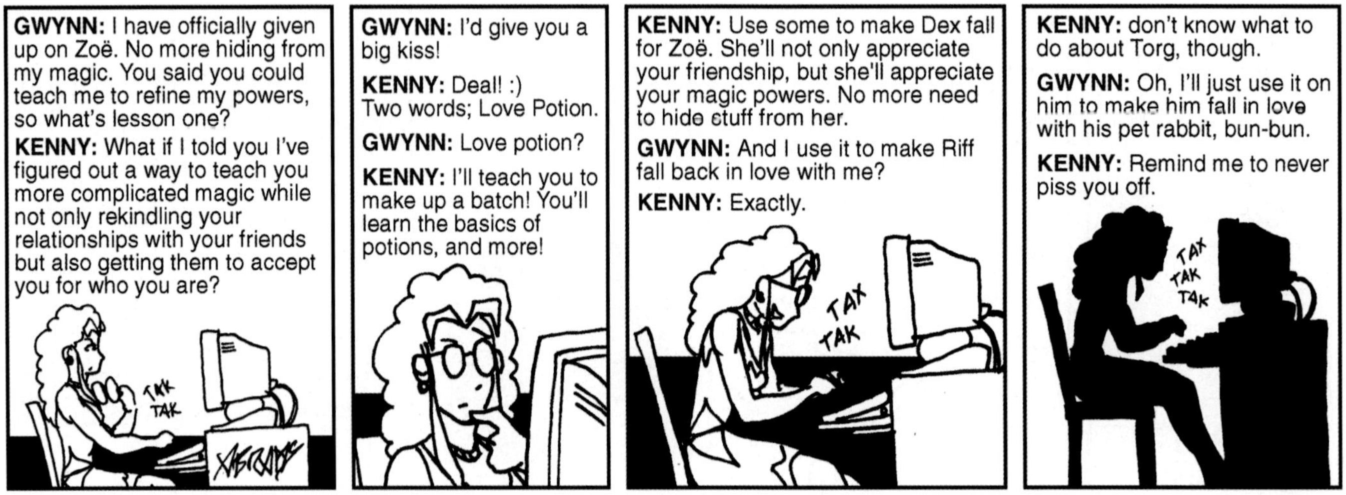
GWYNN: I have officially given up on Zoë. No more hiding from my magic. You said you could teach me to refine my powers, so what's lesson one?
KENNY: What if I told you I've figured out a way to teach you more complicated magic while not only rekindling your relationships with your friends but also getting them to accept you for who you are?
TAK TAK
GWYNN: I'd give you a big kiss!
KENNY: Deal! :) Two words; Love Potion.
GWYNN: Love potion?
KENNY: I'll teach you to make up a batch! You'll learn the basics of potions, and more!
KENNY: Use some to make Dex fall for Zoë. She'll not only appreciate your friendship, but she'll appreciate your magic powers. No more need to hide stuff from her.
GWYNN: And I use it to make Riff fall back in love with me?
KENNY: Exactly.
TAK TAK
KENNY: don't know what to do about Torg, though.
GWYNN: Oh, I'll just use it on him to make him fall in love with his pet rabbit, bun-bun.
KENNY: Remind me to never piss you off.
TAK TAK TAK

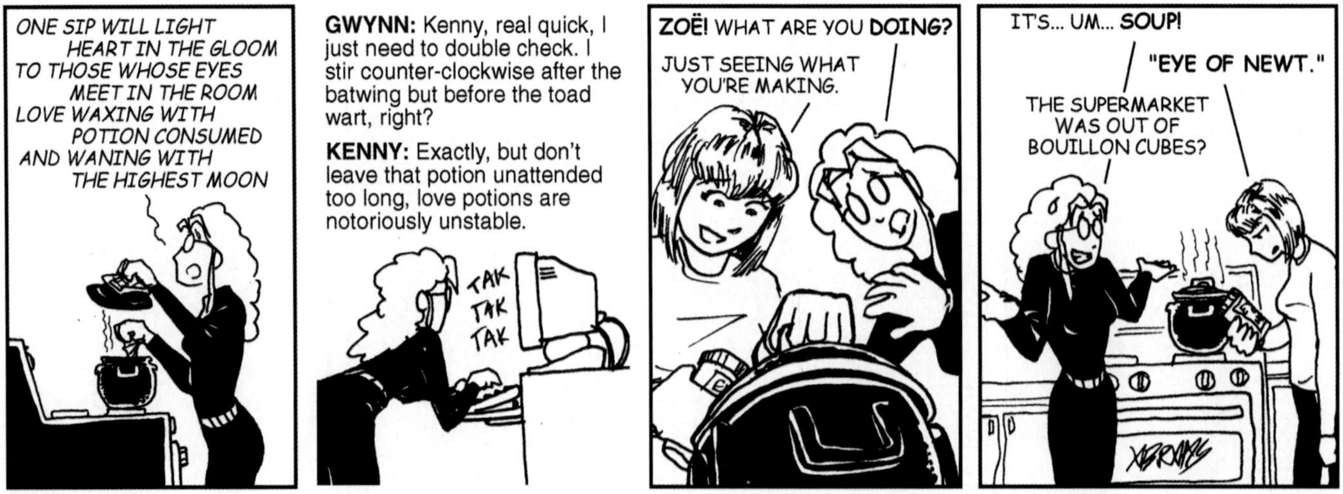
ONE SIP WILL LIGHT HEART IN THE GLOOM
TO THOSE WHOSE EYES MEET IN THE ROOM
LOVE WAXING WITH POTION CONSUMED
AND WANING WITH THE HIGHEST MOON
GWYNN: Kenny, real quick, I just need to double check. I stir counter-clockwise after the batwing but before the toad wart, right?
KENNY: Exactly, but don't leave that potion unattended too long, love potions are notoriously unstable.
TAK TAK TAK
ZOË! WHAT ARE YOU DOING?
JUST SEEING WHAT YOU'RE MAKING.
IT'S... UM... SOUP!
"EYE OF NEWT."
THE SUPERMARKET WAS OUT OF BOUILLON CUBES?

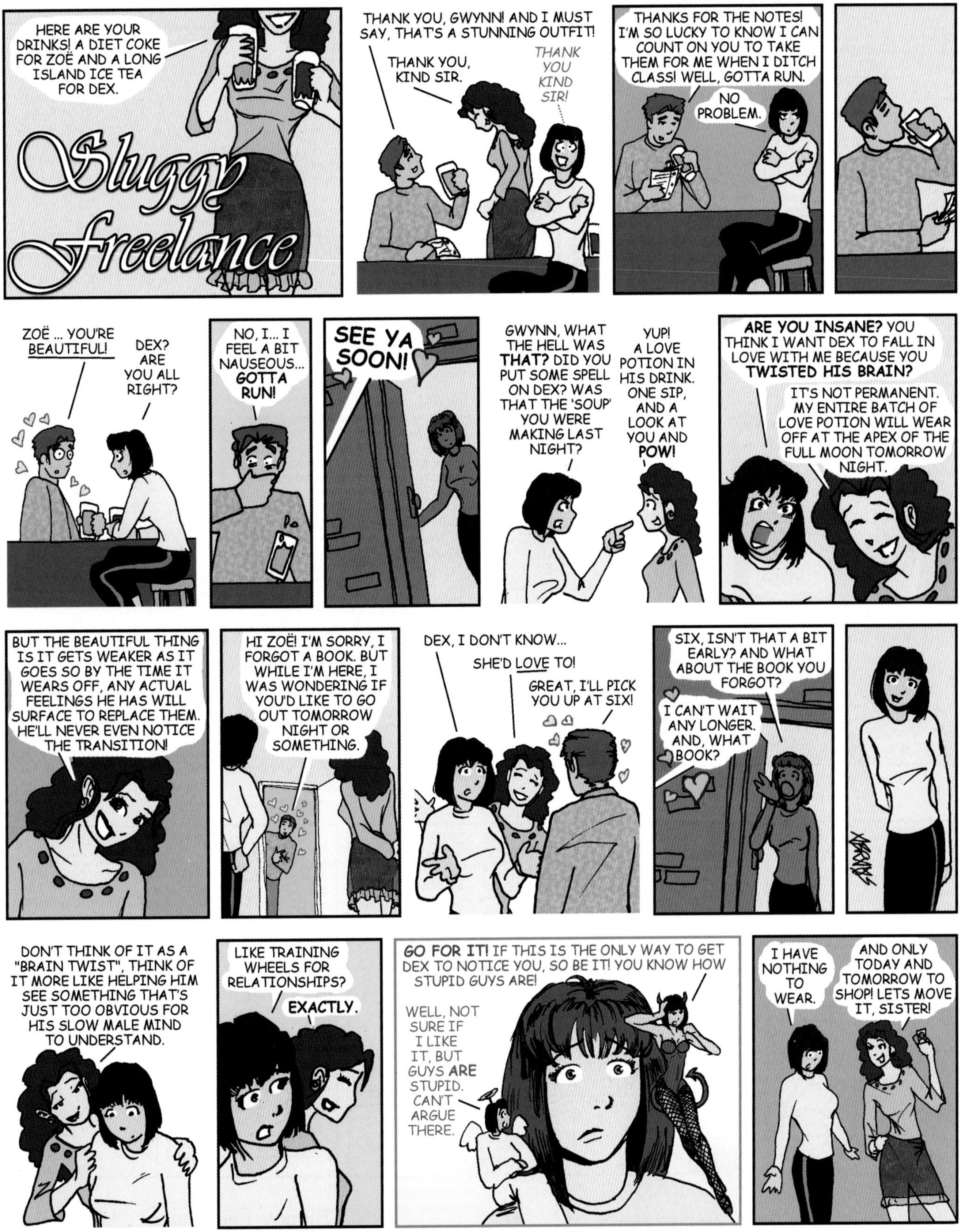
HERE ARE YOUR DRINKS! A DIET COKE FOR ZOË AND A LONG ISLAND ICE TEA FOR DEX.
Sluggy Freelance
THANK YOU, GWYNN! AND I MUST SAY, THAT'S A STUNNING OUTFIT!
THANK YOU, KIND SIR.
THANK YOU KIND SIR!
THANKS FOR THE NOTES! I'M SO LUCKY TO KNOW I CAN COUNT ON YOU TO TAKE THEM FOR ME WHEN I DITCH CLASS! WELL, GOTTA RUN.
NO PROBLEM.
ZOË ... YOU'RE BEAUTIFUL!
DEX? ARE YOU ALL RIGHT?
NO, I... I FEEL A BIT NAUSEOUS... GOTTA RUN!
SEE YA SOON!
GWYNN, WHAT THE HELL WAS THAT? DID YOU PUT SOME SPELL ON DEX? WAS THAT THE 'SOUP' YOU WERE MAKING LAST NIGHT?
YUP! A LOVE POTION IN HIS DRINK. ONE SIP, AND A LOOK AT YOU AND POW!
ARE YOU INSANE? YOU THINK I WANT DEX TO FALL IN LOVE WITH ME BECAUSE YOU TWISTED HIS BRAIN?
IT'S NOT PERMANENT. MY ENTIRE BATCH OF LOVE POTION WILL WEAR OFF AT THE APEX OF THE FULL MOON TOMORROW NIGHT.
BUT THE BEAUTIFUL THING IS IT GETS WEAKER AS IT GOES SO BY THE TIME IT WEARS OFF, ANY ACTUAL FEELINGS HE HAS WILL SURFACE TO REPLACE THEM. HE'LL NEVER EVEN NOTICE THE TRANSITION!
HI ZOË! I'M SORRY, I FORGOT A BOOK. BUT WHILE I'M HERE, I WAS WONDERING IF YOU'D LIKE TO GO OUT TOMORROW NIGHT OR SOMETHING.
DEX, I DON'T KNOW...
SHE'D LOVE TO!
GREAT, I'LL PICK YOU UP AT SIX!
SIX, ISN'T THAT A BIT EARLY? AND WHAT ABOUT THE BOOK YOU FORGOT?
I CAN'T WAIT ANY LONGER. AND, WHAT BOOK?
DON'T THINK OF IT AS A "BRAIN TWIST", THINK OF IT MORE LIKE HELPING HIM SEE SOMETHING THAT'S JUST TOO OBVIOUS FOR HIS SLOW MALE MIND TO UNDERSTAND.
LIKE TRAINING WHEELS FOR RELATIONSHIPS?
EXACTLY.
GO FOR IT! IF THIS IS THE ONLY WAY TO GET DEX TO NOTICE YOU, SO BE IT! YOU KNOW HOW STUPID GUYS ARE!
WELL, NOT SURE IF I LIKE IT, BUT GUYS ARE STUPID. CAN'T ARGUE THERE.
I HAVE NOTHING TO WEAR.
AND ONLY TODAY AND TOMORROW TO SHOP! LETS MOVE IT, SISTER!

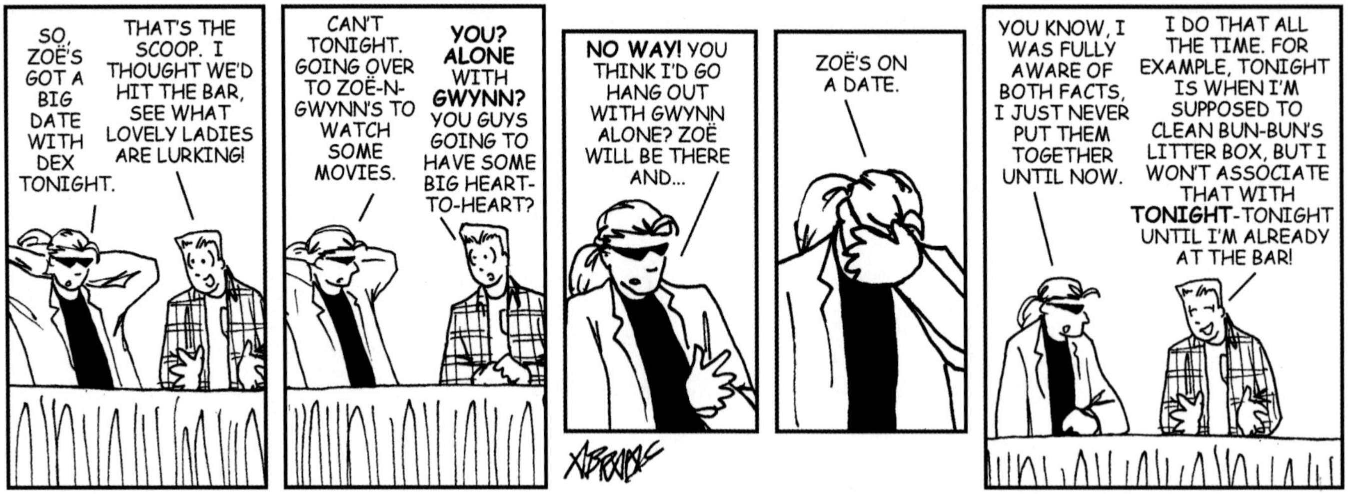
SO, ZOË'S GOT A BIG DATE WITH DEX TONIGHT.
THAT'S THE SCOOP. I THOUGHT WE'D HIT THE BAR, SEE WHAT LOVELY LADIES ARE LURKING!
CAN'T TONIGHT. GOING OVER TO ZOË-N-GWYNN'S TO WATCH SOME MOVIES.
YOU? ALONE WITH GWYNN? YOU GUYS GOING TO HAVE SOME BIG HEART-TO-HEART?
NO WAY! YOU THINK I'D GO HANG OUT WITH GWYNN ALONE? ZOË WILL BE THERE AND...
ZOË'S ON A DATE.
YOU KNOW, I WAS FULLY AWARE OF BOTH FACTS, I JUST NEVER PUT THEM TOGETHER UNTIL NOW.
I DO THAT ALL THE TIME. FOR EXAMPLE, TONIGHT IS WHEN I'M SUPPOSED TO CLEAN BUN-BUN'S LITTER BOX, BUT I WON'T ASSOCIATE THAT WITH TONIGHT-TONIGHT UNTIL I'M ALREADY AT THE BAR!

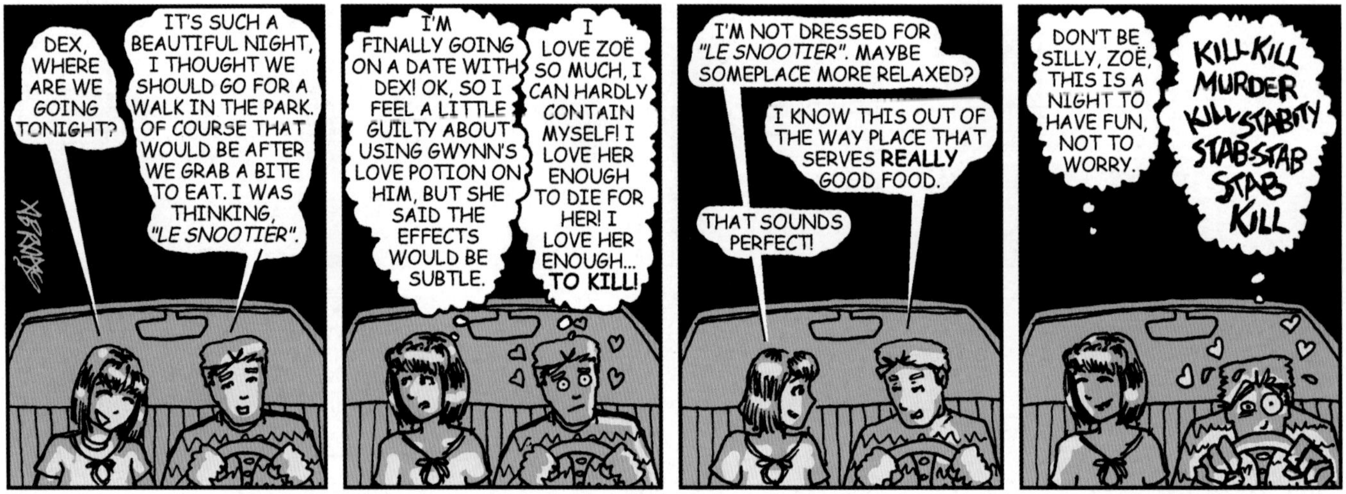
DEX, WHERE ARE WE GOING TONIGHT?
IT'S SUCH A BEAUTIFUL NIGHT, I THOUGHT WE SHOULD GO FOR A WALK IN THE PARK. OF COURSE THAT WOULD BE AFTER WE GRAB A BITE TO EAT. I WAS THINKING, "LE SNOOTIER".
I'M FINALLY GOING ON A DATE WITH DEX! OK, SO I FEEL A LITTLE GUILTY ABOUT USING GWYNN'S LOVE POTION ON HIM, BUT SHE SAID THE EFFECTS WOULD BE SUBTLE.
I LOVE ZOË SO MUCH, I CAN HARDLY CONTAIN MYSELF! I LOVE HER ENOUGH TO DIE FOR HER! I LOVE HER ENOUGH... TO KILL!
I'M NOT DRESSED FOR "LE SNOOTIER". MAYBE SOMEPLACE MORE RELAXED?
I KNOW THIS OUT OF THE WAY PLACE THAT SERVES REALLY GOOD FOOD.
THAT SOUNDS PERFECT!
DON'T BE SILLY, ZOË, THIS IS A NIGHT TO HAVE FUN, NOT TO WORRY.
KILL-KILL MURDER KILL-STABITY STAB-STAB STAB KILL

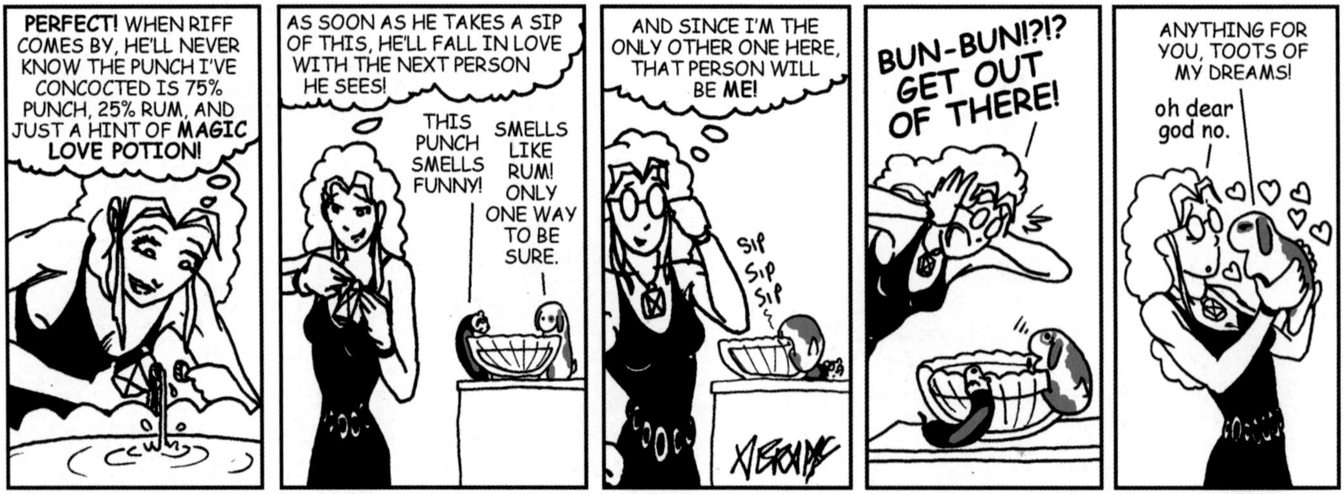
PERFECT! WHEN RIFF COMES BY, HE'LL NEVER KNOW THE PUNCH I'VE CONCOCTED IS 75% PUNCH, 25% RUM, AND JUST A HINT OF MAGIC LOVE POTION!
AS SOON AS HE TAKES A SIP OF THIS, HE'LL FALL IN LOVE WITH THE NEXT PERSON HE SEES!
THIS PUNCH SMELLS FUNNY!
SMELLS LIKE RUM! ONLY ONE WAY TO BE SURE.
AND SINCE I'M THE ONLY OTHER ONE HERE, THAT PERSON WILL BE ME!
SIP SIP SIP
BUN-BUN!?!? GET OUT OF THERE!
ANYTHING FOR YOU, TOOTS OF MY DREAMS!
oh dear god no.

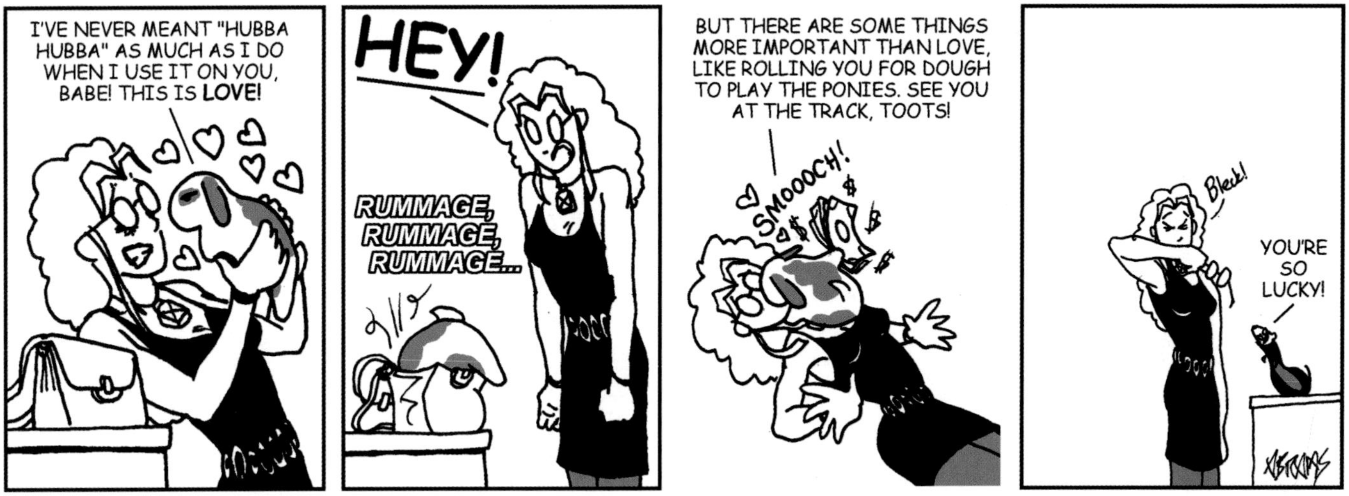
I'VE NEVER MEANT "HUBBA HUBBA" AS MUCH AS I DO WHEN I USE IT ON YOU, BABE! THIS IS LOVE!
HEY!
RUMMAGE, RUMMAGE, RUMMAGE...
BUT THERE ARE SOME THINGS MORE IMPORTANT THAN LOVE, LIKE ROLLING YOU FOR DOUGH TO PLAY THE PONIES. SEE YOU AT THE TRACK, TOOTS!
SMOOOCH!
Bleck!
YOU'RE SO LUCKY!

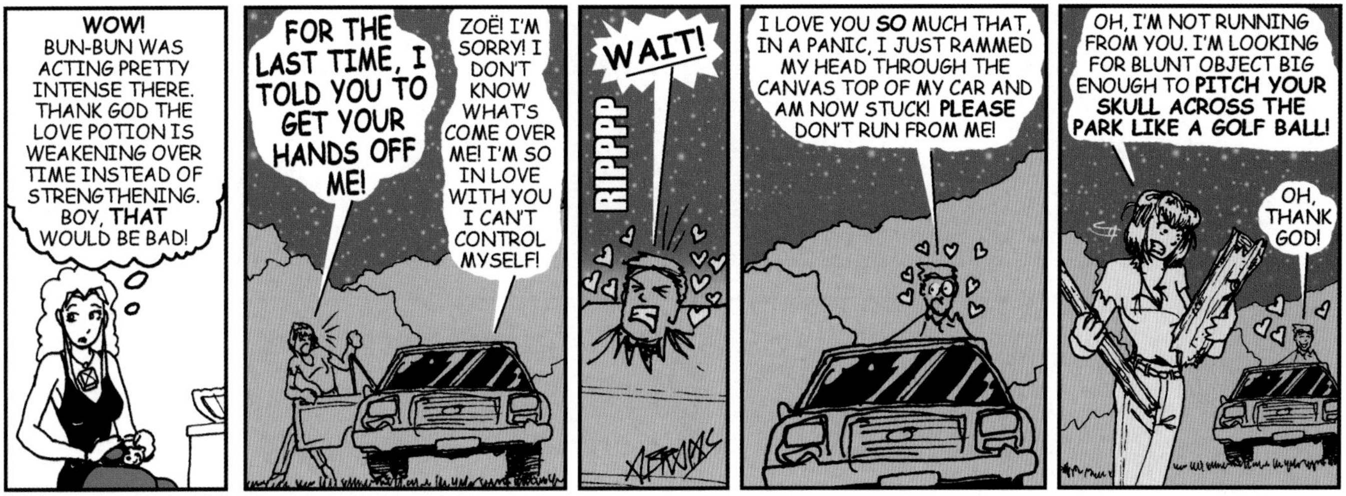
WOW! BUN-BUN WAS ACTING PRETTY INTENSE THERE. THANK GOD THE LOVE POTION IS WEAKENING OVER TIME INSTEAD OF STRENGTHENING. BOY, THAT WOULD BE BAD!
FOR THE LAST TIME, I TOLD YOU TO GET YOUR HANDS OFF ME!
ZOË! I'M SORRY! I DON'T KNOW WHAT'S COME OVER ME! I'M SO IN LOVE WITH YOU I CAN'T CONTROL MYSELF!
RIPPPP
WAIT!
I LOVE YOU SO MUCH THAT, IN A PANIC, I JUST RAMMED MY HEAD THROUGH THE CANVAS TOP OF MY CAR AND AM NOW STUCK! PLEASE DON'T RUN FROM ME!
OH, I'M NOT RUNNING FROM YOU. I'M LOOKING FOR BLUNT OBJECT BIG ENOUGH TO PITCH YOUR SKULL ACROSS THE PARK LIKE A GOLF BALL!
OH, THANK GOD!

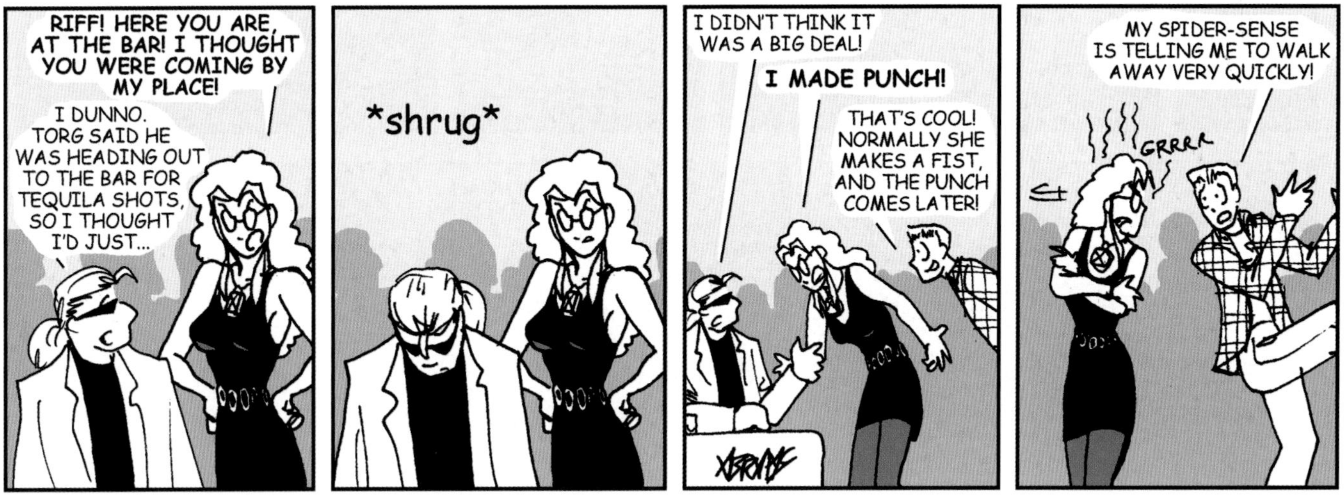
RIFF! HERE YOU ARE, AT THE BAR! I THOUGHT YOU WERE COMING BY MY PLACE!
I DUNNO. TORG SAID HE WAS HEADING OUT TO THE BAR FOR TEQUILA SHOTS, SO I THOUGHT I'D JUST...
shrug
I DIDN'T THINK IT WAS A BIG DEAL!
I MADE PUNCH!
THAT'S COOL! NORMALLY SHE MAKES A FIST, AND THE PUNCH COMES LATER!
GRRRR
MY SPIDER-SENSE IS TELLING ME TO WALK AWAY VERY QUICKLY!

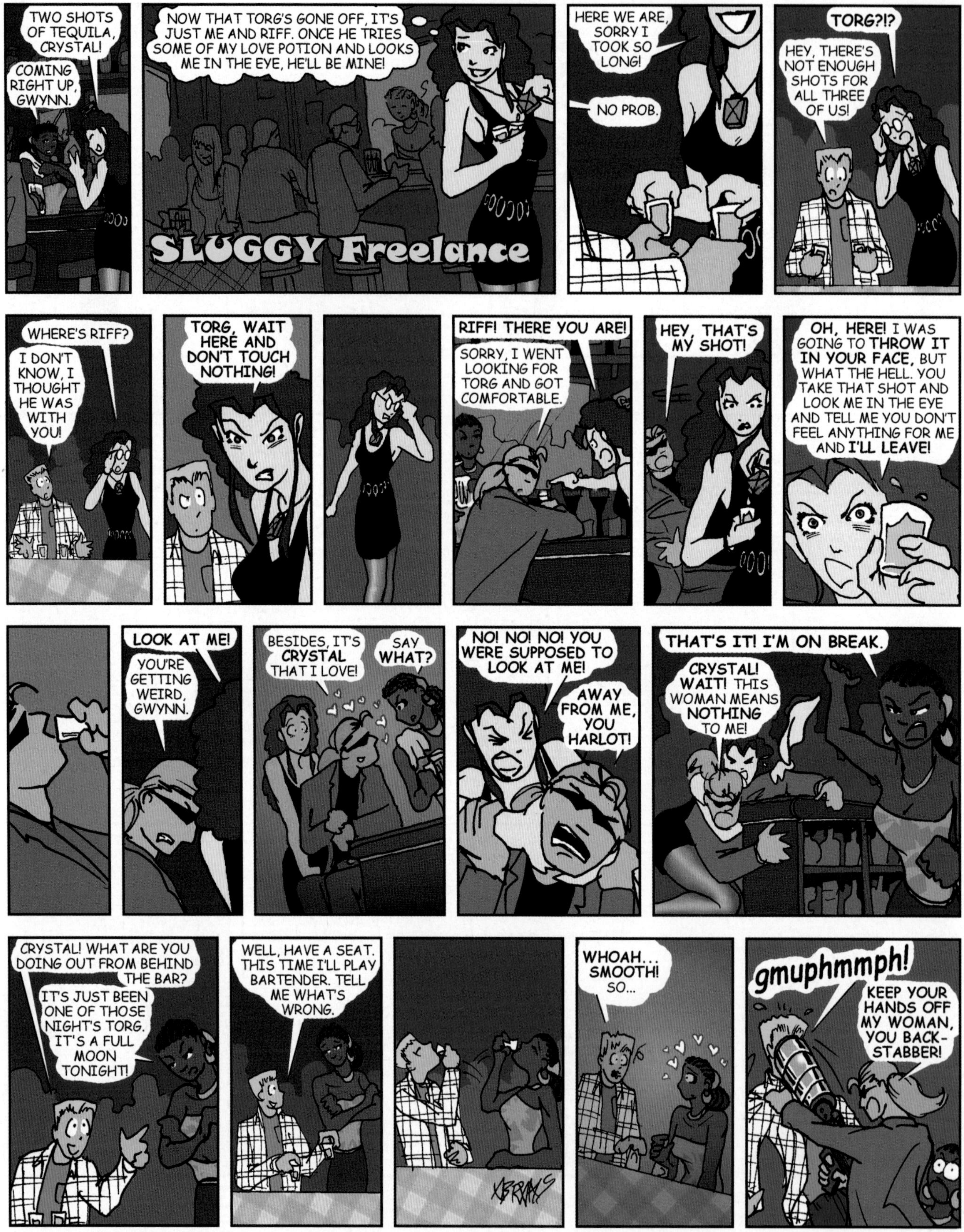

TWO SHOTS OF TEQUILA, CRYSTAL!
COMING RIGHT UP, GWYNN.
NOW THAT TORG'S GONE OFF, IT'S JUST ME AND RIFF. ONCE HE TRIES SOME OF MY LOVE POTION AND LOOKS ME IN THE EYE, HE'LL BE MINE!
SLUGGY Freelance
HERE WE ARE, SORRY I TOOK SO LONG!
NO PROB.
TORG?!?
HEY, THERE'S NOT ENOUGH SHOTS FOR ALL THREE OF US!
WHERE'S RIFF?
I DON'T KNOW, I THOUGHT HE WAS WITH YOU!
TORG, WAIT HERE AND DON'T TOUCH NOTHING!
RIFF! THERE YOU ARE!
SORRY, I WENT LOOKING FOR TORG AND GOT COMFORTABLE.
HEY, THAT'S MY SHOT!
OH, HERE! I WAS GOING TO THROW IT IN YOUR FACE, BUT WHAT THE HELL. YOU TAKE THAT SHOT AND LOOK ME IN THE EYE AND TELL ME YOU DON'T FEEL ANYTHING FOR ME AND I'LL LEAVE!
LOOK AT ME!
YOU'RE GETTING WEIRD, GWYNN.
BESIDES, IT'S CRYSTAL THAT I LOVE!
SAY WHAT?
NO! NO! NO! YOU WERE SUPPOSED TO LOOK AT ME!
AWAY FROM ME, YOU HARLOT!
THAT'S IT! I'M ON BREAK.
CRYSTAL! WAIT! THIS WOMAN MEANS NOTHING TO ME!
CRYSTAL! WHAT ARE YOU DOING OUT FROM BEHIND THE BAR?
IT'S JUST BEEN ONE OF THOSE NIGHT'S TORG. IT'S A FULL MOON TONIGHT!
WELL, HAVE A SEAT. THIS TIME I'LL PLAY BARTENDER. TELL ME WHAT'S WRONG.
WHOAH... SMOOTH! SO...
gmuphmmph!
KEEP YOUR HANDS OFF MY WOMAN, YOU BACK-STABBER!

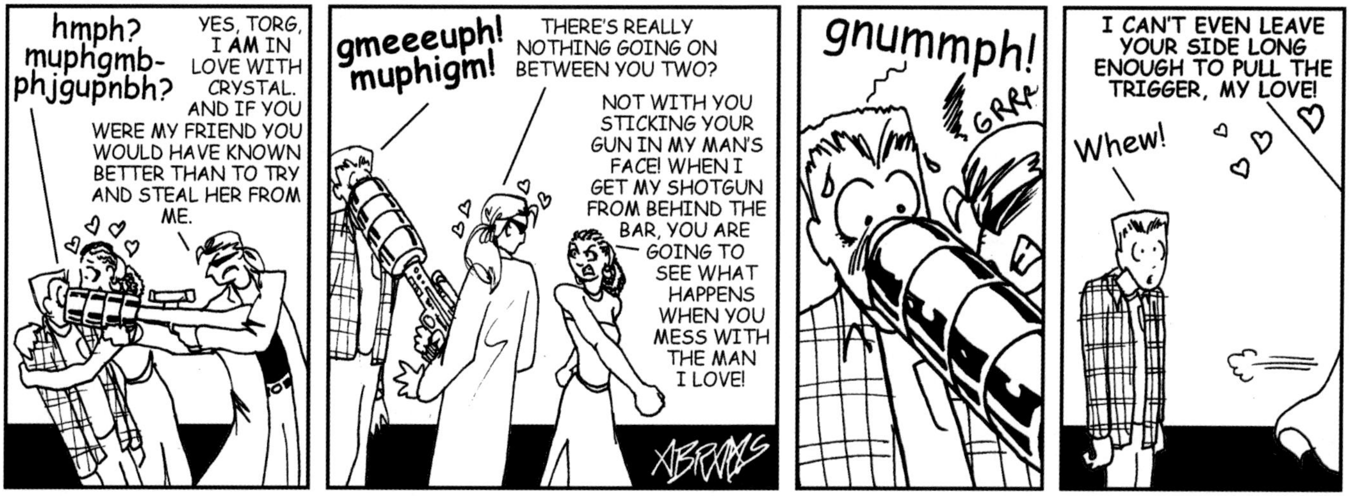
hmph? muphgmb-phjgupnbh?
YES, TORG, I **AM** IN LOVE WITH CRYSTAL. AND IF YOU WERE MY FRIEND YOU WOULD HAVE KNOWN BETTER THAN TO TRY AND STEAL HER FROM ME.
gmeeeuph! muphigm!
THERE'S REALLY NOTHING GOING ON BETWEEN YOU TWO?
NOT WITH YOU STICKING YOUR GUN IN MY MAN'S FACE! WHEN I GET MY SHOTGUN FROM BEHIND THE BAR, YOU ARE GOING TO SEE WHAT HAPPENS WHEN YOU MESS WITH THE MAN I LOVE!
gnummph!
I CAN'T EVEN LEAVE YOUR SIDE LONG ENOUGH TO PULL THE TRIGGER, MY LOVE!
Whew!

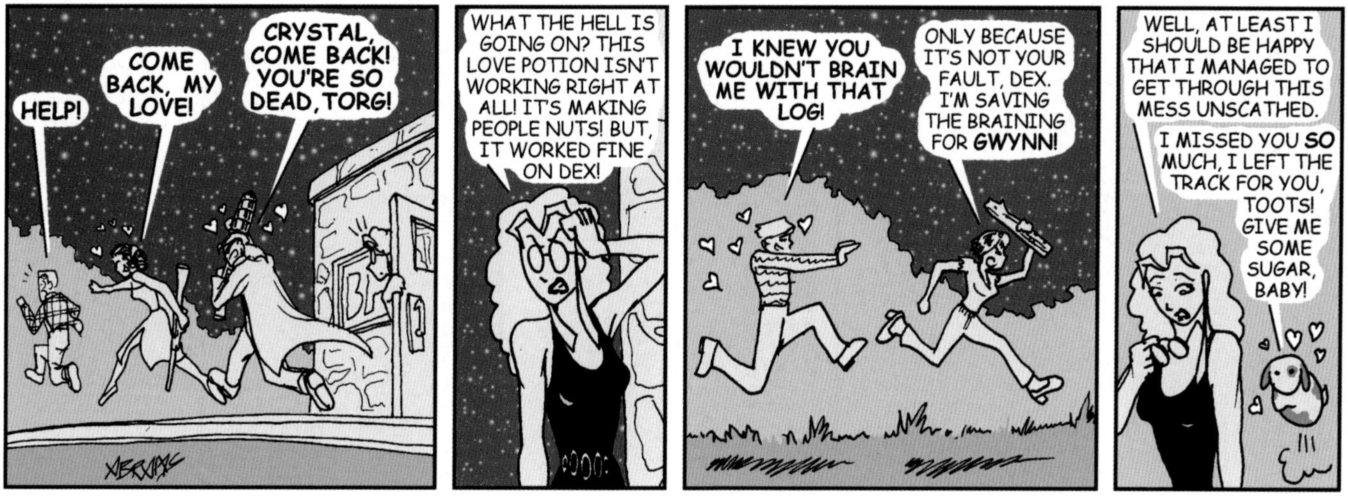
HELP!
COME BACK, MY LOVE!
CRYSTAL, COME BACK! YOU'RE SO DEAD, TORG!
WHAT THE HELL IS GOING ON? THIS LOVE POTION ISN'T WORKING RIGHT AT ALL! IT'S MAKING PEOPLE NUTS! BUT, IT WORKED FINE ON DEX!
I KNEW YOU WOULDN'T BRAIN ME WITH THAT LOG!
ONLY BECAUSE IT'S NOT YOUR FAULT, DEX. I'M SAVING THE BRAINING FOR **GWYNN!**
WELL, AT LEAST I SHOULD BE HAPPY THAT I MANAGED TO GET THROUGH THIS MESS UNSCATHED.
I MISSED YOU **SO** MUCH, I LEFT THE TRACK FOR YOU, TOOTS! GIVE ME SOME SUGAR, BABY!

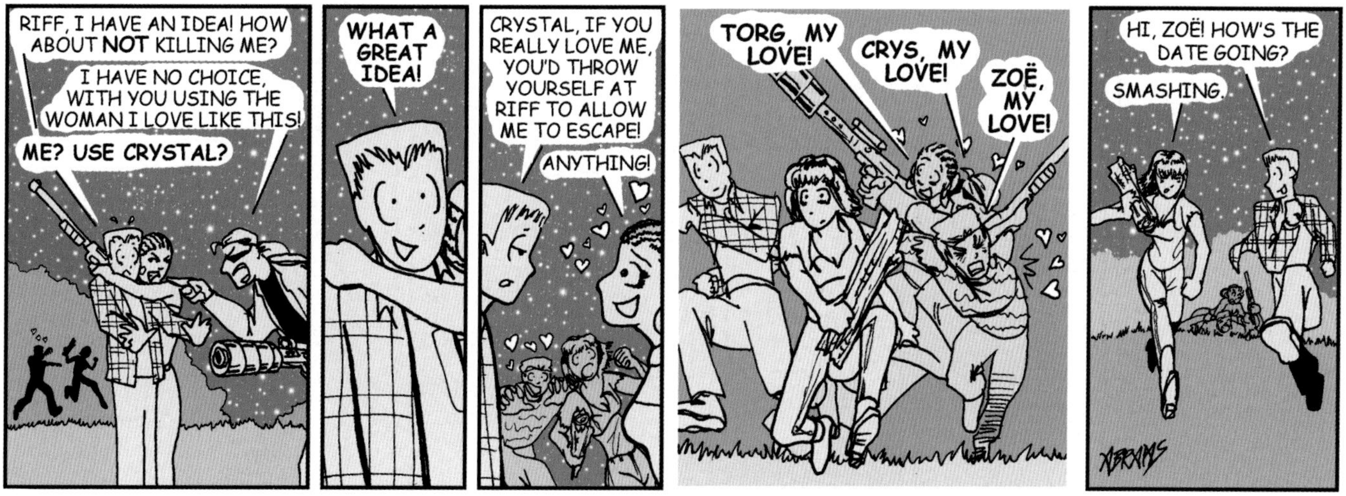
RIFF, I HAVE AN IDEA! HOW ABOUT **NOT** KILLING ME?
I HAVE NO CHOICE, WITH YOU USING THE WOMAN I LOVE LIKE THIS!
ME? USE CRYSTAL?
WHAT A GREAT IDEA!
CRYSTAL, IF YOU REALLY LOVE ME, YOU'D THROW YOURSELF AT RIFF TO ALLOW ME TO ESCAPE!
ANYTHING!
TORG, MY LOVE!
CRYS, MY LOVE!
ZOË, MY LOVE!
HI, ZOË! HOW'S THE DATE GOING?
SMASHING.

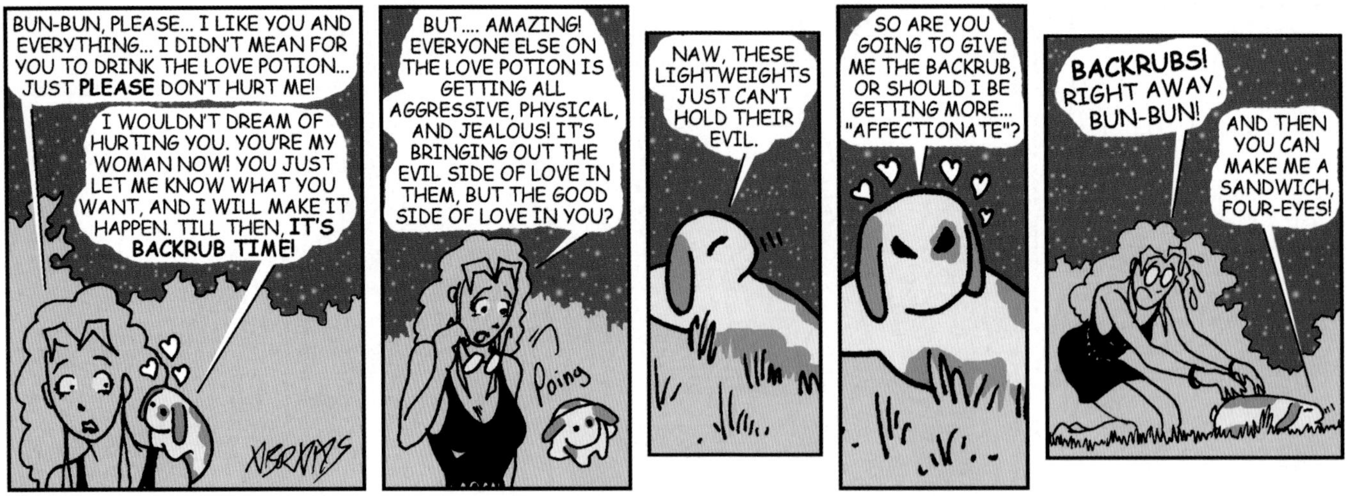
BUN-BUN, PLEASE... I LIKE YOU AND EVERYTHING... I DIDN'T MEAN FOR YOU TO DRINK THE LOVE POTION... JUST PLEASE DON'T HURT ME!
I WOULDN'T DREAM OF HURTING YOU. YOU'RE MY WOMAN NOW! YOU JUST LET ME KNOW WHAT YOU WANT, AND I WILL MAKE IT HAPPEN. TILL THEN, IT'S BACKRUB TIME!
BUT.... AMAZING! EVERYONE ELSE ON THE LOVE POTION IS GETTING ALL AGGRESSIVE, PHYSICAL, AND JEALOUS! IT'S BRINGING OUT THE EVIL SIDE OF LOVE IN THEM, BUT THE GOOD SIDE OF LOVE IN YOU?
Poing
NAW, THESE LIGHTWEIGHTS JUST CAN'T HOLD THEIR EVIL.
SO ARE YOU GOING TO GIVE ME THE BACKRUB, OR SHOULD I BE GETTING MORE... "AFFECTIONATE"?
BACKRUBS! RIGHT AWAY, BUN-BUN!
AND THEN YOU CAN MAKE ME A SANDWICH, FOUR-EYES!

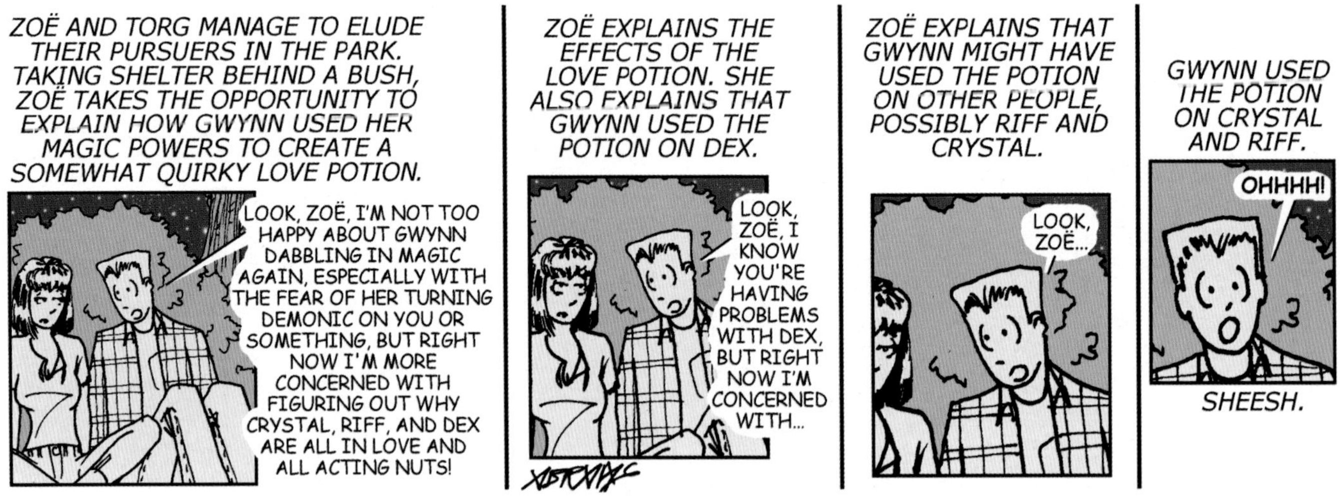
ZOË AND TORG MANAGE TO ELUDE THEIR PURSUERS IN THE PARK. TAKING SHELTER BEHIND A BUSH, ZOË TAKES THE OPPORTUNITY TO EXPLAIN HOW GWYNN USED HER MAGIC POWERS TO CREATE A SOMEWHAT QUIRKY LOVE POTION.
LOOK, ZOË, I'M NOT TOO HAPPY ABOUT GWYNN DABBLING IN MAGIC AGAIN, ESPECIALLY WITH THE FEAR OF HER TURNING DEMONIC ON YOU OR SOMETHING, BUT RIGHT NOW I'M MORE CONCERNED WITH FIGURING OUT WHY CRYSTAL, RIFF, AND DEX ARE ALL IN LOVE AND ALL ACTING NUTS!
ZOË EXPLAINS THE EFFECTS OF THE LOVE POTION. SHE ALSO EXPLAINS THAT GWYNN USED THE POTION ON DEX.
LOOK, ZOË, I KNOW YOU'RE HAVING PROBLEMS WITH DEX, BUT RIGHT NOW I'M CONCERNED WITH...
ZOË EXPLAINS THAT GWYNN MIGHT HAVE USED THE POTION ON OTHER PEOPLE, POSSIBLY RIFF AND CRYSTAL.
LOOK, ZOË...
GWYNN USED THE POTION ON CRYSTAL AND RIFF.
OHHHH!
SHEESH.

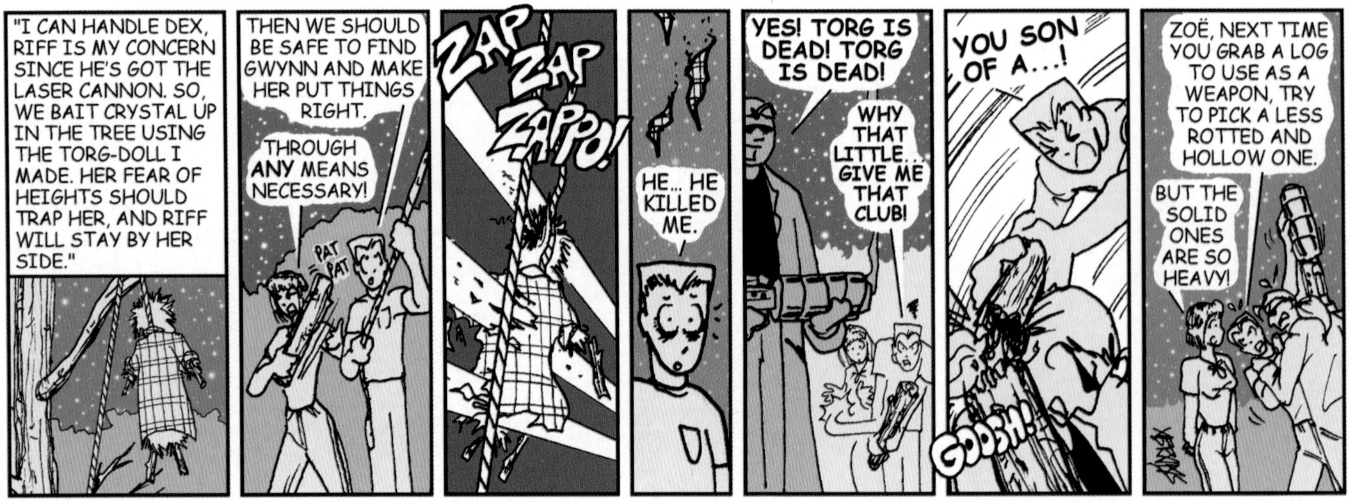
"I CAN HANDLE DEX, RIFF IS MY CONCERN SINCE HE'S GOT THE LASER CANNON. SO, WE BAIT CRYSTAL UP IN THE TREE USING THE TORG-DOLL I MADE. HER FEAR OF HEIGHTS SHOULD TRAP HER, AND RIFF WILL STAY BY HER SIDE."
THEN WE SHOULD BE SAFE TO FIND GWYNN AND MAKE HER PUT THINGS RIGHT.
THROUGH ANY MEANS NECESSARY!
PAT PAT
ZAP ZAP ZAPPO!
HE... HE KILLED ME.
YES! TORG IS DEAD! TORG IS DEAD!
WHY THAT LITTLE... GIVE ME THAT CLUB!
YOU SON OF A...!
GOOSH!
ZOË, NEXT TIME YOU GRAB A LOG TO USE AS A WEAPON, TRY TO PICK A LESS ROTTED AND HOLLOW ONE.
BUT THE SOLID ONES ARE SO HEAVY!

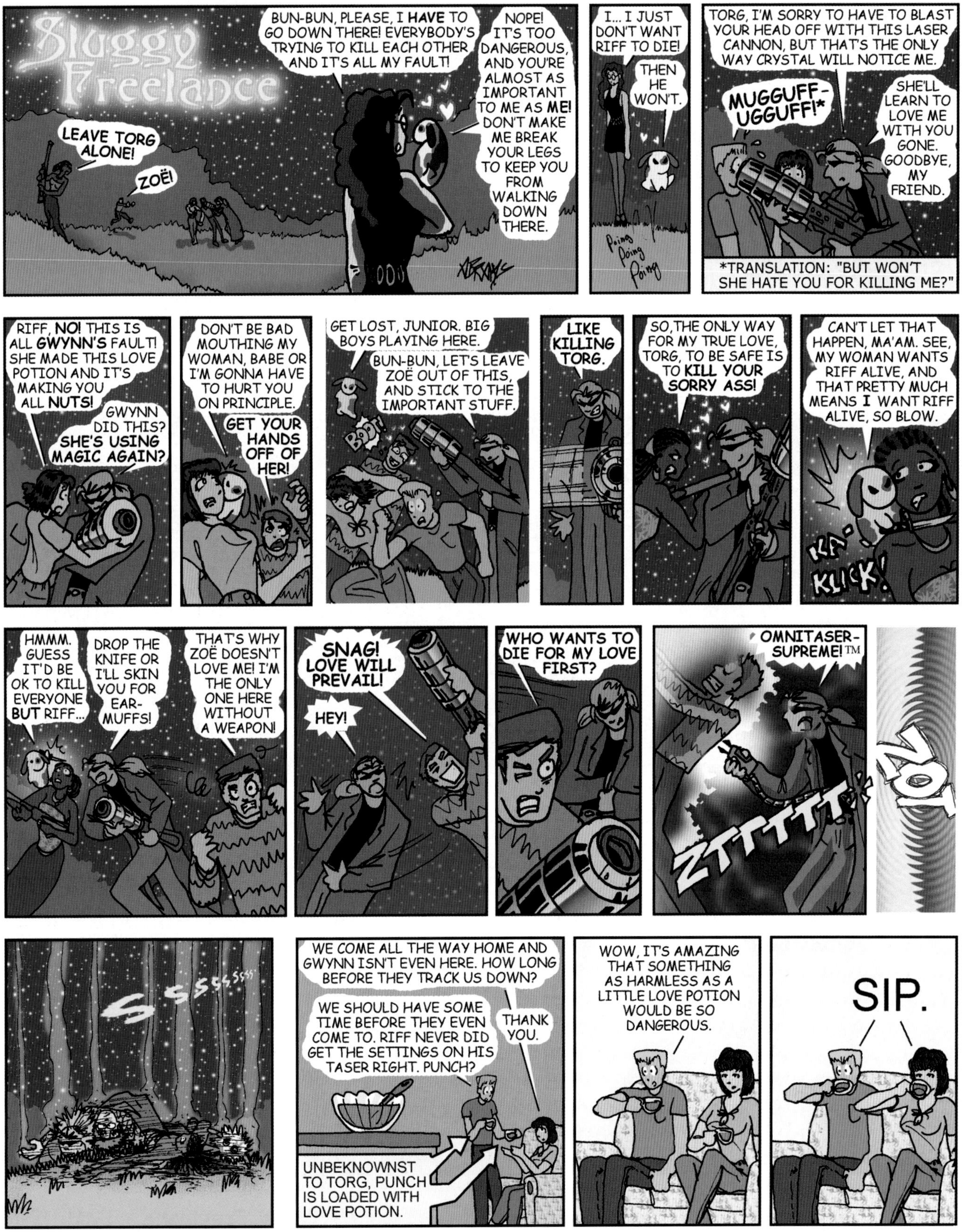
Sluggy Freelance
LEAVE TORG ALONE!
ZOË!
BUN-BUN, PLEASE, I HAVE TO GO DOWN THERE! EVERYBODY'S TRYING TO KILL EACH OTHER AND IT'S ALL MY FAULT!
NOPE! IT'S TOO DANGEROUS, AND YOU'RE ALMOST AS IMPORTANT TO ME AS ME! DON'T MAKE ME BREAK YOUR LEGS TO KEEP YOU FROM WALKING DOWN THERE.
I... I JUST DON'T WANT RIFF TO DIE!
THEN HE WON'T.
Poing Poing Poing
TORG, I'M SORRY TO HAVE TO BLAST YOUR HEAD OFF WITH THIS LASER CANNON, BUT THAT'S THE ONLY WAY CRYSTAL WILL NOTICE ME.
MUGGUFF-UGGUFF!*
SHE'LL LEARN TO LOVE ME WITH YOU GONE. GOODBYE, MY FRIEND.
*TRANSLATION: "BUT WON'T SHE HATE YOU FOR KILLING ME?"
RIFF, NO! THIS IS ALL GWYNN'S FAULT! SHE MADE THIS LOVE POTION AND IT'S MAKING YOU ALL NUTS!
GWYNN DID THIS? SHE'S USING MAGIC AGAIN?
DON'T BE BAD MOUTHING MY WOMAN, BABE OR I'M GONNA HAVE TO HURT YOU ON PRINCIPLE.
GET YOUR HANDS OFF OF HER!
GET LOST, JUNIOR. BIG BOYS PLAYING HERE.
BUN-BUN, LET'S LEAVE ZOË OUT OF THIS, AND STICK TO THE IMPORTANT STUFF.
BOOT
LIKE KILLING TORG.
SO, THE ONLY WAY FOR MY TRUE LOVE, TORG, TO BE SAFE IS TO KILL YOUR SORRY ASS!
CAN'T LET THAT HAPPEN, MA'AM. SEE, MY WOMAN WANTS RIFF ALIVE, AND THAT PRETTY MUCH MEANS I WANT RIFF ALIVE, SO BLOW.
KA-KLICK!
HMMM. GUESS IT'D BE OK TO KILL EVERYONE BUT RIFF...
DROP THE KNIFE OR I'LL SKIN YOU FOR EAR-MUFFS!
THAT'S WHY ZOË DOESN'T LOVE ME! I'M THE ONLY ONE HERE WITHOUT A WEAPON!
SNAG! LOVE WILL PREVAIL!
HEY!
WHO WANTS TO DIE FOR MY LOVE FIRST?
OMNITASER-SUPREME!™
ZTTTTTT!
ZOT
S S S S S S S S
WE COME ALL THE WAY HOME AND GWYNN ISN'T EVEN HERE. HOW LONG BEFORE THEY TRACK US DOWN?
WE SHOULD HAVE SOME TIME BEFORE THEY EVEN COME TO. RIFF NEVER DID GET THE SETTINGS ON HIS TASER RIGHT. PUNCH?
THANK YOU.
UNBEKNOWNST TO TORG, PUNCH IS LOADED WITH LOVE POTION.
WOW, IT'S AMAZING THAT SOMETHING AS HARMLESS AS A LITTLE LOVE POTION WOULD BE SO DANGEROUS.
SIP.

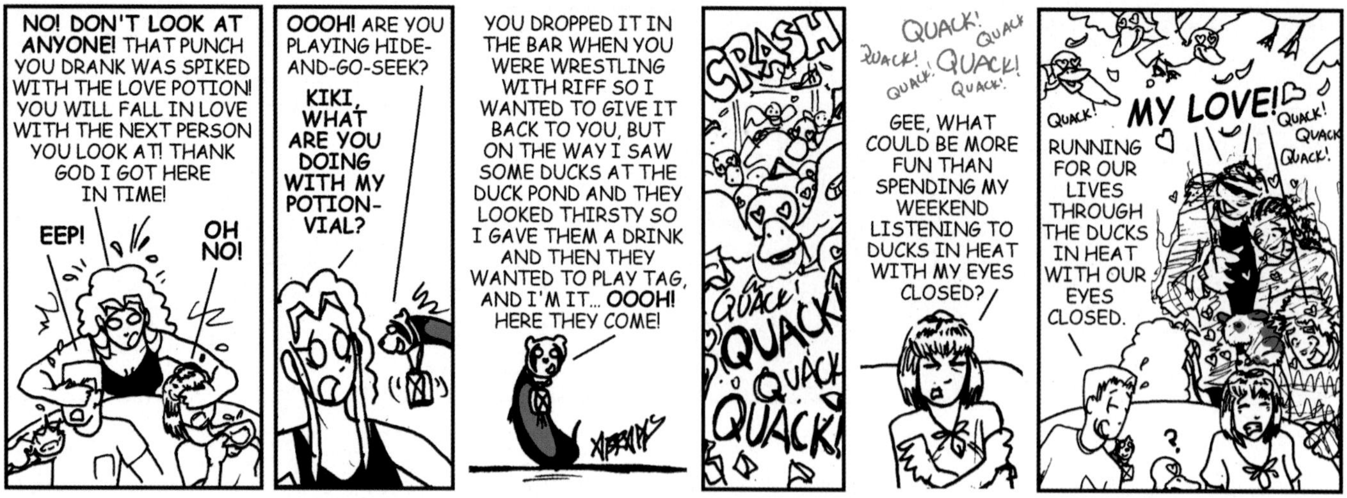
NO! DON'T LOOK AT ANYONE! THAT PUNCH YOU DRANK WAS SPIKED WITH THE LOVE POTION! YOU WILL FALL IN LOVE WITH THE NEXT PERSON YOU LOOK AT! THANK GOD I GOT HERE IN TIME!
EEP!
OH NO!
OOOH! ARE YOU PLAYING HIDE-AND-GO-SEEK?
KIKI, WHAT ARE YOU DOING WITH MY POTION-VIAL?
YOU DROPPED IT IN THE BAR WHEN YOU WERE WRESTLING WITH RIFF SO I WANTED TO GIVE IT BACK TO YOU, BUT ON THE WAY I SAW SOME DUCKS AT THE DUCK POND AND THEY LOOKED THIRSTY SO I GAVE THEM A DRINK AND THEN THEY WANTED TO PLAY TAG, AND I'M IT... OOOH! HERE THEY COME!
CRASH
QUACK! QUACK! QUACK! QUACK!
QUACK! QUACK! QUACK! QUACK! QUACK! QUACK! QUACK!
GEE, WHAT COULD BE MORE FUN THAN SPENDING MY WEEKEND LISTENING TO DUCKS IN HEAT WITH MY EYES CLOSED?
MY LOVE!
QUACK! QUACK! QUACK! QUACK!
RUNNING FOR OUR LIVES THROUGH THE DUCKS IN HEAT WITH OUR EYES CLOSED.

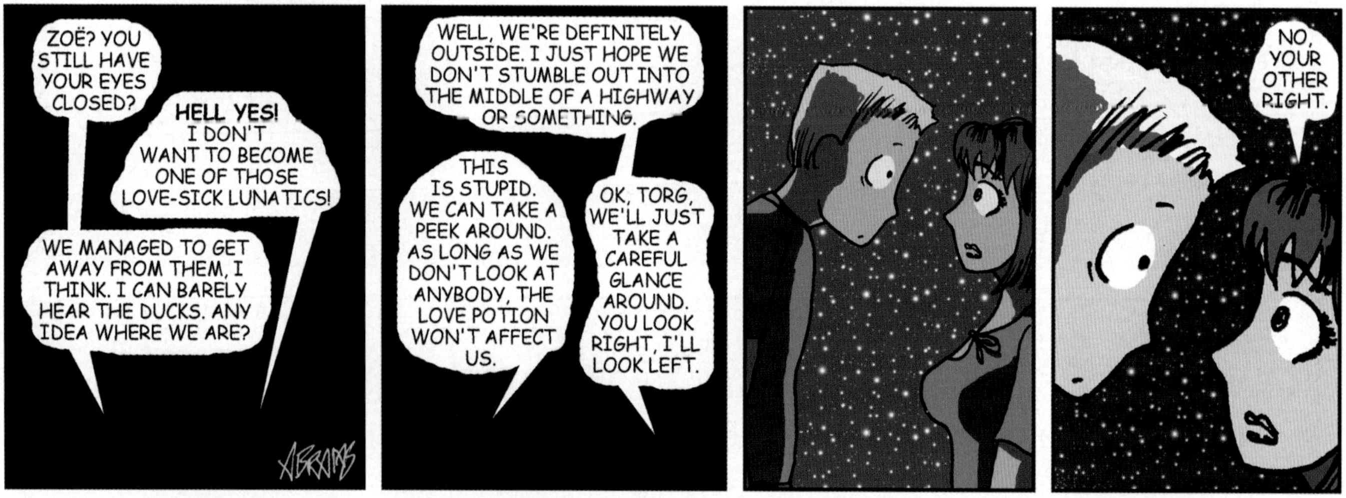
ZOË? YOU STILL HAVE YOUR EYES CLOSED?
HELL YES! I DON'T WANT TO BECOME ONE OF THOSE LOVE-SICK LUNATICS!
WE MANAGED TO GET AWAY FROM THEM, I THINK. I CAN BARELY HEAR THE DUCKS. ANY IDEA WHERE WE ARE?
WELL, WE'RE DEFINITELY OUTSIDE. I JUST HOPE WE DON'T STUMBLE OUT INTO THE MIDDLE OF A HIGHWAY OR SOMETHING.
THIS IS STUPID. WE CAN TAKE A PEEK AROUND. AS LONG AS WE DON'T LOOK AT ANYBODY, THE LOVE POTION WON'T AFFECT US.
OK, TORG, WE'LL JUST TAKE A CAREFUL GLANCE AROUND. YOU LOOK RIGHT, I'LL LOOK LEFT.
NO, YOUR OTHER RIGHT.

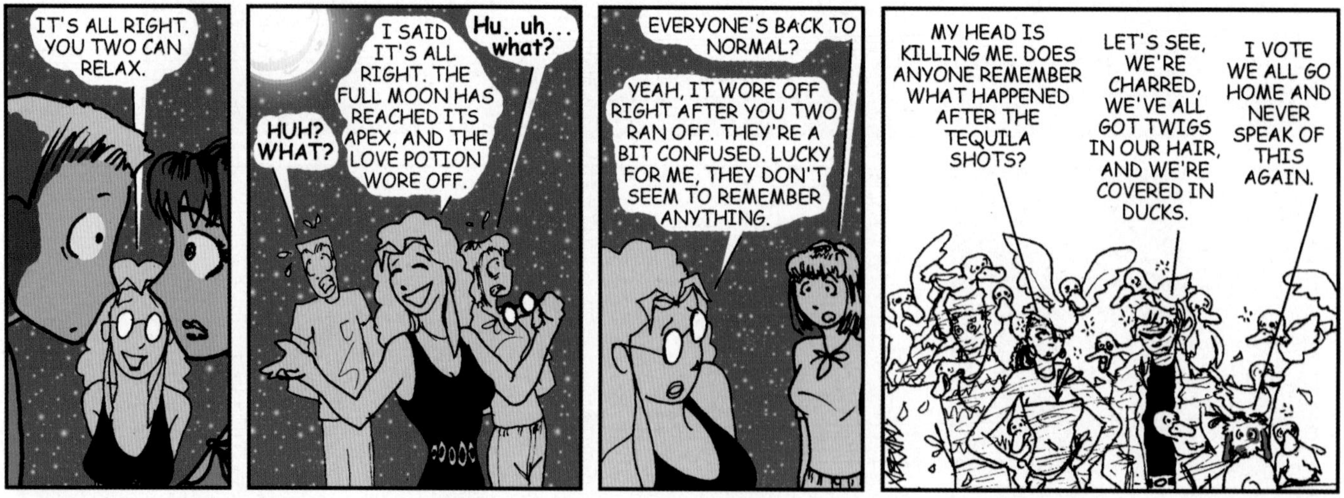
IT'S ALL RIGHT. YOU TWO CAN RELAX.
HUH? WHAT?
I SAID IT'S ALL RIGHT. THE FULL MOON HAS REACHED ITS APEX, AND THE LOVE POTION WORE OFF.
Hu..uh... what?
EVERYONE'S BACK TO NORMAL?
YEAH, IT WORE OFF RIGHT AFTER YOU TWO RAN OFF. THEY'RE A BIT CONFUSED. LUCKY FOR ME, THEY DON'T SEEM TO REMEMBER ANYTHING.
MY HEAD IS KILLING ME. DOES ANYONE REMEMBER WHAT HAPPENED AFTER THE TEQUILA SHOTS?
LET'S SEE, WE'RE CHARRED, WE'VE ALL GOT TWIGS IN OUR HAIR, AND WE'RE COVERED IN DUCKS.
I VOTE WE ALL GO HOME AND NEVER SPEAK OF THIS AGAIN.

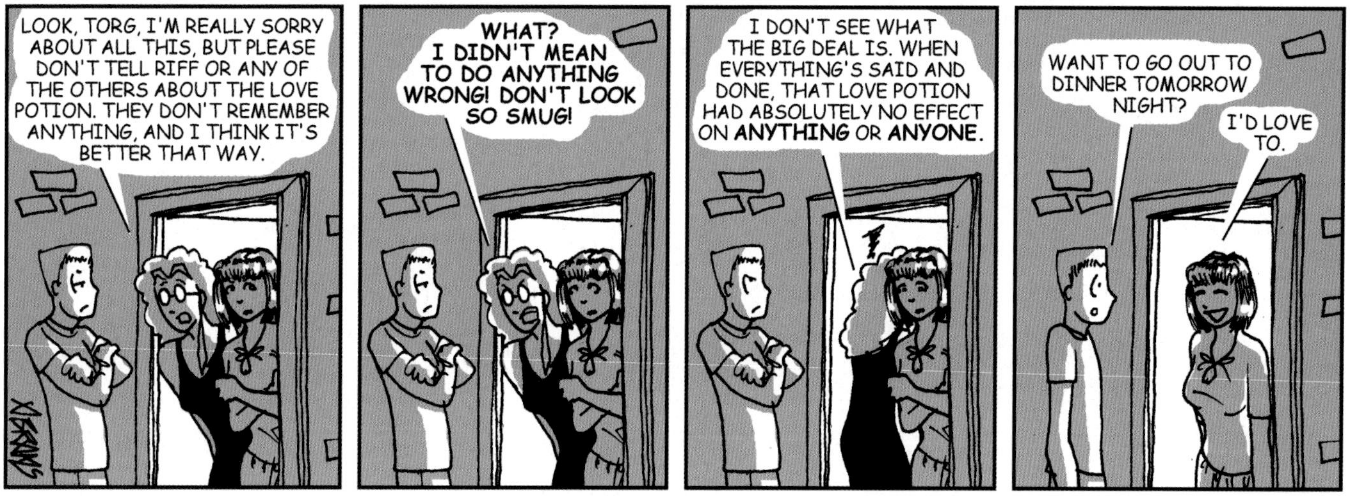
LOOK, TORG, I'M REALLY SORRY ABOUT ALL THIS, BUT PLEASE DON'T TELL RIFF OR ANY OF THE OTHERS ABOUT THE LOVE POTION. THEY DON'T REMEMBER ANYTHING, AND I THINK IT'S BETTER THAT WAY.
WHAT? I DIDN'T MEAN TO DO ANYTHING WRONG! DON'T LOOK SO SMUG!
I DON'T SEE WHAT THE BIG DEAL IS. WHEN EVERYTHING'S SAID AND DONE, THAT LOVE POTION HAD ABSOLUTELY NO EFFECT ON ANYTHING OR ANYONE.
WANT TO GO OUT TO DINNER TOMORROW NIGHT?
I'D LOVE TO.

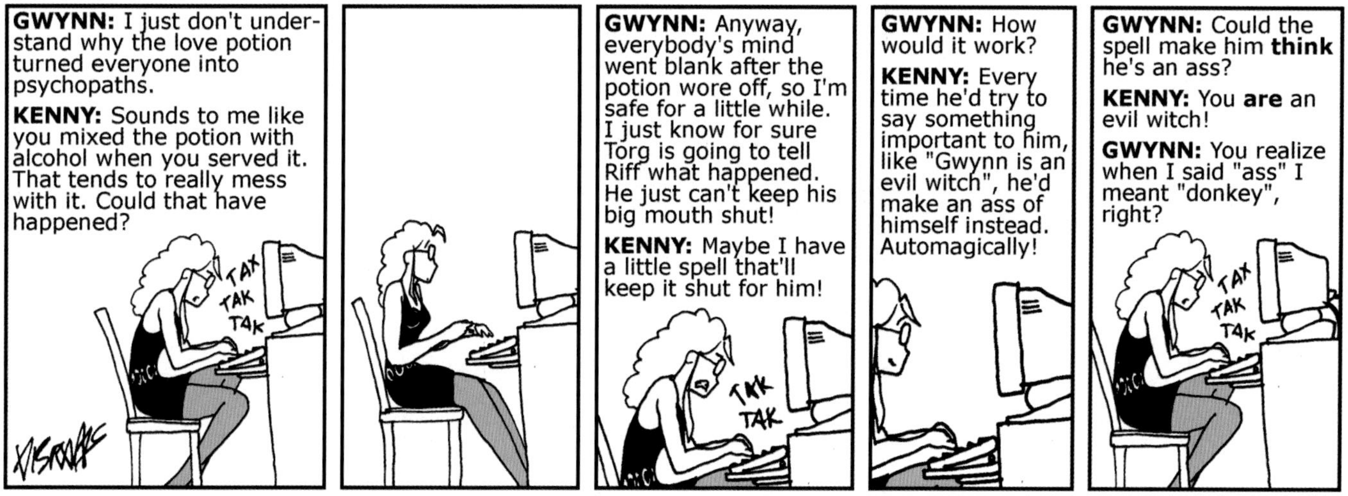
GWYNN: I just don't understand why the love potion turned everyone into psychopaths.
KENNY: Sounds to me like you mixed the potion with alcohol when you served it. That tends to really mess with it. Could that have happened?
TAK TAK TAK
GWYNN: Anyway, everybody's mind went blank after the potion wore off, so I'm safe for a little while. I just know for sure Torg is going to tell Riff what happened. He just can't keep his big mouth shut!
KENNY: Maybe I have a little spell that'll keep it shut for him!
TAK TAK
GWYNN: How would it work?
KENNY: Every time he'd try to say something important to him, like "Gwynn is an evil witch", he'd make an ass of himself instead. Automagically!
GWYNN: Could the spell make him think he's an ass?
KENNY: You are an evil witch!
GWYNN: You realize when I said "ass" I meant "donkey", right?
TAK TAK TAK

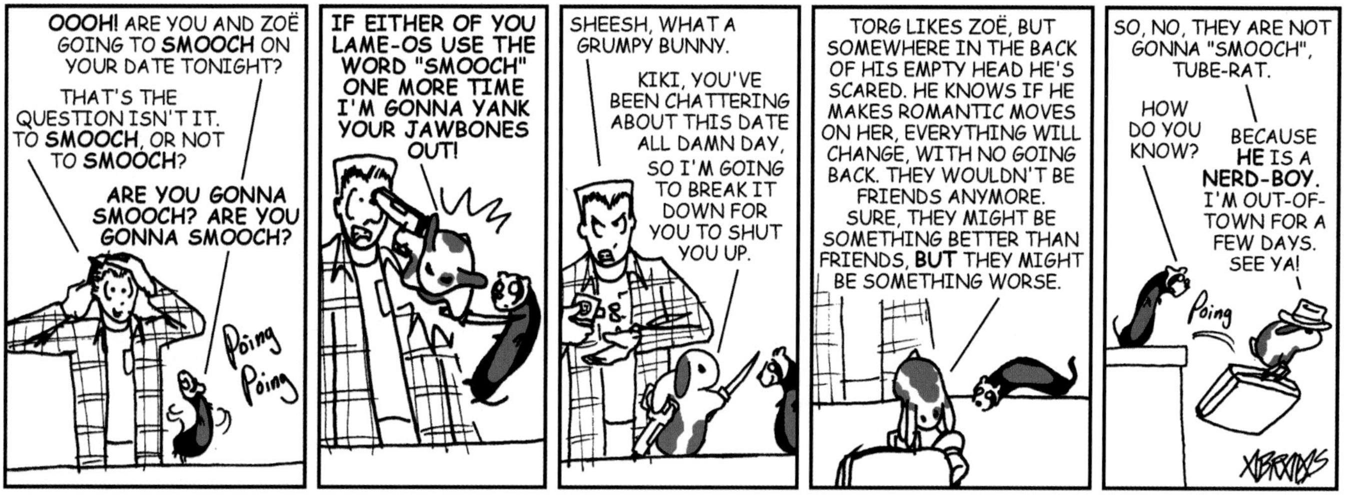
OOOH! ARE YOU AND ZOË GOING TO SMOOCH ON YOUR DATE TONIGHT?
THAT'S THE QUESTION ISN'T IT. TO SMOOCH, OR NOT TO SMOOCH?
ARE YOU GONNA SMOOCH? ARE YOU GONNA SMOOCH?
Poing Poing
IF EITHER OF YOU LAME-OS USE THE WORD "SMOOCH" ONE MORE TIME I'M GONNA YANK YOUR JAWBONES OUT!
SHEESH, WHAT A GRUMPY BUNNY.
KIKI, YOU'VE BEEN CHATTERING ABOUT THIS DATE ALL DAMN DAY, SO I'M GOING TO BREAK IT DOWN FOR YOU TO SHUT YOU UP.
TORG LIKES ZOË, BUT SOMEWHERE IN THE BACK OF HIS EMPTY HEAD HE'S SCARED. HE KNOWS IF HE MAKES ROMANTIC MOVES ON HER, EVERYTHING WILL CHANGE, WITH NO GOING BACK. THEY WOULDN'T BE FRIENDS ANYMORE. SURE, THEY MIGHT BE SOMETHING BETTER THAN FRIENDS, BUT THEY MIGHT BE SOMETHING WORSE.
SO, NO, THEY ARE NOT GONNA "SMOOCH", TUBE-RAT.
HOW DO YOU KNOW?
BECAUSE HE IS A NERD-BOY. I'M OUT-OF-TOWN FOR A FEW DAYS. SEE YA!
Poing

I, AGAIN, APOLOGIZE FOR KEEPING YOU WAITING, BUT I WANTED TO MAKE SURE WE HAVE ENOUGH DISHES FOR YOU TO WASH TO COVER YOUR BILL. WE HAVE CREATED QUITE A MOUNTAIN OF THEM FOR YOU. IT'S RATHER BREATHTAKING.

LOOK, SPARKY, I DIDN'T MEAN TO SKIP OUT ON THE CHECK LAST TIME...

OH, MY, YES. YOU MUST HAVE SPOTTED THE "TRASH-SIGNAL" IN THE SKY. OFF TO FIGHT CRIME IN THE "TRASH-MOBILE".

DON'T WORRY, I HAVE A CREDIT CARD.

THIS MEAL IS "ON THE HOUSE" IF YOU CAN EXPLAIN WHY A WOMAN OF YOUR OBVIOUS QUALITY WOULD BE SEEN WITH THE LIKES OF "CLETUS" HERE.

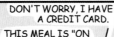

I'M A QUALITY PIECE OF MEAT, HUH? HOW DO YOU KNOW I'M QUALITY? YOU HAVEN'T CHECKED MY TEETH YET.

OOOOOOH!

MY APOLOGIES, MADAM! I MEANT NO...

HA-HAH! IS YOUR FACE RED! WELL, OK, IT'S ACTUALLY STILL PALE.

HE SEEMS TO REALLY LIKE YOU!

I THINK I'VE DEVELOPED QUITE THE REPUTATION HERE!

IS THIS WHERE YOU BRING ALL YOUR HIGH-QUALITY DATES?

YOU KNOW ME! I'M QUITE THE LADIES MAN!

WHY IS MY HEART RACING? IT'S JUST ZOË! IT'S JUST A DATE WITH ZOË. NO BIG DEAL.

HE'S SCARED. HE KNOWS IF HE MAKES ROMANTIC MOVES ON HER, EVERYTHING WILL CHANGE, WITH NO GOING BACK. THEY WOULDN'T BE FRIENDS ANYMORE. SURE, THEY MIGHT BE SOMETHING BETTER THAN FRIENDS, BUT THEY MIGHT BE SOMETHING WORSE

BUN-BUN'S RIGHT. WHETHER TONIGHT, OR A MONTH DOWN THE ROAD, I'M GOING TO SCREW THIS RELATIONSHIP UP. I ALWAYS DO. MAYBE IT'S FOR THE BEST THAT THIS NEVER TURNS SERIOUS AT ALL.

TORG? ARE YOU ALRIGHT? YOU JUST SORT-OF ZONED OUT THERE.

I'M SORRY. I WAS JUST THINKING AND MY BRAIN DERAILED.

THAT'S ALL RIGHT.

BUT ZOË SEEMS REALLY HAPPY TO BE HERE WITH ME. I CAN'T REMEMBER THE LAST TIME SHE LOOKED SO... GOD, SHE'S PRETTY

SO, NO, THEY ARE NOT GONNA "SMOOCH", TUBE-RAT.

HOW DO YOU KNOW?

BECAUSE HE IS A NERD-BOY.

POING

SCREW BUN-BUN. MAYBE I'M JUST THINKING TOO HARD ABOUT IT ALL. MAYBE IT'S TIME I LET EVERYTHING RIDE AND JUST LEAN OVER AND GIVE ZOË A BIG...

Sluggy Freelance

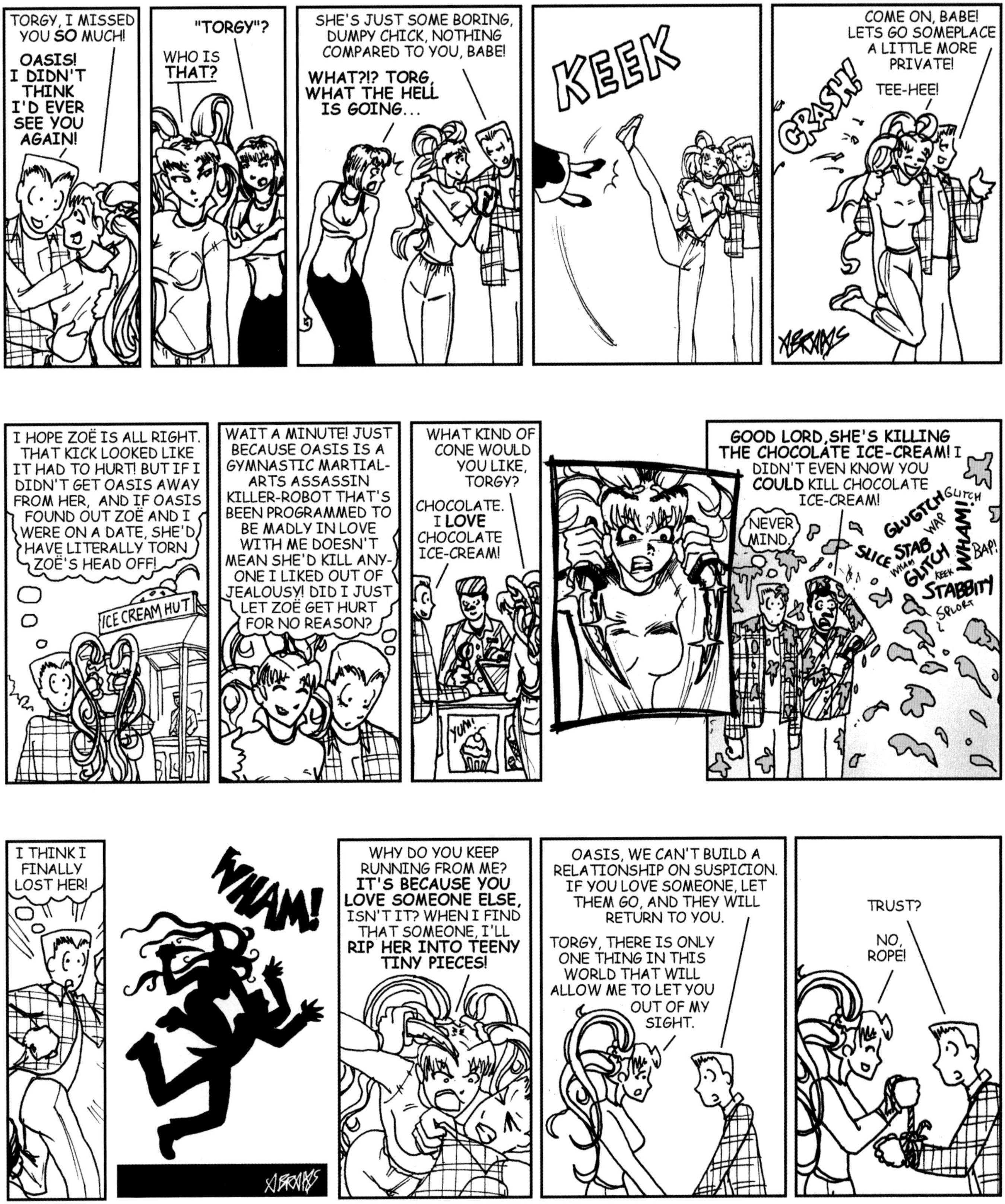
TORGY, I MISSED YOU SO MUCH!
OASIS! I DIDN'T THINK I'D EVER SEE YOU AGAIN!
"TORGY"?
WHO IS THAT?
SHE'S JUST SOME BORING, DUMPY CHICK, NOTHING COMPARED TO YOU, BABE!
WHAT?!? TORG, WHAT THE HELL IS GOING...
KEEK
COME ON, BABE! LETS GO SOMEPLACE A LITTLE MORE PRIVATE!
CRASH!
TEE-HEE!
I HOPE ZOË IS ALL RIGHT. THAT KICK LOOKED LIKE IT HAD TO HURT! BUT IF I DIDN'T GET OASIS AWAY FROM HER, AND IF OASIS FOUND OUT ZOË AND I WERE ON A DATE, SHE'D HAVE LITERALLY TORN ZOË'S HEAD OFF!
ICE CREAM HUT
WAIT A MINUTE! JUST BECAUSE OASIS IS A GYMNASTIC MARTIAL-ARTS ASSASSIN KILLER-ROBOT THAT'S BEEN PROGRAMMED TO BE MADLY IN LOVE WITH ME DOESN'T MEAN SHE'D KILL ANY-ONE I LIKED OUT OF JEALOUSY! DID I JUST LET ZOË GET HURT FOR NO REASON?
WHAT KIND OF CONE WOULD YOU LIKE, TORGY?
CHOCOLATE. I LOVE CHOCOLATE ICE-CREAM!
YUM!
GOOD LORD, SHE'S KILLING THE CHOCOLATE ICE-CREAM! I DIDN'T EVEN KNOW YOU COULD KILL CHOCOLATE ICE-CREAM!
NEVER MIND.
GLUGTCH GLITCH WAP SLICE STAB WHAM GLITCH WHAM! BAP! KEEK STABBITY SPLORT
I THINK I FINALLY LOST HER!
WHAM!
WHY DO YOU KEEP RUNNING FROM ME? IT'S BECAUSE YOU LOVE SOMEONE ELSE, ISN'T IT? WHEN I FIND THAT SOMEONE, I'LL RIP HER INTO TEENY TINY PIECES!
OASIS, WE CAN'T BUILD A RELATIONSHIP ON SUSPICION. IF YOU LOVE SOMEONE, LET THEM GO, AND THEY WILL RETURN TO YOU.
TORGY, THERE IS ONLY ONE THING IN THIS WORLD THAT WILL ALLOW ME TO LET YOU OUT OF MY SIGHT.
TRUST?
NO, ROPE!

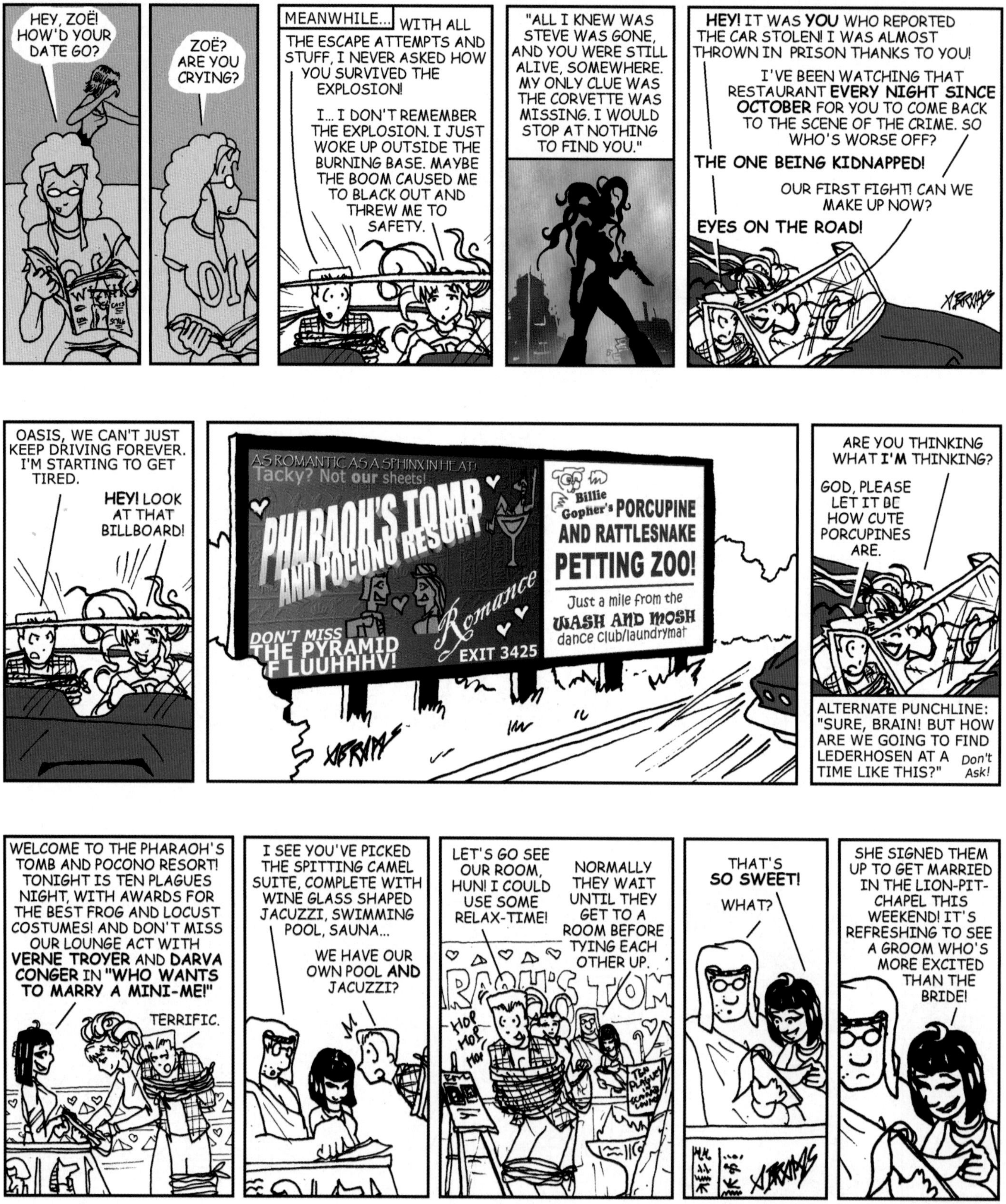

HEY, ZOË! HOW'D YOUR DATE GO?
ZOË? ARE YOU CRYING?
MEANWHILE...
WITH ALL THE ESCAPE ATTEMPTS AND STUFF, I NEVER ASKED HOW YOU SURVIVED THE EXPLOSION!
I... I DON'T REMEMBER THE EXPLOSION. I JUST WOKE UP OUTSIDE THE BURNING BASE. MAYBE THE BOOM CAUSED ME TO BLACK OUT AND THREW ME TO SAFETY.
"ALL I KNEW WAS STEVE WAS GONE, AND YOU WERE STILL ALIVE, SOMEWHERE. MY ONLY CLUE WAS THE CORVETTE WAS MISSING. I WOULD STOP AT NOTHING TO FIND YOU."
HEY! IT WAS YOU WHO REPORTED THE CAR STOLEN! I WAS ALMOST THROWN IN PRISON THANKS TO YOU!
I'VE BEEN WATCHING THAT RESTAURANT EVERY NIGHT SINCE OCTOBER FOR YOU TO COME BACK TO THE SCENE OF THE CRIME. SO WHO'S WORSE OFF?
THE ONE BEING KIDNAPPED!
OUR FIRST FIGHT! CAN WE MAKE UP NOW?
EYES ON THE ROAD!
OASIS, WE CAN'T JUST KEEP DRIVING FOREVER. I'M STARTING TO GET TIRED.
HEY! LOOK AT THAT BILLBOARD!
AS ROMANTIC AS A SPHINX IN HEAT!
Tacky? Not our sheets!
PHARAOH'S TOMB AND POCONO RESORT
Romance
DON'T MISS THE PYRAMID F LUUHHHV!
EXIT 3425
Billie Gopher's PORCUPINE AND RATTLESNAKE PETTING ZOO!
Just a mile from the WASH AND MOSH dance club/laundrymat
ARE YOU THINKING WHAT I'M THINKING?
GOD, PLEASE LET IT BE HOW CUTE PORCUPINES ARE.
ALTERNATE PUNCHLINE: "SURE, BRAIN! BUT HOW ARE WE GOING TO FIND LEDERHOSEN AT A TIME LIKE THIS?"
Don't Ask!
WELCOME TO THE PHARAOH'S TOMB AND POCONO RESORT! TONIGHT IS TEN PLAGUES NIGHT, WITH AWARDS FOR THE BEST FROG AND LOCUST COSTUMES! AND DON'T MISS OUR LOUNGE ACT WITH VERNE TROYER AND DARVA CONGER IN "WHO WANTS TO MARRY A MINI-ME!"
TERRIFIC.
I SEE YOU'VE PICKED THE SPITTING CAMEL SUITE, COMPLETE WITH WINE GLASS SHAPED JACUZZI, SWIMMING POOL, SAUNA...
WE HAVE OUR OWN POOL AND JACUZZI?
LET'S GO SEE OUR ROOM, HUN! I COULD USE SOME RELAX-TIME!
NORMALLY THEY WAIT UNTIL THEY GET TO A ROOM BEFORE TYING EACH OTHER UP.
HOP HOP HOP
TEN PLAGUES
THAT'S SO SWEET!
WHAT?
SHE SIGNED THEM UP TO GET MARRIED IN THE LION-PIT-CHAPEL THIS WEEKEND! IT'S REFRESHING TO SEE A GROOM WHO'S MORE EXCITED THAN THE BRIDE!

PREVIOUS TO ZOË AND TORG'S DATE...

GWYNN: Ok, Kenny. I've got everything needed. You're sure this spell will work right?

KENNY: Torg will be unable to tell anyone about your magic powers, or anything else important to him, until you cancel the spell in person.

OASIS IS OFF GRABBING FOOD, I COULD TRY TO MAKE A BREAK FOR IT. WHO AM I KIDDING, SHE'D NAB ME IN A MINUTE. IF I PROVE TO OASIS THAT SHE'S A ROBOT, IT MIGHT DISTRACT HER ENOUGH FOR ME TO GET AWAY. BUT THE TRUTH MIGHT CRUSH HER. FOR SOME REASON I DON'T WANT TO DO THAT.

Sluggy Freelance

AND LOW THIS CURSE UPON BE SENT, WHEN NEED TO SPEAK ENLIGHTENMENT. IN PLACE OF SECRETS YET UNLENT, BRAY THE DONKEY'S WORD NOT MEANT.

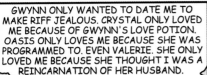

GWYNN ONLY WANTED TO DATE ME TO MAKE RIFF JEALOUS. CRYSTAL ONLY LOVED ME BECAUSE OF GWYNN'S LOVE POTION. OASIS ONLY LOVES ME BECAUSE SHE WAS PROGRAMMED TO. EVEN VALERIE. SHE ONLY LOVED ME BECAUSE SHE THOUGHT I WAS A REINCARNATION OF HER HUSBAND.

NOBODY EVER CARED ABOUT ME FOR ME.

ZOË. HOW COULD I BE SO STUPID? RIGHT IN FRONT OF MY FACE THE WHOLE TIME. I HAVE TO TELL HER HOW I FEEL!

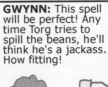

GWYNN: This spell will be perfect! Any time Torg tries to spill the beans, he'll think he's a jackass. How fitting!

RING-G-G

ZOË, I HAVE TO TELL YOU SOMETHING VERY IMPORTANT! HEE HEE! HAW HAW! HEE HAW

click

YOU TREAT ME LIKE DIRT ON OUR "DATE" AND THEN YOU CALL TO LAUGH IN MY FACE? **YOU GO TO HELL!**

HEE HAW! HEE HAW! HEE HAW! HEE HAW!

TORGY? WHAT'S WRONG?

SUB JNA

WHAT THE HECK JUST HAPPENED? LOOK AT YOUR EARS!

WHAT'S HAPPENING TO ME?

WE'LL NEED TO FIX THAT BEFORE THE WEDDING PHOTOS!

WEDDING... ...PHOTOS?

SURPRISE! WE'RE GETTING MARRIED!

GOOD GOD! WHETHER IT CRUSHES HER OR NOT, I MUST TELL HER SHE'S A ROBOT NOW!

OASIS! YOU'RE HEE HAW! HEE HAW! HEE HAW! HEE HAW! HEE HAW!

I KNEW YOU'D BE EXCITED!

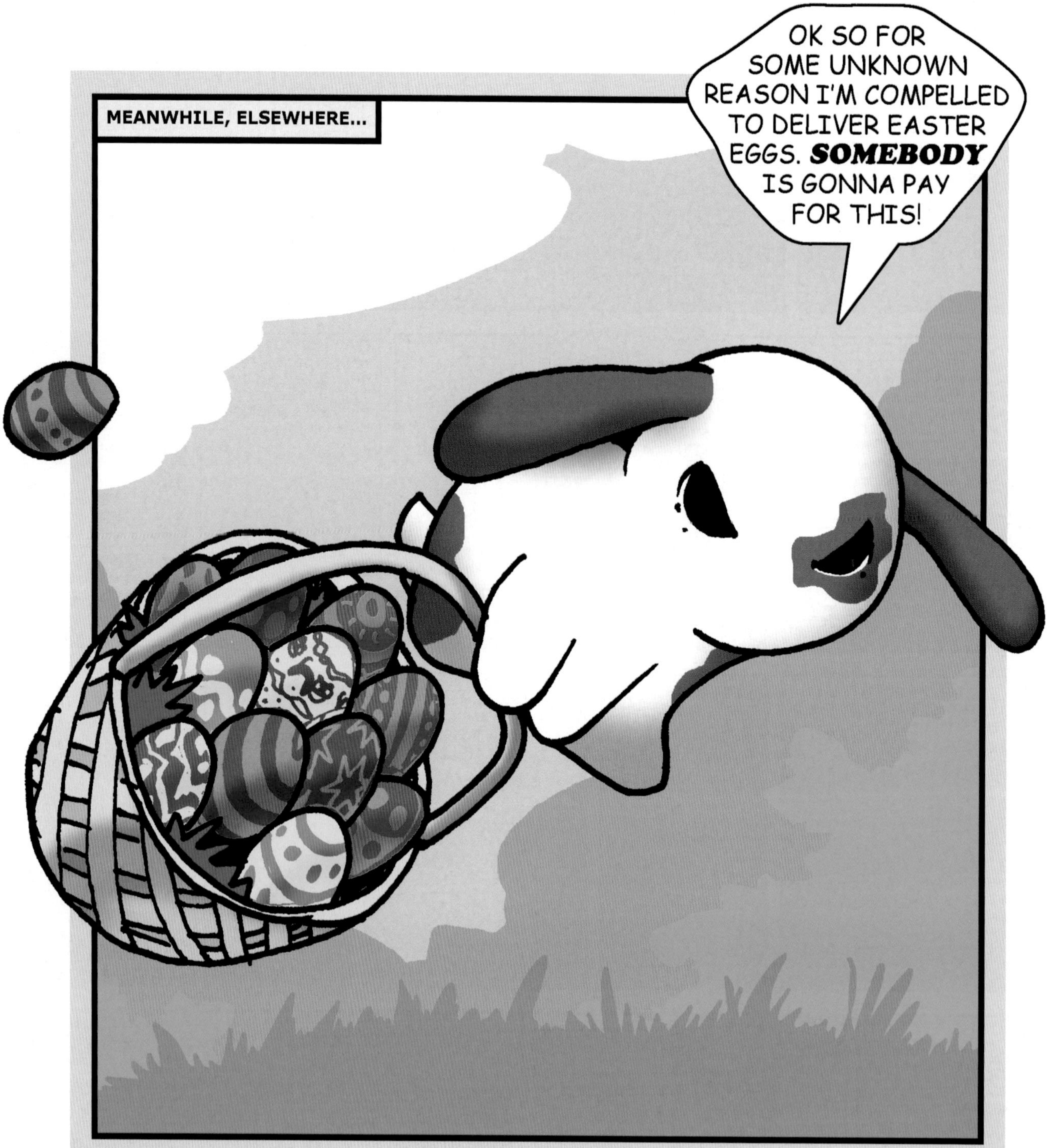
MEANWHILE, ELSEWHERE...
OK SO FOR SOME UNKNOWN REASON I'M COMPELLED TO DELIVER EASTER EGGS. SOMEBODY IS GONNA PAY FOR THIS!

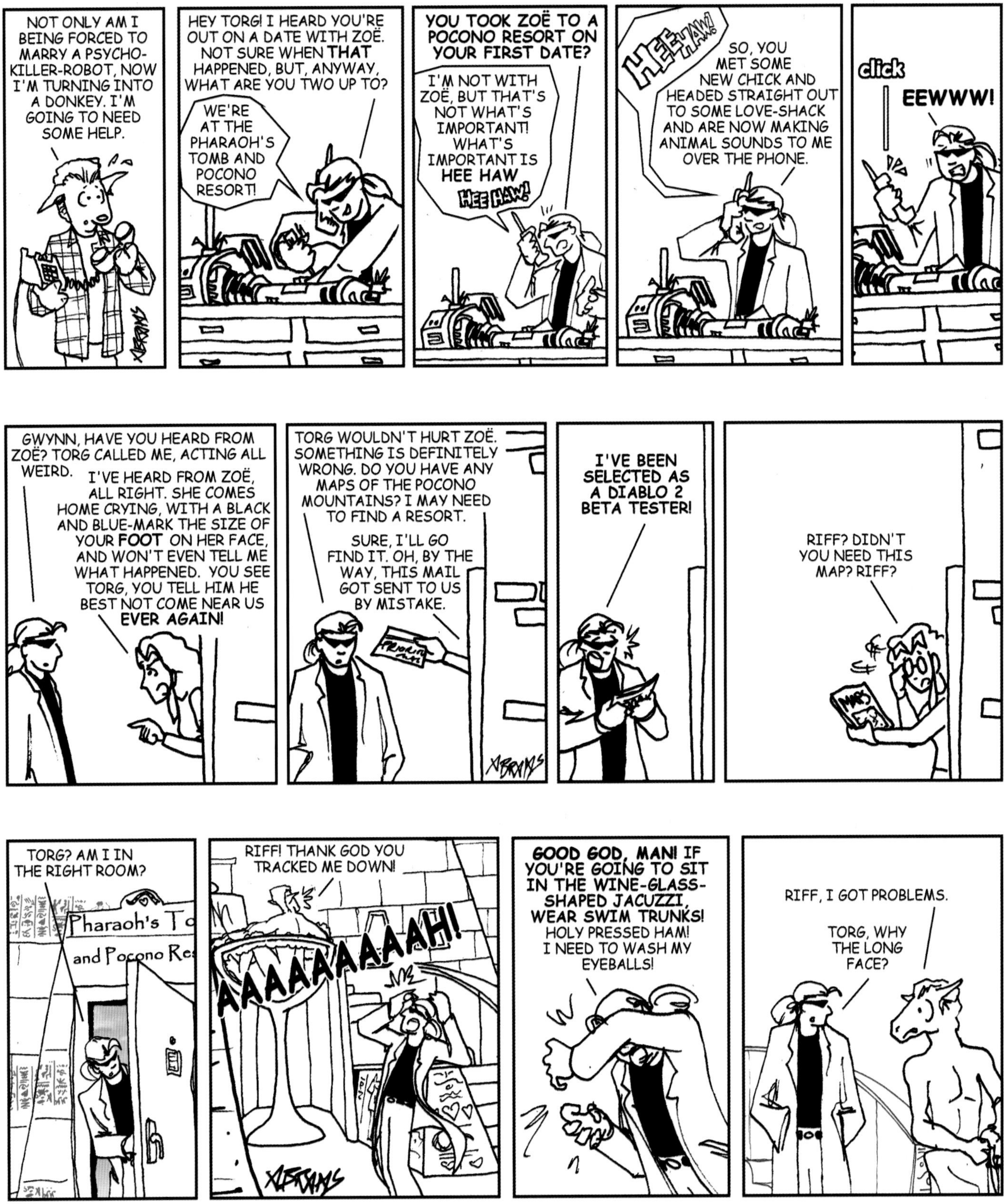
NOT ONLY AM I BEING FORCED TO MARRY A PSYCHO-KILLER-ROBOT, NOW I'M TURNING INTO A DONKEY. I'M GOING TO NEED SOME HELP.
HEY TORG! I HEARD YOU'RE OUT ON A DATE WITH ZOË. NOT SURE WHEN THAT HAPPENED, BUT, ANYWAY, WHAT ARE YOU TWO UP TO?
WE'RE AT THE PHARAOH'S TOMB AND POCONO RESORT!
YOU TOOK ZOË TO A POCONO RESORT ON YOUR FIRST DATE?
I'M NOT WITH ZOË, BUT THAT'S NOT WHAT'S IMPORTANT! WHAT'S IMPORTANT IS HEE HAW
HEE HAW!
HEE HAW!
SO, YOU MET SOME NEW CHICK AND HEADED STRAIGHT OUT TO SOME LOVE-SHACK AND ARE NOW MAKING ANIMAL SOUNDS TO ME OVER THE PHONE.
click
EEWWW!
GWYNN, HAVE YOU HEARD FROM ZOË? TORG CALLED ME, ACTING ALL WEIRD.
I'VE HEARD FROM ZOË, ALL RIGHT. SHE COMES HOME CRYING, WITH A BLACK AND BLUE-MARK THE SIZE OF YOUR FOOT ON HER FACE, AND WON'T EVEN TELL ME WHAT HAPPENED. YOU SEE TORG, YOU TELL HIM HE BEST NOT COME NEAR US EVER AGAIN!
TORG WOULDN'T HURT ZOË. SOMETHING IS DEFINITELY WRONG. DO YOU HAVE ANY MAPS OF THE POCONO MOUNTAINS? I MAY NEED TO FIND A RESORT.
SURE, I'LL GO FIND IT. OH, BY THE WAY, THIS MAIL GOT SENT TO US BY MISTAKE.
I'VE BEEN SELECTED AS A DIABLO 2 BETA TESTER!
RIFF? DIDN'T YOU NEED THIS MAP? RIFF?
MAPS
TORG? AM I IN THE RIGHT ROOM?
Pharaoh's To
and Pocono Re
RIFF! THANK GOD YOU TRACKED ME DOWN!
AAAAAAAAAAH!
GOOD GOD, MAN! IF YOU'RE GOING TO SIT IN THE WINE-GLASS-SHAPED JACUZZI, WEAR SWIM TRUNKS!
HOLY PRESSED HAM! I NEED TO WASH MY EYEBALLS!
RIFF, I GOT PROBLEMS.
TORG, WHY THE LONG FACE?

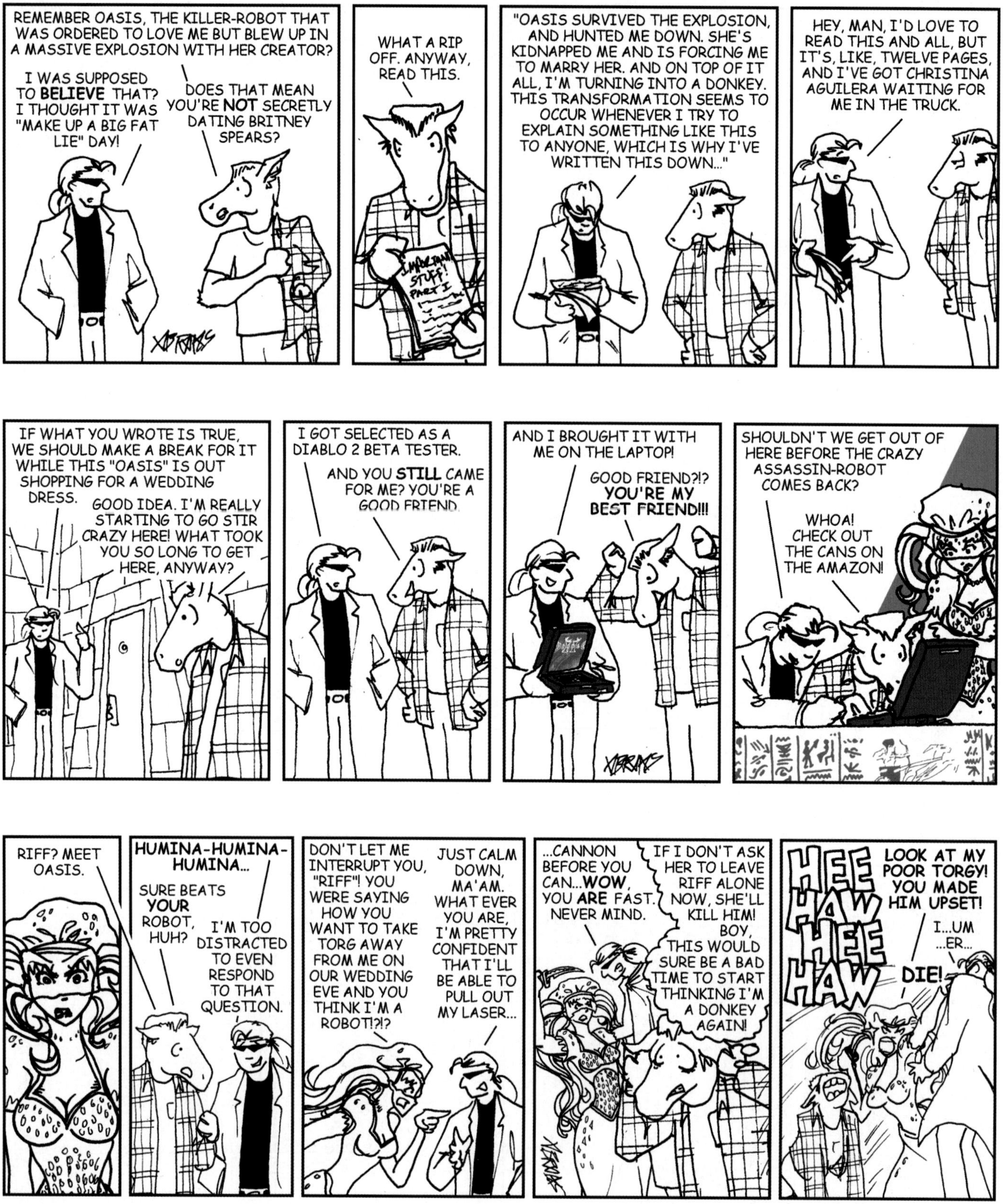

REMEMBER OASIS, THE KILLER-ROBOT THAT WAS ORDERED TO LOVE ME BUT BLEW UP IN A MASSIVE EXPLOSION WITH HER CREATOR?
I WAS SUPPOSED TO **BELIEVE** THAT? I THOUGHT IT WAS "MAKE UP A BIG FAT LIE" DAY!
DOES THAT MEAN YOU'RE **NOT** SECRETLY DATING BRITNEY SPEARS?
WHAT A RIP OFF. ANYWAY, READ THIS.
IMPORTANT STUFF! PART I
"OASIS SURVIVED THE EXPLOSION, AND HUNTED ME DOWN. SHE'S KIDNAPPED ME AND IS FORCING ME TO MARRY HER. AND ON TOP OF IT ALL, I'M TURNING INTO A DONKEY. THIS TRANSFORMATION SEEMS TO OCCUR WHENEVER I TRY TO EXPLAIN SOMETHING LIKE THIS TO ANYONE, WHICH IS WHY I'VE WRITTEN THIS DOWN..."
HEY, MAN, I'D LOVE TO READ THIS AND ALL, BUT IT'S, LIKE, TWELVE PAGES, AND I'VE GOT CHRISTINA AGUILERA WAITING FOR ME IN THE TRUCK.
IF WHAT YOU WROTE IS TRUE, WE SHOULD MAKE A BREAK FOR IT WHILE THIS "OASIS" IS OUT SHOPPING FOR A WEDDING DRESS.
GOOD IDEA. I'M REALLY STARTING TO GO STIR CRAZY HERE! WHAT TOOK YOU SO LONG TO GET HERE, ANYWAY?
I GOT SELECTED AS A DIABLO 2 BETA TESTER.
AND YOU **STILL** CAME FOR ME? YOU'RE A GOOD FRIEND.
AND I BROUGHT IT WITH ME ON THE LAPTOP!
GOOD FRIEND?!? **YOU'RE MY BEST FRIEND!!!**
SHOULDN'T WE GET OUT OF HERE BEFORE THE CRAZY ASSASSIN-ROBOT COMES BACK?
WHOA! CHECK OUT THE CANS ON THE AMAZON!
RIFF? MEET OASIS.
HUMINA-HUMINA-HUMINA...
SURE BEATS **YOUR** ROBOT, HUH?
I'M TOO DISTRACTED TO EVEN RESPOND TO THAT QUESTION.
DON'T LET ME INTERRUPT YOU, "RIFF"! YOU WERE SAYING HOW YOU WANT TO TAKE TORG AWAY FROM ME ON OUR WEDDING EVE AND YOU THINK I'M A ROBOT!?!?
JUST CALM DOWN, MA'AM. WHAT EVER YOU ARE, I'M PRETTY CONFIDENT THAT I'LL BE ABLE TO PULL OUT MY LASER...
...CANNON BEFORE YOU CAN...**WOW**, YOU **ARE** FAST. NEVER MIND.
IF I DON'T ASK HER TO LEAVE RIFF ALONE NOW, SHE'LL KILL HIM! BOY, THIS WOULD SURE BE A BAD TIME TO START THINKING I'M A DONKEY AGAIN!
HEE HAW HEE HAW
LOOK AT MY POOR TORGY! YOU MADE HIM UPSET!
I...UM ...ER...
DIE!

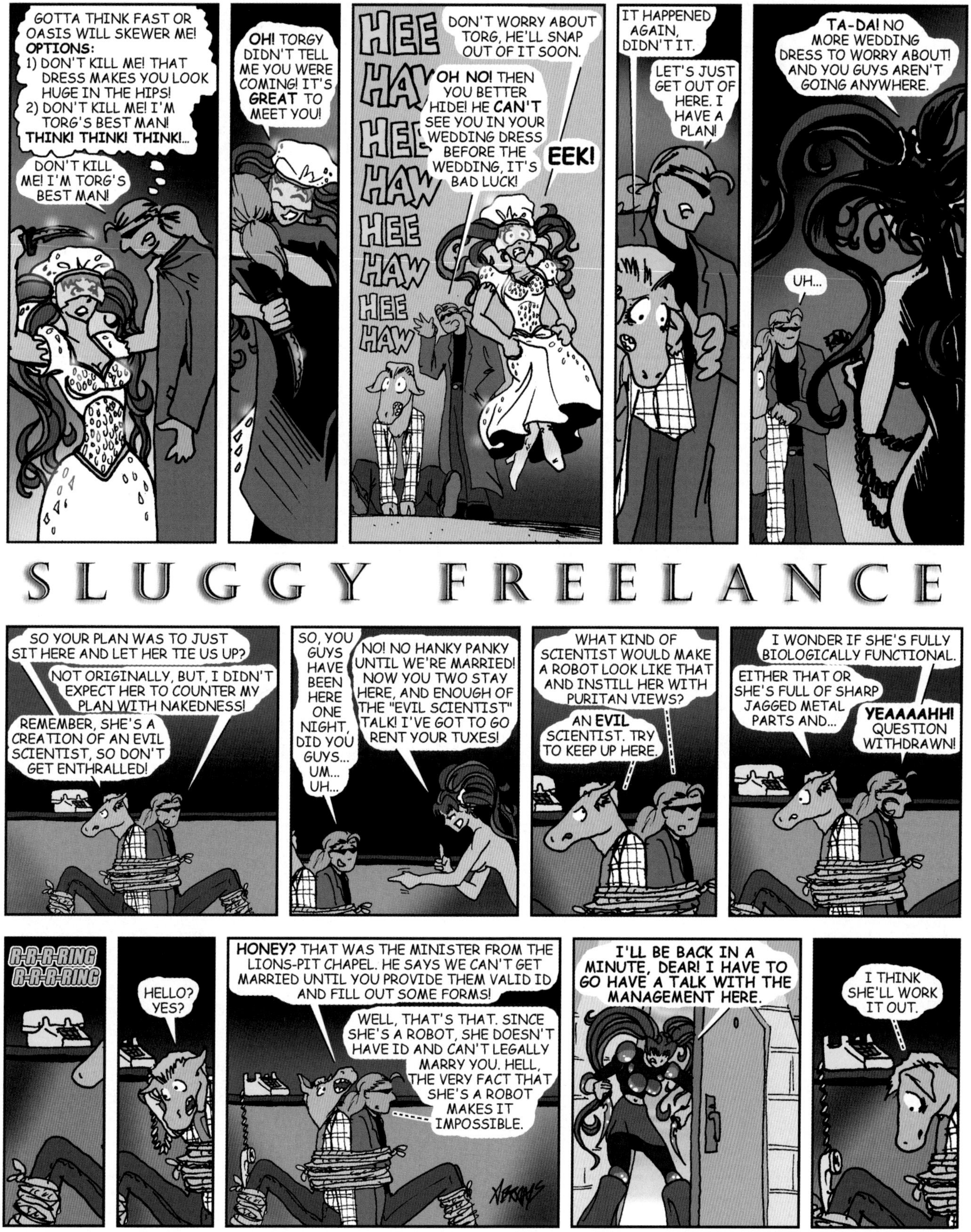
GOTTA THINK FAST OR OASIS WILL SKEWER ME! **OPTIONS:** 1) DON'T KILL ME! THAT DRESS MAKES YOU LOOK HUGE IN THE HIPS! 2) DON'T KILL ME! I'M TORG'S BEST MAN! **THINK! THINK! THINK!...**
DON'T KILL ME! I'M TORG'S BEST MAN!
OH! TORGY DIDN'T TELL ME YOU WERE COMING! IT'S **GREAT** TO MEET YOU!
HEE HAW HEE HAW HEE HAW HEE HAW
DON'T WORRY ABOUT TORG, HE'LL SNAP OUT OF IT SOON.
OH NO! THEN YOU BETTER HIDE! HE **CAN'T** SEE YOU IN YOUR WEDDING DRESS BEFORE THE WEDDING, IT'S BAD LUCK!
EEK!
IT HAPPENED AGAIN, DIDN'T IT.
LET'S JUST GET OUT OF HERE. I HAVE A PLAN!
TA-DA! NO MORE WEDDING DRESS TO WORRY ABOUT! AND YOU GUYS AREN'T GOING ANYWHERE.
UH...
SLUGGY FREELANCE
SO YOUR PLAN WAS TO JUST SIT HERE AND LET HER TIE US UP?
NOT ORIGINALLY, BUT, I DIDN'T EXPECT HER TO COUNTER MY PLAN WITH NAKEDNESS!
REMEMBER, SHE'S A CREATION OF AN EVIL SCIENTIST, SO DON'T GET ENTHRALLED!
SO, YOU GUYS HAVE BEEN HERE ONE NIGHT, DID YOU GUYS... UM... UH...
NO! NO HANKY PANKY UNTIL WE'RE MARRIED! NOW YOU TWO STAY HERE, AND ENOUGH OF THE "EVIL SCIENTIST" TALK! I'VE GOT TO GO RENT YOUR TUXES!
WHAT KIND OF SCIENTIST WOULD MAKE A ROBOT LOOK LIKE THAT AND INSTILL HER WITH PURITAN VIEWS?
AN **EVIL** SCIENTIST. TRY TO KEEP UP HERE.
I WONDER IF SHE'S FULLY BIOLOGICALLY FUNCTIONAL.
EITHER THAT OR SHE'S FULL OF SHARP JAGGED METAL PARTS AND...
YEAAAAHH! QUESTION WITHDRAWN!
R-R-R-RING R-R-R-RING
HELLO? YES?
HONEY? THAT WAS THE MINISTER FROM THE LIONS-PIT CHAPEL. HE SAYS WE CAN'T GET MARRIED UNTIL YOU PROVIDE THEM VALID ID AND FILL OUT SOME FORMS!
WELL, THAT'S THAT. SINCE SHE'S A ROBOT, SHE DOESN'T HAVE ID AND CAN'T LEGALLY MARRY YOU. HELL, THE VERY FACT THAT SHE'S A ROBOT MAKES IT IMPOSSIBLE.
I'LL BE BACK IN A MINUTE, DEAR! I HAVE TO GO HAVE A TALK WITH THE MANAGEMENT HERE.
I THINK SHE'LL WORK IT OUT.

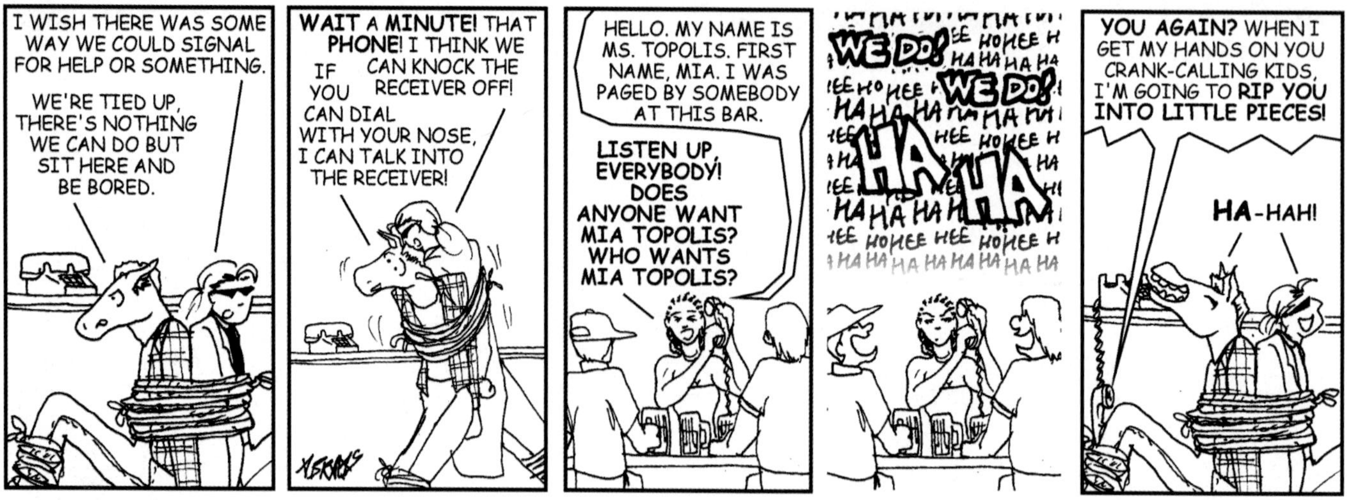
I WISH THERE WAS SOME WAY WE COULD SIGNAL FOR HELP OR SOMETHING.
WE'RE TIED UP, THERE'S NOTHING WE CAN DO BUT SIT HERE AND BE BORED.
WAIT A MINUTE! THAT PHONE! I THINK WE CAN KNOCK THE RECEIVER OFF!
IF YOU CAN DIAL WITH YOUR NOSE, I CAN TALK INTO THE RECEIVER!
HELLO. MY NAME IS MS. TOPOLIS. FIRST NAME, MIA. I WAS PAGED BY SOMEBODY AT THIS BAR.
LISTEN UP, EVERYBODY! DOES ANYONE WANT MIA TOPOLIS? WHO WANTS MIA TOPOLIS?
WE DO!
WE DO!
HA HA
YOU AGAIN? WHEN I GET MY HANDS ON YOU CRANK-CALLING KIDS, I'M GOING TO RIP YOU INTO LITTLE PIECES!
HA-HAH!

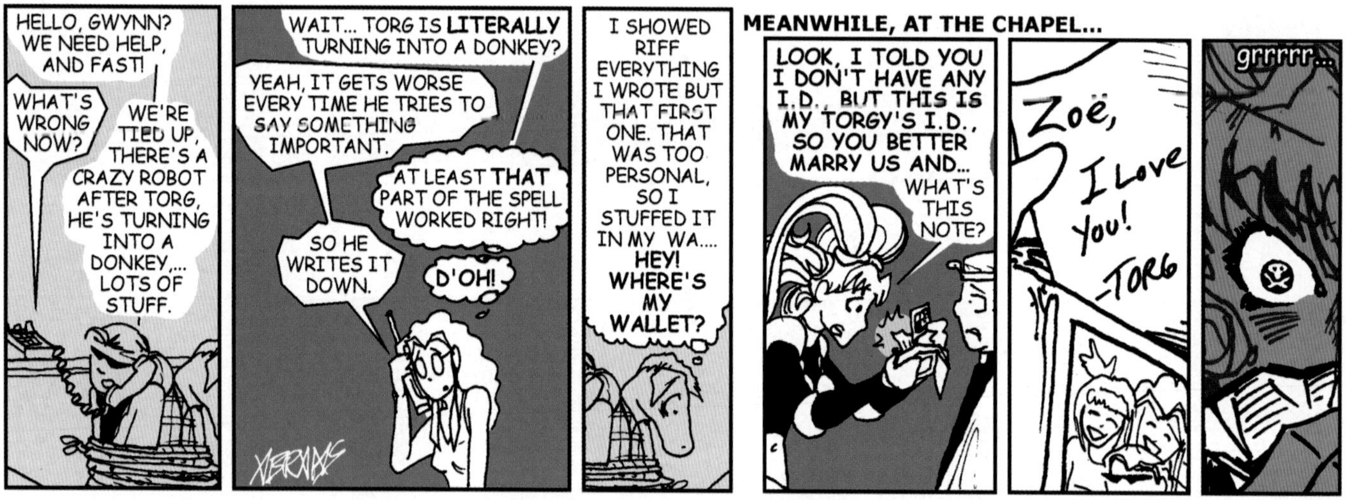
HELLO, GWYNN? WE NEED HELP, AND FAST!
WHAT'S WRONG NOW?
WE'RE TIED UP, THERE'S A CRAZY ROBOT AFTER TORG, HE'S TURNING INTO A DONKEY,... LOTS OF STUFF.
WAIT... TORG IS LITERALLY TURNING INTO A DONKEY?
YEAH, IT GETS WORSE EVERY TIME HE TRIES TO SAY SOMETHING IMPORTANT.
SO HE WRITES IT DOWN.
AT LEAST THAT PART OF THE SPELL WORKED RIGHT!
D'OH!
I SHOWED RIFF EVERYTHING I WROTE BUT THAT FIRST ONE. THAT WAS TOO PERSONAL, SO I STUFFED IT IN MY WA.... HEY! WHERE'S MY WALLET?
MEANWHILE, AT THE CHAPEL...
LOOK, I TOLD YOU I DON'T HAVE ANY I.D., BUT THIS IS MY TORGY'S I.D., SO YOU BETTER MARRY US AND...
WHAT'S THIS NOTE?
Zoë, I Love You! -TORG
grrrrr...

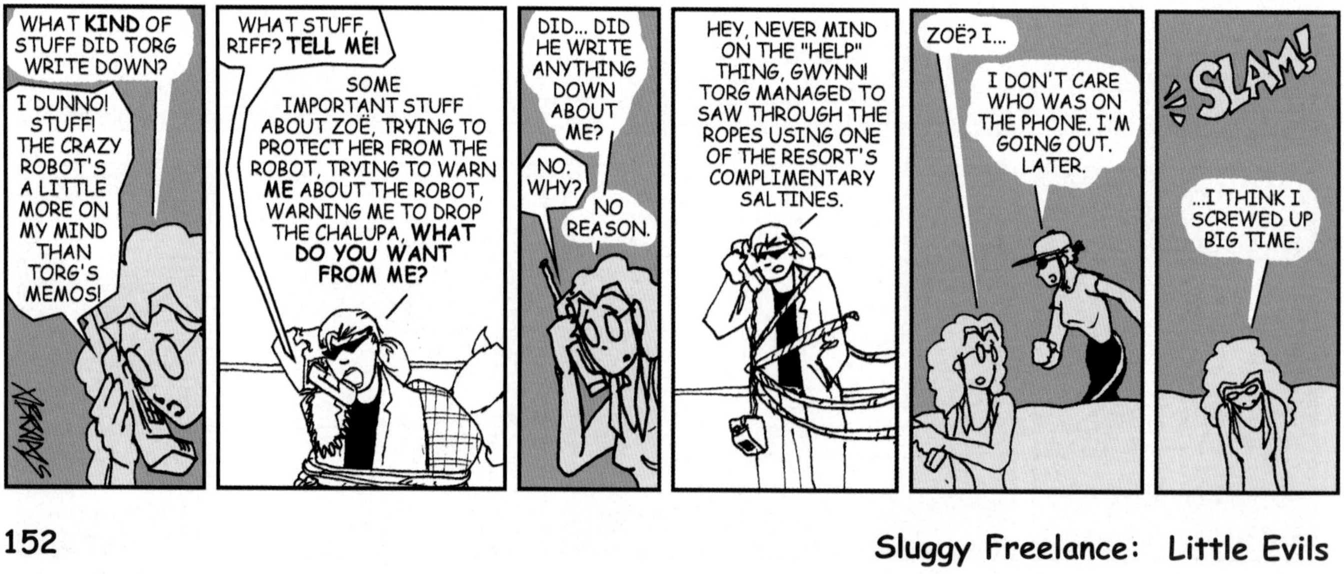
WHAT KIND OF STUFF DID TORG WRITE DOWN?
I DUNNO! STUFF! THE CRAZY ROBOT'S A LITTLE MORE ON MY MIND THAN TORG'S MEMOS!
WHAT STUFF, RIFF? TELL ME!
SOME IMPORTANT STUFF ABOUT ZOË, TRYING TO PROTECT HER FROM THE ROBOT, TRYING TO WARN ME ABOUT THE ROBOT, WARNING ME TO DROP THE CHALUPA, WHAT DO YOU WANT FROM ME?
DID... DID HE WRITE ANYTHING DOWN ABOUT ME?
NO. WHY?
NO REASON.
HEY, NEVER MIND ON THE "HELP" THING, GWYNN! TORG MANAGED TO SAW THROUGH THE ROPES USING ONE OF THE RESORT'S COMPLIMENTARY SALTINES.
ZOË? I...
I DON'T CARE WHO WAS ON THE PHONE. I'M GOING OUT. LATER.
SLAM!
...I THINK I SCREWED UP BIG TIME.

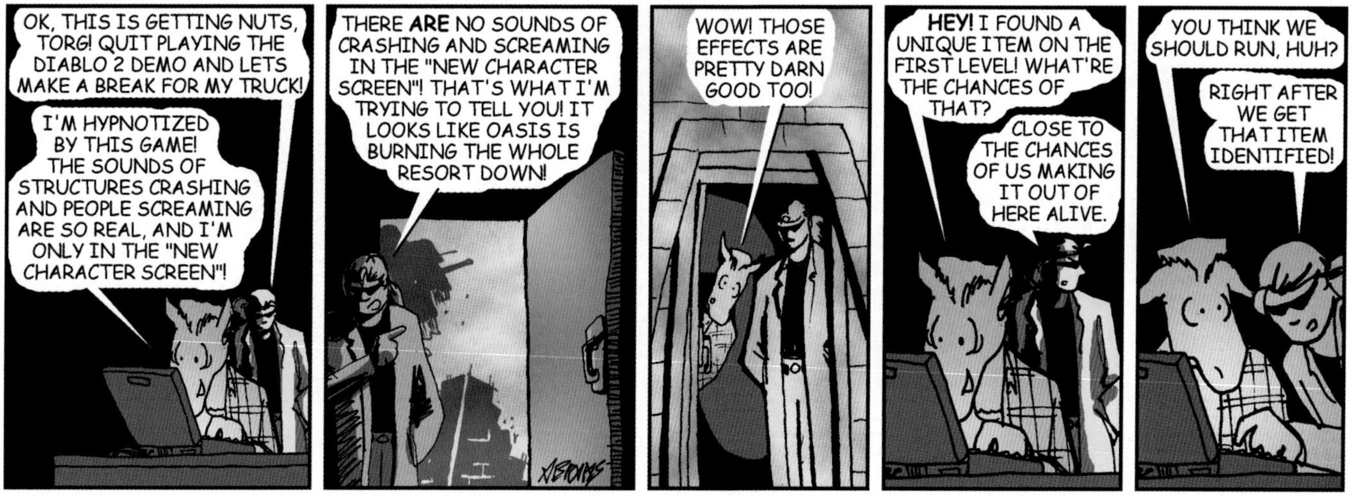
OK, THIS IS GETTING NUTS, TORG! QUIT PLAYING THE DIABLO 2 DEMO AND LETS MAKE A BREAK FOR MY TRUCK!
I'M HYPNOTIZED BY THIS GAME! THE SOUNDS OF STRUCTURES CRASHING AND PEOPLE SCREAMING ARE SO REAL, AND I'M ONLY IN THE "NEW CHARACTER SCREEN"!
THERE ARE NO SOUNDS OF CRASHING AND SCREAMING IN THE "NEW CHARACTER SCREEN"! THAT'S WHAT I'M TRYING TO TELL YOU! IT LOOKS LIKE OASIS IS BURNING THE WHOLE RESORT DOWN!
WOW! THOSE EFFECTS ARE PRETTY DARN GOOD TOO!
HEY! I FOUND A UNIQUE ITEM ON THE FIRST LEVEL! WHAT'RE THE CHANCES OF THAT?
CLOSE TO THE CHANCES OF US MAKING IT OUT OF HERE ALIVE.
YOU THINK WE SHOULD RUN, HUH?
RIGHT AFTER WE GET THAT ITEM IDENTIFIED!

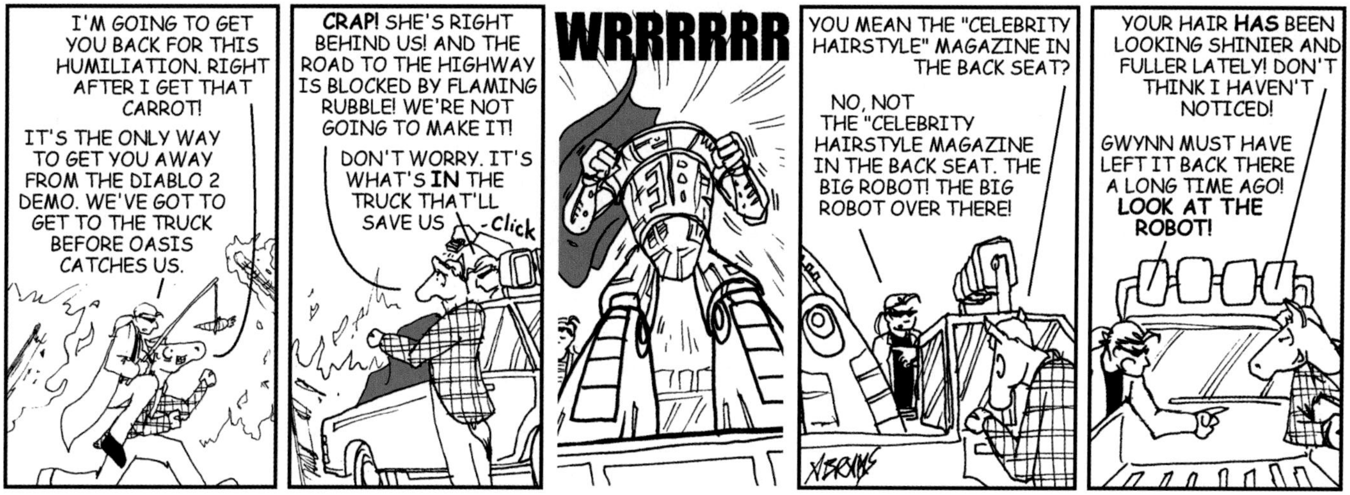
I'M GOING TO GET YOU BACK FOR THIS HUMILIATION. RIGHT AFTER I GET THAT CARROT!
IT'S THE ONLY WAY TO GET YOU AWAY FROM THE DIABLO 2 DEMO. WE'VE GOT TO GET TO THE TRUCK BEFORE OASIS CATCHES US.
CRAP! SHE'S RIGHT BEHIND US! AND THE ROAD TO THE HIGHWAY IS BLOCKED BY FLAMING RUBBLE! WE'RE NOT GOING TO MAKE IT!
DON'T WORRY. IT'S WHAT'S IN THE TRUCK THAT'LL SAVE US
-Click
WRRRRRR
YOU MEAN THE "CELEBRITY HAIRSTYLE" MAGAZINE IN THE BACK SEAT?
NO, NOT THE "CELEBRITY HAIRSTYLE MAGAZINE IN THE BACK SEAT. THE BIG ROBOT! THE BIG ROBOT OVER THERE!
YOUR HAIR HAS BEEN LOOKING SHINIER AND FULLER LATELY! DON'T THINK I HAVEN'T NOTICED!
GWYNN MUST HAVE LEFT IT BACK THERE A LONG TIME AGO! LOOK AT THE ROBOT!

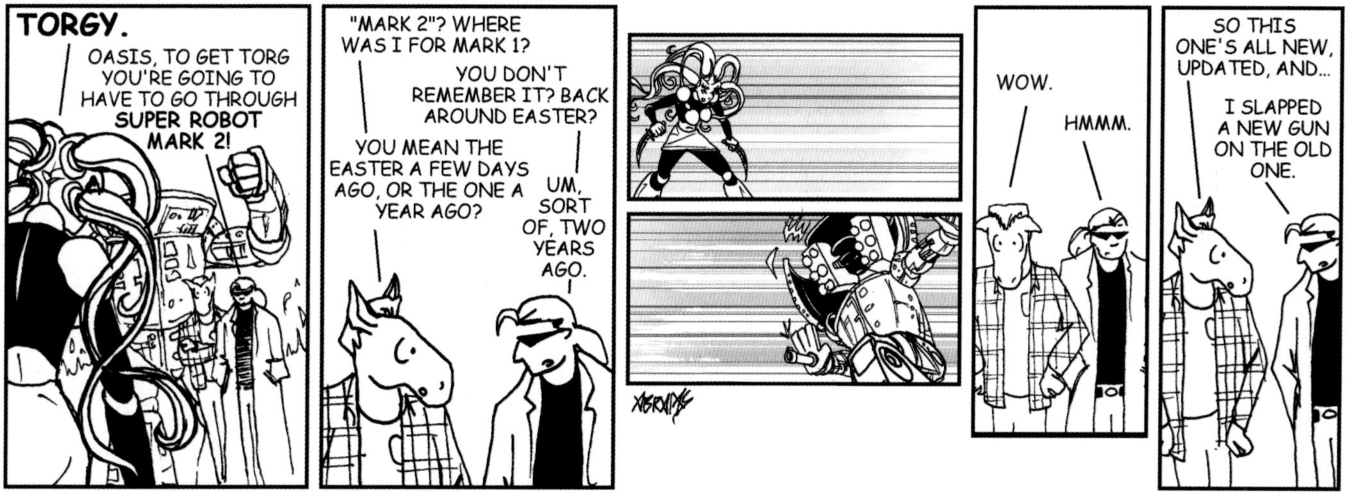
TORGY.
OASIS, TO GET TORG YOU'RE GOING TO HAVE TO GO THROUGH SUPER ROBOT MARK 2!
"MARK 2"? WHERE WAS I FOR MARK 1?
YOU DON'T REMEMBER IT? BACK AROUND EASTER?
YOU MEAN THE EASTER A FEW DAYS AGO, OR THE ONE A YEAR AGO?
UM, SORT OF, TWO YEARS AGO.
WOW.
HMMM.
SO THIS ONE'S ALL NEW, UPDATED, AND...
I SLAPPED A NEW GUN ON THE OLD ONE.

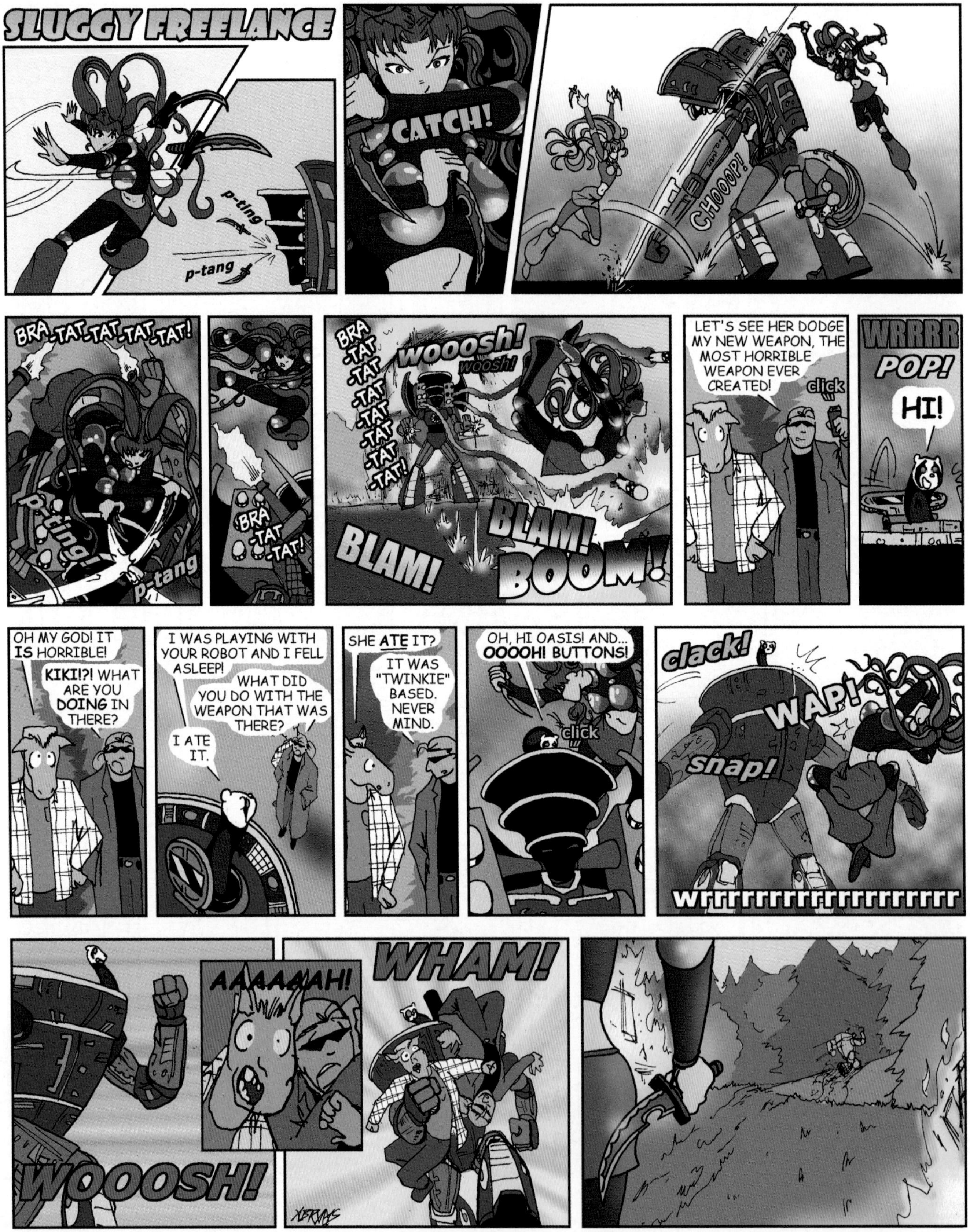
SLUGGY FREELANCE
p-ting
p-tang
CATCH!
CHOOOP!
BRA-TAT-TAT-TAT-TAT!
p-ting!
p-tang
BRA
-TAT
-TAT!
BRA
-TAT
-TAT
-TAT
-TAT
-TAT
-TAT
-TAT
-TAT!
wooosh!
woosh!
BLAM!
BLAM!
BOOM!
LET'S SEE HER DODGE MY NEW WEAPON, THE MOST HORRIBLE WEAPON EVER CREATED!
click
WRRRR
POP!
HI!
OH MY GOD! IT IS HORRIBLE!
KIKI!?! WHAT ARE YOU DOING IN THERE?
I WAS PLAYING WITH YOUR ROBOT AND I FELL ASLEEP!
WHAT DID YOU DO WITH THE WEAPON THAT WAS THERE?
I ATE IT.
SHE ATE IT?
IT WAS "TWINKIE" BASED. NEVER MIND.
OH, HI OASIS! AND... OOOOH! BUTTONS!
click
clack!
WAP!
snap!
wrrrrrrrrrrrrrrrrrrr
AAAAAAH!
WHAM!
WOOOSH!

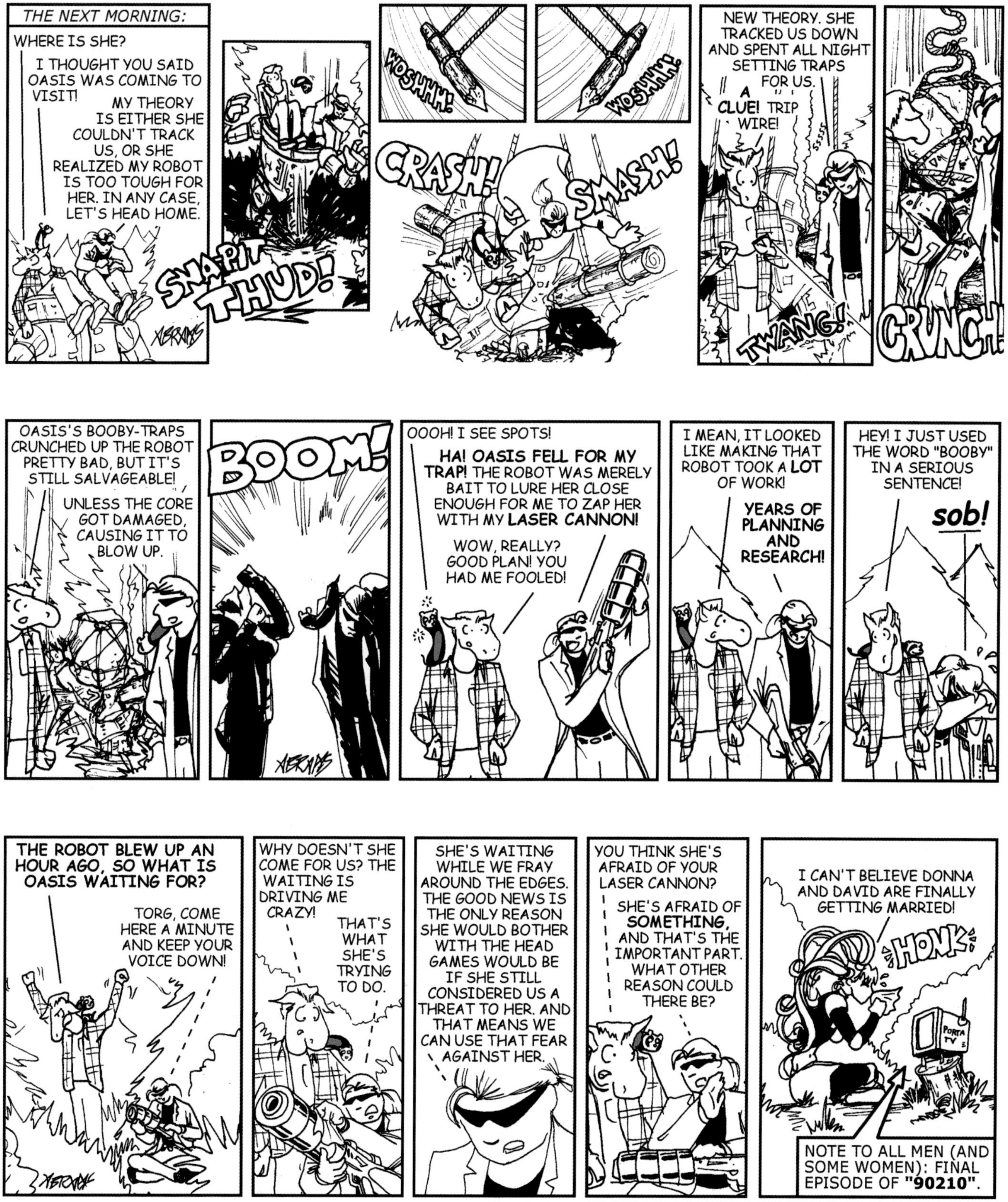
THE NEXT MORNING:
WHERE IS SHE?
I THOUGHT YOU SAID OASIS WAS COMING TO VISIT!
MY THEORY IS EITHER SHE COULDN'T TRACK US, OR SHE REALIZED MY ROBOT IS TOO TOUGH FOR HER. IN ANY CASE, LET'S HEAD HOME.
SNAP!
THUD!
WOSHHH!
WOSHHH!
CRASH!
SMASH!
NEW THEORY. SHE TRACKED US DOWN AND SPENT ALL NIGHT SETTING TRAPS FOR US.
A CLUE! TRIP WIRE!
TWANG!
CRUNCH!
OASIS'S BOOBY-TRAPS CRUNCHED UP THE ROBOT PRETTY BAD, BUT IT'S STILL SALVAGEABLE!
UNLESS THE CORE GOT DAMAGED, CAUSING IT TO BLOW UP.
BOOM!
OOOH! I SEE SPOTS!
HA! OASIS FELL FOR MY TRAP! THE ROBOT WAS MERELY BAIT TO LURE HER CLOSE ENOUGH FOR ME TO ZAP HER WITH MY LASER CANNON!
WOW, REALLY? GOOD PLAN! YOU HAD ME FOOLED!
I MEAN, IT LOOKED LIKE MAKING THAT ROBOT TOOK A LOT OF WORK!
YEARS OF PLANNING AND RESEARCH!
HEY! I JUST USED THE WORD "BOOBY" IN A SERIOUS SENTENCE!
sob!
THE ROBOT BLEW UP AN HOUR AGO, SO WHAT IS OASIS WAITING FOR?
TORG, COME HERE A MINUTE AND KEEP YOUR VOICE DOWN!
WHY DOESN'T SHE COME FOR US? THE WAITING IS DRIVING ME CRAZY!
THAT'S WHAT SHE'S TRYING TO DO.
SHE'S WAITING WHILE WE FRAY AROUND THE EDGES. THE GOOD NEWS IS THE ONLY REASON SHE WOULD BOTHER WITH THE HEAD GAMES WOULD BE IF SHE STILL CONSIDERED US A THREAT TO HER. AND THAT MEANS WE CAN USE THAT FEAR AGAINST HER.
YOU THINK SHE'S AFRAID OF YOUR LASER CANNON?
SHE'S AFRAID OF SOMETHING, AND THAT'S THE IMPORTANT PART. WHAT OTHER REASON COULD THERE BE?
I CAN'T BELIEVE DONNA AND DAVID ARE FINALLY GETTING MARRIED!
HONK!
PORTA TV
NOTE TO ALL MEN (AND SOME WOMEN): FINAL EPISODE OF "90210".

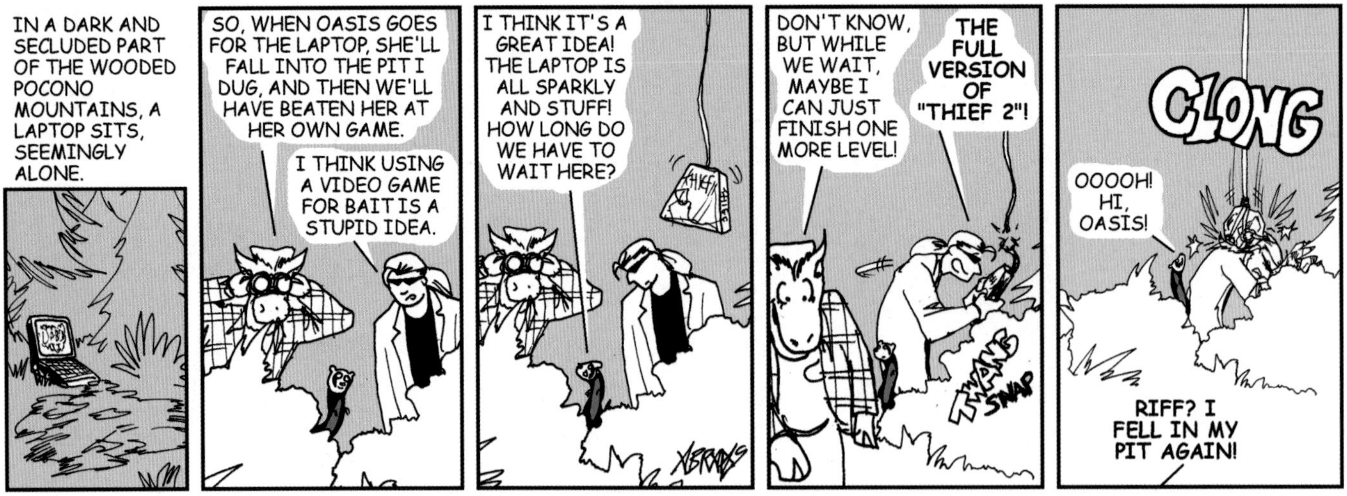
IN A DARK AND SECLUDED PART OF THE WOODED POCONO MOUNTAINS, A LAPTOP SITS, SEEMINGLY ALONE.
SO, WHEN OASIS GOES FOR THE LAPTOP, SHE'LL FALL INTO THE PIT I DUG, AND THEN WE'LL HAVE BEATEN HER AT HER OWN GAME.
I THINK USING A VIDEO GAME FOR BAIT IS A STUPID IDEA.
I THINK IT'S A GREAT IDEA! THE LAPTOP IS ALL SPARKLY AND STUFF! HOW LONG DO WE HAVE TO WAIT HERE?
DON'T KNOW, BUT WHILE WE WAIT, MAYBE I CAN JUST FINISH ONE MORE LEVEL!
THE FULL VERSION OF "THIEF 2"!
TWANG
SNAP
CLONG
OOOOH! HI, OASIS!
RIFF? I FELL IN MY PIT AGAIN!

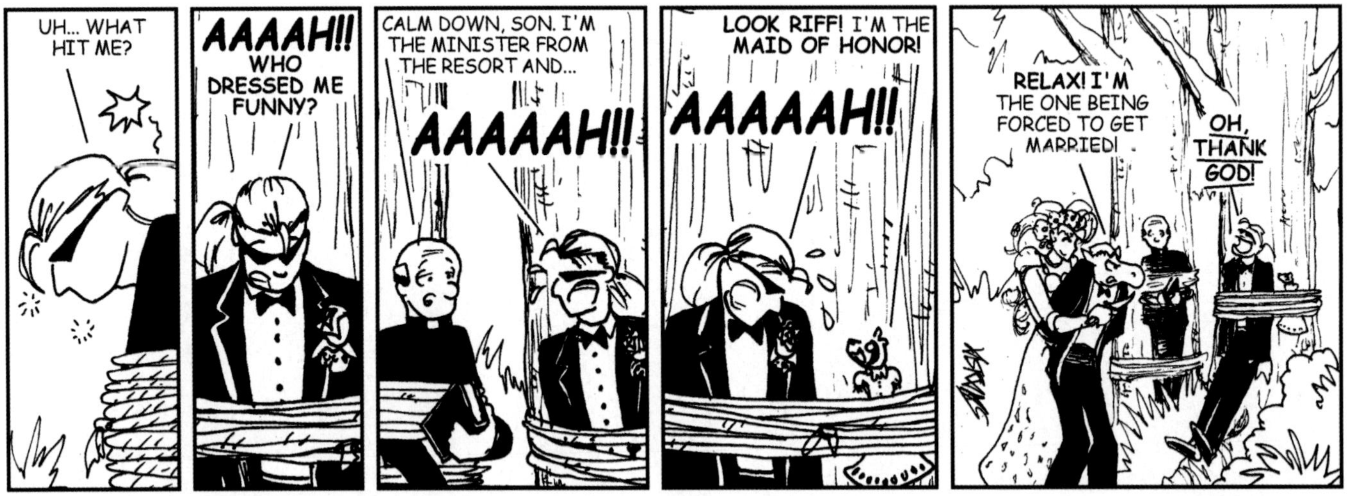
UH... WHAT HIT ME?
AAAAH!! WHO DRESSED ME FUNNY?
CALM DOWN, SON. I'M THE MINISTER FROM THE RESORT AND...
AAAAAH!!
LOOK RIFF! I'M THE MAID OF HONOR!
AAAAAH!!
RELAX! I'M THE ONE BEING FORCED TO GET MARRIED!
OH, THANK GOD!

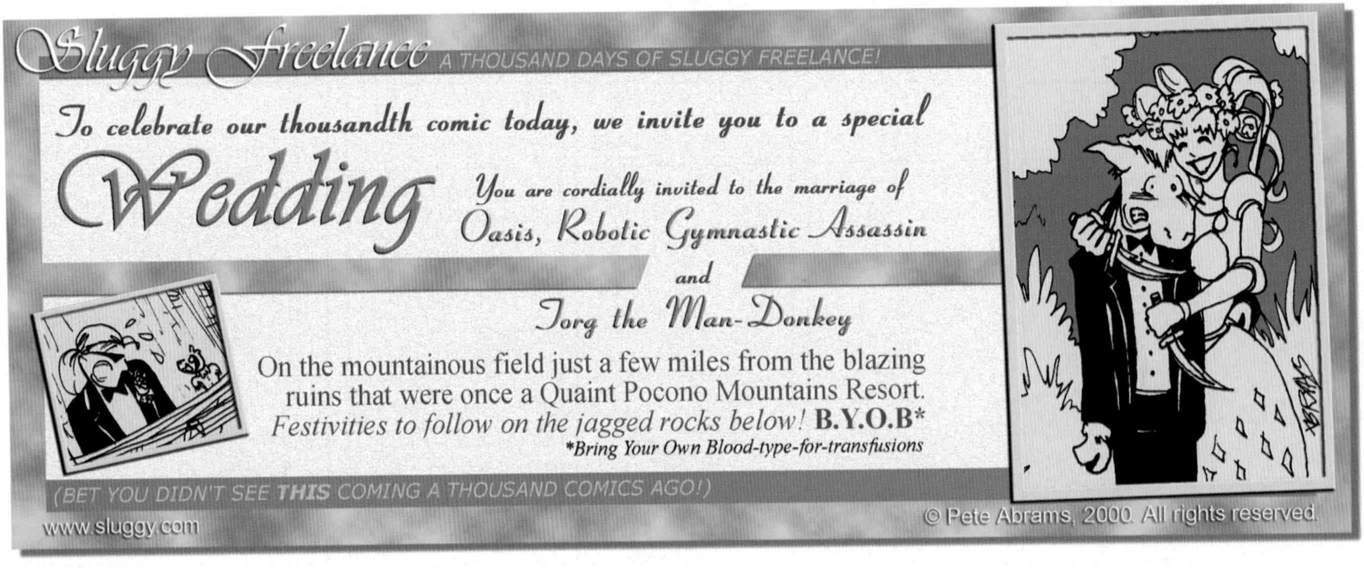
Sluggy Freelance
A THOUSAND DAYS OF SLUGGY FREELANCE!
To celebrate our thousandth comic today, we invite you to a special
Wedding
You are cordially invited to the marriage of
Oasis, Robotic Gymnastic Assassin
and
Torg the Man-Donkey
On the mountainous field just a few miles from the blazing ruins that were once a Quaint Pocono Mountains Resort.
Festivities to follow on the jagged rocks below! B.Y.O.B*
*Bring Your Own Blood-type-for-transfusions
(BET YOU DIDN'T SEE THIS COMING A THOUSAND COMICS AGO!)
www.sluggy.com
© Pete Abrams, 2000. All rights reserved.

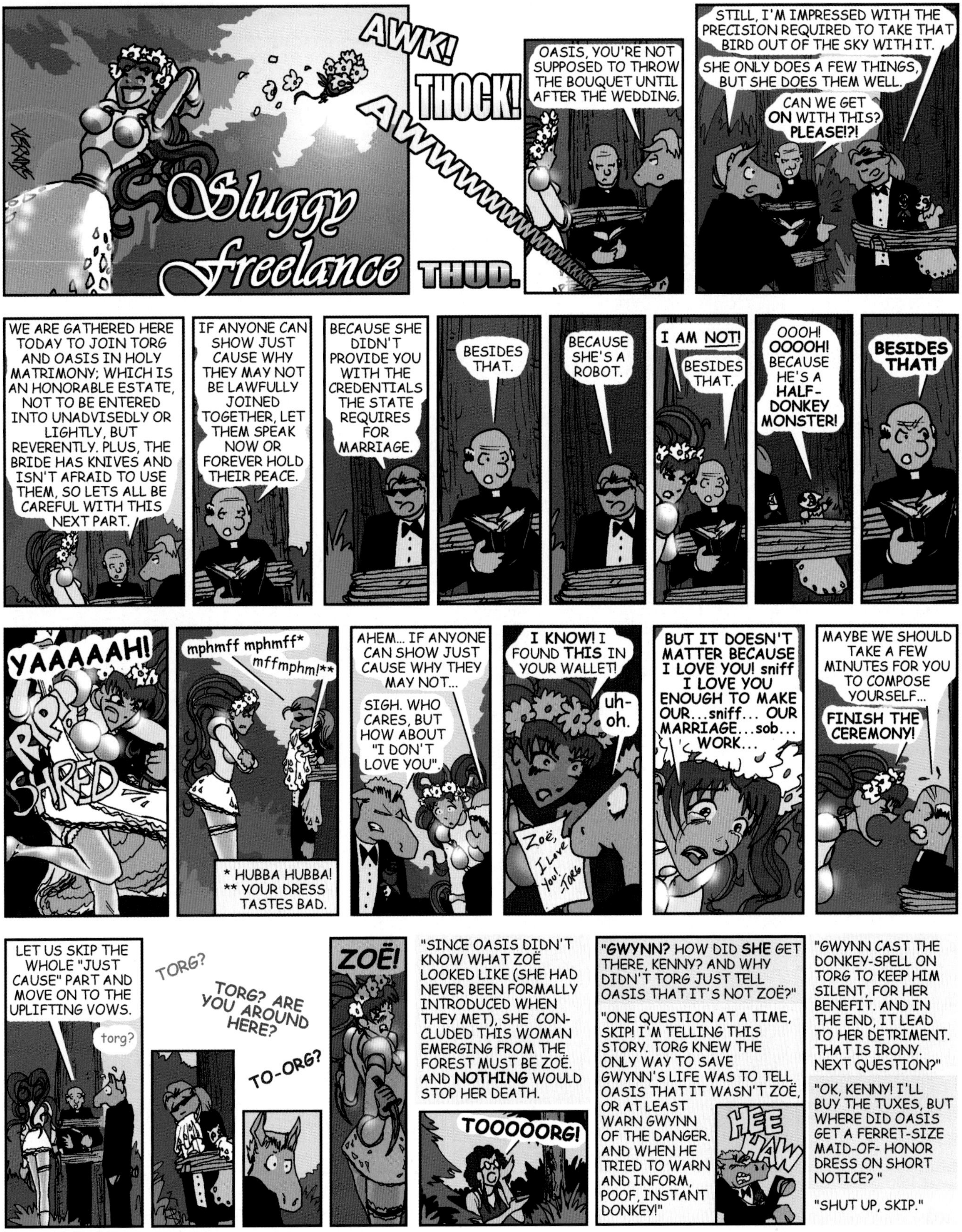
Sluggy freelance
AWK!
THOCK!
AWWWWWWWWWKKKK
THUD.
OASIS, YOU'RE NOT SUPPOSED TO THROW THE BOUQUET UNTIL AFTER THE WEDDING.
STILL, I'M IMPRESSED WITH THE PRECISION REQUIRED TO TAKE THAT BIRD OUT OF THE SKY WITH IT.
SHE ONLY DOES A FEW THINGS, BUT SHE DOES THEM WELL.
CAN WE GET ON WITH THIS? PLEASE!?!
WE ARE GATHERED HERE TODAY TO JOIN TORG AND OASIS IN HOLY MATRIMONY; WHICH IS AN HONORABLE ESTATE, NOT TO BE ENTERED INTO UNADVISEDLY OR LIGHTLY, BUT REVERENTLY. PLUS, THE BRIDE HAS KNIVES AND ISN'T AFRAID TO USE THEM, SO LETS ALL BE CAREFUL WITH THIS NEXT PART.
IF ANYONE CAN SHOW JUST CAUSE WHY THEY MAY NOT BE LAWFULLY JOINED TOGETHER, LET THEM SPEAK NOW OR FOREVER HOLD THEIR PEACE.
BECAUSE SHE DIDN'T PROVIDE YOU WITH THE CREDENTIALS THE STATE REQUIRES FOR MARRIAGE.
BESIDES THAT.
BECAUSE SHE'S A ROBOT.
I AM NOT!
BESIDES THAT.
OOOH! OOOOH! BECAUSE HE'S A HALF-DONKEY MONSTER!
BESIDES THAT!
YAAAAAH!
RIP
SHRED
mphmff mphmff*
mffmphm!**
* HUBBA HUBBA!
** YOUR DRESS TASTES BAD.
AHEM... IF ANYONE CAN SHOW JUST CAUSE WHY THEY MAY NOT...
SIGH. WHO CARES, BUT HOW ABOUT "I DON'T LOVE YOU".
I KNOW! I FOUND THIS IN YOUR WALLET!
uh-oh.
Zoë, I Love You! -TORG
BUT IT DOESN'T MATTER BECAUSE I LOVE YOU! sniff I LOVE YOU ENOUGH TO MAKE OUR...sniff... OUR MARRIAGE...sob... WORK...
MAYBE WE SHOULD TAKE A FEW MINUTES FOR YOU TO COMPOSE YOURSELF...
FINISH THE CEREMONY!
LET US SKIP THE WHOLE "JUST CAUSE" PART AND MOVE ON TO THE UPLIFTING VOWS.
torg?
TORG?
TORG? ARE YOU AROUND HERE?
TO-ORG?
ZOË!
"SINCE OASIS DIDN'T KNOW WHAT ZOË LOOKED LIKE (SHE HAD NEVER BEEN FORMALLY INTRODUCED WHEN THEY MET), SHE CONCLUDED THIS WOMAN EMERGING FROM THE FOREST MUST BE ZOË. AND NOTHING WOULD STOP HER DEATH.
TOOOOORG!
"GWYNN? HOW DID SHE GET THERE, KENNY? AND WHY DIDN'T TORG JUST TELL OASIS THAT IT'S NOT ZOË?"
"ONE QUESTION AT A TIME, SKIP! I'M TELLING THIS STORY. TORG KNEW THE ONLY WAY TO SAVE GWYNN'S LIFE WAS TO TELL OASIS THAT IT WASN'T ZOË, OR AT LEAST WARN GWYNN OF THE DANGER. AND WHEN HE TRIED TO WARN AND INFORM, POOF, INSTANT DONKEY!"
HEE HAW
"GWYNN CAST THE DONKEY-SPELL ON TORG TO KEEP HIM SILENT, FOR HER BENEFIT. AND IN THE END, IT LEAD TO HER DETRIMENT. THAT IS IRONY. NEXT QUESTION?"
"OK, KENNY! I'LL BUY THE TUXES, BUT WHERE DID OASIS GET A FERRET-SIZE MAID-OF- HONOR DRESS ON SHORT NOTICE? "
"SHUT UP, SKIP."

"KENNY, HOW DID GWYNN FIND TORG, RIFF, AND KIKI?"

"ONCE GWYNN **GOT** TO THE RESORT, SHE KNEW ENOUGH MAGIC TO USE TORG'S HAIR (LEFT OVER FROM PREVIOUS SPELLS) TO FASHION A "TORG-COMPASS". IT LEAD HER THROUGH THE WOODS RIGHT TO THE ILL-FATED WEDDING CEREMONY. HOW SHE GOT **TO** THE RESORT INVOLVED A FORTUNATE COINCIDENCE."

I WAS WRONG. I MISJUDGED TORG, AND NOW HE'S CURSED. KENNY SAID I HAVE TO CANCEL THE CURSE IN PERSON, AND I WOULD... IF I ONLY HAD THE SLIGHTEST CLUE HOW TO FIND THEM. RIFF GOT OFF THE PHONE TOO QUICKLY, IT WASN'T MY FAULT! WHAT AM I SUPPOSED TO DO? ASK AROUND IF ANYONE'S SEEN A MAN-DONKEY? MY ONLY CLUE IS THAT THEY'RE AT SOME QUAINT POCONO MOUNTAINS RESORT.

Yawn!

QWIRKY WALTONS, HERE, LIVE FROM PHARAOH'S TOMB RESORT WHICH IS NOW ABLAZE. NO ONE IS SURE THE CAUSE OF THE DESTRUCTION, BUT FIRE FIGHTERS ARE TRYING TO KEEP THE BLAZE FROM SPREADING TO THE SURROUNDING WOODS OF THIS **"QUAINT POCONO MOUNTAINS RESORT"**.

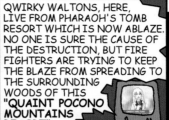

THE ONLY THING STRANGER THAN THE PANIC STRICKEN BLAZE OF VERNE TROYER AND DARVA CONGER STREAKING ACROSS THE BURNING RUINS LIKE A ROMAN CANDLE, WAS THIS SHOT OF A COSTUMED BEAUTY CHASING WHAT CAN ONLY BE DESCRIBED AS A **MAN-DONKEY!**

YES, IT WAS DEFINITELY A MAN-DONKEY.

ALL RIGHT! ALL RIGHT! I'M GOING!

"WHERE WAS I? OH YES. OASIS ON THE MOVE TO SLAUGHTER THE UNSUSPECTING GWYNN, WHILE TORG "GALLOPS" IN TO WARN HER OF THE DANGER, A WARNING SHE CAN'T UNDERSTAND."

TORG?!? THIS IS WORSE THAN I THOUGHT!

HEEHAW

"WITH THE ELEMENT OF SURPRISE ON OASIS'S SIDE, GWYNN NEVER HAD A CHANCE."

DON'T WORRY, I CAN FIX THIS IN A JIFFY!

"OASIS MOVED LIKE A SILENT DANCER. THE FIRST STAB-WOUND WAS BUT A LEAD-IN FOR THE KILLING BLOW TO ARRIVE A SPLIT SECOND LATER."

"BUT OASIS WAS ALSO CAUGHT OFF GUARD, TORG USING HIS DONKEY-FORM TO ITS BEST OFFENSIVE USE."

WHAM!

"THAT'S WHEN THINGS GOT INTERESTING."

WAP
WAP

MY CLOTHES ARE RIPPED AND COVERED IN BLOOD.

DO YOU KNOW HOW EXPENSIVE THIS BLOUSE IS?

TORGY? WHY ARE YOU LEAVING?

OASIS'S WEDDING IS RUINED, KNIVES ARE FLYING, GWYNN'S PUPILS HAVE OMINOUSLY VANISHED AND SHE'S HAVING CLOTHES-ISSUES, ... THERE ARE JUST **SO MANY** REASONS TO RUN FOR MY LIFE, I'M HAVING TROUBLE SETTLING ON JUST ONE!

Sluggy Freelance: Little Evils

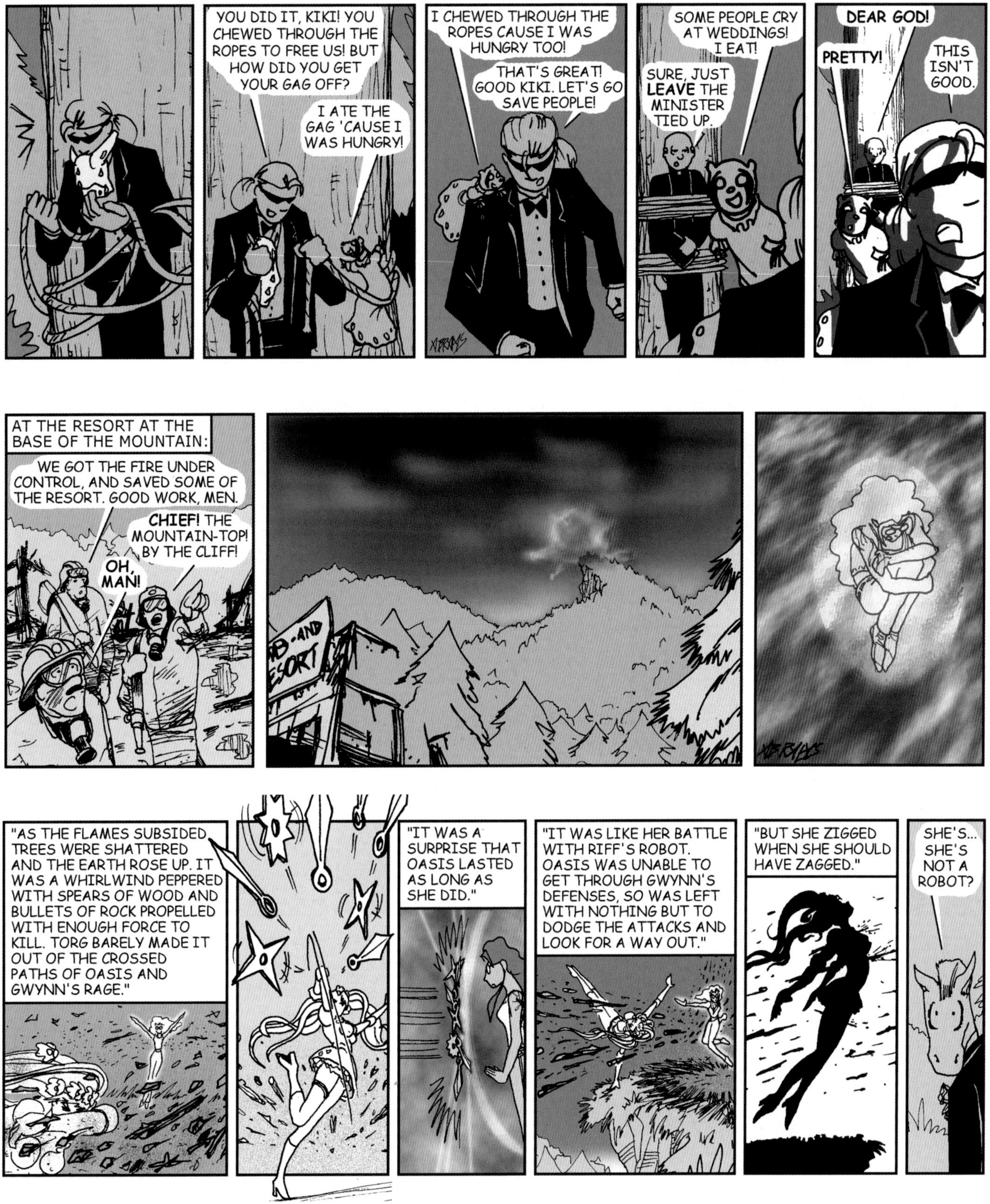
YOU DID IT, KIKI! YOU CHEWED THROUGH THE ROPES TO FREE US! BUT HOW DID YOU GET YOUR GAG OFF?
I ATE THE GAG 'CAUSE I WAS HUNGRY!
I CHEWED THROUGH THE ROPES CAUSE I WAS HUNGRY TOO!
THAT'S GREAT! GOOD KIKI. LET'S GO SAVE PEOPLE!
SOME PEOPLE CRY AT WEDDINGS! I EAT!
SURE, JUST LEAVE THE MINISTER TIED UP.
DEAR GOD!
PRETTY!
THIS ISN'T GOOD.
AT THE RESORT AT THE BASE OF THE MOUNTAIN:
WE GOT THE FIRE UNDER CONTROL, AND SAVED SOME OF THE RESORT. GOOD WORK, MEN.
CHIEF! THE MOUNTAIN-TOP! BY THE CLIFF!
OH, MAN!
"AS THE FLAMES SUBSIDED, TREES WERE SHATTERED AND THE EARTH ROSE UP. IT WAS A WHIRLWIND PEPPERED WITH SPEARS OF WOOD AND BULLETS OF ROCK PROPELLED WITH ENOUGH FORCE TO KILL. TORG BARELY MADE IT OUT OF THE CROSSED PATHS OF OASIS AND GWYNN'S RAGE."
"IT WAS A SURPRISE THAT OASIS LASTED AS LONG AS SHE DID."
"IT WAS LIKE HER BATTLE WITH RIFF'S ROBOT. OASIS WAS UNABLE TO GET THROUGH GWYNN'S DEFENSES, SO WAS LEFT WITH NOTHING BUT TO DODGE THE ATTACKS AND LOOK FOR A WAY OUT."
"BUT SHE ZIGGED WHEN SHE SHOULD HAVE ZAGGED."
SHE'S... SHE'S NOT A ROBOT?

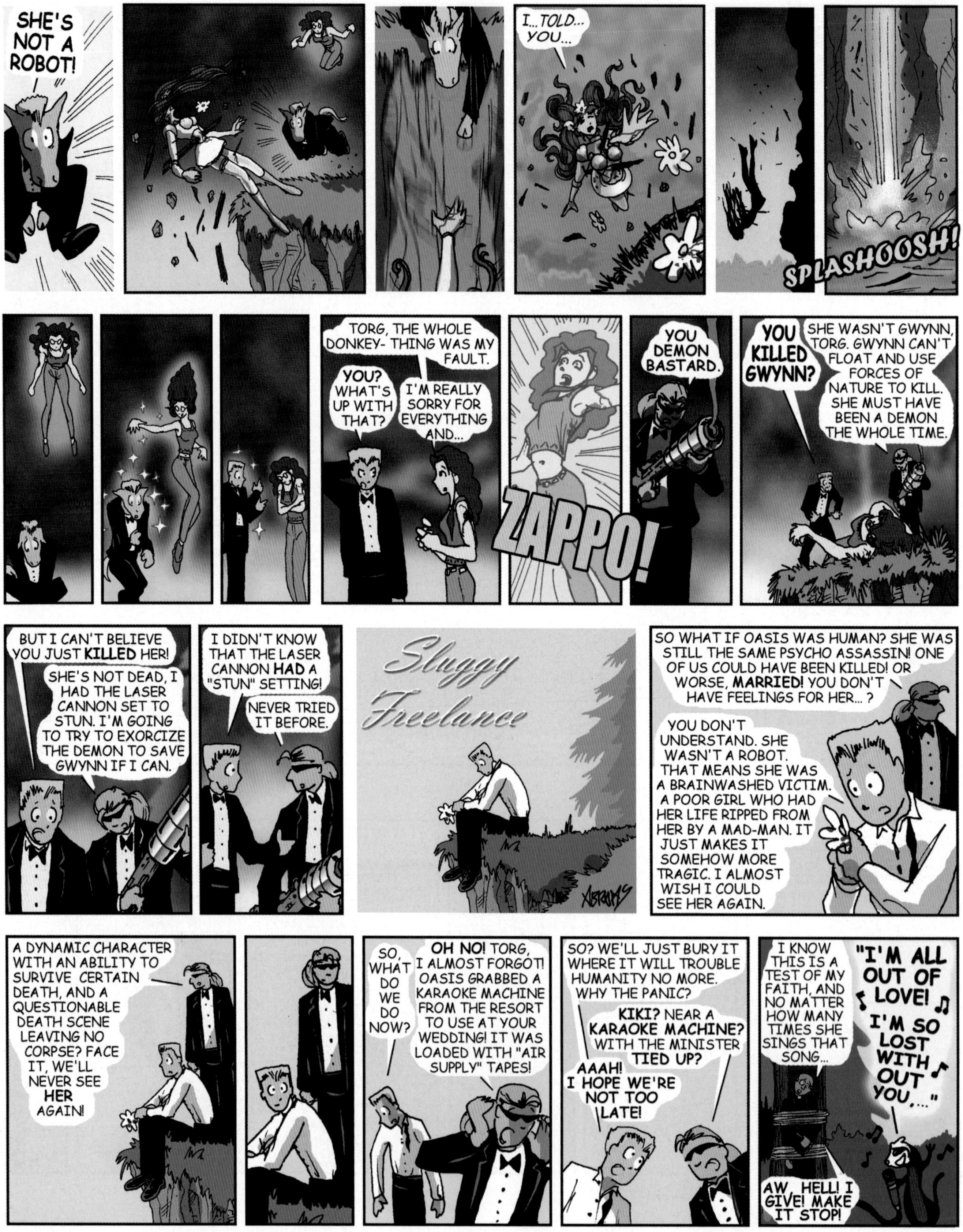
SHE'S NOT A ROBOT!
I... TOLD... YOU...
SPLASHOOSH!
TORG, THE WHOLE DONKEY- THING WAS MY FAULT.
YOU? WHAT'S UP WITH THAT?
I'M REALLY SORRY FOR EVERYTHING AND...
ZAPPO!
YOU DEMON BASTARD.
YOU KILLED GWYNN?
SHE WASN'T GWYNN, TORG. GWYNN CAN'T FLOAT AND USE FORCES OF NATURE TO KILL. SHE MUST HAVE BEEN A DEMON THE WHOLE TIME.
BUT I CAN'T BELIEVE YOU JUST KILLED HER!
SHE'S NOT DEAD, I HAD THE LASER CANNON SET TO STUN. I'M GOING TO TRY TO EXORCIZE THE DEMON TO SAVE GWYNN IF I CAN.
I DIDN'T KNOW THAT THE LASER CANNON HAD A "STUN" SETTING!
NEVER TRIED IT BEFORE.
Sluggy Freelance
SO WHAT IF OASIS WAS HUMAN? SHE WAS STILL THE SAME PSYCHO ASSASSIN! ONE OF US COULD HAVE BEEN KILLED! OR WORSE, MARRIED! YOU DON'T HAVE FEELINGS FOR HER... ?
YOU DON'T UNDERSTAND. SHE WASN'T A ROBOT. THAT MEANS SHE WAS A BRAINWASHED VICTIM. A POOR GIRL WHO HAD HER LIFE RIPPED FROM HER BY A MAD-MAN. IT JUST MAKES IT SOMEHOW MORE TRAGIC. I ALMOST WISH I COULD SEE HER AGAIN.
A DYNAMIC CHARACTER WITH AN ABILITY TO SURVIVE CERTAIN DEATH, AND A QUESTIONABLE DEATH SCENE LEAVING NO CORPSE? FACE IT, WE'LL NEVER SEE HER AGAIN!
SO, WHAT DO WE DO NOW?
OH NO! TORG, I ALMOST FORGOT! OASIS GRABBED A KARAOKE MACHINE FROM THE RESORT TO USE AT YOUR WEDDING! IT WAS LOADED WITH "AIR SUPPLY" TAPES!
SO? WE'LL JUST BURY IT WHERE IT WILL TROUBLE HUMANITY NO MORE. WHY THE PANIC?
KIKI? NEAR A KARAOKE MACHINE? WITH THE MINISTER TIED UP?
AAAH! I HOPE WE'RE NOT TOO LATE!
I KNOW THIS IS A TEST OF MY FAITH, AND NO MATTER HOW MANY TIMES SHE SINGS THAT SONG...
"I'M ALL OUT OF LOVE! I'M SO LOST WITH OUT YOU,..."
AW, HELL! I GIVE! MAKE IT STOP!

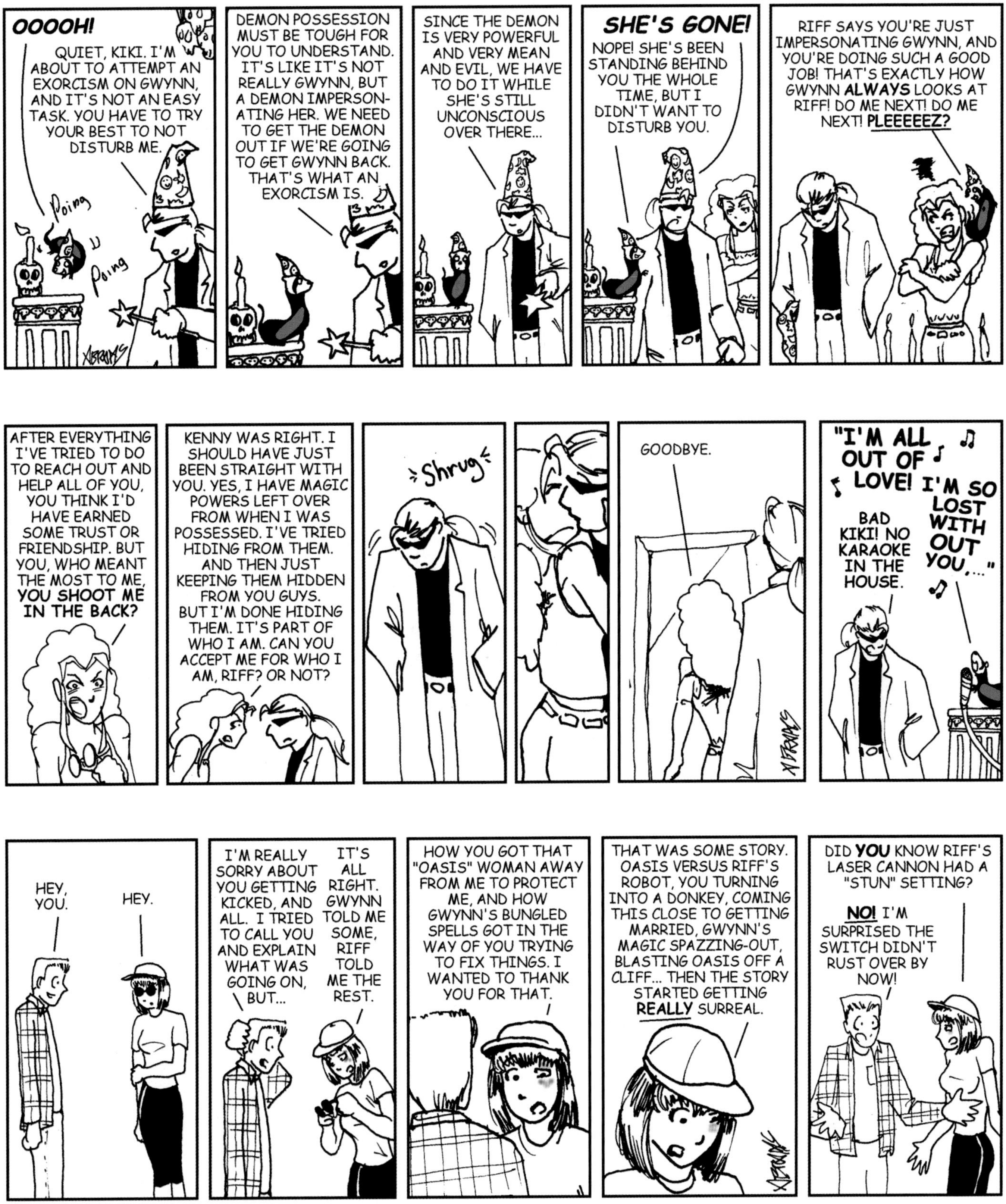
OOOOH!
QUIET, KIKI. I'M ABOUT TO ATTEMPT AN EXORCISM ON GWYNN, AND IT'S NOT AN EASY TASK. YOU HAVE TO TRY YOUR BEST TO NOT DISTURB ME.
Poing
Poing
DEMON POSSESSION MUST BE TOUGH FOR YOU TO UNDERSTAND. IT'S LIKE IT'S NOT REALLY GWYNN, BUT A DEMON IMPERSONATING HER. WE NEED TO GET THE DEMON OUT IF WE'RE GOING TO GET GWYNN BACK. THAT'S WHAT AN EXORCISM IS.
SINCE THE DEMON IS VERY POWERFUL AND VERY MEAN AND EVIL, WE HAVE TO DO IT WHILE SHE'S STILL UNCONSCIOUS OVER THERE...
SHE'S GONE!
NOPE! SHE'S BEEN STANDING BEHIND YOU THE WHOLE TIME, BUT I DIDN'T WANT TO DISTURB YOU.
RIFF SAYS YOU'RE JUST IMPERSONATING GWYNN, AND YOU'RE DOING SUCH A GOOD JOB! THAT'S EXACTLY HOW GWYNN ALWAYS LOOKS AT RIFF! DO ME NEXT! DO ME NEXT! PLEEEEEZ?
AFTER EVERYTHING I'VE TRIED TO DO TO REACH OUT AND HELP ALL OF YOU, YOU THINK I'D HAVE EARNED SOME TRUST OR FRIENDSHIP. BUT YOU, WHO MEANT THE MOST TO ME, YOU SHOOT ME IN THE BACK?
KENNY WAS RIGHT. I SHOULD HAVE JUST BEEN STRAIGHT WITH YOU. YES, I HAVE MAGIC POWERS LEFT OVER FROM WHEN I WAS POSSESSED. I'VE TRIED HIDING FROM THEM. AND THEN JUST KEEPING THEM HIDDEN FROM YOU GUYS. BUT I'M DONE HIDING THEM. IT'S PART OF WHO I AM. CAN YOU ACCEPT ME FOR WHO I AM, RIFF? OR NOT?
Shrug
GOODBYE.
"I'M ALL OUT OF LOVE! I'M SO LOST WITH OUT YOU,..."
BAD KIKI! NO KARAOKE IN THE HOUSE.
HEY, YOU.
HEY.
I'M REALLY SORRY ABOUT YOU GETTING KICKED, AND ALL. I TRIED TO CALL YOU AND EXPLAIN WHAT WAS GOING ON, BUT...
IT'S ALL RIGHT. GWYNN TOLD ME SOME, RIFF TOLD ME THE REST.
HOW YOU GOT THAT "OASIS" WOMAN AWAY FROM ME TO PROTECT ME, AND HOW GWYNN'S BUNGLED SPELLS GOT IN THE WAY OF YOU TRYING TO FIX THINGS. I WANTED TO THANK YOU FOR THAT.
THAT WAS SOME STORY. OASIS VERSUS RIFF'S ROBOT, YOU TURNING INTO A DONKEY, COMING THIS CLOSE TO GETTING MARRIED, GWYNN'S MAGIC SPAZZING-OUT, BLASTING OASIS OFF A CLIFF... THEN THE STORY STARTED GETTING REALLY SURREAL.
DID YOU KNOW RIFF'S LASER CANNON HAD A "STUN" SETTING?
NO! I'M SURPRISED THE SWITCH DIDN'T RUST OVER BY NOW!

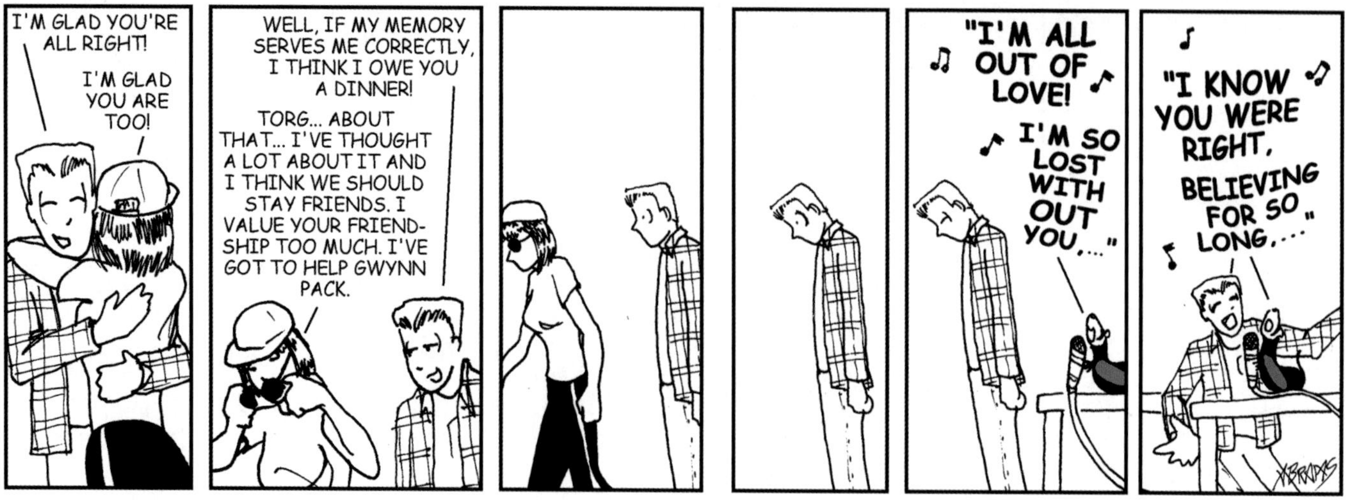
I'M GLAD YOU'RE ALL RIGHT!
I'M GLAD YOU ARE TOO!
WELL, IF MY MEMORY SERVES ME CORRECTLY, I THINK I OWE YOU A DINNER!
TORG... ABOUT THAT... I'VE THOUGHT A LOT ABOUT IT AND I THINK WE SHOULD STAY FRIENDS. I VALUE YOUR FRIENDSHIP TOO MUCH. I'VE GOT TO HELP GWYNN PACK.
"I'M ALL OUT OF LOVE! I'M SO LOST WITH OUT YOU,..."
"I KNOW YOU WERE RIGHT, BELIEVING FOR SO LONG,..."

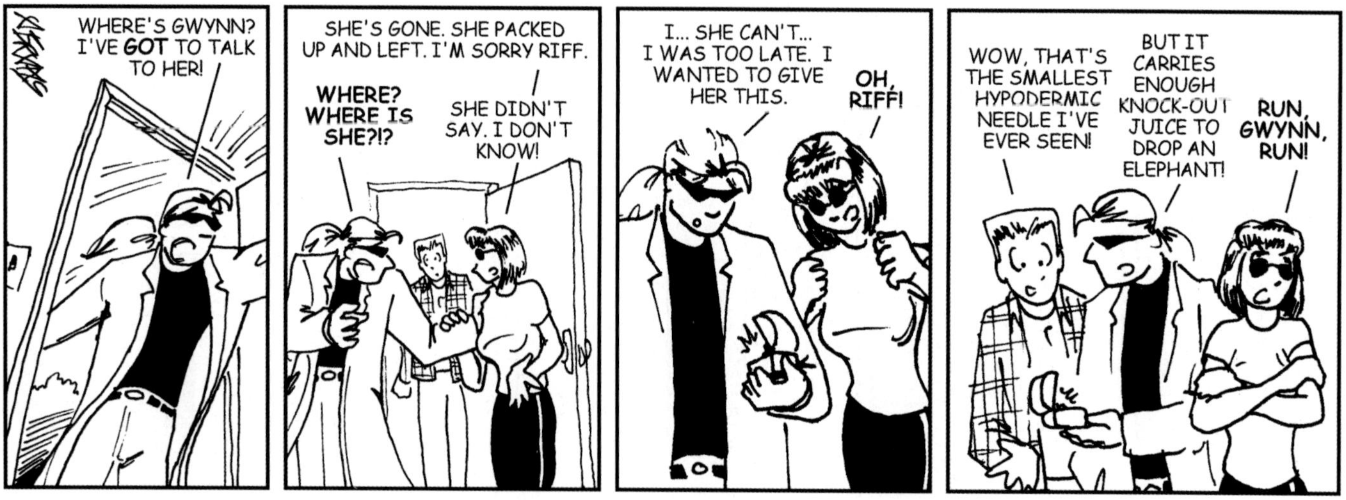
WHERE'S GWYNN? I'VE **GOT** TO TALK TO HER!
SHE'S GONE. SHE PACKED UP AND LEFT. I'M SORRY RIFF.
WHERE? WHERE IS SHE?!?
SHE DIDN'T SAY. I DON'T KNOW!
I... SHE CAN'T... I WAS TOO LATE. I WANTED TO GIVE HER THIS.
OH, RIFF!
WOW, THAT'S THE SMALLEST HYPODERMIC NEEDLE I'VE EVER SEEN!
BUT IT CARRIES ENOUGH KNOCK-OUT JUICE TO DROP AN ELEPHANT!
RUN, GWYNN, RUN!

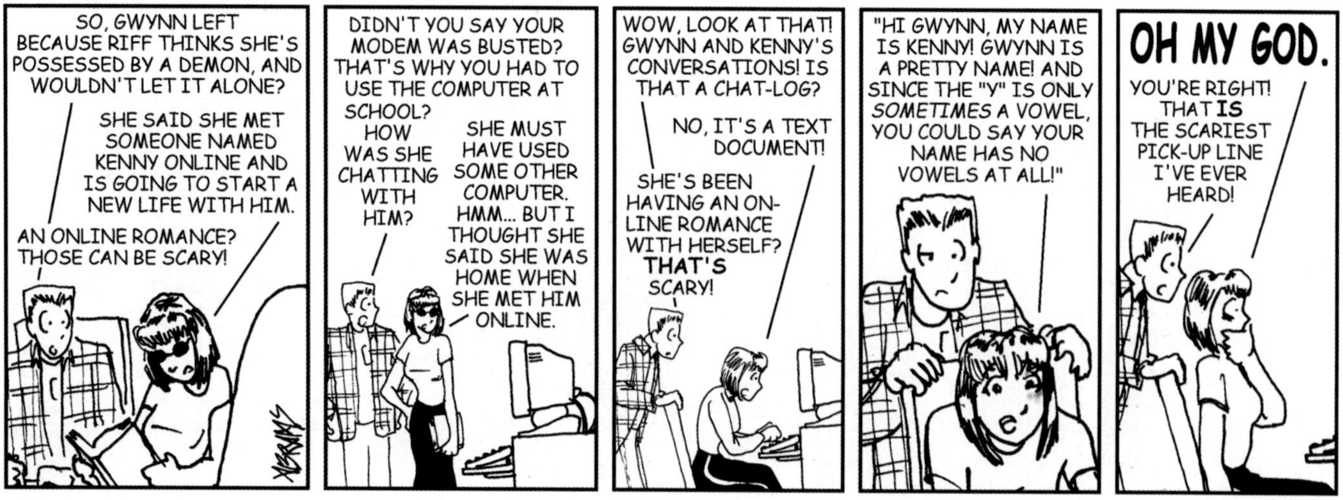
SO, GWYNN LEFT BECAUSE RIFF THINKS SHE'S POSSESSED BY A DEMON, AND WOULDN'T LET IT ALONE?
SHE SAID SHE MET SOMEONE NAMED KENNY ONLINE AND IS GOING TO START A NEW LIFE WITH HIM.
AN ONLINE ROMANCE? THOSE CAN BE SCARY!
DIDN'T YOU SAY YOUR MODEM WAS BUSTED? THAT'S WHY YOU HAD TO USE THE COMPUTER AT SCHOOL? HOW WAS SHE CHATTING WITH HIM?
SHE MUST HAVE USED SOME OTHER COMPUTER. HMM... BUT I THOUGHT SHE SAID SHE WAS HOME WHEN SHE MET HIM ONLINE.
WOW, LOOK AT THAT! GWYNN AND KENNY'S CONVERSATIONS! IS THAT A CHAT-LOG?
NO, IT'S A TEXT DOCUMENT!
SHE'S BEEN HAVING AN ON-LINE ROMANCE WITH HERSELF? **THAT'S** SCARY!
"HI GWYNN, MY NAME IS KENNY! GWYNN IS A PRETTY NAME! AND SINCE THE "Y" IS ONLY *SOMETIMES* A VOWEL, YOU COULD SAY YOUR NAME HAS NO VOWELS AT ALL!"
OH MY GOD.
YOU'RE RIGHT! THAT **IS** THE SCARIEST PICK-UP LINE I'VE EVER HEARD!

WHAT'S WRONG? THIS "KENNY" TURNS GWYNN AGAINST US AND TOWARDS USING HER POWERS, AND COMMENTS THAT HER NAME HAS NO VOWELS! TORG, **THINK**!

BUT THERE **IS** NO KENNY! IT WAS ALL IN GWYNN'S HEAD!

...OH! ....ohno.

RIFF WAS RIGHT!

KIZKE.

MAYBE IT'S NOT TOO LATE! DO YOU KNOW WHERE SHE WENT?

NO! SHE DIDN'T TELL ME, AND I DIDN'T ASK, BECAUSE... I WANTED HER GONE. **WHAT HAVE I DONE?**

AND WE HAVE REACHED THE TIME FOR THE RECAP AND SUMMATION.

Sluggy Freelance

A LONG TIME AGO I RIPPED GWYNN'S SOUL FROM HER, AND TOOK IT WITH ME WHEN I WAS SENT TO THE PAST.

"WHEN I WAS DESTROYED BY *THAT INFURIATING ZOË,* ALL THE SOULS I HAD COLLECTED WERE SIMILARLY RIPPED FROM ME. SOME, LIKE GWYNN, TOOK PARTS OF ME BACK WITH THEM. GWYNN GOT A SENTIENT PART."

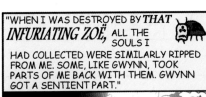

AND I'VE BEEN TRYING TO REBUILD MY STRENGTH EVER SINCE.

YOU MUST BE POWERFUL, KENNY! YOU CAN ACTUALLY REGENERATE YOURSELF FROM ONLY A SMALL PIECE!

"IT WAS NOT EASY! THE MORE SHE USED MY POWERS, THE STRONGER I BECAME, BUT BOTH HER AND I HAD TO BE CAREFUL OF DISCOVERY, SO IT TOOK MUCH TIME AND PATIENCE. *I HATE PATIENCE!*"

"AFTER A WHILE I WAS ABLE TO EXERT MINOR CONTROL OVER HER *PERCEPTION.* USING A TRICK WITH *AUTOMATIC WRITING,* I WAS ABLE TO MAKE HER THINK SHE WAS CHATTING WITH SOMEONE ON LINE WHEN SHE WAS ACTUALLY TYPING FOR *BOTH* OF US."

"I PLAYED THE ROLE OF A KINDRED SPIRIT WHO HAD ALSO BEEN LEFT WITH RESIDUAL POWERS AFTER POSSESSION. I STARTED ENCOURAGING HER TO USE HER POWERS MORE, AND GIVING HER INEFFECTUAL SPELLS TO DRIVE A *WEDGE* BETWEEN THE PEOPLE SHE LOVED AND THE PEOPLE WHO LOVED HER."

"BUT THIS *"OASIS"* WAS AN AMAZING STROKE OF GOOD FORTUNE! THE RAGE AND POWER SHE UNLEASHED OUT OF GWYNN WAS ENOUGH FOR ME TO START *REALLY* DRIVING HER DECISIONS!"

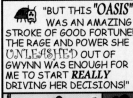

"NOW THAT I'VE GOTTEN HER AWAY FROM HER FRIENDS, IT SHOULD BE NO TIME BEFORE I'LL START FEELING MYSELF AGAIN. *AND BE ABLE TO COME BACK AND eXTRACT MY REVENGE on* RIFFY, TORG, *AND ZOË!*"

THAT **IS** A GREAT STORY, KENNY! ALL KINDS OF GOOD FORTUNE! AND I GUESS THE FINAL ONE IS THAT GWYNN WOULD HAPPEN TO SIT NEXT TO THE ONLY OTHER DEMON-POSSESSED PERSON ON THE TRAIN, ALLOWING US TO EXCHANGE STORIES!

AND WHAT IS *YOUR* STORY, SKIP?

BOB, HERE, GOT A UNIQUE BAZOOKA-JOE COMIC WITH HIS GUM. A PRINTING ERROR CAUSED THE WORDS OF THE COMIC TO BLUR INTO THE EXACT WORDING OF RUNES OF EVIL POWER.

WHEN HE READ THE COMIC OUT LOUD (BECAUSE HE DIDN'T GET IT), POOF! I POSSESSED HIM. GOOD STORY, HUH, KENNY?

AH, THAT'S A GOOD STORY TOO, SKIP. BUT PLEASE, LET'S NOT CALL EACH OTHER BY OUR FALSENAMES. MY TRUENAME IS K'Z'K!

MY TRUENAME IS "SKIPPY"!

SKIPPY THE DEMON.

YEP!

AND YOU HIDE YOUR TRUENAME BY CALLING YOURSELF SKIP. I *LIKE* IT.

HEY! "K'Z'K"? K'Z'K THE VOWELESS? K'Z'K *THE SOUL COLLECTOR?* YOU'RE ONE OF THE **BIG** ONES! WEREN'T YOU SUPPOSED TO ENSLAVE AND DESTROY THE WORLD?

I WILL.

fin.

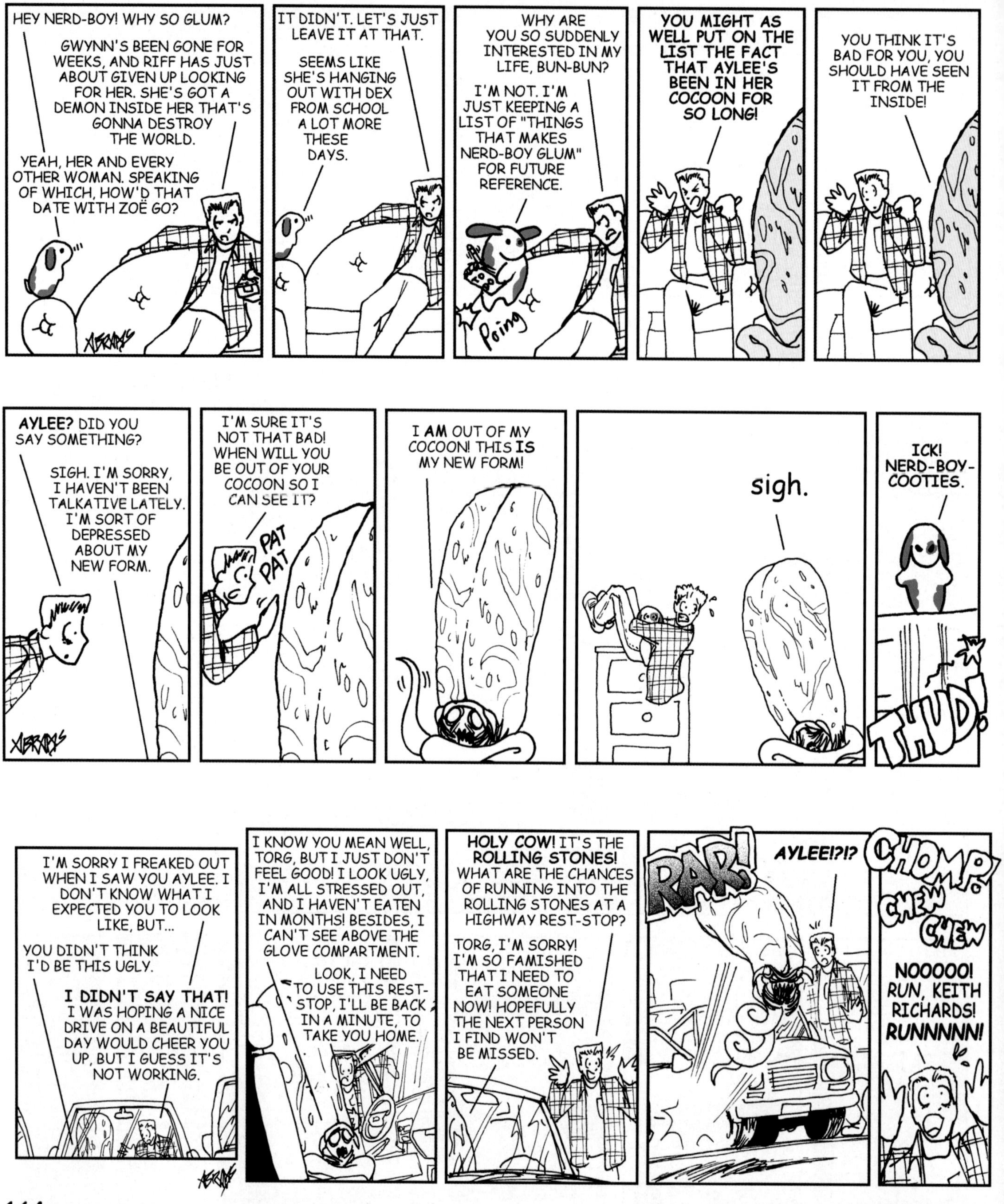
HEY NERD-BOY! WHY SO GLUM?
GWYNN'S BEEN GONE FOR WEEKS, AND RIFF HAS JUST ABOUT GIVEN UP LOOKING FOR HER. SHE'S GOT A DEMON INSIDE HER THAT'S GONNA DESTROY THE WORLD.
YEAH, HER AND EVERY OTHER WOMAN. SPEAKING OF WHICH, HOW'D THAT DATE WITH ZOË GO?
IT DIDN'T. LET'S JUST LEAVE IT AT THAT.
SEEMS LIKE SHE'S HANGING OUT WITH DEX FROM SCHOOL A LOT MORE THESE DAYS.
WHY ARE YOU SO SUDDENLY INTERESTED IN MY LIFE, BUN-BUN?
I'M NOT. I'M JUST KEEPING A LIST OF "THINGS THAT MAKES NERD-BOY GLUM" FOR FUTURE REFERENCE.
Poing
YOU MIGHT AS WELL PUT ON THE LIST THE FACT THAT AYLEE'S BEEN IN HER COCOON FOR SO LONG!
YOU THINK IT'S BAD FOR YOU, YOU SHOULD HAVE SEEN IT FROM THE INSIDE!
AYLEE? DID YOU SAY SOMETHING?
SIGH. I'M SORRY, I HAVEN'T BEEN TALKATIVE LATELY. I'M SORT OF DEPRESSED ABOUT MY NEW FORM.
I'M SURE IT'S NOT THAT BAD! WHEN WILL YOU BE OUT OF YOUR COCOON SO I CAN SEE IT?
PAT PAT
I AM OUT OF MY COCOON! THIS IS MY NEW FORM!
sigh.
ICK! NERD-BOY-COOTIES.
THUD!
I'M SORRY I FREAKED OUT WHEN I SAW YOU AYLEE. I DON'T KNOW WHAT I EXPECTED YOU TO LOOK LIKE, BUT...
YOU DIDN'T THINK I'D BE THIS UGLY.
I DIDN'T SAY THAT! I WAS HOPING A NICE DRIVE ON A BEAUTIFUL DAY WOULD CHEER YOU UP, BUT I GUESS IT'S NOT WORKING.
I KNOW YOU MEAN WELL, TORG, BUT I JUST DON'T FEEL GOOD! I LOOK UGLY, I'M ALL STRESSED OUT, AND I HAVEN'T EATEN IN MONTHS! BESIDES, I CAN'T SEE ABOVE THE GLOVE COMPARTMENT.
LOOK, I NEED TO USE THIS REST-STOP, I'LL BE BACK IN A MINUTE, TO TAKE YOU HOME.
HOLY COW! IT'S THE ROLLING STONES! WHAT ARE THE CHANCES OF RUNNING INTO THE ROLLING STONES AT A HIGHWAY REST-STOP?
TORG, I'M SORRY! I'M SO FAMISHED THAT I NEED TO EAT SOMEONE NOW! HOPEFULLY THE NEXT PERSON I FIND WON'T BE MISSED.
RAR!
AYLEE!?!?
CHOMP!
CHEW
CHEW
NOOOOO! RUN, KEITH RICHARDS! RUNNNNN!

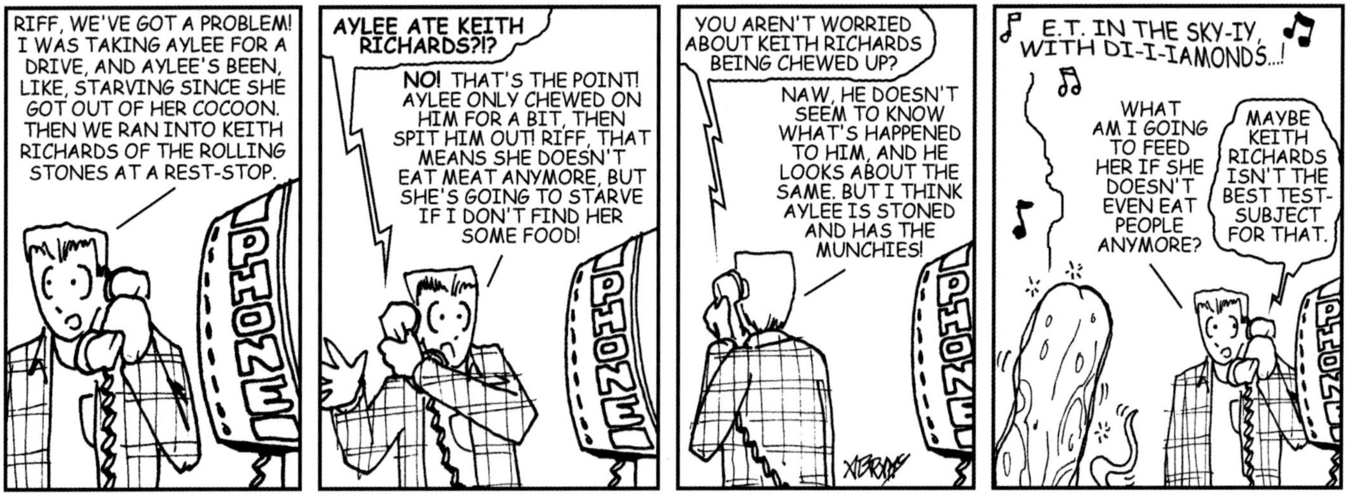
RIFF, WE'VE GOT A PROBLEM! I WAS TAKING AYLEE FOR A DRIVE, AND AYLEE'S BEEN, LIKE, STARVING SINCE SHE GOT OUT OF HER COCOON. THEN WE RAN INTO KEITH RICHARDS OF THE ROLLING STONES AT A REST-STOP.
PHONE
AYLEE ATE KEITH RICHARDS?!?
NO! THAT'S THE POINT! AYLEE ONLY CHEWED ON HIM FOR A BIT, THEN SPIT HIM OUT! RIFF, THAT MEANS SHE DOESN'T EAT MEAT ANYMORE, BUT SHE'S GOING TO STARVE IF I DON'T FIND HER SOME FOOD!
PHONE
YOU AREN'T WORRIED ABOUT KEITH RICHARDS BEING CHEWED UP?
NAW, HE DOESN'T SEEM TO KNOW WHAT'S HAPPENED TO HIM, AND HE LOOKS ABOUT THE SAME. BUT I THINK AYLEE IS STONED AND HAS THE MUNCHIES!
PHONE
E.T. IN THE SKY-IY, WITH DI-I-IAMONDS...!
WHAT AM I GOING TO FEED HER IF SHE DOESN'T EVEN EAT PEOPLE ANYMORE?
MAYBE KEITH RICHARDS ISN'T THE BEST TEST-SUBJECT FOR THAT.
PHONE

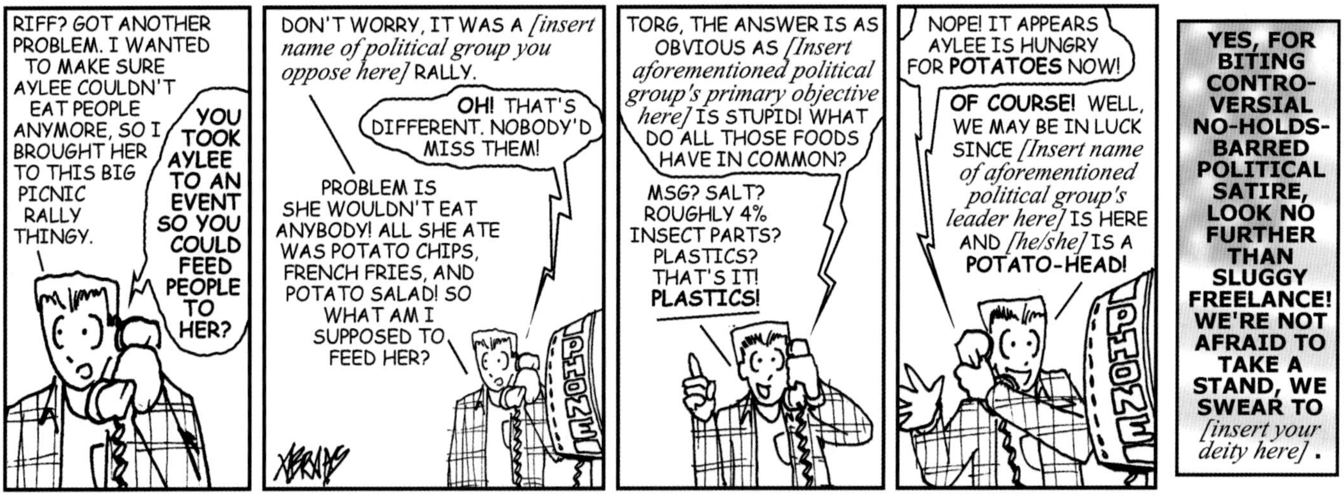
RIFF? GOT ANOTHER PROBLEM. I WANTED TO MAKE SURE AYLEE COULDN'T EAT PEOPLE ANYMORE, SO I BROUGHT HER TO THIS BIG PICNIC RALLY THINGY.
YOU TOOK AYLEE TO AN EVENT SO YOU COULD FEED PEOPLE TO HER?
DON'T WORRY, IT WAS A *[insert name of political group you oppose here]* RALLY.
OH! THAT'S DIFFERENT. NOBODY'D MISS THEM!
PROBLEM IS SHE WOULDN'T EAT ANYBODY! ALL SHE ATE WAS POTATO CHIPS, FRENCH FRIES, AND POTATO SALAD! SO WHAT AM I SUPPOSED TO FEED HER?
PHONE
TORG, THE ANSWER IS AS OBVIOUS AS *[Insert aforementioned political group's primary objective here]* IS STUPID! WHAT DO ALL THOSE FOODS HAVE IN COMMON?
MSG? SALT? ROUGHLY 4% INSECT PARTS? PLASTICS? THAT'S IT! **PLASTICS!**
NOPE! IT APPEARS AYLEE IS HUNGRY FOR **POTATOES** NOW!
OF COURSE! WELL, WE MAY BE IN LUCK SINCE *[Insert name of aforementioned political group's leader here]* IS HERE AND *[he/she]* IS A **POTATO-HEAD!**
PHONE
YES, FOR BITING CONTRO-VERSIAL NO-HOLDS-BARRED POLITICAL SATIRE, LOOK NO FURTHER THAN SLUGGY FREELANCE! WE'RE NOT AFRAID TO TAKE A STAND, WE SWEAR TO *[insert your deity here]* **.**

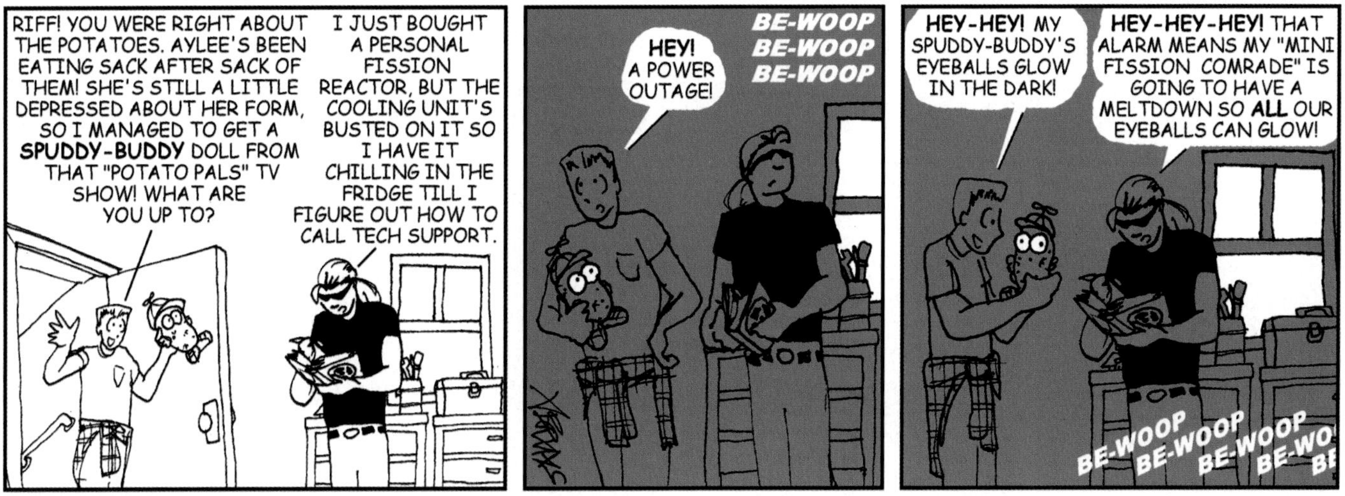
RIFF! YOU WERE RIGHT ABOUT THE POTATOES. AYLEE'S BEEN EATING SACK AFTER SACK OF THEM! SHE'S STILL A LITTLE DEPRESSED ABOUT HER FORM, SO I MANAGED TO GET A **SPUDDY-BUDDY** DOLL FROM THAT "POTATO PALS" TV SHOW! WHAT ARE YOU UP TO?
I JUST BOUGHT A PERSONAL FISSION REACTOR, BUT THE COOLING UNIT'S BUSTED ON IT SO I HAVE IT CHILLING IN THE FRIDGE TILL I FIGURE OUT HOW TO CALL TECH SUPPORT.
BE-WOOP BE-WOOP BE-WOOP
HEY! A POWER OUTAGE!
HEY-HEY! MY SPUDDY-BUDDY'S EYEBALLS GLOW IN THE DARK!
HEY-HEY-HEY! THAT ALARM MEANS MY "MINI FISSION COMRADE" IS GOING TO HAVE A MELTDOWN SO **ALL** OUR EYEBALLS CAN GLOW!
BE-WOOP BE-WOOP BE-WOOP

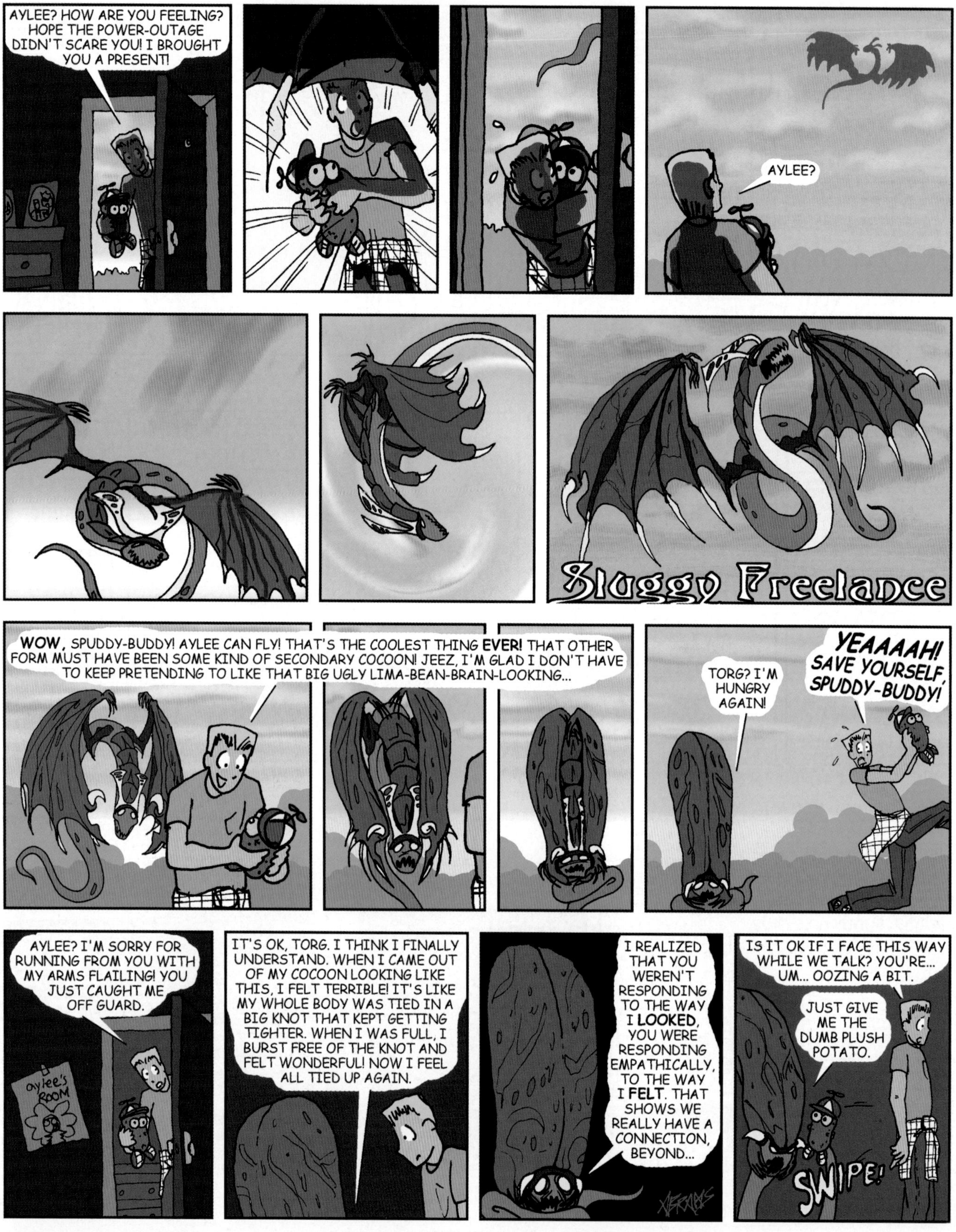

AYLEE? HOW ARE YOU FEELING? HOPE THE POWER-OUTAGE DIDN'T SCARE YOU! I BROUGHT YOU A PRESENT!
AYLEE?
Sluggy Freelance
WOW, SPUDDY-BUDDY! AYLEE CAN FLY! THAT'S THE COOLEST THING EVER! THAT OTHER FORM MUST HAVE BEEN SOME KIND OF SECONDARY COCOON! JEEZ, I'M GLAD I DON'T HAVE TO KEEP PRETENDING TO LIKE THAT BIG UGLY LIMA-BEAN-BRAIN-LOOKING...
TORG? I'M HUNGRY AGAIN!
YEAAAAH! SAVE YOURSELF, SPUDDY-BUDDY!
AYLEE? I'M SORRY FOR RUNNING FROM YOU WITH MY ARMS FLAILING! YOU JUST CAUGHT ME OFF GUARD.
aylee's ROOM
IT'S OK, TORG. I THINK I FINALLY UNDERSTAND. WHEN I CAME OUT OF MY COCOON LOOKING LIKE THIS, I FELT TERRIBLE! IT'S LIKE MY WHOLE BODY WAS TIED IN A BIG KNOT THAT KEPT GETTING TIGHTER. WHEN I WAS FULL, I BURST FREE OF THE KNOT AND FELT WONDERFUL! NOW I FEEL ALL TIED UP AGAIN.
I REALIZED THAT YOU WEREN'T RESPONDING TO THE WAY I LOOKED, YOU WERE RESPONDING EMPATHICALLY, TO THE WAY I FELT. THAT SHOWS WE REALLY HAVE A CONNECTION, BEYOND...
IS IT OK IF I FACE THIS WAY WHILE WE TALK? YOU'RE... UM... OOZING A BIT.
JUST GIVE ME THE DUMB PLUSH POTATO.
SWIPE!

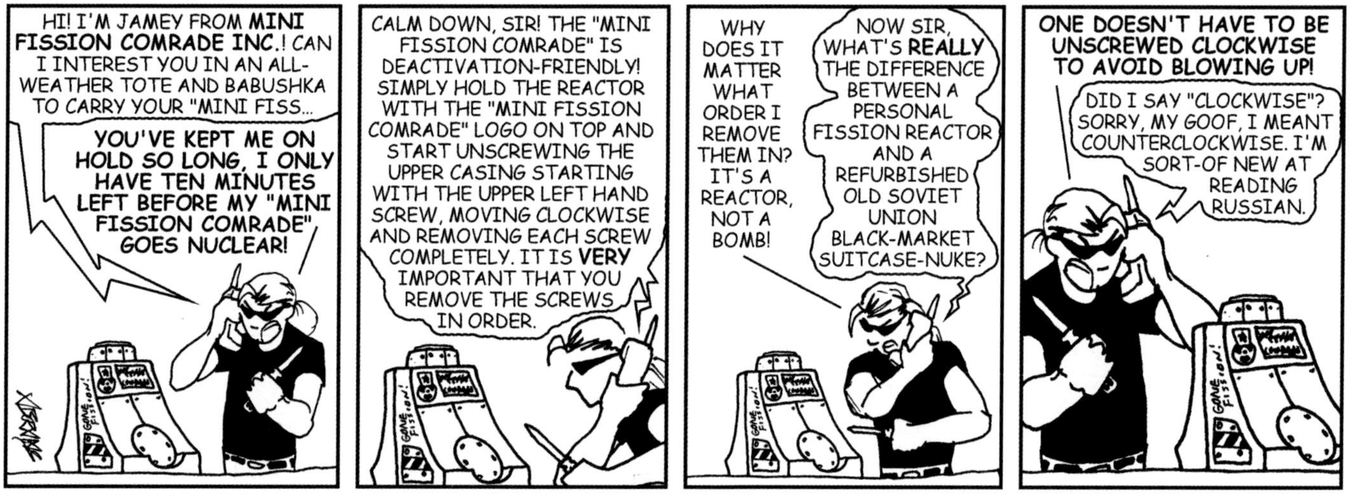
HI! I'M JAMEY FROM **MINI FISSION COMRADE INC.**! CAN I INTEREST YOU IN AN ALL-WEATHER TOTE AND BABUSHKA TO CARRY YOUR "MINI FISS...
YOU'VE KEPT ME ON HOLD SO LONG, I ONLY HAVE TEN MINUTES LEFT BEFORE MY "MINI FISSION COMRADE" GOES NUCLEAR!
CALM DOWN, SIR! THE "MINI FISSION COMRADE" IS DEACTIVATION-FRIENDLY! SIMPLY HOLD THE REACTOR WITH THE "MINI FISSION COMRADE" LOGO ON TOP AND START UNSCREWING THE UPPER CASING STARTING WITH THE UPPER LEFT HAND SCREW, MOVING CLOCKWISE AND REMOVING EACH SCREW COMPLETELY. IT IS **VERY** IMPORTANT THAT YOU REMOVE THE SCREWS IN ORDER.
WHY DOES IT MATTER WHAT ORDER I REMOVE THEM IN? IT'S A REACTOR, NOT A BOMB!
NOW SIR, WHAT'S **REALLY** THE DIFFERENCE BETWEEN A PERSONAL FISSION REACTOR AND A REFURBISHED OLD SOVIET UNION BLACK-MARKET SUITCASE-NUKE?
ONE DOESN'T HAVE TO BE UNSCREWED CLOCKWISE TO AVOID BLOWING UP!
DID I SAY "CLOCKWISE"? SORRY, MY GOOF, I MEANT COUNTERCLOCKWISE. I'M SORT-OF NEW AT READING RUSSIAN.

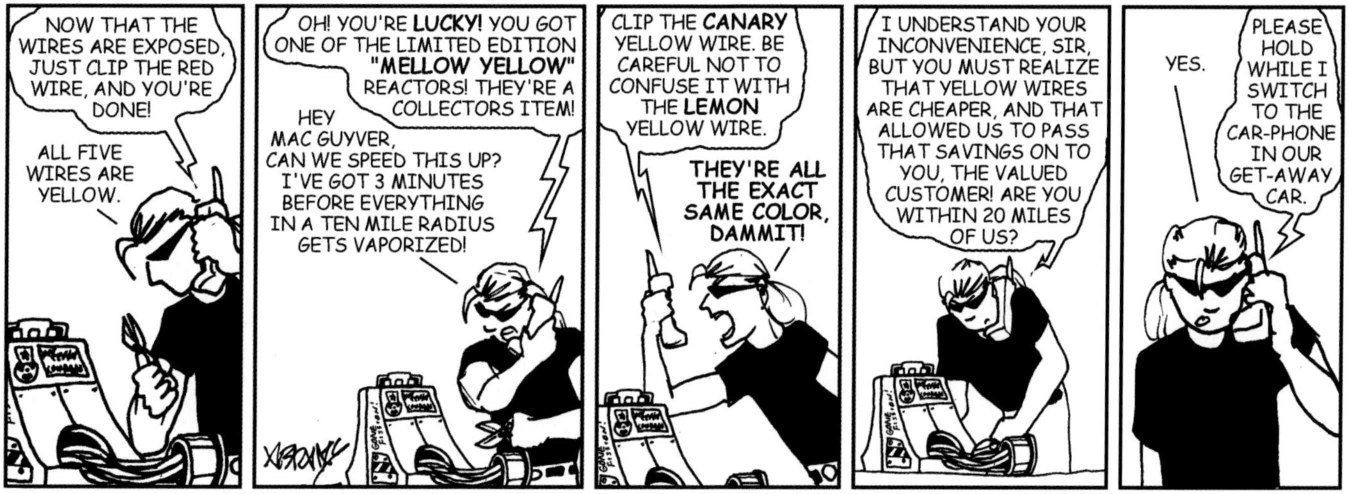
NOW THAT THE WIRES ARE EXPOSED, JUST CLIP THE RED WIRE, AND YOU'RE DONE!
ALL FIVE WIRES ARE YELLOW.
OH! YOU'RE **LUCKY!** YOU GOT ONE OF THE LIMITED EDITION **"MELLOW YELLOW"** REACTORS! THEY'RE A COLLECTORS ITEM!
HEY MAC GUYVER, CAN WE SPEED THIS UP? I'VE GOT 3 MINUTES BEFORE EVERYTHING IN A TEN MILE RADIUS GETS VAPORIZED!
CLIP THE **CANARY** YELLOW WIRE. BE CAREFUL NOT TO CONFUSE IT WITH THE **LEMON** YELLOW WIRE.
THEY'RE ALL THE EXACT SAME COLOR, DAMMIT!
I UNDERSTAND YOUR INCONVENIENCE, SIR, BUT YOU MUST REALIZE THAT YELLOW WIRES ARE CHEAPER, AND THAT ALLOWED US TO PASS THAT SAVINGS ON TO YOU, THE VALUED CUSTOMER! ARE YOU WITHIN 20 MILES OF US?
YES.
PLEASE HOLD WHILE I SWITCH TO THE CAR-PHONE IN OUR GET-AWAY CAR.

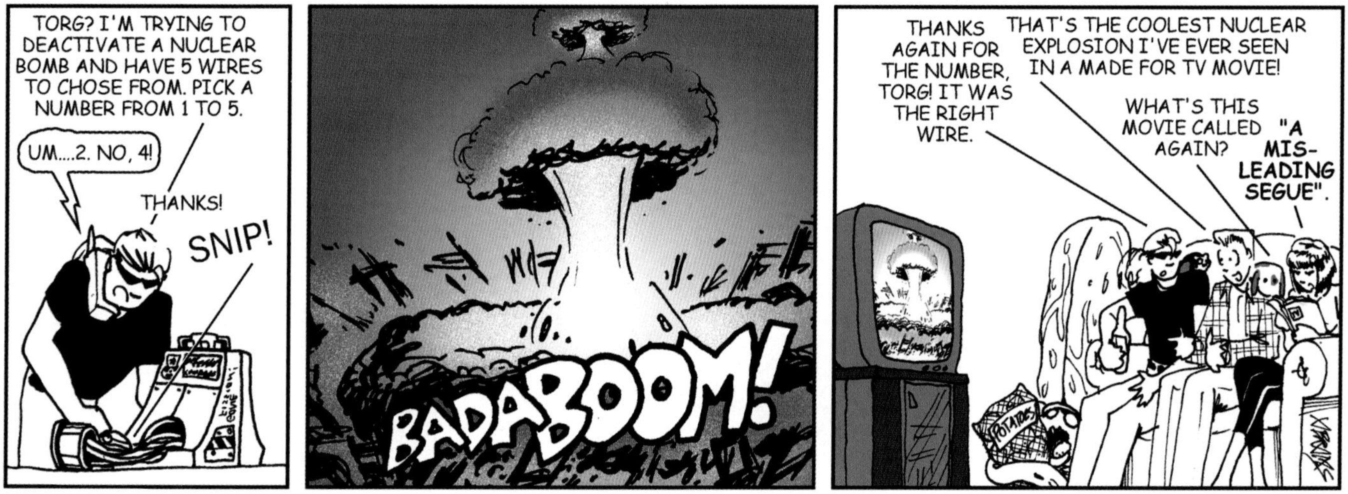
TORG? I'M TRYING TO DEACTIVATE A NUCLEAR BOMB AND HAVE 5 WIRES TO CHOSE FROM. PICK A NUMBER FROM 1 TO 5.
UM....2. NO, 4!
THANKS!
SNIP!
BADABOOM!
THANKS AGAIN FOR THE NUMBER, TORG! IT WAS THE RIGHT WIRE.
THAT'S THE COOLEST NUCLEAR EXPLOSION I'VE EVER SEEN IN A MADE FOR TV MOVIE!
WHAT'S THIS MOVIE CALLED AGAIN?
"A MIS-LEADING SEGUE".

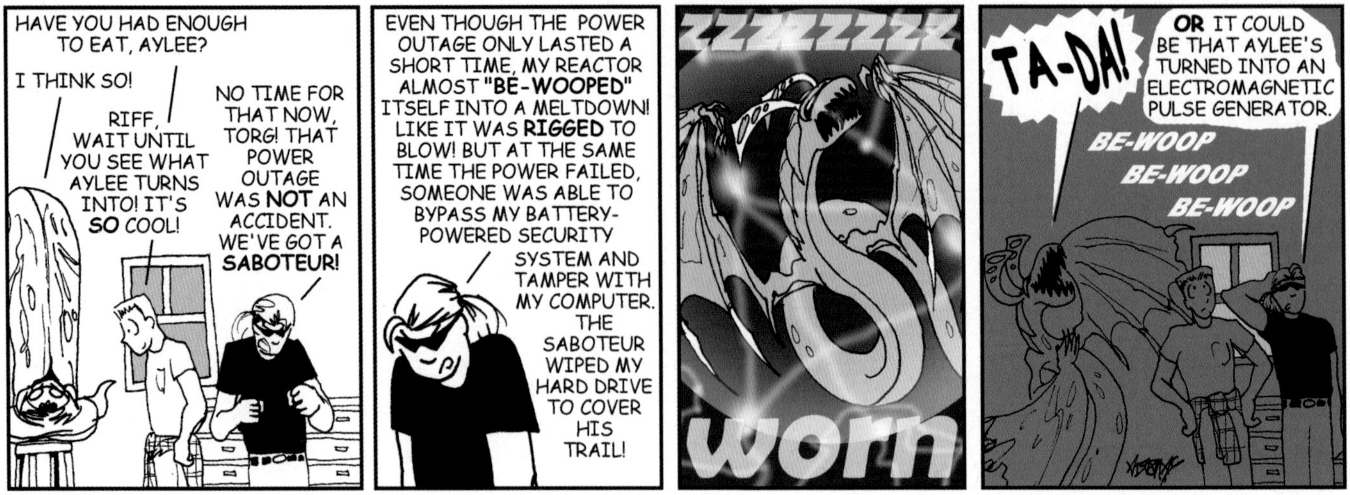
HAVE YOU HAD ENOUGH TO EAT, AYLEE?
I THINK SO!
RIFF, WAIT UNTIL YOU SEE WHAT AYLEE TURNS INTO! IT'S **SO** COOL!
NO TIME FOR THAT NOW, TORG! THAT POWER OUTAGE WAS **NOT** AN ACCIDENT. WE'VE GOT A **SABOTEUR!**
EVEN THOUGH THE POWER OUTAGE ONLY LASTED A SHORT TIME, MY REACTOR ALMOST **"BE-WOOPED"** ITSELF INTO A MELTDOWN! LIKE IT WAS **RIGGED** TO BLOW! BUT AT THE SAME TIME THE POWER FAILED, SOMEONE WAS ABLE TO BYPASS MY BATTERY-POWERED SECURITY SYSTEM AND TAMPER WITH MY COMPUTER. THE SABOTEUR WIPED MY HARD DRIVE TO COVER HIS TRAIL!
ZZZZZZZZ
worn
TA-DA!
OR IT COULD BE THAT AYLEE'S TURNED INTO AN ELECTROMAGNETIC PULSE GENERATOR.
BE-WOOP
BE-WOOP
BE-WOOP

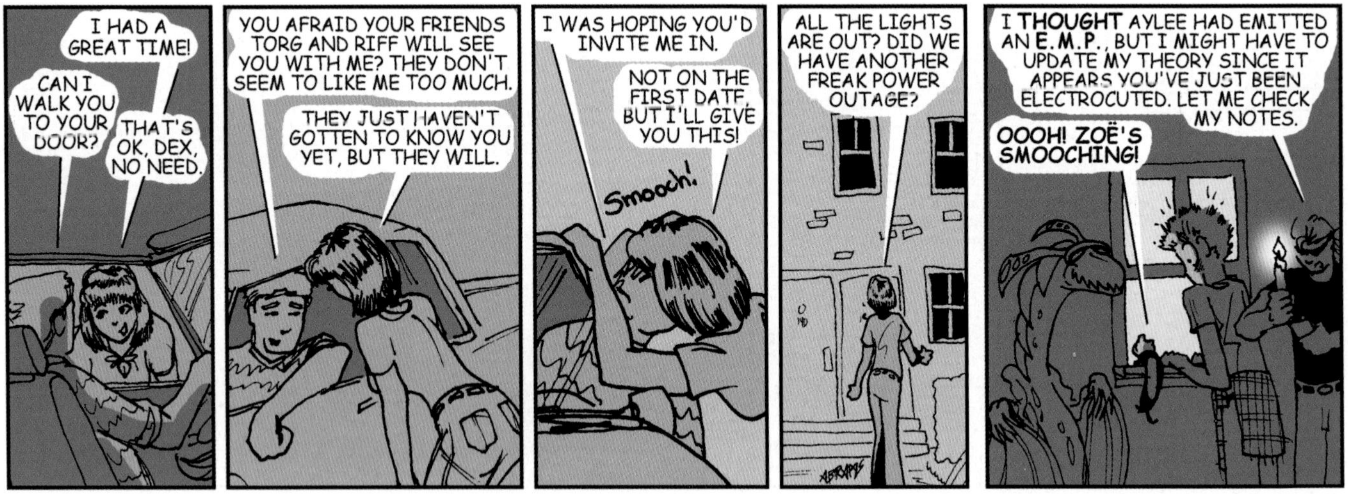
CAN I WALK YOU TO YOUR DOOR?
I HAD A GREAT TIME!
THAT'S OK, DEX, NO NEED.
YOU AFRAID YOUR FRIENDS TORG AND RIFF WILL SEE YOU WITH ME? THEY DON'T SEEM TO LIKE ME TOO MUCH.
THEY JUST HAVEN'T GOTTEN TO KNOW YOU YET, BUT THEY WILL.
I WAS HOPING YOU'D INVITE ME IN.
NOT ON THE FIRST DATE, BUT I'LL GIVE YOU THIS!
Smooch!
ALL THE LIGHTS ARE OUT? DID WE HAVE ANOTHER FREAK POWER OUTAGE?
I **THOUGHT** AYLEE HAD EMITTED AN **E.M.P.**, BUT I MIGHT HAVE TO UPDATE MY THEORY SINCE IT APPEARS YOU'VE JUST BEEN ELECTROCUTED. LET ME CHECK MY NOTES.
OOOH! ZOË'S SMOOCHING!

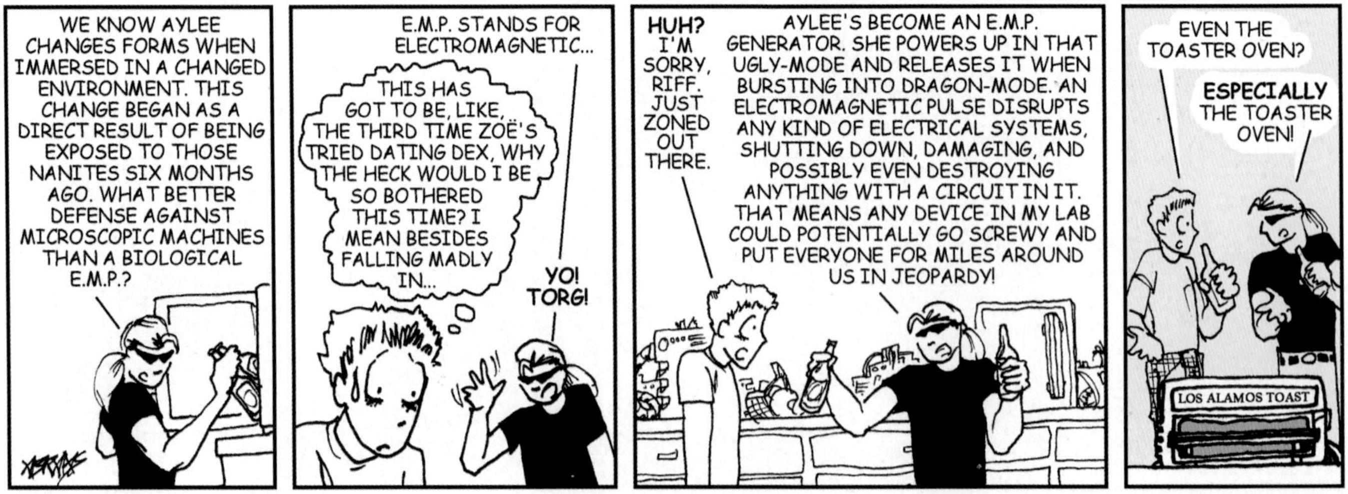
WE KNOW AYLEE CHANGES FORMS WHEN IMMERSED IN A CHANGED ENVIRONMENT. THIS CHANGE BEGAN AS A DIRECT RESULT OF BEING EXPOSED TO THOSE NANITES SIX MONTHS AGO. WHAT BETTER DEFENSE AGAINST MICROSCOPIC MACHINES THAN A BIOLOGICAL E.M.P.?
E.M.P. STANDS FOR ELECTROMAGNETIC...
THIS HAS GOT TO BE, LIKE, THE THIRD TIME ZOË'S TRIED DATING DEX, WHY THE HECK WOULD I BE SO BOTHERED THIS TIME? I MEAN BESIDES FALLING MADLY IN...
YO! TORG!
HUH? I'M SORRY, RIFF. JUST ZONED OUT THERE.
AYLEE'S BECOME AN E.M.P. GENERATOR. SHE POWERS UP IN THAT UGLY-MODE AND RELEASES IT WHEN BURSTING INTO DRAGON-MODE. AN ELECTROMAGNETIC PULSE DISRUPTS ANY KIND OF ELECTRICAL SYSTEMS, SHUTTING DOWN, DAMAGING, AND POSSIBLY EVEN DESTROYING ANYTHING WITH A CIRCUIT IN IT. THAT MEANS ANY DEVICE IN MY LAB COULD POTENTIALLY GO SCREWY AND PUT EVERYONE FOR MILES AROUND US IN JEOPARDY!
EVEN THE TOASTER OVEN?
ESPECIALLY THE TOASTER OVEN!
LOS ALAMOS TOAST

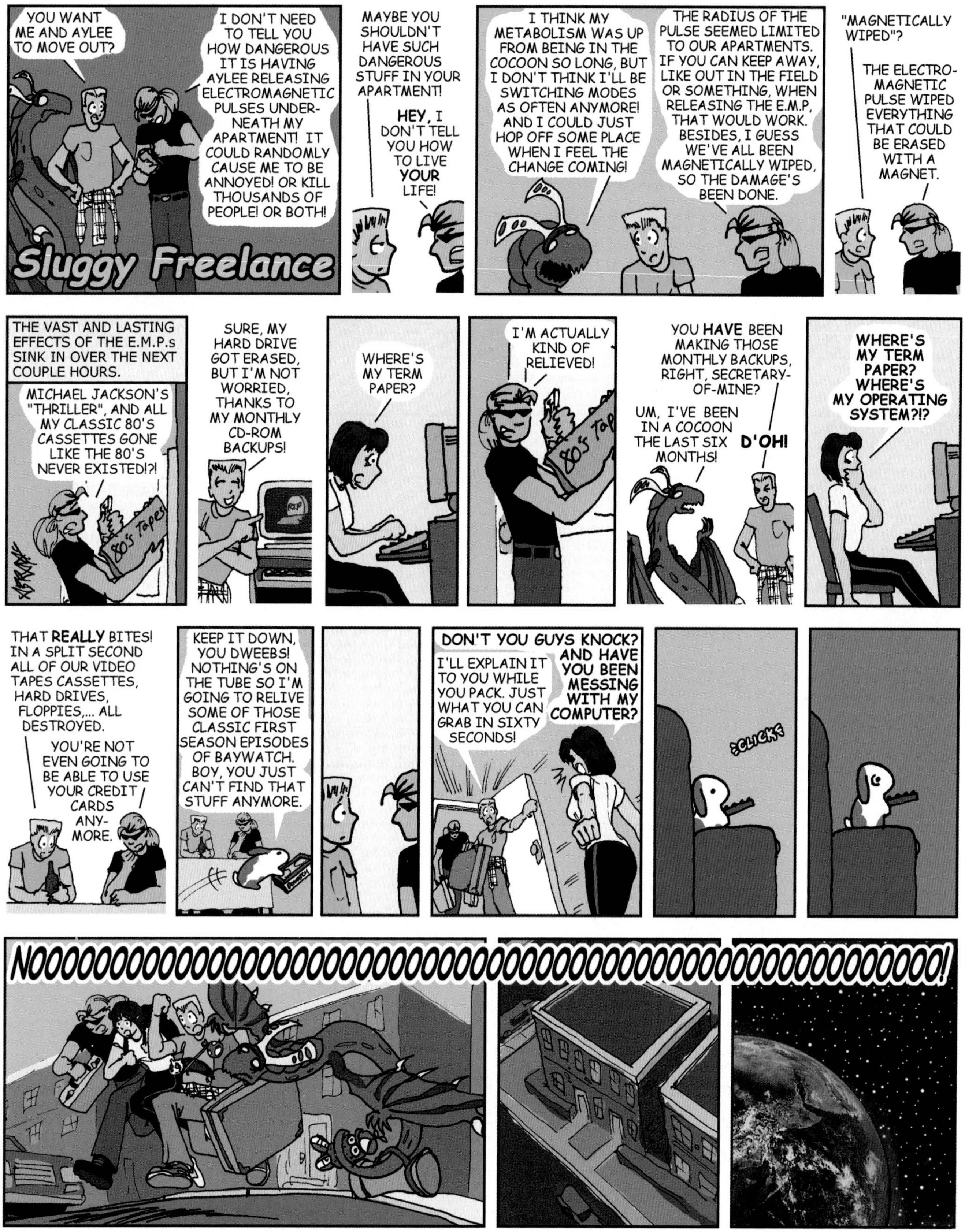
YOU WANT ME AND AYLEE TO MOVE OUT?
I DON'T NEED TO TELL YOU HOW DANGEROUS IT IS HAVING AYLEE RELEASING ELECTROMAGNETIC PULSES UNDERNEATH MY APARTMENT! IT COULD RANDOMLY CAUSE ME TO BE ANNOYED! OR KILL THOUSANDS OF PEOPLE! OR BOTH!
Sluggy Freelance
MAYBE YOU SHOULDN'T HAVE SUCH DANGEROUS STUFF IN YOUR APARTMENT!
HEY, I DON'T TELL YOU HOW TO LIVE YOUR LIFE!
I THINK MY METABOLISM WAS UP FROM BEING IN THE COCOON SO LONG, BUT I DON'T THINK I'LL BE SWITCHING MODES AS OFTEN ANYMORE! AND I COULD JUST HOP OFF SOME PLACE WHEN I FEEL THE CHANGE COMING!
THE RADIUS OF THE PULSE SEEMED LIMITED TO OUR APARTMENTS. IF YOU CAN KEEP AWAY, LIKE OUT IN THE FIELD OR SOMETHING, WHEN RELEASING THE E.M.P, THAT WOULD WORK. BESIDES, I GUESS WE'VE ALL BEEN MAGNETICALLY WIPED, SO THE DAMAGE'S BEEN DONE.
"MAGNETICALLY WIPED"?
THE ELECTROMAGNETIC PULSE WIPED EVERYTHING THAT COULD BE ERASED WITH A MAGNET.
THE VAST AND LASTING EFFECTS OF THE E.M.P.s SINK IN OVER THE NEXT COUPLE HOURS.
MICHAEL JACKSON'S "THRILLER", AND ALL MY CLASSIC 80'S CASSETTES GONE LIKE THE 80'S NEVER EXISTED!?!
80's Tapes
SURE, MY HARD DRIVE GOT ERASED, BUT I'M NOT WORRIED, THANKS TO MY MONTHLY CD-ROM BACKUPS!
WHERE'S MY TERM PAPER?
I'M ACTUALLY KIND OF RELIEVED!
YOU HAVE BEEN MAKING THOSE MONTHLY BACKUPS, RIGHT, SECRETARY-OF-MINE?
UM, I'VE BEEN IN A COCOON THE LAST SIX MONTHS!
D'OH!
WHERE'S MY TERM PAPER? WHERE'S MY OPERATING SYSTEM?!?
THAT REALLY BITES! IN A SPLIT SECOND ALL OF OUR VIDEO TAPES CASSETTES, HARD DRIVES, FLOPPIES,... ALL DESTROYED.
YOU'RE NOT EVEN GOING TO BE ABLE TO USE YOUR CREDIT CARDS ANYMORE.
KEEP IT DOWN, YOU DWEEBS! NOTHING'S ON THE TUBE SO I'M GOING TO RELIVE SOME OF THOSE CLASSIC FIRST SEASON EPISODES OF BAYWATCH. BOY, YOU JUST CAN'T FIND THAT STUFF ANYMORE.
DON'T YOU GUYS KNOCK? AND HAVE YOU BEEN MESSING WITH MY COMPUTER?
I'LL EXPLAIN IT TO YOU WHILE YOU PACK. JUST WHAT YOU CAN GRAB IN SIXTY SECONDS!
CLICK
NOOOOOOOOOOOOOOOOOOOOOOOOOOOOOOOOOOOOOOOOOOOOOOOOOOOOOOOOOOOO!

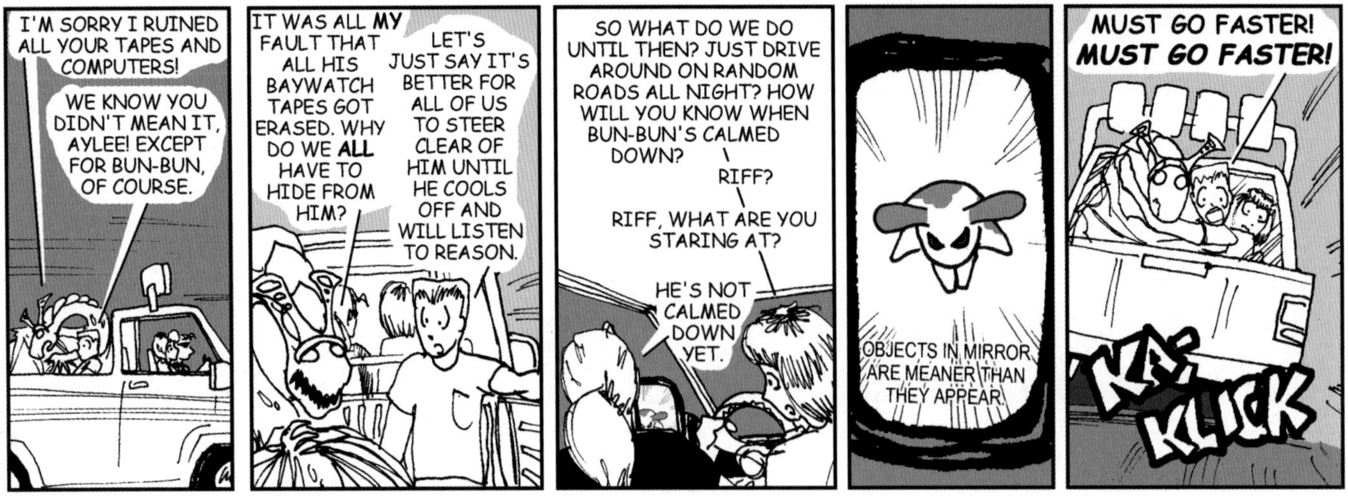
I'M SORRY I RUINED ALL YOUR TAPES AND COMPUTERS!
WE KNOW YOU DIDN'T MEAN IT, AYLEE! EXCEPT FOR BUN-BUN, OF COURSE.
IT WAS ALL MY FAULT THAT ALL HIS BAYWATCH TAPES GOT ERASED. WHY DO WE ALL HAVE TO HIDE FROM HIM?
LET'S JUST SAY IT'S BETTER FOR ALL OF US TO STEER CLEAR OF HIM UNTIL HE COOLS OFF AND WILL LISTEN TO REASON.
SO WHAT DO WE DO UNTIL THEN? JUST DRIVE AROUND ON RANDOM ROADS ALL NIGHT? HOW WILL YOU KNOW WHEN BUN-BUN'S CALMED DOWN?
RIFF?
RIFF, WHAT ARE YOU STARING AT?
HE'S NOT CALMED DOWN YET.
OBJECTS IN MIRROR ARE MEANER THAN THEY APPEAR
MUST GO FASTER! MUST GO FASTER!
KA-KLICK

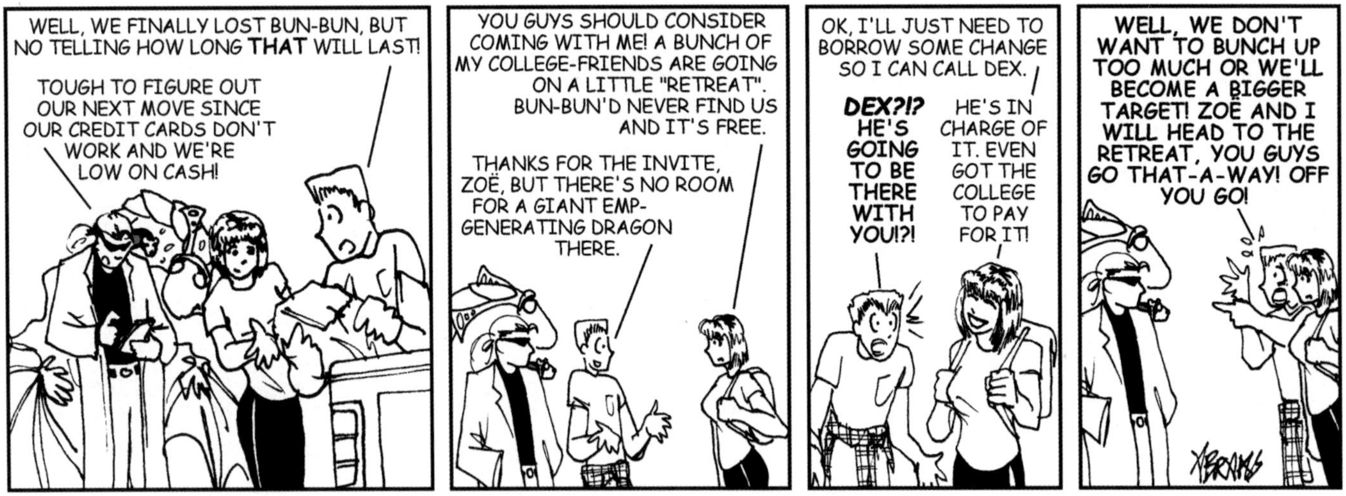
WELL, WE FINALLY LOST BUN-BUN, BUT NO TELLING HOW LONG THAT WILL LAST!
TOUGH TO FIGURE OUT OUR NEXT MOVE SINCE OUR CREDIT CARDS DON'T WORK AND WE'RE LOW ON CASH!
YOU GUYS SHOULD CONSIDER COMING WITH ME! A BUNCH OF MY COLLEGE-FRIENDS ARE GOING ON A LITTLE "RETREAT". BUN-BUN'D NEVER FIND US AND IT'S FREE.
THANKS FOR THE INVITE, ZOË, BUT THERE'S NO ROOM FOR A GIANT EMP-GENERATING DRAGON THERE.
OK, I'LL JUST NEED TO BORROW SOME CHANGE SO I CAN CALL DEX.
DEX?!? HE'S GOING TO BE THERE WITH YOU!?!
HE'S IN CHARGE OF IT. EVEN GOT THE COLLEGE TO PAY FOR IT!
WELL, WE DON'T WANT TO BUNCH UP TOO MUCH OR WE'LL BECOME A BIGGER TARGET! ZOË AND I WILL HEAD TO THE RETREAT, YOU GUYS GO THAT-A-WAY! OFF YOU GO!

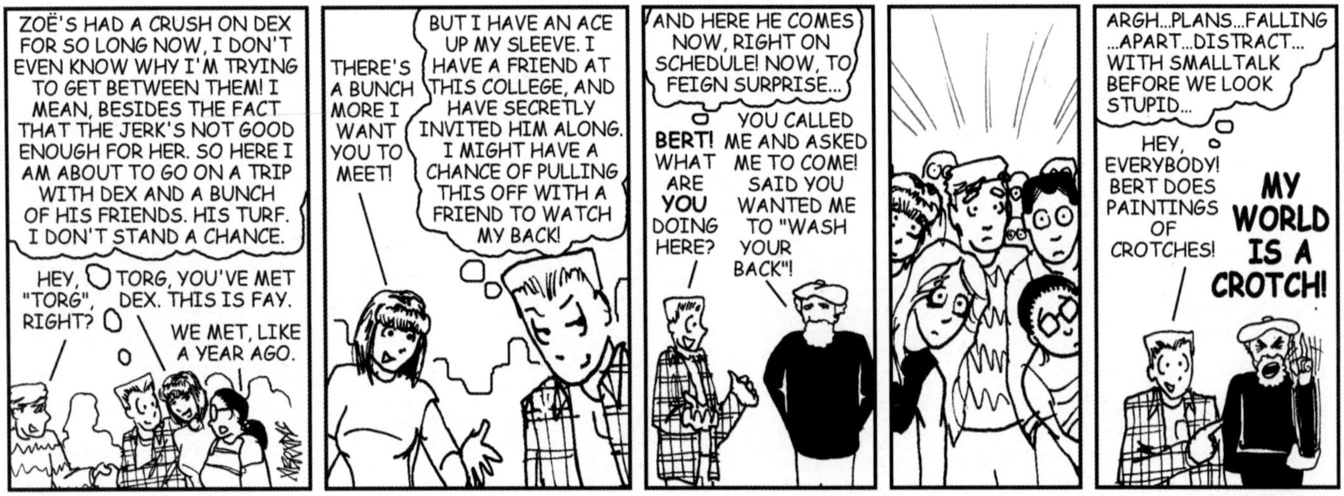
ZOË'S HAD A CRUSH ON DEX FOR SO LONG NOW, I DON'T EVEN KNOW WHY I'M TRYING TO GET BETWEEN THEM! I MEAN, BESIDES THE FACT THAT THE JERK'S NOT GOOD ENOUGH FOR HER. SO HERE I AM ABOUT TO GO ON A TRIP WITH DEX AND A BUNCH OF HIS FRIENDS. HIS TURF. I DON'T STAND A CHANCE.
HEY, "TORG", RIGHT?
TORG, YOU'VE MET DEX. THIS IS FAY.
WE MET, LIKE A YEAR AGO.
THERE'S A BUNCH MORE I WANT YOU TO MEET!
BUT I HAVE AN ACE UP MY SLEEVE. I HAVE A FRIEND AT THIS COLLEGE, AND HAVE SECRETLY INVITED HIM ALONG. I MIGHT HAVE A CHANCE OF PULLING THIS OFF WITH A FRIEND TO WATCH MY BACK!
AND HERE HE COMES NOW, RIGHT ON SCHEDULE! NOW, TO FEIGN SURPRISE...
BERT! WHAT ARE YOU DOING HERE?
YOU CALLED ME AND ASKED ME TO COME! SAID YOU WANTED ME TO "WASH YOUR BACK"!
ARGH...PLANS...FALLING ...APART...DISTRACT... WITH SMALLTALK BEFORE WE LOOK STUPID...
HEY, EVERYBODY! BERT DOES PAINTINGS OF CROTCHES!
MY WORLD IS A CROTCH!

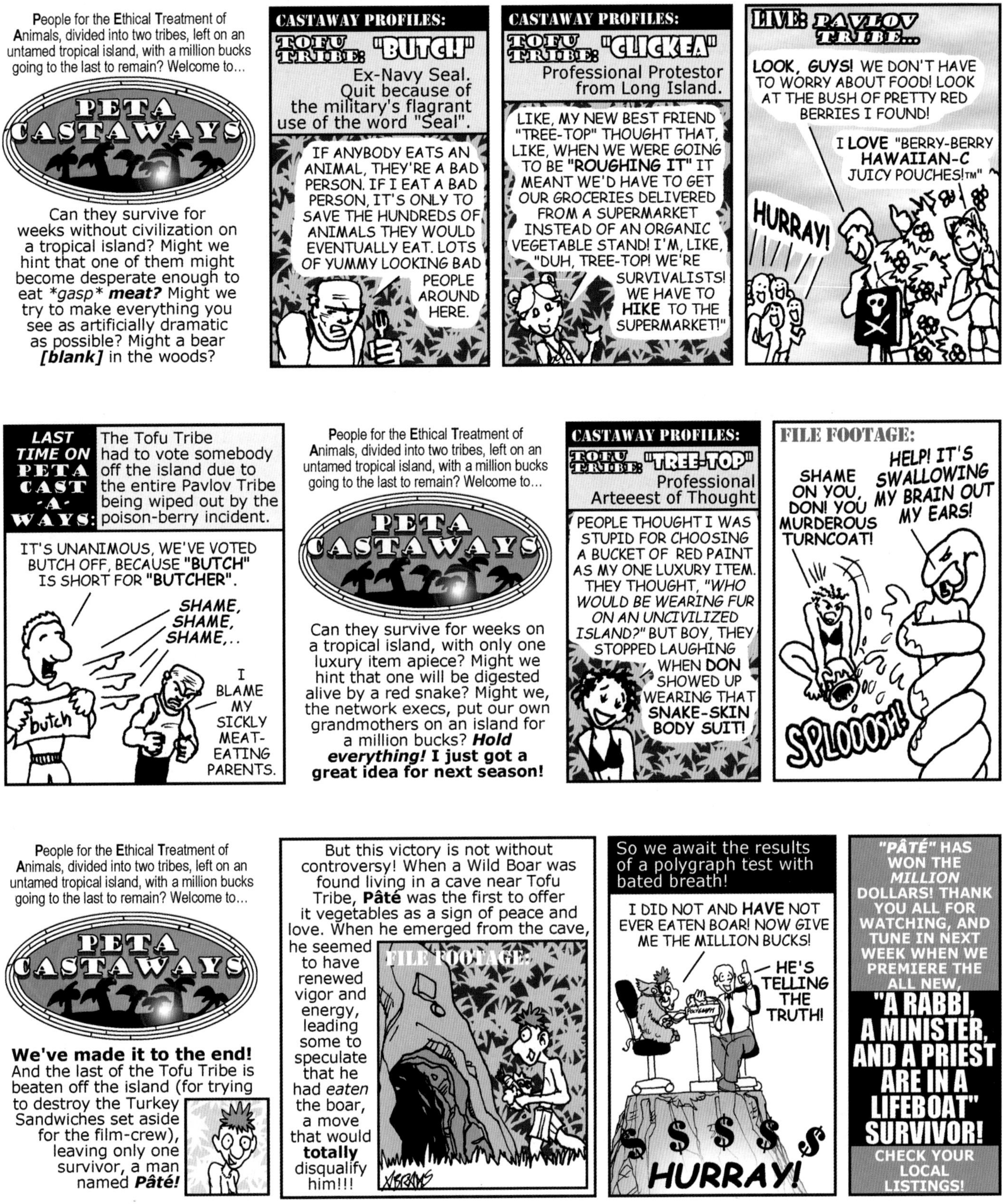
People for the Ethical Treatment of Animals, divided into two tribes, left on an untamed tropical island, with a million bucks going to the last to remain? Welcome to…
PETA CASTAWAYS
Can they survive for weeks without civilization on a tropical island? Might we hint that one of them might become desperate enough to eat *gasp* meat? Might we try to make everything you see as artificially dramatic as possible? Might a bear [blank] in the woods?
CASTAWAY PROFILES:
TOFU TRIBE: "BUTCH"
Ex-Navy Seal. Quit because of the military's flagrant use of the word "Seal".
IF ANYBODY EATS AN ANIMAL, THEY'RE A BAD PERSON. IF I EAT A BAD PERSON, IT'S ONLY TO SAVE THE HUNDREDS OF ANIMALS THEY WOULD EVENTUALLY EAT. LOTS OF YUMMY LOOKING BAD PEOPLE AROUND HERE.
CASTAWAY PROFILES:
TOFU TRIBE: "CLICKEA"
Professional Protestor from Long Island.
LIKE, MY NEW BEST FRIEND "TREE-TOP" THOUGHT THAT, LIKE, WHEN WE WERE GOING TO BE "ROUGHING IT" IT MEANT WE'D HAVE TO GET OUR GROCERIES DELIVERED FROM A SUPERMARKET INSTEAD OF AN ORGANIC VEGETABLE STAND! I'M, LIKE, "DUH, TREE-TOP! WE'RE SURVIVALISTS! WE HAVE TO HIKE TO THE SUPERMARKET!"
LIVE: PAVLOV TRIBE…
LOOK, GUYS! WE DON'T HAVE TO WORRY ABOUT FOOD! LOOK AT THE BUSH OF PRETTY RED BERRIES I FOUND!
I LOVE "BERRY-BERRY HAWAIIAN-C JUICY POUCHES!™"
HURRAY!
LAST TIME ON PETA CAST-A-WAYS:
The Tofu Tribe had to vote somebody off the island due to the entire Pavlov Tribe being wiped out by the poison-berry incident.
IT'S UNANIMOUS, WE'VE VOTED BUTCH OFF, BECAUSE "BUTCH" IS SHORT FOR "BUTCHER".
SHAME, SHAME, SHAME,..
I BLAME MY SICKLY MEAT-EATING PARENTS.
butch
People for the Ethical Treatment of Animals, divided into two tribes, left on an untamed tropical island, with a million bucks going to the last to remain? Welcome to…
PETA CASTAWAYS
Can they survive for weeks on a tropical island, with only one luxury item apiece? Might we hint that one will be digested alive by a red snake? Might we, the network execs, put our own grandmothers on an island for a million bucks? Hold everything! I just got a great idea for next season!
CASTAWAY PROFILES:
TOFU TRIBE: "TREE-TOP"
Professional Arteeest of Thought
PEOPLE THOUGHT I WAS STUPID FOR CHOOSING A BUCKET OF RED PAINT AS MY ONE LUXURY ITEM. THEY THOUGHT, "WHO WOULD BE WEARING FUR ON AN UNCIVILIZED ISLAND?" BUT BOY, THEY STOPPED LAUGHING WHEN DON SHOWED UP WEARING THAT SNAKE-SKIN BODY SUIT!
FILE FOOTAGE:
SHAME ON YOU, DON! YOU MURDEROUS TURNCOAT!
HELP! IT'S SWALLOWING MY BRAIN OUT MY EARS!
SPLOOOSH!
People for the Ethical Treatment of Animals, divided into two tribes, left on an untamed tropical island, with a million bucks going to the last to remain? Welcome to…
PETA CASTAWAYS
We've made it to the end! And the last of the Tofu Tribe is beaten off the island (for trying to destroy the Turkey Sandwiches set aside for the film-crew), leaving only one survivor, a man named Pâté!
But this victory is not without controversy! When a Wild Boar was found living in a cave near Tofu Tribe, Pâté was the first to offer it vegetables as a sign of peace and love. When he emerged from the cave, he seemed to have renewed vigor and energy, leading some to speculate that he had eaten the boar, a move that would totally disqualify him!!!
FILE FOOTAGE:
So we await the results of a polygraph test with bated breath!
I DID NOT AND HAVE NOT EVER EATEN BOAR! NOW GIVE ME THE MILLION BUCKS!
HE'S TELLING THE TRUTH!
HURRAY!
"PÂTÉ" HAS WON THE MILLION DOLLARS! THANK YOU ALL FOR WATCHING, AND TUNE IN NEXT WEEK WHEN WE PREMIERE THE ALL NEW,
"A RABBI, A MINISTER, AND A PRIEST ARE IN A LIFEBOAT" SURVIVOR!
CHECK YOUR LOCAL LISTINGS!

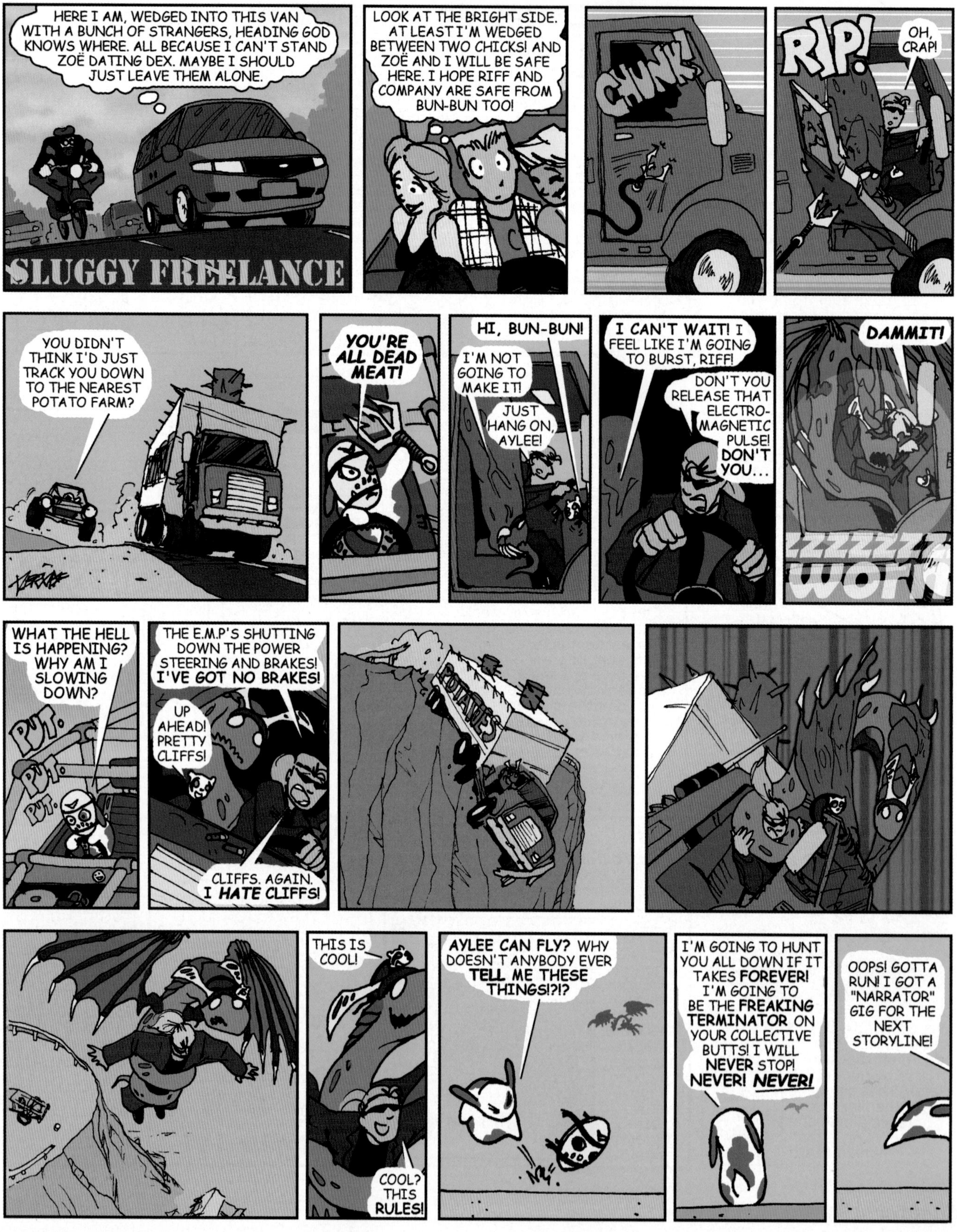
HERE I AM, WEDGED INTO THIS VAN WITH A BUNCH OF STRANGERS, HEADING GOD KNOWS WHERE. ALL BECAUSE I CAN'T STAND ZOË DATING DEX. MAYBE I SHOULD JUST LEAVE THEM ALONE.
SLUGGY FREELANCE
LOOK AT THE BRIGHT SIDE. AT LEAST I'M WEDGED BETWEEN TWO CHICKS! AND ZOË AND I WILL BE SAFE HERE. I HOPE RIFF AND COMPANY ARE SAFE FROM BUN-BUN TOO!
CHUNK!
RIP!
OH, CRAP!
YOU DIDN'T THINK I'D JUST TRACK YOU DOWN TO THE NEAREST POTATO FARM?
YOU'RE ALL DEAD MEAT!
HI, BUN-BUN!
I'M NOT GOING TO MAKE IT!
JUST HANG ON, AYLEE!
I CAN'T WAIT! I FEEL LIKE I'M GOING TO BURST, RIFF!
DON'T YOU RELEASE THAT ELECTRO-MAGNETIC PULSE! DON'T YOU...
DAMMIT!
ZZZZZZ
WOM
WHAT THE HELL IS HAPPENING? WHY AM I SLOWING DOWN?
PUT.
PUT.
PUT.
THE E.M.P'S SHUTTING DOWN THE POWER STEERING AND BRAKES! I'VE GOT NO BRAKES!
UP AHEAD! PRETTY CLIFFS!
CLIFFS. AGAIN. I HATE CLIFFS!
POTATOES
THIS IS COOL!
COOL? THIS RULES!
AYLEE CAN FLY? WHY DOESN'T ANYBODY EVER TELL ME THESE THINGS!?!?
I'M GOING TO HUNT YOU ALL DOWN IF IT TAKES FOREVER! I'M GOING TO BE THE FREAKING TERMINATOR ON YOUR COLLECTIVE BUTTS! I WILL NEVER STOP! NEVER! NEVER!
OOPS! GOTTA RUN! I GOT A "NARRATOR" GIG FOR THE NEXT STORYLINE!

KITTEN

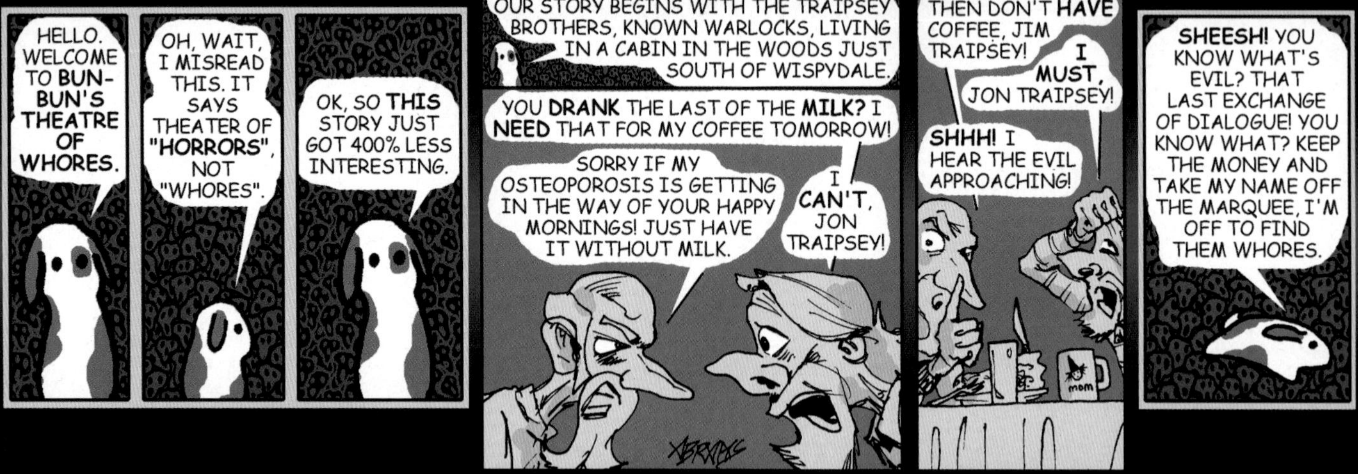
HELLO. WELCOME TO **BUN-BUN'S THEATRE OF WHORES**.
OH, WAIT, I MISREAD THIS. IT SAYS THEATER OF **"HORRORS"**, NOT "WHORES".
OK, SO **THIS** STORY JUST GOT 400% LESS INTERESTING.
OUR STORY BEGINS WITH THE TRAIPSEY BROTHERS, KNOWN WARLOCKS, LIVING IN A CABIN IN THE WOODS JUST SOUTH OF WISPYDALE.
YOU **DRANK** THE LAST OF THE **MILK?** I **NEED** THAT FOR MY COFFEE TOMORROW!
SORRY IF MY OSTEOPOROSIS IS GETTING IN THE WAY OF YOUR HAPPY MORNINGS! JUST HAVE IT WITHOUT MILK.
I **CAN'T**, JON TRAIPSEY!
THEN DON'T **HAVE** COFFEE, JIM TRAIPSEY!
I **MUST**, JON TRAIPSEY!
SHHH! I HEAR THE EVIL APPROACHING!
SHEESH! YOU KNOW WHAT'S EVIL? THAT LAST EXCHANGE OF DIALOGUE! YOU KNOW WHAT? KEEP THE MONEY AND TAKE MY NAME OFF THE MARQUEE, I'M OFF TO FIND THEM WHORES.

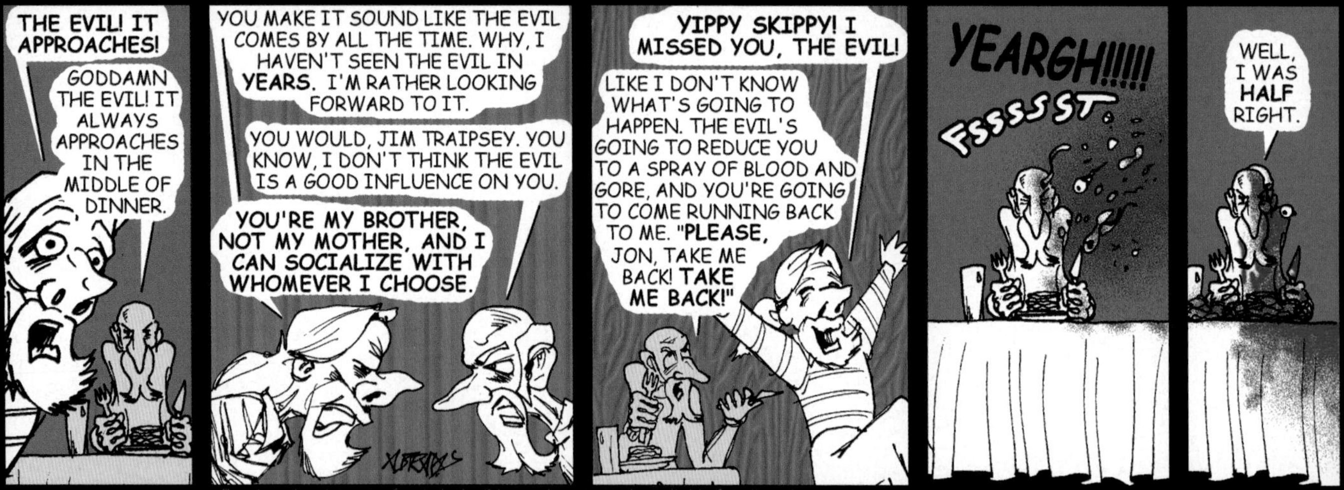
THE EVIL! IT APPROACHES!
GODDAMN THE EVIL! IT ALWAYS APPROACHES IN THE MIDDLE OF DINNER.
YOU MAKE IT SOUND LIKE THE EVIL COMES BY ALL THE TIME. WHY, I HAVEN'T SEEN THE EVIL IN **YEARS**. I'M RATHER LOOKING FORWARD TO IT.
YOU WOULD, JIM TRAIPSEY. YOU KNOW, I DON'T THINK THE EVIL IS A GOOD INFLUENCE ON YOU.
YOU'RE MY BROTHER, NOT MY MOTHER, AND I CAN SOCIALIZE WITH WHOMEVER I CHOOSE.
YIPPY SKIPPY! I MISSED YOU, THE EVIL!
LIKE I DON'T KNOW WHAT'S GOING TO HAPPEN. THE EVIL'S GOING TO REDUCE YOU TO A SPRAY OF BLOOD AND GORE, AND YOU'RE GOING TO COME RUNNING BACK TO ME. **"PLEASE,** JON, TAKE ME BACK! **TAKE ME BACK!"**
YEARGH!!!!!!
FSSSSST
WELL, I WAS **HALF** RIGHT.

Due to extensive use of red pixels, this comic may not be suitable for all audiences.

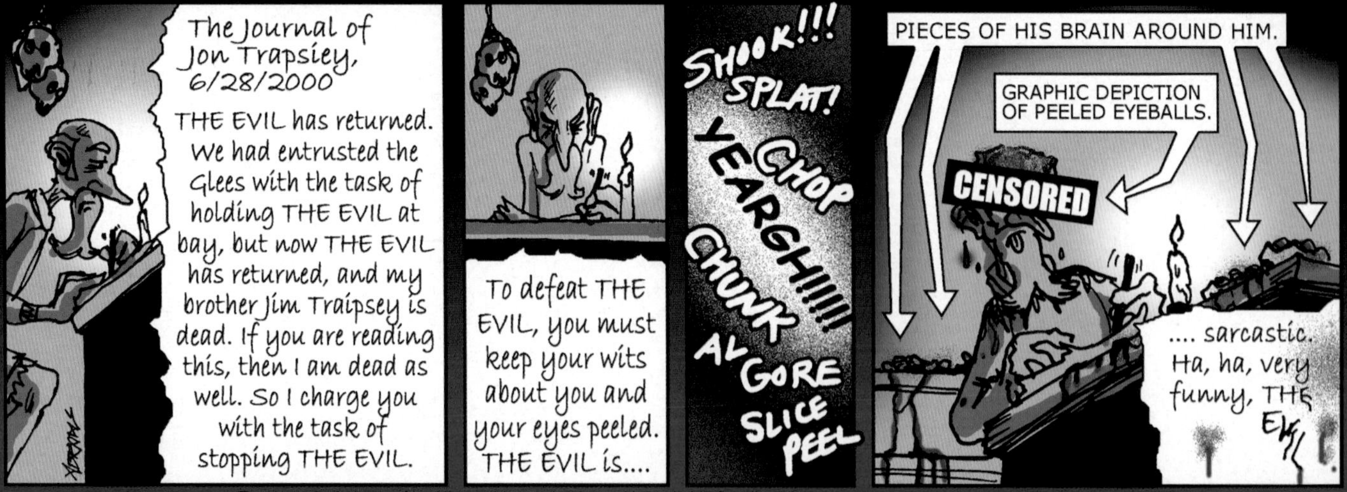
The Journal of Jon Trapsiey, 6/28/2000
THE EVIL has returned. We had entrusted the Glees with the task of holding THE EVIL at bay, but now THE EVIL has returned, and my brother Jim Traipsey is dead. If you are reading this, then I am dead as well. So I charge you with the task of stopping THE EVIL.
To defeat THE EVIL, you must keep your wits about you and your eyes peeled. THE EVIL is....
SHOOK!!!
SPLAT!
CHOP
YEARGH!!!!!!!
CHUNK
AV
GORE
SLICE
PEEL
PIECES OF HIS BRAIN AROUND HIM.
GRAPHIC DEPICTION OF PEELED EYEBALLS.
CENSORED
.... sarcastic. Ha, ha, very funny, THE EVIL

Due to repeated use of bad puns, this comic may not be suitable for all audiences.

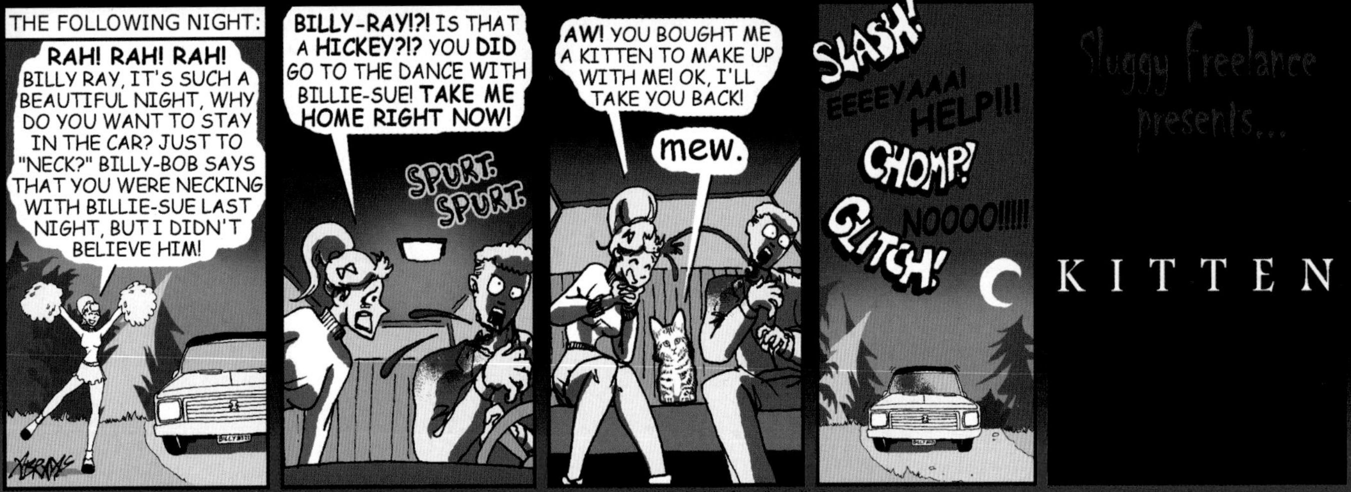
THE FOLLOWING NIGHT:
RAH! RAH! RAH! BILLY RAY, IT'S SUCH A BEAUTIFUL NIGHT, WHY DO YOU WANT TO STAY IN THE CAR? JUST TO "NECK?" BILLY-BOB SAYS THAT YOU WERE NECKING WITH BILLIE-SUE LAST NIGHT, BUT I DIDN'T BELIEVE HIM!
BILLY-RAY!?! IS THAT A HICKEY?!? YOU DID GO TO THE DANCE WITH BILLIE-SUE! TAKE ME HOME RIGHT NOW!
SPURT. SPURT.
AW! YOU BOUGHT ME A KITTEN TO MAKE UP WITH ME! OK, I'LL TAKE YOU BACK!
mew.
SLASH!
EEEEYAAA! HELP!!!
CHOMP!
NOOOO!!!!!
GLITCH!
Sluggy Freelance presents...
KITTEN

Due to repeated use of the name "Billy", this comic may not be suitable for all audiences.

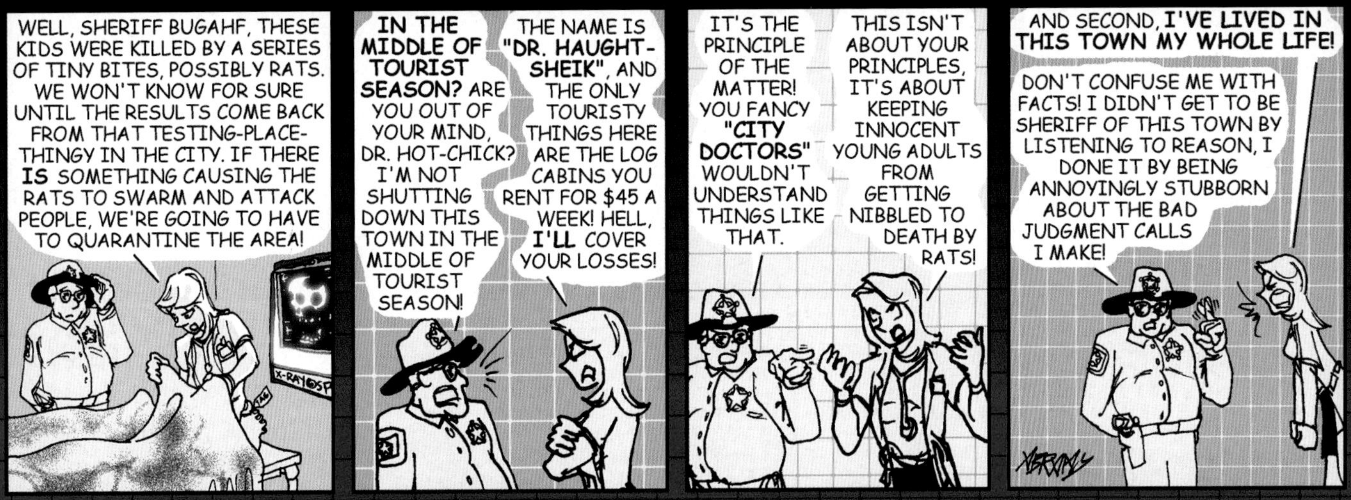
WELL, SHERIFF BUGAHF, THESE KIDS WERE KILLED BY A SERIES OF TINY BITES, POSSIBLY RATS. WE WON'T KNOW FOR SURE UNTIL THE RESULTS COME BACK FROM THAT TESTING-PLACE-THINGY IN THE CITY. IF THERE IS SOMETHING CAUSING THE RATS TO SWARM AND ATTACK PEOPLE, WE'RE GOING TO HAVE TO QUARANTINE THE AREA!
IN THE MIDDLE OF TOURIST SEASON? ARE YOU OUT OF YOUR MIND, DR. HOT-CHICK? I'M NOT SHUTTING DOWN THIS TOWN IN THE MIDDLE OF TOURIST SEASON!
THE NAME IS "DR. HAUGHT-SHEIK", AND THE ONLY TOURISTY THINGS HERE ARE THE LOG CABINS YOU RENT FOR $45 A WEEK! HELL, I'LL COVER YOUR LOSSES!
IT'S THE PRINCIPLE OF THE MATTER! YOU FANCY "CITY DOCTORS" WOULDN'T UNDERSTAND THINGS LIKE THAT.
THIS ISN'T ABOUT YOUR PRINCIPLES, IT'S ABOUT KEEPING INNOCENT YOUNG ADULTS FROM GETTING NIBBLED TO DEATH BY RATS!
AND SECOND, I'VE LIVED IN THIS TOWN MY WHOLE LIFE!
DON'T CONFUSE ME WITH FACTS! I DIDN'T GET TO BE SHERIFF OF THIS TOWN BY LISTENING TO REASON, I DONE IT BY BEING ANNOYINGLY STUBBORN ABOUT THE BAD JUDGMENT CALLS I MAKE!

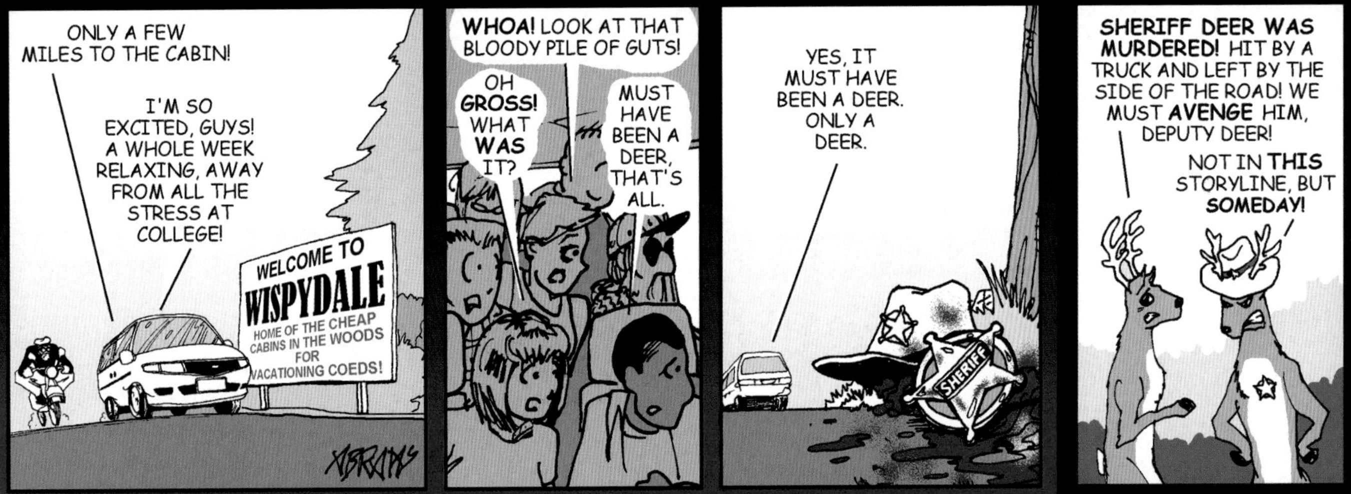
ONLY A FEW MILES TO THE CABIN!
I'M SO EXCITED, GUYS! A WHOLE WEEK RELAXING, AWAY FROM ALL THE STRESS AT COLLEGE!
WELCOME TO WISPYDALE
HOME OF THE CHEAP CABINS IN THE WOODS FOR VACATIONING COEDS!
WHOA! LOOK AT THAT BLOODY PILE OF GUTS!
OH GROSS! WHAT WAS IT?
MUST HAVE BEEN A DEER, THAT'S ALL.
YES, IT MUST HAVE BEEN A DEER. ONLY A DEER.
SHERIFF
SHERIFF DEER WAS MURDERED! HIT BY A TRUCK AND LEFT BY THE SIDE OF THE ROAD! WE MUST AVENGE HIM, DEPUTY DEER!
NOT IN THIS STORYLINE, BUT SOMEDAY!

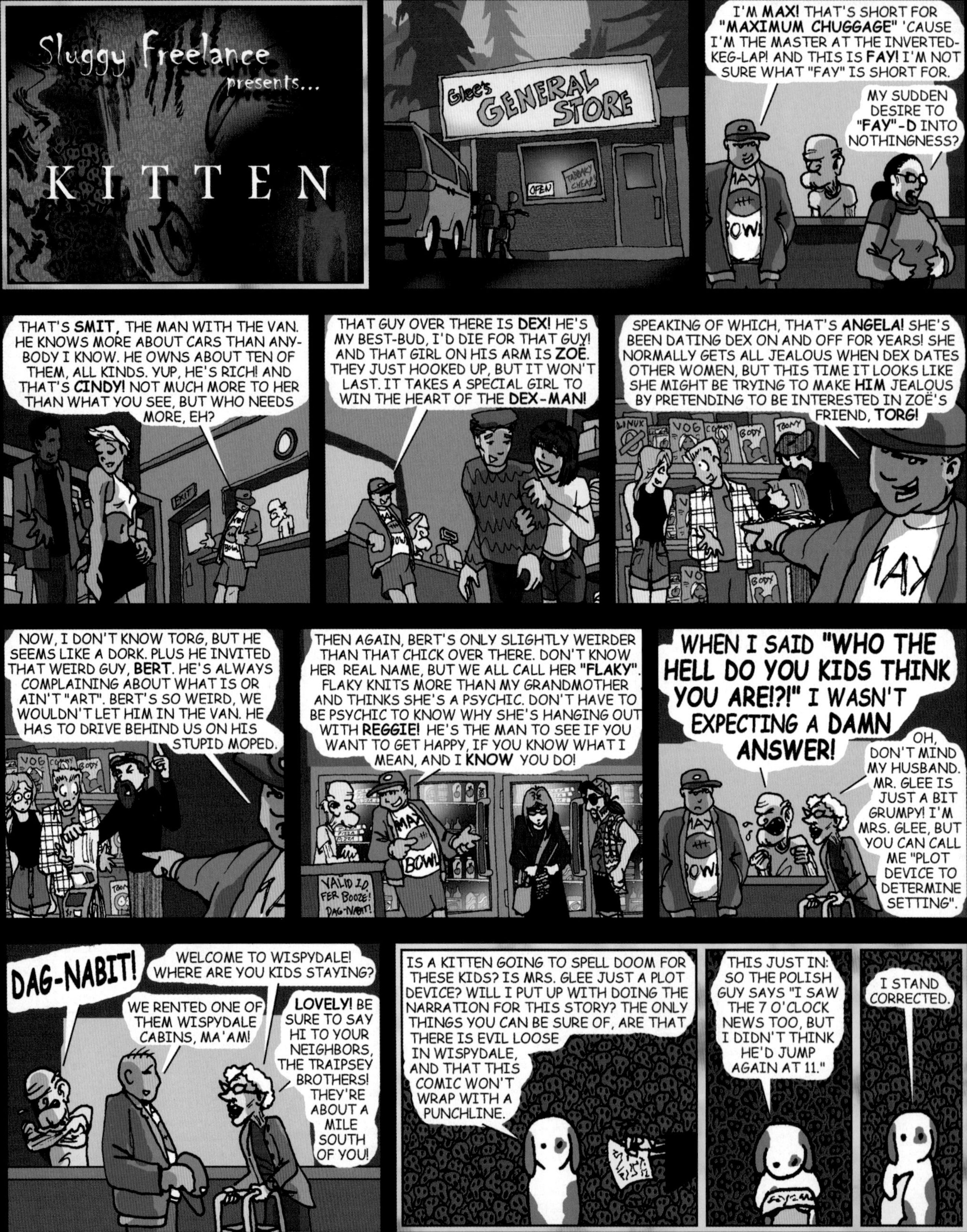
Sluggy Freelance
presents...
KITTEN
Glee's GENERAL STORE
OPEN
TABACKY CHEAP
I'M MAX! THAT'S SHORT FOR "MAXIMUM CHUGGAGE" 'CAUSE I'M THE MASTER AT THE INVERTED-KEG-LAP! AND THIS IS FAY! I'M NOT SURE WHAT "FAY" IS SHORT FOR.
MY SUDDEN DESIRE TO "FAY"-D INTO NOTHINGNESS?
THAT'S SMIT, THE MAN WITH THE VAN. HE KNOWS MORE ABOUT CARS THAN ANYBODY I KNOW. HE OWNS ABOUT TEN OF THEM, ALL KINDS. YUP, HE'S RICH! AND THAT'S CINDY! NOT MUCH MORE TO HER THAN WHAT YOU SEE, BUT WHO NEEDS MORE, EH?
EXIT
THAT GUY OVER THERE IS DEX! HE'S MY BEST-BUD, I'D DIE FOR THAT GUY! AND THAT GIRL ON HIS ARM IS ZOË. THEY JUST HOOKED UP, BUT IT WON'T LAST. IT TAKES A SPECIAL GIRL TO WIN THE HEART OF THE DEX-MAN!
SPEAKING OF WHICH, THAT'S ANGELA! SHE'S BEEN DATING DEX ON AND OFF FOR YEARS! SHE NORMALLY GETS ALL JEALOUS WHEN DEX DATES OTHER WOMEN, BUT THIS TIME IT LOOKS LIKE SHE MIGHT BE TRYING TO MAKE HIM JEALOUS BY PRETENDING TO BE INTERESTED IN ZOË'S FRIEND, TORG!
NOW, I DON'T KNOW TORG, BUT HE SEEMS LIKE A DORK. PLUS HE INVITED THAT WEIRD GUY, BERT. HE'S ALWAYS COMPLAINING ABOUT WHAT IS OR AIN'T "ART". BERT'S SO WEIRD, WE WOULDN'T LET HIM IN THE VAN. HE HAS TO DRIVE BEHIND US ON HIS STUPID MOPED.
THEN AGAIN, BERT'S ONLY SLIGHTLY WEIRDER THAN THAT CHICK OVER THERE. DON'T KNOW HER REAL NAME, BUT WE ALL CALL HER "FLAKY". FLAKY KNITS MORE THAN MY GRANDMOTHER AND THINKS SHE'S A PSYCHIC. DON'T HAVE TO BE PSYCHIC TO KNOW WHY SHE'S HANGING OUT WITH REGGIE! HE'S THE MAN TO SEE IF YOU WANT TO GET HAPPY, IF YOU KNOW WHAT I MEAN, AND I KNOW YOU DO!
VALID I.D. FER BOOZE! DAG-NABIT!
WHEN I SAID "WHO THE HELL DO YOU KIDS THINK YOU ARE!?!" I WASN'T EXPECTING A DAMN ANSWER!
OH, DON'T MIND MY HUSBAND. MR. GLEE IS JUST A BIT GRUMPY! I'M MRS. GLEE, BUT YOU CAN CALL ME "PLOT DEVICE TO DETERMINE SETTING".
DAG-NABIT!
WELCOME TO WISPYDALE! WHERE ARE YOU KIDS STAYING?
WE RENTED ONE OF THEM WISPYDALE CABINS, MA'AM!
LOVELY! BE SURE TO SAY HI TO YOUR NEIGHBORS, THE TRAIPSEY BROTHERS! THEY'RE ABOUT A MILE SOUTH OF YOU!
IS A KITTEN GOING TO SPELL DOOM FOR THESE KIDS? IS MRS. GLEE JUST A PLOT DEVICE? WILL I PUT UP WITH DOING THE NARRATION FOR THIS STORY? THE ONLY THINGS YOU CAN BE SURE OF, ARE THAT THERE IS EVIL LOOSE IN WISPYDALE, AND THAT THIS COMIC WON'T WRAP WITH A PUNCHLINE.
THIS JUST IN: SO THE POLISH GUY SAYS "I SAW THE 7 O'CLOCK NEWS TOO, BUT I DIDN'T THINK HE'D JUMP AGAIN AT 11."
I STAND CORRECTED.

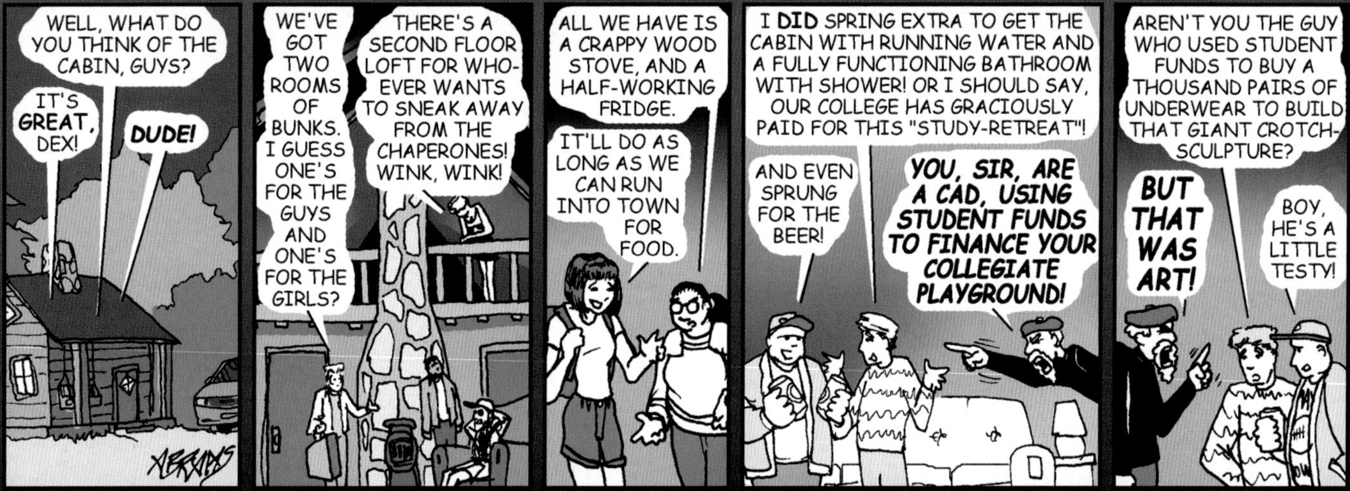
WELL, WHAT DO YOU THINK OF THE CABIN, GUYS?
IT'S GREAT, DEX!
DUDE!
WE'VE GOT TWO ROOMS OF BUNKS. I GUESS ONE'S FOR THE GUYS AND ONE'S FOR THE GIRLS?
THERE'S A SECOND FLOOR LOFT FOR WHO-EVER WANTS TO SNEAK AWAY FROM THE CHAPERONES! WINK, WINK!
ALL WE HAVE IS A CRAPPY WOOD STOVE, AND A HALF-WORKING FRIDGE.
IT'LL DO AS LONG AS WE CAN RUN INTO TOWN FOR FOOD.
I DID SPRING EXTRA TO GET THE CABIN WITH RUNNING WATER AND A FULLY FUNCTIONING BATHROOM WITH SHOWER! OR I SHOULD SAY, OUR COLLEGE HAS GRACIOUSLY PAID FOR THIS "STUDY-RETREAT"!
AND EVEN SPRUNG FOR THE BEER!
YOU, SIR, ARE A CAD, USING STUDENT FUNDS TO FINANCE YOUR COLLEGIATE PLAYGROUND!
AREN'T YOU THE GUY WHO USED STUDENT FUNDS TO BUY A THOUSAND PAIRS OF UNDERWEAR TO BUILD THAT GIANT CROTCH-SCULPTURE?
BUT THAT WAS ART!
BOY, HE'S A LITTLE TESTY!

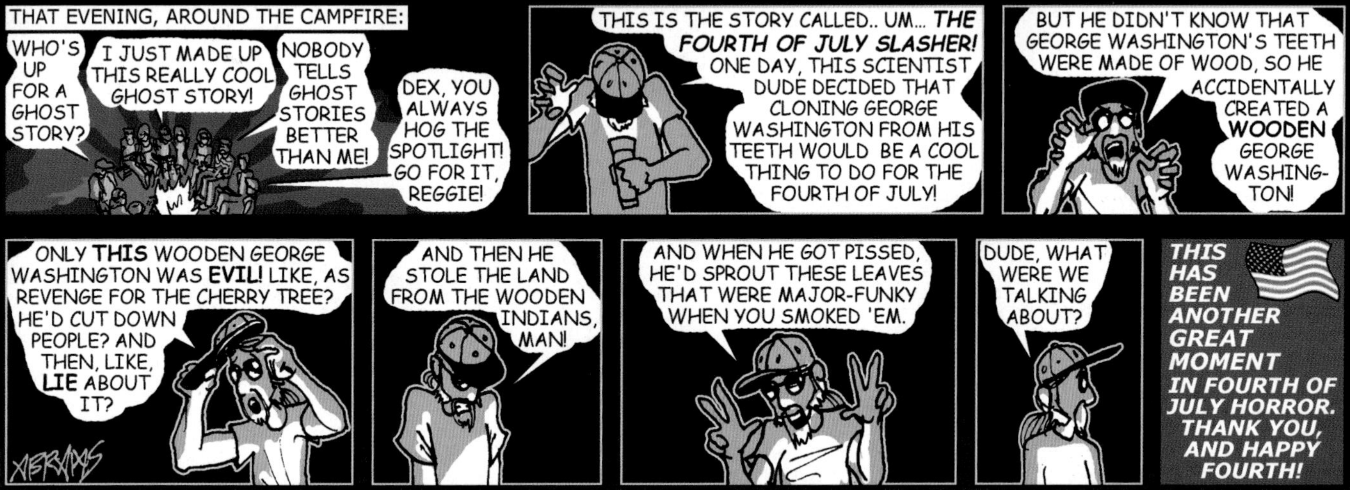
THAT EVENING, AROUND THE CAMPFIRE:
WHO'S UP FOR A GHOST STORY?
I JUST MADE UP THIS REALLY COOL GHOST STORY!
NOBODY TELLS GHOST STORIES BETTER THAN ME!
DEX, YOU ALWAYS HOG THE SPOTLIGHT! GO FOR IT, REGGIE!
THIS IS THE STORY CALLED.. UM... THE FOURTH OF JULY SLASHER! ONE DAY, THIS SCIENTIST DUDE DECIDED THAT CLONING GEORGE WASHINGTON FROM HIS TEETH WOULD BE A COOL THING TO DO FOR THE FOURTH OF JULY!
BUT HE DIDN'T KNOW THAT GEORGE WASHINGTON'S TEETH WERE MADE OF WOOD, SO HE ACCIDENTALLY CREATED A WOODEN GEORGE WASHING-TON!
ONLY THIS WOODEN GEORGE WASHINGTON WAS EVIL! LIKE, AS REVENGE FOR THE CHERRY TREE? HE'D CUT DOWN PEOPLE? AND THEN, LIKE, LIE ABOUT IT?
AND THEN HE STOLE THE LAND FROM THE WOODEN INDIANS, MAN!
AND WHEN HE GOT PISSED, HE'D SPROUT THESE LEAVES THAT WERE MAJOR-FUNKY WHEN YOU SMOKED 'EM.
DUDE, WHAT WERE WE TALKING ABOUT?
THIS HAS BEEN ANOTHER GREAT MOMENT IN FOURTH OF JULY HORROR. THANK YOU, AND HAPPY FOURTH!

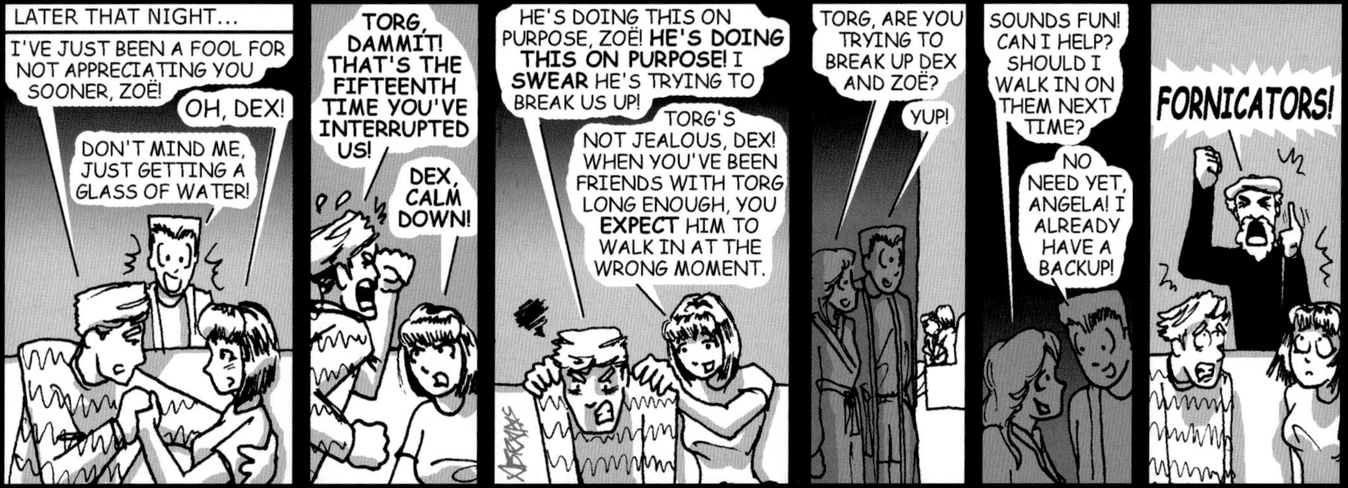
LATER THAT NIGHT...
I'VE JUST BEEN A FOOL FOR NOT APPRECIATING YOU SOONER, ZOË!
OH, DEX!
DON'T MIND ME, JUST GETTING A GLASS OF WATER!
TORG, DAMMIT! THAT'S THE FIFTEENTH TIME YOU'VE INTERRUPTED US!
DEX, CALM DOWN!
HE'S DOING THIS ON PURPOSE, ZOË! HE'S DOING THIS ON PURPOSE! I SWEAR HE'S TRYING TO BREAK US UP!
TORG'S NOT JEALOUS, DEX! WHEN YOU'VE BEEN FRIENDS WITH TORG LONG ENOUGH, YOU EXPECT HIM TO WALK IN AT THE WRONG MOMENT.
TORG, ARE YOU TRYING TO BREAK UP DEX AND ZOË?
YUP!
SOUNDS FUN! CAN I HELP? SHOULD I WALK IN ON THEM NEXT TIME?
NO NEED YET, ANGELA! I ALREADY HAVE A BACKUP!
FORNICATORS!

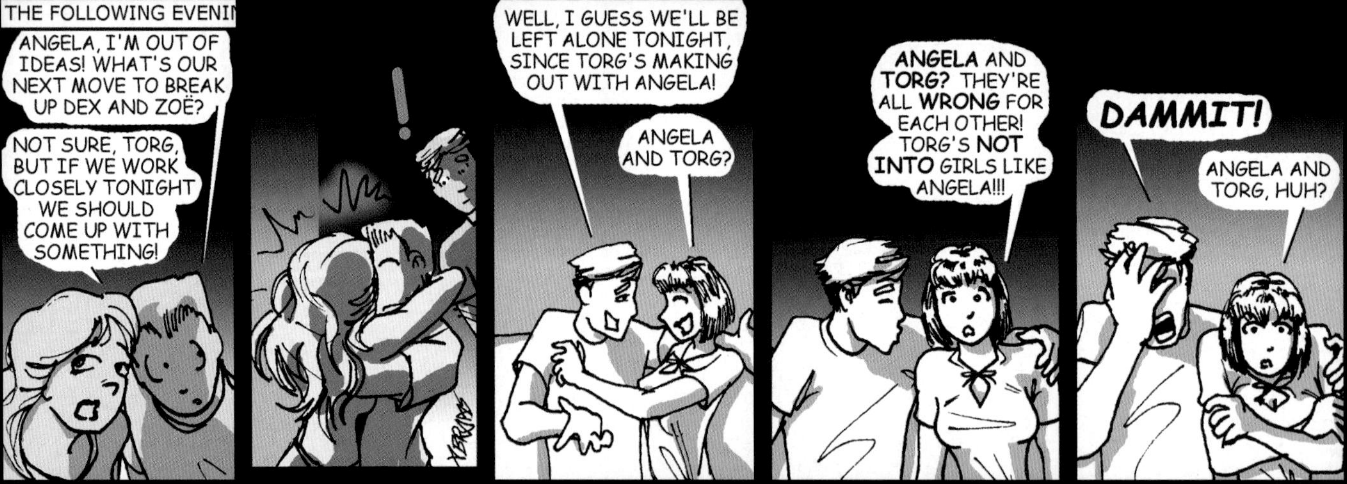
THE FOLLOWING EVENI
ANGELA, I'M OUT OF IDEAS! WHAT'S OUR NEXT MOVE TO BREAK UP DEX AND ZOË?
NOT SURE, TORG, BUT IF WE WORK CLOSELY TONIGHT WE SHOULD COME UP WITH SOMETHING!
!
WELL, I GUESS WE'LL BE LEFT ALONE TONIGHT, SINCE TORG'S MAKING OUT WITH ANGELA!
ANGELA AND TORG?
ANGELA AND TORG? THEY'RE ALL WRONG FOR EACH OTHER! TORG'S NOT INTO GIRLS LIKE ANGELA!!!
DAMMIT!
ANGELA AND TORG, HUH?

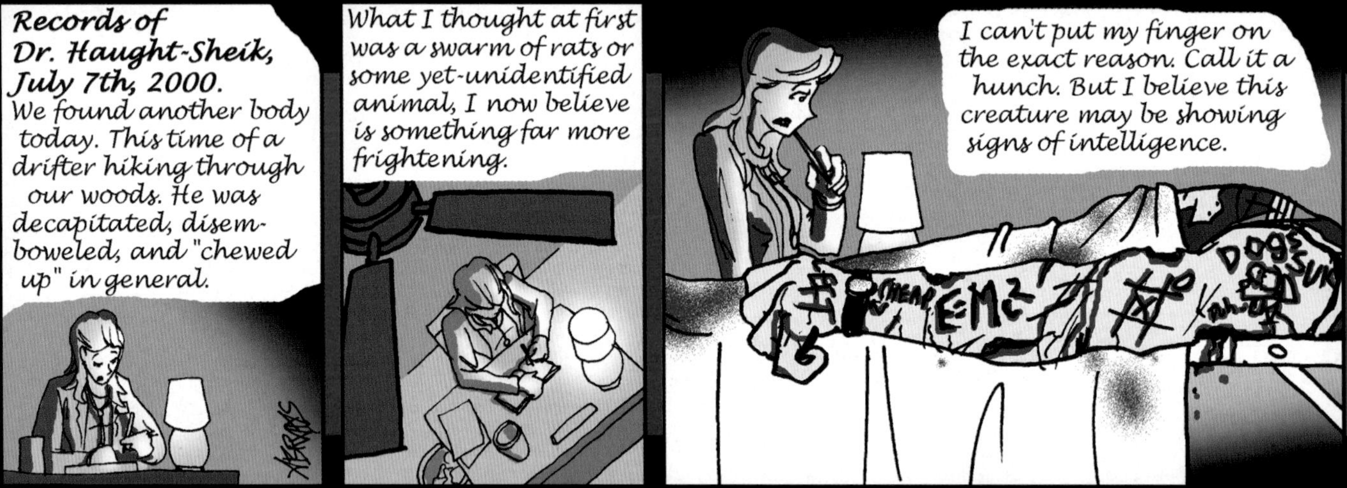
Records of Dr. Haught-Sheik, July 7th, 2000.
We found another body today. This time of a drifter hiking through our woods. He was decapitated, disemboweled, and "chewed up" in general.
What I thought at first was a swarm of rats or some yet-unidentified animal, I now believe is something far more frightening.
I can't put my finger on the exact reason. Call it a hunch. But I believe this creature may be showing signs of intelligence.
E=MC²

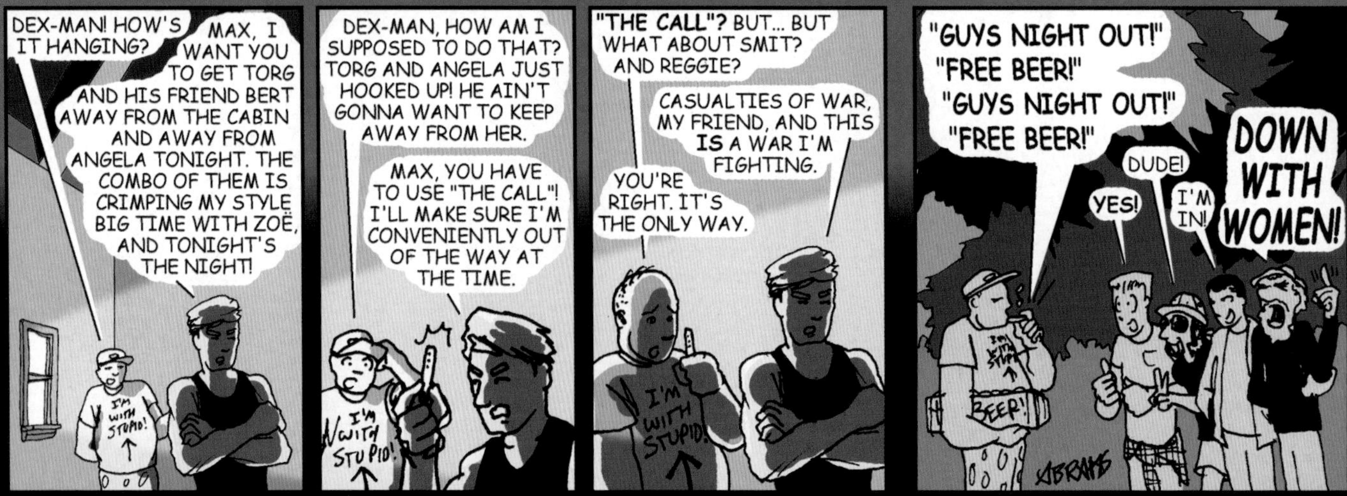
DEX-MAN! HOW'S IT HANGING?
MAX, I WANT YOU TO GET TORG AND HIS FRIEND BERT AWAY FROM THE CABIN AND AWAY FROM ANGELA TONIGHT. THE COMBO OF THEM IS CRIMPING MY STYLE BIG TIME WITH ZOË, AND TONIGHT'S THE NIGHT!
I'M WITH STUPID!
DEX-MAN, HOW AM I SUPPOSED TO DO THAT? TORG AND ANGELA JUST HOOKED UP! HE AIN'T GONNA WANT TO KEEP AWAY FROM HER.
MAX, YOU HAVE TO USE "THE CALL"! I'LL MAKE SURE I'M CONVENIENTLY OUT OF THE WAY AT THE TIME.
"THE CALL"? BUT... BUT WHAT ABOUT SMIT? AND REGGIE?
CASUALTIES OF WAR, MY FRIEND, AND THIS IS A WAR I'M FIGHTING.
YOU'RE RIGHT. IT'S THE ONLY WAY.
"GUYS NIGHT OUT!"
"FREE BEER!"
"GUYS NIGHT OUT!"
"FREE BEER!"
DUDE!
YES!
I'M IN!
DOWN WITH WOMEN!
BEER!

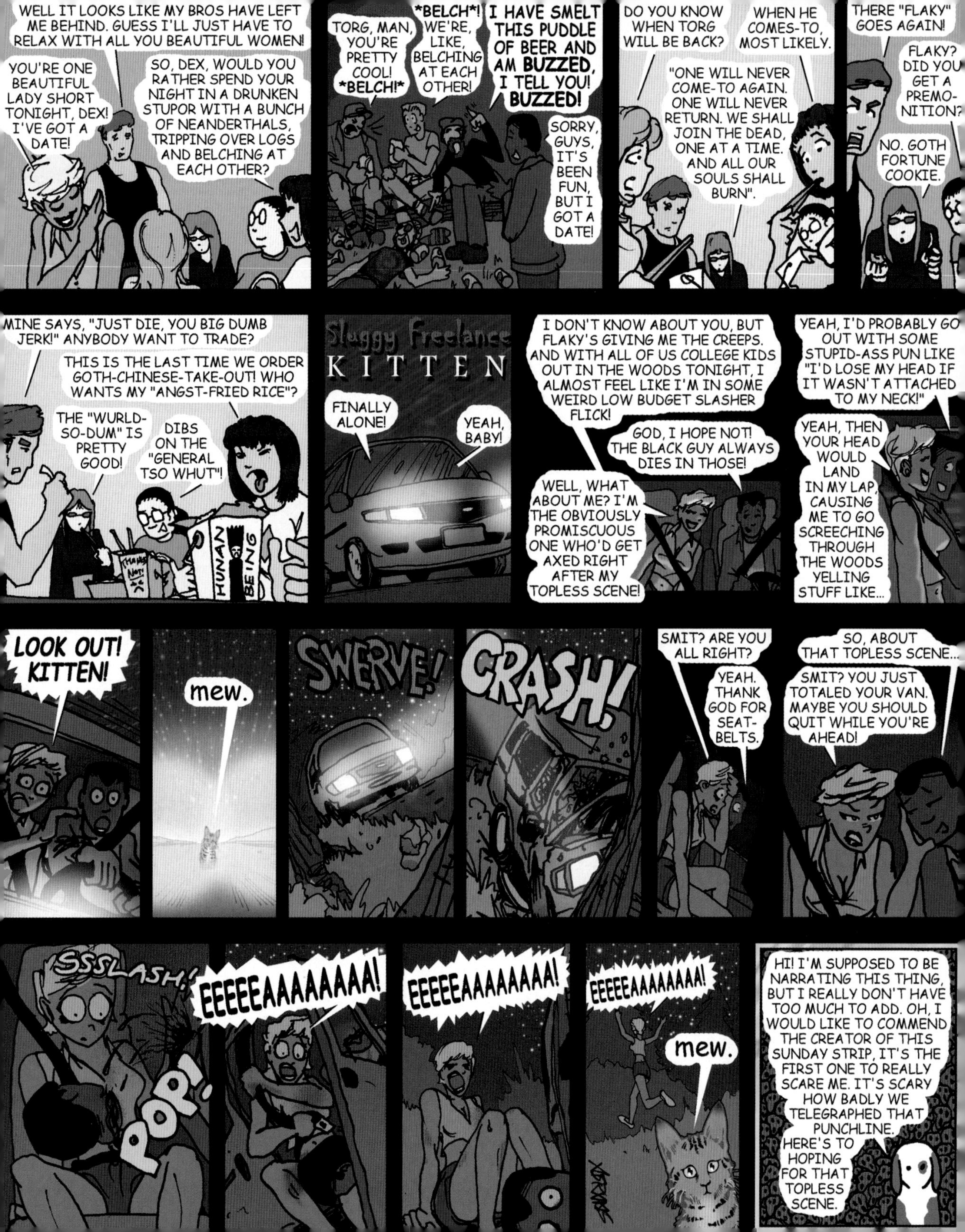
WELL IT LOOKS LIKE MY BROS HAVE LEFT ME BEHIND. GUESS I'LL JUST HAVE TO RELAX WITH ALL YOU BEAUTIFUL WOMEN!
YOU'RE ONE BEAUTIFUL LADY SHORT TONIGHT, DEX! I'VE GOT A DATE!
SO, DEX, WOULD YOU RATHER SPEND YOUR NIGHT IN A DRUNKEN STUPOR WITH A BUNCH OF NEANDERTHALS, TRIPPING OVER LOGS AND BELCHING AT EACH OTHER?
TORG, MAN, YOU'RE PRETTY COOL! *BELCH!*
BELCH! WE'RE, LIKE, BELCHING AT EACH OTHER!
I HAVE SMELT THIS PUDDLE OF BEER AND AM BUZZED, I TELL YOU! BUZZED!
SORRY, GUYS, IT'S BEEN FUN, BUT I GOT A DATE!
DO YOU KNOW WHEN TORG WILL BE BACK?
WHEN HE COMES-TO, MOST LIKELY.
"ONE WILL NEVER COME-TO AGAIN. ONE WILL NEVER RETURN. WE SHALL JOIN THE DEAD, ONE AT A TIME. AND ALL OUR SOULS SHALL BURN".
THERE "FLAKY" GOES AGAIN!
FLAKY? DID YOU GET A PREMONITION?
NO. GOTH FORTUNE COOKIE.
MINE SAYS, "JUST DIE, YOU BIG DUMB JERK!" ANYBODY WANT TO TRADE?
THIS IS THE LAST TIME WE ORDER GOTH-CHINESE-TAKE-OUT! WHO WANTS MY "ANGST-FRIED RICE"?
THE "WURLD-SO-DUM" IS PRETTY GOOD!
DIBS ON THE "GENERAL TSO WHUT"!
THANKS NOT!
HUNAN BEING
Sluggy Freelance
KITTEN
FINALLY ALONE!
YEAH, BABY!
I DON'T KNOW ABOUT YOU, BUT FLAKY'S GIVING ME THE CREEPS. AND WITH ALL OF US COLLEGE KIDS OUT IN THE WOODS TONIGHT, I ALMOST FEEL LIKE I'M IN SOME WEIRD LOW BUDGET SLASHER FLICK!
GOD, I HOPE NOT! THE BLACK GUY ALWAYS DIES IN THOSE!
WELL, WHAT ABOUT ME? I'M THE OBVIOUSLY PROMISCUOUS ONE WHO'D GET AXED RIGHT AFTER MY TOPLESS SCENE!
YEAH, I'D PROBABLY GO OUT WITH SOME STUPID-ASS PUN LIKE "I'D LOSE MY HEAD IF IT WASN'T ATTACHED TO MY NECK!"
YEAH, THEN YOUR HEAD WOULD LAND IN MY LAP, CAUSING ME TO GO SCREECHING THROUGH THE WOODS YELLING STUFF LIKE...
LOOK OUT! KITTEN!
mew.
SWERVE!
CRASH!
SMIT? ARE YOU ALL RIGHT?
YEAH. THANK GOD FOR SEAT-BELTS.
SO, ABOUT THAT TOPLESS SCENE...
SMIT? YOU JUST TOTALED YOUR VAN. MAYBE YOU SHOULD QUIT WHILE YOU'RE AHEAD!
SSSLASH!
POP!
EEEEEAAAAAAAA!
EEEEEAAAAAAAA!
EEEEEAAAAAAAA!
mew.
HI! I'M SUPPOSED TO BE NARRATING THIS THING, BUT I REALLY DON'T HAVE TOO MUCH TO ADD. OH, I WOULD LIKE TO COMMEND THE CREATOR OF THIS SUNDAY STRIP, IT'S THE FIRST ONE TO REALLY SCARE ME. IT'S SCARY HOW BADLY WE TELEGRAPHED THAT PUNCHLINE.
HERE'S TO HOPING FOR THAT TOPLESS SCENE.

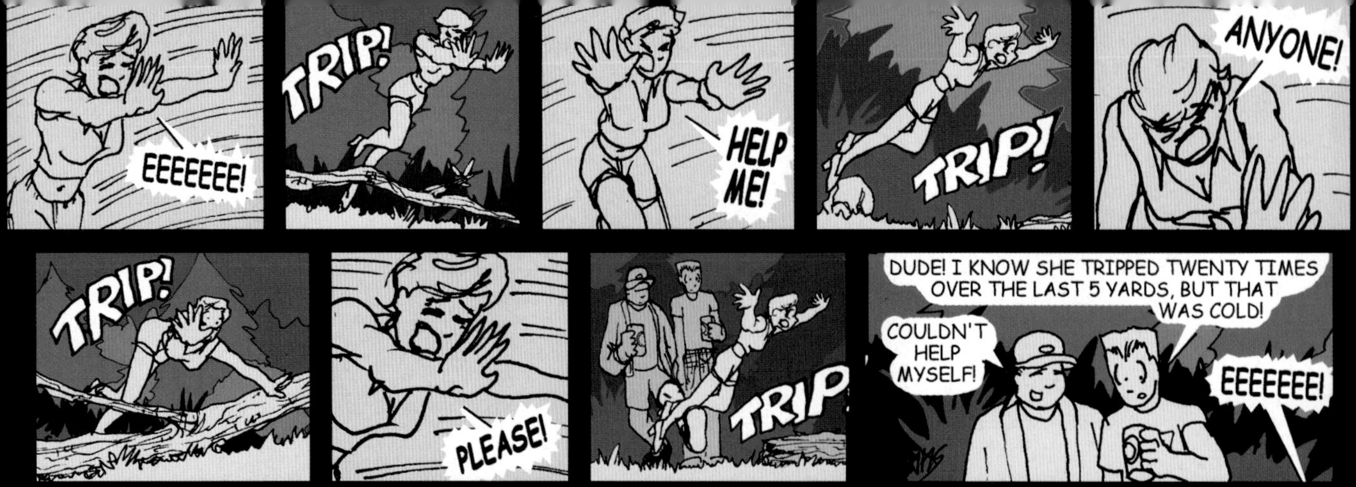
EEEEEEE!
TRIP!
HELP ME!
TRIP!
ANYONE!
TRIP!
PLEASE!
TRIP!
DUDE! I KNOW SHE TRIPPED TWENTY TIMES OVER THE LAST 5 YARDS, BUT THAT WAS COLD!
COULDN'T HELP MYSELF!
EEEEEEE!

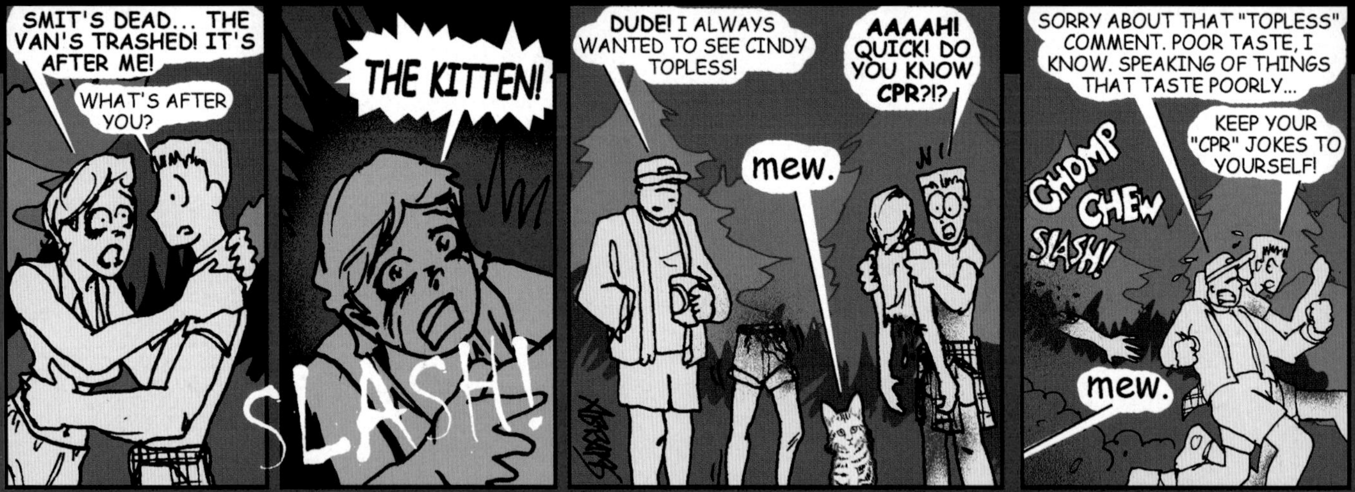
SMIT'S DEAD... THE VAN'S TRASHED! IT'S AFTER ME!
WHAT'S AFTER YOU?
THE KITTEN!
SLASH!
DUDE! I ALWAYS WANTED TO SEE CINDY TOPLESS!
AAAAH! QUICK! DO YOU KNOW CPR?!?
mew.
SORRY ABOUT THAT "TOPLESS" COMMENT. POOR TASTE, I KNOW. SPEAKING OF THINGS THAT TASTE POORLY...
KEEP YOUR "CPR" JOKES TO YOURSELF!
CHOMP
CHEW
SLASH!
mew.

Due to gratuitous topless scenes, this comic may not be suitable for all audiences.

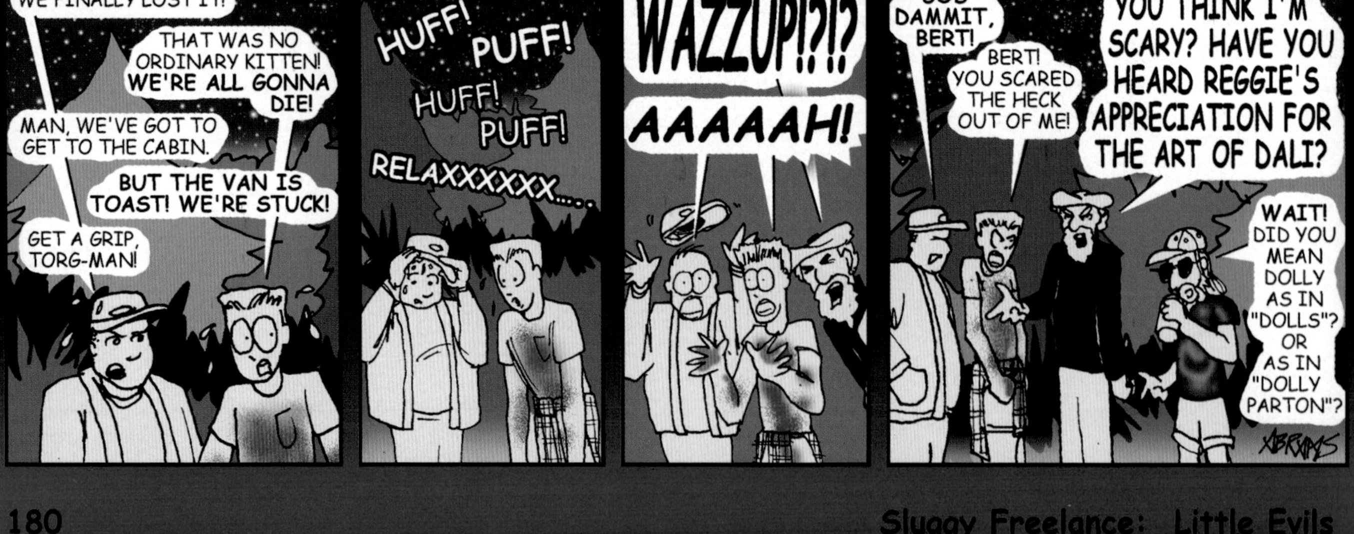
WE FINALLY LOST IT!
THAT WAS NO ORDINARY KITTEN! WE'RE ALL GONNA DIE!
MAN, WE'VE GOT TO GET TO THE CABIN.
BUT THE VAN IS TOAST! WE'RE STUCK!
GET A GRIP, TORG-MAN!
HUFF! PUFF!
HUFF! PUFF!
RELAXXXXXX.....
WAZZUP!?!?
AAAAAH!
GOD DAMMIT, BERT!
BERT! YOU SCARED THE HECK OUT OF ME!
YOU THINK I'M SCARY? HAVE YOU HEARD REGGIE'S APPRECIATION FOR THE ART OF DALI?
WAIT! DID YOU MEAN DOLLY AS IN "DOLLS"? OR AS IN "DOLLY PARTON"?

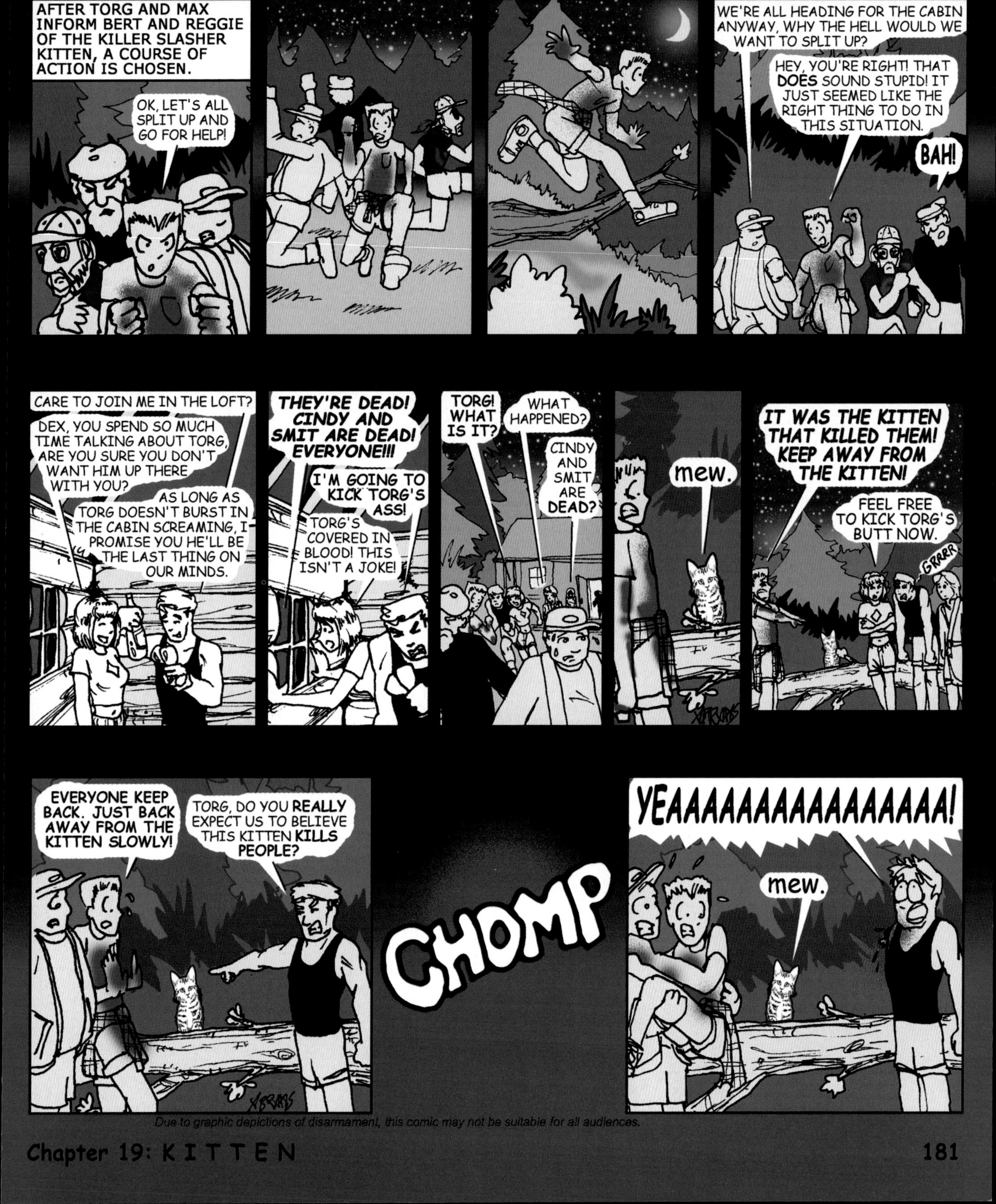
AFTER TORG AND MAX INFORM BERT AND REGGIE OF THE KILLER SLASHER KITTEN, A COURSE OF ACTION IS CHOSEN.
OK, LET'S ALL SPLIT UP AND GO FOR HELP!
WE'RE ALL HEADING FOR THE CABIN ANYWAY, WHY THE HELL WOULD WE WANT TO SPLIT UP?
HEY, YOU'RE RIGHT! THAT DOES SOUND STUPID! IT JUST SEEMED LIKE THE RIGHT THING TO DO IN THIS SITUATION.
BAH!
CARE TO JOIN ME IN THE LOFT?
DEX, YOU SPEND SO MUCH TIME TALKING ABOUT TORG, ARE YOU SURE YOU DON'T WANT HIM UP THERE WITH YOU?
AS LONG AS TORG DOESN'T BURST IN THE CABIN SCREAMING, I PROMISE YOU HE'LL BE THE LAST THING ON OUR MINDS.
THEY'RE DEAD! CINDY AND SMIT ARE DEAD! EVERYONE!!!
I'M GOING TO KICK TORG'S ASS!
TORG'S COVERED IN BLOOD! THIS ISN'T A JOKE!
TORG! WHAT IS IT?
WHAT HAPPENED?
CINDY AND SMIT ARE DEAD?
mew.
IT WAS THE KITTEN THAT KILLED THEM! KEEP AWAY FROM THE KITTEN!
FEEL FREE TO KICK TORG'S BUTT NOW.
GRRRR
EVERYONE KEEP BACK. JUST BACK AWAY FROM THE KITTEN SLOWLY!
TORG, DO YOU REALLY EXPECT US TO BELIEVE THIS KITTEN KILLS PEOPLE?
CHOMP
YEAAAAAAAAAAAAAAA!
mew.

Due to graphic depictions of disarmament, this comic may not be suitable for all audiences.

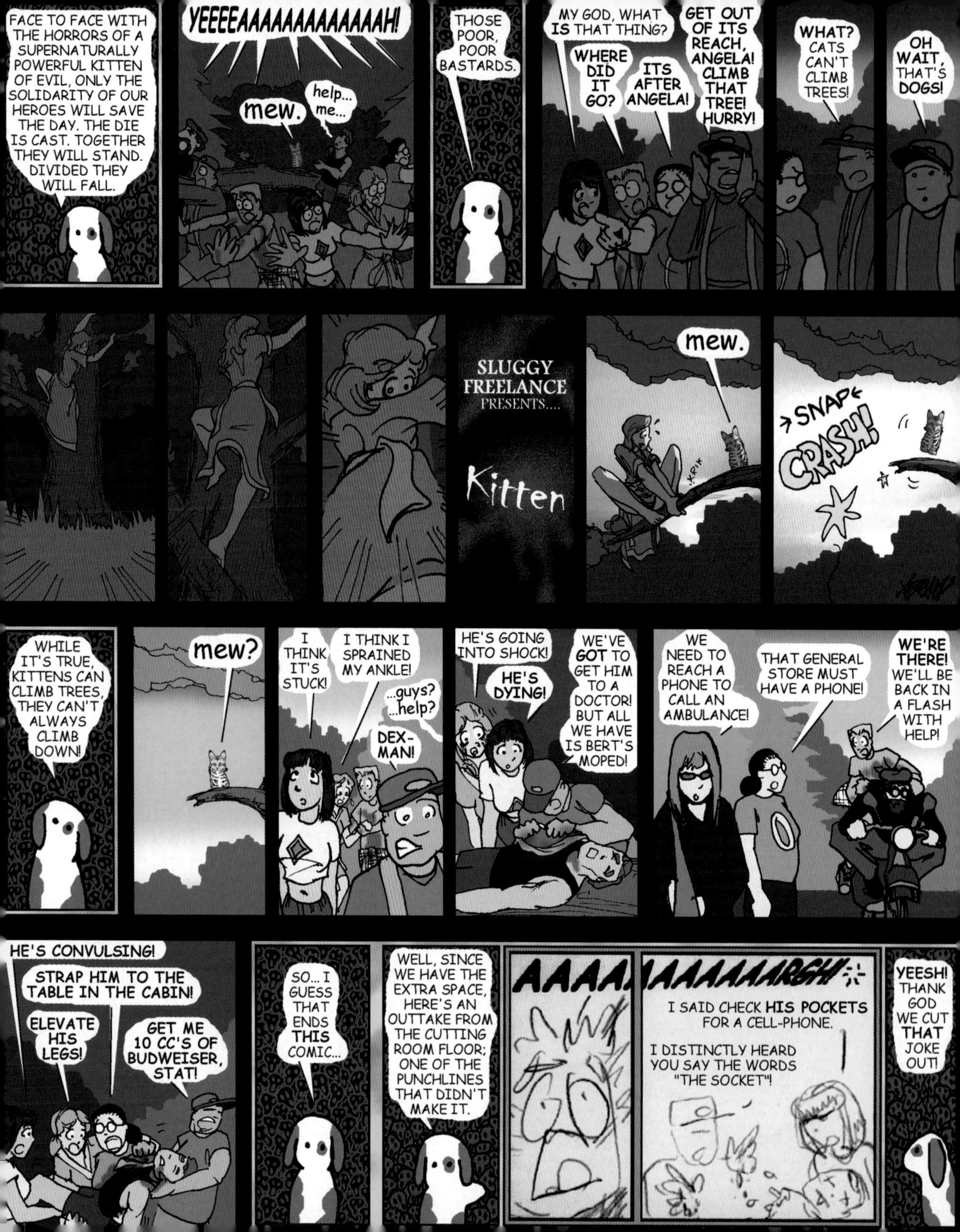

FACE TO FACE WITH THE HORRORS OF A SUPERNATURALLY POWERFUL KITTEN OF EVIL, ONLY THE SOLIDARITY OF OUR HEROES WILL SAVE THE DAY. THE DIE IS CAST. TOGETHER THEY WILL STAND. DIVIDED THEY WILL FALL.
YEEEEAAAAAAAAAAAAAH!
mew.
help... me...
THOSE POOR, POOR BASTARDS.
MY GOD, WHAT IS THAT THING?
WHERE DID IT GO?
ITS AFTER ANGELA!
GET OUT OF ITS REACH, ANGELA! CLIMB THAT TREE! HURRY!
WHAT? CATS CAN'T CLIMB TREES!
OH WAIT, THAT'S DOGS!
SLUGGY FREELANCE PRESENTS....
Kitten
mew.
KRIK
SNAP
CRASH!
WHILE IT'S TRUE, KITTENS CAN CLIMB TREES, THEY CAN'T ALWAYS CLIMB DOWN!
mew?
I THINK IT'S STUCK!
I THINK I SPRAINED MY ANKLE!
...guys? ...help?
DEX-MAN!
HE'S GOING INTO SHOCK!
HE'S DYING!
WE'VE GOT TO GET HIM TO A DOCTOR! BUT ALL WE HAVE IS BERT'S MOPED!
WE NEED TO REACH A PHONE TO CALL AN AMBULANCE!
THAT GENERAL STORE MUST HAVE A PHONE!
WE'RE THERE! WE'LL BE BACK IN A FLASH WITH HELP!
HE'S CONVULSING!
STRAP HIM TO THE TABLE IN THE CABIN!
ELEVATE HIS LEGS!
GET ME 10 CC'S OF BUDWEISER, STAT!
SO... I GUESS THAT ENDS THIS COMIC...
WELL, SINCE WE HAVE THE EXTRA SPACE, HERE'S AN OUTTAKE FROM THE CUTTING ROOM FLOOR; ONE OF THE PUNCHLINES THAT DIDN'T MAKE IT.
AAAAAAAAAAAAARGH!
I SAID CHECK HIS POCKETS FOR A CELL-PHONE.
I DISTINCTLY HEARD YOU SAY THE WORDS "THE SOCKET"!
YEESH! THANK GOD WE CUT THAT JOKE OUT!

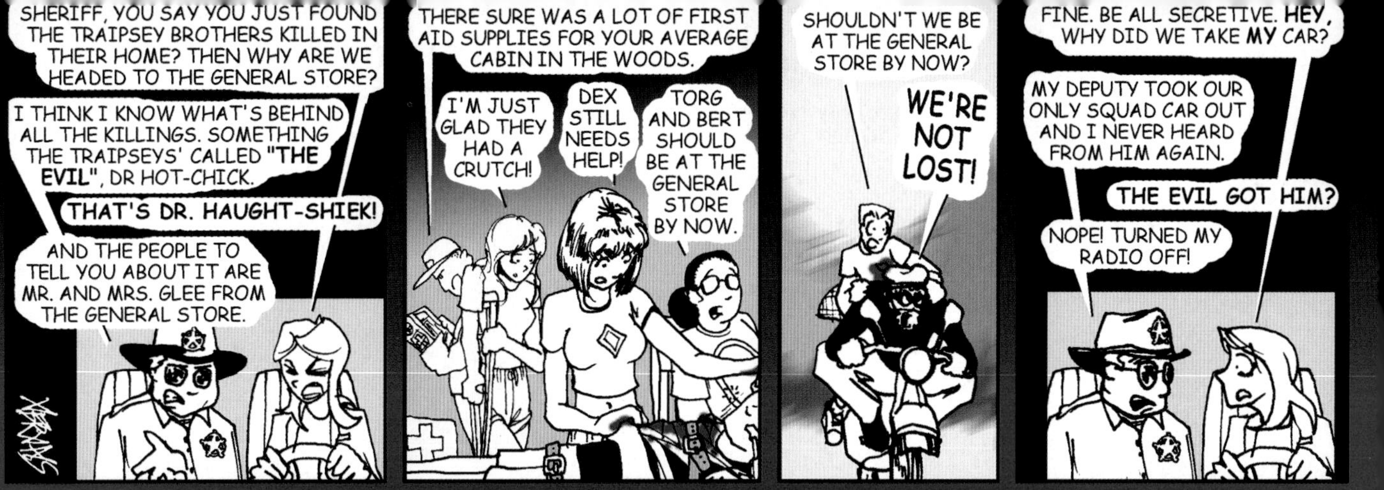
SHERIFF, YOU SAY YOU JUST FOUND THE TRAIPSEY BROTHERS KILLED IN THEIR HOME? THEN WHY ARE WE HEADED TO THE GENERAL STORE?
I THINK I KNOW WHAT'S BEHIND ALL THE KILLINGS. SOMETHING THE TRAIPSEYS' CALLED "THE EVIL", DR HOT-CHICK.
THAT'S DR. HAUGHT-SHIEK!
AND THE PEOPLE TO TELL YOU ABOUT IT ARE MR. AND MRS. GLEE FROM THE GENERAL STORE.
THERE SURE WAS A LOT OF FIRST AID SUPPLIES FOR YOUR AVERAGE CABIN IN THE WOODS.
I'M JUST GLAD THEY HAD A CRUTCH!
DEX STILL NEEDS HELP!
TORG AND BERT SHOULD BE AT THE GENERAL STORE BY NOW.
SHOULDN'T WE BE AT THE GENERAL STORE BY NOW?
WE'RE NOT LOST!
FINE. BE ALL SECRETIVE. HEY, WHY DID WE TAKE MY CAR?
MY DEPUTY TOOK OUR ONLY SQUAD CAR OUT AND I NEVER HEARD FROM HIM AGAIN.
THE EVIL GOT HIM?
NOPE! TURNED MY RADIO OFF!

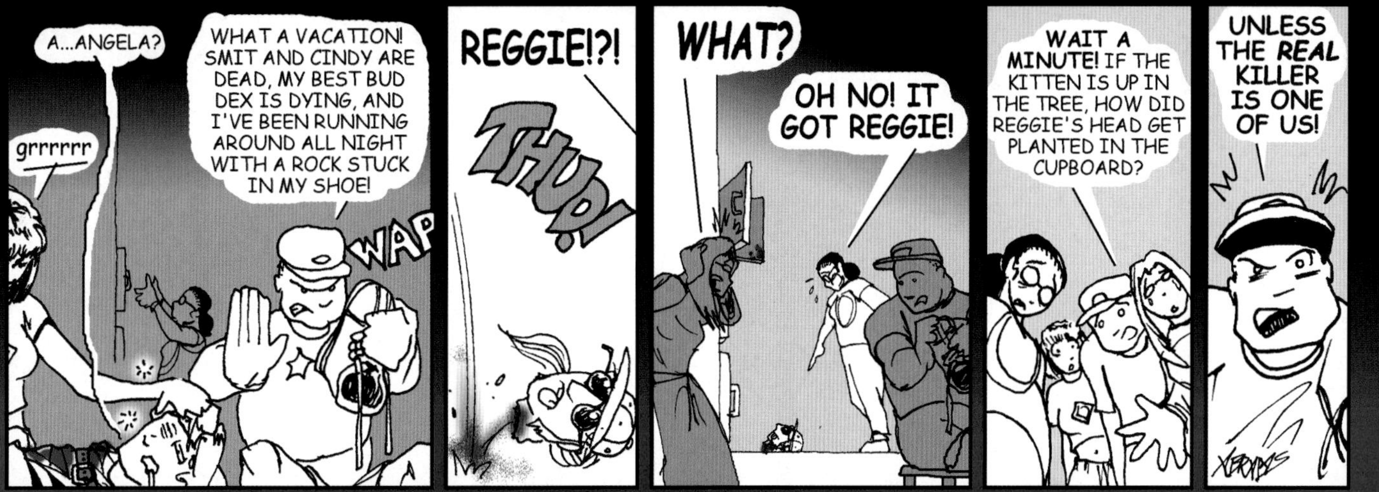
A...ANGELA?
grrrrrr
WHAT A VACATION! SMIT AND CINDY ARE DEAD, MY BEST BUD DEX IS DYING, AND I'VE BEEN RUNNING AROUND ALL NIGHT WITH A ROCK STUCK IN MY SHOE!
WAP
REGGIE!?!
THUD!
WHAT?
OH NO! IT GOT REGGIE!
WAIT A MINUTE! IF THE KITTEN IS UP IN THE TREE, HOW DID REGGIE'S HEAD GET PLANTED IN THE CUPBOARD?
UNLESS THE REAL KILLER IS ONE OF US!

Due to manipulative head-games, this comic may not be suitable for all audiences.

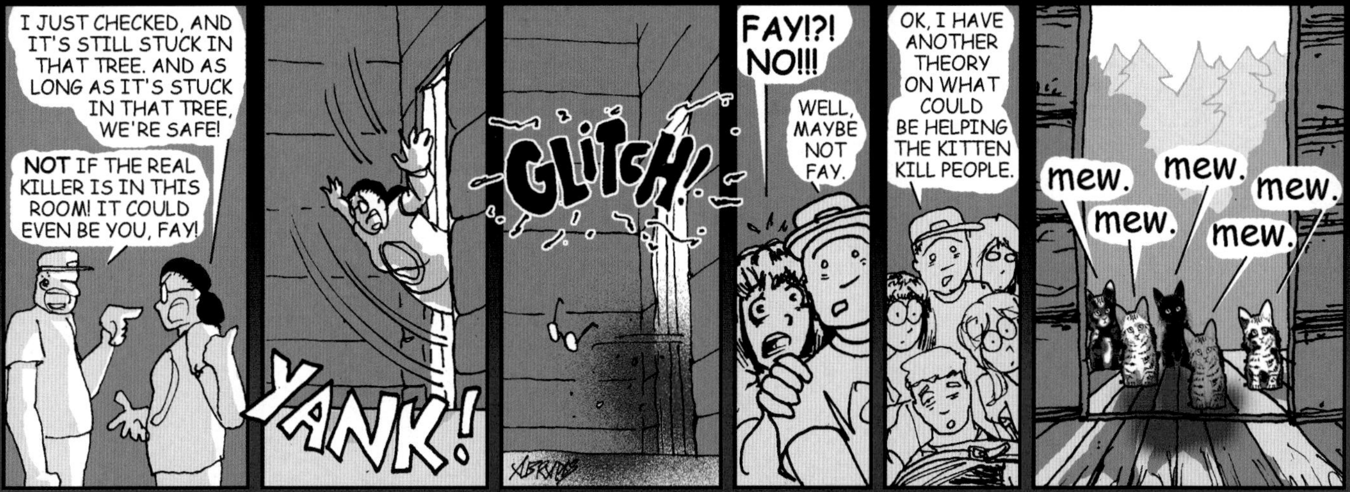
I JUST CHECKED, AND IT'S STILL STUCK IN THAT TREE. AND AS LONG AS IT'S STUCK IN THAT TREE, WE'RE SAFE!
NOT IF THE REAL KILLER IS IN THIS ROOM! IT COULD EVEN BE YOU, FAY!
YANK!
GLITCH!
FAY!?! NO!!!
WELL, MAYBE NOT FAY.
OK, I HAVE ANOTHER THEORY ON WHAT COULD BE HELPING THE KITTEN KILL PEOPLE.
mew.
mew.
mew.
mew.
mew.

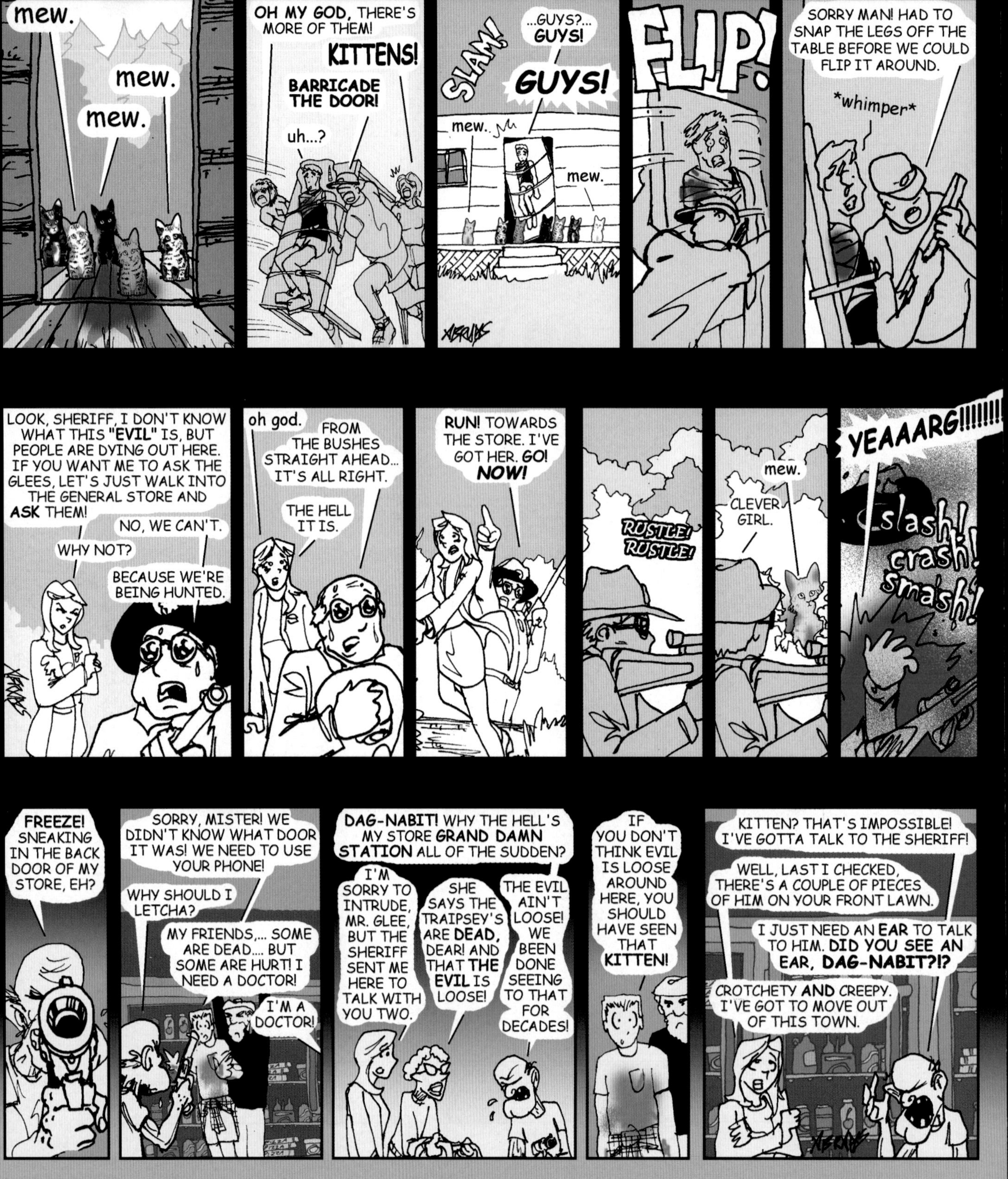

mew.
mew.
mew.
OH MY GOD, THERE'S MORE OF THEM!
KITTENS!
BARRICADE THE DOOR!
uh...?
SLAM!
...GUYS?... GUYS!
GUYS!
mew.
mew.
FLIP!
SORRY MAN! HAD TO SNAP THE LEGS OFF THE TABLE BEFORE WE COULD FLIP IT AROUND.
whimper
LOOK, SHERIFF, I DON'T KNOW WHAT THIS "EVIL" IS, BUT PEOPLE ARE DYING OUT HERE. IF YOU WANT ME TO ASK THE GLEES, LET'S JUST WALK INTO THE GENERAL STORE AND ASK THEM!
NO, WE CAN'T.
WHY NOT?
BECAUSE WE'RE BEING HUNTED.
oh god.
FROM THE BUSHES STRAIGHT AHEAD... IT'S ALL RIGHT.
THE HELL IT IS.
RUN! TOWARDS THE STORE. I'VE GOT HER. GO! NOW!
RUSTLE! RUSTLE!
mew.
CLEVER GIRL.
YEAAARG!!!!!!!
slash! crash! smash!
FREEZE! SNEAKING IN THE BACK DOOR OF MY STORE, EH?
SORRY, MISTER! WE DIDN'T KNOW WHAT DOOR IT WAS! WE NEED TO USE YOUR PHONE!
WHY SHOULD I LETCHA?
MY FRIENDS,... SOME ARE DEAD.... BUT SOME ARE HURT! I NEED A DOCTOR!
I'M A DOCTOR!
DAG-NABIT! WHY THE HELL'S MY STORE GRAND DAMN STATION ALL OF THE SUDDEN?
I'M SORRY TO INTRUDE, MR. GLEE, BUT THE SHERIFF SENT ME HERE TO TALK WITH YOU TWO.
SHE SAYS THE TRAIPSEY'S ARE DEAD, DEAR! AND THAT THE EVIL IS LOOSE!
THE EVIL AIN'T LOOSE! WE BEEN DONE SEEING TO THAT FOR DECADES!
IF YOU DON'T THINK EVIL IS LOOSE AROUND HERE, YOU SHOULD HAVE SEEN THAT KITTEN!
KITTEN? THAT'S IMPOSSIBLE! I'VE GOTTA TALK TO THE SHERIFF!
WELL, LAST I CHECKED, THERE'S A COUPLE OF PIECES OF HIM ON YOUR FRONT LAWN.
I JUST NEED AN EAR TO TALK TO HIM. DID YOU SEE AN EAR, DAG-NABIT?!?
CROTCHETY AND CREEPY. I'VE GOT TO MOVE OUT OF THIS TOWN.

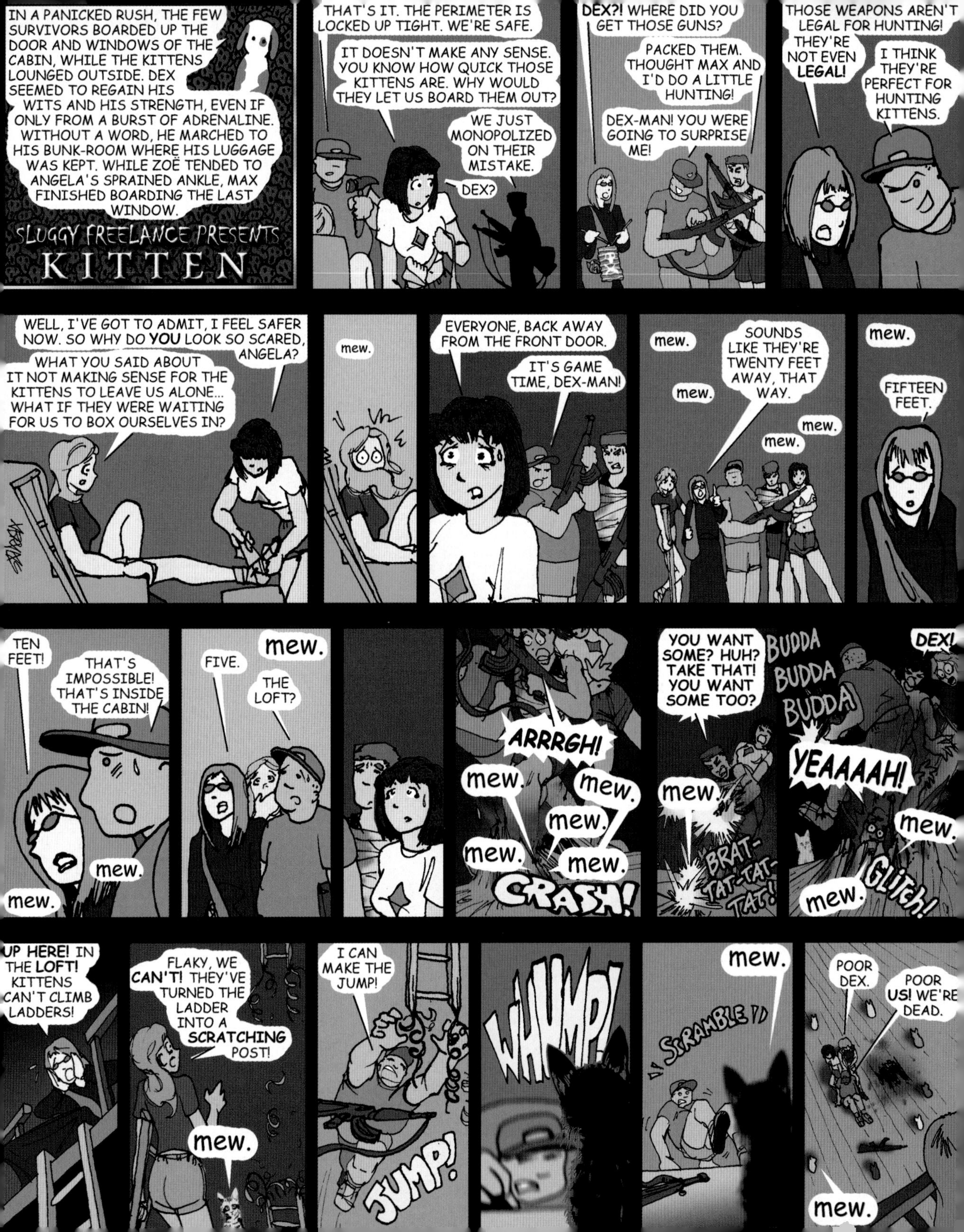
IN A PANICKED RUSH, THE FEW SURVIVORS BOARDED UP THE DOOR AND WINDOWS OF THE CABIN, WHILE THE KITTENS LOUNGED OUTSIDE. DEX SEEMED TO REGAIN HIS WITS AND HIS STRENGTH, EVEN IF ONLY FROM A BURST OF ADRENALINE. WITHOUT A WORD, HE MARCHED TO HIS BUNK-ROOM WHERE HIS LUGGAGE WAS KEPT. WHILE ZOË TENDED TO ANGELA'S SPRAINED ANKLE, MAX FINISHED BOARDING THE LAST WINDOW.
SLUGGY FREELANCE PRESENTS
KITTEN
THAT'S IT. THE PERIMETER IS LOCKED UP TIGHT. WE'RE SAFE.
IT DOESN'T MAKE ANY SENSE. YOU KNOW HOW QUICK THOSE KITTENS ARE. WHY WOULD THEY LET US BOARD THEM OUT?
WE JUST MONOPOLIZED ON THEIR MISTAKE.
DEX?
DEX?! WHERE DID YOU GET THOSE GUNS?
PACKED THEM. THOUGHT MAX AND I'D DO A LITTLE HUNTING!
DEX-MAN! YOU WERE GOING TO SURPRISE ME!
THOSE WEAPONS AREN'T LEGAL FOR HUNTING!
THEY'RE NOT EVEN LEGAL!
I THINK THEY'RE PERFECT FOR HUNTING KITTENS.
WELL, I'VE GOT TO ADMIT, I FEEL SAFER NOW. SO WHY DO YOU LOOK SO SCARED, ANGELA?
WHAT YOU SAID ABOUT IT NOT MAKING SENSE FOR THE KITTENS TO LEAVE US ALONE... WHAT IF THEY WERE WAITING FOR US TO BOX OURSELVES IN?
mew.
EVERYONE, BACK AWAY FROM THE FRONT DOOR.
IT'S GAME TIME, DEX-MAN!
mew.
mew.
SOUNDS LIKE THEY'RE TWENTY FEET AWAY, THAT WAY.
mew.
mew.
mew.
FIFTEEN FEET.
TEN FEET!
THAT'S IMPOSSIBLE! THAT'S INSIDE THE CABIN!
mew.
mew.
mew.
FIVE.
THE LOFT?
ARRRGH!
mew.
mew.
mew.
mew.
mew.
CRASH!
YOU WANT SOME? HUH? TAKE THAT! YOU WANT SOME TOO?
mew.
BRAT-TAT-TAT-TAT!
BUDDA BUDDA BUDDA
YEAAAAH!
DEX!
mew.
mew.
GLITCH!
UP HERE! IN THE LOFT! KITTENS CAN'T CLIMB LADDERS!
FLAKY, WE CAN'T! THEY'VE TURNED THE LADDER INTO A SCRATCHING POST!
mew.
I CAN MAKE THE JUMP!
JUMP!
WHUMP!
SCRAMBLE
mew.
POOR DEX.
POOR US! WE'RE DEAD.
mew.

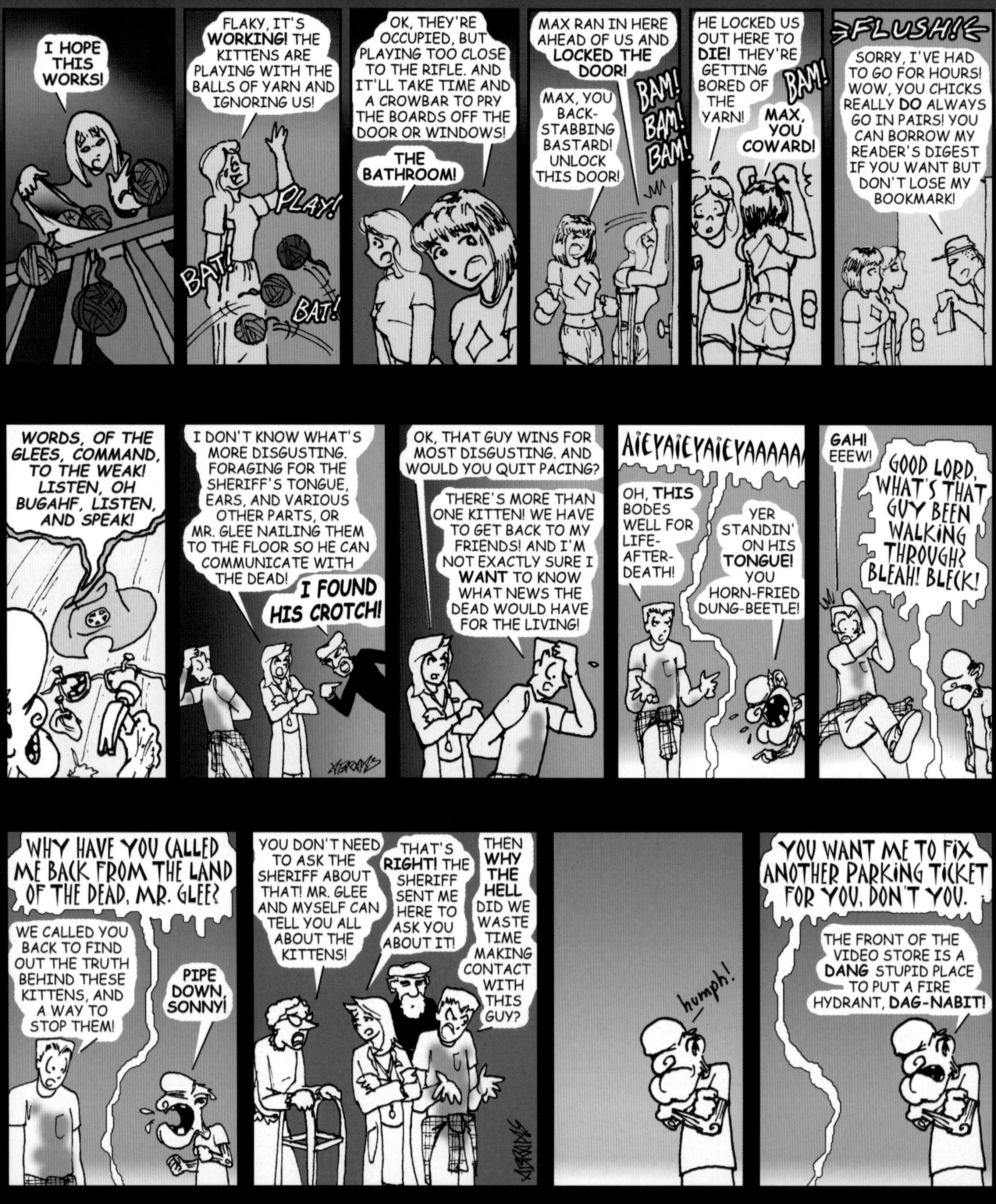
I HOPE THIS WORKS!
FLAKY, IT'S WORKING! THE KITTENS ARE PLAYING WITH THE BALLS OF YARN AND IGNORING US!
PLAY!
BAT!
BAT!
OK, THEY'RE OCCUPIED, BUT PLAYING TOO CLOSE TO THE RIFLE. AND IT'LL TAKE TIME AND A CROWBAR TO PRY THE BOARDS OFF THE DOOR OR WINDOWS!
THE BATHROOM!
MAX RAN IN HERE AHEAD OF US AND LOCKED THE DOOR!
MAX, YOU BACK-STABBING BASTARD! UNLOCK THIS DOOR!
BAM! BAM! BAM!
HE LOCKED US OUT HERE TO DIE! THEY'RE GETTING BORED OF THE YARN!
BAM!
MAX, YOU COWARD!
FLUSH!
SORRY, I'VE HAD TO GO FOR HOURS! WOW, YOU CHICKS REALLY DO ALWAYS GO IN PAIRS! YOU CAN BORROW MY READER'S DIGEST IF YOU WANT BUT DON'T LOSE MY BOOKMARK!
WORDS, OF THE GLEES, COMMAND, TO THE WEAK! LISTEN, OH BUGAHF, LISTEN, AND SPEAK!
I DON'T KNOW WHAT'S MORE DISGUSTING. FORAGING FOR THE SHERIFF'S TONGUE, EARS, AND VARIOUS OTHER PARTS, OR MR. GLEE NAILING THEM TO THE FLOOR SO HE CAN COMMUNICATE WITH THE DEAD!
I FOUND HIS CROTCH!
OK, THAT GUY WINS FOR MOST DISGUSTING. AND WOULD YOU QUIT PACING?
THERE'S MORE THAN ONE KITTEN! WE HAVE TO GET BACK TO MY FRIENDS! AND I'M NOT EXACTLY SURE I WANT TO KNOW WHAT NEWS THE DEAD WOULD HAVE FOR THE LIVING!
AIEYAIEYAIEYAAAAA
OH, THIS BODES WELL FOR LIFE-AFTER-DEATH!
YER STANDIN' ON HIS TONGUE! YOU HORN-FRIED DUNG-BEETLE!
GAH! EEEW!
GOOD LORD, WHAT'S THAT GUY BEEN WALKING THROUGH? BLEAH! BLECK!
WHY HAVE YOU CALLED ME BACK FROM THE LAND OF THE DEAD, MR. GLEE?
WE CALLED YOU BACK TO FIND OUT THE TRUTH BEHIND THESE KITTENS, AND A WAY TO STOP THEM!
PIPE DOWN, SONNY!
YOU DON'T NEED TO ASK THE SHERIFF ABOUT THAT! MR. GLEE AND MYSELF CAN TELL YOU ALL ABOUT THE KITTENS!
THAT'S RIGHT! THE SHERIFF SENT ME HERE TO ASK YOU ABOUT IT!
THEN WHY THE HELL DID WE WASTE TIME MAKING CONTACT WITH THIS GUY?
humph!
YOU WANT ME TO FIX ANOTHER PARKING TICKET FOR YOU, DON'T YOU.
THE FRONT OF THE VIDEO STORE IS A DANG STUPID PLACE TO PUT A FIRE HYDRANT, DAG-NABIT!

IT LOOKS LIKE MOST OF THE KITTENS HAVE GROUPED AROUND THE BATHROOM DOOR! ARE YOU GUYS OK?
mew.
mew.
mew.
mew.
WE'RE FINE! THE KITTENS ARE KEEPING AWAY FROM THE WATER. WE'RE SAFE AS LONG AS WE STAY IN THE SHOWER STALL.
ARE WE GOING TO HAVE TO STAY HERE FOREVER? THIS IS A NIGHTMARE!
FOR ME, PERSONALLY, SHARING A SHOWER WITH TWO BEAUTIFUL WOMEN PRETTY MUCH COMPLETES MY LIFE LONG DREAM!
FAY DESERVED BETTER THAN TO DIE LIKE THAT! WE ALL DO!
THE WAY THEY TOOK DEX'S ARM! THEN THEY CHOSE HIM TO DIE! THEY'RE JUST PLAYING WITH US NOW! TORG AND BERT WOULD HAVE BEEN BACK BY NOW IF... IF........
DON'T YOU EVEN SAY TORG'S DEAD! DON'T YOU SAY IT!
I DON'T WANT TO DIE!
HEY FLAKY, THINGS ARE GETTING EMOTIONAL HERE! YOU'RE PSYCHIC! HOW ABOUT PREDICTING A HAPPY FUTURE FOR US?
I CAN'T SEE BEYOND MY OWN FATE! AND MY OWN FATE IS... NOOOOOOOOOOOOO!
GOD! NOOOOOOOOOOOO
SIGH, VERY UPLIFTING, FLAKY! THERE, THERE, YOU TWO. EVERYTHING'S GOING TO BE ALL RIGHT!
HUG!
MAX, GET YOUR HANDS OFF OUR BUTTS.
WELL THERE GOES THE OLD "VULNERABLE CHICKS ARE EASY" THEORY!
WE'RE GOING BACK FOR MY FRIENDS. ARE YOU COMING OR NOT, DR. HOT-CHEEKS?
THE NAME IS DR. HAUGHT-SHEIK!
I'M THROUGH FOOLING AROUND. UNLESS YOU WANT F.E.M.A., THE NATIONAL GUARD, AND EVERY BIG-SHOT I CAN MUSTER BREATHING DOWN YOUR NECKS, YOU BETTER JUST TELL ME WHAT THE HELL IS GOING ON WITH THESE KITTENS! THE SHORT VERSION!
THE KITTENS ARE THE CHILDREN OF THE DEVIL. ME AND A BUNCH OF MY FELLOW SATAN-WORSHIPPERS TEND TO 'EM. AND NOW SOME IMPOSTER KITTENS ARE ATTACKIN' PEOPLE TO GET SATAN'S KIDS IN TROUBLE, AND I AIMS TA KNOW WHY!
POOR LITTLE KIDS OF SATAN!
OK, LET'S TRY THE LONG VERSION.

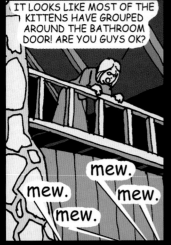

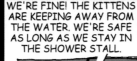

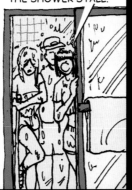

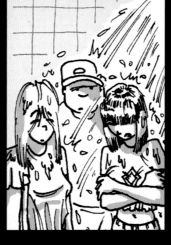

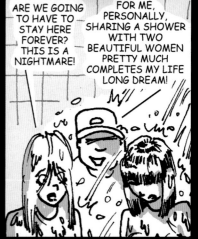

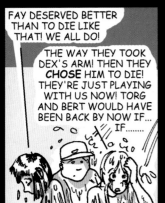

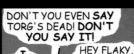

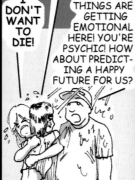

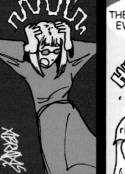

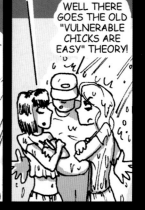

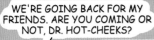

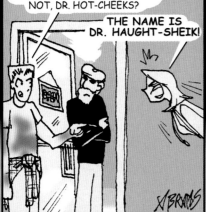

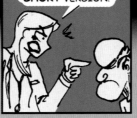

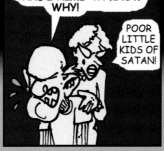

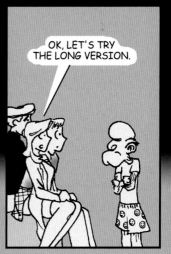

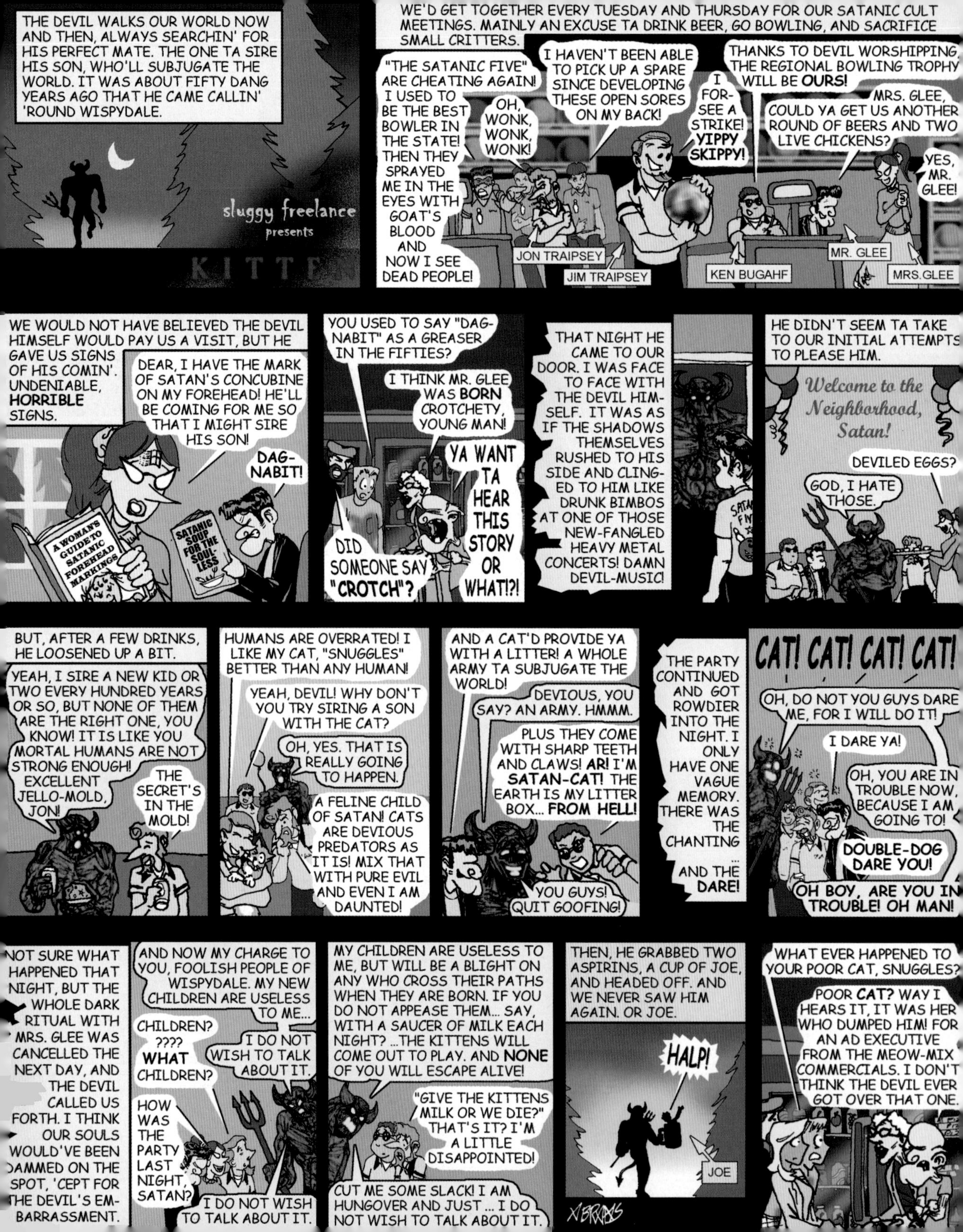

THE DEVIL WALKS OUR WORLD NOW AND THEN, ALWAYS SEARCHIN' FOR HIS PERFECT MATE. THE ONE TA SIRE HIS SON, WHO'LL SUBJUGATE THE WORLD. IT WAS ABOUT FIFTY DANG YEARS AGO THAT HE CAME CALLIN' 'ROUND WISPYDALE.
sluggy freelance presents
KITTEN
WE'D GET TOGETHER EVERY TUESDAY AND THURSDAY FOR OUR SATANIC CULT MEETINGS. MAINLY AN EXCUSE TA DRINK BEER, GO BOWLING, AND SACRIFICE SMALL CRITTERS.
"THE SATANIC FIVE" ARE CHEATING AGAIN! I USED TO BE THE BEST BOWLER IN THE STATE! THEN THEY SPRAYED ME IN THE EYES WITH GOAT'S BLOOD AND NOW I SEE DEAD PEOPLE!
OH, WONK, WONK, WONK!
I HAVEN'T BEEN ABLE TO PICK UP A SPARE SINCE DEVELOPING THESE OPEN SORES ON MY BACK!
I FOR-SEE A STRIKE! YIPPY SKIPPY!
THANKS TO DEVIL WORSHIPPING THE REGIONAL BOWLING TROPHY WILL BE OURS!
MRS. GLEE, COULD YA GET US ANOTHER ROUND OF BEERS AND TWO LIVE CHICKENS?
YES, MR. GLEE!
JON TRAIPSEY
JIM TRAIPSEY
KEN BUGAHF
MR. GLEE
MRS.GLEE
WE WOULD NOT HAVE BELIEVED THE DEVIL HIMSELF WOULD PAY US A VISIT, BUT HE GAVE US SIGNS OF HIS COMIN'. UNDENIABLE, HORRIBLE SIGNS.
DEAR, I HAVE THE MARK OF SATAN'S CONCUBINE ON MY FOREHEAD! HE'LL BE COMING FOR ME SO THAT I MIGHT SIRE HIS SON!
DAG-NABIT!
A WOMAN'S GUIDE TO SATANIC FOREHEAD MARKINGS
SATANIC SOUP FOR THE SOUL-LESS
YOU USED TO SAY "DAG-NABIT" AS A GREASER IN THE FIFTIES?
I THINK MR. GLEE WAS BORN CROTCHETY, YOUNG MAN!
YA WANT TA HEAR THIS STORY OR WHAT!?!
DID SOMEONE SAY "CROTCH"?
THAT NIGHT HE CAME TO OUR DOOR. I WAS FACE TO FACE WITH THE DEVIL HIM-SELF. IT WAS AS IF THE SHADOWS THEMSELVES RUSHED TO HIS SIDE AND CLING-ED TO HIM LIKE DRUNK BIMBOS AT ONE OF THOSE NEW-FANGLED HEAVY METAL CONCERTS! DAMN DEVIL-MUSIC!
HE DIDN'T SEEM TA TAKE TO OUR INITIAL ATTEMPTS TO PLEASE HIM.
Welcome to the Neighborhood, Satan!
DEVILED EGGS?
GOD, I HATE THOSE.
BUT, AFTER A FEW DRINKS, HE LOOSENED UP A BIT.
YEAH, I SIRE A NEW KID OR TWO EVERY HUNDRED YEARS OR SO, BUT NONE OF THEM ARE THE RIGHT ONE, YOU KNOW! IT IS LIKE YOU MORTAL HUMANS ARE NOT STRONG ENOUGH! EXCELLENT JELLO-MOLD, JON!
THE SECRET'S IN THE MOLD!
HUMANS ARE OVERRATED! I LIKE MY CAT, "SNUGGLES" BETTER THAN ANY HUMAN!
YEAH, DEVIL! WHY DON'T YOU TRY SIRING A SON WITH THE CAT?
OH, YES. THAT IS REALLY GOING TO HAPPEN.
A FELINE CHILD OF SATAN! CATS ARE DEVIOUS PREDATORS AS IT IS! MIX THAT WITH PURE EVIL AND EVEN I AM DAUNTED!
AND A CAT'D PROVIDE YA WITH A LITTER! A WHOLE ARMY TA SUBJUGATE THE WORLD!
DEVIOUS, YOU SAY? AN ARMY. HMMM.
PLUS THEY COME WITH SHARP TEETH AND CLAWS! AR! I'M SATAN-CAT! THE EARTH IS MY LITTER BOX... FROM HELL!
YOU GUYS! QUIT GOOFING!
THE PARTY CONTINUED AND GOT ROWDIER INTO THE NIGHT. I ONLY HAVE ONE VAGUE MEMORY. THERE WAS THE CHANTING ... AND THE DARE!
CAT! CAT! CAT! CAT!
OH, DO NOT YOU GUYS DARE ME, FOR I WILL DO IT!
I DARE YA!
OH, YOU ARE IN TROUBLE NOW, BECAUSE I AM GOING TO!
DOUBLE-DOG DARE YOU!
OH BOY, ARE YOU IN TROUBLE! OH MAN!
NOT SURE WHAT HAPPENED THAT NIGHT, BUT THE WHOLE DARK RITUAL WITH MRS. GLEE WAS CANCELLED THE NEXT DAY, AND THE DEVIL CALLED US FORTH. I THINK OUR SOULS WOULD'VE BEEN DAMMED ON THE SPOT, 'CEPT FOR THE DEVIL'S EM-BARRASSMENT.
AND NOW MY CHARGE TO YOU, FOOLISH PEOPLE OF WISPYDALE. MY NEW CHILDREN ARE USELESS TO ME...
CHILDREN? ???? WHAT CHILDREN?
I DO NOT WISH TO TALK ABOUT IT.
HOW WAS THE PARTY LAST NIGHT, SATAN?
I DO NOT WISH TO TALK ABOUT IT.
MY CHILDREN ARE USELESS TO ME, BUT WILL BE A BLIGHT ON ANY WHO CROSS THEIR PATHS WHEN THEY ARE BORN. IF YOU DO NOT APPEASE THEM... SAY, WITH A SAUCER OF MILK EACH NIGHT? ...THE KITTENS WILL COME OUT TO PLAY. AND NONE OF YOU WILL ESCAPE ALIVE!
"GIVE THE KITTENS MILK OR WE DIE?" THAT'S IT? I'M A LITTLE DISAPPOINTED!
CUT ME SOME SLACK! I AM HUNGOVER AND JUST ... I DO NOT WISH TO TALK ABOUT IT.
THEN, HE GRABBED TWO ASPIRINS, A CUP OF JOE, AND HEADED OFF. AND WE NEVER SAW HIM AGAIN. OR JOE.
HALP!
JOE
WHAT EVER HAPPENED TO YOUR POOR CAT, SNUGGLES?
POOR CAT? WAY I HEARS IT, IT WAS HER WHO DUMPED HIM! FOR AN AD EXECUTIVE FROM THE MEOW-MIX COMMERCIALS. I DON'T THINK THE DEVIL EVER GOT OVER THAT ONE.

SO THAT'S THE STORY. A SHORT TIME LATER THE KITTENS WERE BORN. THERE WERE SIX PLUS SIX PLUS SIX OF THEM, AND JIM TRAIPSEY NAMED THE WHOLE LITTER **"THE EVIL"**, AFTER HIS MOTHER. AND WE'VE BEEN TAKING CARE OF THEM EVER SINCE.

SO YOU SEE, THAT'S WHY SATAN'S KITTENS CANNOT BE RESPONSIBLE FOR ALL THE KILLINGS! NOT A NIGHT GOES BY THAT MY WIFE AND I DON'T PUT OUT SAUCERS OF MILK FOR THEM, AS PER SATAN'S REQUEST.

AND THEY'RE HEALTHIER SINCE IT'S NOT REAL MILK!

WHAT?!?

I JUST SWITCHED US TO SOY-MILK LAST WEEK! TOTALLY NON-DAIRY!

SOY MILK!
HAPPY COW SOY SOY SOY
SOY MILK

ALICIA SILVERSTONE RECOMMENDS IT!

DAG-DOUBLE-NABIT.

WHY, MRS. GLEE?!? WHY DID YOU SWITCH OUR MILK FOR THAT SOY-MILK CRAP?

FOR YOUR BLOOD PRESSURE, DEAR!

mew.

Glitch!

FSSSSSSSSSSSSSSSSSSS

YOU CUT BACK ON **SODIUM** FOR BLOOD PRESSURE.

I ALWAYS MIX THOSE UP! WHERE'D MR. GLEE GO?

WOW! HIS BLOOD WAS UNDER QUITE A LOT OF PRESSURE!

EVERYONE, RUN FOR IT! I'LL HOLD IT OFF WITH THIS TWO-BY-FOUR!

mew.

WHAM! WHAM! WHAM! WHAM!

TORG! NO! THAT'S NOT ONE OF THE CHILDREN-OF-SATAN KITTENS! THAT'S MY PET KITTEN!

OH!

OH, BOY DO I FEEL LOUSY!

WAIT A MINUTE! NO, I'M WRONG, TITIAN WOULDN'T EAT ME LIKE THIS.

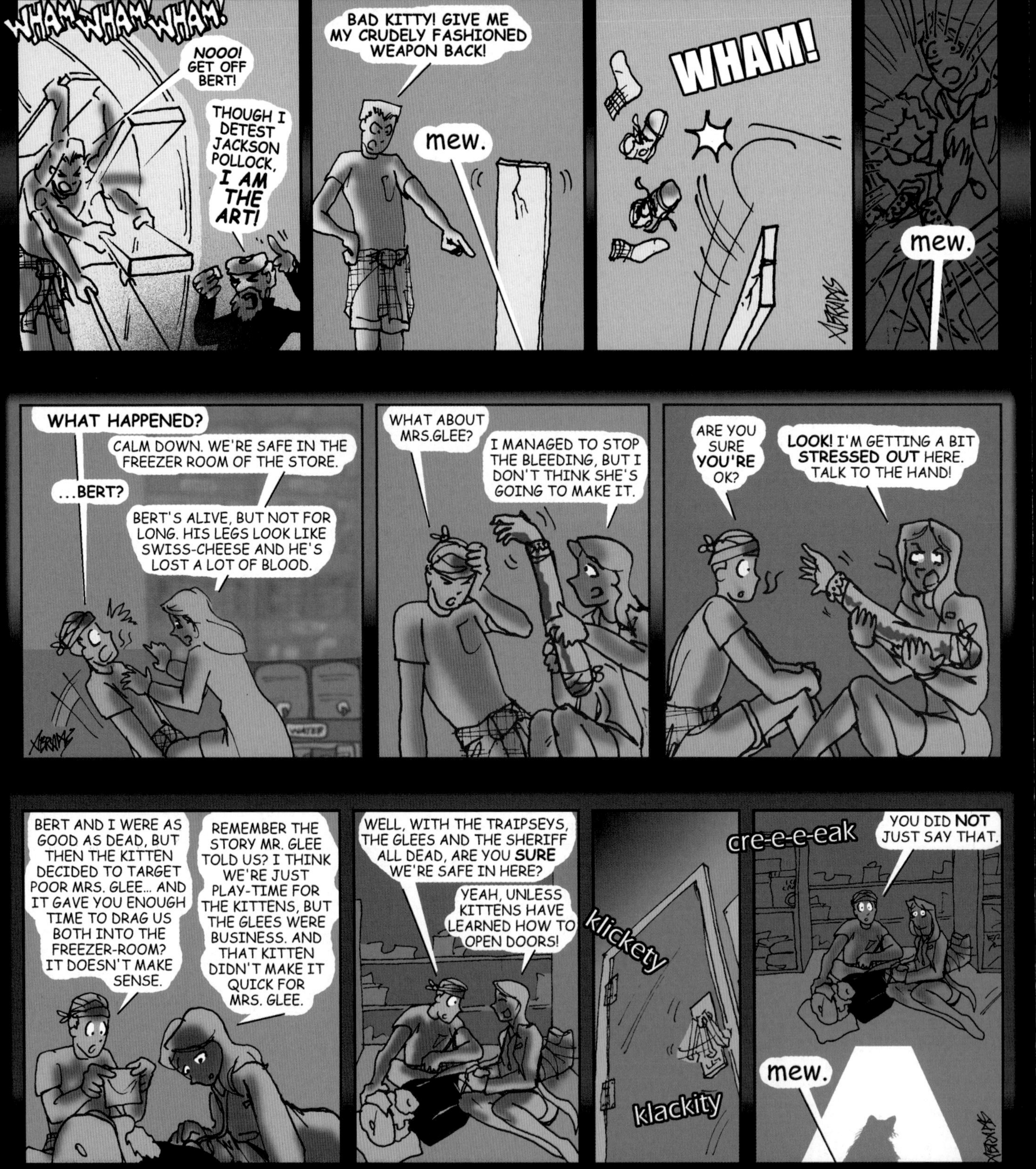
WHAM WHAM WHAM!
NOOO! GET OFF BERT!
THOUGH I DETEST JACKSON POLLOCK, I AM THE ART!
BAD KITTY! GIVE ME MY CRUDELY FASHIONED WEAPON BACK!
mew.
WHAM!
mew.
WHAT HAPPENED?
CALM DOWN. WE'RE SAFE IN THE FREEZER ROOM OF THE STORE.
...BERT?
BERT'S ALIVE, BUT NOT FOR LONG. HIS LEGS LOOK LIKE SWISS-CHEESE AND HE'S LOST A LOT OF BLOOD.
WHAT ABOUT MRS.GLEE?
I MANAGED TO STOP THE BLEEDING, BUT I DON'T THINK SHE'S GOING TO MAKE IT.
ARE YOU SURE YOU'RE OK?
LOOK! I'M GETTING A BIT STRESSED OUT HERE. TALK TO THE HAND!
BERT AND I WERE AS GOOD AS DEAD, BUT THEN THE KITTEN DECIDED TO TARGET POOR MRS. GLEE... AND IT GAVE YOU ENOUGH TIME TO DRAG US BOTH INTO THE FREEZER-ROOM? IT DOESN'T MAKE SENSE.
REMEMBER THE STORY MR. GLEE TOLD US? I THINK WE'RE JUST PLAY-TIME FOR THE KITTENS, BUT THE GLEES WERE BUSINESS. AND THAT KITTEN DIDN'T MAKE IT QUICK FOR MRS. GLEE.
WELL, WITH THE TRAIPSEYS, THE GLEES AND THE SHERIFF ALL DEAD, ARE YOU SURE WE'RE SAFE IN HERE?
YEAH, UNLESS KITTENS HAVE LEARNED HOW TO OPEN DOORS!
klickety
klackity
cre-e-e-eak
YOU DID NOT JUST SAY THAT.
mew.

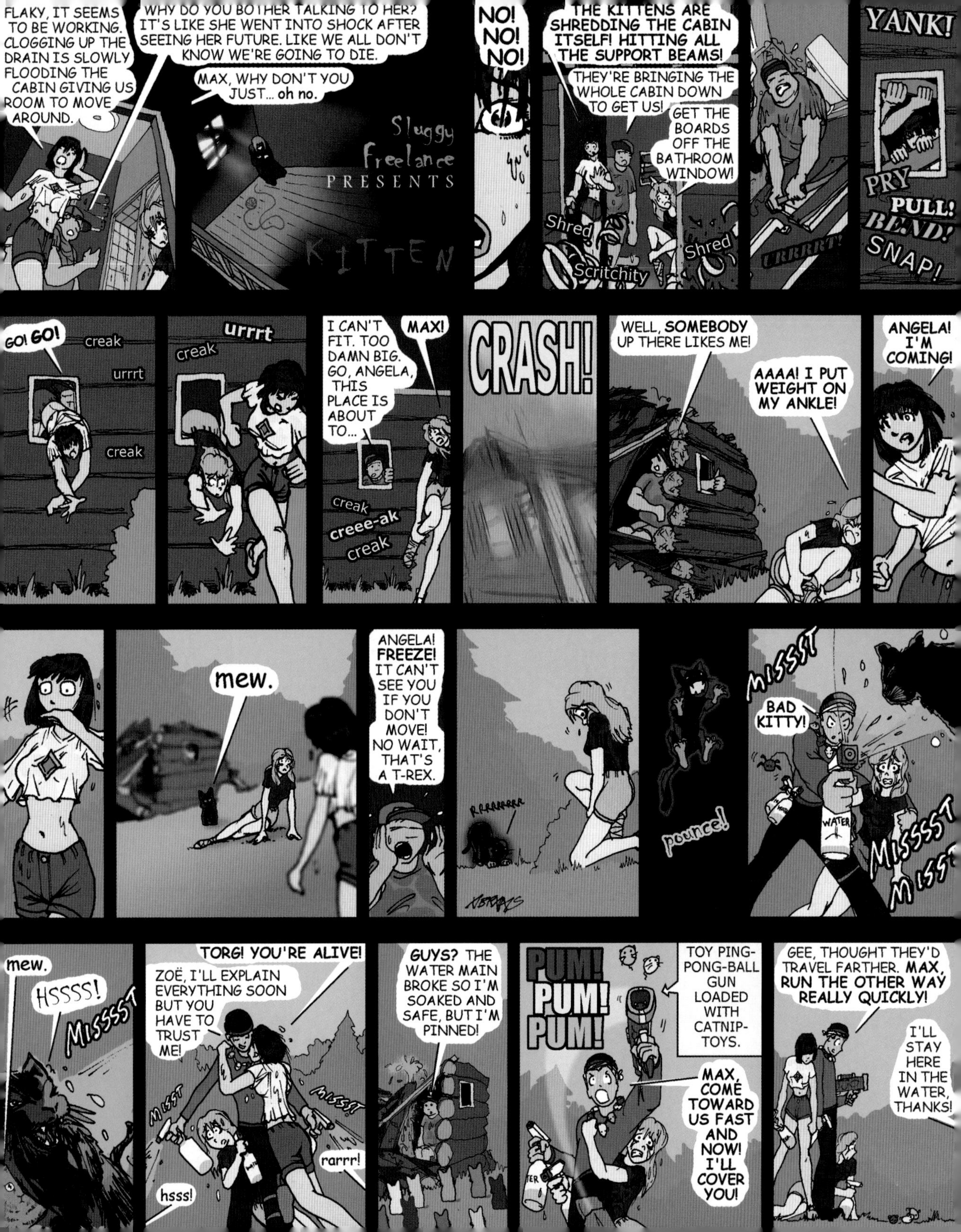

FLAKY, IT SEEMS TO BE WORKING. CLOGGING UP THE DRAIN IS SLOWLY FLOODING THE CABIN GIVING US ROOM TO MOVE AROUND.
WHY DO YOU BOTHER TALKING TO HER? IT'S LIKE SHE WENT INTO SHOCK AFTER SEEING HER FUTURE. LIKE WE ALL DON'T KNOW WE'RE GOING TO DIE.
MAX, WHY DON'T YOU JUST... oh no.
Sluggy Freelance
PRESENTS
KITTEN
NO! NO! NO!
THE KITTENS ARE SHREDDING THE CABIN ITSELF! HITTING ALL THE SUPPORT BEAMS!
THEY'RE BRINGING THE WHOLE CABIN DOWN TO GET US!
GET THE BOARDS OFF THE BATHROOM WINDOW!
Shred
Scritchity
Shred
URRRRT!
YANK!
PRY
PULL!
BEND!
SNAP!
GO! GO!
creak
urrrt
creak
urrrt
creak
I CAN'T FIT. TOO DAMN BIG. GO, ANGELA, THIS PLACE IS ABOUT TO...
MAX!
creak
creee-ak
creak
CRASH!
WELL, SOMEBODY UP THERE LIKES ME!
AAAA! I PUT WEIGHT ON MY ANKLE!
ANGELA! I'M COMING!
mew.
ANGELA! FREEZE! IT CAN'T SEE YOU IF YOU DON'T MOVE! NO WAIT, THAT'S A T-REX.
RRRRRRRRR
pounce!
MISSST
BAD KITTY!
WATER
MISSSST
MISST
mew.
HSSSS!
MISSSST
TORG! YOU'RE ALIVE!
ZOË, I'LL EXPLAIN EVERYTHING SOON BUT YOU HAVE TO TRUST ME!
MISST
MISSST
hsss!
rarrr!
GUYS? THE WATER MAIN BROKE SO I'M SOAKED AND SAFE, BUT I'M PINNED!
PUM! PUM! PUM!
TOY PING-PONG-BALL GUN LOADED WITH CATNIP-TOYS.
MAX, COME TOWARD US FAST AND NOW! I'LL COVER YOU!
GEE, THOUGHT THEY'D TRAVEL FARTHER. MAX, RUN THE OTHER WAY REALLY QUICKLY!
I'LL STAY HERE IN THE WATER, THANKS!

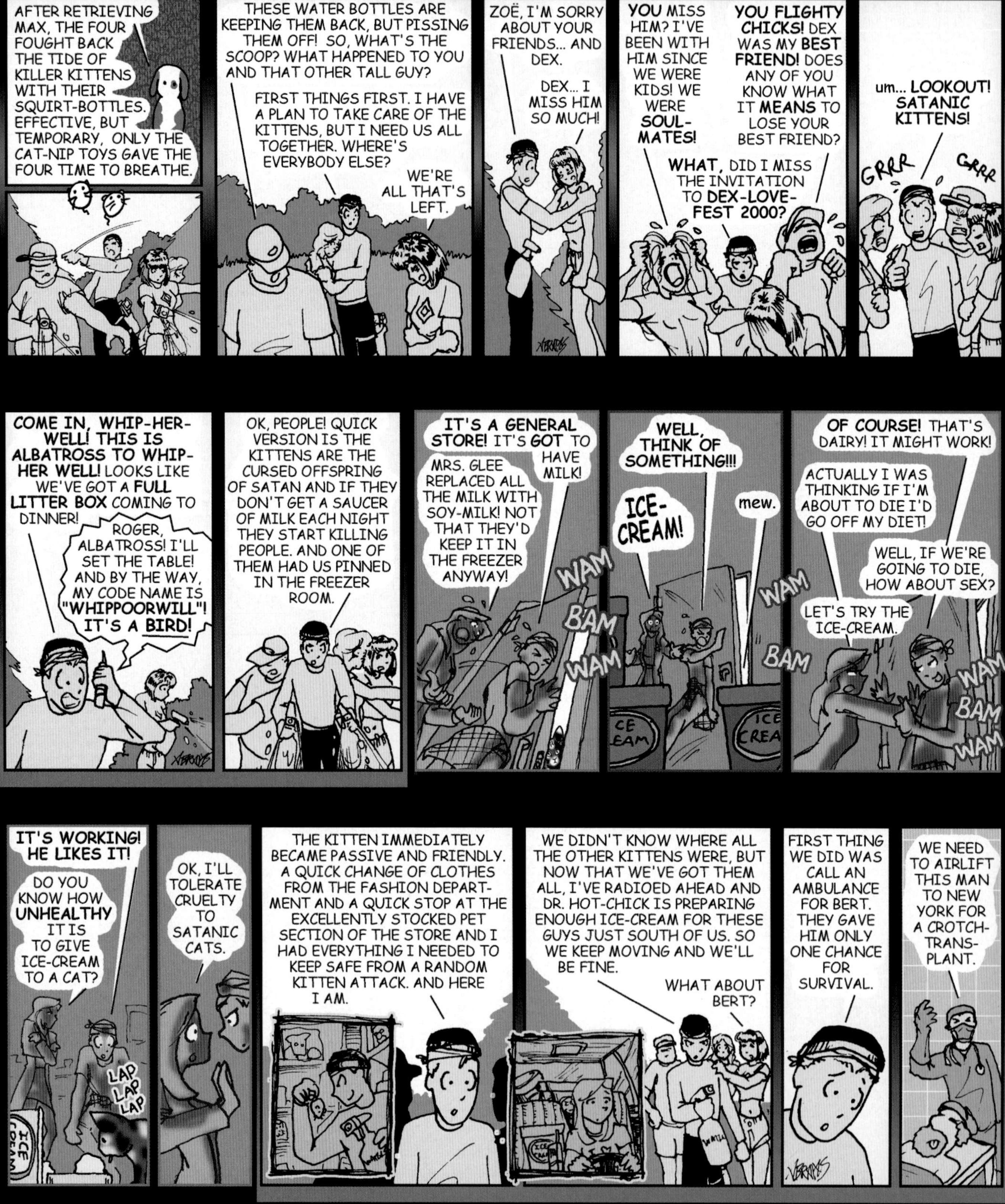
AFTER RETRIEVING MAX, THE FOUR FOUGHT BACK THE TIDE OF KILLER KITTENS WITH THEIR SQUIRT-BOTTLES. EFFECTIVE, BUT TEMPORARY, ONLY THE CAT-NIP TOYS GAVE THE FOUR TIME TO BREATHE.
THESE WATER BOTTLES ARE KEEPING THEM BACK, BUT PISSING THEM OFF! SO, WHAT'S THE SCOOP? WHAT HAPPENED TO YOU AND THAT OTHER TALL GUY?
FIRST THINGS FIRST. I HAVE A PLAN TO TAKE CARE OF THE KITTENS, BUT I NEED US ALL TOGETHER. WHERE'S EVERYBODY ELSE?
WE'RE ALL THAT'S LEFT.
ZOË, I'M SORRY ABOUT YOUR FRIENDS... AND DEX.
DEX... I MISS HIM SO MUCH!
YOU MISS HIM? I'VE BEEN WITH HIM SINCE WE WERE KIDS! WE WERE SOUL-MATES!
YOU FLIGHTY CHICKS! DEX WAS MY BEST FRIEND! DOES ANY OF YOU KNOW WHAT IT MEANS TO LOSE YOUR BEST FRIEND?
WHAT, DID I MISS THE INVITATION TO DEX-LOVE-FEST 2000?
um... LOOKOUT! SATANIC KITTENS!
GRRR
GRRR
COME IN, WHIP-HER-WELL! THIS IS ALBATROSS TO WHIP-HER WELL! LOOKS LIKE WE'VE GOT A FULL LITTER BOX COMING TO DINNER!
ROGER, ALBATROSS! I'LL SET THE TABLE! AND BY THE WAY, MY CODE NAME IS "WHIPPOORWILL"! IT'S A BIRD!
OK, PEOPLE! QUICK VERSION IS THE KITTENS ARE THE CURSED OFFSPRING OF SATAN AND IF THEY DON'T GET A SAUCER OF MILK EACH NIGHT THEY START KILLING PEOPLE. AND ONE OF THEM HAD US PINNED IN THE FREEZER ROOM.
IT'S A GENERAL STORE! IT'S GOT TO HAVE MILK!
MRS. GLEE REPLACED ALL THE MILK WITH SOY-MILK! NOT THAT THEY'D KEEP IT IN THE FREEZER ANYWAY!
WAM
BAM
WAM
WELL, THINK OF SOMETHING!!!
ICE-CREAM!
mew.
WAM
BAM
OF COURSE! THAT'S DAIRY! IT MIGHT WORK!
ACTUALLY I WAS THINKING IF I'M ABOUT TO DIE I'D GO OFF MY DIET!
WELL, IF WE'RE GOING TO DIE, HOW ABOUT SEX?
LET'S TRY THE ICE-CREAM.
WAM
BAM
WAM
IT'S WORKING! HE LIKES IT!
DO YOU KNOW HOW UNHEALTHY IT IS TO GIVE ICE-CREAM TO A CAT?
LAP
LAP
LAP
OK, I'LL TOLERATE CRUELTY TO SATANIC CATS.
THE KITTEN IMMEDIATELY BECAME PASSIVE AND FRIENDLY. A QUICK CHANGE OF CLOTHES FROM THE FASHION DEPARTMENT AND A QUICK STOP AT THE EXCELLENTLY STOCKED PET SECTION OF THE STORE AND I HAD EVERYTHING I NEEDED TO KEEP SAFE FROM A RANDOM KITTEN ATTACK. AND HERE I AM.
WE DIDN'T KNOW WHERE ALL THE OTHER KITTENS WERE, BUT NOW THAT WE'VE GOT THEM ALL, I'VE RADIOED AHEAD AND DR. HOT-CHICK IS PREPARING ENOUGH ICE-CREAM FOR THESE GUYS JUST SOUTH OF US. SO WE KEEP MOVING AND WE'LL BE FINE.
WHAT ABOUT BERT?
FIRST THING WE DID WAS CALL AN AMBULANCE FOR BERT. THEY GAVE HIM ONLY ONE CHANCE FOR SURVIVAL.
WE NEED TO AIRLIFT THIS MAN TO NEW YORK FOR A CROTCH-TRANSPLANT.

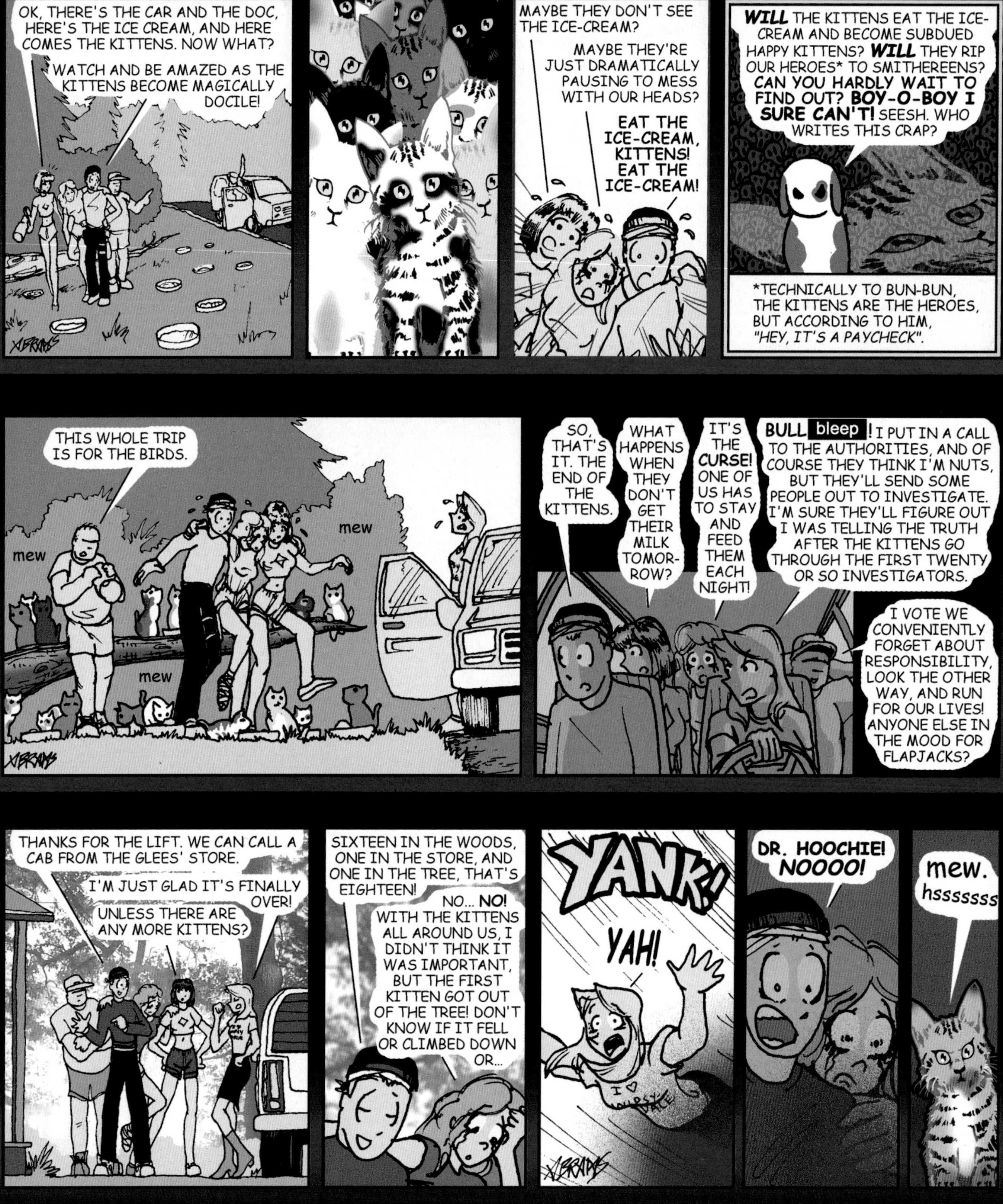

OK, THERE'S THE CAR AND THE DOC, HERE'S THE ICE CREAM, AND HERE COMES THE KITTENS. NOW WHAT?
WATCH AND BE AMAZED AS THE KITTENS BECOME MAGICALLY DOCILE!
MAYBE THEY DON'T SEE THE ICE-CREAM?
MAYBE THEY'RE JUST DRAMATICALLY PAUSING TO MESS WITH OUR HEADS?
EAT THE ICE-CREAM, KITTENS! EAT THE ICE-CREAM!
WILL THE KITTENS EAT THE ICE-CREAM AND BECOME SUBDUED HAPPY KITTENS? WILL THEY RIP OUR HEROES* TO SMITHEREENS? CAN YOU HARDLY WAIT TO FIND OUT? BOY-O-BOY I SURE CAN'T! SEESH. WHO WRITES THIS CRAP?
*TECHNICALLY TO BUN-BUN, THE KITTENS ARE THE HEROES, BUT ACCORDING TO HIM, "HEY, IT'S A PAYCHECK".
THIS WHOLE TRIP IS FOR THE BIRDS.
mew
mew
mew
SO, THAT'S IT. THE END OF THE KITTENS.
WHAT HAPPENS WHEN THEY DON'T GET THEIR MILK TOMORROW?
IT'S THE CURSE! ONE OF US HAS TO STAY AND FEED THEM EACH NIGHT!
BULL bleep! I PUT IN A CALL TO THE AUTHORITIES, AND OF COURSE THEY THINK I'M NUTS, BUT THEY'LL SEND SOME PEOPLE OUT TO INVESTIGATE. I'M SURE THEY'LL FIGURE OUT I WAS TELLING THE TRUTH AFTER THE KITTENS GO THROUGH THE FIRST TWENTY OR SO INVESTIGATORS.
I VOTE WE CONVENIENTLY FORGET ABOUT RESPONSIBILITY, LOOK THE OTHER WAY, AND RUN FOR OUR LIVES! ANYONE ELSE IN THE MOOD FOR FLAPJACKS?
THANKS FOR THE LIFT. WE CAN CALL A CAB FROM THE GLEES' STORE.
I'M JUST GLAD IT'S FINALLY OVER!
UNLESS THERE ARE ANY MORE KITTENS?
SIXTEEN IN THE WOODS, ONE IN THE STORE, AND ONE IN THE TREE, THAT'S EIGHTEEN!
NO... NO! WITH THE KITTENS ALL AROUND US, I DIDN'T THINK IT WAS IMPORTANT, BUT THE FIRST KITTEN GOT OUT OF THE TREE! DON'T KNOW IF IT FELL OR CLIMBED DOWN OR...
YANK!
YAH!
DR. HOOCHIE! NOOOO!
mew.
hssssss

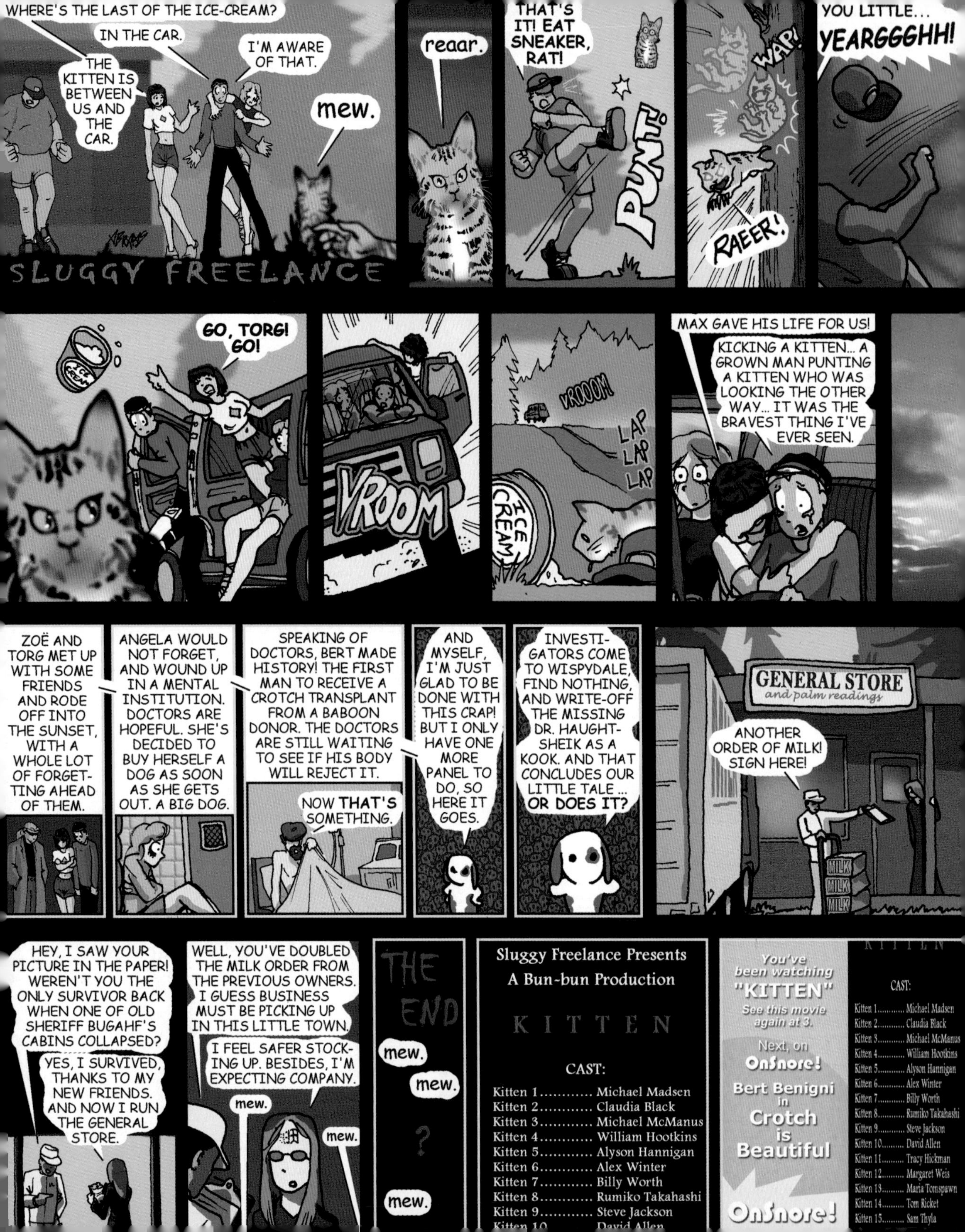
WHERE'S THE LAST OF THE ICE-CREAM?
IN THE CAR.
THE KITTEN IS BETWEEN US AND THE CAR.
I'M AWARE OF THAT.
mew.
SLUGGY FREELANCE
reaar.
THAT'S IT! EAT SNEAKER, RAT!
PUNT!
WAP!
RAEER!
YOU LITTLE... YEARGGGHH!
GO, TORG! GO!
ICE CREAM
VROOM
VROOOM
LAP LAP LAP
ICE CREAM
MAX GAVE HIS LIFE FOR US!
KICKING A KITTEN... A GROWN MAN PUNTING A KITTEN WHO WAS LOOKING THE OTHER WAY... IT WAS THE BRAVEST THING I'VE EVER SEEN.
ZOË AND TORG MET UP WITH SOME FRIENDS AND RODE OFF INTO THE SUNSET, WITH A WHOLE LOT OF FORGETTING AHEAD OF THEM.
ANGELA WOULD NOT FORGET, AND WOUND UP IN A MENTAL INSTITUTION. DOCTORS ARE HOPEFUL. SHE'S DECIDED TO BUY HERSELF A DOG AS SOON AS SHE GETS OUT. A BIG DOG.
SPEAKING OF DOCTORS, BERT MADE HISTORY! THE FIRST MAN TO RECEIVE A CROTCH TRANSPLANT FROM A BABOON DONOR. THE DOCTORS ARE STILL WAITING TO SEE IF HIS BODY WILL REJECT IT.
NOW THAT'S SOMETHING.
AND MYSELF, I'M JUST GLAD TO BE DONE WITH THIS CRAP! BUT I ONLY HAVE ONE MORE PANEL TO DO, SO HERE IT GOES.
INVESTIGATORS COME TO WISPYDALE, FIND NOTHING, AND WRITE-OFF THE MISSING DR. HAUGHT-SHEIK AS A KOOK. AND THAT CONCLUDES OUR LITTLE TALE ... OR DOES IT?
GENERAL STORE
and palm readings
ANOTHER ORDER OF MILK! SIGN HERE!
MILK
MILK
MILK
HEY, I SAW YOUR PICTURE IN THE PAPER! WEREN'T YOU THE ONLY SURVIVOR BACK WHEN ONE OF OLD SHERIFF BUGAHF'S CABINS COLLAPSED?
YES, I SURVIVED, THANKS TO MY NEW FRIENDS. AND NOW I RUN THE GENERAL STORE.
WELL, YOU'VE DOUBLED THE MILK ORDER FROM THE PREVIOUS OWNERS. I GUESS BUSINESS MUST BE PICKING UP IN THIS LITTLE TOWN.
I FEEL SAFER STOCKING UP. BESIDES, I'M EXPECTING COMPANY.
mew.
mew.
THE END
?
mew.
mew.
mew.
Sluggy Freelance Presents
A Bun-bun Production
KITTEN
CAST:
Kitten 1............ Michael Madsen
Kitten 2............ Claudia Black
Kitten 3............ Michael McManus
Kitten 4............ William Hootkins
Kitten 5............ Alyson Hannigan
Kitten 6............ Alex Winter
Kitten 7............ Billy Worth
Kitten 8............ Rumiko Takahashi
Kitten 9............ Steve Jackson
You've been watching "KITTEN"
See this movie again at 3.
Next, on OnSnore!
Bert Benigni in Crotch is Beautiful
OnSnore!
CAST:
Kitten 1........... Michael Madsen
Kitten 2........... Claudia Black
Kitten 3........... Michael McManus
Kitten 4........... William Hootkins
Kitten 5........... Alyson Hannigan
Kitten 6........... Alex Winter
Kitten 7........... Billy Worth
Kitten 8........... Rumiko Takahashi
Kitten 9........... Steve Jackson
Kitten 10.......... David Allen
Kitten 11.......... Tracy Hickman
Kitten 12.......... Margaret Weis
Kitten 13.......... Maria Tomspawn
Kitten 14.......... Tom Ricket
Kitten 15.......... Sam Thyla

SLUGGY FREELANCE

GEE, ZOË! SORRY YOUR BOYFRIEND GOT EATEN BY KITTENS!

IT'S FUNNY WHEN **HE** SAYS IT!

Chapter 19: K I T T E N

195

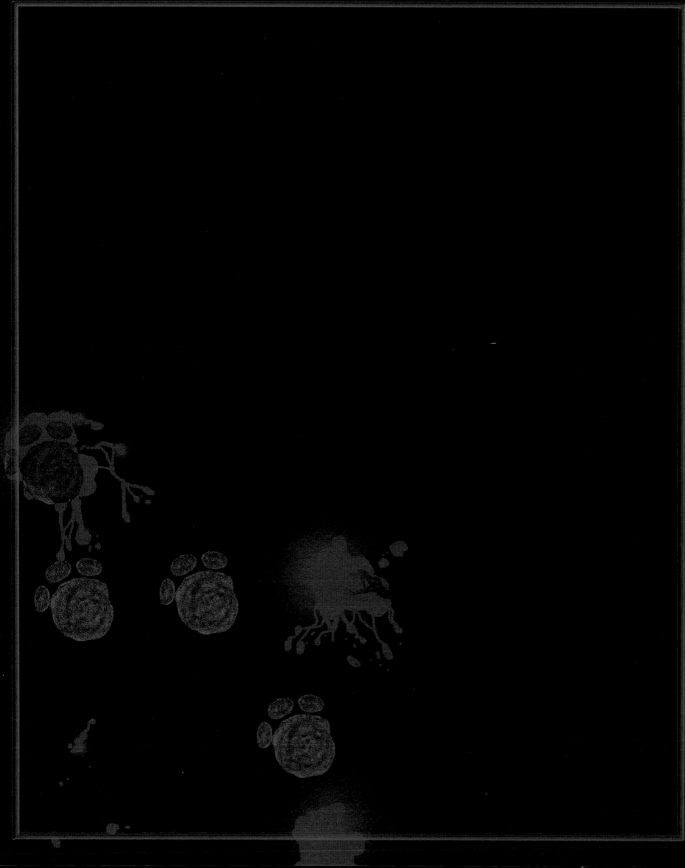

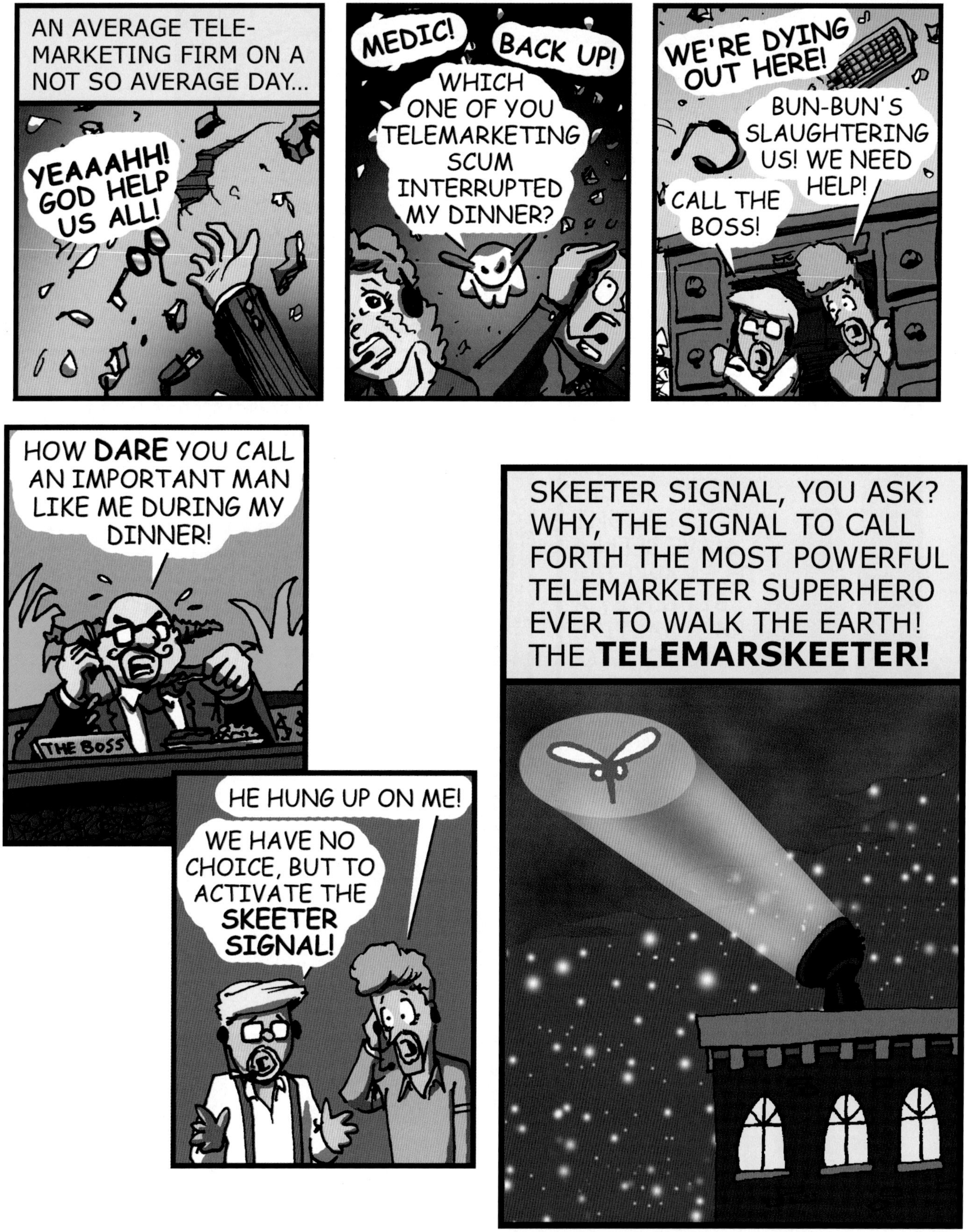
AN AVERAGE TELE-MARKETING FIRM ON A NOT SO AVERAGE DAY...
YEAAAHH! GOD HELP US ALL!
MEDIC!
BACK UP!
WHICH ONE OF YOU TELEMARKETING SCUM INTERRUPTED MY DINNER?
WE'RE DYING OUT HERE!
BUN-BUN'S SLAUGHTERING US! WE NEED HELP!
CALL THE BOSS!
HOW DARE YOU CALL AN IMPORTANT MAN LIKE ME DURING MY DINNER!
THE BOSS
HE HUNG UP ON ME!
WE HAVE NO CHOICE, BUT TO ACTIVATE THE SKEETER SIGNAL!
SKEETER SIGNAL, YOU ASK? WHY, THE SIGNAL TO CALL FORTH THE MOST POWERFUL TELEMARKETER SUPERHERO EVER TO WALK THE EARTH! THE TELEMARSKEETER!

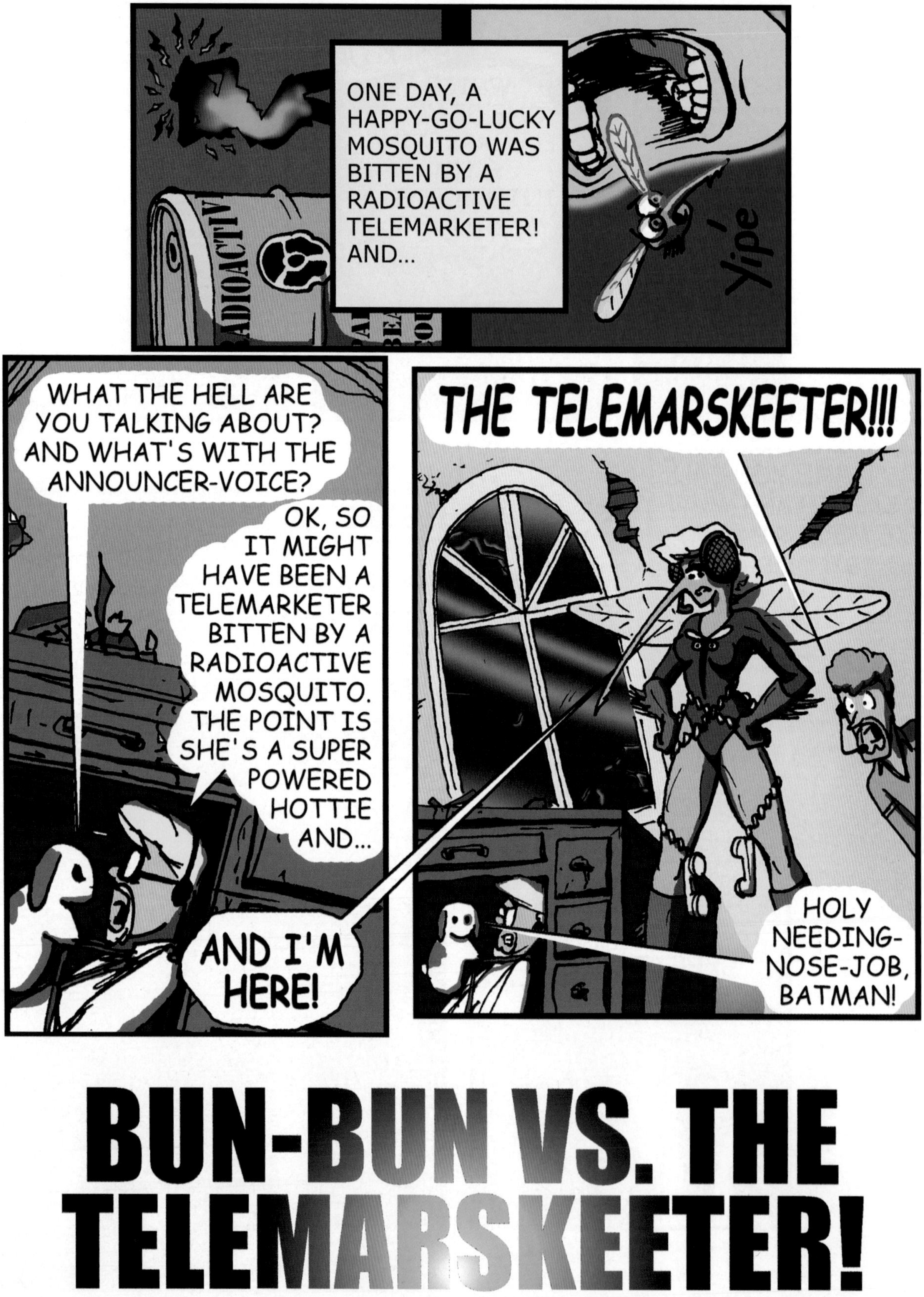
ONE DAY, A HAPPY-GO-LUCKY MOSQUITO WAS BITTEN BY A RADIOACTIVE TELEMARKETER! AND...
Yipe
WHAT THE HELL ARE YOU TALKING ABOUT? AND WHAT'S WITH THE ANNOUNCER-VOICE?
OK, SO IT MIGHT HAVE BEEN A TELEMARKETER BITTEN BY A RADIOACTIVE MOSQUITO. THE POINT IS SHE'S A SUPER POWERED HOTTIE AND...
THE TELEMARSKEETER!!!
AND I'M HERE!
HOLY NEEDING-NOSE-JOB, BATMAN!

BUN-BUN VS. THE TELEMARSKEETER!

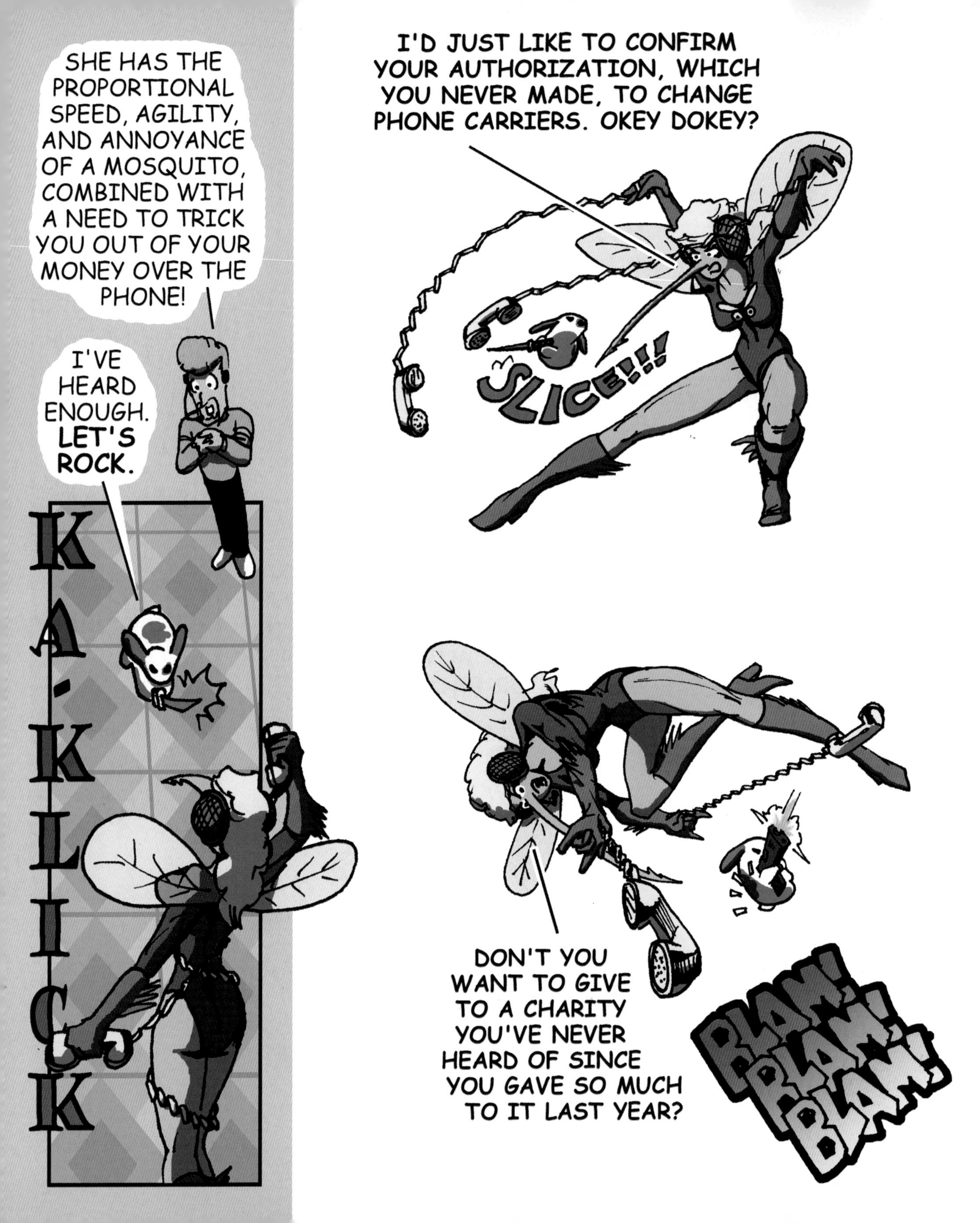
SHE HAS THE PROPORTIONAL SPEED, AGILITY, AND ANNOYANCE OF A MOSQUITO, COMBINED WITH A NEED TO TRICK YOU OUT OF YOUR MONEY OVER THE PHONE!
I'VE HEARD ENOUGH. LET'S ROCK.
KA-KLICK
I'D JUST LIKE TO CONFIRM YOUR AUTHORIZATION, WHICH YOU NEVER MADE, TO CHANGE PHONE CARRIERS. OKEY DOKEY?
SLICE!!!
DON'T YOU WANT TO GIVE TO A CHARITY YOU'VE NEVER HEARD OF SINCE YOU GAVE SO MUCH TO IT LAST YEAR?
BLAM! BLAM! BLAM!

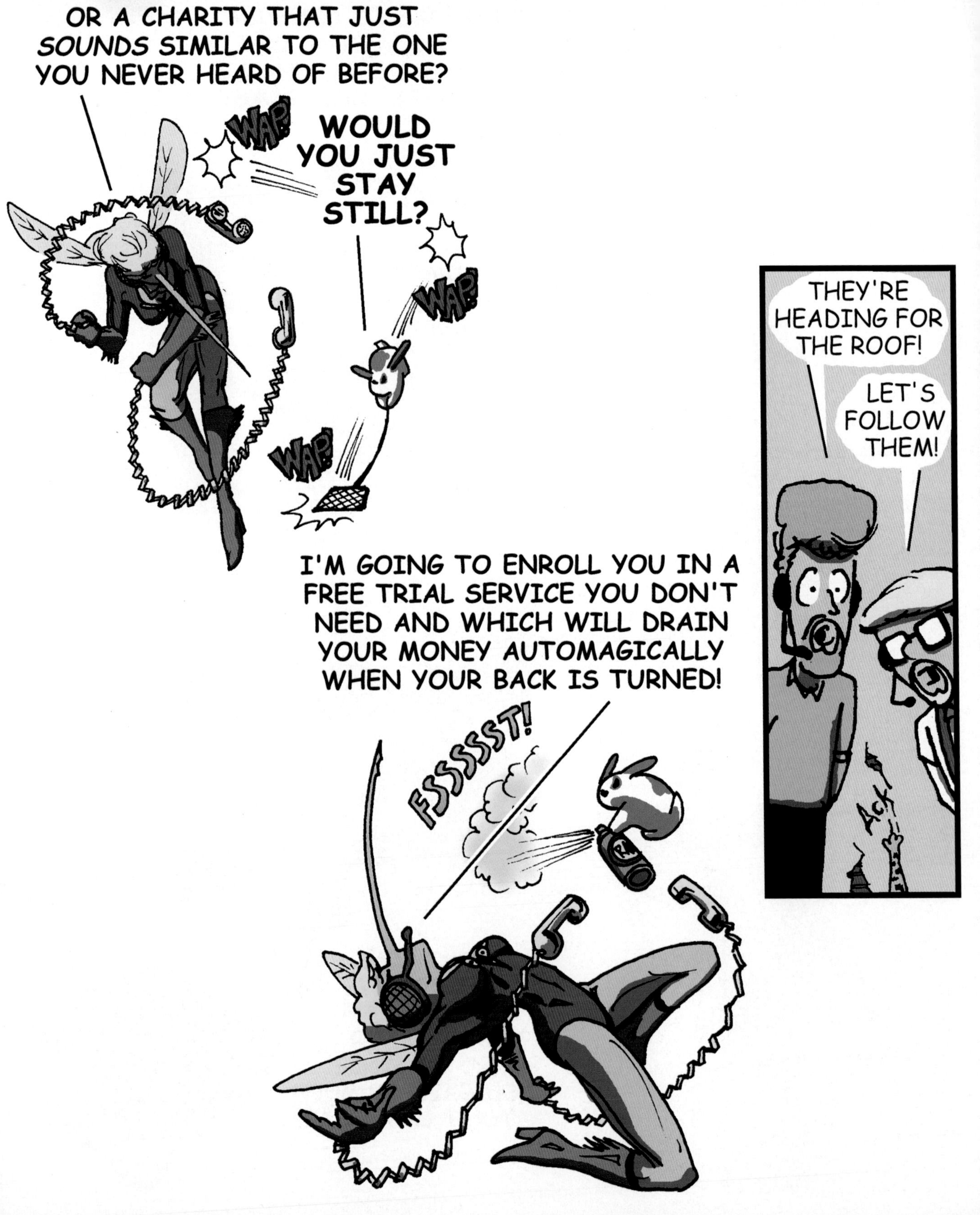
OR A CHARITY THAT JUST *SOUNDS* SIMILAR TO THE ONE YOU NEVER HEARD OF BEFORE?
WAP!
WOULD YOU JUST STAY STILL?
WAP!
WAP!
I'M GOING TO ENROLL YOU IN A FREE TRIAL SERVICE YOU DON'T NEED AND WHICH WILL DRAIN YOUR MONEY AUTOMAGICALLY WHEN YOUR BACK IS TURNED!
FSSSSST!
THEY'RE HEADING FOR THE ROOF!
LET'S FOLLOW THEM!
ACK

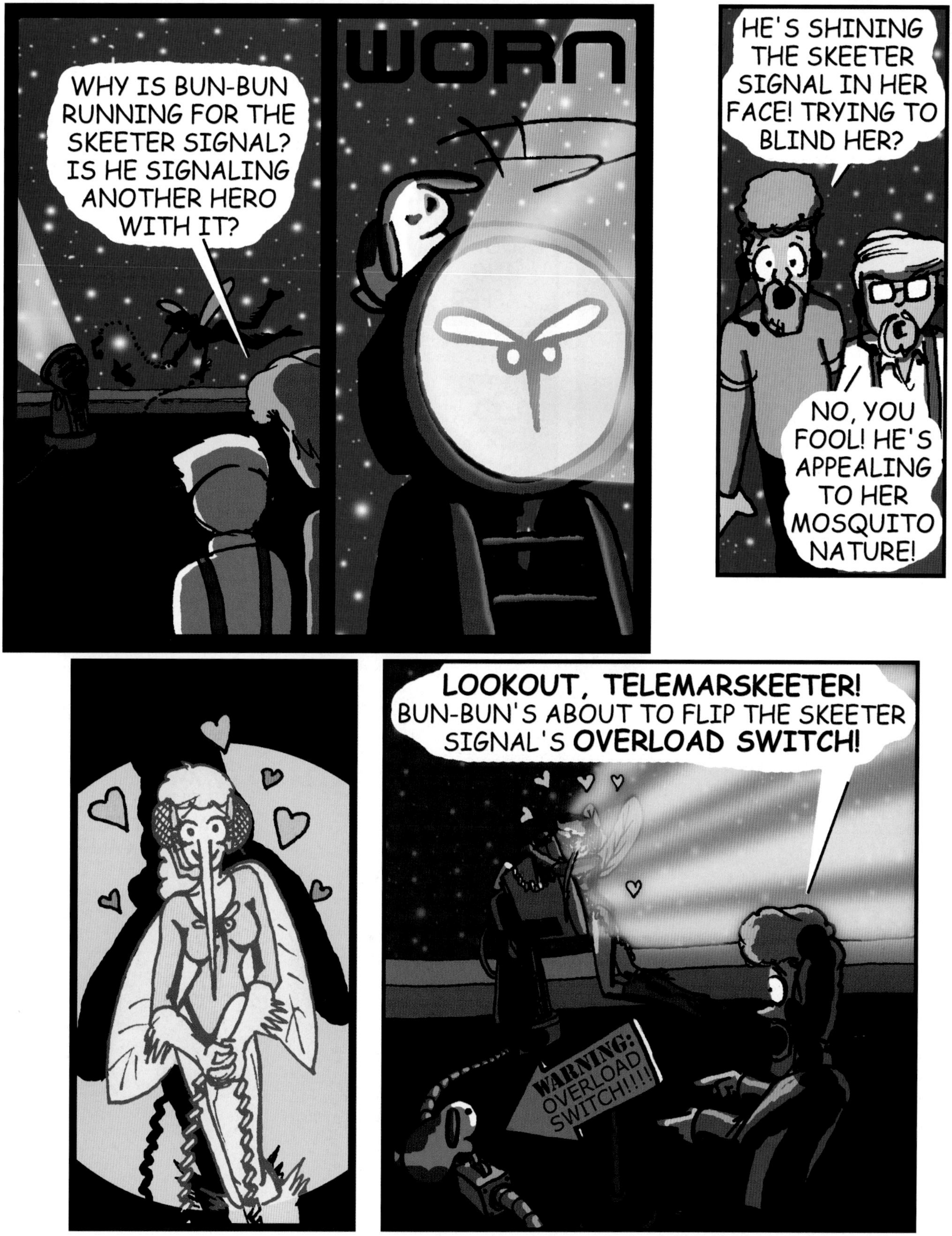
WHY IS BUN-BUN RUNNING FOR THE SKEETER SIGNAL? IS HE SIGNALING ANOTHER HERO WITH IT?
WORN
HE'S SHINING THE SKEETER SIGNAL IN HER FACE! TRYING TO BLIND HER?
NO, YOU FOOL! HE'S APPEALING TO HER MOSQUITO NATURE!
LOOKOUT, TELEMARSKEETER! BUN-BUN'S ABOUT TO FLIP THE SKEETER SIGNAL'S OVERLOAD SWITCH!
WARNING: OVERLOAD SWITCH!!!!

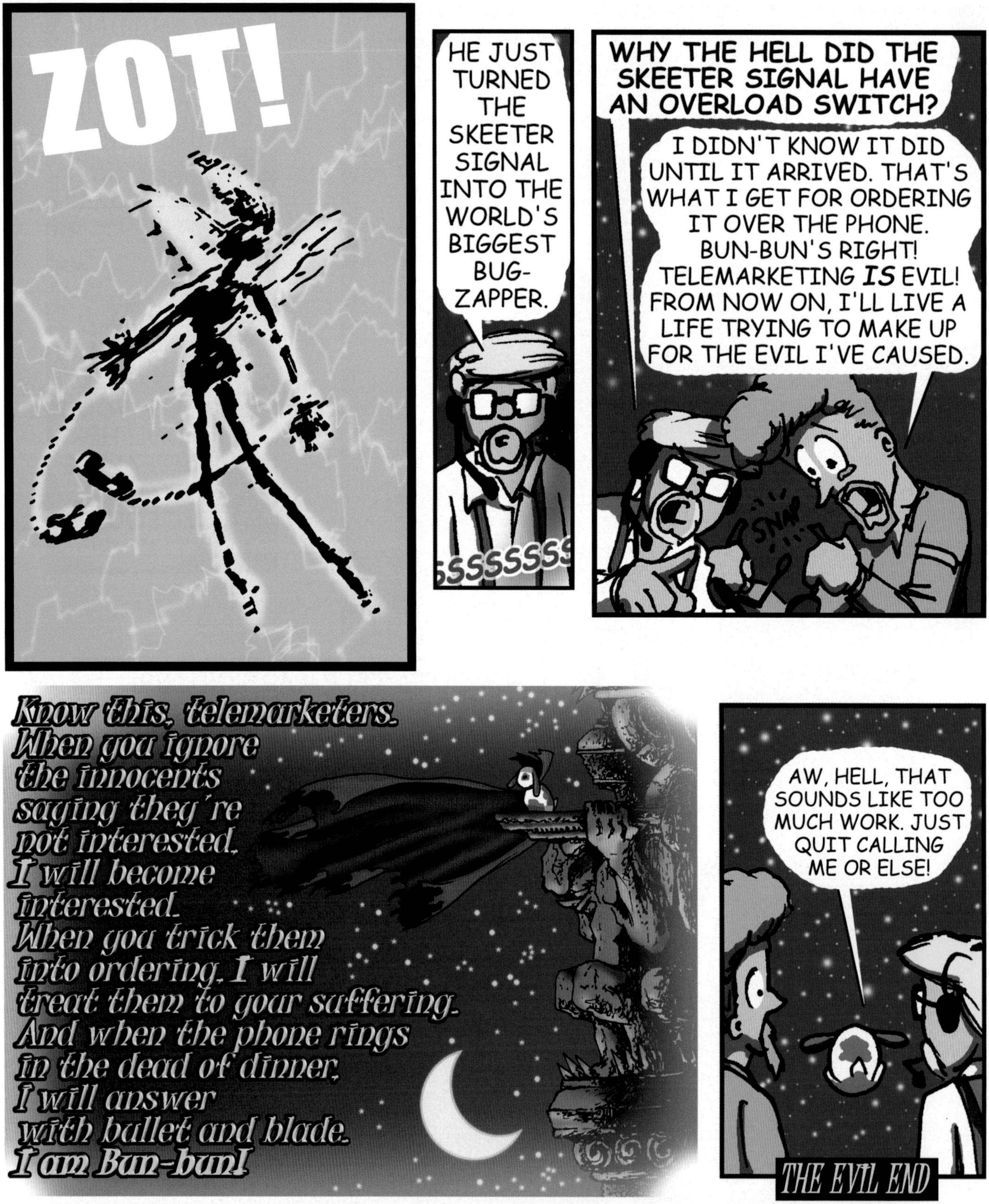
ZOT!
HE JUST TURNED THE SKEETER SIGNAL INTO THE WORLD'S BIGGEST BUG-ZAPPER.
SSSSSSSS
WHY THE HELL DID THE SKEETER SIGNAL HAVE AN OVERLOAD SWITCH?
I DIDN'T KNOW IT DID UNTIL IT ARRIVED. THAT'S WHAT I GET FOR ORDERING IT OVER THE PHONE. BUN-BUN'S RIGHT! TELEMARKETING IS EVIL! FROM NOW ON, I'LL LIVE A LIFE TRYING TO MAKE UP FOR THE EVIL I'VE CAUSED.
SNAP
Know this, telemarketers. When you ignore the innocents saying they're not interested, I will become interested. When you trick them into ordering, I will treat them to your suffering. And when the phone rings in the dead of dinner, I will answer with bullet and blade. I am Bun-bun!
AW, HELL, THAT SOUNDS LIKE TOO MUCH WORK. JUST QUIT CALLING ME OR ELSE!
THE EVIL END

SLUGGY FREELANCE BOOK 6
THE BUG, THE WITCH, AND THE ROBOT
by Pete Abrams

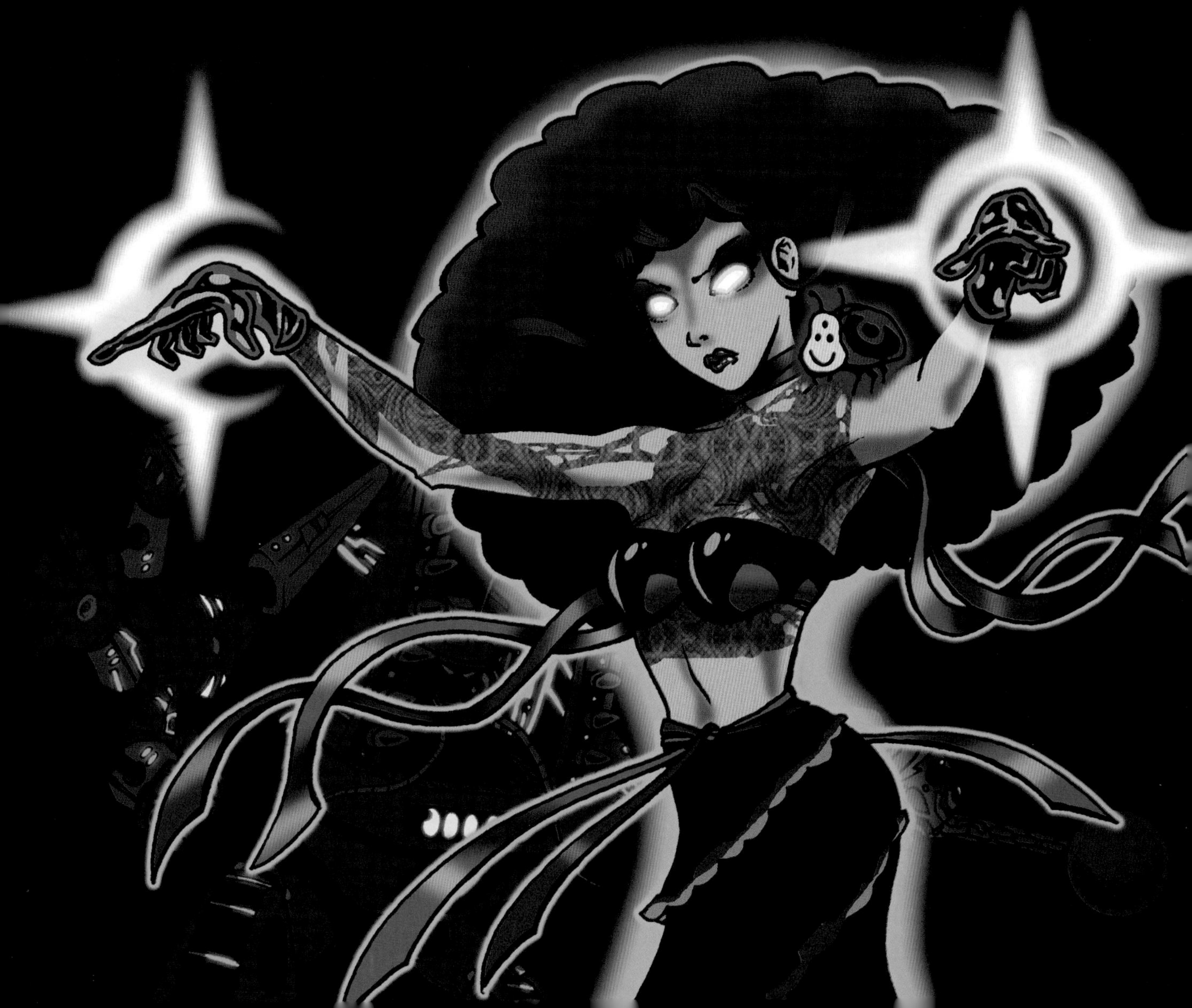

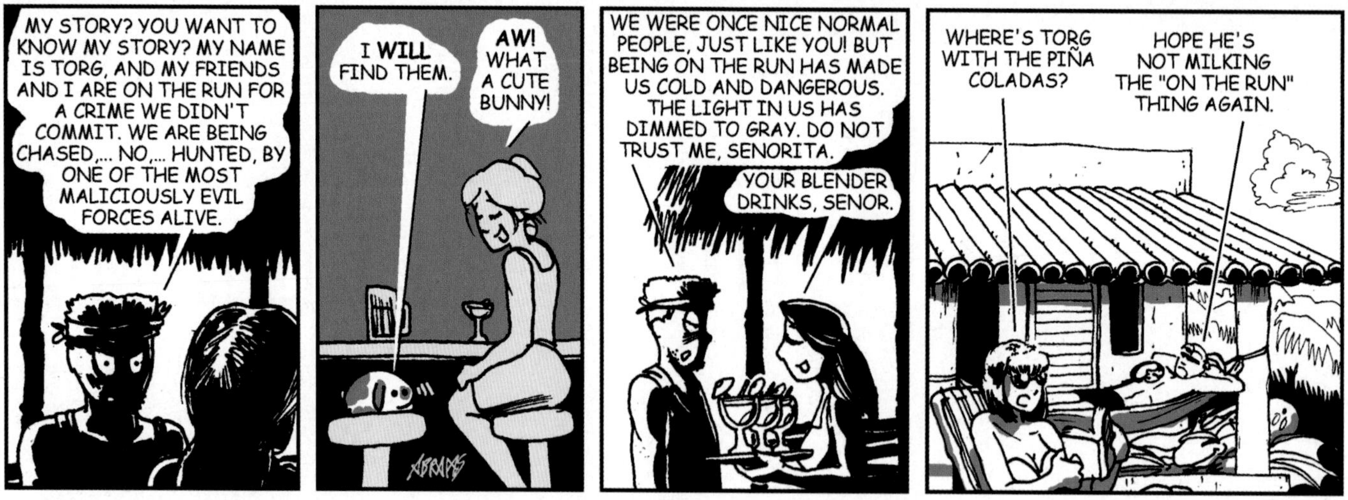
MY STORY? YOU WANT TO KNOW MY STORY? MY NAME IS TORG, AND MY FRIENDS AND I ARE ON THE RUN FOR A CRIME WE DIDN'T COMMIT. WE ARE BEING CHASED,... NO,... HUNTED, BY ONE OF THE MOST MALICIOUSLY EVIL FORCES ALIVE.
I WILL FIND THEM.
AW! WHAT A CUTE BUNNY!
WE WERE ONCE NICE NORMAL PEOPLE, JUST LIKE YOU! BUT BEING ON THE RUN HAS MADE US COLD AND DANGEROUS. THE LIGHT IN US HAS DIMMED TO GRAY. DO NOT TRUST ME, SENORITA.
YOUR BLENDER DRINKS, SENOR.
WHERE'S TORG WITH THE PIÑA COLADAS?
HOPE HE'S NOT MILKING THE "ON THE RUN" THING AGAIN.

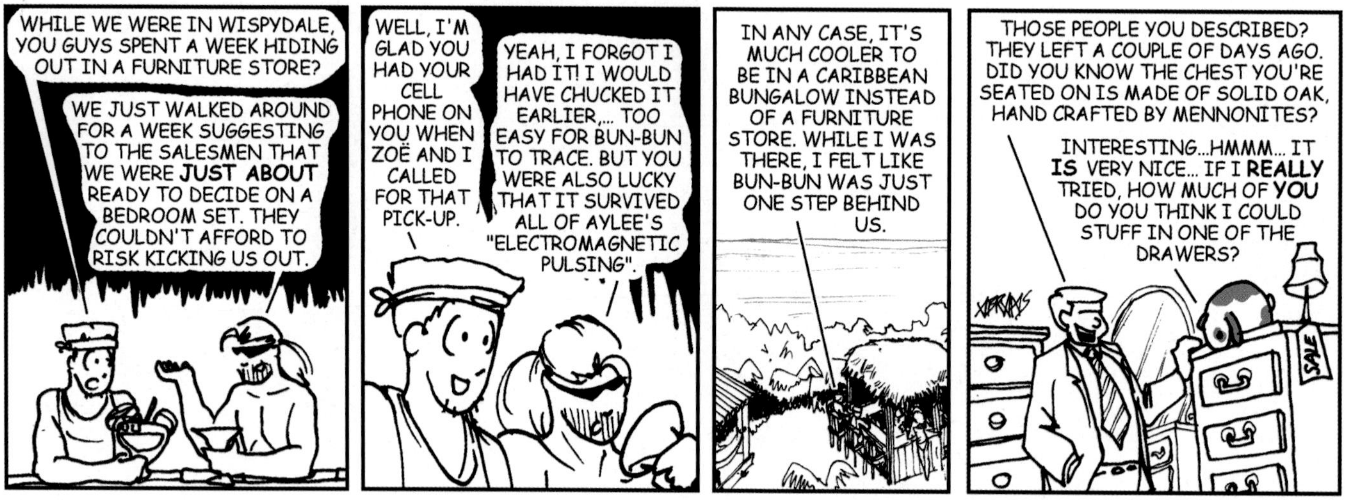
WHILE WE WERE IN WISPYDALE, YOU GUYS SPENT A WEEK HIDING OUT IN A FURNITURE STORE?
WE JUST WALKED AROUND FOR A WEEK SUGGESTING TO THE SALESMEN THAT WE WERE JUST ABOUT READY TO DECIDE ON A BEDROOM SET. THEY COULDN'T AFFORD TO RISK KICKING US OUT.
WELL, I'M GLAD YOU HAD YOUR CELL PHONE ON YOU WHEN ZOË AND I CALLED FOR THAT PICK-UP.
YEAH, I FORGOT I HAD IT! I WOULD HAVE CHUCKED IT EARLIER,... TOO EASY FOR BUN-BUN TO TRACE. BUT YOU WERE ALSO LUCKY THAT IT SURVIVED ALL OF AYLEE'S "ELECTROMAGNETIC PULSING".
IN ANY CASE, IT'S MUCH COOLER TO BE IN A CARIBBEAN BUNGALOW INSTEAD OF A FURNITURE STORE. WHILE I WAS THERE, I FELT LIKE BUN-BUN WAS JUST ONE STEP BEHIND US.
THOSE PEOPLE YOU DESCRIBED? THEY LEFT A COUPLE OF DAYS AGO. DID YOU KNOW THE CHEST YOU'RE SEATED ON IS MADE OF SOLID OAK, HAND CRAFTED BY MENNONITES?
INTERESTING...HMMM... IT IS VERY NICE... IF I REALLY TRIED, HOW MUCH OF YOU DO YOU THINK I COULD STUFF IN ONE OF THE DRAWERS?
SALE

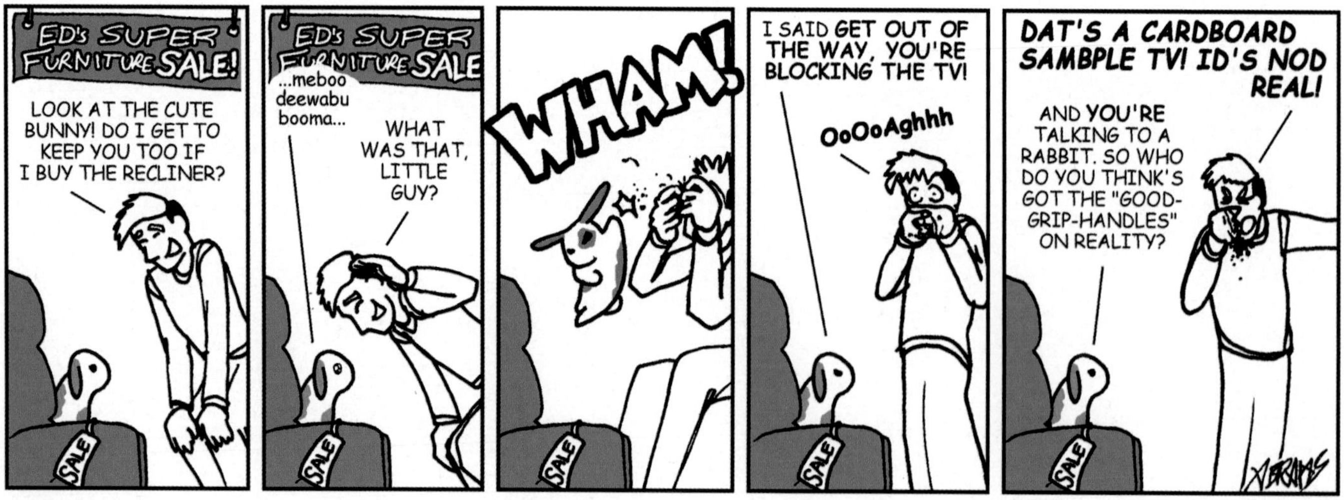
ED's SUPER FURNITURE SALE!
LOOK AT THE CUTE BUNNY! DO I GET TO KEEP YOU TOO IF I BUY THE RECLINER?
SALE
...meboo deewabu booma...
WHAT WAS THAT, LITTLE GUY?
WHAM!
I SAID GET OUT OF THE WAY, YOU'RE BLOCKING THE TV!
OoOoAghhh
DAT'S A CARDBOARD SAMBPLE TV! ID'S NOD REAL!
AND YOU'RE TALKING TO A RABBIT. SO WHO DO YOU THINK'S GOT THE "GOOD-GRIP-HANDLES" ON REALITY?

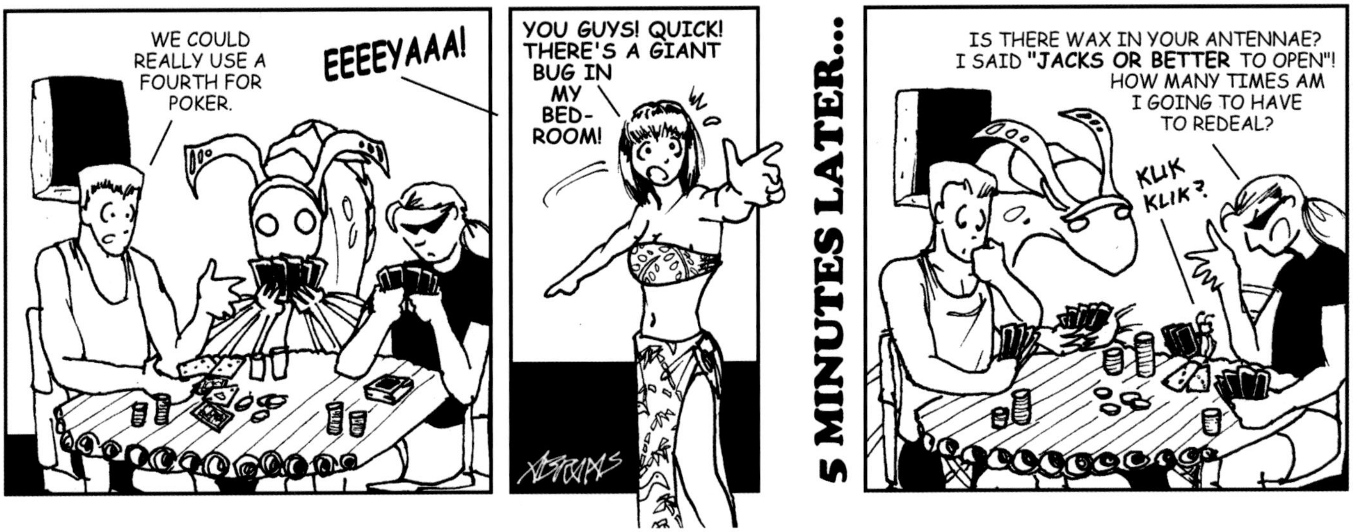
WE COULD REALLY USE A FOURTH FOR POKER.
EEEEYAAA!
YOU GUYS! QUICK! THERE'S A GIANT BUG IN MY BED-ROOM!
5 MINUTES LATER...
IS THERE WAX IN YOUR ANTENNAE? I SAID "JACKS OR BETTER TO OPEN"! HOW MANY TIMES AM I GOING TO HAVE TO REDEAL?
KLIK KLIK?

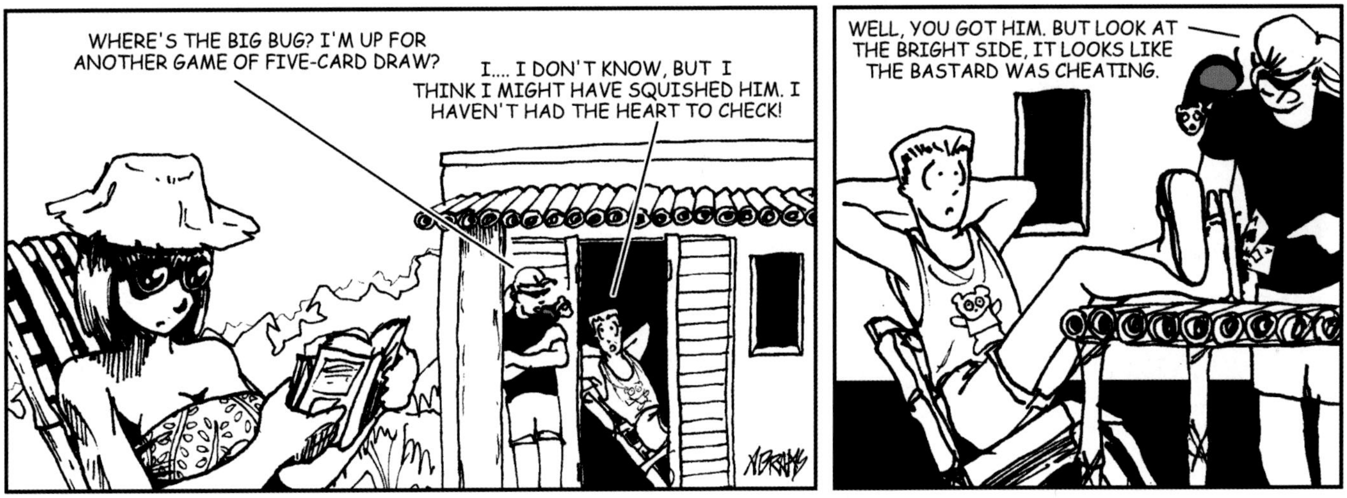
WHERE'S THE BIG BUG? I'M UP FOR ANOTHER GAME OF FIVE-CARD DRAW?
I.... I DON'T KNOW, BUT I THINK I MIGHT HAVE SQUISHED HIM. I HAVEN'T HAD THE HEART TO CHECK!
WELL, YOU GOT HIM. BUT LOOK AT THE BRIGHT SIDE, IT LOOKS LIKE THE BASTARD WAS CHEATING.

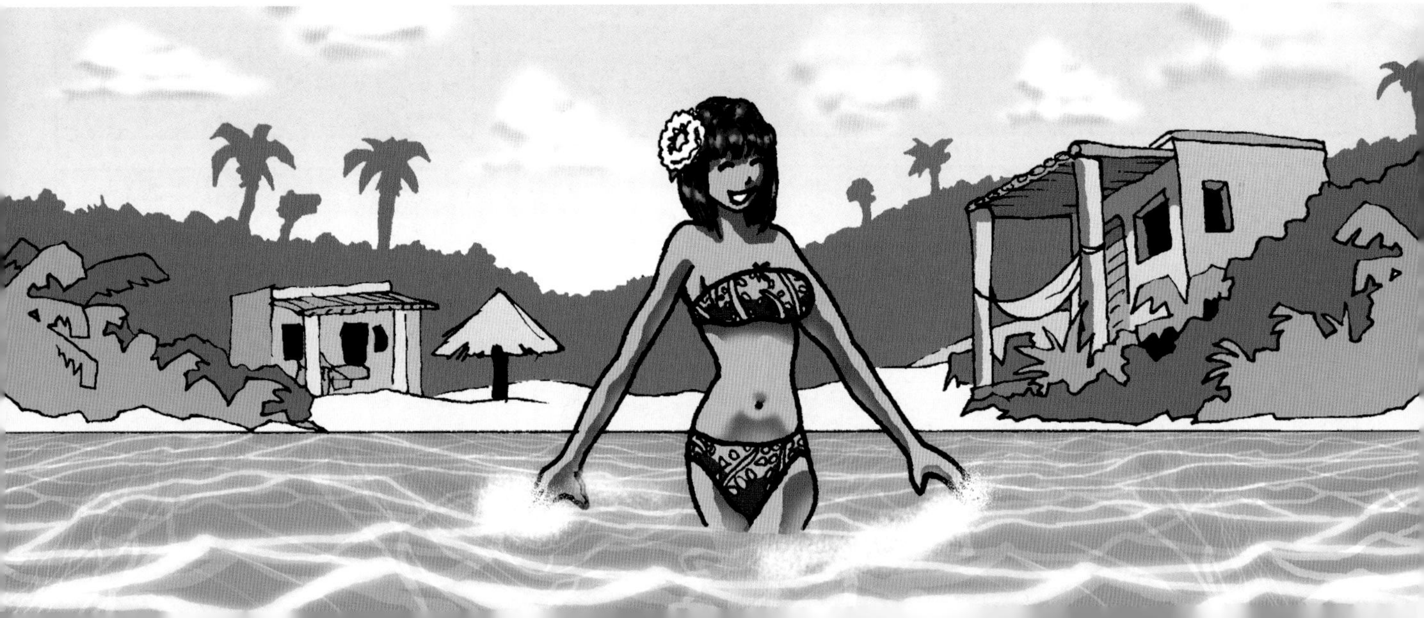

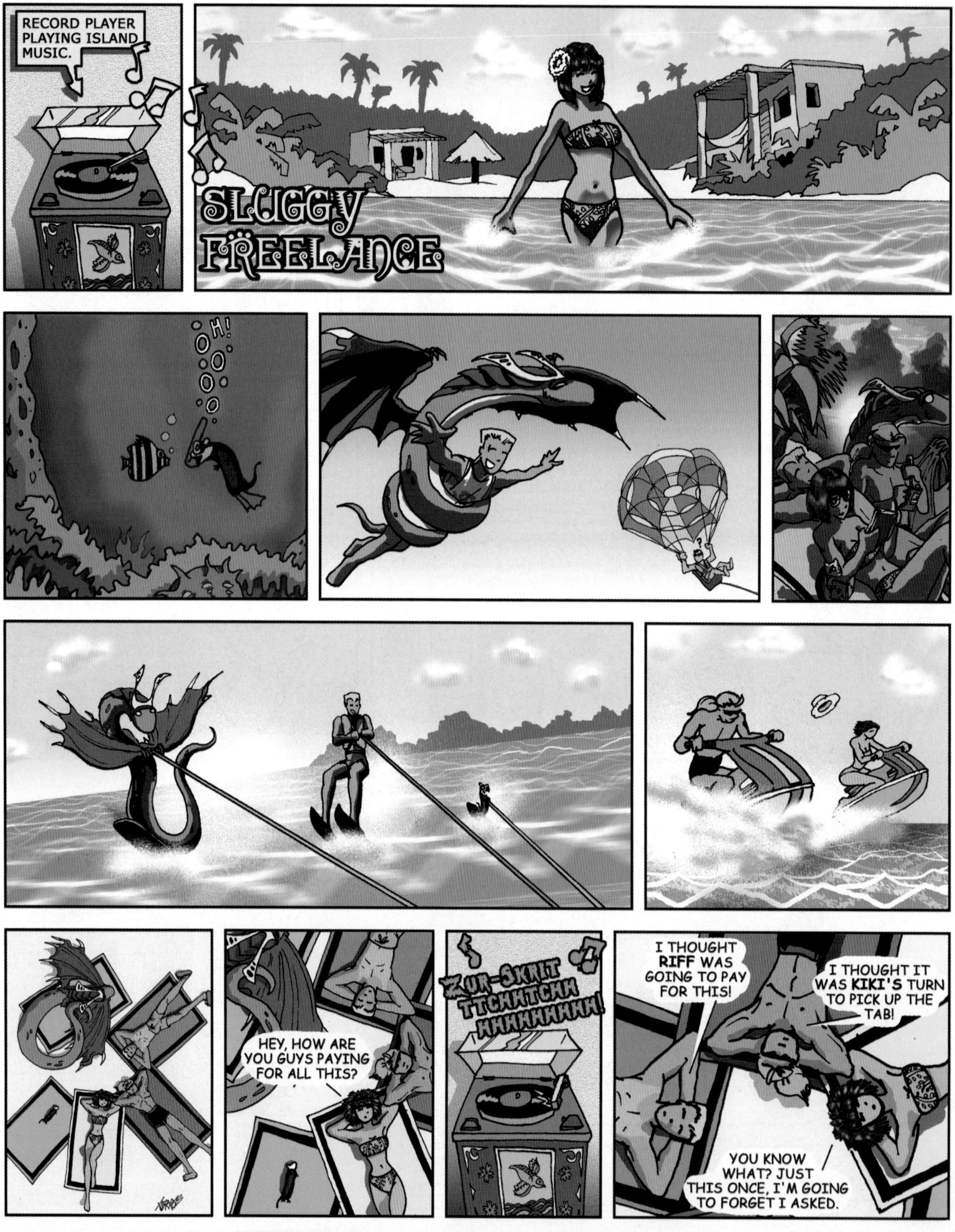
RECORD PLAYER PLAYING ISLAND MUSIC.
SLUGGY FREELANCE
OH!
HEY, HOW ARE YOU GUYS PAYING FOR ALL THIS?
ZUR-SKRIT TTCHHTCHH HHHHHHHHH!
I THOUGHT RIFF WAS GOING TO PAY FOR THIS!
I THOUGHT IT WAS KIKI'S TURN TO PICK UP THE TAB!
YOU KNOW WHAT? JUST THIS ONCE, I'M GOING TO FORGET I ASKED.

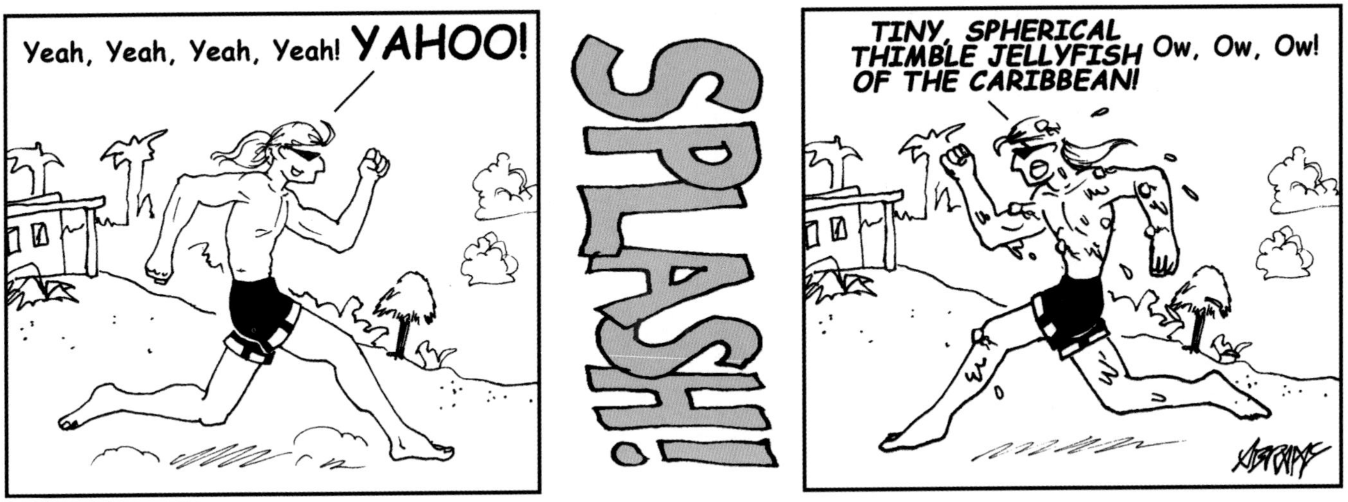
Yeah, Yeah, Yeah, Yeah! YAHOO!
SPLASH!
TINY, SPHERICAL THIMBLE JELLYFISH OF THE CARIBBEAN!
Ow, Ow, Ow!

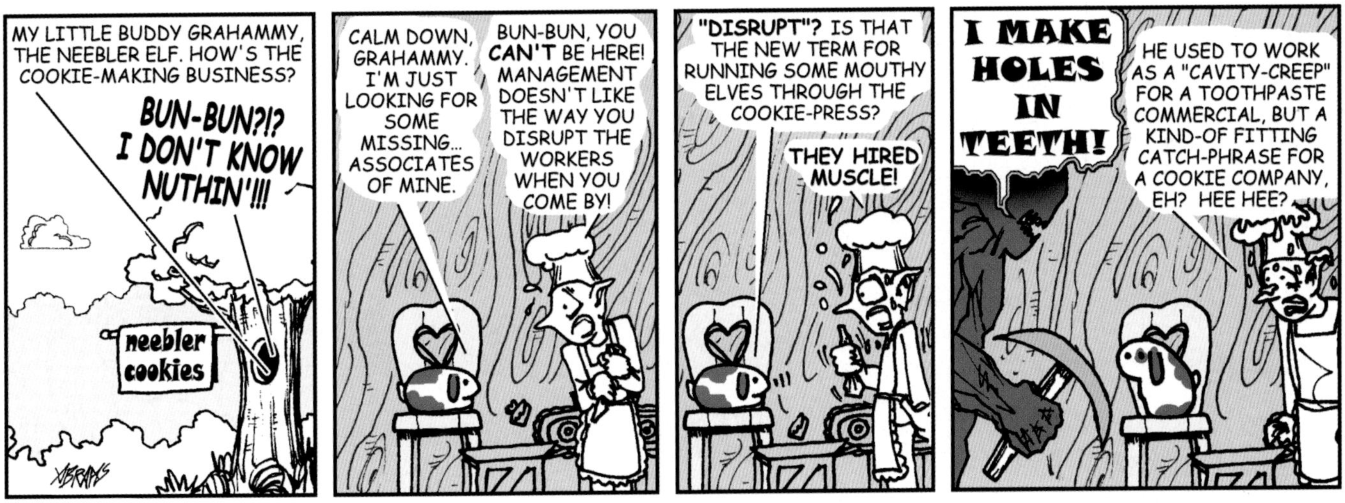
MY LITTLE BUDDY GRAHAMMY, THE NEEBLER ELF. HOW'S THE COOKIE-MAKING BUSINESS?
BUN-BUN?!? I DON'T KNOW NUTHIN'!!!
neebler cookies
CALM DOWN, GRAHAMMY. I'M JUST LOOKING FOR SOME MISSING... ASSOCIATES OF MINE.
BUN-BUN, YOU CAN'T BE HERE! MANAGEMENT DOESN'T LIKE THE WAY YOU DISRUPT THE WORKERS WHEN YOU COME BY!
"DISRUPT"? IS THAT THE NEW TERM FOR RUNNING SOME MOUTHY ELVES THROUGH THE COOKIE-PRESS?
THEY HIRED MUSCLE!
I MAKE HOLES IN TEETH!
HE USED TO WORK AS A "CAVITY-CREEP" FOR A TOOTHPASTE COMMERCIAL, BUT A KIND-OF FITTING CATCH-PHRASE FOR A COOKIE COMPANY, EH? HEE HEE?

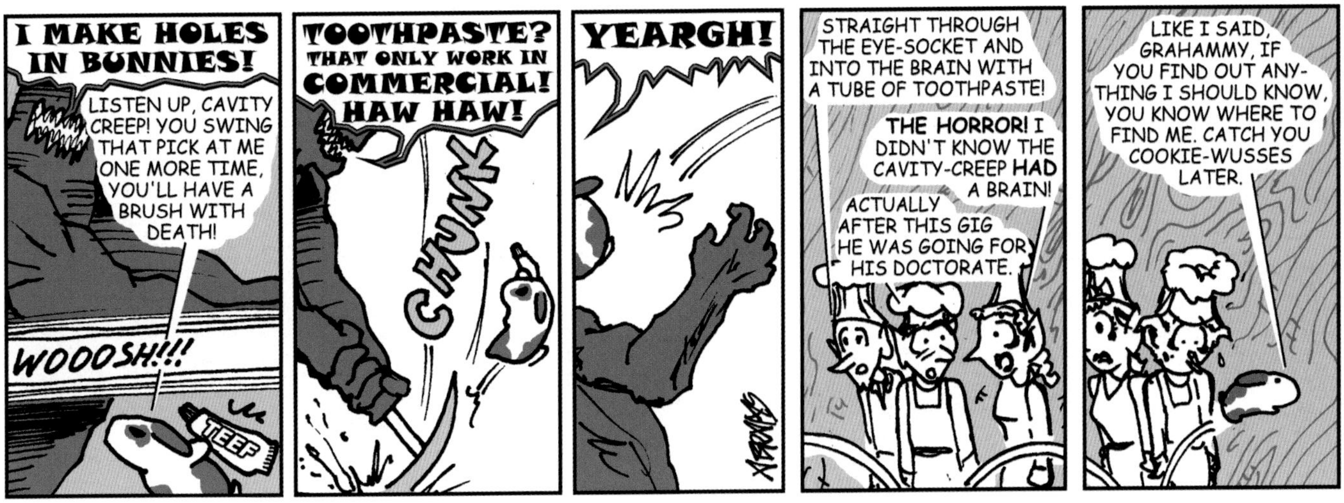
I MAKE HOLES IN BUNNIES!
LISTEN UP, CAVITY CREEP! YOU SWING THAT PICK AT ME ONE MORE TIME, YOU'LL HAVE A BRUSH WITH DEATH!
WOOOSH!!!
TEEF
TOOTHPASTE? THAT ONLY WORK IN COMMERCIAL! HAW HAW!
CHUNK
YEARGH!
STRAIGHT THROUGH THE EYE-SOCKET AND INTO THE BRAIN WITH A TUBE OF TOOTHPASTE!
THE HORROR! I DIDN'T KNOW THE CAVITY-CREEP HAD A BRAIN!
ACTUALLY AFTER THIS GIG HE WAS GOING FOR HIS DOCTORATE.
LIKE I SAID, GRAHAMMY, IF YOU FIND OUT ANY-THING I SHOULD KNOW, YOU KNOW WHERE TO FIND ME. CATCH YOU COOKIE-WUSSES LATER.

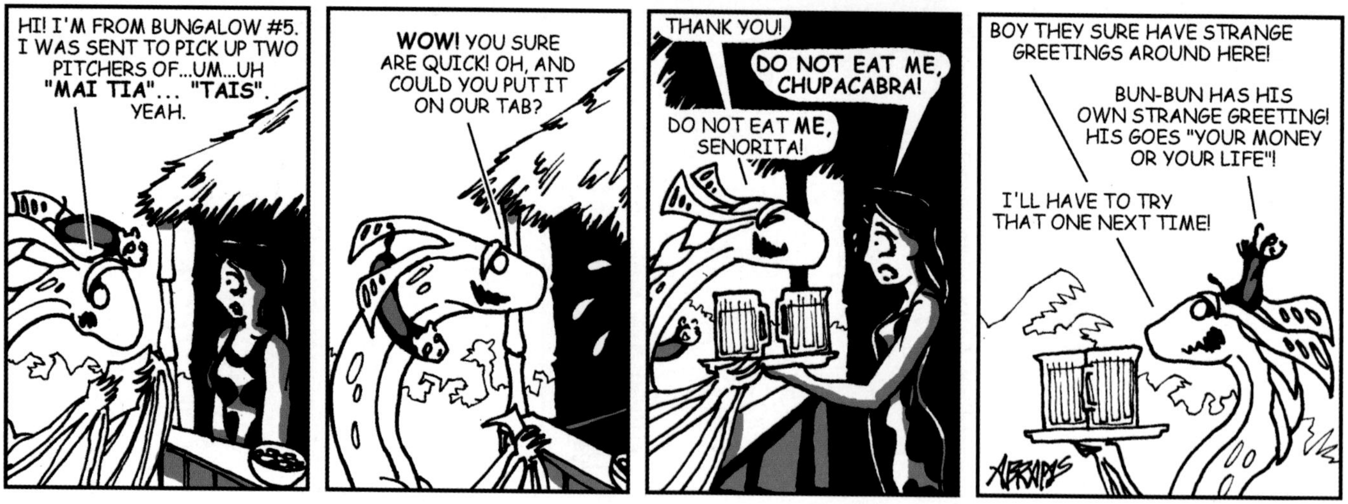

HI! I'M FROM BUNGALOW #5. I WAS SENT TO PICK UP TWO PITCHERS OF...UM...UH "MAI TIA"... "TAIS". YEAH.
WOW! YOU SURE ARE QUICK! OH, AND COULD YOU PUT IT ON OUR TAB?
THANK YOU!
DO NOT EAT ME, CHUPACABRA!
DO NOT EAT ME, SENORITA!
BOY THEY SURE HAVE STRANGE GREETINGS AROUND HERE!
BUN-BUN HAS HIS OWN STRANGE GREETING! HIS GOES "YOUR MONEY OR YOUR LIFE"!
I'LL HAVE TO TRY THAT ONE NEXT TIME!

OFFICIAL SLUGGY FREELANCE THIRD ANNIVERSARY COMIC

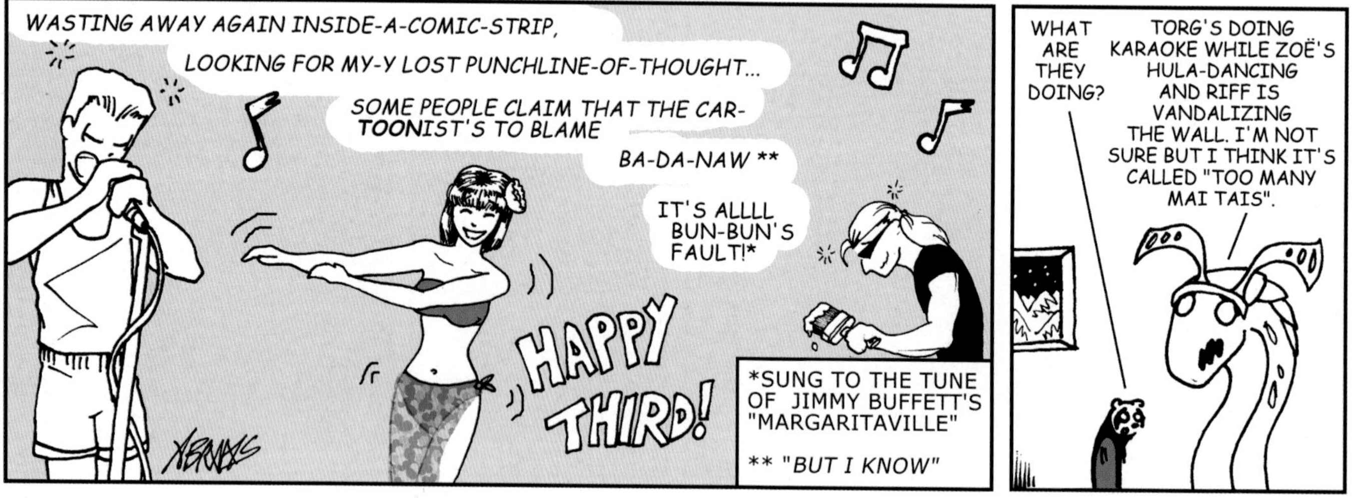

WASTING AWAY AGAIN INSIDE-A-COMIC-STRIP,
LOOKING FOR MY-Y LOST PUNCHLINE-OF-THOUGHT...
SOME PEOPLE CLAIM THAT THE CAR-TOONIST'S TO BLAME
BA-DA-NAW **
IT'S ALLLL BUN-BUN'S FAULT!*
HAPPY THIRD!
*SUNG TO THE TUNE OF JIMMY BUFFETT'S "MARGARITAVILLE"
** "BUT I KNOW"
WHAT ARE THEY DOING?
TORG'S DOING KARAOKE WHILE ZOË'S HULA-DANCING AND RIFF IS VANDALIZING THE WALL. I'M NOT SURE BUT I THINK IT'S CALLED "TOO MANY MAI TAIS".

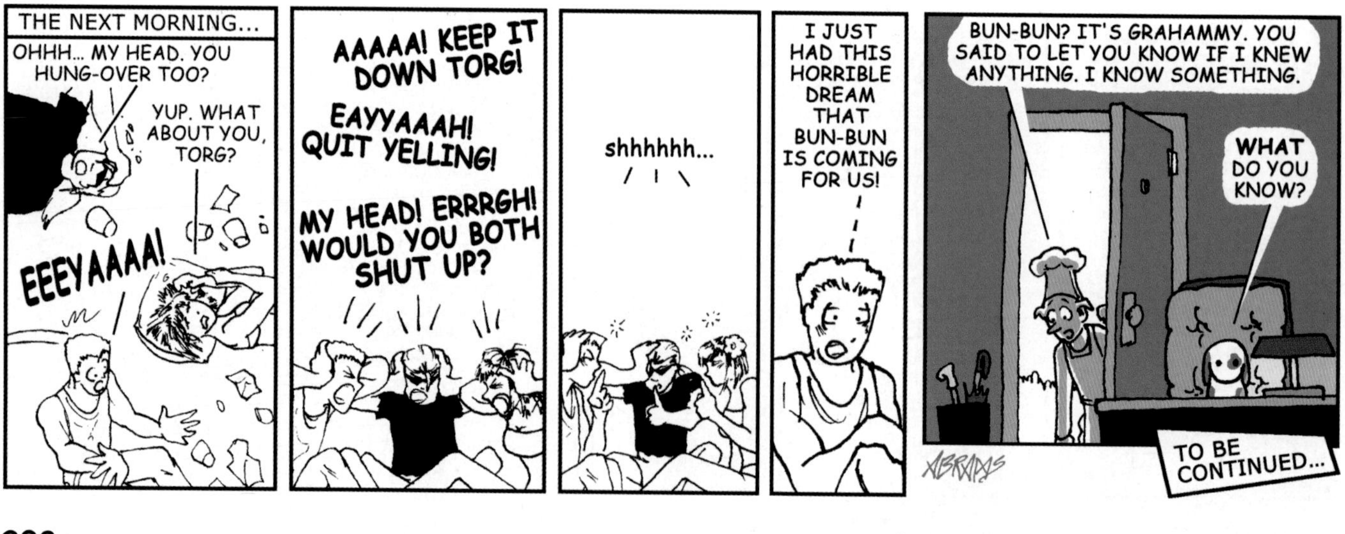

THE NEXT MORNING...
OHHH... MY HEAD. YOU HUNG-OVER TOO?
YUP. WHAT ABOUT YOU, TORG?
EEEYAAAA!
AAAAA! KEEP IT DOWN TORG!
EAYYAAAH! QUIT YELLING!
MY HEAD! ERRRGH! WOULD YOU BOTH SHUT UP?
shhhhhh...
I JUST HAD THIS HORRIBLE DREAM THAT BUN-BUN IS COMING FOR US!
BUN-BUN? IT'S GRAHAMMY. YOU SAID TO LET YOU KNOW IF I KNEW ANYTHING. I KNOW SOMETHING.
WHAT DO YOU KNOW?
TO BE CONTINUED...

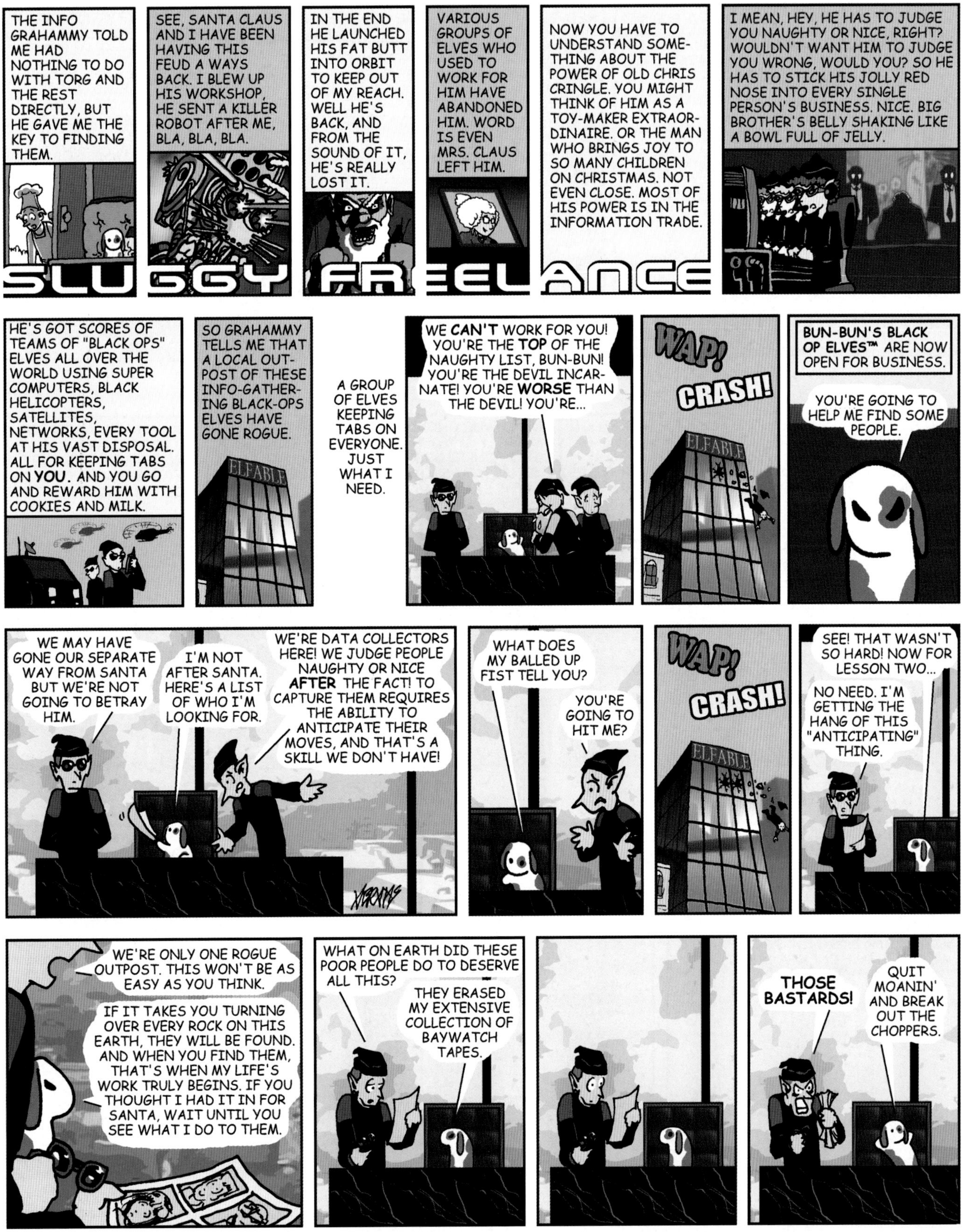
THE INFO GRAHAMMY TOLD ME HAD NOTHING TO DO WITH TORG AND THE REST DIRECTLY, BUT HE GAVE ME THE KEY TO FINDING THEM.
SEE, SANTA CLAUS AND I HAVE BEEN HAVING THIS FEUD A WAYS BACK. I BLEW UP HIS WORKSHOP, HE SENT A KILLER ROBOT AFTER ME, BLA, BLA, BLA.
IN THE END HE LAUNCHED HIS FAT BUTT INTO ORBIT TO KEEP OUT OF MY REACH. WELL HE'S BACK, AND FROM THE SOUND OF IT, HE'S REALLY LOST IT.
VARIOUS GROUPS OF ELVES WHO USED TO WORK FOR HIM HAVE ABANDONED HIM. WORD IS EVEN MRS. CLAUS LEFT HIM.
NOW YOU HAVE TO UNDERSTAND SOMETHING ABOUT THE POWER OF OLD CHRIS CRINGLE. YOU MIGHT THINK OF HIM AS A TOY-MAKER EXTRAORDINAIRE. OR THE MAN WHO BRINGS JOY TO SO MANY CHILDREN ON CHRISTMAS. NOT EVEN CLOSE. MOST OF HIS POWER IS IN THE INFORMATION TRADE.
I MEAN, HEY, HE HAS TO JUDGE YOU NAUGHTY OR NICE, RIGHT? WOULDN'T WANT HIM TO JUDGE YOU WRONG, WOULD YOU? SO HE HAS TO STICK HIS JOLLY RED NOSE INTO EVERY SINGLE PERSON'S BUSINESS. NICE. BIG BROTHER'S BELLY SHAKING LIKE A BOWL FULL OF JELLY.
SLUGGY FREELANCE
HE'S GOT SCORES OF TEAMS OF "BLACK OPS" ELVES ALL OVER THE WORLD USING SUPER COMPUTERS, BLACK HELICOPTERS, SATELLITES, NETWORKS, EVERY TOOL AT HIS VAST DISPOSAL. ALL FOR KEEPING TABS ON YOU. AND YOU GO AND REWARD HIM WITH COOKIES AND MILK.
SO GRAHAMMY TELLS ME THAT A LOCAL OUTPOST OF THESE INFO-GATHERING BLACK-OPS ELVES HAVE GONE ROGUE.
ELFABLE
A GROUP OF ELVES KEEPING TABS ON EVERYONE. JUST WHAT I NEED.
WE CAN'T WORK FOR YOU! YOU'RE THE TOP OF THE NAUGHTY LIST, BUN-BUN! YOU'RE THE DEVIL INCARNATE! YOU'RE WORSE THAN THE DEVIL! YOU'RE...
WAP!
CRASH!
ELFABLE
BUN-BUN'S BLACK OP ELVES™ ARE NOW OPEN FOR BUSINESS.
YOU'RE GOING TO HELP ME FIND SOME PEOPLE.
WE MAY HAVE GONE OUR SEPARATE WAY FROM SANTA BUT WE'RE NOT GOING TO BETRAY HIM.
I'M NOT AFTER SANTA. HERE'S A LIST OF WHO I'M LOOKING FOR.
WE'RE DATA COLLECTORS HERE! WE JUDGE PEOPLE NAUGHTY OR NICE AFTER THE FACT! TO CAPTURE THEM REQUIRES THE ABILITY TO ANTICIPATE THEIR MOVES, AND THAT'S A SKILL WE DON'T HAVE!
WHAT DOES MY BALLED UP FIST TELL YOU?
YOU'RE GOING TO HIT ME?
WAP!
CRASH!
ELFABLE
SEE! THAT WASN'T SO HARD! NOW FOR LESSON TWO...
NO NEED. I'M GETTING THE HANG OF THIS "ANTICIPATING" THING.
WE'RE ONLY ONE ROGUE OUTPOST. THIS WON'T BE AS EASY AS YOU THINK.
IF IT TAKES YOU TURNING OVER EVERY ROCK ON THIS EARTH, THEY WILL BE FOUND. AND WHEN YOU FIND THEM, THAT'S WHEN MY LIFE'S WORK TRULY BEGINS. IF YOU THOUGHT I HAD IT IN FOR SANTA, WAIT UNTIL YOU SEE WHAT I DO TO THEM.
WHAT ON EARTH DID THESE POOR PEOPLE DO TO DESERVE ALL THIS?
THEY ERASED MY EXTENSIVE COLLECTION OF BAYWATCH TAPES.
THOSE BASTARDS!
QUIT MOANIN' AND BREAK OUT THE CHOPPERS.

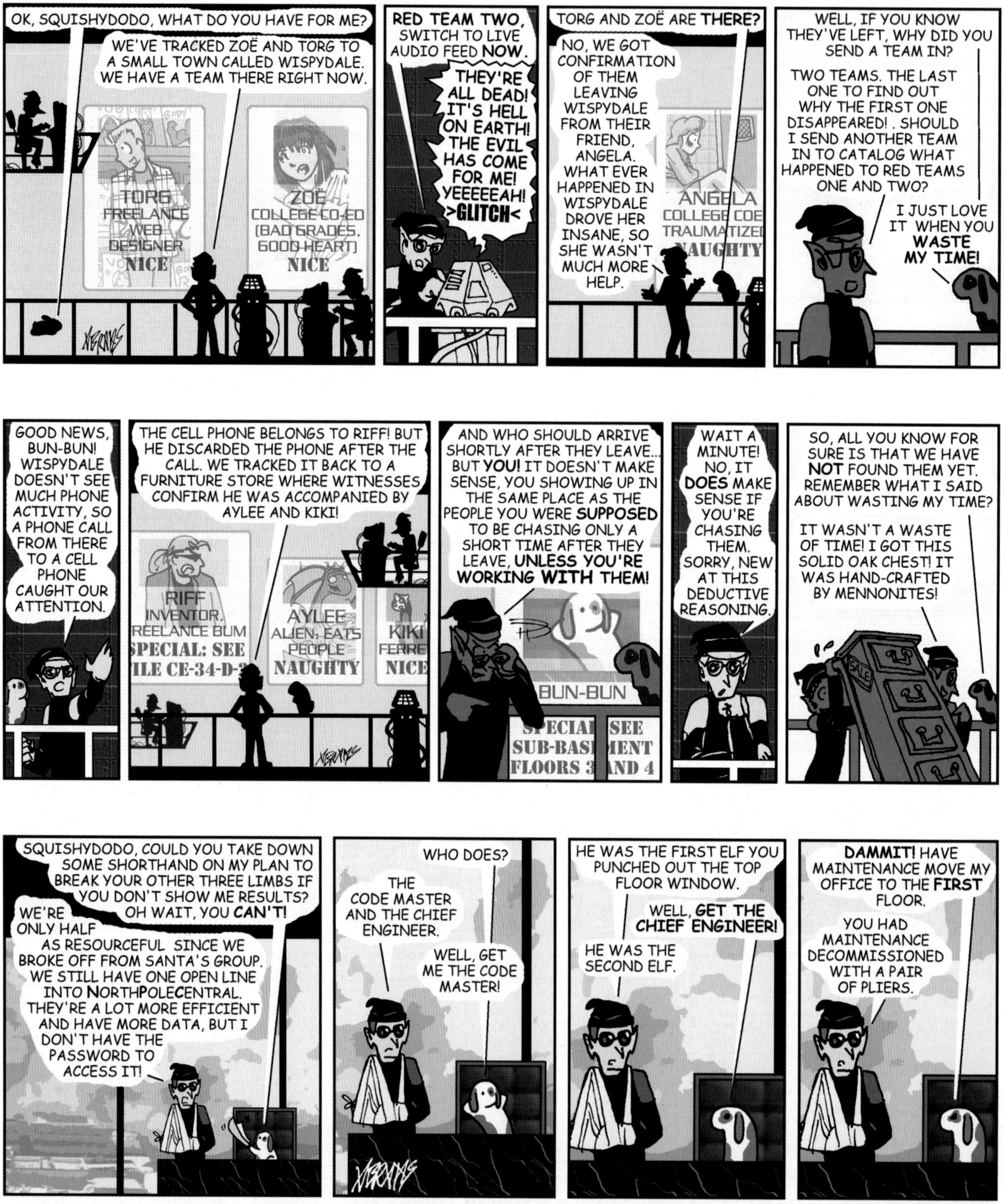

OK, SQUISHYDODO, WHAT DO YOU HAVE FOR ME?
WE'VE TRACKED ZOË AND TORG TO A SMALL TOWN CALLED WISPYDALE. WE HAVE A TEAM THERE RIGHT NOW.
TORG FREELANCE WEB DESIGNER NICE
ZOË COLLEGE CO-ED [BAD GRADES, GOOD HEART] NICE
RED TEAM TWO, SWITCH TO LIVE AUDIO FEED NOW.
THEY'RE ALL DEAD! IT'S HELL ON EARTH! THE EVIL HAS COME FOR ME! YEEEEEAH! >GLITCH<
TORG AND ZOË ARE THERE?
NO, WE GOT CONFIRMATION OF THEM LEAVING WISPYDALE FROM THEIR FRIEND, ANGELA. WHAT EVER HAPPENED IN WISPYDALE DROVE HER INSANE, SO SHE WASN'T MUCH MORE HELP.
ANGELA COLLEGE COED TRAUMATIZED NAUGHTY
WELL, IF YOU KNOW THEY'VE LEFT, WHY DID YOU SEND A TEAM IN?
TWO TEAMS. THE LAST ONE TO FIND OUT WHY THE FIRST ONE DISAPPEARED! . SHOULD I SEND ANOTHER TEAM IN TO CATALOG WHAT HAPPENED TO RED TEAMS ONE AND TWO?
I JUST LOVE IT WHEN YOU WASTE MY TIME!
GOOD NEWS, BUN-BUN! WISPYDALE DOESN'T SEE MUCH PHONE ACTIVITY, SO A PHONE CALL FROM THERE TO A CELL PHONE CAUGHT OUR ATTENTION.
THE CELL PHONE BELONGS TO RIFF! BUT HE DISCARDED THE PHONE AFTER THE CALL. WE TRACKED IT BACK TO A FURNITURE STORE WHERE WITNESSES CONFIRM HE WAS ACCOMPANIED BY AYLEE AND KIKI!
RIFF INVENTOR, FREELANCE BUM SPECIAL: SEE FILE CE-34-D-3
AYLEE ALIEN: EATS PEOPLE NAUGHTY
KIKI FERRET NICE
AND WHO SHOULD ARRIVE SHORTLY AFTER THEY LEAVE... BUT YOU! IT DOESN'T MAKE SENSE, YOU SHOWING UP IN THE SAME PLACE AS THE PEOPLE YOU WERE SUPPOSED TO BE CHASING ONLY A SHORT TIME AFTER THEY LEAVE, UNLESS YOU'RE WORKING WITH THEM!
BUN-BUN
SPECIAL: SEE SUB-BASEMENT FLOORS 3 AND 4
WAIT A MINUTE! NO, IT DOES MAKE SENSE IF YOU'RE CHASING THEM. SORRY, NEW AT THIS DEDUCTIVE REASONING.
SO, ALL YOU KNOW FOR SURE IS THAT WE HAVE NOT FOUND THEM YET. REMEMBER WHAT I SAID ABOUT WASTING MY TIME?
IT WASN'T A WASTE OF TIME! I GOT THIS SOLID OAK CHEST! IT WAS HAND-CRAFTED BY MENNONITES!
SALE
SQUISHYDODO, COULD YOU TAKE DOWN SOME SHORTHAND ON MY PLAN TO BREAK YOUR OTHER THREE LIMBS IF YOU DON'T SHOW ME RESULTS? OH WAIT, YOU CAN'T!
WE'RE ONLY HALF AS RESOURCEFUL SINCE WE BROKE OFF FROM SANTA'S GROUP. WE STILL HAVE ONE OPEN LINE INTO NORTHPOLECENTRAL. THEY'RE A LOT MORE EFFICIENT AND HAVE MORE DATA, BUT I DON'T HAVE THE PASSWORD TO ACCESS IT!
WHO DOES?
THE CODE MASTER AND THE CHIEF ENGINEER.
WELL, GET ME THE CODE MASTER!
HE WAS THE FIRST ELF YOU PUNCHED OUT THE TOP FLOOR WINDOW.
WELL, GET THE CHIEF ENGINEER!
HE WAS THE SECOND ELF.
DAMMIT! HAVE MAINTENANCE MOVE MY OFFICE TO THE FIRST FLOOR.
YOU HAD MAINTENANCE DECOMMISSIONED WITH A PAIR OF PLIERS.

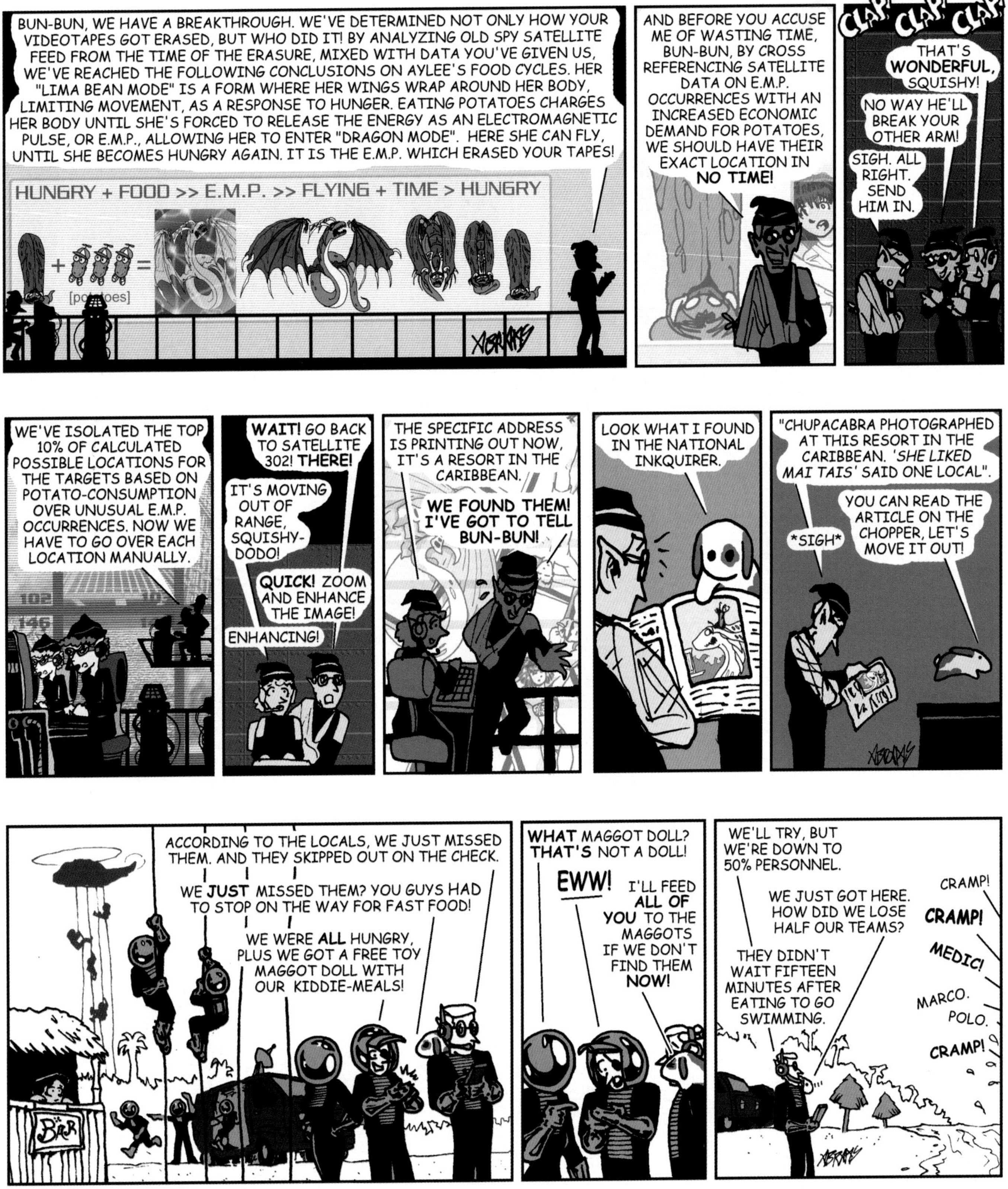

BUN-BUN, WE HAVE A BREAKTHROUGH. WE'VE DETERMINED NOT ONLY HOW YOUR VIDEOTAPES GOT ERASED, BUT WHO DID IT! BY ANALYZING OLD SPY SATELLITE FEED FROM THE TIME OF THE ERASURE, MIXED WITH DATA YOU'VE GIVEN US, WE'VE REACHED THE FOLLOWING CONCLUSIONS ON AYLEE'S FOOD CYCLES. HER "LIMA BEAN MODE" IS A FORM WHERE HER WINGS WRAP AROUND HER BODY, LIMITING MOVEMENT, AS A RESPONSE TO HUNGER. EATING POTATOES CHARGES HER BODY UNTIL SHE'S FORCED TO RELEASE THE ENERGY AS AN ELECTROMAGNETIC PULSE, OR E.M.P., ALLOWING HER TO ENTER "DRAGON MODE". HERE SHE CAN FLY, UNTIL SHE BECOMES HUNGRY AGAIN. IT IS THE E.M.P. WHICH ERASED YOUR TAPES!
HUNGRY + FOOD >> E.M.P. >> FLYING + TIME > HUNGRY
[potatoes]
AND BEFORE YOU ACCUSE ME OF WASTING TIME, BUN-BUN, BY CROSS REFERENCING SATELLITE DATA ON E.M.P. OCCURRENCES WITH AN INCREASED ECONOMIC DEMAND FOR POTATOES, WE SHOULD HAVE THEIR EXACT LOCATION IN NO TIME!
CLAP! CLAP! CLAP!
THAT'S WONDERFUL, SQUISHY!
NO WAY HE'LL BREAK YOUR OTHER ARM!
SIGH. ALL RIGHT. SEND HIM IN.
WE'VE ISOLATED THE TOP 10% OF CALCULATED POSSIBLE LOCATIONS FOR THE TARGETS BASED ON POTATO-CONSUMPTION OVER UNUSUAL E.M.P. OCCURRENCES. NOW WE HAVE TO GO OVER EACH LOCATION MANUALLY.
WAIT! GO BACK TO SATELLITE 302! THERE!
IT'S MOVING OUT OF RANGE, SQUISHY-DODO!
QUICK! ZOOM AND ENHANCE THE IMAGE!
ENHANCING!
THE SPECIFIC ADDRESS IS PRINTING OUT NOW, IT'S A RESORT IN THE CARIBBEAN.
WE FOUND THEM! I'VE GOT TO TELL BUN-BUN!
LOOK WHAT I FOUND IN THE NATIONAL INKQUIRER.
"CHUPACABRA PHOTOGRAPHED AT THIS RESORT IN THE CARIBBEAN. 'SHE LIKED MAI TAIS' SAID ONE LOCAL".
SIGH
YOU CAN READ THE ARTICLE ON THE CHOPPER, LET'S MOVE IT OUT!
ACCORDING TO THE LOCALS, WE JUST MISSED THEM. AND THEY SKIPPED OUT ON THE CHECK.
WE JUST MISSED THEM? YOU GUYS HAD TO STOP ON THE WAY FOR FAST FOOD!
WE WERE ALL HUNGRY, PLUS WE GOT A FREE TOY MAGGOT DOLL WITH OUR KIDDIE-MEALS!
BAR
WHAT MAGGOT DOLL? THAT'S NOT A DOLL!
EWW!
I'LL FEED ALL OF YOU TO THE MAGGOTS IF WE DON'T FIND THEM NOW!
WE'LL TRY, BUT WE'RE DOWN TO 50% PERSONNEL.
WE JUST GOT HERE. HOW DID WE LOSE HALF OUR TEAMS?
THEY DIDN'T WAIT FIFTEEN MINUTES AFTER EATING TO GO SWIMMING.
CRAMP!
CRAMP!
MEDIC!
MARCO.
POLO.
CRAMP!

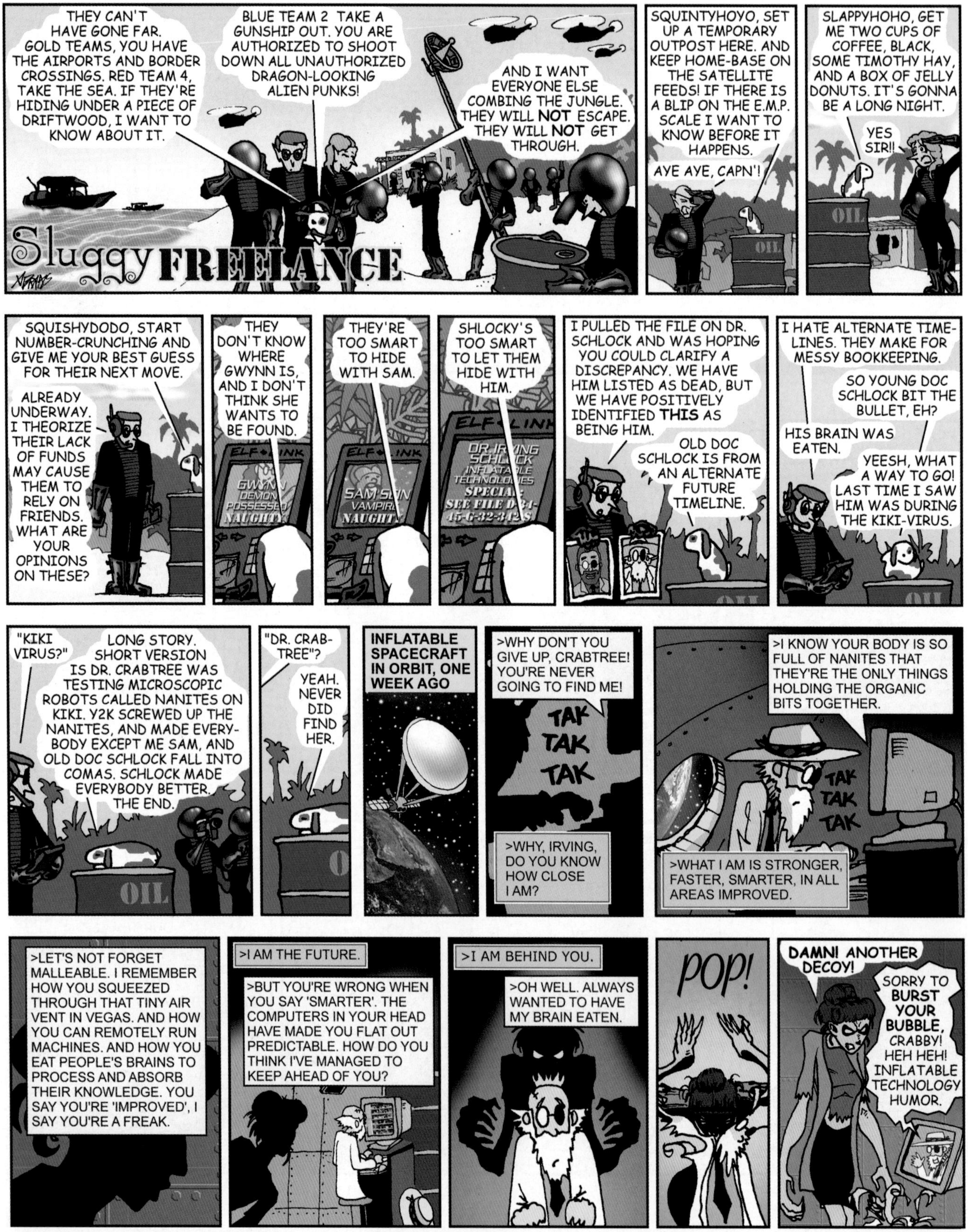

THEY CAN'T HAVE GONE FAR. GOLD TEAMS, YOU HAVE THE AIRPORTS AND BORDER CROSSINGS. RED TEAM 4, TAKE THE SEA. IF THEY'RE HIDING UNDER A PIECE OF DRIFTWOOD, I WANT TO KNOW ABOUT IT.
BLUE TEAM 2 TAKE A GUNSHIP OUT. YOU ARE AUTHORIZED TO SHOOT DOWN ALL UNAUTHORIZED DRAGON-LOOKING ALIEN PUNKS!
AND I WANT EVERYONE ELSE COMBING THE JUNGLE. THEY WILL **NOT** ESCAPE. THEY WILL **NOT** GET THROUGH.
Sluggy FREELANCE
SQUINTYHOYO, SET UP A TEMPORARY OUTPOST HERE. AND KEEP HOME-BASE ON THE SATELLITE FEEDS! IF THERE IS A BLIP ON THE E.M.P. SCALE I WANT TO KNOW BEFORE IT HAPPENS.
AYE AYE, CAPN'!
OIL
SLAPPYHOHO, GET ME TWO CUPS OF COFFEE, BLACK, SOME TIMOTHY HAY, AND A BOX OF JELLY DONUTS. IT'S GONNA BE A LONG NIGHT.
YES SIR!!
OIL
SQUISHYDODO, START NUMBER-CRUNCHING AND GIVE ME YOUR BEST GUESS FOR THEIR NEXT MOVE.
ALREADY UNDERWAY. I THEORIZE THEIR LACK OF FUNDS MAY CAUSE THEM TO RELY ON FRIENDS. WHAT ARE YOUR OPINIONS ON THESE?
THEY DON'T KNOW WHERE GWYNN IS, AND I DON'T THINK SHE WANTS TO BE FOUND.
THEY'RE TOO SMART TO HIDE WITH SAM.
SHLOCKY'S TOO SMART TO LET THEM HIDE WITH HIM.
I PULLED THE FILE ON DR. SCHLOCK AND WAS HOPING YOU COULD CLARIFY A DISCREPANCY. WE HAVE HIM LISTED AS DEAD, BUT WE HAVE POSITIVELY IDENTIFIED **THIS** AS BEING HIM.
OLD DOC SCHLOCK IS FROM AN ALTERNATE FUTURE TIMELINE.
I HATE ALTERNATE TIME-LINES. THEY MAKE FOR MESSY BOOKKEEPING.
SO YOUNG DOC SCHLOCK BIT THE BULLET, EH?
HIS BRAIN WAS EATEN.
YEESH, WHAT A WAY TO GO! LAST TIME I SAW HIM WAS DURING THE KIKI-VIRUS.
"KIKI VIRUS?"
LONG STORY. SHORT VERSION IS DR. CRABTREE WAS TESTING MICROSCOPIC ROBOTS CALLED NANITES ON KIKI. Y2K SCREWED UP THE NANITES, AND MADE EVERY-BODY EXCEPT ME SAM, AND OLD DOC SCHLOCK FALL INTO COMAS. SCHLOCK MADE EVERYBODY BETTER. THE END.
OIL
"DR. CRAB-TREE"?
YEAH. NEVER DID FIND HER.
INFLATABLE SPACECRAFT IN ORBIT, ONE WEEK AGO
>WHY DON'T YOU GIVE UP, CRABTREE! YOU'RE NEVER GOING TO FIND ME!
TAK TAK TAK
>WHY, IRVING, DO YOU KNOW HOW CLOSE I AM?
>I KNOW YOUR BODY IS SO FULL OF NANITES THAT THEY'RE THE ONLY THINGS HOLDING THE ORGANIC BITS TOGETHER.
TAK TAK TAK
>WHAT I AM IS STRONGER, FASTER, SMARTER, IN ALL AREAS IMPROVED.
>LET'S NOT FORGET MALLEABLE. I REMEMBER HOW YOU SQUEEZED THROUGH THAT TINY AIR VENT IN VEGAS. AND HOW YOU CAN REMOTELY RUN MACHINES. AND HOW YOU EAT PEOPLE'S BRAINS TO PROCESS AND ABSORB THEIR KNOWLEDGE. YOU SAY YOU'RE 'IMPROVED', I SAY YOU'RE A FREAK.
>I AM THE FUTURE.
>BUT YOU'RE WRONG WHEN YOU SAY 'SMARTER'. THE COMPUTERS IN YOUR HEAD HAVE MADE YOU FLAT OUT PREDICTABLE. HOW DO YOU THINK I'VE MANAGED TO KEEP AHEAD OF YOU?
>I AM BEHIND YOU.
>OH WELL. ALWAYS WANTED TO HAVE MY BRAIN EATEN.
POP!
DAMN! ANOTHER DECOY!
SORRY TO **BURST YOUR BUBBLE,** CRABBY! HEH HEH! INFLATABLE TECHNOLOGY HUMOR.

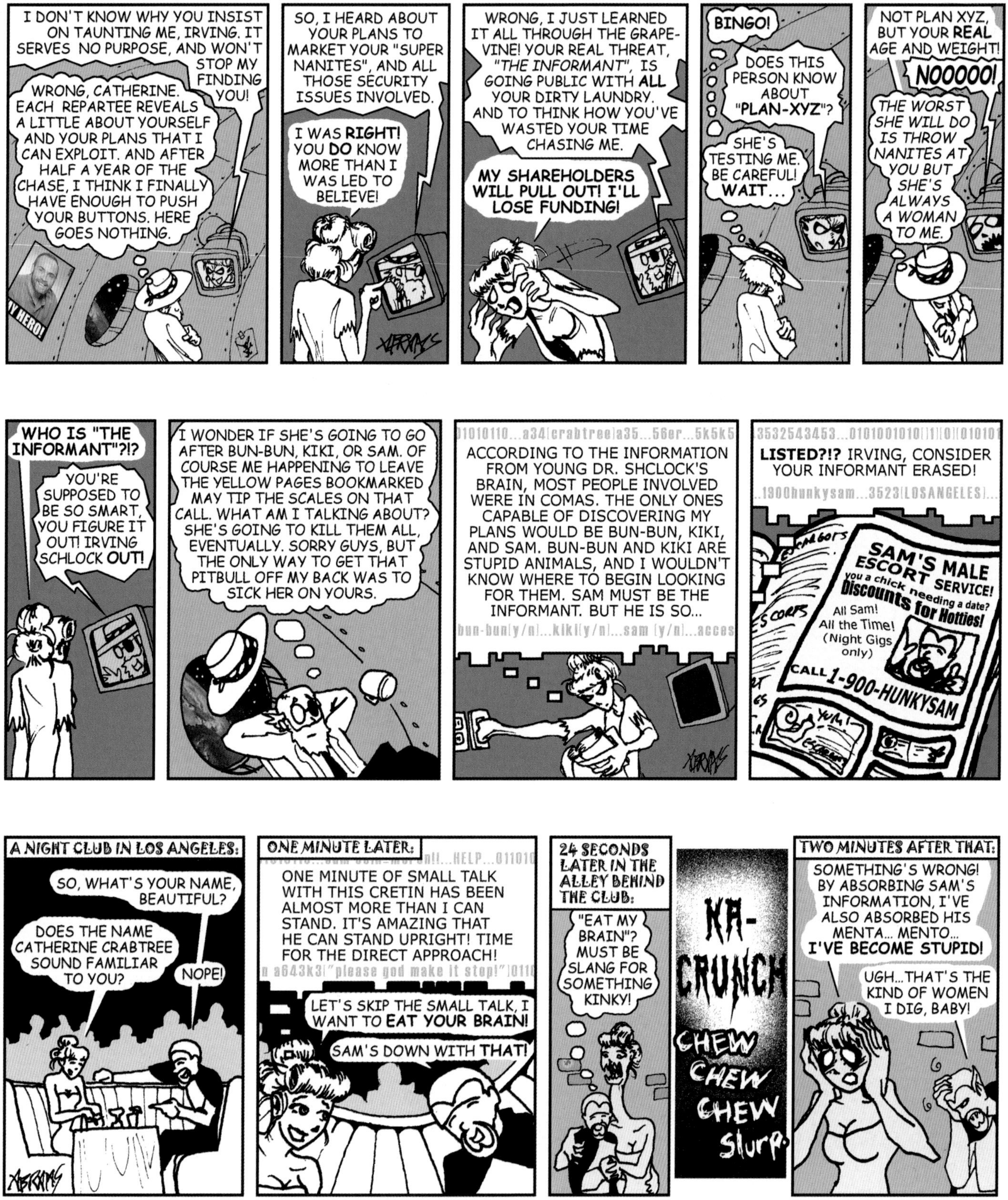
I DON'T KNOW WHY YOU INSIST ON TAUNTING ME, IRVING. IT SERVES NO PURPOSE, AND WON'T STOP MY FINDING YOU!
WRONG, CATHERINE. EACH REPARTEE REVEALS A LITTLE ABOUT YOURSELF AND YOUR PLANS THAT I CAN EXPLOIT. AND AFTER HALF A YEAR OF THE CHASE, I THINK I FINALLY HAVE ENOUGH TO PUSH YOUR BUTTONS. HERE GOES NOTHING.
SO, I HEARD ABOUT YOUR PLANS TO MARKET YOUR "SUPER NANITES", AND ALL THOSE SECURITY ISSUES INVOLVED.
I WAS **RIGHT**! YOU **DO** KNOW MORE THAN I WAS LED TO BELIEVE!
WRONG, I JUST LEARNED IT ALL THROUGH THE GRAPE-VINE! YOUR REAL THREAT, *"THE INFORMANT"*, IS GOING PUBLIC WITH **ALL** YOUR DIRTY LAUNDRY. AND TO THINK HOW YOU'VE WASTED YOUR TIME CHASING ME.
MY SHAREHOLDERS WILL PULL OUT! I'LL LOSE FUNDING!
BINGO!
DOES THIS PERSON KNOW ABOUT "**PLAN-XYZ**"?
SHE'S TESTING ME. BE CAREFUL! **WAIT**...
NOT PLAN XYZ, BUT YOUR **REAL** AGE AND WEIGHT!
NOOOOO!
THE WORST SHE WILL DO IS THROW NANITES AT YOU BUT SHE'S ALWAYS A WOMAN TO ME.
WHO IS "THE INFORMANT"?!?
YOU'RE SUPPOSED TO BE SO SMART, YOU FIGURE IT OUT! IRVING SCHLOCK **OUT!**
I WONDER IF SHE'S GOING TO GO AFTER BUN-BUN, KIKI, OR SAM. OF COURSE ME HAPPENING TO LEAVE THE YELLOW PAGES BOOKMARKED MAY TIP THE SCALES ON THAT CALL. WHAT AM I TALKING ABOUT? SHE'S GOING TO KILL THEM ALL, EVENTUALLY. SORRY GUYS, BUT THE ONLY WAY TO GET THAT PITBULL OFF MY BACK WAS TO SICK HER ON YOURS.
01010110...a34[crabtree]a35...56er...5k5k5
ACCORDING TO THE INFORMATION FROM YOUNG DR. SHCLOCK'S BRAIN, MOST PEOPLE INVOLVED WERE IN COMAS. THE ONLY ONES CAPABLE OF DISCOVERING MY PLANS WOULD BE BUN-BUN, KIKI, AND SAM. BUN-BUN AND KIKI ARE STUPID ANIMALS, AND I WOULDN'T KNOW WHERE TO BEGIN LOOKING FOR THEM. SAM MUST BE THE INFORMANT. BUT HE IS SO...
bun-bun[y/n]...kiki[y/n]...sam [y/n]...acces
3532543453...0101001010[1]1[0][010101
LISTED?!? IRVING, CONSIDER YOUR INFORMANT ERASED!
..1300hunkysam...3523[LOSANGELES]...
SAM'S MALE ESCORT SERVICE!
you a chick needing a date?
Discounts for Hotties!
All Sam! All the Time! (Night Gigs only)
CALL 1-900-HUNKYSAM
A NIGHT CLUB IN LOS ANGELES:
SO, WHAT'S YOUR NAME, BEAUTIFUL?
DOES THE NAME CATHERINE CRABTREE SOUND FAMILIAR TO YOU?
NOPE!
ONE MINUTE LATER:
ONE MINUTE OF SMALL TALK WITH THIS CRETIN HAS BEEN ALMOST MORE THAN I CAN STAND. IT'S AMAZING THAT HE CAN STAND UPRIGHT! TIME FOR THE DIRECT APPROACH!
n a643k3["please god make it stop!"]011
LET'S SKIP THE SMALL TALK, I WANT TO **EAT YOUR BRAIN!**
SAM'S DOWN WITH **THAT!**
24 SECONDS LATER IN THE ALLEY BEHIND THE CLUB:
"EAT MY BRAIN"? MUST BE SLANG FOR SOMETHING KINKY!
KA-CRUNCH
CHEW CHEW CHEW Slurp
TWO MINUTES AFTER THAT:
SOMETHING'S WRONG! BY ABSORBING SAM'S INFORMATION, I'VE ALSO ABSORBED HIS MENTA... MENTO... **I'VE BECOME STUPID!**
UGH...THAT'S THE KIND OF WOMEN I DIG, BABY!

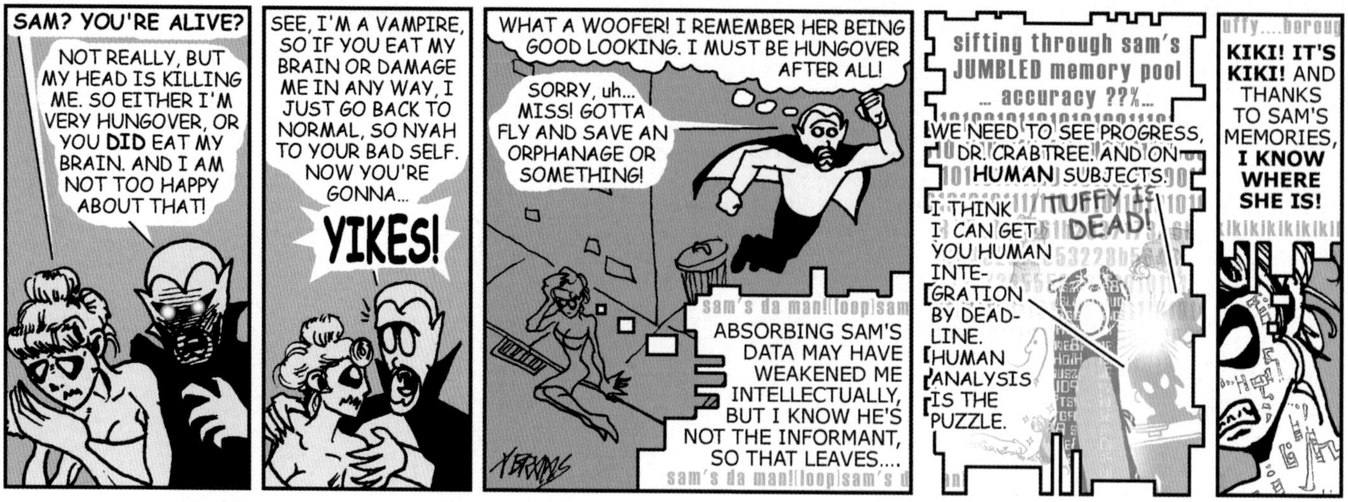
SAM? YOU'RE ALIVE?
NOT REALLY, BUT MY HEAD IS KILLING ME. SO EITHER I'M VERY HUNGOVER, OR YOU DID EAT MY BRAIN. AND I AM NOT TOO HAPPY ABOUT THAT!
SEE, I'M A VAMPIRE, SO IF YOU EAT MY BRAIN OR DAMAGE ME IN ANY WAY, I JUST GO BACK TO NORMAL, SO NYAH TO YOUR BAD SELF. NOW YOU'RE GONNA...
YIKES!
WHAT A WOOFER! I REMEMBER HER BEING GOOD LOOKING. I MUST BE HUNGOVER AFTER ALL!
SORRY, uh... MISS! GOTTA FLY AND SAVE AN ORPHANAGE OR SOMETHING!
sam's da man!(loop)sam
ABSORBING SAM'S DATA MAY HAVE WEAKENED ME INTELLECTUALLY, BUT I KNOW HE'S NOT THE INFORMANT, SO THAT LEAVES....
sam's da man!(loop)sam's d
sifting through sam's JUMBLED memory pool ... accuracy ??%...
WE NEED TO SEE PROGRESS, DR. CRABTREE. AND ON HUMAN SUBJECTS.
TUFFY IS DEAD!
I THINK I CAN GET YOU HUMAN INTE-GRATION BY DEAD-LINE. HUMAN ANALYSIS IS THE PUZZLE.
KIKI! IT'S KIKI! AND THANKS TO SAM'S MEMORIES, I KNOW WHERE SHE IS!
kikikikikikikiki

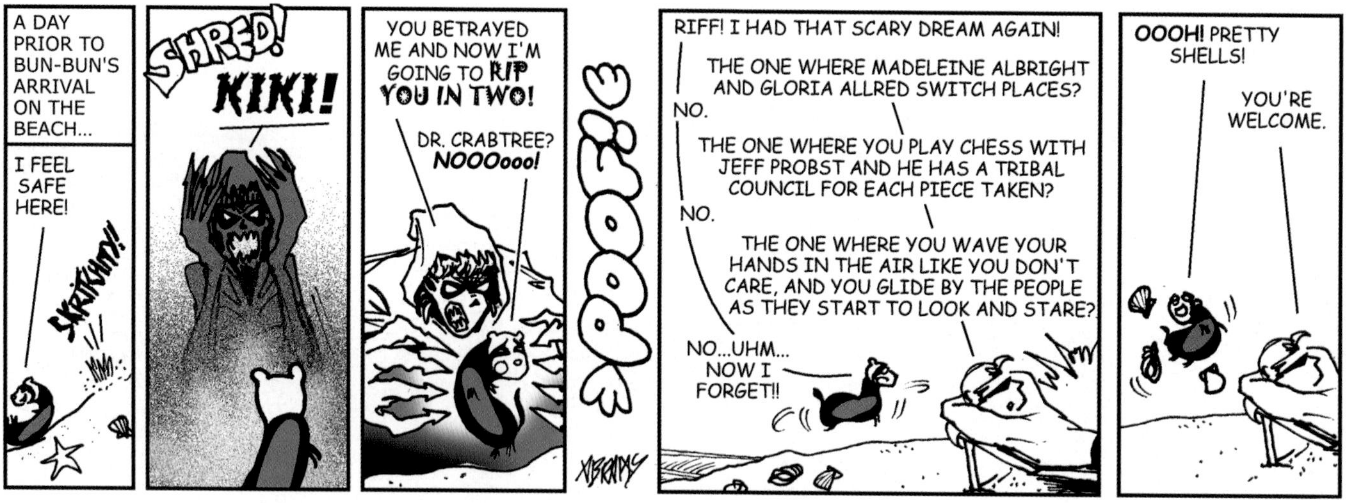
A DAY PRIOR TO BUN-BUN'S ARRIVAL ON THE BEACH...
I FEEL SAFE HERE!
SKRITCH!
SHRED!
KIKI!
YOU BETRAYED ME AND NOW I'M GOING TO RIP YOU IN TWO!
DR. CRABTREE? NOOOooo!
POOF!
RIFF! I HAD THAT SCARY DREAM AGAIN!
THE ONE WHERE MADELEINE ALBRIGHT AND GLORIA ALLRED SWITCH PLACES?
NO.
THE ONE WHERE YOU PLAY CHESS WITH JEFF PROBST AND HE HAS A TRIBAL COUNCIL FOR EACH PIECE TAKEN?
NO.
THE ONE WHERE YOU WAVE YOUR HANDS IN THE AIR LIKE YOU DON'T CARE, AND YOU GLIDE BY THE PEOPLE AS THEY START TO LOOK AND STARE?
NO...UHM... NOW I FORGET!!
OOOH! PRETTY SHELLS!
YOU'RE WELCOME.

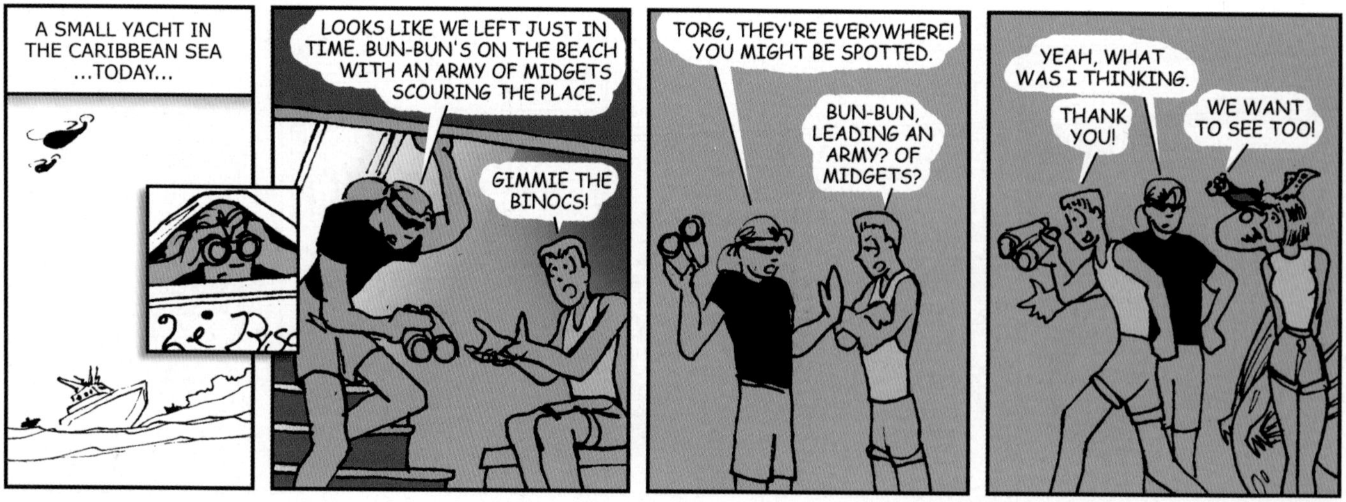
A SMALL YACHT IN THE CARIBBEAN SEA ...TODAY...
LOOKS LIKE WE LEFT JUST IN TIME. BUN-BUN'S ON THE BEACH WITH AN ARMY OF MIDGETS SCOURING THE PLACE.
GIMMIE THE BINOCS!
TORG, THEY'RE EVERYWHERE! YOU MIGHT BE SPOTTED.
BUN-BUN, LEADING AN ARMY? OF MIDGETS?
YEAH, WHAT WAS I THINKING.
THANK YOU!
WE WANT TO SEE TOO!

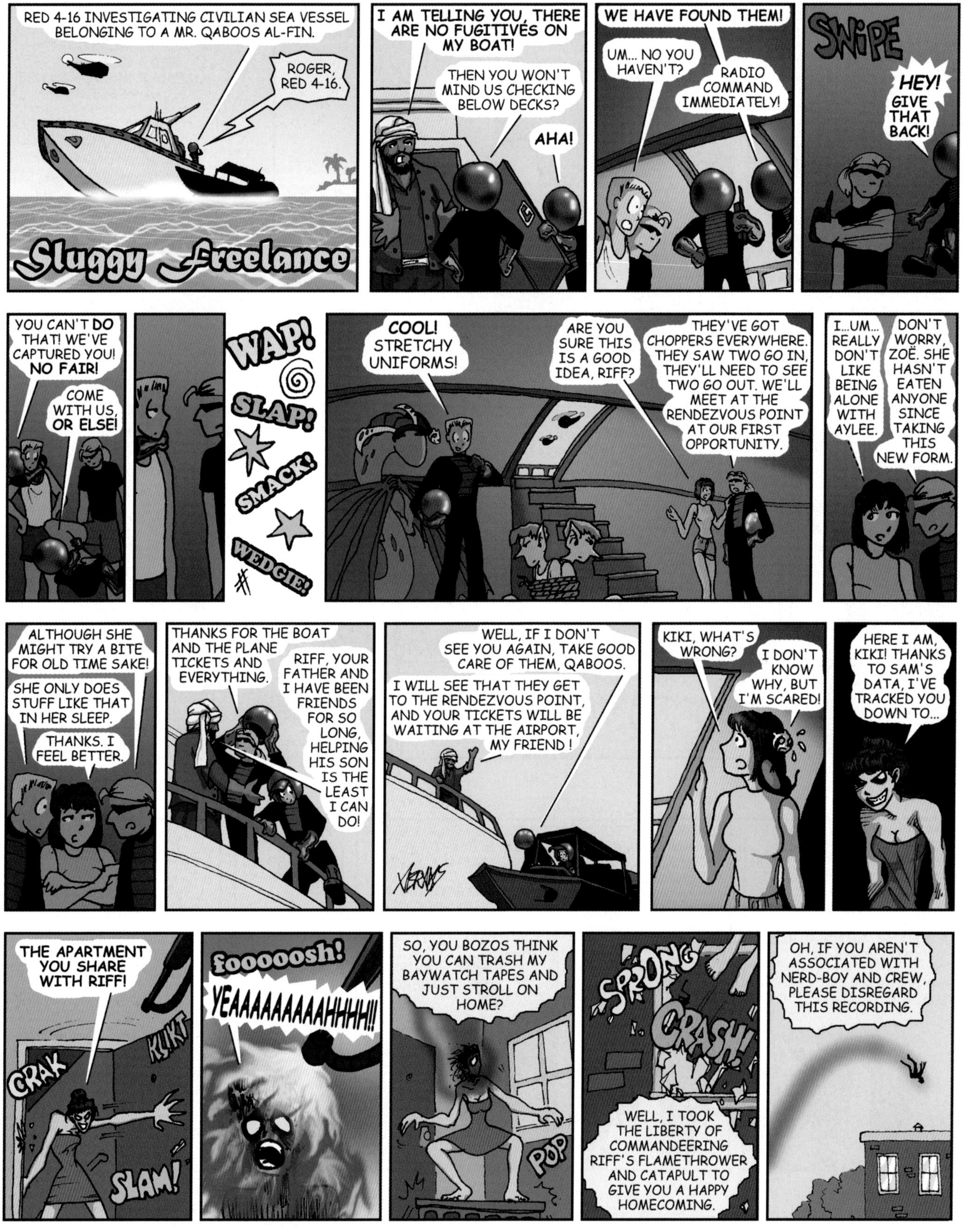
RED 4-16 INVESTIGATING CIVILIAN SEA VESSEL BELONGING TO A MR. QABOOS AL-FIN.
ROGER, RED 4-16.
Sluggy Freelance
I AM TELLING YOU, THERE ARE NO FUGITIVES ON MY BOAT!
THEN YOU WON'T MIND US CHECKING BELOW DECKS?
AHA!
WE HAVE FOUND THEM!
UM... NO YOU HAVEN'T?
RADIO COMMAND IMMEDIATELY!
SNIPE
HEY! GIVE THAT BACK!
YOU CAN'T DO THAT! WE'VE CAPTURED YOU! NO FAIR!
COME WITH US, OR ELSE!
WAP!
SLAP!
SMACK!
WEDGIE!
COOL! STRETCHY UNIFORMS!
ARE YOU SURE THIS IS A GOOD IDEA, RIFF?
THEY'VE GOT CHOPPERS EVERYWHERE. THEY SAW TWO GO IN, THEY'LL NEED TO SEE TWO GO OUT. WE'LL MEET AT THE RENDEZVOUS POINT AT OUR FIRST OPPORTUNITY.
I...UM... REALLY DON'T LIKE BEING ALONE WITH AYLEE.
DON'T WORRY, ZOË. SHE HASN'T EATEN ANYONE SINCE TAKING THIS NEW FORM.
ALTHOUGH SHE MIGHT TRY A BITE FOR OLD TIME SAKE!
SHE ONLY DOES STUFF LIKE THAT IN HER SLEEP.
THANKS. I FEEL BETTER.
THANKS FOR THE BOAT AND THE PLANE TICKETS AND EVERYTHING.
RIFF, YOUR FATHER AND I HAVE BEEN FRIENDS FOR SO LONG, HELPING HIS SON IS THE LEAST I CAN DO!
WELL, IF I DON'T SEE YOU AGAIN, TAKE GOOD CARE OF THEM, QABOOS.
I WILL SEE THAT THEY GET TO THE RENDEZVOUS POINT, AND YOUR TICKETS WILL BE WAITING AT THE AIRPORT, MY FRIEND !
KIKI, WHAT'S WRONG?
I DON'T KNOW WHY, BUT I'M SCARED!
HERE I AM, KIKI! THANKS TO SAM'S DATA, I'VE TRACKED YOU DOWN TO...
THE APARTMENT YOU SHARE WITH RIFF!
CRAK
KLIKT
SLAM!
foooooosh!
YEAAAAAAAAHHHH!!
SO, YOU BOZOS THINK YOU CAN TRASH MY BAYWATCH TAPES AND JUST STROLL ON HOME?
POP
SPROING
CRASH!
WELL, I TOOK THE LIBERTY OF COMMANDEERING RIFF'S FLAMETHROWER AND CATAPULT TO GIVE YOU A HAPPY HOMECOMING.
OH, IF YOU AREN'T ASSOCIATED WITH NERD-BOY AND CREW, PLEASE DISREGARD THIS RECORDING.

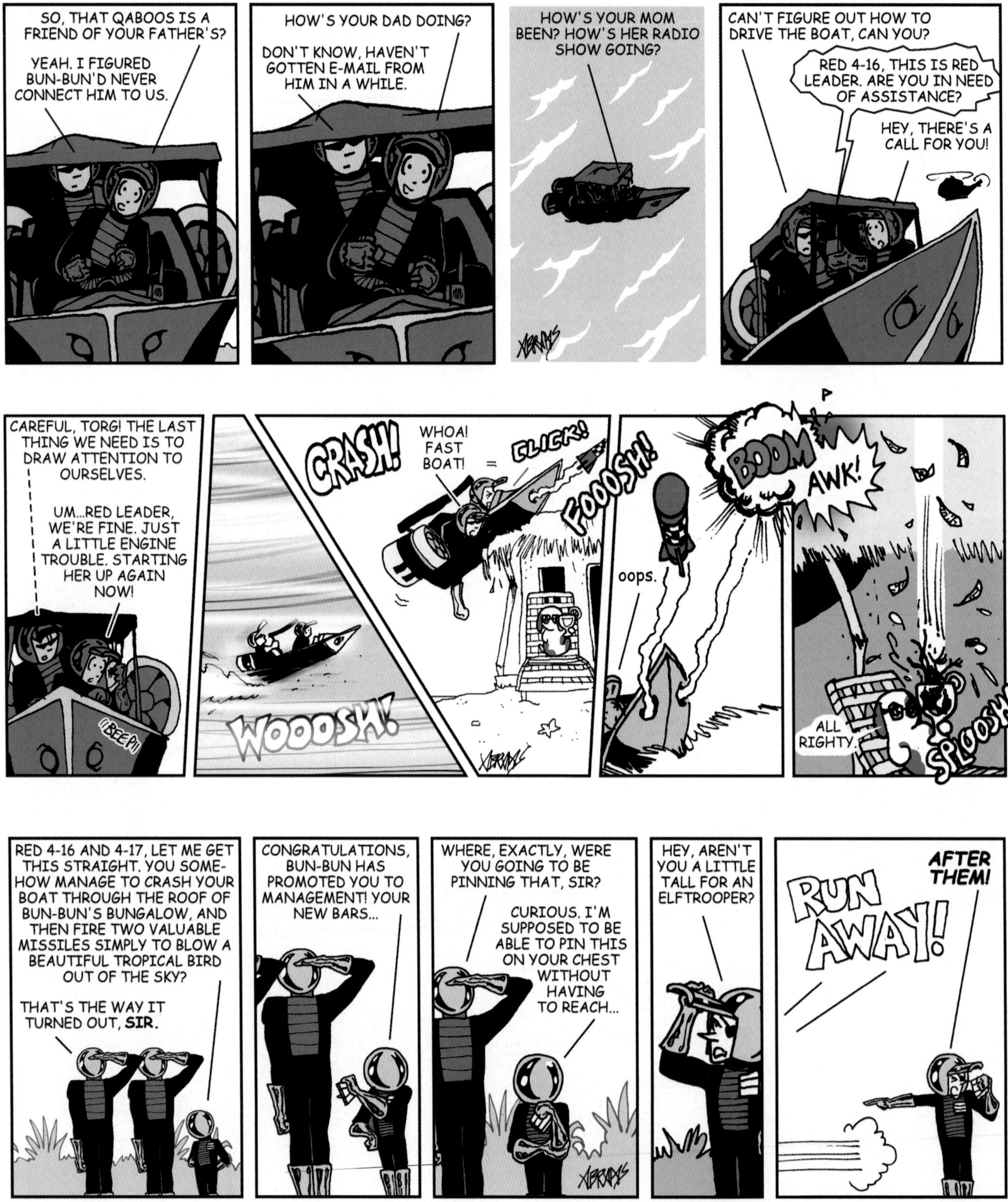
SO, THAT QABOOS IS A FRIEND OF YOUR FATHER'S?
YEAH. I FIGURED BUN-BUN'D NEVER CONNECT HIM TO US.
HOW'S YOUR DAD DOING?
DON'T KNOW, HAVEN'T GOTTEN E-MAIL FROM HIM IN A WHILE.
HOW'S YOUR MOM BEEN? HOW'S HER RADIO SHOW GOING?
CAN'T FIGURE OUT HOW TO DRIVE THE BOAT, CAN YOU?
RED 4-16, THIS IS RED LEADER. ARE YOU IN NEED OF ASSISTANCE?
HEY, THERE'S A CALL FOR YOU!
CAREFUL, TORG! THE LAST THING WE NEED IS TO DRAW ATTENTION TO OURSELVES.
UM...RED LEADER, WE'RE FINE. JUST A LITTLE ENGINE TROUBLE. STARTING HER UP AGAIN NOW!
BEEP!
WOOOSH!
CRASH!
WHOA! FAST BOAT!
CLICK!
FOOOSH!
oops.
BOOM
AWK!
ALL RIGHTY.
SPLOOSH!
RED 4-16 AND 4-17, LET ME GET THIS STRAIGHT. YOU SOMEHOW MANAGE TO CRASH YOUR BOAT THROUGH THE ROOF OF BUN-BUN'S BUNGALOW, AND THEN FIRE TWO VALUABLE MISSILES SIMPLY TO BLOW A BEAUTIFUL TROPICAL BIRD OUT OF THE SKY?
THAT'S THE WAY IT TURNED OUT, **SIR.**
CONGRATULATIONS, BUN-BUN HAS PROMOTED YOU TO MANAGEMENT! YOUR NEW BARS...
WHERE, EXACTLY, WERE YOU GOING TO BE PINNING THAT, SIR?
CURIOUS. I'M SUPPOSED TO BE ABLE TO PIN THIS ON YOUR CHEST WITHOUT HAVING TO REACH...
HEY, AREN'T YOU A LITTLE TALL FOR AN ELFTROOPER?
RUN AWAY!
AFTER THEM!

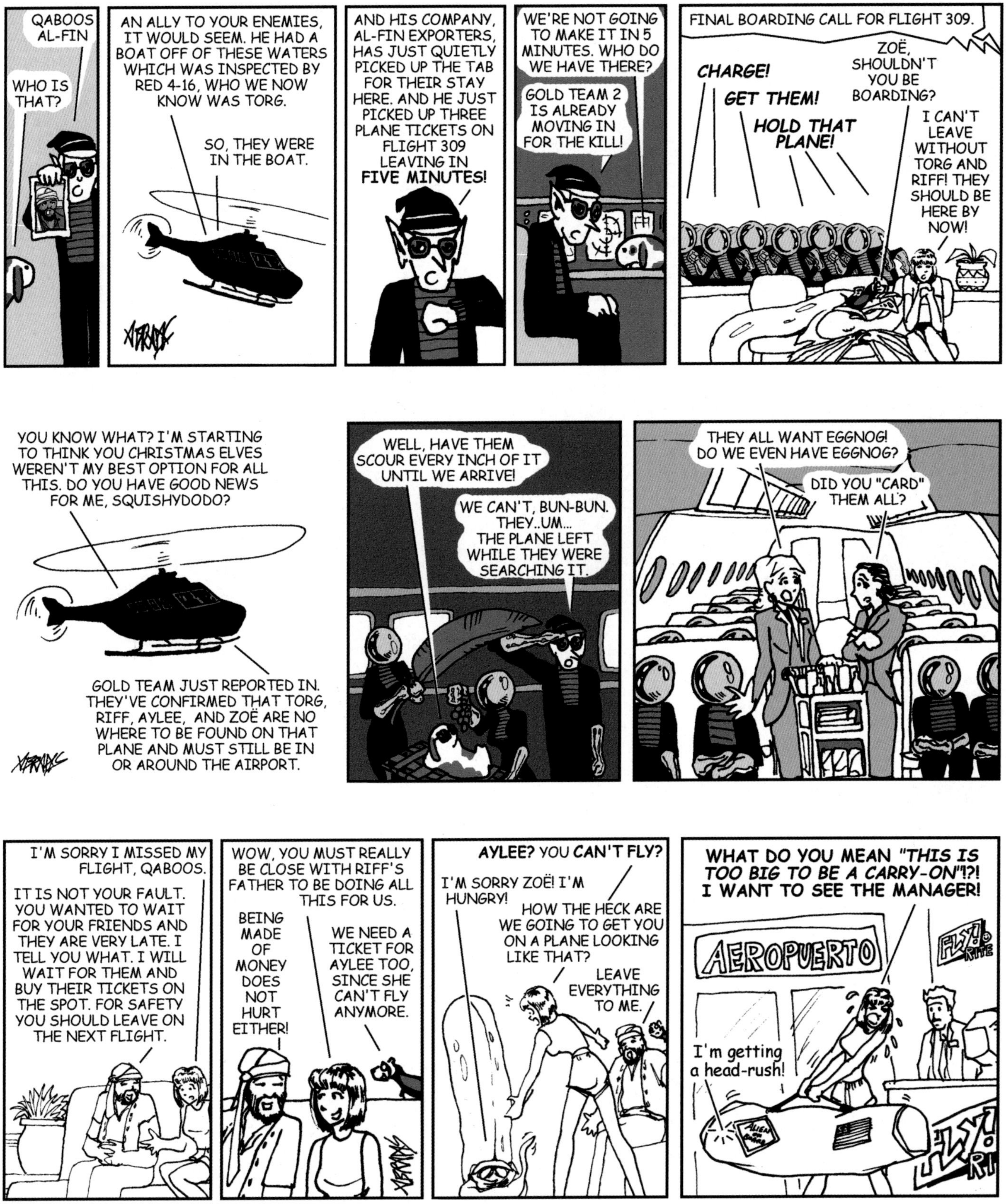
WHO IS THAT?
QABOOS AL-FIN
AN ALLY TO YOUR ENEMIES, IT WOULD SEEM. HE HAD A BOAT OFF OF THESE WATERS WHICH WAS INSPECTED BY RED 4-16, WHO WE NOW KNOW WAS TORG.
SO, THEY WERE IN THE BOAT.
AND HIS COMPANY, AL-FIN EXPORTERS, HAS JUST QUIETLY PICKED UP THE TAB FOR THEIR STAY HERE. AND HE JUST PICKED UP THREE PLANE TICKETS ON FLIGHT 309 LEAVING IN **FIVE MINUTES!**
WE'RE NOT GOING TO MAKE IT IN 5 MINUTES. WHO DO WE HAVE THERE?
GOLD TEAM 2 IS ALREADY MOVING IN FOR THE KILL!
FINAL BOARDING CALL FOR FLIGHT 309.
CHARGE!
GET THEM!
HOLD THAT PLANE!
ZOË, SHOULDN'T YOU BE BOARDING?
I CAN'T LEAVE WITHOUT TORG AND RIFF! THEY SHOULD BE HERE BY NOW!
YOU KNOW WHAT? I'M STARTING TO THINK YOU CHRISTMAS ELVES WEREN'T MY BEST OPTION FOR ALL THIS. DO YOU HAVE GOOD NEWS FOR ME, SQUISHYDODO?
GOLD TEAM JUST REPORTED IN. THEY'VE CONFIRMED THAT TORG, RIFF, AYLEE, AND ZOË ARE NO WHERE TO BE FOUND ON THAT PLANE AND MUST STILL BE IN OR AROUND THE AIRPORT.
WELL, HAVE THEM SCOUR EVERY INCH OF IT UNTIL WE ARRIVE!
WE CAN'T, BUN-BUN. THEY..UM... THE PLANE LEFT WHILE THEY WERE SEARCHING IT.
THEY ALL WANT EGGNOG! DO WE EVEN HAVE EGGNOG?
DID YOU "CARD" THEM ALL?
I'M SORRY I MISSED MY FLIGHT, QABOOS.
IT IS NOT YOUR FAULT. YOU WANTED TO WAIT FOR YOUR FRIENDS AND THEY ARE VERY LATE. I TELL YOU WHAT. I WILL WAIT FOR THEM AND BUY THEIR TICKETS ON THE SPOT. FOR SAFETY YOU SHOULD LEAVE ON THE NEXT FLIGHT.
WOW, YOU MUST REALLY BE CLOSE WITH RIFF'S FATHER TO BE DOING ALL THIS FOR US.
BEING MADE OF MONEY DOES NOT HURT EITHER!
WE NEED A TICKET FOR AYLEE TOO, SINCE SHE CAN'T FLY ANYMORE.
AYLEE? YOU **CAN'T FLY?**
I'M SORRY ZOË! I'M HUNGRY!
HOW THE HECK ARE WE GOING TO GET YOU ON A PLANE LOOKING LIKE THAT?
LEAVE EVERYTHING TO ME.
WHAT DO YOU MEAN *"THIS IS TOO BIG TO BE A CARRY-ON"*!?! I WANT TO SEE THE MANAGER!
AEROPUERTO
FLY! RITE
I'm getting a head-rush!

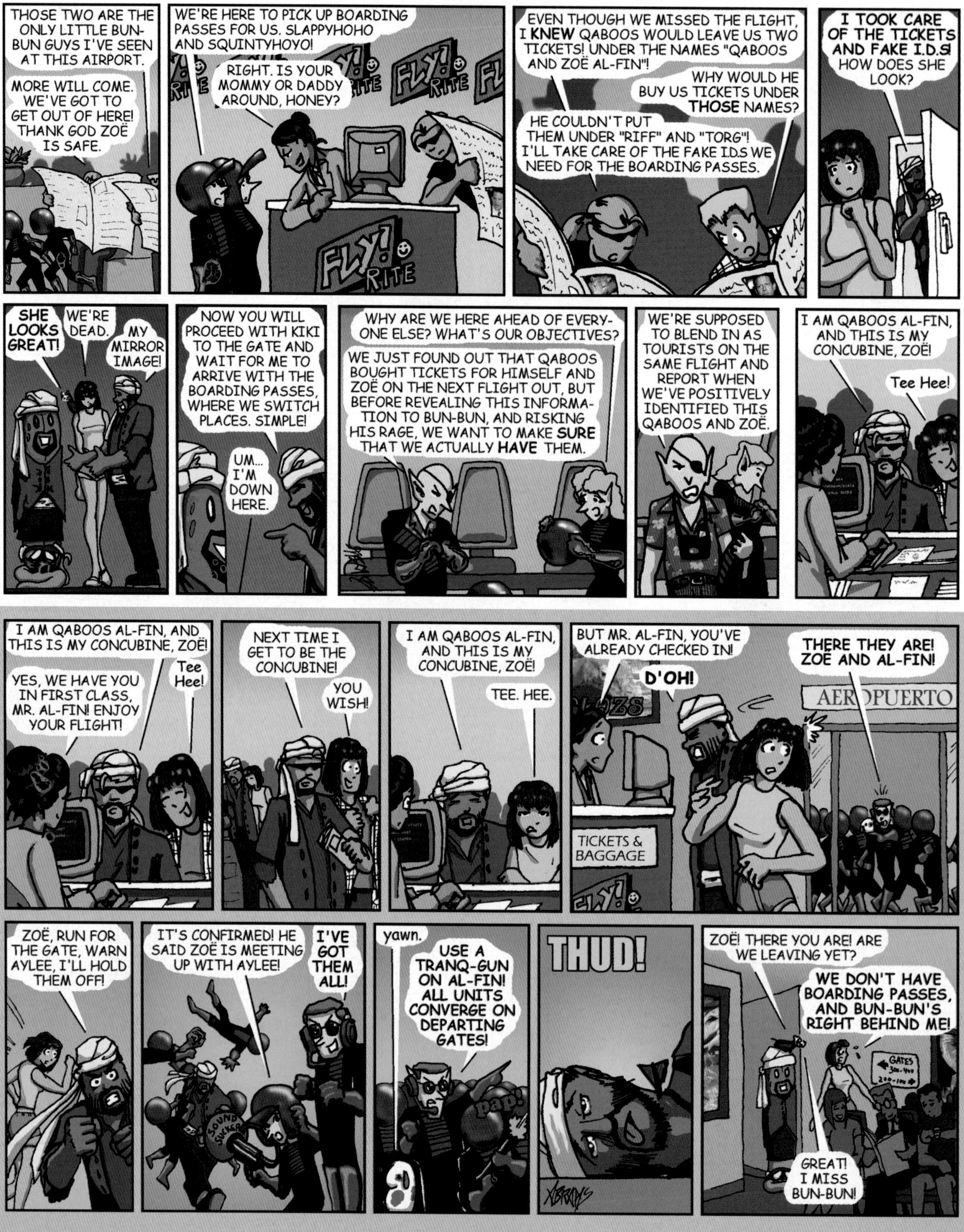
THOSE TWO ARE THE ONLY LITTLE BUN-BUN GUYS I'VE SEEN AT THIS AIRPORT.
MORE WILL COME. WE'VE GOT TO GET OUT OF HERE! THANK GOD ZOË IS SAFE.
WE'RE HERE TO PICK UP BOARDING PASSES FOR US. SLAPPYHOHO AND SQUINTYHOYO!
RIGHT. IS YOUR MOMMY OR DADDY AROUND, HONEY?
FLY! RITE
EVEN THOUGH WE MISSED THE FLIGHT, I KNEW QABOOS WOULD LEAVE US TWO TICKETS! UNDER THE NAMES "QABOOS AND ZOË AL-FIN"!
WHY WOULD HE BUY US TICKETS UNDER THOSE NAMES?
HE COULDN'T PUT THEM UNDER "RIFF" AND "TORG"! I'LL TAKE CARE OF THE FAKE I.D.S WE NEED FOR THE BOARDING PASSES.
I TOOK CARE OF THE TICKETS AND FAKE I.D.S! HOW DOES SHE LOOK?
SHE LOOKS GREAT!
WE'RE DEAD.
MY MIRROR IMAGE!
NOW YOU WILL PROCEED WITH KIKI TO THE GATE AND WAIT FOR ME TO ARRIVE WITH THE BOARDING PASSES, WHERE WE SWITCH PLACES. SIMPLE!
UM... I'M DOWN HERE.
WHY ARE WE HERE AHEAD OF EVERYONE ELSE? WHAT'S OUR OBJECTIVES?
WE JUST FOUND OUT THAT QABOOS BOUGHT TICKETS FOR HIMSELF AND ZOË ON THE NEXT FLIGHT OUT, BUT BEFORE REVEALING THIS INFORMATION TO BUN-BUN, AND RISKING HIS RAGE, WE WANT TO MAKE SURE THAT WE ACTUALLY HAVE THEM.
WE'RE SUPPOSED TO BLEND IN AS TOURISTS ON THE SAME FLIGHT AND REPORT WHEN WE'VE POSITIVELY IDENTIFIED THIS QABOOS AND ZOË.
I AM QABOOS AL-FIN, AND THIS IS MY CONCUBINE, ZOË!
Tee Hee!
I AM QABOOS AL-FIN, AND THIS IS MY CONCUBINE, ZOË!
Tee Hee!
YES, WE HAVE YOU IN FIRST CLASS, MR. AL-FIN! ENJOY YOUR FLIGHT!
NEXT TIME I GET TO BE THE CONCUBINE!
YOU WISH!
I AM QABOOS AL-FIN, AND THIS IS MY CONCUBINE, ZOË!
TEE. HEE.
BUT MR. AL-FIN, YOU'VE ALREADY CHECKED IN!
D'OH!
THERE THEY ARE! ZOË AND AL-FIN!
AEROPUERTO
TICKETS & BAGGAGE
ZOË, RUN FOR THE GATE, WARN AYLEE, I'LL HOLD THEM OFF!
IT'S CONFIRMED! HE SAID ZOË IS MEETING UP WITH AYLEE!
I'VE GOT THEM ALL!
SOUND SUCKER
yawn.
USE A TRANQ-GUN ON AL-FIN! ALL UNITS CONVERGE ON DEPARTING GATES!
pap!
THUD!
ZOË! THERE YOU ARE! ARE WE LEAVING YET?
WE DON'T HAVE BOARDING PASSES, AND BUN-BUN'S RIGHT BEHIND ME!
GATES
GREAT! I MISS BUN-BUN!

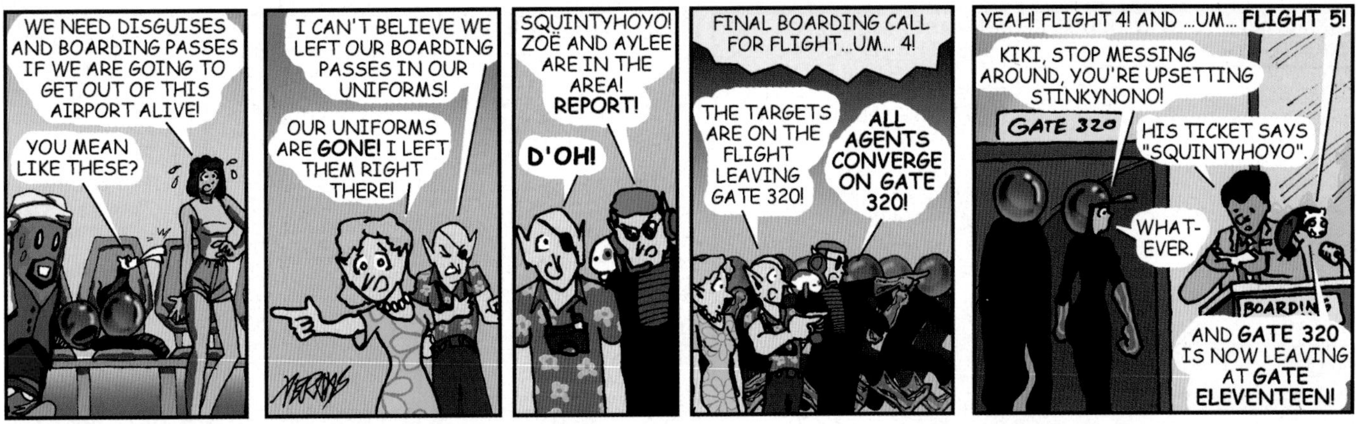
WE NEED DISGUISES AND BOARDING PASSES IF WE ARE GOING TO GET OUT OF THIS AIRPORT ALIVE!
YOU MEAN LIKE THESE?
I CAN'T BELIEVE WE LEFT OUR BOARDING PASSES IN OUR UNIFORMS!
OUR UNIFORMS ARE GONE! I LEFT THEM RIGHT THERE!
SQUINTYHOYO! ZOË AND AYLEE ARE IN THE AREA! REPORT!
D'OH!
FINAL BOARDING CALL FOR FLIGHT...UM... 4!
THE TARGETS ARE ON THE FLIGHT LEAVING GATE 320!
ALL AGENTS CONVERGE ON GATE 320!
YEAH! FLIGHT 4! AND ...UM... FLIGHT 5!
KIKI, STOP MESSING AROUND, YOU'RE UPSETTING STINKYNONO!
GATE 320
HIS TICKET SAYS "SQUINTYHOYO".
WHAT-EVER.
BOARDING
AND GATE 320 IS NOW LEAVING AT GATE ELEVENTEEN!

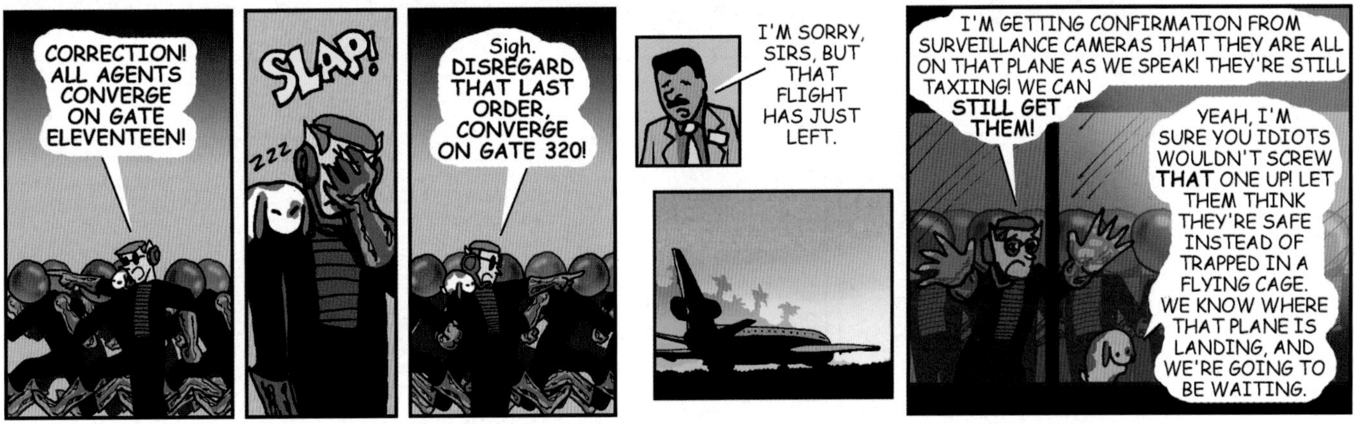
CORRECTION! ALL AGENTS CONVERGE ON GATE ELEVENTEEN!
SLAP!
ZZZ
Sigh. DISREGARD THAT LAST ORDER, CONVERGE ON GATE 320!
I'M SORRY, SIRS, BUT THAT FLIGHT HAS JUST LEFT.
I'M GETTING CONFIRMATION FROM SURVEILLANCE CAMERAS THAT THEY ARE ALL ON THAT PLANE AS WE SPEAK! THEY'RE STILL TAXIING! WE CAN STILL GET THEM!
YEAH, I'M SURE YOU IDIOTS WOULDN'T SCREW THAT ONE UP! LET THEM THINK THEY'RE SAFE INSTEAD OF TRAPPED IN A FLYING CAGE. WE KNOW WHERE THAT PLANE IS LANDING, AND WE'RE GOING TO BE WAITING.

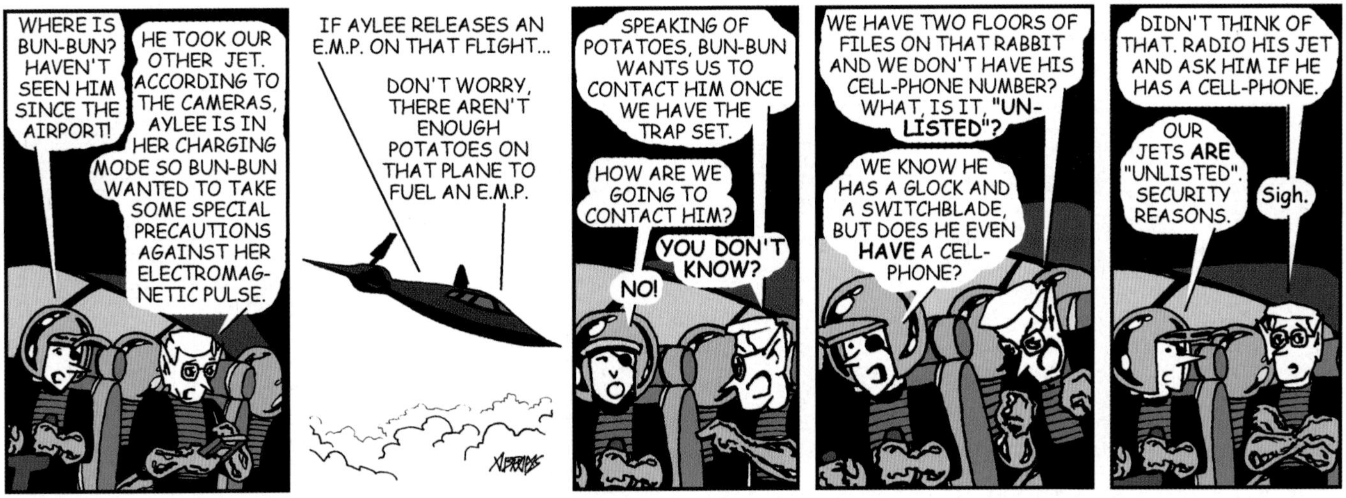
WHERE IS BUN-BUN? HAVEN'T SEEN HIM SINCE THE AIRPORT!
HE TOOK OUR OTHER JET. ACCORDING TO THE CAMERAS, AYLEE IS IN HER CHARGING MODE SO BUN-BUN WANTED TO TAKE SOME SPECIAL PRECAUTIONS AGAINST HER ELECTROMAG-NETIC PULSE.
IF AYLEE RELEASES AN E.M.P. ON THAT FLIGHT...
DON'T WORRY, THERE AREN'T ENOUGH POTATOES ON THAT PLANE TO FUEL AN E.M.P.
SPEAKING OF POTATOES, BUN-BUN WANTS US TO CONTACT HIM ONCE WE HAVE THE TRAP SET.
HOW ARE WE GOING TO CONTACT HIM?
YOU DON'T KNOW?
NO!
WE HAVE TWO FLOORS OF FILES ON THAT RABBIT AND WE DON'T HAVE HIS CELL-PHONE NUMBER? WHAT, IS IT, "UN-LISTED"?
WE KNOW HE HAS A GLOCK AND A SWITCHBLADE, BUT DOES HE EVEN HAVE A CELL-PHONE?
DIDN'T THINK OF THAT. RADIO HIS JET AND ASK HIM IF HE HAS A CELL-PHONE.
OUR JETS ARE "UNLISTED". SECURITY REASONS.
Sigh.

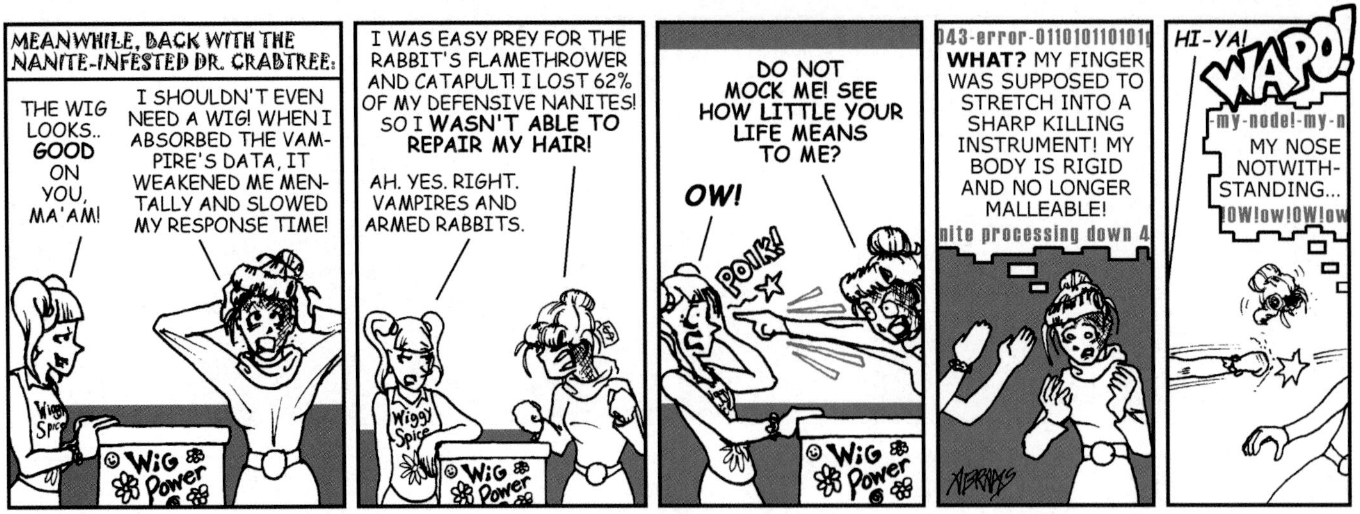
MEANWHILE, BACK WITH THE NANITE-INFESTED DR. CRABTREE:
THE WIG LOOKS.. GOOD ON YOU, MA'AM!
I SHOULDN'T EVEN NEED A WIG! WHEN I ABSORBED THE VAMPIRE'S DATA, IT WEAKENED ME MENTALLY AND SLOWED MY RESPONSE TIME!
Wiggy Spice
WiG Power
I WAS EASY PREY FOR THE RABBIT'S FLAMETHROWER AND CATAPULT! I LOST 62% OF MY DEFENSIVE NANITES! SO I WASN'T ABLE TO REPAIR MY HAIR!
AH. YES. RIGHT. VAMPIRES AND ARMED RABBITS.
DO NOT MOCK ME! SEE HOW LITTLE YOUR LIFE MEANS TO ME?
OW!
POIK!
043-error-011010110101
WHAT? MY FINGER WAS SUPPOSED TO STRETCH INTO A SHARP KILLING INSTRUMENT! MY BODY IS RIGID AND NO LONGER MALLEABLE!
nite processing down 4
HI-YA!
WAPO!
-my-node!-my-n
MY NOSE NOTWITH-STANDING...
OW!ow!OW!ow

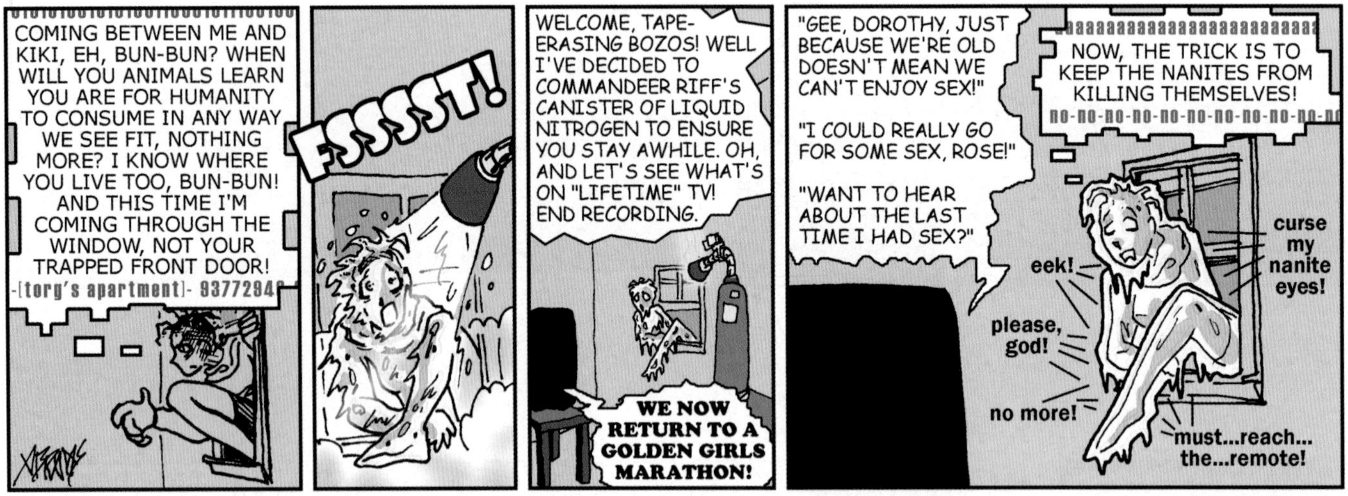
COMING BETWEEN ME AND KIKI, EH, BUN-BUN? WHEN WILL YOU ANIMALS LEARN YOU ARE FOR HUMANITY TO CONSUME IN ANY WAY WE SEE FIT, NOTHING MORE? I KNOW WHERE YOU LIVE TOO, BUN-BUN! AND THIS TIME I'M COMING THROUGH THE WINDOW, NOT YOUR TRAPPED FRONT DOOR!
-[torg's apartment]- 9377294
FSSSST!
WELCOME, TAPE-ERASING BOZOS! WELL I'VE DECIDED TO COMMANDEER RIFF'S CANISTER OF LIQUID NITROGEN TO ENSURE YOU STAY AWHILE. OH, AND LET'S SEE WHAT'S ON "LIFETIME" TV! END RECORDING.
WE NOW RETURN TO A GOLDEN GIRLS MARATHON!
"GEE, DOROTHY, JUST BECAUSE WE'RE OLD DOESN'T MEAN WE CAN'T ENJOY SEX!"
"I COULD REALLY GO FOR SOME SEX, ROSE!"
"WANT TO HEAR ABOUT THE LAST TIME I HAD SEX?"
aaaaaaaaaaaaaaaaaaaaaaaaa
NOW, THE TRICK IS TO KEEP THE NANITES FROM KILLING THEMSELVES!
no-no-no-no-no-no-no-no-no-no
eek!
curse my nanite eyes!
please, god!
no more!
must...reach... the...remote!

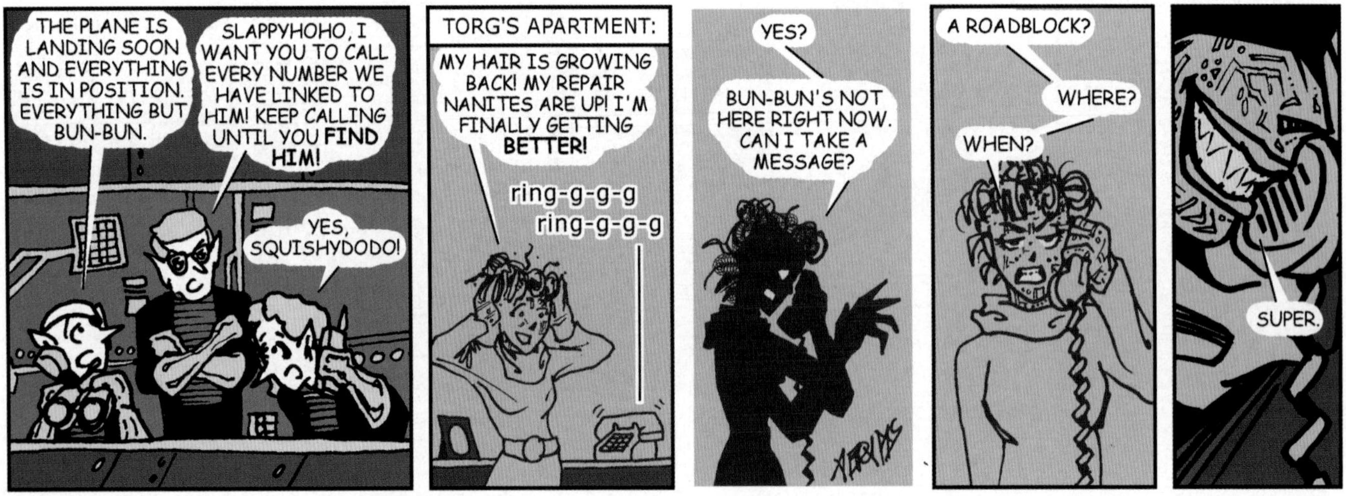
THE PLANE IS LANDING SOON AND EVERYTHING IS IN POSITION. EVERYTHING BUT BUN-BUN.
SLAPPYHOHO, I WANT YOU TO CALL EVERY NUMBER WE HAVE LINKED TO HIM! KEEP CALLING UNTIL YOU FIND HIM!
YES, SQUISHYDODO!
TORG'S APARTMENT:
MY HAIR IS GROWING BACK! MY REPAIR NANITES ARE UP! I'M FINALLY GETTING BETTER!
ring-g-g-g
ring-g-g-g
YES?
BUN-BUN'S NOT HERE RIGHT NOW. CAN I TAKE A MESSAGE?
A ROADBLOCK?
WHERE?
WHEN?
SUPER.

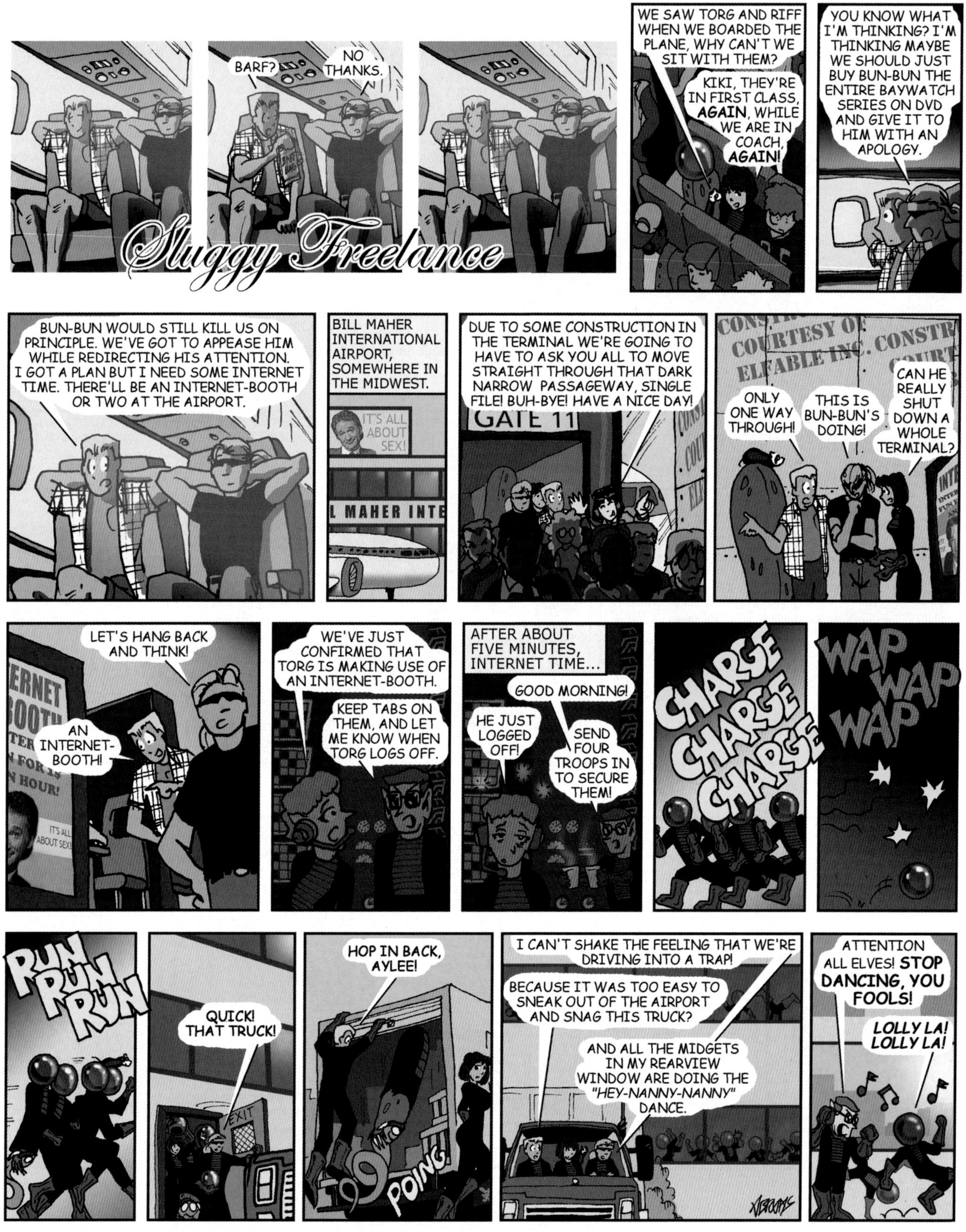

Sluggy Freelance
BARF?
NO THANKS.
WE SAW TORG AND RIFF WHEN WE BOARDED THE PLANE, WHY CAN'T WE SIT WITH THEM?
KIKI, THEY'RE IN FIRST CLASS, **AGAIN**, WHILE WE ARE IN COACH, **AGAIN**!
YOU KNOW WHAT I'M THINKING? I'M THINKING MAYBE WE SHOULD JUST BUY BUN-BUN THE ENTIRE BAYWATCH SERIES ON DVD AND GIVE IT TO HIM WITH AN APOLOGY.
BUN-BUN WOULD STILL KILL US ON PRINCIPLE. WE'VE GOT TO APPEASE HIM WHILE REDIRECTING HIS ATTENTION. I GOT A PLAN BUT I NEED SOME INTERNET TIME. THERE'LL BE AN INTERNET-BOOTH OR TWO AT THE AIRPORT.
BILL MAHER INTERNATIONAL AIRPORT, SOMEWHERE IN THE MIDWEST.
IT'S ALL ABOUT SEX!
L MAHER INTE
DUE TO SOME CONSTRUCTION IN THE TERMINAL WE'RE GOING TO HAVE TO ASK YOU ALL TO MOVE STRAIGHT THROUGH THAT DARK NARROW PASSAGEWAY, SINGLE FILE! BUH-BYE! HAVE A NICE DAY!
GATE 11
COURTESY OF ELFABLE INC.
ONLY ONE WAY THROUGH!
THIS IS BUN-BUN'S DOING!
CAN HE REALLY SHUT DOWN A WHOLE TERMINAL?
LET'S HANG BACK AND THINK!
AN INTERNET-BOOTH!
IT'S ALL ABOUT SEX!
WE'VE JUST CONFIRMED THAT TORG IS MAKING USE OF AN INTERNET-BOOTH.
KEEP TABS ON THEM, AND LET ME KNOW WHEN TORG LOGS OFF.
AFTER ABOUT FIVE MINUTES, INTERNET TIME...
GOOD MORNING!
HE JUST LOGGED OFF!
SEND FOUR TROOPS IN TO SECURE THEM!
CHARGE CHARGE CHARGE
WAP WAP WAP
RUN RUN RUN
QUICK! THAT TRUCK!
EXIT
HOP IN BACK, AYLEE!
POING
I CAN'T SHAKE THE FEELING THAT WE'RE DRIVING INTO A TRAP!
BECAUSE IT WAS TOO EASY TO SNEAK OUT OF THE AIRPORT AND SNAG THIS TRUCK?
AND ALL THE MIDGETS IN MY REARVIEW WINDOW ARE DOING THE *"HEY-NANNY-NANNY"* DANCE.
ATTENTION ALL ELVES! **STOP DANCING, YOU FOOLS!**
LOLLY LA! LOLLY LA!

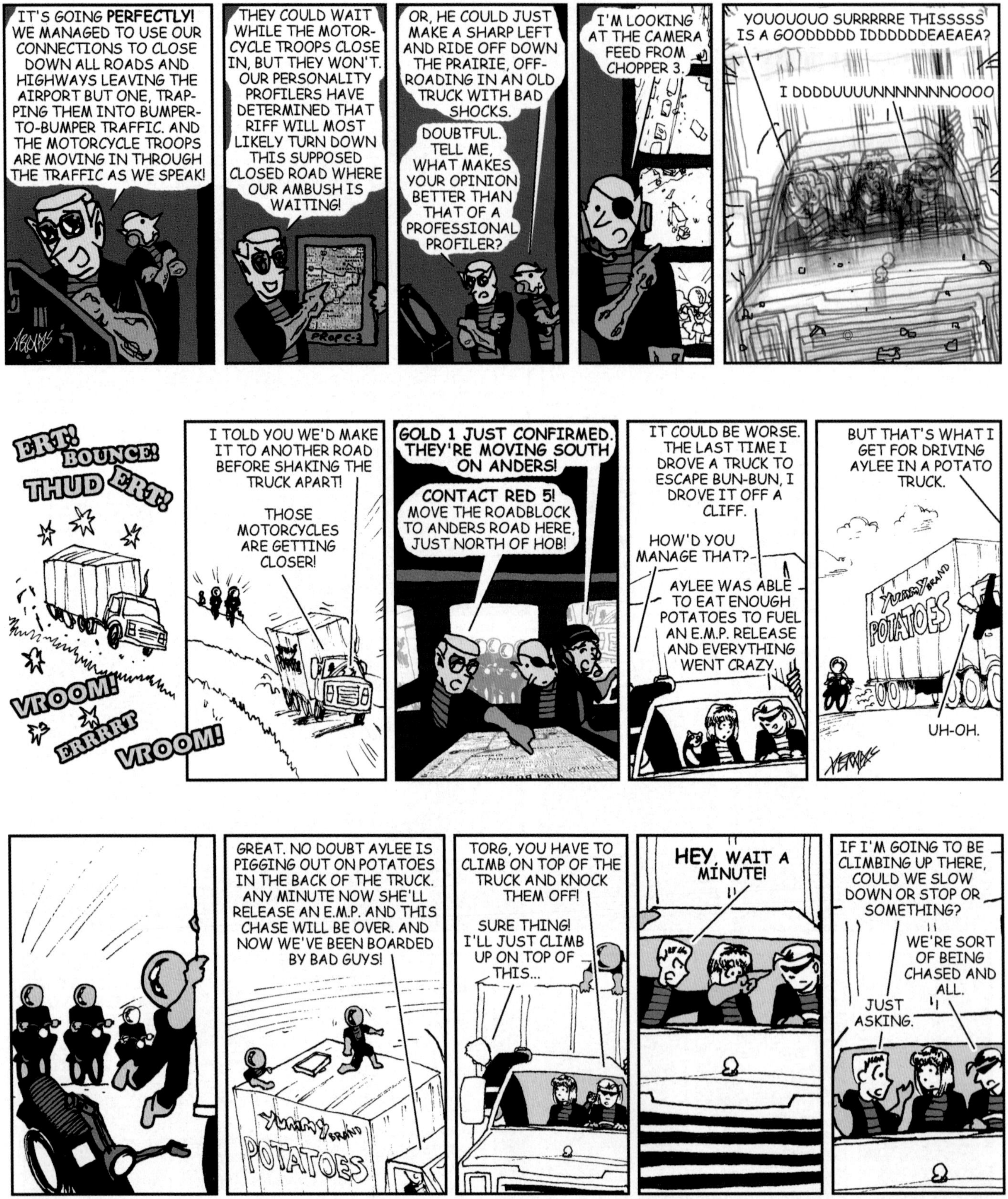
IT'S GOING PERFECTLY! WE MANAGED TO USE OUR CONNECTIONS TO CLOSE DOWN ALL ROADS AND HIGHWAYS LEAVING THE AIRPORT BUT ONE, TRAPPING THEM INTO BUMPER-TO-BUMPER TRAFFIC. AND THE MOTORCYCLE TROOPS ARE MOVING IN THROUGH THE TRAFFIC AS WE SPEAK!
THEY COULD WAIT WHILE THE MOTORCYCLE TROOPS CLOSE IN, BUT THEY WON'T. OUR PERSONALITY PROFILERS HAVE DETERMINED THAT RIFF WILL MOST LIKELY TURN DOWN THIS SUPPOSED CLOSED ROAD WHERE OUR AMBUSH IS WAITING!
PROP C-3
OR, HE COULD JUST MAKE A SHARP LEFT AND RIDE OFF DOWN THE PRAIRIE, OFF-ROADING IN AN OLD TRUCK WITH BAD SHOCKS.
DOUBTFUL. TELL ME, WHAT MAKES YOUR OPINION BETTER THAN THAT OF A PROFESSIONAL PROFILER?
I'M LOOKING AT THE CAMERA FEED FROM CHOPPER 3.
YOUOUOUO SURRRRRE THISSSSS IS A GOODDDDD IDDDDDDEAEAEA?
I DDDDUUUUNNNNNNNOOOO
ERT! BOUNCE! THUD ERT!
VROOM! ERRRRT VROOM!
I TOLD YOU WE'D MAKE IT TO ANOTHER ROAD BEFORE SHAKING THE TRUCK APART!
THOSE MOTORCYCLES ARE GETTING CLOSER!
GOLD 1 JUST CONFIRMED. THEY'RE MOVING SOUTH ON ANDERS!
CONTACT RED 5! MOVE THE ROADBLOCK TO ANDERS ROAD HERE, JUST NORTH OF HOB!
IT COULD BE WORSE. THE LAST TIME I DROVE A TRUCK TO ESCAPE BUN-BUN, I DROVE IT OFF A CLIFF.
HOW'D YOU MANAGE THAT?
AYLEE WAS ABLE TO EAT ENOUGH POTATOES TO FUEL AN E.M.P. RELEASE AND EVERYTHING WENT CRAZY.
BUT THAT'S WHAT I GET FOR DRIVING AYLEE IN A POTATO TRUCK.
YUMMY BRAND POTATOES
UH-OH.
GREAT. NO DOUBT AYLEE IS PIGGING OUT ON POTATOES IN THE BACK OF THE TRUCK. ANY MINUTE NOW SHE'LL RELEASE AN E.M.P. AND THIS CHASE WILL BE OVER. AND NOW WE'VE BEEN BOARDED BY BAD GUYS!
YUMMY BRAND POTATOES
TORG, YOU HAVE TO CLIMB ON TOP OF THE TRUCK AND KNOCK THEM OFF!
SURE THING! I'LL JUST CLIMB UP ON TOP OF THIS...
HEY, WAIT A MINUTE!
IF I'M GOING TO BE CLIMBING UP THERE, COULD WE SLOW DOWN OR STOP OR SOMETHING?
WE'RE SORT OF BEING CHASED AND ALL.
JUST ASKING.

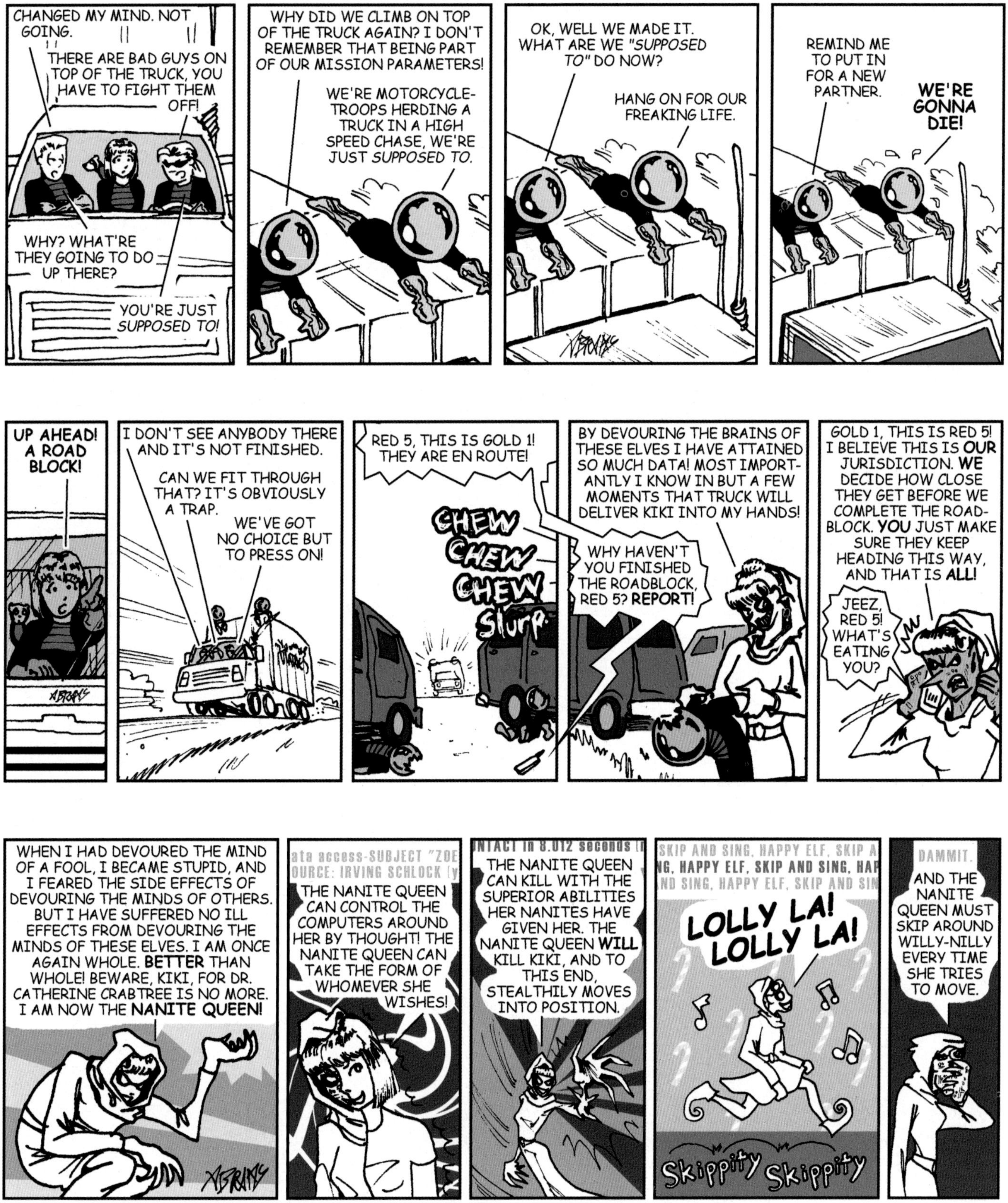

CHANGED MY MIND. NOT GOING.
THERE ARE BAD GUYS ON TOP OF THE TRUCK, YOU HAVE TO FIGHT THEM OFF!
WHY? WHAT'RE THEY GOING TO DO UP THERE?
YOU'RE JUST *SUPPOSED TO!*
WHY DID WE CLIMB ON TOP OF THE TRUCK AGAIN? I DON'T REMEMBER THAT BEING PART OF OUR MISSION PARAMETERS!
WE'RE MOTORCYCLE-TROOPS HERDING A TRUCK IN A HIGH SPEED CHASE, WE'RE JUST *SUPPOSED TO.*
OK, WELL WE MADE IT. WHAT ARE WE *"SUPPOSED TO"* DO NOW?
HANG ON FOR OUR FREAKING LIFE.
REMIND ME TO PUT IN FOR A NEW PARTNER.
WE'RE GONNA DIE!
UP AHEAD! A ROAD BLOCK!
I DON'T SEE ANYBODY THERE AND IT'S NOT FINISHED.
CAN WE FIT THROUGH THAT? IT'S OBVIOUSLY A TRAP.
WE'VE GOT NO CHOICE BUT TO PRESS ON!
RED 5, THIS IS GOLD 1! THEY ARE EN ROUTE!
CHEW CHEW CHEW Slurp.
WHY HAVEN'T YOU FINISHED THE ROADBLOCK, RED 5? **REPORT!**
BY DEVOURING THE BRAINS OF THESE ELVES I HAVE ATTAINED SO MUCH DATA! MOST IMPORTANTLY I KNOW IN BUT A FEW MOMENTS THAT TRUCK WILL DELIVER KIKI INTO MY HANDS!
GOLD 1, THIS IS RED 5! I BELIEVE THIS IS **OUR** JURISDICTION. **WE** DECIDE HOW CLOSE THEY GET BEFORE WE COMPLETE THE ROAD-BLOCK. **YOU** JUST MAKE SURE THEY KEEP HEADING THIS WAY, AND THAT IS **ALL!**
JEEZ, RED 5! WHAT'S EATING YOU?
WHEN I HAD DEVOURED THE MIND OF A FOOL, I BECAME STUPID, AND I FEARED THE SIDE EFFECTS OF DEVOURING THE MINDS OF OTHERS. BUT I HAVE SUFFERED NO ILL EFFECTS FROM DEVOURING THE MINDS OF THESE ELVES. I AM ONCE AGAIN WHOLE. **BETTER** THAN WHOLE! BEWARE, KIKI, FOR DR. CATHERINE CRABTREE IS NO MORE. I AM NOW THE **NANITE QUEEN!**
THE NANITE QUEEN CAN CONTROL THE COMPUTERS AROUND HER BY THOUGHT! THE NANITE QUEEN CAN TAKE THE FORM OF WHOMEVER SHE WISHES!
THE NANITE QUEEN CAN KILL WITH THE SUPERIOR ABILITIES HER NANITES HAVE GIVEN HER. THE NANITE QUEEN **WILL** KILL KIKI, AND TO THIS END, STEALTHILY MOVES INTO POSITION.
LOLLY LA! LOLLY LA!
Skippity Skippity
DAMMIT.
AND THE NANITE QUEEN MUST SKIP AROUND WILLY-NILLY EVERY TIME SHE TRIES TO MOVE.

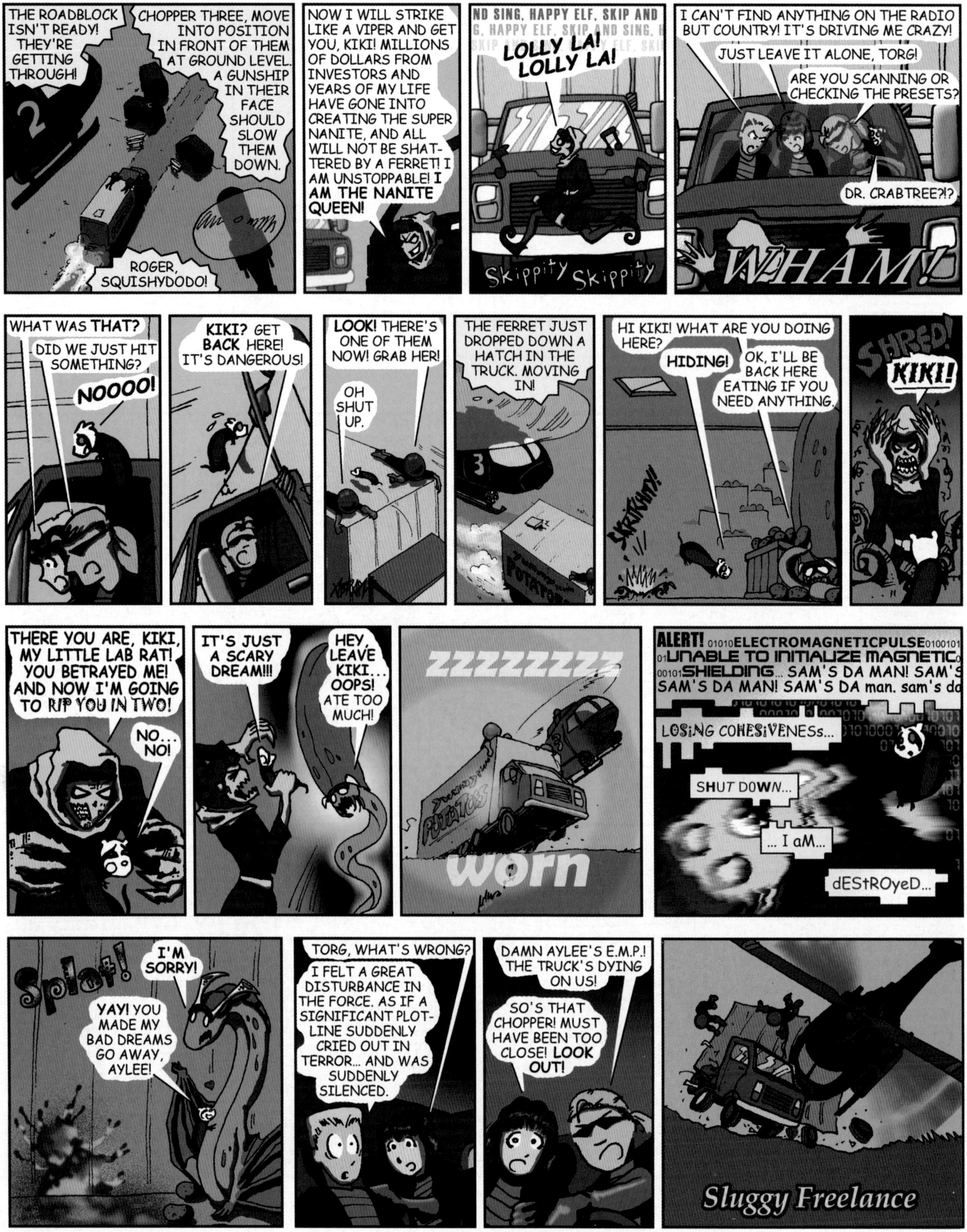
THE ROADBLOCK ISN'T READY! THEY'RE GETTING THROUGH!
CHOPPER THREE, MOVE INTO POSITION IN FRONT OF THEM AT GROUND LEVEL. A GUNSHIP IN THEIR FACE SHOULD SLOW THEM DOWN.
ROGER, SQUISHYDODO!
NOW I WILL STRIKE LIKE A VIPER AND GET YOU, KIKI! MILLIONS OF DOLLARS FROM INVESTORS AND YEARS OF MY LIFE HAVE GONE INTO CREATING THE SUPER NANITE, AND ALL WILL NOT BE SHATTERED BY A FERRET! I AM UNSTOPPABLE! I AM THE NANITE QUEEN!
ND SING, HAPPY ELF, SKIP AND
LOLLY LA! LOLLY LA!
Skippity Skippity
I CAN'T FIND ANYTHING ON THE RADIO BUT COUNTRY! IT'S DRIVING ME CRAZY!
JUST LEAVE IT ALONE, TORG!
ARE YOU SCANNING OR CHECKING THE PRESETS?
DR. CRABTREE?!?
WHAM!
WHAT WAS THAT?
DID WE JUST HIT SOMETHING?
NOOOO!
KIKI? GET BACK HERE! IT'S DANGEROUS!
LOOK! THERE'S ONE OF THEM NOW! GRAB HER!
OH SHUT UP.
THE FERRET JUST DROPPED DOWN A HATCH IN THE TRUCK. MOVING IN!
HI KIKI! WHAT ARE YOU DOING HERE?
HIDING!
OK, I'LL BE BACK HERE EATING IF YOU NEED ANYTHING.
SKRITCHITY!
SHRED!
KIKI!
THERE YOU ARE, KIKI, MY LITTLE LAB RAT! YOU BETRAYED ME! AND NOW I'M GOING TO RIP YOU IN TWO!
NO... NO!
IT'S JUST A SCARY DREAM!!!
HEY, LEAVE KIKI... OOPS! ATE TOO MUCH!
ZZZZZZZZ
worn
ALERT! 01010ELECTROMAGNETICPULSE0100101
01UNABLE TO INITIALIZE MAGNETIC
00101SHIELDING... SAM'S DA MAN! SAM'S
SAM'S DA MAN! SAM'S DA man. sam's da
LOSiNG COHESiVENESs...
SHUT DOWN...
... I aM...
dEStROyeD...
Splat!
I'M SORRY!
YAY! YOU MADE MY BAD DREAMS GO AWAY, AYLEE!
TORG, WHAT'S WRONG?
I FELT A GREAT DISTURBANCE IN THE FORCE. AS IF A SIGNIFICANT PLOTLINE SUDDENLY CRIED OUT IN TERROR... AND WAS SUDDENLY SILENCED.
DAMN AYLEE'S E.M.P.! THE TRUCK'S DYING ON US!
SO'S THAT CHOPPER! MUST HAVE BEEN TOO CLOSE! LOOK OUT!
Sluggy Freelance

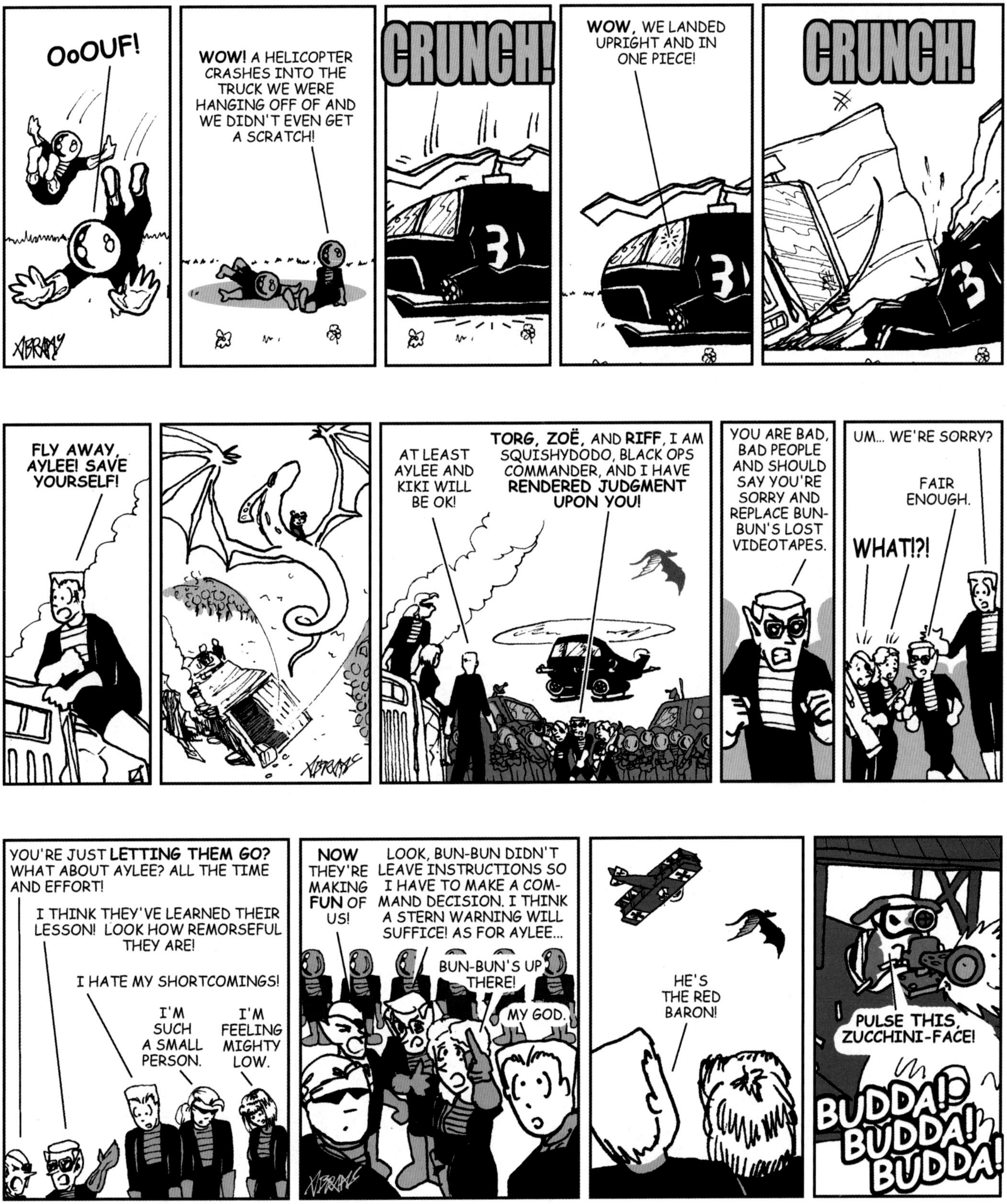
OoOUF!
WOW! A HELICOPTER CRASHES INTO THE TRUCK WE WERE HANGING OFF OF AND WE DIDN'T EVEN GET A SCRATCH!
CRUNCH!
WOW, WE LANDED UPRIGHT AND IN ONE PIECE!
CRUNCH!
FLY AWAY, AYLEE! SAVE YOURSELF!
AT LEAST AYLEE AND KIKI WILL BE OK!
TORG, ZOË, AND RIFF, I AM SQUISHYDODO, BLACK OPS COMMANDER, AND I HAVE RENDERED JUDGMENT UPON YOU!
YOU ARE BAD, BAD PEOPLE AND SHOULD SAY YOU'RE SORRY AND REPLACE BUN-BUN'S LOST VIDEOTAPES.
WHAT!?!
FAIR ENOUGH.
UM... WE'RE SORRY?
YOU'RE JUST LETTING THEM GO? WHAT ABOUT AYLEE? ALL THE TIME AND EFFORT!
I THINK THEY'VE LEARNED THEIR LESSON! LOOK HOW REMORSEFUL THEY ARE!
I HATE MY SHORTCOMINGS!
I'M SUCH A SMALL PERSON.
I'M FEELING MIGHTY LOW.
NOW THEY'RE MAKING FUN OF US!
LOOK, BUN-BUN DIDN'T LEAVE INSTRUCTIONS SO I HAVE TO MAKE A COMMAND DECISION. I THINK A STERN WARNING WILL SUFFICE! AS FOR AYLEE...
BUN-BUN'S UP THERE!
MY GOD.
HE'S THE RED BARON!
PULSE THIS, ZUCCHINI-FACE!
BUDDA! BUDDA! BUDDA!

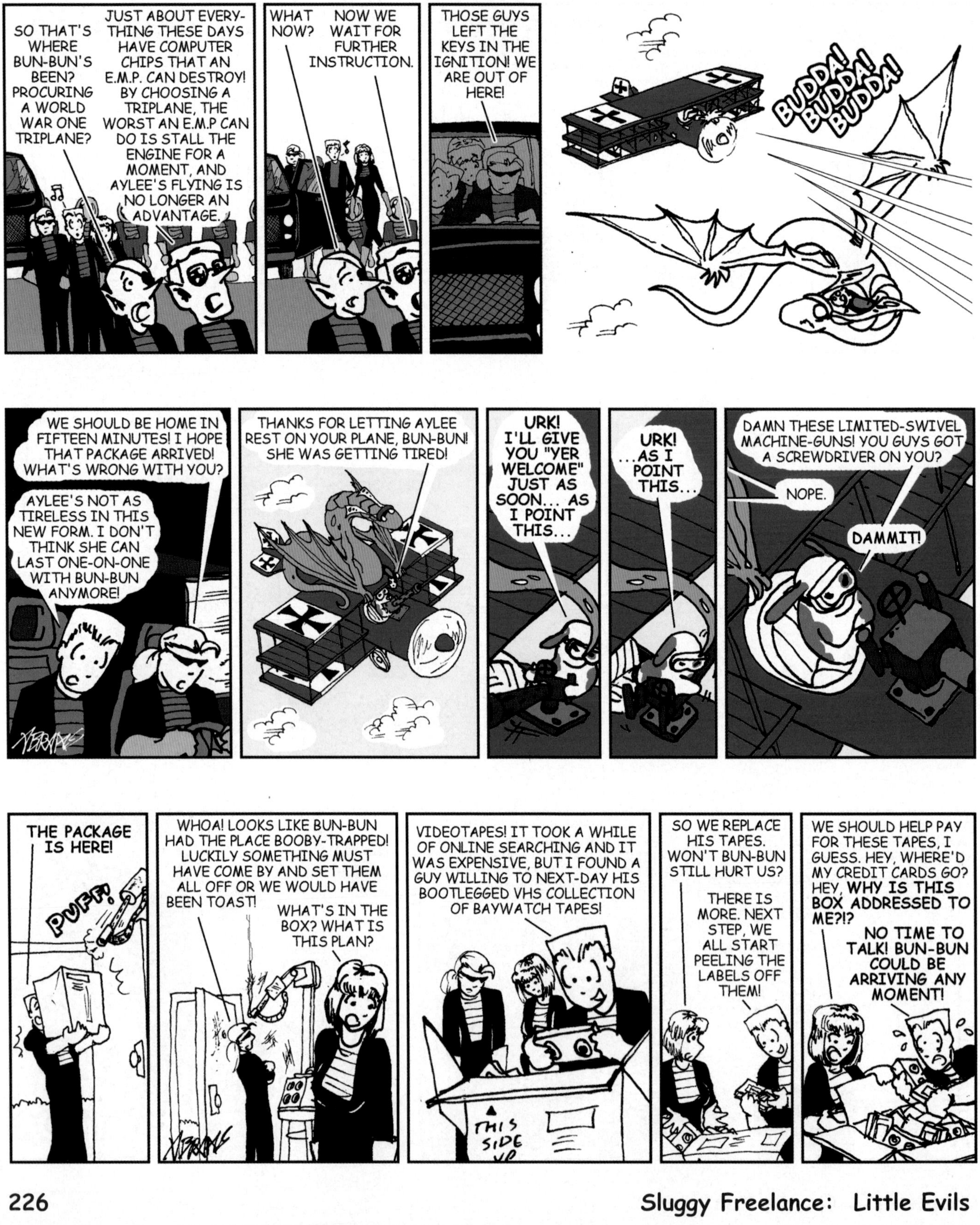
SO THAT'S WHERE BUN-BUN'S BEEN? PROCURING A WORLD WAR ONE TRIPLANE?
JUST ABOUT EVERYTHING THESE DAYS HAVE COMPUTER CHIPS THAT AN E.M.P. CAN DESTROY! BY CHOOSING A TRIPLANE, THE WORST AN E.M.P CAN DO IS STALL THE ENGINE FOR A MOMENT, AND AYLEE'S FLYING IS NO LONGER AN ADVANTAGE.
WHAT NOW?
NOW WE WAIT FOR FURTHER INSTRUCTION.
THOSE GUYS LEFT THE KEYS IN THE IGNITION! WE ARE OUT OF HERE!
BUDDA! BUDDA! BUDDA!
WE SHOULD BE HOME IN FIFTEEN MINUTES! I HOPE THAT PACKAGE ARRIVED! WHAT'S WRONG WITH YOU?
AYLEE'S NOT AS TIRELESS IN THIS NEW FORM. I DON'T THINK SHE CAN LAST ONE-ON-ONE WITH BUN-BUN ANYMORE!
THANKS FOR LETTING AYLEE REST ON YOUR PLANE, BUN-BUN! SHE WAS GETTING TIRED!
URK! I'LL GIVE YOU "YER WELCOME" JUST AS SOON... AS I POINT THIS...
URK! ...AS I POINT THIS...
DAMN THESE LIMITED-SWIVEL MACHINE-GUNS! YOU GUYS GOT A SCREWDRIVER ON YOU?
NOPE.
DAMMIT!
THE PACKAGE IS HERE!
PUFF!
WHOA! LOOKS LIKE BUN-BUN HAD THE PLACE BOOBY-TRAPPED! LUCKILY SOMETHING MUST HAVE COME BY AND SET THEM ALL OFF OR WE WOULD HAVE BEEN TOAST!
WHAT'S IN THE BOX? WHAT IS THIS PLAN?
VIDEOTAPES! IT TOOK A WHILE OF ONLINE SEARCHING AND IT WAS EXPENSIVE, BUT I FOUND A GUY WILLING TO NEXT-DAY HIS BOOTLEGGED VHS COLLECTION OF BAYWATCH TAPES!
THIS SIDE UP
SO WE REPLACE HIS TAPES. WON'T BUN-BUN STILL HURT US?
THERE IS MORE. NEXT STEP, WE ALL START PEELING THE LABELS OFF THEM!
WE SHOULD HELP PAY FOR THESE TAPES, I GUESS. HEY, WHERE'D MY CREDIT CARDS GO? HEY, WHY IS THIS BOX ADDRESSED TO ME?!?
NO TIME TO TALK! BUN-BUN COULD BE ARRIVING ANY MOMENT!

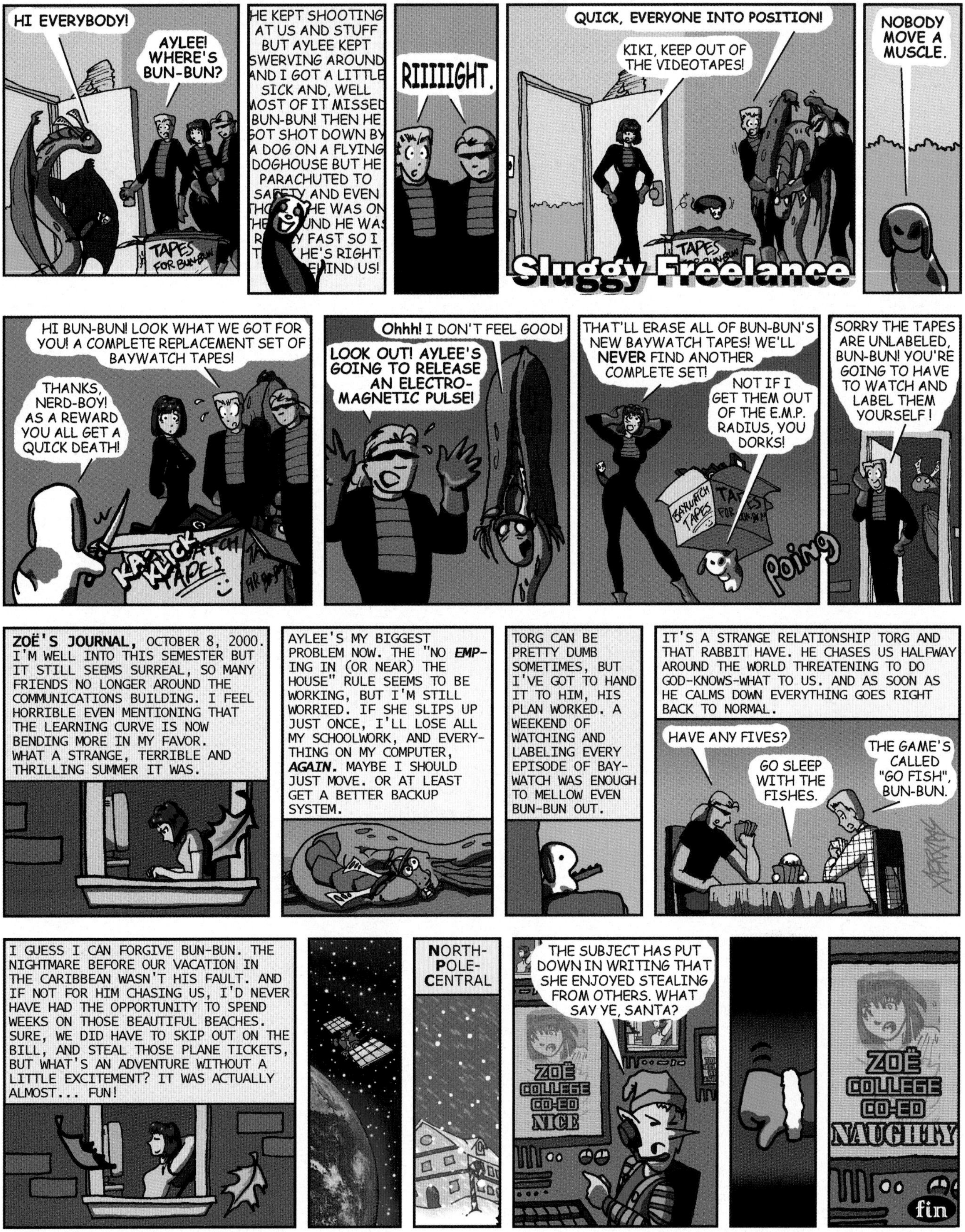

HI EVERYBODY!
AYLEE! WHERE'S BUN-BUN?
TAPES FOR BUN-BUN
HE KEPT SHOOTING AT US AND STUFF BUT AYLEE KEPT SWERVING AROUND AND I GOT A LITTLE SICK AND, WELL MOST OF IT MISSED BUN-BUN! THEN HE GOT SHOT DOWN BY A DOG ON A FLYING DOGHOUSE BUT HE PARACHUTED TO SAFETY AND EVEN THO HE WAS ON THE GROUND HE WAS REALLY FAST SO I THINK HE'S RIGHT BEHIND US!
RIIIIIGHT.
QUICK, EVERYONE INTO POSITION!
KIKI, KEEP OUT OF THE VIDEOTAPES!
TAPES FOR BUN-BUN
Sluggy Freelance
NOBODY MOVE A MUSCLE.
HI BUN-BUN! LOOK WHAT WE GOT FOR YOU! A COMPLETE REPLACEMENT SET OF BAYWATCH TAPES!
THANKS, NERD-BOY! AS A REWARD YOU ALL GET A QUICK DEATH!
KA-KLICK
Ohhh! I DON'T FEEL GOOD!
LOOK OUT! AYLEE'S GOING TO RELEASE AN ELECTRO-MAGNETIC PULSE!
THAT'LL ERASE ALL OF BUN-BUN'S NEW BAYWATCH TAPES! WE'LL NEVER FIND ANOTHER COMPLETE SET!
NOT IF I GET THEM OUT OF THE E.M.P. RADIUS, YOU DORKS!
BAYWATCH TAPES
poing
SORRY THE TAPES ARE UNLABELED, BUN-BUN! YOU'RE GOING TO HAVE TO WATCH AND LABEL THEM YOURSELF!
ZOË'S JOURNAL, OCTOBER 8, 2000. I'M WELL INTO THIS SEMESTER BUT IT STILL SEEMS SURREAL, SO MANY FRIENDS NO LONGER AROUND THE COMMUNICATIONS BUILDING. I FEEL HORRIBLE EVEN MENTIONING THAT THE LEARNING CURVE IS NOW BENDING MORE IN MY FAVOR. WHAT A STRANGE, TERRIBLE AND THRILLING SUMMER IT WAS.
AYLEE'S MY BIGGEST PROBLEM NOW. THE "NO EMPING IN (OR NEAR) THE HOUSE" RULE SEEMS TO BE WORKING, BUT I'M STILL WORRIED. IF SHE SLIPS UP JUST ONCE, I'LL LOSE ALL MY SCHOOLWORK, AND EVERYTHING ON MY COMPUTER, AGAIN. MAYBE I SHOULD JUST MOVE. OR AT LEAST GET A BETTER BACKUP SYSTEM.
TORG CAN BE PRETTY DUMB SOMETIMES, BUT I'VE GOT TO HAND IT TO HIM, HIS PLAN WORKED. A WEEKEND OF WATCHING AND LABELING EVERY EPISODE OF BAYWATCH WAS ENOUGH TO MELLOW EVEN BUN-BUN OUT.
IT'S A STRANGE RELATIONSHIP TORG AND THAT RABBIT HAVE. HE CHASES US HALFWAY AROUND THE WORLD THREATENING TO DO GOD-KNOWS-WHAT TO US. AND AS SOON AS HE CALMS DOWN EVERYTHING GOES RIGHT BACK TO NORMAL.
HAVE ANY FIVES?
GO SLEEP WITH THE FISHES.
THE GAME'S CALLED "GO FISH", BUN-BUN.
I GUESS I CAN FORGIVE BUN-BUN. THE NIGHTMARE BEFORE OUR VACATION IN THE CARIBBEAN WASN'T HIS FAULT. AND IF NOT FOR HIM CHASING US, I'D NEVER HAVE HAD THE OPPORTUNITY TO SPEND WEEKS ON THOSE BEAUTIFUL BEACHES. SURE, WE DID HAVE TO SKIP OUT ON THE BILL, AND STEAL THOSE PLANE TICKETS, BUT WHAT'S AN ADVENTURE WITHOUT A LITTLE EXCITEMENT? IT WAS ACTUALLY ALMOST... FUN!
NORTH-POLE-CENTRAL
THE SUBJECT HAS PUT DOWN IN WRITING THAT SHE ENJOYED STEALING FROM OTHERS. WHAT SAY YE, SANTA?
ZOË COLLEGE CO-ED NICE
ZOË COLLEGE CO-ED NAUGHTY
fin

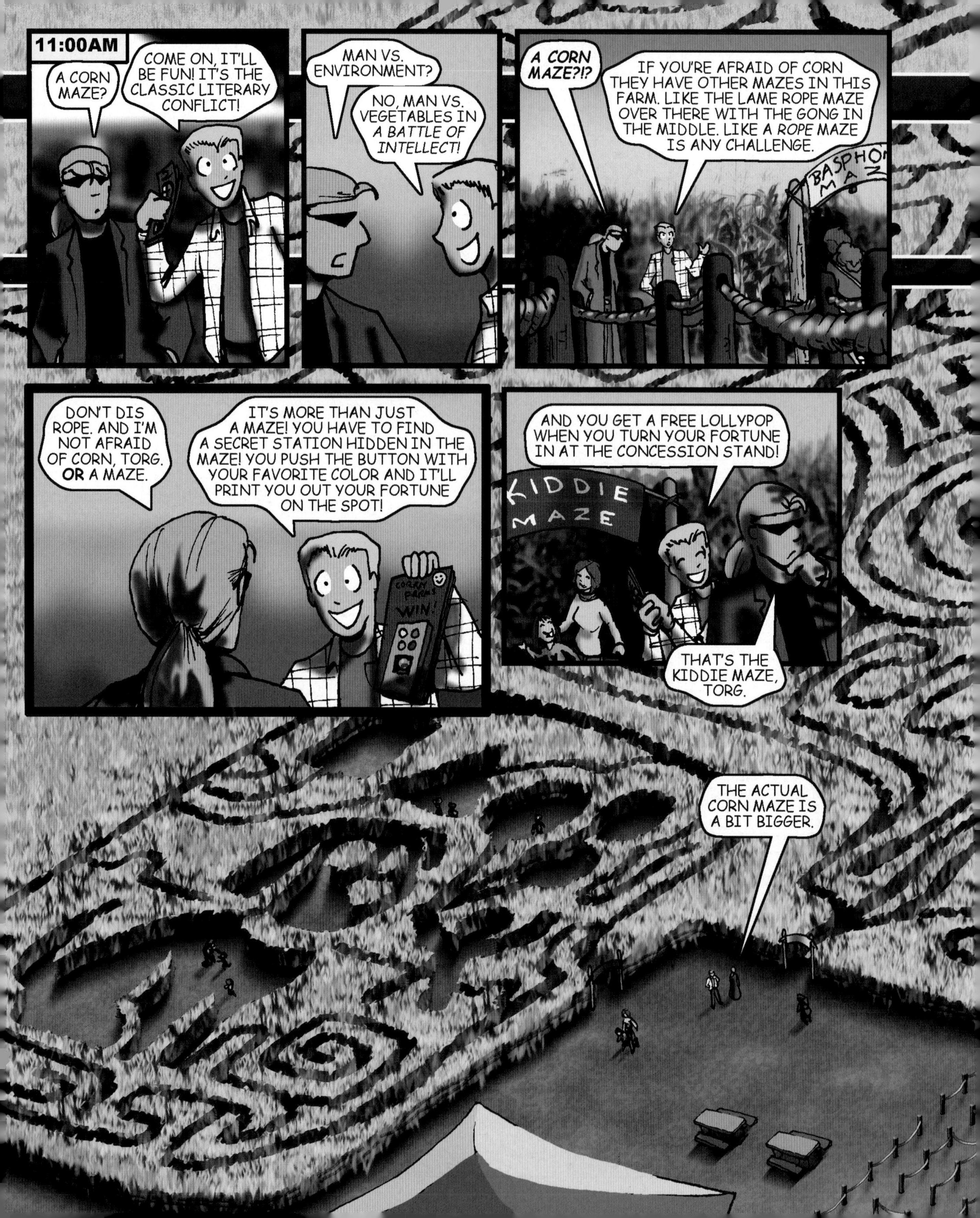
11:00AM
A CORN MAZE?
COME ON, IT'LL BE FUN! IT'S THE CLASSIC LITERARY CONFLICT!
MAN VS. ENVIRONMENT?
NO, MAN VS. VEGETABLES IN A BATTLE OF INTELLECT!
A CORN MAZE?!?
IF YOU'RE AFRAID OF CORN THEY HAVE OTHER MAZES IN THIS FARM. LIKE THE LAME ROPE MAZE OVER THERE WITH THE GONG IN THE MIDDLE. LIKE A ROPE MAZE IS ANY CHALLENGE.
DON'T DIS ROPE. AND I'M NOT AFRAID OF CORN, TORG. OR A MAZE.
IT'S MORE THAN JUST A MAZE! YOU HAVE TO FIND A SECRET STATION HIDDEN IN THE MAZE! YOU PUSH THE BUTTON WITH YOUR FAVORITE COLOR AND IT'LL PRINT YOU OUT YOUR FORTUNE ON THE SPOT!
WIN!
AND YOU GET A FREE LOLLYPOP WHEN YOU TURN YOUR FORTUNE IN AT THE CONCESSION STAND!
KIDDIE MAZE
THAT'S THE KIDDIE MAZE, TORG.
THE ACTUAL CORN MAZE IS A BIT BIGGER.

SLUGGY FREELANCE PRESENTS...

THE MAIZE OF MADNESS

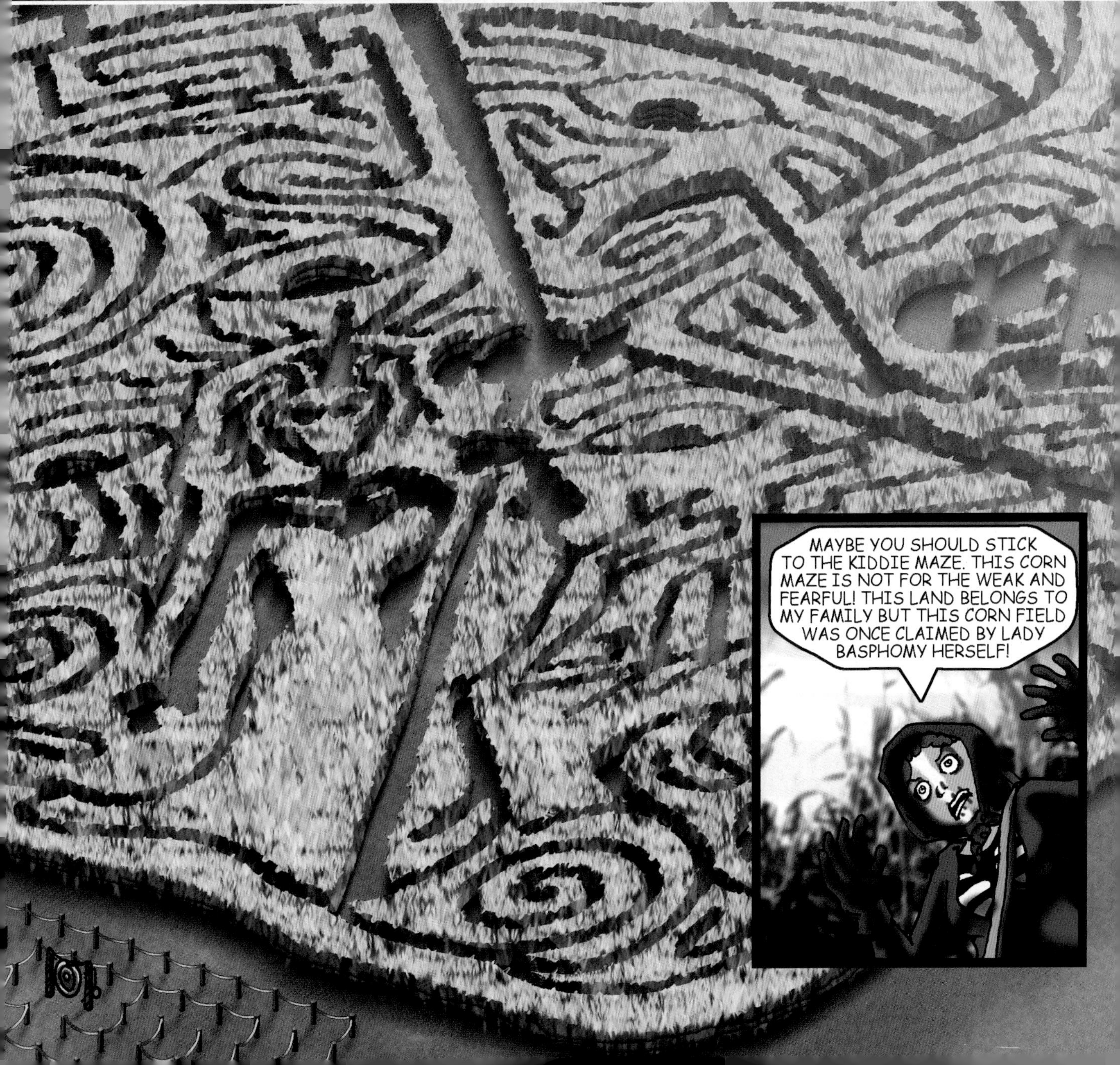
MAYBE YOU SHOULD STICK TO THE KIDDIE MAZE. THIS CORN MAZE IS NOT FOR THE WEAK AND FEARFUL! THIS LAND BELONGS TO MY FAMILY BUT THIS CORN FIELD WAS ONCE CLAIMED BY LADY BASPHOMY HERSELF!

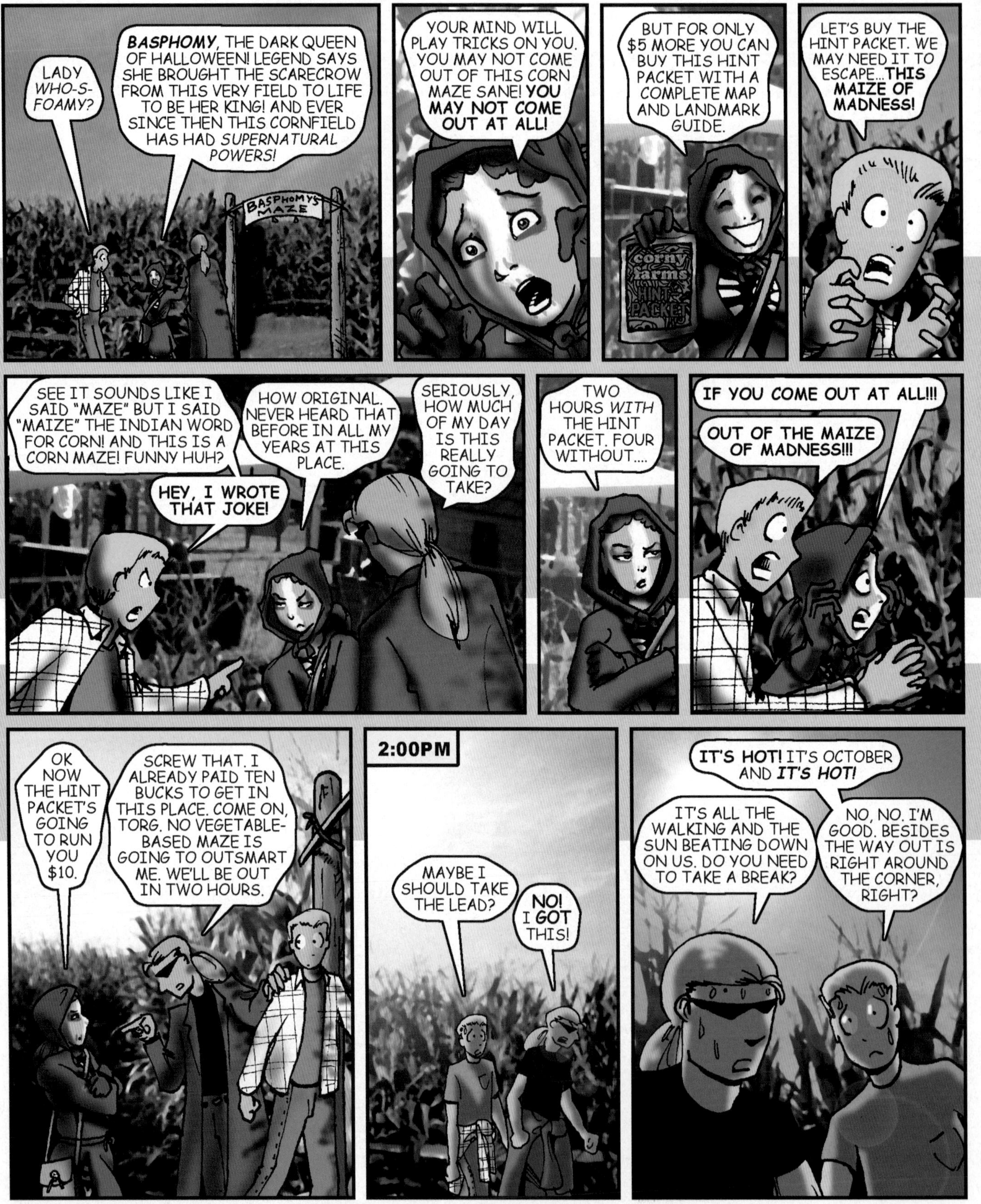
LADY WHO-S-FOAMY?
BASPHOMY, THE DARK QUEEN OF HALLOWEEN! LEGEND SAYS SHE BROUGHT THE SCARECROW FROM THIS VERY FIELD TO LIFE TO BE HER KING! AND EVER SINCE THEN THIS CORNFIELD HAS HAD SUPERNATURAL POWERS!
BASPHOMY'S MAZE
YOUR MIND WILL PLAY TRICKS ON YOU. YOU MAY NOT COME OUT OF THIS CORN MAZE SANE! YOU MAY NOT COME OUT AT ALL!
BUT FOR ONLY $5 MORE YOU CAN BUY THIS HINT PACKET WITH A COMPLETE MAP AND LANDMARK GUIDE.
corny farms HINT PACKET
LET'S BUY THE HINT PACKET. WE MAY NEED IT TO ESCAPE...THIS MAIZE OF MADNESS!
SEE IT SOUNDS LIKE I SAID "MAZE" BUT I SAID "MAIZE" THE INDIAN WORD FOR CORN! AND THIS IS A CORN MAZE! FUNNY HUH?
HEY, I WROTE THAT JOKE!
HOW ORIGINAL. NEVER HEARD THAT BEFORE IN ALL MY YEARS AT THIS PLACE.
SERIOUSLY, HOW MUCH OF MY DAY IS THIS REALLY GOING TO TAKE?
TWO HOURS WITH THE HINT PACKET. FOUR WITHOUT....
IF YOU COME OUT AT ALL!!!
OUT OF THE MAIZE OF MADNESS!!!
OK NOW THE HINT PACKET'S GOING TO RUN YOU $10.
SCREW THAT. I ALREADY PAID TEN BUCKS TO GET IN THIS PLACE. COME ON, TORG. NO VEGETABLE-BASED MAZE IS GOING TO OUTSMART ME. WE'LL BE OUT IN TWO HOURS.
2:00PM
MAYBE I SHOULD TAKE THE LEAD?
NO! I GOT THIS!
IT'S HOT! IT'S OCTOBER AND IT'S HOT!
IT'S ALL THE WALKING AND THE SUN BEATING DOWN ON US. DO YOU NEED TO TAKE A BREAK?
NO, NO. I'M GOOD. BESIDES THE WAY OUT IS RIGHT AROUND THE CORNER, RIGHT?

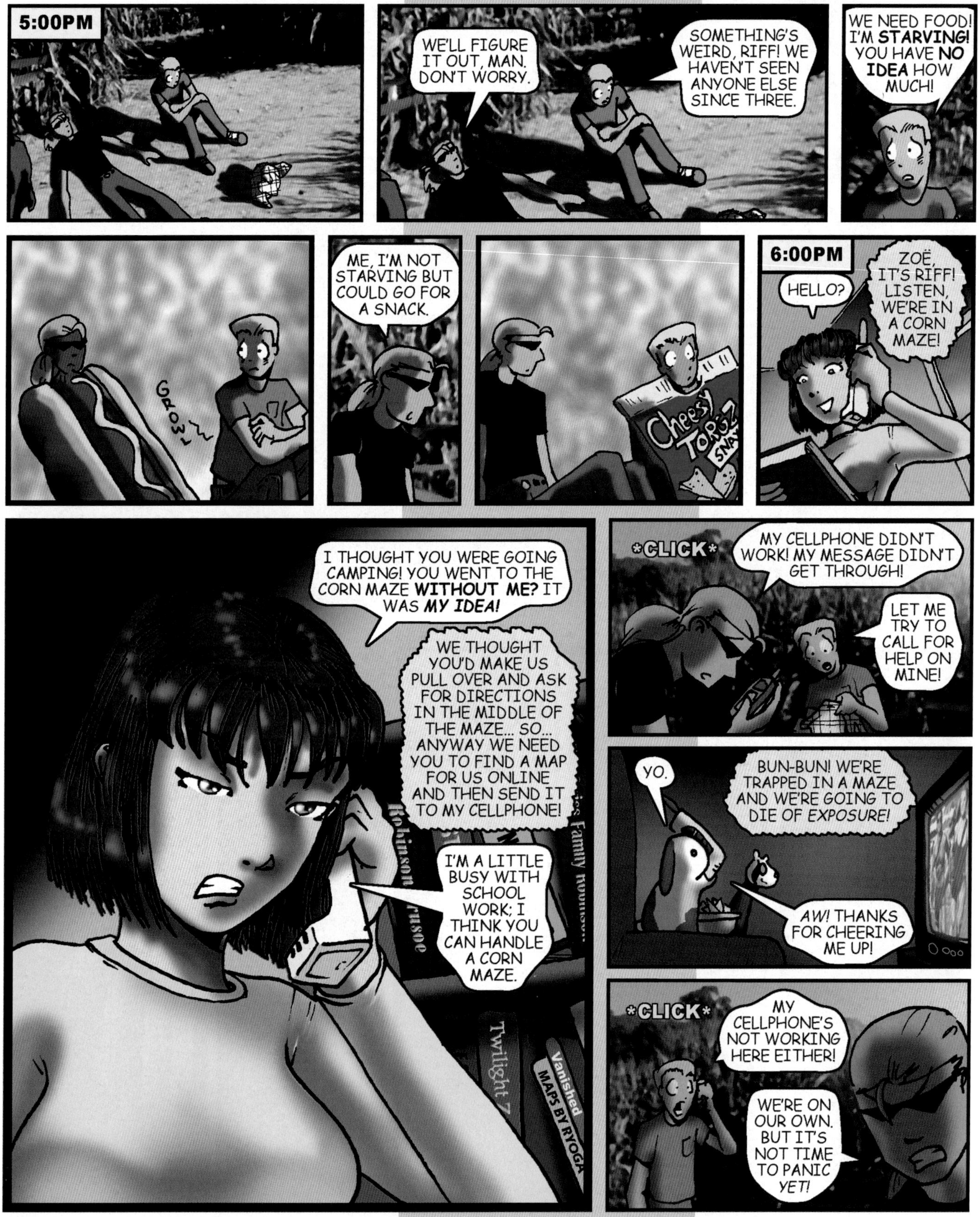
5:00PM
WE'LL FIGURE IT OUT, MAN. DON'T WORRY.
SOMETHING'S WEIRD, RIFF! WE HAVEN'T SEEN ANYONE ELSE SINCE THREE.
WE NEED FOOD! I'M STARVING! YOU HAVE NO IDEA HOW MUCH!
GROWL
ME, I'M NOT STARVING BUT COULD GO FOR A SNACK.
Cheesy TORIZ SNAX
6:00PM
HELLO?
ZOË, IT'S RIFF! LISTEN, WE'RE IN A CORN MAZE!
I THOUGHT YOU WERE GOING CAMPING! YOU WENT TO THE CORN MAZE WITHOUT ME? IT WAS MY IDEA!
WE THOUGHT YOU'D MAKE US PULL OVER AND ASK FOR DIRECTIONS IN THE MIDDLE OF THE MAZE... SO... ANYWAY WE NEED YOU TO FIND A MAP FOR US ONLINE AND THEN SEND IT TO MY CELLPHONE!
I'M A LITTLE BUSY WITH SCHOOL WORK; I THINK YOU CAN HANDLE A CORN MAZE.
Robinson Crusoe
Twilight 7
Vanished
MAPS BY RYOGA
CLICK
MY CELLPHONE DIDN'T WORK! MY MESSAGE DIDN'T GET THROUGH!
LET ME TRY TO CALL FOR HELP ON MINE!
YO.
BUN-BUN! WE'RE TRAPPED IN A MAZE AND WE'RE GOING TO DIE OF EXPOSURE!
AW! THANKS FOR CHEERING ME UP!
CLICK
MY CELLPHONE'S NOT WORKING HERE EITHER!
WE'RE ON OUR OWN. BUT IT'S NOT TIME TO PANIC YET!

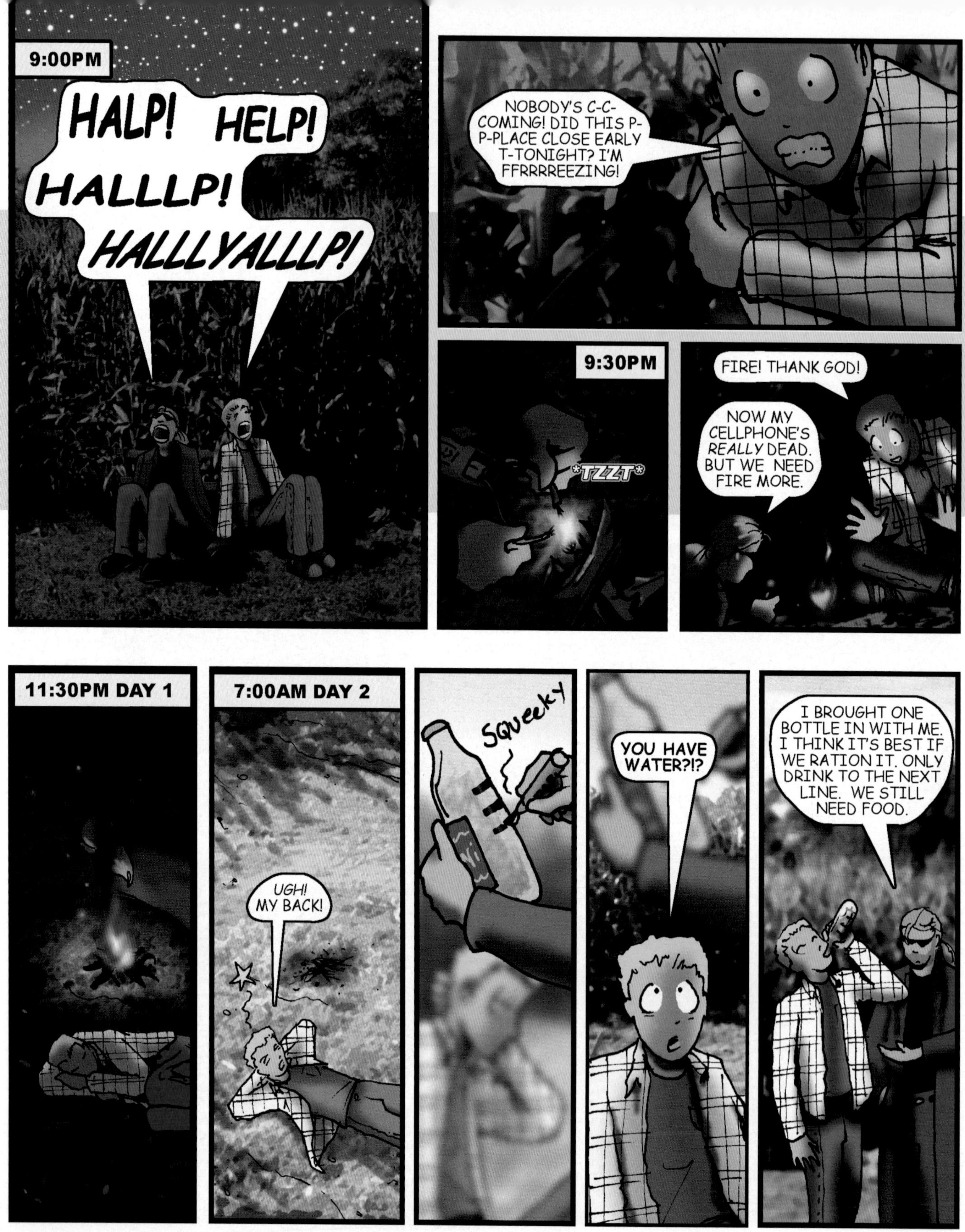
9:00PM
HALP! HELP! HALLLP! HALLLYALLLP!
NOBODY'S C-C-COMING! DID THIS P-P-PLACE CLOSE EARLY T-TONIGHT? I'M FFRRRRREEZING!
9:30PM
TZZT
FIRE! THANK GOD!
NOW MY CELLPHONE'S REALLY DEAD. BUT WE NEED FIRE MORE.
11:30PM DAY 1
7:00AM DAY 2
UGH! MY BACK!
Squeeky
YOU HAVE WATER?!?
I BROUGHT ONE BOTTLE IN WITH ME. I THINK IT'S BEST IF WE RATION IT. ONLY DRINK TO THE NEXT LINE. WE STILL NEED FOOD.

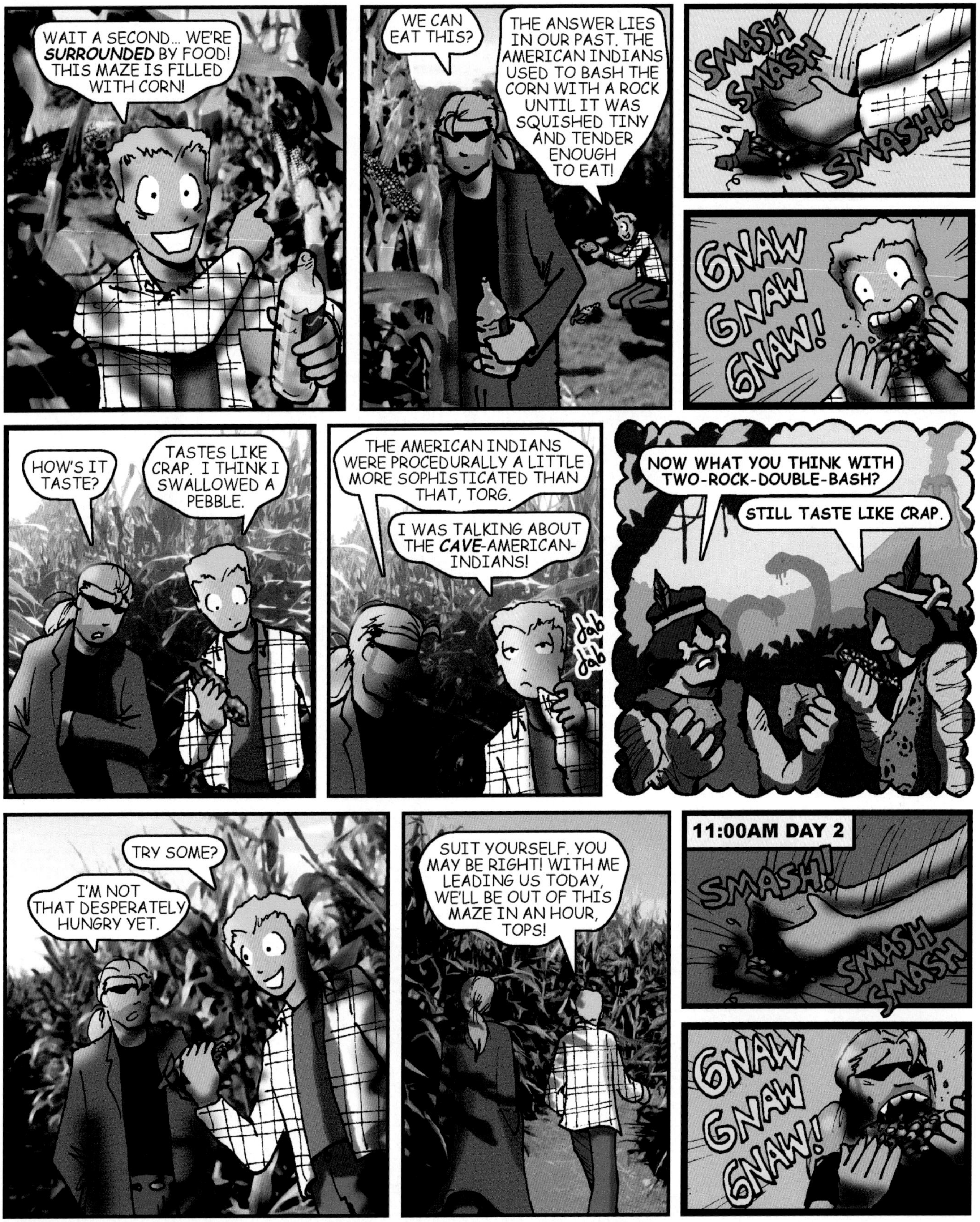
WAIT A SECOND... WE'RE **SURROUNDED** BY FOOD! THIS MAZE IS FILLED WITH CORN!
WE CAN EAT THIS?
THE ANSWER LIES IN OUR PAST. THE AMERICAN INDIANS USED TO BASH THE CORN WITH A ROCK UNTIL IT WAS SQUISHED TINY AND TENDER ENOUGH TO EAT!
SMASH SMASH SMASH!
GNAW GNAW GNAW!
HOW'S IT TASTE?
TASTES LIKE CRAP. I THINK I SWALLOWED A PEBBLE.
THE AMERICAN INDIANS WERE PROCEDURALLY A LITTLE MORE SOPHISTICATED THAN THAT, TORG.
I WAS TALKING ABOUT THE **CAVE**-AMERICAN-INDIANS!
dab dab
NOW WHAT YOU THINK WITH TWO-ROCK-DOUBLE-BASH?
STILL TASTE LIKE CRAP.
TRY SOME?
I'M NOT THAT DESPERATELY HUNGRY YET.
SUIT YOURSELF. YOU MAY BE RIGHT! WITH ME LEADING US TODAY, WE'LL BE OUT OF THIS MAZE IN AN HOUR, TOPS!
11:00AM DAY 2
SMASH! SMASH SMASH!
GNAW GNAW GNAW!

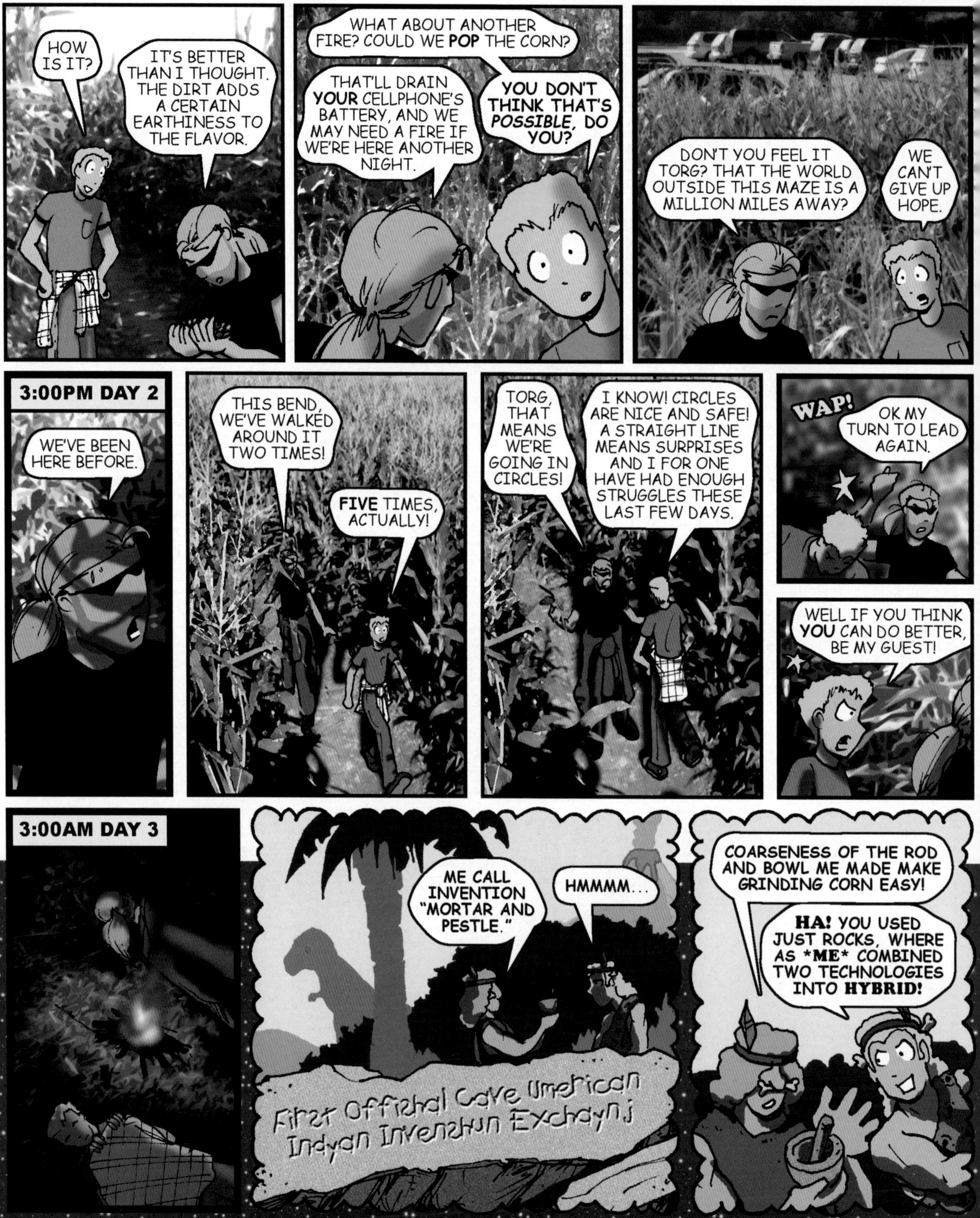
HOW IS IT?
IT'S BETTER THAN I THOUGHT. THE DIRT ADDS A CERTAIN EARTHINESS TO THE FLAVOR.
WHAT ABOUT ANOTHER FIRE? COULD WE POP THE CORN?
THAT'LL DRAIN YOUR CELLPHONE'S BATTERY, AND WE MAY NEED A FIRE IF WE'RE HERE ANOTHER NIGHT.
YOU DON'T THINK THAT'S POSSIBLE, DO YOU?
DON'T YOU FEEL IT TORG? THAT THE WORLD OUTSIDE THIS MAZE IS A MILLION MILES AWAY?
WE CAN'T GIVE UP HOPE.
3:00PM DAY 2
WE'VE BEEN HERE BEFORE.
THIS BEND, WE'VE WALKED AROUND IT TWO TIMES!
FIVE TIMES, ACTUALLY!
TORG, THAT MEANS WE'RE GOING IN CIRCLES!
I KNOW! CIRCLES ARE NICE AND SAFE! A STRAIGHT LINE MEANS SURPRISES AND I FOR ONE HAVE HAD ENOUGH STRUGGLES THESE LAST FEW DAYS.
WAP!
OK MY TURN TO LEAD AGAIN.
WELL IF YOU THINK YOU CAN DO BETTER, BE MY GUEST!
3:00AM DAY 3
ME CALL INVENTION "MORTAR AND PESTLE."
HMMMM...
First Offishal Cave Umerican Indyan Invenshun Exchaynj
COARSENESS OF THE ROD AND BOWL ME MADE MAKE GRINDING CORN EASY!
HA! YOU USED JUST ROCKS, WHERE AS *ME* COMBINED TWO TECHNOLOGIES INTO HYBRID!

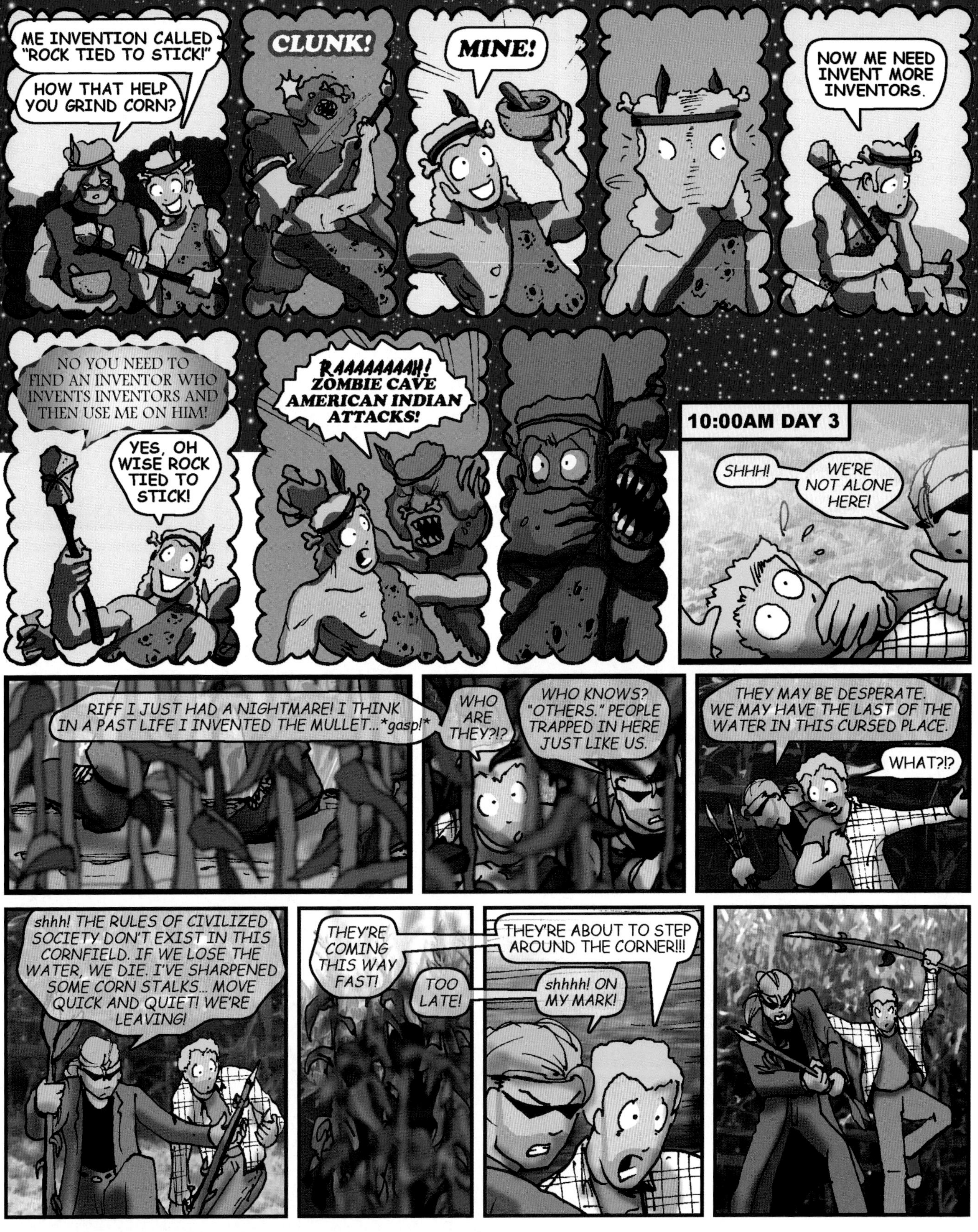
ME INVENTION CALLED "ROCK TIED TO STICK!"
HOW THAT HELP YOU GRIND CORN?
CLUNK!
MINE!
NOW ME NEED INVENT MORE INVENTORS.
NO YOU NEED TO FIND AN INVENTOR WHO INVENTS INVENTORS AND THEN USE ME ON HIM!
YES, OH WISE ROCK TIED TO STICK!
RAAAAAAAAH! ZOMBIE CAVE AMERICAN INDIAN ATTACKS!
10:00AM DAY 3
SHHH!
WE'RE NOT ALONE HERE!
RIFF I JUST HAD A NIGHTMARE! I THINK IN A PAST LIFE I INVENTED THE MULLET... *gasp!*
WHO ARE THEY?!?
WHO KNOWS? "OTHERS." PEOPLE TRAPPED IN HERE JUST LIKE US.
THEY MAY BE DESPERATE. WE MAY HAVE THE LAST OF THE WATER IN THIS CURSED PLACE.
WHAT?!?
shhh! THE RULES OF CIVILIZED SOCIETY DON'T EXIST IN THIS CORNFIELD. IF WE LOSE THE WATER, WE DIE. I'VE SHARPENED SOME CORN STALKS... MOVE QUICK AND QUIET! WE'RE LEAVING!
THEY'RE COMING THIS WAY FAST!
THEY'RE ABOUT TO STEP AROUND THE CORNER!!!
TOO LATE!
shhhh! ON MY MARK!

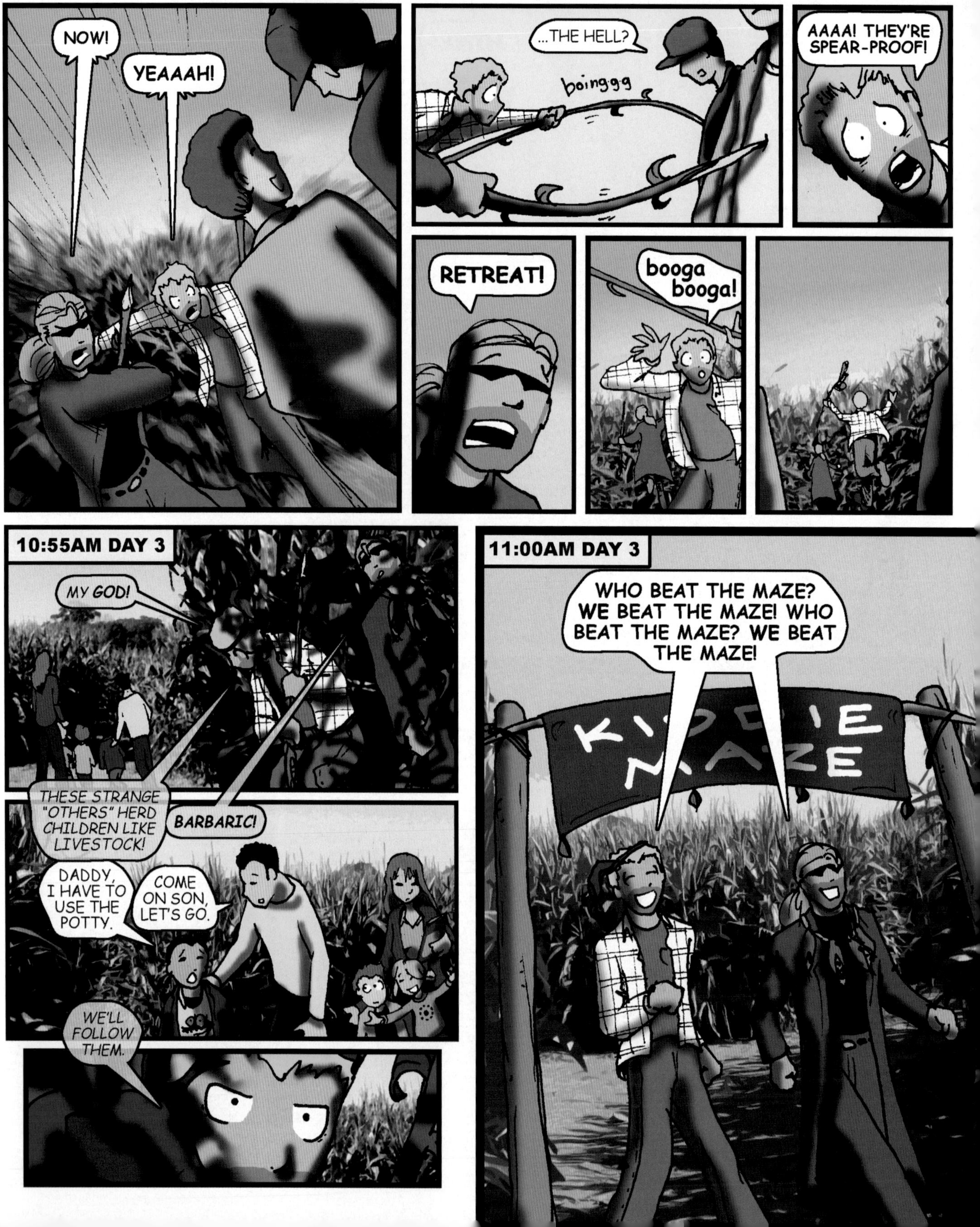
NOW!
YEAAAH!
...THE HELL?
boinggg
AAAA! THEY'RE SPEAR-PROOF!
RETREAT!
booga booga!
10:55AM DAY 3
MY GOD!
THESE STRANGE "OTHERS" HERD CHILDREN LIKE LIVESTOCK!
BARBARIC!
DADDY, I HAVE TO USE THE POTTY.
COME ON SON, LET'S GO.
WE'LL FOLLOW THEM.
11:00AM DAY 3
WHO BEAT THE MAZE? WE BEAT THE MAZE! WHO BEAT THE MAZE? WE BEAT THE MAZE!
KIDDIE MAZE

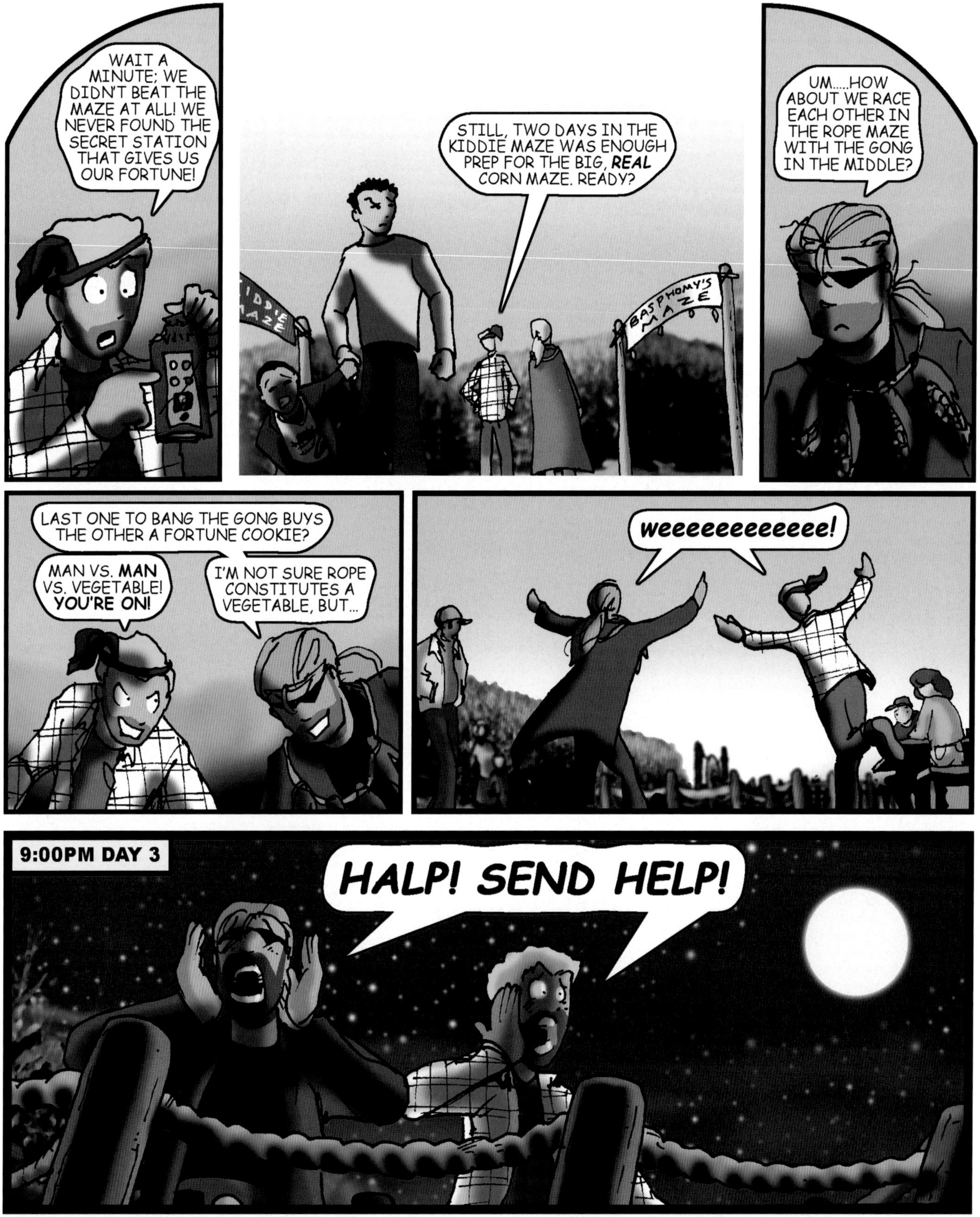
WAIT A MINUTE; WE DIDN'T BEAT THE MAZE AT ALL! WE NEVER FOUND THE SECRET STATION THAT GIVES US OUR FORTUNE!
STILL, TWO DAYS IN THE KIDDIE MAZE WAS ENOUGH PREP FOR THE BIG, **REAL** CORN MAZE. READY?
KIDDIE MAZE
BASPHOMY'S MAZE
UM.....HOW ABOUT WE RACE EACH OTHER IN THE ROPE MAZE WITH THE GONG IN THE MIDDLE?
LAST ONE TO BANG THE GONG BUYS THE OTHER A FORTUNE COOKIE?
MAN VS. **MAN** VS. VEGETABLE! **YOU'RE ON!**
I'M NOT SURE ROPE CONSTITUTES A VEGETABLE, BUT...
weeeeeeeeeeee!
9:00PM DAY 3
HALP! SEND HELP!

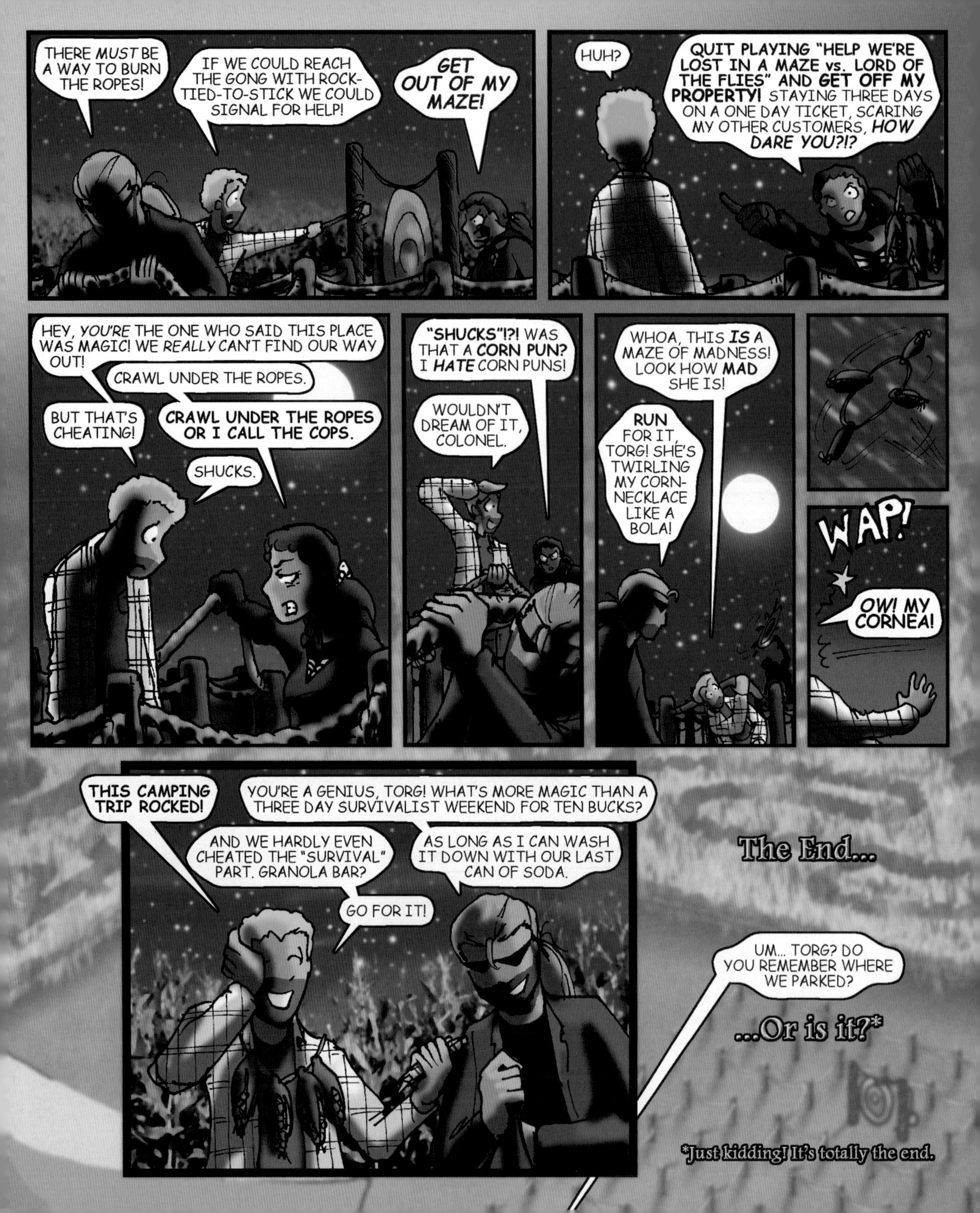

THERE MUST BE A WAY TO BURN THE ROPES!
IF WE COULD REACH THE GONG WITH ROCK-TIED-TO-STICK WE COULD SIGNAL FOR HELP!
GET OUT OF MY MAZE!
HUH?
QUIT PLAYING "HELP WE'RE LOST IN A MAZE vs. LORD OF THE FLIES" AND GET OFF MY PROPERTY! STAYING THREE DAYS ON A ONE DAY TICKET, SCARING MY OTHER CUSTOMERS, HOW DARE YOU?!?
HEY, YOU'RE THE ONE WHO SAID THIS PLACE WAS MAGIC! WE REALLY CAN'T FIND OUR WAY OUT!
CRAWL UNDER THE ROPES.
BUT THAT'S CHEATING!
CRAWL UNDER THE ROPES OR I CALL THE COPS.
SHUCKS.
"SHUCKS"!?! WAS THAT A CORN PUN? I HATE CORN PUNS!
WOULDN'T DREAM OF IT, COLONEL.
WHOA, THIS IS A MAZE OF MADNESS! LOOK HOW MAD SHE IS!
RUN FOR IT, TORG! SHE'S TWIRLING MY CORN-NECKLACE LIKE A BOLA!
WAP!
OW! MY CORNEA!
THIS CAMPING TRIP ROCKED!
YOU'RE A GENIUS, TORG! WHAT'S MORE MAGIC THAN A THREE DAY SURVIVALIST WEEKEND FOR TEN BUCKS?
AND WE HARDLY EVEN CHEATED THE "SURVIVAL" PART. GRANOLA BAR?
AS LONG AS I CAN WASH IT DOWN WITH OUR LAST CAN OF SODA.
GO FOR IT!
The End...
UM... TORG? DO YOU REMEMBER WHERE WE PARKED?
...Or is it?*
*Just kidding! It's totally the end.

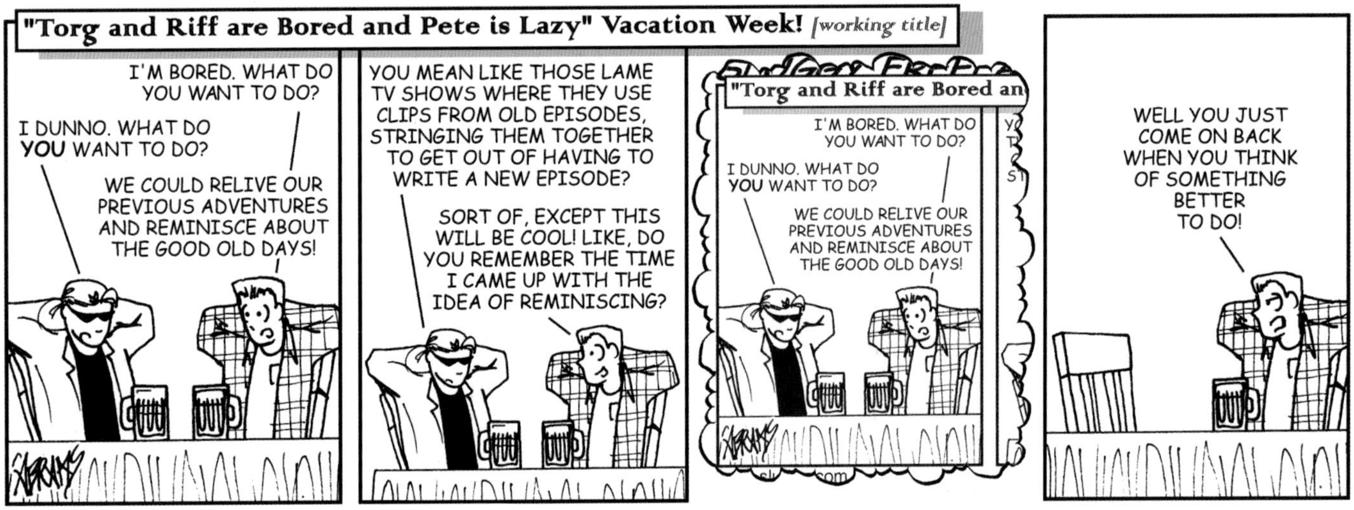
"Torg and Riff are Bored and Pete is Lazy" Vacation Week! [working title]
I'M BORED. WHAT DO YOU WANT TO DO?
I DUNNO. WHAT DO **YOU** WANT TO DO?
WE COULD RELIVE OUR PREVIOUS ADVENTURES AND REMINISCE ABOUT THE GOOD OLD DAYS!
YOU MEAN LIKE THOSE LAME TV SHOWS WHERE THEY USE CLIPS FROM OLD EPISODES, STRINGING THEM TOGETHER TO GET OUT OF HAVING TO WRITE A NEW EPISODE?
SORT OF, EXCEPT THIS WILL BE COOL! LIKE, DO YOU REMEMBER THE TIME I CAME UP WITH THE IDEA OF REMINISCING?
"Torg and Riff are Bored an
I'M BORED. WHAT DO YOU WANT TO DO?
I DUNNO. WHAT DO **YOU** WANT TO DO?
WE COULD RELIVE OUR PREVIOUS ADVENTURES AND REMINISCE ABOUT THE GOOD OLD DAYS!
WELL YOU JUST COME ON BACK WHEN YOU THINK OF SOMETHING BETTER TO DO!

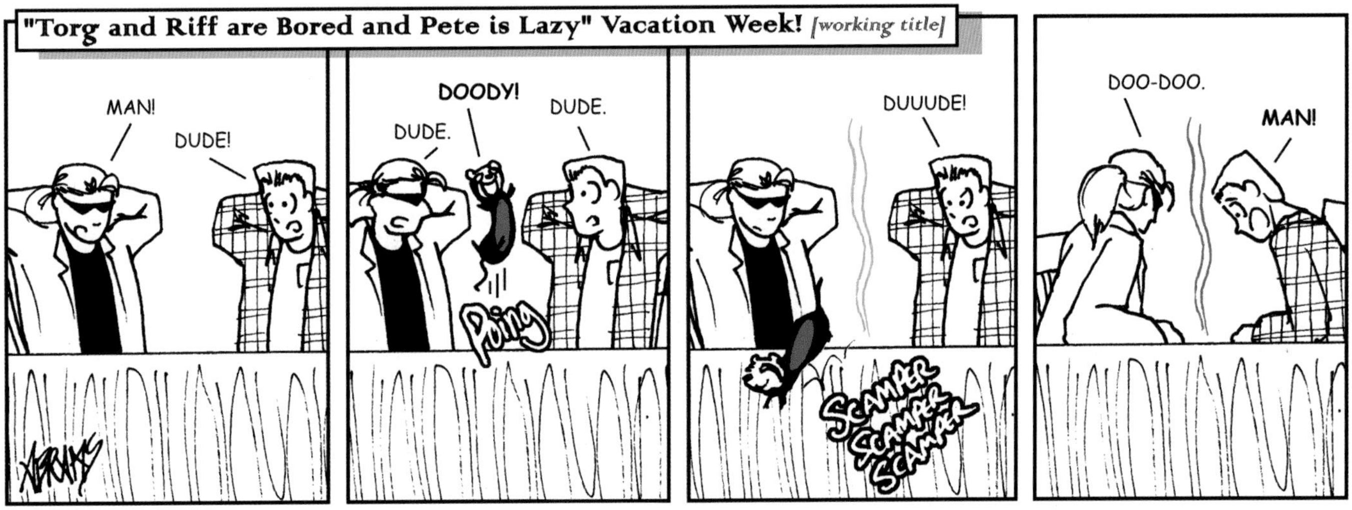
"Torg and Riff are Bored and Pete is Lazy" Vacation Week! [working title]
MAN!
DUDE!
DUDE.
DOODY!
DUDE.
Poing
DUUUDE!
SCAMPER SCAMPER SCAMPER
DOO-DOO.
MAN!

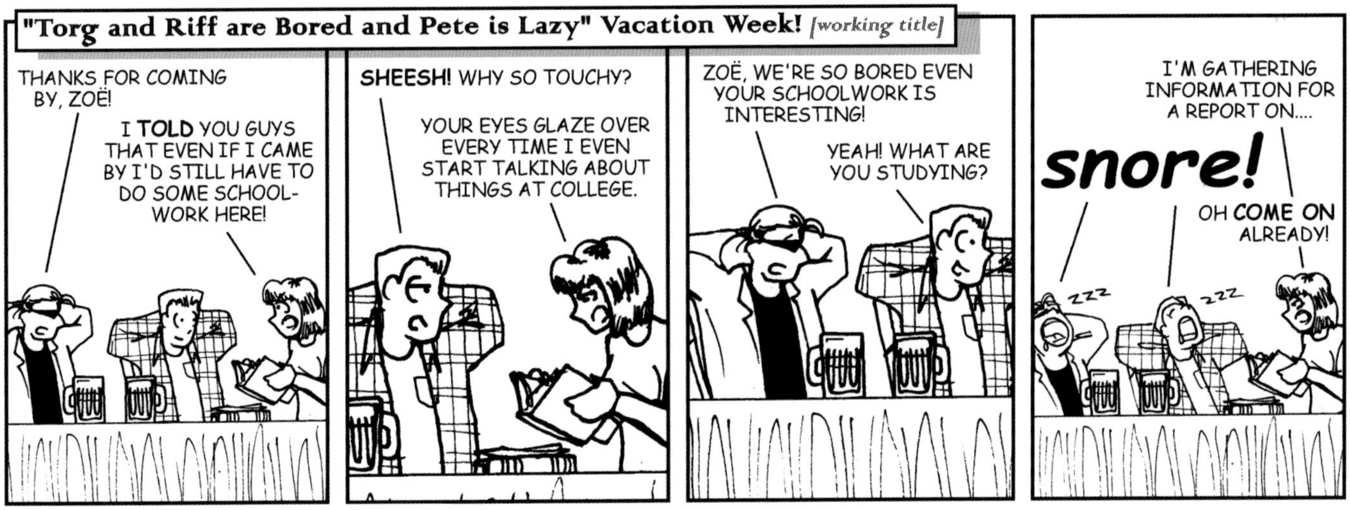
"Torg and Riff are Bored and Pete is Lazy" Vacation Week! [working title]
THANKS FOR COMING BY, ZOË!
I **TOLD** YOU GUYS THAT EVEN IF I CAME BY I'D STILL HAVE TO DO SOME SCHOOL-WORK HERE!
SHEESH! WHY SO TOUCHY?
YOUR EYES GLAZE OVER EVERY TIME I EVEN START TALKING ABOUT THINGS AT COLLEGE.
ZOË, WE'RE SO BORED EVEN YOUR SCHOOLWORK IS INTERESTING!
YEAH! WHAT ARE YOU STUDYING?
I'M GATHERING INFORMATION FOR A REPORT ON....
snore!
ZZZ
ZZZ
OH **COME ON** ALREADY!

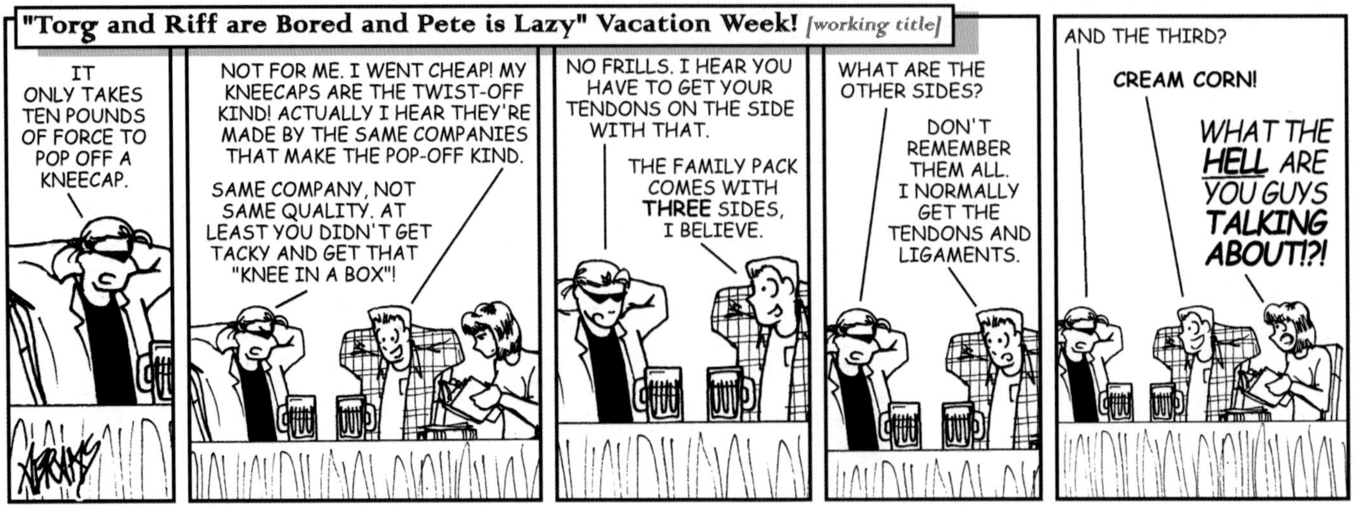
"Torg and Riff are Bored and Pete is Lazy" Vacation Week! [working title]
IT ONLY TAKES TEN POUNDS OF FORCE TO POP OFF A KNEECAP.
NOT FOR ME. I WENT CHEAP! MY KNEECAPS ARE THE TWIST-OFF KIND! ACTUALLY I HEAR THEY'RE MADE BY THE SAME COMPANIES THAT MAKE THE POP-OFF KIND.
SAME COMPANY, NOT SAME QUALITY. AT LEAST YOU DIDN'T GET TACKY AND GET THAT "KNEE IN A BOX"!
NO FRILLS. I HEAR YOU HAVE TO GET YOUR TENDONS ON THE SIDE WITH THAT.
THE FAMILY PACK COMES WITH THREE SIDES, I BELIEVE.
WHAT ARE THE OTHER SIDES?
DON'T REMEMBER THEM ALL. I NORMALLY GET THE TENDONS AND LIGAMENTS.
AND THE THIRD?
CREAM CORN!
WHAT THE HELL ARE YOU GUYS TALKING ABOUT!?!

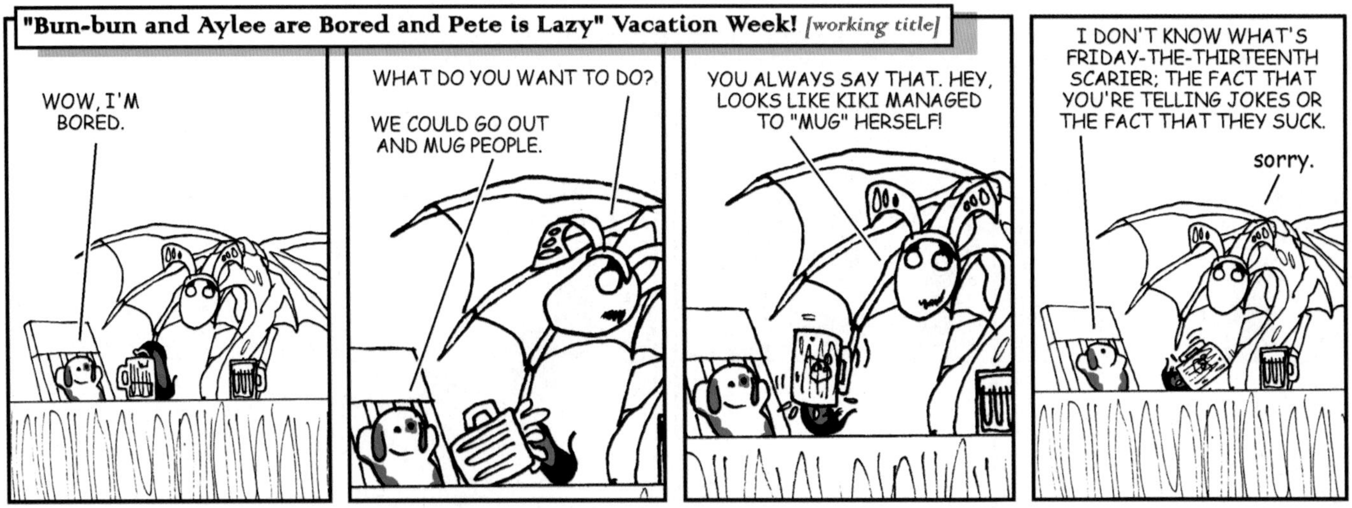
"Bun-bun and Aylee are Bored and Pete is Lazy" Vacation Week! [working title]
WOW, I'M BORED.
WHAT DO YOU WANT TO DO?
WE COULD GO OUT AND MUG PEOPLE.
YOU ALWAYS SAY THAT. HEY, LOOKS LIKE KIKI MANAGED TO "MUG" HERSELF!
I DON'T KNOW WHAT'S FRIDAY-THE-THIRTEENTH SCARIER; THE FACT THAT YOU'RE TELLING JOKES OR THE FACT THAT THEY SUCK.
sorry.

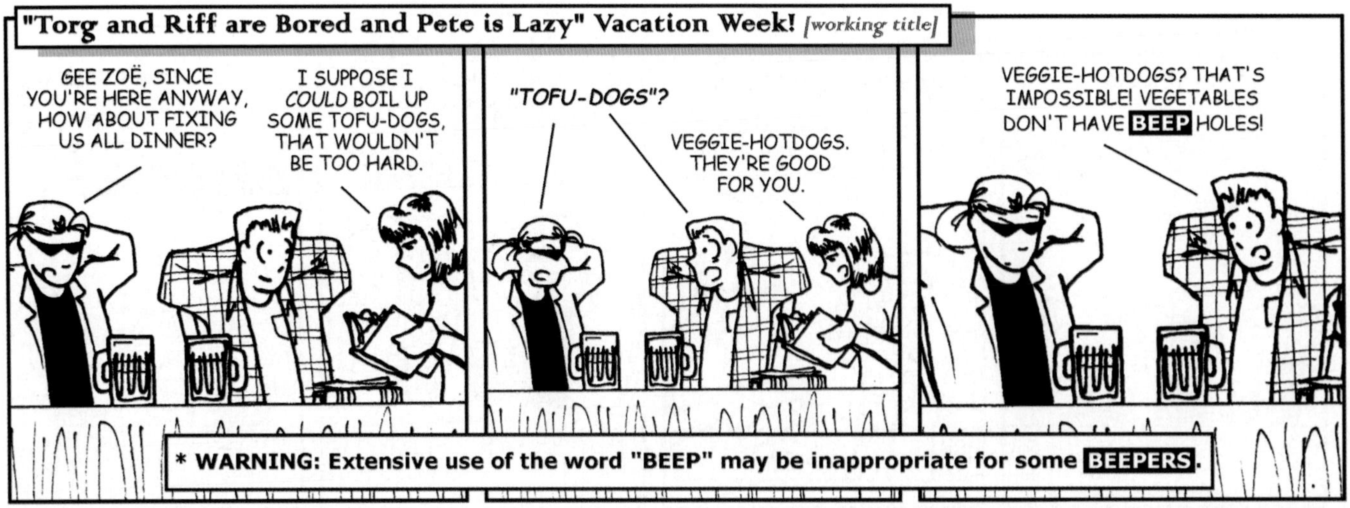
"Torg and Riff are Bored and Pete is Lazy" Vacation Week! [working title]
GEE ZOË, SINCE YOU'RE HERE ANYWAY, HOW ABOUT FIXING US ALL DINNER?
I SUPPOSE I COULD BOIL UP SOME TOFU-DOGS, THAT WOULDN'T BE TOO HARD.
"TOFU-DOGS"?
VEGGIE-HOTDOGS. THEY'RE GOOD FOR YOU.
VEGGIE-HOTDOGS? THAT'S IMPOSSIBLE! VEGETABLES DON'T HAVE BEEP HOLES!
* WARNING: Extensive use of the word "BEEP" may be inappropriate for some BEEPERS.

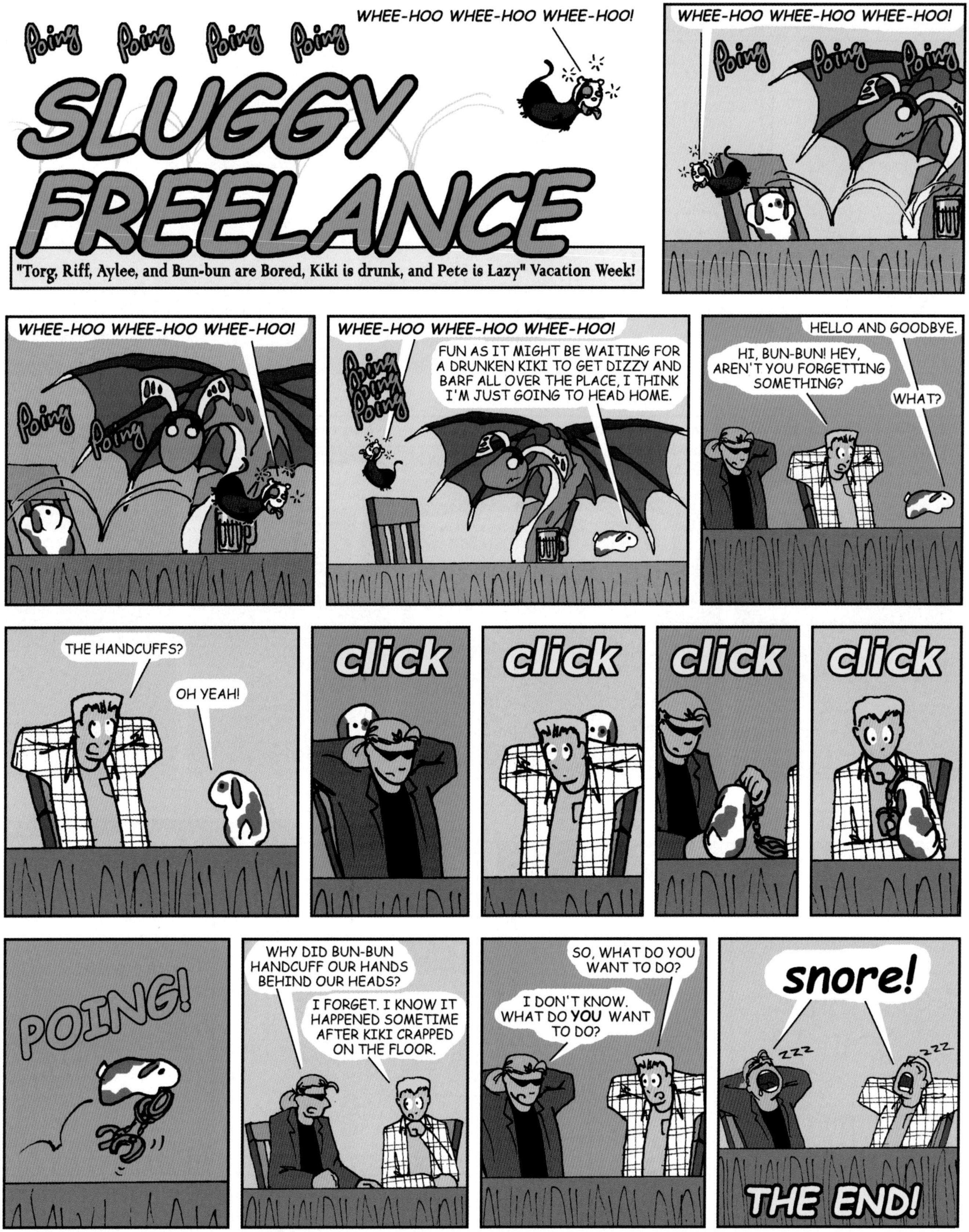

Poing Poing Poing Poing
WHEE-HOO WHEE-HOO WHEE-HOO!
SLUGGY FREELANCE
"Torg, Riff, Aylee, and Bun-bun are Bored, Kiki is drunk, and Pete is Lazy" Vacation Week!
WHEE-HOO WHEE-HOO WHEE-HOO!
Poing Poing Poing
WHEE-HOO WHEE-HOO WHEE-HOO!
Poing Poing
WHEE-HOO WHEE-HOO WHEE-HOO!
Poing Poing Poing
FUN AS IT MIGHT BE WAITING FOR A DRUNKEN KIKI TO GET DIZZY AND BARF ALL OVER THE PLACE, I THINK I'M JUST GOING TO HEAD HOME.
HELLO AND GOODBYE.
HI, BUN-BUN! HEY, AREN'T YOU FORGETTING SOMETHING?
WHAT?
THE HANDCUFFS?
OH YEAH!
click
click
click
click
POING!
WHY DID BUN-BUN HANDCUFF OUR HANDS BEHIND OUR HEADS?
I FORGET. I KNOW IT HAPPENED SOMETIME AFTER KIKI CRAPPED ON THE FLOOR.
SO, WHAT DO YOU WANT TO DO?
I DON'T KNOW. WHAT DO **YOU** WANT TO DO?
snore!
ZZZ
ZZZ
THE END!

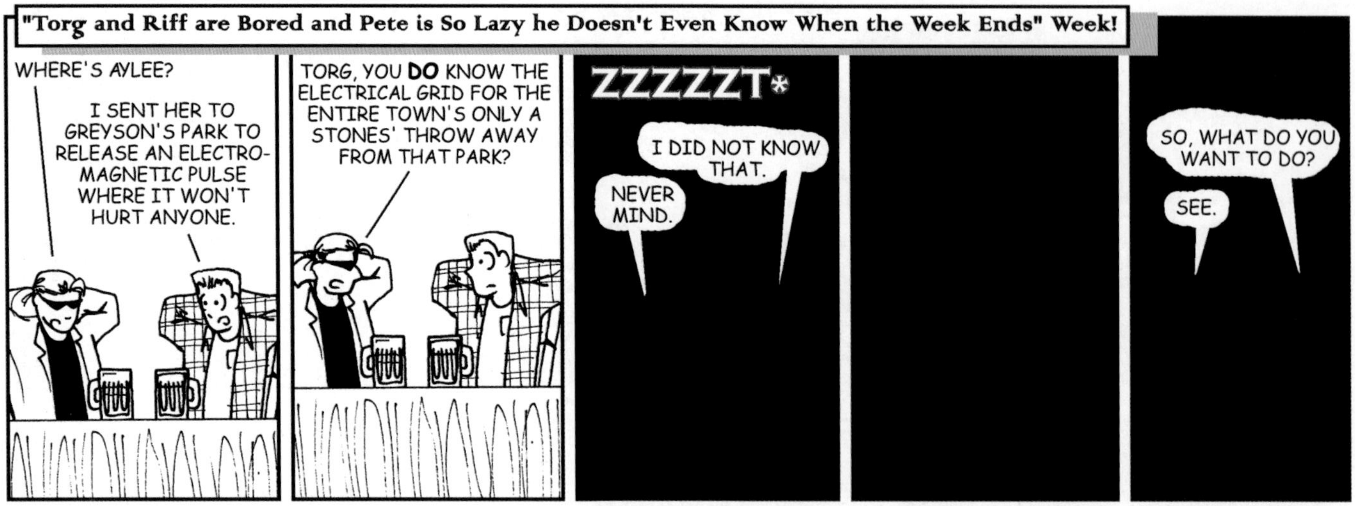
"Torg and Riff are Bored and Pete is So Lazy he Doesn't Even Know When the Week Ends" Week!
WHERE'S AYLEE?
I SENT HER TO GREYSON'S PARK TO RELEASE AN ELECTRO-MAGNETIC PULSE WHERE IT WON'T HURT ANYONE.
TORG, YOU DO KNOW THE ELECTRICAL GRID FOR THE ENTIRE TOWN'S ONLY A STONES' THROW AWAY FROM THAT PARK?
ZZZZZT*
I DID NOT KNOW THAT.
NEVER MIND.
SO, WHAT DO YOU WANT TO DO?
SEE.

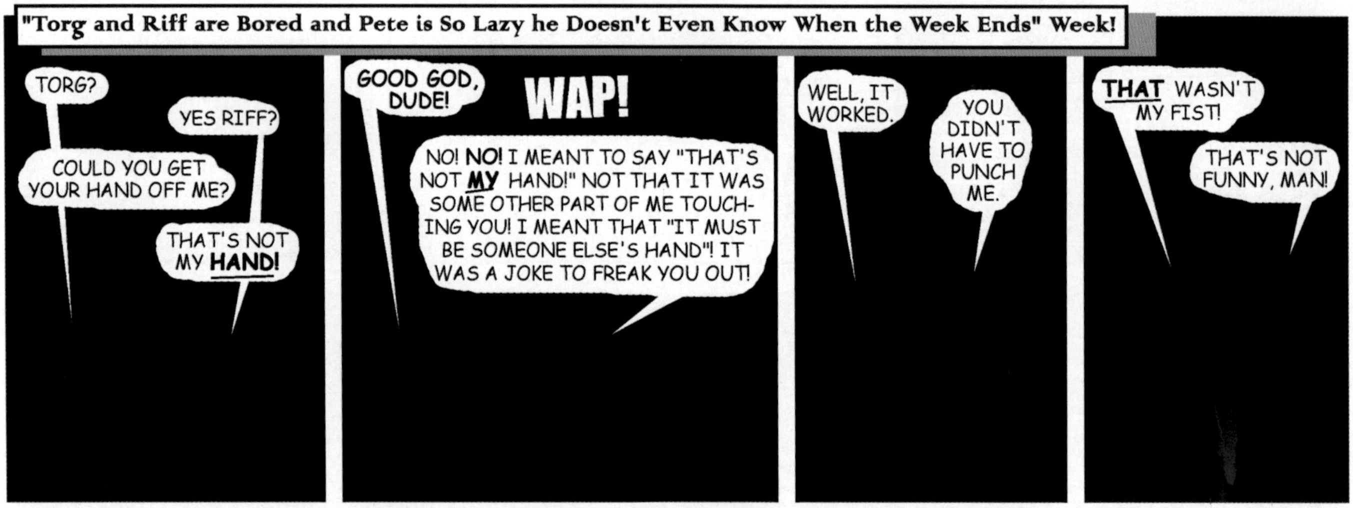
"Torg and Riff are Bored and Pete is So Lazy he Doesn't Even Know When the Week Ends" Week!
TORG?
YES RIFF?
COULD YOU GET YOUR HAND OFF ME?
THAT'S NOT MY HAND!
GOOD GOD, DUDE!
WAP!
NO! NO! I MEANT TO SAY "THAT'S NOT MY HAND!" NOT THAT IT WAS SOME OTHER PART OF ME TOUCH-ING YOU! I MEANT THAT "IT MUST BE SOMEONE ELSE'S HAND"! IT WAS A JOKE TO FREAK YOU OUT!
WELL, IT WORKED.
YOU DIDN'T HAVE TO PUNCH ME.
THAT WASN'T MY FIST!
THAT'S NOT FUNNY, MAN!

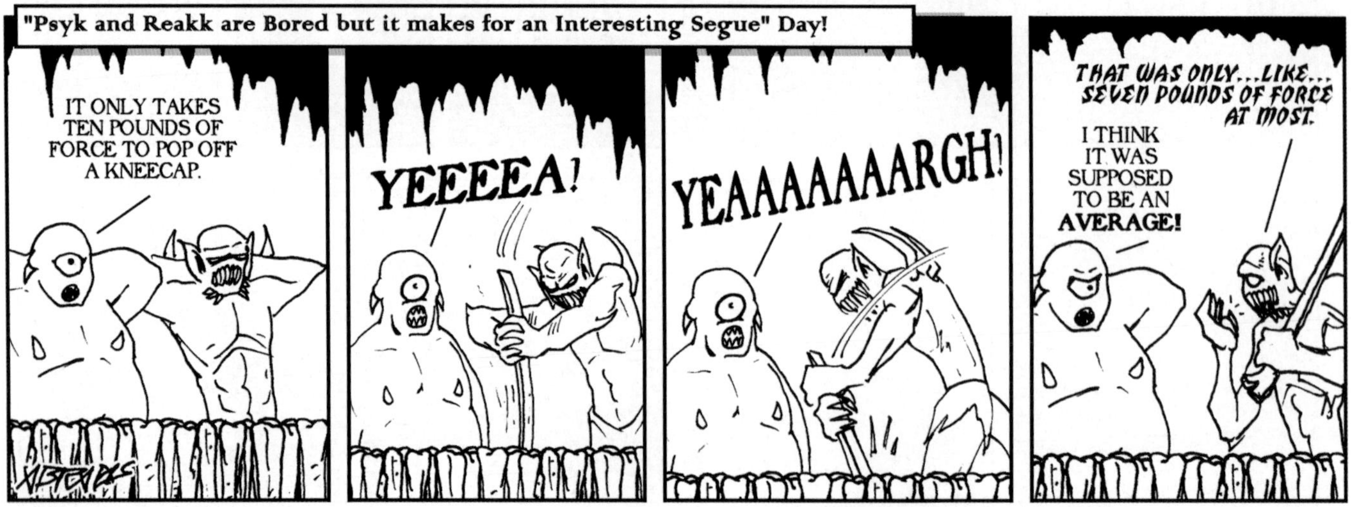
"Psyk and Reakk are Bored but it makes for an Interesting Segue" Day!
IT ONLY TAKES TEN POUNDS OF FORCE TO POP OFF A KNEECAP.
YEEEEA!
YEAAAAAAARGH!
THAT WAS ONLY...LIKE... SEVEN POUNDS OF FORCE AT MOST.
I THINK IT WAS SUPPOSED TO BE AN AVERAGE!

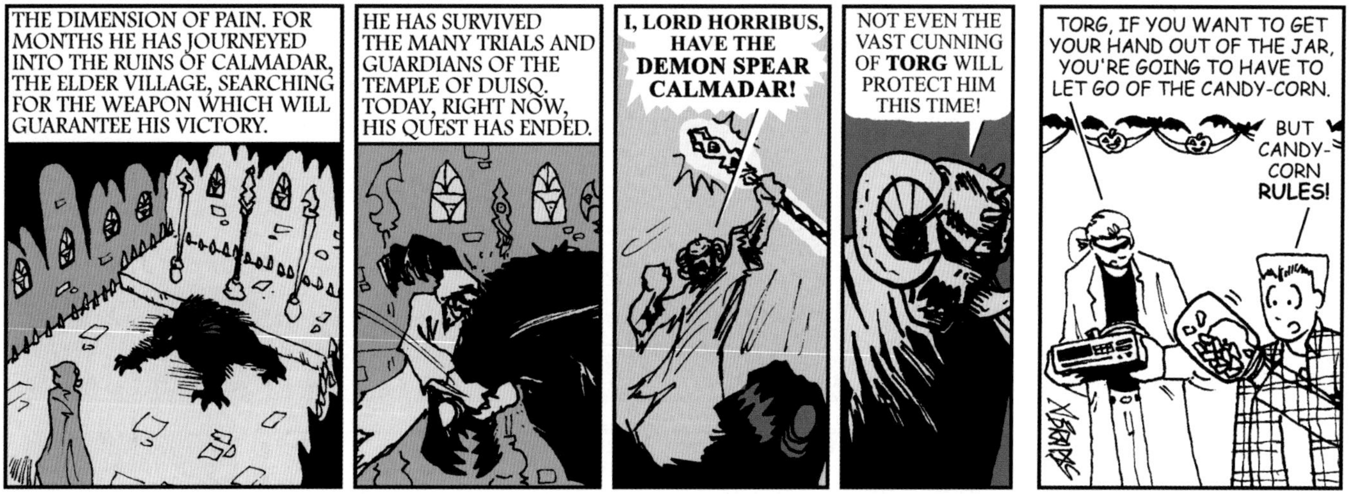
THE DIMENSION OF PAIN. FOR MONTHS HE HAS JOURNEYED INTO THE RUINS OF CALMADAR, THE ELDER VILLAGE, SEARCHING FOR THE WEAPON WHICH WILL GUARANTEE HIS VICTORY.
HE HAS SURVIVED THE MANY TRIALS AND GUARDIANS OF THE TEMPLE OF DUISQ. TODAY, RIGHT NOW, HIS QUEST HAS ENDED.
I, LORD HORRIBUS, HAVE THE DEMON SPEAR CALMADAR!
NOT EVEN THE VAST CUNNING OF TORG WILL PROTECT HIM THIS TIME!
TORG, IF YOU WANT TO GET YOUR HAND OUT OF THE JAR, YOU'RE GOING TO HAVE TO LET GO OF THE CANDY-CORN.
BUT CANDY-CORN RULES!

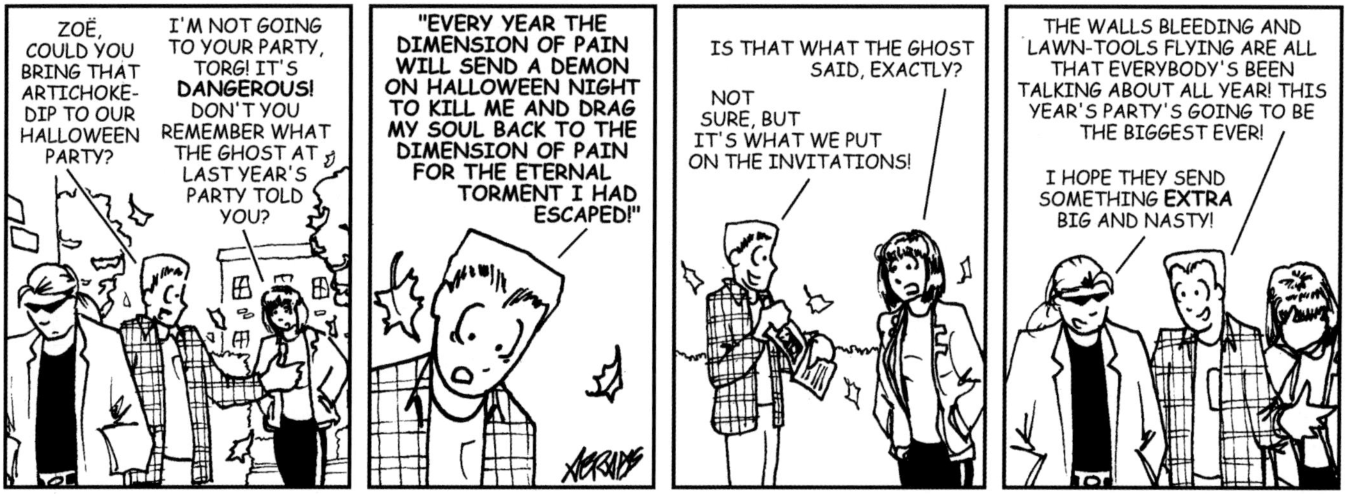
ZOË, COULD YOU BRING THAT ARTICHOKE-DIP TO OUR HALLOWEEN PARTY?
I'M NOT GOING TO YOUR PARTY, TORG! IT'S DANGEROUS! DON'T YOU REMEMBER WHAT THE GHOST AT LAST YEAR'S PARTY TOLD YOU?
"EVERY YEAR THE DIMENSION OF PAIN WILL SEND A DEMON ON HALLOWEEN NIGHT TO KILL ME AND DRAG MY SOUL BACK TO THE DIMENSION OF PAIN FOR THE ETERNAL TORMENT I HAD ESCAPED!"
IS THAT WHAT THE GHOST SAID, EXACTLY?
NOT SURE, BUT IT'S WHAT WE PUT ON THE INVITATIONS!
THE WALLS BLEEDING AND LAWN-TOOLS FLYING ARE ALL THAT EVERYBODY'S BEEN TALKING ABOUT ALL YEAR! THIS YEAR'S PARTY'S GOING TO BE THE BIGGEST EVER!
I HOPE THEY SEND SOMETHING EXTRA BIG AND NASTY!

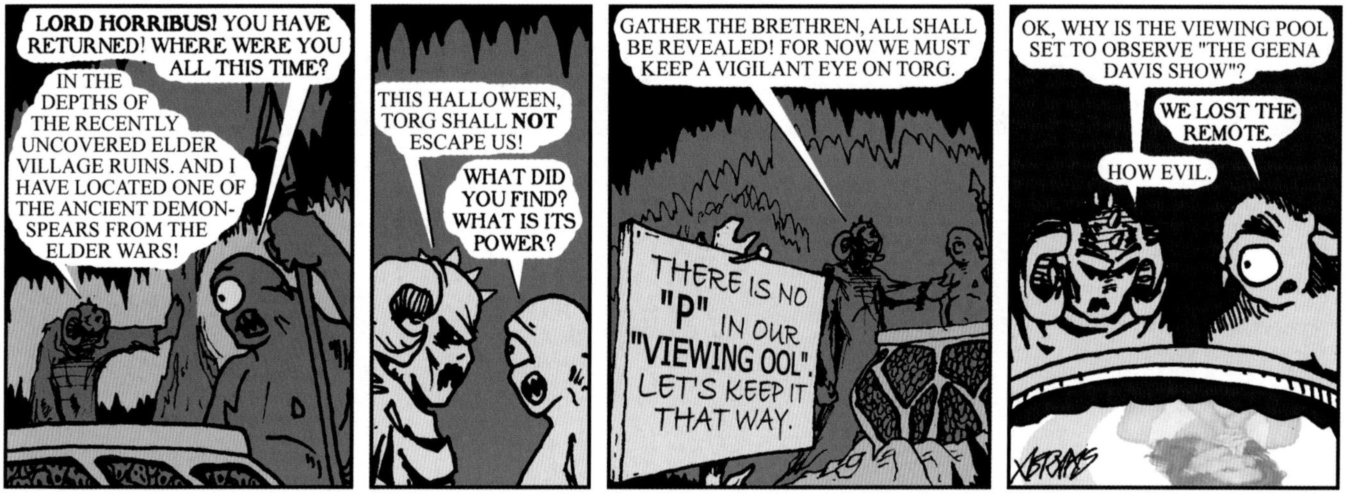
LORD HORRIBUS! YOU HAVE RETURNED! WHERE WERE YOU ALL THIS TIME?
IN THE DEPTHS OF THE RECENTLY UNCOVERED ELDER VILLAGE RUINS. AND I HAVE LOCATED ONE OF THE ANCIENT DEMON-SPEARS FROM THE ELDER WARS!
THIS HALLOWEEN, TORG SHALL NOT ESCAPE US!
WHAT DID YOU FIND? WHAT IS ITS POWER?
GATHER THE BRETHREN, ALL SHALL BE REVEALED! FOR NOW WE MUST KEEP A VIGILANT EYE ON TORG.
THERE IS NO "P" IN OUR "VIEWING OOL". LET'S KEEP IT THAT WAY.
OK, WHY IS THE VIEWING POOL SET TO OBSERVE "THE GEENA DAVIS SHOW"?
WE LOST THE REMOTE.
HOW EVIL.

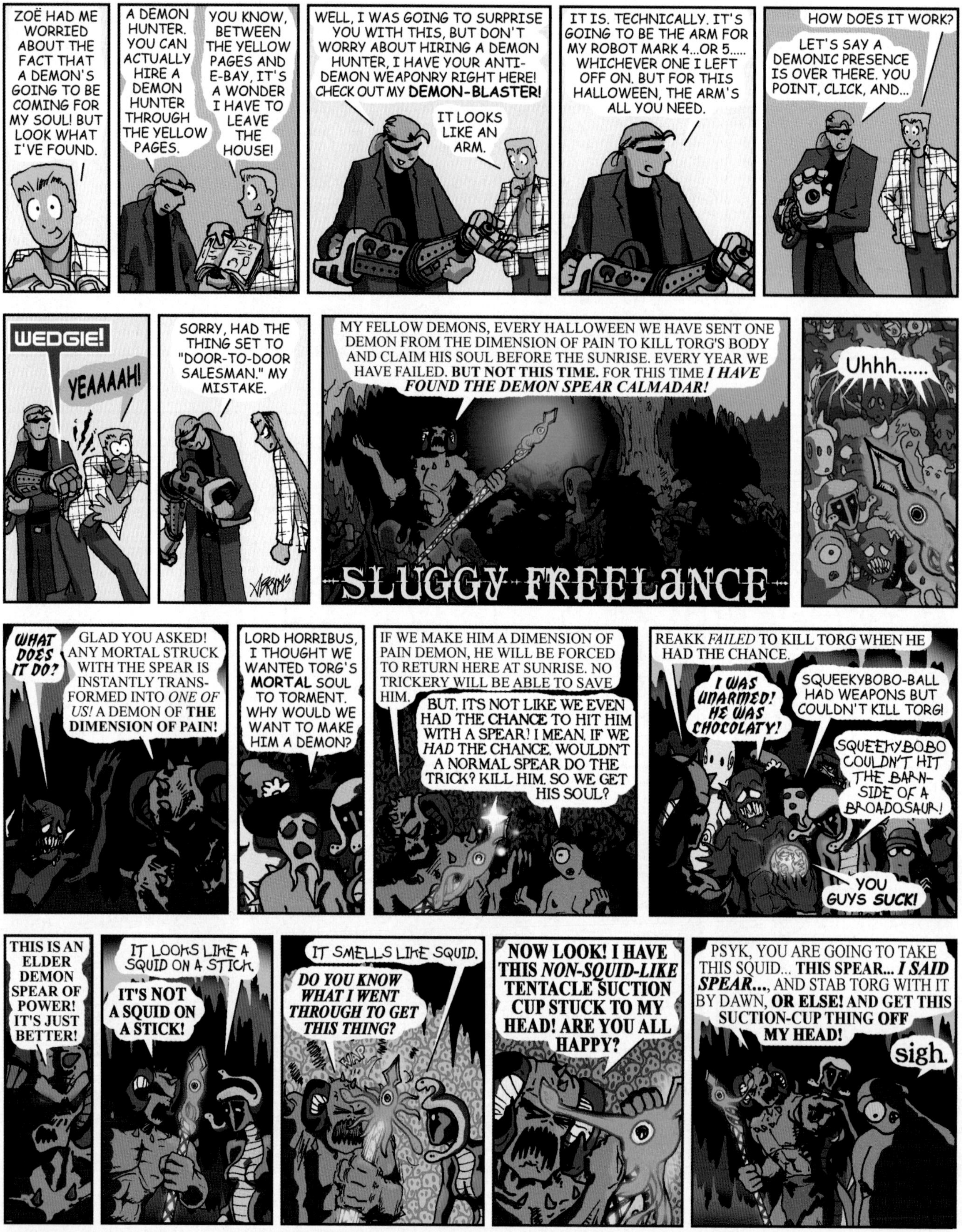
ZOË HAD ME WORRIED ABOUT THE FACT THAT A DEMON'S GOING TO BE COMING FOR MY SOUL! BUT LOOK WHAT I'VE FOUND.
A DEMON HUNTER. YOU CAN ACTUALLY HIRE A DEMON HUNTER THROUGH THE YELLOW PAGES.
YOU KNOW, BETWEEN THE YELLOW PAGES AND E-BAY, IT'S A WONDER I HAVE TO LEAVE THE HOUSE!
WELL, I WAS GOING TO SURPRISE YOU WITH THIS, BUT DON'T WORRY ABOUT HIRING A DEMON HUNTER, I HAVE YOUR ANTI-DEMON WEAPONRY RIGHT HERE! CHECK OUT MY DEMON-BLASTER!
IT LOOKS LIKE AN ARM.
IT IS. TECHNICALLY. IT'S GOING TO BE THE ARM FOR MY ROBOT MARK 4...OR 5..... WHICHEVER ONE I LEFT OFF ON. BUT FOR THIS HALLOWEEN, THE ARM'S ALL YOU NEED.
HOW DOES IT WORK?
LET'S SAY A DEMONIC PRESENCE IS OVER THERE. YOU POINT, CLICK, AND...
WEDGIE!
YEAAAAH!
SORRY, HAD THE THING SET TO "DOOR-TO-DOOR SALESMAN." MY MISTAKE.
MY FELLOW DEMONS, EVERY HALLOWEEN WE HAVE SENT ONE DEMON FROM THE DIMENSION OF PAIN TO KILL TORG'S BODY AND CLAIM HIS SOUL BEFORE THE SUNRISE. EVERY YEAR WE HAVE FAILED. BUT NOT THIS TIME. FOR THIS TIME I HAVE FOUND THE DEMON SPEAR CALMADAR!
SLUGGY FREELANCE
Uhhh......
WHAT DOES IT DO?
GLAD YOU ASKED! ANY MORTAL STRUCK WITH THE SPEAR IS INSTANTLY TRANS-FORMED INTO ONE OF US! A DEMON OF THE DIMENSION OF PAIN!
LORD HORRIBUS, I THOUGHT WE WANTED TORG'S MORTAL SOUL TO TORMENT. WHY WOULD WE WANT TO MAKE HIM A DEMON?
IF WE MAKE HIM A DIMENSION OF PAIN DEMON, HE WILL BE FORCED TO RETURN HERE AT SUNRISE. NO TRICKERY WILL BE ABLE TO SAVE HIM.
BUT, IT'S NOT LIKE WE EVEN HAD THE CHANCE TO HIT HIM WITH A SPEAR! I MEAN, IF WE HAD THE CHANCE, WOULDN'T A NORMAL SPEAR DO THE TRICK? KILL HIM, SO WE GET HIS SOUL?
REAKK FAILED TO KILL TORG WHEN HE HAD THE CHANCE.
I WAS UNARMED! HE WAS CHOCOLATY!
SQUEEKYBOBO-BALL HAD WEAPONS BUT COULDN'T KILL TORG!
SQUEEKYBOBO COULDN'T HIT THE BARN-SIDE OF A BROADOSAUR!
YOU GUYS SUCK!
THIS IS AN ELDER DEMON SPEAR OF POWER! IT'S JUST BETTER!
IT LOOKS LIKE A SQUID ON A STICK.
IT'S NOT A SQUID ON A STICK!
IT SMELLS LIKE SQUID.
DO YOU KNOW WHAT I WENT THROUGH TO GET THIS THING?
NOW LOOK! I HAVE THIS NON-SQUID-LIKE TENTACLE SUCTION CUP STUCK TO MY HEAD! ARE YOU ALL HAPPY?
PSYK, YOU ARE GOING TO TAKE THIS SQUID... THIS SPEAR... I SAID SPEAR..., AND STAB TORG WITH IT BY DAWN, OR ELSE! AND GET THIS SUCTION-CUP THING OFF MY HEAD!
sigh.

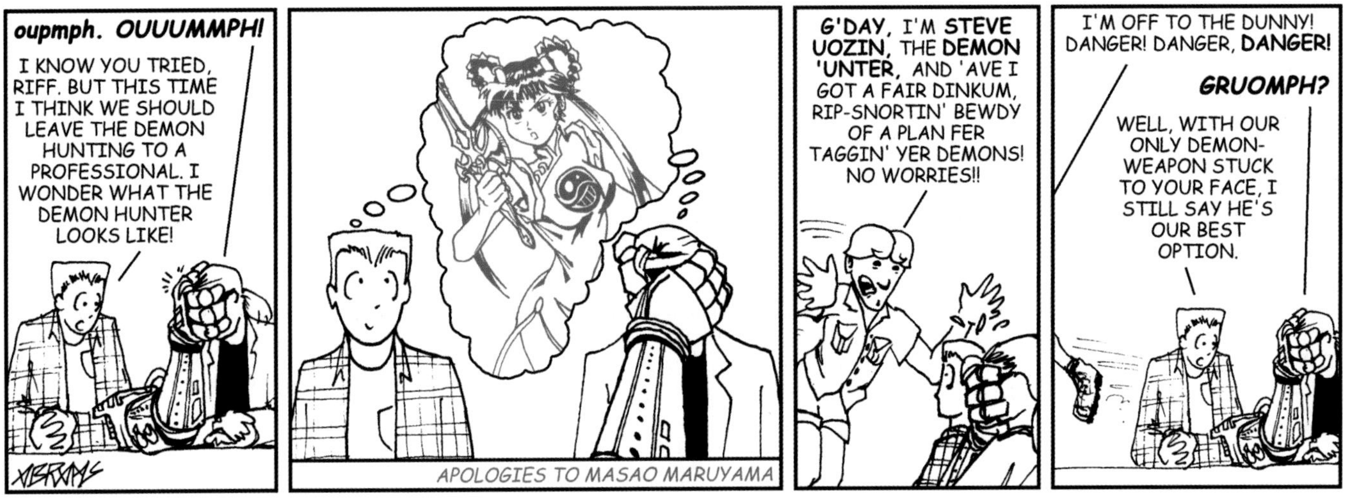
oupmph. OUUUMMPH!
I KNOW YOU TRIED, RIFF. BUT THIS TIME I THINK WE SHOULD LEAVE THE DEMON HUNTING TO A PROFESSIONAL. I WONDER WHAT THE DEMON HUNTER LOOKS LIKE!
APOLOGIES TO MASAO MARUYAMA
G'DAY, I'M STEVE UOZIN, THE DEMON 'UNTER, AND 'AVE I GOT A FAIR DINKUM, RIP-SNORTIN' BEWDY OF A PLAN FER TAGGIN' YER DEMONS! NO WORRIES!!
I'M OFF TO THE DUNNY! DANGER! DANGER, DANGER!
GRUOMPH?
WELL, WITH OUR ONLY DEMON-WEAPON STUCK TO YOUR FACE, I STILL SAY HE'S OUR BEST OPTION.

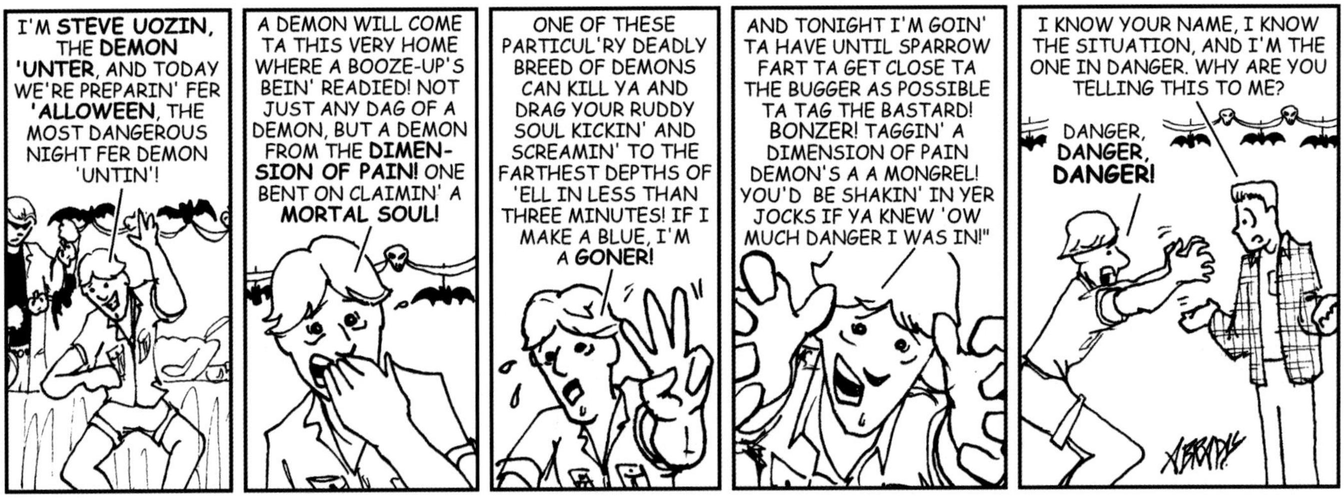
I'M STEVE UOZIN, THE DEMON 'UNTER, AND TODAY WE'RE PREPARIN' FER 'ALLOWEEN, THE MOST DANGEROUS NIGHT FER DEMON 'UNTIN'!
A DEMON WILL COME TA THIS VERY HOME WHERE A BOOZE-UP'S BEIN' READIED! NOT JUST ANY DAG OF A DEMON, BUT A DEMON FROM THE DIMEN-SION OF PAIN! ONE BENT ON CLAIMIN' A MORTAL SOUL!
ONE OF THESE PARTICUL'RY DEADLY BREED OF DEMONS CAN KILL YA AND DRAG YOUR RUDDY SOUL KICKIN' AND SCREAMIN' TO THE FARTHEST DEPTHS OF 'ELL IN LESS THAN THREE MINUTES! IF I MAKE A BLUE, I'M A GONER!
AND TONIGHT I'M GOIN' TA HAVE UNTIL SPARROW FART TA GET CLOSE TA THE BUGGER AS POSSIBLE TA TAG THE BASTARD! BONZER! TAGGIN' A DIMENSION OF PAIN DEMON'S A A MONGREL! YOU'D BE SHAKIN' IN YER JOCKS IF YA KNEW 'OW MUCH DANGER I WAS IN!"
I KNOW YOUR NAME, I KNOW THE SITUATION, AND I'M THE ONE IN DANGER. WHY ARE YOU TELLING THIS TO ME?
DANGER, DANGER, DANGER!

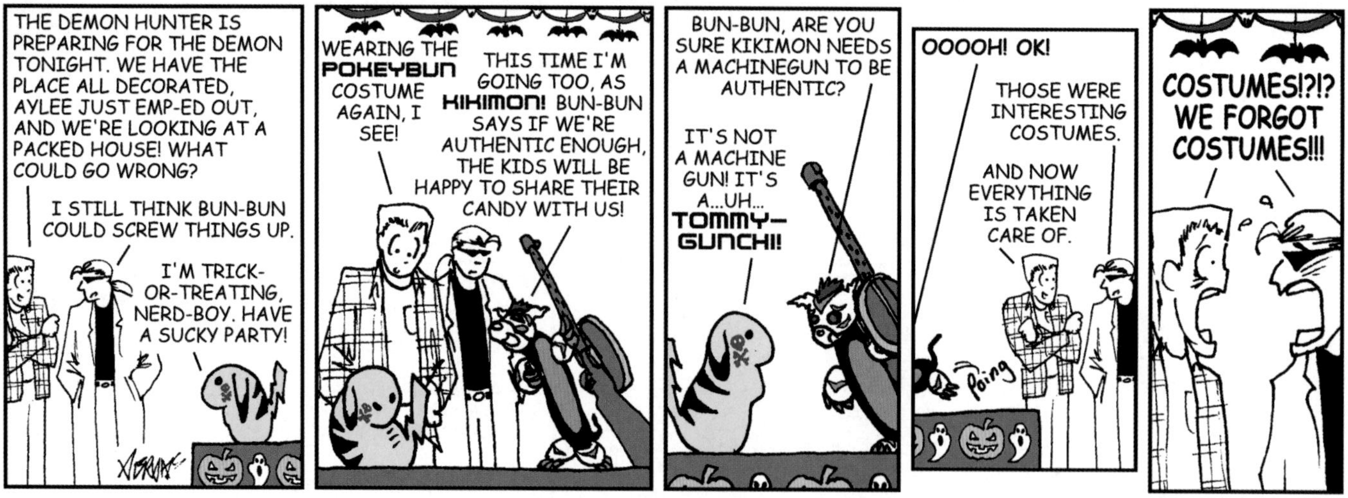
THE DEMON HUNTER IS PREPARING FOR THE DEMON TONIGHT. WE HAVE THE PLACE ALL DECORATED, AYLEE JUST EMP-ED OUT, AND WE'RE LOOKING AT A PACKED HOUSE! WHAT COULD GO WRONG?
I STILL THINK BUN-BUN COULD SCREW THINGS UP.
I'M TRICK-OR-TREATING, NERD-BOY. HAVE A SUCKY PARTY!
WEARING THE POKEYBUN COSTUME AGAIN, I SEE!
THIS TIME I'M GOING TOO, AS KIKIMON! BUN-BUN SAYS IF WE'RE AUTHENTIC ENOUGH, THE KIDS WILL BE HAPPY TO SHARE THEIR CANDY WITH US!
BUN-BUN, ARE YOU SURE KIKIMON NEEDS A MACHINEGUN TO BE AUTHENTIC?
IT'S NOT A MACHINE GUN! IT'S A...UH... TOMMY-GUNCHI!!
OOOOH! OK!
Poing
THOSE WERE INTERESTING COSTUMES.
AND NOW EVERYTHING IS TAKEN CARE OF.
COSTUMES!?!? WE FORGOT COSTUMES!!!

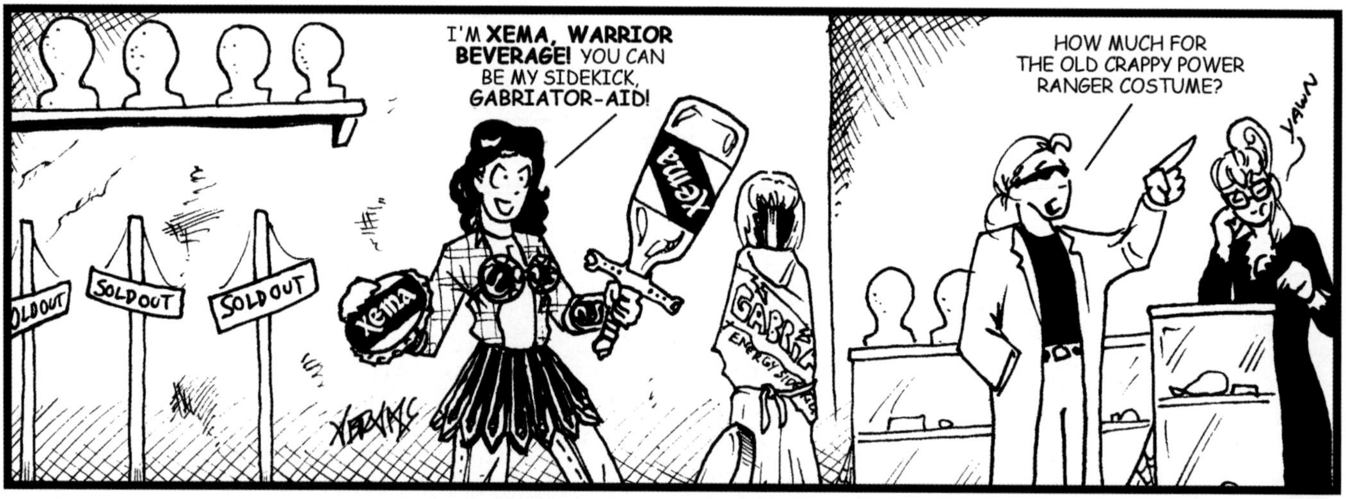
SOLD OUT
SOLD OUT
SOLD OUT
I'M XEMA, WARRIOR BEVERAGE! YOU CAN BE MY SIDEKICK, GABRIATOR-AID!
Xema
Xema
HOW MUCH FOR THE OLD CRAPPY POWER RANGER COSTUME?
YAWN

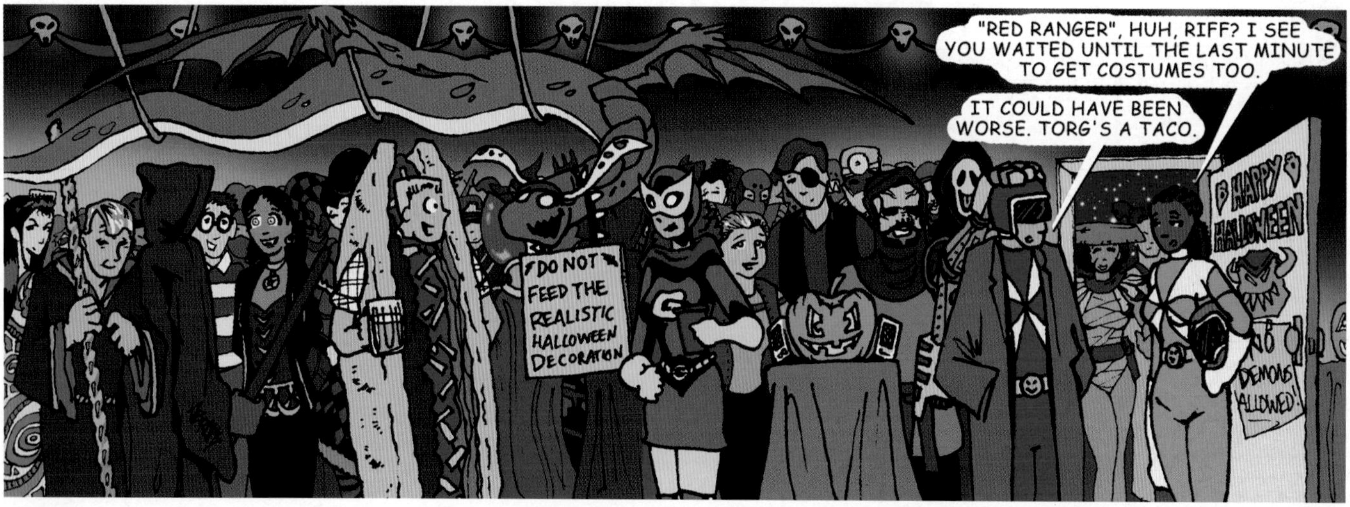
"RED RANGER", HUH, RIFF? I SEE YOU WAITED UNTIL THE LAST MINUTE TO GET COSTUMES TOO.
IT COULD HAVE BEEN WORSE. TORG'S A TACO.
DO NOT FEED THE REALISTIC HALLOWEEN DECORATION
HAPPY HALLOWEEN
DEMONS ALLOWED!

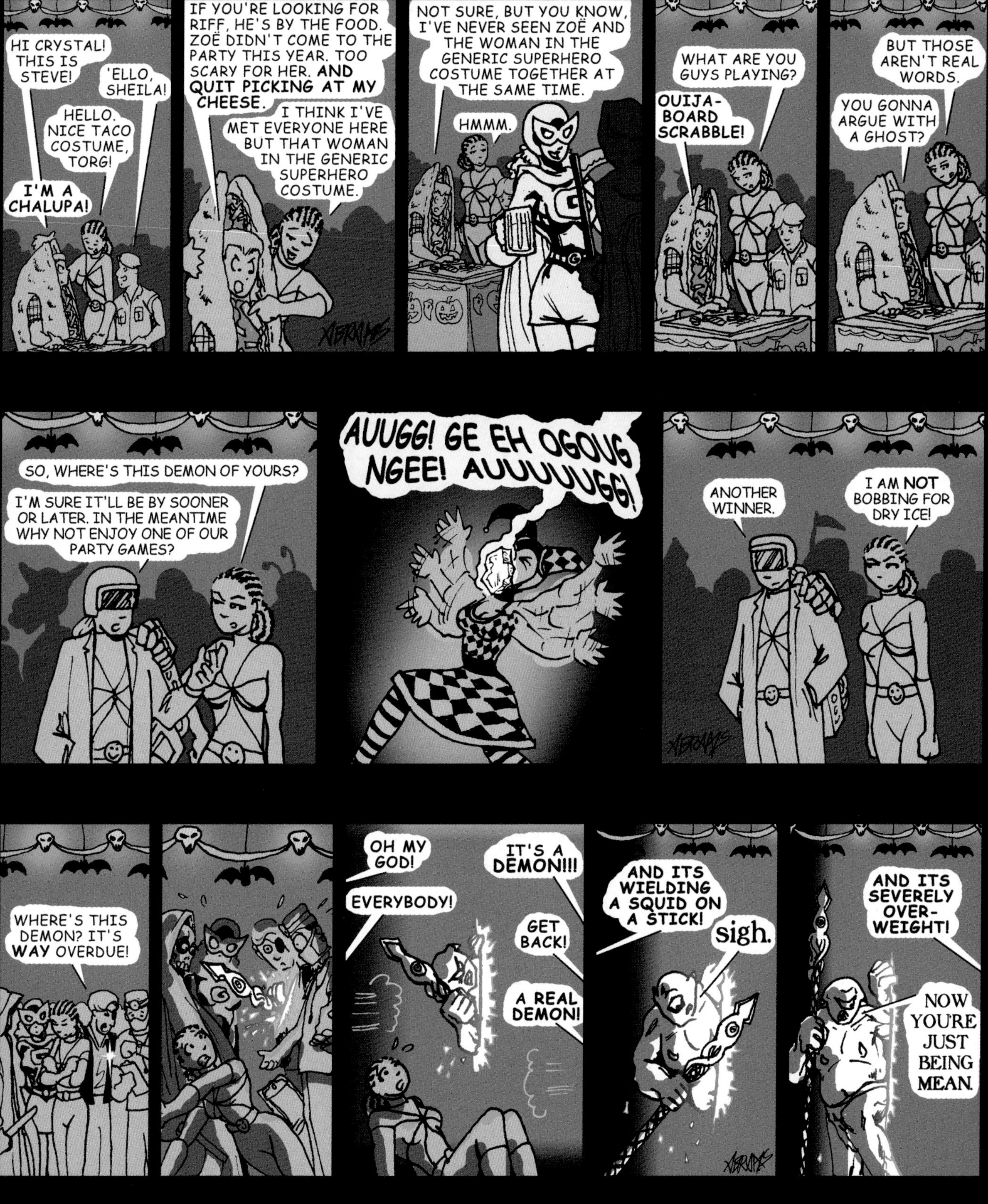
HI CRYSTAL! THIS IS STEVE!
'ELLO, SHEILA!
HELLO. NICE TACO COSTUME, TORG!
I'M A CHALUPA!
IF YOU'RE LOOKING FOR RIFF, HE'S BY THE FOOD. ZOË DIDN'T COME TO THE PARTY THIS YEAR. TOO SCARY FOR HER. AND QUIT PICKING AT MY CHEESE.
I THINK I'VE MET EVERYONE HERE BUT THAT WOMAN IN THE GENERIC SUPERHERO COSTUME.
NOT SURE, BUT YOU KNOW, I'VE NEVER SEEN ZOË AND THE WOMAN IN THE GENERIC SUPERHERO COSTUME TOGETHER AT THE SAME TIME.
HMMM.
WHAT ARE YOU GUYS PLAYING?
OUIJA-BOARD SCRABBLE!
BUT THOSE AREN'T REAL WORDS.
YOU GONNA ARGUE WITH A GHOST?
SO, WHERE'S THIS DEMON OF YOURS?
I'M SURE IT'LL BE BY SOONER OR LATER. IN THE MEANTIME WHY NOT ENJOY ONE OF OUR PARTY GAMES?
AUUGG! GE EH OGOUG NGEE! AUUUUUGG!
ANOTHER WINNER.
I AM NOT BOBBING FOR DRY ICE!
WHERE'S THIS DEMON? IT'S WAY OVERDUE!
OH MY GOD!
EVERYBODY!
IT'S A DEMON!!!
GET BACK!
A REAL DEMON!
AND ITS WIELDING A SQUID ON A STICK!
sigh.
AND ITS SEVERELY OVER-WEIGHT!
NOW YOU'RE JUST BEING MEAN.

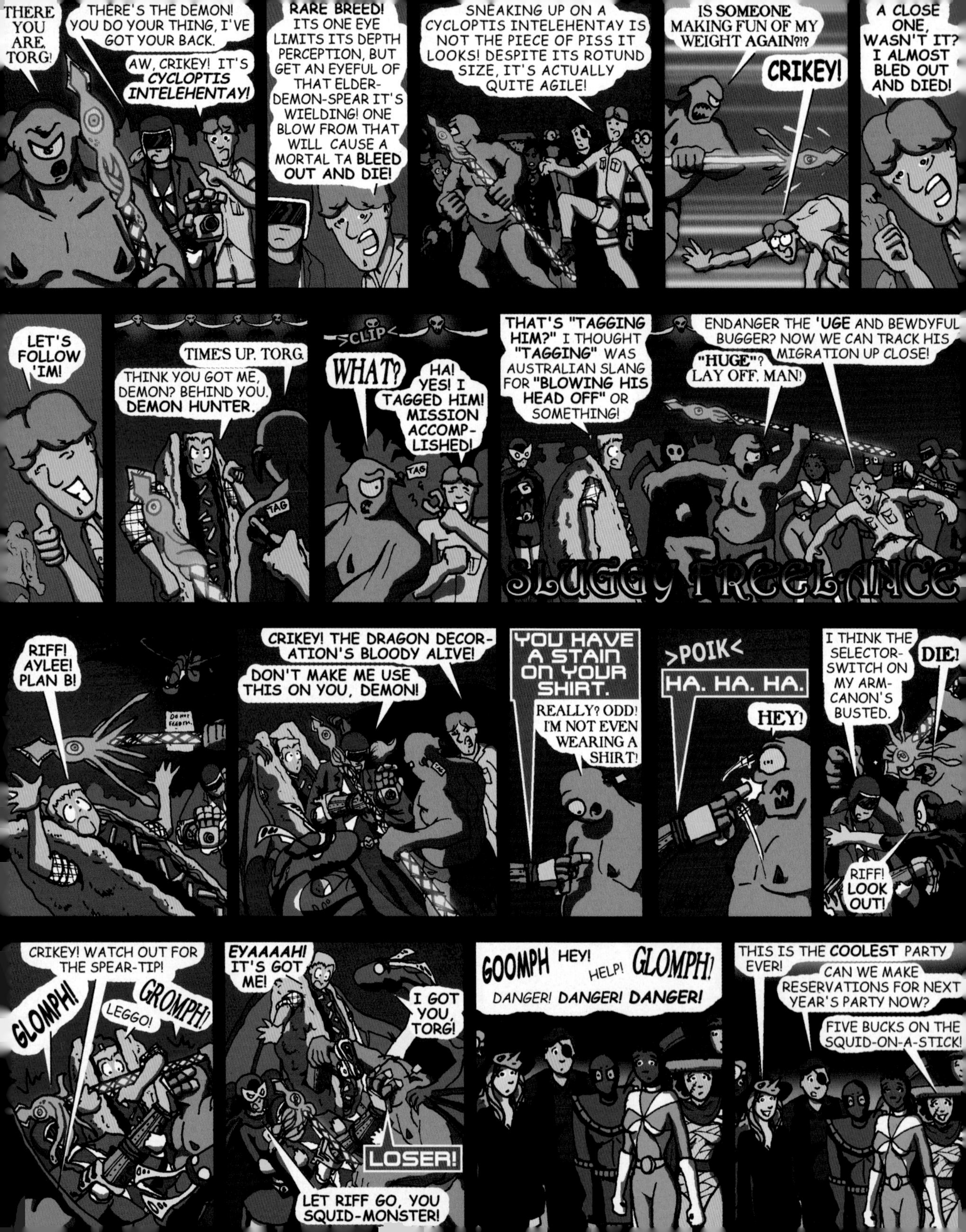
THERE YOU ARE, TORG!
THERE'S THE DEMON! YOU DO YOUR THING, I'VE GOT YOUR BACK.
AW, CRIKEY! IT'S CYCLOPTIS INTELEHENTAY!
RARE BREED! ITS ONE EYE LIMITS ITS DEPTH PERCEPTION, BUT GET AN EYEFUL OF THAT ELDER-DEMON-SPEAR IT'S WIELDING! ONE BLOW FROM THAT WILL CAUSE A MORTAL TA BLEED OUT AND DIE!
SNEAKING UP ON A CYCLOPTIS INTELEHENTAY IS NOT THE PIECE OF PISS IT LOOKS! DESPITE ITS ROTUND SIZE, IT'S ACTUALLY QUITE AGILE!
IS SOMEONE MAKING FUN OF MY WEIGHT AGAIN?!?
CRIKEY!
A CLOSE ONE, WASN'T IT? I ALMOST BLED OUT AND DIED!
LET'S FOLLOW 'IM!
TIME'S UP, TORG.
THINK YOU GOT ME, DEMON? BEHIND YOU. DEMON HUNTER.
TAG
>CLIP<
WHAT?
HA! YES! I TAGGED HIM! MISSION ACCOMPLISHED!
TAG
THAT'S "TAGGING HIM?" I THOUGHT "TAGGING" WAS AUSTRALIAN SLANG FOR "BLOWING HIS HEAD OFF" OR SOMETHING!
ENDANGER THE 'UGE AND BEWDYFUL BUGGER? NOW WE CAN TRACK HIS MIGRATION UP CLOSE!
"HUGE"? LAY OFF, MAN!
SLUGGY FREELANCE
RIFF! AYLEE! PLAN B!
DO NOT FEED TH...
CRIKEY! THE DRAGON DECORATION'S BLOODY ALIVE!
DON'T MAKE ME USE THIS ON YOU, DEMON!
YOU HAVE A STAIN ON YOUR SHIRT.
REALLY? ODD! I'M NOT EVEN WEARING A SHIRT!
>POIK<
HA. HA. HA.
HEY!
I THINK THE SELECTOR-SWITCH ON MY ARM-CANON'S BUSTED.
DIE!
RIFF! LOOK OUT!
CRIKEY! WATCH OUT FOR THE SPEAR-TIP!
GLOMPH!
LEGGO!
GROMPH!
EYAAAAH! IT'S GOT ME!
I GOT YOU, TORG!
LOSER!
LET RIFF GO, YOU SQUID-MONSTER!
GOOMPH
HEY!
HELP!
GLOMPH!
DANGER! DANGER! DANGER!
THIS IS THE COOLEST PARTY EVER!
CAN WE MAKE RESERVATIONS FOR NEXT YEAR'S PARTY NOW?
FIVE BUCKS ON THE SQUID-ON-A-STICK!

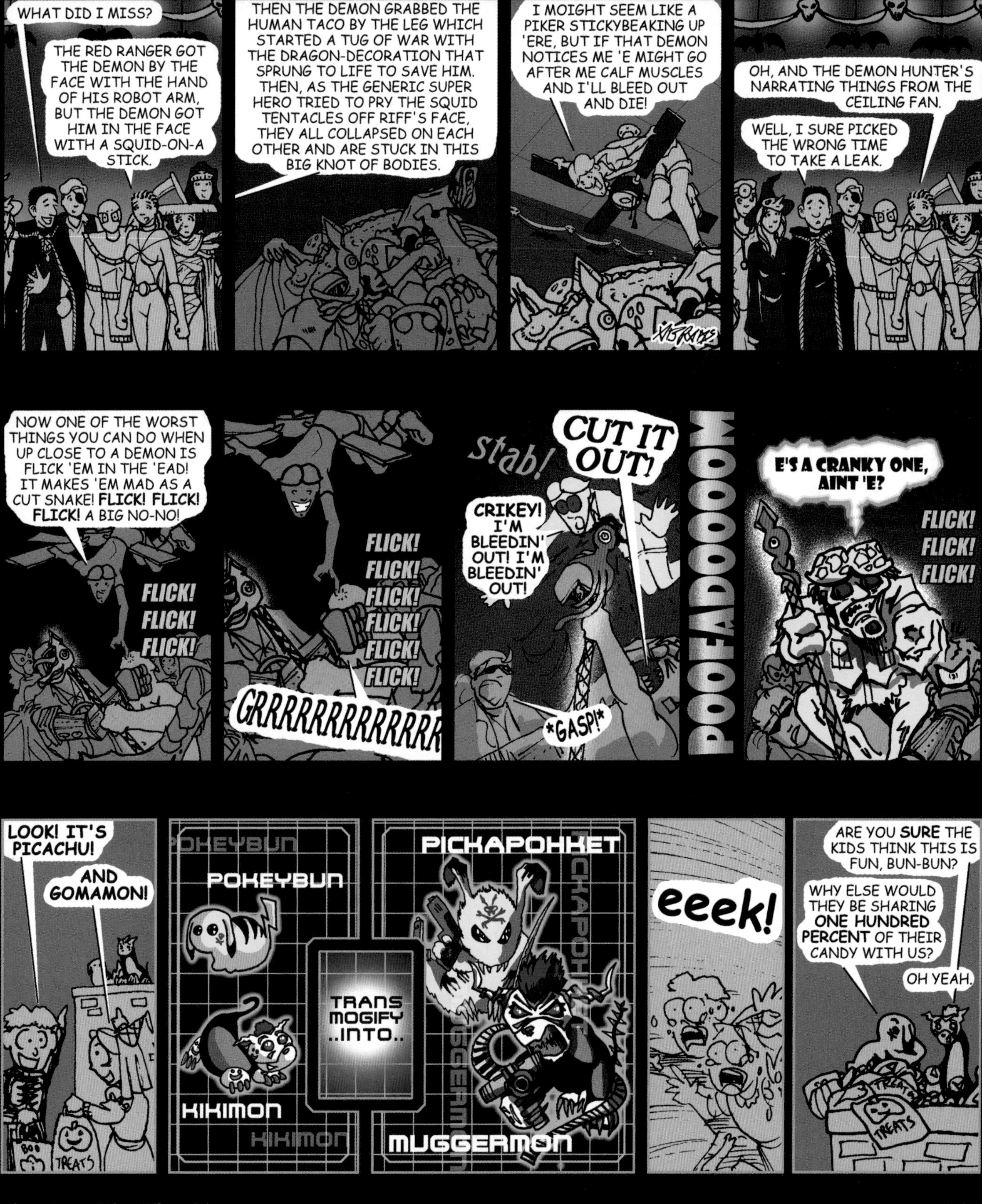
WHAT DID I MISS?
THE RED RANGER GOT THE DEMON BY THE FACE WITH THE HAND OF HIS ROBOT ARM, BUT THE DEMON GOT HIM IN THE FACE WITH A SQUID-ON-A STICK.
THEN THE DEMON GRABBED THE HUMAN TACO BY THE LEG WHICH STARTED A TUG OF WAR WITH THE DRAGON-DECORATION THAT SPRUNG TO LIFE TO SAVE HIM. THEN, AS THE GENERIC SUPER HERO TRIED TO PRY THE SQUID TENTACLES OFF RIFF'S FACE, THEY ALL COLLAPSED ON EACH OTHER AND ARE STUCK IN THIS BIG KNOT OF BODIES.
I MOIGHT SEEM LIKE A PIKER STICKYBEAKING UP 'ERE, BUT IF THAT DEMON NOTICES ME 'E MIGHT GO AFTER ME CALF MUSCLES AND I'LL BLEED OUT AND DIE!
OH, AND THE DEMON HUNTER'S NARRATING THINGS FROM THE CEILING FAN.
WELL, I SURE PICKED THE WRONG TIME TO TAKE A LEAK.
NOW ONE OF THE WORST THINGS YOU CAN DO WHEN UP CLOSE TO A DEMON IS FLICK 'EM IN THE 'EAD! IT MAKES 'EM MAD AS A CUT SNAKE! **FLICK! FLICK! FLICK!** A BIG NO-NO!
FLICK! FLICK! FLICK!
FLICK! FLICK! FLICK! FLICK! FLICK! FLICK!
GRRRRRRRRRRRRR
stab!
CUT IT OUT!
CRIKEY! I'M BLEEDIN' OUT! I'M BLEEDIN' OUT!
GASP!
POOFADOOOOOM
E'S A CRANKY ONE, AINT 'E?
FLICK! FLICK! FLICK!
LOOK! IT'S PICACHU!
AND GOMAMON!
BOO
TREATS
POKEYBUN
POKEYBUN
KIKIMON
KIKIMON
TRANS MOGIFY ..INTO..
PICKAPOHKET
PICKAPOHKET
MUGGERMON
MUGGERMON
eeek!
ARE YOU **SURE** THE KIDS THINK THIS IS FUN, BUN-BUN?
WHY ELSE WOULD THEY BE SHARING **ONE HUNDRED PERCENT** OF THEIR CANDY WITH US?
OH YEAH.
TREATS
TREATS

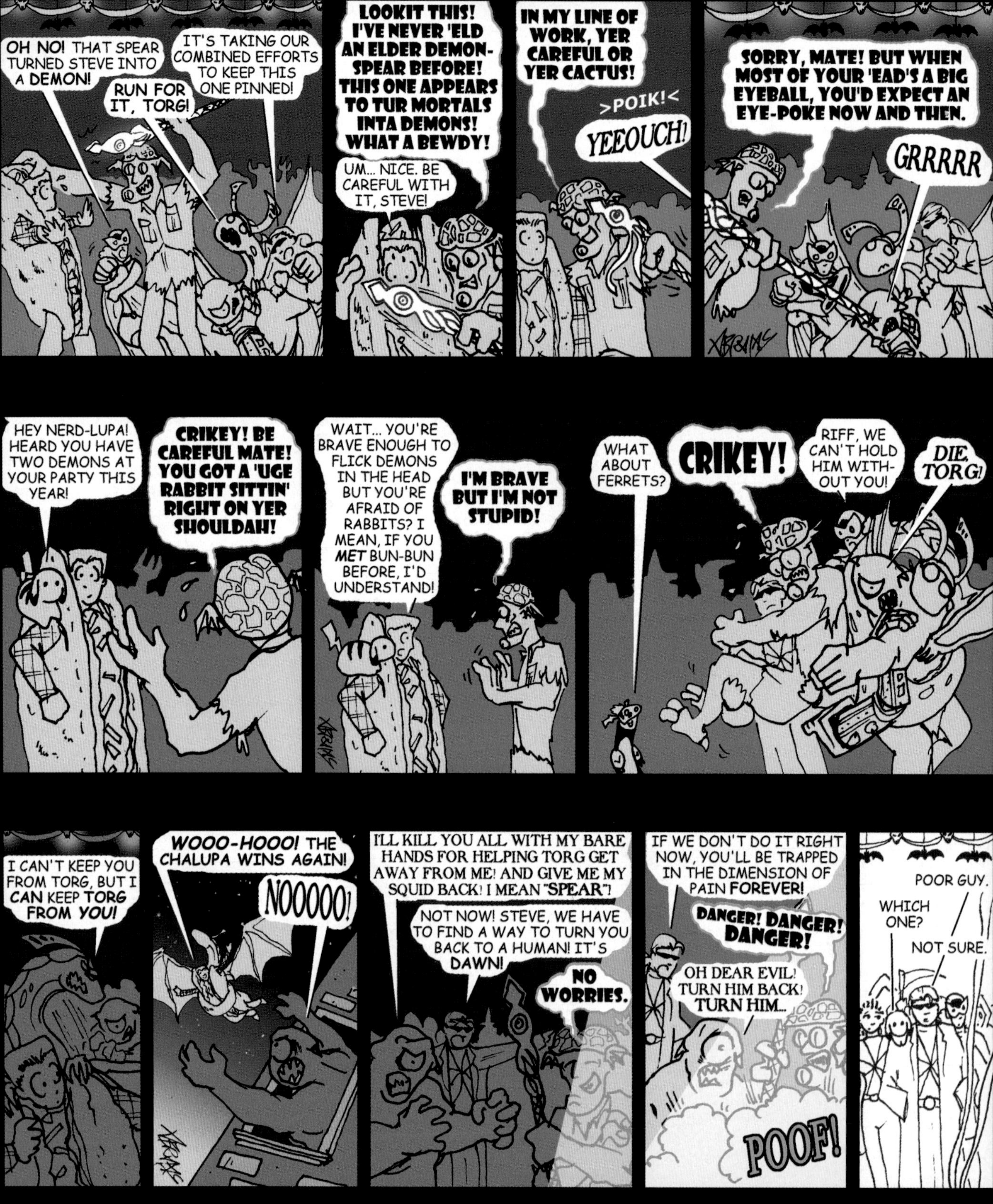
OH NO! THAT SPEAR TURNED STEVE INTO A DEMON!
IT'S TAKING OUR COMBINED EFFORTS TO KEEP THIS ONE PINNED!
RUN FOR IT, TORG!
LOOKIT THIS! I'VE NEVER 'ELD AN ELDER DEMON-SPEAR BEFORE! THIS ONE APPEARS TO TUR MORTALS INTA DEMONS! WHAT A BEWDY!
UM... NICE. BE CAREFUL WITH IT, STEVE!
IN MY LINE OF WORK, YER CAREFUL OR YER CACTUS!
>POIK!<
YEEOUCH!
SORRY, MATE! BUT WHEN MOST OF YOUR 'EAD'S A BIG EYEBALL, YOU'D EXPECT AN EYE-POKE NOW AND THEN.
GRRRRR
HEY NERD-LUPA! HEARD YOU HAVE TWO DEMONS AT YOUR PARTY THIS YEAR!
CRIKEY! BE CAREFUL MATE! YOU GOT A 'UGE RABBIT SITTIN' RIGHT ON YER SHOULDAH!
WAIT... YOU'RE BRAVE ENOUGH TO FLICK DEMONS IN THE HEAD BUT YOU'RE AFRAID OF RABBITS? I MEAN, IF YOU MET BUN-BUN BEFORE, I'D UNDERSTAND!
I'M BRAVE BUT I'M NOT STUPID!
WHAT ABOUT FERRETS?
CRIKEY!
RIFF, WE CAN'T HOLD HIM WITH-OUT YOU!
DIE, TORG!
I CAN'T KEEP YOU FROM TORG, BUT I CAN KEEP TORG FROM YOU!
WOOO-HOOO! THE CHALUPA WINS AGAIN!
NOOOOO!
I'LL KILL YOU ALL WITH MY BARE HANDS FOR HELPING TORG GET AWAY FROM ME! AND GIVE ME MY SQUID BACK! I MEAN "SPEAR"!
NOT NOW! STEVE, WE HAVE TO FIND A WAY TO TURN YOU BACK TO A HUMAN! IT'S DAWN!
NO WORRIES.
IF WE DON'T DO IT RIGHT NOW, YOU'LL BE TRAPPED IN THE DIMENSION OF PAIN FOREVER!
DANGER! DANGER! DANGER!
OH DEAR EVIL! TURN HIM BACK! TURN HIM...
POOF!
POOR GUY.
WHICH ONE?
NOT SURE.

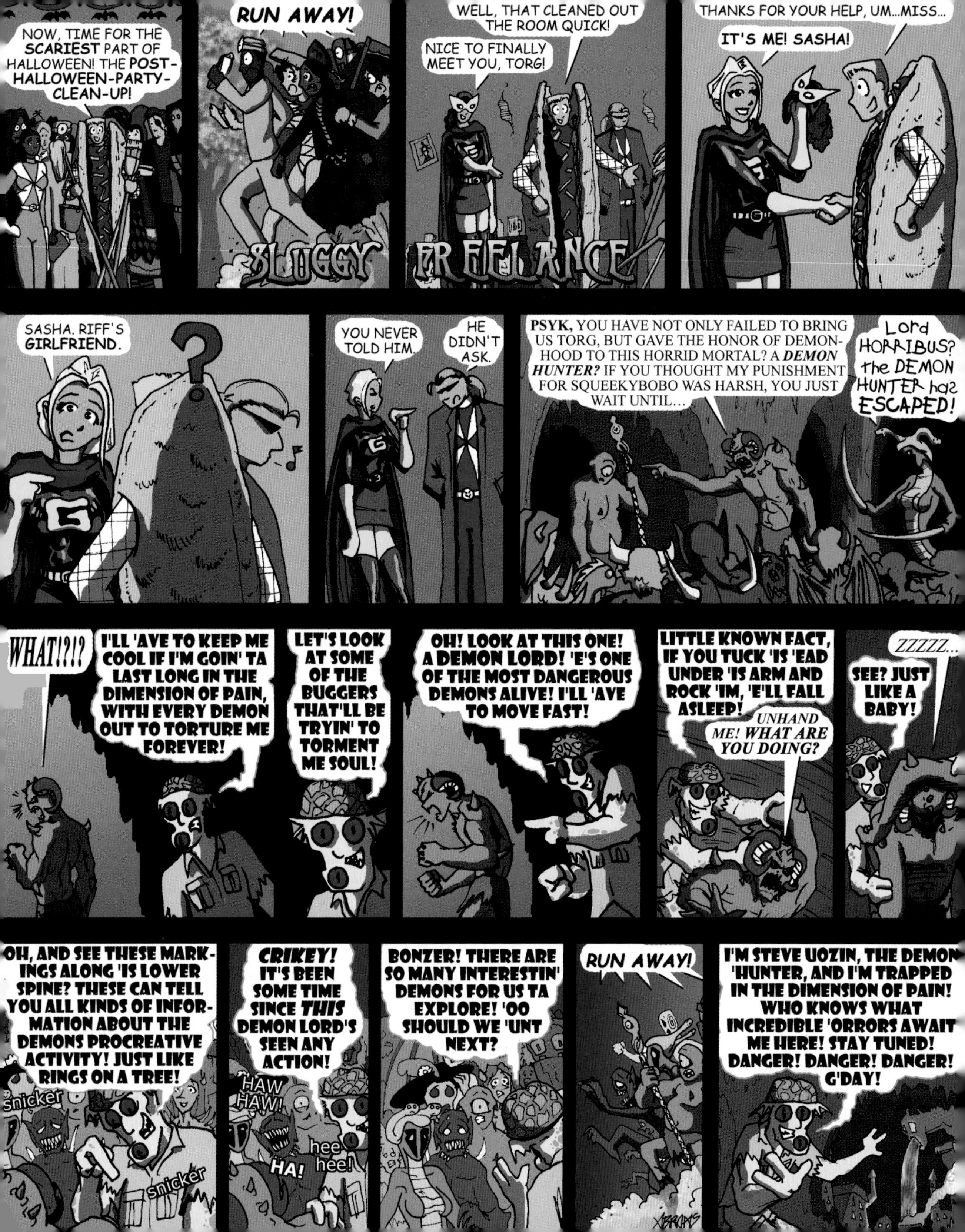
NOW, TIME FOR THE SCARIEST PART OF HALLOWEEN! THE POST-HALLOWEEN-PARTY-CLEAN-UP!
RUN AWAY!
SLUGGY FREELANCE
WELL, THAT CLEANED OUT THE ROOM QUICK!
NICE TO FINALLY MEET YOU, TORG!
THANKS FOR YOUR HELP, UM...MISS...
IT'S ME! SASHA!
SASHA. RIFF'S GIRLFRIEND.
?
YOU NEVER TOLD HIM.
HE DIDN'T ASK.
PSYK, YOU HAVE NOT ONLY FAILED TO BRING US TORG, BUT GAVE THE HONOR OF DEMON-HOOD TO THIS HORRID MORTAL? A DEMON HUNTER? IF YOU THOUGHT MY PUNISHMENT FOR SQUEEKYBOBO WAS HARSH, YOU JUST WAIT UNTIL…
Lord HORRIBUS? the DEMON HUNTER has ESCAPED!
WHAT!?!?
I'LL 'AVE TO KEEP ME COOL IF I'M GOIN' TA LAST LONG IN THE DIMENSION OF PAIN, WITH EVERY DEMON OUT TO TORTURE ME FOREVER!
LET'S LOOK AT SOME OF THE BUGGERS THAT'LL BE TRYIN' TO TORMENT ME SOUL!
OH! LOOK AT THIS ONE! A DEMON LORD! 'E'S ONE OF THE MOST DANGEROUS DEMONS ALIVE! I'LL 'AVE TO MOVE FAST!
LITTLE KNOWN FACT, IF YOU TUCK 'IS 'EAD UNDER 'IS ARM AND ROCK 'IM, 'E'LL FALL ASLEEP!
UNHAND ME! WHAT ARE YOU DOING?
ZZZZZ...
SEE? JUST LIKE A BABY!
OH, AND SEE THESE MARKINGS ALONG 'IS LOWER SPINE? THESE CAN TELL YOU ALL KINDS OF INFORMATION ABOUT THE DEMONS PROCREATIVE ACTIVITY! JUST LIKE RINGS ON A TREE!
snicker
snicker
CRIKEY! IT'S BEEN SOME TIME SINCE THIS DEMON LORD'S SEEN ANY ACTION!
HAW HAW!
HA!
hee hee!
BONZER! THERE ARE SO MANY INTERESTIN' DEMONS FOR US TA EXPLORE! 'OO SHOULD WE 'UNT NEXT?
RUN AWAY!
I'M STEVE UOZIN, THE DEMON 'HUNTER, AND I'M TRAPPED IN THE DIMENSION OF PAIN! WHO KNOWS WHAT INCREDIBLE 'ORRORS AWAIT ME HERE! STAY TUNED! DANGER! DANGER! DANGER! G'DAY!

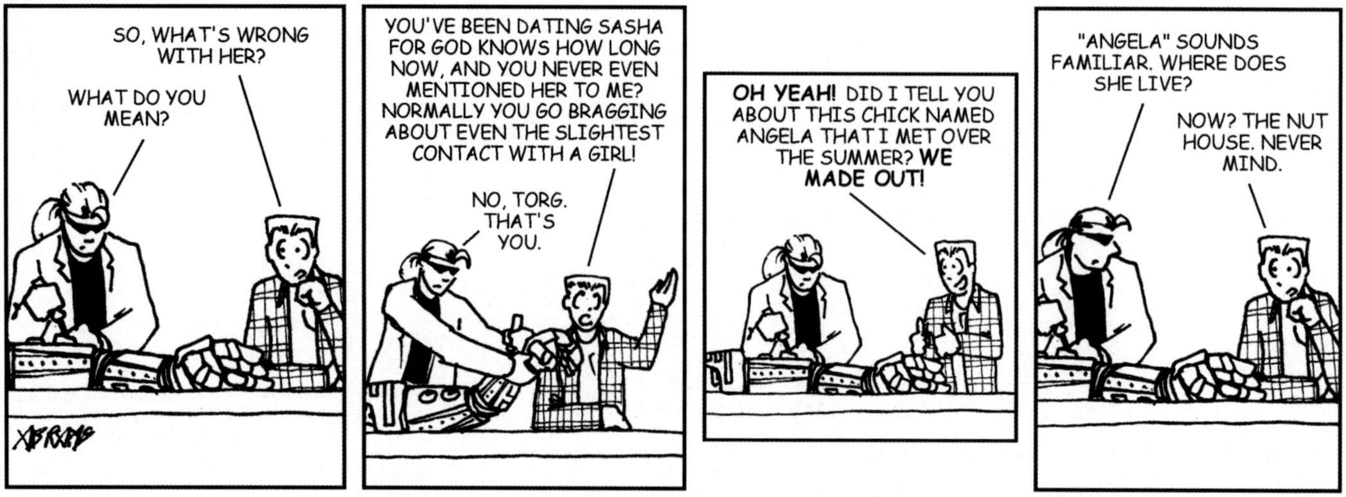
SO, WHAT'S WRONG WITH HER?
WHAT DO YOU MEAN?
YOU'VE BEEN DATING SASHA FOR GOD KNOWS HOW LONG NOW, AND YOU NEVER EVEN MENTIONED HER TO ME? NORMALLY YOU GO BRAGGING ABOUT EVEN THE SLIGHTEST CONTACT WITH A GIRL!
NO, TORG. THAT'S YOU.
OH YEAH! DID I TELL YOU ABOUT THIS CHICK NAMED ANGELA THAT I MET OVER THE SUMMER? WE MADE OUT!
"ANGELA" SOUNDS FAMILIAR. WHERE DOES SHE LIVE?
NOW? THE NUT HOUSE. NEVER MIND.

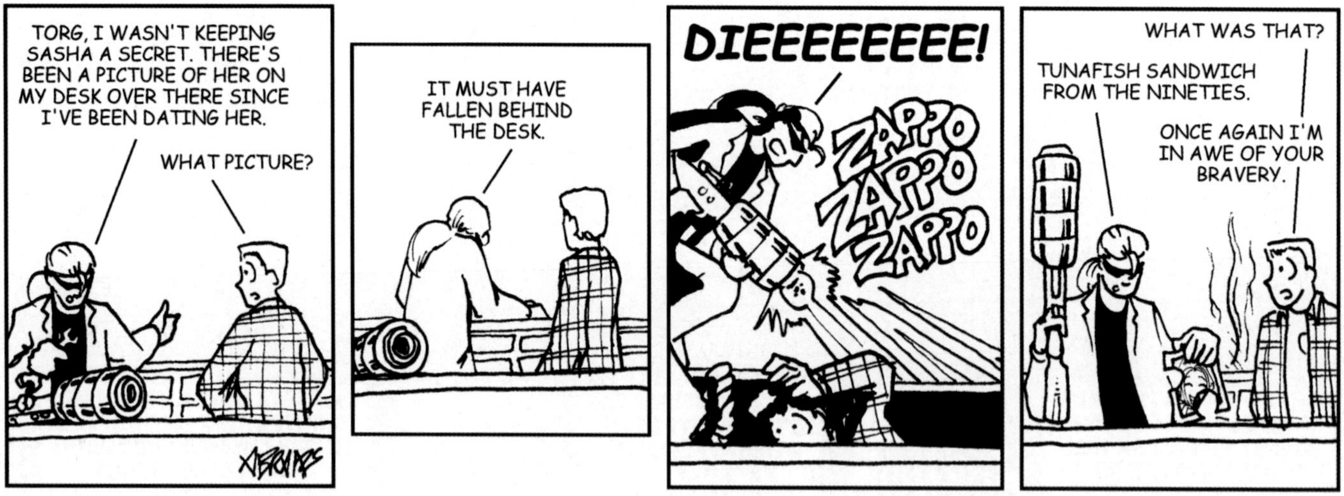
TORG, I WASN'T KEEPING SASHA A SECRET. THERE'S BEEN A PICTURE OF HER ON MY DESK OVER THERE SINCE I'VE BEEN DATING HER.
WHAT PICTURE?
IT MUST HAVE FALLEN BEHIND THE DESK.
DIEEEEEEEEE!
ZAPPO ZAPPO ZAPPO
WHAT WAS THAT?
TUNAFISH SANDWICH FROM THE NINETIES.
ONCE AGAIN I'M IN AWE OF YOUR BRAVERY.

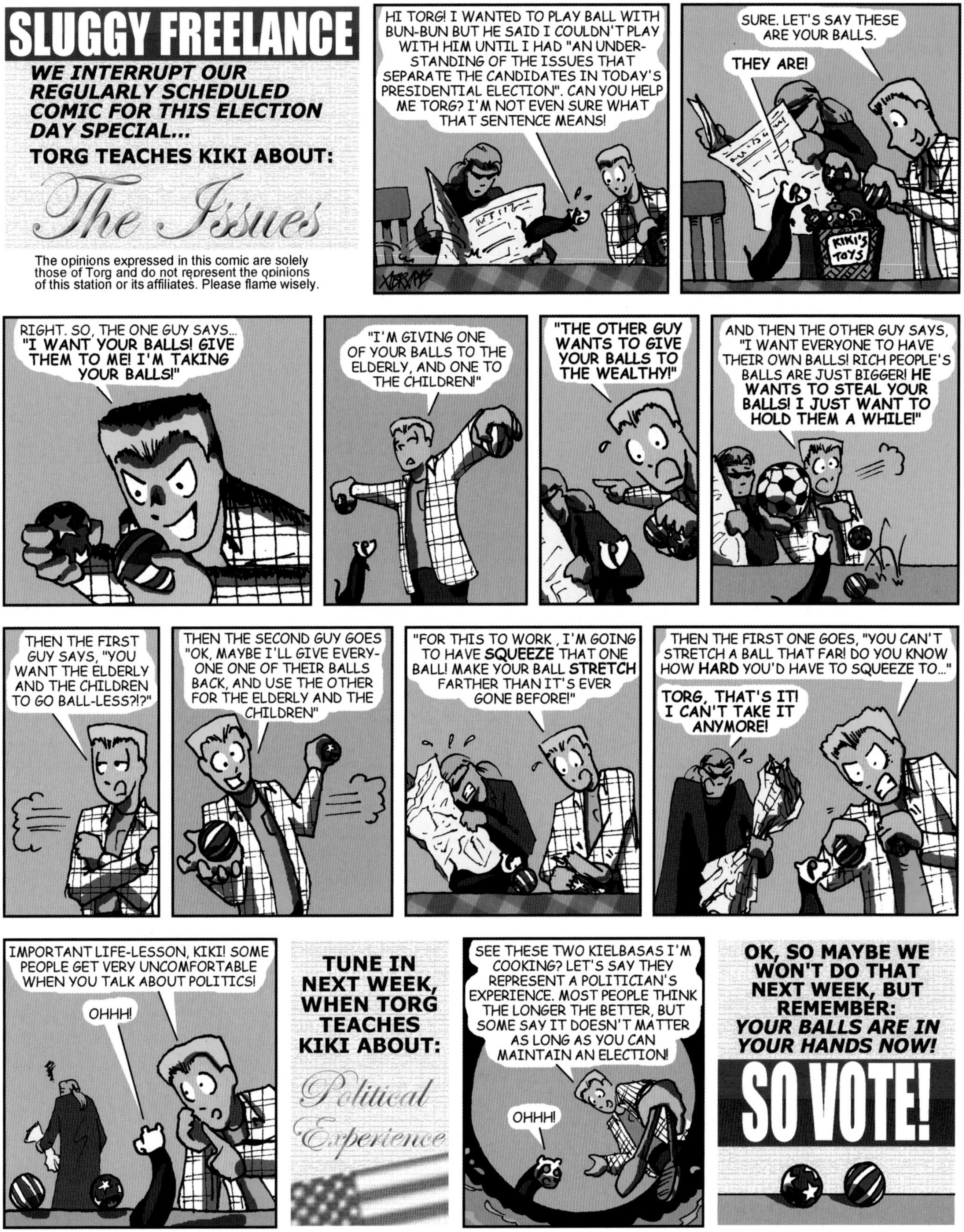
SLUGGY FREELANCE
WE INTERRUPT OUR REGULARLY SCHEDULED COMIC FOR THIS ELECTION DAY SPECIAL...
TORG TEACHES KIKI ABOUT:
The Issues
The opinions expressed in this comic are solely those of Torg and do not represent the opinions of this station or its affiliates. Please flame wisely.
HI TORG! I WANTED TO PLAY BALL WITH BUN-BUN BUT HE SAID I COULDN'T PLAY WITH HIM UNTIL I HAD "AN UNDER-STANDING OF THE ISSUES THAT SEPARATE THE CANDIDATES IN TODAY'S PRESIDENTIAL ELECTION". CAN YOU HELP ME TORG? I'M NOT EVEN SURE WHAT THAT SENTENCE MEANS!
SURE. LET'S SAY THESE ARE YOUR BALLS.
THEY ARE!
RIGHT. SO, THE ONE GUY SAYS... "I WANT YOUR BALLS! GIVE THEM TO ME! I'M TAKING YOUR BALLS!"
"I'M GIVING ONE OF YOUR BALLS TO THE ELDERLY, AND ONE TO THE CHILDREN!"
"THE OTHER GUY WANTS TO GIVE YOUR BALLS TO THE WEALTHY!"
AND THEN THE OTHER GUY SAYS, "I WANT EVERYONE TO HAVE THEIR OWN BALLS! RICH PEOPLE'S BALLS ARE JUST BIGGER! HE WANTS TO STEAL YOUR BALLS! I JUST WANT TO HOLD THEM A WHILE!"
THEN THE FIRST GUY SAYS, "YOU WANT THE ELDERLY AND THE CHILDREN TO GO BALL-LESS?!?"
THEN THE SECOND GUY GOES "OK, MAYBE I'LL GIVE EVERY-ONE ONE OF THEIR BALLS BACK, AND USE THE OTHER FOR THE ELDERLY AND THE CHILDREN"
"FOR THIS TO WORK , I'M GOING TO HAVE SQUEEZE THAT ONE BALL! MAKE YOUR BALL STRETCH FARTHER THAN IT'S EVER GONE BEFORE!"
THEN THE FIRST ONE GOES, "YOU CAN'T STRETCH A BALL THAT FAR! DO YOU KNOW HOW HARD YOU'D HAVE TO SQUEEZE TO..."
TORG, THAT'S IT! I CAN'T TAKE IT ANYMORE!
IMPORTANT LIFE-LESSON, KIKI! SOME PEOPLE GET VERY UNCOMFORTABLE WHEN YOU TALK ABOUT POLITICS!
OHHH!
TUNE IN NEXT WEEK, WHEN TORG TEACHES KIKI ABOUT:
Political Experience
SEE THESE TWO KIELBASAS I'M COOKING? LET'S SAY THEY REPRESENT A POLITICIAN'S EXPERIENCE. MOST PEOPLE THINK THE LONGER THE BETTER, BUT SOME SAY IT DOESN'T MATTER AS LONG AS YOU CAN MAINTAIN AN ELECTION!
OHHH!
OK, SO MAYBE WE WON'T DO THAT NEXT WEEK, BUT REMEMBER: YOUR BALLS ARE IN YOUR HANDS NOW!
SO VOTE!

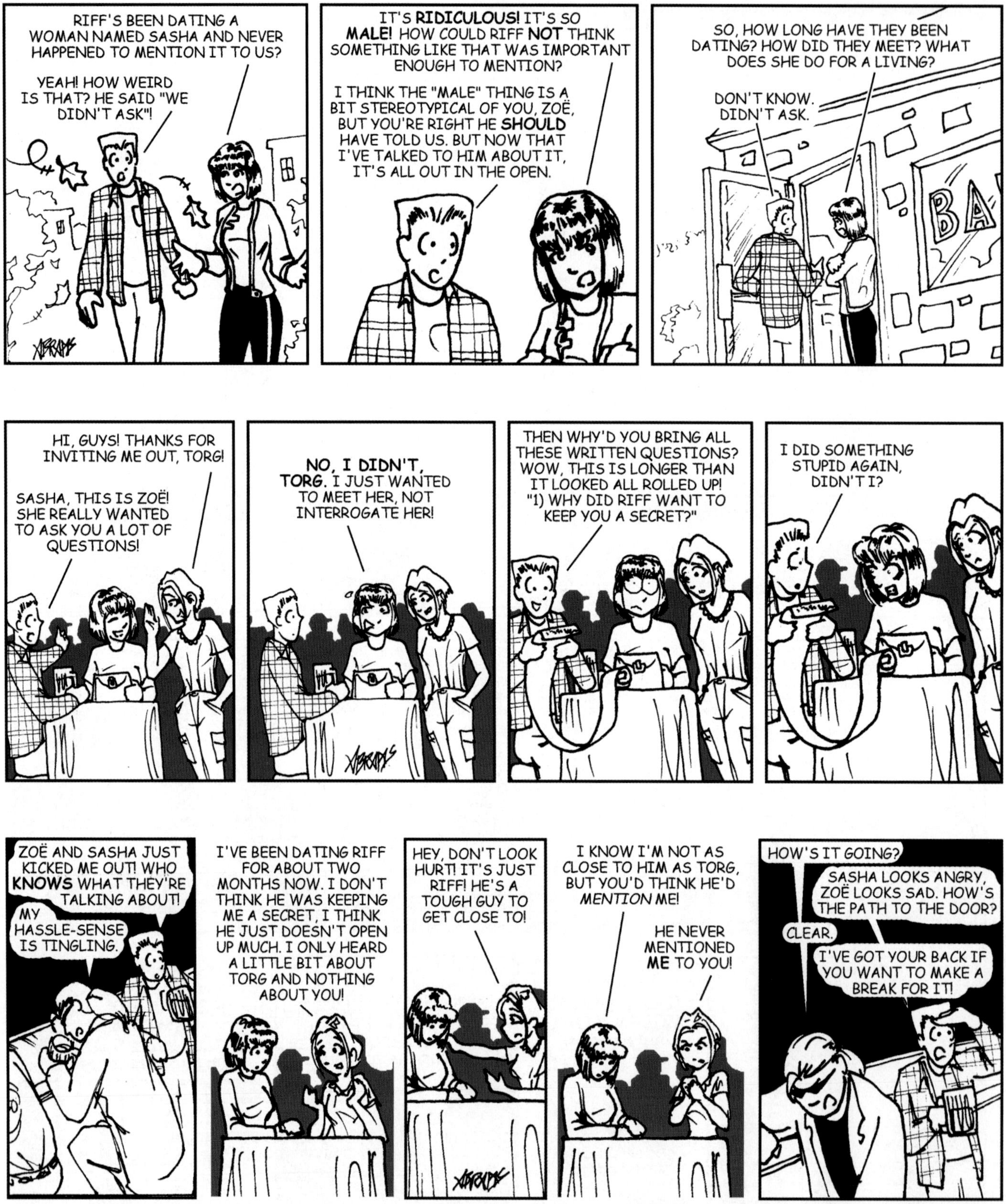
RIFF'S BEEN DATING A WOMAN NAMED SASHA AND NEVER HAPPENED TO MENTION IT TO US?
YEAH! HOW WEIRD IS THAT? HE SAID "WE DIDN'T ASK"!
IT'S RIDICULOUS! IT'S SO MALE! HOW COULD RIFF NOT THINK SOMETHING LIKE THAT WAS IMPORTANT ENOUGH TO MENTION?
I THINK THE "MALE" THING IS A BIT STEREOTYPICAL OF YOU, ZOË, BUT YOU'RE RIGHT HE SHOULD HAVE TOLD US. BUT NOW THAT I'VE TALKED TO HIM ABOUT IT, IT'S ALL OUT IN THE OPEN.
SO, HOW LONG HAVE THEY BEEN DATING? HOW DID THEY MEET? WHAT DOES SHE DO FOR A LIVING?
DON'T KNOW. DIDN'T ASK.
HI, GUYS! THANKS FOR INVITING ME OUT, TORG!
SASHA, THIS IS ZOË! SHE REALLY WANTED TO ASK YOU A LOT OF QUESTIONS!
NO, I DIDN'T, TORG. I JUST WANTED TO MEET HER, NOT INTERROGATE HER!
THEN WHY'D YOU BRING ALL THESE WRITTEN QUESTIONS? WOW, THIS IS LONGER THAN IT LOOKED ALL ROLLED UP! "1) WHY DID RIFF WANT TO KEEP YOU A SECRET?"
I DID SOMETHING STUPID AGAIN, DIDN'T I?
ZOË AND SASHA JUST KICKED ME OUT! WHO KNOWS WHAT THEY'RE TALKING ABOUT!
MY HASSLE-SENSE IS TINGLING.
I'VE BEEN DATING RIFF FOR ABOUT TWO MONTHS NOW. I DON'T THINK HE WAS KEEPING ME A SECRET, I THINK HE JUST DOESN'T OPEN UP MUCH. I ONLY HEARD A LITTLE BIT ABOUT TORG AND NOTHING ABOUT YOU!
HEY, DON'T LOOK HURT! IT'S JUST RIFF! HE'S A TOUGH GUY TO GET CLOSE TO!
I KNOW I'M NOT AS CLOSE TO HIM AS TORG, BUT YOU'D THINK HE'D MENTION ME!
HE NEVER MENTIONED ME TO YOU!
HOW'S IT GOING?
SASHA LOOKS ANGRY, ZOË LOOKS SAD. HOW'S THE PATH TO THE DOOR?
CLEAR.
I'VE GOT YOUR BACK IF YOU WANT TO MAKE A BREAK FOR IT!

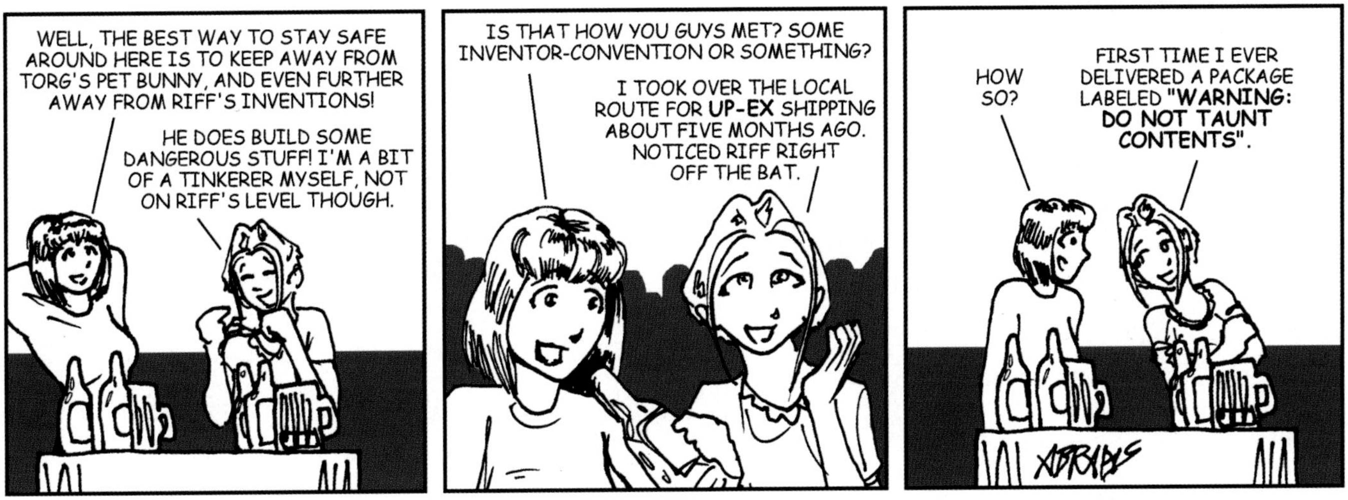
WELL, THE BEST WAY TO STAY SAFE AROUND HERE IS TO KEEP AWAY FROM TORG'S PET BUNNY, AND EVEN FURTHER AWAY FROM RIFF'S INVENTIONS!
HE DOES BUILD SOME DANGEROUS STUFF! I'M A BIT OF A TINKERER MYSELF, NOT ON RIFF'S LEVEL THOUGH.
IS THAT HOW YOU GUYS MET? SOME INVENTOR-CONVENTION OR SOMETHING?
I TOOK OVER THE LOCAL ROUTE FOR UP-EX SHIPPING ABOUT FIVE MONTHS AGO. NOTICED RIFF RIGHT OFF THE BAT.
HOW SO?
FIRST TIME I EVER DELIVERED A PACKAGE LABELED "WARNING: DO NOT TAUNT CONTENTS".

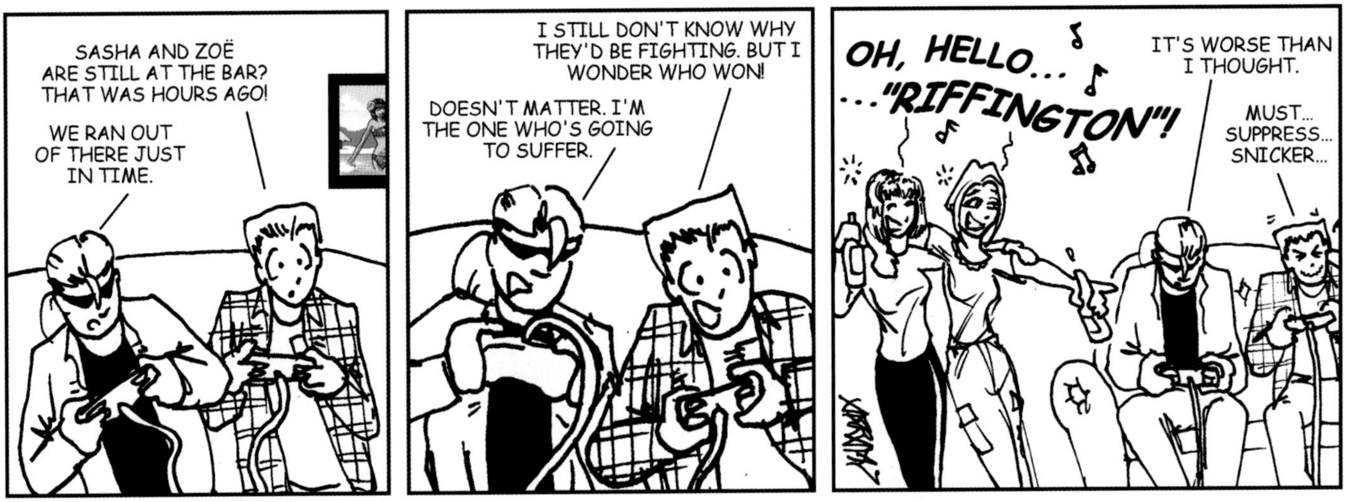
SASHA AND ZOË ARE STILL AT THE BAR? THAT WAS HOURS AGO!
WE RAN OUT OF THERE JUST IN TIME.
I STILL DON'T KNOW WHY THEY'D BE FIGHTING. BUT I WONDER WHO WON!
DOESN'T MATTER. I'M THE ONE WHO'S GOING TO SUFFER.
OH, HELLO... ..."RIFFINGTON"!
IT'S WORSE THAN I THOUGHT.
MUST... SUPPRESS... SNICKER...

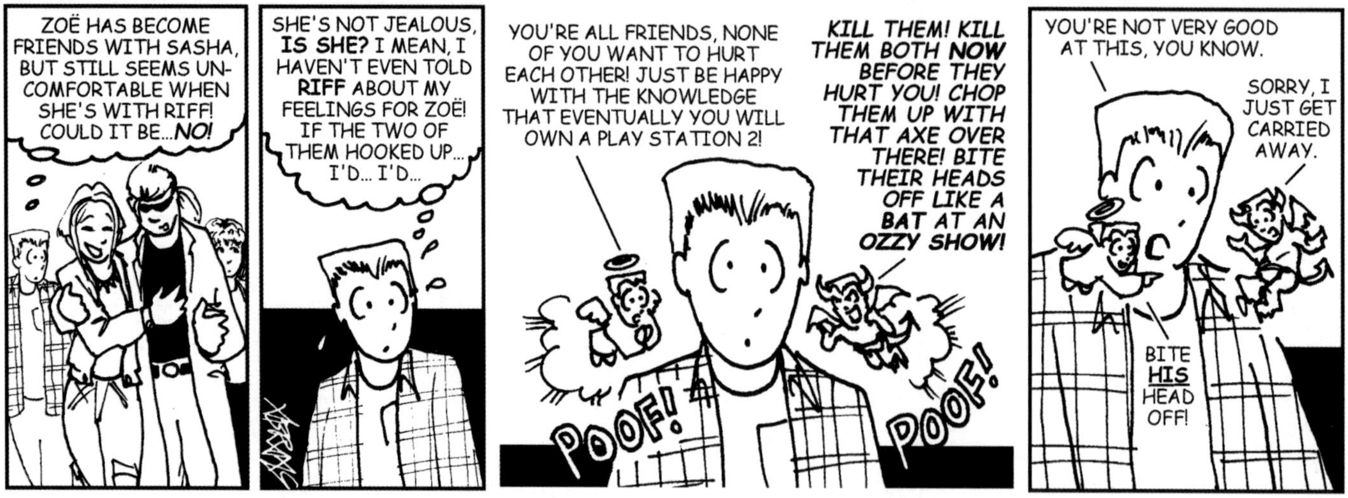
ZOË HAS BECOME FRIENDS WITH SASHA, BUT STILL SEEMS UN-COMFORTABLE WHEN SHE'S WITH RIFF! COULD IT BE...NO!
SHE'S NOT JEALOUS, IS SHE? I MEAN, I HAVEN'T EVEN TOLD RIFF ABOUT MY FEELINGS FOR ZOË! IF THE TWO OF THEM HOOKED UP... I'D... I'D...
YOU'RE ALL FRIENDS, NONE OF YOU WANT TO HURT EACH OTHER! JUST BE HAPPY WITH THE KNOWLEDGE THAT EVENTUALLY YOU WILL OWN A PLAY STATION 2!
KILL THEM! KILL THEM BOTH NOW BEFORE THEY HURT YOU! CHOP THEM UP WITH THAT AXE OVER THERE! BITE THEIR HEADS OFF LIKE A BAT AT AN OZZY SHOW!
POOF!
POOF!
YOU'RE NOT VERY GOOD AT THIS, YOU KNOW.
SORRY, I JUST GET CARRIED AWAY.
BITE HIS HEAD OFF!

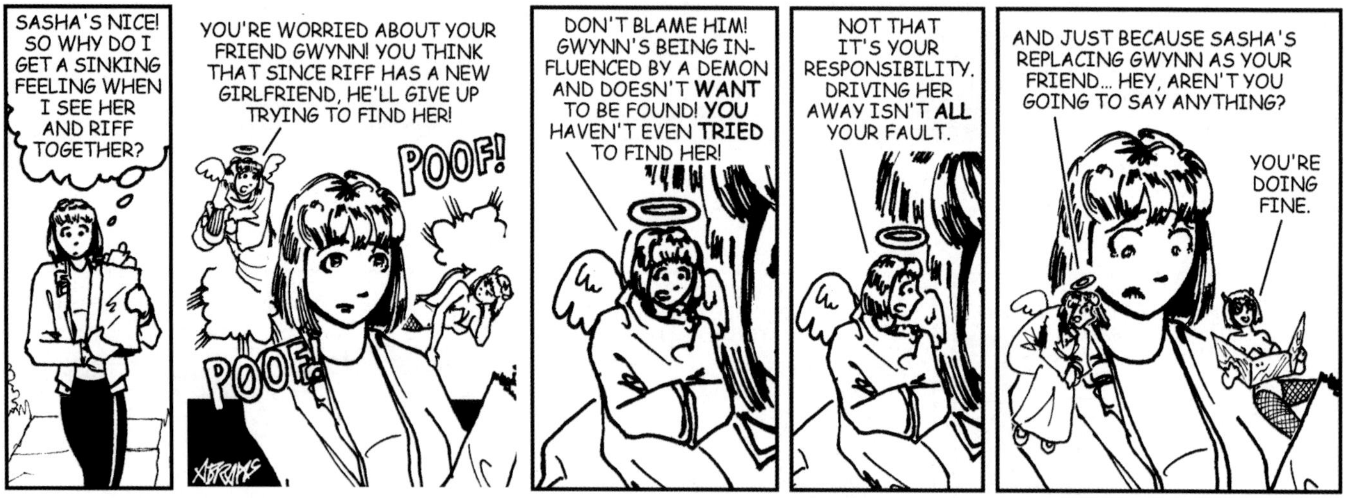
SASHA'S NICE! SO WHY DO I GET A SINKING FEELING WHEN I SEE HER AND RIFF TOGETHER?
YOU'RE WORRIED ABOUT YOUR FRIEND GWYNN! YOU THINK THAT SINCE RIFF HAS A NEW GIRLFRIEND, HE'LL GIVE UP TRYING TO FIND HER!
POOF!
POOF!
DON'T BLAME HIM! GWYNN'S BEING IN-FLUENCED BY A DEMON AND DOESN'T WANT TO BE FOUND! YOU HAVEN'T EVEN TRIED TO FIND HER!
NOT THAT IT'S YOUR RESPONSIBILITY. DRIVING HER AWAY ISN'T ALL YOUR FAULT.
AND JUST BECAUSE SASHA'S REPLACING GWYNN AS YOUR FRIEND... HEY, AREN'T YOU GOING TO SAY ANYTHING?
YOU'RE DOING FINE.

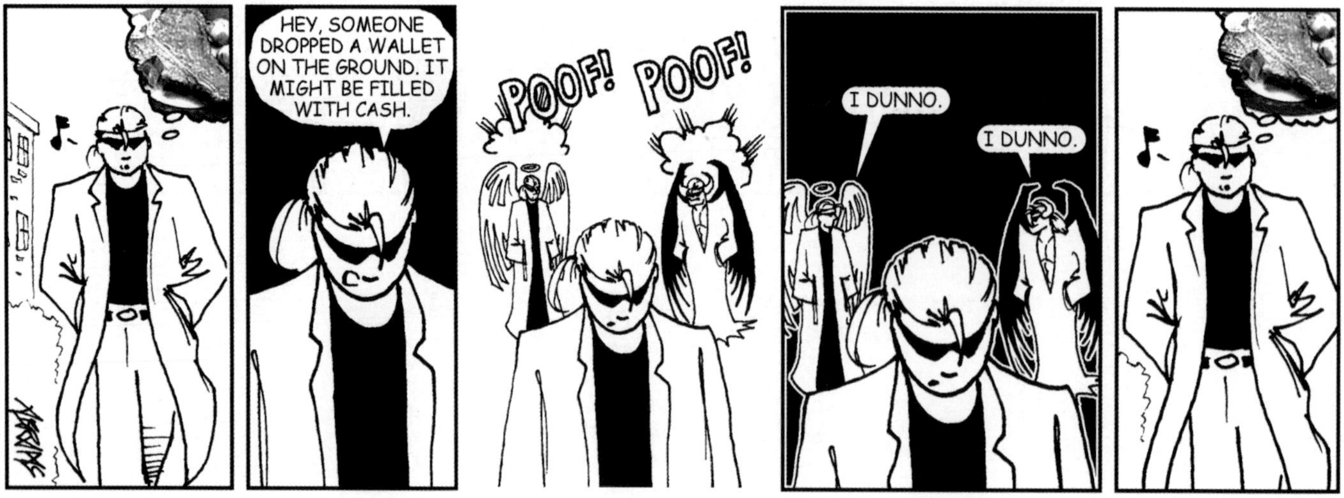
HEY, SOMEONE DROPPED A WALLET ON THE GROUND. IT MIGHT BE FILLED WITH CASH.
POOF!
POOF!
I DUNNO.
I DUNNO.

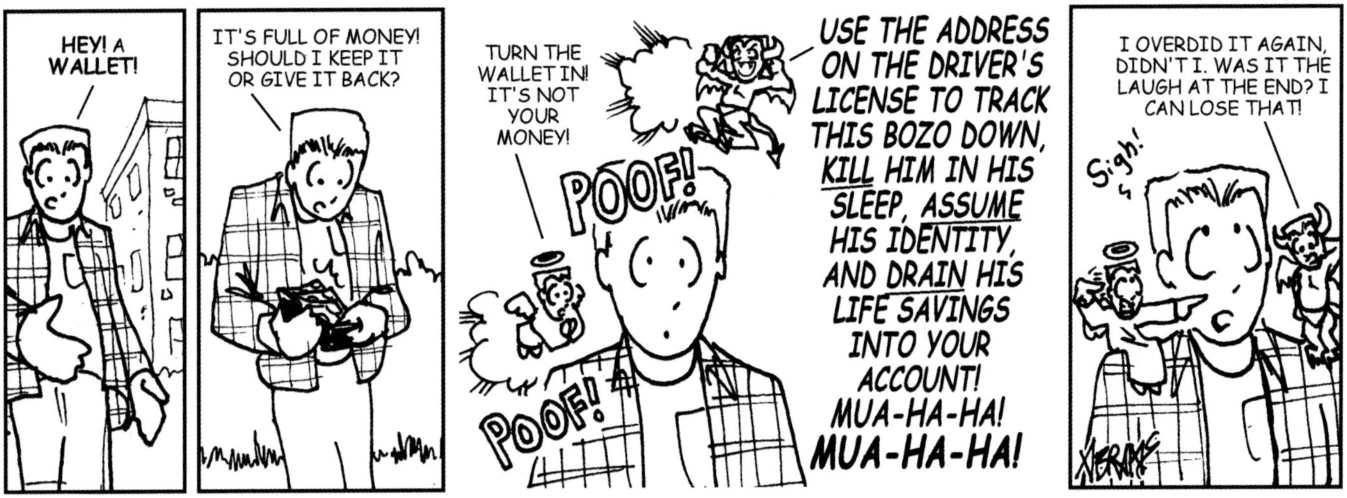

HEY! A WALLET!
IT'S FULL OF MONEY! SHOULD I KEEP IT OR GIVE IT BACK?
TURN THE WALLET IN! IT'S NOT YOUR MONEY!
POOF!
POOF!
USE THE ADDRESS ON THE DRIVER'S LICENSE TO TRACK THIS BOZO DOWN, KILL HIM IN HIS SLEEP, ASSUME HIS IDENTITY, AND DRAIN HIS LIFE SAVINGS INTO YOUR ACCOUNT! MUA-HA-HA! MUA-HA-HA!
Sigh!
I OVERDID IT AGAIN, DIDN'T I. WAS IT THE LAUGH AT THE END? I CAN LOSE THAT!

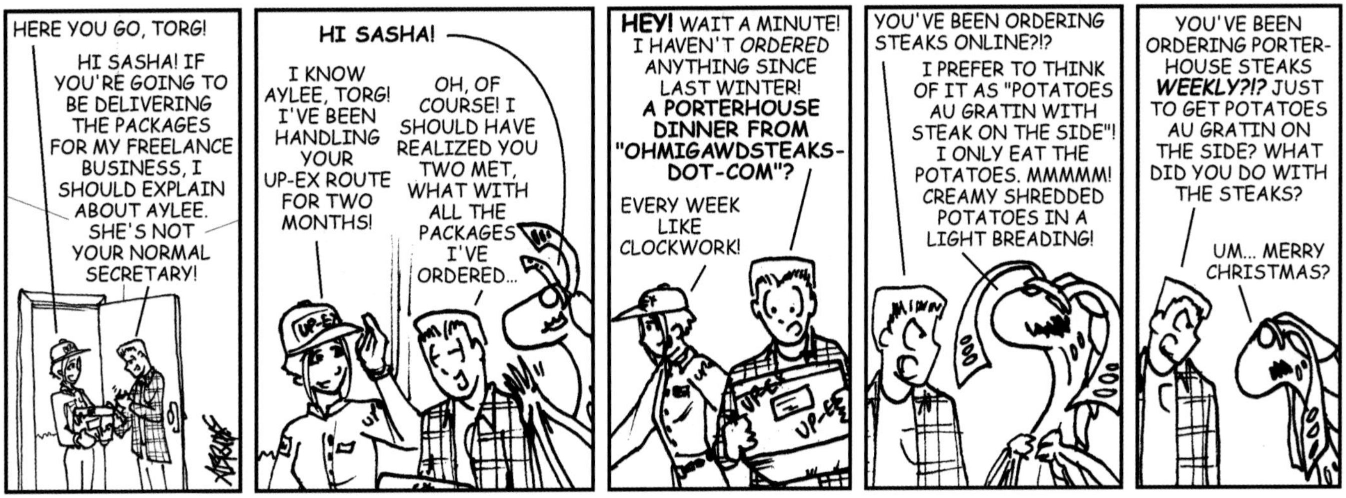

HERE YOU GO, TORG!
HI SASHA! IF YOU'RE GOING TO BE DELIVERING THE PACKAGES FOR MY FREELANCE BUSINESS, I SHOULD EXPLAIN ABOUT AYLEE. SHE'S NOT YOUR NORMAL SECRETARY!
HI SASHA!
I KNOW AYLEE, TORG! I'VE BEEN HANDLING YOUR UP-EX ROUTE FOR TWO MONTHS!
OH, OF COURSE! I SHOULD HAVE REALIZED YOU TWO MET, WHAT WITH ALL THE PACKAGES I'VE ORDERED...
UP-EX
HEY! WAIT A MINUTE! I HAVEN'T ORDERED ANYTHING SINCE LAST WINTER! A PORTERHOUSE DINNER FROM "OHMIGAWDSTEAKS-DOT-COM"?
EVERY WEEK LIKE CLOCKWORK!
UP-EX
YOU'VE BEEN ORDERING STEAKS ONLINE?!?
I PREFER TO THINK OF IT AS "POTATOES AU GRATIN WITH STEAK ON THE SIDE"! I ONLY EAT THE POTATOES. MMMMM! CREAMY SHREDDED POTATOES IN A LIGHT BREADING!
YOU'VE BEEN ORDERING PORTER-HOUSE STEAKS WEEKLY?!? JUST TO GET POTATOES AU GRATIN ON THE SIDE? WHAT DID YOU DO WITH THE STEAKS?
UM... MERRY CHRISTMAS?

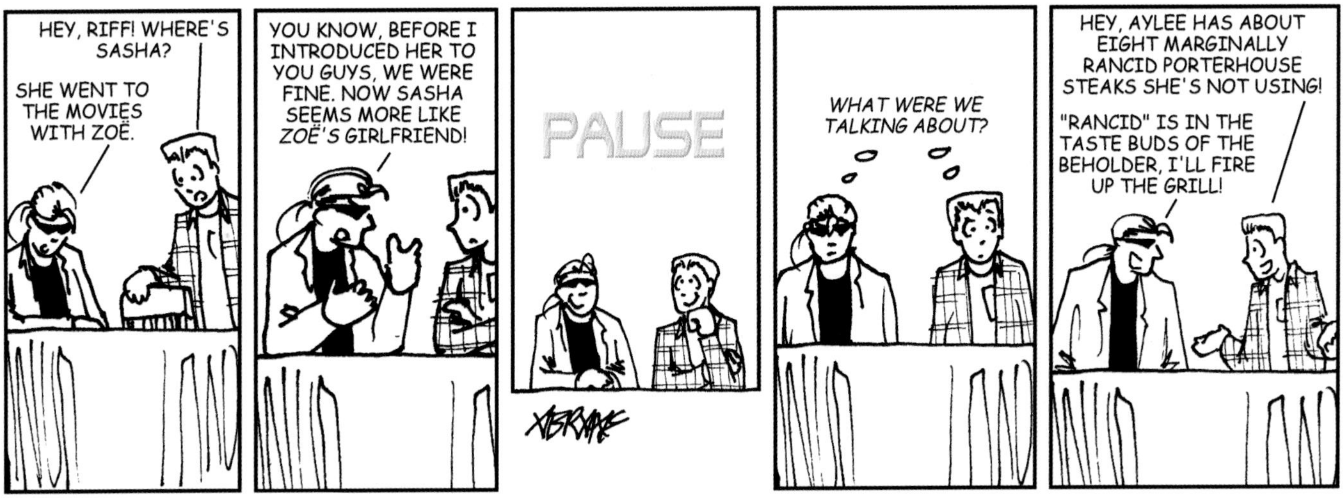

HEY, RIFF! WHERE'S SASHA?
SHE WENT TO THE MOVIES WITH ZOË.
YOU KNOW, BEFORE I INTRODUCED HER TO YOU GUYS, WE WERE FINE. NOW SASHA SEEMS MORE LIKE ZOË'S GIRLFRIEND!
PAUSE
WHAT WERE WE TALKING ABOUT?
HEY, AYLEE HAS ABOUT EIGHT MARGINALLY RANCID PORTERHOUSE STEAKS SHE'S NOT USING!
"RANCID" IS IN THE TASTE BUDS OF THE BEHOLDER. I'LL FIRE UP THE GRILL!

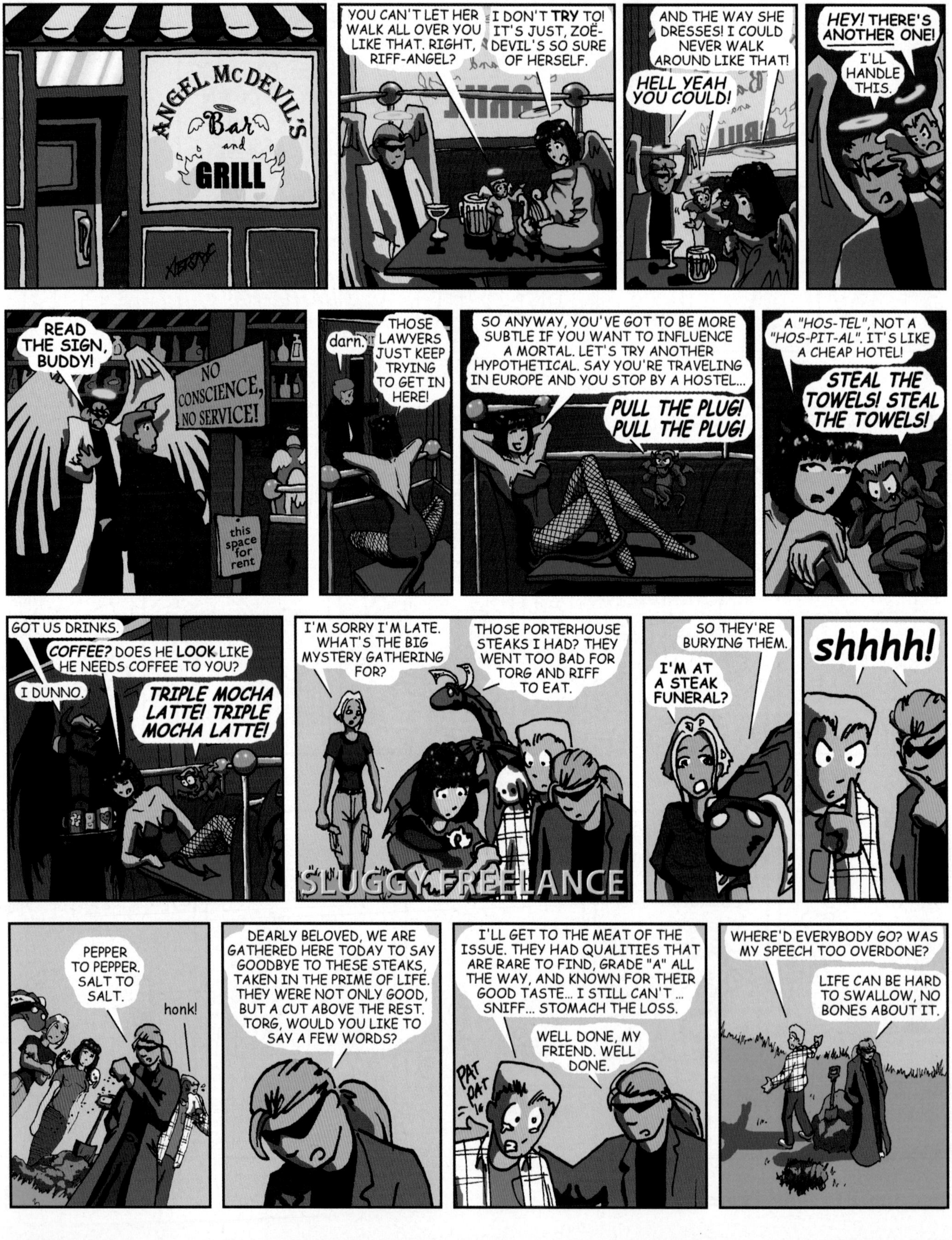
ANGEL McDEVIL'S
Bar and GRILL
YOU CAN'T LET HER WALK ALL OVER YOU LIKE THAT. RIGHT, RIFF-ANGEL?
I DON'T TRY TO! IT'S JUST, ZOË-DEVIL'S SO SURE OF HERSELF.
AND THE WAY SHE DRESSES! I COULD NEVER WALK AROUND LIKE THAT!
HELL YEAH YOU COULD!
HEY! THERE'S ANOTHER ONE!
I'LL HANDLE THIS.
READ THE SIGN, BUDDY!
NO CONSCIENCE, NO SERVICE!
this space for rent
darn.
THOSE LAWYERS JUST KEEP TRYING TO GET IN HERE!
SO ANYWAY, YOU'VE GOT TO BE MORE SUBTLE IF YOU WANT TO INFLUENCE A MORTAL. LET'S TRY ANOTHER HYPOTHETICAL. SAY YOU'RE TRAVELING IN EUROPE AND YOU STOP BY A HOSTEL...
PULL THE PLUG! PULL THE PLUG!
A "HOS-TEL", NOT A "HOS-PIT-AL". IT'S LIKE A CHEAP HOTEL!
STEAL THE TOWELS! STEAL THE TOWELS!
GOT US DRINKS.
COFFEE? DOES HE LOOK LIKE HE NEEDS COFFEE TO YOU?
I DUNNO.
TRIPLE MOCHA LATTE! TRIPLE MOCHA LATTE!
I'M SORRY I'M LATE. WHAT'S THE BIG MYSTERY GATHERING FOR?
THOSE PORTERHOUSE STEAKS I HAD? THEY WENT TOO BAD FOR TORG AND RIFF TO EAT.
SLUGGY FREELANCE
SO THEY'RE BURYING THEM.
I'M AT A STEAK FUNERAL?
shhhh!
PEPPER TO PEPPER. SALT TO SALT.
honk!
DEARLY BELOVED, WE ARE GATHERED HERE TODAY TO SAY GOODBYE TO THESE STEAKS, TAKEN IN THE PRIME OF LIFE. THEY WERE NOT ONLY GOOD, BUT A CUT ABOVE THE REST. TORG, WOULD YOU LIKE TO SAY A FEW WORDS?
I'LL GET TO THE MEAT OF THE ISSUE. THEY HAD QUALITIES THAT ARE RARE TO FIND, GRADE "A" ALL THE WAY, AND KNOWN FOR THEIR GOOD TASTE... I STILL CAN'T ... SNIFF... STOMACH THE LOSS.
WELL DONE, MY FRIEND. WELL DONE.
PAT PAT
WHERE'D EVERYBODY GO? WAS MY SPEECH TOO OVERDONE?
LIFE CAN BE HARD TO SWALLOW, NO BONES ABOUT IT.

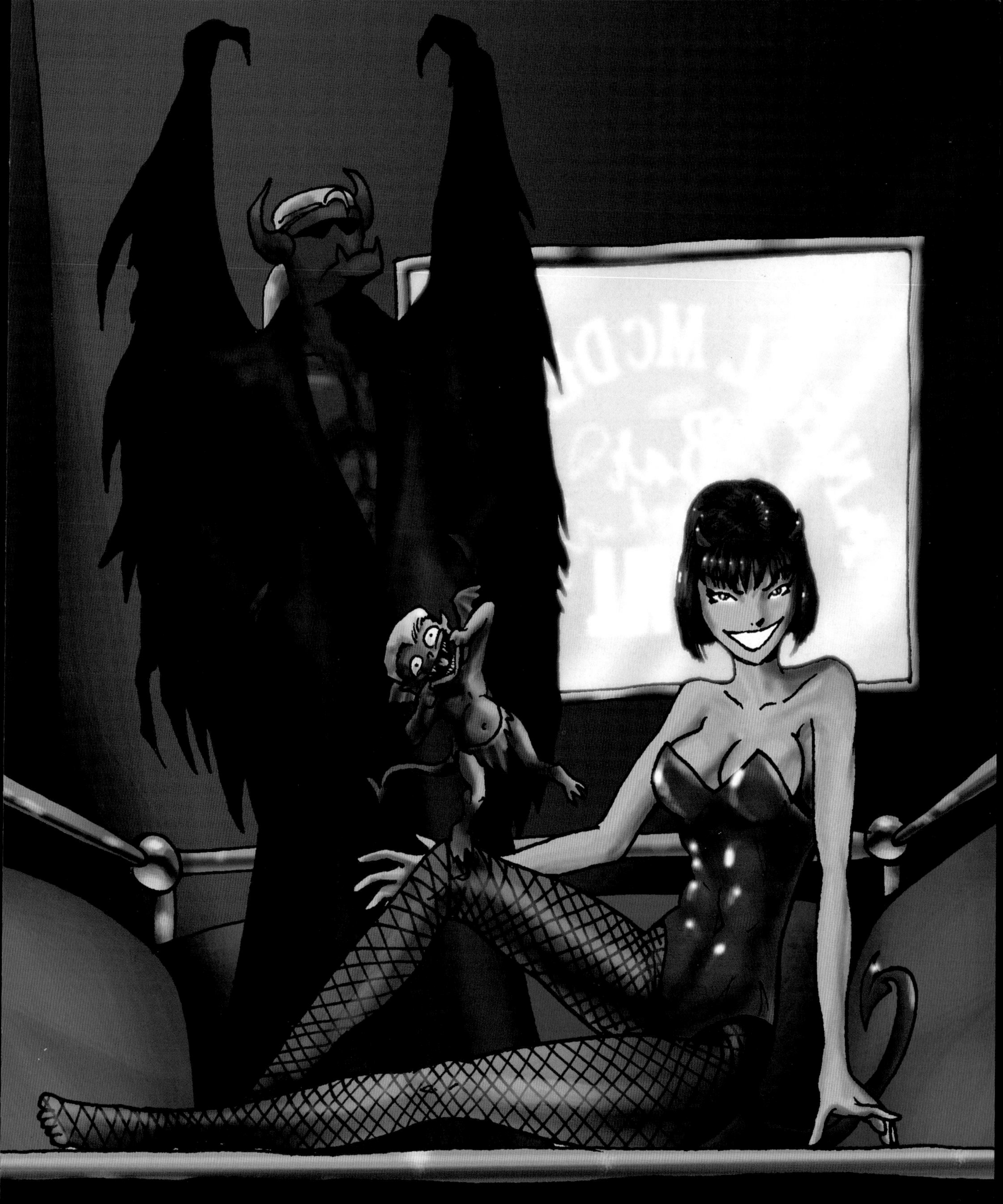

IT'S ALL GONE WRONG, AND SQUISHYDODO IS TO BLAME. I WAS WRONG TO EVER TRUST HIM. AND NOW HE CONTROLS ENOUGH **RSR GAS** TO DESTROY US ALL. BUT THERE IS ANOTHER WHO CAN SAVE THE DAY.

SQUINTYHOYO! NO!

"IT ALL STARTED WITH THE DISTRESS CALL".

MRS. CLAUS?

SQUISHYDODO? PLEASE HELP ME! IT'S **SANTA!** WE DON'T HAVE LONG! SEND A RESCUE TEAM TO **NORTHPOLECENTRAL** BEFORE IT'S TOO...

SIGNAL TERMINATED

YEAEE-EAAAH!

MRS. CLAUS!

SLAPPYHOHO! PUT ME THROUGH TO SANTA'S WORKSHOP!

CAN'T GET THROUGH! IT'S LIKE **NORTHPOLECENTRAL** HAS GONE... DEAD!

PREPARE THE CHOPPERS! SQUINTYHOYO? PREPARE THE REVERB, I'M ABOUT TO MAKE A STATEMENT OF POWER!

ATTENTION, **BLACK OP ELVES!** WE HAVE A PLEA FOR HELP ON A DANGEROUS MISSION. AND THOUGH **NONE OF US MAY SURVIVE** WE MUST TRY TO RESCUE CHRISTMAS AND ATTEMPT... *THE RESCUE MISSION TO THE NORTH POLE!*

MIXER

YOU WERE SUPPOSED TO REVERB THE "RESCUE MISSION TO THE NORTH POLE" PART.

SORRY, **MY BAD.**

BEFORE WE REACH THE NORTH POLE, I WANT ALL BLUE TEAM ELVES TO REVIEW THIS TIMELINE I'VE CODENAMED **"OPERATION RECAP"**

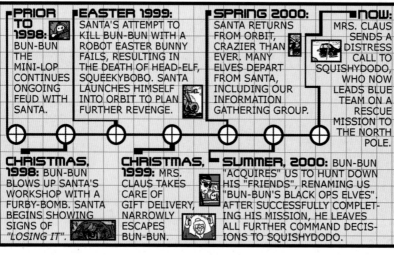

PRIOR TO 1998: BUN-BUN THE MINI-LOP CONTINUES ONGOING FEUD WITH SANTA.

EASTER 1999: SANTA'S ATTEMPT TO KILL BUN-BUN WITH A ROBOT EASTER BUNNY FAILS, RESULTING IN THE DEATH OF HEAD-ELF, SQUEEKYBOBO. SANTA LAUNCHES HIMSELF INTO ORBIT TO PLAN FURTHER REVENGE.

SPRING 2000: SANTA RETURNS FROM ORBIT, CRAZIER THAN EVER. MANY ELVES DEPART FROM SANTA, INCLUDING OUR INFORMATION GATHERING GROUP.

NOW: MRS. CLAUS SENDS A DISTRESS CALL TO SQUISHYDODO, WHO NOW LEADS BLUE TEAM ON A RESCUE MISSION TO THE NORTH POLE.

CHRISTMAS, 1998: BUN-BUN BLOWS UP SANTA'S WORKSHOP WITH A FURBY-BOMB. SANTA BEGINS SHOWING SIGNS OF *"LOSING IT".*

CHRISTMAS, 1999: MRS. CLAUS TAKES CARE OF GIFT DELIVERY, NARROWLY ESCAPES BUN-BUN.

SUMMER, 2000: BUN-BUN "ACQUIRES" US TO HUNT DOWN HIS "FRIENDS", RENAMING US "BUN-BUN'S BLACK OPS ELVES". AFTER SUCCESSFULLY COMPLETING HIS MISSION, HE LEAVES ALL FURTHER COMMAND DECISIONS TO SQUISHYDODO.

ANY QUESTIONS?

SQUISHYDODO, **SIR!** WHAT ARE OUR MISSION PARAMETERS? ARE WE TO RESCUE JUST MRS. CLAUS? SANTA? OTHER ELVES? WHAT OPPOSITION ARE WE EXPECTING?

GOOD QUESTION, SQUINTYHOYO! I REFER EVERYONE TO THE POST-IT NOTE I'VE CODENAMED **"OPERATION I-DUNNO"**

EVERYBODY LISTEN UP. OUR SITUATION HAS CHANGED. A NASTY BLIZZARD IS HEADING OUR WAY. THE WINDS ARE ALREADY TOO STRONG FOR THE CHOPPERS TO LAND.

WE'RE GOING TO HAVE TO MAKE A DROP, AT WHICH POINT THE CHOPPERS WILL HAVE TO TURN BACK. DUE TO THE WHITEOUT CONDITIONS, WE'LL BE OUT OF CONTACT AND UNABLE TO BE EXTRACTED FOR 24 TO 48 HOURS.

OUR PRECISION PILOTS WILL FIGHT AGAINST THE WINDS TO HOLD POSITION AT EXACTLY 35 FEET OFF THE GROUND, WHERE WE WILL DO A RAPPELLING DIVE USING EXACTLY 34 FEET OF ROPE. WE HAVE NO MARGIN OF ERROR HERE.

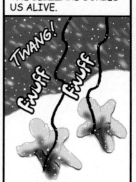

WE MUST HIT THE GROUND RUNNING, AND REACH SANTA'S WORKSHOP ON FOOT BEFORE THE BLIZZARD BURIES US ALIVE.

TWANG!
FWUFF
FWUFF

ANY QUESTIONS?

WHO SWITCHED OUR ROPE FOR BUNGEE CORD?

I THOUGHT BUNGEE'D BE FUNNER.

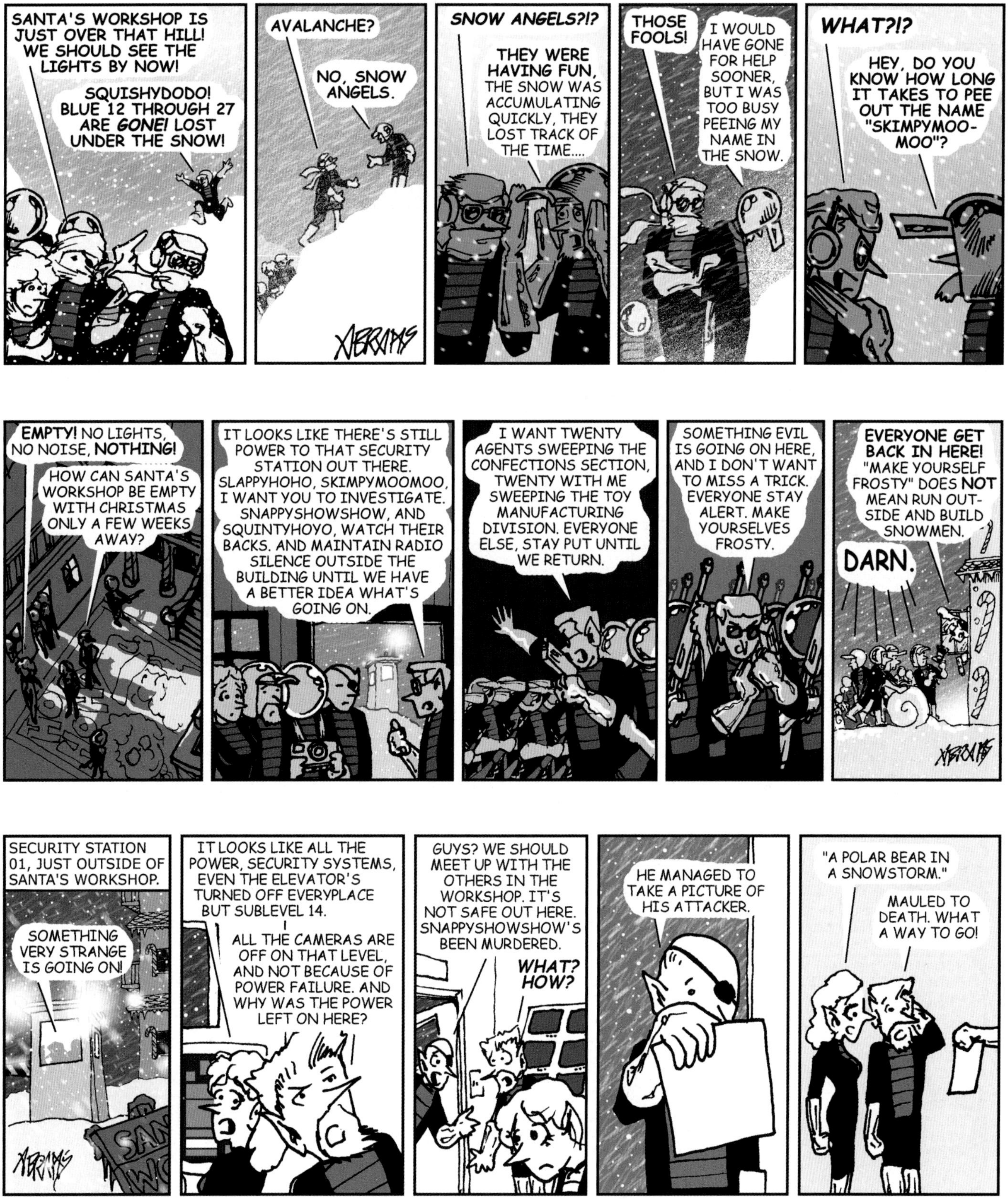
SANTA'S WORKSHOP IS JUST OVER THAT HILL! WE SHOULD SEE THE LIGHTS BY NOW!
SQUISHYDODO! BLUE 12 THROUGH 27 ARE GONE! LOST UNDER THE SNOW!
AVALANCHE?
NO, SNOW ANGELS.
SNOW ANGELS?!?
THEY WERE HAVING FUN, THE SNOW WAS ACCUMULATING QUICKLY, THEY LOST TRACK OF THE TIME....
THOSE FOOLS!
I WOULD HAVE GONE FOR HELP SOONER, BUT I WAS TOO BUSY PEEING MY NAME IN THE SNOW.
WHAT?!?
HEY, DO YOU KNOW HOW LONG IT TAKES TO PEE OUT THE NAME "SKIMPYMOO-MOO"?
EMPTY! NO LIGHTS, NO NOISE, NOTHING!
HOW CAN SANTA'S WORKSHOP BE EMPTY WITH CHRISTMAS ONLY A FEW WEEKS AWAY?
IT LOOKS LIKE THERE'S STILL POWER TO THAT SECURITY STATION OUT THERE. SLAPPYHOHO, SKIMPYMOOMOO, I WANT YOU TO INVESTIGATE. SNAPPYSHOWSHOW, AND SQUINTYHOYO, WATCH THEIR BACKS. AND MAINTAIN RADIO SILENCE OUTSIDE THE BUILDING UNTIL WE HAVE A BETTER IDEA WHAT'S GOING ON.
I WANT TWENTY AGENTS SWEEPING THE CONFECTIONS SECTION, TWENTY WITH ME SWEEPING THE TOY MANUFACTURING DIVISION. EVERYONE ELSE, STAY PUT UNTIL WE RETURN.
SOMETHING EVIL IS GOING ON HERE, AND I DON'T WANT TO MISS A TRICK. EVERYONE STAY ALERT. MAKE YOURSELVES FROSTY.
EVERYONE GET BACK IN HERE! "MAKE YOURSELF FROSTY" DOES NOT MEAN RUN OUT-SIDE AND BUILD SNOWMEN.
DARN.
SECURITY STATION 01, JUST OUTSIDE OF SANTA'S WORKSHOP.
SOMETHING VERY STRANGE IS GOING ON!
IT LOOKS LIKE ALL THE POWER, SECURITY SYSTEMS, EVEN THE ELEVATOR'S TURNED OFF EVERYPLACE BUT SUBLEVEL 14.
ALL THE CAMERAS ARE OFF ON THAT LEVEL, AND NOT BECAUSE OF POWER FAILURE. AND WHY WAS THE POWER LEFT ON HERE?
GUYS? WE SHOULD MEET UP WITH THE OTHERS IN THE WORKSHOP. IT'S NOT SAFE OUT HERE. SNAPPYSHOWSHOW'S BEEN MURDERED.
WHAT? HOW?
HE MANAGED TO TAKE A PICTURE OF HIS ATTACKER.
"A POLAR BEAR IN A SNOWSTORM."
MAULED TO DEATH. WHAT A WAY TO GO!

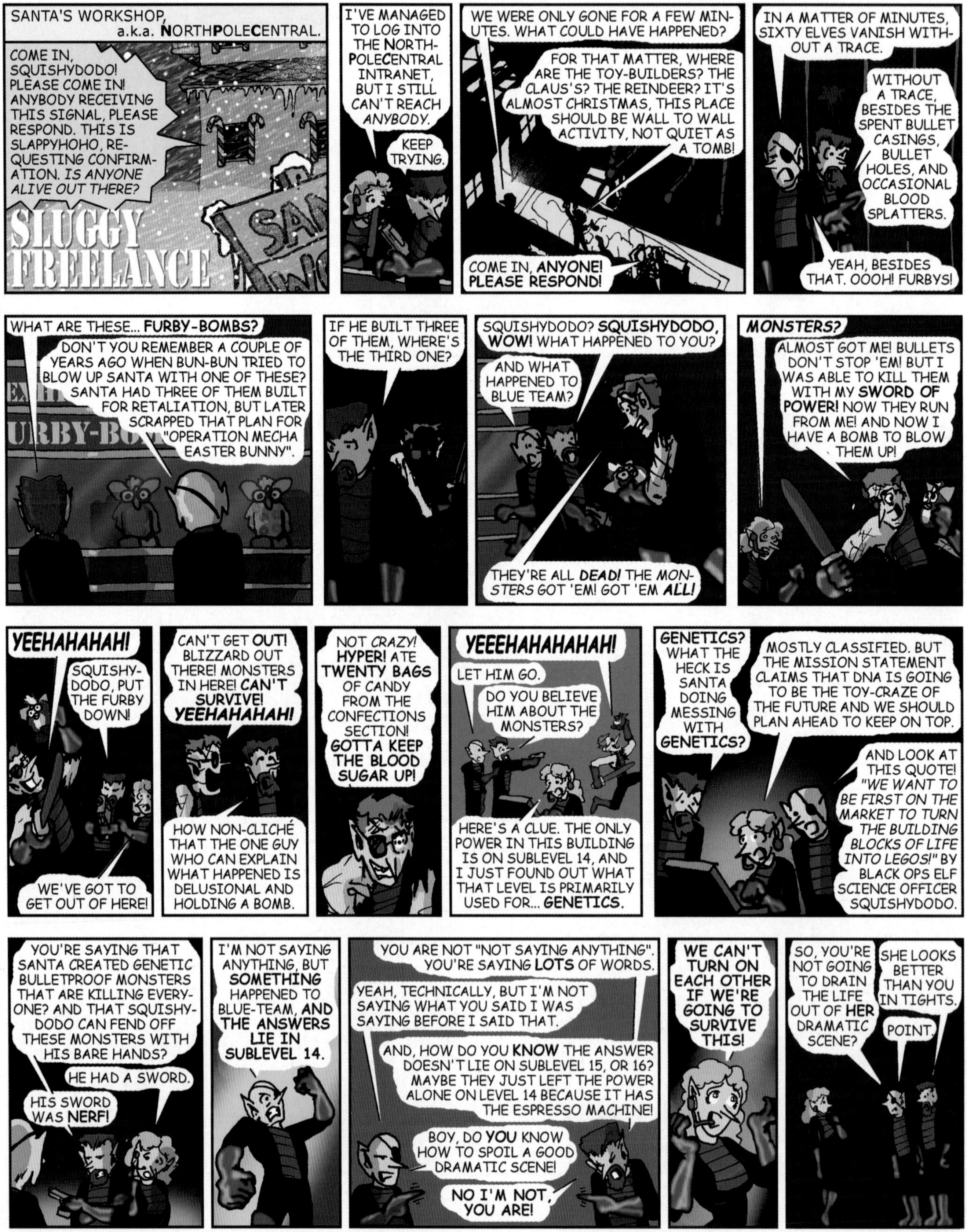
SANTA'S WORKSHOP, a.k.a. NORTHPOLECENTRAL.
COME IN, SQUISHYDODO! PLEASE COME IN! ANYBODY RECEIVING THIS SIGNAL, PLEASE RESPOND. THIS IS SLAPPYHOHO, REQUESTING CONFIRMATION. IS ANYONE ALIVE OUT THERE?
SLUGGY FREELANCE
I'VE MANAGED TO LOG INTO THE NORTHPOLECENTRAL INTRANET, BUT I STILL CAN'T REACH ANYBODY.
KEEP TRYING.
WE WERE ONLY GONE FOR A FEW MINUTES. WHAT COULD HAVE HAPPENED?
FOR THAT MATTER, WHERE ARE THE TOY-BUILDERS? THE CLAUS'S? THE REINDEER? IT'S ALMOST CHRISTMAS, THIS PLACE SHOULD BE WALL TO WALL ACTIVITY, NOT QUIET AS A TOMB!
COME IN, ANYONE! PLEASE RESPOND!
IN A MATTER OF MINUTES, SIXTY ELVES VANISH WITHOUT A TRACE.
WITHOUT A TRACE, BESIDES THE SPENT BULLET CASINGS, BULLET HOLES, AND OCCASIONAL BLOOD SPLATTERS.
YEAH, BESIDES THAT. OOOH! FURBYS!
WHAT ARE THESE... FURBY-BOMBS?
DON'T YOU REMEMBER A COUPLE OF YEARS AGO WHEN BUN-BUN TRIED TO BLOW UP SANTA WITH ONE OF THESE? SANTA HAD THREE OF THEM BUILT FOR RETALIATION, BUT LATER SCRAPPED THAT PLAN FOR "OPERATION MECHA EASTER BUNNY".
IF HE BUILT THREE OF THEM, WHERE'S THE THIRD ONE?
SQUISHYDODO? SQUISHYDODO, WOW! WHAT HAPPENED TO YOU?
AND WHAT HAPPENED TO BLUE TEAM?
THEY'RE ALL DEAD! THE MONSTERS GOT 'EM! GOT 'EM ALL!
MONSTERS?
ALMOST GOT ME! BULLETS DON'T STOP 'EM! BUT I WAS ABLE TO KILL THEM WITH MY SWORD OF POWER! NOW THEY RUN FROM ME! AND NOW I HAVE A BOMB TO BLOW THEM UP!
YEEHAHAHAH!
SQUISHYDODO, PUT THE FURBY DOWN!
WE'VE GOT TO GET OUT OF HERE!
CAN'T GET OUT! BLIZZARD OUT THERE! MONSTERS IN HERE! CAN'T SURVIVE! YEEHAHAHAH!
HOW NON-CLICHÉ THAT THE ONE GUY WHO CAN EXPLAIN WHAT HAPPENED IS DELUSIONAL AND HOLDING A BOMB.
NOT CRAZY! HYPER! ATE TWENTY BAGS OF CANDY FROM THE CONFECTIONS SECTION! GOTTA KEEP THE BLOOD SUGAR UP!
YEEEHAHAHAHAH!
LET HIM GO.
DO YOU BELIEVE HIM ABOUT THE MONSTERS?
HERE'S A CLUE. THE ONLY POWER IN THIS BUILDING IS ON SUBLEVEL 14, AND I JUST FOUND OUT WHAT THAT LEVEL IS PRIMARILY USED FOR... GENETICS.
GENETICS? WHAT THE HECK IS SANTA DOING MESSING WITH GENETICS?
MOSTLY CLASSIFIED. BUT THE MISSION STATEMENT CLAIMS THAT DNA IS GOING TO BE THE TOY-CRAZE OF THE FUTURE AND WE SHOULD PLAN AHEAD TO KEEP ON TOP.
AND LOOK AT THIS QUOTE! "WE WANT TO BE FIRST ON THE MARKET TO TURN THE BUILDING BLOCKS OF LIFE INTO LEGOS!" BY BLACK OPS ELF SCIENCE OFFICER SQUISHYDODO.
YOU'RE SAYING THAT SANTA CREATED GENETIC BULLETPROOF MONSTERS THAT ARE KILLING EVERYONE? AND THAT SQUISHYDODO CAN FEND OFF THESE MONSTERS WITH HIS BARE HANDS?
HE HAD A SWORD.
HIS SWORD WAS NERF!
I'M NOT SAYING ANYTHING, BUT SOMETHING HAPPENED TO BLUE-TEAM, AND THE ANSWERS LIE IN SUBLEVEL 14.
YOU ARE NOT "NOT SAYING ANYTHING". YOU'RE SAYING LOTS OF WORDS.
YEAH, TECHNICALLY, BUT I'M NOT SAYING WHAT YOU SAID I WAS SAYING BEFORE I SAID THAT.
AND, HOW DO YOU KNOW THE ANSWER DOESN'T LIE ON SUBLEVEL 15, OR 16? MAYBE THEY JUST LEFT THE POWER ALONE ON LEVEL 14 BECAUSE IT HAS THE ESPRESSO MACHINE!
BOY, DO YOU KNOW HOW TO SPOIL A GOOD DRAMATIC SCENE!
NO I'M NOT, YOU ARE!
WE CAN'T TURN ON EACH OTHER IF WE'RE GOING TO SURVIVE THIS!
SO, YOU'RE NOT GOING TO DRAIN THE LIFE OUT OF HER DRAMATIC SCENE?
SHE LOOKS BETTER THAN YOU IN TIGHTS.
POINT.

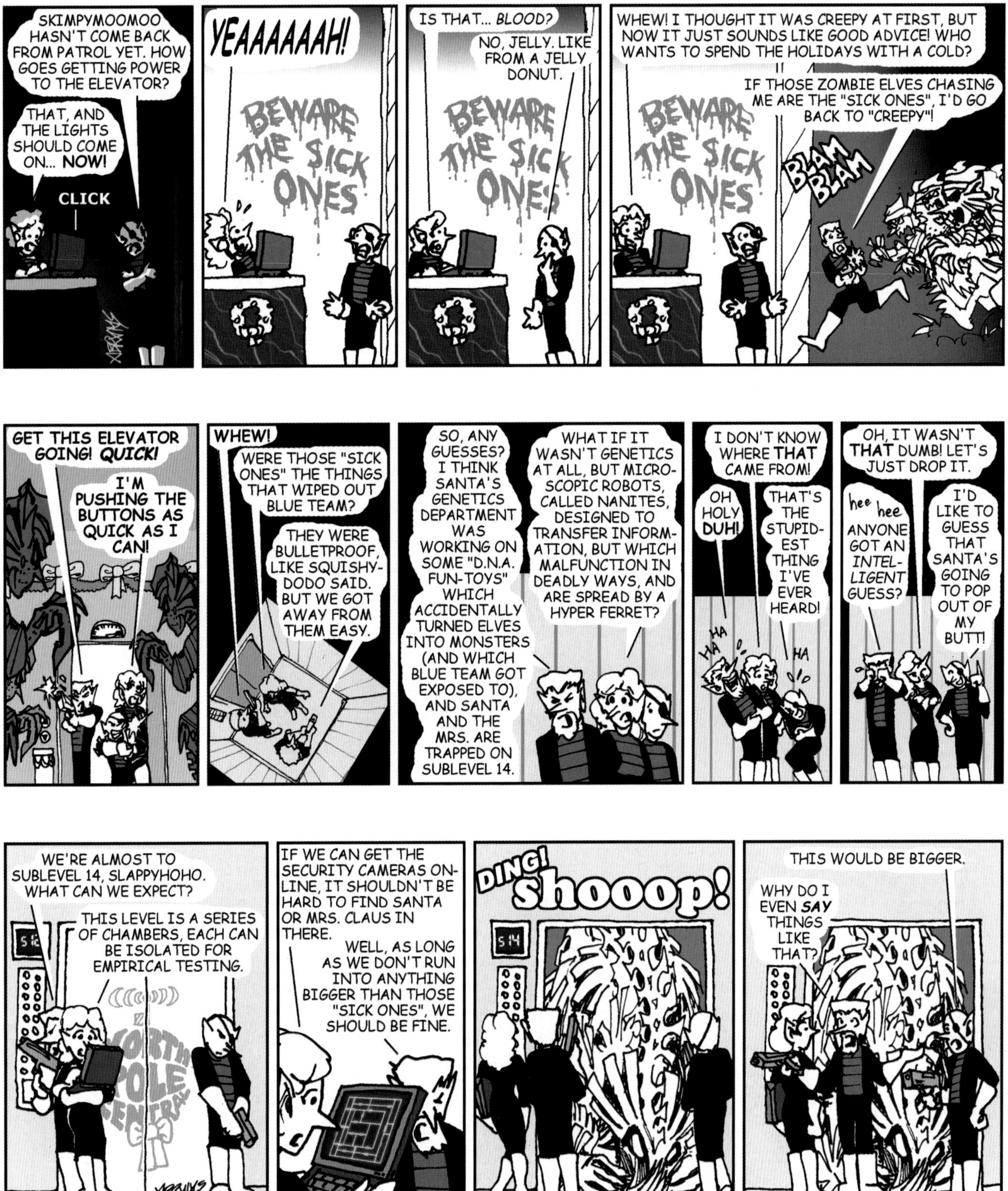
SKIMPYMOOMOO HASN'T COME BACK FROM PATROL YET. HOW GOES GETTING POWER TO THE ELEVATOR?
THAT, AND THE LIGHTS SHOULD COME ON... NOW!
CLICK
YEAAAAAAH!
BEWARE THE SICK ONES
IS THAT... BLOOD?
NO, JELLY. LIKE FROM A JELLY DONUT.
BEWARE THE SICK ONES
WHEW! I THOUGHT IT WAS CREEPY AT FIRST, BUT NOW IT JUST SOUNDS LIKE GOOD ADVICE! WHO WANTS TO SPEND THE HOLIDAYS WITH A COLD?
IF THOSE ZOMBIE ELVES CHASING ME ARE THE "SICK ONES", I'D GO BACK TO "CREEPY"!
BEWARE THE SICK ONES
BLAM BLAM
GET THIS ELEVATOR GOING! QUICK!
I'M PUSHING THE BUTTONS AS QUICK AS I CAN!
WHEW!
WERE THOSE "SICK ONES" THE THINGS THAT WIPED OUT BLUE TEAM?
THEY WERE BULLETPROOF, LIKE SQUISHYDODO SAID. BUT WE GOT AWAY FROM THEM EASY.
SO, ANY GUESSES? I THINK SANTA'S GENETICS DEPARTMENT WAS WORKING ON SOME "D.N.A. FUN-TOYS" WHICH ACCIDENTALLY TURNED ELVES INTO MONSTERS (AND WHICH BLUE TEAM GOT EXPOSED TO), AND SANTA AND THE MRS. ARE TRAPPED ON SUBLEVEL 14.
WHAT IF IT WASN'T GENETICS AT ALL, BUT MICROSCOPIC ROBOTS, CALLED NANITES, DESIGNED TO TRANSFER INFORMATION, BUT WHICH MALFUNCTION IN DEADLY WAYS, AND ARE SPREAD BY A HYPER FERRET?
I DON'T KNOW WHERE THAT CAME FROM!
OH HOLY DUH!
THAT'S THE STUPIDEST THING I'VE EVER HEARD!
HA HA
HA
OH, IT WASN'T THAT DUMB! LET'S JUST DROP IT.
hee hee ANYONE GOT AN INTELLIGENT GUESS?
I'D LIKE TO GUESS THAT SANTA'S GOING TO POP OUT OF MY BUTT!
WE'RE ALMOST TO SUBLEVEL 14, SLAPPYHOHO. WHAT CAN WE EXPECT?
THIS LEVEL IS A SERIES OF CHAMBERS, EACH CAN BE ISOLATED FOR EMPIRICAL TESTING.
NORTH POLE CENTRAL
IF WE CAN GET THE SECURITY CAMERAS ONLINE, IT SHOULDN'T BE HARD TO FIND SANTA OR MRS. CLAUS IN THERE.
WELL, AS LONG AS WE DON'T RUN INTO ANYTHING BIGGER THAN THOSE "SICK ONES", WE SHOULD BE FINE.
DING!
shooop!
S14
THIS WOULD BE BIGGER.
WHY DO I EVEN SAY THINGS LIKE THAT?

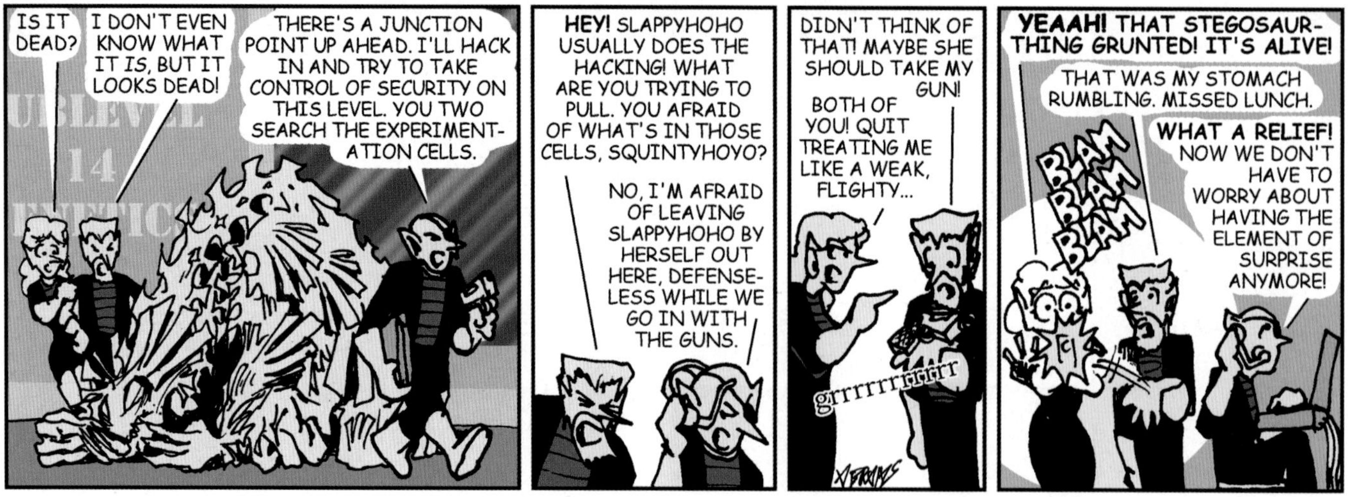
IS IT DEAD?
I DON'T EVEN KNOW WHAT IT *IS*, BUT IT LOOKS DEAD!
THERE'S A JUNCTION POINT UP AHEAD. I'LL HACK IN AND TRY TO TAKE CONTROL OF SECURITY ON THIS LEVEL. YOU TWO SEARCH THE EXPERIMENT-ATION CELLS.
HEY! SLAPPYHOHO USUALLY DOES THE HACKING! WHAT ARE YOU TRYING TO PULL. YOU AFRAID OF WHAT'S IN THOSE CELLS, SQUINTYHOYO?
NO, I'M AFRAID OF LEAVING SLAPPYHOHO BY HERSELF OUT HERE, DEFENSE-LESS WHILE WE GO IN WITH THE GUNS.
DIDN'T THINK OF THAT! MAYBE SHE SHOULD TAKE MY GUN!
BOTH OF YOU! QUIT TREATING ME LIKE A WEAK, FLIGHTY...
grrrrrrrrrrr
YEAAH! THAT STEGOSAUR-THING GRUNTED! IT'S ALIVE!
THAT WAS MY STOMACH RUMBLING. MISSED LUNCH.
BLAM BLAM BLAM
WHAT A RELIEF! NOW WE DON'T HAVE TO WORRY ABOUT HAVING THE ELEMENT OF SURPRISE ANYMORE!

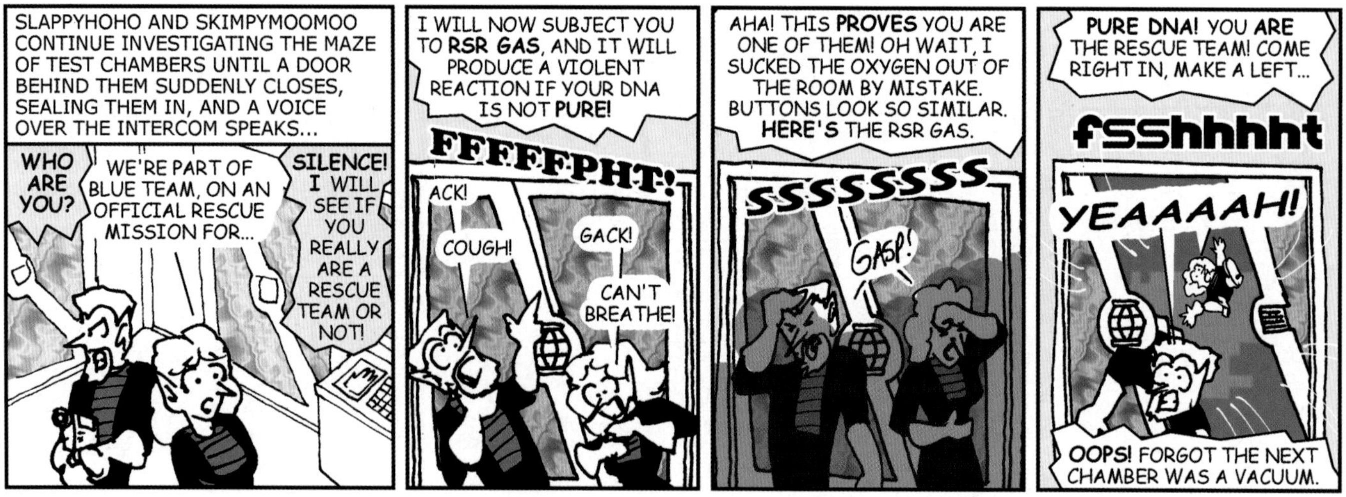
SLAPPYHOHO AND SKIMPYMOOMOO CONTINUE INVESTIGATING THE MAZE OF TEST CHAMBERS UNTIL A DOOR BEHIND THEM SUDDENLY CLOSES, SEALING THEM IN, AND A VOICE OVER THE INTERCOM SPEAKS...
WHO ARE YOU?
WE'RE PART OF BLUE TEAM, ON AN OFFICIAL RESCUE MISSION FOR...
SILENCE! I WILL SEE IF YOU REALLY ARE A RESCUE TEAM OR NOT!
I WILL NOW SUBJECT YOU TO **RSR GAS**, AND IT WILL PRODUCE A VIOLENT REACTION IF YOUR DNA IS NOT **PURE!**
FFFFFPHT!
ACK!
COUGH!
GACK!
CAN'T BREATHE!
AHA! THIS **PROVES** YOU ARE ONE OF THEM! OH WAIT, I SUCKED THE OXYGEN OUT OF THE ROOM BY MISTAKE. BUTTONS LOOK SO SIMILAR. **HERE'S** THE RSR GAS.
SSSSSSSS
GASP!
PURE DNA! YOU **ARE** THE RESCUE TEAM! COME RIGHT IN, MAKE A LEFT...
fsshhhht
YEAAAAH!
OOPS! FORGOT THE NEXT CHAMBER WAS A VACUUM.

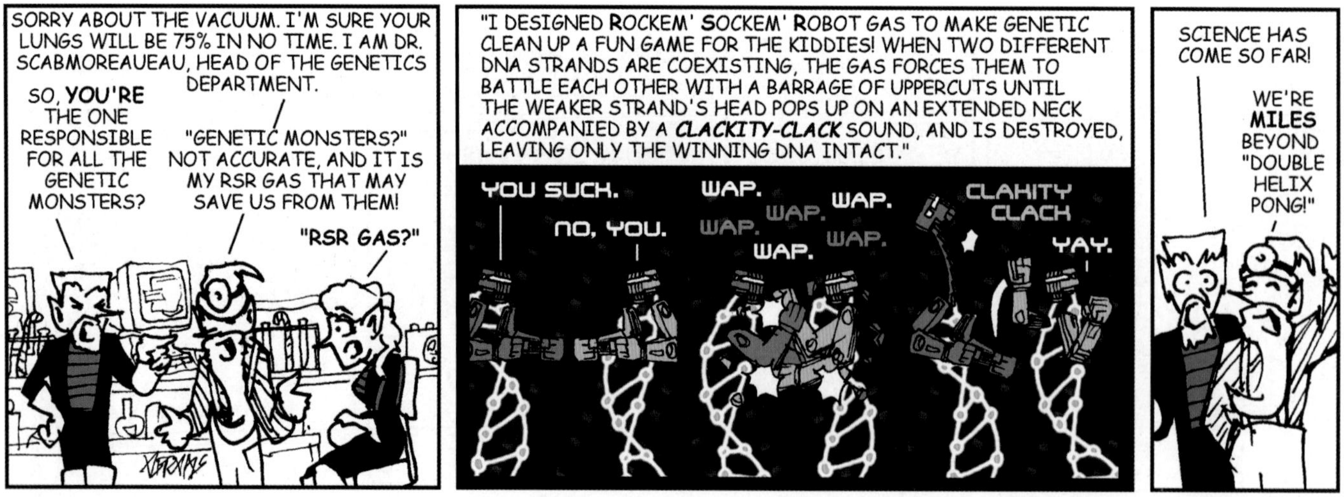
SORRY ABOUT THE VACUUM. I'M SURE YOUR LUNGS WILL BE 75% IN NO TIME. I AM DR. SCABMOREAUEAU, HEAD OF THE GENETICS DEPARTMENT.
SO, **YOU'RE** THE ONE RESPONSIBLE FOR ALL THE GENETIC MONSTERS?
"GENETIC MONSTERS?" NOT ACCURATE, AND IT IS MY RSR GAS THAT MAY SAVE US FROM THEM!
"RSR GAS?"
"I DESIGNED **R**OCKEM' **S**OCKEM' **R**OBOT GAS TO MAKE GENETIC CLEAN UP A FUN GAME FOR THE KIDDIES! WHEN TWO DIFFERENT DNA STRANDS ARE COEXISTING, THE GAS FORCES THEM TO BATTLE EACH OTHER WITH A BARRAGE OF UPPERCUTS UNTIL THE WEAKER STRAND'S HEAD POPS UP ON AN EXTENDED NECK ACCOMPANIED BY A ***CLACKITY-CLACK*** SOUND, AND IS DESTROYED, LEAVING ONLY THE WINNING DNA INTACT."
YOU SUCK.
NO, YOU.
WAP. WAP. WAP. WAP. WAP. WAP.
CLAKITY CLACK
YAY.
SCIENCE HAS COME SO FAR!
WE'RE **MILES** BEYOND "DOUBLE HELIX PONG!"

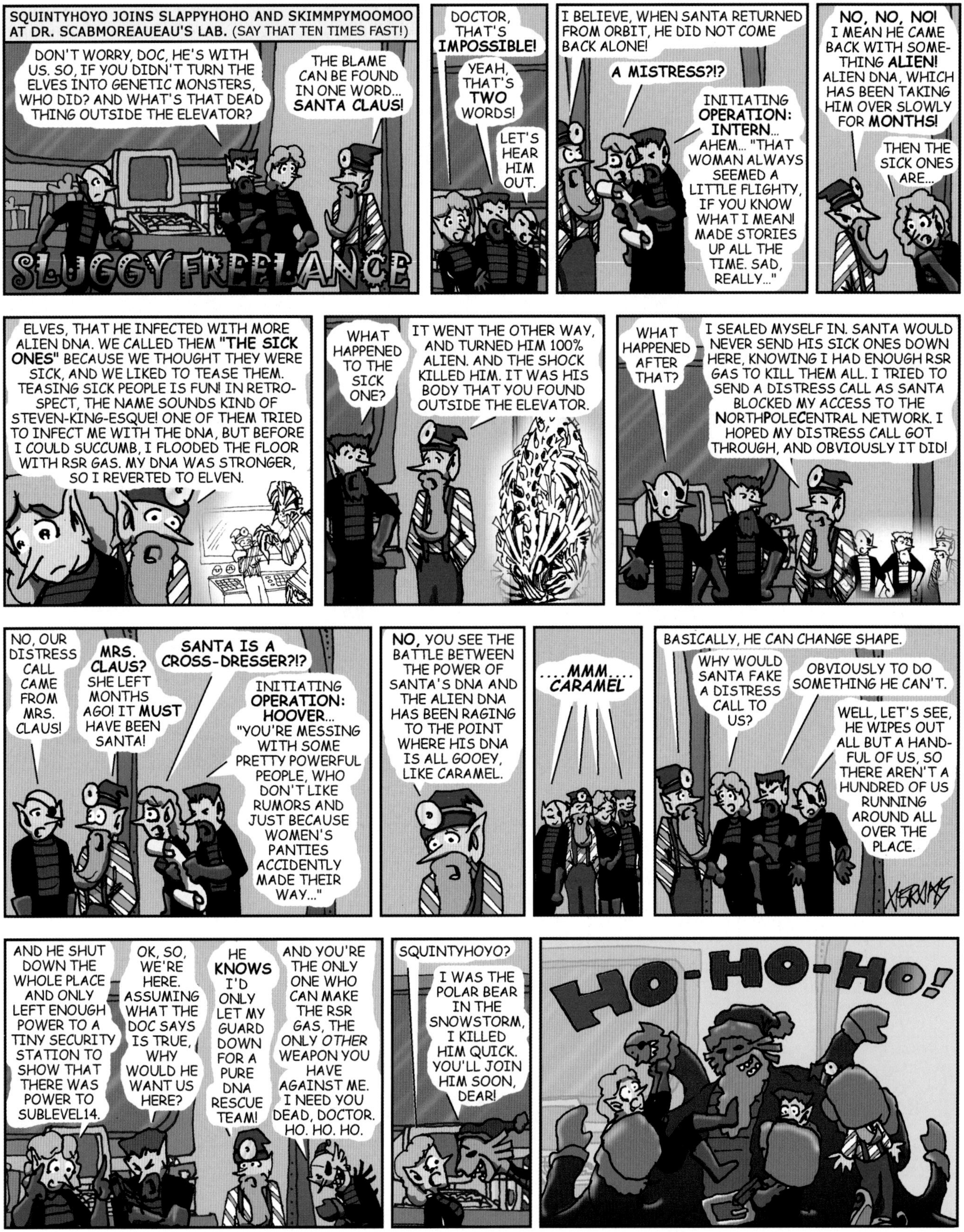
SQUINTYHOYO JOINS SLAPPYHOHO AND SKIMMPYMOOMOO AT DR. SCABMOREAUEAU'S LAB. (SAY THAT TEN TIMES FAST!)
DON'T WORRY, DOC, HE'S WITH US. SO, IF YOU DIDN'T TURN THE ELVES INTO GENETIC MONSTERS, WHO DID? AND WHAT'S THAT DEAD THING OUTSIDE THE ELEVATOR?
THE BLAME CAN BE FOUND IN ONE WORD... SANTA CLAUS!
SLUGGY FREELANCE
DOCTOR, THAT'S IMPOSSIBLE!
YEAH, THAT'S TWO WORDS!
LET'S HEAR HIM OUT.
I BELIEVE, WHEN SANTA RETURNED FROM ORBIT, HE DID NOT COME BACK ALONE!
A MISTRESS?!?
INITIATING OPERATION: INTERN... AHEM... "THAT WOMAN ALWAYS SEEMED A LITTLE FLIGHTY, IF YOU KNOW WHAT I MEAN! MADE STORIES UP ALL THE TIME. SAD, REALLY..."
NO, NO, NO! I MEAN HE CAME BACK WITH SOME-THING ALIEN! ALIEN DNA, WHICH HAS BEEN TAKING HIM OVER SLOWLY FOR MONTHS!
THEN THE SICK ONES ARE...
ELVES, THAT HE INFECTED WITH MORE ALIEN DNA. WE CALLED THEM "THE SICK ONES" BECAUSE WE THOUGHT THEY WERE SICK, AND WE LIKED TO TEASE THEM. TEASING SICK PEOPLE IS FUN! IN RETRO-SPECT, THE NAME SOUNDS KIND OF STEVEN-KING-ESQUE! ONE OF THEM TRIED TO INFECT ME WITH THE DNA, BUT BEFORE I COULD SUCCUMB, I FLOODED THE FLOOR WITH RSR GAS. MY DNA WAS STRONGER, SO I REVERTED TO ELVEN.
WHAT HAPPENED TO THE SICK ONE?
IT WENT THE OTHER WAY, AND TURNED HIM 100% ALIEN. AND THE SHOCK KILLED HIM. IT WAS HIS BODY THAT YOU FOUND OUTSIDE THE ELEVATOR.
WHAT HAPPENED AFTER THAT?
I SEALED MYSELF IN. SANTA WOULD NEVER SEND HIS SICK ONES DOWN HERE, KNOWING I HAD ENOUGH RSR GAS TO KILL THEM ALL. I TRIED TO SEND A DISTRESS CALL AS SANTA BLOCKED MY ACCESS TO THE NORTHPOLECENTRAL NETWORK. I HOPED MY DISTRESS CALL GOT THROUGH, AND OBVIOUSLY IT DID!
NO, OUR DISTRESS CALL CAME FROM MRS. CLAUS!
MRS. CLAUS? SHE LEFT MONTHS AGO! IT MUST HAVE BEEN SANTA!
SANTA IS A CROSS-DRESSER?!?
INITIATING OPERATION: HOOVER... "YOU'RE MESSING WITH SOME PRETTY POWERFUL PEOPLE, WHO DON'T LIKE RUMORS AND JUST BECAUSE WOMEN'S PANTIES ACCIDENTLY MADE THEIR WAY..."
NO, YOU SEE THE BATTLE BETWEEN THE POWER OF SANTA'S DNA AND THE ALIEN DNA HAS BEEN RAGING TO THE POINT WHERE HIS DNA IS ALL GOOEY, LIKE CARAMEL.
....MMM.... CARAMEL
BASICALLY, HE CAN CHANGE SHAPE.
WHY WOULD SANTA FAKE A DISTRESS CALL TO US?
OBVIOUSLY TO DO SOMETHING HE CAN'T.
WELL, LET'S SEE, HE WIPES OUT ALL BUT A HAND-FUL OF US, SO THERE AREN'T A HUNDRED OF US RUNNING AROUND ALL OVER THE PLACE.
AND HE SHUT DOWN THE WHOLE PLACE AND ONLY LEFT ENOUGH POWER TO A TINY SECURITY STATION TO SHOW THAT THERE WAS POWER TO SUBLEVEL14.
OK, SO, WE'RE HERE. ASSUMING WHAT THE DOC SAYS IS TRUE, WHY WOULD HE WANT US HERE?
HE KNOWS I'D ONLY LET MY GUARD DOWN FOR A PURE DNA RESCUE TEAM!
AND YOU'RE THE ONLY ONE WHO CAN MAKE THE RSR GAS, THE ONLY OTHER WEAPON YOU HAVE AGAINST ME. I NEED YOU DEAD, DOCTOR. HO. HO. HO.
SQUINTYHOYO?
I WAS THE POLAR BEAR IN THE SNOWSTORM, I KILLED HIM QUICK. YOU'LL JOIN HIM SOON, DEAR!
HO-HO-HO!

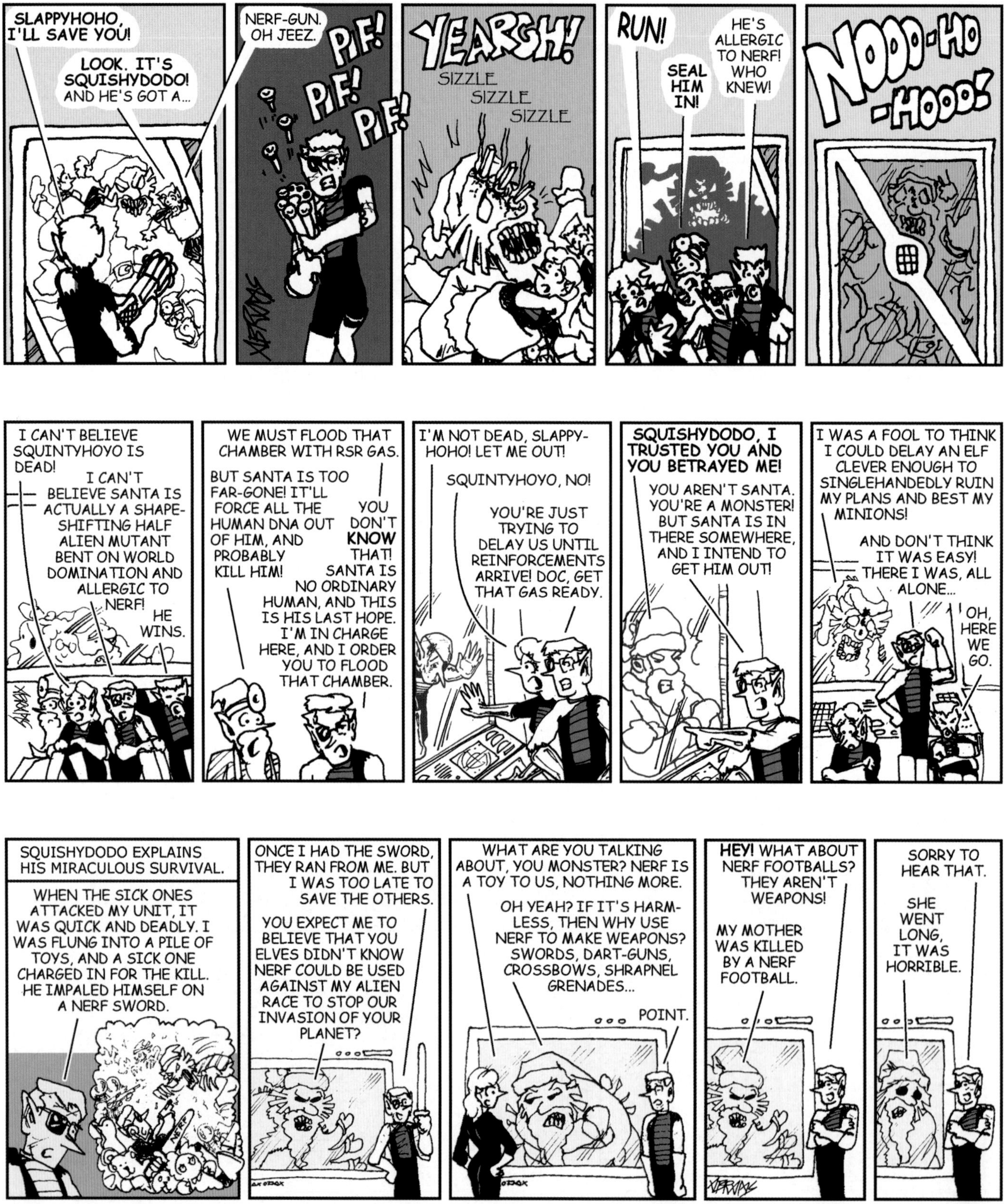

SLAPPYHOHO, I'LL SAVE YOU!
LOOK. IT'S SQUISHYDODO! AND HE'S GOT A...
NERF-GUN. OH JEEZ.
PIF! PIF! PIF!
YEARGH!
SIZZLE SIZZLE SIZZLE
RUN!
SEAL HIM IN!
HE'S ALLERGIC TO NERF! WHO KNEW!
NOOO-HO-HOOO!
I CAN'T BELIEVE SQUINTYHOYO IS DEAD!
I CAN'T BELIEVE SANTA IS ACTUALLY A SHAPE-SHIFTING HALF ALIEN MUTANT BENT ON WORLD DOMINATION AND ALLERGIC TO NERF!
HE WINS.
WE MUST FLOOD THAT CHAMBER WITH RSR GAS.
BUT SANTA IS TOO FAR-GONE! IT'LL FORCE ALL THE HUMAN DNA OUT OF HIM, AND PROBABLY KILL HIM!
YOU DON'T KNOW THAT! SANTA IS NO ORDINARY HUMAN, AND THIS IS HIS LAST HOPE. I'M IN CHARGE HERE, AND I ORDER YOU TO FLOOD THAT CHAMBER.
I'M NOT DEAD, SLAPPY-HOHO! LET ME OUT!
SQUINTYHOYO, NO!
YOU'RE JUST TRYING TO DELAY US UNTIL REINFORCEMENTS ARRIVE! DOC, GET THAT GAS READY.
SQUISHYDODO, I TRUSTED YOU AND YOU BETRAYED ME!
YOU AREN'T SANTA. YOU'RE A MONSTER! BUT SANTA IS IN THERE SOMEWHERE, AND I INTEND TO GET HIM OUT!
I WAS A FOOL TO THINK I COULD DELAY AN ELF CLEVER ENOUGH TO SINGLEHANDEDLY RUIN MY PLANS AND BEST MY MINIONS!
AND DON'T THINK IT WAS EASY! THERE I WAS, ALL ALONE...
OH, HERE WE GO.
SQUISHYDODO EXPLAINS HIS MIRACULOUS SURVIVAL.
WHEN THE SICK ONES ATTACKED MY UNIT, IT WAS QUICK AND DEADLY. I WAS FLUNG INTO A PILE OF TOYS, AND A SICK ONE CHARGED IN FOR THE KILL. HE IMPALED HIMSELF ON A NERF SWORD.
ONCE I HAD THE SWORD, THEY RAN FROM ME. BUT I WAS TOO LATE TO SAVE THE OTHERS.
YOU EXPECT ME TO BELIEVE THAT YOU ELVES DIDN'T KNOW NERF COULD BE USED AGAINST MY ALIEN RACE TO STOP OUR INVASION OF YOUR PLANET?
WHAT ARE YOU TALKING ABOUT, YOU MONSTER? NERF IS A TOY TO US, NOTHING MORE.
OH YEAH? IF IT'S HARMLESS, THEN WHY USE NERF TO MAKE WEAPONS? SWORDS, DART-GUNS, CROSSBOWS, SHRAPNEL GRENADES...
POINT.
HEY! WHAT ABOUT NERF FOOTBALLS? THEY AREN'T WEAPONS!
MY MOTHER WAS KILLED BY A NERF FOOTBALL.
SORRY TO HEAR THAT.
SHE WENT LONG, IT WAS HORRIBLE.

AFTER A LONG AND TIRESOME DEBATE...
WAIT A MINUTE. SO NOBODY KNOWS WE ARE HERE AND THAT WE ARE SUSCEPTIBLE TO NERF WEAPONRY EXCEPT YOU FOUR?
...YES!
AND SINCE YOU GUYS ARE THE ONLY ONES WHO KNOW OF THE RSR GAS, IF WE KILL YOU FOUR, THERE WILL BE NOTHING TO STOP MY COMMANDING OFFICER FROM ISSUING THE ORDER TO START THE INVASION!
...
YES! FINALLY HE GETS IT!
WE WENT AFTER SANTA CLAUS BECAUSE WE THOUGHT HE WAS YOUR CHIEF WEAPONS DISTRIBUTOR, EACH YEAR INDOCTRINATING A NEW GENERATION INTO NERF COMBAT TRAINING! BOY ARE OUR FACES RED!
HAHA!
...
BOY, FOR A SUPERIOR RACE, YOU SURE ARE SLOW!
WAIT A MINUTE! DID YOU SAY SOMETHING ABOUT A "COMMANDING OFFICER"?
SO THERE'S ANOTHER BOSS! DOC, I WANT YOU TO FLOOD THIS FLOOR WITH RSR ASAP. SKIMPY, LOAD THE NERF DART GUN. MUTATED RUDOLPH THE-RED-NOSED-REINDEER, I WANT YOU ON RECON...
ROAR
UH-OH!
RUDOLPH IS THE ALIEN COMMANDER? DOC! FLOOD THE FLOOR WITH RSR GAS NOW!
I CAN'T! THEY'VE DISABLED THE CONTROLS IN THIS CHAMBER!
WE'VE BEEN CONTROLLING THIS INSTALLATION THE WHOLE TIME, FOOLS! NOW OUR PLAN CAN MOVE FORWARD! AFTER WE KILL YOU, WE WILL EVACUATE ON SANTA'S SLEIGH! THEN WE WILL DETONATE THE ROOM OF EXPLOSIVES WE PUT ON SUBLEVEL 1, CAUSING THIS WHOLE BUILDING TO COLLAPSE, COVERING OUR TRAIL AND ENSURING ALL THE RSR GAS IS DESTROYED.
AND THEN WE CAN SIGNAL THE INVASION TO COMMENCE!
SINCE I WON'T BE ALIVE ON CHRISTMAS, I'LL HAVE TO GIVE YOU YOUR GIFT NOW!
A GIFT? FOR ME?
A FLATULENT FRANNY DOLL! WITH REAL METHANE!
AND WHAT HAPPENED THEN...? WELL...THE OPS-ELVES WILL SAY, THE COMMANDER'S ALIEN HEART MUTATED WITH CHRISTMAS DNA!
PHERT-T-T-T...
WAIT A MINUTE! THAT'S NOT METHANE! THAT'S...
"RSR GAS."
AND THIS ISN'T A REAL FLATULENT FRANNY DOLL!
IT'S A KNOCK-OFF FROM HONG KONG.
NOOO!! CURSE THE LIES OF CHRISTMAS!
YEARGH!
I WILL SAVE YOU, COMMANDER!
SANTA'S ABOUT TO SUCK ALL THE OXYGEN OUT OF OUR CHAMBER!
WHAT DO WE DO?
VENTILATE THAT GLASS AND EXPOSE HIM TO THE RSR GAS!
PIF! PIF! PIF!
WAP
WAP
WAP
BLAM BLAM BLAM
PERHAPS IN THIS CASE REAL GUNS MIGHT WORK BETTER.
SHOW-OFF.
YEARGH!

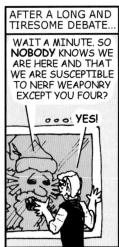

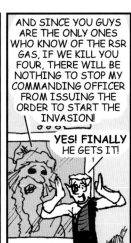

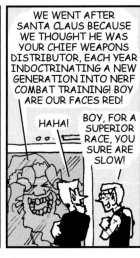

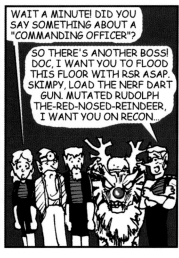

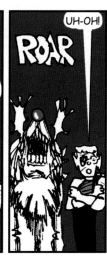

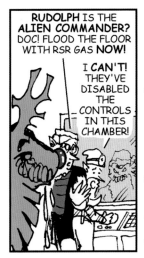

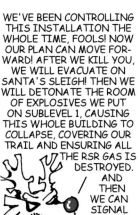

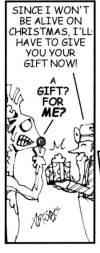

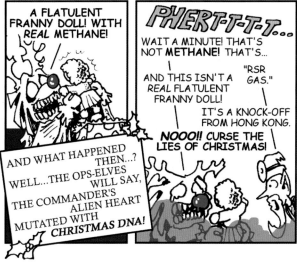

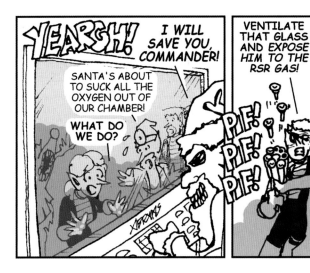

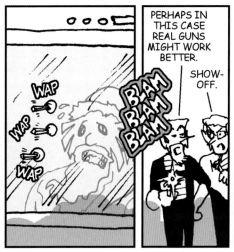

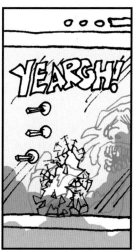

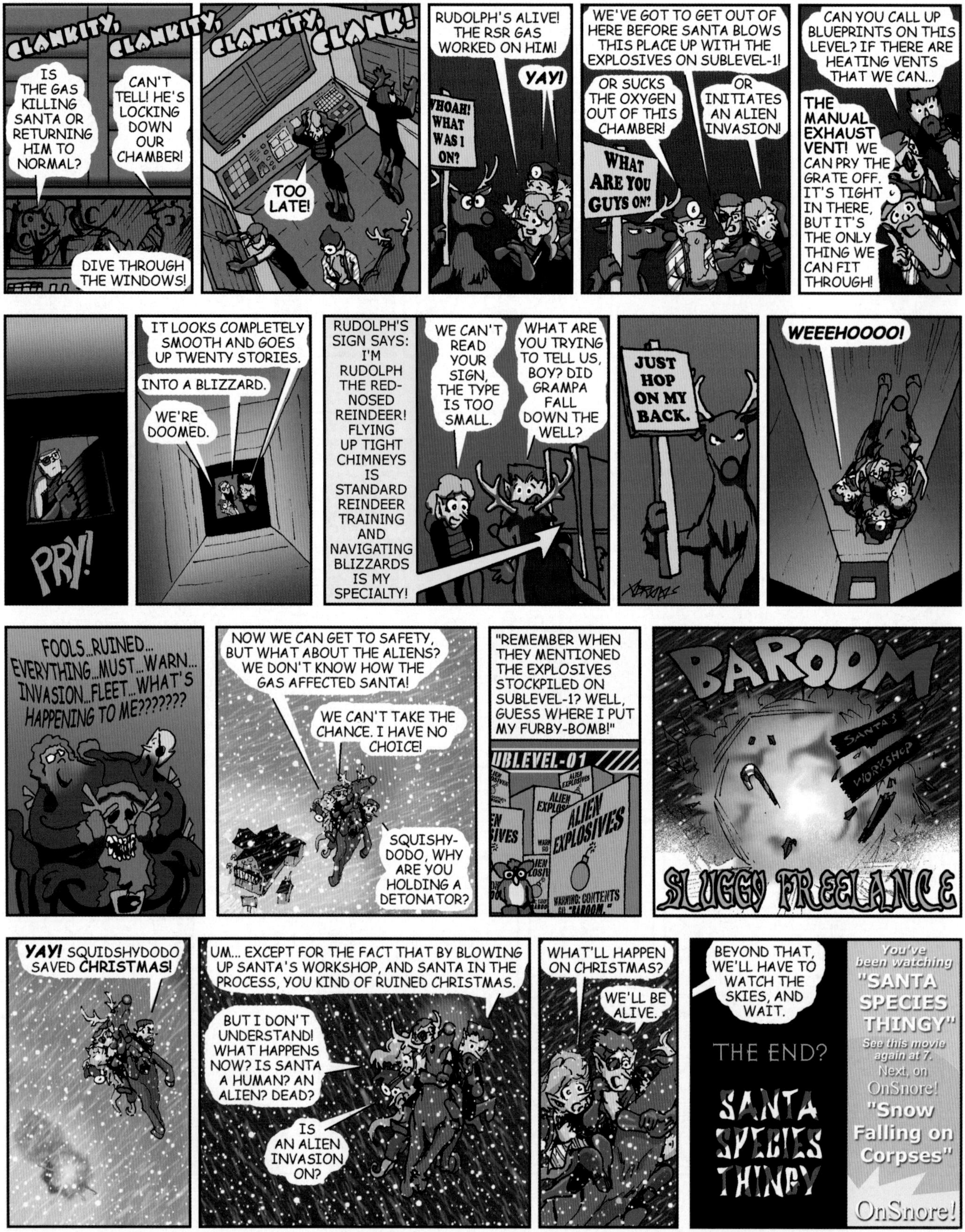
CLANKITY, CLANKITY,
IS THE GAS KILLING SANTA OR RETURNING HIM TO NORMAL?
CAN'T TELL! HE'S LOCKING DOWN OUR CHAMBER!
DIVE THROUGH THE WINDOWS!
CLANKITY, CLANK!
TOO LATE!
RUDOLPH'S ALIVE! THE RSR GAS WORKED ON HIM!
YAY!
WHOAH! WHAT WAS I ON?
WE'VE GOT TO GET OUT OF HERE BEFORE SANTA BLOWS THIS PLACE UP WITH THE EXPLOSIVES ON SUBLEVEL-1!
OR SUCKS THE OXYGEN OUT OF THIS CHAMBER!
OR INITIATES AN ALIEN INVASION!
WHAT ARE YOU GUYS ON?
CAN YOU CALL UP BLUEPRINTS ON THIS LEVEL? IF THERE ARE HEATING VENTS THAT WE CAN...
THE MANUAL EXHAUST VENT! WE CAN PRY THE GRATE OFF. IT'S TIGHT IN THERE, BUT IT'S THE ONLY THING WE CAN FIT THROUGH!
PRY!
IT LOOKS COMPLETELY SMOOTH AND GOES UP TWENTY STORIES.
INTO A BLIZZARD.
WE'RE DOOMED.
RUDOLPH'S SIGN SAYS: I'M RUDOLPH THE RED-NOSED REINDEER! FLYING UP TIGHT CHIMNEYS IS STANDARD REINDEER TRAINING AND NAVIGATING BLIZZARDS IS MY SPECIALTY!
WE CAN'T READ YOUR SIGN, THE TYPE IS TOO SMALL.
WHAT ARE YOU TRYING TO TELL US, BOY? DID GRAMPA FALL DOWN THE WELL?
JUST HOP ON MY BACK.
WEEEHOOOO!
FOOLS...RUINED... EVERYTHING...MUST...WARN... INVASION...FLEET...WHAT'S HAPPENING TO ME???????
NOW WE CAN GET TO SAFETY, BUT WHAT ABOUT THE ALIENS? WE DON'T KNOW HOW THE GAS AFFECTED SANTA!
WE CAN'T TAKE THE CHANCE. I HAVE NO CHOICE!
SQUISHY-DODO, WHY ARE YOU HOLDING A DETONATOR?
"REMEMBER WHEN THEY MENTIONED THE EXPLOSIVES STOCKPILED ON SUBLEVEL-1? WELL, GUESS WHERE I PUT MY FURBY-BOMB!"
SUBLEVEL-01
ALIEN EXPLOSIVES
WARNING: CONTENTS GO "BAROOM."
BAROOM
SANTA'S WORKSHOP
SLUGGY FREELANCE
YAY! SQUIDSHYDODO SAVED CHRISTMAS!
UM... EXCEPT FOR THE FACT THAT BY BLOWING UP SANTA'S WORKSHOP, AND SANTA IN THE PROCESS, YOU KIND OF RUINED CHRISTMAS.
BUT I DON'T UNDERSTAND! WHAT HAPPENS NOW? IS SANTA A HUMAN? AN ALIEN? DEAD?
IS AN ALIEN INVASION ON?
WHAT'LL HAPPEN ON CHRISTMAS?
WE'LL BE ALIVE.
BEYOND THAT, WE'LL HAVE TO WATCH THE SKIES, AND WAIT.
THE END?
SANTA SPECIES THINGY
You've been watching "SANTA SPECIES THINGY"
See this movie again at 7.
Next, on OnSnore!
"Snow Falling on Corpses"
OnSnore!

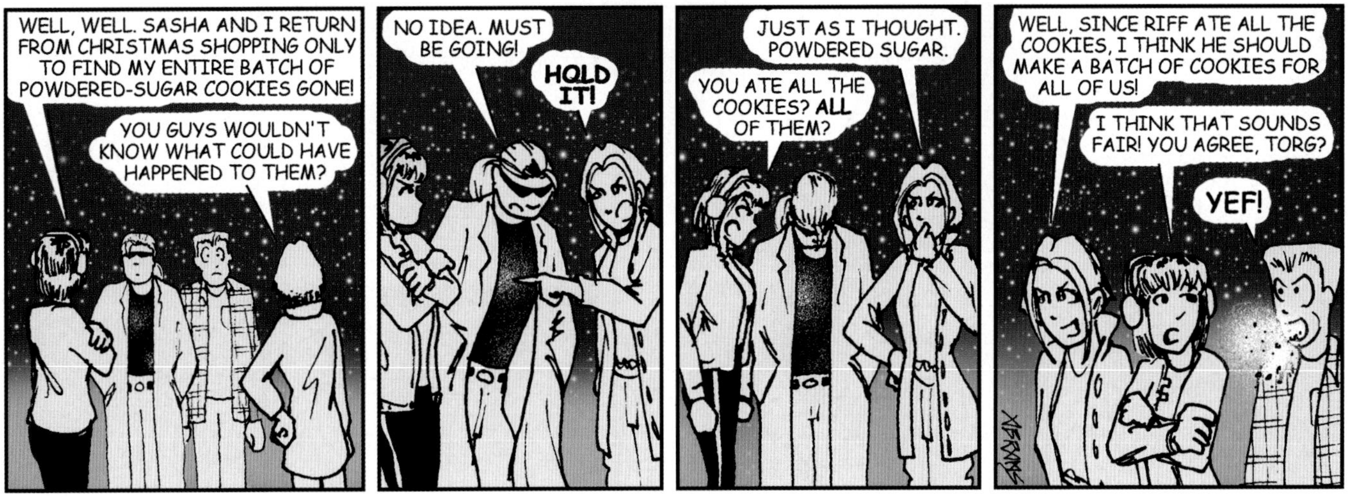
WELL, WELL. SASHA AND I RETURN FROM CHRISTMAS SHOPPING ONLY TO FIND MY ENTIRE BATCH OF POWDERED-SUGAR COOKIES GONE!
YOU GUYS WOULDN'T KNOW WHAT COULD HAVE HAPPENED TO THEM?
NO IDEA. MUST BE GOING!
HOLD IT!
JUST AS I THOUGHT. POWDERED SUGAR.
YOU ATE ALL THE COOKIES? ALL OF THEM?
WELL, SINCE RIFF ATE ALL THE COOKIES, I THINK HE SHOULD MAKE A BATCH OF COOKIES FOR ALL OF US!
I THINK THAT SOUNDS FAIR! YOU AGREE, TORG?
YEF!

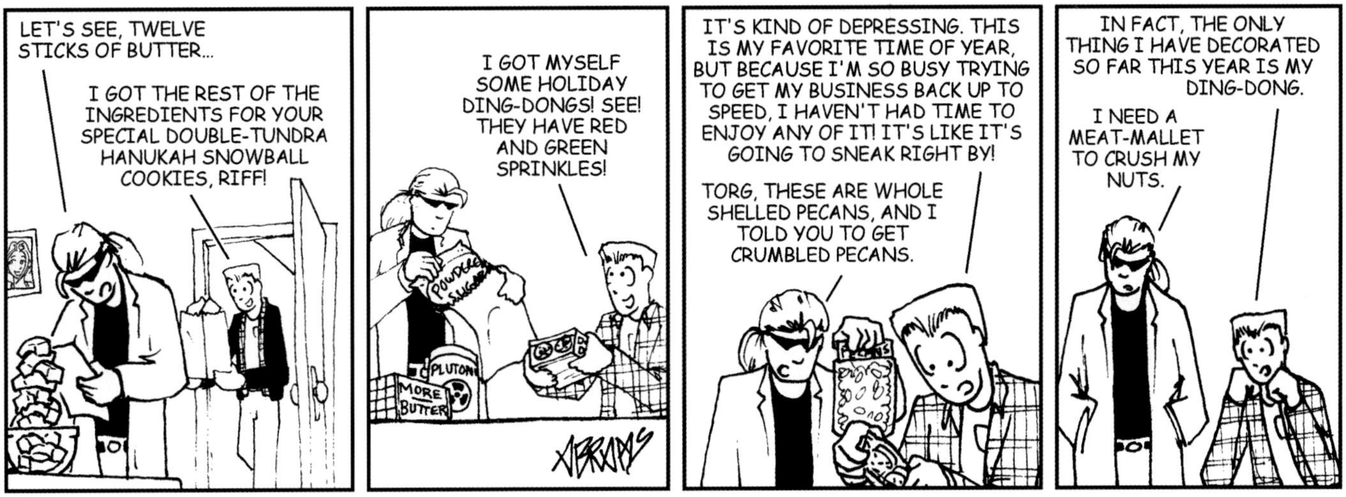
LET'S SEE, TWELVE STICKS OF BUTTER...
I GOT THE REST OF THE INGREDIENTS FOR YOUR SPECIAL DOUBLE-TUNDRA HANUKAH SNOWBALL COOKIES, RIFF!
I GOT MYSELF SOME HOLIDAY DING-DONGS! SEE! THEY HAVE RED AND GREEN SPRINKLES!
MORE BUTTER
IT'S KIND OF DEPRESSING. THIS IS MY FAVORITE TIME OF YEAR, BUT BECAUSE I'M SO BUSY TRYING TO GET MY BUSINESS BACK UP TO SPEED, I HAVEN'T HAD TIME TO ENJOY ANY OF IT! IT'S LIKE IT'S GOING TO SNEAK RIGHT BY!
TORG, THESE ARE WHOLE SHELLED PECANS, AND I TOLD YOU TO GET CRUMBLED PECANS.
I NEED A MEAT-MALLET TO CRUSH MY NUTS.
IN FACT, THE ONLY THING I HAVE DECORATED SO FAR THIS YEAR IS MY DING-DONG.

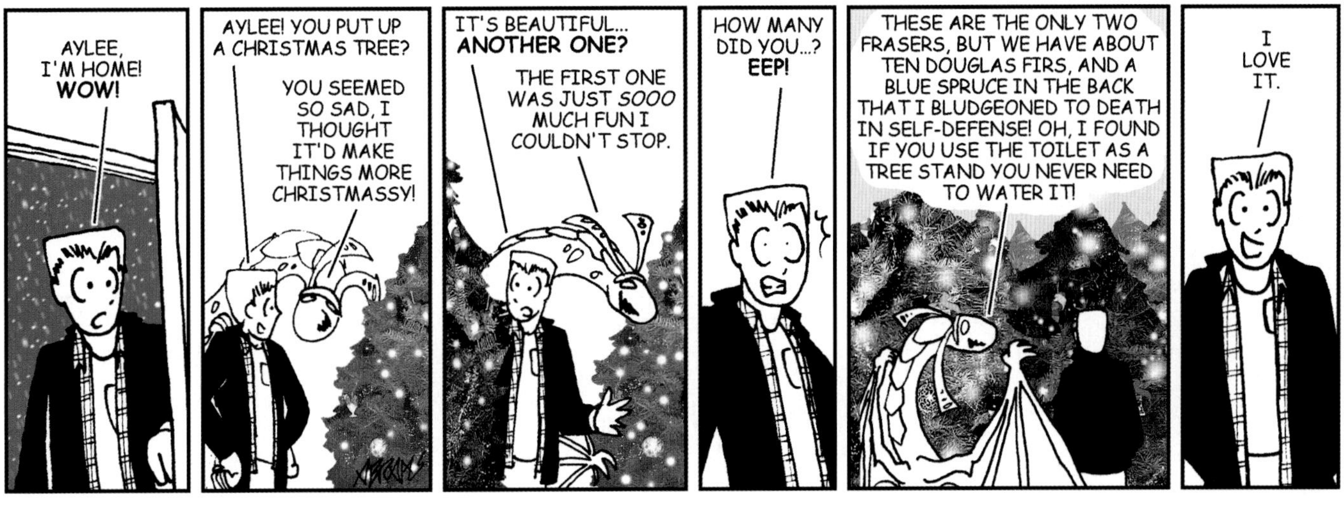
AYLEE, I'M HOME! WOW!
AYLEE! YOU PUT UP A CHRISTMAS TREE?
YOU SEEMED SO SAD, I THOUGHT IT'D MAKE THINGS MORE CHRISTMASSY!
IT'S BEAUTIFUL... ANOTHER ONE?
THE FIRST ONE WAS JUST SOOO MUCH FUN I COULDN'T STOP.
HOW MANY DID YOU...? EEP!
THESE ARE THE ONLY TWO FRASERS, BUT WE HAVE ABOUT TEN DOUGLAS FIRS, AND A BLUE SPRUCE IN THE BACK THAT I BLUDGEONED TO DEATH IN SELF-DEFENSE! OH, I FOUND IF YOU USE THE TOILET AS A TREE STAND YOU NEVER NEED TO WATER IT!
I LOVE IT.

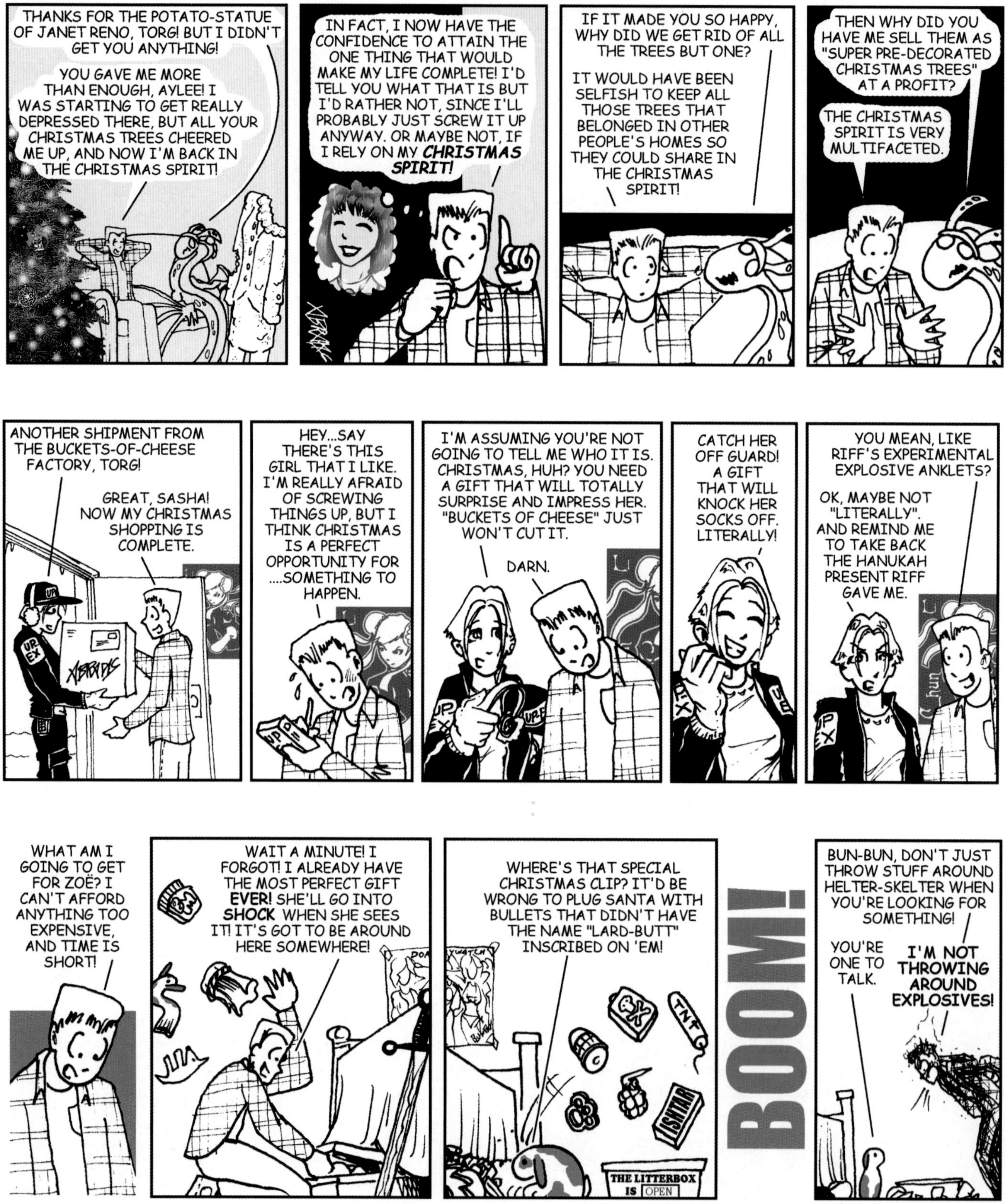
THANKS FOR THE POTATO-STATUE OF JANET RENO, TORG! BUT I DIDN'T GET YOU ANYTHING!
YOU GAVE ME MORE THAN ENOUGH, AYLEE! I WAS STARTING TO GET REALLY DEPRESSED THERE, BUT ALL YOUR CHRISTMAS TREES CHEERED ME UP, AND NOW I'M BACK IN THE CHRISTMAS SPIRIT!
IN FACT, I NOW HAVE THE CONFIDENCE TO ATTAIN THE ONE THING THAT WOULD MAKE MY LIFE COMPLETE! I'D TELL YOU WHAT THAT IS BUT I'D RATHER NOT, SINCE I'LL PROBABLY JUST SCREW IT UP ANYWAY. OR MAYBE NOT, IF I RELY ON MY CHRISTMAS SPIRIT!
IF IT MADE YOU SO HAPPY, WHY DID WE GET RID OF ALL THE TREES BUT ONE?
IT WOULD HAVE BEEN SELFISH TO KEEP ALL THOSE TREES THAT BELONGED IN OTHER PEOPLE'S HOMES SO THEY COULD SHARE IN THE CHRISTMAS SPIRIT!
THEN WHY DID YOU HAVE ME SELL THEM AS "SUPER PRE-DECORATED CHRISTMAS TREES" AT A PROFIT?
THE CHRISTMAS SPIRIT IS VERY MULTIFACETED.
ANOTHER SHIPMENT FROM THE BUCKETS-OF-CHEESE FACTORY, TORG!
GREAT, SASHA! NOW MY CHRISTMAS SHOPPING IS COMPLETE.
HEY...SAY THERE'S THIS GIRL THAT I LIKE. I'M REALLY AFRAID OF SCREWING THINGS UP, BUT I THINK CHRISTMAS IS A PERFECT OPPORTUNITY FOR ....SOMETHING TO HAPPEN.
I'M ASSUMING YOU'RE NOT GOING TO TELL ME WHO IT IS. CHRISTMAS, HUH? YOU NEED A GIFT THAT WILL TOTALLY SURPRISE AND IMPRESS HER. "BUCKETS OF CHEESE" JUST WON'T CUT IT.
DARN.
CATCH HER OFF GUARD! A GIFT THAT WILL KNOCK HER SOCKS OFF. LITERALLY!
YOU MEAN, LIKE RIFF'S EXPERIMENTAL EXPLOSIVE ANKLETS?
OK, MAYBE NOT "LITERALLY". AND REMIND ME TO TAKE BACK THE HANUKAH PRESENT RIFF GAVE ME.
WHAT AM I GOING TO GET FOR ZOË? I CAN'T AFFORD ANYTHING TOO EXPENSIVE, AND TIME IS SHORT!
WAIT A MINUTE! I FORGOT! I ALREADY HAVE THE MOST PERFECT GIFT EVER! SHE'LL GO INTO SHOCK WHEN SHE SEES IT! IT'S GOT TO BE AROUND HERE SOMEWHERE!
WHERE'S THAT SPECIAL CHRISTMAS CLIP? IT'D BE WRONG TO PLUG SANTA WITH BULLETS THAT DIDN'T HAVE THE NAME "LARD-BUTT" INSCRIBED ON 'EM!
TNT
ISHTAR
THE LITTERBOX IS OPEN
BOOM!
BUN-BUN, DON'T JUST THROW STUFF AROUND HELTER-SKELTER WHEN YOU'RE LOOKING FOR SOMETHING!
YOU'RE ONE TO TALK.
I'M NOT THROWING AROUND EXPLOSIVES!

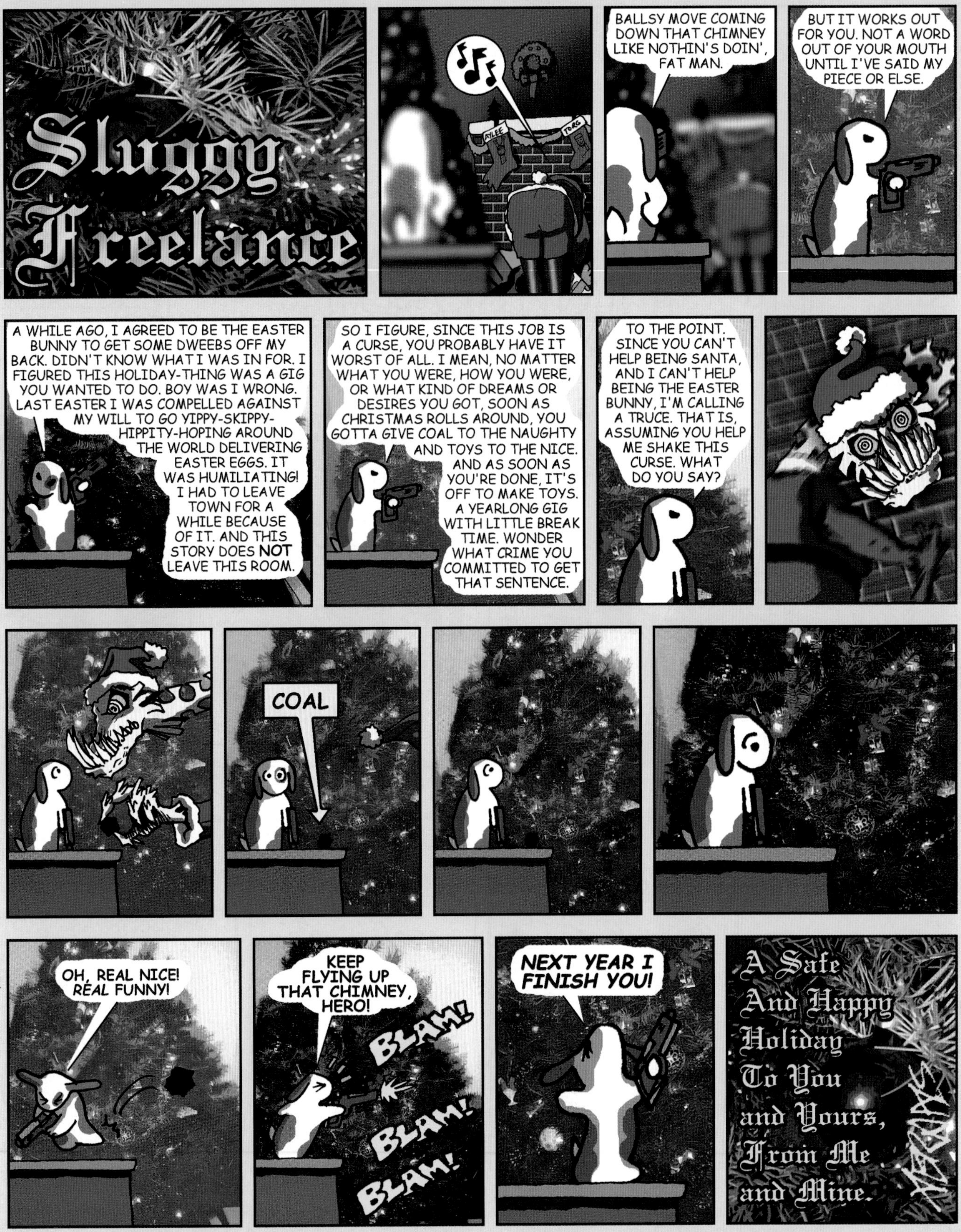
Sluggy Freelance
AYLEE
TORG
BALLSY MOVE COMING DOWN THAT CHIMNEY LIKE NOTHIN'S DOIN', FAT MAN.
BUT IT WORKS OUT FOR YOU. NOT A WORD OUT OF YOUR MOUTH UNTIL I'VE SAID MY PIECE OR ELSE.
A WHILE AGO, I AGREED TO BE THE EASTER BUNNY TO GET SOME DWEEBS OFF MY BACK. DIDN'T KNOW WHAT I WAS IN FOR. I FIGURED THIS HOLIDAY-THING WAS A GIG YOU WANTED TO DO. BOY WAS I WRONG. LAST EASTER I WAS COMPELLED AGAINST MY WILL TO GO YIPPY-SKIPPY-HIPPITY-HOPING AROUND THE WORLD DELIVERING EASTER EGGS. IT WAS HUMILIATING! I HAD TO LEAVE TOWN FOR A WHILE BECAUSE OF IT. AND THIS STORY DOES NOT LEAVE THIS ROOM.
SO I FIGURE, SINCE THIS JOB IS A CURSE, YOU PROBABLY HAVE IT WORST OF ALL. I MEAN, NO MATTER WHAT YOU WERE, HOW YOU WERE, OR WHAT KIND OF DREAMS OR DESIRES YOU GOT, SOON AS CHRISTMAS ROLLS AROUND, YOU GOTTA GIVE COAL TO THE NAUGHTY AND TOYS TO THE NICE. AND AS SOON AS YOU'RE DONE, IT'S OFF TO MAKE TOYS. A YEARLONG GIG WITH LITTLE BREAK TIME. WONDER WHAT CRIME YOU COMMITTED TO GET THAT SENTENCE.
TO THE POINT. SINCE YOU CAN'T HELP BEING SANTA, AND I CAN'T HELP BEING THE EASTER BUNNY, I'M CALLING A TRUCE. THAT IS, ASSUMING YOU HELP ME SHAKE THIS CURSE. WHAT DO YOU SAY?
COAL
OH, REAL NICE! REAL FUNNY!
KEEP FLYING UP THAT CHIMNEY, HERO!
BLAM!
BLAM!
BLAM!
NEXT YEAR I FINISH YOU!
A Safe And Happy Holiday To You and Yours, From Me and Mine.

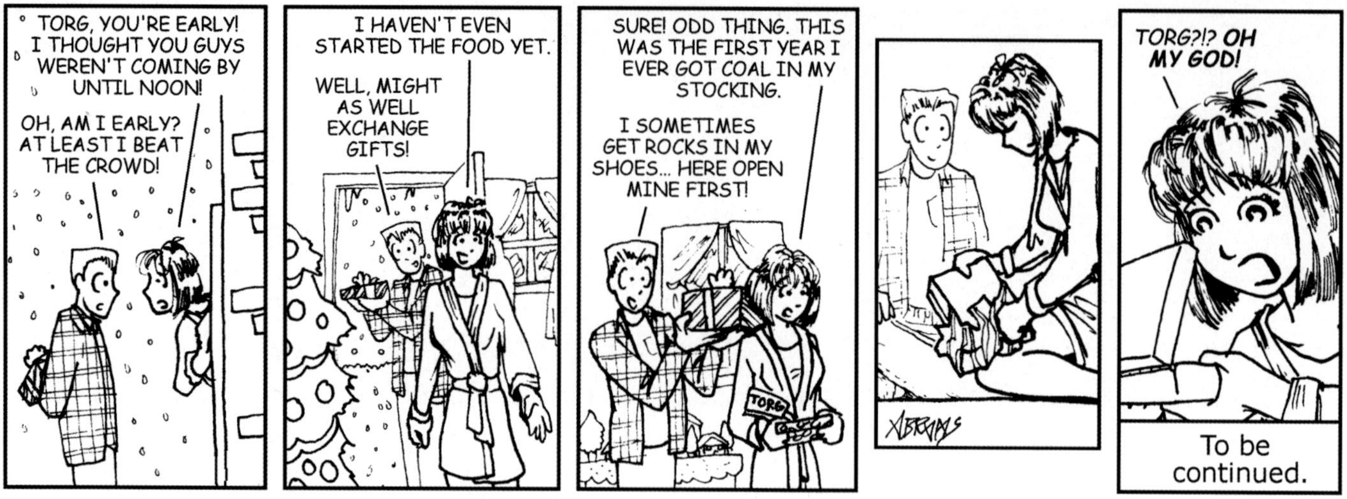
TORG, YOU'RE EARLY! I THOUGHT YOU GUYS WEREN'T COMING BY UNTIL NOON!
OH, AM I EARLY? AT LEAST I BEAT THE CROWD!
I HAVEN'T EVEN STARTED THE FOOD YET.
WELL, MIGHT AS WELL EXCHANGE GIFTS!
SURE! ODD THING. THIS WAS THE FIRST YEAR I EVER GOT COAL IN MY STOCKING.
I SOMETIMES GET ROCKS IN MY SHOES... HERE OPEN MINE FIRST!
TORG
TORG?!? OH MY GOD!
To be continued.

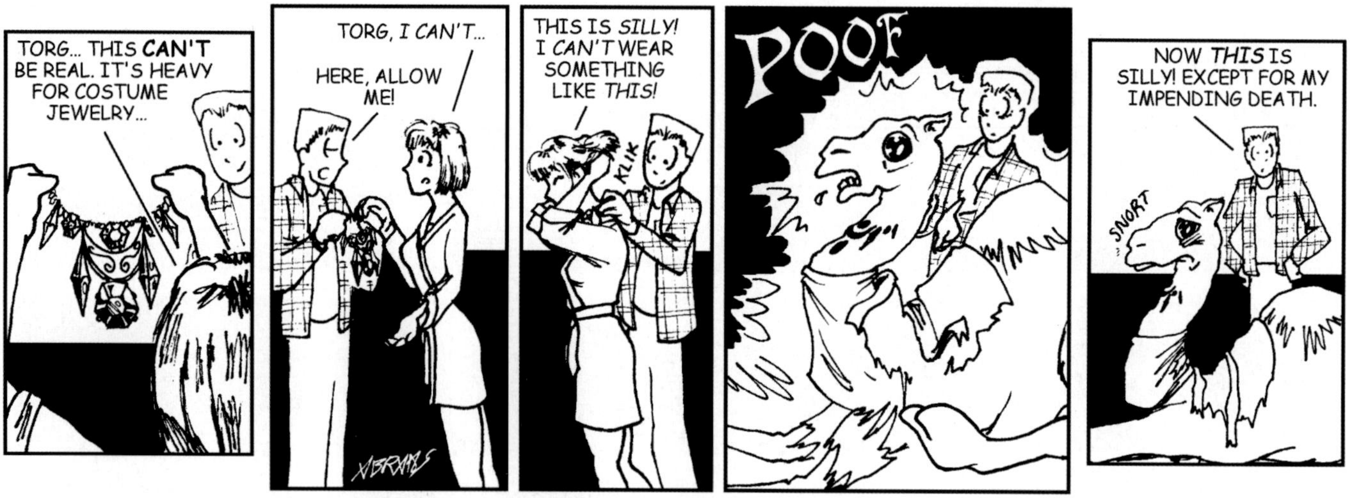
TORG... THIS CAN'T BE REAL. IT'S HEAVY FOR COSTUME JEWELRY...
TORG, I CAN'T...
HERE, ALLOW ME!
THIS IS SILLY! I CAN'T WEAR SOMETHING LIKE THIS!
KLIK
POOF
NOW THIS IS SILLY! EXCEPT FOR MY IMPENDING DEATH.
SNORT

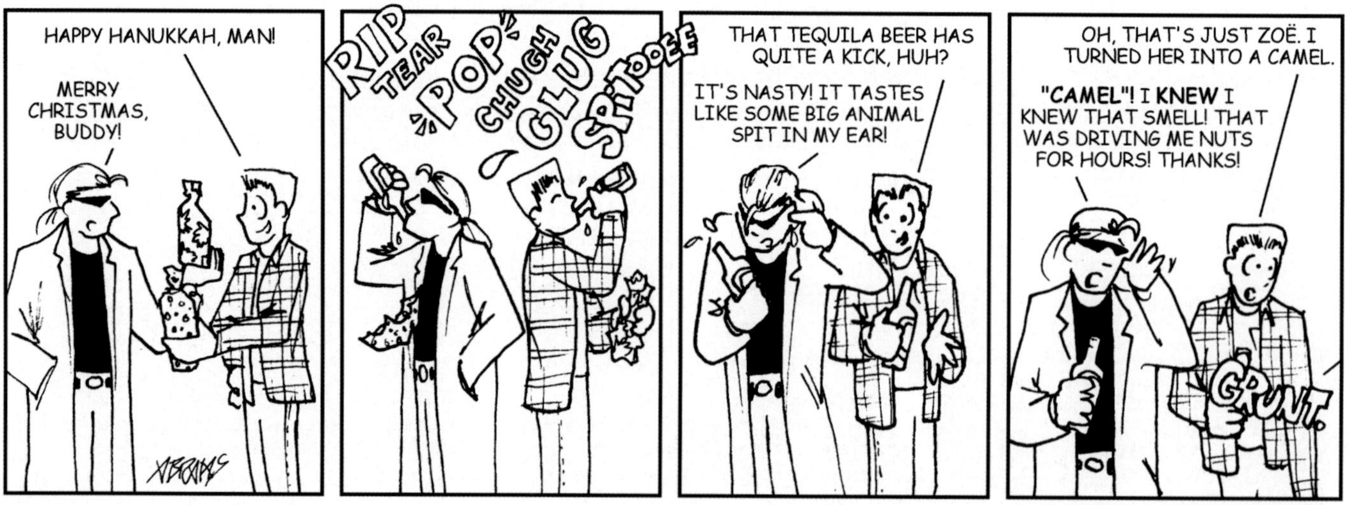
HAPPY HANUKKAH, MAN!
MERRY CHRISTMAS, BUDDY!
RIP
TEAR
POP
CHUGH
GLUG
SPITOOEE
THAT TEQUILA BEER HAS QUITE A KICK, HUH?
IT'S NASTY! IT TASTES LIKE SOME BIG ANIMAL SPIT IN MY EAR!
OH, THAT'S JUST ZOË. I TURNED HER INTO A CAMEL.
"CAMEL"! I KNEW I KNEW THAT SMELL! THAT WAS DRIVING ME NUTS FOR HOURS! THANKS!
GRUNT

YOU TOOK JEWELRY FROM THAT PYRAMID IN TUNISIA TWO YEARS AGO?

HOW WAS I SUPPOSED TO KNOW IT'D BE CURSED AND TURN ZOË INTO A CAMEL?

I DON'T REMEMBER ANY TREASURE. HOW, WHEN, AND WHERE DID YOU FIND IT?

IT WAS WHILE LARA KROFT-MACARONI-AND-CHEESE ™ WAS HELPING US OUT OF THE PYRAMID. YOU WERE ASKING HER HOW TO DO THE DEEP KNEE-BENDS NEEDED TO PASS THE RAZOR-PENDULUMS AHEAD.

munch munch

WOW! GUYS, LOOK AT THIS! IT'LL MAKE A GREAT GIFT FOR SOMEONE I CARE ABOUT SOMEDAY!

COULD YOU SHOW ME AGAIN?

BLIMEY! ROIGHT! THIS ISN'T ANUVVER EXCUSE TER HAVE A LOOK AT ME BUM, IS IT?

I DON'T REMEMBER THAT AT ALL.

IT WAS RIGHT AFTER YOU ASKED HER TO DEMONSTRATE PROPER FORM FOR BOUNCING UP AND DOWN A LOT.

OH YEAH!

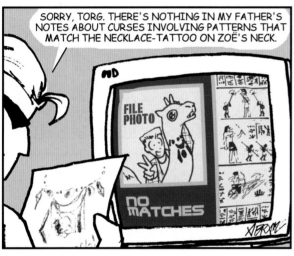

SORRY, TORG. THERE'S NOTHING IN MY FATHER'S NOTES ABOUT CURSES INVOLVING PATTERNS THAT MATCH THE NECKLACE-TATTOO ON ZOË'S NECK.

FILE PHOTO

NO MATCHES

IT'S BEEN A WEEK! ZOË'S GOING TO HATE ME FOREVER! AND PEOPLE ARE GOING TO START NOTICING HER GONE WHEN HER NEXT SEMESTER STARTS!

JUST TELL THEM WHATEVER YOU TOLD SASHA. SHE SEEMS OK WITH THE SITCH.

WELL, SHE'S OPEN MINDED ENOUGH TO KNOW THE TRUTH! MOSTLY.

GEE, ZOË, I'M SORRY YOU'RE STILL A CAMEL. BUT YOU REALLY SHOULD HAVE KNOWN BETTER THAN TO MESS WITH CURSED ARTIFACTS YOU STOLE FROM A MUMMY'S TOMB.

GRUMPH

SNORT

HAPPY NEW YEAR! WHAT'S UP?

WHAT A HELL-WEEK THIS HAS BEEN AT UP-EX! I'VE BEEN DELIVERING PACKAGES FOR WEEKS STRAIGHT! I'M SO READY FOR THIS NEW YEAR'S EVE PARTY!

I'M BUN-BUN!

OH-NO! THEY WARNED ME ABOUT YOU! BEFORE YOU KICK MY BUTT FOR UNLOADING MY PROBLEMS ON YOU, JUST KEEP IN MIND THAT I AM AN OVERWORKED PSEUDO-POSTAL-WORKER.

Smooch!

I JUST KISSED A GIRL NAMED ...SOMETHING... I LOVE ALL YOU GUYS! I'M THE EASTER BUNNY!

DID YOU JUST SEE A DRUNKEN RABBIT HOP BY WITH MY BOTTLE OF 151-RUM?

YOU'RE SO LUCKY!

Chapter 21: The Hunt

SANTA SPECIES THINGY

EPILOGUE

SLUGGY FREELANCE

SORRY FOR THE D.N.A. TESTING, MRS. CLAUS, BUT WE HAVE TO BE SURE!

I UNDERSTAND, DEAR. THESE ARE DANGEROUS TIMES.

THE GOOD NEWS IS IT APPEARS CHRISTMAS WENT OFF FLAWLESSLY. AT LEAST ON THE SURFACE.

DESPITE MY HUSBAND'S MUTATED D.N.A., IT APPEARS THE CHRISTMAS SPIRIT WON OUT. I ASSUME THE CLARION-CALL FOR AN ALIEN INVASION FAILED TO SOUND?

WE KNOW THE ALIENS ARE VULNERABLE TO NERF WEAPONS AND RSR GAS, WHICH WE'RE PRODUCING AS WE SPEAK. I DOUBT THE ALIENS WILL MAKE A MOVE UNTIL THEY HAVE A SURE WIN. WE JUST HAVE TO KEEP THEM UNSURE.

THIS YEAR, 2001, IS GOING TO BE AN IMPORTANT YEAR FOR US. PERHAPS THE **MOST** IMPORTANT.

WE HAVE MUCH TO DO. I HAVE BEEN IN CONTACT WITH THE OTHER SPLINTER GROUPS OF SURVIVING ELVES. THEY ARE LOOKING TO ME FOR LEADERSHIP. I AM LOOKING TO YOU.

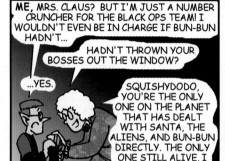

ME, MRS. CLAUS? BUT I'M JUST A NUMBER CRUNCHER FOR THE BLACK OPS TEAM! I WOULDN'T EVEN BE IN CHARGE IF BUN-BUN HADN'T...

HADN'T THROWN YOUR BOSSES OUT THE WINDOW?

...YES.

SQUISHYDODO, YOU'RE THE ONLY ONE ON THE PLANET THAT HAS DEALT WITH SANTA, THE ALIENS, AND BUN-BUN DIRECTLY. THE ONLY ONE STILL ALIVE, I SHOULD SAY. I CAN THINK OF NO ONE BETTER TO LEAD.

WELL, I'M OFF TO BERMUDA, QUITE THE NEW YEAR'S EVE BLAST GOING THERE. YOU MUST HAVE PLANS TOO!

MAYBE I **DO.**

IN FACT, I NOW HAVE THE CONFIDENCE TO ATTAIN THE ONE THING THAT WOULD MAKE MY LIFE COMPLETE! I'D TELL YOU WHAT THAT IS BUT I'D RATHER NOT, SINCE I'LL PROBABLY JUST SCREW IT UP ANYWAY. OR MAYBE NOT, IF I RELY ON MY **NEW YEAR'S SPIRIT!**

HELLO?

HI, SLAPPYHOHO! I WAS THINKING IF YOU DIDN'T HAVE PLANS TONIGHT THAT WE COULD....

HA-HA! GOTCHA! THIS IS MY VIDEO ANSWERING MACHINE! PLEASE LEAVE A MESSAGE AT THE BEEP! *BEEEEP!*

OH!... UM... HI... HAPPY NEW YEAR! I'LL SEE YOU ON TUESDAY.

WOW! **I** DON'T EVEN HAVE A VIDEO ANSWERING MACHINE!

click

THANK GOD HE BOUGHT IT! I FEEL HORRIBLE LYING TO SQUISHYDODO, BUT MY HEART BELONGS TO ANOTHER, WHO DOESN'T KNOW HOW I FEEL.

I MISS SQUINTYHOYO. HE'D TELL ME I WAS AN IDIOT FOR MAKING THE FIRST MOVE. "IT'S NEW YEAR'S EVE! HE PROBABLY HAS PLANS," HE'D SAY.

BUT THEN HE'D TELL ME TO DO IT ANYWAY, SO HERE I GO!

BLACK OPS GRUNT BARRACKS

KNOCK! KNOCK!

SLAPPYHOHO?

SKIMPYMOOMOO!....?

WHAT BRINGS YOU AROUND?

UM... NOTHING? IT'S STRANGE SEEING YOU OUT OF UNIFORM...

YOU'RE STARING AT ME FUNNY, **AREN'T YOU?** STARING AT MY **SKIMPY MOO-MOO!**

NO! NO, NOT AT ALL!

OH GREAT! HEY, I WAS WONDERING IF YOU WANTED TO JOIN ME AT SPOCKEAR-CLUB TONIGHT!

OH, I CAN'T! I HAVE A DATE WITH SQUISHYDODO! I JUST WANTED TO SAY... HAPPY NEW YEAR! SEE YOU TUESDAY!

HA! SHOT DOWN AGAIN!

LIKE **YOU'VE** GOT NO PROBLEMS GETTING DATES, STINKYPOOPOO!

HAPPY NEW YEAR!

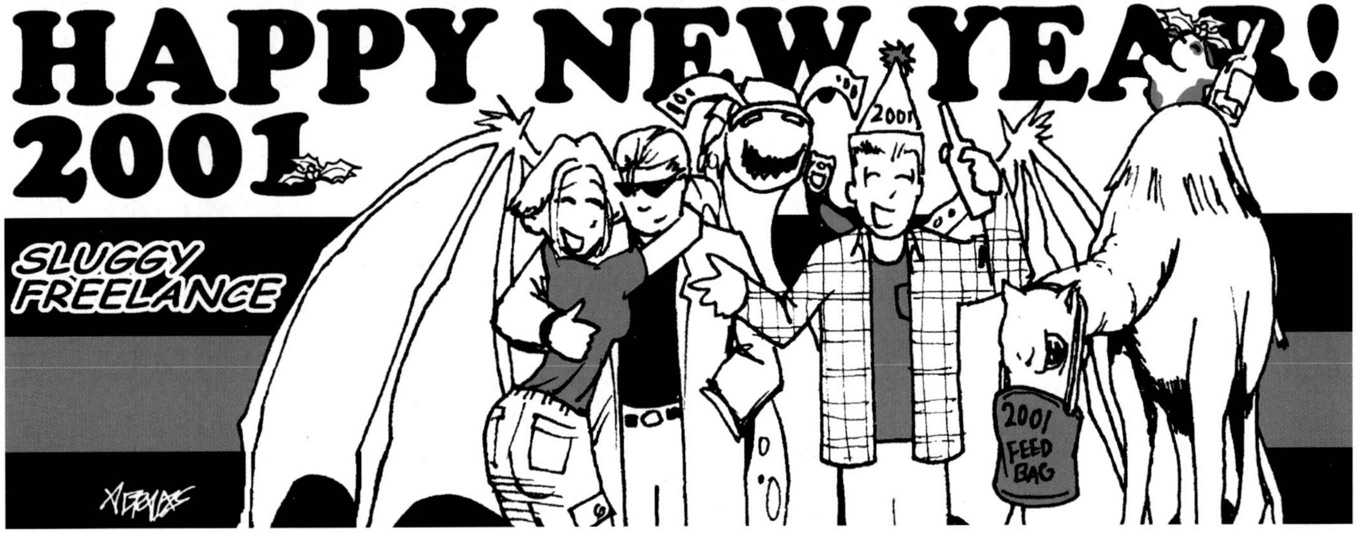
HAPPY NEW YEAR!
2001
SLUGGY FREELANCE
2001
2001 FEED BAG

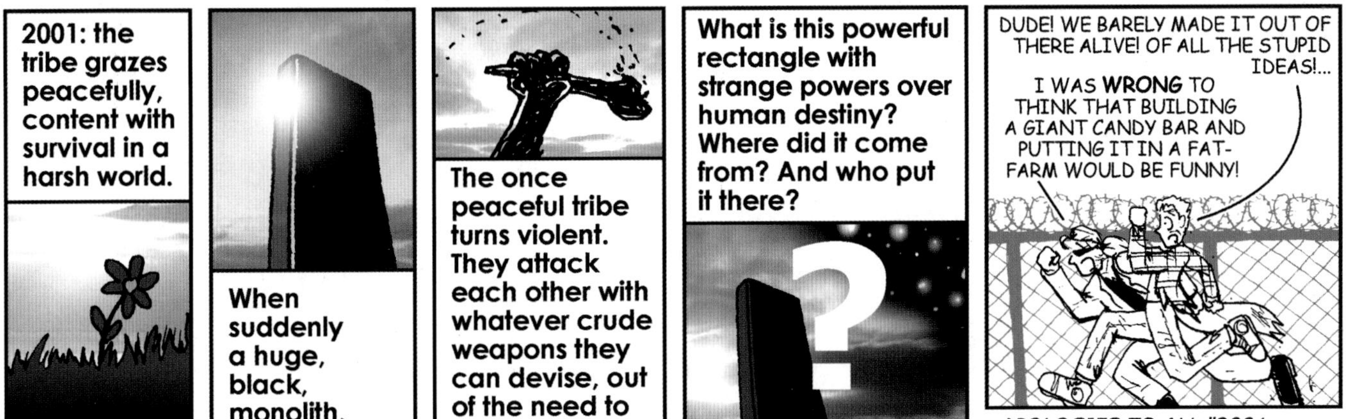
2001: the tribe grazes peacefully, content with survival in a harsh world.
When suddenly a huge, black, monolith, appears in their den.
The once peaceful tribe turns violent. They attack each other with whatever crude weapons they can devise, out of the need to possess the monolithic slab.
What is this powerful rectangle with strange powers over human destiny? Where did it come from? And who put it there?
?
DUDE! WE BARELY MADE IT OUT OF THERE ALIVE! OF ALL THE STUPID IDEAS!...
I WAS **WRONG** TO THINK THAT BUILDING A GIANT CANDY BAR AND PUTTING IT IN A FAT-FARM WOULD BE FUNNY!

APOLOGIES TO ALL "2001: A SPACE ODYSSEY" FANS AND EVERYONE IN FAT-FARMS.

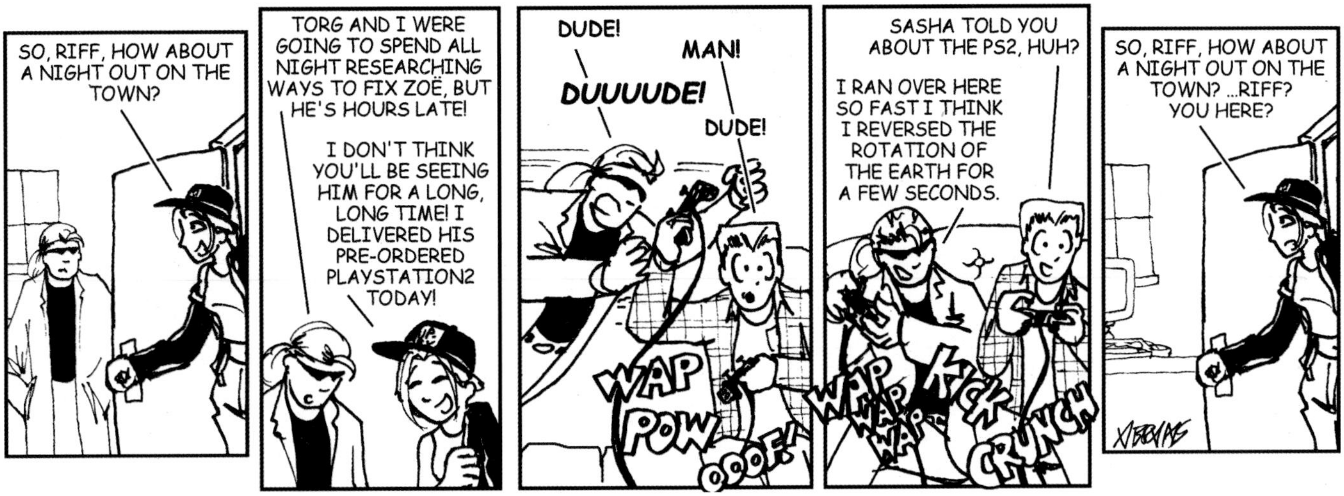
SO, RIFF, HOW ABOUT A NIGHT OUT ON THE TOWN?
TORG AND I WERE GOING TO SPEND ALL NIGHT RESEARCHING WAYS TO FIX ZOË, BUT HE'S HOURS LATE!
I DON'T THINK YOU'LL BE SEEING HIM FOR A LONG, LONG TIME! I DELIVERED HIS PRE-ORDERED PLAYSTATION2 TODAY!
DUDE!
MAN!
DUUUUDE!
DUDE!
WAP
POW
OOOF!
SASHA TOLD YOU ABOUT THE PS2, HUH?
I RAN OVER HERE SO FAST I THINK I REVERSED THE ROTATION OF THE EARTH FOR A FEW SECONDS.
WAP
WAP
WAP
KICK
CRUNCH
SO, RIFF, HOW ABOUT A NIGHT OUT ON THE TOWN? ...RIFF? YOU HERE?

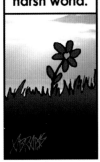

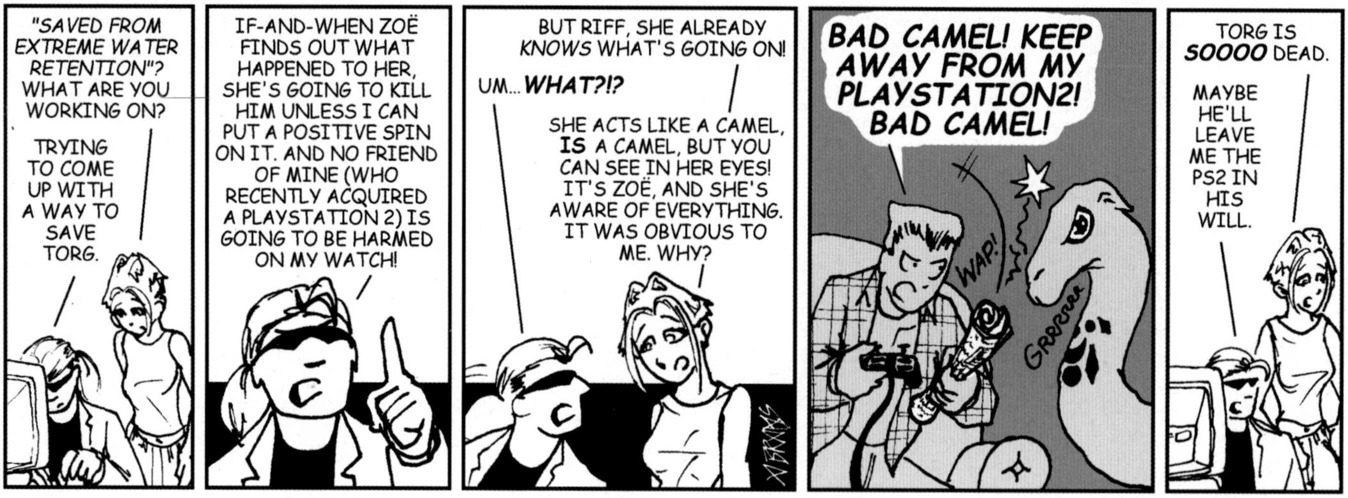
"SAVED FROM EXTREME WATER RETENTION"? WHAT ARE YOU WORKING ON?
TRYING TO COME UP WITH A WAY TO SAVE TORG.
IF-AND-WHEN ZOË FINDS OUT WHAT HAPPENED TO HER, SHE'S GOING TO KILL HIM UNLESS I CAN PUT A POSITIVE SPIN ON IT. AND NO FRIEND OF MINE (WHO RECENTLY ACQUIRED A PLAYSTATION 2) IS GOING TO BE HARMED ON MY WATCH!
BUT RIFF, SHE ALREADY KNOWS WHAT'S GOING ON!
UM... WHAT?!?
SHE ACTS LIKE A CAMEL, IS A CAMEL, BUT YOU CAN SEE IN HER EYES! IT'S ZOË, AND SHE'S AWARE OF EVERYTHING. IT WAS OBVIOUS TO ME. WHY?
BAD CAMEL! KEEP AWAY FROM MY PLAYSTATION2! BAD CAMEL!
WAP!
GRRRRRR
TORG IS SOOOO DEAD.
MAYBE HE'LL LEAVE ME THE PS2 IN HIS WILL.

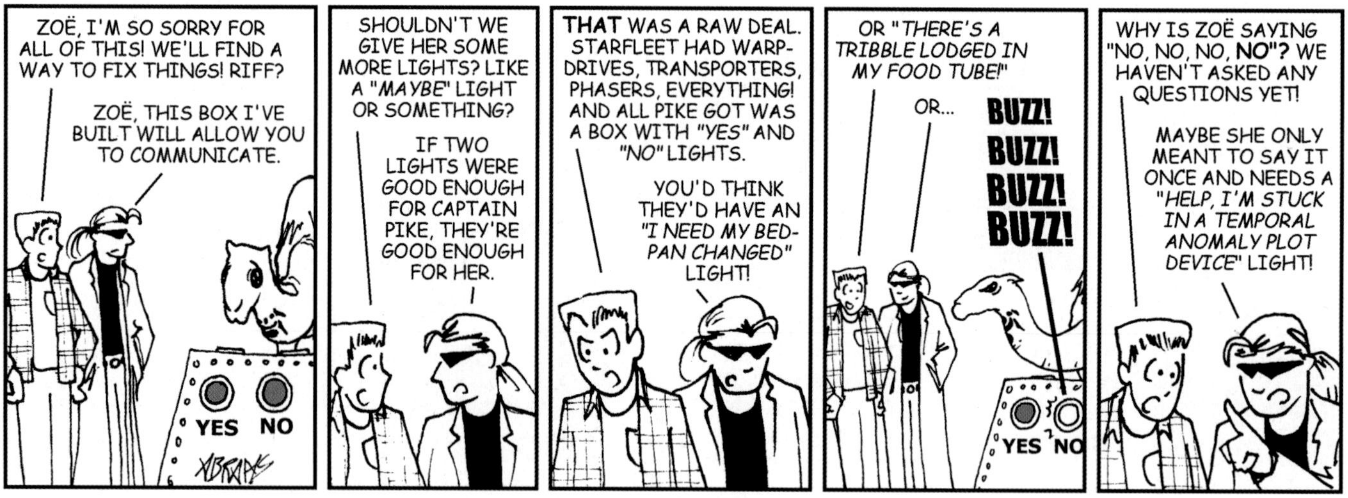
ZOË, I'M SO SORRY FOR ALL OF THIS! WE'LL FIND A WAY TO FIX THINGS! RIFF?
ZOË, THIS BOX I'VE BUILT WILL ALLOW YOU TO COMMUNICATE.
YES NO
SHOULDN'T WE GIVE HER SOME MORE LIGHTS? LIKE A "MAYBE" LIGHT OR SOMETHING?
IF TWO LIGHTS WERE GOOD ENOUGH FOR CAPTAIN PIKE, THEY'RE GOOD ENOUGH FOR HER.
THAT WAS A RAW DEAL. STARFLEET HAD WARP-DRIVES, TRANSPORTERS, PHASERS, EVERYTHING! AND ALL PIKE GOT WAS A BOX WITH "YES" AND "NO" LIGHTS.
YOU'D THINK THEY'D HAVE AN "I NEED MY BED-PAN CHANGED" LIGHT!
OR "THERE'S A TRIBBLE LODGED IN MY FOOD TUBE!"
OR...
BUZZ! BUZZ! BUZZ! BUZZ!
YES NO
WHY IS ZOË SAYING "NO, NO, NO, NO"? WE HAVEN'T ASKED ANY QUESTIONS YET!
MAYBE SHE ONLY MEANT TO SAY IT ONCE AND NEEDS A "HELP, I'M STUCK IN A TEMPORAL ANOMALY PLOT DEVICE" LIGHT!

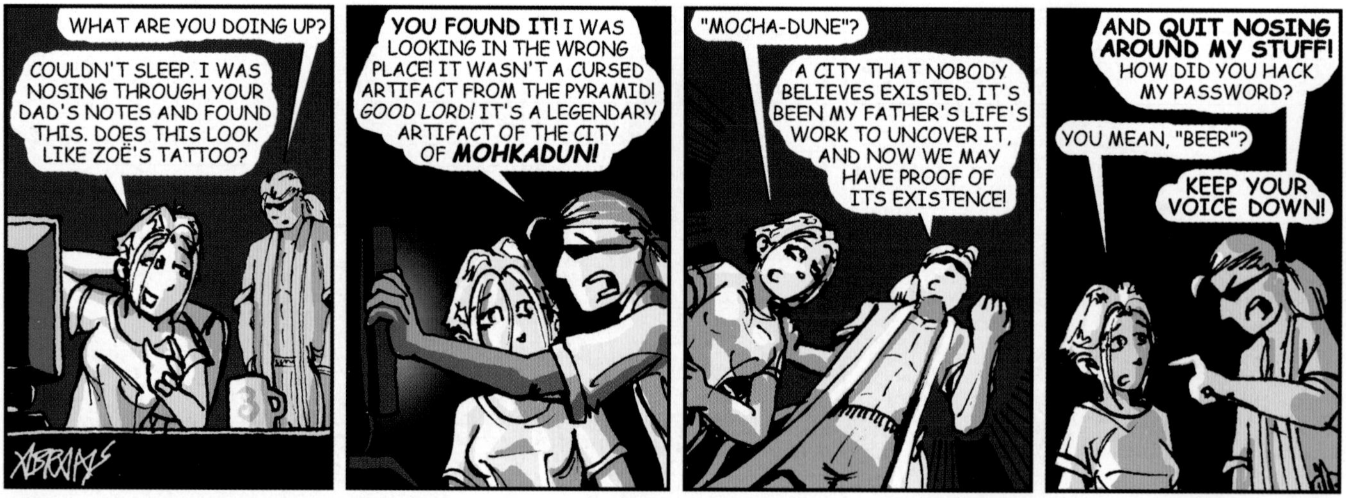
WHAT ARE YOU DOING UP?
COULDN'T SLEEP. I WAS NOSING THROUGH YOUR DAD'S NOTES AND FOUND THIS. DOES THIS LOOK LIKE ZOË'S TATTOO?
YOU FOUND IT! I WAS LOOKING IN THE WRONG PLACE! IT WASN'T A CURSED ARTIFACT FROM THE PYRAMID! GOOD LORD! IT'S A LEGENDARY ARTIFACT OF THE CITY OF MOHKADUN!
"MOCHA-DUNE"?
A CITY THAT NOBODY BELIEVES EXISTED. IT'S BEEN MY FATHER'S LIFE'S WORK TO UNCOVER IT, AND NOW WE MAY HAVE PROOF OF ITS EXISTENCE!
AND QUIT NOSING AROUND MY STUFF! HOW DID YOU HACK MY PASSWORD?
YOU MEAN, "BEER"?
KEEP YOUR VOICE DOWN!

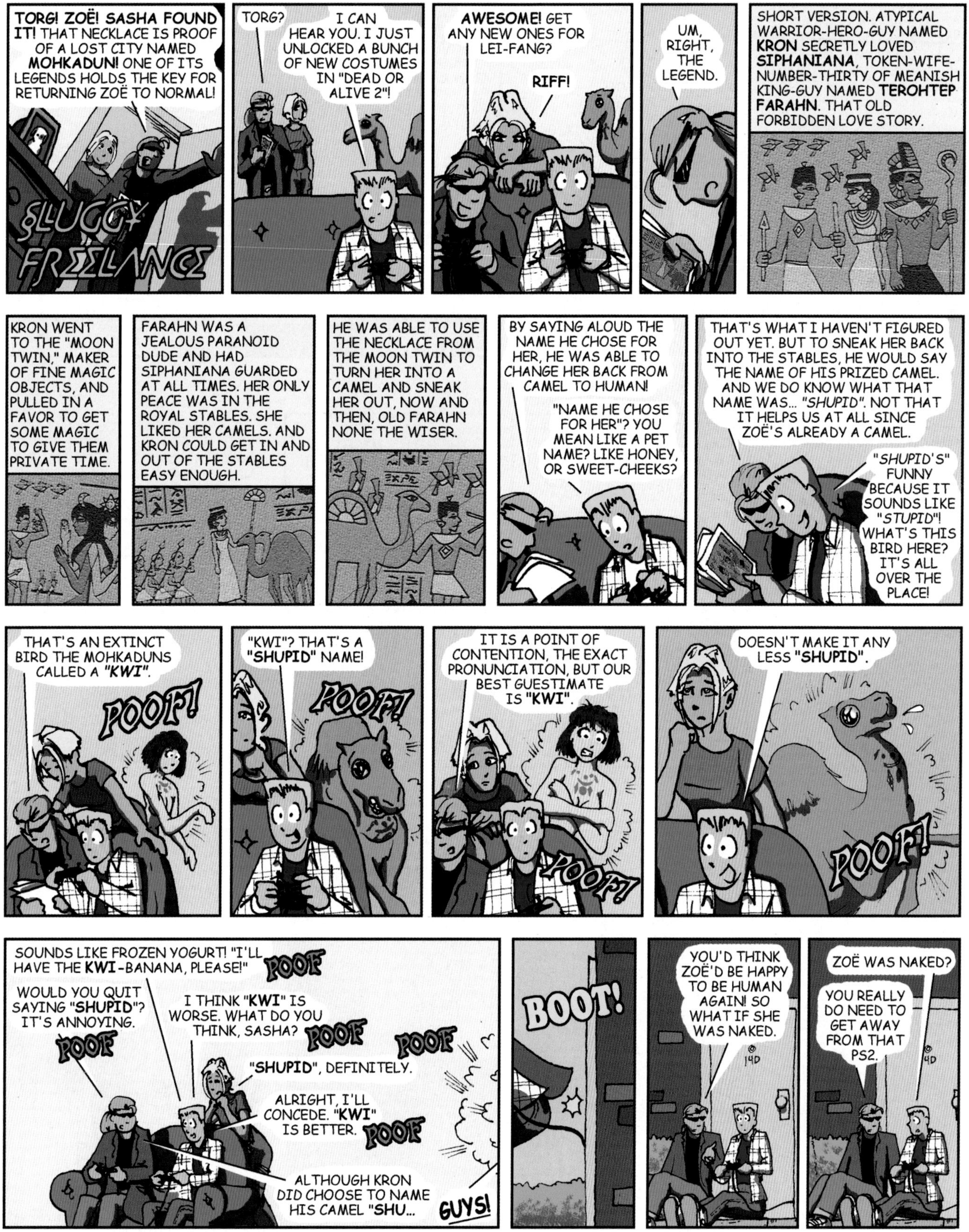
TORG! ZOË! SASHA FOUND IT! THAT NECKLACE IS PROOF OF A LOST CITY NAMED MOHKADUN! ONE OF ITS LEGENDS HOLDS THE KEY FOR RETURNING ZOË TO NORMAL!
SLUGGY FREELANCE
TORG?
I CAN HEAR YOU. I JUST UNLOCKED A BUNCH OF NEW COSTUMES IN "DEAD OR ALIVE 2"!
AWESOME! GET ANY NEW ONES FOR LEI-FANG?
RIFF!
UM, RIGHT, THE LEGEND.
SHORT VERSION. ATYPICAL WARRIOR-HERO-GUY NAMED KRON SECRETLY LOVED SIPHANIANA, TOKEN-WIFE-NUMBER-THIRTY OF MEANISH KING-GUY NAMED TEROHTEP FARAHN. THAT OLD FORBIDDEN LOVE STORY.
KRON WENT TO THE "MOON TWIN," MAKER OF FINE MAGIC OBJECTS, AND PULLED IN A FAVOR TO GET SOME MAGIC TO GIVE THEM PRIVATE TIME.
FARAHN WAS A JEALOUS PARANOID DUDE AND HAD SIPHANIANA GUARDED AT ALL TIMES. HER ONLY PEACE WAS IN THE ROYAL STABLES. SHE LIKED HER CAMELS. AND KRON COULD GET IN AND OUT OF THE STABLES EASY ENOUGH.
HE WAS ABLE TO USE THE NECKLACE FROM THE MOON TWIN TO TURN HER INTO A CAMEL AND SNEAK HER OUT, NOW AND THEN, OLD FARAHN NONE THE WISER.
BY SAYING ALOUD THE NAME HE CHOSE FOR HER, HE WAS ABLE TO CHANGE HER BACK FROM CAMEL TO HUMAN!
"NAME HE CHOSE FOR HER"? YOU MEAN LIKE A PET NAME? LIKE HONEY, OR SWEET-CHEEKS?
THAT'S WHAT I HAVEN'T FIGURED OUT YET. BUT TO SNEAK HER BACK INTO THE STABLES, HE WOULD SAY THE NAME OF HIS PRIZED CAMEL. AND WE DO KNOW WHAT THAT NAME WAS... "SHUPID". NOT THAT IT HELPS US AT ALL SINCE ZOË'S ALREADY A CAMEL.
"SHUPID'S" FUNNY BECAUSE IT SOUNDS LIKE "STUPID"! WHAT'S THIS BIRD HERE? IT'S ALL OVER THE PLACE!
THAT'S AN EXTINCT BIRD THE MOHKADUNS CALLED A "KWI".
POOF!
"KWI"? THAT'S A "SHUPID" NAME!
POOF!
IT IS A POINT OF CONTENTION, THE EXACT PRONUNCIATION, BUT OUR BEST GUESTIMATE IS "KWI".
POOF!
DOESN'T MAKE IT ANY LESS "SHUPID".
POOF!
SOUNDS LIKE FROZEN YOGURT! "I'LL HAVE THE KWI-BANANA, PLEASE!"
POOF
WOULD YOU QUIT SAYING "SHUPID"? IT'S ANNOYING.
POOF
I THINK "KWI" IS WORSE. WHAT DO YOU THINK, SASHA?
POOF
POOF
"SHUPID", DEFINITELY.
ALRIGHT, I'LL CONCEDE. "KWI" IS BETTER.
POOF
ALTHOUGH KRON DID CHOOSE TO NAME HIS CAMEL "SHU...
GUYS!
BOOT!
YOU'D THINK ZOË'D BE HAPPY TO BE HUMAN AGAIN! SO WHAT IF SHE WAS NAKED.
ZOË WAS NAKED?
YOU REALLY DO NEED TO GET AWAY FROM THAT PS2.

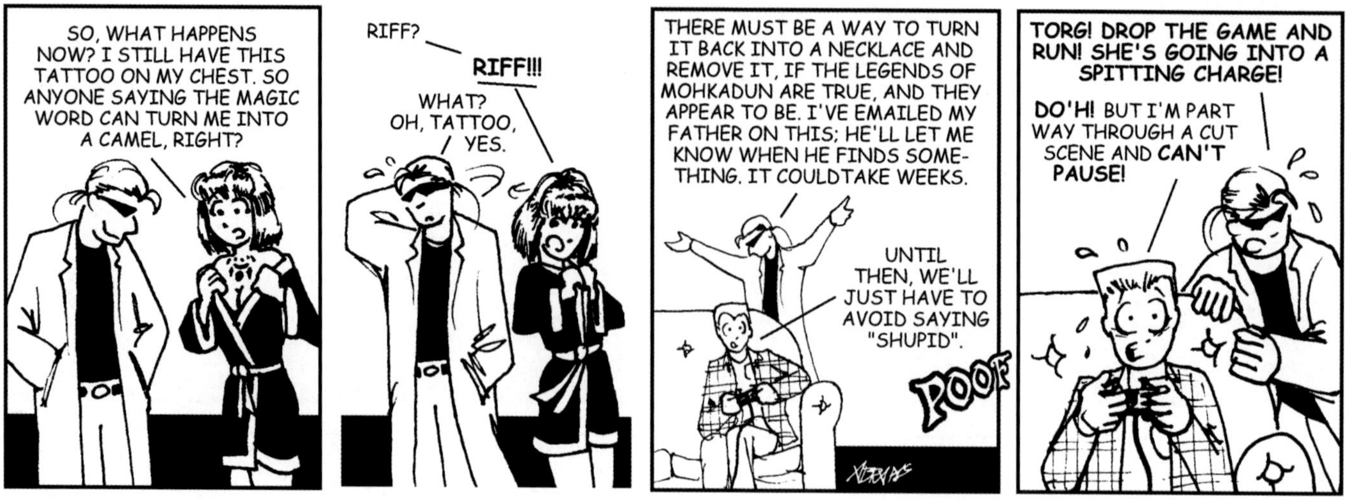
SO, WHAT HAPPENS NOW? I STILL HAVE THIS TATTOO ON MY CHEST. SO ANYONE SAYING THE MAGIC WORD CAN TURN ME INTO A CAMEL, RIGHT?
RIFF?
RIFF!!!
WHAT? OH, TATTOO, YES.
THERE MUST BE A WAY TO TURN IT BACK INTO A NECKLACE AND REMOVE IT, IF THE LEGENDS OF MOHKADUN ARE TRUE, AND THEY APPEAR TO BE. I'VE EMAILED MY FATHER ON THIS; HE'LL LET ME KNOW WHEN HE FINDS SOME-THING. IT COULDTAKE WEEKS.
UNTIL THEN, WE'LL JUST HAVE TO AVOID SAYING "SHUPID".
POOF
TORG! DROP THE GAME AND RUN! SHE'S GOING INTO A SPITTING CHARGE!
DO'H! BUT I'M PART WAY THROUGH A CUT SCENE AND CAN'T PAUSE!

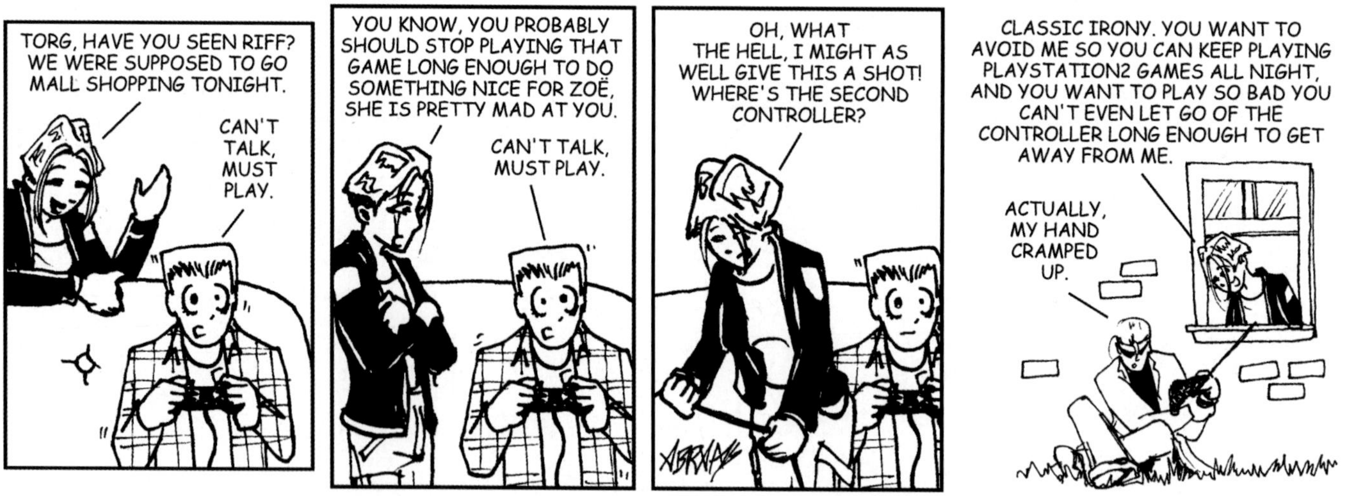
TORG, HAVE YOU SEEN RIFF? WE WERE SUPPOSED TO GO MALL SHOPPING TONIGHT.
CAN'T TALK, MUST PLAY.
YOU KNOW, YOU PROBABLY SHOULD STOP PLAYING THAT GAME LONG ENOUGH TO DO SOMETHING NICE FOR ZOË, SHE IS PRETTY MAD AT YOU.
CAN'T TALK, MUST PLAY.
OH, WHAT THE HELL, I MIGHT AS WELL GIVE THIS A SHOT! WHERE'S THE SECOND CONTROLLER?
CLASSIC IRONY. YOU WANT TO AVOID ME SO YOU CAN KEEP PLAYING PLAYSTATION2 GAMES ALL NIGHT, AND YOU WANT TO PLAY SO BAD YOU CAN'T EVEN LET GO OF THE CONTROLLER LONG ENOUGH TO GET AWAY FROM ME.
ACTUALLY, MY HAND CRAMPED UP.

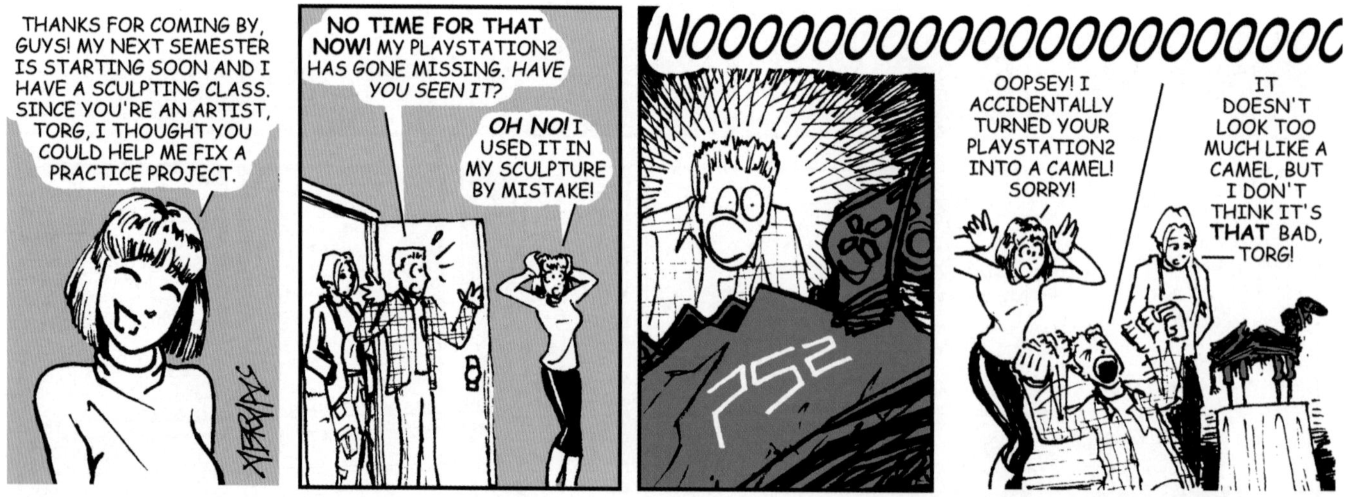
THANKS FOR COMING BY, GUYS! MY NEXT SEMESTER IS STARTING SOON AND I HAVE A SCULPTING CLASS. SINCE YOU'RE AN ARTIST, TORG, I THOUGHT YOU COULD HELP ME FIX A PRACTICE PROJECT.
NO TIME FOR THAT NOW! MY PLAYSTATION2 HAS GONE MISSING. HAVE YOU SEEN IT?
OH NO! I USED IT IN MY SCULPTURE BY MISTAKE!
NOOOOOOOOOOOOOOOOOOOOOOO
PS2
OOPSEY! I ACCIDENTALLY TURNED YOUR PLAYSTATION2 INTO A CAMEL! SORRY!
IT DOESN'T LOOK TOO MUCH LIKE A CAMEL, BUT I DON'T THINK IT'S THAT BAD, TORG!

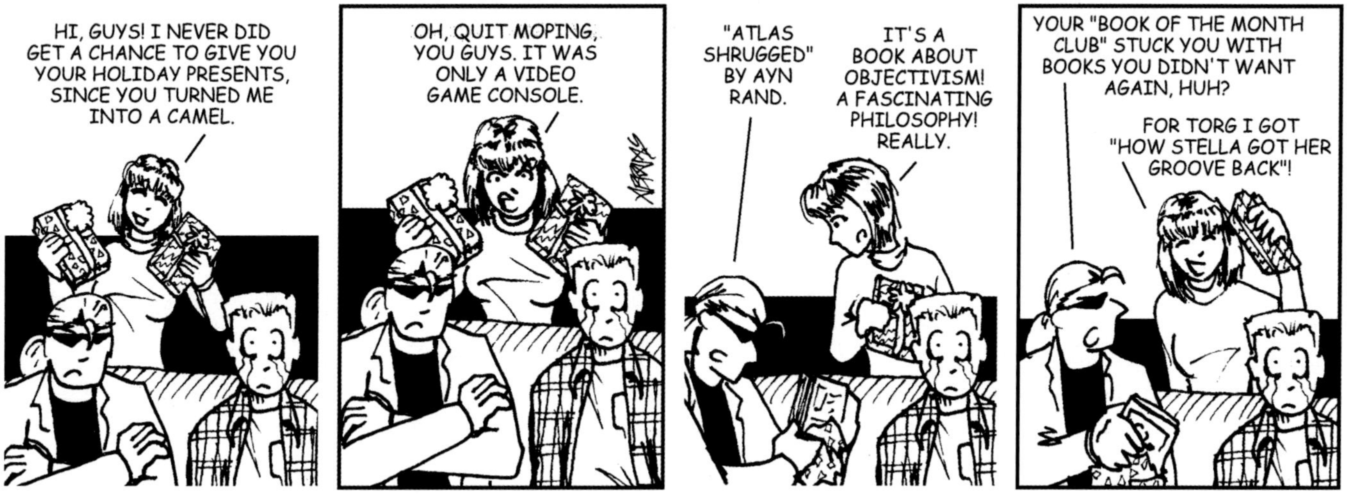
HI, GUYS! I NEVER DID GET A CHANCE TO GIVE YOU YOUR HOLIDAY PRESENTS, SINCE YOU TURNED ME INTO A CAMEL.
OH, QUIT MOPING, YOU GUYS. IT WAS ONLY A VIDEO GAME CONSOLE.
"ATLAS SHRUGGED" BY AYN RAND.
IT'S A BOOK ABOUT OBJECTIVISM! A FASCINATING PHILOSOPHY! REALLY.
YOUR "BOOK OF THE MONTH CLUB" STUCK YOU WITH BOOKS YOU DIDN'T WANT AGAIN, HUH?
FOR TORG I GOT "HOW STELLA GOT HER GROOVE BACK"!

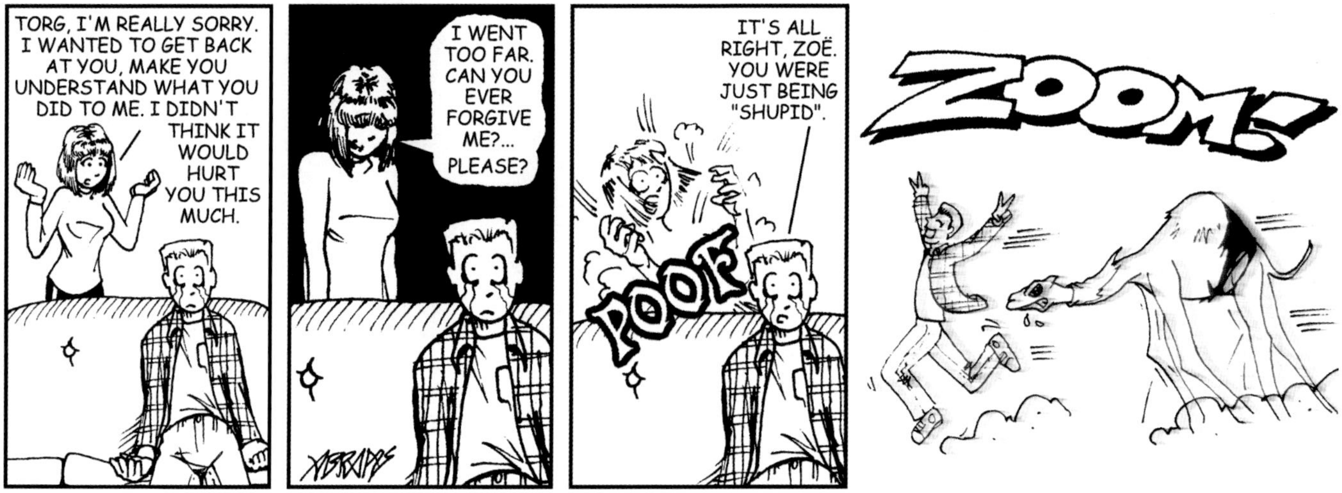
TORG, I'M REALLY SORRY. I WANTED TO GET BACK AT YOU, MAKE YOU UNDERSTAND WHAT YOU DID TO ME. I DIDN'T THINK IT WOULD HURT YOU THIS MUCH.
I WENT TOO FAR. CAN YOU EVER FORGIVE ME?... PLEASE?
IT'S ALL RIGHT, ZOË. YOU WERE JUST BEING "SHUPID".
POOF
ZOOM!

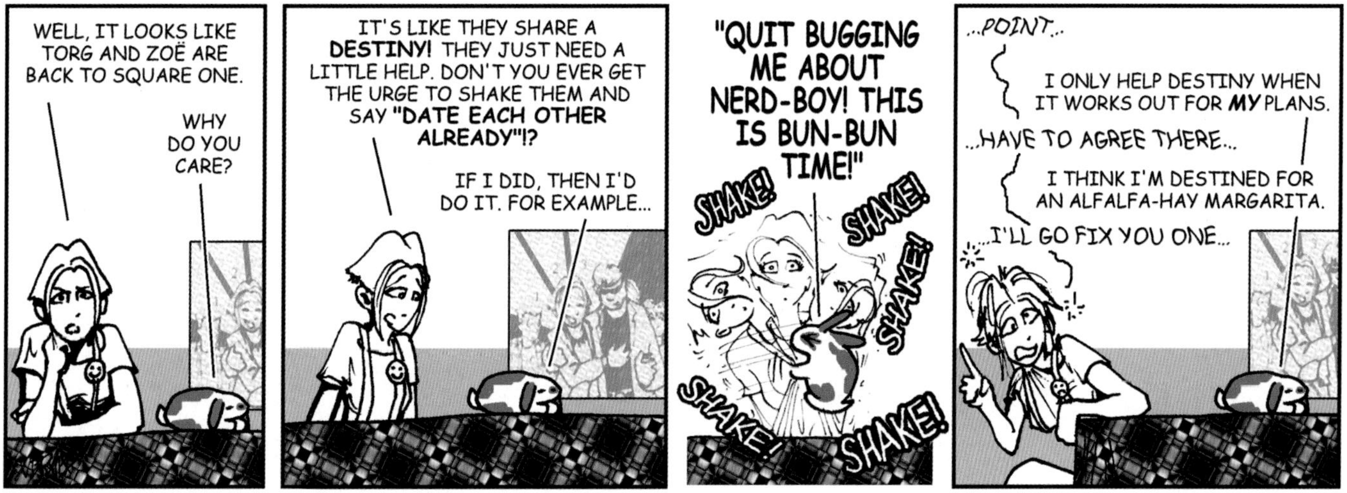
WELL, IT LOOKS LIKE TORG AND ZOË ARE BACK TO SQUARE ONE.
WHY DO YOU CARE?
IT'S LIKE THEY SHARE A **DESTINY!** THEY JUST NEED A LITTLE HELP. DON'T YOU EVER GET THE URGE TO SHAKE THEM AND SAY **"DATE EACH OTHER ALREADY"!?**
IF I DID, THEN I'D DO IT. FOR EXAMPLE...
"QUIT BUGGING ME ABOUT NERD-BOY! THIS IS BUN-BUN TIME!"
SHAKE! SHAKE! SHAKE! SHAKE! SHAKE! SHAKE!
...POINT...
I ONLY HELP DESTINY WHEN IT WORKS OUT FOR **MY** PLANS.
...HAVE TO AGREE THERE...
I THINK I'M DESTINED FOR AN ALFALFA-HAY MARGARITA.
...I'LL GO FIX YOU ONE...

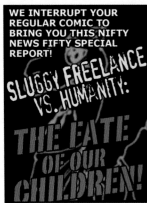

WE INTERRUPT YOUR REGULAR COMIC TO BRING YOU THIS NIFTY NEWS FIFTY SPECIAL REPORT!
SLUGGY FREELANCE VS. HUMANITY: THE FATE OF OUR CHILDREN!
THIS IS A NIFTY NEWS FIFTY SPECIAL REPORT, I'M STONE JOHNSON. IN RECENT WEEKS THE ONLINE COMIC STRIP "SLUGGY FREELANCE" HAS BEEN INVOLVED WITH A STORYLINE THAT WAS INNOCENT ENOUGH ON THE SURFACE.
STONE JOHNSON NIFTY NEWS 50
INNOCENT, THAT IS, IF YOU DON'T TAKE INTO ACCOUNT THEIR *INSIDIOUS PLAN* TO MAKE CURSED ARTIFACTS SEEM HAPPY, AND FUN! CURSED ARTIFACTS THAT CAN TAKE OUR CHILDREN'S LIVES! THEIR VERY SOULS! MAKE THEIR EYEBALLS BLEED! HOW, YOU ASK? WHAT SPOKES-PERSON COULD MAKE CURSED ARTIFACTS "COOL"? I GIVE YOU... **ZO CAMEL.**
ZO CAMEL! THE TRUTH OF THEIR ATTEMPT TO MARKET CURSED ARTIFACTS TO YOUR CHILDREN IS SO OBVIOUS THAT I HAVE NO NEED OF PROOF, AND MY CREED AS AN UNBIASED JOURNALIST GIVES ME NO CHOICE BUT TO REPORT IT.
ZO CAMEL
ZO CAMEL BAD! NIFTY NEWS 50
HOW FAR HAVE WE FALLEN AS A SOCIETY WHEN WE ALLOW SUCH SHENANIGANS ALL IN THE NAME OF MONEY? HAVE WE NO INTEGRITY? ARE WE SO SHALLOW? JUST BECAUSE IT'S A FACT THAT CUTE ANIMALS EQUAL CASH, SHOULD THEY BE EVERY-WHERE? THERE IS MORE TO LIFE THAN...
THE NEWS BROADCAST HAS BEEN INTERRUPTED DUE TO TECHNICAL DIFFICULTIES.
PLEASE STAND BY!
SORRY FOR THE INTERRUPTION, LADIES AND GENTLEMAN! THIS IS NEWSEY POOCHIE REPORTING FOR NIFTY NEWS FIFTY! OUR NEW TOP STORY, A SERIAL KILLER IS ON THE LOOSE AND...
NOT VERY KNIFE!
NEWSEY POOCHIE NIFTY NEWS 50
HOLD ON! THIS JUST IN! OUR PARENT COMPANY HAS JUST PURCHASED THE **CHOCO-LISHUS BAR COMPANY™!** WE GO LIVE TO ANOTHER CUTE ANIMAL!
LIVE
HI NEWSEY! THIS IS KANGAPANDEROO RE-PORTING THAT THE ENTIRE POPULATION OF THIS EN-TIRE EARTH AGREES THAT CHOCO-LISHUS BARS ™ ARE THE MOST DELICIOUS CHOCOLATE-LIKE BARS *EVER!* BACK TO YOU, NEWSEY POOCHIE!
KANGAPANDEROO NIFTY NEWS 50
MORE BREAKING NEWS! DUE TO POOR FACT-CHECKING BY STONE JOHNSON, WHO WE SHOULD POINT OUT HAS BEEN FIRED FROM THIS VERY STATION UNDER MYSTERIOUS CIRCUMSTANCES...
VERY MYSTERIOUS! NEVER DID TRUST HIM MUCH! JUST **ONE** OF THE REASONS THIS FINE NETWORK CANNED HIS BUTT!
...DUE TO POOR FACT-CHECKING BY THIS OBVIOUS SERVANT OF THE DEVIL, HE WAS IN ERROR TO SUGGEST THAT HAVING CUTE ANIMALS HOST NETWORK NEWS MEANT AN INCREASE IN PROFITS! A MEMO JUST ISSUED FORM THE **TRUSTWORTHY STATISTICS OF AMERICA** INDICATE THE MOST PROFITABLE HOST WOULD BE...
NO... THIS **CAN'T** BE RIGHT! HISTORICALLY, THE AMAZONS HAVE BEEN OUT OF EXISTENCE FOR THOUSANDS OF YEARS! AND THE TERM "SCANTILY CLAD" IS DEFINED IN WEBSTER'S DICTIONARY AS...
Duh!
THE NEWS BROADCAST HAS BEEN INTERRUPTED DUE TO TECHNICAL DIFFICULTIES.
PLEASE STAND BY!
HI! I'M AMY THE MASKED AMAZON WITH TONIGHT'S TOP STORY: MY BIKINI WAX LINES, AND HOW NOT SEEING THEM CAN HARM YOUR CHILDREN. WE'LL BE BACK AFTER A WORD FROM OUR SPONSORS, NOT TO BE CONFUSED WITH THE WORD FROM OUR SPONSORS WE'RE ALREADY GIVING YOU!
AMY'S A HIT!
MASKED AMAZON AMY NIFTY NEWS 50
NIFTY NEWS 50
WHEN TRUTH GIVES YOU LEMONS, WE MAKE LEMON-FLAVORED BEVERAGES.

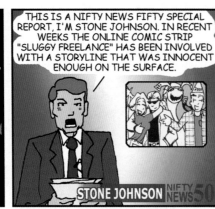

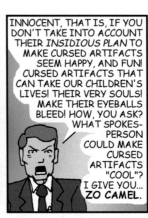

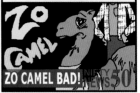

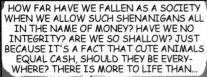

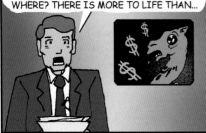

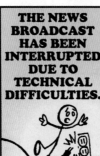

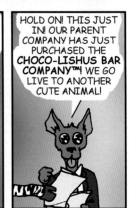

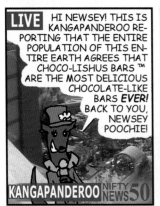

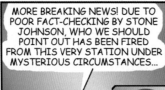

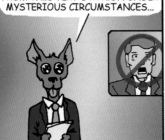

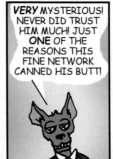

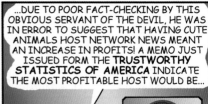

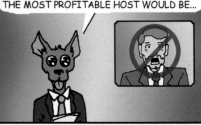

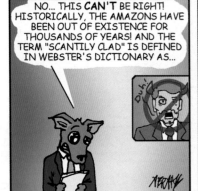

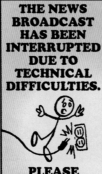

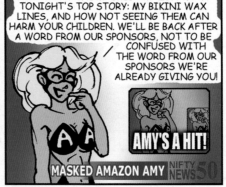

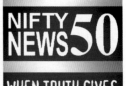

SLUGGY FREELANCE
KIKI
SHRUGGED

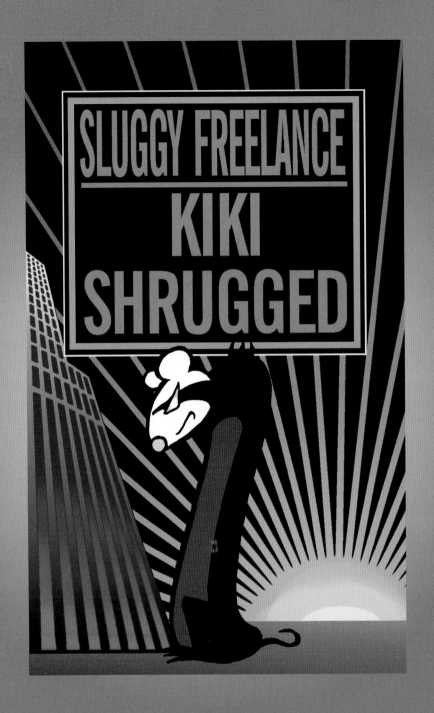

January 15th to January 21st, 2001, Ian McDonald, of the webcomic Bruno the Bandit (www.brunothebandit.com), agreed to fill in for me for a week. He also created this nifty cover for his run and gave me permission to use it. The script was his original creation, poking playful fun at Objectivism. It has often been debated whether this and future guest artist weeks are considered "canon."

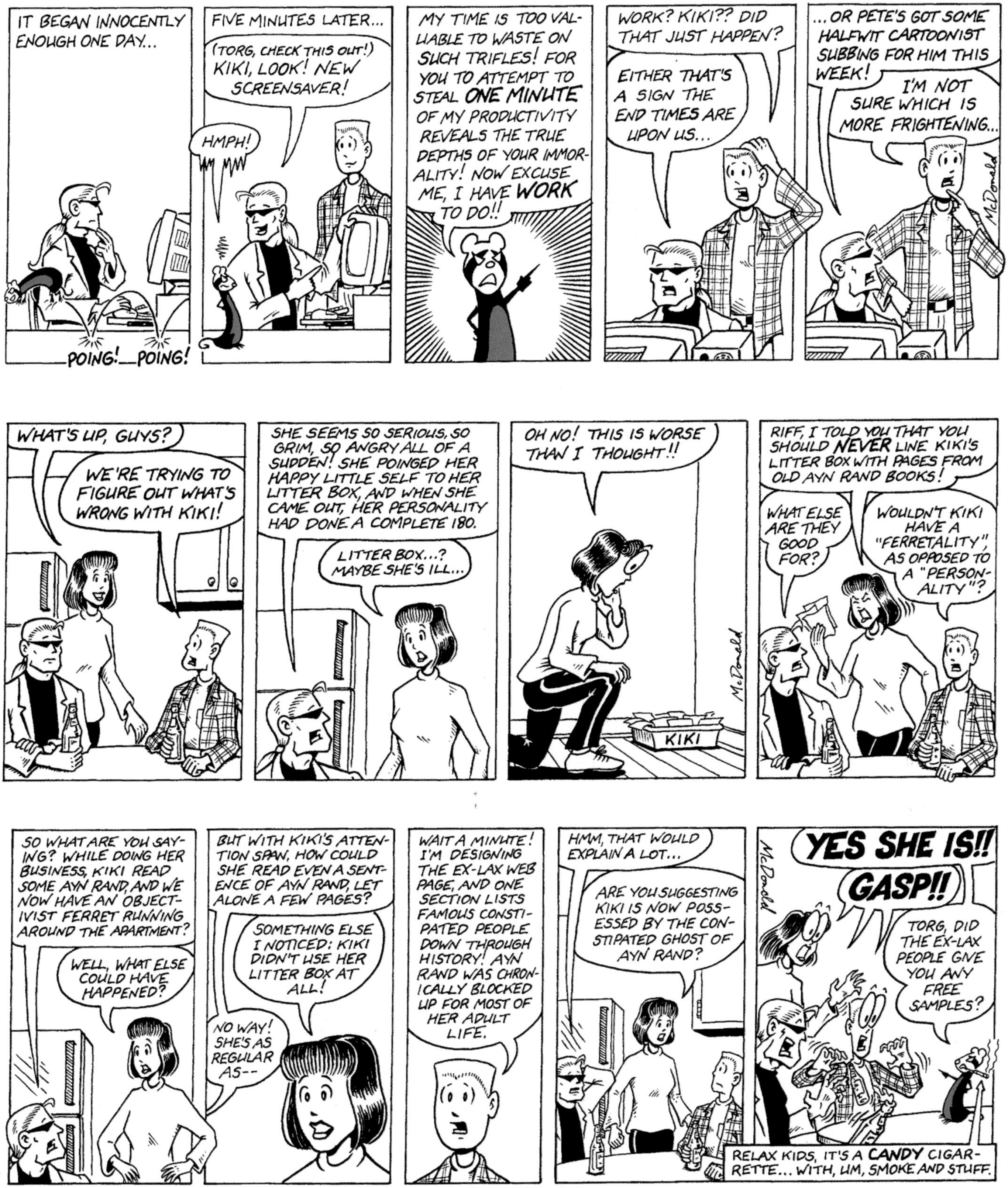
IT BEGAN INNOCENTLY ENOUGH ONE DAY...
POING! POING!
FIVE MINUTES LATER...
(TORG, CHECK THIS OUT!) KIKI, LOOK! NEW SCREENSAVER!
HMPH!
MY TIME IS TOO VALUABLE TO WASTE ON SUCH TRIFLES! FOR YOU TO ATTEMPT TO STEAL ONE MINUTE OF MY PRODUCTIVITY REVEALS THE TRUE DEPTHS OF YOUR IMMORALITY! NOW EXCUSE ME, I HAVE WORK TO DO!!
WORK? KIKI?? DID THAT JUST HAPPEN?
EITHER THAT'S A SIGN THE END TIMES ARE UPON US...
...OR PETE'S GOT SOME HALFWIT CARTOONIST SUBBING FOR HIM THIS WEEK!
I'M NOT SURE WHICH IS MORE FRIGHTENING...
WHAT'S UP, GUYS?
WE'RE TRYING TO FIGURE OUT WHAT'S WRONG WITH KIKI!
SHE SEEMS SO SERIOUS, SO GRIM, SO ANGRY ALL OF A SUDDEN! SHE POINGED HER HAPPY LITTLE SELF TO HER LITTER BOX, AND WHEN SHE CAME OUT, HER PERSONALITY HAD DONE A COMPLETE 180.
LITTER BOX...? MAYBE SHE'S ILL...
OH NO! THIS IS WORSE THAN I THOUGHT!!
KIKI
RIFF, I TOLD YOU THAT YOU SHOULD NEVER LINE KIKI'S LITTER BOX WITH PAGES FROM OLD AYN RAND BOOKS!
WHAT ELSE ARE THEY GOOD FOR?
WOULDN'T KIKI HAVE A "FERRETALITY", AS OPPOSED TO A "PERSONALITY"?
SO WHAT ARE YOU SAYING? WHILE DOING HER BUSINESS, KIKI READ SOME AYN RAND, AND WE NOW HAVE AN OBJECTIVIST FERRET RUNNING AROUND THE APARTMENT?
WELL, WHAT ELSE COULD HAVE HAPPENED?
BUT WITH KIKI'S ATTENTION SPAN, HOW COULD SHE READ EVEN A SENTENCE OF AYN RAND, LET ALONE A FEW PAGES?
SOMETHING ELSE I NOTICED: KIKI DIDN'T USE HER LITTER BOX AT ALL!
NO WAY! SHE'S AS REGULAR AS--
WAIT A MINUTE! I'M DESIGNING THE EX-LAX WEB PAGE, AND ONE SECTION LISTS FAMOUS CONSTIPATED PEOPLE DOWN THROUGH HISTORY! AYN RAND WAS CHRONICALLY BLOCKED UP FOR MOST OF HER ADULT LIFE.
HMM, THAT WOULD EXPLAIN A LOT...
ARE YOU SUGGESTING KIKI IS NOW POSSESSED BY THE CONSTIPATED GHOST OF AYN RAND?
YES SHE IS!!
GASP!!
TORG, DID THE EX-LAX PEOPLE GIVE YOU ANY FREE SAMPLES?
RELAX KIDS, IT'S A CANDY CIGARRETTE... WITH, UM, SMOKE AND STUFF.

THIS CREATURE WHOM I NOW POSSESS HAPPENED TO GLANCE AT A PAGE OF MY WORK AS SHE WAS ABOUT TO GO POTTY! ONE GLANCE WAS ALL IT TOOK FOR ME TO MAKE MY MOVE!
MY RESTLESS SPIRIT HAS HAUNTED THE PAGES OF MY WORK! BUT NOW, THANKS TO THIS BEAST, I'M BACK!
BUT WHY? SHE'S AN INNOCENT LITTLE CREATURE! SHE--
SHE HAS FOUND A BETTER CALLING: TO BE A FERRET OF THE MIND!
AND NOW, I'M OFF TO GET BILL GATES' AID TO FORM A NEW SOCIETY! ONE IN WHICH REASON AND ENLIGHTENED SELF-INTEREST REIGN SUPREME! ONE IN WHICH THERE IS NO ROOM FOR ALTRUISM, COLLECTIVISM, OR MYSTICISM! DON'T WAIT UP FOR ME!
POING. POING.
SO, YOU UP FOR A GAME OF DIABLO 2?
AS ALWAYS!
GUYS!!
NEXT DAY, AT MICROSOFT H.Q....
ATTORNEY GENERAL ON LINE ONE, SIR!
NO!! I CAN'T LET BILL CUT A DEAL WITH THE GOVERNMENT! WHAT CAN I DO...?
I'LL TAKE IT!
MR. GATES, THE NEW ADMINISTRATION WISHES TO PUT THE GOVERNMENT'S FIGHT WITH YOU BEHIND US. WE FEEL WE HAVE A SOLUTION TO BENEFIT ALL PARTIES.
I'M LISTENING...
WELL, FIRST OF ALL--
AACK! THERE'S A %☆$#@ FERRET IN MY PANTS!!
?
ARE... ARE YOU COMING ON TO ME??
AIIEEE!! IT TALKS!!
SIR, I NEED TO SPEAK WITH YOU!
MR. GATES, YOU ARE HUMANITY'S LAST, BEST HOPE! IT IS YOU WHO MUST LEAD OUR BEST AND BRIGHTEST AWAY FROM THIS VILE, CORRUPT EXCUSE FOR A SOCIETY. A SOCIETY THAT USES YOUR INNOVATIVE THINKING, WHILE AT THE SAME TIME, PUNISHES YOU FOR IT! LET US LEAVE THE MOOCHERS AND MYSTICS BEHIND!
YOU MAKE A LOT OF SENSE... FOR A FERRET.
BUT THE GOVERNMENT WAS READY TO MAKE A DEAL! PERHAPS I CAN SAVE MICROSOFT FROM BEING SPLIT UP!
WITH YOUR OUTBURST ON THE PHONE JUST NOW, FORGET IT. THEY NOW SEE YOU AS THE ÜBERGEEK DAVID KORESH, AND MICROSOFT AS THE NEXT BRANCH DAVIDIAN COMPOUND!
I DARESAY THE TANKS ARE ON THEIR WAY TO FLATTEN THIS PLACE AS WE SPEAK!
NONSENSE! I'LL MAKE A RETURN CALL, AND--
BOOOM!!!
PERHAPS WE SHOULD CONTINUE THIS DISCUSSION IN MY ESCAPE POD, KIKI!
SOUNDS LIKE A PLAN...
RESISTANCE IS FUTILE!
RRRUMBLE!!

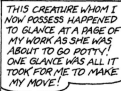

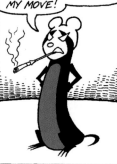

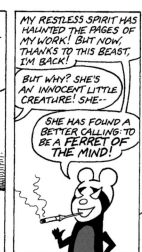

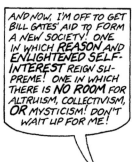

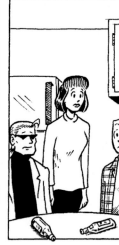

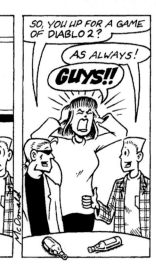

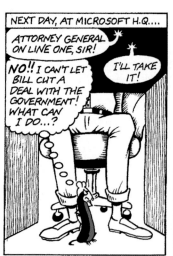

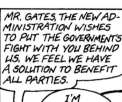

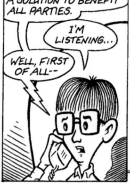

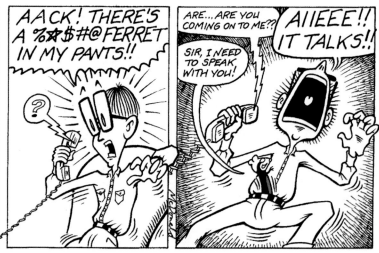

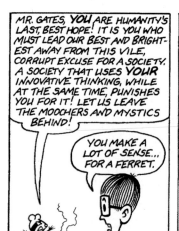

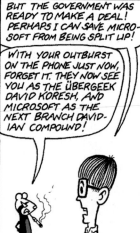

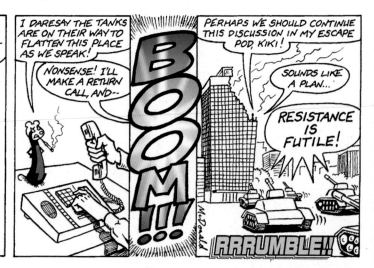

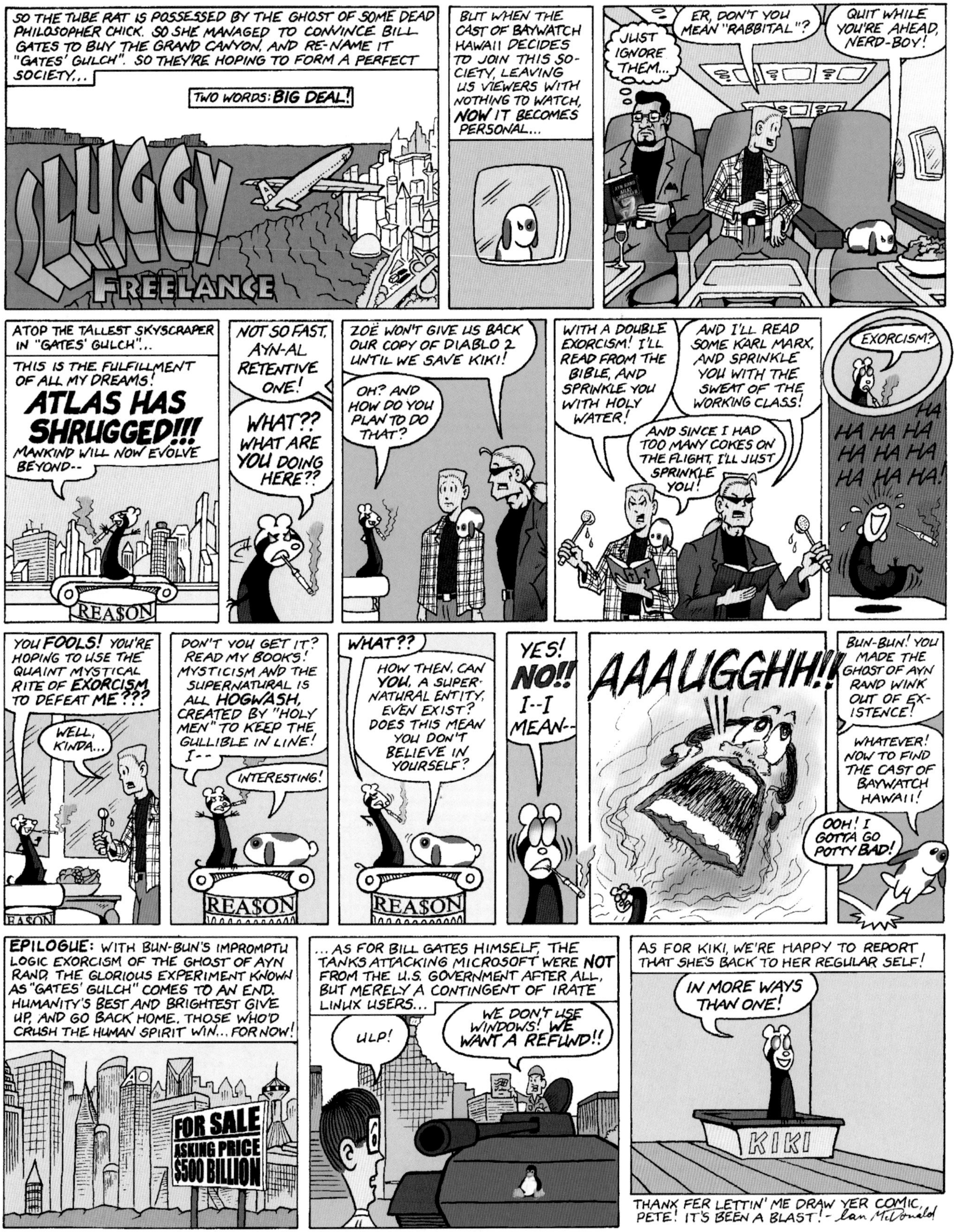
SO THE TUBE RAT IS POSSESSED BY THE GHOST OF SOME DEAD PHILOSOPHER CHICK. SO SHE MANAGED TO CONVINCE BILL GATES TO BUY THE GRAND CANYON, AND RE-NAME IT "GATES' GULCH". SO THEY'RE HOPING TO FORM A PERFECT SOCIETY...
TWO WORDS: BIG DEAL!
SLUGGY
FREELANCE
BUT WHEN THE CAST OF BAYWATCH HAWAII DECIDES TO JOIN THIS SOCIETY, LEAVING US VIEWERS WITH NOTHING TO WATCH, NOW IT BECOMES PERSONAL...
JUST IGNORE THEM...
ER, DON'T YOU MEAN "RABBITAL"?
QUIT WHILE YOU'RE AHEAD, NERD-BOY!
ATOP THE TALLEST SKYSCRAPER IN "GATES' GULCH"...
THIS IS THE FULFILLMENT OF ALL MY DREAMS! ATLAS HAS SHRUGGED!!! MANKIND WILL NOW EVOLVE BEYOND--
REA$ON
NOT SO FAST, AYN-AL RETENTIVE ONE!
WHAT?? WHAT ARE YOU DOING HERE??
ZOË WON'T GIVE US BACK OUR COPY OF DIABLO 2 UNTIL WE SAVE KIKI!
OH? AND HOW DO YOU PLAN TO DO THAT?
WITH A DOUBLE EXORCISM! I'LL READ FROM THE BIBLE, AND SPRINKLE YOU WITH HOLY WATER!
AND I'LL READ SOME KARL MARX, AND SPRINKLE YOU WITH THE SWEAT OF THE WORKING CLASS!
AND SINCE I HAD TOO MANY COKES ON THE FLIGHT, I'LL JUST SPRINKLE YOU!
EXORCISM?
HA HA HA HA HA HA HA HA HA HA HA!
YOU FOOLS! YOU'RE HOPING TO USE THE QUAINT MYSTICAL RITE OF EXORCISM TO DEFEAT ME???
WELL, KINDA...
DON'T YOU GET IT? READ MY BOOKS! MYSTICISM AND THE SUPERNATURAL IS ALL HOGWASH, CREATED BY "HOLY MEN" TO KEEP THE GULLIBLE IN LINE! I--
INTERESTING!
REA$ON
WHAT??
HOW THEN, CAN YOU, A SUPERNATURAL ENTITY, EVEN EXIST? DOES THIS MEAN YOU DON'T BELIEVE IN YOURSELF?
REA$ON
YES! NO!! I--I MEAN--
AAAUGGHH!!
BUN-BUN! YOU MADE THE GHOST OF AYN RAND WINK OUT OF EXISTENCE!
WHATEVER! NOW TO FIND THE CAST OF BAYWATCH HAWAII!
OOH! I GOTTA GO POTTY BAD!
EPILOGUE: WITH BUN-BUN'S IMPROMPTU LOGIC EXORCISM OF THE GHOST OF AYN RAND, THE GLORIOUS EXPERIMENT KNOWN AS "GATES' GULCH" COMES TO AN END. HUMANITY'S BEST AND BRIGHTEST GIVE UP, AND GO BACK HOME. THOSE WHO'D CRUSH THE HUMAN SPIRIT WIN... FOR NOW!
FOR SALE
ASKING PRICE
$500 BILLION
...AS FOR BILL GATES HIMSELF, THE TANKS ATTACKING MICROSOFT WERE NOT FROM THE U.S. GOVERNMENT AFTER ALL, BUT MERELY A CONTINGENT OF IRATE LINUX USERS...
ULP!
WE DON'T USE WINDOWS! WE WANT A REFUND!!
AS FOR KIKI, WE'RE HAPPY TO REPORT THAT SHE'S BACK TO HER REGULAR SELF!
IN MORE WAYS THAN ONE!
KIKI
THANX FER LETTIN' ME DRAW YER COMIC, PETE! IT'S BEEN A BLAST! - Ian McDonald

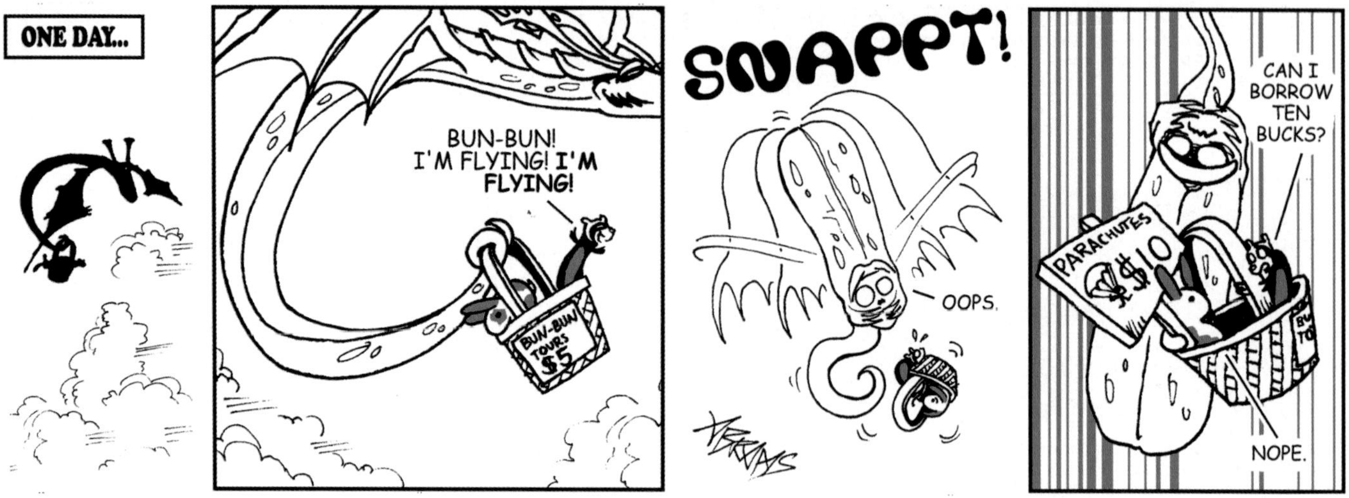
ONE DAY...
BUN-BUN! I'M FLYING! I'M FLYING!
BUN-BUN TOURS $5
SNAPPT!
OOPS.
CAN I BORROW TEN BUCKS?
PARACHUTES $10
NOPE.

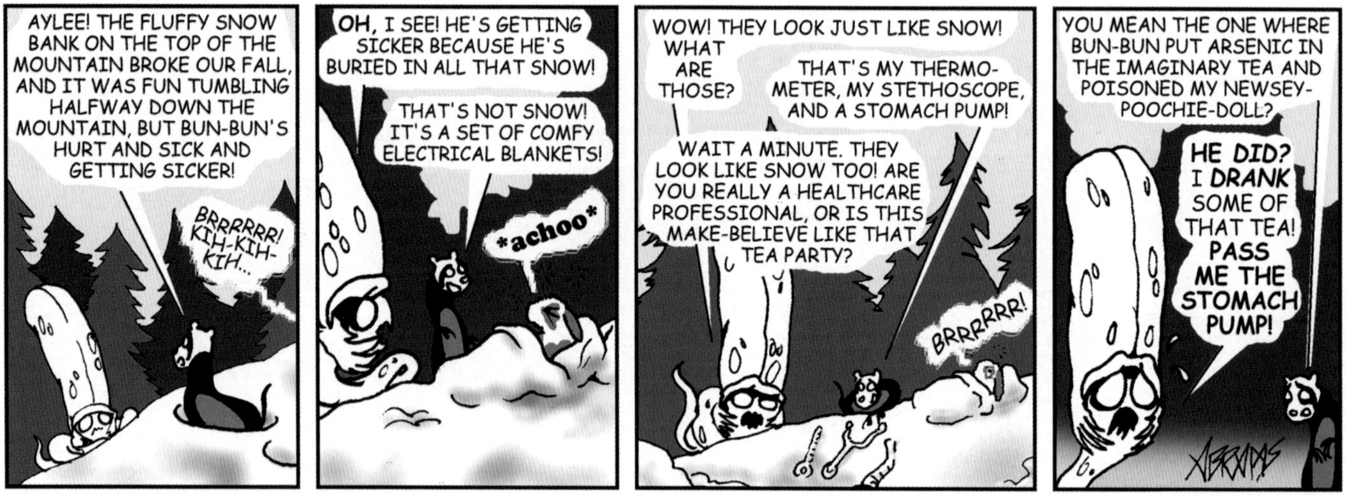
AYLEE! THE FLUFFY SNOW BANK ON THE TOP OF THE MOUNTAIN BROKE OUR FALL, AND IT WAS FUN TUMBLING HALFWAY DOWN THE MOUNTAIN, BUT BUN-BUN'S HURT AND SICK AND GETTING SICKER!
BRRRRRR! KIH-KIH-KIH...
OH, I SEE! HE'S GETTING SICKER BECAUSE HE'S BURIED IN ALL THAT SNOW!
THAT'S NOT SNOW! IT'S A SET OF COMFY ELECTRICAL BLANKETS!
achoo
WOW! THEY LOOK JUST LIKE SNOW! WHAT ARE THOSE?
THAT'S MY THERMOMETER, MY STETHOSCOPE, AND A STOMACH PUMP!
WAIT A MINUTE. THEY LOOK LIKE SNOW TOO! ARE YOU REALLY A HEALTHCARE PROFESSIONAL, OR IS THIS MAKE-BELIEVE LIKE THAT TEA PARTY?
BRRRRRR!
YOU MEAN THE ONE WHERE BUN-BUN PUT ARSENIC IN THE IMAGINARY TEA AND POISONED MY NEWSEY-POOCHIE-DOLL?
HE DID? I DRANK SOME OF THAT TEA! PASS ME THE STOMACH PUMP!

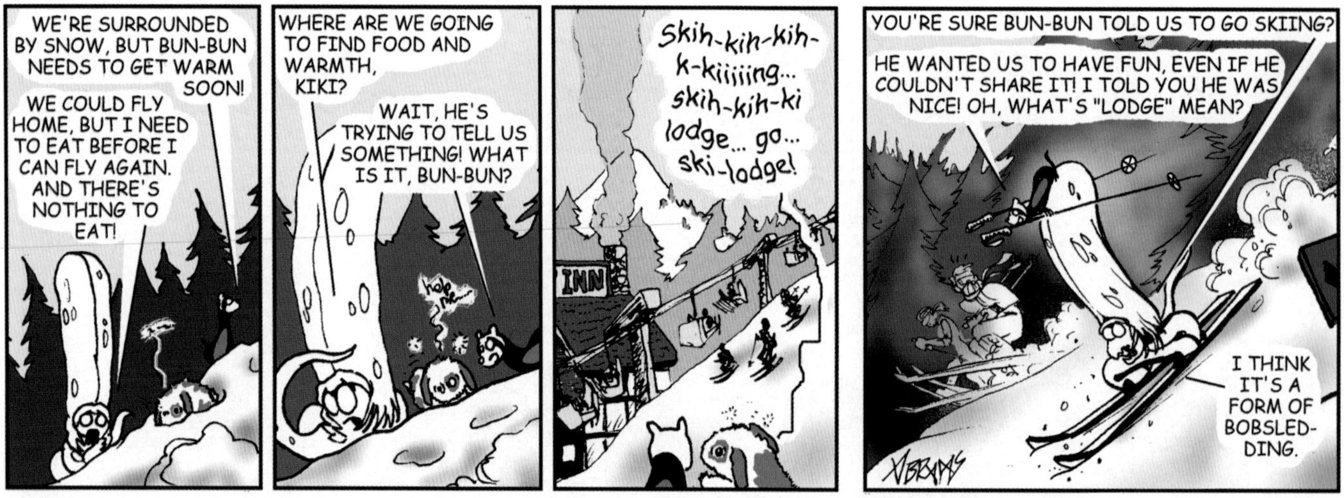
WE'RE SURROUNDED BY SNOW, BUT BUN-BUN NEEDS TO GET WARM SOON!
WE COULD FLY HOME, BUT I NEED TO EAT BEFORE I CAN FLY AGAIN. AND THERE'S NOTHING TO EAT!
WHERE ARE WE GOING TO FIND FOOD AND WARMTH, KIKI?
WAIT, HE'S TRYING TO TELL US SOMETHING! WHAT IS IT, BUN-BUN?
Skih-kih-kih-k-kiiiiing... skih-kih-ki lodge... go... ski-lodge!
INN
YOU'RE SURE BUN-BUN TOLD US TO GO SKIING?
HE WANTED US TO HAVE FUN, EVEN IF HE COULDN'T SHARE IT! I TOLD YOU HE WAS NICE! OH, WHAT'S "LODGE" MEAN?
I THINK IT'S A FORM OF BOBSLEDDING.

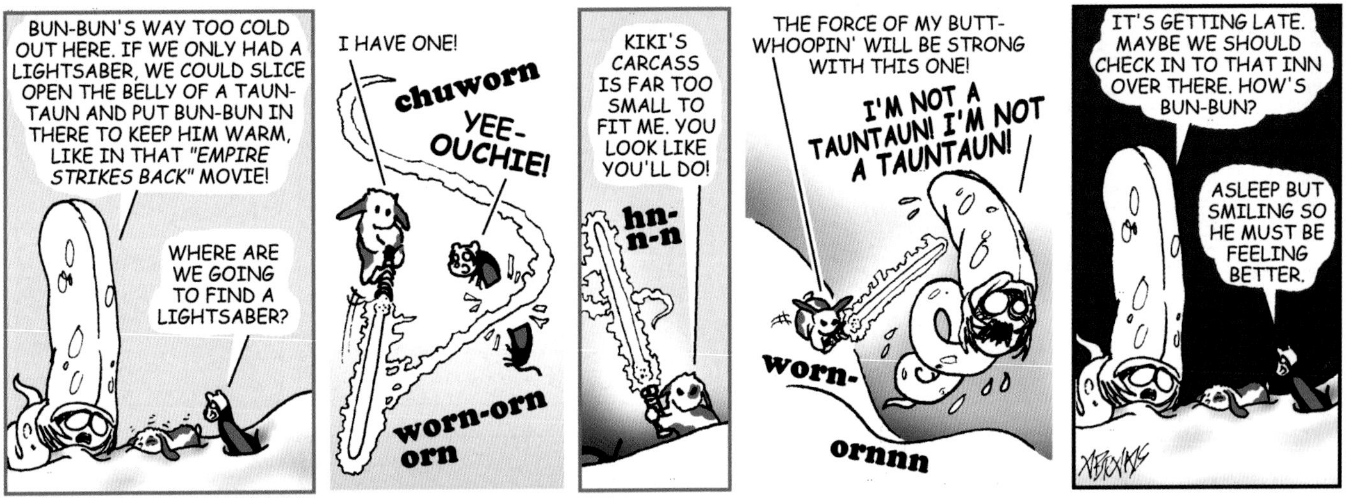
BUN-BUN'S WAY TOO COLD OUT HERE. IF WE ONLY HAD A LIGHTSABER, WE COULD SLICE OPEN THE BELLY OF A TAUN-TAUN AND PUT BUN-BUN IN THERE TO KEEP HIM WARM, LIKE IN THAT "EMPIRE STRIKES BACK" MOVIE!
WHERE ARE WE GOING TO FIND A LIGHTSABER?
I HAVE ONE!
chuworn
YEE-OUCHIE!
worn-orn orn
KIKI'S CARCASS IS FAR TOO SMALL TO FIT ME. YOU LOOK LIKE YOU'LL DO!
hn-n-n
THE FORCE OF MY BUTT-WHOOPIN' WILL BE STRONG WITH THIS ONE!
I'M NOT A TAUNTAUN! I'M NOT A TAUNTAUN!
worn-ornnn
IT'S GETTING LATE. MAYBE WE SHOULD CHECK IN TO THAT INN OVER THERE. HOW'S BUN-BUN?
ASLEEP BUT SMILING SO HE MUST BE FEELING BETTER.

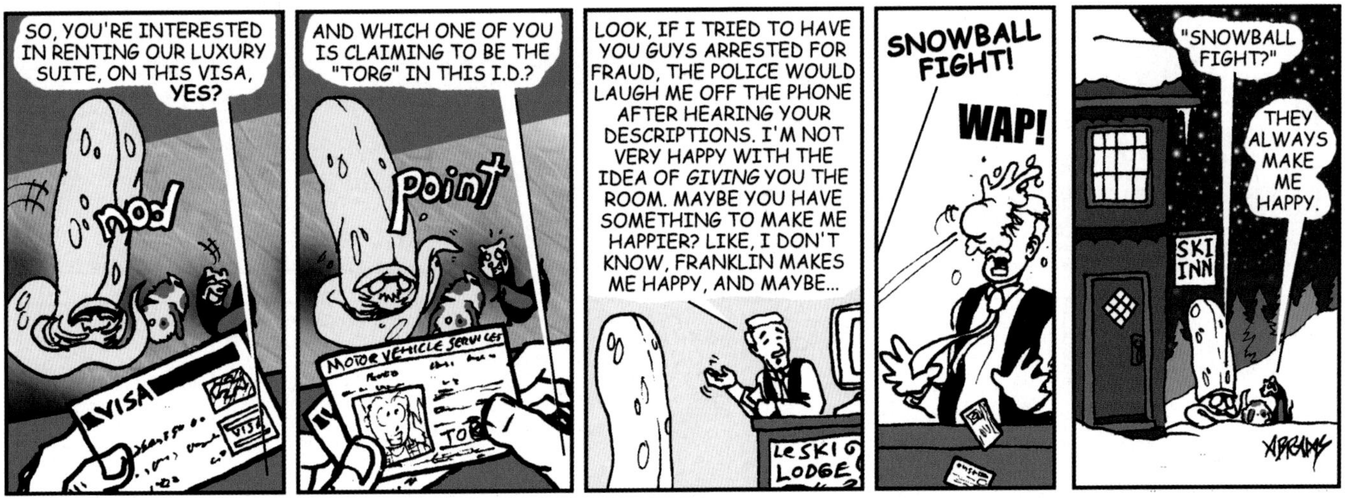
SO, YOU'RE INTERESTED IN RENTING OUR LUXURY SUITE, ON THIS VISA, YES?
nod
VISA
AND WHICH ONE OF YOU IS CLAIMING TO BE THE "TORG" IN THIS I.D.?
point
MOTOR VEHICLE SERVICES
LOOK, IF I TRIED TO HAVE YOU GUYS ARRESTED FOR FRAUD, THE POLICE WOULD LAUGH ME OFF THE PHONE AFTER HEARING YOUR DESCRIPTIONS. I'M NOT VERY HAPPY WITH THE IDEA OF GIVING YOU THE ROOM. MAYBE YOU HAVE SOMETHING TO MAKE ME HAPPIER? LIKE, I DON'T KNOW, FRANKLIN MAKES ME HAPPY, AND MAYBE...
Le SKI LODGE
SNOWBALL FIGHT!
WAP!
"SNOWBALL FIGHT?"
THEY ALWAYS MAKE ME HAPPY.
SKI INN

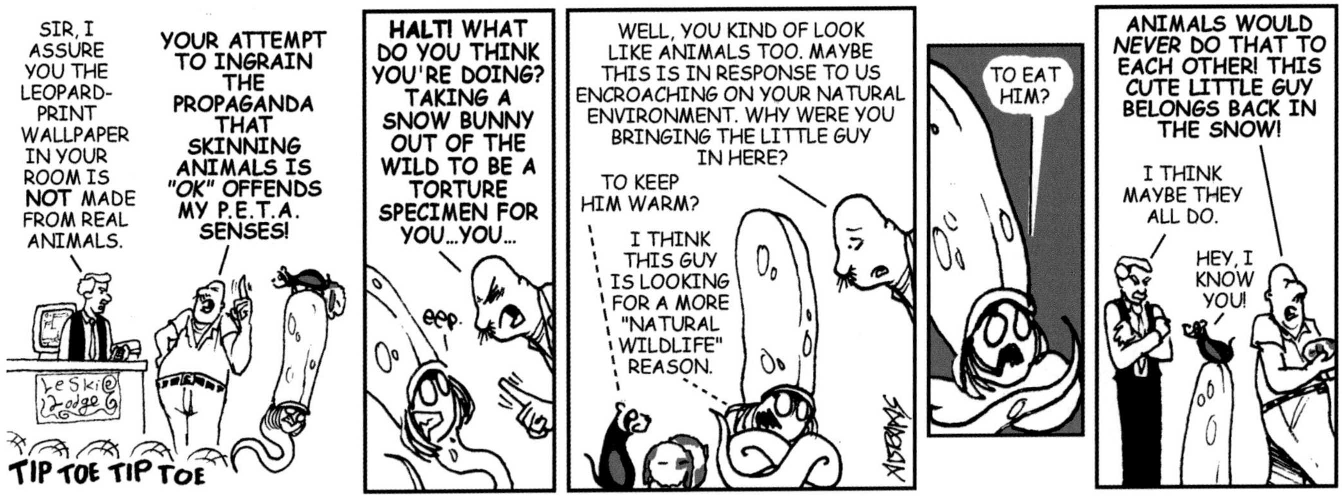
SIR, I ASSURE YOU THE LEOPARD-PRINT WALLPAPER IN YOUR ROOM IS NOT MADE FROM REAL ANIMALS.
YOUR ATTEMPT TO INGRAIN THE PROPAGANDA THAT SKINNING ANIMALS IS "OK" OFFENDS MY P.E.T.A. SENSES!
Le Ski Lodge
TIP TOE TIP TOE
HALT! WHAT DO YOU THINK YOU'RE DOING? TAKING A SNOW BUNNY OUT OF THE WILD TO BE A TORTURE SPECIMEN FOR YOU...YOU...
eep.
WELL, YOU KIND OF LOOK LIKE ANIMALS TOO. MAYBE THIS IS IN RESPONSE TO US ENCROACHING ON YOUR NATURAL ENVIRONMENT. WHY WERE YOU BRINGING THE LITTLE GUY IN HERE?
TO KEEP HIM WARM?
I THINK THIS GUY IS LOOKING FOR A MORE "NATURAL WILDLIFE" REASON.
TO EAT HIM?
ANIMALS WOULD NEVER DO THAT TO EACH OTHER! THIS CUTE LITTLE GUY BELONGS BACK IN THE SNOW!
I THINK MAYBE THEY ALL DO.
HEY, I KNOW YOU!

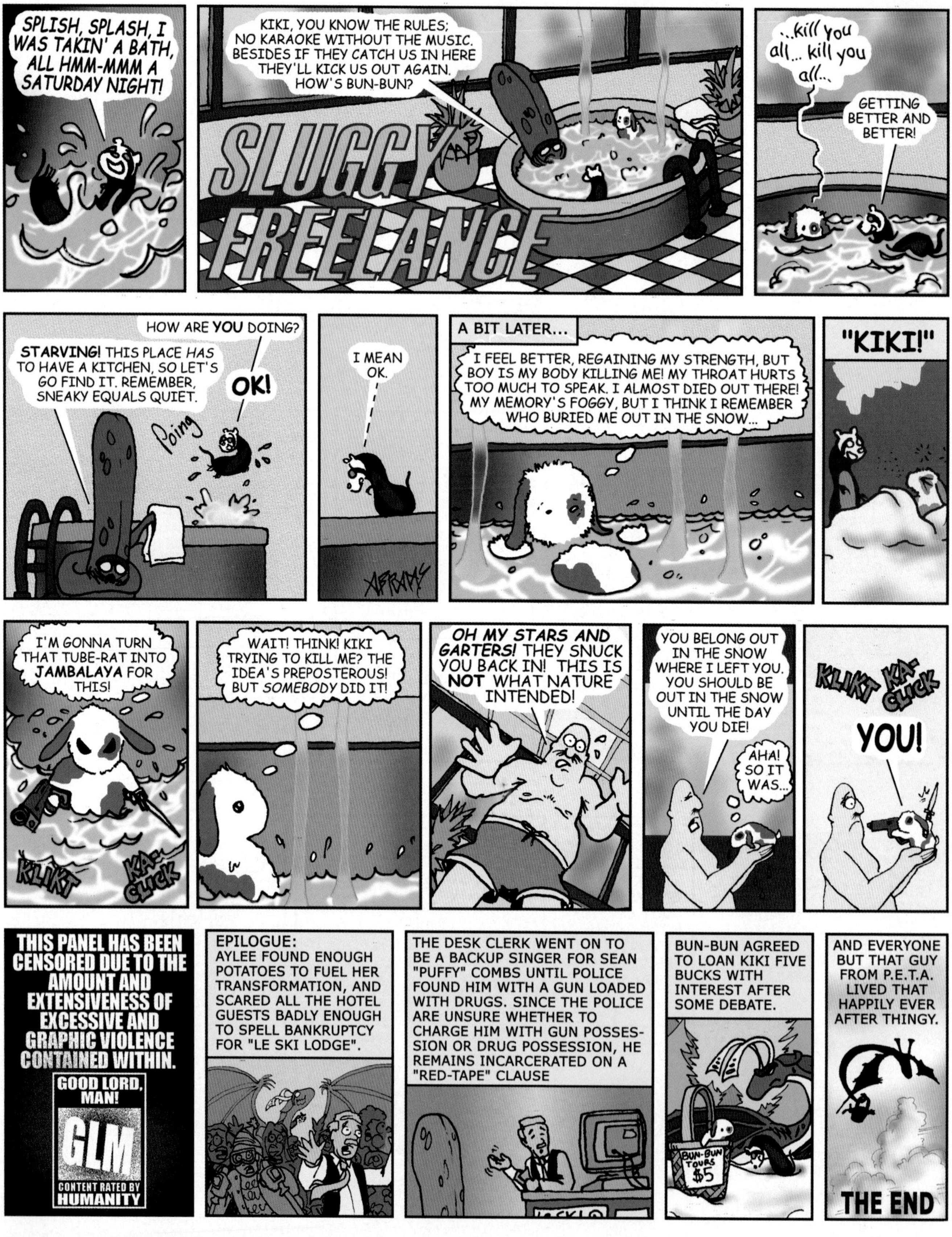
SPLISH, SPLASH, I WAS TAKIN' A BATH, ALL HMM-MMM A SATURDAY NIGHT!
KIKI, YOU KNOW THE RULES; NO KARAOKE WITHOUT THE MUSIC. BESIDES IF THEY CATCH US IN HERE THEY'LL KICK US OUT AGAIN. HOW'S BUN-BUN?
SLUGGY FREELANCE
..kill you all... kill you all...
GETTING BETTER AND BETTER!
HOW ARE YOU DOING?
STARVING! THIS PLACE HAS TO HAVE A KITCHEN, SO LET'S GO FIND IT. REMEMBER, SNEAKY EQUALS QUIET.
OK!
Poing
I MEAN OK.
A BIT LATER...
I FEEL BETTER, REGAINING MY STRENGTH, BUT BOY IS MY BODY KILLING ME! MY THROAT HURTS TOO MUCH TO SPEAK. I ALMOST DIED OUT THERE! MY MEMORY'S FOGGY, BUT I THINK I REMEMBER WHO BURIED ME OUT IN THE SNOW...
"KIKI!"
I'M GONNA TURN THAT TUBE-RAT INTO JAMBALAYA FOR THIS!
KLIKT
KA-CLICK
WAIT! THINK! KIKI TRYING TO KILL ME? THE IDEA'S PREPOSTEROUS! BUT SOMEBODY DID IT!
OH MY STARS AND GARTERS! THEY SNUCK YOU BACK IN! THIS IS NOT WHAT NATURE INTENDED!
YOU BELONG OUT IN THE SNOW WHERE I LEFT YOU. YOU SHOULD BE OUT IN THE SNOW UNTIL THE DAY YOU DIE!
AHA! SO IT WAS...
KLIKT
KA-CLICK
YOU!
THIS PANEL HAS BEEN CENSORED DUE TO THE AMOUNT AND EXTENSIVENESS OF EXCESSIVE AND GRAPHIC VIOLENCE CONTAINED WITHIN.
GOOD LORD, MAN!
GLM
CONTENT RATED BY HUMANITY
EPILOGUE: AYLEE FOUND ENOUGH POTATOES TO FUEL HER TRANSFORMATION, AND SCARED ALL THE HOTEL GUESTS BADLY ENOUGH TO SPELL BANKRUPTCY FOR "LE SKI LODGE".
THE DESK CLERK WENT ON TO BE A BACKUP SINGER FOR SEAN "PUFFY" COMBS UNTIL POLICE FOUND HIM WITH A GUN LOADED WITH DRUGS. SINCE THE POLICE ARE UNSURE WHETHER TO CHARGE HIM WITH GUN POSSESSION OR DRUG POSSESSION, HE REMAINS INCARCERATED ON A "RED-TAPE" CLAUSE
BUN-BUN AGREED TO LOAN KIKI FIVE BUCKS WITH INTEREST AFTER SOME DEBATE.
BUN-BUN TOURS $5
AND EVERYONE BUT THAT GUY FROM P.E.T.A. LIVED THAT HAPPILY EVER AFTER THINGY.
THE END

The Bug, The Witch, and The Robot.

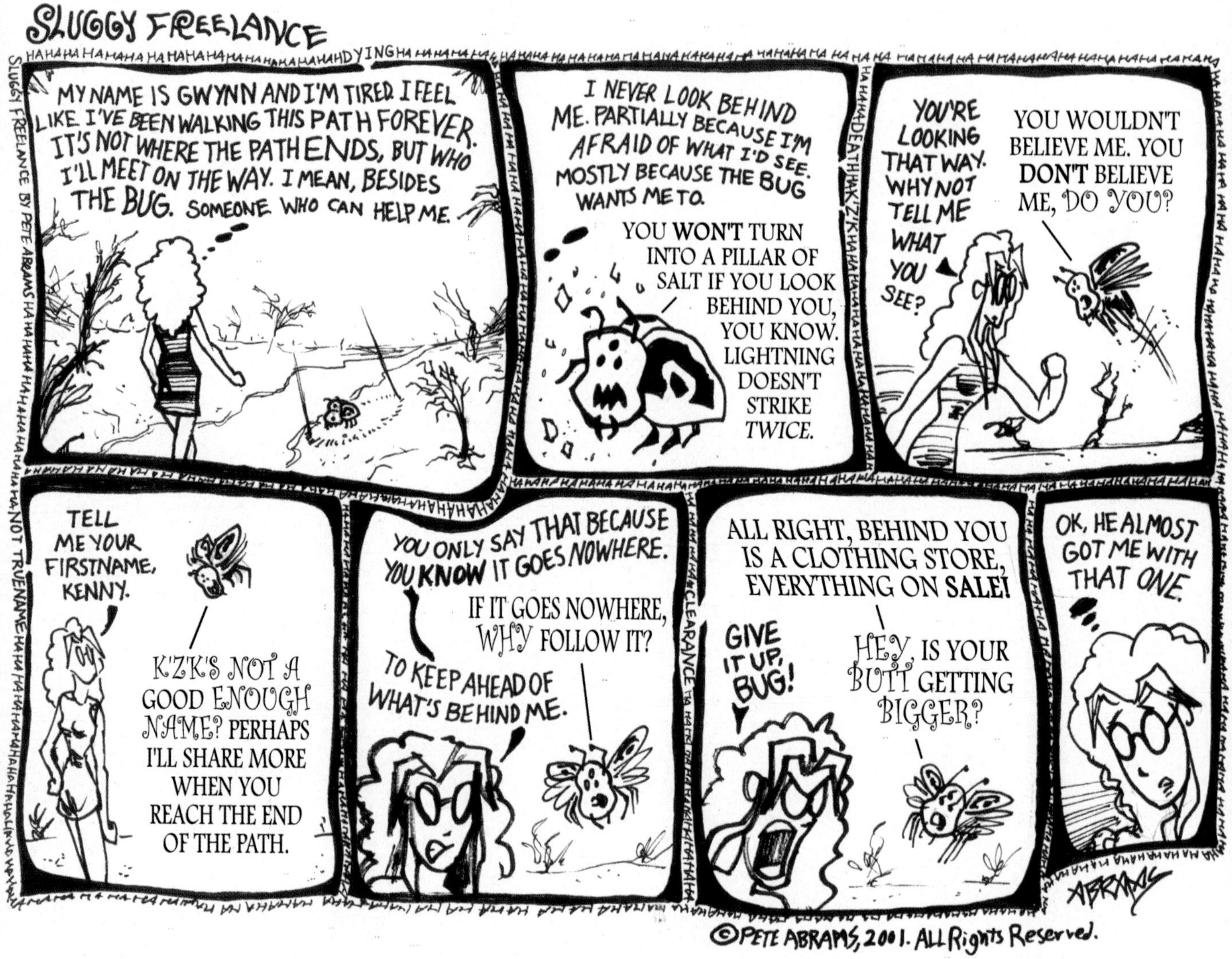
SLUGGY FREELANCE
MY NAME IS GWYNN AND I'M TIRED. I FEEL LIKE I'VE BEEN WALKING THIS PATH FOREVER. IT'S NOT WHERE THE PATH ENDS, BUT WHO I'LL MEET ON THE WAY. I MEAN, BESIDES THE BUG. SOMEONE WHO CAN HELP ME.
I NEVER LOOK BEHIND ME. PARTIALLY BECAUSE I'M AFRAID OF WHAT I'D SEE. MOSTLY BECAUSE THE BUG WANTS ME TO.
YOU WON'T TURN INTO A PILLAR OF SALT IF YOU LOOK BEHIND YOU, YOU KNOW. LIGHTNING DOESN'T STRIKE TWICE.
YOU'RE LOOKING THAT WAY. WHY NOT TELL ME WHAT YOU SEE?
YOU WOULDN'T BELIEVE ME. YOU DON'T BELIEVE ME, DO YOU?
TELL ME YOUR FIRSTNAME, KENNY.
K'Z'K'S NOT A GOOD ENOUGH NAME? PERHAPS I'LL SHARE MORE WHEN YOU REACH THE END OF THE PATH.
YOU ONLY SAY THAT BECAUSE YOU KNOW IT GOES NOWHERE.
IF IT GOES NOWHERE, WHY FOLLOW IT?
TO KEEP AHEAD OF WHAT'S BEHIND ME.
ALL RIGHT, BEHIND YOU IS A CLOTHING STORE, EVERYTHING ON SALE!
GIVE IT UP, BUG!
HEY, IS YOUR BUTT GETTING BIGGER?
OK, HE ALMOST GOT ME WITH THAT ONE.
ABRAMS
©PETE ABRAMS, 2001. ALL Rights Reserved.

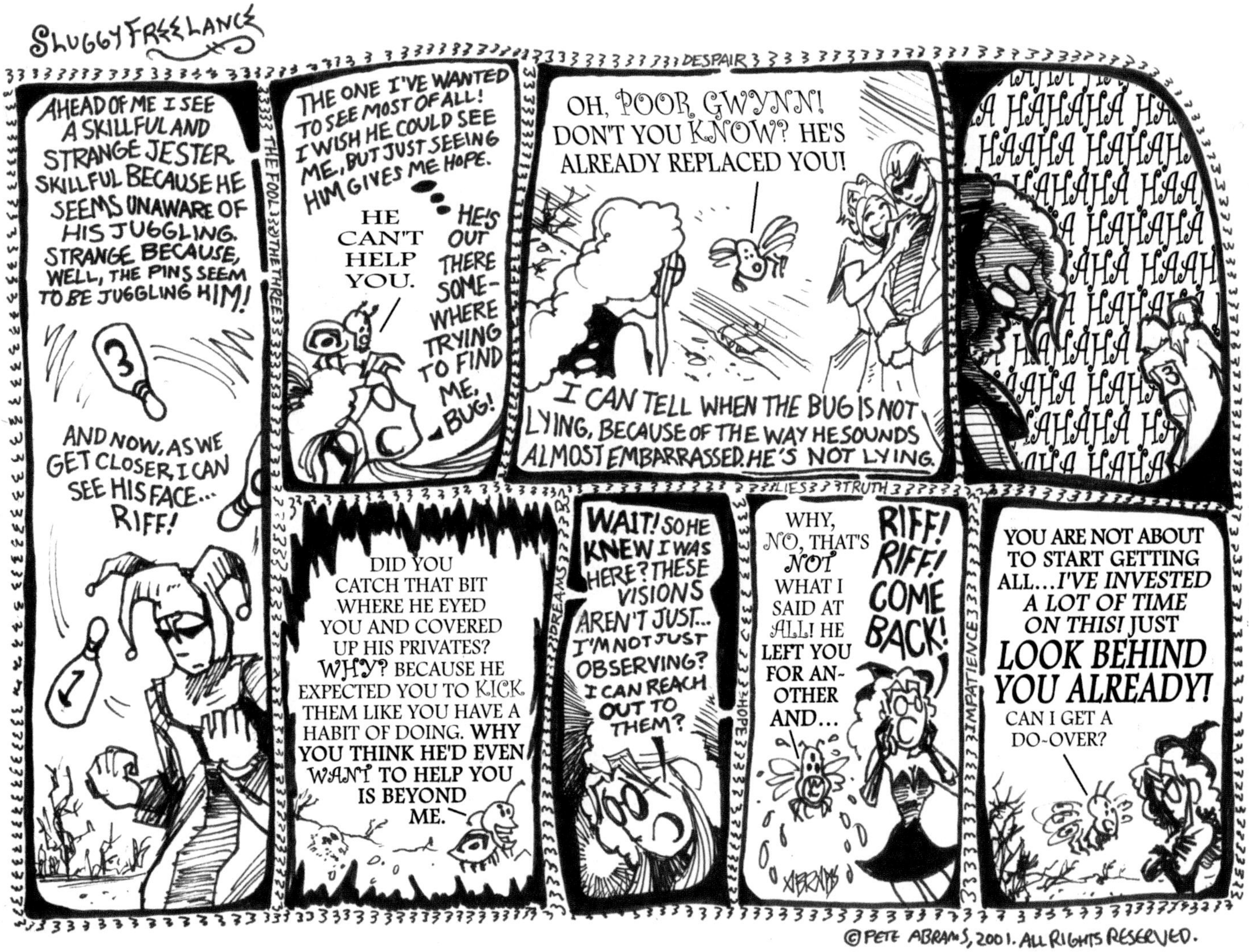
SLUGGY FREELANCE
AHEAD OF ME I SEE A SKILLFUL AND STRANGE JESTER. SKILLFUL BECAUSE HE SEEMS UNAWARE OF HIS JUGGLING. STRANGE BECAUSE, WELL, THE PINS SEEM TO BE JUGGLING HIM!
AND NOW, AS WE GET CLOSER, I CAN SEE HIS FACE... RIFF!
THE FOOL
THE THREE
THE ONE I'VE WANTED TO SEE MOST OF ALL! I WISH HE COULD SEE ME, BUT JUST SEEING HIM GIVES ME HOPE.
HE CAN'T HELP YOU.
HE'S OUT THERE SOME-WHERE TRYING TO FIND ME, BUG!
DESPAIR
OH, POOR GWYNN! DON'T YOU KNOW? HE'S ALREADY REPLACED YOU!
I CAN TELL WHEN THE BUG IS NOT LYING, BECAUSE OF THE WAY HE SOUNDS ALMOST EMBARRASSED. HE'S NOT LYING.
HAHAHA HAHAHA HAHAHA HAHAHA
LIES
TRUTH
DID YOU CATCH THAT BIT WHERE HE EYED YOU AND COVERED UP HIS PRIVATES? WHY? BECAUSE HE EXPECTED YOU TO KICK THEM LIKE YOU HAVE A HABIT OF DOING. WHY YOU THINK HE'D EVEN WANT TO HELP YOU IS BEYOND ME.
DREAMS
WAIT! SO HE KNEW I WAS HERE? THESE VISIONS AREN'T JUST... I'M NOT JUST OBSERVING? I CAN REACH OUT TO THEM?
HOPE
WHY, NO, THAT'S NOT WHAT I SAID AT ALL! HE LEFT YOU FOR AN-OTHER AND...
RIFF! RIFF! COME BACK!
IMPATIENCE
YOU ARE NOT ABOUT TO START GETTING ALL... I'VE INVESTED A LOT OF TIME ON THIS! JUST LOOK BEHIND YOU ALREADY!
CAN I GET A DO-OVER?
ABRAMS
©PETE ABRAMS, 2001. ALL RIGHTS RESERVED.

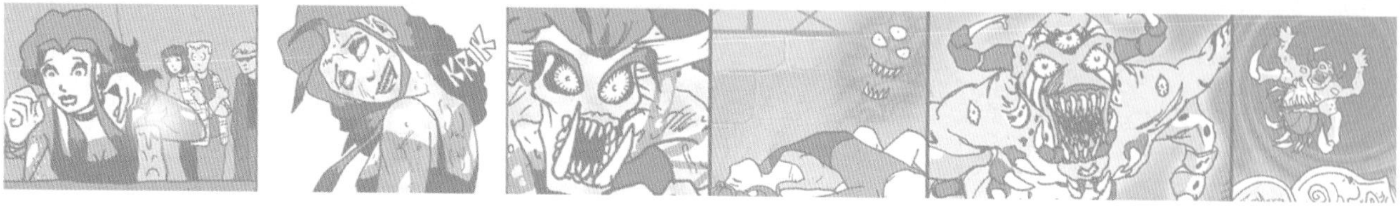

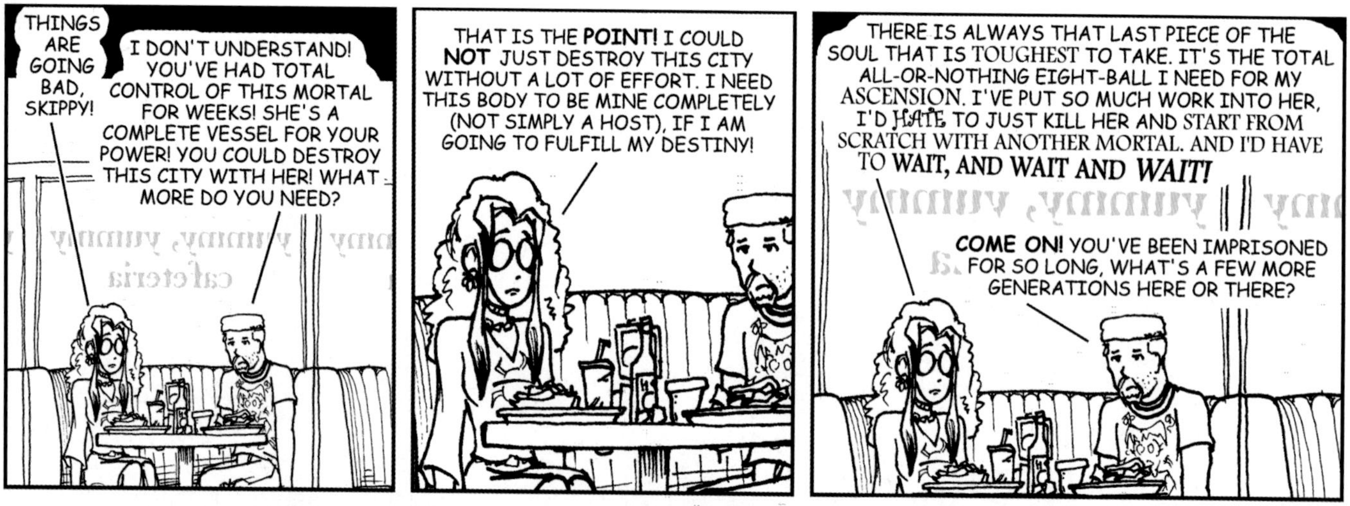

THINGS ARE GOING BAD, SKIPPY!
I DON'T UNDERSTAND! YOU'VE HAD TOTAL CONTROL OF THIS MORTAL FOR WEEKS! SHE'S A COMPLETE VESSEL FOR YOUR POWER! YOU COULD DESTROY THIS CITY WITH HER! WHAT MORE DO YOU NEED?
THAT IS THE POINT! I COULD NOT JUST DESTROY THIS CITY WITHOUT A LOT OF EFFORT. I NEED THIS BODY TO BE MINE COMPLETELY (NOT SIMPLY A HOST), IF I AM GOING TO FULFILL MY DESTINY!
THERE IS ALWAYS THAT LAST PIECE OF THE SOUL THAT IS TOUGHEST TO TAKE. IT'S THE TOTAL ALL-OR-NOTHING EIGHT-BALL I NEED FOR MY ASCENSION. I'VE PUT SO MUCH WORK INTO HER, I'D HATE TO JUST KILL HER AND START FROM SCRATCH WITH ANOTHER MORTAL. AND I'D HAVE TO WAIT, AND WAIT AND WAIT!
COME ON! YOU'VE BEEN IMPRISONED FOR SO LONG, WHAT'S A FEW MORE GENERATIONS HERE OR THERE?

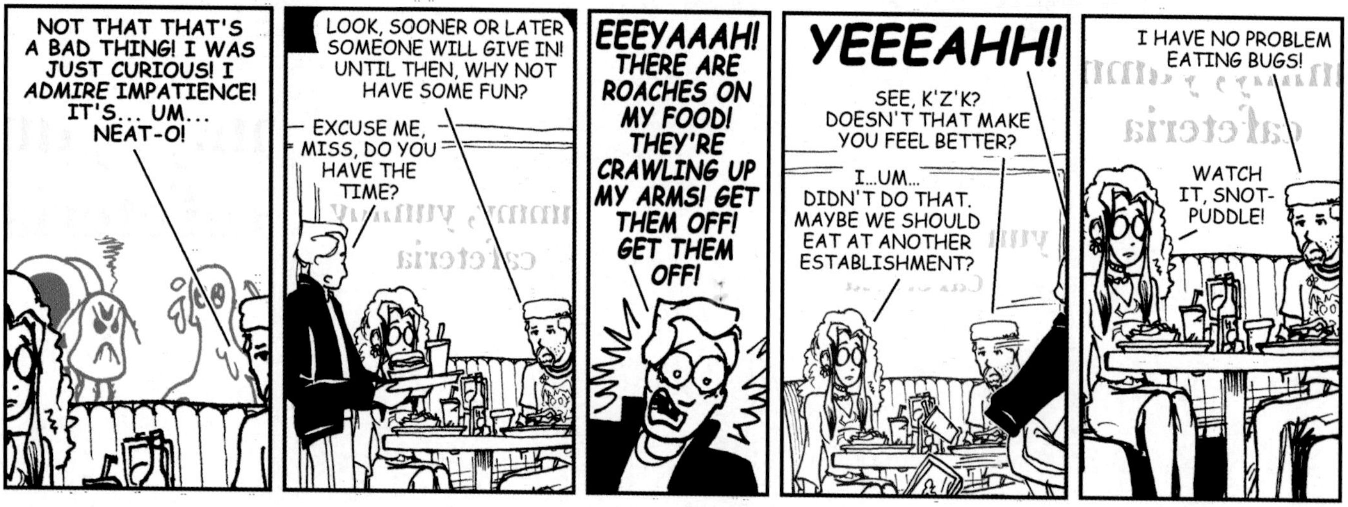

NOT THAT THAT'S A BAD THING! I WAS JUST CURIOUS! I ADMIRE IMPATIENCE! IT'S... UM... NEAT-O!
LOOK, SOONER OR LATER SOMEONE WILL GIVE IN! UNTIL THEN, WHY NOT HAVE SOME FUN?
EXCUSE ME, MISS, DO YOU HAVE THE TIME?
EEEYAAAH! THERE ARE ROACHES ON MY FOOD! THEY'RE CRAWLING UP MY ARMS! GET THEM OFF! GET THEM OFF!
YEEEAHH!
SEE, K'Z'K? DOESN'T THAT MAKE YOU FEEL BETTER?
I...UM... DIDN'T DO THAT. MAYBE WE SHOULD EAT AT ANOTHER ESTABLISHMENT?
I HAVE NO PROBLEM EATING BUGS!
WATCH IT, SNOT-PUDDLE!

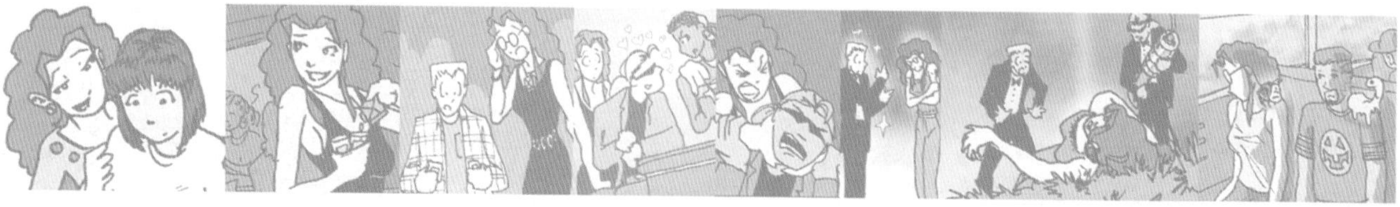

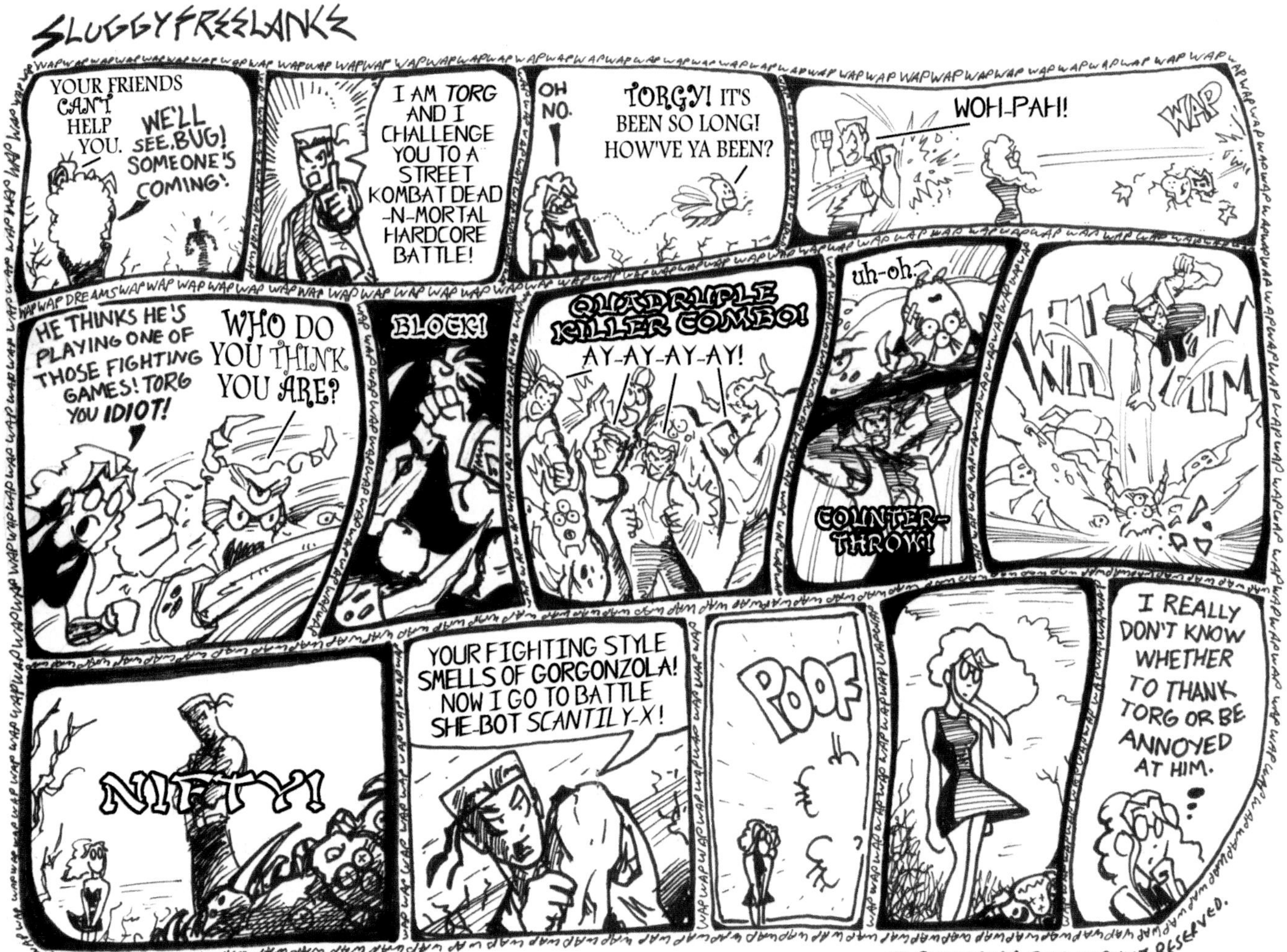
SLUGGY FREELANCE
YOUR FRIENDS CAN'T HELP YOU.
WE'LL SEE, BUG! SOMEONE'S COMING!
I AM TORG AND I CHALLENGE YOU TO A STREET KOMBAT DEAD-N-MORTAL HARDCORE BATTLE!
OH NO.
TORGY! IT'S BEEN SO LONG! HOW'VE YA BEEN?
WOH-PAH!
WAP
HE THINKS HE'S PLAYING ONE OF THOSE FIGHTING GAMES! TORG YOU IDIOT!
WHO DO YOU THINK YOU ARE?
BLOCK!
QUADRUPLE KILLER COMBO!
AY-AY-AY-AY!
uh-oh.
COUNTER-THROW!
NIFTY!
YOUR FIGHTING STYLE SMELLS OF GORGONZOLA! NOW I GO TO BATTLE SHE-BOT SCANTILY-X!
POOF
I REALLY DON'T KNOW WHETHER TO THANK TORG OR BE ANNOYED AT HIM.

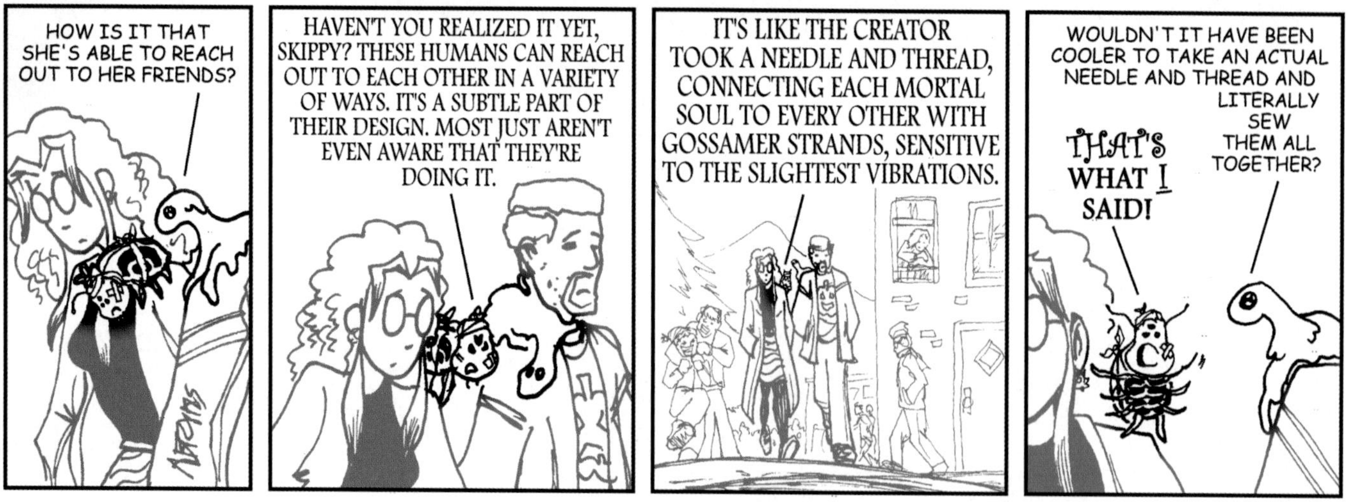
HOW IS IT THAT SHE'S ABLE TO REACH OUT TO HER FRIENDS?
HAVEN'T YOU REALIZED IT YET, SKIPPY? THESE HUMANS CAN REACH OUT TO EACH OTHER IN A VARIETY OF WAYS. IT'S A SUBTLE PART OF THEIR DESIGN. MOST JUST AREN'T EVEN AWARE THAT THEY'RE DOING IT.
IT'S LIKE THE CREATOR TOOK A NEEDLE AND THREAD, CONNECTING EACH MORTAL SOUL TO EVERY OTHER WITH GOSSAMER STRANDS, SENSITIVE TO THE SLIGHTEST VIBRATIONS.
WOULDN'T IT HAVE BEEN COOLER TO TAKE AN ACTUAL NEEDLE AND THREAD AND LITERALLY SEW THEM ALL TOGETHER?
THAT'S WHAT I SAID!

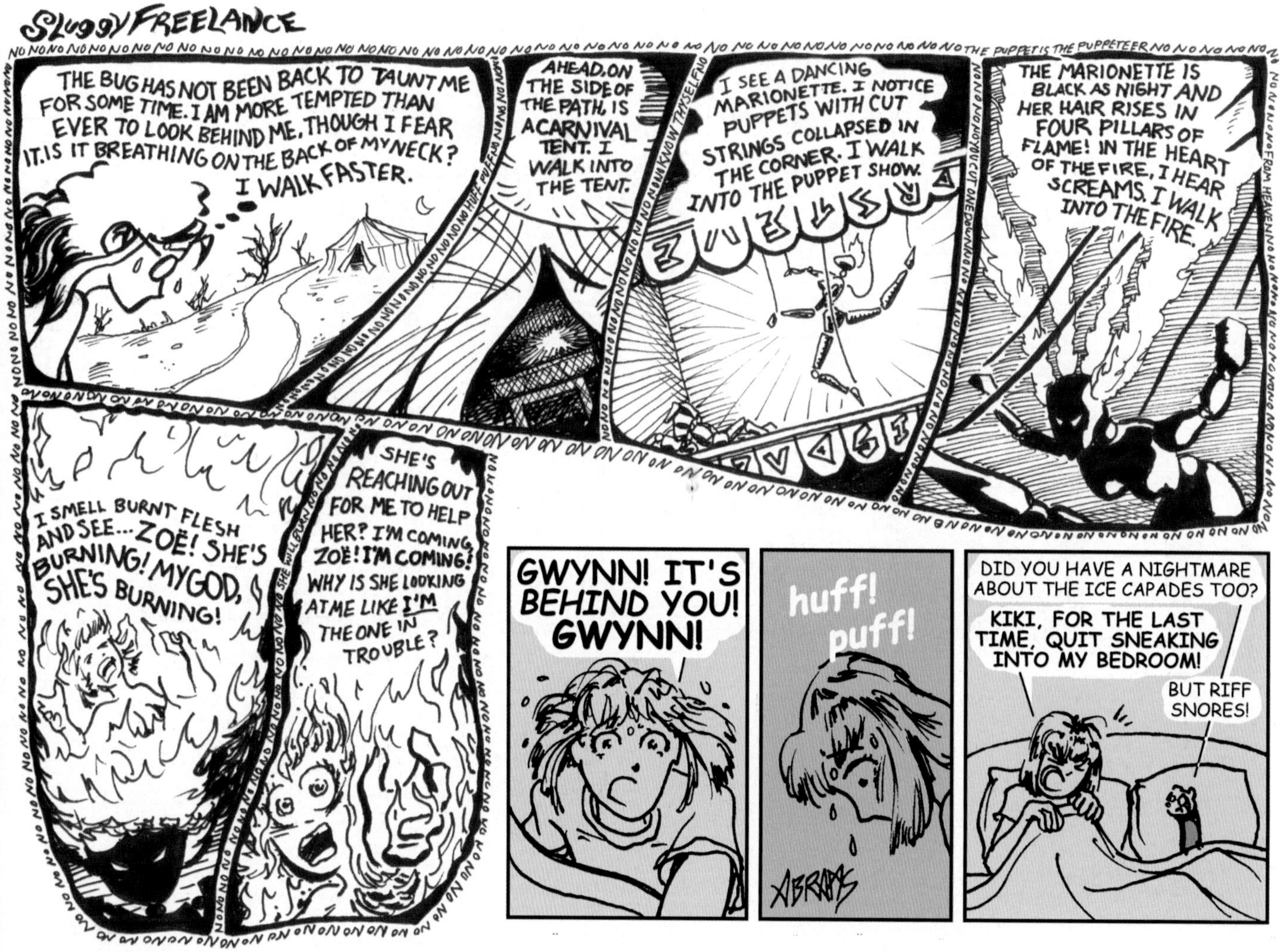
SLUGGY FREELANCE
THE PUPPET IS THE PUPPETEER
THE BUG HAS NOT BEEN BACK TO TAUNT ME FOR SOME TIME. I AM MORE TEMPTED THAN EVER TO LOOK BEHIND ME, THOUGH I FEAR IT. IS IT BREATHING ON THE BACK OF MY NECK?
I WALK FASTER.
AHEAD, ON THE SIDE OF THE PATH, IS A CARNIVAL TENT. I WALK INTO THE TENT.
I SEE A DANCING MARIONETTE. I NOTICE PUPPETS WITH CUT STRINGS COLLAPSED IN THE CORNER. I WALK INTO THE PUPPET SHOW.
THE MARIONETTE IS BLACK AS NIGHT AND HER HAIR RISES IN FOUR PILLARS OF FLAME! IN THE HEART OF THE FIRE, I HEAR SCREAMS. I WALK INTO THE FIRE.
I SMELL BURNT FLESH AND SEE... ZOË! SHE'S BURNING! MY GOD, SHE'S BURNING!
SHE'S REACHING OUT FOR ME TO HELP HER? I'M COMING, ZOË! I'M COMING!
WHY IS SHE LOOKING AT ME LIKE I'M THE ONE IN TROUBLE?
GWYNN! IT'S BEHIND YOU! GWYNN!
huff! puff!
DID YOU HAVE A NIGHTMARE ABOUT THE ICE CAPADES TOO?
KIKI, FOR THE LAST TIME, QUIT SNEAKING INTO MY BEDROOM!
BUT RIFF SNORES!

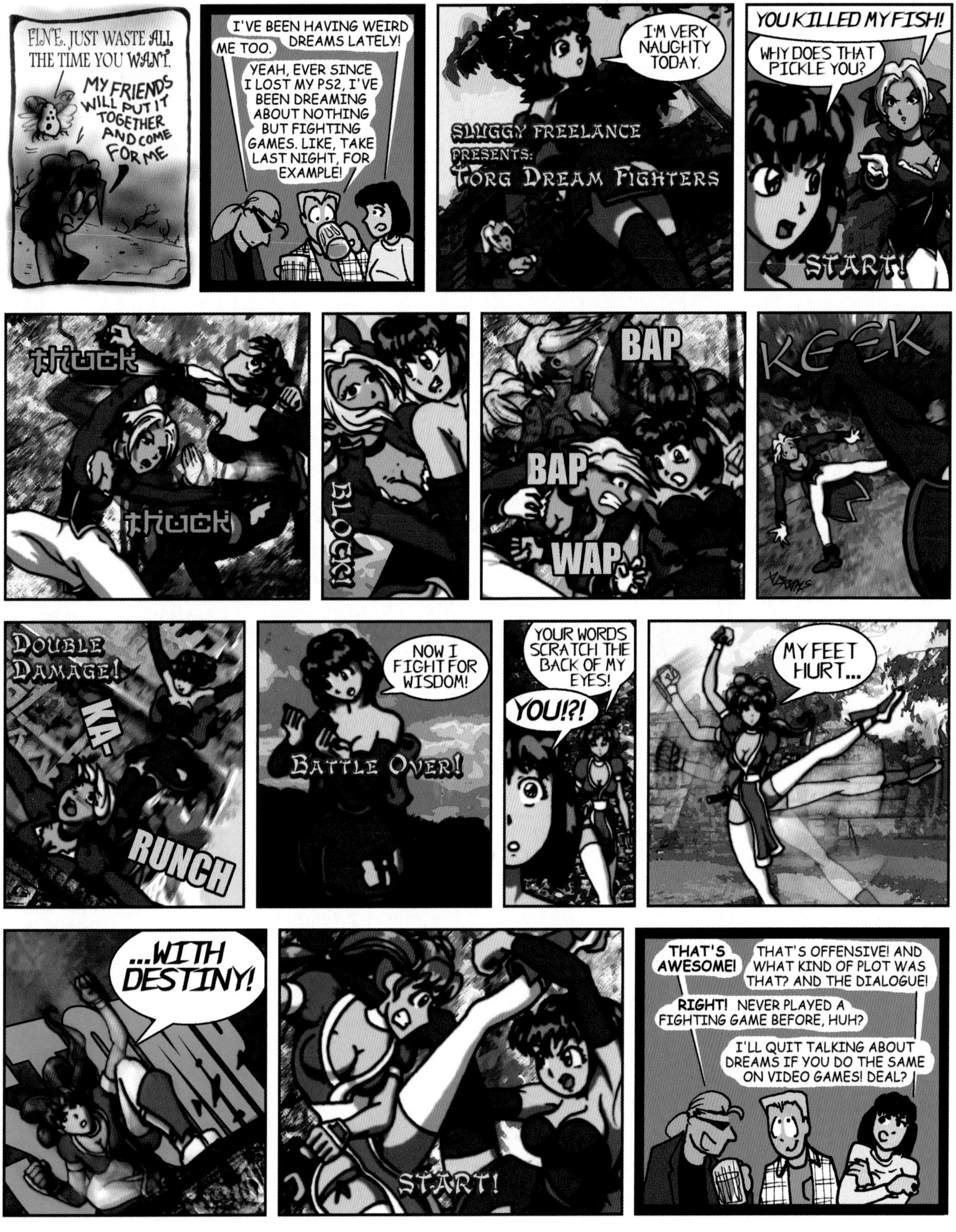
FINE. JUST WASTE ALL THE TIME YOU WANT.
MY FRIENDS WILL PUT IT TOGETHER AND COME FOR ME
I'VE BEEN HAVING WEIRD DREAMS LATELY!
ME TOO.
YEAH, EVER SINCE I LOST MY PS2, I'VE BEEN DREAMING ABOUT NOTHING BUT FIGHTING GAMES. LIKE, TAKE LAST NIGHT, FOR EXAMPLE!
I'M VERY NAUGHTY TODAY.
SLUGGY FREELANCE PRESENTS:
TORG DREAM FIGHTERS
YOU KILLED MY FISH!
WHY DOES THAT PICKLE YOU?
START!
THUCK
THUCK
BLOCK!
BAP
BAP
WAP
KEEK
DOUBLE DAMAGE!
KA-
RUNCH
NOW I FIGHT FOR WISDOM!
BATTLE OVER!
YOUR WORDS SCRATCH THE BACK OF MY EYES!
YOU!?!
MY FEET HURT...
...WITH DESTINY!
START!
THAT'S AWESOME!
THAT'S OFFENSIVE! AND WHAT KIND OF PLOT WAS THAT? AND THE DIALOGUE!
RIGHT! NEVER PLAYED A FIGHTING GAME BEFORE, HUH?
I'LL QUIT TALKING ABOUT DREAMS IF YOU DO THE SAME ON VIDEO GAMES! DEAL?

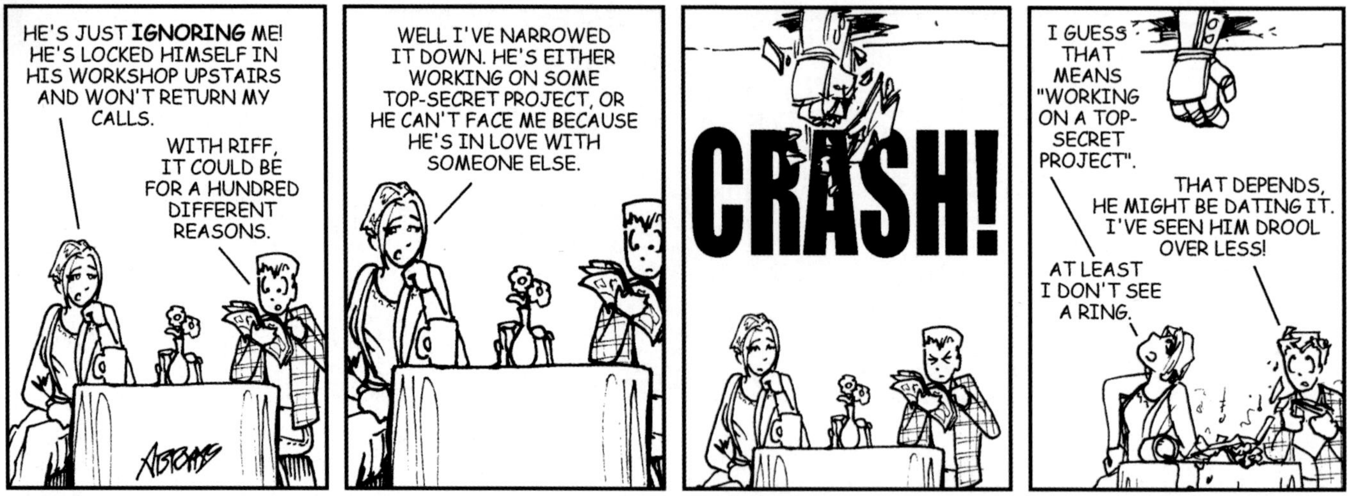
HE'S JUST IGNORING ME! HE'S LOCKED HIMSELF IN HIS WORKSHOP UPSTAIRS AND WON'T RETURN MY CALLS.
WITH RIFF, IT COULD BE FOR A HUNDRED DIFFERENT REASONS.
WELL I'VE NARROWED IT DOWN. HE'S EITHER WORKING ON SOME TOP-SECRET PROJECT, OR HE CAN'T FACE ME BECAUSE HE'S IN LOVE WITH SOMEONE ELSE.
CRASH!
I GUESS THAT MEANS "WORKING ON A TOP-SECRET PROJECT".
THAT DEPENDS, HE MIGHT BE DATING IT. I'VE SEEN HIM DROOL OVER LESS!
AT LEAST I DON'T SEE A RING.

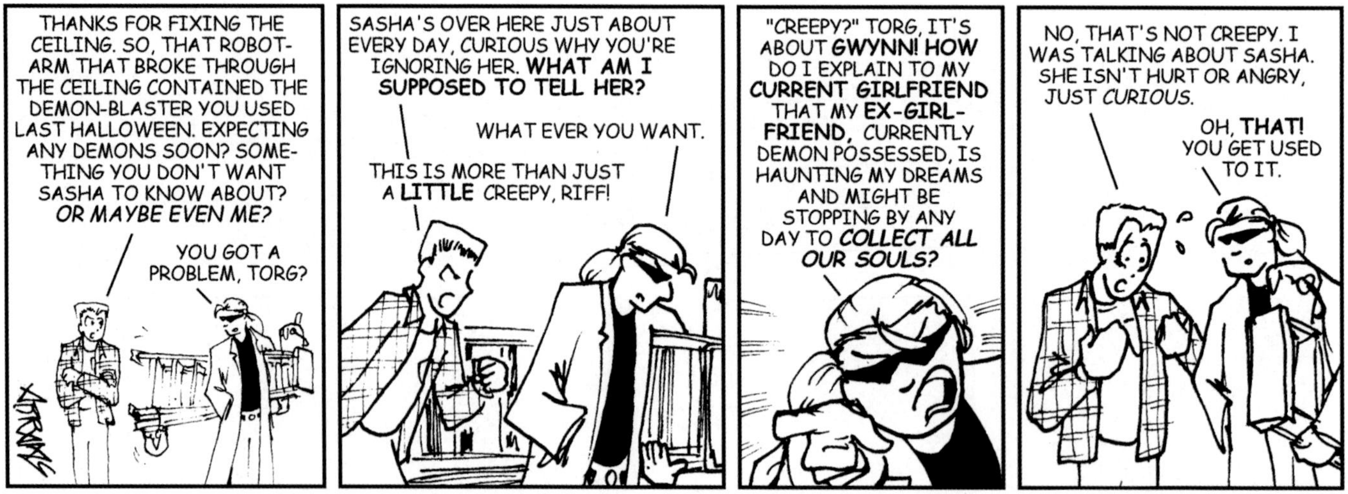
THANKS FOR FIXING THE CEILING. SO, THAT ROBOT-ARM THAT BROKE THROUGH THE CEILING CONTAINED THE DEMON-BLASTER YOU USED LAST HALLOWEEN. EXPECTING ANY DEMONS SOON? SOME-THING YOU DON'T WANT SASHA TO KNOW ABOUT? OR MAYBE EVEN ME?
YOU GOT A PROBLEM, TORG?
SASHA'S OVER HERE JUST ABOUT EVERY DAY, CURIOUS WHY YOU'RE IGNORING HER. WHAT AM I SUPPOSED TO TELL HER?
WHAT EVER YOU WANT.
THIS IS MORE THAN JUST A LITTLE CREEPY, RIFF!
"CREEPY?" TORG, IT'S ABOUT GWYNN! HOW DO I EXPLAIN TO MY CURRENT GIRLFRIEND THAT MY EX-GIRL-FRIEND, CURRENTLY DEMON POSSESSED, IS HAUNTING MY DREAMS AND MIGHT BE STOPPING BY ANY DAY TO COLLECT ALL OUR SOULS?
NO, THAT'S NOT CREEPY. I WAS TALKING ABOUT SASHA. SHE ISN'T HURT OR ANGRY, JUST CURIOUS.
OH, THAT! YOU GET USED TO IT.

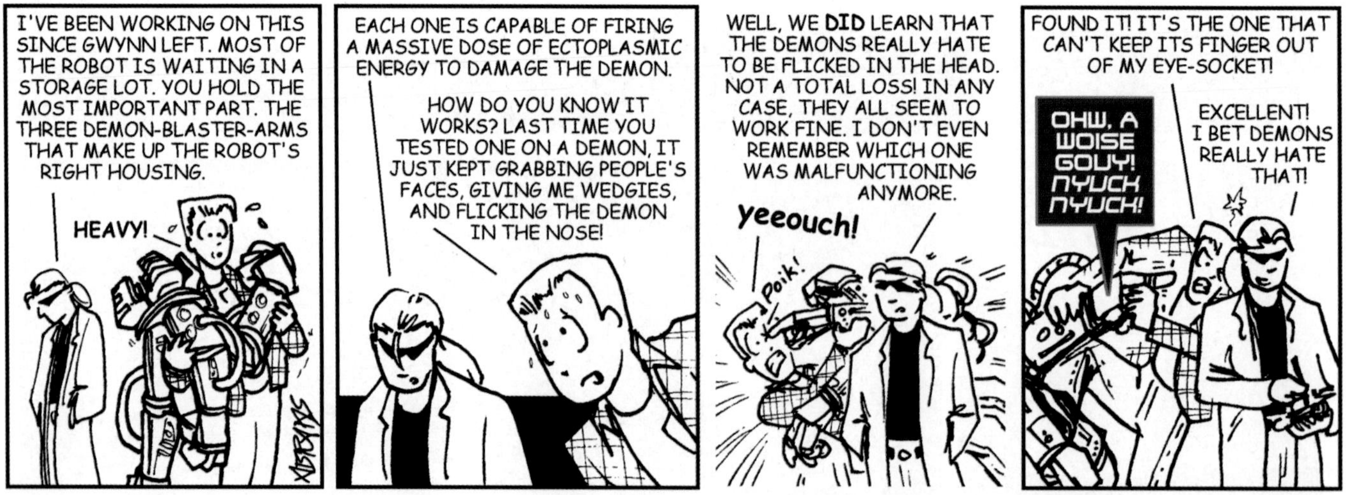
I'VE BEEN WORKING ON THIS SINCE GWYNN LEFT. MOST OF THE ROBOT IS WAITING IN A STORAGE LOT. YOU HOLD THE MOST IMPORTANT PART. THE THREE DEMON-BLASTER-ARMS THAT MAKE UP THE ROBOT'S RIGHT HOUSING.
HEAVY!
EACH ONE IS CAPABLE OF FIRING A MASSIVE DOSE OF ECTOPLASMIC ENERGY TO DAMAGE THE DEMON.
HOW DO YOU KNOW IT WORKS? LAST TIME YOU TESTED ONE ON A DEMON, IT JUST KEPT GRABBING PEOPLE'S FACES, GIVING ME WEDGIES, AND FLICKING THE DEMON IN THE NOSE!
WELL, WE DID LEARN THAT THE DEMONS REALLY HATE TO BE FLICKED IN THE HEAD. NOT A TOTAL LOSS! IN ANY CASE, THEY ALL SEEM TO WORK FINE. I DON'T EVEN REMEMBER WHICH ONE WAS MALFUNCTIONING ANYMORE.
yeeouch!
Poik!
FOUND IT! IT'S THE ONE THAT CAN'T KEEP ITS FINGER OUT OF MY EYE-SOCKET!
OHW, A WOISE GOUY! NYUCK NYUCK!
EXCELLENT! I BET DEMONS REALLY HATE THAT!

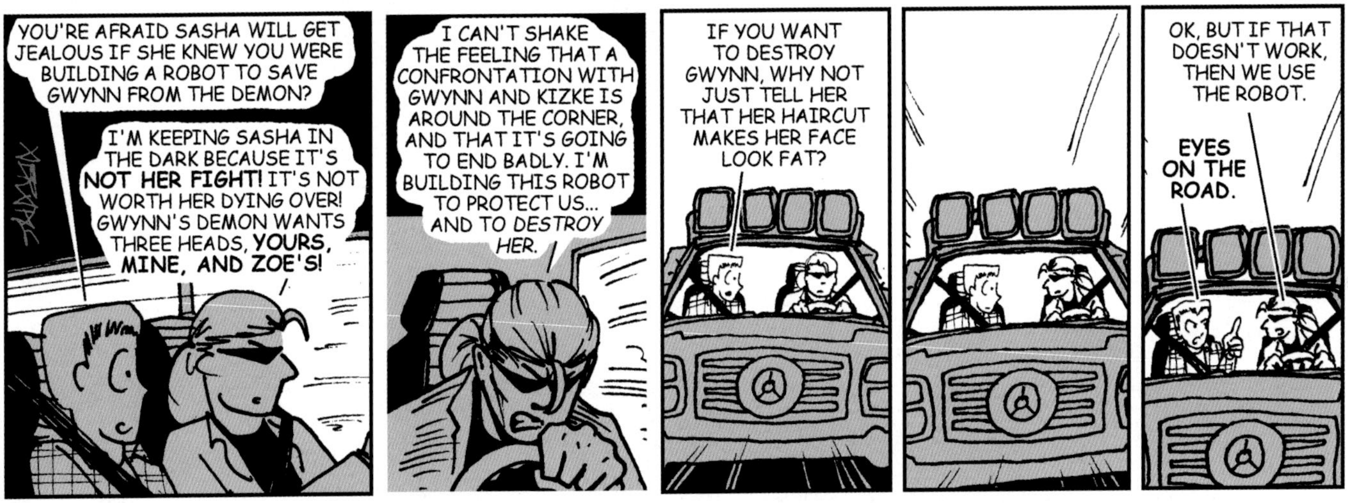

YOU'RE AFRAID SASHA WILL GET JEALOUS IF SHE KNEW YOU WERE BUILDING A ROBOT TO SAVE GWYNN FROM THE DEMON?
I'M KEEPING SASHA IN THE DARK BECAUSE IT'S NOT HER FIGHT! IT'S NOT WORTH HER DYING OVER! GWYNN'S DEMON WANTS THREE HEADS, YOURS, MINE, AND ZOE'S!
I CAN'T SHAKE THE FEELING THAT A CONFRONTATION WITH GWYNN AND KIZKE IS AROUND THE CORNER, AND THAT IT'S GOING TO END BADLY. I'M BUILDING THIS ROBOT TO PROTECT US... AND TO DESTROY HER.
IF YOU WANT TO DESTROY GWYNN, WHY NOT JUST TELL HER THAT HER HAIRCUT MAKES HER FACE LOOK FAT?
OK, BUT IF THAT DOESN'T WORK, THEN WE USE THE ROBOT.
EYES ON THE ROAD.

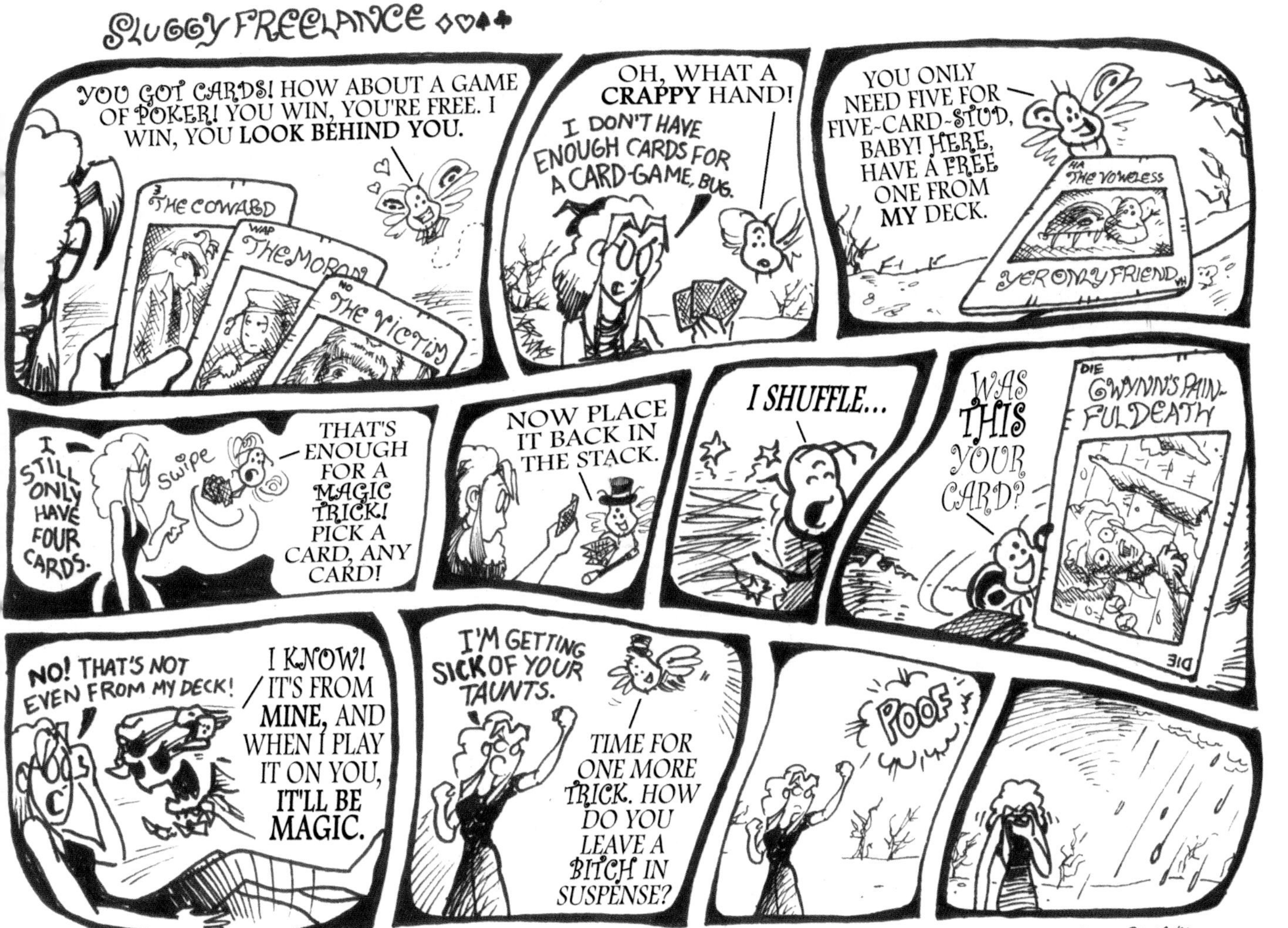

SLUGGY FREELANCE
YOU GOT CARDS! HOW ABOUT A GAME OF POKER! YOU WIN, YOU'RE FREE. I WIN, YOU LOOK BEHIND YOU.
THE COWARD
THE MORON
THE VICTIM
OH, WHAT A CRAPPY HAND!
I DON'T HAVE ENOUGH CARDS FOR A CARD-GAME, BUG.
YOU ONLY NEED FIVE FOR FIVE-CARD-STUD, BABY! HERE, HAVE A FREE ONE FROM MY DECK.
THE VOWELESS
YER ONLY FRIEND
I STILL ONLY HAVE FOUR CARDS.
SWIPE
THAT'S ENOUGH FOR A MAGIC TRICK! PICK A CARD, ANY CARD!
NOW PLACE IT BACK IN THE STACK.
I SHUFFLE...
WAS THIS YOUR CARD?
GWYNN'S PAINFUL DEATH
NO! THAT'S NOT EVEN FROM MY DECK!
I KNOW! IT'S FROM MINE, AND WHEN I PLAY IT ON YOU, IT'LL BE MAGIC.
I'M GETTING SICK OF YOUR TAUNTS.
TIME FOR ONE MORE TRICK. HOW DO YOU LEAVE A BITCH IN SUSPENSE?
POOF

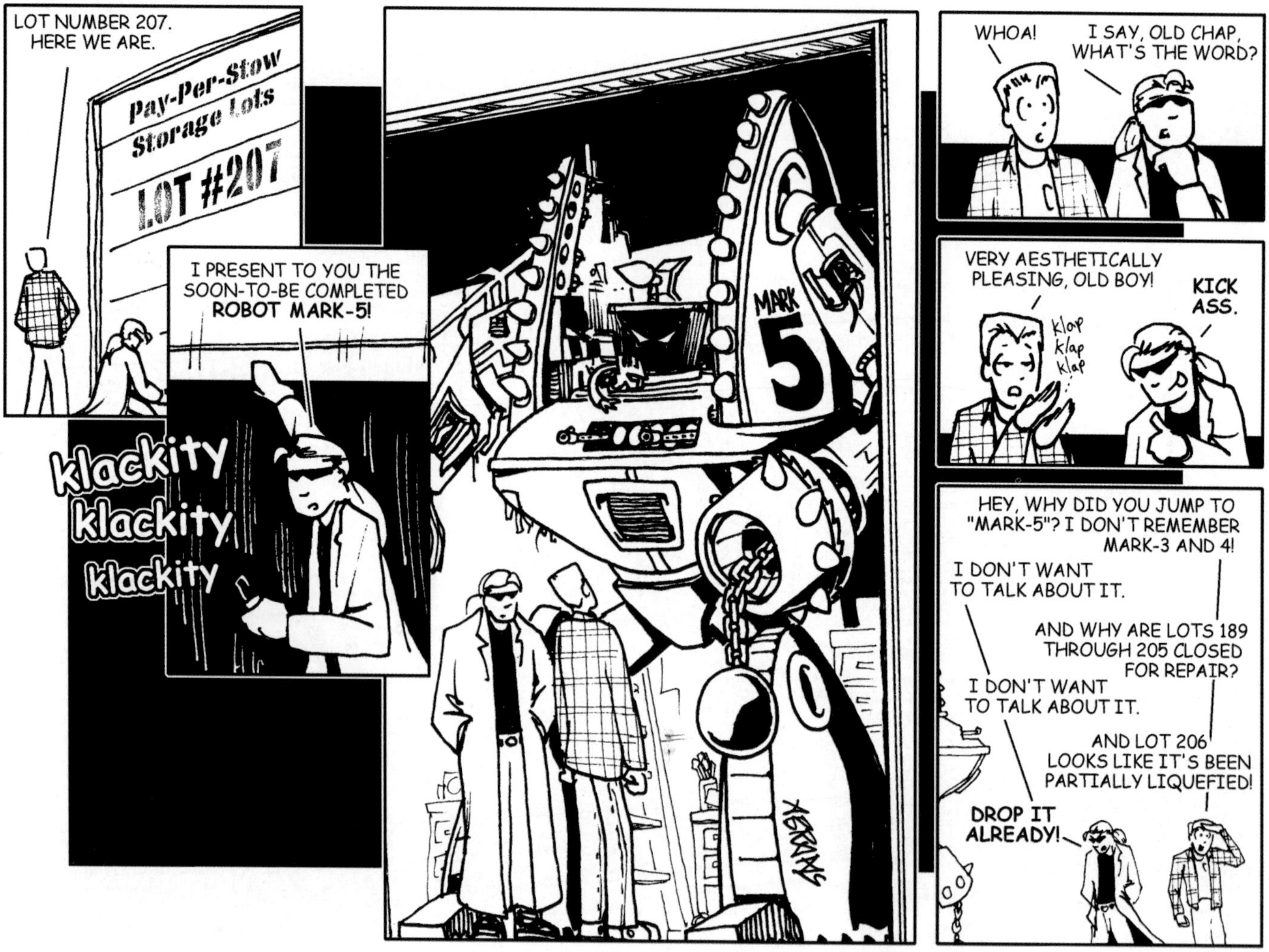

LOT NUMBER 207.
HERE WE ARE.
Pay-Per-Stow
Storage Lots
LOT #207
I PRESENT TO YOU THE SOON-TO-BE COMPLETED ROBOT MARK-5!
klackity
klackity
klackity
MARK 5
WHOA!
I SAY, OLD CHAP, WHAT'S THE WORD?
VERY AESTHETICALLY PLEASING, OLD BOY!
klap
klap
klap
KICK ASS.
HEY, WHY DID YOU JUMP TO "MARK-5"? I DON'T REMEMBER MARK-3 AND 4!
I DON'T WANT TO TALK ABOUT IT.
AND WHY ARE LOTS 189 THROUGH 205 CLOSED FOR REPAIR?
I DON'T WANT TO TALK ABOUT IT.
AND LOT 206 LOOKS LIKE IT'S BEEN PARTIALLY LIQUEFIED!
DROP IT ALREADY!

RIFF, I CAN'T TAKE THIS MUCH LONGER! WHY WON'T YOU LOOK AT ME? STOP WALLING ME OUT!
Sluggy FREELANCE
THE ROBOT IS FULLY ARMORED IN HEAT-TREATED, TRIPLE-FOLDED TITANIUM. IT CAN RESIST HIGH-POWERED ARTILLERY BLASTS OR A POINT-BLANK SENATE ETHICS COMMITTEE HEARING.
IS THAT ENOUGH TO BE DEMON PROOF?
WELL, I'M HOPING ANY DEMON WON'T GET CLOSE ENOUGH! BESIDES THE MULTIPLE FIREARMS, MISSILES, DEMON-BLASTERS, AND SPIKE WEAPONRY, THIS BABY IS ALSO PACKING THE LATEST INCARNATION OF MY OMNITASER SUPREME! EXTENDING TENDRILS MAKE IT A RANGED ATTACK.
TZ-Z-Z-Z-ZT!
DID YOU FIND A WAY TO MODULATE THE POWER LEVEL, SO IT'S NOT AS DANGEROUS?
HELL NO!
EXCELLENT! WHAT'S THIS?
WHEN ACTIVATED, IT QUICKLY CYCLES THROUGH EVERY HOLY SYMBOL OF EVERY MAJOR RELIGION IN CASE THE DEMON HAS WEAKNESSES TO ONE.
WOH-SHAT
FLICKETY FLICKETY FLICKETY
IT STOPPED ON RICKY MARTIN!
IT'S TOTALLY RANDOM BUT I SWEAR IT HAS FAVORITES.
WHAT'S THE BALL AND CHAIN DO?
WELL, THE ROBOT CAN SHOOT OR SWING THE BALL INTO THE AIR AND TRY TO CATCH IT BACK IN THE CUP. Y'KNOW, IN CASE THE ROBOT GETS BORED WAITING FOR THE DEMON.
THAT RULES! CAN WE PLAY IT MANUALLY?
TORG, IT'S NOT A TOY.
HEY, I JUST NOTICED ALL THE LARGE CIRCULAR HOLES IN THE CEILING.
WELL IT IS A TOY, BUT IT'S NOT AS EASY AS IT LOOKS.
I SEE YOU'VE ALSO ARMED IT WITH THE DIMENSIONAL FLUX AGITATOR. I GUESS THAT WOULD MAKE IT A QUICK BATTLE, TO JUST BLAST THE DEMON INTO SOME RANDOM DIMENSION.
TORG, I CAN'T RELEASE A DEMON OF KIZKE'S POWER ON SOME RANDOM, POSSIBLY DEFENSELESS, UNSUSPECTING DIMENSION. BUT IT CAN BE USED CREATIVELY; SUCH AS TO ZAP THE GROUND OUT FROM UNDER THE DEMON, OR AS AN EMERGENCY ESCAPE DEVICE FOR THE PILOT.
PILOT? I THOUGHT THIS WAS A ROBOT!
WELL, YES, BUT I DESIGNED IT TO HOLD ONE OR TWO OF US FOR PROTECTION, AND CAN BE PILOTED FROM THE INSIDE IF WE HAVE PROBLEMS WITH THE ROBOT'S ARTIFICIAL INTELLIGENCE. IT'S THE LAST MAJOR TASK I HAVE TO FINISH.
MARK 5
HOW MUCH TIME DO YOU NEED ON THE A.I.?
THIS IS WHERE IT'S AT SO FAR...
WAAAAAAAAAAAAA
BEEP
"THE HORSE SAYS NEEEEEEEEEIGHHHHHHHH!"
YOU USED YOUR OLD "SEE-'N-SAY"?
I'M WORKING ON A BUDGET HERE!

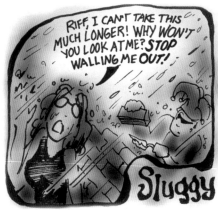

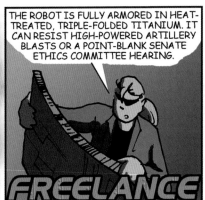

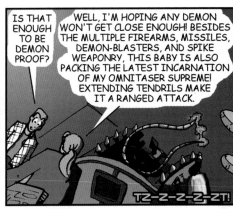

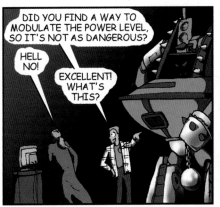

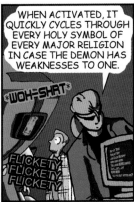

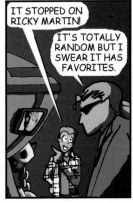

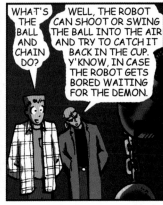

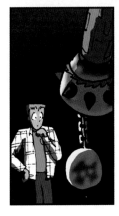

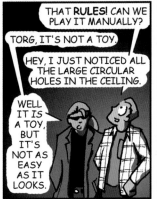

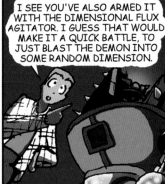

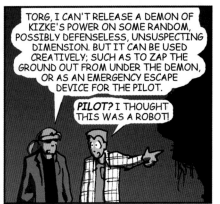

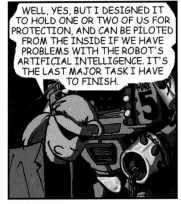

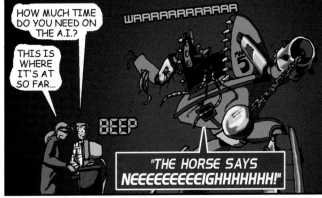

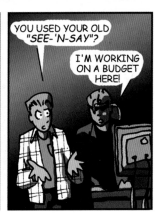

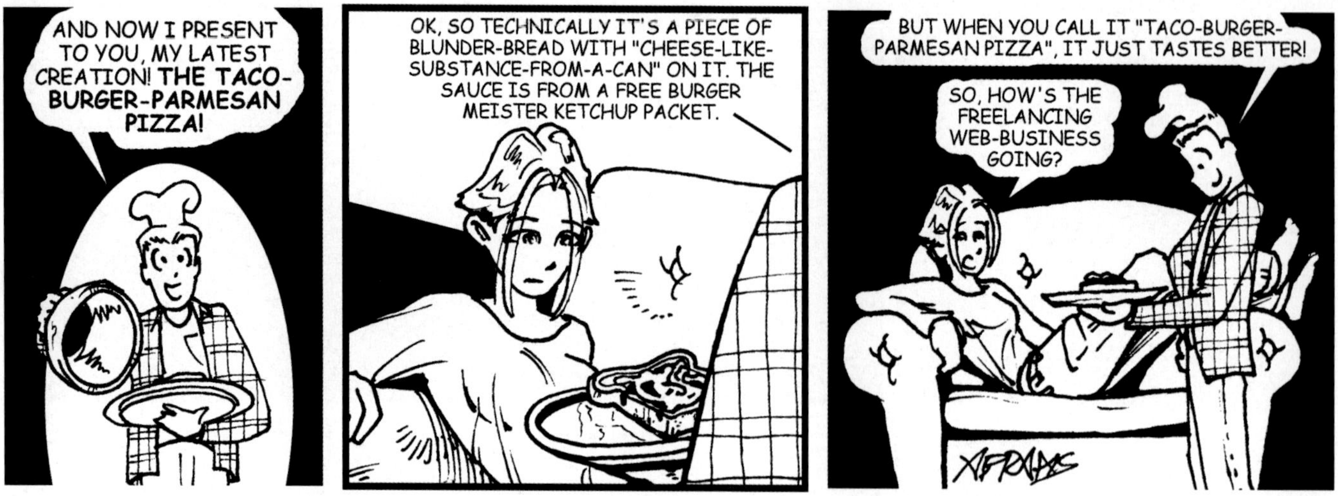
AND NOW I PRESENT TO YOU, MY LATEST CREATION! **THE TACO-BURGER-PARMESAN PIZZA!**
OK, SO TECHNICALLY IT'S A PIECE OF BLUNDER-BREAD WITH "CHEESE-LIKE-SUBSTANCE-FROM-A-CAN" ON IT. THE SAUCE IS FROM A FREE BURGER MEISTER KETCHUP PACKET.
BUT WHEN YOU CALL IT "TACO-BURGER-PARMESAN PIZZA", IT JUST TASTES BETTER!
SO, HOW'S THE FREELANCING WEB-BUSINESS GOING?

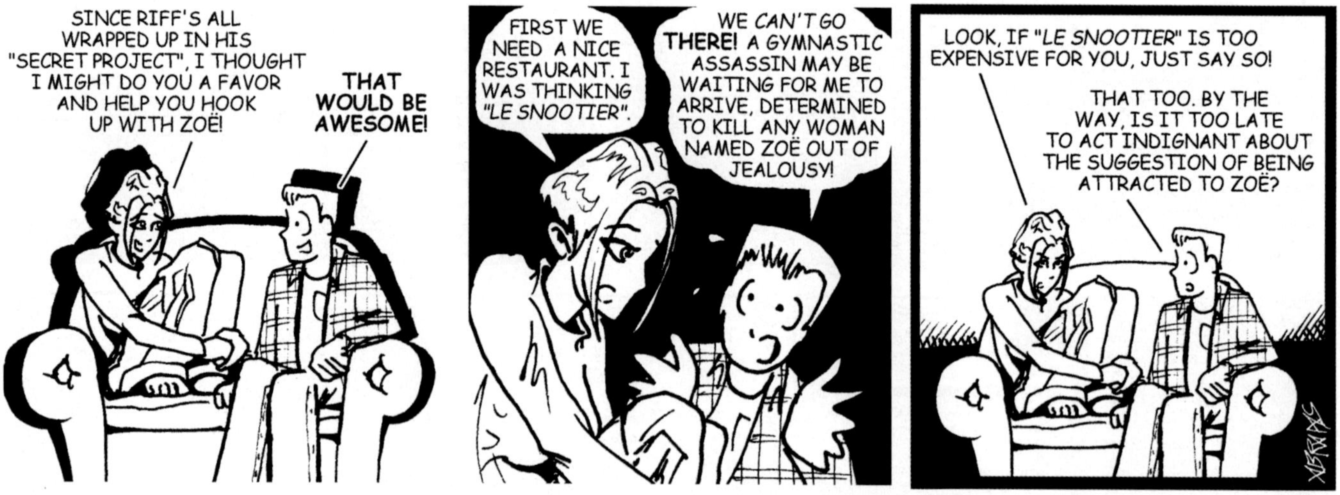
SINCE RIFF'S ALL WRAPPED UP IN HIS "SECRET PROJECT", I THOUGHT I MIGHT DO YOU A FAVOR AND HELP YOU HOOK UP WITH ZOË!
THAT WOULD BE AWESOME!
FIRST WE NEED A NICE RESTAURANT. I WAS THINKING *"LE SNOOTIER"*.
WE *CAN'T* GO **THERE!** A GYMNASTIC ASSASSIN MAY BE WAITING FOR ME TO ARRIVE, DETERMINED TO KILL ANY WOMAN NAMED ZOË OUT OF JEALOUSY!
LOOK, IF "*LE SNOOTIER*" IS TOO EXPENSIVE FOR YOU, JUST SAY SO!
THAT TOO. BY THE WAY, IS IT TOO LATE TO ACT INDIGNANT ABOUT THE SUGGESTION OF BEING ATTRACTED TO ZOË?

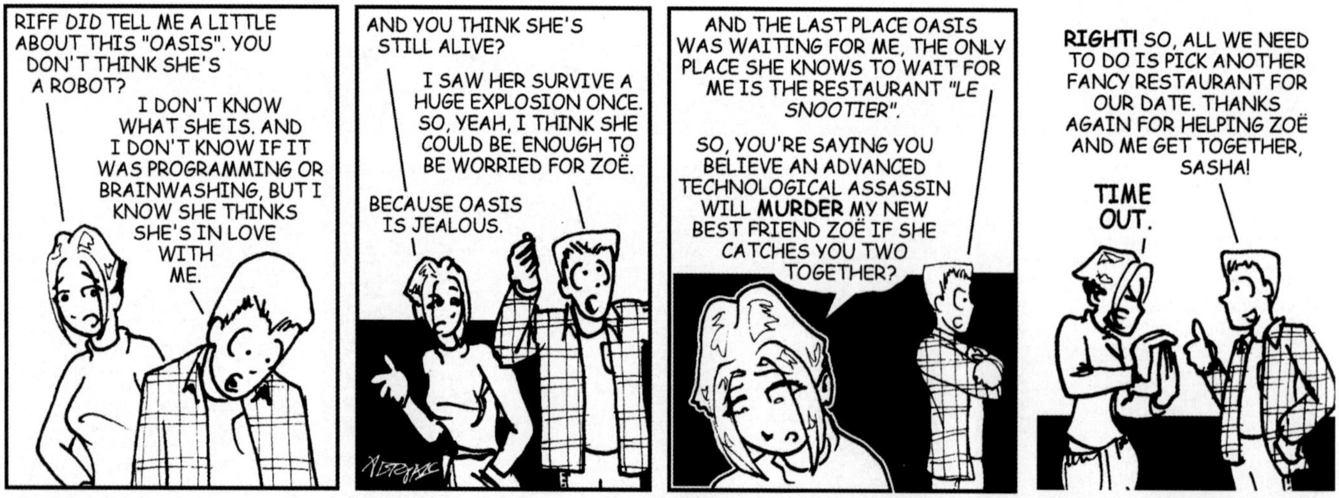
RIFF *DID* TELL ME A LITTLE ABOUT THIS "OASIS". YOU DON'T THINK SHE'S A ROBOT?
I DON'T KNOW WHAT SHE IS. AND I DON'T KNOW IF IT WAS PROGRAMMING OR BRAINWASHING, BUT I KNOW SHE THINKS SHE'S IN LOVE WITH ME.
AND YOU THINK SHE'S STILL ALIVE?
I SAW HER SURVIVE A HUGE EXPLOSION ONCE. SO, YEAH, I THINK SHE COULD BE. ENOUGH TO BE WORRIED FOR ZOË.
BECAUSE OASIS IS JEALOUS.
AND THE LAST PLACE OASIS WAS WAITING FOR ME, THE ONLY PLACE SHE KNOWS TO WAIT FOR ME IS THE RESTAURANT *"LE SNOOTIER"*.
SO, YOU'RE SAYING YOU BELIEVE AN ADVANCED TECHNOLOGICAL ASSASSIN WILL **MURDER** MY NEW BEST FRIEND ZOË IF SHE CATCHES YOU TWO TOGETHER?
RIGHT! SO, ALL WE NEED TO DO IS PICK ANOTHER FANCY RESTAURANT FOR OUR DATE. THANKS AGAIN FOR HELPING ZOË AND ME GET TOGETHER, SASHA!
TIME OUT.

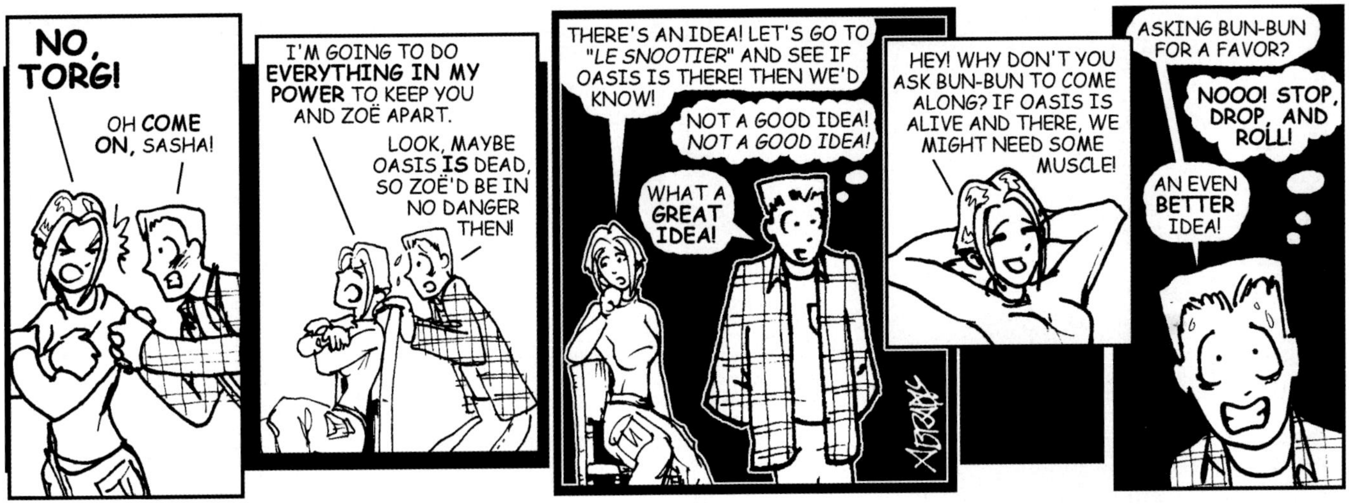
NO, TORG!
OH COME ON, SASHA!
I'M GOING TO DO EVERYTHING IN MY POWER TO KEEP YOU AND ZOË APART.
LOOK, MAYBE OASIS IS DEAD, SO ZOË'D BE IN NO DANGER THEN!
THERE'S AN IDEA! LET'S GO TO "LE SNOOTIER" AND SEE IF OASIS IS THERE! THEN WE'D KNOW!
NOT A GOOD IDEA! NOT A GOOD IDEA!
WHAT A GREAT IDEA!
HEY! WHY DON'T YOU ASK BUN-BUN TO COME ALONG? IF OASIS IS ALIVE AND THERE, WE MIGHT NEED SOME MUSCLE!
ASKING BUN-BUN FOR A FAVOR?
NOOO! STOP, DROP, AND ROLL!
AN EVEN BETTER IDEA!

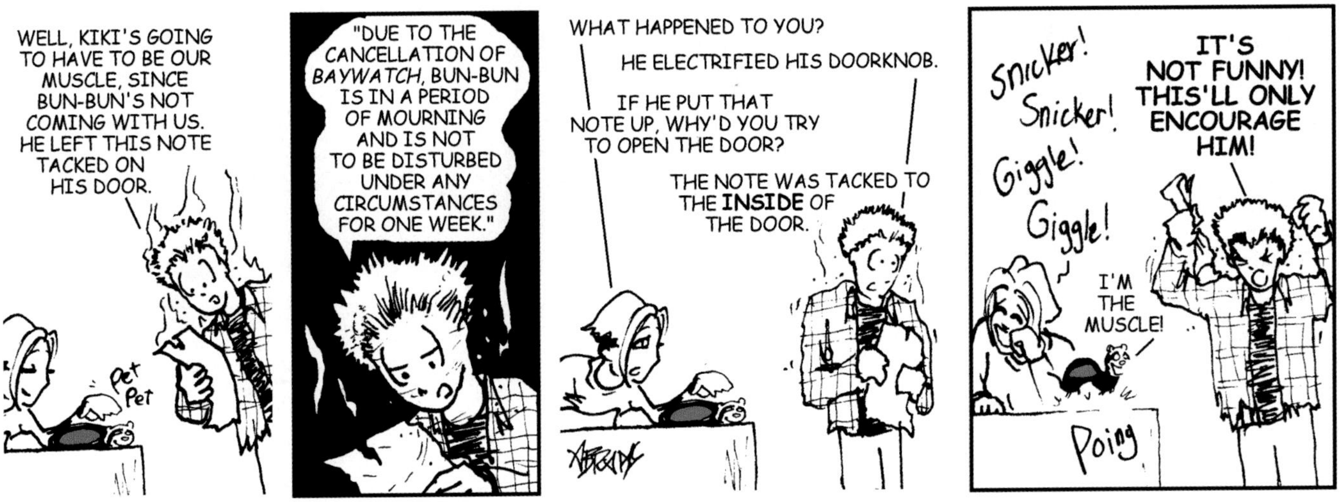
WELL, KIKI'S GOING TO HAVE TO BE OUR MUSCLE, SINCE BUN-BUN'S NOT COMING WITH US. HE LEFT THIS NOTE TACKED ON HIS DOOR.
Pet Pet
"DUE TO THE CANCELLATION OF BAYWATCH, BUN-BUN IS IN A PERIOD OF MOURNING AND IS NOT TO BE DISTURBED UNDER ANY CIRCUMSTANCES FOR ONE WEEK."
WHAT HAPPENED TO YOU?
HE ELECTRIFIED HIS DOORKNOB.
IF HE PUT THAT NOTE UP, WHY'D YOU TRY TO OPEN THE DOOR?
THE NOTE WAS TACKED TO THE INSIDE OF THE DOOR.
Snicker! Snicker! Giggle! Giggle!
IT'S NOT FUNNY! THIS'LL ONLY ENCOURAGE HIM!
I'M THE MUSCLE!
Poing

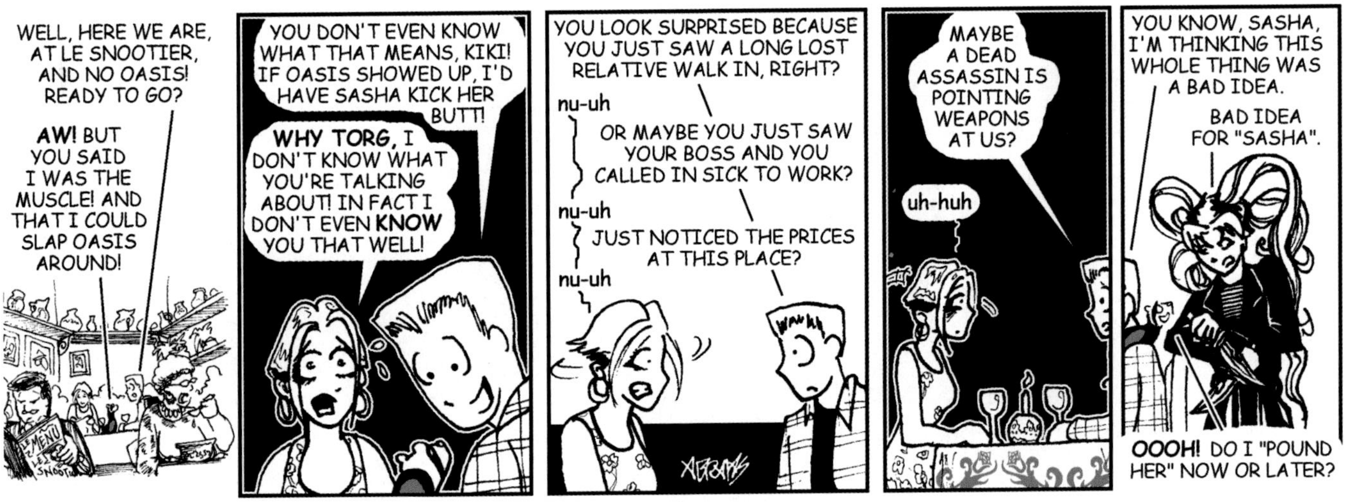
WELL, HERE WE ARE, AT LE SNOOTIER, AND NO OASIS! READY TO GO?
AW! BUT YOU SAID I WAS THE MUSCLE! AND THAT I COULD SLAP OASIS AROUND!
YOU DON'T EVEN KNOW WHAT THAT MEANS, KIKI! IF OASIS SHOWED UP, I'D HAVE SASHA KICK HER BUTT!
WHY TORG, I DON'T KNOW WHAT YOU'RE TALKING ABOUT! IN FACT I DON'T EVEN KNOW YOU THAT WELL!
YOU LOOK SURPRISED BECAUSE YOU JUST SAW A LONG LOST RELATIVE WALK IN, RIGHT?
nu-uh
OR MAYBE YOU JUST SAW YOUR BOSS AND YOU CALLED IN SICK TO WORK?
nu-uh
JUST NOTICED THE PRICES AT THIS PLACE?
nu-uh
MAYBE A DEAD ASSASSIN IS POINTING WEAPONS AT US?
uh-huh
YOU KNOW, SASHA, I'M THINKING THIS WHOLE THING WAS A BAD IDEA.
BAD IDEA FOR "SASHA".
OOOH! DO I "POUND HER" NOW OR LATER?

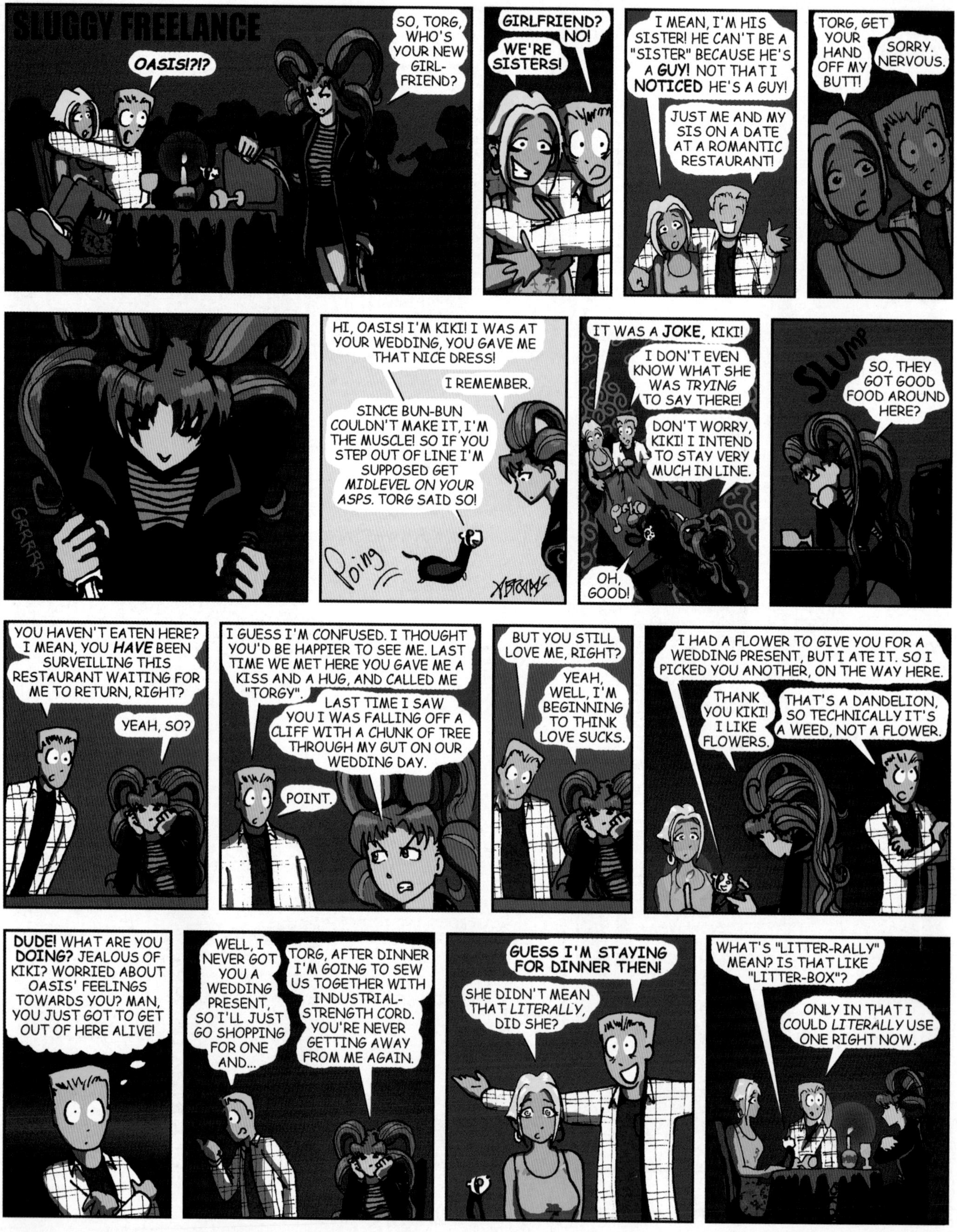
SLUGGY FREELANCE
OASIS!?!?
SO, TORG, WHO'S YOUR NEW GIRL-FRIEND?
GIRLFRIEND? NO!
WE'RE SISTERS!
I MEAN, I'M HIS SISTER! HE CAN'T BE A "SISTER" BECAUSE HE'S A GUY! NOT THAT I NOTICED HE'S A GUY!
JUST ME AND MY SIS ON A DATE AT A ROMANTIC RESTAURANT!
TORG, GET YOUR HAND OFF MY BUTT!
SORRY. NERVOUS.
GRRRRR
HI, OASIS! I'M KIKI! I WAS AT YOUR WEDDING, YOU GAVE ME THAT NICE DRESS!
I REMEMBER.
SINCE BUN-BUN COULDN'T MAKE IT, I'M THE MUSCLE! SO IF YOU STEP OUT OF LINE I'M SUPPOSED GET MIDLEVEL ON YOUR ASPS. TORG SAID SO!
Poing
IT WAS A JOKE, KIKI!
I DON'T EVEN KNOW WHAT SHE WAS TRYING TO SAY THERE!
DON'T WORRY, KIKI! I INTEND TO STAY VERY MUCH IN LINE.
OH, GOOD!
SLUMP
SO, THEY GOT GOOD FOOD AROUND HERE?
YOU HAVEN'T EATEN HERE? I MEAN, YOU HAVE BEEN SURVEILLING THIS RESTAURANT WAITING FOR ME TO RETURN, RIGHT?
YEAH, SO?
I GUESS I'M CONFUSED. I THOUGHT YOU'D BE HAPPIER TO SEE ME. LAST TIME WE MET HERE YOU GAVE ME A KISS AND A HUG, AND CALLED ME "TORGY".
LAST TIME I SAW YOU I WAS FALLING OFF A CLIFF WITH A CHUNK OF TREE THROUGH MY GUT ON OUR WEDDING DAY.
POINT.
BUT YOU STILL LOVE ME, RIGHT?
YEAH, WELL, I'M BEGINNING TO THINK LOVE SUCKS.
I HAD A FLOWER TO GIVE YOU FOR A WEDDING PRESENT, BUT I ATE IT. SO I PICKED YOU ANOTHER, ON THE WAY HERE.
THANK YOU KIKI! I LIKE FLOWERS.
THAT'S A DANDELION, SO TECHNICALLY IT'S A WEED, NOT A FLOWER.
DUDE! WHAT ARE YOU DOING? JEALOUS OF KIKI? WORRIED ABOUT OASIS' FEELINGS TOWARDS YOU? MAN, YOU JUST GOT TO GET OUT OF HERE ALIVE!
WELL, I NEVER GOT YOU A WEDDING PRESENT, SO I'LL JUST GO SHOPPING FOR ONE AND...
TORG, AFTER DINNER I'M GOING TO SEW US TOGETHER WITH INDUSTRIAL-STRENGTH CORD. YOU'RE NEVER GETTING AWAY FROM ME AGAIN.
GUESS I'M STAYING FOR DINNER THEN!
SHE DIDN'T MEAN THAT LITERALLY, DID SHE?
WHAT'S "LITTER-RALLY" MEAN? IS THAT LIKE "LITTER-BOX"?
ONLY IN THAT I COULD LITERALLY USE ONE RIGHT NOW.

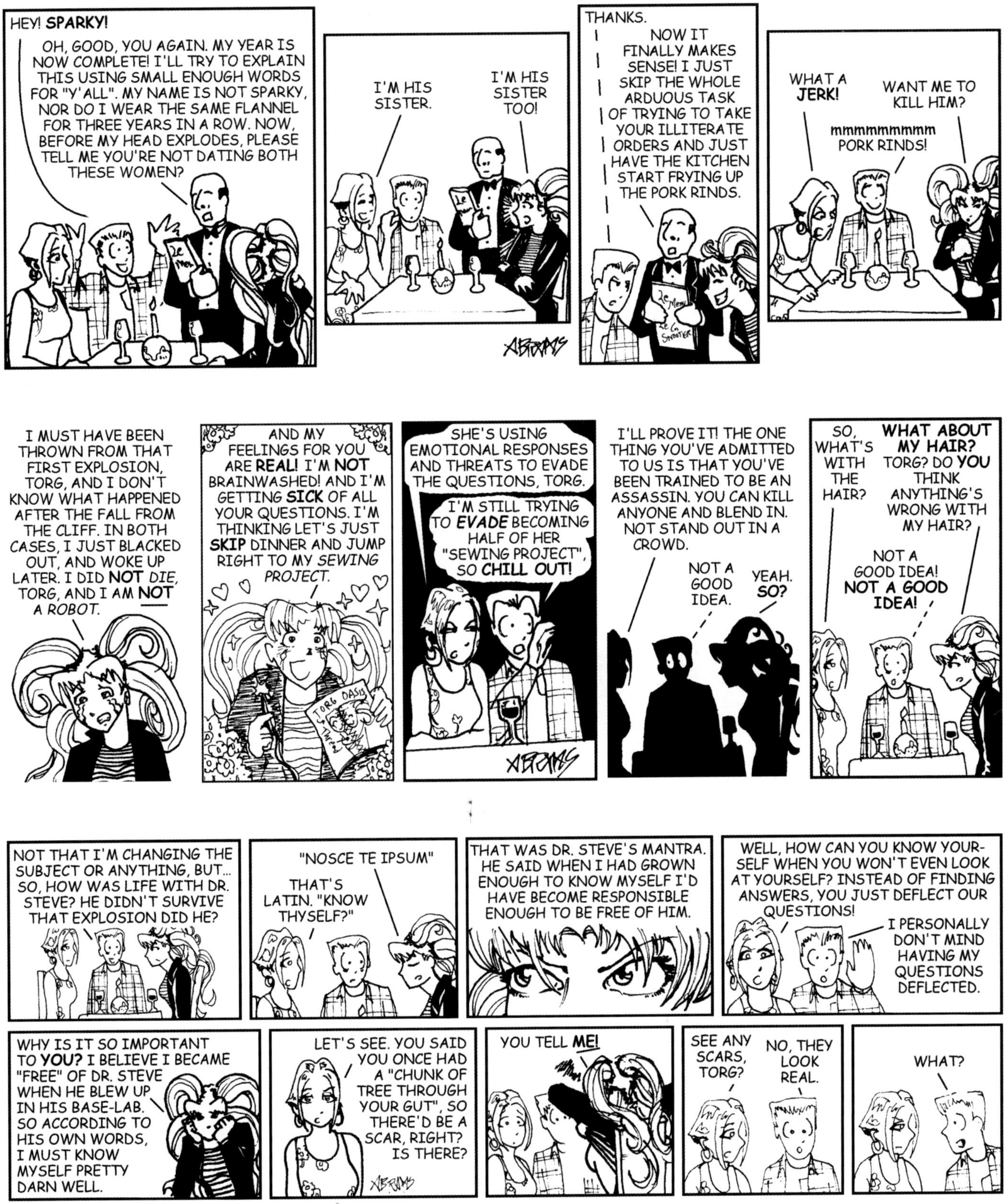
HEY! **SPARKY!**
OH, GOOD, YOU AGAIN. MY YEAR IS NOW COMPLETE! I'LL TRY TO EXPLAIN THIS USING SMALL ENOUGH WORDS FOR "Y'ALL". MY NAME IS NOT SPARKY, NOR DO I WEAR THE SAME FLANNEL FOR THREE YEARS IN A ROW. NOW, BEFORE MY HEAD EXPLODES, PLEASE TELL ME YOU'RE NOT DATING BOTH THESE WOMEN?
I'M HIS SISTER.
I'M HIS SISTER TOO!
THANKS.
NOW IT FINALLY MAKES SENSE! I JUST SKIP THE WHOLE ARDUOUS TASK OF TRYING TO TAKE YOUR ILLITERATE ORDERS AND JUST HAVE THE KITCHEN START FRYING UP THE PORK RINDS.
WHAT A **JERK!**
WANT ME TO KILL HIM?
mmmmmmmmmm PORK RINDS!
ABRAMS
I MUST HAVE BEEN THROWN FROM THAT FIRST EXPLOSION, TORG, AND I DON'T KNOW WHAT HAPPENED AFTER THE FALL FROM THE CLIFF. IN BOTH CASES, I JUST BLACKED OUT, AND WOKE UP LATER. I DID **NOT** *DIE*, TORG, AND I AM **NOT** *A ROBOT*.
AND MY FEELINGS FOR YOU ARE **REAL!** I'M **NOT** BRAINWASHED! AND I'M GETTING **SICK** OF ALL YOUR QUESTIONS. I'M THINKING LET'S JUST **SKIP** DINNER AND JUMP RIGHT TO MY *SEWING PROJECT*.
SHE'S USING EMOTIONAL RESPONSES AND THREATS TO EVADE THE QUESTIONS, TORG.
I'M STILL TRYING TO ***EVADE*** BECOMING HALF OF HER "SEWING PROJECT", SO **CHILL OUT!**
ABRAMS
I'LL PROVE IT! THE ONE THING YOU'VE ADMITTED TO US IS THAT YOU'VE BEEN TRAINED TO BE AN ASSASSIN. YOU CAN KILL ANYONE AND BLEND IN. NOT STAND OUT IN A CROWD.
NOT A GOOD IDEA.
YEAH. **SO?**
SO, WHAT'S WITH THE HAIR?
WHAT ABOUT MY HAIR? TORG? DO **YOU** THINK ANYTHING'S WRONG WITH MY HAIR?
NOT A GOOD IDEA! **NOT A GOOD IDEA!**
NOT THAT I'M CHANGING THE SUBJECT OR ANYTHING, BUT... SO, HOW WAS LIFE WITH DR. STEVE? HE DIDN'T SURVIVE THAT EXPLOSION DID HE?
"NOSCE TE IPSUM"
THAT'S LATIN. "KNOW THYSELF?"
THAT WAS DR. STEVE'S MANTRA. HE SAID WHEN I HAD GROWN ENOUGH TO KNOW MYSELF I'D HAVE BECOME RESPONSIBLE ENOUGH TO BE FREE OF HIM.
WELL, HOW CAN YOU KNOW YOURSELF WHEN YOU WON'T EVEN LOOK AT YOURSELF? INSTEAD OF FINDING ANSWERS, YOU JUST DEFLECT OUR QUESTIONS!
I PERSONALLY DON'T MIND HAVING MY QUESTIONS DEFLECTED.
WHY IS IT SO IMPORTANT TO **YOU?** I BELIEVE I BECAME "FREE" OF DR. STEVE WHEN HE BLEW UP IN HIS BASE-LAB. SO ACCORDING TO HIS OWN WORDS, I MUST KNOW MYSELF PRETTY DARN WELL.
LET'S SEE. YOU SAID YOU ONCE HAD A "CHUNK OF TREE THROUGH YOUR GUT", SO THERE'D BE A SCAR, RIGHT? IS THERE?
ABRAMS
YOU TELL **ME!**
SEE ANY SCARS, TORG?
NO, THEY LOOK REAL.
WHAT?

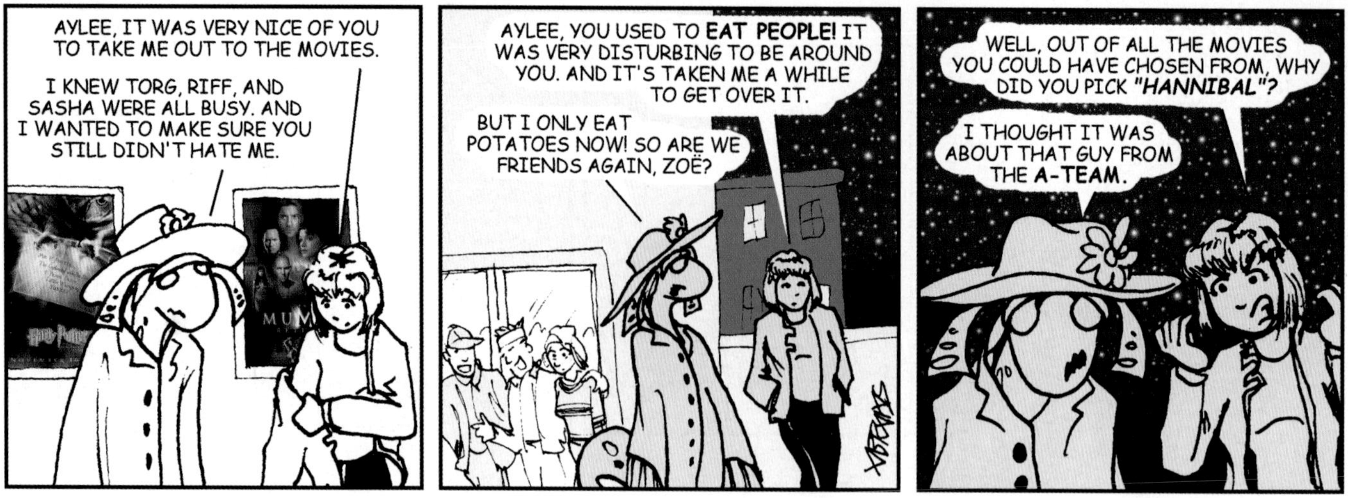
AYLEE, IT WAS VERY NICE OF YOU TO TAKE ME OUT TO THE MOVIES.
I KNEW TORG, RIFF, AND SASHA WERE ALL BUSY. AND I WANTED TO MAKE SURE YOU STILL DIDN'T HATE ME.
AYLEE, YOU USED TO **EAT PEOPLE!** IT WAS VERY DISTURBING TO BE AROUND YOU. AND IT'S TAKEN ME A WHILE TO GET OVER IT.
BUT I ONLY EAT POTATOES NOW! SO ARE WE FRIENDS AGAIN, ZOË?
WELL, OUT OF ALL THE MOVIES YOU COULD HAVE CHOSEN FROM, WHY DID YOU PICK ***"HANNIBAL"?***
I THOUGHT IT WAS ABOUT THAT GUY FROM THE **A-TEAM.**

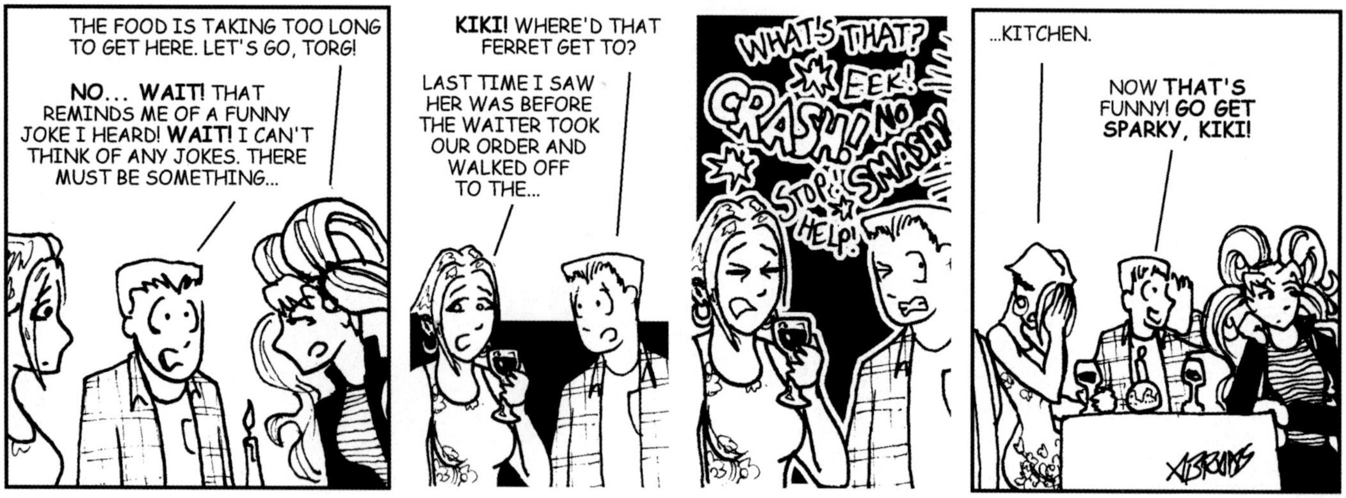
THE FOOD IS TAKING TOO LONG TO GET HERE. LET'S GO, TORG!
NO... WAIT! THAT REMINDS ME OF A FUNNY JOKE I HEARD! **WAIT!** I CAN'T THINK OF ANY JOKES. THERE MUST BE SOMETHING...
KIKI! WHERE'D THAT FERRET GET TO?
LAST TIME I SAW HER WAS BEFORE THE WAITER TOOK OUR ORDER AND WALKED OFF TO THE...
WHAT'S THAT?
EEK!
CRASH!
NO
SMASH!
STOP!
HELP!
...KITCHEN.
NOW **THAT'S** FUNNY! **GO GET SPARKY, KIKI!**

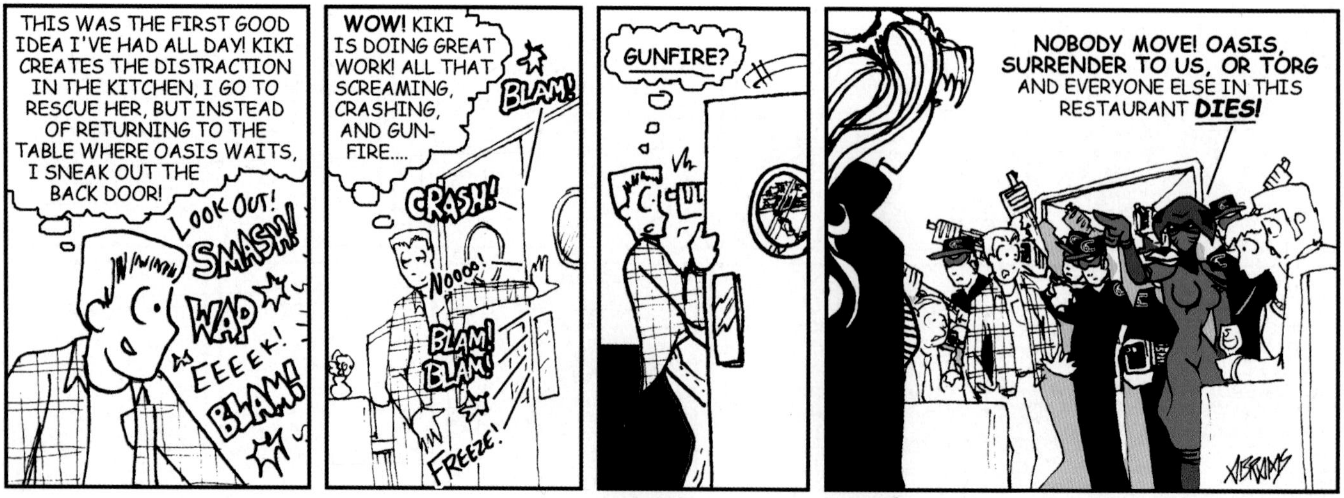
THIS WAS THE FIRST GOOD IDEA I'VE HAD ALL DAY! KIKI CREATES THE DISTRACTION IN THE KITCHEN, I GO TO RESCUE HER, BUT INSTEAD OF RETURNING TO THE TABLE WHERE OASIS WAITS, I SNEAK OUT THE BACK DOOR!
LOOK OUT!
SMASH!
WAP
EEEEK!
BLAM!
WOW! KIKI IS DOING GREAT WORK! ALL THAT SCREAMING, CRASHING, AND GUN-FIRE....
BLAM!
CRASH!
Noooo!
BLAM! BLAM!
FREEZE!
GUNFIRE?
NOBODY MOVE! OASIS, SURRENDER TO US, OR TORG AND EVERYONE ELSE IN THIS RESTAURANT **DIES!**

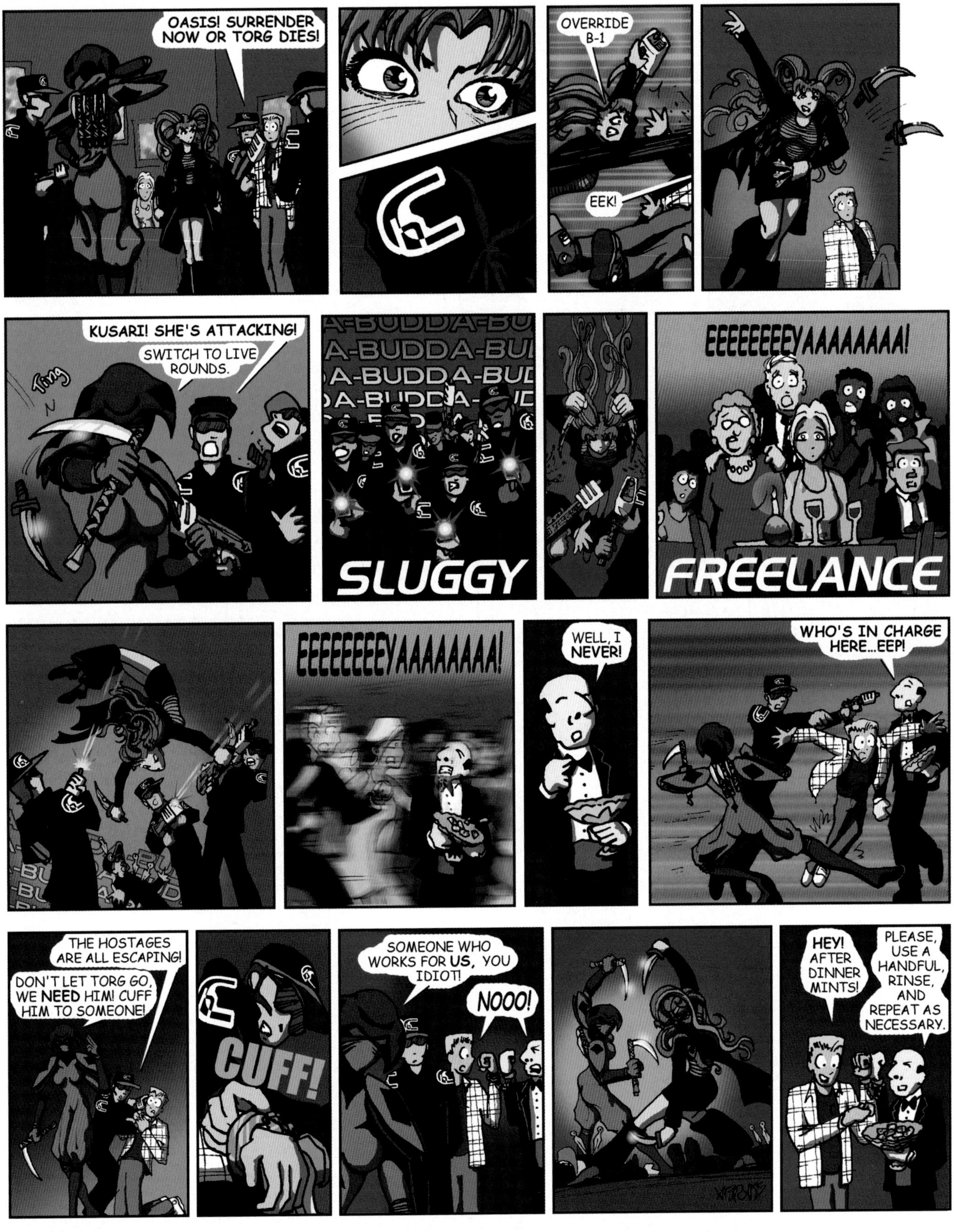
OASIS! SURRENDER NOW OR TORG DIES!
OVERRIDE B-1
EEK!
KUSARI! SHE'S ATTACKING!
SWITCH TO LIVE ROUNDS.
Tong
A-BUDDA-BUDDA-BUDDA-BUDDA-BU
SLUGGY
EEEEEEEEYAAAAAAAA!
FREELANCE
EEEEEEEEYAAAAAAAA!
WELL, I NEVER!
WHO'S IN CHARGE HERE...EEP!
THE HOSTAGES ARE ALL ESCAPING!
DON'T LET TORG GO, WE NEED HIM! CUFF HIM TO SOMEONE!
CUFF!
SOMEONE WHO WORKS FOR US, YOU IDIOT!
NOOO!
HEY! AFTER DINNER MINTS!
PLEASE, USE A HANDFUL, RINSE, AND REPEAT AS NECESSARY.

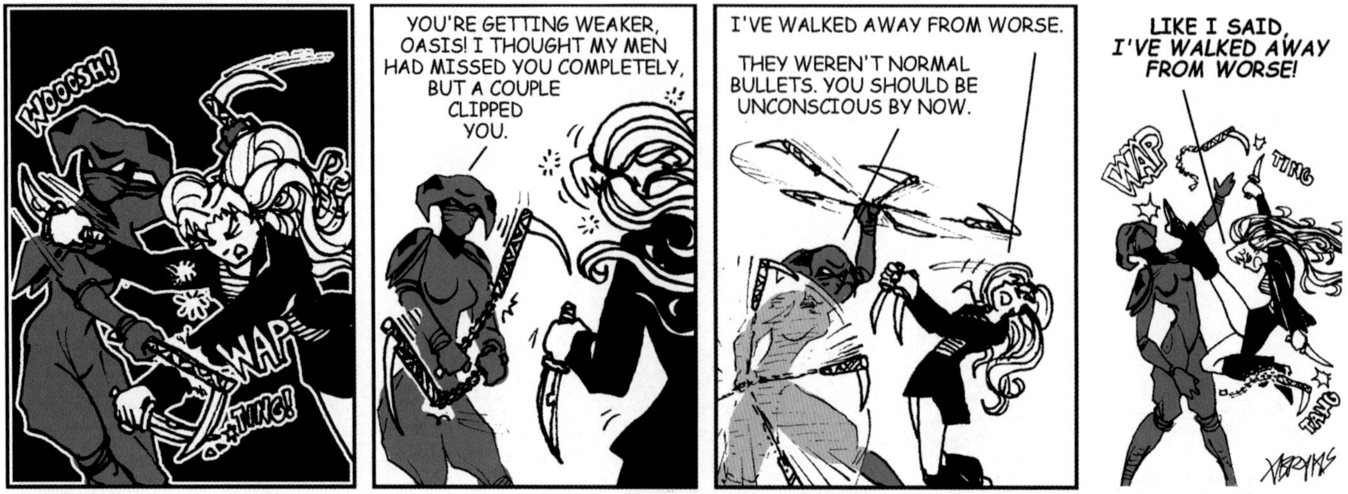
WOOOSH!
WAP
TING!
YOU'RE GETTING WEAKER, OASIS! I THOUGHT MY MEN HAD MISSED YOU COMPLETELY, BUT A COUPLE CLIPPED YOU.
I'VE WALKED AWAY FROM WORSE.
THEY WEREN'T NORMAL BULLETS. YOU SHOULD BE UNCONSCIOUS BY NOW.
LIKE I SAID, *I'VE WALKED AWAY FROM WORSE!*
WAP
TING

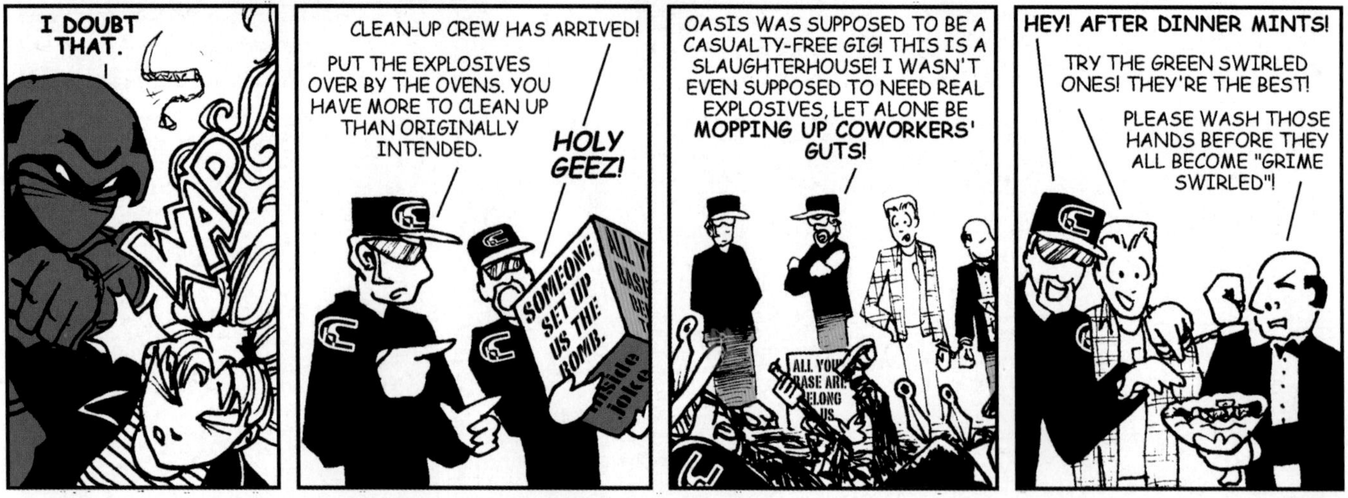
I DOUBT THAT.
WAP
CLEAN-UP CREW HAS ARRIVED!
PUT THE EXPLOSIVES OVER BY THE OVENS. YOU HAVE MORE TO CLEAN UP THAN ORIGINALLY INTENDED.
HOLY GEEZ!
SOMEONE SET UP US THE BOMB.
inside joke
OASIS WAS SUPPOSED TO BE A CASUALTY-FREE GIG! THIS IS A SLAUGHTERHOUSE! I WASN'T EVEN SUPPOSED TO NEED REAL EXPLOSIVES, LET ALONE BE **MOPPING UP COWORKERS' GUTS!**
HEY! AFTER DINNER MINTS!
TRY THE GREEN SWIRLED ONES! THEY'RE THE BEST!
PLEASE WASH THOSE HANDS BEFORE THEY ALL BECOME "GRIME SWIRLED"!

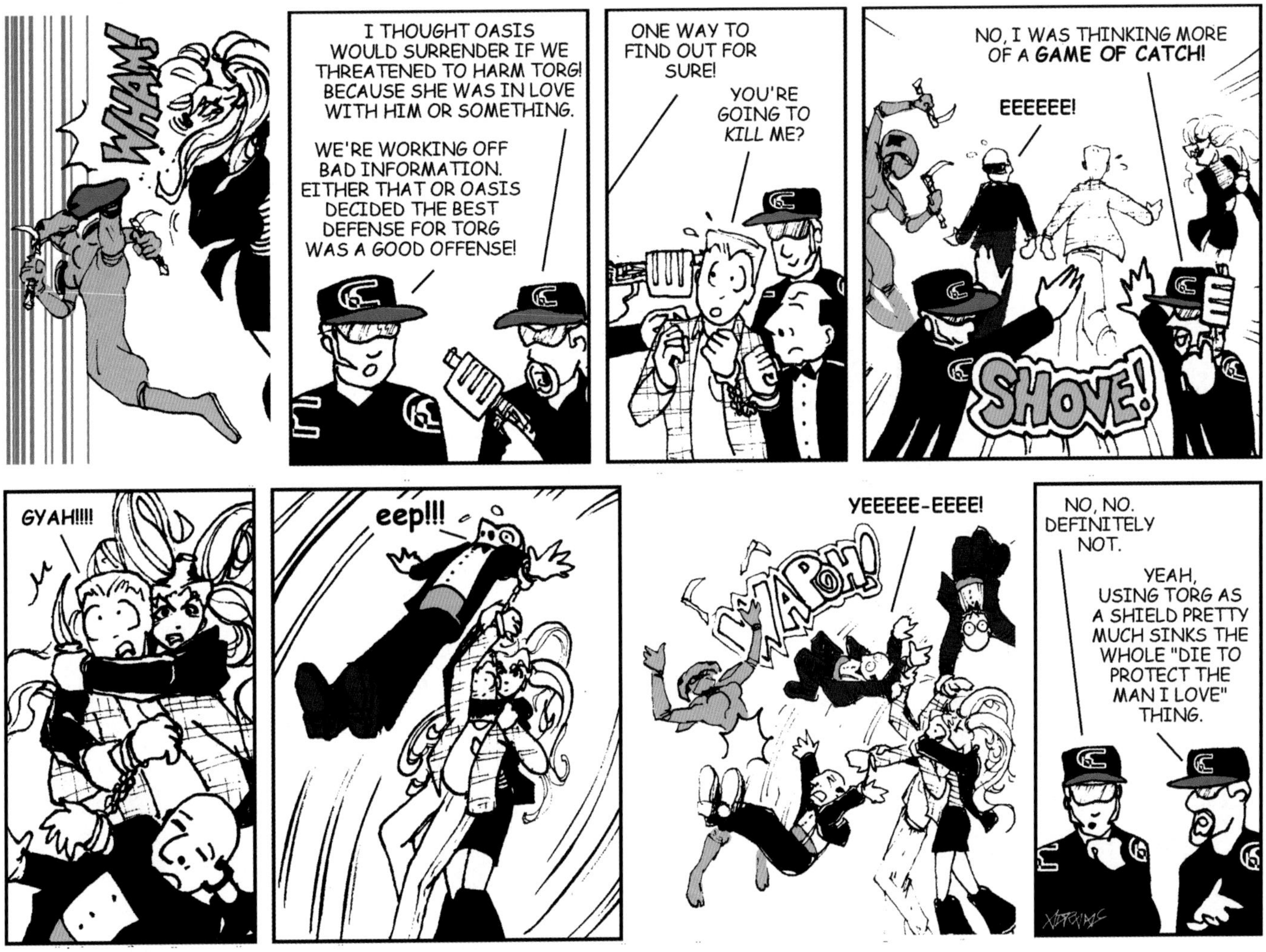
WHAM!
I THOUGHT OASIS WOULD SURRENDER IF WE THREATENED TO HARM TORG! BECAUSE SHE WAS IN LOVE WITH HIM OR SOMETHING.
WE'RE WORKING OFF BAD INFORMATION. EITHER THAT OR OASIS DECIDED THE BEST DEFENSE FOR TORG WAS A GOOD OFFENSE!
ONE WAY TO FIND OUT FOR SURE!
YOU'RE GOING TO KILL ME?
NO, I WAS THINKING MORE OF A **GAME OF CATCH!**
EEEEEE!
SHOVE!
GYAH!!!!
eep!!!
YEEEEE-EEEE!
WAPOH!
NO, NO. DEFINITELY NOT.
YEAH, USING TORG AS A SHIELD PRETTY MUCH SINKS THE WHOLE "DIE TO PROTECT THE MAN I LOVE" THING.

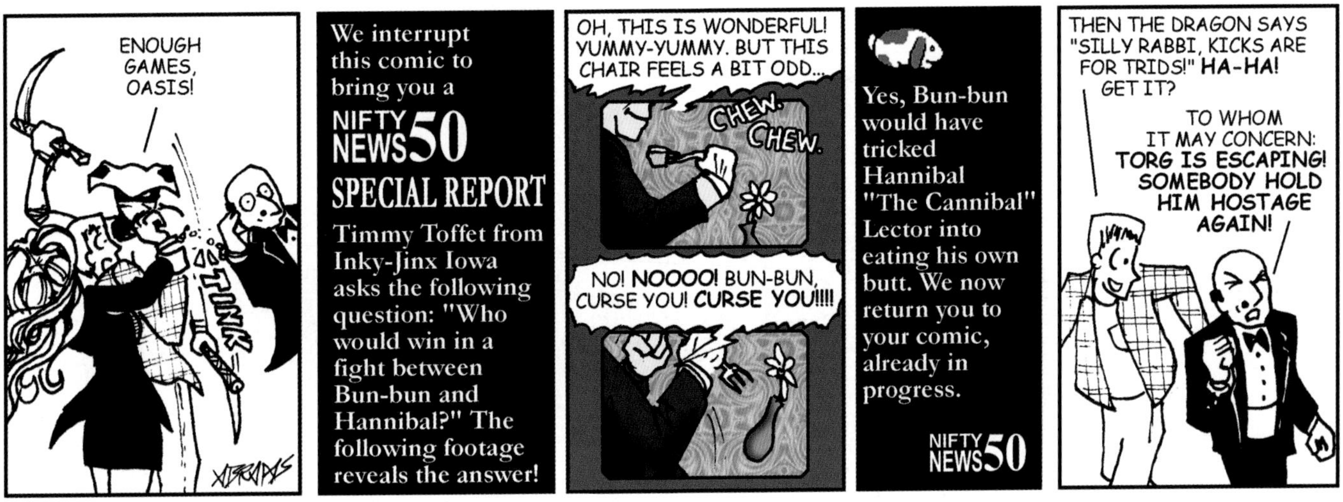
ENOUGH GAMES, OASIS!
TINK
We interrupt this comic to bring you a
NIFTY NEWS 50
SPECIAL REPORT
Timmy Toffet from Inky-Jinx Iowa asks the following question: "Who would win in a fight between Bun-bun and Hannibal?" The following footage reveals the answer!
OH, THIS IS WONDERFUL! YUMMY-YUMMY. BUT THIS CHAIR FEELS A BIT ODD...
CHEW. CHEW.
NO! **NOOOO!** BUN-BUN, CURSE YOU! **CURSE YOU!!!!**
Yes, Bun-bun would have tricked Hannibal "The Cannibal" Lector into eating his own butt. We now return you to your comic, already in progress.
NIFTY NEWS 50
THEN THE DRAGON SAYS "SILLY RABBI, KICKS ARE FOR TRIDS!" **HA-HA!** GET IT?
TO WHOM IT MAY CONCERN: **TORG IS ESCAPING! SOMEBODY HOLD HIM HOSTAGE AGAIN!**

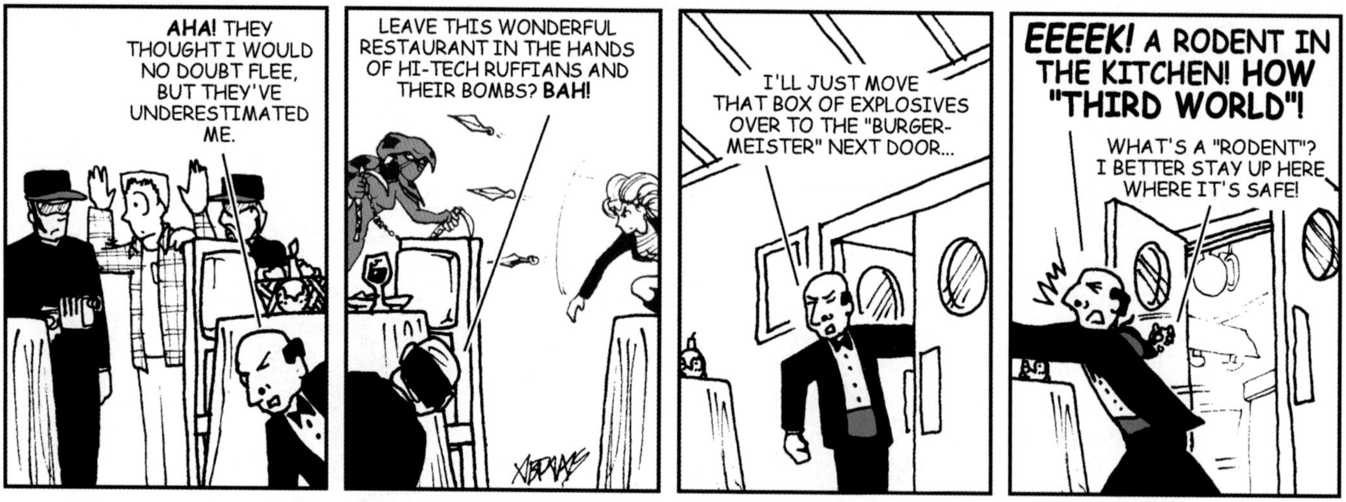
AHA! THEY THOUGHT I WOULD NO DOUBT FLEE, BUT THEY'VE UNDERESTIMATED ME.
LEAVE THIS WONDERFUL RESTAURANT IN THE HANDS OF HI-TECH RUFFIANS AND THEIR BOMBS? BAH!
I'LL JUST MOVE THAT BOX OF EXPLOSIVES OVER TO THE "BURGER-MEISTER" NEXT DOOR...
EEEEK! A RODENT IN THE KITCHEN! HOW "THIRD WORLD"!
WHAT'S A "RODENT"? I BETTER STAY UP HERE WHERE IT'S SAFE!

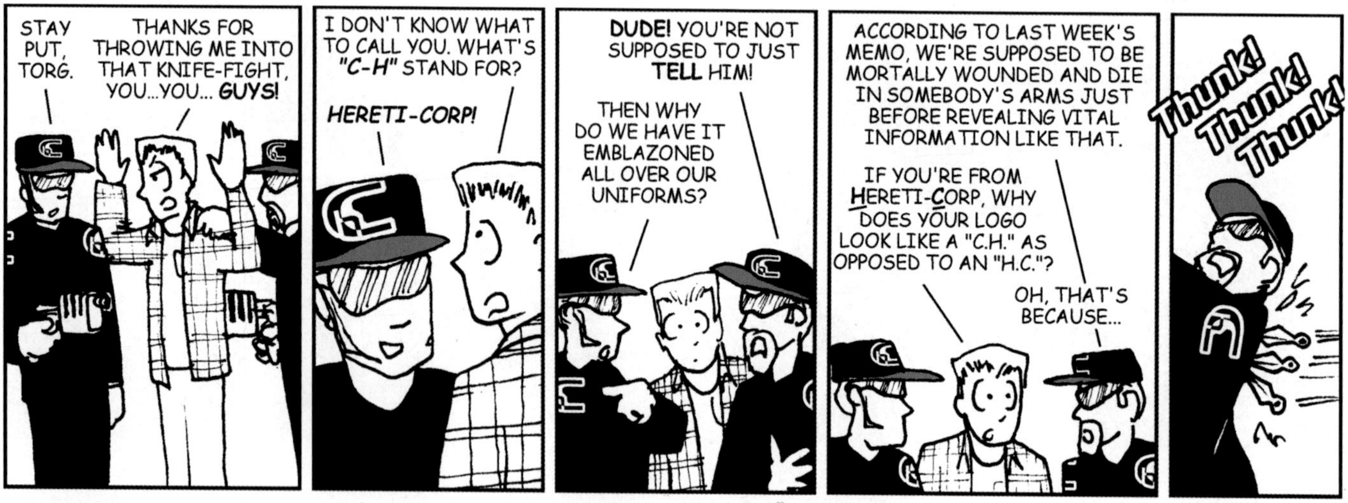
STAY PUT, TORG.
THANKS FOR THROWING ME INTO THAT KNIFE-FIGHT, YOU...YOU... GUYS!
I DON'T KNOW WHAT TO CALL YOU. WHAT'S "C-H" STAND FOR?
HERETI-CORP!
DUDE! YOU'RE NOT SUPPOSED TO JUST TELL HIM!
THEN WHY DO WE HAVE IT EMBLAZONED ALL OVER OUR UNIFORMS?
ACCORDING TO LAST WEEK'S MEMO, WE'RE SUPPOSED TO BE MORTALLY WOUNDED AND DIE IN SOMEBODY'S ARMS JUST BEFORE REVEALING VITAL INFORMATION LIKE THAT.
IF YOU'RE FROM HERETI-CORP, WHY DOES YOUR LOGO LOOK LIKE A "C.H." AS OPPOSED TO AN "H.C."?
OH, THAT'S BECAUSE...
Thunk! Thunk! Thunk!

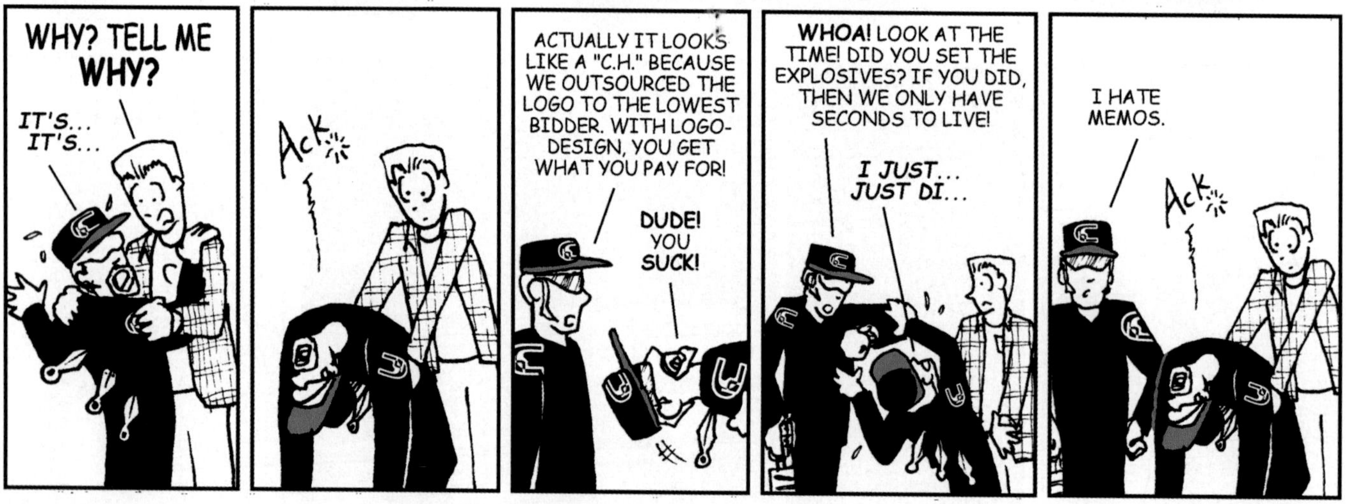
WHY? TELL ME WHY?
IT'S... IT'S...
Ack
ACTUALLY IT LOOKS LIKE A "C.H." BECAUSE WE OUTSOURCED THE LOGO TO THE LOWEST BIDDER. WITH LOGO-DESIGN, YOU GET WHAT YOU PAY FOR!
DUDE! YOU SUCK!
WHOA! LOOK AT THE TIME! DID YOU SET THE EXPLOSIVES? IF YOU DID, THEN WE ONLY HAVE SECONDS TO LIVE!
I JUST... JUST DI...
I HATE MEMOS.
Ack

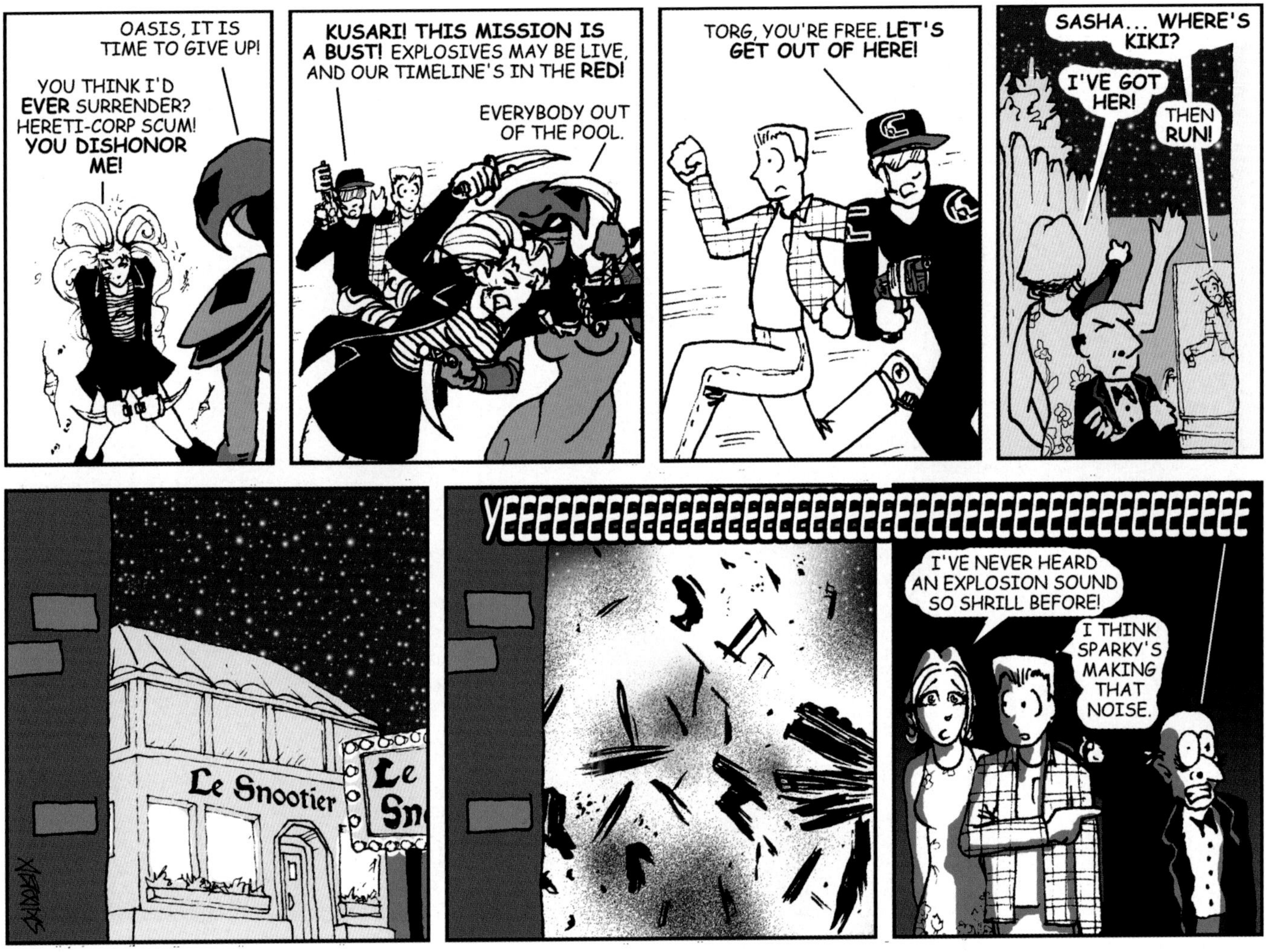
OASIS, IT IS TIME TO GIVE UP!
YOU THINK I'D **EVER** SURRENDER? HERETI-CORP SCUM! **YOU DISHONOR ME!**
KUSARI! THIS MISSION IS A BUST! EXPLOSIVES MAY BE LIVE, AND OUR TIMELINE'S IN THE **RED!**
EVERYBODY OUT OF THE POOL.
TORG, YOU'RE FREE. **LET'S GET OUT OF HERE!**
SASHA... WHERE'S KIKI?
I'VE GOT HER!
THEN **RUN!**
Le Snootier
YEEEEEEEEEEEEEEEEEEEEEEEEEEEEEEEEEEEEEEEEEEEEEE
I'VE NEVER HEARD AN EXPLOSION SOUND SO SHRILL BEFORE!
I THINK SPARKY'S MAKING THAT NOISE.

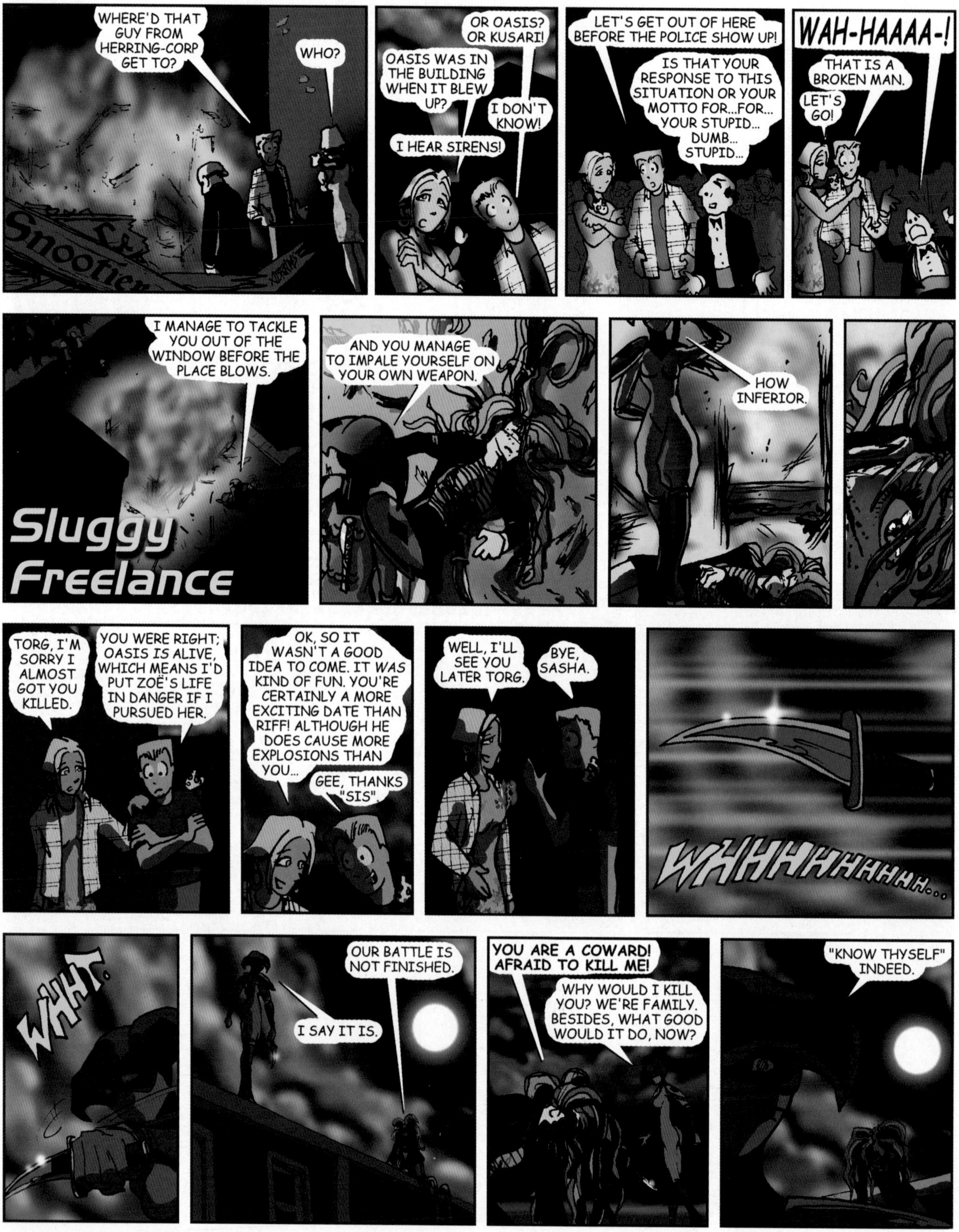
WHERE'D THAT GUY FROM HERRING-CORP GET TO?
WHO?
Snootier
OR OASIS? OR KUSARI!
OASIS WAS IN THE BUILDING WHEN IT BLEW UP?
I DON'T KNOW!
I HEAR SIRENS!
LET'S GET OUT OF HERE BEFORE THE POLICE SHOW UP!
IS THAT YOUR RESPONSE TO THIS SITUATION OR YOUR MOTTO FOR...FOR... YOUR STUPID... DUMB... STUPID...
WAH-HAAAA-!
THAT IS A BROKEN MAN.
LET'S GO!
I MANAGE TO TACKLE YOU OUT OF THE WINDOW BEFORE THE PLACE BLOWS.
Sluggy Freelance
AND YOU MANAGE TO IMPALE YOURSELF ON YOUR OWN WEAPON.
HOW INFERIOR.
TORG, I'M SORRY I ALMOST GOT YOU KILLED.
YOU WERE RIGHT; OASIS *IS* ALIVE, WHICH MEANS I'D PUT ZOË'S LIFE IN DANGER IF I PURSUED HER.
OK, SO IT WASN'T A GOOD IDEA TO COME. IT *WAS* KIND OF FUN. YOU'RE CERTAINLY A MORE EXCITING DATE THAN RIFF! ALTHOUGH HE DOES CAUSE MORE EXPLOSIONS THAN YOU...
GEE, THANKS "SIS".
WELL, I'LL SEE YOU LATER TORG.
BYE, SASHA.
WHHHHHHHHH...
WHHT.
OUR BATTLE IS NOT FINISHED.
I SAY IT IS.
YOU ARE A COWARD! AFRAID TO KILL ME!
WHY WOULD I KILL YOU? WE'RE FAMILY. BESIDES, WHAT GOOD WOULD IT DO, NOW?
"KNOW THYSELF" INDEED.

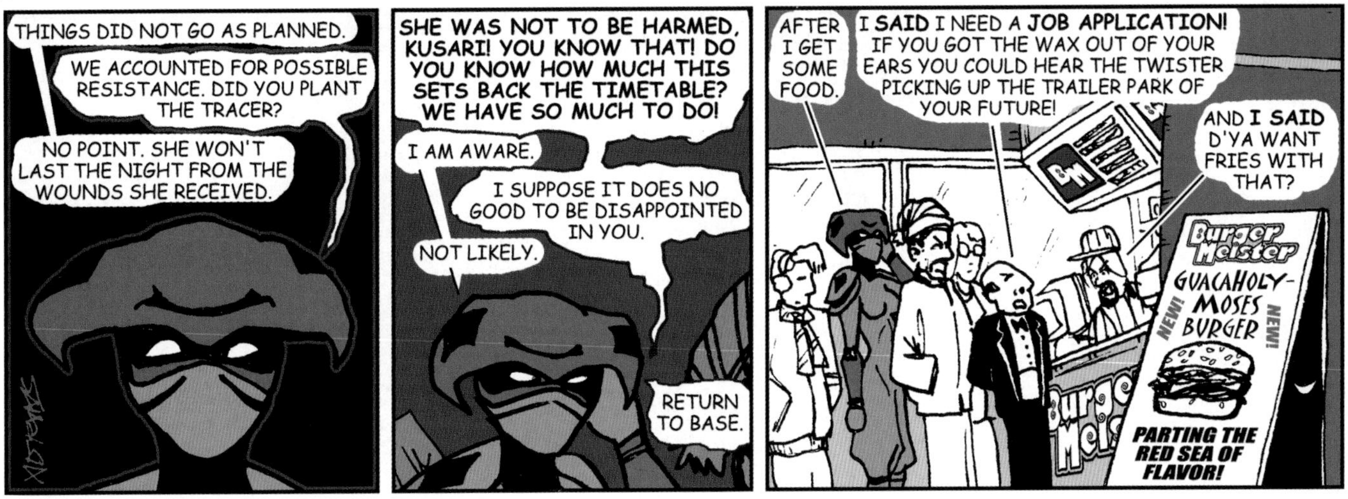
THINGS DID NOT GO AS PLANNED.
WE ACCOUNTED FOR POSSIBLE RESISTANCE. DID YOU PLANT THE TRACER?
NO POINT. SHE WON'T LAST THE NIGHT FROM THE WOUNDS SHE RECEIVED.
SHE WAS NOT TO BE HARMED, KUSARI! YOU KNOW THAT! DO YOU KNOW HOW MUCH THIS SETS BACK THE TIMETABLE? WE HAVE SO MUCH TO DO!
I AM AWARE.
I SUPPOSE IT DOES NO GOOD TO BE DISAPPOINTED IN YOU.
NOT LIKELY.
RETURN TO BASE.
AFTER I GET SOME FOOD.
I SAID I NEED A JOB APPLICATION! IF YOU GOT THE WAX OUT OF YOUR EARS YOU COULD HEAR THE TWISTER PICKING UP THE TRAILER PARK OF YOUR FUTURE!
AND I SAID D'YA WANT FRIES WITH THAT?
Burger Meister
GUACAHOLY-MOSES BURGER
NEW!
NEW!
PARTING THE RED SEA OF FLAVOR!

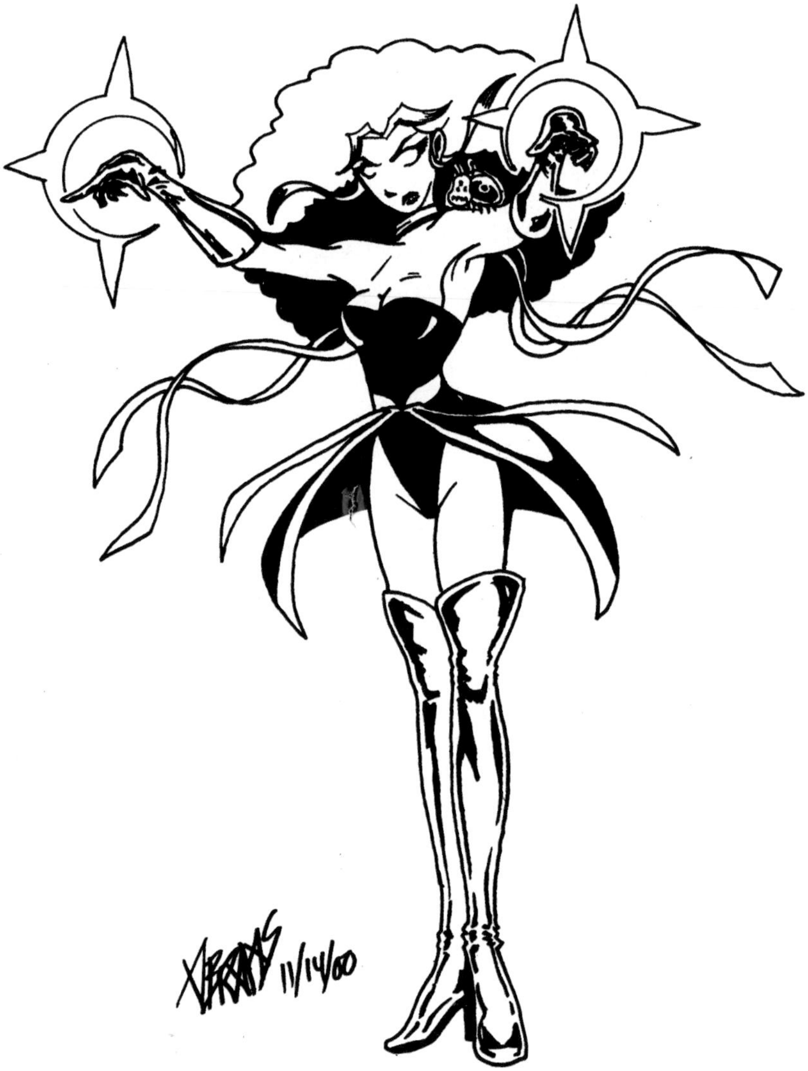
11/14/00

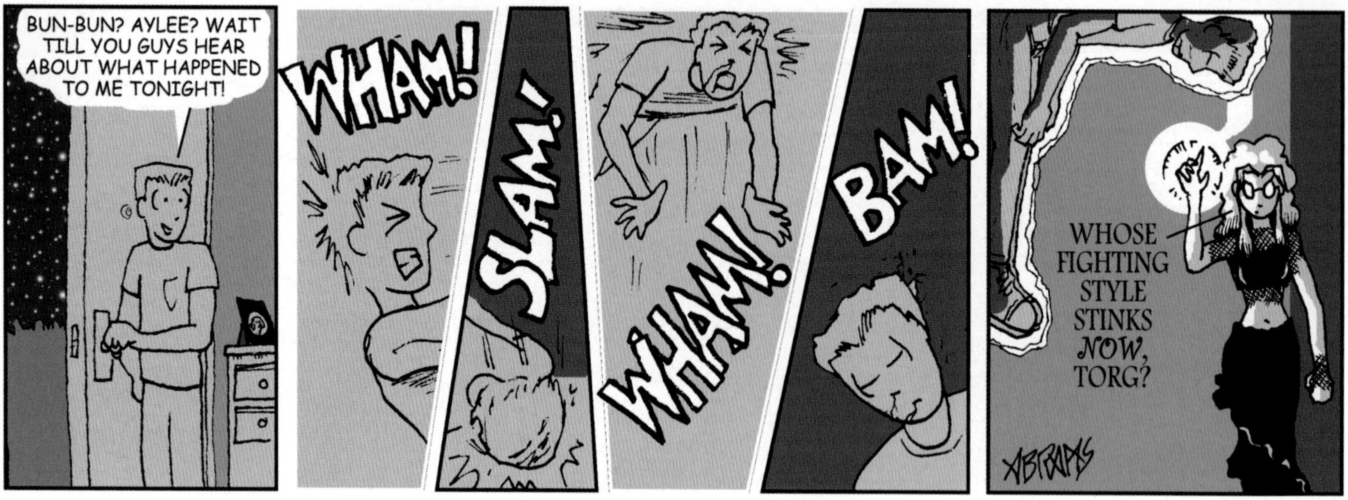
BUN-BUN? AYLEE? WAIT TILL YOU GUYS HEAR ABOUT WHAT HAPPENED TO ME TONIGHT!
WHAM!
SLAM!
WHAM!
BAM!
WHOSE FIGHTING STYLE STINKS NOW, TORG?

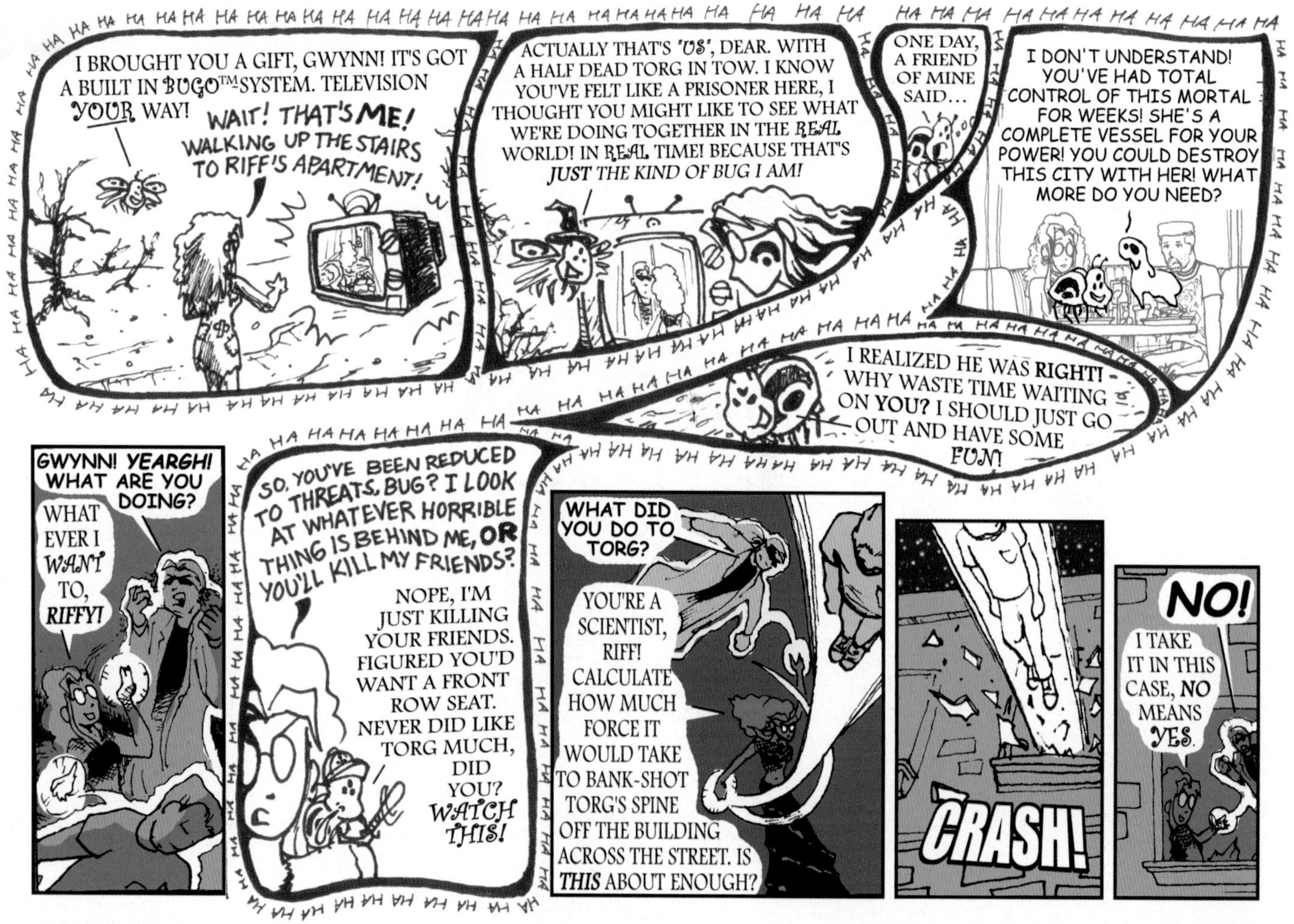
I BROUGHT YOU A GIFT, GWYNN! IT'S GOT A BUILT IN BUGO™ SYSTEM. TELEVISION YOUR WAY!
WAIT! THAT'S ME! WALKING UP THE STAIRS TO RIFF'S APARTMENT!
ACTUALLY THAT'S 'US', DEAR. WITH A HALF DEAD TORG IN TOW. I KNOW YOU'VE FELT LIKE A PRISONER HERE, I THOUGHT YOU MIGHT LIKE TO SEE WHAT WE'RE DOING TOGETHER IN THE REAL WORLD! IN REAL TIME! BECAUSE THAT'S JUST THE KIND OF BUG I AM!
ONE DAY, A FRIEND OF MINE SAID…
I DON'T UNDERSTAND! YOU'VE HAD TOTAL CONTROL OF THIS MORTAL FOR WEEKS! SHE'S A COMPLETE VESSEL FOR YOUR POWER! YOU COULD DESTROY THIS CITY WITH HER! WHAT MORE DO YOU NEED?
I REALIZED HE WAS RIGHT! WHY WASTE TIME WAITING ON YOU? I SHOULD JUST GO OUT AND HAVE SOME FUN!
GWYNN! YEARGH! WHAT ARE YOU DOING?
WHAT EVER I WANT TO, RIFFY!
SO, YOU'VE BEEN REDUCED TO THREATS, BUG? I LOOK AT WHATEVER HORRIBLE THING IS BEHIND ME, OR YOU'LL KILL MY FRIENDS?
NOPE, I'M JUST KILLING YOUR FRIENDS. FIGURED YOU'D WANT A FRONT ROW SEAT. NEVER DID LIKE TORG MUCH, DID YOU? WATCH THIS!
WHAT DID YOU DO TO TORG?
YOU'RE A SCIENTIST, RIFF! CALCULATE HOW MUCH FORCE IT WOULD TAKE TO BANK-SHOT TORG'S SPINE OFF THE BUILDING ACROSS THE STREET. IS THIS ABOUT ENOUGH?
CRASH!
NO!
I TAKE IT IN THIS CASE, NO MEANS YES.

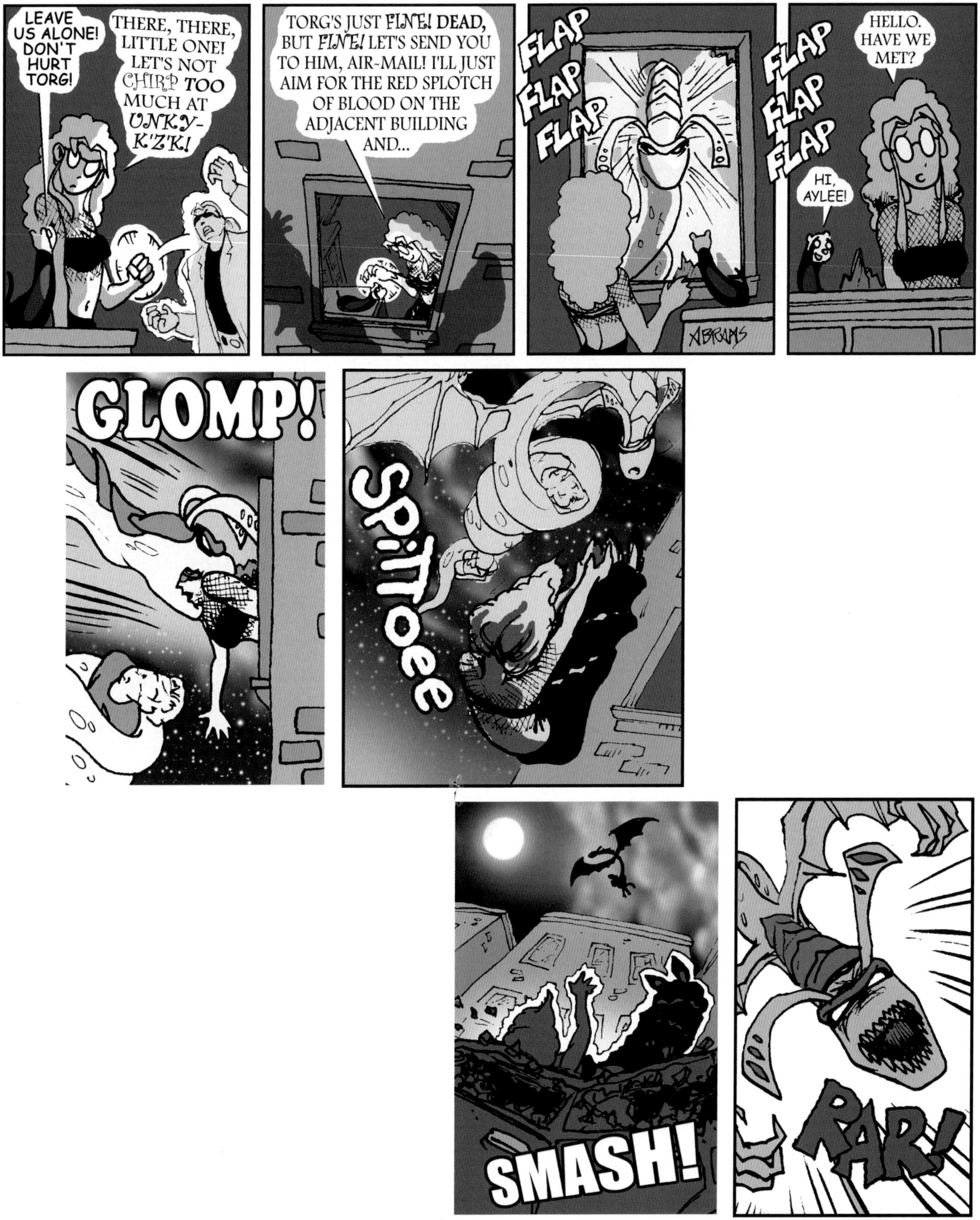

LEAVE US ALONE! DON'T HURT TORG!
THERE, THERE, LITTLE ONE! LET'S NOT CHIRP TOO MUCH AT UNKY-K'Z'K!
TORG'S JUST FINE! DEAD, BUT FINE! LET'S SEND YOU TO HIM, AIR-MAIL! I'LL JUST AIM FOR THE RED SPLOTCH OF BLOOD ON THE ADJACENT BUILDING AND...
FLAP FLAP FLAP
ABRAMS
FLAP FLAP FLAP
HELLO. HAVE WE MET?
HI, AYLEE!
GLOMP!
SPITOEE
SMASH!
RAR!

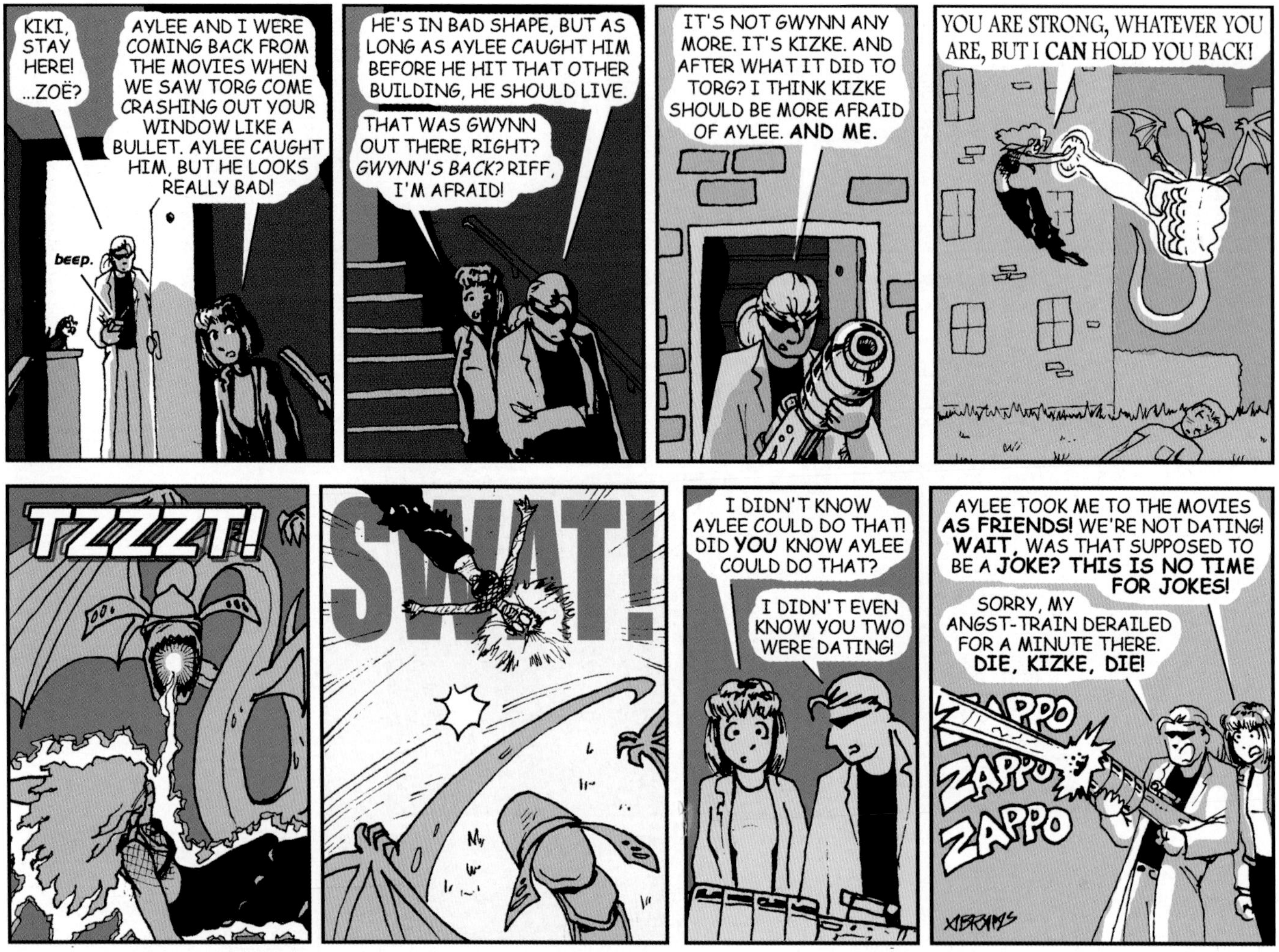
KIKI, STAY HERE! ...ZOË?
AYLEE AND I WERE COMING BACK FROM THE MOVIES WHEN WE SAW TORG COME CRASHING OUT YOUR WINDOW LIKE A BULLET. AYLEE CAUGHT HIM, BUT HE LOOKS REALLY BAD!
beep.
HE'S IN BAD SHAPE, BUT AS LONG AS AYLEE CAUGHT HIM BEFORE HE HIT THAT OTHER BUILDING, HE SHOULD LIVE.
THAT WAS GWYNN OUT THERE, RIGHT? GWYNN'S BACK? RIFF, I'M AFRAID!
IT'S NOT GWYNN ANY MORE. IT'S KIZKE. AND AFTER WHAT IT DID TO TORG? I THINK KIZKE SHOULD BE MORE AFRAID OF AYLEE. AND ME.
YOU ARE STRONG, WHATEVER YOU ARE, BUT I CAN HOLD YOU BACK!
TZZZZT!
SWAT!
I DIDN'T KNOW AYLEE COULD DO THAT! DID YOU KNOW AYLEE COULD DO THAT?
I DIDN'T EVEN KNOW YOU TWO WERE DATING!
AYLEE TOOK ME TO THE MOVIES AS FRIENDS! WE'RE NOT DATING! WAIT, WAS THAT SUPPOSED TO BE A JOKE? THIS IS NO TIME FOR JOKES!
SORRY, MY ANGST-TRAIN DERAILED FOR A MINUTE THERE. DIE, KIZKE, DIE!
ZAPPO
ZAPPO
ZAPPO
ABRAMS

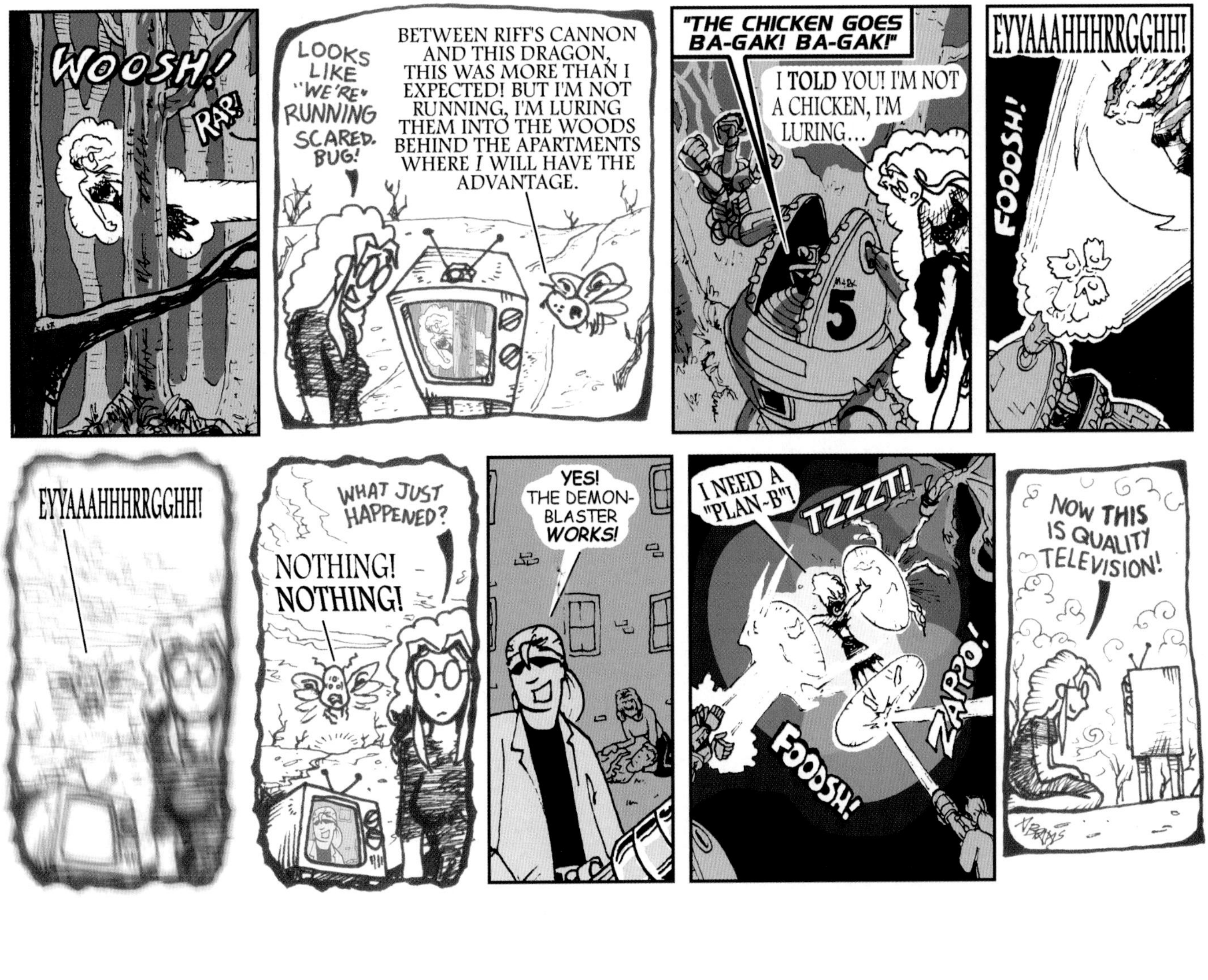
WOOSH!
RAP!
LOOKS LIKE "WE'RE" RUNNING SCARED. BUG!
BETWEEN RIFF'S CANNON AND THIS DRAGON, THIS WAS MORE THAN I EXPECTED! BUT I'M NOT RUNNING, I'M LURING THEM INTO THE WOODS BEHIND THE APARTMENTS WHERE *I* WILL HAVE THE ADVANTAGE.
"THE CHICKEN GOES BA-GAK! BA-GAK!"
I **TOLD** YOU! I'M NOT A CHICKEN, I'M LURING…
5
EYYAAAHHHRRGGHH!
FOOOSH!
EYYAAAHHHRRGGHH!
WHAT JUST HAPPENED?
NOTHING! **NOTHING!**
YES! THE DEMON-BLASTER **WORKS!**
I NEED A "PLAN-B"!
TZZZT!
FOOOSH!
ZAPPO!
NOW **THIS** IS QUALITY TELEVISION!

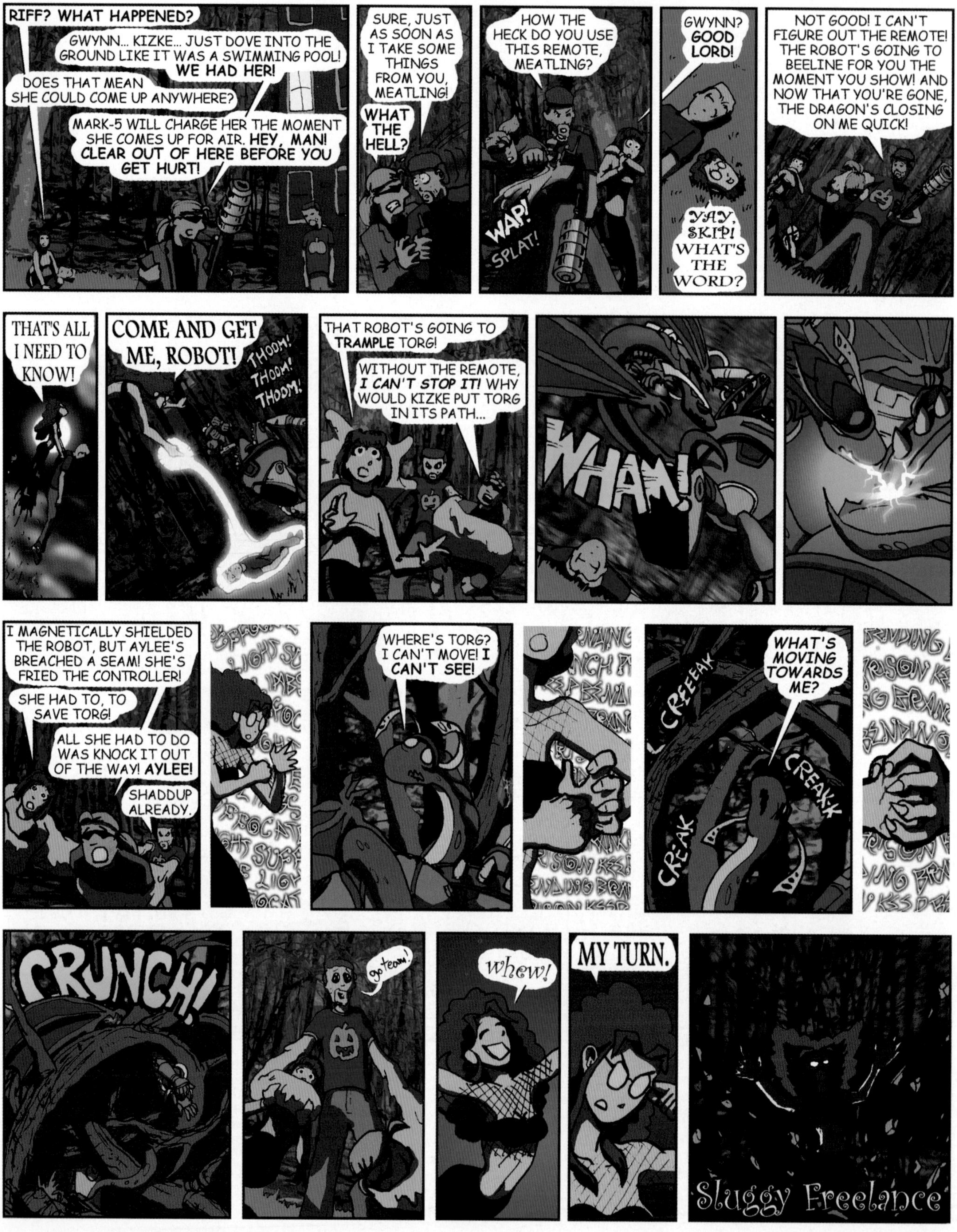

RIFF? WHAT HAPPENED?
GWYNN... KIZKE... JUST DOVE INTO THE GROUND LIKE IT WAS A SWIMMING POOL! WE HAD HER!
DOES THAT MEAN SHE COULD COME UP ANYWHERE?
MARK-5 WILL CHARGE HER THE MOMENT SHE COMES UP FOR AIR. HEY, MAN! CLEAR OUT OF HERE BEFORE YOU GET HURT!
SURE, JUST AS SOON AS I TAKE SOME THINGS FROM YOU, MEATLING!
WHAT THE HELL?
WAP!
SPLAT!
HOW THE HECK DO YOU USE THIS REMOTE, MEATLING?
GWYNN? GOOD LORD!
YAY, SKIP! WHAT'S THE WORD?
NOT GOOD! I CAN'T FIGURE OUT THE REMOTE! THE ROBOT'S GOING TO BEELINE FOR YOU THE MOMENT YOU SHOW! AND NOW THAT YOU'RE GONE, THE DRAGON'S CLOSING ON ME QUICK!
THAT'S ALL I NEED TO KNOW!
COME AND GET ME, ROBOT!
THOOM! THOOM! THOOM!
THAT ROBOT'S GOING TO TRAMPLE TORG!
WITHOUT THE REMOTE, I CAN'T STOP IT! WHY WOULD KIZKE PUT TORG IN ITS PATH...
WHAM!
I MAGNETICALLY SHIELDED THE ROBOT, BUT AYLEE'S BREACHED A SEAM! SHE'S FRIED THE CONTROLLER!
SHE HAD TO, TO SAVE TORG!
ALL SHE HAD TO DO WAS KNOCK IT OUT OF THE WAY! AYLEE!
SHADDUP ALREADY.
WHERE'S TORG? I CAN'T MOVE! I CAN'T SEE!
CREEEAK
WHAT'S MOVING TOWARDS ME?
CREAKK
CREAK
CRUNCH!
go team!
whew!
MY TURN.
Sluggy Freelance

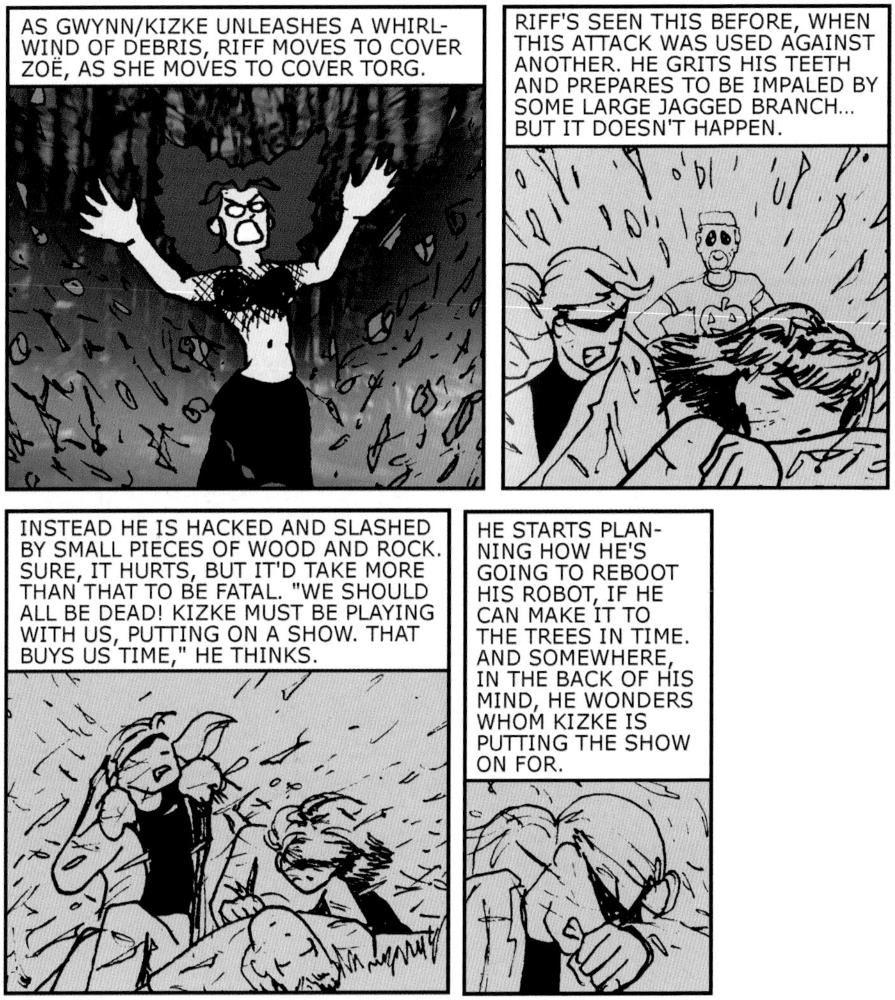
AS GWYNN/KIZKE UNLEASHES A WHIRLWIND OF DEBRIS, RIFF MOVES TO COVER ZOË, AS SHE MOVES TO COVER TORG.
RIFF'S SEEN THIS BEFORE, WHEN THIS ATTACK WAS USED AGAINST ANOTHER. HE GRITS HIS TEETH AND PREPARES TO BE IMPALED BY SOME LARGE JAGGED BRANCH... BUT IT DOESN'T HAPPEN.
INSTEAD HE IS HACKED AND SLASHED BY SMALL PIECES OF WOOD AND ROCK. SURE, IT HURTS, BUT IT'D TAKE MORE THAN THAT TO BE FATAL. "WE SHOULD ALL BE DEAD! KIZKE MUST BE PLAYING WITH US, PUTTING ON A SHOW. THAT BUYS US TIME," HE THINKS.
HE STARTS PLANNING HOW HE'S GOING TO REBOOT HIS ROBOT, IF HE CAN MAKE IT TO THE TREES IN TIME. AND SOMEWHERE, IN THE BACK OF HIS MIND, HE WONDERS WHOM KIZKE IS PUTTING THE SHOW ON FOR.

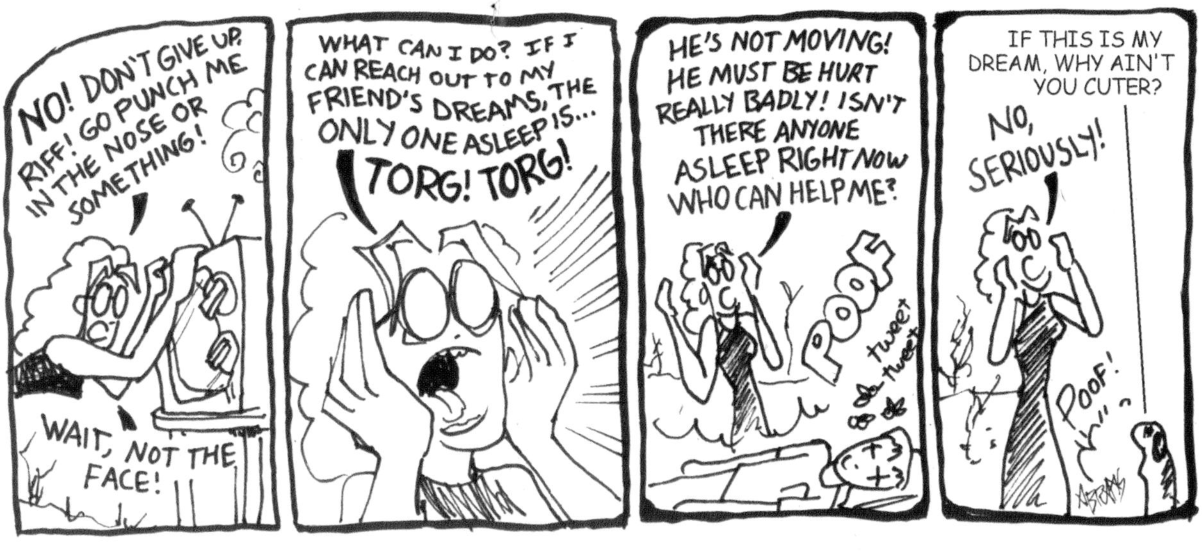
NO! DON'T GIVE UP. RIFF! GO PUNCH ME IN THE NOSE OR SOMETHING!
WAIT, NOT THE FACE!
WHAT CAN I DO? IF I CAN REACH OUT TO MY FRIEND'S DREAMS, THE ONLY ONE ASLEEP IS...
TORG! TORG!
HE'S NOT MOVING! HE MUST BE HURT REALLY BADLY! ISN'T THERE ANYONE ASLEEP RIGHT NOW WHO CAN HELP ME?
POOF
tweet tweet
IF THIS IS MY DREAM, WHY AIN'T YOU CUTER?
NO, SERIOUSLY!
POOF!

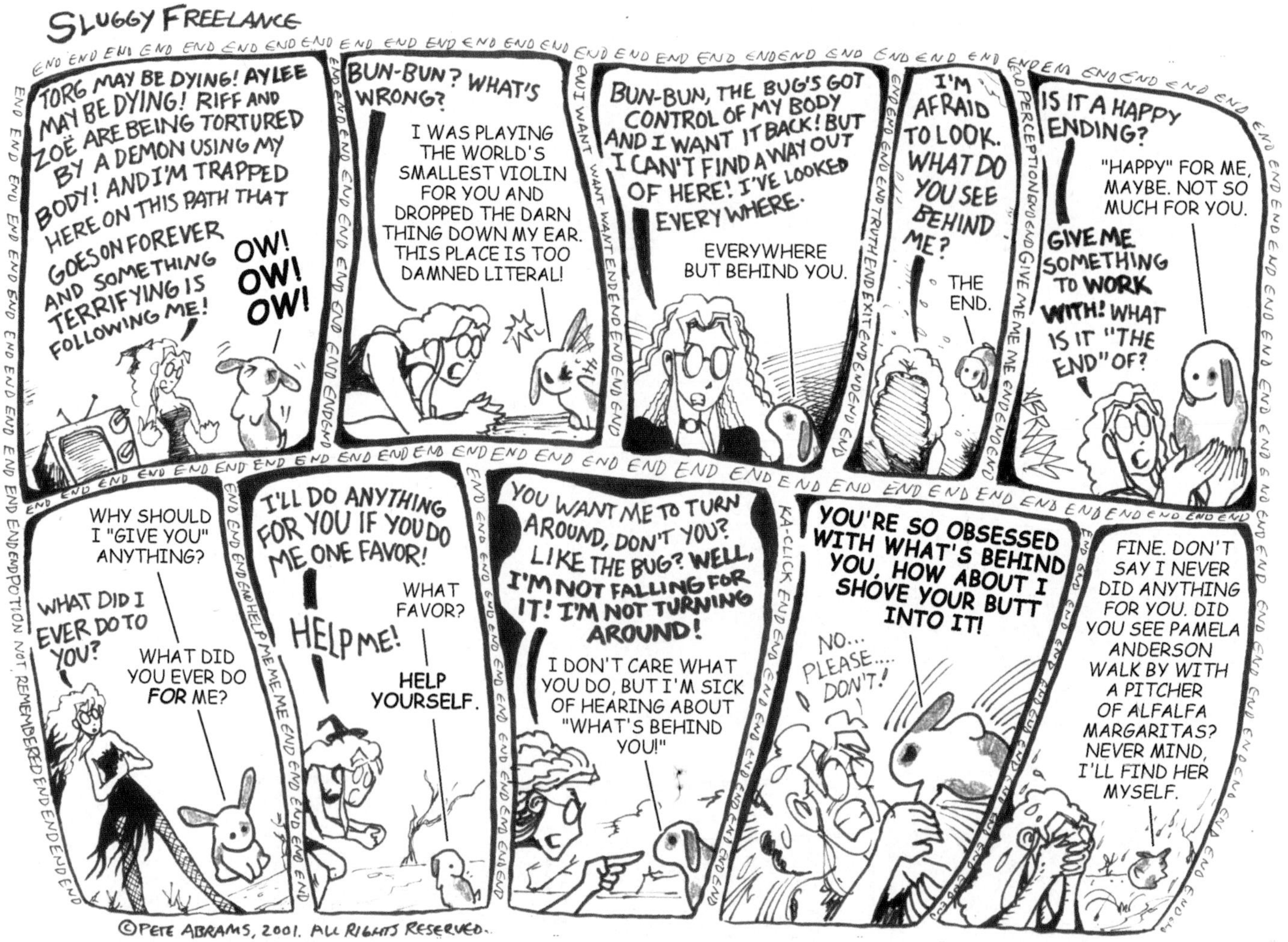
SLUGGY FREELANCE
TORG MAY BE DYING! AYLEE MAY BE DYING! RIFF AND ZOË ARE BEING TORTURED BY A DEMON USING MY BODY! AND I'M TRAPPED HERE ON THIS PATH THAT GOES ON FOREVER AND SOMETHING TERRIFYING IS FOLLOWING ME!
OW! OW! OW!
BUN-BUN? WHAT'S WRONG?
I WAS PLAYING THE WORLD'S SMALLEST VIOLIN FOR YOU AND DROPPED THE DARN THING DOWN MY EAR. THIS PLACE IS TOO DAMNED LITERAL!
BUN-BUN, THE BUG'S GOT CONTROL OF MY BODY AND I WANT IT BACK! BUT I CAN'T FIND A WAY OUT OF HERE! I'VE LOOKED EVERYWHERE.
EVERYWHERE BUT BEHIND YOU.
I'M AFRAID TO LOOK. WHAT DO YOU SEE BEHIND ME?
THE END.
IS IT A HAPPY ENDING?
"HAPPY" FOR ME, MAYBE. NOT SO MUCH FOR YOU.
GIVE ME SOMETHING TO WORK WITH! WHAT IS IT "THE END" OF?
WHY SHOULD I "GIVE YOU" ANYTHING?
WHAT DID I EVER DO TO YOU?
WHAT DID YOU EVER DO FOR ME?
I'LL DO ANYTHING FOR YOU IF YOU DO ME ONE FAVOR!
WHAT FAVOR?
HELP ME!
HELP YOURSELF.
YOU WANT ME TO TURN AROUND, DON'T YOU? LIKE THE BUG? WELL, I'M NOT FALLING FOR IT! I'M NOT TURNING AROUND!
I DON'T CARE WHAT YOU DO, BUT I'M SICK OF HEARING ABOUT "WHAT'S BEHIND YOU!"
KA-CLICK
YOU'RE SO OBSESSED WITH WHAT'S BEHIND YOU, HOW ABOUT I SHOVE YOUR BUTT INTO IT!
NO... PLEASE.... DON'T!
FINE. DON'T SAY I NEVER DID ANYTHING FOR YOU. DID YOU SEE PAMELA ANDERSON WALK BY WITH A PITCHER OF ALFALFA MARGARITAS? NEVER MIND, I'LL FIND HER MYSELF.

GWYNN TURNED AROUND.

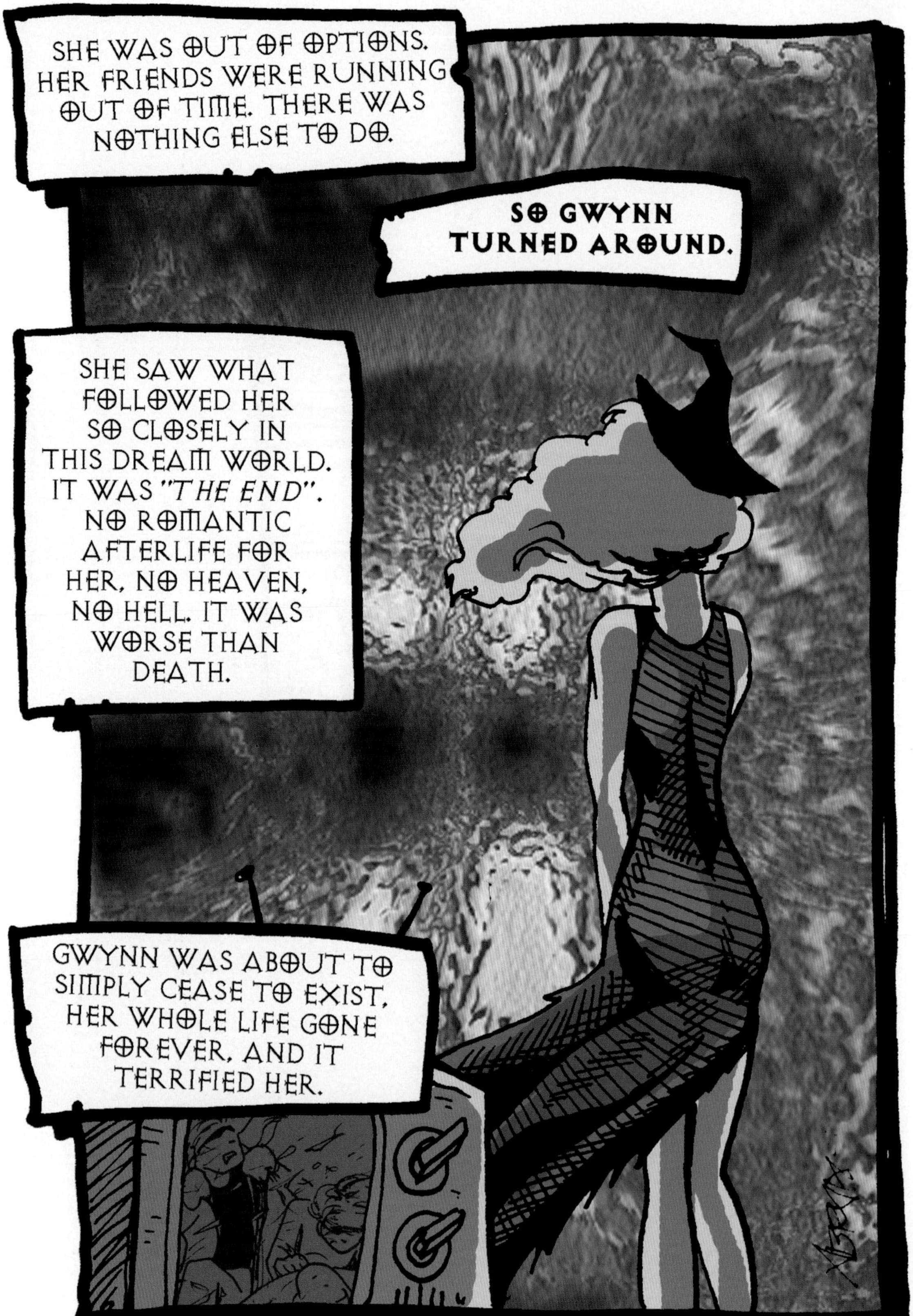
SHE WAS OUT OF OPTIONS. HER FRIENDS WERE RUNNING OUT OF TIME. THERE WAS NOTHING ELSE TO DO.
SO GWYNN TURNED AROUND.
SHE SAW WHAT FOLLOWED HER SO CLOSELY IN THIS DREAM WORLD. IT WAS "THE END". NO ROMANTIC AFTERLIFE FOR HER, NO HEAVEN, NO HELL. IT WAS WORSE THAN DEATH.
GWYNN WAS ABOUT TO SIMPLY CEASE TO EXIST, HER WHOLE LIFE GONE FOREVER, AND IT TERRIFIED HER.

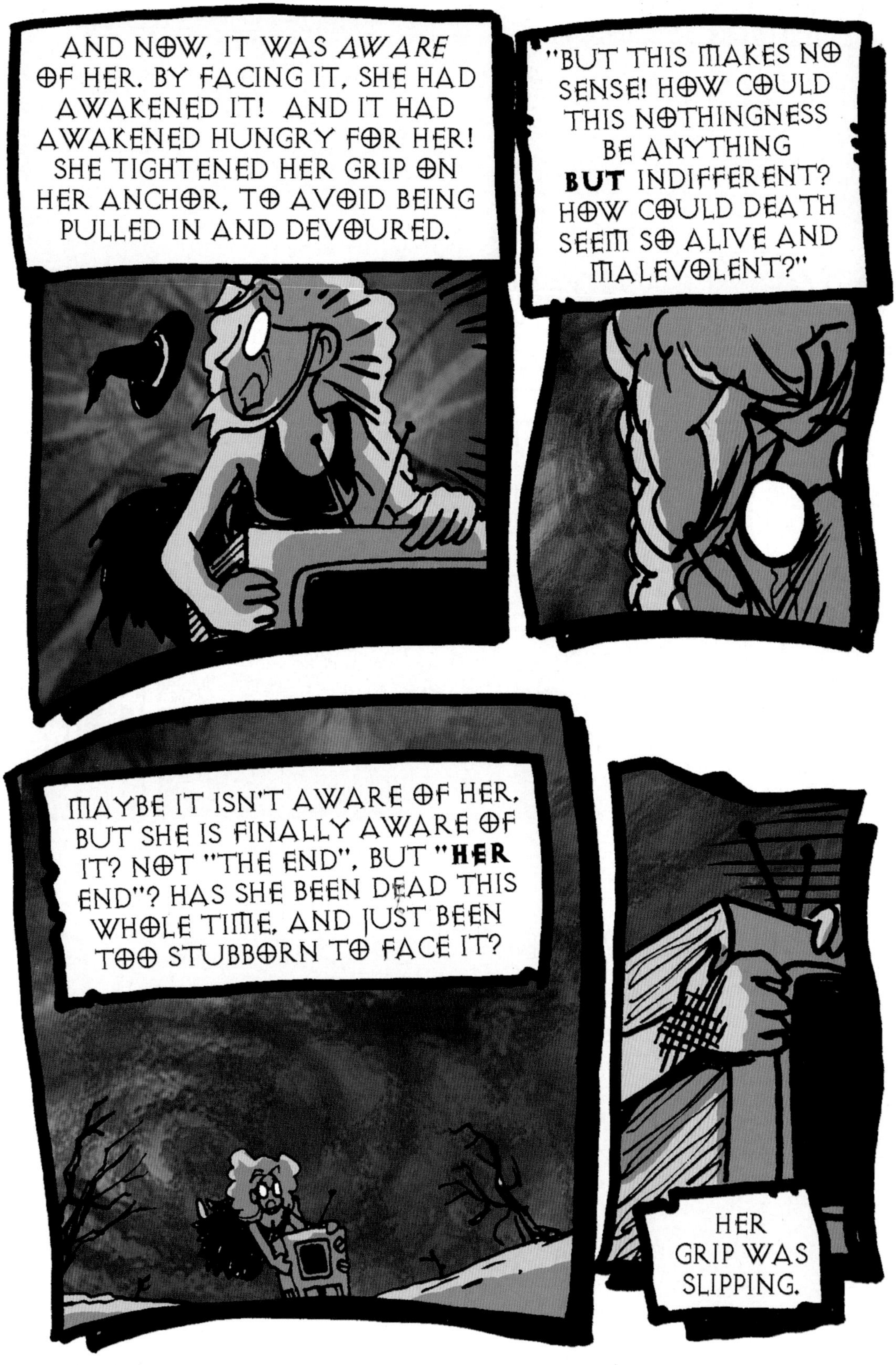
AND NOW, IT WAS *AWARE* OF HER. BY FACING IT, SHE HAD AWAKENED IT! AND IT HAD AWAKENED HUNGRY FOR HER! SHE TIGHTENED HER GRIP ON HER ANCHOR, TO AVOID BEING PULLED IN AND DEVOURED.
"BUT THIS MAKES NO SENSE! HOW COULD THIS NOTHINGNESS BE ANYTHING **BUT** INDIFFERENT? HOW COULD DEATH SEEM SO ALIVE AND MALEVOLENT?"
MAYBE IT ISN'T AWARE OF HER, BUT SHE IS FINALLY AWARE OF IT? NOT "THE END", BUT "**HER** END"? HAS SHE BEEN DEAD THIS WHOLE TIME, AND JUST BEEN TOO STUBBORN TO FACE IT?
HER GRIP WAS SLIPPING.

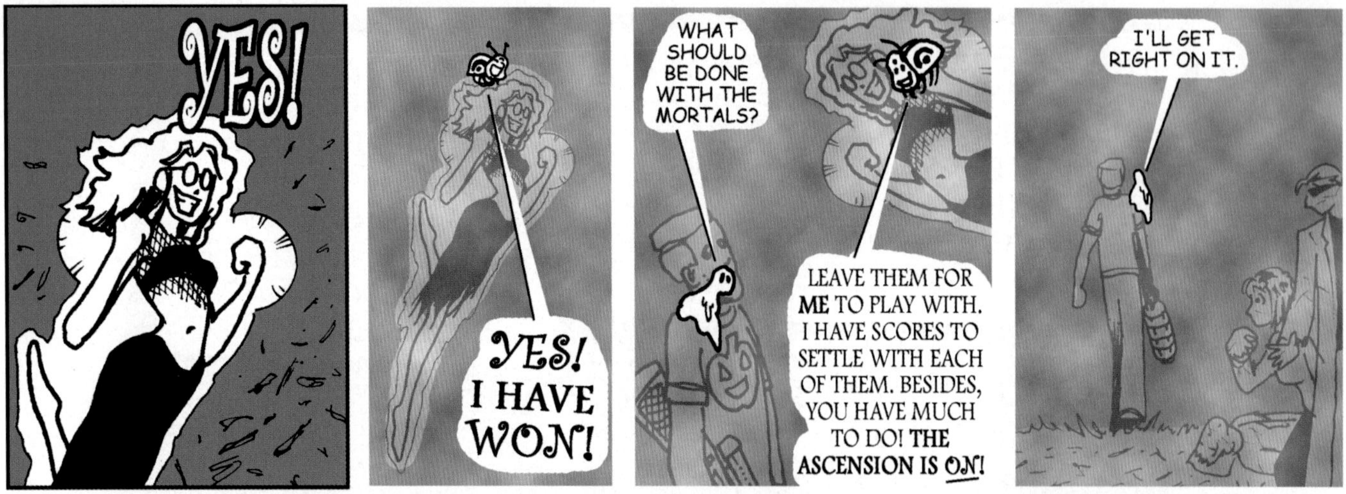
YES!
YES! I HAVE WON!
WHAT SHOULD BE DONE WITH THE MORTALS?
LEAVE THEM FOR ME TO PLAY WITH. I HAVE SCORES TO SETTLE WITH EACH OF THEM. BESIDES, YOU HAVE MUCH TO DO! THE ASCENSION IS ON!
I'LL GET RIGHT ON IT.

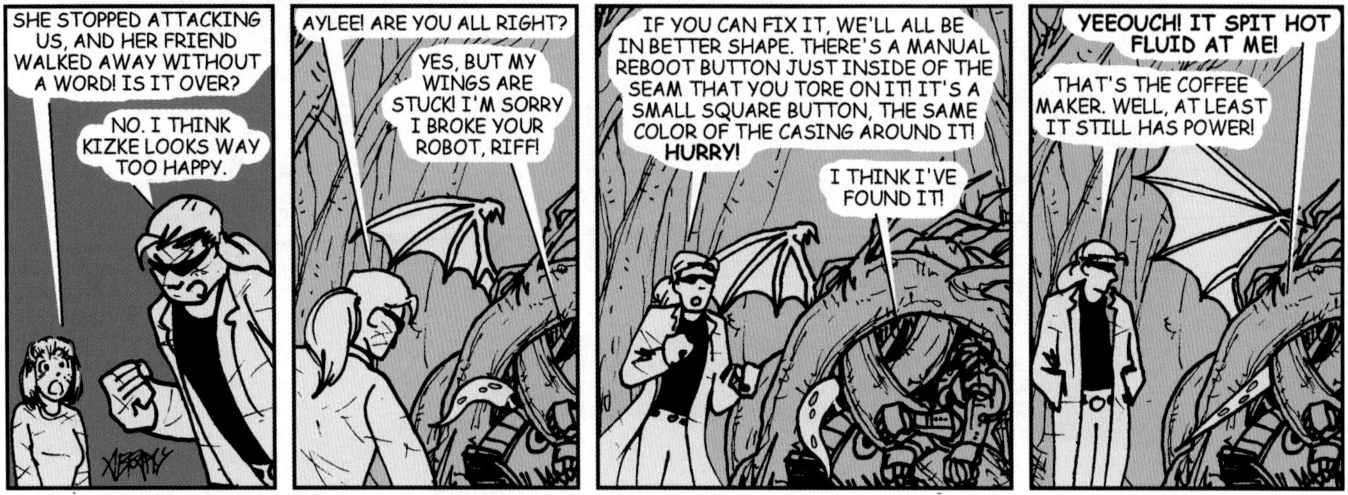
SHE STOPPED ATTACKING US, AND HER FRIEND WALKED AWAY WITHOUT A WORD! IS IT OVER?
NO. I THINK KIZKE LOOKS WAY TOO HAPPY.
AYLEE! ARE YOU ALL RIGHT?
YES, BUT MY WINGS ARE STUCK! I'M SORRY I BROKE YOUR ROBOT, RIFF!
IF YOU CAN FIX IT, WE'LL ALL BE IN BETTER SHAPE. THERE'S A MANUAL REBOOT BUTTON JUST INSIDE OF THE SEAM THAT YOU TORE ON IT! IT'S A SMALL SQUARE BUTTON, THE SAME COLOR OF THE CASING AROUND IT! HURRY!
I THINK I'VE FOUND IT!
YEEOUCH! IT SPIT HOT FLUID AT ME!
THAT'S THE COFFEE MAKER. WELL, AT LEAST IT STILL HAS POWER!

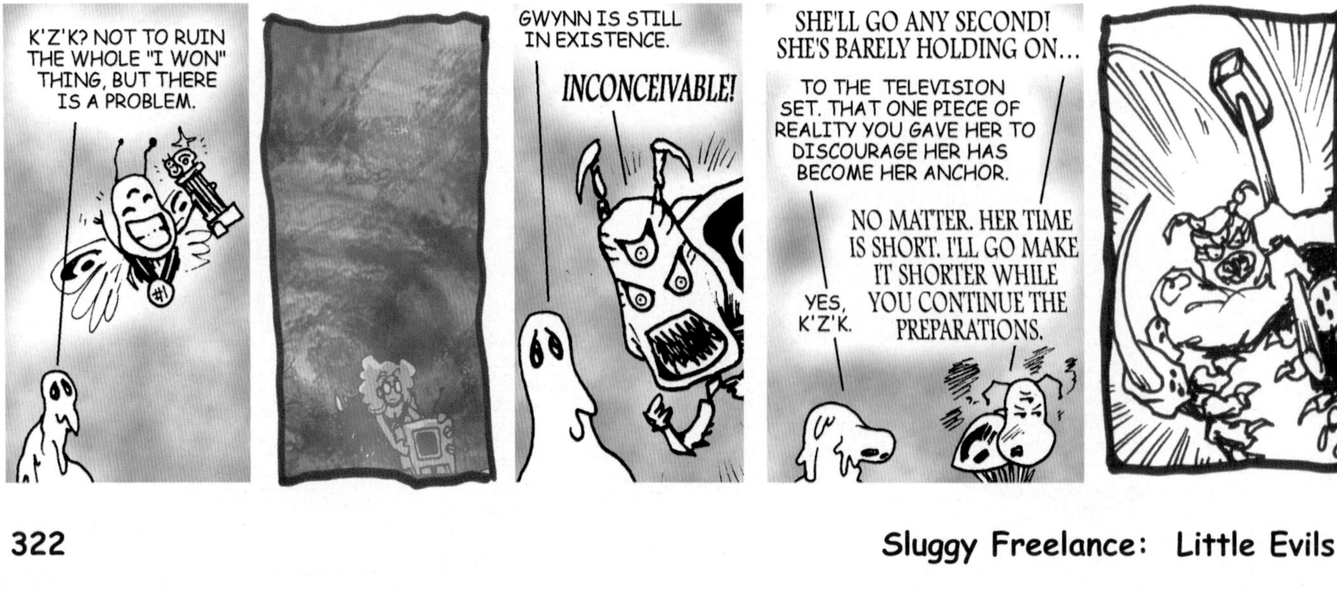
K'Z'K? NOT TO RUIN THE WHOLE "I WON" THING, BUT THERE IS A PROBLEM.
#1
GWYNN IS STILL IN EXISTENCE.
INCONCEIVABLE!
SHE'LL GO ANY SECOND! SHE'S BARELY HOLDING ON...
TO THE TELEVISION SET. THAT ONE PIECE OF REALITY YOU GAVE HER TO DISCOURAGE HER HAS BECOME HER ANCHOR.
YES, K'Z'K.
NO MATTER. HER TIME IS SHORT. I'LL GO MAKE IT SHORTER WHILE YOU CONTINUE THE PREPARATIONS.

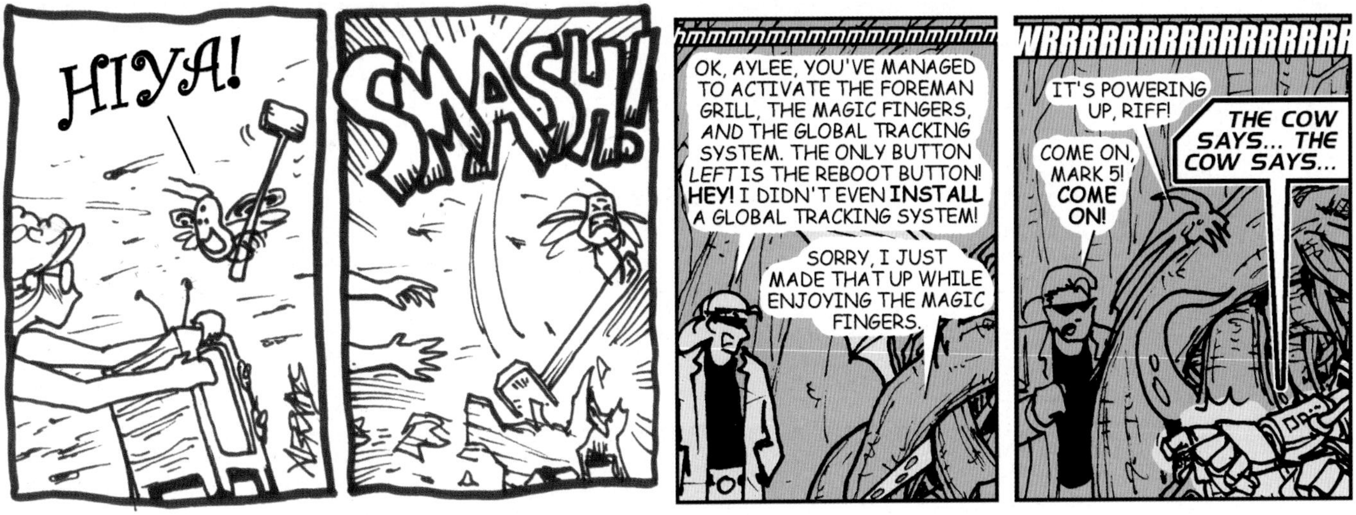
HIYA!
SMASH!
hmmmmmmmmmmmmmmmmm
OK, AYLEE, YOU'VE MANAGED TO ACTIVATE THE FOREMAN GRILL, THE MAGIC FINGERS, AND THE GLOBAL TRACKING SYSTEM. THE ONLY BUTTON *LEFT* IS THE REBOOT BUTTON! **HEY!** I DIDN'T EVEN **INSTALL** A GLOBAL TRACKING SYSTEM!
SORRY, I JUST MADE THAT UP WHILE ENJOYING THE MAGIC FINGERS.
WRRRRRRRRRRRRRRRR
IT'S POWERING UP, RIFF!
COME ON, MARK 5! **COME ON!**
THE COW SAYS... THE COW SAYS...

"Whoever fights monsters should see to it that in the process he does not become a monster. And when you look into the abyss, the abyss also looks into you."
- Nietzsche

"Facing terror isn't *half* as fun as sharing it."
-Bun-bun

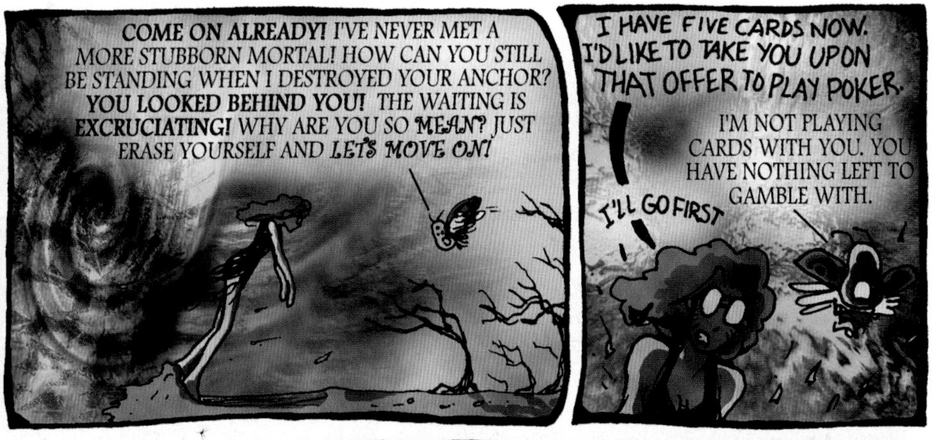
COME ON ALREADY! I'VE NEVER MET A MORE STUBBORN MORTAL! HOW CAN YOU STILL BE STANDING WHEN I DESTROYED YOUR ANCHOR? **YOU LOOKED BEHIND YOU!** THE WAITING IS **EXCRUCIATING!** WHY ARE YOU SO *MEAN?* JUST ERASE YOURSELF AND *LET'S MOVE ON!*
I HAVE FIVE CARDS NOW. I'D LIKE TO TAKE YOU UP ON THAT OFFER TO PLAY POKER.
I'M NOT PLAYING CARDS WITH YOU. YOU HAVE NOTHING LEFT TO GAMBLE WITH.
I'LL GO FIRST

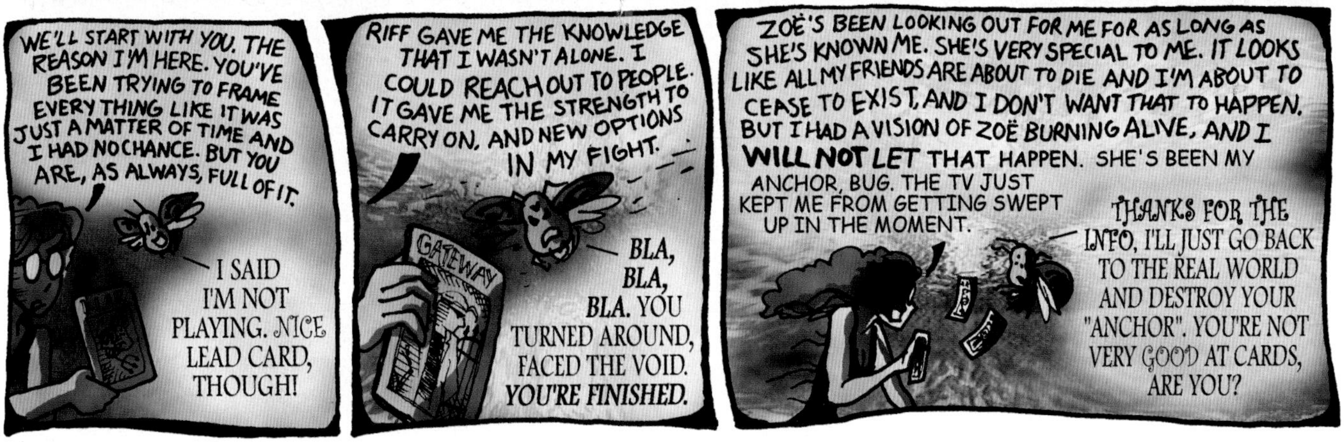
WE'LL START WITH YOU. THE REASON I'M HERE. YOU'VE BEEN TRYING TO FRAME EVERYTHING LIKE IT WAS JUST A MATTER OF TIME AND I HAD NO CHANCE. BUT YOU ARE, AS ALWAYS, FULL OF IT.
I SAID I'M NOT PLAYING. NICE LEAD CARD, THOUGH!
RIFF GAVE ME THE KNOWLEDGE THAT I WASN'T ALONE. I COULD REACH OUT TO PEOPLE. IT GAVE ME THE STRENGTH TO CARRY ON, AND NEW OPTIONS IN MY FIGHT.
GATEWAY
BLA, BLA, BLA. YOU TURNED AROUND, FACED THE VOID. *YOU'RE FINISHED.*
ZOË'S BEEN LOOKING OUT FOR ME FOR AS LONG AS SHE'S KNOWN ME. SHE'S VERY SPECIAL TO ME. IT LOOKS LIKE ALL MY FRIENDS ARE ABOUT TO DIE AND I'M ABOUT TO CEASE TO EXIST, AND I DON'T WANT THAT TO HAPPEN. BUT I HAD A VISION OF ZOË BURNING ALIVE, AND I **WILL NOT LET** THAT HAPPEN. SHE'S BEEN MY ANCHOR, BUG. THE TV JUST KEPT ME FROM GETTING SWEPT UP IN THE MOMENT.
THANKS FOR THE INFO, I'LL JUST GO BACK TO THE REAL WORLD AND DESTROY YOUR "ANCHOR". YOU'RE NOT VERY GOOD AT CARDS, ARE YOU?

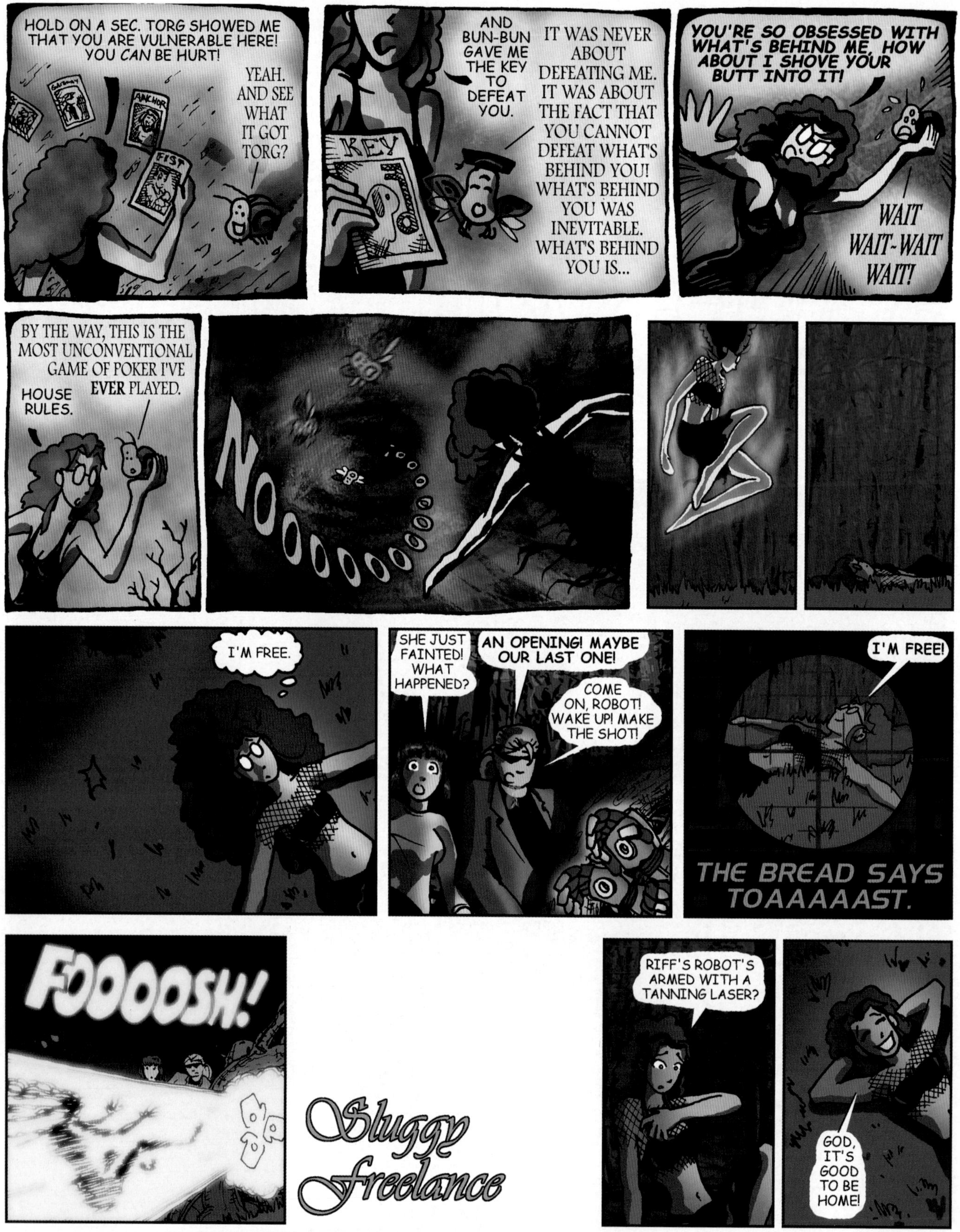
HOLD ON A SEC. TORG SHOWED ME THAT YOU ARE VULNERABLE HERE! YOU CAN BE HURT!
ANCHOR
FIST
YEAH. AND SEE WHAT IT GOT TORG?
KEY
AND BUN-BUN GAVE ME THE KEY TO DEFEAT YOU.
IT WAS NEVER ABOUT DEFEATING ME. IT WAS ABOUT THE FACT THAT YOU CANNOT DEFEAT WHAT'S BEHIND YOU! WHAT'S BEHIND YOU WAS INEVITABLE. WHAT'S BEHIND YOU IS...
YOU'RE SO OBSESSED WITH WHAT'S BEHIND ME, HOW ABOUT I SHOVE YOUR BUTT INTO IT!
WAIT WAIT~WAIT WAIT!
BY THE WAY, THIS IS THE MOST UNCONVENTIONAL GAME OF POKER I'VE EVER PLAYED.
HOUSE RULES.
NOOOOOOOOOOOOO
I'M FREE.
SHE JUST FAINTED! WHAT HAPPENED?
AN OPENING! MAYBE OUR LAST ONE!
COME ON, ROBOT! WAKE UP! MAKE THE SHOT!
I'M FREE!
THE BREAD SAYS TOAAAAAST.
FOOOOSH!
Sluggy Freelance
RIFF'S ROBOT'S ARMED WITH A TANNING LASER?
GOD, IT'S GOOD TO BE HOME!

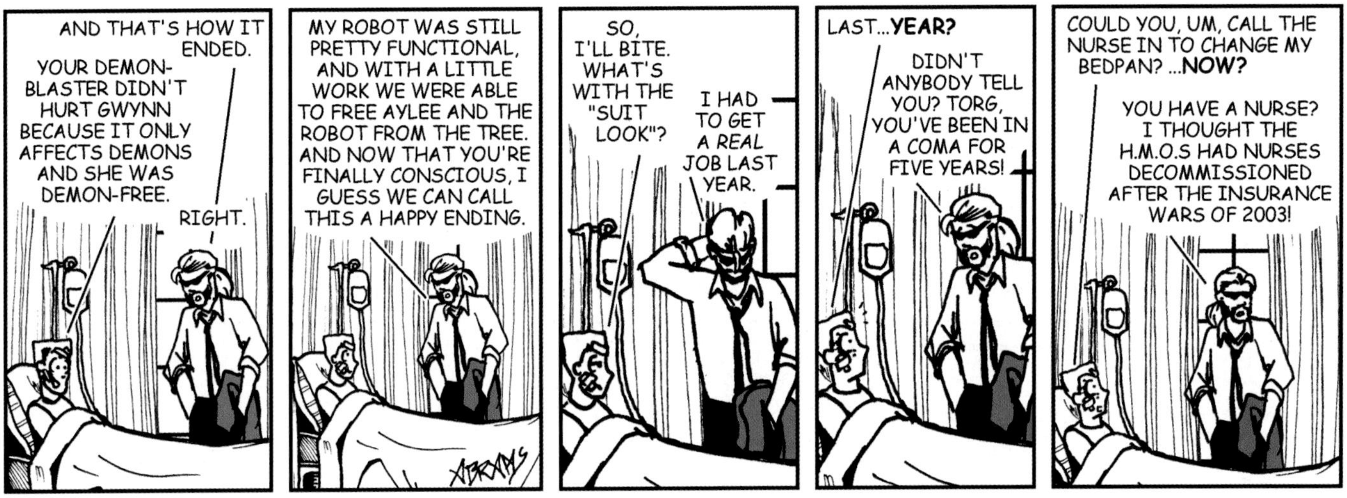
AND THAT'S HOW IT ENDED.
YOUR DEMON-BLASTER DIDN'T HURT GWYNN BECAUSE IT ONLY AFFECTS DEMONS AND SHE WAS DEMON-FREE.
RIGHT.
MY ROBOT WAS STILL PRETTY FUNCTIONAL, AND WITH A LITTLE WORK WE WERE ABLE TO FREE AYLEE AND THE ROBOT FROM THE TREE. AND NOW THAT YOU'RE FINALLY CONSCIOUS, I GUESS WE CAN CALL THIS A HAPPY ENDING.
SO, I'LL BITE. WHAT'S WITH THE "SUIT LOOK"?
I HAD TO GET A *REAL* JOB LAST YEAR.
LAST...**YEAR?**
DIDN'T ANYBODY TELL YOU? TORG, YOU'VE BEEN IN A COMA FOR FIVE YEARS!
COULD YOU, UM, CALL THE NURSE IN TO CHANGE MY BEDPAN? ...**NOW?**
YOU HAVE A NURSE? I THOUGHT THE H.M.O.S HAD NURSES DECOMMISSIONED AFTER THE INSURANCE WARS OF 2003!

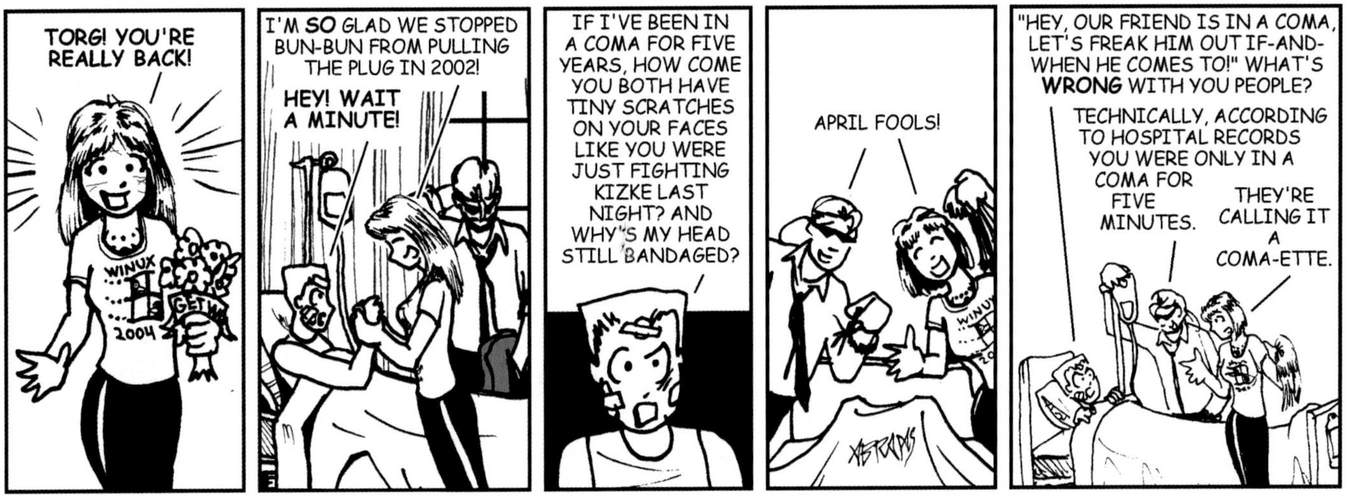
TORG! YOU'RE REALLY BACK!
WINUX
2004
I'M **SO** GLAD WE STOPPED BUN-BUN FROM PULLING THE PLUG IN 2002!
HEY! WAIT A MINUTE!
IF I'VE BEEN IN *A COMA* FOR FIVE YEARS, HOW COME YOU BOTH HAVE TINY SCRATCHES ON YOUR FACES LIKE YOU WERE JUST FIGHTING KIZKE LAST NIGHT? AND WHY'S MY HEAD STILL BANDAGED?
APRIL FOOLS!
"HEY, OUR FRIEND IS IN A *COMA*, LET'S FREAK HIM OUT IF-AND-WHEN HE COMES TO!" WHAT'S **WRONG** WITH YOU PEOPLE?
TECHNICALLY, ACCORDING TO HOSPITAL RECORDS YOU WERE ONLY IN A COMA FOR FIVE MINUTES.
THEY'RE CALLING IT A COMA-ETTE.

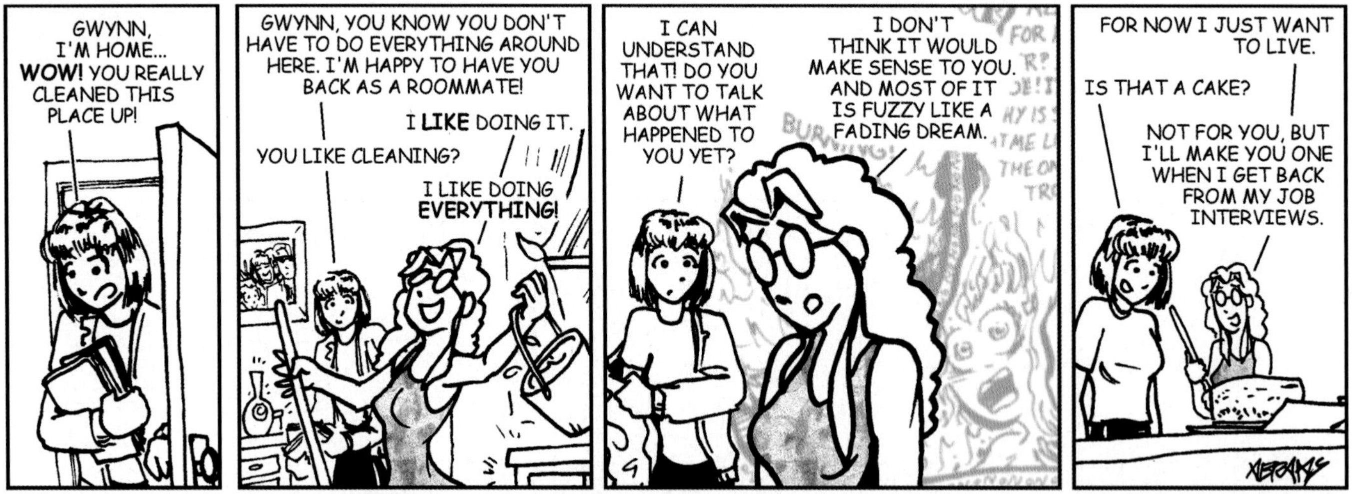
GWYNN, I'M HOME... **WOW!** YOU REALLY CLEANED THIS PLACE UP!
GWYNN, YOU KNOW YOU DON'T HAVE TO DO EVERYTHING AROUND HERE. I'M HAPPY TO HAVE YOU BACK AS A ROOMMATE!
I **LIKE** DOING IT.
YOU LIKE CLEANING?
I LIKE DOING **EVERYTHING!**
I CAN UNDERSTAND THAT! DO YOU WANT TO TALK ABOUT WHAT HAPPENED TO YOU YET?
I DON'T THINK IT WOULD MAKE SENSE TO YOU. AND MOST OF IT IS FUZZY LIKE A FADING DREAM.
FOR NOW I JUST WANT TO LIVE.
IS THAT A CAKE?
NOT FOR YOU, BUT I'LL MAKE YOU ONE WHEN I GET BACK FROM MY JOB INTERVIEWS.

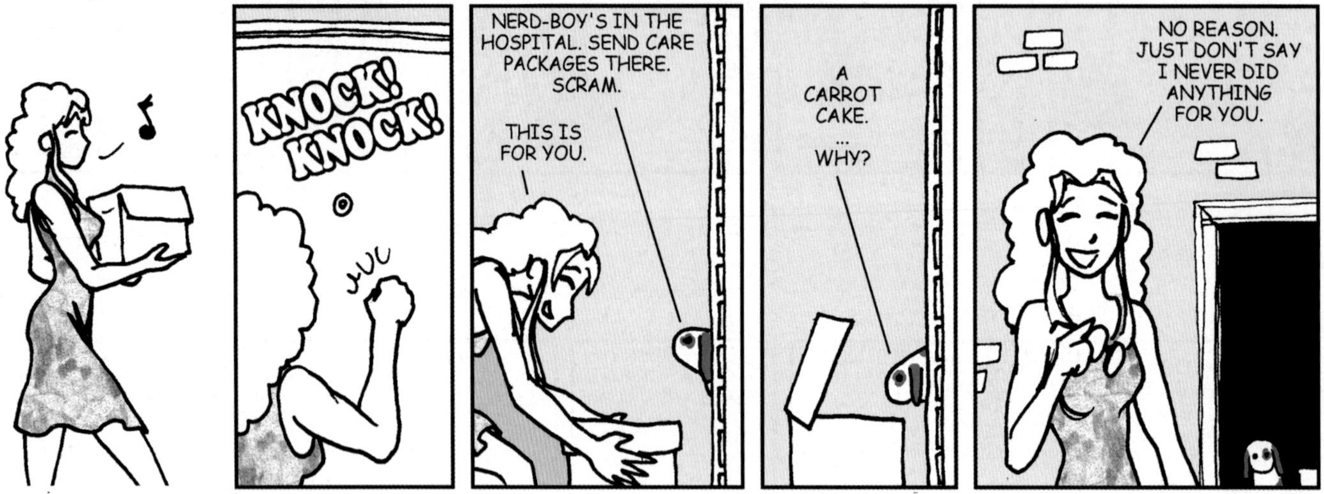
KNOCK! KNOCK!
NERD-BOY'S IN THE HOSPITAL. SEND CARE PACKAGES THERE. SCRAM.
THIS IS FOR YOU.
A CARROT CAKE. ... WHY?
NO REASON. JUST DON'T SAY I NEVER DID ANYTHING FOR YOU.

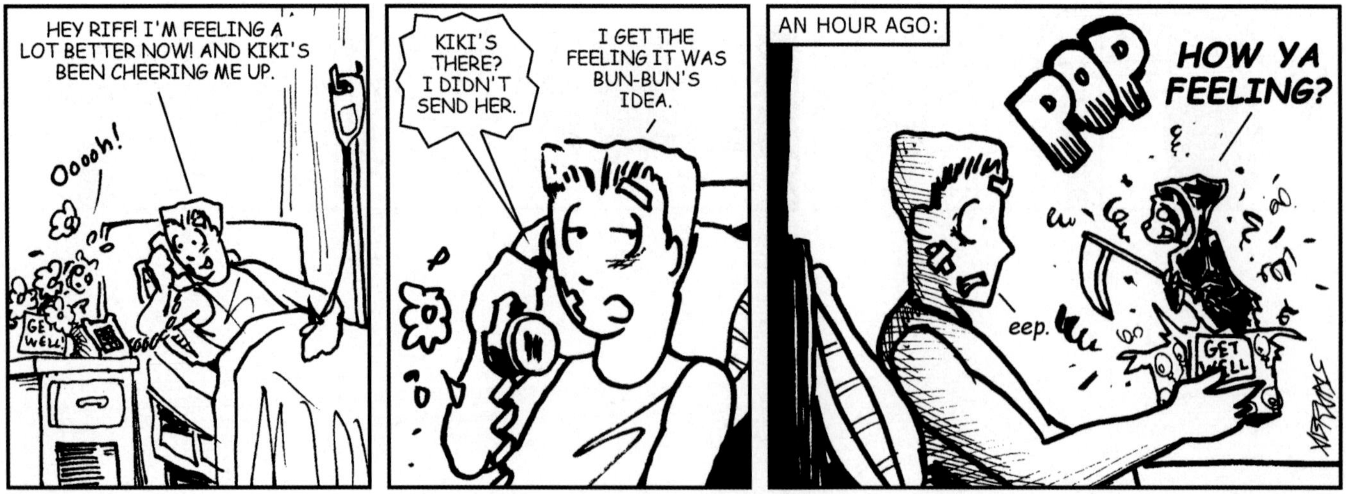
HEY RIFF! I'M FEELING A LOT BETTER NOW! AND KIKI'S BEEN CHEERING ME UP.
Ooooh!
KIKI'S THERE? I DIDN'T SEND HER.
I GET THE FEELING IT WAS BUN-BUN'S IDEA.
AN HOUR AGO:
POP
HOW YA FEELING?
eep.
GET WELL

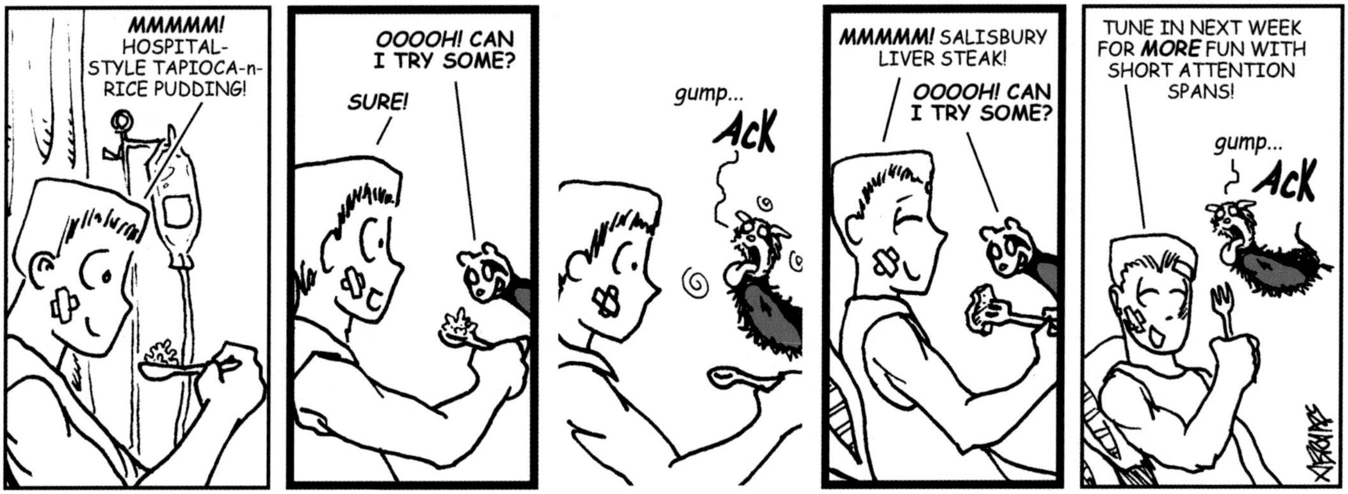
MMMMM! HOSPITAL-STYLE TAPIOCA-n-RICE PUDDING!
OOOOH! CAN I TRY SOME?
SURE!
gump...
ACK
MMMMM! SALISBURY LIVER STEAK!
OOOOH! CAN I TRY SOME?
TUNE IN NEXT WEEK FOR ***MORE*** FUN WITH SHORT ATTENTION SPANS!
gump...
ACK

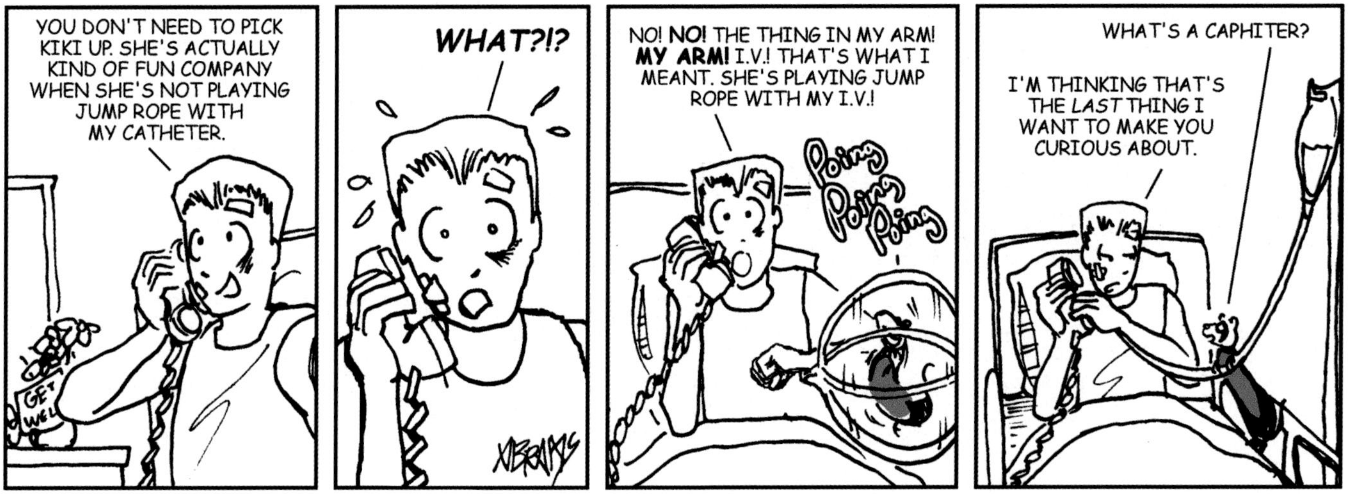
YOU DON'T NEED TO PICK KIKI UP. SHE'S ACTUALLY KIND OF FUN COMPANY WHEN SHE'S NOT PLAYING JUMP ROPE WITH MY CATHETER.
GET WELL
WHAT?!?
NO! **NO!** THE THING IN MY ARM! **MY ARM!** I.V.! THAT'S WHAT I MEANT. SHE'S PLAYING JUMP ROPE WITH MY I.V.!
Poing Poing Poing
WHAT'S A CAPHITER?
I'M THINKING THAT'S THE *LAST* THING I WANT TO MAKE YOU CURIOUS ABOUT.

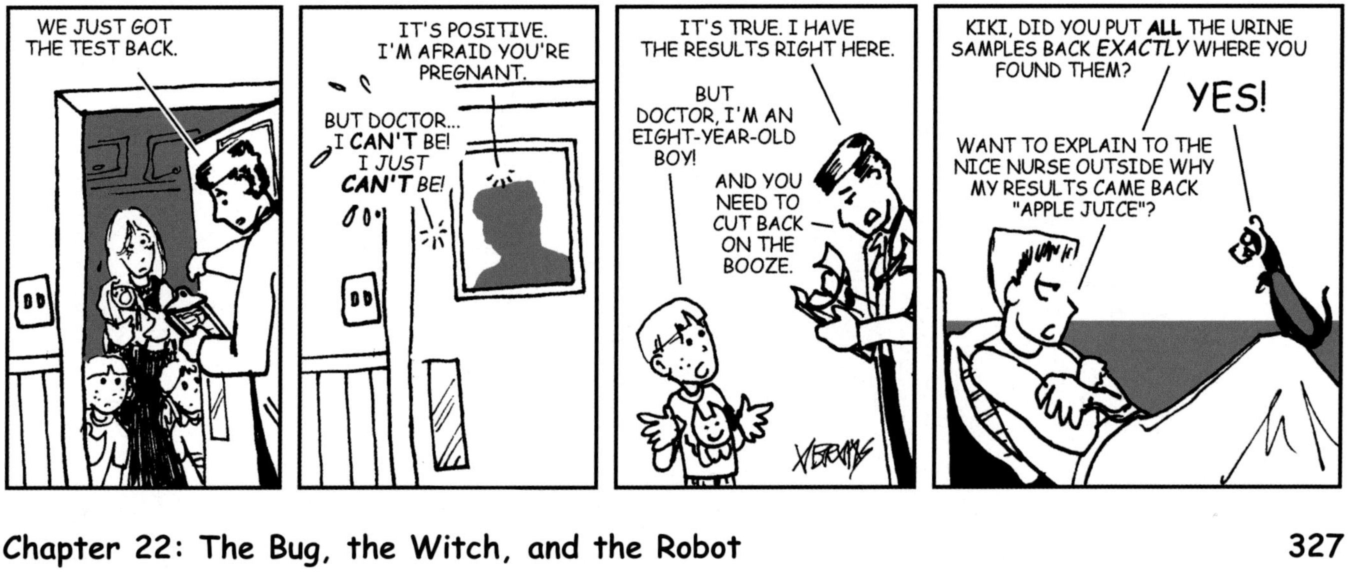
WE JUST GOT THE TEST BACK.
IT'S POSITIVE. I'M AFRAID YOU'RE PREGNANT.
BUT DOCTOR... I **CAN'T** BE! I *JUST* ***CAN'T*** BE!
IT'S TRUE. I HAVE THE RESULTS RIGHT HERE.
BUT DOCTOR, I'M AN EIGHT-YEAR-OLD BOY!
AND YOU NEED TO CUT BACK ON THE BOOZE.
KIKI, DID YOU PUT **ALL** THE URINE SAMPLES BACK ***EXACTLY*** WHERE YOU FOUND THEM?
YES!
WANT TO EXPLAIN TO THE NICE NURSE OUTSIDE WHY MY RESULTS CAME BACK "APPLE JUICE"?

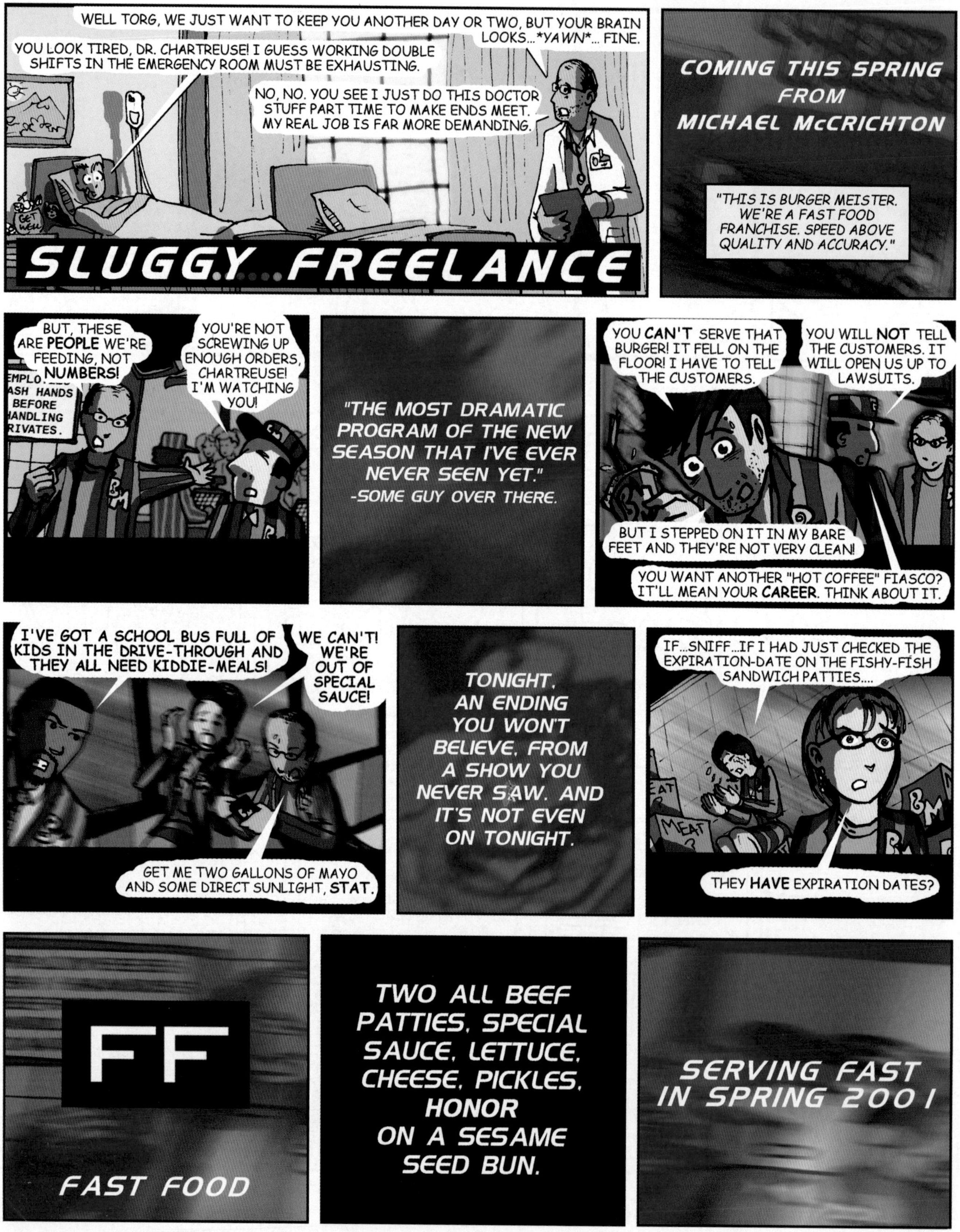

WELL TORG, WE JUST WANT TO KEEP YOU ANOTHER DAY OR TWO, BUT YOUR BRAIN LOOKS... *YAWN*... FINE.
YOU LOOK TIRED, DR. CHARTREUSE! I GUESS WORKING DOUBLE SHIFTS IN THE EMERGENCY ROOM MUST BE EXHAUSTING.
NO, NO. YOU SEE I JUST DO THIS DOCTOR STUFF PART TIME TO MAKE ENDS MEET. MY REAL JOB IS FAR MORE DEMANDING.
SLUGGY FREELANCE
COMING THIS SPRING FROM MICHAEL McCRICHTON
"THIS IS BURGER MEISTER. WE'RE A FAST FOOD FRANCHISE. SPEED ABOVE QUALITY AND ACCURACY."
BUT, THESE ARE PEOPLE WE'RE FEEDING, NOT NUMBERS!
YOU'RE NOT SCREWING UP ENOUGH ORDERS, CHARTREUSE! I'M WATCHING YOU!
"THE MOST DRAMATIC PROGRAM OF THE NEW SEASON THAT I'VE EVER NEVER SEEN YET."
-SOME GUY OVER THERE.
YOU CAN'T SERVE THAT BURGER! IT FELL ON THE FLOOR! I HAVE TO TELL THE CUSTOMERS.
YOU WILL NOT TELL THE CUSTOMERS. IT WILL OPEN US UP TO LAWSUITS.
BUT I STEPPED ON IT IN MY BARE FEET AND THEY'RE NOT VERY CLEAN!
YOU WANT ANOTHER "HOT COFFEE" FIASCO? IT'LL MEAN YOUR CAREER. THINK ABOUT IT.
I'VE GOT A SCHOOL BUS FULL OF KIDS IN THE DRIVE-THROUGH AND THEY ALL NEED KIDDIE-MEALS!
WE CAN'T! WE'RE OUT OF SPECIAL SAUCE!
GET ME TWO GALLONS OF MAYO AND SOME DIRECT SUNLIGHT, STAT.
TONIGHT, AN ENDING YOU WON'T BELIEVE, FROM A SHOW YOU NEVER SAW. AND IT'S NOT EVEN ON TONIGHT.
IF...SNIFF...IF I HAD JUST CHECKED THE EXPIRATION-DATE ON THE FISHY-FISH SANDWICH PATTIES....
THEY HAVE EXPIRATION DATES?
FF
FAST FOOD
TWO ALL BEEF PATTIES, SPECIAL SAUCE, LETTUCE, CHEESE, PICKLES, HONOR ON A SESAME SEED BUN.
SERVING FAST IN SPRING 2001

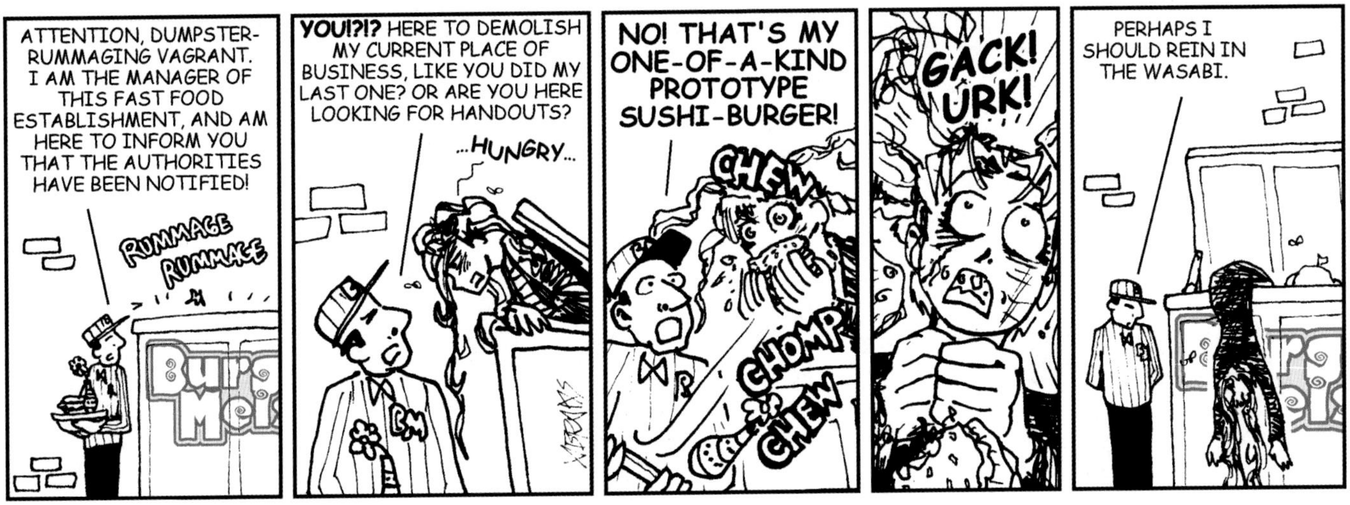
ATTENTION, DUMPSTER-RUMMAGING VAGRANT. I AM THE MANAGER OF THIS FAST FOOD ESTABLISHMENT, AND AM HERE TO INFORM YOU THAT THE AUTHORITIES HAVE BEEN NOTIFIED!
RUMMAGE RUMMAGE
YOU!?!? HERE TO DEMOLISH MY CURRENT PLACE OF BUSINESS, LIKE YOU DID MY LAST ONE? OR ARE YOU HERE LOOKING FOR HANDOUTS?
...HUNGRY...
NO! THAT'S MY ONE-OF-A-KIND PROTOTYPE SUSHI-BURGER!
CHEW
CHOMP
CHEW
GACK! URK!
PERHAPS I SHOULD REIN IN THE WASABI.

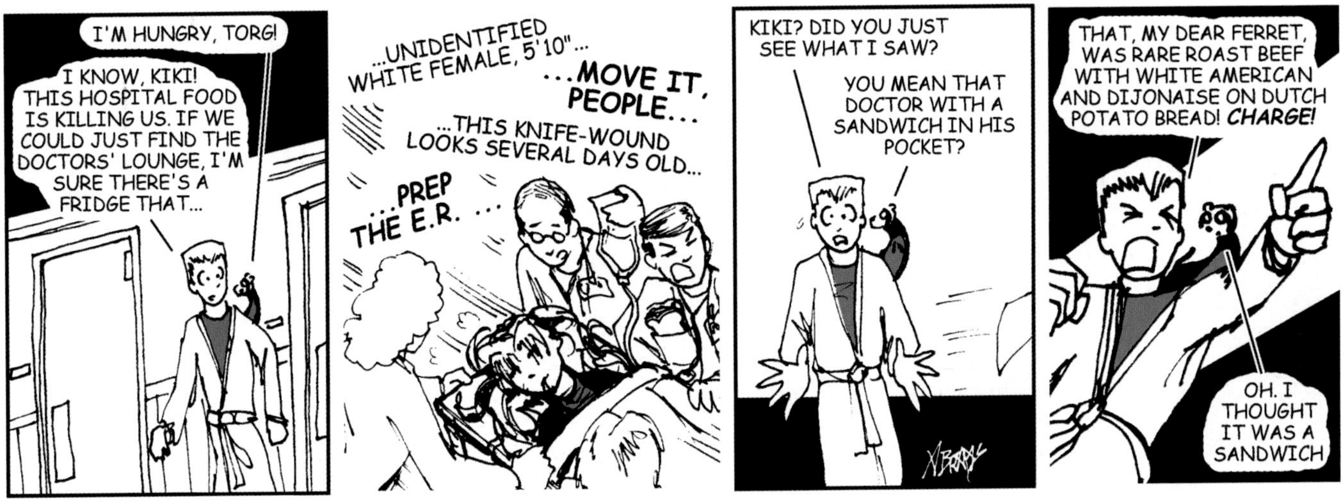
I'M HUNGRY, TORG!
I KNOW, KIKI! THIS HOSPITAL FOOD IS KILLING US. IF WE COULD JUST FIND THE DOCTORS' LOUNGE, I'M SURE THERE'S A FRIDGE THAT...
...UNIDENTIFIED WHITE FEMALE, 5'10"...
...MOVE IT, PEOPLE...
...THIS KNIFE-WOUND LOOKS SEVERAL DAYS OLD...
...PREP THE E.R. ...
KIKI? DID YOU JUST SEE WHAT I SAW?
YOU MEAN THAT DOCTOR WITH A SANDWICH IN HIS POCKET?
THAT, MY DEAR FERRET, WAS RARE ROAST BEEF WITH WHITE AMERICAN AND DIJONAISE ON DUTCH POTATO BREAD! CHARGE!
OH. I THOUGHT IT WAS A SANDWICH

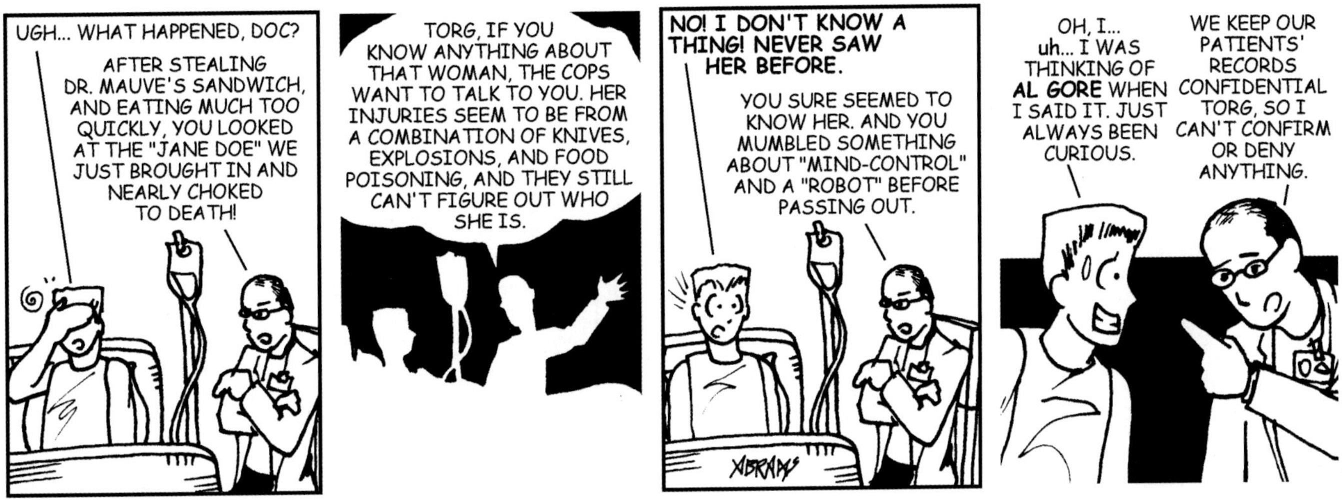
UGH... WHAT HAPPENED, DOC?
AFTER STEALING DR. MAUVE'S SANDWICH, AND EATING MUCH TOO QUICKLY, YOU LOOKED AT THE "JANE DOE" WE JUST BROUGHT IN AND NEARLY CHOKED TO DEATH!
TORG, IF YOU KNOW ANYTHING ABOUT THAT WOMAN, THE COPS WANT TO TALK TO YOU. HER INJURIES SEEM TO BE FROM A COMBINATION OF KNIVES, EXPLOSIONS, AND FOOD POISONING, AND THEY STILL CAN'T FIGURE OUT WHO SHE IS.
NO! I DON'T KNOW A THING! NEVER SAW HER BEFORE.
YOU SURE SEEMED TO KNOW HER. AND YOU MUMBLED SOMETHING ABOUT "MIND-CONTROL" AND A "ROBOT" BEFORE PASSING OUT.
OH, I... uh... I WAS THINKING OF AL GORE WHEN I SAID IT. JUST ALWAYS BEEN CURIOUS.
WE KEEP OUR PATIENTS' RECORDS CONFIDENTIAL TORG, SO I CAN'T CONFIRM OR DENY ANYTHING.

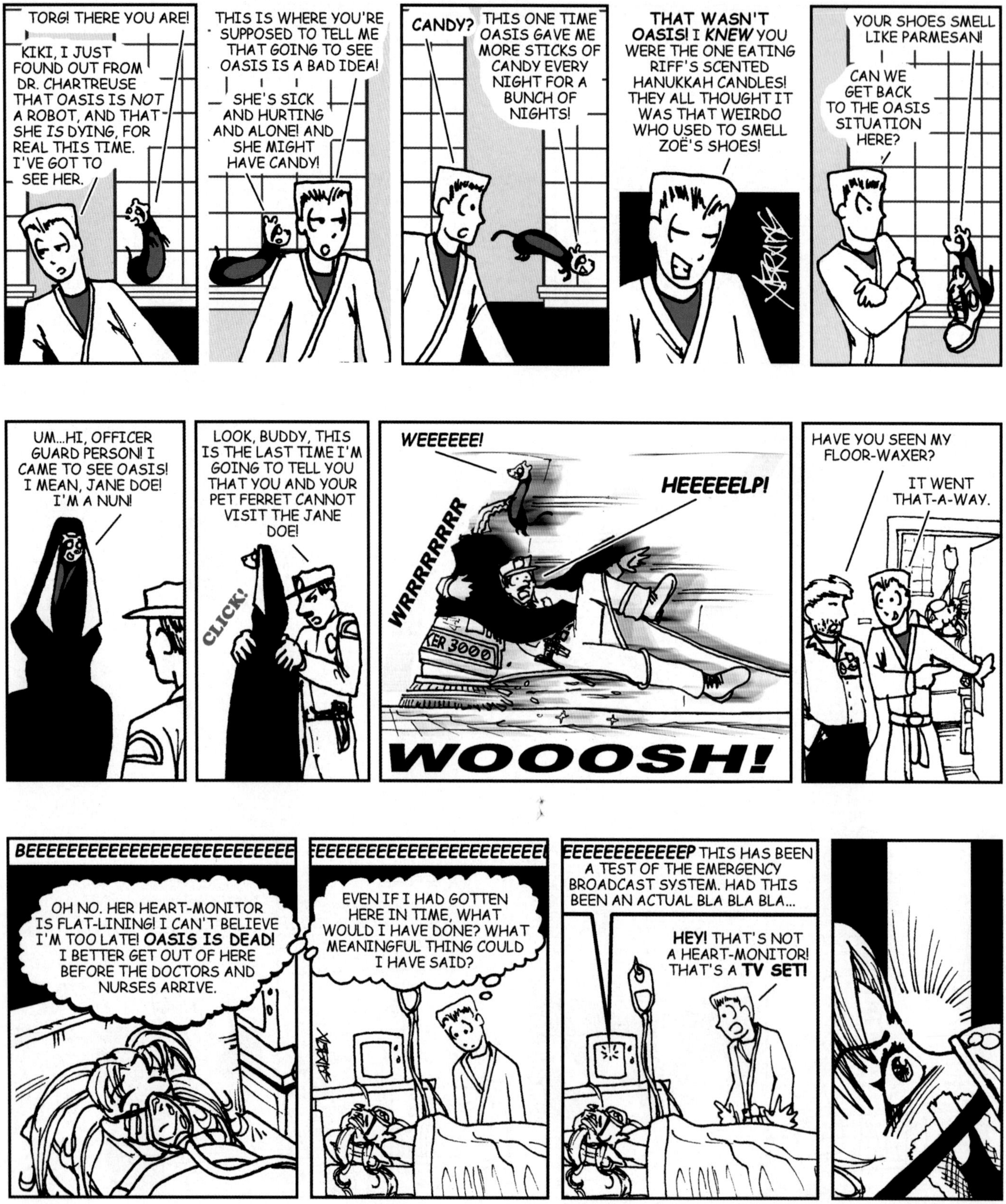

TORG! THERE YOU ARE!
KIKI, I JUST FOUND OUT FROM DR. CHARTREUSE THAT OASIS IS *NOT* A ROBOT, AND THAT SHE *IS* DYING, FOR REAL THIS TIME. I'VE GOT TO SEE HER.
THIS IS WHERE YOU'RE SUPPOSED TO TELL ME THAT GOING TO SEE OASIS IS A BAD IDEA!
SHE'S SICK AND HURTING AND ALONE! AND SHE MIGHT HAVE CANDY!
CANDY?
THIS ONE TIME OASIS GAVE ME MORE STICKS OF CANDY EVERY NIGHT FOR A BUNCH OF NIGHTS!
THAT WASN'T OASIS! I ***KNEW*** YOU WERE THE ONE EATING RIFF'S SCENTED HANUKKAH CANDLES! THEY ALL THOUGHT IT WAS THAT WEIRDO WHO USED TO SMELL ZOË'S SHOES!
YOUR SHOES SMELL LIKE PARMESAN!
CAN WE GET BACK TO THE OASIS SITUATION HERE?
UM...HI, OFFICER GUARD PERSON! I CAME TO SEE OASIS! I MEAN, JANE DOE! I'M A NUN!
LOOK, BUDDY, THIS IS THE LAST TIME I'M GOING TO TELL YOU THAT YOU AND YOUR PET FERRET CANNOT VISIT THE JANE DOE!
CLICK!
WEEEEEE!
HEEEEELP!
WRRRRRRRR
WOOOSH!
HAVE YOU SEEN MY FLOOR-WAXER?
IT WENT THAT-A-WAY.
BEEEEEEEEEEEEEEEEEEEEEEEEE
OH NO. HER HEART-MONITOR IS FLAT-LINING! I CAN'T BELIEVE I'M TOO LATE! **OASIS IS DEAD!** I BETTER GET OUT OF HERE BEFORE THE DOCTORS AND NURSES ARRIVE.
EEEEEEEEEEEEEEEEEEEEEEEEE
EVEN IF I HAD GOTTEN HERE IN TIME, WHAT WOULD I HAVE DONE? WHAT MEANINGFUL THING COULD I HAVE SAID?
EEEEEEEEEEEEP THIS HAS BEEN A TEST OF THE EMERGENCY BROADCAST SYSTEM. HAD THIS BEEN AN ACTUAL BLA BLA BLA...
HEY! THAT'S NOT A HEART-MONITOR! THAT'S A **TV SET!**

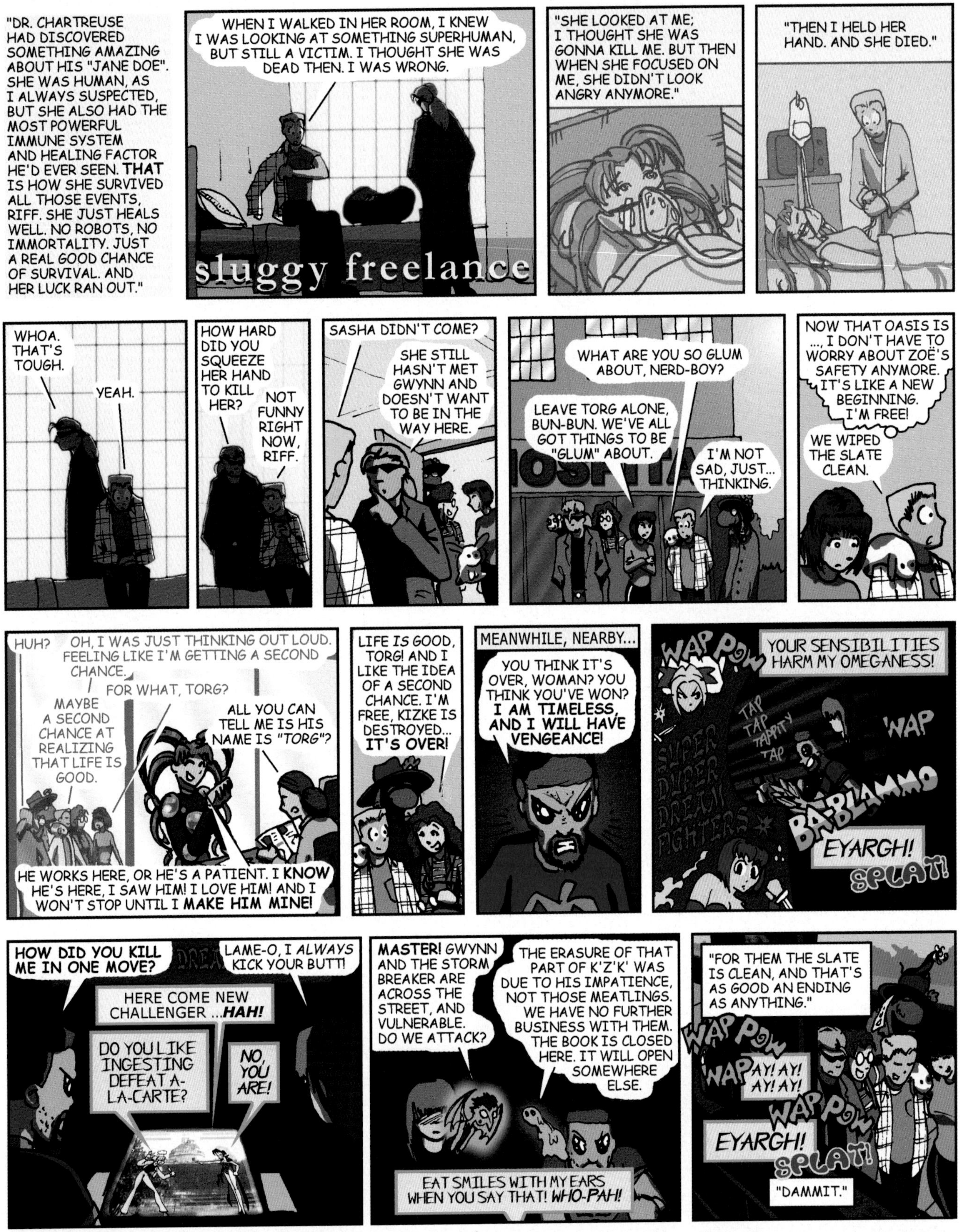
"DR. CHARTREUSE HAD DISCOVERED SOMETHING AMAZING ABOUT HIS "JANE DOE". SHE WAS HUMAN, AS I ALWAYS SUSPECTED, BUT SHE ALSO HAD THE MOST POWERFUL IMMUNE SYSTEM AND HEALING FACTOR HE'D EVER SEEN. THAT IS HOW SHE SURVIVED ALL THOSE EVENTS, RIFF. SHE JUST HEALS WELL. NO ROBOTS, NO IMMORTALITY. JUST A REAL GOOD CHANCE OF SURVIVAL. AND HER LUCK RAN OUT."
WHEN I WALKED IN HER ROOM, I KNEW I WAS LOOKING AT SOMETHING SUPERHUMAN, BUT STILL A VICTIM. I THOUGHT SHE WAS DEAD THEN. I WAS WRONG.
sluggy freelance
"SHE LOOKED AT ME; I THOUGHT SHE WAS GONNA KILL ME. BUT THEN WHEN SHE FOCUSED ON ME, SHE DIDN'T LOOK ANGRY ANYMORE."
"THEN I HELD HER HAND. AND SHE DIED."
WHOA. THAT'S TOUGH.
YEAH.
HOW HARD DID YOU SQUEEZE HER HAND TO KILL HER?
NOT FUNNY RIGHT NOW, RIFF.
SASHA DIDN'T COME?
SHE STILL HASN'T MET GWYNN AND DOESN'T WANT TO BE IN THE WAY HERE.
WHAT ARE YOU SO GLUM ABOUT, NERD-BOY?
LEAVE TORG ALONE, BUN-BUN. WE'VE ALL GOT THINGS TO BE "GLUM" ABOUT.
I'M NOT SAD, JUST... THINKING.
NOW THAT OASIS IS ..., I DON'T HAVE TO WORRY ABOUT ZOË'S SAFETY ANYMORE. IT'S LIKE A NEW BEGINNING. I'M FREE!
WE WIPED THE SLATE CLEAN.
HUH?
OH, I WAS JUST THINKING OUT LOUD. FEELING LIKE I'M GETTING A SECOND CHANCE.
FOR WHAT, TORG?
MAYBE A SECOND CHANCE AT REALIZING THAT LIFE IS GOOD.
ALL YOU CAN TELL ME IS HIS NAME IS "TORG"?
HE WORKS HERE, OR HE'S A PATIENT. I KNOW HE'S HERE, I SAW HIM! I LOVE HIM! AND I WON'T STOP UNTIL I MAKE HIM MINE!
LIFE IS GOOD, TORG! AND I LIKE THE IDEA OF A SECOND CHANCE. I'M FREE, KIZKE IS DESTROYED... IT'S OVER!
MEANWHILE, NEARBY...
YOU THINK IT'S OVER, WOMAN? YOU THINK YOU'VE WON? I AM TIMELESS, AND I WILL HAVE VENGEANCE!
WAP POW
YOUR SENSIBILITIES HARM MY OMEGANESS!
TAP TAP TAPPITY TAP
WAP
SUPER DUPER DREAM FIGHTERS
BABLAMMO
EYARGH!
SPLAT!
HOW DID YOU KILL ME IN ONE MOVE?
LAME-O, I ALWAYS KICK YOUR BUTT!
HERE COME NEW CHALLENGER ...HAH!
DO YOU LIKE INGESTING DEFEAT A-LA-CARTE?
NO, YOU ARE!
MASTER! GWYNN AND THE STORM BREAKER ARE ACROSS THE STREET, AND VULNERABLE. DO WE ATTACK?
THE ERASURE OF THAT PART OF K'Z'K' WAS DUE TO HIS IMPATIENCE, NOT THOSE MEATLINGS. WE HAVE NO FURTHER BUSINESS WITH THEM. THE BOOK IS CLOSED HERE. IT WILL OPEN SOMEWHERE ELSE.
EAT SMILES WITH MY EARS WHEN YOU SAY THAT! WHO-PAH!
"FOR THEM THE SLATE IS CLEAN, AND THAT'S AS GOOD AN ENDING AS ANYTHING."
WAP POW
WAP
AY! AY! AY! AY!
WAP POW
EYARGH!
SPLAT!
"DAMMIT."

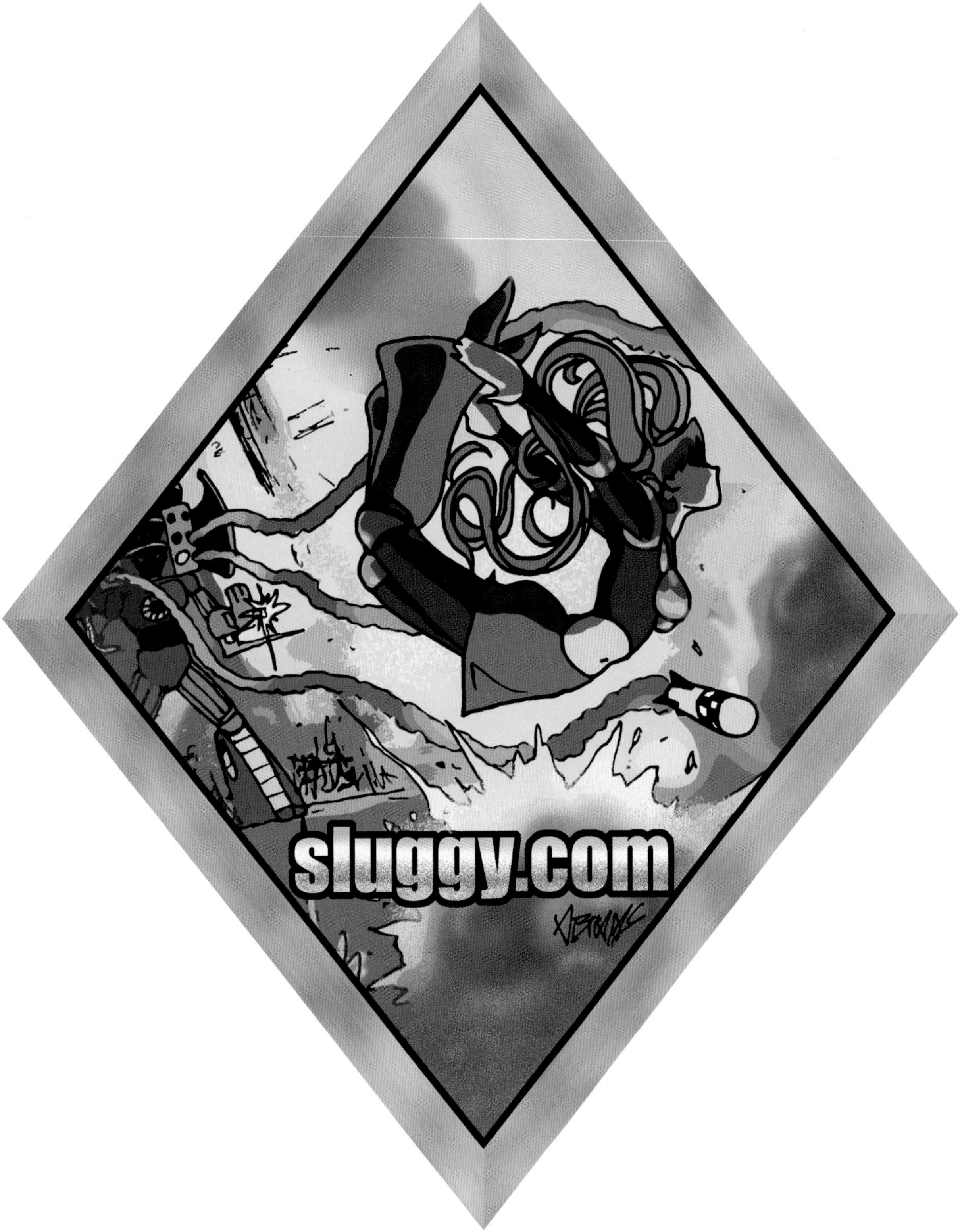
sluggy.com

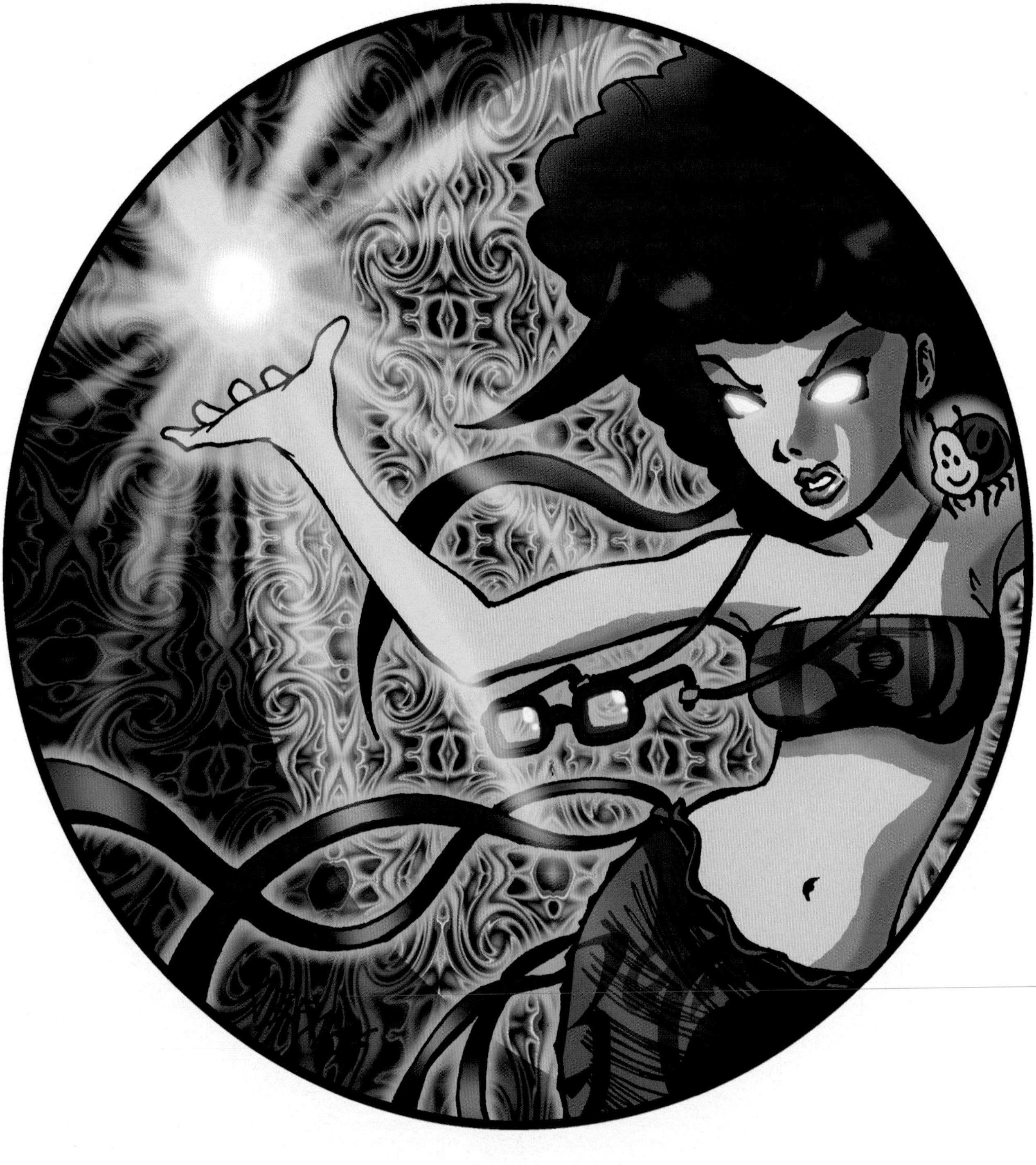

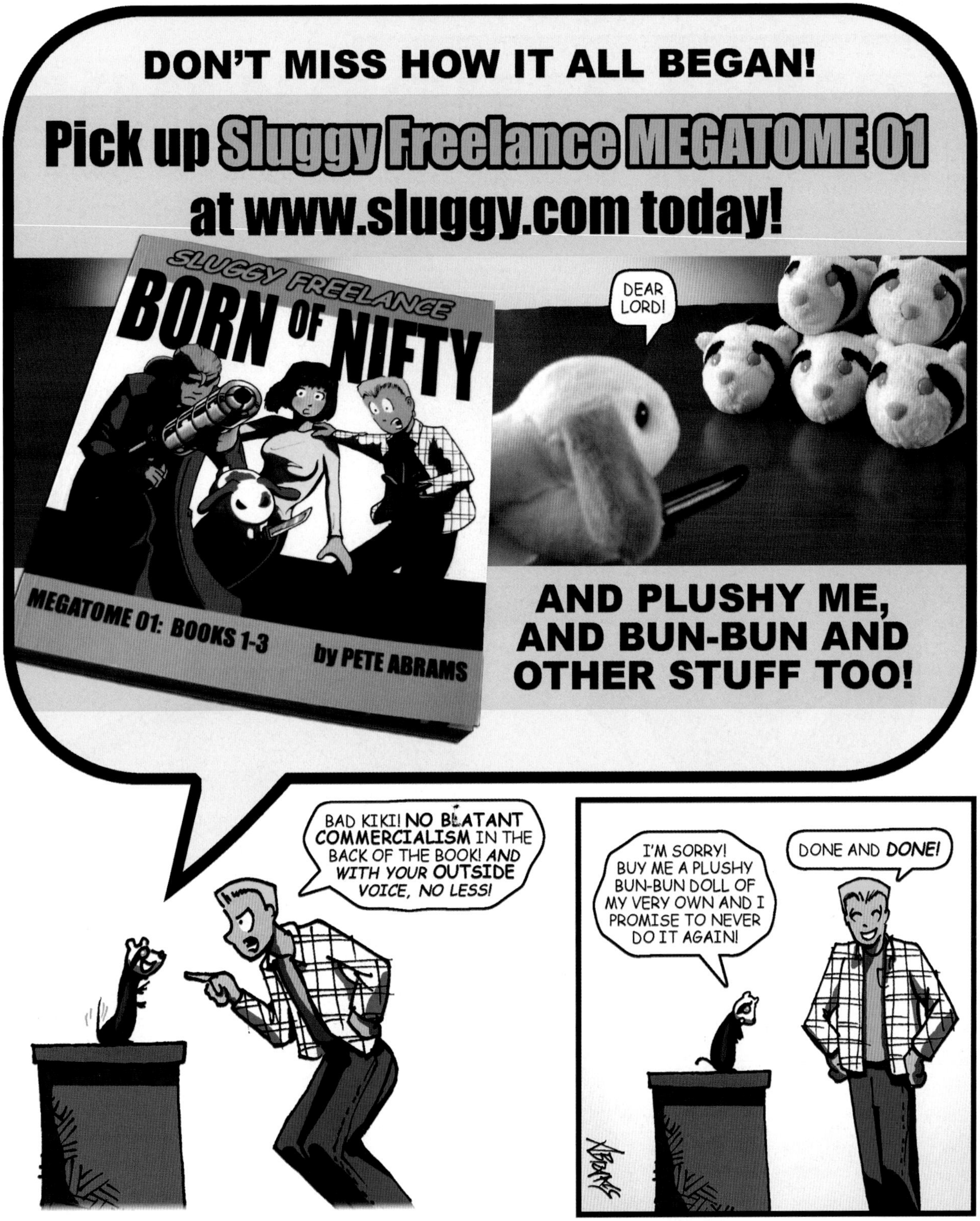
DON'T MISS HOW IT ALL BEGAN!
Pick up Sluggy Freelance MEGATOME 01
at www.sluggy.com today!
SLUGGY FREELANCE
BORN OF NIFTY
MEGATOME 01: BOOKS 1-3
by PETE ABRAMS
DEAR LORD!
AND PLUSHY ME, AND BUN-BUN AND OTHER STUFF TOO!
BAD KIKI! NO BLATANT COMMERCIALISM IN THE BACK OF THE BOOK! AND WITH YOUR OUTSIDE VOICE, NO LESS!
I'M SORRY! BUY ME A PLUSHY BUN-BUN DOLL OF MY VERY OWN AND I PROMISE TO NEVER DO IT AGAIN!
DONE AND DONE!

SLUGGY FREELANCE

WWW.SLUGGY.COM

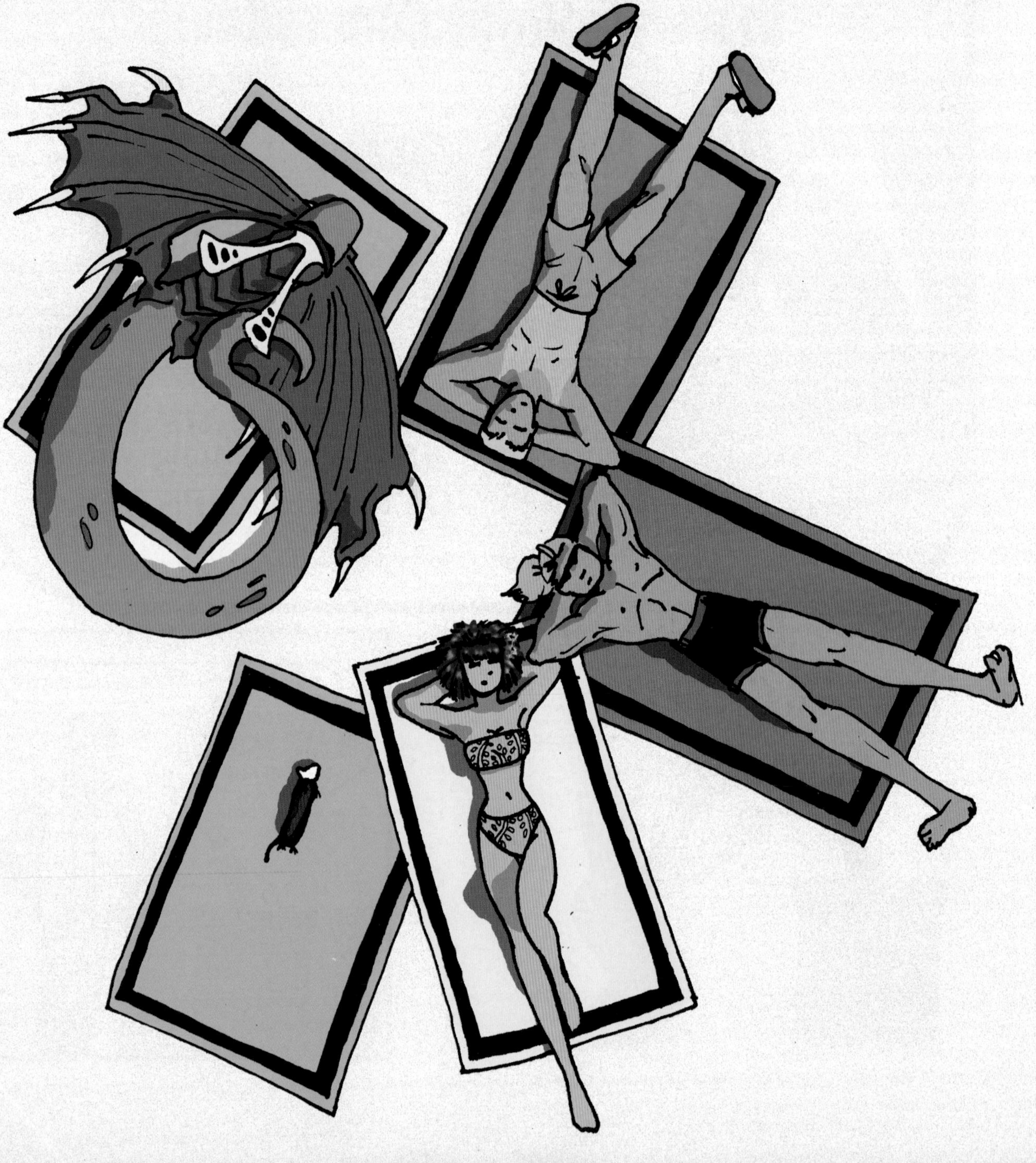